Sambhaji

Vishwas Patil is one of the most acclaimed Marathi writers today. He has written iconic novels like *Mahanayak*, *Chandramukhi*, *Pangira*, *Zadazadati*, *Panipat*, *Sambhaji*, *Nagkeshar* and *Lust for Lalbaug*. He has received the Priyadarshini National Award, the Vikhe Patil Award and the Sahitya Akademi Award for *Zadazadati* and the Gadkari Award for *Mahanayak*. In 2020, he was awarded the prestigious Dr Indira Goswami (Mamoni Raisom Goswami) National Literature Award. *Panipat* has received thirty-eight awards since its publication in 1988 and was recently released as an English translation by Eka. *Nagkeshar* is being made into a television serial.

Vikrant Pande has published ten translations from Marathi into English, namely Ranjit Desai's *Raja Ravi Varma*, *Shivaji: The Great Maratha* (*Shriman Yogi*) and *Karna: The Great Warrior* (*Radheya*), N.S. Inamdar's *Rau: The Love Story of Bajirao-Mastani* and *Shahenshah: The Story of Aurangzeb,* Milind Bokil's *Shala*, V.P. Kale's *Karmachari* and Ratnakar Matkari's collection of horror short stories titled *Darkness*. His translation of Girish Kuber's *Tatayan* as *The Tatas: How a Family Built a Business and a Nation* bagged the Gaja Capital Best Business Book Award 2019. His most recent translation is Kaka Vidhate's *Duryodhan* which was released by Eka. Vikrant's forthcoming translations include Anita Padhye's biography of Goldie Anand (Manjul Prakashan). He is also working on a book capturing 200 years of the State Bank of India, being published by Westland.

Vikrant is a graduate of IIM Bangalore and after spending nearly twenty-five years in corporate sector is now a full-time writer and translator. He resides in Vadodara.

Sambhaji

VISHWAS PATIL

Translated from the Marathi by
VIKRANT PANDE

eka

eka

First published in Marathi as *Sambhaji* in 2006 by Mehta Publishing House

First published in English as *Sambhaji* in 2020 by Eka, an imprint of Westland Publications Private Limited, by an arrangement with Mehta Publishing House

Published in English in 2022 by Eka, an imprint of Westland Books, a division of Nasadiya Technologies Private Limited

No. 269/2B, First Floor, 'Irai Arul', Vimalraj Street, Nethaji Nagar, Allappakkam Main Road, Maduravoyal, Chennai 600095

ISBN: 9789395767316

10 9 8 7 6 5 4 3

This is a work of fiction. Names, characters, organisations, places, events and incidents are either products of the author's imagination or used fictitiously.

Typeset by Jojy Philip, New Delhi 110015

Printed at Gopsons Papers Pvt. Ltd

ONE

The Unknown Danger

1

It was past midnight but Godavari was wide awake. She could hear the cool wind as it ruffled the leaves of the trees in the nearby wood, and the constant drumming of the peepal seeds falling on the roof of the house. Even the cows seemed unable to sleep tonight; she could hear them move about restlessly in the cowshed.

Godu tossed and turned in her bed. She wore the green bangles of a new bride. It had only been a month since she was married. The house was silent except for the rhythmic snoring of her mother-in-law who slept in the next room. Godu's husband had not come in yet.

After a while, Godu got up and stepped outside her room to peep into the garden. A mashaal, stuck on a pillar, burnt brightly as Trayamabakrao, Godu's father-in-law, and her husband Niwasrao, sat engrossed in a serious discussion. There were three other strangers; men Godu had not seen before. Trayambakrao, after all, was a Deshpande who managed the affairs of twelve villages.

'Looks like my father-in-law is trying to sort out some petty misunderstanding,' Godu concluded, trying to convince herself that the nocturnal assembly in the garden was of no importance.

Yet she could not dismiss the feeling of unease that came over her tonight. What kind of politics people indulge in, she wondered. Her village was near Mahad and her uncle, Annaji Datto Prabhunikar, was one of the Ashta Pradhan, the prestigious council of ministers in Chhattrapati Shivaji's court. Godu had visited her uncle many times as a child and had been to Pachad and Raigad often. She had grown up listening to military campaigns being planned and to tales of victorious battles. The sun, the moon and Shivaji—Godu believed they would live forever!

She remembered an event from her childhood. She was visiting some relatives with her family when they heard the tragic news of Tanaji Malsure's death. He had fallen in battle while trying to save the Kondana fort. The fort had been recaptured but the lion was dead! Shivaji had named the fortress Sinhagad in memory of Tanaji.

'Tanaji is dead! The palanquin carrying his body is coming this way. Shivaji Maharaj himself is one of the palanquin bearers!' One of her cousins, a boy, came rushing in excitedly. All the boys wanted to pay their last respects to Tanaji. In a moment,they started running across the woods to see the procession. Soon, they heard someone following them. Turning around, they saw it was eight-year-old Godu!

Godu recalled that evening with vivid clarity. She could barely look at the crestfallen face of Shivaji Maharaj, the way he walked beside the palanquin with drooping shoulders. He had lost his most precious lieutenant. Men from villages on the route were joining the procession in droves. Soon, it was a caravan of more than two thousand people. It was a sight Godu would never forget. Nor could she ever forget the way her heart ached seeing the Chattrapati's face. He was devastated!

It was very late but Godu was still restless, her nerves on edge. She got up once more to look at the assembly in the garden. They were huddled together around a fire—their voices softer now, taking on a tone of conspiracy. Godu was suddenly alert. She listened intently.

Trayambakrao said, suddenly laughing out aloud, 'That's it! Just another day to go! Tomorrow is Holi … the festival will provide the spark we need to end the Bhosale might. Forty of our daredevils are out there, spread all over. As soon as Shivaji reaches the square to celebrate Holi, our men will fire the cannons at the Tiger gate. In the garb of playing with colours, we would have finished Shivaji off!'

'Are you sure everything is going according to plan?' Niwasrao asked nervously.

'I have had discussions with Khan sahab at Bahadurgad. Twelve of his men in disguise are already at the fort. The moment the cannons are fired, signalling the end of Shivaji, the Mughal troops hiding in the woods will stream in. The capture of Raigad will be a fitting snub to the so-called Maratha Empire!'

In the light of the fire, Godu could see the flame of vengeance burning in Tryambakrao's eyes. The men around him were mesmerised as they listened to his fiery words outline his confident plan.

Trayambakrao flung his shawl around his shoulders in a single movement and tied his hair with a flourish. He was already celebrating a victory which was yet to be his.

Godu's mouth went dry. She had heard every word her father-in-law had spoken and the message was loud and clear. Worried that her nervous breathing may be heard in the silence of the night, she pushed the edge of her pallu into her mouth and rushed towards the back door.

Soon, she was out in the open. A cool breeze blew, almost as if it was pushing her to run faster. Entering the stable, she was able to spot Pakhru in an instant, even among the seventy or eighty horses there. She was astride her favourite horse in a single smooth move. Spurring the beast, she raced across the woods towards Raigad.

Nothing was going to stop Godu tonight. The thorny bushes which brushed her limbs, the low branches which she ducked as she galloped through the woods—nothing!

'Come on, dear!' She spurred Pakhru, eager not to lose time.

She reached Pachad just before dawn. Now the silhouette of the Konkan Diva mountain was clearly outlined against the paling sky. The peaks were slowly becoming visible. Sunrise was still sometime away. Pachad was soon left behind as Godu continued her ride. Soon, in the faint pre-dawn light, she could see the main entrance of the Raigad fort.

'Did you hear the neighing of the horses?' Niwasrao asked, frowning, not long after Godu had left. He had heard some noise from the direction of the stables.

Suddenly everyone was alert. Yes, they too had heard. Trayambakrao's men rushed to the stable and found the door open. Pakhru was missing. It was obvious! Godu had bolted with Pakhru.

'I know that bitch is Shivaji's devotee. I am sure she has overheard our plans and rushed to Raigad!' Trayambakrao screamed.

There was no time to lose. Soon, the men were astride their horses and galloping towards Raigad. The only way to prevent disaster was to find a way to overtake Godu.

The horses were soon foaming at their mouths as their riders spurred them relentlessly.

2

Now that the fort's entrance was in sight, Godu breathed a little easy. Riding up to the great doors, she stopped the horse. Both she and Pakhru were sweating, exhausted from the long and frantic ride. Jumping down, Godu rushed towards the gate, shouting.

'Open the door! Open the door, please! There is a conspiracy!'

Her shrill voice cut through the cold morning air. Two guards peered over the ramparts above and saw a young girl running towards the gate. Her face was scratched and bleeding, and her crumpled saree told of a long journey on horseback. She screamed once more, at the top of her voice, 'Dada, please open the door. I have to meet Maharaj right away! It's urgent. Please!'

'Who are you? Don't you know the rules?'

'But, dada …'

'The fortkeeper will come at seven. Only then can the doors be opened. Not before, do you get it?'

The guard's voice carried a steely edge. Who the hell was this wisp of a girl demanding that the doors of Raigad fort be opened? And that too to meet Maharaj!

'It would be too late by then! Maharaj's life is in danger! Please, I beg of you. Let me in!'

The guards laughed. All her screams and supplications fell on deaf ears. After a while they started mocking her. They were used to such raving madwomen, wandering about like ghosts in the early hours of the day, they said jokingly.

Godu really was raving mad by now. There was no way she was going to let the guards decide! She had to find a way to get the news to Maharaj. Realising that she was wasting her time there, she moved away quietly from the gate. A plan had formed in her mind.

In her childhood she had heard of a daring woman who had once climbed down the walls of the fort. It so happened that the fort had closed its doors for the evening. The woman, a milk-seller, was trapped inside as she was not allowed to leave the fort once the doors were closed. That was the rule. But she had to find a way out to breastfeed her hungry child, who she knew would be crying in her hut in the village below. She managed to climb down the steep walls, reaching the base of the fort, and had become a legend thereafter.

Godu was now desperately searching for a way to climb up. There had to be one! Soon she noticed holes made at regular intervals in the rock to allow the rainwater to flow out. It was enough for her! Soon, she was climbing up the steep rock face. Her face, arms, and legs were bruised.

Her saree was half-torn. But she did not care. All she wanted was to meet Maharaj!

The sky was brightening now, the darkness slowly receding. Preparations for the festival were to begin at dawn. The trumpets and horns were ready. The elephants had been decked for the occasion, and people had begun to gather on the ramparts clad in their finest clothes. A few guards, with swords at their waists and spears in their hands, stood outside Maharaj's room.

Suddenly they saw a dishevelled young woman rushing towards them. She fell at their feet and pleaded,

'I need to meet Maharaj! Please, take me to Maharaj!'

She was insistent. The guards were at their wits' end. Where had she come from? Who was she?

'Why do you want to meet Maharaj?'

At that moment, they heard the sound of hooves behind them. A handsome man astride a horse looked at Godu curiously. She stared at the finely sculpted face, framed by long hair that flowed down to his shoulders. His nose was aquiline, the eyes dark and deeply penetrating. A faint beard and a thick moustache enhanced his manly persona. Was he the Yuvraj? She was mesmerised.

The guards ran up to him, saluting,

'Shambhu Raje! Sambhaji Raje!'

Sambhaji was followed by Jotyaji Kesarkar, Kavi Kalash and Jagderao. Along with them rode a man of the Mahar caste, called Rayappa. He did not wear the kind of turban which Sambhaji and the others sported, but had tied a cloth around his head. Although he was dressed like an ordinary farmer, his thick whiskers and his tall, dark and solidly built body added a distinct personality to his looks. His horse drew up beside Sambhaji and Kavi Kalash's.

Yuvraj would normally be in a jovial mood on the day of Holi but he seemed jaded today. It was apparent that he had not slept the previous night. The truth of the matter was that he had had a premonition of sorts and now his alert eyes looked around, trying to find the source of his restlessness.

Sambhaji pulled the reins of his horse when he heard Godu shouting at the guards, 'Mahraj's life is in danger; why don't you listen to me? I want to meet him.'

The moment Godu recognised Yuvraj, she turned to him and cried, 'Yuvraj … Yuvraj … our Maharaj is in trouble. His life is in danger …'

Sambhaji exchanged glances with Jotyaji and Rayappa. Then he said in a low voice,

'Let us not make a fuss here. Get the woman to come with us. We will talk to her in private.'

Sambhaji turned his horse in the direction of his quarters. His men followed, escorting Godu.

Once he was seated in his chamber, Sambhaji allowed Godu to narrate what she had heard the previous night—the details of the plot her father-in-law and his men had hatched. He believed that she was telling the truth. Sambhaji said, turning to Kavi,

'Now do you believe me, Kaviraj, when I say I had a strong premonition that something untoward was to happen?'

'I believe you. But we have checked all the main points on the fort. There is nothing to worry about.'

'You cannot be sure of that, Kaviraj. Abasaheb believes in being safe and alert all the times. Ensure that the father-son duo are apprehended. Send your men to their village. I want them arrested today.'

'As you command, Rajan,' the men said and walked backwards a few steps before exiting the room. At that moment Yesubai walked in.

Godu had been standing at the edge of the room, just inside the door. She was shivering with excitement and fear. Sambhaji looked at her and said to Yesubai, 'Give her some nice clothes to wear. I feel she has averted a disaster today. But her life could be in danger. I put her in your care.'

3

It was a bright and sunny morning. There was festivity in the air of Raigad. The crowds were already flocking to Shivaji Maharaj's palace. Amidst the celebrations, Trayambakrao and Niwasrao entered the fort, looking rather terrified. They knew that were Godu to reach before them and talk to Maharaj, they would not escape the death penalty. And that meant being thrown over the cliff. The very thought shook them to the core.

Trayambakrao asked a guard standing near the entrance, 'Did you see a young woman, newly married, wearing a saffron-coloured saree with a yellow blouse?' He spoke in whispers lest someone else hear them.

'Yes, I did see a woman of that description. Shambhu Raje took her to his quarters.'

That meant Godu had probably spoken to Yuvraj! Trayambakrao smiled. It was a golden opportunity to cast aspersions on the character of the young bride. And it would be easy to smear Yuvraj's name by alleging that it was he who had mesmerised and lured her to the fort. He was a known womaniser. Or so people believed.

All Trayambakrao wanted now was to escape death. He was willing to go any lengths to avoid that.

They rushed towards Sambhaji's quarters. But by the time they reached his door, their confidence had vanished. It was akin to entering a lion's den. Would they be able to stand before him and accuse him of making off with their new bride? No! It was better to speak to Maharaj. He was likelier to fall for such rumours.

They headed to Maharaj's palace instead. The crowds outside were swelling by the minute. Maharaj was expected to emerge and visit the Jagdeeshwar temple for a darshan any moment now. Trayambakrao set his plan in motion.

He started shouting, 'My daughter-in-law! She has been kidnapped by Yuvraj!'

'My wife! Where shall I go now?' Niwasrao followed suit.

Both father and son were shouting at the top of their voices. Niwasrao wailed loudly for added effect.

The people around them could not believe what they were hearing. Here were two men alleging that Yuvraj Sambhaji, the heir to Shivaji's throne, had actually kidnapped someone's wife! And these men had the guts to shout these accusations in front of Maharaj's palace? It was unbelievable!

Seeing the crowd's reaction, the father-son duo increased their pitch. 'Do you realise,' they said to no one in particular, 'that this is happening in the very court of justice? Where should poor people like us go then? What faith would we have in those who rule? Do the men in power have the right to do anything with us mere mortals?'

'Hey you!' A guard shouted. 'Be warned, you are inviting death. Don't you think twice before making such allegations?'

'And what proof do you have?' Someone else butted in.

'You want proof? Go to Yuvraj's quarters and see for yourself. You will find my wife has been caged there!'

'What exactly happened?' Another man asked, curious.

'Let me tell you,' Niwasrao said, stepping forward. 'A few days back Yuvraj had gone for shikaar near our village when he spotted my wife at the edge of the lake. He coveted her as soon as he set eyes on her. And as we feared, he sent his men to our house the next day and they literally dragged her to Raigad.'

'What are we poor souls supposed to do?' Trayambakrao wailed.

Suddenly the crowds parted. A palanquin had arrived. As they waited to see who it was,the palanquin was lowered to the ground and Prahlad Niraji, one of the Ashta Pradhan, stepped out. It did not take more than a few seconds for his keen ears to ascertain the situation. Niraji wondered why Yuvraj had chosen the pious day of Holi to carry out such a vile act. How would Maharaj react?

Niraji hurriedly entered the palace and stepped into Maharaj's private quarters. For once he even forgot to salute his Maharaj, so eager was he to tell what he had heard. By then Kazi Mullah, one of the judges in Shivaji's court, had arrived too. The Wadkar father and son were called in. Trayambakrao was not one to waste such an opportunity. He fell forward, and banging his head on Shivaji's feet, started sobbing.

'Maharaj, we are doomed! How do we live if the Yuvraj himself behaves in such a manner? How is this different from the Mughals who forcefully take any young and good-looking woman who catches their eye into their harems?'

'Khamosh!' Shivaji's voice rang across the room. 'Trayambakrao, please reign in your tongue. Be careful of what you are alleging.'

Shivaji's face was stern. He was dressed for the occasion,and ready to celebrate Holi with his men. Little had he imagined that the stain of such an allegation would soil his festive attire even before the celebrations began.

Shambhu Raje's stepmothers, Soyrabai and Putalabai, had arrived from Pachad especially to celebrate the festival. Putalabai loved Sambhaji dearly. Soyrabai was about to leave for the pooja with Shivaji Maharaj when Trayambakrao and Niwasrao entered the private chamber. She was dressed in an exquisitely embroidered saree. A beautiful necklace of pearls, a gold cummerbund, and a lovely shawl draped around her shoulders completed her attire. Shivaji had plans to present her with a special diamond which he had got from a jeweller at Poladpur.

As Yuvraj's character was being assassinated, she smiled contemptuously. But Trayambakrao's words had left Shivaji and Putalabai downcast.

A few months back, Raigad was rife with rumours linking Yuvraj with Annaji Datto's daughter Hansa. It had troubled Shivaji no end. Why did Shambhu behave so? Shivaji, who had the courage to face enemies as formidable as Aurangzeb, was forced to bend his head in shame today. He was desperately trying to rein in his emotions. Was Shambhu at fault? Or was he being accused falsely?

However he had no choice but to take action as would be deemed fit. He could not afford to be seen as being biased towards anyone. He said, turning towards Trayambakrao,

'Listen! Let the celebrations get over. We will then go over the matter. Rest assured that the guilty, whosoever they may be, will be punished.'

Shivaji hesitated before leaving the room. After a thought, he conferred with Kazi Mullahsahab for a while. He was a trusted aide, someone Shivaji had absolute faith in. Kazi Mullah was reputed to be a fair and incorruptible judge amongst the Marathas. Shivaji, having shared his thoughts, walked out of his quarters to join the crowds who had been waiting for him so eagerly.

Putalabai, glancing in the direction of Sambhaji's quarters, could barely hold back her tears. She was clearly worried.

4

Never before on the day of Holi in Raigad had one felt stained even before the colours were thrown. People everywhere gossiped. 'How did Yuvraj dare to do such a thing? In broad daylight, he had the temerity to pick up a married woman, throw her on his horse and bring her here!'

'Well, nothing surprising about it. It is an age-old tradition for Maharajas, isn't it? To pick up whomsoever they fancy and despoil her.'

The celebrations subsided as the day drew to a close. As the sun was setting in the western sky, Shivaji sat in his chamber, his face faintly creased with anxiety. Despite his agitation, he maintained a calm demeanour. After deliberating for a while, Maharaj said to one of the guards in attendance, 'Ask Shambhu Raje to present himself immediately.'

Trayambakrao and Niwasrao sat in a corner of the room. Their drama continued. The way they wept and made themselves look like meek victims was truly worthy of applause. Anyone would have believed them! Now they turned to see Sambhaji entering.

He walked in with firm but slow steps, touching the emerald necklace he wore. How handsome he looked, with his fair complexion, broad forehead, arched eyebrows, and lively, shining eyes! Anyone present would have been impressed seeing the two most powerful men in the Maratha Empire in that room. Shivaji and his son Sambhaji clearly stood apart from the rest in their attire, bearing and personality. It was the meeting of the moon and the sun, a poet would have surmised.

But the air was fraught with tension. Yuvraj, looking at his father, was taken aback seeing the mixture of agony and anger in his eyes. Sambhaji's close confidantes, Rayappa and Jotyaji Kesarkar were no less distraught. They had never expected Sambhaji to be charged with such an allegation. In a few moments Yesubai entered, followed by a young woman clad in a simple yet elegant saree. The father-son duo was now clearly nervous. They had not anticipated that Godu would be there. Shivaji himself was surprised. He had not expected Yesubai to accompany Sambhaji. As for her companion, Shivaji surmised that she was the lady in question, the one the Wadkars claimed his son had abducted.

Shivaji asked, 'Yesubai, what brings you here?'

Yesubai hesitated for a moment, taking some time to frame an answer. Mistaking her silence for guilt, Shivaji thundered,

'Are you unaware that Yuvraj has managed to keep you in the dark about his doings? Please bear in mind—Shambhu's crime cannot go unpunished. A father may turn a blind eye but a king cannot allow his affection to come in the way.'

The room reverberated with the sound of Shivaji's deep and firm voice.

Yesubai was tongue-tied. Sambhaji looked at the carpet, insulted by the way his father had spoken. Their reactions encouraged Trayambakrao. He stood up and said,

'Maharaj, I want my daughter-in-law back.'

'Maharaj, my wife! Please give her back to me!' Niwasrao pitched in for added effect.

Shivaji threw an angry glance at Sambhaji and erupted,

'What a pity! What a tragedy! If a common man feels that his wife or daughter or daughter-in-law is not safe, then we need to question the very purpose of our existence. What are we here for?'

Sambhaji and Yesubai were speechless, unable to summon the words to counter Maharaj. Shivaji's words echoed in the silence of the chamber. Godu could not bear it anymore. She felt suffocated by the truth that remained unspoken. Rushing towards Shivaji, she fell at his feet and cried,

'Maharaj! Let me speak! This is all a conspiracy.'

Before Trayambakrao and Niwasrao could react, she continued,

'Maharaj, my father-in-law and my husband—they are not as innocent as they pretend to be. I swear on the name of Bhawani Mata, Maharaj. These two had planned to kill you today. The plot was to assassinate you while you were on your way to the temple!'

'You mean they planned to attack me? That too, here at Raigad?'

Shivaji smiled incredulousy at the thought. Even the guards standing next to Maharaj smiled. No one could bring themselves to believe what Godu had just said. Trayambakrao, encouraged by Shivaji's response, said,

'Maharaj, do you see the influence Yuvraj has had on her? For the rich and the powerful, all this is play, but poor people like us have to bear the consequences of their games, Maharaj.'

Shivaji did not doubt Sambhaji's courage or his capabilities but certain snippets of gossip and rumour had found their way to his ears, indicating a blot on his son's character. Several of his ministers and confidantes had hinted at Sambhaji's penchant for good-looking women. They had, in direct or indirect ways, suggested that Yuvraj was something of a philanderer.

Just then, a little commotion outside the door attracted the attention of the guards. Before they could bar his way, Annaji Datto entered. He was about sixty-five years of age and there was a solemn weight to his personality, despite his simple attire and the way he had casually thrown his shawl around his shoulders

He said, bending low in mujra, 'I beg your pardon, Maharaj, for coming in unannounced and without permission.'

He hesitated for a moment as he looked at Sambhaji. The fact that they did not like each other was evident. Wiping his forehead he said, 'Raje, Trayambakrao is a close relative of mine. And Godavari is my niece.'

Looking at Godu, Annaji could barely restrain his tears. The memory of his only daughter Hansa was too painful to bear. She had been the darling of his household and the apple of his eye. Annaji could not have imagined life without his daughter. Hansa had been married for barely a month or so when, on her way home for a brief stay, she had visited the royal household. What happened there was unknown but she had returned hurt and unhappy. After a day or so, Hansa's body was found in a well outside Pachad. It was a tragedy which Annaji had not been able to reconcile with.

Her death spawned a myriad of rumours. Some said she had been raped while a few believed she had suffered some form of mental torture which had led to her suicide. Most were pointing fingers at Shambhu Raje. Annaji firmly believed that Yuvraj was responsible for Hansa's death. It had been two years since Hansa's death but seeing Godu had reawakened the memory, bringing tears in its wake.

With Annaji's entry, the tense atmosphere in Shivaji's chamber tautened almost to breaking point. Even the judge Prahlad Niraji, a man of equanimity, was taken aback at his sudden arrival. As for Trayambakrao, he continued his drama. Removing his turban, he placed it at Shivaji's feet. 'Maharaj, please allow this poor man to take his daughter-in-law back.'

Annaji, encouraged by Trayambakrao's words, said, 'Maharaj, it was you who had ordered that the daughter-in-law of the Subedar of Kalyan was to be treated with grace and dignity after the Mughal Subedar and the caravan with his treasure had been captured. I have seen such great days. Anyway, what's the point in speaking of the past now ...'

He deliberately left his sentence hanging.

Shivaji looked at Yesubai. He was surprised to see that she was unaffected by Annaji's words. On the contrary, she seemed ready to counter them.

Yesubai said, 'Annaji, it is not right to accuse someone without an iota of proof. And speaking of dignity—Yuvraj cares as much for a woman's dignity as anyone else.'

It was apparent that Annaji was chastised by her words, but Shivaji interrupted. 'Yesubai, you might be blind to your husband's flaws, but as a father I know my son well.'

Surprisingly, despite being the topic of discussion, Sambhaji had remained silent until then. He did not want to argue with his father in public, and he was aware of the political intrigue and gossip-mongering which was aimed at creating a gap between him and Maharaj. But now he could not stay quiet anymore and erupted,

'Abasaheb, I feel sad that I am being labelled a criminal when I have done nothing wrong. I urge you to look into the matter first. If you find me guilty, I will accept whatever punishment you deem fit. You will be surprised to learn that there was indeed a plan to fire the cannons while others were bursting crackers. Your life was in danger, Abasaheb. That is why Godu, without caring for her own safety, rushed all the way to Raigad to inform you. But now she is being made to look like a fool and I am being accused of having kidnapped her.'

Annaji was not one to keep quiet. He said, 'Shambhu Raje, one cannot go by hearsay or assumptions. We need proof.'

At that moment Mullah Haider, a close confidante of Maharaj, entered. He said, saluting quickly,

'Maharaj, as you had instructed, I have carried out an inspection of the ammunition and gunpowder at the Lion Gate. It was certainly not meant for the fireworks. It was for firing the cannons.'

All present in the room, with the exception of Trayambakrao, Niwasrao and Godu, were stunned. The fact that such a thing had happened in Raigad, the very heart of the kingdom, the capital of Hindavi Swaraj that was Shivaji's dream of a land ruled by its own, was disturbing at the very least. Mullah Haider further described how the guards had accosted five or six suspicious-looking men who were seen loitering around the gate. When the guards gave a chase, the miscreants had managed to run towards Bhawani Point and jump over the wall into the bushes below. The search for them was still on, Mullah Haider said.

Within a few minutes, Kanhojirao entered and said, 'Maharaj, the bodies of four of the men who had jumped have been found. From the way they were dressed, they look like Pathans. No one has seen them before.'

Shivaji's face relaxed now. He looked at Godu, his expression clearly showing gratitude. He was now convinced that there had indeed been a conspiracy to kill him.

He turned to Sambhaji and said, 'If this was so important, I wonder why you did not inform me before rushing towards the Lion Gate.'

'It was my duty to first ensure that the cannons were safe, Maharaj. It was a question of your life,' Sambhaji said.

Shivaji now turned his gaze on the Wadkars. They were clearly rattled, and knew their game was up. But they waited with bated breath to hear what Maharaj would say. Annaji too realised that Godu had spoken the truth. All eyes were now on Shivaji.

He said, 'Annaji, this is a serious matter. It needs to be investigated thoroughly. Meanwhile, arrest these two and throw them into the temporary prison.'

Before the father and son could react, the guards had already pointed their spears at them. There was no escape for them now.

Annaji turned to Godu and said, putting his hand on her shoulder, 'Dear, you have been through a terrible ordeal. Come, let us go to your aunt's place.'

Godu brushed his hand aside, saying, 'I don't want to go anywhere. I am tired of all my relatives. Enough of it!'

Shivaji was disturbed by Godu's response. He was indebted to her; she had risked her life to save his. He would, on any other day, have taken his necklace off his breast and gifted it to her. But today was different. Although the Wadkars were clearly at fault, he did not want to offend Annaji. He was one of the Ashta Pradhan, his key council of ministers, and it would not do to insult him publicly.

But what should he do with Godu? Shivaji was confused. She had clearly refused Annaji's invitation. Finally, he said,

'Godu is not a child. Let her decide for herself.'

Godu too was confused. Where would she go? She stood rooted to her spot, not knowing what she should say. She looked at Sambhaji once and then turned towards Yesubai, who stood with a grace, poise and dignity that reminded Godu of the butter lamp burning steadily in the temple. Rushing towards her, she hugged her affectionately and said, 'Ranisaheb, take me into your fold! I am willing to work as your slave, do whatever task you wish. Only, please give me shelter!'

For a moment, Yesubai did not know how to react. A little while ago, everyone had labelled her husband as the one who had kidnapped her. And now the same woman was embracing her, pleading with her. Yesubai gently caressed Godu's face, saying, 'As you say, Godu. Till we find a place for you, you can stay at my servants' quarters.'

Yesubai gestured to one of the guards to take Godu to the queen's quarters. Annaji was expecting Maharaj to react, but to his surprise, Shivaji did not say anything. He was already deep in conversation with Mullah Haider, instructing him to get to the heart of the conspiracy and uncover the truth. Realising that Shivaji was not in a mood to discuss the matter with him, Annaji walked away in a huff.

5

Only Sambhaji, Yesubai and Maharaj himself now remained in Shivaji's private chambers. Shivaji looked at Sambhaji who could sense the hurt in his father's eyes. He said, 'Please pardon me, Abasaheb. I have given you a lot of trouble. But I wish you would believe that I was in no way connected with this incident.'

'Shambhu, you are the Yuvraj of the Hindavi Swaraj. And you are now nineteen years of age. I wish you to behave responsibly, as befits the position you hold.'

'Abasaheb, how is it fair to treat someone as a criminal when he has not committed any crime? But leave all that aside for the moment! I am more worried that the security at Raigad is so lax.'

'What do you mean?'

'How come the main door of the fort can be opened at any time of the night, especially when Maharaj is at Raigad?'

Shivaji was amused at his allegation. 'What are you saying, son? Once the doors closed, they are not opened till the next morning. Not even a worm can enter.'

'If that be the case, how are Annaji and his kin accusing my men of having left the fort and kidnapped the girl in the night? How could they have come in once the doors had been closed?'

Shivaji threw a surprised glance at Sambhaji. He realised something was amiss. Then Sambhaji said, 'Maharaj, it is my fate, unfortunately, that you barely hear me. And on the other hand, the doors of Raigad are opened for people to come in and go at their will.'

Shivaji's heart, pierced by these words, grew fonder towards his son. He knew Sambhaji was hurt.

He said, putting a loving hand on his shoulder, 'Don't take it to heart, my son. I will investigate the matter.'

'Maharaj, I wish you understood that everyone is conspiring to ensure you hate me … that you don't trust me and my words.'

Shivaji asked Sambhaji to sit next to him while he continued to caress his shoulder. 'I will look into the matter, Shambhu. But I want you to understand that my ministers have worked with me for the last forty years, toiling day and night. They have sacrificed themselves to the cause of the

Swaraj, and I urge you to show them some respect. You are the Yuvraj and it is not becoming of you to throw these allegations at them. You need to change your attitude, else …'

'Else, what?' Sambhaji did not utter the words but his raised eyebrows conveyed the question.

'I will have to find a way to live without you, Yuvraj.'

Sambhaji had not expected such a response from his father. He felt literally uprooted, as a small tree would be swept away by a great flood. Tears gathered in his eyes. He said, 'Abasaheb, the very thought of being sent away is intolerable. I can bear the pain of being trampled by an elephant, but I cannot even imagine being separated from you.'

Sambhaji remembered his grandmother's words. Jijabai used to say, 'Shambhu bal, please stay in Shivba's shadows.' It was like a mantra that he had taken to heart. But things had changed now. Shivaji Raje, whom the world loved, and who cared for his Swaraj, had no time for his own son. Sambhaji's voice quivered with emotion as he said, 'Abasaheb, I have one fault for sure.'

'And what is that?' Shivaji asked, unable to read his son's heart.

'You may be able to survive without me, but it would be impossible for Sambhaji to live without the loving protection of Shivaji Raje. I suppose that is my only fault.'

In his heart, Shivaji knew that he was being unnecessarily harsh. Sambhaji had never seen his mother. Jijabai, who had raised him, too had died a few years ago. As for Shivaji himself, Sambhaji had been the apple of his eye till his coronation.

As a young prince he had shown his administrative skills while managing the Jagir of Kolar in Karnatak. It was a testament to his diplomatic abilities that the emissaries of the French, the Portuguese and the English would first meet Sambhaji before presenting themselves in Shivaji's court. Seeing his intelligence and charm, these envoys had often commented that he was already a step ahead of his father and that he would be the next Shivaji.

That very son was today, somehow, estranged from him. Shivaji knew that something needed to be done to bridge the gap. Lost in thought, he did not realise that Sambhaji and Yesubai had quietly left the room and were walking away. When he got up to hug his son affectionately, all he could hear were their receding footsteps.

Shivaji sat down with a deep sigh.

6

Rayappa was at his post, guarding the main entrance of the fort, when sometime in the late afternoon, a heavily decorated palanquin stopped at the doors. It was accompanied by Bhaskar Thakur and two firangi soldiers. The Subedar waved his hand, asking Rayappa to allow them to proceed. But Rayappa stood in the way and asked, 'Who are you? Who do you want to meet?'

'Let them go, Rayappa! They are Ramji Thakur's men, here to meet Annaji Pant.' It was evident that the Subedar had been expecting the party.

Rayappa was a little confused as he had not been given any notice of their arrival. 'Guests of Ramji Thakur, the emissary from Goa? Should they not meet Raje first?'

'So what if they want to meet Annaji?'

'But there are no orders to let them pass, Subedar.'

'Rayappa, why are you being so adamant? In any case, Maharaj is not in Raigad!'

'In that case, should they not meet Yuvraj?'

Rayappa was a seasoned guard and a man who had grown up in the wild. He could sense danger intuitively. He wondered why the Portuguese emissary's guests would want to meet Annaji Datto, the treasurer and chief revenue officer, instead of Raje; and that too without prior intimation to anyone. He directed the guests to meet Yuvraj.

Sambhaji greeted the guests and asked in a harsh tone,

'Tell me the truth. What are you carrying in this box?'

The clerk accompanying the palanquin blurted out, 'There are two pearl necklaces. They have been sent by Ramji Thakur from Goa.'

'Who are they for?'

'For Annaji Pant.'

'A gift?'

'Not exactly … it is …' The clerk was stammering. 'It so happened that when our emissary had met Shivaji on behalf of the Portuguese Viceroy, he had presented Raje with lavish gifts. Annaji Pant and Moropant Peshwa later wrote to our emissary and threatened him with dire consequences if he did not give anything to them. That is why we were carrying this for him.'

Sambhaji said grimly, 'I will accept this on their behalf.' He turned to Kavi Kalash, the poet, who stood next to him. Kavi Kalash was a Brahmin from Kannauj, a friend and an advisor to Yuvraj. He was a tall, well-built man in his thirties with shoulder-length hair, an impeccably groomed moustache and fair complexion. Sambhaji said to him, 'Please give them a receipt and ask them to return to Goa immediately.'

'Rajan, what do you plan to do now?'

'Well, let the person who commissioned the gift ask for it and I will give the pearls to him,' Sambhaji said, laughing loudly.

That evening Annaji's younger brother, Somaji Datto, came to meet Sambhaji.

'Yuvraj, a couple of months ago, my brother had sent a messenger to Goa with some money to get a few pearl necklaces made. I believe the same have been delivered to you.'

'Oh, is that so? A man had indeed come from Goa, but he said he was the emissary's clerk and not the jeweller. Since when have jewellers started using the emissary's office to deliver goods, I wonder?'

Somaji wiped his forehead with his angavastram nervously. He knew his bluff had been called.

Sambhaji thundered, 'Let Annaji Kaka know that I am aware of the whole affair! Shivaji Raje never takes a single gift for himself, as you well know, but deposits them in the royal treasury. While your brother complained to the Goan ambassador, demanding a personal favour. What a disgrace! Everything here belongs to the Hindavi Swaraj. It is no one's personal property, not even the king's! I would like to know where Annaji planned to deposit this gift? Not in the royal treasury, for sure!'

Somaji Datto had no answer. He took his leave with a hasty salute without daring to look at Sambhaji. After that, no one from Annaji's household came asking for the jewels.

A few days later, Shivaji Raje invited his ministers to the palace for a meal. Those in attendance were Annaji, Moropant, Rahuji Somnath, Balaji Avaji and Shambhu Raje.

Balaji Avaji was a close confidante, almost a friend, of Shivaji. Moropant was an old man now, bent a little at the waist. But his energy and enthusiasm were the same as before. Shivaji had often depended on Moropant and Annaji for the success of some of his most ambitious and dangerous missions. But they had their own misgivings about each other.

Annaji was generally a man of few words, but on this occasion he was unable to hold himself back.

'Maharaj, the firangi jewellers are experts in their trade. That is why I had sent some money in advance to get a few pearl necklaces made.'

'I heard about it,' Shivaji Raje said, nodding his head.

'But Shambhu Raje was so enamoured of the necklaces that he decided to keep them for himself,' Annaji said.

Sambhaji, undeterred by the taunt, said, 'Well, you have got the receipt. The necklaces have been deposited in the royal treasury. You may verify this for yourself.'

That shut Annaji up. But Sambhaji's blood boiled. Unwilling to tolerate the insults anymore, he said, looking at his father, 'Abasaheb, it is my firm belief that our ministers should not deal directly with the emissaries and other agents of the firangis or any other kingdom. It has certain repercussions.'

The council of ministers was taken aback. They had not expected Sambhaji to accuse them in such a direct manner. Shivaji's lack of comment made them even more restless.

The next day Annaji invited the other ministers to his quarters, ostensibly for a game of chess. Naturally, the topic of discussion was the fearless way in which Sambhaji had spoken against the ministers. The Ashta Pradhan were not a little offended by his audacious criticism of their methods of working. What upset them even more was the fact that their freedom would now be curtailed. Sambhaji had shown himself to be unusually alert in matters of administration which till date had been left entirely to the jurisdiction of the ministers concerned.

7

It was a pleasant evening, and Sambhaji and Yesubai sat on a swing in the pretty garden adjoining the small wooded area behind their haveli. It had been many days since they had enjoyed such solitude together.

Yesubai said softly, 'May I say something?'

She continued, without waiting for his reply, 'A king's word is final. He has the ultimate power of decision when it comes to matters of state. But does that mean a king can take every beautiful girl he fancies and put her in his zenankhana? Would that be right?'

'What are you blabbering? We are not Mughals! This happens in the realm of the Sultans. not in Shivaji's kingdom.'

'Are you sure?' Yesubai asked smiling. Her eyes conveyed different emotions though, those of anger and hurt.

'Yesubai, what do you want to say? Don't speak in riddles,' Sambhaji frowned.

'Annaji Datto Prabhunikar is a pillar of Abasaheb's kingdom. What did you achieve by torturing his beautiful and innocent daughter Hansa?'

'Yesu, do you realise what you are alleging?'

'I am only repeating what people are saying in the streets.'

Sambhaji was stunned by Yesubai's words. She had the same power in her voice as Jijabai. Despite his impulsive, short-tempered nature, he decided not to react, and remained silent.

Yesubai was a year or so younger than Sambhaji but she had already earned a place in the royal household through her genuine affection and dedication to the people around her. While Soyrabai and the other queens kept to their quarters in the palace, Yesu had managed to carve a niche for herself.

Sambhaji thought of the events that had brought Yesubai to Raigad, many years ago. Shringarpur was a small kingdom, nestled in the Konkan mountains near Sangameshwar. Suryarao Surve, the local ruler, considered himself the sovereign lord of the territory and ruled in a manner befitting an emperor. He had under his control the ports of Dabhol and Sangameshwar, and had managed to capture and loot more than a hundred ships, intercepting the vessels en route to Mecca, Madina and other distant destinations. Suryarao Surve was Yesubai's maternal grandfather. Her father, Pilajirao Shirke, was an important sardar in Suryarao's court.

When Shivaji announced his desire to form a Hindavi Swaraj, many like Suryarao openly opposed it. They believed they were superior to the Marathas and yet they did not hesitate to stoop low and kowtow to the Mughals. Suryarao hated Shivaji and, forming an alliance with the Mores who controlled the Jawli area, he had often fought against Shivaji's forces. When Siddi Johar had surrounded Panhala, it was Suryarao who came forward to provide local support to the Mughal sardar.

Shivaji had confronted Suryarao during his campaign in Talkonkan, and announced his willingness to pardon his mistakes. He wanted to give the ruler of Shringarpur one last chance to join the Swaraj. But Suryarao had responded with a snub that was beyond endurance. Shivaji consequently marched on Shringarpur himself.

Suryarao had no option but to flee in order to save his skin. Even as she witnessed her grandfather run for his life, seven-year-old Yesu had stared in awe at Shivaji's magnificent personality. Her father Pilajirao, however, did not run away. He had long been a silent admirer of Shivaji and received the Maratha leader as befit his stature.

While the loot captured from the fort was being counted, Shivaji remarked, 'I have seen many a treasury, but the way the silver and gold vessels have been kept, especially those used for worship, shows the hand of a very diligent lady.'

'Maharaj, you are right! It is my daughter Yesu who is responsible for the upkeep.'

Maharaj turned to see the young girl looking at him. She had been peeping from behind a door all the while, watching the proceedings.

Shivaji had put a loving hand on her head and blessed her. Then he said, looking at Pilajirao, 'I am so incensed at your father-in-law that I feel like burning down half of Shringarpur but your daughter has mesmerised me. Please keep all the wealth for yourself. All I ask in return is the most precious thing from your palace—your daughter as my daughter-in-law!'

Overwhelmed, Pilajirao fell at Shivaji's feet and wept in gratitude. 'Maharaj, I am a traitor. We don't deserve to be treated with such affection. You will find many girls who are far more capable and beautiful than my Yesu.'

'You are mistaken, Pilajirao. I can recognise the value of a jewel when I see one.'

Many events unfolded in a few days. Sambhaji and Yesu were engaged to be married, and Raje's daughter Nanibai, also known as Rajkunwar, was married to Pilaji's son Ganoji.

Yesu soon moved to Raigad. The two young newly-weds would sit with the pandits and learn their lessons together. They were more like friends than husband and wife. Their relationship was thus cemented long before they realised that they had a conjugal relationship as well.

Ever since she had come to Raigad, Yesubai had struggled to manage the two strong and often opposing personalities in her life. On one hand was her father-in-law, who was loved and respected everywhere as a wise and cautious people's king. On the other hand her husband, despite his capabilities, was more famous for his blunt and often politically incorrect way of confronting the most influential and esteemed ministers at Raje's durbar.

Yesubai's direct accusation regarding Hansa had stunned Sambhaji. He said, recovering after a while, 'Yesu, if I was enamoured of a girl, I would have married her. There is no dearth of space here to build another mahal.'

'But Yuvraj, she is Annaji Pant's daughter. She was, I mean …'

'People enjoy gossiping and I cannot stop them.'

'Well, I have been told by Rayappa and Jotyaji that you are even careful not to bathe in the open while on a campaign. I believe women have only to see your handsome face and manly figure once to fall hopelessly in love with you. The girls who come to the rivers to fill their pots swoon and fall down … I believe it has happened a few times.'

'It seems you are quite aware of many things. Where is the need for me to clarify?'

Yesu smiled. Sambhaji continued, 'If I wanted to take pleasure in amorous activities, I would find a place far away from Raigad. What can I do if some Hansa fell in love with me? How am I responsible for it? You know only too well that she literally chased me. I had known her since she was a child. But she was a grown-up girl when she came here, on the way to Pachad for a visit, the first after her marriage. She was exceptionally attractive, no doubt. But from the moment I realised that she had grown into a young woman, I stayed away from her. I avoided meeting her. Annaji Pant was after all like my father's elder brother.'

'So you were aware of what was likely to happen?'

'Annaji Pant himself was aware that Hansa was enamoured of me. It was the reason he had got her married in the first place.'

Sambhaji paused before he continued, 'I was in my private chamber, engrossed in writing a letter, when Hansa entered. The guards had been given strict instructions not to allow anyone in but she fooled them by saying I had invited her. She came in and embraced me. Then she started showering kisses on my face. I pushed her away and slapped her hard, shouting, "Have you gone mad? What is wrong with you? You are Pant's daughter and a married woman at that." She laughed hysterically and said, trying to hold my hand, "I am here to dedicate myself to you. Me, my soul, my body … they are all yours." I pulled my hand back and said, "You idiot! You are not in your senses."

'She refused to go away; I slapped her hard once but her madness had reached its peak. Laughing, she said, "Raje, love makes a person go blind. I am like the moth attracted to a lamp, one that does not care if it gets burnt."

'I asked her what she wanted and she said, "My husband is no one compared to you. Raje, I am longing for you. I need you. Just once, please take me in your arms."

'I realised she was not going to give up without a fight. I tried putting some sense in her head but she was beyond reason. Then she put her arms around my waist. I pushed her away again, with such force that she hit her head and began bleeding. She was hurt, but the most terrible wound was in her eyes. As she stepped out of my quarters, I could see that she was sobbing. She said, turning towards me at the door, "Raje, I will wait for you for three days. If you don't come to me, I swear, you will see my dead body."

'Hansa rushed out. At that moment, her mother happened to see her leave my quarters. Naturally, her hair, her saree, her entire appearance was dishevelled. After that, even if I had tried to tell my side of the story, no one would have believed it. They all assumed that I had tried to force myself on her. Yet even I had never imagined that she would kill herself. After four days, her corpse was found in a well in Pachad. Everyone believed that I had committed the unpardonable crime of violating a married woman, that I was responsible for her death. I am innocent, but I have had to suffer taunts and accusations in silence ever since. That's the truth, Yesu!'

The same night, after dinner, Sambhaji asked Yesu, 'So what have you decided to do about Godu?'

'Where can the poor girl go?' Yesu said, 'She cannot go back to her father's place or to her in-laws'. Let her stay at the servants' quarters here.'

8

Godavari had never seen such a magnificent palace. Her husband's house, where she had stayed after her marriage, was large but only modest in comparison to the palace here in Raigad with its great chandeliers, the waist-high lamps and vast chambers. It was almost heaven, she thought.

They had found room for her at the servants' quarters behind Yesubai's palace but she had become Yesu's shadow, never leaving her side, whether in the kitchen, the pooja room, or the garden. Godu had become indispensible to Yesubai too. She was a bundle of energy, always ready for any chore with her radiant smile. Soon, she was the talk of the servants' quarters, for most of them felt jealous of the way she had become the Yuvrani's confidante.

Shivaji had fortified the wall which Godu had climbed to get into the fort. Raigad was now completely secure, invulnerable to enemy incursions. This meant that Godu had become the talk of the town too. And not all of it was in her praise.

'That Godu seems to be a daredevil! Look at the way her poor husband and father-in-law, who came to lodge a complaint, have been thrown into the jail, while she enjoys the luxuries of Yuvraj's palace. First, she mesmerised Yuvraj, and now she has managed to become Yesubai's confidante. Wonder how she manages all this!' Such were the comments heard on the streets.

Rayappa, overhearing the gossip, found it hard to tolerate. Everywhere in Raigad, people were openly talking of Yuvraj and his household. He made his way to Sambhaji's quarters, determined to do something about it, but knew that he could not bluntly state what he had heard on the streets. Yuvraj approached most matters in a direct and no-nonsense manner but he had a quick temper, sensitive to such aspersions cast on his conduct.

Stepping into Sambhaji's chamber, Rayappa said, finally finding his voice, 'Yuvraj, people out there are gossiping unnecessarily, and I don't like it!'

'What about?'

'About Godu, and the way she has mesmerised you and Yesubai Ranisarkar.'

Sambhaji did not react immediately. But while having his meal that afternoon, he asked his wife again, 'What do you think we should do about Godu?'

'Let her stay here,' Yesubai said, smiling. 'Such a sweet girl, and she has really become my right hand ...'

'Yesu, you are large-hearted and innocent. But what about all the talk on the streets? They don't care whether they are talking about a poor man or a prince. When it comes to gossip, they don't discriminate ...'

Yesubai looked into Sambhaji's eyes and said, 'But you know the truth, don't you? She risked her life and her family ties to come here and save

Maharaj's life. We cannot punish her for that.' She continued in a low voice, 'Only the other day, Maharaj saheb was enquiring about her and whether she was being taken good care of.'

A few days later, a secret message sent by the Wadkar duo in prison to Aurangzeb's 'milk brother', Bahadur Khan Kolkatash was intercepted. Aurangzeb and Kolkatash had been fed by the same wet nurse. It said: '*As discussed before please see that we are released quickly. We need your help.*' It had finally come to light that the Wadkar father and son were, in fact, traitors. They were speedily despatched to the ill-famed dungeons in the Lingana fort. Godu's innocence, and the fact that she had risked everything to save Maharaj's life, was now proven beyond a doubt.

Yesubai said, 'Godu, we owe a lot to your selfless courage. You did not care for your life or your reputation when you acted as you did, only for the future of our Swaraj. You are truly a hero.'

Godu was overwhelmed. 'Vahinisaheb, Shivaji Raje is our God! We would do anything for him.'

Yesubai looked at Sambhaji and said, 'Yuvraj, had her in-laws not accused you of having kidnapped her, Shivaji Maharaj would have taken out a procession in her honour today.'

The days passed rapidly.

Ananji Datto was rattled by the fact that his close relatives had turned out to be traitors. To save face, he once again requested Godu to stay with his family but she refused.

Sambhaji's sister Ranubai, who came visiting from Wai, was impressed with the way Godu managed her chores. But before she left, she said to her sister-in-law in a confidential tone,

'Yesu, no doubt this Godu is really efficient in her work. But she is so young and good-looking! Whatever you say, she is a married woman, and the fact that she stays with you has already got tongues wagging. You need to do something about it.'

Gradually, Yesubai began to realise that she needed to make plans for Godu's future. She asked her one day, 'Godu, have you thought about your future life?'

'What can I say, Vahinisaheb? My husband turned out to be a traitor. What future can I possibly think of?'

'Why not get married again?'

'Married? Well, I can think of only one person ...'

'And who is that?'

Godu glanced at Sambhaji Raje before staring into the deep blue sky. She let out a heavy sigh.

Sambhaji asked gently, 'Godu, are you in love with someone?'

Godu nodded her head absently but refused to answer the question.

A few days later, she came to Yesubai and said, 'Ranisaheb, can I take some time to visit my aunt who lives in the valley beyond the fort? She is old and all alone. I thought I could spend a few days with her.'

'Why not? It's a good idea!'

Sambhaji instructed the headman of Sarvat, the village Godu was to visit, 'She is to be provided with everything she requires. Your expenses will be reimbursed from the state treasury.'

The next day, Godu was packed and ready to leave. Only before stepping out of the palace did she look at Sambhaji once, a brief glance, and then, nodding her head absently, she set out on her journey.

9

Balaji Avaji, one of Shivaji's secretaries, was waiting for Maharaj to arrive when Sambhaji walked in. He said, looking at Yuvraj, 'I am told that you are making really life difficult for the Ashta Pradhan these days. Is that so?'

'Why do you ask, Balaji Kaka? Have I erred in any way? Whatever I do or object to, is for the benefit of Swaraj,' Sambhaji said, his tone a little defensive.

'No, I didn't mean that … but …' Balaji hesitated. 'Yuvraj, sometimes your matter-of-fact tone is taken as accusatory. It does not suit a young man of your age. Rulers must learn not to confront their ministers unnecessarily. One should tread carefully, that is all.'

Balaji was a man of ripe years and a seasoned minister of Shivaji's court. Sambhaji, careful not to offend him, merely nodded. Balaji said, holding the young man's hand affectionately in his, 'Yuvraj, I didn't mean to hurt you. The blood spilt on mother earth in a battle is washed away by the rains but the repercussions of what the clerks write on paper in ink can be felt for generations. I just want you to be careful.'

TWO

Emotional Discord

1

For the first time since his coronation, Shivaji was planning a military campaign in Karnatak. Maharaj and Sambhaji were set to leave with an army of nearly forty thousand foot-soldiers and twenty thousand cavalry.

A campaign of this size required preparations on a massive scale. Eighteen factories at the base of the fort were producing weapons and other equipment. Shivaji was overseeing the war effort himself and would often ask Sambhaji to update him on various matters.

Shivaji's questions were relentless. To keep up with them, Sambhaji would get up at the crack of dawn and hurry to the base. Rayappa, the loyal soldier, would be there even before Sambhaji arrived. The evenings would turn into nights as Sambhaji pored over letters carrying military intelligence from strategic Maratha posts across Shivaji's kingdom. Yesubai would often wait until the small hours for her husband to return.

Much to his satisfaction, Shivaji could finally see in Sambhaji a diligent and responsible Yuvraj who was equal to the challenges heaped on his shoulders every day. Balaji Pant helped Sambhaji at each step, ensuring that he did not slip up or fall behind in his duties. Sambhaji's friends too were excited about the upcoming campaign and gratified by the way Maharaj had entrusted various important tasks to their beloved Yuvraj.

It had been out of sheer curiosity that Jotyaji Kesarkar had first come to meet Sambhaji. A single meeting had been enough to convert his curiosity to loyalty. In no time, he had become one of Sambhaji's closest and most cherished friends. Once, on a hunt, Sambhaji had shot at a wild boar but the arrow missed its target. Rayappa, a very young man then, had charged at the boar, putting himself between the Yuvraj and mortal danger. Despite being grievously wounded, he held on to the beast and killed it with his bare hands. Since then, he too had been more a friend than a servitor to the Yuvraj, following him like a shadow and guarding him with his life. Among all his companions and advisors, only Kavi Kalash was older than Sambhaji by about ten years.

Outside his inner circle, Sambhaji already had a large and devoted following among the youth of the kingdom. His mere presence next to

Shivaji Maharaj during the coronation had trebled his popularity, and the young men around Raigad flocked to him afterwards. Impressed by Sambhaji's brave and affable nature, many had volunteered to join the Maratha army, increasing its strength.

From this enthusiastic crowd of new recruits, Sambhaji had gradually carved an elite force of his own. They followed the Yuvraj on his inspection tours and he supervised their training himself. Sambhaji would often challenge his men to run up to the top of Konkan Diva fort from the base. It was a sheer climb of nearly four thousand feet that tested the endurance as well as the courage of the youth who attempted it.

Sambhaji would spend his leisure hours with his men too, sometimes fishing in the clear waters of Kalganga or enjoying a lazy swim in Banganga. On these occasions, Yuvraj was often seen showing his skills with the gauntlet sword or dancing with the lezim cymbals, much to the entertainment of the poor folk of these parts who gathered to watch. For them, it was a matter of pride and delight to have the crown prince of the Swaraj visit their villages and attend their humble ceremonies.

Some of Shivaji's senior courtiers and ministers were critical of Sambhaji's friendly nature. They had complained to the Maharaj that it was not becoming of Yuvraj to roam around so freely and meet people from all castes, especially the lower ones.

Shivaji, for his part, was happy that his son was mixing with the ryots and not behaving like a typical Yuvraj. It was evidence that he had the ability to gather men around him. He said, when he met Sambhaji at his chambers one day, 'Yuvraj, I am happy to know that you are roaming the kingdom in search of gems. The Swaraj has need of such loyal and dedicated men. Carry on with your good work.' Sambhaji was thrilled to receive his father's endorsement. So, despite their best efforts, his father's advisors had not managed to corrupt his mind against him yet!

2

Annaji Datto was one of the high-ranking sardars of Shivaji's court who resented Sambhaji's popularity and his proximity to the common people. As head of the royal treasury, he disapproved of the way men from all backgrounds were able to approach the Yuvraj with their troubles and get away with a waiver on their taxes.

'If the people start meeting the Yuvraj in person to get respite from paying their dues, how are we to run the Empire?' He complained to Moropant Peshwa. 'Why is the Yuvraj interfering in the matters of finance?'

Morpopant laughed, much to the chagrin of Annaji. He clarified, seeing Annaji raise a questioning eyebrow, 'Annaji, Yuvraj is responsible for the ryots. It is quite right on his part to listen to the people, his subjects, isn't it? After all, he is the crown prince of the Swaraj.'

'I knew you would say so. You are always justifying his actions.'

'I do not support Yuvraj blindly. Just take the case of the men who had come from Vishalgad the other day, asking for permission to dam a stream nearby so that their fields could be watered properly. You might object to the expense but it was a reasonable request. Look Annaji, this is bound to happen when new blood takes over. You must learn to accept such changes and move on.'

Annaji was not convinced. He said in a taunting manner, 'Today he has diverted a stream. Tomorrow he may talk of building dams on the rivers. What then?'

'Well, I am told Shambhu Raje is planning to discuss quite a few matters of importance while on campaign in the Karnatak.'

'I am not surprised,' Annaji scoffed. 'He is influenced in all this new thinking by the poet Kalash. I don't see much difference between a poet and a buffalo, frankly speaking.'

Annaji recalled Moropant asking Shivaji Raje only a few days ago, 'Raje, is Yuvraj coming with you on the campaign?'

Shivaji had answered, smiling, 'Of course! He is a young man now and there is no point in making him sit here in Raigad when he can learn so much on the battlefield.'

Balaji Avaji had added, 'After all, Yuvraj is of age. It is the right time for him to learn the art of warfare, not to mention what goes into the planning of such a large campaign.'

Annaji did not like Balaji trying to score a point, but he had held his tongue. It seemed inevitable now that Raje would take Sambhaji with him. It was something Annaji had wanted to prevent at all cost. That Sambhaji would outshine all others on the field of battle and impress Maharaj with his bravery and skill was a foregone conclusion. Annaji was disturbed by these thoughts. He stepped out of his office, and almost of their own accord, his feet turned towards Soyrabai's palace.

Annaji had shifted his residence to Raigad a few months earlier. He was ageing and it was difficult for him to ride up to the fort everyday. The death of Hansa, his daughter, was the final straw. Pachad did not feel like home anymore.

Annaji's formidable personality was enhanced by his tall, heavy build and dusky complexion. His smart turban and dangling earrings made heads turn as he strode confidently into the administrative office at Raigad each day. As a young man, he had impressed Maharaj with his bravery, acumen and dedication to the Swaraj, and he had risen quickly to become one of the Ashta Pradhan. He was the principal correspondent for the Maratha Empire as well as the minister in charge of the treasury. He ran his office like a tight ship. The clerks, fearing his temper, worked hard to meet his meticulous standards.

Annaji had rendered many years of faithful service to the Swaraj. At Pratapgad, when Shivaji had gone to meet Afzal Khan, he had left Jijabai and the young Sambhaji in Annaji's care. While Maharaj was away in Agra for negotiations with Aurangzeb, a large part of the administrative responsibilities of the kingdom were managed by Annaji. He was at the forefront of the battles which captured the Panhala and Rangana forts. It was no wonder that he occupied pride of place amongst Shivaji's sardars.

However, Sambhaji was a young, dynamic and blunt man, unschooled as yet in the art of diplomacy, particularly when it came to dealing with the senior ministers of the Swaraj. And when he started looking into matters of revenue collection, raising questions about the management of the treasury in his straightforward manner, Annaji began to sit up and take notice, not a little alarmed.

For instance, it was customary for the emissaries of the English, Dutch and Portuguese companies, when they came to pay their respects to Shivaji, to bring expensive gifts for Annaji, Moropant and Rahuji Somnath. In fact, at times, Annaji even sent his men to collect his 'dues'. On several occasions, Sambhaji had pointed out discrepancies between the revenue collected in the Konkan region and the amount deposited in the treasury, much to the embarrassment of Annaji.

Evidently, as the kingdom grew, so did the expectations and aspirations of the men running it. It was not that Shivaji was unaware of the fact that some of his courtiers enriched themselves at the expense of the Swaraj.

However he would ignore minor transgressions, keeping in mind the dedication and loyalty of the men concerned, and the role they had played in building the Maratha Empire over the years.

For Sambhaji, on the other hand, it was a question of ethics and integrity, and his blood would boil when he came across such deliberate lapses. Consequently, he had accused Annaji of stealing from the royal treasury—publicly, and in no uncertain terms.

Unfortunately, these events had led to Annaji distancing himself from Yuvraj. Moreover, the tragic death of Hansa had added fuel to fire. Annaji squarely blamed Shambhu Raje for his daughter's suicide, and it was apparent that his dislike had grown to implacable hatred.

3

Soyrabai welcomed Annaji into her private chambers. Each recognised the other as an ally; their objective was the same although their paths were rather different. Soyrabai had often said, while talking to Annaji, 'I wish Rajaram was the eldest son, not Sambhaji. It would have been perfect, don't you think?'

'Maharani saheb, age is not the only factor to be considered while choosing a successor to the throne. There are instances where even a pregnant queen has been made to sit on the throne and rule in the name of the would-be prince. Rajaram saheb is no longer a child; he is nearly seven now.'

Annaji's fertile mind imagined the coronation of Rajaram and a smile appeared on his face.

Soyrabai said, 'Well, it is good that both father and son are going on a long campaign. We can at least breathe easy in Raigad for a few months.'

'Not at all, Maharani saheb. You are totally mistaken!' Annaji's bitterness was evident in his tone. 'Pardon my saying so, Maharani saheb, but you live in a dreamworld. This campaign would be the perfect opportunity for Sambhaji to show his valour and add more feathers to his cap. He will showcase his capabilities as the rightful successor to Maharaj!'

Soyrabai, disturbed by Annaji's assessment of the situation, fanned herself with her pallu and wiped the beads of sweat from her forehead. 'This does not portend well, Annaji.'

'But tell me, Maharani saheb,' Annaji challenged her, 'Am I responsible for this? My hands are tied. But maybe *you* could have done something about it ...' He deliberately left the statement hanging for effect.

Soyrabai instantly remembered the day Maharaj had asked her to look into the circumstances that had led to Hansa's death. Yuvaraj was openly accused of having molested Hansa, triggering her suicide. It was no easy task, this investigation. On one hand was Annaji, Hansa's father, third in the hierarchy of the Ashta Pradhan, close confidante of Shivaji, and a loyal sardar of the Swaraj. On the other was Shivaji's eldest son, Yuvraj himself.

Annaji said, reminding Soyrabai of the task she had been entrusted with, 'You were given a God-sent opportunity. Had you concluded that Yuvraj was responsible for Hansa's death, the matter would have been settled once and for all.'

But Soyrabai had been loyal to the task assigned to her by Maharaj. She had taken great care to speak to all the witnesses, even inspecting the well where Hansa had ended her life. All the evidence she had gathered suggested that Hansa had gone to meet Sambhaji of her own volition.

Soyrabai recalled vividly what Sambhaji said when she had questioned him about Hansa's death, 'Maasaheb, my palace is surrounded by temples on all sides. There is a tulsi plant right in the courtyard. There is an image of Ganesh on every door. Can you imagine me engaging in such a vile act—molesting a young woman, at my private quarters? Would I commit such a heinous crime in the presence of divinity?'

'Shambhu Raje, tell me whether you are guilty or not,' she had said to him.

'Not to mention the fact that the guards and servants, and several of my men, are always around! Maasaheb, I would be a fool if I were to force myself on a woman in my palace. And lest you forget: I am a lion's cub!'

Soyrabai had presented her findings to Maharaj. He had let out a deep sigh of relief when they confirmed Sambhaji's innocence. However, he had asked Soyrabai, 'Ranisaheb, had he been found guilty, how would you have reacted?'

Soyrabai had said, without a moment's hesitation, 'I would have been saddened by the fact that a father so revered by the masses has such a lecherous son. But I would have asked Maharaj to give him the death penalty and set a new standard for justice and good governance in the Swaraj.'

Raje smiled. Soyrabai asked, 'Why did you assign this task to me when you have esteemed judges like Kazi Haidar in your court, a man known for his judicial acumen?'

Raje answered with a smile, 'It was a very delicate matter, Ranisaheb. And I was sure you would not allow your emotions to influence your judgement. I was confident that you would conduct an impartial investigation.'

Recalling Shivaji's words, Soyrabai now said, looking at Annaji, 'I am convinced that Hansa was in love with Yuvraj, and when he did not entertain her overtures, she decided to end her life. That is the truth, Annaji.'

'Whatever you may say, Maharani saheb, I cannot forget the fact that I lost my only daughter because of Sambhaji, that he and only he is responsible for her death. He is a curse on our family. I can never forgive him.'

'What do you think I could have done, Pant?'

'Ranisaheb, had you thought of the coronation of Rajaram, I am sure the scales of justice could have been induced to tilt the other way.'

'Why did you not advise me to do so then?'

'Knowing your ambitious nature, I was sure that you would not waste such a golden chance to remove the thorn from your path. I never imagined you would do otherwise.'

'In any case, this is a rather fruitless discussion,' Annaji said, coming back to the issue at hand, 'Maharani saheb, it would be best if Yuvraj does not accompany Maharaj on the Karnatak campaign. You must find a way to prevent him from going.'

'But it is decided, Pant. Maharaj has made that clear to me,' Soyrabai said, with a sigh. 'Like day follows night, the Yuvraj too has to follow in the footsteps of his father: those were Raje's words.'

But Annaji was not one to give up so easily. He lowered his voice, his tone becoming conspiratorial, 'There is a way out!'

Soyrabai threw a surprised glance at him as he continued, 'You remember Maharaj had once spoken of breaking the empire up into two regions—Karnatak and Raigad? What you must do, Ranisaheb, is sow the seeds of partition in Raje's mind. Then, let Maharaj decide whether he wants to divide the Swaraj, or take Yuvraj with him. If we still don't manage to stop Yuvraj from going, be assured that he will return with the confidence to take over the entire Swaraj. And there will be no place left, not even a small hut, for you and Rajaram saheb to take shelter in.'

4

Soyrabai walked towards Shivaji Maharaj's chambers. There had been a time when Shambhu Raje was Soyrabai's favourite. After the death of Jijabai, it was she who had taken Shambhu under her care and given him all the tenderness and affection of a mother. But now with her own son growing up, and Shambhu Raje proving himself to be a capable young man eligible to succeed Shivaji on the throne, the threat her stepson posed to Rajaram's chances of ruling the Swaraj was becoming more and more evident to Soyrabai. Rajaram, on the other hand, was an innocent child who worshipped his elder brother and spent every minute he could in the company of Yuvraj.

Soyrabai watched worried as Sambhaji's prowess and popularity grew by the day. The very sight of him perturbed her these days, and her forehead would crease anxiously at the mere mention of him.

Shivaji was relaxing in his private chambers when Soyrabai entered and sat on the edge of his bed. After some small talk, she ventured, 'Swami, it is difficult to control a firebrand like Shambhu Raje when you are not around.'

Shivaji smiled and said, 'Oh, are you suggesting I take him with me on the campaign?'

Soyrabai was taken aback. She wondered if she had misspoken. 'Not at all! I didn't mean that. What I am trying to say is that he tends to rub people the wrong way. If misunderstandings were to erupt in your absence, it will be difficult to resolve them.'

Shivaji was silent for a while. Then he said, 'Tell me Ranisaheb, do you want me to take him with me or are you suggesting that he stay back?'

'Swami, the fact of the matter is that he does create a lot of headaches for all of us.'

Shivaji said, sighing sadly, 'I know. Even Annaji and Rahuji are not happy with him and they too have pleaded that he not be left behind at Raigad. They don't seem to see eye to eye with Shambhu.'

'The last thing I want is for Shambhu Raje and the ministers to start fighting amongst themselves. I have a suggestion …'

Seeing her hesitate, Shivaji said, 'Please speak freely.'

'You once spoke of dividing the kingdom in two halves?'

'Don't mention that, Ranisaheb,' Shivaji interrupted her, raising a hand. There was an edge to his voice as he continued, 'The very thought of breaking up the Hindavi Swaraj is not only painful but also ludicrous. It is not just an empire. It stands for the sacrifices of thousands of Maratha men, and the blessings of our elders, our gods and goddesses. How can I even think of splitting it into two parts?'

Soyrabai blurted out, 'Maharaj, lest you forget, you have two sons.'

'I am aware, Ranisaheb! Whosoever shows his mettle and his calibre would be chosen as the successor. It is as simple at that!'

'Maharaj, isn't that unfair? Is Shambhu Raje entitled to all the opportunities? Why don't you take Rajaram on your campaign instead? Let him also learn.'

'Do you realise how young he is?'

Soyrabai burst into tears. Shivaji did not know how to react.

She said, sobbing, 'Maharaj, either you divide the kingdom and hand over a part to Rajaram or don't take Shambhu Ṛaje to Karnatak. If you cannot make a choice, then the only option for me is to forsake water and food and fast unto death.'

Shivaji Raje managed to convince Soyrabai not to take such extreme steps. She left for her quarters after a while. A worried Shivaji sat alone in his chamber. The emotional drama which Soyrabai had just staged had left him feeling drained and slightly feverish. He summoned Balaji Chitnis to share his thoughts.

Chitnis heard him out and said, 'Maharaj, I would advise you not to give much credence to her threats. If you wish to take Shambhu Raje with you, don't think twice. Please go ahead as planned.'

Shivaji had a despondent look as he replied, 'One may spend an entire lifetime with a woman and yet not be able to read her mind. I am surprised and worried at the way Maharani saheb has put forth her demands today.'

'Maharaj!'

'Look at the timing, Chitnis. I am to leave for the campaign in a few days. I cannot delay my departure because of this domestic discord. This is a terrible dilemma. God knows what other difficult choices are in store for me!'

5

Yesubai hurried to her quarters when she was told that Shambhu Raje had returned earlier than expected. A weary Sambhaji was resting in his bed when Yesubai entered. He seemed dejected.

Yesu said softly, 'You know, Jijabai used to say, "The relationship between Shivba and Shambhu is a unique one. They do not need to talk to each other to communicate!"'

Sambhaji responded with a deep sigh but did not say anything. Yesubai put her hand on his shoulder and said, 'You must be tired. After all, the preparation for the Karnatak campaign involves a lot of work, and you leave in a few days, is that right?'

'You believe I should go?'

'Of course! After all, it's the first big campaign after the coronation, and a chance for you showcase your skills. Even as a young lad, you were with him in Agra when he planned the escape from Aurangzeb's prison. Now you are the successor to the throne of Hindavi Swaraj! Should you not work shoulder to shoulder with Maharaj ...?'

Shambhu stood up suddenly and said, stopping Yesubai mid-sentence, 'Enough! Don't build castles in the air, Yesu. I am told that Abasaheb has decided not to take me along with him.'

'I cannot believe it!' exclaimed Yesubai, dejected at Sambhaji's words.

Sambhaji did not elaborate. He paced the room like a wounded lion, hands knotted behind his back and lost in his thoughts. Knowing her husband was deeply hurt, Yesu did not pursue the matter. Sambhaji continued to pace up and down for two hours, until his legs began to hurt. The lamps had nearly burnt themselves out but sleep still eluded him.

Yesubai said, when Sambhaji finally sat down on the edge of the bed, 'I feel Maharaj saheb has taken the right decision.'

'How can you say that?'

'After all, someone responsible needs to stay behind and look after Raigad. Just think, the treasury has crores of hons in it. Does Maharaj's decision not make sense?'

'Well ... I don't think it is as simple as you make it out to be. But I don't want to discuss it right now. I have a splitting headache.'

Yesubai knew Sambhaji's dismissive manner concealed a distraught mind. As for Sambhaji, he was quite unable to control his emotions. Thoughts raced through his mind. He racked his brains, wondered why his father had decided not to take him. It was not that Sambhaji was unfamiliar with the territory. In fact, as a young boy, he had been given charge of Kolar and Chikkabelapur as a Jagirdar.

He remembered a conversation with his father about the southern provinces. Shivaji Maharaj had said, 'My father, Shahaji Maharaj, governed the Bengaluru province and he had played an important role in earning the city its pride of place. Later, my stepbrother Ekoji Raje made the mistake of shifting his headquarters to Tanjavur.'

'I am told the provinces of Tanjavur, Tiruchirappalli and Jinji are very fertile. Aren't they?'

'That is true, but the fact that he shifted his base to Tanjavur allowed the king of Mysore, Chikkadevaraja, to run riot. We have lost a lot of revenue from the provinces of Karnatak and other southern territories. We need to find a way to retrieve and secure them.'

Recalling these talks with Shivaji, Shambhu had been tremendously excited about the campaign in Karnatak until the new orders came. He was deeply hurt and disappointed to learn that he would not be a part of it.

Finally, Shambhu's tired body could no longer stay awake and he fell into a deep sleep. But Yesubai, still sitting on the edge of the cot, had a worried look on her face. Her forehead was creased with anxiety as she wondered what had made Maharaj change his mind.

6

Annaji Datto and Soyrabai, with their jealous intrigues, had managed to stab Sambhaji in the back. Petty politics had played a winning hand, and all Sambhaji could do was pace his room like a lion wounded in battle. Sambhaji's close confidantes, Kavi Kalash, Jotyaji Kesarkar, Krishnaji Kank and others, stayed close to Yuvraj, worried that Shivaji's decision not to take him on the campaign had affected him tremendously. As for Yesubai, she was trying her best to ensure Sambhaji did not develop any ill feeling for his father.

She said, trying to pacify him, 'What's so sacrosanct about this campaign? There will be many more. And it is not that he has ordered you to be imprisoned here in Raigad.'

'Yesu, the very air in Raigad has become poisonous with the kind of politics and backstabbing which is going on. I feel suffocated here.'

Sambhaji waited eagerly to hear from Balaji Avaji who was at that very moment conferring with Maharaj about the latest plans for the campaign. He was hoping that Balaji would be able to convince Maharaj to reverse his decision. It was late in the night when Balaji stepped into Sambhaji's quarters.

He said, without further ado, 'Maharaj has advised that till he returns from his campaign, Yuvraj should stay put at Shringarpur.'

Sambhaji turned sharply towards Balaji, tears gathering in his eyes. 'That means he does not even want me to stay at Raigad!'

Balaji and Yesubai hardly knew how to react. Sambhaji said, 'Balaji Kaka, it is an age-old tradition for the Yuvraj to manage the throne in the absence of the king, isn't it? I was hoping, when Maharaj spoke of my accompanying him on the campaign, to get a chance to spend some time with him and learn a few things. That is not to be. But now, I am being asked to leave Raigad! And the reins of the capital will be entrusted to the hands of a mere sardar like Rahuji Somnath who hates me. I wonder what kind of politics is going on and why Maharaj has fallen prey to it.'

He paused as if to collect himself and continued, 'I feel orphaned and impoverished, despite having a father like Maharaj saheb and a treasury worth crores of hons. I am being exiled to Shringarpur as if I were some kind of criminal!'

'Yuvraj, hasn't the Maharaj given you the sole responsibility of managing the South Konkan region?'

'And the Prabhavali province,' Yesubai added.

'Enough! All this is to save face, to make the world think that he has not treated me badly. Such small mercies do not change the reality, Yesu. Nor does it soothe my wounded feelings in the least.'

Sambhaji remembered the night he and his father had planned their escape from captivity in Agra. Shivaji Maharaj, worried about Sambhaji's safety, had said, to Hiroji. 'I may be able to ride all the way to the Deccan, but I am worried about my son. How do I leave Shambhu, the apple of my eye, my dearest, to fate?'

His father had sobbed at the very thought of leaving him behind. However Maharaj had no choice but to make the hard decision to leave for the Deccan on his own while his son took a different route. That had been the only way to secure the future of the Hindavi Swaraj.

Recalling those events brought fresh tears to Sambhaji's eyes. He said, 'I get goosebumps each time I think of that night. His warm hug, the tears in his eyes, his angst—I will never forget, for as long as I live.'

Yesubai said, smiling, 'When you have such a father, why would you ever feel dejected and lonely?'

'Yesu, I don't care if I am captured and killed by enemies. But it hurts when people you consider your own stab you in the back. Faced with a difficult choice, Maharaj left a seven-year-old son to fend for himself, back in Agra. Today, when I am eighteen and capable of assisting him in an important campaign, I am being asked to stay behind. And packed off to Shringarpur, because Soyrabai Matushree is worried that I will be a nuisance if I stay at Raigad. Their entire effort is to ensure I don't have a chair to sit on—forget the throne!'

He said, almost choking with emotion, 'What hurts me most is that Abasaheb, who trusts the lowly soldier guarding the gates of Raigad, is not willing to trust his own son. The very thought is killing me.'

7

Sambhaji entered Shivaji's chamber and said, bending low in mujra, 'Abasaheb, please bless me. As you have commanded, I am leaving for Shringarpur.'

For a moment, Shivaji Raje was taken aback. Then he said, placing his hands on his son's shoulders, 'What's the hurry, Shambhu? Wait for a day. I have to leave for Karnatak and we can travel upto Sangameshwar together.'

The next day, the departure of Shivaji Raje and Sambhaji was announced by the horns and trumpets. Once they reached Pachad at the base of Raigad, they turned to look up at the fort. A huge army of nearly twenty thousand cavalry and forty thousand foot-soldiers awaited the command from Shivaji Raje to move forward. It had been a long time since the Marathas had waged a campaign of this magnitude, and the men seemed restless, eager to march forward.

On such occasions, Jijabai would have accompanied them till Pachad to bless Raje before he set out on a new campaign. Her death, soon after the coronation, had deeply affected Raje. He directed his men towards her mausoleum to pay his respects. At a respectful distance stood Suryaji Malsure, Baji Sarjerao, Yesaji Kank, Sarfoji Gaekwad, Anandrao and many others sardars. They waited patiently as Shivaji spent a long time at the grave. He could feel his mother's presence there and he sorely missed her blessings.

Shivaji recalled the day they had left for Agra. The treaty of Purandar, signed with Mirza Jai Singh and Diler Khan, had forced them to make the trip to pay their respects to the Mughal emperor Aurangzeb. Before their departure, Shivaji had spent time training Sambhaji in the art of using the sword and the spear. He had also coached him on how to behave in the Mughal court and other matters of ettiquette.

When they were about to leave, Jijabai had asked, her voice choking with emotion, 'Shivba, is it necessary to take this young lad with you? Are you not being cruel?'

Shivaji had replied, 'Maasaheb, the treaty forces me to. I have no choice.'

He had stood watching Jijabai hug Sambhaji who refused to leave his grandmother's embrace. It was a poignant moment, but Shivaji had grown restless and said, 'Maasaheb, I have a duty to fulfil. Please let Sambhaji go now. Do you remember how you had blessed me when I set out to meet Afzal Khan? You knew the dangers that awaited me; yet you had given me your good wishes smilingly, urging me to kill that demon.'

Jijabai said, 'Raje, you will understand my emotions when you become a grandfather.'

'Maasaheb, I can understand your emotions. But an eaglet, if it has to soar high in the air, must learn to live with the dangers of flying. How else will it develop strong wings?'

Shivaji could hear Jijabai's voice ask him, as he sat near the grave, 'What happened to your eaglet, Shivba? Why are you leaving your brave and valorous son in Shringarpur instead of taking him with you?'

Shivaji's angst was palpable. He knew he was making a mistake, yet he felt helpless. He asked Sambhaji to ride with him for a while. At Sangameshwar, they parted ways after crossing the river Shastri. Yuvraj took the route for Shringarpur while Shivaji turned towards Karnatak.

Before departing, Sambhaji said, 'Abasaheb, you have just recovered from a long illness. I feel I should be by your side on this campaign. But you are not asking me to join you. I could have been of great service to you, yet you choose not to take my help.'

'Shambhu, please be patient. Things will turn out fine.'

'Abasaheb, it is difficult for me to accept the fact that you are going to war in the southern provinces, at your age, while I—capable in every way of leading our troops—must stay put in Shringarpur. But it seems I have no choice but to obey your command.'

Raje was acutely aware that Sambhaji's pride had been deeply hurt by his decision. He said, 'The Yuvraj has recourse if he feels some injustice has been done to him. But what if the King himself feels that he is being tried? Who does he reach out to?'

'Abasaheb, maybe the fault lies in my stars. But it appears that the pens of the clerks and the whispers of others are more capable of taking revenge than the swords of bravehearts which are left to rust.'

'Shambhu, you are still young. Let the matter rest!'

'Abasaheb, I was only eight years of age when I attended Aurangzeb's court with you. I was made a Mughal mansabdar before I turned ten. And now, when I am nearly twenty, I am labelled as an ignoramus and somebody who can easily be abandoned! How is that fair, Abasaheb?'

Shivaji could sense the helplessness Sambhaji was experiencing. Desperate to make amends before parting, he said, 'Shambhu, it was a deliberate decision not to take you along on this campaign. Please try to understand. If something were to happen to me, I need you to take charge. Don't you realise that?'

Sambhaji's laughter surprised Shivaji. He replied, before his father could react, 'The rest of the army and the treasury is at Raigad while I am being banished to Shringarpur. I wonder how I am to protect the kingdom.'

Shivaji held Sambhaji's hand in his and squeezed it gently, saying, 'Remember this, Shambhu; Raigad is not safe for you at present. For many reasons, I cannot allow you to remain there right now. I want to protect my son from danger. Please bear that in mind. You are dear to me.'

Sambhaji suddenly realised his father was suffering from the strain of being unable to speak his mind, and undergoing the same kind of torment as him.

Shivaji said, 'Shambhu, at Shringarpur you will have a lot of time to be with yourself. Use that time to make friends with the sons of the soil, the ryots, and others around you. Learn to understand people better. And remember—there are many amongst us, men with no ethics whatsoever, who, for the smallest of selfish gains, will not hesitate to destroy their king or endanger their kingdom.'

THREE

Shringarpur

1

Shringarpur was a bustling town nestled at the base of the great Sahyadri mountains. Once the capital of Suryarao Surve, it had since Shivaji's conquest been entrusted to the stewardship of Pilajirao Shirke, Sambhaji's father-in-law. Nearly twenty thousand people lived there. There were around sixty havelis in the town, big and small, belonging to the sardars who worked under Shirke.

Shivaji had built a spacious palace next to the residence of the Shirkes, where Sambhaji, Yesubai and Durgadevi, another of Sambhaji's wives, stayed. In front of the palace was a garden, and next to it was another haveli, occupied by Kavi Kalash, Yuvraj's friend and mentor.

Shringarpur had become famous as a Hindu shrine and many pandits, sadhus and others interested in the art of tantra had made it their home. In a cave high up in the mountains, en route to the Prachitgad fort, lived a tantric guru known as Shivayogi. Kavi Kalash and Sambhaji were frequent visitors, and they consulted him on various matters. Prachitgad was a new fort built by Shivaji which overlooked the territory of Shringarpur. Many tantriks and Brahmins had taken up residence at the fort and in the caves nearby.

Finding Sambhaji in low spirits one day, Yesubai said, 'I am quite confident that everything would be fine once my father-in-law returns from Karnatak.

'And till then?'

'Till then? Well, why not enjoy the beauty of Shringarpur? We have Kavi Kalash with us. You can spend time working on your poetry.'

Sambhaji was too despondent even to respond. Yesubai was trying her best to humour Sambhaji while somehow managing to keep her own emotions at bay. She had not forgotten the victorious glance which Soyrabai had thrown at her in Raigad just as she was about to get into the palanquin that would carry her to Shringarpur. But Yesubai had deliberately erased these insults from her memory, and devoted all her energy to lifting her husband's spirits. She was aware of his direct and simple nature—

compassionate at heart yet capable of taking tough decisions, wise but with a short temper that bristled at any kind of injustice.

Yesubai had learnt to deal with uncertainties and troubles since her childhood. She was barely six when she was married to Sambhaji. Sambhaji was a young lad of eight or nine then.

Having signed the treaty of Purandar, Shivaji had been forced to travel with Sambhaji to Agra and present himself in Aurangzeb's durbar. It had been months since their departure for the Mughal capital, much to the anxiety and consternation of Jijabai. She would spend all her time in prayer, and performed various abhisheks and poojas at the temple. Yesubai was a mute participant in all these activities. Sometimes, she would pray quietly at the grave of Saibai, Sambhaji's mother.

The air was heavy with gossip and rumours. It was becoming increasingly clear that Aurangzeb had played a dirty trick, and that the lives of Shivaji and Sambhaji were now in his hands. Would Shivaji be sent on a campaign to Kandahar, where death was inevitable? Had he been put under house arrest? There were no clear answers. The rumours continued to multiply, making Jijabai more and more anxious.

After many months had passed, one day, a group of mendicants called Gosavis arrived at the palace door, demanding to meet the queen mother. A guard came to Jijabai's chambers, saluted and said, 'Aajisaheb, one of the Gosavis is insisting on meeting you and says he will not leave till he has received your blessings.'

Jijabai nodded in acquiescence. Soon, a curly-haired, fair and handsome Gosavi entered and approached Jijabai to put his head reverently on her feet. He said, tears falling down his cheeks, 'Aausaheb!' It was Shivaji! Jijabai's joy knew no bounds and she embraced him, saying, 'Shivba!'

Shivaji had finally managed to find a way to escape from Agra. But where was Sambhaji? Jijabai looked behind her son but all she could see were the smiling mendicants that formed the rest of the party. The young lad was missing!

While all the trumpets, horns, drums and cannons of Raigad announced the return of Shivaji, the question on everyone's mind was about Sambhaji. Where was Yuvraj? What had happened to him? Yesubai looked at Shivaji, wild with anticipation, but kept quiet, waiting for Jijabai to ask the question.

'Shivba, why are you alone? Where is Shambhu Raje?'

Shivaji turned to face his mother and said hesitatingly, 'Maasaheb, let us talk of it in the evening. I will speak to you in private.'

Shivaji's hesitant and vague reply tortured Yesu. All kinds of thoughts and fears flashed through her mind in quick succession. Where was her husband? Was he safe?

On the third day after his arrival, Shivaji sat in his private quarters with Jijabai and his queens. He stretched his hands towards Yesu. 'Come, dear. Come and sit with me,' Raje lovingly asked her to sit on his lap. The little seven-year-old, wearing a traditional nine-yard saree, looked like a doll dressed up for a play. Raje caressed her forehead and then, in a sudden movement, wiped the sindoor off her forehead.

Everyone present gasped in surprise! No one spoke but the message was clear: Sambhaji would never come back. Jijabai burst out sobbing, 'Bal Raje!' In an instant, the palace was cloaked in sadness. Shivaji said, 'Yesu, it was an unfortunate accident. While we were running away from Agra, he fell from his horse in a jungle and succumbed to his injuries.'

Pilajirao and his family reached Raigad the next day. It was a tragedy which broke their heart—their young daughter, widowed, at the tender age of seven. Shivaji tried consoling them as best he could. The ryots came in droves to meet their beloved Shivaji but they would burst into tears the moment they heard of Sambhaji's fate. Soyrabai, not yet a mother, was heartbroken too. She had looked after Sambhaji since Saibai's death, and loved him dearly.

Shivaji prepared for Sambhaji's last rites. Messages of condolence reached Raigad from all over— from Jaipur in the north to Jinji in the south. Shivaji performed the rites, feeding hundreds of Brahmins and mendicants. As for Yesu, she had literally collapsed under the weight of her sorrow. She said to her mother, once the ceremonies were over, 'Maasaheb, I would like to commit sati. I want to join my husband. He was my friend, my playmate and my soulmate. What will I do without him?'

Yesu had no idea what sati meant. Surprisingly, her parents seemed to accept the decision—even to encourage it. Shivaji, on the other hand, was greatly disturbed.

He said, 'My dear, don't worry. Things will be fine.'

'How will things be fine when he is gone?' asked Yesu.

Shivaji struggled to find an answer. He simply folded his hands as he would when praying to Bhawani. The sight was heart-rending. Here was Shivaji pleading with Yesu! How was he to console the poor child? Yet somehow, he managed to convince her not to take the extreme step of committing sati.

The days passed by rapidly. Yesu would be overcome with grief at the mere sight of the clouds in the sky that matched the white saree which she now wore as a widow. She spent most of her time in the temple, praying.

One day, the cannons of Raigad roared, shattering the peace of the morning. It had been two months and eight days since Shivaji's return. Yesubai ran out of her quarters, fearing the worst. Was there an attack on Raigad? But the trumpets, horns and drums followed. It was a celebration!

A confused Yesubai stepped out on the street. Then she saw Soyrabai rushing towards her quarters, with a bowl of sugar in her hand. Beaming with joy, she hugged Yesubai and said, 'Our Shambhu Bal has returned. Our Bal Raje is safe!' The news was too much for Yesu to bear, and she collapsed on the floor.

Visaji Pant, Kashi Pant and Krishnaji Pant, the Trimal brothers, had risked their lives to get Sambhaji to Raigad all the way from Mathura. They had faced terrible dangers at each step. With them was Kavi Kalash, then a twenty-year-old youth.

Raje called for a special durbar in honour of the Trimal brothers, and bestowed upon them the title of Vishwasrao. They were given expensive gifts, including an elephant, a royal palanquin, and clothes befitting men of royal stature.

Visaji Pant said, accepting the gifts with humility, 'Raje, I am Moropant Peshwa's brother-in-law. It is our honour to serve under you for the cause of Swaraj.'

The Trimal brothers were then invited to partake of a special meal in Raje's company. They were overjoyed by the respect being accorded to them.

As the meal progressed, Raje asked Visaji, 'Pant, you must have faced a lot of problems en route. How did you manage to keep your disguise?'

'Raje, it was difficult. We had put a sacred thread on Yuvraj to make him look like a young Brahmin. With his long hair and his lovely eyes, childlike and innocent, he looked just like our nephew,' Visaji Pant smiled at the memory. 'But Maharaj, your escape from the clutches of the Badshah had created quite a furore. We were being questioned at all the check points and had to bribe several officials. Besides, Yuvraj, with his beautiful face, was attracting a lot of attention and curiosity. That was when we decided to dress him up like a girl. We put some jewellery on him and decorated his eyes with kohl. Travelling as our 'maid', he was much safer!'

Yesu, imagining her husband in the guise of a girl, could not contain her laughter, much to the amusement of the grown-ups present. Soon afterwards, the Trimal brothers took their leave. Kavi Kalash, who had become a close friend and confidante of Yuvraj, decided to stay back.

As soon as the brothers left, Raje's queens erupted. They had believed that Yuvraj was dead and participated in his last rites, grieving terribly. It had been revealed to them that Raje was aware of the truth all along. Yet he had chosen to go along with the charade. Soyrabai was so upset that she refused to speak. As for Jijabai, she turned her penetrating stare on Shivaji, which Raje did not dare to meet.

He said, finally finding his voice, 'I had no other choice, Aausaheb! I knew Aurangzeb was furious and would leave no stone unturned to find us. The news of Yuvraj's death was the only piece of misinformation likely to slacken the Mughals in their hunt.

'But you went ahead and performed his last rites!'

'Maasaheb, I am acutely aware that it was a cruel and heartless act, as far as you were concerned. But believe me … that was the only way to ensure Yuvraj's safe return. Had I not made that decision, we may have had to, God forbid, perform the ceremony in reality.'

The very thought made Jijabai shudder. She said, hugging Shambhu Raje, 'Shivba, don't make me go through such an ordeal ever again. When you indulge in such politics, it is I who must suffer the consequences!'

2

Shringarpur transformed itself in the rains. A dense fog would envelop the valley after a heavy downpour, covering everything in its wake. The river Shastri, emerging out of the mountains near the Prachitgad fort, tumbled down the steep slopes, dancing merrily to the tunes of the numerous waterfalls on its way. Never had the Sahyadris been more beautiful! Yuvraj was often mesmerised as he stood by the windows of his palace which faced the imposing fortress, watching the showers.

The monsoon months were indeed an ideal time for Kavi Kalash and Yuvraj to compose poems, but the soldier in Sambhaji was not going to be satisfied simply by penning verses on the beauty of the rains. He decided to set up five akharas where the youth of the region would be trained in the art of wrestling and body building. Soon, the akharas became a popular gathering place for young boys and girls.

Sambhaji learnt from one of the firangi sailors who had come from the port of Rajapur that the English troops were quite unlike the Maratha army. While the Marathas would spend entire months during the monsoon tending to their crops, and fight for the army during the months that remained, the English troops had full-time soldiers, ready for a campaign any time of the year. Sambhaji decided to set up a standing cavalry of two thousand mounted men and purchased the finest horses from Dabhol and Rajapur. His plan was to create a 'Shringarpuri cavalry' which would be known across the Maratha Empire.

Sambhaji deliberately chose men from the lower castes. The young recruits were proud to be a part of Yuvraj's cavalry and committed wholeheartedly to their rigorous training, which commenced soon enough in right earnest. The men would vie with each other, riding their mounts up the steep slopes of Prachitgad. It was a daunting task which challenged the toughest of them. But they were a determined lot and would race to reach the top, crossing deep ravines, muddy fields and dense woods. Curious villagers would gather in crowds to watch the training.

As expected, it was not long before Sambhaji received a note from Rahuji Somnath. It questioned Yuvraj's act of creating a new army in the absence of Shivaji Maharaj and without taking the permission from those in charge at Raigad.

Kavi Kalash replied, saying, 'Please be informed that Yuvraj deserves the title he was given when he sat with Maharaj at the coronation. He has powers equivalent to those of the Ashta Pradhan. The army he is setting up is for the benefit of the Swaraj. His actions and decisions are hardly out of place.'

Sambhaji, however, was hurt by the fact that even this well-meaning endeavour, to recruit the people of Shringarpur to the Maratha army and make them feel they were a part of the Swaraj, was being seen with a jaundiced eye. He said, feeling dejected, 'I am training cavalrymen and setting up akharas to teach people the art of wrestling. I am not opening zenankhanas. I wonder why they fail to understand such simple acts. In what way am I working against the Swaraj?'

During those days at Shringarpur, Sambhaji would often stand at the highest point of Prachitgad and look at the river Warna in the distance.

Beyond it was Panhalgad, and in the same line of vision although far beyond his ken, were Bijapur and the southern province of Karnatak. He would gaze wistfully at the horizon, sighing deeply and wondering where his father was at that moment, while he stood alone on the ramparts of the fort.

Like a calf waiting for its mother to return in the evening, like the lover waiting for her companion to arrive, or the devotee who climbs the steps to a temple to worship his God—a range of emotions would rush through Sambhaji's heart. He was desperate to meet his father. But he knew the wait would be long. He would go only when he was called for.

Yesubai was pregnant and the child was growing rapidly in her womb. Sambhaji had made up his mind to return to Raigad only after the child was born. He would pray at the Jagdeeshwar temple and then meet Maharaj.

3

The monsoon progressed steadily, changing the topography of Shringarpur. More than half the territory was covered with dense jungles while numerous waterfalls cascaded down the steep slopes of Prachitgad. The rice fields shone in the mild sunlight and wild flowers lit up the shades of the rainforest.

Kavi Kalash was the son of Muralidhar Shastri of Prayag. His real name was Umaji Pandit but by the time he was a youth of twenty, he had participated in various literary competitions and made a name for himself as a poet as well as a scholar of Sanskrit and Braj Bhasha. It was because he had reached the zenith, the 'kalash', of his poetic abilities at an early age that he was given the title of Kavi Kalash.

Muralidhar Shastri had attracted the wrath of the Mughal throne for having composed and sung paeans in praise of Shivaji. One day, when Kalash returned from his morning prayers, his father said, 'You need to leave immediately for Agra. I have received news that Shivaji Maharaj and his son Sambhaji have been summoned to Agra, and I fear that Aurangzeb may have some tricks up his sleeve. We cannot trust the Mughal Emperor to play straight … he might try to arrest Maharaj. I am too old to make the journey. But you need to leave right away.'

As Kalash took his leave, Shastri said, 'Remember, we owe a lot to the Bhosale family. Do whatever it takes to help them. The Hindus of this land look to Shivaji Maharaj as their saviour, and we cannot let him down in his hour of need.'

Kalash reached Agra and presented himself to Shivaji. Impressed with his mastery over Sanskrit, Maharaj asked him to tutor Sambhaji. Kalash and Shambhu were ten years apart in age but became instant friends. Sambhaji's love for poetry and languages made Kalash's job easy. Soon, the pair were inseparable.

On the eve of his escape from Agra, a tearful Shivaji had told Kalash, 'I am going away but I leave a part of myself behind. Take care of him!' He took off a diamond ring he was wearing and gave it to Kalash.

Kalash stayed on in Agra for a few days with Saxena, a friend of his. Soon after Shivaji's departure, they were arrested on suspicion of involvement in his escape and asked to leave town. Kalash then made his way to Mathura, where his grandfather lived. Sambhaji was already there, dressed as a Brahmin boy, under the care of the Trimal brothers. Kalash went with Sambhaji to their house and, when the Trimal brothers decided to leave for the Deccan, Kalash joined them on their journey.

Travelling with Kalash gave Sambhaji the opportunity to understand and develop his passion for literature, Sanskrit classics and poetry. He decided that he would write verses under the pen-name of Nrupashambhu. Kavi Kalash became his best friend, critic and guru.

In the daytime, at Shringarpur, Kalash would help Sambhaji in his official duties, including correspondence on various matters of state. The evenings were devoted to poetry and discussing the classics. The two got along as well as they had when they met almost a decade earlier, mixing work and pleasure with ease.

The serene beauty of Shringarpur helped Sambhaji to refine his poetic skills, and it was during his sojourn there that he started writing Budhabhushanam in Sanskrit. Gradually, in the stimulating company of Kavi Kalash and Keshav Pandit, Sambhaji began to get over the fact that his father had not taken him along on the Karnatak campaign.

4

Yesubai sat at the window of her bedchamber, enjoying the beauty of Prachitgad bathed in the light of the morning sun. She was taken by surprise when she felt Yuvraj's hand on her shoulder. He said, 'You seem to be lost in your thoughts. What happened?'

'Whenever I see the huge tree guarding the gorge, I am reminded of Maharaj. Whether in Raigad or Shringarpur, his presence is felt everywhere.'

'Well, it was his keen eye that spotted a gem here in Shringarpur,' Sambhaji said, much to the embarrassment of Yesubai who blushed pink. Sambhaji was referring to the proposal of marriage that Shivaji had made to Yesu's father.

Late that night, Sambhaji lay on his bed. But sleep eluded him as his eyes strayed towards the open windows. In the distance, he could see the dark silhouette of the mighty Prachitgad fort. In the dense jungles below, torches glowed intermittently. Sambhaji knew his men were patrolling the forest and guarding the road to the fort. Then he heard horses. The sound of their hooves stopped at the gates of the palace.

Before the messenger reached the palace, Sambhaji came out. The tall lamps that were lit at dusk continued to burn, albeit weakly, on the verandah. Kavi Kalash, ever alert, already stood quietly in a corner. The messenger approached, escorted by the guards. Sambhaji looked closely at the man; he appeared to be a Mughal soldier in his fifties. The guards saluted smartly, seeing Yuvraj arrive.

Sambhaji looked at Kalash, who addressed the messenger, 'What is this about?'

'It is a message from Diler Khan, Raje saheb,' the old man said.

Sambhaji was careful not to show his reaction although he was not particularly surprised to hear that a mighty Mughal sardar like Diler Khan had reached out to him. Khan, in his sixties, was a tall, well-built Rohilla Pathan and a seasoned soldier who had fought many a battle from the Ganga in the north to the Bhima and the Kaveri in the south. His bravery and devotion to the Mughal cause matched his religious zeal and his belief in cruelty as a means of gaining his ends. It was he who had brought Muazzam, the Shahzada who had tried to usurp his father Aurangzeb's throne, to his knees. He was no less skilful in the diplomatic negotiations of the durbar. Diler Khan had been given the Subedari of the Deccan a couple of years ago and had since been making frantic efforts to win Sambhaji over.

Sambhaji muttered a silent prayer before asking Kalash to read the message aloud. Kalash nodded and read:

'Rajadhiraj Sher Shamsher Sambhaji Raje Bhosale,

I don't need to tell the poet in you that when a man extends his hand of friendship he has already burnt away the cobwebs of enmity from his heart. I am sure you are aware that a lotus blooms in a lake and nowhere else. A lion cub too shows its beauty in the dense jungles and not in a zoo. I am thus tempted to ask you—why has a Maratha Shahzada like you decided to confine himself in the dark caves of Shringarpur? I believe that you have been kept away from Raigad. Despite being the son of Shivaji Bhosale himself, you are neglected and deprived of his love and affection.

You are familiar with enmity of the Mughals but you have not experienced their friendship. Had we not been true to our vows of friendship, we would not have been able to maintain relations with the Rajputs for three generations. I request you therefore to consider my proposal without any doubt or suspicion. Don't reject my offer of friendship. If you accept, please be assured that if you ever need my assistance of any kind, all you need to do is send word. Don't hesitate whether it is day or night. This old man will not spare any effort to give you all the help we can provide.'

Kavi Kalash paused, wondering if Diler Khan was being earnest in his offer. Amused by Diler Khan's desperate attempt to take advantage of the situation, Sambhaji burst out laughing. The very fact that the Mughal Subedar of the Deccan was now speaking of pure and disinterested friendship with the Yuvraj of the Maratha Empire was ironic, if not utterly ridiculous.

Nevertheless, an uneasy silence reigned in Sambhaji's quarters for the remainder of the night. The messenger waited patiently outside to take his message back to Diler Khan. Sambhaji decided that it was best not to answer in a hurry and resolved to confront the issue the next morning.

The next day, wearied by his long wait in the humid Shringarpur weather, the messenger sent several reminders to Sambhaji, asking humbly for his reply. That afternoon, Sambhaji finally said, summoning the messenger, 'Please convey my answer to Diler Khan—like the river which cannot flow back to its origin, the very thought of a friendship between a

Mughal Subedar and Shivaji's son is impossible. It not merely foolish to wish for it—it is sheer madness.'

5

It was well past noon when the palanquins carrying Sambhaji and Yesubai reached the coast near Sangameshwar. The bright sun reflected on the waters, the fishing boats gently bobbing in the sea, the swaying palm trees—all added to the charm of the afternoon. Sambhaji loved the ancient town which was situated at the confluence of the rivers Varuna and Alaknanda. It was said that the Lord Parshuram had built numerous temples here. So had the Chalukya king, Karna, who made it the capital of his kingdom. The Adilshahi sultan of Bijapur once had a subedar stationed here who later moved to the Deccan when the Hindavi Swaraj expanded and threatened his existence.

Enamoured with the beauty of the place, Sambhaji decided to construct a palace at Sangameshwar and gave orders for the work to commence immediately. 'It will help me to keep an eye on the movement from Goa and Kolhapur, he said, 'while I enjoy the natural beauty of this coast.'

Sambhaji, aiming to reach Shringarpur before nightfall, decided to ride back. But it was already growing dark as he and Kavi Kalash sped through the woods close behind a few men who rode with lighted torches. As they passed a small village, a group of nearly two hundred men and women came forward. They all clamoured to meet Yuvraj. Sensing the urgency of the matter, Sambhaji pulled the reins of his horse.

'Yuvraj,' one of the men began, 'please help us. Save us!'

'What happened?'

'Sarkar, how are we to survive if you take away our fields?'

'Whose orders are those?' Sambhaji asked, signalling to Kavi to read the papers which the old man held out in his hands. The province of Prabhavali was under Sambhaji's direct supervision and he wondered how such a directive had come from Raigad without his permission.

'We have not been able to pay our dues for a few years due to poor harvests. Now they have issued orders, attaching our land to the treasury,' the old man said.

'The orders have come from Rahuji Somnath. Based on specific instructions given by Annaji Datto, it says,' Kavi Kalash said, his eyes moving swiftly over the documents.

The old man stepped forward to touch Sambhaji's feet, 'Sarkar, our crops have failed for the past seven years. Many of our men have committed suicide out of sheer frustration. Please have pity on us, Sarkar!'

Sambhaji looked at the weak, shrivelled men and women; it was clear to him that the villagers were desperate and that they were not lying. Without a moment's hesitation, he summoned the thanedar of Sangameshwar. When the man arrived, he said, 'I am exempting these people from paying any taxes or dues, past and present. Please issue the orders immediately.'

The villagers were astounded at the instant decision taken by the Yuvraj. They nearly danced in joy as they blessed his kind heart.

That evening, as Sambhaji sat relaxing in his room, Kavi Kalash came in and suggested, 'Yuvraj, don't you think we should inform Raigad of your orders, for their records?'

'Why? Do you think I made the wrong decision?'

'We should not give the head of the royal treasury a reason to object to your decision. Is it not wise to explain why we have issued such orders?'

Sambhaji erupted, 'I am the Subedar of Prabhavali and I have the authority to waive the taxes. And, in case you forget, I am the Yuvraj! It is my duty and privilege to give instant relief and justice to the ryots, especially those who are suffering. Don't you think so?'

Kavi Kalash smiled, unperturbed, and said, 'Yuvraj, I know I don't have a right to lecture you on these matters but I am advising you as a friend, based on my experience. The walls of the durbar are porous; the winds of rumours and gossip blow through them incessantly. In the current situation, when those in charge at Raigad are waiting to find fault with you, is it not prudent to send a note to the treasury, explaining the rationale behind our decision?'

6

Days turned into months, but the routines of Yuvraj and his household at Shringarpur hardly changed. One morning, Balaji Avaji arrived from

Raigad. He was the official responsible for all of Shivaji's correspondence. His slim, tall figure, not to mention the energetic pace at which he climbed the twenty-odd steps to the palace in one go, belied his sixty years. While Yesubai welcomed him with a respectful namaskar, Sambhaji hugged him affectionately and asked, a little surprised, 'Balaji Kaka, what brings you here?'

'Shambhu Raje, it has been months since Shivaji Raje left for Karnatak. There is no fun at Raigad without him; hence I thought I might spend a few days here with you.'

Balaji Avaji was one of the few handpicked men like Hambirrao, Yesaji Kank, Hiroji Farzand, Annaji Datto and Moropant Pingle, who had been with Shivaji since the beginning. Daredevils like Tanaji and Bajiprabhu Deshpande, beloved of Maharaj, had died martyrs in the service of the Hindavi Swaraj.

Balaji's association with Shivaji had begun with a tragedy spawned by an unfortunate coincidence. His father, Avaji Hari Chitre, was a prominent official at the court of Siddi Babshikhan in Janjira, infamous for his cruelty and the way he treated the common man. Meanwhile, Avaji rapidly rose to the position of Diwan due to his dedication and hard work, arousing the jealousy of the Muslim sardars of the Janjira court.

The Siddi was ailing when Avaji had taken leave to visit his family deity in Jejuri. On his return he found that the Siddi's health had deteriorated further. This gave the Muslim sardars a chance to spread the rumour that Avaji had gone to Jejuri to pray for the Siddi's death. As luck would have it, Siddi Babshikhan died, and his young successor was led to believe that the tragedy was caused by Avaji's black magic. Despite Avaji's ardent pleas of innocence, he was forced to drink poison along with his brother Khandoji. Then their bodies were tied together and thrown into the ocean.

The cruel young Sultan did not stop at that, and decreed that Avaji's three sons Balaji, Chimnaji and Shyamji, as well as his wife Rakhmabai, be sent to Persia as slaves. They were rounded up and put on a ship. Luckily, near Rajapur, the winds changed their direction and the ship was forced to dock. It was Rakhamabai's good fortune that her brother Visaji Shankar was a trader stationed at Rajapur, and he managed to cajole, bribe and finally convince the sailors to release his sister and her sons.

Balaji was only eleven years old. But he had already heard stories of Shivaji's efforts to create a Hindavi Swaraj and was impressed by his valour and determination. One day, he composed and sent a letter to Shivaji in his neat cursive handwriting, 'It would be my honour, Raje, to serve under you as a soldier for the cause of the Swaraj.'

Luckily, Raje was visiting Rajapur then and wanted to meet the brave young boy who had written the letter. Soon afterwards he inducted Balaji into his army. Rakhmabai was worried about her son's safety, as she was yet to recover from the terrible and torturous death of her husband. However Raje gave his word to Rakhmabai, saying, 'Mother, you have three sons. Please consider me as your fourth one. For as long as your son takes care of the Swaraj, I promise to take care of your son.'

Balaji rose swiftly in the ranks owing to his dedication and integrity. Despite opposition from the Brahmins in Shivaji's court, he was given the title of Chitnis, personal secretary to Shivaji, responsible for all the correspondence and paper work of the Empire. Eventually he came to be known as Balaji Avaji Chitnis. All the important forts of the Hindavi Swaraj were entrusted to Balaji's supervision. He appointed capable men from his community, the Prabhus—also known as Chandraseniya Kayastha Prabhu—to manage the forts. This was widely resented by the Brahmins who felt that the Prabhus were growing arrogant and misusing their powers.

Amongst the Ashta Pradhan, Moropant Pingle and Annaji Datto were on least friendly terms with Balaji Avaji. But neither of them had the temerity to openly state their differences in the presence of Shivaji Raje. The reality behind their pretence of cordiality was very different, of course.

Balaji Avaji had always felt a deep affection for Sambhaji. He could empathise with the fact that Sambhaji had grown up without the loving presence of a mother while his father had constantly been away on one campaign or another. He was one of the few men in Shivaji's council of ministers who invariably acted in the Yuvraj's best interests.

His support was based on genuine respect: he was impressed by the way Sambhaji had run offices of the empire in Raigad under Shivaji's direction. Even earlier, Sambhaji had earned his spurs by proving himself an able administrator by the way he had governed the provinces of Kolar and Chikkabelapur, not to mention the success of the daredevil military campaigns he had conducted at Raibagh, Golconda and Akola, going right up to the borders of Goa. The Yuvraj had even managed to get a large booty for the Swaraj after extending a hand of friendship to Diwan Madanna of the Qutbshahi regime.

Yuvraj and Yesubai were overjoyed to receive Balaji Avaji at Shringarpur after a gap of many months. That evening, at dinner, Balaji asked, 'Where is that kapalik, the practitioner of black magic?'

'To whom are you referring?' Sambhaji asked, puzzled.

'The one who has mesmerised you. The one whose scheming mind is poisoning your thoughts. The one who sits on a wet buffalo skin and meditates.'

Sambhaji realised that Balaji was speaking of Kavi Kalash. He smiled, looking at Yesubai, before he replied, 'It seems that you too have been influenced by others in your opinions, Balaji.'

'He is manipulating people with his tantric practices. He kills animals for his sacrifices and eats all kinds of meat. He is a bad influence, Yuvraj.'

'Balaji Kaka, you are being misled. There are different ways of practising your faith. The tantric practices by themselves are not bad. It is a way of praying to Shakti. After all, our family deity, Tulja Bhawani Mata, is depicted holding a sword in her hand to kill her enemies and wipe out all evil. She requires blood as an offering from her devotees, doesn't she?' Sambhaji smiled and continued, 'In this vitiated atmosphere, when everyone is against me, don't I need someone who can protect me from the evil eye?'

'Shambhu Raje, the elder Maharaj never went looking for such support.'

'I am surprised you say that, Balaji Kaka. When Maharaj was not satisfied with the coronation ceremony supervised by Gaga Bhatt, he had invited the Gosavi Nischalgiri to perform various tantric rites. Don't forget that Nischalgiri was later given a place to stay at Sangameshwar, on Raje's orders.'

Balaji suddenly said, 'I did not know you were so eager to take your place on the throne.'

'What are you saying, Kaka? Why would I even imagine myself on the throne when Abasaheb is alive? Am I a Mughal or a Sultan's son to dream of overthrowing his father?'

'I am told you had a kalashabhishek performed.'

'Kakasaheb, you are not aware of the events that drove me to perform this ceremony to ward off the evil eye. I have seen a horse die suddenly for no reason. Lemons pierced with needles and dolls have been found in the palace grounds. Allegations against me multiply; all kinds of malicious gossip is being peddled about me and my behaviour—it was all becoming too much. If I am to serve the Swaraj as my father might wish, I need peace.'

Balaji Avaji was not impressed by Sambhaji's explanation. He persisted, 'Peace! What kind of peace are you looking for, Yuvraj? When do you expect to find it—when Shivaji Raje is no more?'

Unable to tolerate such accusations, Sambhaji shouted, rising from his seat, 'What kind of nonsense is this, Kaka?'

'Yuvraj, you don't realise the enormity of your act. The kalabhishek ceremony is performed only by someone who wishes the death of the one who sits on the throne. News of your ceremony has spread far and wide, and people have sent messages to Shivaji Raje. Annaji Datto, Rahuji Somnath, Soryabai Maharani, and many others are very upset..' Balaji Avaji wiped his face with his angavastram and continued, 'When I heard all this, it pierced my heart and I could not stay put at Raigad. I had to see you!'

Sambhaji said, with a lump in his throat, 'What a pity! I wonder why these vile people are out to spread such malicious rumours about me. What do they have against me? Now I realise it is a good thing that I am so far away from Raigad. What an irony that in the land of greats like Tukaram and Samarth Ramdas, we still entertain such petty and selfish thoughts!' Overcome with emotion, Sambhaji nearly collapsed on the floor. Balaji Avaji rushed to help him up and made him sit on a chair.

Sambhaji was deeply hurt. He had never imagined that the conspiracy against him would reach such proportions. He said as Balaji brought him a tumbler of water,'Balaji Kaka, isn't it a pity that the men holding high posts in the Swaraj indulge in dirty politics of the basest level?'

Balaji had known Sambhaji since childhood. Yuvraj had always spoken his mind. He had a strong sense of justice, and treated everyone around him as they deserved to be treated. He was blunt and rude with those who behaved in a similar manner, and could be most compassionate and soft-spoken with those who merited such kindness. Balaji knew his clear and transparent mind inside out.

He said, trying to soothe Sambhaji, 'Yuvraj, people are not blaming you. They feel that you have been influenced by Kalash who is playing with your emotions and manipulating you.'

'I don't think so. It may look like they are criticising Kalash but their taunts are most certainly directed at me.'

'Shambhu Raje, just ignore them. Even today, many of the so-called high-caste Brahmins and Marathas are not willing even to recognise Shivaji Raje as a Kshatriya. In fact, they had openly protested before Raje was coronated. They claimed that ever since Lord Parshuram decimated all the Kshatriyas, there were none left and hence Shivaji Raje could not claim to be one! To prove the naysayers wrong, it was I who had gone all the way to the north to prove that Raje's ancestors belonged to the Sisodiya family of Rajputana.'

'Why don't people like Annaji Datto understand this?'

'Yuvraj, you must recognise the fact that Annaji Datto has been an efficient Pradhan. He has fought many battles with Raje and served the Swaraj well. It is he who oversees the collection of the revenue that maintains the empire. Of course, it is a different story that he was tempted to keep a part of the revenue for himself. Despite his capabilities, it is evident that he is not an entirely honest man. But above all, remember this: Annaji believes that there are no real Kshatriyas in the kingdom, whether among the Marathas or the Prabhus.' Balaji paused before he said, 'I myself have had to suffer many insults silently, Shambhu Raje. When I needed to perform my son's thread ceremony, it was Annaji who raised objections. I appealed to Moropant Pingle for justice, only to find that he had already been biased by Annaji's opinion. Finally, I managed somehow to convince Gaga Bhatt to perform the ceremony, against the wishes of these so-called Brahmins.'

Balaji stayed at Shringarpur for two days, conversing at length with Yuvraj and Yesubai. It was clear to Sambhaji that the people acting against him and Kavi Kalash were trying their best to poison Shivaji Raje's mind. The ministers were also blaming him for having waived the taxes of the Prabhavali peasants.

Regarding his decision, Sambhaji said, 'Kaka, these people have been plagued by torrential rains and floods for the past eight years. For the same reason, they are also in debt to local moneylenders. They are in no position to pay taxes. Isn't it fair that in such a situation we waive their dues and reduce their burden?'

'Yuvraj, your heart and its motives are as pure and transparent as the flowing stream. But your enemies are spreading the rumour that you are out to undo whatever Raje has done. They have already sent several messages to Maharaj, complaining about your actions, twisting the truth to serve their purposes.'

'I am not bothered about their plots and plans,' Sambhaji said confidently. 'Let Abasaheb return. I will tell him the truth and I am sure he will only pat me on the back for the way I have conducted myself and the affairs of the kingdom during these past months.'

However, when Balaji Avaji took his leave, the Yuvraj was despondent again. 'I did not bother when these people found a way to stop me from joining Abasaheb in the Karnatak campaign. I did not complain when I was asked to leave Raigad and stay at Shringarpur. I was even accused of molesting a girl and driving her to suicide. I took all that in my stride, but now they accuse me of performing some tantric acts against my own father! I cannot take it any more … I feel …'

Sambhaji could not continue. He was overwhelmed with emotion. He said, after taking a deep breath, 'Kaka, let them say what they have to. But I tell you—to fulfil Abasaheb's dream, for the Swaraj—I am willing to sacrifice myself anytime, anywhere. That is my promise!'

7

Memories of the elder Maharaj flooded Sambhaji's mind. Images of Raigad troubled him. He said to his wife, sighing deeply,

'How things change with time. There were times when Soyrabai, playing with me in my childhood, would turn into a small child herself. She would often fight with Jijabai on my behalf. Later …'

'What happened later?'

'Well, it seems the very walls of the palace changed their colour ever since the first cries of baby Rajaram reverberated there.'

'Yuvraj, don't you remember the grand celebration when Maharaj was coronated? The way he introduced you as Yuvraj of the Swaraj and the heir apparent! On that occasion, even Soyrabai, Shivaji Raje's chief consort, had not objected to it!'

'Well, that may be true … but I distinctly remember her growing cold towards me since that day.'

Yesubai said, rubbing Sambhaji's palm affectionately, 'What's the point in getting upset like this? Maharaj saheb, who considers me his daughter, will surely never forget you—his own flesh and blood.'

'Yesu, understand this—Shambhu is not going to get justice in his father's palace. Many are waiting to put a black mark on my character whenever possible. There is literally a contest amongst them to label me as cruel, drunkard, wayward, arrogant, vagabond, womaniser—in short, as one who is not fit to be Yuvraj.'

'Yuvraj, have faith in the Lord.'

'I pray to several gods and goddesses each day but, in truth, there is no God higher than Shivaji. I shelter in his shade, like that of a massive banyan tree. However there are evil souls who would not only deny me refuge under the tree but uproot my very identity!'

Yesubai could sense the growing restlessness in Sambhaji. He could barely sleep. The deep sighs he let out at intervals spoke of the inner turmoil he was experiencing. The baseless allegations churned out by the Raigad faction were beginning to test his self-esteem and hurt his ego; his usually poetic and peaceful mind seethed with violent rage nowadays. Yesubai, in her maturity and wisdom, tried her best to curb these destructive passions.

'Yuvraj, the elder Maharaj has spent all his life trying to build the Swaraj that you are destined to rule. Why don't you go to him, tell your side of the story? Or, at the very least, meet Annaji and speak to him.'

'What's the point? Is he going to listen? Ever since Hansa took her life, he blames me for it. And to top it all, Godu turned out to be his brother-in-law's daughter. Things have taken such a turn that wisdom seems to be hiding its face in darkness.'

These anxious thoughts refused to leave Sambhaji's mind. He was awake till the wee hours of the morning.

The next morning, as Yuvraj rose a little late, he found Kavi Kalash waiting for him with the thanedar of Sangameshwar. After a long journey on horseback, the man was sweating and out of breath. He said, before Sambhaji could speak,

'Yuvraj, everything is topsy-turvy. Yesterday, riders came from Raigad and confiscated the poor farmers' milk yielding cows; even their utensils!'

'What for?' Sambhaji exclaimed, unable to believe his ears. Kalash was quiet, looking down at the floor.

'Oh, I see!' Sambhaji said suddenly, nodding his head. 'It is because I had issued orders to waive their dues.'

'Yes, Sarkar,' the thanedar said hesitatingly. 'I tried explaining to them that those were your direct orders and that the farmers were really distressed but they said ...'

'Please go on. Don't hesitate.'

'They said ... Shambhu Raje is not the one on the throne. When he is, we will salute him.'

'I see!' Sambhaji said, at a loss for words. Then he said, reining in his emotions, 'Tell the emissaries from Raigad not to trouble the poor farmers, and that I will take responsibility for the loans they have forfeited.'

'They don't seem to be in a mood to listen, Raje. I tried, but ...'

'Go on!'

'They said that if Raje had intended Yuvraj's orders to be followed, he would have handed over the charge of Raigad to him before leaving for Karnatak. He would not have been banished to the jungles of Shringarpur, the way we throw small pebbles out while cleaning rice.'

The thanedar seemed relieved that he had spelt out every word he had heard. Sambhaji's face, however, was creased with pain, and Yesubai and Kalash were clearly dejected. They could not believe that Yuvraj was being openly insulted in this manner.

Sambhaji finally said to Kalash, in a cold and dry voice, 'Kaviraj, take a platoon of a thousand soldiers and leave for Sangameshwar right away. Capture Rahuji Somnath's official and his other men, and throw them in the prison here at Shringarpur.'

That day, before the sun set in the western sky, Kavi Kalash had carried out Yuvraj's orders. Sambhaji said, when Kalash reported to him after completing the task,

'Let those fellows suffer from hunger and thirst. Don't show any pity on them.'

Annaji Datto was the Subedar of Prabhawali earlier and had ruled with an iron hand, caring a damn about the troubles faced by the ryots. The fact that someone like Yuvraj had arrived and shown the revenue officials their true place was a matter of celebration for the ryots and residents of Shringarpur.

Sambhaji said to Yesubai that night, 'At last, things are changing!

Yesubai took his hand gently and put it on her belly, saying, 'Well, I am worried about the changes happening here too. Please be careful. Act with restraint till the elder Maharaj returns.'

FOUR

The Revolt

1

Not long after Balaji Avaji's visit, Ranubai Akkasaheb and her entourage reached Shringapur. Ranubai Jadhav was excited by the news that her younger brother was going to be a father soon. Sambhaji had lost his mother when he was only two years old but he had been showered with love by three sisters. The eldest, Sakwarbai alias Sakhubai, was married to Mahadji Nimbalkar of Phaltan, the middle sister Ranubai married into the Jadhav family of Wai, and the youngest, Ambikabai, was married to Harji Mahadik of Tarale near Satara. All three were older than Shambhu. While Sambhaji had mostly lavished his love on Ambikabai, it was Ranubai who had really cared for Sambhaji.

It happened when Sambhaji was nearly one and a half years of age. Running on the ramparts of Raigad, he had stumbled and would have fallen into the deep ravine overlooked by the fort, had it not been for Ranubai who rushed to the spot and held him by his legs, hurting her own knees badly in the process. Saibai had said that day, as she hugged Shambhu tightly, 'Ranu, our Bal Raje is brave, but aggressive and a little rash in nature. He tends to acts without thinking sometimes. I may not be there to look after him always, but I wish you would take care of him, my dear!'

It was dark when Sambhaji reached his quarters the day Ranubai arrived. Yesubai welcomed him with a smile and said, pointing to the inner room,

'Guess, who has come to visit us today?'

A lady sat near the shrine inside. When she heard Sambhaji's footsteps, she turned. It was Godu! She blushed seeing Yuvraj. How much she had changed, Sambhaji thought! The slim, petite figure was the same but the face, framed by long tresses, had lost all its charm. Faint dark circles below the eyes suggested anxiety and lack of sleep. Before Sambhaji could speak, she said, 'Raje, ever since you stopped the revenue officials from collecting their dues, your name is being besmirched at Raigad. The senior officials are spreading all kinds of gossip.'

'Let it be, Godu! These pen soldiers can only do so much damage.'

'Yuvraj, a soldier like you might not be able to estimate the kind of damage these paper-pushers are capable of causing.' Godu stopped for a moment, realising that she may have spoken more than what she should have. She said, 'Rahuji Pant, under guidance of Annaji Kaka, has sent a note to the elder Maharaj, blaming you for creating obstacles in their work. They have recommended that you be arrested for this crime!'

'Godu, are you sure of what you just said?' Yesubai asked.

'Baisaheb, they have gone further and suggested that if Yuvraj cannot be arrested, the title of 'Yuvraj' and all associated benefits may be removed till such time as the elder Maharaj returns. They have sent three reminders to Shivaji Raje since then.'

Sambhaji closed his eyes, muttering Bhawani's name. He said, after a pause, 'Godu, you have our thanks for bringing us the news. But I wonder why my spies have not been able to give me this information.'

Yesubai said later, while discussing the matter with Sambhaji, 'Yuvraj, I am confident of your father's intelligence and his large-hearted nature. Knowing his keen sense of justice, I would not be worried. He is not going to punish his son without a thorough investigation.'

The next day, Sambhaji and Kavi Kalash visited a few villages where they had planted mango saplings some weeks earlier. After enjoying a homemade meal with the villagers, they were returning to Shringarpur when they spotted a royal palanquin crossing the dry bed of a river. As per Yesubai's orders, the palanquin was carrying Godu to the village of Sarwat. Sambhaji stopped the palanquin to speak to Godu while the men stood at a respectful distance.

Sambhaji asked, 'Godu, what has become of your husband and father-in-law?'

'They are dead as far as I am concerned. The day they planned a revolt against the Swaraj, they were dead to me. I pray you don't raise this topic again; it troubles me to speak of it.'

Sambhaji said, a little hesitantly, 'Godu, why don't you think of getting married again?'

'There is only one person in the world that I can marry!' Her eyes shone as she spoke.

'Well, why don't you then? I am sure that person knows how much you love him.'

'God only knows!' Godu said, in a soft voice. 'But I know that his wife is Lakshmi in human form. I cannot afford to hurt her.'

Raigad's constant interference and the deliberate attempts to besmirch his name were disconcerting for Sambhaji. But now he was increasingly preoccupied with the news from Karnatak. He frequently received messages describing the success of the campaign. The entire city of Hyderabad had poured itself on the streets to welcome Shivaji Maharaj. Qutb Shah of Golconda had welcomed him with open arms. Men like Dhanaji Jadhav, Nagoji Jedhe and Hambirrao Mohite had shown unparalleled valour on the field of battle. The footsteps of the Maratha soldiers echoed even on Jinji fort, signalling the extent of the spread of Maratha might. Naturally, Yuvraj was ecstatic upon hearing such success stories.

Yesubai remarked, referring to the officials captured by Sambhaji for trying to extort revenue from the farmers of Prabhavali, 'Raje, it seems you cannot remain angry for long! I am told you released the men within two days and that you ensured they had adequate food and money for their travel back to Raigad!'

Sambhaji merely smiled in response.

Two days after Godu's departure, Diler Khan's emissary arrived at Shringarpur again. The moment Sambhaji read Mughal Subedar's message, he said, his anger evident,

'Has the old Khan gone senile?'

The message read:

'Rustam-e-Dakhan-Sambhajiraje!

I request you to meet me in my camp. Badshah Aurangzeb is keen to capture the whole country including the Deccan. Please pardon me as I don't intend to poke my nose into your family matters. Yet, I can undertand your pain. Your father's affection seems to be veering towards Soyrabai and Rajaram. The officials at Raigad look at you with suspicion. Instead of putting up with these insults and managing the tiny territory you have been given charge of, I wish you would accept the hand of friendship I extend to you. One day, Alamgir will march on the Deccan and our fortunes will shine.'

Sambhaji said, 'We must reply. I don't want my silence to be taken as a mute acceptance of his offer.'

'What shall we say, Raje?' Kavi Kalash inquired.

Sambhaji dictated the reply,

> *'Khansaheb, I must thank Allah for your kind wishes and your concern for my welfare. You are right about the situation at Raigad which has created a rift in the family. But that need not give you any reason to feel elated. When he departed for Karnatak, my father left the kingdom in the hands of his most trusted officials and his Yuvraj. And you are now suggesting I betray his trust! Khansaheb, I am lucky to have the blessings of a father like Shivaji. How can I think of leaving the shade of a mighty tree to take shelter in your tent?'*

Sambhaji was in tears as he dictated the message. Kalash could feel the intense love Sambhaji had for his father and the Swaraj. As Kalash was about to tie the messenger bag, Sambhaji suddenly said, 'Wait! I want to add a few more lines.'

Sambhaji dictated, '*Dilerji, if you and your Badshah are truly impressed with my valour, I would like to join forces with you and present a new territory to the Badshah.*'

'My intention is not to break ties with Diler Khan but to keep the conversation going,' Sambhaji explained to Kalash.

'Raje, why engage in a discussion with someone like him?'

Sambhaji's face darkened for a moment. Then he said, trying to smile while he let out a deep sigh, 'We never know what destiny has in store for us.'

2

Yesubai stood on the terrace, looking in the direction of Sangameshwar. She was observing a group of cavalrymen who were approaching the haveli. Squinting her eyes, she was able to see the saffron flag held aloft by the man leading the group. She smiled. A few days back, they had received information that Shivaji Raje had returned to Panhalgad after nearly two years. They were waiting desperately for an invitation from the elder Maharaj.

Kavi Kalash and his men rushed to receive the mounted soldiers. The entire party at Shringarpur— Sardar Vishwanath, Ranubai and Yuvraj— were eager to meet Shivaji Raje. Even Pilaji Shirke, despite his failing health, was waiting for the invitation. The excitement and expectation in the air was palpable. Sambhaji came into the hall, acknowledging the mujras of the messengers, and said to Kalash,

'Please read the message.'

He began, '*My dear Shambhu, I rushed to Panhalgad after completing the campaign at Karnatak. The very thought of meeting you and embracing you with affection spurred my horse. But ...*'

Kavi Kalash stopped for a moment. A strange fear gripped him. He was worried that the next line might not be to Yuvraj's liking. Sambhaji said, his voice ringing loud and clear, 'Please continue; whatever it may be.'

> *'But ... I heard of your daredevil acts. Yuvraj, you are a man of twenty-two years and not a young boy anymore. I am surprised at your lack of wisdom. You have pardoned people who have not paid their dues for eight years. Moreover you have arrested and threatened officials who were doing their duty. You have insulted my Ashta Pradhan. These are men who have fought shoulder to shoulder with me for the past twenty or thirty years. You have, without considering their age, their contributions to the Swaraj and their place in the hierarchy of my court, insulted them. I know you are eager to meet me but let it be clear—don't bother to show your face to me!'*

As he read, Kalash's face was pale from surprise, fear and sadness. His hand, holding the letter, trembled. The others present did not know how to react. Sambhaji himself felt as he was drowning in an ocean of sadness. His discomfiture was unnerving to watch. He signalled to Kalash to continue, but Yesubai screamed, 'Stop!' she said in a tear-filled voice, 'Enough! Enough, Kaviraj! I don't want to listen to a single word more.'

'Why should he stop?' Sambhaji's voice had steadied itself. 'The words are those of Shivaprabhu. Don't stop, Kaviraj. Those present should hear everything lest this too gives rise to unnecessary and vicious gossip. Let us all hear what is written.'

Kalash continued, '*I suggest you don't go about destroying the Swaraj and insulting my men. Please don't interfere in the work the officials are doing. I hope you will heed my advice if there is an iota of wisdom left in you. Instead of meeting me at Panhalgad, please go to Sajjangad and spend some time in the company of Ramdas Swami. I hope his presence would drive some sense into you, teaching you a few things about good manners and the conduct that becomes a prince of your standing. Take Swami's blessings, and change your ways before it is too late.'*

No one dared to speak. After a while, each of them left without saying a word. Only Sambhaji remained, seated in his chair like a rock, unable to move, while Kalash stood silently next to him. After a long silence, Yuvraj said with a sigh, 'Look at the way Diler Khan praises my wisdom. Sometimes it seems to me that my own blood relations are blind! And many a time the enemy speaks the truth.'

'Raje, don't give up your hopes so easily,' Kalash tried to console him.

'Have I done anything wrong? After being separated from him for nearly twenty months, I was desperate to meet Abasaheb. He had promised me to meet me after returning from Karnatak, to discuss the allegations against me with an open and patient mind. But now ...'

'Yuvraj?'

'But now there is no invitation, no discussion! Not a single word of love! And I have been declared a criminal without being given a chance to prove my innocence.'

Sambhaji was in deep agony. He retired to his bedchamber, refusing to have his lunch. Soon, it was evening. Shadows lengthened in the garden outside. Yesubai came in with a tray of food, hoping to persuade him to eat, but to her surprise and dismay, Sambhaji waved it away. He lay on the bed with his face buried in the pillow. But rest offered no solace. He felt that he was burning all over.

Looking up at the chandelier suspended from the ceiling, he felt that his life too was hanging by a thread. He said, banging his fist on the bedpost, 'Yesu, I was sure that the cunning officials and clerks of Raigad would carry their accusations to Maharaj. They have the support of Annaji Datto. That man has spent half his life spreading malice against me. After all, his complaints serve to deflect Maharaj's attention from his own deficiencies.'

'What do you mean?'

'The Maharaj would have, on his return from Karnatak, asked why the campaign at Janjira did not succeed. So he must have started a litany of allegations against me, diverting the topic of discussion elsewhere. That way he kills two birds with one stone!'

Yesubai stepped forward to touch Sambhaji's forehead which seemed to be burning with fever. She said, 'This too will pass. Have some patience.'

'How much patience can I show? While the officials are pouring in with their complaints, Soyrabai Ranisaheb does not miss a chance to increase the rancour against me. I have no one left and no place to go. My father has abandoned me and Raigad has closed its doors on my face!'

Sambhaji's opponents were working overtime, as his spies informed him with their regular updates. The Ashta Pradhan were suggesting that the Hindavi Swaraj be divided into two parts—that Raigad and twelve other provinces be given to Rajaram while the difficult terrain of Jinji was to be relegated to Sambhaji. There were rumours that Shivaji Raje too was thinking along similar lines.

Sambhaji's exile at Shringarpur seemed endless, with no solution in sight. To make matters worse, he received another message from Diler Khan, rubbing salt into his exposed wounds. It said:

> *'My dear unfortunate Shahzada! The officials at Raigad have succeeded in their task. I wonder what you are waiting for! Isn't the Badshah's camp closer and more convenient than going all the way to the far-flung Jinji? You may come to me without any doubt or fear in your heart. My shamiana is itching to offer you our famed hospitality.'*

Despite the annoyance Sambhaji felt on reading these words, Diler Khan's latest missive set him thinking. The moon and star symbols on the distant mosque seemed to be inviting him. After all, his own gods were silent these days.

Diler Khan, the man who was extending his hand in friendship, was no ordinary sardar after all. He had earned his spurs in Aurangzeb's durbar. And he was courting Sambhaji as if his life depended on it.

In reality, Diler Khan dreamt day and night of the moment Alamgir would put an aigrette of honour in his turban. There was no one who could challenge Aurangzeb's supremacy from Kabul and Kandahar in the north-west to the Bay of Bengal in the east. But there was a formidable foe in the South. Aurangzeb had often said in private that the only enemy worth his steel was Shivaji. A single vision—the Emperor's reaction when he, Diler Khan, presented Sambhaji, his sworn enemy's son, in the Mughal durbar—had consumed the old Pathan for the past two years. His spies had been feeding him with accurate and timely information on the developments in Raigad, and he knew that Sambhaji was troubled of late by his father's attitude.

For his own reasons, Sambhaji too made diplomatic overtures to the Mughal sardar. He began by sending Jotyaji Kesarkar into Diler Khan's territory to get a first-hand report of the situation. Yesubai, when she came to know of it, was deeply worried that Jotyaji had been sent on such a dangerous mission. She entered Sambhaji's quarters as he was about to start his daily pooja.

Yesu said, her voice full of entreaty, 'Yuvraj, it is not wise to be so reckless. You must exhibit some restraint.'

Sambhaji said, ignoring Yesubai's request, 'You may say or believe whatever you want but the Swaraj does not need Sambhaji anymore.'

'Does that mean you must go and put your head in Diler Khan's lap?' Yesubai fumed. 'I am sure you have not forgotten that it was the same demon Diler Khan who did not hesitate to behead Murarbaji when he seized Purandar. Yuvraj, please show some restraint. Think!'

'What am I supposed to do sitting here? I may be the Yuvraj but I am barred from the campaigns. I am not allowed to stay in my own palace. I cannot raise my own cavalry nor even solve the simplest of problems which the ryots face. Am I to spend the rest of my life discussing philosophy at Sajjangad?'

'Yuvraj, I beg of you, listen to what I am saying. Consider Ramdas Swami as your saviour. The pious and serene atmosphere of Sajjangad would cleanse your mind of toxins. You will find a way out of this darkness,' Yesubai said, her voice quivering.

For a moment Sambhaji was lost in his thoughts. Soon a pall of sadness spread over his face and he said, his voice trembling, 'Yesu, I don't know why I am in the clutches of a strange fear all the time. We were to visit Abasaheb this coming month, with our little one. I would have put the heir to the Swaraj at his feet! Now, I am worried Abasaheb may give the order for me to be chained and thrown into a dungeon before that.'

'How dark your thoughts are! I am surprised you don't have an iota of affection or respect for your great father. It is not right, Yuvraj,' Yesubai reprimanded her husband.

Sambhaji said, gulping down his doubts and distress, 'I wonder why Abasaheb had to send that letter through the royal messengers. I would not have felt so bad if he had summoned me in person and skinned me!'

Yesubai was only a month away from delivering the child. But the pain of watching her husband suffer was far greater than the troubles of her pregnancy. She requested Ranubai akkasaheb to ask Sambhaji's other wife to come down to Shringarpur.

When Durgabai arrived at Shringarpur, Yesubai received her warmly, saying, 'Durgavati, Yuvraj is in a delicate state of mind. The next few weeks are critical. I cannot run behind Yuvraj with a pregnancy entering the ninth month. Please see that you take good care of him.'

Durgabai nodded, holding Yesubai's hand in hers, 'Your word is my command, Akkasaheb.'

Once the Jadhavs of Supe had invited Sambhaji to their home. When he sat down to the dinner prepared in his honour, his eyes fell on their pretty daughter Durga. Sambhaji was enamoured of her in no time. She was not as tall, slim and beautiful as Yesubai but her short and slightly plump stature was endearing. She did not have the doe eyes of Yesubai but her narrow slanted eyes had the power to enchant a man in their very first glance. Unlike Yesubai, who was talkative, Durga was quiet and reserved by nature.

Sambhaji's visits to Supe and Baramati had increased after he saw Durga a couple of times. He would often, on the pretext of a hunting expedition, reach the Jadav haveli at lunchtime. Seeing through her husband's antics, it was Yesubai herself who proposed idea of the marriage to Sambhaji. She said to her husband, 'Keep in mind that this proposal is in my own best interest. It is not possible for me alone to manage a burning ember like you. I need someone to assist me!'

One night Sambhaji sat writing for a long time. He did not seem to want to his clerk or Kavi Kalash around. Yesubai, sleeping fitfully, noticed that Yuvraj had been at his writing table for many hours. It was nearly dawn when he stood up, stretched and lay on the bed with a sigh.

Yesubai rose and went over to the table. Several crumpled pieces of paper lay on it. Then she noticed a royal messenger bag beside them. Yesu instantly recognised the Mughal seal of Aurangzeb. Unable to contain her curiosity, she read the contents. It was a message from Diler Khan on behalf of Shah Alam, Aurangzeb's son, who had taken charge as the Subedar of the Deccan. The message urged Sambhaji to join hands with them without any apprehension. Yesubai realised Sambhaji was contemplating the next steps. That morning, Sambhaji woke up to find a tearful Yesubai at his feet. She said, as soon as he opened his eyes, 'Yuvraj,

I beg of you. Don't take such hasty decisions. Don't strangle Shivaji Raje's dream of Swaraj just because you are upset with a few officials at Raigad. It would be disaster!'

'You are blind to the fact that I am being made to look like a fool. The decision had already been made at Raigad: Rajaram will get twelve provinces and Raigad while I will be banished to Jinji.'

Yesubai wiped her tears and said, looking into Sambhaji's eyes, 'Let the kingdom go, if it has to! Since when did a brave soldier, a poet and a scholar like you start coveting power? Yuvraj, tell me; what will you choose if you have to—between fourteen provinces on the one hand and a father like Shivaji Raje on the other?'

'You know the answer. Why do you keep repeating the question? You know very well that without Shivaji Raje and his dreams for the Swaraj, Sambhaji cannot live for even a moment. But what about the fact that the king who has such love and affection for his ryots has none left today for his own son?'

Yesubai was silent. Her tears had dried on her cheeks. As for Sambhaji's grief, it was beyond mere tears. Yesu said in a soft voice, 'Yuvraj, I am deeply worried by the way you are being treated. But try to imagine the elder Maharaj's state of mind if he were to learn that you have joined hands with the enemy. He would be shattered!'

That night a fever raged in Yesubai's body. The physician prepared a strong medicine which Sambhaji made Yesu drink. Sambhaji knew the reason for her illness. He said, gently touching Yesubai's cheeks with his fingers, 'Don't worry so much. Your excessive anxiety is causing all this. It's not that the world is going to come to an end if I go over to the enemy camp. Have I not been to the Mughal court as a young boy, holding Abasaheb's hand? I have been appointed a Mughal mansabdar twice.'

Yesubai tried to smile, saying, 'Your visit to Agra was part of Maharaj's political game plan.'

'How long will I remain quiet? What will the officials think of me? They will say that I have no spine, that I am scared! Yesu, there is only way for me to remove this stain from my reputation. I need to show them that I can make my moves intelligently and once again gain my father's trust and confidence.'

Yesubai was not convinced. Sambhaji revealed his plan, 'The idea is to enter into the enemy camp with a gesture of friendship and then defeat them at the appropriate time.'

'Yuvraj, Diler Khan is no ordinary fish. He is a crocodile.'

'And you think I am an infant suckling his mother's milk? I am the son of Shivaji, the one who will become the scourge of the Mughals!'

Both were awake the whole night. Yesubai continued to insist that Sambhaji should not join the Mughal camp. Her fever, her weak voice and her pale face indicated an agitated state of mind, putting brakes on Sambhaji's determination to act immediately. Finally, using her womanhood and her deep bond with Sambhaji, she appealed to him, placing his hand on her heart, 'Yuvraj, make a promise to me—the one who has walked all the way with you.'

'Ask.'

'First honour Maharaj's wish and visit Sajjangad. Decide on the next steps after you take the blessings of Swami Samarth.'

'I promise.'

3

Sambhaji was all set to journey on a bold new path. The lovely Mahadev temple at Shringarpur was overflowing with his friends. The sky was overcast with dark clouds. They began the prayers, led by priests who sat bare-bodied chanting the mantras. The pooja lasted more than an hour. As the men streamed out, Kavi Kalash and Sambhaji remained in the sanctum sanctorum.

Kalash said, 'Maharaj, I have been with you like a shadow ever since Agra. You are everything to me—my home, my kingdom.'

Sambhaji smiled and said, 'You are the soothing shadow of the tree of knowledge. You are more than a friend—rather, my most trusted advisor.'

'Shall I come along with you then?'

'No. Not this time,' Sambhaji said. 'I don't want you to be blamed for my departure. They will say you performed some tantric ritual to influence my mind and persuade me to join the Mughals.'

Kalash smiled dejectedly. His sadness at Sambhaji's impending departure was evident. Yuvraj said, trying to console him, 'In fact, if you stay back it would be a great help for me to keep an eye on the people here. And I promise to ask you to come to me when I need help.'

'As you command,' Kalash said. 'But Yuvraj, I won't be surprised if some people instigate the elder Maharaj to throw me out of the kingdom.'

'Don't be worried about that. Shivaji Raje is aware of who you are. Remember that it was he who chose you as my advisor in Agra. If he had believed some of the rumours people are trying to spread about you, he would have ordered your execution long back.'

Kalash, overcome by emotion, could barely speak. He said finally, holding Sambhaji's hand, 'Take care, Maharaj.'

The clouds were threatening to pour when Sambhaji set out from Shringarpur, accompanied by nearly two thousand five hundred horsemen. Yesubai, Ranubai akkabsaheb and Durgabai, in their respective palanquins, went till the borders of Shringarpur to see him off. Kalash was in tears as Sambhaji bid him farewell. Yesubai's palanquin had been set down below a large jamun tree. That she was at an advanced stage of her pregnancy was evident from her bloated face and sunken eyes. Tears streamed down her cheeks, the collyrium leaving black lines on her fair face. Sambhaji tried wiping it off with the edge of his shawl.

Ranubai took leave of Durgabai, instructing her to look after Yesu's health. Sambhaji tried to persuade his sister to stay on but she said, 'Shambhu Raje, I will accompany you till the gates of Sajjangad, whence I will leave for Wai.'

Yesubai said, seeing Sambhaji's worried face, 'Don't worry about me. What matters is that Swami will help clear your mind at Sajjangad. These days shall pass.'

'Don't stay at Shringarpur for long. Leave for Panhalgad when you can.'

'Why do you say that?'

'Haven't you heard? Abasaheb is exhausted from the long campaign in Karnatak. Shouldn't someone from the family be there to look after his health?'

Yesubai's tears vanished, replaced by a smile that spoke volumes of her pride in her husband.

4

Only a person with self-respect and dignity can understand how difficult it is to suffer indignity and slander. The humiliations of the past months caught up with Sambhaji on his long ride. When he reached the gates of Sajjangad, his head was aching so badly that he felt the only way to reduce the pain was either to bang his head against a stone or surrender it at the feet of someone like Samarth Ramdas.

Krishnaji Bhaskar and Vasudev Balkrishna, the officials at the gate, received Sambhaji warmly. Yuvraj asked if he might pay his respects to the Swami at his ashram before retiring to the palace in Sajjangad. But misfortune seemed to be following Sambhaji everywhere. He was informed that Swamiji had left for Kolhapur the previous day and was not expected to return for a fortnight.

During the weeks that followed, Sambhaji tried his best to keep his mind occupied. Accompanied by his guards, he walked to the temple of Hanuman situated in a corner of the fort every day and offered his prayers. Like a kite whose string had been cut off, he roamed the ramparts without any purpose. At times he would sit near the ashram and meditate for hours.

One day a Gosavi named Sadanand came from a nearby village to meet Sambhaji with a request to resume the annual donation which used to be given to the ashram there. Sambhaji, gladdened by an opportunity to look into administrative matters, asked him to come back the next day. That night at dinner, Ranubai, who was staying in Sajjangad for a few weeks, asked her brother, 'You still harbour feelings of anger against Abasaheb, don't you?'

'Have you realised how long it has been since Abasaheb returned from Karnatak? Six months now! A father does not bother for six months to meet his twenty-year-old son. Isn't that strange? And when I request a meeting, there is no response. What crime have I committed to deserve such treatment? Why is Shivaji Raje, famed for his affection and compassion for the world at large, so stingy when it comes to his own son? I am not a mute unfeeling stone, am I?'

The next day he met Sadanand Gosavi and said, 'I understand that you deserve the donation you were getting earlier. But my hands are tied. However I shall write to Annaji Datto today, conveying your request.'

Sadanand Gosavi's face fell. He said, hastily saluting, 'I did not come here expecting this. Yuvraj, it would be done if you put merely your seal on the paper …'

'Listen! I cannot interfere in matters of administration. I am sending my recommendation today. You will meet Annaji after a few days.'

'As you command,' he said, and left.

More than a month had passed since Sambhaji arrived in Sajjangad, but Swami Samarth Ramdas had not returned to the fort. Tired of wandering around Sajjangad and neighbouring Parli, Yuvraj was growing restless. He had enquired many times with the Swami's disciples and the officials of the fort but he did not get a satisfactory answer.

After a few weeks, Sadanand Gosavi returned to Sajjangad. Meeting Sambhaji, he said, 'I spent three weeks at the base of Raigad, waiting for permission to meet Annaji Datto. But all I got were vague excuses. Finally, when I confronted Annaji, he said, "Our king is in Panhalgad and not Sajjangad." That is when I came to know the truth.'

'What truth?'

'That the elder Maharaj does not trust you. The clerks these days not only ignore your orders but don't even read them.'

Sadanand did not realise but he had just dropped a burning coal on a haystack. Sambhaji's face was red with anger. He asked all the lower officials to leave and ordered Vasudev Balkrishna to present himself. Upon being questioned by Sambhaji, Balkrishna said, his voice quivering with fear, 'Yuvraj, Sadanand is not entirely wrong. We have been instructed to ignore, as far as possible, any orders given by you.'

'Are these instructions in writing?'

'No. Just oral.'

'Are they from Panhalgad? From Abasaheb?'

'No … but they are from Raigad … from Rahuji Somnath and other officials.'

'So what have you decided?'

'Sarkar, we are mere servants. When we received oral instructions from Raigad, we sent a messenger to Maharaj in Panhalgad for clarifications. Despite waiting for four days, our messenger did not receive any clarity from Maharaj. What are we to assume?'

Sambhaji responded with a dejected smile and retired to his quarters. He said, looking at Ranubai, 'I have been in Sajjangad for nearly two months now. There is no sign of Samarth. What crime have I committed for Maharaj to ignore me in this manner? Even Samarth seems to be ignoring me! Despite being Yuvraj, I do not have the power even to resolve a simple administrative matter. If neither my people nor my king need me, I will be better off in a foreign land.'

'Shambhu, please restrain yourself. This calamity will soon pass.'

That afternoon Subedar Kheloji Naik Bhange from Mahuli came to meet Sambhaji. Kheloji was in his seventies but had the energy and enthusiasm of a teenager. His loyalty to the elder Maharaj and affection for Sambhaji knew no bounds.

Sambhaji said to him, 'Tomorrow is an auspicious day and I would like to come to Mahuli for a holy dip. But let that be a secret.'

5

It was 3 December 1678.

The next morning, Sambhaji and three hundred of his cavalrymen left for Mahuli. By the time the sun rose, they had reached the banks of the Krishna. The rivers Krishna and Venna meet at Mahuli. They also marked the boundary of the Hindavi Swaraj. The far bank was under the control of Adilshah of Bijapur. The Rahimatpur post in his kingdom was close to Mahuli.

A large crowd of worshippers had gathered at the banks of the sangam for the auspicious bath, including many sanyasis. Kheloji Naik was more than happy to receive Yuvraj. He bowed low in mujra, welcoming Sambhaji.

As the religious rites were being performed, Sambhaji's mind was preoccupied. He constantly glanced at the eastern boundary of the rivers. Soon, it was bright and sunny. As the rivers did not run deep at this time of year, many worshippers crossed to the other side, wading in waist-deep water. Sambhaji took his holy dip in one of the many pools created by the dry weather in the river bed.

All of a sudden, there was a movement in the grass on the other bank. A green flag appeared for a brief moment, as if signalling something, and vanished. Kheloji had noticed the flag but considering it part of a routine patrol in the enemy territory, he chose to ignore it. However, Sambhaji quickly climbed out of the pool and put on his clothes. The moment he put on his headgear, Kheloji, seeing his aquiline nose, fair complexion and shining eyes, was reminded of the elder Maharaj. Lost in trance, he continued to stare at Yuvraj.

At that moment, Sambhaji mounted his horse and spurred it. It shot forward like an arrow. Kheloji stared at the galloping horse, unable to believe his eyes. Instead of turning towards Parli, Sambhaji was crossing the river into enemy territory.

Sambhaji's men spurred their horses too, following him. In the distance, Kheloji could see a line of Mughal soldiers on the other bank. Seeing Sambhaji enter the river they shouted, raising their spears and flags in the air, 'Jay Shambhuraja! Allah-o-Akbar!'

The shouts of the Mughals hurt Kheloji's ears; his heart refused to believe what he was hearing. He jumped into the water and, with his naked sword glinting in the sun, shouted, 'Shambhu Raje! Where are you going?'

Sambhaji turned to look at Kheloji. He said, in a tortured voice, 'Khelojibaba, everything is over. Our paths must separate henceforth!'

'What are you blabbering, Yuvraj? These are the words of an enemy! Can the son of Shivaji be under the care of Diler Khan? Enough of this, Yuvraj! Don't take another step. Just turn back.'

Sambhaji turned his horse and was surprised to see nearly thirty or forty Maratha soldiers in the water, hard on his heels. Worried that they would surround him and stop him from going over to the other side, he unsheathed his sword and prepared to fight. But Kheloji, without thinking of his own safety, stepped forward. Folding his hands in supplication, he pleaded, 'Dear Yuvraj, don't do that! Shambhuraja, this act of yours would break Shivba's heart into pieces!'

Sambhaji, taking water from the Krishna in his palms, thundered, 'I take an oath with Krishna as my witness. I shall let you know, at the appropriate time, who Sambhaji really is! I shall conquer the world and return to accept your salutes.'

The Maratha warriors scrambled to obstruct Sambhaji and his men with shouts of 'Stop, stop!' Soon, a hand-to-hand combat ensued.

Kheloji was standing near Sambhaji's horse, and before Sambhaji could react, the old man lunged at him. Had the old man managed to hug him at that moment, saying 'Shambhubal!', Sambhaji would have been forced to let his sword fall in the river. But he succeeded in avoiding Kheloji's embrace, and rushed towards the other bank. The bank was steep and the horse, unable to jump over, came to a halt, raising its forelegs in vain.

Sambhaji spurred him and pulled the reins tight, to no avail. The poor animal bled from its nose as it tried desperately to climb. In a few minutes, Sambhaji's horse collapsed and fell with a thud. Sambhaji managed to save himself from being crushed as he jumped off the horse's back in the nick of time and rolled out of the way.

The Mughals on the bank welcomed Sambhaji with 'Aaiye, Yuvraj, jaldi aaiye!' Sambhaji turned to see Kheloji being surrounded and restrained by a few Mughal soldiers.

As for Sambhaji's horse, its chest had been split open by its broken ribs. It lay on the bank, bleeding and drawing its final breaths. Sambhaji could not bear to see his favourite horse in such agony. Ignoring the helping hand of a Mughal soldier, he ran back to his horse and took out a water bag tied to the saddle. He poured a little water in the horse's mouth. Soon, the horse stretched its legs and, in a few moments, was still.

Sambhaji climbed the steep bank and walked into enemy territory. But he was troubled by a sudden fear as he took his first few steps. He wondered if these were inauspicious signs of things to come. Was he going in the right direction? Was his decision wise? But he had nowhere else to go. The territory he had left behind—its forests, fields, men, palaces—they were no longer his!

He did not know what awaited him but, after all, a man was known by his bold deeds and daredevil attitude. His father had had the courage to revolt against Adilshah when he was still a vassal in the Shah's service. Sambhaji believed that he could create a name for himself and then return victorious to his father to take his blessings. He had no other option at this moment but to jump into the mouth of the golden fish called Diler Khan.

6

It was an extraordinary day for the Mughal soldiers. The Yuvraj of the Maratha Empire was riding with them. The news that Sambhaji had joined them was cause for elation throughout the Mughal dominion from the Delhi Durbar to the Deccan.

As for Sambhaji, the farther they journeyed into Adilshahi territory, the more nervous he felt. It was beginning to dawn on him that there was a thin line between daredevilry and a risk which could turn out fatal. At the village of Vathar, Diler Khan's Subedar Ikhlas Khan waited for Sambhaji with a cavalry, nearly two thousand strong. They greeted Sambhaji warmly.

They crossed the river Neera, while Diler Khan paced in eager anticipation in his tent at the Kurkumbh, the Mughal outpost. Things were moving the way he had planned, but he did not trust the Marathas and had therefore sent Ikhlas Khan to meet and greet Sambhaji first. He recalled how Shivaji had entered the Lal Mahal in Pune and maimed his friend Shaista Khan, cutting off his fingers. Shaista Khan had often wept, showing his disfigured hand, whenever he recalled that unfortunate incident. The story of how Shivaji had killed Afzal Khan, tearing his chest open and then beheading him, had been told many times over. It was no wonder, then, that Diler Khan was circumspect, despite the friendly tones of Sambhaji's recent letters. He still suspected that this was a ploy by the father-son duo to deceive and overthrow him.

Yet, he was happy when a messenger brought news that Shivaji's son had joined the Mughals a couple of hours ago and was already on his way. The joy exceeded even the sadistic pleasure he felt when he had beheaded Murarbaji at Purandhar and wiped his bloodstained hands on his embroidered coat.

Diler Khan turned to look outside his tent where an approaching cloud of dust announced Sambhaji's arrival. In a few moments they entered his range of vision. The sight brought tears of joy to Diler Khan's eyes. Sitting atop a richly decorated elephant in a howdah were Ikhlas Khan and Sambhaji. As he stared at the rapidly approaching elephant, Diler Khan noticed that Sambhaji resembled Shivaji very closely.

The servants following the elephant rushed to set up a ladder and were about to climb up when Diler Khan, with a wave of his hand, dismissed them. He climbed up the ladder himself to welcome Sambhaji. 'Aayiye … the pride of the Deccan, Sher Sambhaji! Welcome!' Diler Khan, beside himself at the way things had turned out, felt the kind of joy he would have experienced upon meeting a long-lost brother.

There was a feast that afternoon with a spread of delicacies which included kebabs specially made for the occasion. Diler Khan was nearly forty years older than Sambhaji but the two spoke to each other as if they were childhood friends. Despite the show of friendship and happiness by Sambhaji, Diler Khan's keen eye did not miss the tinge of melancholy on young prince's face. He said, encouragingly, 'Yuvraj, the all-powerful

Alamgir is really pleased with you. What is there to fear when you have his blessings?'

The two conferred that afternoon. Diler Khan was careful in word and deed to ensure that the proud son of Shivaji, quick to take offence, did not find him wanting in hospitality or tact. He did not want to mar what promised to be the beginning of a great alliance. He said, pacifying Sambhaji, 'Shahzade, don't worry even one bit! A bright future awaits you. Your brother Diler Khan is fully aware of the way you have been insulted at Raigad.'

Sambhaji fell silent. Diler Khan said, taking Sambhaji's hand, 'Don't make the mistake of taking decisions prompted by the heart. A king must ensure that his parents, friends and close confidantes are all in his control before taking any step. It is quite natural that your stepmother Soyrabai would demand the thone for her son. And after all, even Dashrath could not refuse his favourite queen!'

Sambhaji said, taken by surprise, 'It seems you have studied the Ramayana …'

'If you want to rule a place, it is important to understand the weather there, isn't it? One should be aware of the gods and goddesses there. But let me assure you—the Badshah of Hindustan, Aurangzeb, is deeply concerned about your welfare.'

'Thank you, Khan saheb.'

'I tell you, Shahzade: do not feel guilty for having left your family. In your puranas, you have examples of Ravan fighting with his brother, Yudhishtir with his uncle Shakuni. Why, our own Alamgir Aurangzeb had to revolt against his father. There is no victory without war and no glory without victory.'

7

Diler Khan knew he had a long way to travel. He was worried that Shivaji Raje might, in order to save his son, come marching against him. Taking necessary precautions, he ordered the camp to pack up and move. Sambhaji's throat went dry when he heard they were approaching Bahadurgad. Diler Khan sensed the change on Sambhaji's face and wondered why the Yuvraj had suddenly become tense. The troops crossed the Sahyadris and soon the flat plains on the banks of the river Bhima were visible from a distance.

Aurangzeb had earlier appointed his 'milk brother' Bahadur Khan Kolkatash Jafarjung the Subedar of the Deccan. He had built a strong fort on the banks of the Bhima at Pedgaon and christened it Bahadurgad. Sambhaji had heard of the fort, namesake of the Sultan's brother, for the first time during the coronation of Shivaji Raje. Maharaj had also received information that a huge treasure worth at least a crore hons as well as two hundred of the choicest Arabian horses were being held at the fort. It was a mouth-watering prospect for the Marathas.

One day, Bahadur Khan received news of a Maratha force, nearly two thousand strong, approaching the fort from the western side. He smiled. He had deliberately kept vigil at the western gates quite lax to fool the Marathas. Consequently, the Maratha soldiers were able to enter the fort quite easily, only to find thousands of well-armed Mughal soldiers waiting for them within the walls. The Marathas ran for their lives, much to the amusement of Bahadur Khan, whose men chased them as they crossed the narrow Saraswati river and entered the territories of Jalalpur and Shedgaon. The Mughals continued their chase.

The fort, meanwhile, was left almost unguarded, and only women, children and servants remained inside. There were not enough soldiers left even to shut the twelve heavy doors. Just when the people of Bahadurgad had relaxed their guard, out of nowhere, seven thousand Maratha soldiers, who had been hiding in the woods nearby, attacked the fort. The Marathas faced no resistance whatsoever, and soon, they were marching away with two hundred horses and the contents of the fort's treasury. The wily Shivaji had once again scored over the mighty Mughals. Bahadur Khan had been made to look like a fool.

As he neared the fort, Sambhaji was under tremendous pressure. He wondered whether his plans would make the Maratha Empire stronger or destroy it. With the river Bhima on his right, he could see the distant ramparts of Bahadurgad clearly. Trumpets, horns and drums welcomed him with great gusto. Diler Khan sat proudly with Sambhaji in the howdah. A large bustling town was visible within the strong, heavily guarded walls of the fort. Sambhaji could see the moon and stars, symbol of Aurangzeb, fluttering on the battlements and on the rooftops of havelis.

The fort was a symbol of the arrogance of the Mughals. From these strong walls and ramparts, they believed they could look down with contempt at the Deccan kings. The residents of Bahadurgad had often seen sardars from the Deccan arriving with their necks bowed, carrying trays of gems and jewellery as a token of their acceptance of Mughal suzerainty. Many of these sardars were welcomed with a whiplash and treated like slaves. But the scene today was very different. Men, women and children assembled on the terraces and rooftops to see who was being felicitated with such fanfare and who was arriving on a howdah with all the pomp meant for a Mughal Badshah.

Sambhaji, despite the grandeur of his reception at Bahadurgad, was not comfortable. An inkling of something being amiss constantly irked him. He wondered whether it was his victory or defeat to arrive here amidst such pageantry, saluting and receiving salutes while entering an enemy camp. To moisten his dry throat, he gulped down water from a camelskin pouch. Yet, his nervousness did not abate.

The fort, built on flat land, was spread over nearly six hundred acres, a section of its walls looking out over the confluence of the rivers Saraswati and Bhima. Sambhaji, who was used to the Maratha hill forts, was reminded by Bahadurgad of his childhood stay in Agra and its tall havelis, mosques and temple spires. The town had a population of nearly seventy thousand which included ryots, soldiers, Arabs, Persians, Muslims from the Deccan, and Maratha soldiers, not to mention the Mughals, who were at the top of the social hierarchy.

At the centre of the town was a square palace built by Bahadur Khan. The palace was made of teak and decorated with flying banners, buntings and flags which fluttered in the wind. There were no drapes covering the windows though and people sitting in the Diwan-e-Aam could see the silvery Bhima flowing in the distance. Sambhaji was to be a guest at the palace today.

8

The celebrations, with firecrackers bursting all around him as he climbed the steps to the palace with Bahadur Khan, reminded Sambhaji of Diwali. He felt as if even the huge oil lamps, lit in his honour, were shouting with joy, 'Look! Shivaji's son has joined hands with the Mughals!'

The palace singers sang paeans in praise of Sambhaji as he was presented with fine clothes and jewellery. Sambhaji glanced at the sardars in attendance. An old sardar with his white flowing beard attracted his attention. His attire was that of the Mughals, but he was a Maratha! As Sambhaji's eyes met him, he turned his face away with a look of hatred. Sambhaji recognised Bajaji Naik's son Mahadji who was married to his elder sister Sakhubai.

Shivaji's son was being felicitated in Bahadurgad but the town had not forgotten the way Shivaji had fooled Bahadur Khan and looted the fort. Moreover, he had yet another humiliation in store for the Subedar of the Deccan. When Shivaji had left for the extended campaign in Karnatak, he sent a message to Bahadur Khan, with a plea to hand over all his forts in the region to Aurangzeb. It was Shivaji's ploy to ensure that Bahadur Khan would not attack Raigad in his absence. He had pleaded, 'I want peace in my old age. I am happy to surrender all my forts unconditionally.' Aurangzeb, already troubled with the unrest in Kabul and Kandahar, had been delighted when he heard Shivaji's message.

Shivaji's sole condition for his surrender was that he wanted an impression of Aurangzeb's palm as a token of his acceptance. Bahadur Khan had smilingly accepted the condition and sent a note to Delhi. The treaty was to be executed the moment he received the token from Delhi. In the meantime, Khan decided to give some exquisite gifts to Shivaji. He made arrangements for an elephant and a sandalwood palanquin to be delivered to Raigad. While Bahadur Khan was still waiting for the message from Delhi with the Emperor's palmprint, Shivaji returned from his Karnatak campaign and promptly cancelled the treaty to surrender. Once again, Bahadur Khan had been made to look like a fool. Aurangzeb, incensed at Khan's inability to read the Maratha rat's mind, had removed him from the post of Subedar of the Deccan.

While celebrations were in progress, Diler Khan pointed to the richly decorated elephant which had brought them to Bahadurgad and said, 'Shahzade, this is the same elephant which Bahadur Khan had selected as a present for Shivaji. I am going to present it to you today.'

He continued, 'The elephant is lucky to meet the son, if not the father!'

Sambhaji was reminded of his father's bravery and cunning. Diler Khan then stood up, holding a silver tray in his hand. He said, waving a hand towards the sardars in attendance, 'I request Sambhaji's brother-in-law, Mahadji Nimbalkar, to present this token of our appreciation to Shahzada.'

Diler Khan's suggestion was greeted with loud applause from the crowd, forcing Mahadji to get up, albeit with a long face. However, he had a sudden cramp in his back while rising from his seat and was forced to sit down again. Hence Diler Khan had to present the gift of royal clothes himself. He said, addressing the assembly, 'On behalf of Shahenshah Aurangzeb, I declare Sambhaji as a Watandar with seven thousand troops. He is also honoured with the title of Raja. He will be treated henceforth as a king.'

After the ceremony, many including Diler Khan insisted that Sambhaji should sit atop the elephant again. They wanted him to ride to his haveli sitting in the howdah. But Sambhaji declined and walked down to the haveli. His quarters were in the inner wing of the haveli. Soon he realised that Mahadji's rooms were adjacent to his own. Wishing to enquire about his brother-in-law's health before retiring for the night, he entered Mahadji's bedchamber. Despite sensing Sambhaji's presence in his room, Mahadji did not move, nor even bother to get out of bed.

Sambhaji asked, 'How is your health, Daaji?'

'Fine,' Mahadji growled.

'Well, it is natural that you would feel the spasms of a fake sprain.'

Mahadji glared at Sambhaji. He said, spitting into a spittoon, 'Sambha, why did you leave Shivaji and come here? What was your compulsion?'

'I thought it would be nice to follow your footsteps and become a slave.'

'Don't rub salt into my wounds. Sardars like me have been working under others all our lives. But you and your father have a duty towards fulfilling the dream of Swaraj which you have been talking of for so long, for all our sakes.'

Mahadji's words pierced Sambhaji's heart. The brittle smile, which he had carried since the durbar began, vanished. In this beautifully decorated town, resplendent with Mughal wealth, Sambhaji suddenly felt lonely.

After a couple of days, two royal palanquins arrived at Bahadurgad. Anticipating the possibility of a chase and some skirmishes during his escape into Mughal territory, Sambhaji had asked Durgabai to go to the Mughal post of Rahimatpur and stay put there, along with a few loyal servants. Hence he was shocked to see both Durgabai and Ranuakka at Bahadurgad.

He asked, 'What is Akkasaheb doing here? Why is she here, leaving her family and children back at Wai?'

'Shambhu, don't worry about me. In fact, I insisted that I would come along to take care of you.'

'But Akka ...'

'Shambhu, you never got your mother's love. Nor is your grandmother, Jijabai, alive now. Your father has turned his back on you. Shouldn't someone from the family be by your side?'

Overcome by emotion on hearing his sister's words, Sambhaji did not say a word.

Sambhaji's quarters were in a new and beautiful haveli. Behind the haveli was a small house. It was a small but strongly built house where a mysterious prisoner was being kept. It was evident from the fact he was incarcerated alone in an independent house rather than thrown in the Bahadurgad jail with other prisoners, that he was a man of high standing. Inexplicably, Sambhaji was attracted towards the house and would often look at it from the haveli's terrace or his window. But he had never seen or heard the doors being opened. The prisoner inside was being treated like a caged animal, with irons chains around his ankles. Food and water was dropped through the windows.

Sambhaji had seen the prisoner at the windows a few times in daylight or by the light of candles at night. He appeared to be an old Muslim man, probably in his sixties, a little bent, and with beautiful sparkling eyes. Sambhaji soon learnt that his name was Miyan Khan and that he was the former Subedar of Athani. Judging from his demeanour, Sambhaji presumed that he must have been a good man who had fallen on bad times and gotten arrested.

It had been two months since Sambhaji's arrival in Bahadurgad. He was not able to make out what Diler Khan had in mind and began to feel suffocated in the luxuriously furnished haveli. He would toss and turn in his bed at night, fiddling with his necklace which had an image of Bhawani. Memories of his homeland, and especially his father, would often overwhelm him. He recalled the loving eyes of Yesubai with an aching heart. Durgabai and Ranubai watched Sambhaji helplessly, not knowing how to console him. Durgabai could barely sleep at night wondering how she could make her husband more comfortable.

One night, Sambhaji woke up from a terrible dream. It was windy outside and the neem trees swayed in the night breeze. Sambhaji, despite being awake, was still under the influence of the nightmare he had just seen. In the dream, the elephant gifted by Diler Khan was crushing Sambhaji beneath his heavy feet. Sambhaji could clearly see his own bloodstained body as it was ground into the earth.

FIVE

In the Grip of a Python

1

A man from Mahad, under the pretext of selling Maratha-made jewellery, had entered the strongly guarded fortress of Bahadurgad. He possessed the art of glib talk, persuading Durgabai to buy a whole bunch of trinkets. The moment he saw Sambhaji, the jeweller revealed the primary purpose of his visit: he had come as a bearer of glad tidings.

'Yuvraj, you have been blessed by Bhawani. A Lakshmi has been born in your house, and both daughter and mother are fine.'

Sambhaji was overwhelmed hearing the news. He took off his pearl necklace and presented it to the messenger. He also instructed the man to inform his wife that he had gifted two diamond rings from his treasury to his newborn. While he rued the fact that he was not there when Bhawani, his first child, was born, he could barely contain his joy. He wanted to distribute sweets to the villagers sitting on an elephant.

Days passed without much incident at Bahadurgad. Sambhaji often saw Miyan Khan, the Adilshahi nobleman and erstwhile Subedar of Athani, at the window of his prison. He had gathered a great deal of information about the man in the last few months. Miyan Khan had served as a Subedar under Adil Shah of Bijapur but was loyal to the Mughal ruler in Delhi. He would send vital and timely information to Aurangzeb about the affairs of the Deccan but his enemies conspired against him and managed to convince the Emperor that he was a double agent. Aurangzeb, suspicious by nature, sent his troops to Athani and captured Miyan Khan. Khan was then placed under arrest at Bahadurgad.

Sambhaji soon realised that while he was free to move around Bahadurgad as the Yuvraj of the Marathas, there were men who silently stood guard outside his haveli at night. They were keeping an eye, no doubt, on him. Many a time, when Sambhaji had stepped outside the boundaries of the fort to take a dip in the Saraswati, a few soldiers would surround him, albeit under the pretext of protecting him. The same was the case when he would go for long walks along the Bhima.

He bluntly asked Diler Khan once, 'Khan saheb, am I a guest here, or a royal prisoner?'

The old man laughed and said, 'You're not an ordinary man, Sambhaji. You are the Shahzada of the Marathas and we need to protect a gem like you!'

Sambhaji was unable to gauge Diler Khan's plans for him. This made him restless. Meanwhile, Khan had sent the good news of Sambhaji's defection to Delhi but Aurangzeb was not willing to believe it just yet. He wanted to make sure that the man proclaiming himself to be Sambhaji was really so and not someone masquerading as the Yuvraj. He decided to send a few handpicked men to the Deccan for the sole purpose of ascertaining the truth. Both Diler Khan and Sambhaji were playing a guessing game: Khan trying to find out what the Badshah had in mind while Sambhaji tried to read Khan's mind. The days crawled and nights were torturous. Sambhaji's restlessness increased.

One night, Sambhaji observed that Miyan Khan was sitting at the window of his house, his face creased with extreme sorrow. Tears were flowing down his cheeks and he banged his head a few times on the window in distress. The scene was repeated next afternoon and also the next night. Sambhaji suggested to Durgabai, 'When you go for your morning darshan to the temple, why don't you leave a little early when it is still dark and speak to the old man? Take a couple of your loyal maids with you.'

Sambhaji eagerly waited the next morning for Durgabai to return. She said, as soon as she entered the haveli, 'He seems like a gentleman. Aurangzeb has made his life hell, and now he is troubled by a personal tragedy.'

'Why, what happened?'

'His begum died at childbirth, leaving behind two daughters. Miyan Khan brought them up on his own. Six months ago, they were betrothed to the sons of a zamindar of Bijapur. The wedding is to be held a few days from now, but under these circumstances the large dowry he had promised for his daughters would be impossible to pay. He is stuck here in prison and feels it is unlikely that the marriage would take place at all.'

Sambhaji was upset on hearing this but soon a daring plan took shape in his mind. He waited restlessly for nightfall before summoning his cook, Zainuddin and instructing him and two other servants to perform a task.

Sambhaji then went out of the haveli and started bursting crackers, pretending to celebrate the joyous occasion of his daughter's birth. All the guards in the vicinity, attracted to the display of firecrackers, assembled to watch the show. While this was going on, his men were working on opening the door of the house behind the haveli. Soon, Miyan Khan was released and in his place, putting on the chains, sat Zainuddin!

At around midnight, Miyan Khan, who had been hiding at the basement of the haveli, came out and fell at Sambhaji's feet in gratitude. He was in tears.

Sambhaji said, 'I can understand your sorrow. I too am a father of a daughter now. And I haven't even seen her face yet.'

Miyan Khan's happiness knew no bounds. He said, 'I will be back in five days. Don't worry, Shahzade!'

Sambhaji said, 'I have taken this bold step as a father who understands your pain. If I am accused of having released a prisoner of the Mughals without permission, it will be an excuse for Aurangzeb to hang me. Please don't betray my trust.'

'Shambhu Raje, rest assured that I will never do anything to betray the trust you have reposed in me. I pray to Allah that I get a chance to serve you. If that day ever comes, I will make shoes out of my skin and put them on your feet.'

The guards posted outside the prisoner's house soon remarked to each other that the old man was not keeping well. For a few days, he rarely sat at the window and his constant coughing could be heard from outside. After about a week, Zainuddin was back in the kitchen and Miyan Khan was at his window again! Even from a distance, Sambhaji could see the look of contentment on his face. He would bow elaborately every time Sambhaji looked at him.

2

Nearly three months had elapsed since Sambhaji had arrived at Bahadurgad. He felt stifled by the constant surveillance of the guards posted outside his house, and the fact that he was not allowed to mix and meet the other Amirs and Umraos in town. It soon became evident to him that while there were no locks on his door or chains on his feet, he was practically under house arrest! Thankfully, he had Ranubai, Durgabai and loyal servants to keep him company.

As for Diler Khan, he kept up his sweet talk and gave Sambhaji honeyed assurances of all kinds. Sambhaji began to realise that the plan he had devised earlier might not work. On the flat terrain of Bahadurgad, the disciplined Mughal soldiers would clearly have an upper hand, and his initial gamble may not pay off. Each passing day made him more nervous and restless.

Sambhaji was 'free' to move around, but the soldiers who accompanied him everywhere never relaxed their vigil for a moment. Despite his mounting frustration, Sambhaji often took long walks along the the banks of the Bhima. He visited the palace built by Chand Bibi and enjoyed the beauty of the ancient temples on the other side of the river.

The river Bhima took a semicircular turn near Bahadurgad fort. Here, the river was quite deep, an abundant source of water for the residents as well as the troops garrisoned there. Elephants were used to draw water from the river in massive leather bags which would then be poured into a channel that supplied water to the fort.

One day, Sambhaji was riding alongside the river. In the distance, he could see the Saraswasti as it merged with the Bhima. Suddenly, he felt a little giddy and decided to rest for a while. He spotted a pleasant green patch on the river bank where he dismounted. Lying down on a carpet of grass, he was soon lost in a trance which brought some strange visions, as if his mind was playing tricks with him. He woke up sweating profusely and realised that he had been having a nightmare. Unable to understand its meaning, he mounted his horse to return to his haveli.

3

Diler Khan knew that being Subedar of the Deccan was like living on a knife's edge. As a seat of power, it was next only to the Delhi throne. Aurangzeb himself had been Subedar twice, as a prince. He thus had a thorough knowledge of the territory—its terrain, its geopolitics and its challenges. Diler Khan had expected the Badshah to reward him for having wooed Sambhaji, Yuvraj of the Marathas, into house arrest at the Bahadurgad fort. Instead, Aurangzeb had sent his own Shahzada, Muazzam, to the Deccan with instructions to look into the matter and report back to him.

Before long, a messenger arrived at Bahadurgad. As Diler Khan read the Emperor's message, his eyes popped out, as if instead of being invited to a feast, he had been slapped.

'Diler, I am told that you are felicitating Sambhaji every day for some reason or the other. The enemy's son is in our camp. You need to take full advantage of this situation. Use him as a shield and attack the Maratha territories. Create havoc. I want maximum damage inflicted on the enemy.'

Diler Khan was disappointed. He had expected a pat on the back but he had received a rap on his knuckles. He asked his Diwan, Ziya Khan, for his opinion. The latter said, 'Huzoor, the Badshah is very cunning. He wants to kill a few birds with a single stone. Hence, Alampanah feels you should take Sambhaji along in your campaigns against Shivaji, as well as the attacks on Bijapur and Golconda.'

Diler Khan began to realise that it was a golden opportunity to exploit Sambhaji's presence. What the Yuvraj himself felt about it was irrelevant as no one involved, least of all Sambhaji, had the authority to oppose the Badshah's plans. Diler Khan asked his Diwan, 'What, according to you, would make the Badshah happiest? Where should we attack first?'

'Bhupalgad.'

'Why so?'

'It is en route to Bijapur and managed by a powerful fortkeeper. If we take the fort, it would open doors to Bijapur.'

Diler Khan's mind began to work overtime. In the days that followed, he gathered as much information about the fort as possible. Built on flat land, it had once brought the ferocious Shaista Khan to his knees when the daredevil Firangoji Narsala held it for fifty-five days during a Mughal siege. Firangoji was the fortkeeper at Bhupalgad. His administrator was Vithal Bhalerao. Situated at the border of several warring states, the fort had witnessed many conflicts between the Adilshahi troops and the Mughals, as well as between the Marathas and the forces of Bijapur. Bhupalgad had stood like a rock amidst all this. The residents put their faith in the Shiva temple inside the fort, in their ample stock of water and foodgrains, and above all in Firangoji, their fortkeeper.

Plans for the campaign were put in motion and one day, soldiers streamed out of Bahadurgad. The carriages carrying the cannons creaked as they moved slowly through the gates of the fort. The accompanying men, including servants, smiths and traders from the bazaar, followed in a caravan.

A distraught Sambhaji sat in his haveli, unable to control the events that were unfolding around him. Diler Khan had not shared his plans with him. Meanwhile, he had received secret letters from Kalash at Shringarpur and Yesubai at Raigad. The messages were almost identical: 'Yuvraj, don't sit idle. You need to do something. All kinds of rumours are circulating. Many have already declared that you are going to convert and adopt the Muslim religion the way Netaji Palkar did. If you feel you are not getting a chance to show your valour, and unable to find a way out, now is the time to act. The very least you can do is to protect what you have. Don't let that go!'

While Sambhaji sat wondering what he should do, Ziya Khan came into his quarters and said, 'Shahzade, Diler Khan is waiting for you to join him.'

'Ask him to meet me here,' growled Sambhaji.

'How's that possible?' Ziya Khan said. 'He is the Subedar of the Deccan.'

Sambhaji's angry glance silenced Ziya, and the Diwan left. Horns and trumpets were announcing that the troops were already on the move. Soon Diler Khan, already in his armour, came to Sambhaji's haveli. He said, saluting him once, 'Shahzade, we must leave now if we want to reach Bhupalgad in two days.'

'I am not in a mood to visit Bhupalgad,' Sambhaji said.

'But the orders from Badshah Alamgir are clear.'

'Is that so? So Delhi decides which forts we should capture?'

Diler Khan was gentle but adamant. After all, the message from Alamgir was clear: use Sambhaji to inflict maximum damage in enemy territory.

Thus, Sambhaji was compelled to accompany Diler khan on his campaign. Travelling through Baramati, Phaltan and Mandesh, they reached the outskirts of Bhupalgad. Diler Khan had planned his moves very carefully. He was aware of the courage and determination of Firangoji Narsala, who had fought at Chakan with a handful of soldiers, not to mention his valiant defence of Bhupalgad against Alamgir's uncle Shaista Khan.

Diler Khan camped a few miles from the fort. Sambhaji's tent was nearby. Khan called for the Yuvraj that night and said, 'Speak to your compatriot. Ask him to vacate the fort before it turns ugly.'

Sambhaji was aware of Diler Khan's ploy but he was trapped and had no option but to comply. He sent a message through one of his trusted servants, 'The fort is weak and Diler Khan's army is strong. Why put your men at risk, and invite destruction of Abasaheb's fort? Hand it over peacefully and go your way unharmed.'

The next morning a messenger arrived from the fort. Sambhaji read Firangoji's message and then handed it over to Diler Khan without a comment. It said: *'It is not Shivaji's habit to run away without putting up a fight. Why don't you tell your friend that it might be a Mughal tradition to do so?'*

Diler Khan's face turned red with anger. He screamed, 'Is that the way someone replies to a message that seeks peace?'

'Khan saheb, a proud Maratha would behave like one, wouldn't he? Not everyone is a traitor like Sambhaji,' Sambhaji said, his face full of sorrow as he uttered the words.

Diler Khan looked at Sambhaji through his kohl-lined eyes, 'Shahzade, how long will you remain blind to the way you were insulted in Raigad? Despite being the rightful heir to the throne, you are being treated like a criminal. Your father does not take you on campaigns, your stepmother tries her best to prevent you from visiting Raigad, while petty officials and senior administrators find fault in your behaviour and try to shred your reputation to pieces. Even a maid's son is treated better!'

'Does that mean I should die an ignoble death?' Sambhaji growled.

Diler Khan held Sambhaji's hand and said, in a pained voice, 'Shahzade, I am offering you a hand of friendship in your time of trouble yet you still look at me as if I am the enemy.'

Sambhaji did not respond. Within moments, the cannons started firing. Now there was no turning back; the attack on Bhupalgad had begun. Meanwhile, a message from Firangoji meant for Sambhaji was intercepted by Khan's men. It read:

> *'Yuvraj, please go away as soon as possible. If you are in trouble, let us know. We shall fight to death to release you. Please inform immediately.'*

Needless to say, it never reached Sambhaji. Diler Khan muttered, as he watched the message burn in the fire in his tent, 'Allah, you have been merciful.'

The Mughal cannons tried their best to destroy the walls of the fort. The Marathas put up an equally strong resistance. They had launched a counter-attack with stones flung from catapults while showering the enemy troops with arrows. Diler Khan was growing impatient. He said to his chief of artillery, 'Do anything; but give me a breach in the walls. Else, this old man Firangoji will not surrender.'

The cannons slowly advanced amidst the shower of stones and arrows. The artillery troops struggled to protect their heads using metal shields while trying to work the cannons at the same time.

Soon, the Mughal soldiers managed to dig a trench to lay the mines. After lighting the mines, they withdrew in haste. As the blasts shook the fort, the mighty walls of Bhupalgad rattled. A few large boulders came rolling down but the fort stood intact.

Sambhaji was in charge of the attack from the other side of the fort. He instructed his men to attach tall ladders along the walls. But the constant artillery fire, as the men climbed up the ladders, proved fatal. Many fell, and others were singed by fire or succumbed to the rain of arrows unleashed by the Maratha soldiers.

Finally, one of the ramparts crumbled, opening a path for the Mughals to enter the fort. Firangoji had put up a spirited defence but could not hold out against the combined attack of Diler Khan and Sambhaji. Realising that the fort had been taken, many Maratha soldiers ran away. Most of the soldiers were captured and brought back as prisoners.

4

The sun had set. A cool breeze blew. A shattered Bhupalgad was trying to hide its wounds in the darkness of the night. At the Mughal camp outside the fort, Sambhaji and Diler Khan sat in their lamp-lit tents. They watched as nearly seven hundred Maratha warriors were marched down from the fort, hands tied behind their backs. Sambhaji stood up to look at the soldiers. Many of the faces were familiar. Some of them looked at the Yuvraj with suspicion while many openly glared at him. Their contemptuous looks, sharply turned moustaches, and the fire in their eyes—all pierced Sambhaji's heart.

Yet, many of them bowed in mujra. Sambhaji, seeing the jewels of the Swaraj thus humiliated, felt miserable. He said, turning to Diler Khan, 'Where are you taking them, Khan saheb?'

'To the dungeon at Bahadurgad.'

'Please keep in mind, Khan saheb ... they deserve no greater punishment than being jailed.'

The next morning, Sambhaji woke up to the loud sounds of hammers crashing against stone. To his utter surprise, Diler Khan had given orders to break down the walls of Bhupalgad. Aghast at the foolishness of the act, he rushed into the Subedar's tent, saying, 'Khan saheb, what madness is this? Why destroy a strong and beautiful fort which we have captured?'

Diler Khan said, smiling contemptuously, 'What is the point in Mughals guarding a fort which is on the borders of Maratha and Bijapur territories?'

Already dismayed, Sambhaji was further incensed when Diler Khan extended his taunt, 'No point in keeping such spoils. The moment cattle-herding children see these forts, they start dreaming of becoming a king one day!'

A few hours later, Sambhaji went for a darshan at the Shiva temple with Ranubai and Durgabai. As he carelessly kicked a few stones lying around, he could hear the work of the hammers and other tools being used to break down the walls of Bhupalgad. Filled with the agonising guilt of being responsible for destroying what Shivaji had built with the blessings of many generations, Sambhaji's mind reeled and he walked with faltering steps. A chain of unfortunate events had begun, he realised, since the day he had entered the Mughal territory after crossing the Krishna at Mahuli.

On the way, he met a Kazi. The man said, 'Alamgir has committed a crime which will bring shame upon all the people here, irrespective of their caste or creed.'

'Why, what has happened, Kazi miyan?'

'The Badshah is imposing Jizya, a tax on all people who are not Muslims. Such blasphemy would never have been condoned by his father or his grandfather!'

Sambhaji muttered to himself, 'Maybe it's Lord Shiva's way of giving me a hint. What kind of justice can I expect from Aurangzeb if he is willing to penalise thousands of innocent Hindus?'

These were indeed challenging times for Sambhaji. In the cool and dark sanctum sanctorum of the temple, Sambhaji sat silently for a long time, his head resting at the feet of the idol.

Ranubai offered twenty-one coconuts and a gold necklace, requesting the priest, 'This time, please bless my brother with a boy child.' Durgabai blushed while Sambhaji looked at her in surprise. He wondered how he was going to carry this sweet burden amidst all the chaos.

Sambhaji's moment of peace did not last long. Four of his servants came running and said, literally screaming in their excitement, 'Yuvraj! Yuvraj!' Sambhaji sensed urgency in their cries. Surely, there had been some calamity! He asked, picking up his sword, 'What has happened? Tell me!'

One of them blurted out, 'Treachery, Raje! We have been fooled.'

Another began, 'The seven hundred Maratha prisoners of war! They were taken away to Bahadurgad and ...'

'Don't stop! Tell me what happened to them,' Sambhaji cried.

'How do I tell you, Yuvraj,' one of the servants said, tears running down his cheeks. In between sobs, he revealed, 'These devils cut off one hand each of half the soldiers and one foot of the rest. Even animals are not so cruel!'

Sambhaji's rage knew no bounds. He clenched his fists and ground his teeth in anger. He rushed out of the temple and jumped onto his horse in one smooth movement. Spurring his mount, he raced through the jungle, leaping over rocks and steering through the dense undergrowth. His men, following close behind, shouted, 'Yuvraj! Be careful!' But Sambhaji was in no mood to listen. Somehow he managed to reach the Mughal camp without any mishap, halting the horse only when he reached his tent.

The Mughal soldiers who stood guard outside Diler Khan's tent stared at Sambhaji's dishevelled hair and the bloodied hooves of his horse. Sambhaji's eyes were flaming red with anger. He jumped off his horse and screamed, 'Where is that treacherous old man? Where is Diler Khan?'

Diler Khan, who had seen Sambhaji racing down from Bhupalgad, sensed danger. He was hiding like a mouse in a field nearby, with nearly two thousand men around him. He did not have the courage to face the enraged Sambhaji.

'You old coward! Come out!' Sambhaji shouted a few times.

The boiling ocean in Sambhaji's mind took a long time to simmer down. Finally he said to a soldier standing near him, 'Give my message to the old Khan. Just because Sambhaji has joined the Mughals, Shivaji is not finished. Not yet.'

That night Sambhaji was in turmoil. Images of the men in the dungeons of Bahadurgad, their hands and feet broken and severed, their faces full of pain and reproach, appeared in vivid waking dreams. His head literally exploded with these visions, denying him even a single moment's respite. Durgabai and Ranubai sat by his bed, their faces creased with worry. As the night wore on, Sambhaji's restlessness increased. Getting up, he went and picked up a sharp stone lying at a corner of the tent. His wife and sister ran after him in a panic and held onto his arms. He said, trying to get out of their embrace, as the servants rushed in, 'Leave me! Leave me, Akkasaheb.'

'Raje, what are you trying to do?'

Sambhaji slapped his forehead with his palm, saying, 'Ranu Akka, despite the presence of Shivaji's son, seven hundred Marathas lose their limbs to the cruelty of the Mughals. What is the point in me being here if I am not able to stop such heinous acts? Let me cut off these vile and useless hands of mine.'

Durgabai pleaded, 'Raje, please restrain yourself. If you give in to despair, what future remains for the Maratha Swaraj?'

Sambhaji pushed the servants away. But Ranubai held his hands, pleading, 'Please listen to me, my dear! If you decide to cut off your hands, have you thought of what would happen to us? If tomorrow Aurangzeb decides to march on Abasaheb, it is only you, Shambhu Raje, who is capable of cutting off his horse's legs.'

Sambhaji could not take it anymore. He dropped the stone on the floor and walked towards a huge metal pole that stood in the middle of the tent. Hugging the pole, he started banging his head on it. Almost delirious, he screamed, tears streaming down his cheeks, 'Abasaheb, please pardon me! I made a terrible mistake. I have erred!'

5

Even a small scratch inflicted by a mouse on a lion's nose is enough to enrage the noble beast. Sambhaji was not only proud of his land and its people but felt responsible for them. Besides, he was young, barely twenty, and blood boiled in his veins at the thought of the seven hundred Marathas who had been maimed by the Mughals while he had stood by doing nothing.

As for Diler Khan, he was an anxious man these days. It had taken the tireless effort of nearly three years to win Sambhaji over to his side. Now, with a single act, he had irked the lion's cub he had tamed by the sweat of his brow. If Sambhaji was to leave suddenly, Diler Khan would lose the gem which had earned him some respect at the Mughal court in Delhi.

The Mughal troops were still camped outside the walls of Bhupalgad. Sambhaji refused to come out of his quarters and had not touched food or water for three days. He would sit in a trance, barely consenting to drink half a glass of milk. Ranubai and Durgabai were growing more anxious by the day. Meanwhile Diler Khan was trying to devise a way to gauge Sambhaji's state of mind. When Durgabai contracted a fever, Khan used the opportunity to send his hakeem to their tent with instructions to ascertain the situation. He also sent baskets of sweets and fruits, and a honeyed message to the effect that the orders to cut off the hands and legs of the Maratha soldiers had not been issued by him. He conveniently put the blame on his nephew Gairat Khan.

Four days went by. Taking stock of the situation, Diler Khan realised that the lion cub's initial anger may have subsided. Entering Sambhaji's chambers like a thief, he sat at his bedside with the meek air of a penitent sinner. Then he said, with a show of sympathy, 'Raje, it has been a real tragedy. Gairat Khan has disappeared. I have petitioned Alamgir to hang him to death.'

'How does that help anyone? Tomorrow, when these disabled, half-legged and one-armed men return home, people would ask how Shivaji's son, who was standing nearby, could allow this kind of cruelty. What am I supposed to say?'

Diler Khan knew Sambhaji had a sharp mind. He had to think of a convincing answer. Calling Ziya Khan to his tent, he dictated a message to Aurangzeb:

> *'Alampanah, please declare all over Hindustan that Sambhaji is the true ruler of the Marathas. A large number of people who are loyal to Sambhaji are in Shivaji's forces. If the enmity between the father and son increases, we will surely benefit. There would be a split amongst the Marathas. Once that is done, it will only be a matter of time before we seize and ravage their territory.'*

Diler Khan instructed Ziya Khan, 'Tell Sambhaji that I have recommended to Alamgir that he be declared as the Shahenshah of the Marathas.'

Ziya Khan conveyed the message to Sambhaji with all the drama he could muster, and he was disappointed by the Yuvraj's indifferent reaction. Sambhaji knew these were childish attempts to incite him to revolt against Shivaji. Besides, the cruelty of the Mughals towards the Maratha prisoners after the siege of Bhupalgadh was not something he could easily forget. And now they were now trying to take advantage of the rift with his father! He desperately wanted to wring the neck of that wily old Diler Khan. He told Durgabai and Ranubai, 'I can finish that old fox any day but the Mughal soldiers guarding him will hunt me down afterwards.'

One day Diler Khan stomped into Sambhaji's quarters, waving a piece of paper. It was apparently a message from Shivaji which his spies had intercepted. He growled, 'Is this the way a lion like Shivaji deals with his cub? Read this!'

Sambhaji retorted, 'What do you mean? What does Abasaheb say?'

'Listen to the message and judge for yourself. It says, *'Don't be hesitant if Sambhaji attacks. Ensure that each and every fort is protected and fight till the end. Don't be merciful to Sambhaji just because he is my son.'* What kind of language is this for a father to use against his own son?'

Sambhaji laughed sarcastically. 'What else do you expect my father to do? Garland his son who has defected to the enemy camp?'

That shut Diler Khan up. The wily Subedar realised that Sambhaji was growing restless and did not wish to remain in the Mughal camp. That night he stayed awake and composed another urgent message to Aurangzeb. It read:

> *'Jahanpanah, I beg your pardon but I reiterate that the need to declare Sambhaji the Shahenshah of the Marathas. I urgently request you to send out a public notice across the Empire. One such proclamation from you will separate the father and son. The Maratha Empire will be split wide open.'*

Diler Khan waited with bated breath for Aurangzeb's reply but he received no response. He was no longer sure of the course of action he should take with regard to Sambhaji. His Diwan, Ziya Khan, perceived his confusion and suggested at an opportune moment, 'Khansaheb, it is my view that we shouldn't waste any more time. Let us arrest Sambhaji like an ordinary criminal and send him to prison at Agra.'

'How does that help me?'

Ziya Khan said, 'Khansaheb, you will get all the credit. If the Emperor is happy, Diler Khan would be appointed Diwan of the Delhi Durbar, no less!'

Diler Khan laughed at Ziya Khan's suggestion. 'You idiot! This means you have not understood our Alamgir yet. He has no enemies left in the North. If Shivaji and his son, his enemies in the South, are finished off, he will have no need of people like us. And he would treat us with the contempt reserved for dogs and cats.'

'What do we do then?'

'Ziya, we have to ensure we don't break the stick and allow the snake to die. Only then can ordinary servants like us survive. Else, we are finished!'

One evening, just as it was getting dark, Diler Khan went out for a ride with his guards. As he crossed a small hill, he saw a tall figure in the distance standing with a few other men. In the enveloping darkness he was not able to see who it was. Ziya Khan said, 'It is Sambhaji with his men.'

'What is he doing there?'

'Khansaheb, have you forgotten? It has only been fifteen days or so. It is the spot where you ordered the limbs of hundreds of Marathas to be cut off. Sambhaji spends a lot of time in this place ... sometimes in the morning, at times in the evening. Often, he spends the whole day here. I am told he takes the soil in his hands and cries like a child.'

'Sentimental fool!' Diler Khan muttered to himself. 'But what frightens me is that this fool is a tiger too!'

Returning to his camp, Diler Khan said, 'We must move away from this place. It has occupied Sambhaji's mind. He will soon go mad. Let us find a way to keep him engaged elsewhere.'

By now, in order to gain Aurangzeb's favour, Diler Khan had begun taking an interest in the affairs of Bijapur. The Sultanate was weak and vulnerable, basking blindly in its lost glory. Adil Shah had been promised support by Shivaji in the event of a Mughal attack. Meanwhile Diler Khan tried to woo the sardars of the Adilshahi durbar by sending letters of assurance that promised them riches in exchange for shifting their loyalty to the Mughals. Everyone was surprised when he finally managed to catch a big fish like Sarja Khan.

Diler Khan also received a letter from his well-wishers at the Delhi durbar. It warned: *'Diler, don't send recommendations to the Alampanah asking for Sambhaji to be declared as Shahenshah of the Marathas. The Badshah views your excessive praise of Sambhaji with suspicion. He suspects that you have struck an friendship with Sambhaji and that the two of you are planning something together. He worries that you may join forces with the Marathas and revolt. The Badshah is growing old and your letters are making him anxious.'*

Two days later, Diler Khan entered Sambhaji's tent with a broad smile and an outstretched hand of friendship. 'Shambhu Shahzade, you might be thinking that we are against the Marathas and no one else. Well, that is not true. Get ready! We are marching on to Bijapur. I will show you how Diler Khan ravages an Islamic kingdom.'

6

One night, furtive footsteps were heard outside Sambhaji's quarters. It was a spy from Raigad who had managed to find his way through enemy territory and reach Sambhaji without any mishap, bearing a message from Maharaj himself. After holding the message to his forehead reverently for a few moments, Sambhaji started reading it:

> *'Blessings to you, my son. Ever since you have left, my mind has been reeling with all kinds of thoughts and making me restless.*
>
> *'What did you learn when you were being taught the Ramayan by the pandits? Ram left his kingdom and chose to live in the forests to fulfil the promise he had made to his father. But you have gone away, abandoning our precious Swaraj. You chose to join the enemy, considering me an outsider. Without thinking twice, and allowing anger to rule your decisions, you entered the camp of the Mughals. I am tortured by these thoughts.*
>
> *'Recently, I heard of the cruel act of the Mughals wherein our men's limbs were brutally severed. My eyes have been shedding tears of blood since that day. Back in the days when Maratha sardars considered it their religious duty to serve under foreign overlords, I managed to gather ordinary but brave souls like Tanaji, Murarbaji and many others in order to build our Hindavi Swaraj. What a misfortune that the very hands which continue to build the temple of Swaraj are brutally cut off by our enemy!*
>
> *I can understand that you are going through the same pain that I am suffering. Shambhu, there are many people here who hate you and are jealous of you. But If you believe that I am biased and listen to their views alone, you are wrong. Please keep in mind that there are as many who love you dearly and would not think twice to sacrifice their lives for you. How can I, as a king and a father, be blind to them?*

'Let bygones be bygones. Bury your ill-feeling and come out of that hell. Half of Maharashtra is waiting for your return, from the ryots and the sadhus to Shivaji Maharaj. Please return, Yuvraj! Come back immediately. You have a lot of responsibilities to shoulder.

P.S: I am aware that it is not easy to come out of the jaws of a crocodile. But I can help you with that. We are now on friendly terms with the Bijapurkars and they will rush to your aid, should you ask for it. Shambhu bal, leave all your worries behind. Don't let the distance between us remain.'

His father's message, written from the heart, touched Sambhaji deeply. His own heart, troubled by the torture of the Marathas at Bhupalgad, was now consoled in some measure. Like a child overcome by unexpected joy, he excitedly showed the message to Durgabai and Ranubai. But now there was a single thought in his mind: how was he to escape Diler Khan's clutches?

Sambhaji was now receiving messages regularly from the Swaraj. He heard that Adil Shah of Bijapur, discovering the Mughal plan to attack, had sent an urgent request to Shivaji asking for help. Shivaji looked at this as an opportunity to build a strong defence against the Mughals in the Deccan. Besides the impending Mughal attack, Bijapur was reeling under a severe drought in which thousands of men and animals had perished. Shivaji had sent a caravan of two thousand bullocks loaded with grain. Yuvraj sorely missed all the action and rued the fact that he was not there to help.

One day, an incensed Diler Khan stormed into Sambhaji's room and said, 'Shambhu Shahzade, it looks like your father is not in the least bothered about your safety. He has attacked our post at Jalnapur near Aurangabad.'

'What about it?'

'Had the attack been of the kind he launched on Surat with the primary intention of looting, it would not have mattered much. But this has been done deliberately to distract us and reduce our pressure on Bijapur.'

Sambhaji did not bother to reply. His mind was preoccupied with wondering how he and his family could escape the old man's clutches. But to all appearances, he was stuck with Diler Khan for the foreseeable future. Sambhaji did not want to attack Bijapur with Khan. He knew that all efforts made by his father to build an alliance with Adil Shah would go to waste if he was seen there with the Mughal army.

Meanwhile Diler Khan's senior sardars were advising him to 'arrest Sambhaji, tie him up and get him to Aurangabad.' But the old man felt he could not afford to give up the last card he held. He was confused and did not know what to do.

A few days later, a spy came with a message from the Maratha commander Hambirrao Mohite. It said, '*Yuvraj, I have sent a few troops to the jungles near Athani. They are waiting for you. Take their help to escape and return home soon.*'

The message gave Sambhaji some solace. Another night, he received a message from his dear friends Kalash and Jotyaji. It said, 'Shambhu Raje, please be alert! We have intercepted some instructions from Aurangzeb and we fear that your life is in danger. You may be taken prisoner soon. We urge you to act at once. Break the cage and fly!'

Sambhaji was looking for an opportune moment to escape but Diler Khan hovered around him all the time with his eagle eye, hatching his own plans. One afternoon he said, 'Shambhu Shahzade, I want to seize Panhalgad under your command.'

Sambhaji knew exactly what Khan had in mind. 'So you want to repeat what you did in Bhupalgad and use me as a shield to take another Maratha fort, don't you? You wish to defame me once and for all in front of my people.'

'Why bother about your good name any more? You are going to become a Mughal sardar soon. I will take you to Delhi. I will ask the Badshah to gift you a royal armour.'

'Royal armour or a ton of fetters?'

Sambhaji's sharp retort put Diler Khan in a spot. He managed to conceal his surprise but was alert thenceforth, knowing Sambhaji could call his bluff anytime.

7

Keeping Sambhaji by his side, Diler Khan proceeded towards Panhalgad. Sambhaji fumed silently. He had recently learned that it was Diler Khan who had recruited the Wadkar duo to attack Shivaji on the day of Holi while celebrations were on in Raigad. Khan still tried to wear a cloak of courtesy but the devil in him was itching to get out. He looted the villages of Athani and Tikota en route to Bijapur, despite the fact that the villages were populated largely by Muslims. The fact that they were under Adilshahi rule was enough for Diler Khan to wreak havoc on them.

Diler Khan's lawlessness and cruelty reached its peak during the march to Panhalgad as he looted bazaars and killed merchants, burnt standing crops and destroyed forests. Soon, he began to round up men and women from the villages, giving orders for them to stripped and subjected to whiplashes. The desperate cries and pleas of women rent the air. Diler Khan's men raped women and young girls, both Hindus and Muslims. Many were murdered after being tortured and molested. Dead bodies were hung on branches of trees for others to see. Many women, fearing rape, jumped in wells and killed themselves.

Several of the Muslim sardars in Diler Khan's troops were shaken by the way he was conducting himself. But not having the courage to confront Khan, they complained to Sambhaji. An already incensed Sambhaji stormed inside Diler Khan's tent and yelled, 'Are you devil or human? How dare you torture the common man?'

'Shambhu Raje, I hope you are now convinced that I do not differentiate between the Hindus and the Muslims.'

'Are you a Mughal sardar or an ordinary thug? You need to stop this right away, or else ...'

'Or else? What will you do?' Diler Khan laughed mockingly.

Sambhaji's body burned with the thought of revenge. He lay on his bed staring into nothingness. Durgabai and Ranubai were at their wits' end,watching helplessly as Sambhaji moaned, 'Durga, what have I done to myself? Diler Khan will drag me to Panhala, shedding blood every inch of the way. There he will repeat the gory deeds of Bhupalgad and I will be branded as traitor for life.'

A couple of days later, Sambhaji received a secret message from Bahadurgad. Sambhaji was happy to see that it was from Miyan Khan. He had written:

'My dear friend Sambhaji,

I was fortunate to witness the marriage of my daughters, thanks to you. I have two reasons to send you this message. One, I have received the royal orders from Delhi declaring me as innocent. I am going to be released soon. But the other news from Delhi is disturbing. I am informed that you will be arrested in the next few days. The Badshah has ordered five thousand men to march from Aurangabad especially for this purpose. It is Aurangzeb's devilish plan to capture, imprison and torture you. By doing so, he wants to frighten your father, his arch enemy, into submission. Please remember, Diler Khan is Aurangzeb's slave and can never be a true friend to the Marathas. Don't delay even a minute! Shambhu, go! Run away!'

The hair on the back of Sambhaji's neck stood as he read Miyan Khan's epistle. That night, his sleep was troubled by recurring nightmares of the men at Bhupalgad losing their limbs and of his father's grief-stricken face. No! He could not go on with this humiliating existence anymore! To live the life of a slave with the enemy while his illustrious father suffered on his account was unthinkable!

Sambhaji spent the rest of the night sitting in front of the idol of Lord Shiva in his room. Durgabai entered his room and, pressing her tear-laden face to Sambhaji's, wailed,

'Yuvraj, I know you are unable to take bold steps because you are thinking of us. Don't bother about us. We don't care if we die here. It would not make a difference to anyone. But if you survive, Shivaji Raje's Swaraj will flourish.'

Sambhaji wiped his tears and got up with a new sense of determination. Durgabai was in the seventh month of her pregnancy. Sambhaji was overwhelmed with emotion by the spirit of sacrifice she displayed even in this condition without a thought for her own safety. All she cared about was to get Sambhaji back to his father! Sambhaji raised Durgabai to her feet by her shoulders and embraced her passionately.

She said, 'Raje, don't get entangled in my love.'

'Durga, look at my fate! When I left Shringarpur, Yesu was pregnant. And now, you want me to run away from here, when you are carrying a child! How can I even think of leaving you here in this state? It seems I do not have the good fortune to see my children playing on my lap.'

Ranubai stepped closer to Sambhaji and said, putting his hand on her forehead, 'Shambhu, don't think about us. While trying to plan an escape that includes us, you may land up being a prisoner of the Mughals for life. The Jadhavs of Wai will find another daughter-in-law like me, but Shivaji Raje's Swaraj will not get another Sambhaji. Don't waste any more time. You need to leave right away!'

Sambhaji sat on his bed for a long time, brooding and silent. He was uncertain of the next steps. Ranubai gently caressed his back and said,

'Shambhu Raje, you are probably not aware of how much Abasaheb misses you. He often used to tell me: "I would not be worried if Sambhaji was a warrior through and through. But I know he is a poet too! Such people are sensitive! When provoked, they can be as dangerous as a raging bull. But when overcome by emotion, they can get carried away like a waterfall. A king cannot afford to be so. He must hold onto anger and revenge, to be used at the appropriate time. But Shambhu cannot hold anything in his heart. I worry about him!'

'Ranu Akka, Abasaheb is a keen observer of character. And he cares for me so deeply!'

'One day he said, with tears in his eyes, "There is only one person who truly understands his valour, his boyishness as well as his maturity; it is Jijau saheb!" Then Abasaheb said, his voice choking, "I wonder who will be able to understand this mad fellow when I am no longer around!"'

Sambhaji continued to sit on his bed, lost in thought. Ranubai pulled him up, holding his hands, and said,

'Get up, Shambhu Raje! Fate seems to be playing a game with us. Can you imagine Abasaheb's state of mind ever since we crossed the Krishna and came to Mughal territory? I am sure he has not been able to sleep even one night!'

'Why did you come with me, Akkasaheb, against the wishes of everyone?'

'I don't know. I was worried about you, Shambhu. Well, there is no time to waste now! You know what the kings used to do earlier to strengthen their forts? They used to perform human sacrifices! The blood of the sacrificed was mixed with mortar and lime to provide protection. So, I want you to stop caring about your sister and your pregnant wife. If destiny smiles on us, we will meet again. But if we die, the fortress of the Hindavi Swaraj, built by Shivaji and Sambhaji, must stand strong.'

8

Diler Khan had lost his ability to sleep at night. The daredevilry with which Sambhaji had attacked him, the sardar of thousands of Mughal soldiers, had left him nervous. He now realised why Aurangzeb had been warning him to 'arrest the dangerous son of Shiva, bind him in irons and get him to Delhi at the earliest.'

That morning, Munsib Khan had visited the camp to report to Diler Khan along with his nephew Bale Khan. Munsib and his nephew had recently switched loyalties from the Bijapurkars to the Mughals. He commanded a troop of five thousand men. Diler Khan asked, with barely concealed anxiety, 'What news, Munsib?'

'Khansahab, we have followed your instructions and captured the two hundred men who had come from Maratha territory.'

'Very good!'

'We have confiscated their horses and put the men to work at a labour camp.'

Diler Khan was pleased with Munsib Khan's report. He said, caressing his white beard, 'Sambha is hot-blooded. I was really taken aback at the way he reacted the other day …'

'Khan saheb, how long do you intend to keep this firebrand with you?'

'Munsib chacha, tomorrow I am expecting five thousand men from Aurangabad. I will send this ball of fire to Aurangzeb in their company. The world knows that Alamgir is capable of turning a raging fire into water.'

The next day, as they marched ahead, Diler Khan had requested Sambhaji to travel in a howdah next to his own elephant. Diler Khan wanted to buy time, to appease and humour Sambhaji, at least until Aurangzeb's troops reached them.

The huge army lumbered along, crossing a small mountain to the valley beyond. Sambhaji saw a small lake with a stream flowing into it. An old Shiva temple stood nearby. Asking the mahout to stop the elephant, he said to Diler Khan, 'Khan saheb, I have not had a darshan for several days. I suggest we stop here, pray to the Lord, and then move ahead.'

Diler Khan smiled, 'Why do you even ask, Yuvraj? Do finish your prayers while I get some rest.'

While the troops halted in the shade of the trees, Sambhaji moved towards the lake with a few of his trusted men. After praying at the temple, he took a dip in the lake. Watching him, Diler Khan was contented. He wondered if this would be Sambhaji's last bath as a free man.

Sambhaji seemed to be in good spirits. He encouraged his men to take a dip. He appeared to be enjoying himself as he splashed around, swimming with joyous abandon. Munsib Khan's men, seeing that Sambhaji and his men were cavorting around in the water, sat down for lunch. Only a few soldiers stood guard at the edge of the lake.

Soon, Sambhaji noticed that five sanyasis were also taking a bath in the lake. Initially he ignored their chants of 'Jay Shambho', but when they started saying, albeit in a low voice, 'Shambho! Shiva's Shambho!', he looked at them carefully. A shiver went down his spine. One of the sanyasis was Jotyaji and another was Rayappa!

Sambhaji glanced around. Without making it obvious to the guards standing at the edge of the lake, he casually swam towards the sanyasis. Jotyaji said, as he came within earshot, while the others continued to recite mantras, 'There are five horses behind the temple, and fifty of our best men in the woods behind. Raje, we need to make a dash for it!'

Sambhaji now began taking dips in the water, pretending to pray to the sun. The soldiers on guard duty watched him curiously. Finally he took a deep breath and plunged into the water. The soldiers waited for a while, but Sambhaji did not surface. They started shouting, 'Sambhaji has escaped. Sambha bhaag gaya!'

There was a clamour all around. Diler Khan was wild with rage, and Bale Khan, without even waiting for further orders, rushed into the woods with five thousand of his men. Munsib Khan stood next to Diler Khan, smiling. Irritated, Diler Khan asked, 'What is so amusing, Munsib Khan?'

Munsib Khan gave no reply as he mounted and spurred his horse. Diler Khan shouted, 'Wait! Don't bring me his dead body. I want him alive! Else, Shahenshah would never forgive me.'

Munsib Khan and his men gave a chase but Sambhaji had left them far behind. Seeing that Bale Khan and his men were far behind, he spurred his own horse violently and repeatedly.

It was evening; the shadows lengthened in the woods. The sun was about to set behind the mountains, cutting off the last rays of light. Munsib Khan could see a valley below him. Then, in the distance, he saw Sambhaji. He was tied to a tree, next to a fast-flowing stream. More than half of the fifty men who had accompanied Sambhaji were lying dead around him. It was evident that they had had a clash with the men chasing them.

Sambhaji himself showed signs of having fought many men. There were wounds all over his body and his clothes were stained with blood. Bale Khan, sword in hand, was screaming at Sambhaji.

Rushing down the slope, Munsib Khan shouted, 'Beta Bale Khan! Stop! For Allah's sake, stop!'

Sambhaji and Bale Khan continued their angry exchange of words while Munsib Khan ran towards them. Bale Khan was punching Sambhaji in his stomach now and, in his rage, pulled his beard violently. Incensed, Sambhaji spat on Bale Khan's face. Bale Khan, throwing restraint to the wind, raised his sword to split Sambhaji's head in half, when Munsib Khan ran up behind him with a cry, 'Bale Khan, beta!' A spear pierced Bale Khan's back and he crashed to the ground.

Sambhaji and the thousand Mughal soldiers surrounding him were stunned into silence. Munsib Khan sat down on the ground, taking his nephew's head into his lap. He tried to give him a sip of water, but he was dead. Munsib Khan, shattered, started wailing like a child.

A few Mughal sardars came forward and one of them said, incensed at Munsib Khan's cruel act, 'Chacha, in order to save the devil, you killed your own nephew?'

'Yes, he was my nephew, my true friend and only heir. But I ask you: why are you so outraged by sight of a dead body on the ground today?'

'What do you mean?' The sardar asked.

Munsib Khan said, throwing an angry glance at the men around him, 'Have you forgotten how Diler Khan and his men looted Athani and Tikota? Do you not remember how they raped hundreds of women, hanging their bodies on trees for others to see? Many of those helpless women were Muslims! But none of you unsheathed your swords in disgust at sight of Diler Khan's cruel acts!'

The men fell silent while Munsib Khan continued, 'The only man who was truly upset, who literally attacked Diler Khan on behalf of those murdered innocents, was Sambhaji, the lion cub. Not one of you! Why were you silent then? What happened to your manly pride?'

'What is it that you want to say, Chacha?' One of the men asked.

'We made a terrible mistake in betraying Bijapur to join Diler Khan. If one of Aurangzeb's sardars has the temerity to carry out such violent acts against us Muslims, imagine our state when the Badshah himself arrives here!'

The truth of Munsib Khan's words began to dawn on the men and they nodded their heads. Munsib continued, 'I tell you, the greatest enemy of the Shias of the Deccan is the kafir Badshah Aurangzeb. If this devil from Delhi destroys the Maratha Empire, it will only be a matter of time before Golconda and the Bijapur Sultanate are razed to the ground. We forget that it was Shivaji who sent a thousand bullock-cartloads of grain to our land when our land was ravaged by drought last year. We must help to protect Shivaji's Swaraj if we are to protect ourselves from Aurangzeb's cruelty.'

Munsib Khan took a dagger out of his cummerbund and cut the cords which bound Sambhaji to the tree. He instructed his men to offer fresh horses to Sambhaji's surviving men. Patting Sambhaji's back affectionately, he addressed the soldiers, 'We need to ensure that Shivaji's son is safe. If not for anything else, to ensure that we in the Deccan are protected!' Turning to Sambhaji, he said, 'Go, beta! Run away!'

Sambhaji, his robes drenched with blood, hugged Munsib Khan affectionately and took his leave.

Munsib Khan returned to the Mughal camp with his men, wondering what excuse he would give Diler Khan for Sambhaji's escape. A few soldiers carried Bale Khan's corpse. Munsib Khan, looking at his dead nephew, could not stop the tears flowing down his cheeks.

SIX

Jiva Shiva

1

Shivaji's palanquin reached Panhalgad late in the night to the sound of cannons booming at the main gate. Sambhaji was there to welcome him. Father and son hugged each other. Shivaji caressed Sambhaji's face affectionately, his hands trembling. There was so much to say. So much had transpired since they last saw each other. All the bittersweet memories were waiting to be relived. But the long journey had tired the elder Maharaj. Besides, it was not possible for him to bare his heart in the presence of all. It was decided that they would meet the next morning in private.

It had been a month since Sambhaji's arrival at Panhala. But he didn't travel around much. The people were hurt by the knowledge that their valorous and capable Yuvraj had chosen to join the Mughals. The ryots would give him strange looks whenever he went out for a ride. Hence Sambhaji chose to stay indoors as much as possible.

Waiting for the elder Maharaj's arrival was torture for Sambhaji. He had commited the heinous crime of defecting. How was he to face his father now? However the affectionate embrace with which Shivaji Maharaj had greeted him put his mind at rest and gave him a new lease of life.

At dawn the next day, Sambhaji put aside his blanket. The cool breeze of the morning filled the room as soon as he opened the windows. He could hear the tinkling of bells at the distant temple. Sambhaji's mind was transported to Agra, some thirteen years back. He was merely nine years old when he had stood next to his father with pride, a small sword hanging by his waist, at Aurangzeb's durbar.

The invitation to Agra had turned out to be a snub and an insult. Shivaji Raje was given the title of a 'panch hazari', a minor sardar in charge of five thousand troops, which naturally enraged him. Despite Shivaji's obvious displeasure, Badshah Aurangzeb continued to sit on his throne and fiddle with his rosary, his face impassive, as if nothing untoward had happened.

Shivaji had said, as they returned to their haveli that evening, ruffling Sambhaji's hair affectionately, 'Dear, I am worried about you. I wonder how we will escape this place and return home!' Sambhaji recalled how he had promised his father the next morning, as they were about to leave for the durbar, 'Abasaheb, please don't get upset. I promise you … wherever you cannot be present or attend to matters, Shambhu will try his best to fill in for you.'

Sambhaji's recollections were interrupted by a message from Shivaji, instructing him to meet Maharaj at the Mahalakshmi temple. However, an elaborate pooja had been organised to welcome Shivaji, and it was not before afternoon that father and son could be alone together. There was no one else at Maharaj's private chambers now.

Shivaji said, smiling, 'Shambhu, even after you left the Mughals, the thought that you may not return to the Swaraj made me lose my sleep. I was worried that you may hesitate or fear to return here and choose to go elsewhere.'

Sambhaji gulped nervously. His eyelids fluttered for a moment. 'Abasaheb, for a long time I roamed and stumbled through darkness. Then I consoled myself, saying: I am returning to the light; why should I be scared?'

Shivaji Raje sighed, 'I know, Shambhu, that you are a poet first and then our Yuvraj.'

Tears escaped Shivaji's eyes and flowed down his cheeks. He said, in a voice full of pain, 'Shambhu Raje, why have you returned alone?'

'Please pardon me, Abasaheb. I pleaded with Durga and Ranu Akka to leave with me but they refused.'

'I understand why they said so, Shambhu. In the process of trying to save them, you could have got caught. I am sure Bhawani will bless you with the strength and resourcefulness to find a way and release them from captivity.' Shivaji paused before he continued, 'Shambhu, you believe that I made a terrible mistake not taking you along for the campaign in Karnatak, don't you?'

Sambhaji hesitated for a moment and said, 'Yes, Abasaheb, I do! I was a mere lad when you put me in custody with Mirza Raje Jaisingh till the treaty of Purandhar was executed. I was just a child when I attended the Agra durbar as a representative of the Hindavi Swaraj. And I was no more than twelve years of age when you sent me to Shahzada Muazzam as a Mughal mansabdar.'

'You remember everything, don't you?' Shivaji said.

'Let me remind you of a few more instances, Abasaheb. Do you recall the responsibility that was thrust upon me while I was serving under Muazzam?' Shivaji threw a questioning glance at Sambhaji, who continued, 'That of finding a way to convince Muazzam to join us; to make him revolt against his father.'

Shivaji smiled at the memory of the event.

Sambhaji continued, 'Abasaheb, you gave me an enormous responsibility at such a tender age. Yet, you found me unfit to join hands with on the campaign in Karnatak?'

Shivaji's face was pained as he replied, 'Shambhu, the Karnatak campaign was a painful chapter in my life. You will understand this when you are a Chattrapati yourself. Sometimes, in the larger interests of the state and your subjects, you are forced to be unfair to your dear ones. Don't I have that right, Shambhu?'

'I could at least have continued to stay in Raigad.'

Shivaji was silent for a few moments at the mention of Raigad. Then he said, with a heavy sigh, 'Shambhu, Raigad is not the same anymore. Ordinary folks have simple aspirations but those in power want the world in their palm. There is nothing as dangerous as the lust for power! Sons have killed their fathers for it. Mothers have turned against their own sons. I could see such lust sprouting in Raigad! Keeping that in mind, I decided it was best not to allow you to stay there. But I am blessed that you were able to escape the clutches of Diler Khan. And you are lucky to have managed it before Aurangzeb found a way to trap you. I heard of your escape when I was in Jalna. We gathered so much loot on the campaign that the elephants and camels were literally bent with the weight. But thanks to the Lord, I am here and we are together ...'

Shivaji stopped for a moment and Sambhaji asked, 'Why, was there any trouble on the way back here? Did you fall ill?'

'Shambhu, while we were returning, we were attacked at Sangamner by Ranmast Khan, the Mughal sardar who had come from Aurangabad with nearly twenty thousand troops. We were trapped in a gorge. But we were saved by the dense jungle and our valorous Bahirji Naik. The canopy was so thick that it blocked all sunlight. Led by Bahirji, we negotiated our way through the forest for nearly three days and then, bypassing the Mughals stationed at Junnar, we reached the Malshej ghat and journeyed onwards to Raigad.'

Sambhaji listened intently as Shivaji continued, 'Strength alone is not enough. Imagine what would have happened if I had been captured by the Mughals. Shambhu, a man may try as hard as he wants to succeed in his ventures, but without the support of the gods, he is nobody. We are meeting here today by the grace of Jagadamba. But remember! A king has to make harsh decisions for the benefit of his kingdom. If you believe that today I am embracing you affectionately as a father, you are under the wrong impression!'

Sambhaji looked at his father, surprised. Shivaji said, smiling, 'I enquired into the matter of your waiving the dues of the poor farmers. This old man has decided to felicitate the true heir to the kingdom, the one who cares for his people!'

Shivaji said, placing his hands affectionately on Sambhaji's shoulders, 'Aurangzeb has been busy with his campaigns in Kabul and Kandahar … but our spies tell us now that he will surely descend on the Deccan within a year or so with a huge army. We must be prepared and will need to assemble an army of more than a hundred and fifty thousand men to raid territories in Gujarat, Burhanpur and other areas.'

Sambhaji let out a hearty laugh. He said, eyes brimming with pride at his father's foresight, 'Now I know, Abasaheb, why you have been so busy buying ammunition from the firangis for the past few years!'

'Son, the most deadly weapon in my arsenal is you! We were forced to sign the ignominious treaty of Purandar because of sardars like Diler Khan and Mirza Raja Jaisingh. We were humiliated at the Agra durbar, and now, we hear that Aurangzeb himself may march upon the Deccan. We must not forget the fact that he is one of the most powerful emperors in the world today. I don't need an astrologer to tell me that the only man capable of confronting his might is the lion's cub! You, my dear, must fight! Fight with all your strength! And save the jungles, the animals and the common man of the Swaraj from the tyranny of the Mughals!'

Sambhaji instantly fell at his father's feet and said, embracing them, 'Abasaheb, your blessings are enough for me to move mountains.'

Shivaji said, 'Dear Shambhu, all we can do is try our best. We cannot tell where the crooked paths of destiny will take us. Tomorrow, when you confront Aurangzeb, I may or may not be alive, but I am sure my blessings and the fruits of my good deeds will be with you.'

2

Shivaji Raje was meeting his eldest son after nearly three years. Just as a stick cannot break the surface of water, jealous intrigues cannot damage strong bonds of heartfelt affection. Both Shivaji and Sambhaji knew they were a rare combination: a father whose valour was known all over the land and a son who had true potential.

After the reunion at Panhalgad, they wanted to spend as much time as possible talking to each other. Father and son were together nearly every moment of the day—offering prayers at the temple of Bhawani in the morning or overseeing administrative affairs of the Swaraj later in the day. Sometimes they would stand on the fort's ramparts, looking northwards at the distant river Warna or the river Panchaganga and its surrounding territory in the south. As the sun set, Sambhaji and Shivaji often sat gazing at the distant hills of Gajapur and the forests below Vishalgad.

Sambhaji was now literally a devotee of Shivaji. The barriers between the two had melted away like wax. Shivaji had found a dedicated follower, a son who hung on to every word he uttered.

Shivaji said one day, 'Shambhu, Rajaram is your younger brother. You must forget your differences. I pray that Bhawani shows you the way.'

'Abasaheb, if I have your blessings, I am happy to survive on a little rice and milk while serving the Hindavi Swaraj.'

A sudden thought changed Shivaji's mood. He said, 'Shambhu, it is easy to confront an enemy who challenges you with a naked sword. But the foe who claims outwardly to be your friend is more dangerous. I have faced many since childhood. There are Maratha families who have served Adil Shah of Bijapur or the Nizam of Ahmednagar for generations. Look at your own brother-in-law, Mahadji Nimbalkar of Phaltan, who takes pride in being a lackey of the Mughals. The Mores of Jawli are traitors. The Surves of Shringarpur and Ganoji Shirke pretend to be loyal to the Swaraj but their true allegiance is to the Mughals! When Afzal Khan destroyed the idol of Tulja Bhawani with his sword, there were several Maratha sardars who praised him. Not one had the temerity to confront him and avenge the desecration. Forget stopping him; they did not even dare to look him in the eye!'

Sambhaji said, his voice full of admiration, 'You have created a Swaraj despite being surrounded by such people!'

'Son, I am proud when my sword rises to cut off the head of an enemy, but when our own people, our kin turn traitors, my head hangs in shame. In future, Shambhu, you must be wary of selfish Marathas and the Brahmin watandars.'

Shivaji continued, 'Keep in mind that when you rule the country, you must be concerned above all with the poorest of the poor. When I started building the Swaraj, I deliberately distanced myself from power-seekers like the watandars and the jagirdars. Instead I looked after the simple folk, cattle herders and humble farmers, who were willing to give their lives for the cause. I made them shiledars and taught them to fight. That is where a Tanaji and a Murarbaji were born! It is the common man who will remain loyal to us till death!'

'But Abasaheb, not all the landlords holding a watan or a jagir are our arch enemies, are they?'

'But neither are they friends of the ryots. Their first loyalty is to their revenues, their profits, their titles, and the positions they hold.'

Shivaji Raje paused for a few moments and said, holding Sambhaji's hand, 'There were times when the green flag of the Muslims fluttering on the walls of Raigad would pierce Maasaheb's heart. Siddi Johar's flag on the Janjira fort still breaks my heart. I have tried to put the saffron flag on the ramparts there but failed, despite making eight attempts.'

'Is Janjira so crucial?'

'Crucial?' The very thought of capturing Janjira bought a smile to Shivaji's face. He said, clenching his fists, 'Janjira, the fort which controls all the trade by sea! When we capture it, just see how the borders of the Swaraj touch the Ganga and Yamuna!'

The question of dividing the Swaraj arose once more. Maharaj had been falling ill often in the last four years and the senior sardars were a worried lot. Shivaji had, in fact, clarified the issue of succession during his coronation by declaring Sambhaji as the Yuvraj. Sambhaji had governed Raigad for four years before the coronation and had a thorough understanding of its administration, its flaws and challenges, the strengths and weaknesses of its forts as well as their escape routes.

But Soyrabai's ambition with regard to Rajaram had not died down. If Rajaram were to ascend the throne, the sardars supporting Soyrabai, already licking their lips at the thought of this golden opportunity to grab power, would fill their coffers under the guise of teaching the younger Yuvraj the art of administration. No wonder men like Annaji Datto were throwing their weight behind Rajaram and Soyrabai! Sambhaji was a thorn in the flesh for the corrupt sardars backing Soyrabai. On the other hand, the ryots and troops saw Sambhaji as Shivaji's true successor.

Annaji and others were trying to convert Maharaj to the view that Sambhaji should be given charge of the Karnatak region while Raigad should be handed over to Rajaram. Shivaji would smile awkwardly whenever the topic of partition came up. 'Our Swaraj is not a watan, a piece of private property, like those managed by the saranjamdars,' he would say, 'It is a temple built by the blood and toil of thousands. An edifice which stands for the unity, strength and the culture of the Deccan. How does one divide such an entity?'

As for Sambhaji, whenever the topic came up, he would say, 'Abasaheb, I am not power hungry. I am happy with whatever you give me, even if it is just a coconut from the temple. I am content to live my life at your feet.'

The western horizon towards Gajapur and Vishalgad was illumined by the rays of the setting sun. It caught the emerald stone adorning Sambhaji's headgear, which was slightly askew. Shivaji Raje, adjusting his son's turban, said, 'Shambhu, have you ever looked at our throne carefully?'

'Yes, many times; why?'

'I want to talk about it. Elsewhere, the right to the throne is hereditary. But you must know that it is different in the Swaraj.'

'I don't understand you, Abasaheb!'

'Let me explain! Don't be in a hurry to ascend the throne. The next time you go near it, inspect it carefully. Look at the pure seat of power and the five steps leading to it.'

He continued, 'The first step, when you look closely, has hundreds of eyes—like the ones you see in a peacock's tail. They represent the eyes of our people; the common folk. And you would, if you listen carefully, be able to hear the waters of our sacred rivers—the Krishna, the Bhima and the Godavari.'

'When you put your feet on the second step, you would be able to see the three hundred and fifty forts in the Sahyadris. When you look at the ramparts of the forts carefully, you would see stains of the blood our valiant soldiers have shed to capture them.

'On the third step you will get a darshan of Jijausaheb. You will see Aausaheb, and thousands of mothers as well as wives who have gracefully accepted their loss for the cause of Swaraj. You can hear the sound of the bangles breaking from the threshold of every widow's house.

'Be careful when you step on the fourth one! You would be able to hear the devout abhangs of Tukoba and the teachings of Gyaneshwar. You will meet the great saints, Ramdas and many others.

'And when you are on the fifth step, you would feel the tall peaks of the Sahyadris speaking to you, looking at you with great hope and unshakeable devotion. Our past, troubled with unfulfilled dreams, would be looking at you with high expectations. Wounds, still raw, would implore you to heal them. Rays of the rising sun would bless you with the ability to accomplish great deeds which can benefit the Swaraj at large. Shambhu, my dear daredevil, the past, the present and the future would be at your feet, imploring you to reach new heights.

'Once you see the five steps the way I have described them, then and only then, my dear son, should you ask yourself a simple question: are you ready? Do you have the capacity to hold high the unfulfilled dreams and aspirations of the ryots? Can you can handle the enormous responsibilities that will be thrust upon you? If you believe you can, you are most welcome to sit on the throne. But if there is even an iota of doubt in your mind, don't go anywhere near it! You may as well become a sanyasi, renouncing this world!'

3

The festivities of Dusshera and Diwali were in full spate in Raigad. Shivaji was at his capital after a gap of a few years. Adding to the charm of the celebrations was the occasion of Rajaram's marriage. He was nearly ten now.

Moropant Peshwa said to his colleagues as they sat in the office of the administrative council, 'We had all been curious and excited to know which lucky girl would be chosen by the elder Maharaj as his daughter-in-law. We were all happy to hear that it is Prataprao Gujar's daughter.'

'Prataprao is a valiant sardar but he committed a serious offence when he pardoned Bahlol Khan of Bijapur. I recall how angry Shivaji Raje was. Shamed by the elder Maharaj's fury, he had marched on the enemy with only six men in tow and sacrificed his life for the cause of the Swaraj. He is immortal now!' Balaji added.

'No wonder Ramdas Swami calls Raje a "jaanata raja", the one who understands. Shivaji Raje has never forgotten Prataprao's sacrifice and has now shown his gratitude by choosing his daughter to be Rajaram Raje's bride.'

'Well friends, we never have had any doubts about the character, vision, or the ability to dispense justice as far as the elder Maharaj is concerned,' Annaji Datto said, leaving a part of his sentence deliberately unsaid. It was clear to the others present what he wanted to convey.

Shivaji Maharaj was busy at the queens' quarters, supervising arrangements for the wedding. Balaji Avaji asked Moropant Peshwa in a low voice, 'Pant, is it true, what I am hearing?'

'What did you hear?'

'That Sambhaji Raje and Yesubai have not been invited for the wedding.'

'Well, unfortunately, it is true,' Moropant said dejectedly.

Balaji Avaji was saddened by the news. He said, 'Doesn't custom say that one must not forget one's kin during marriage and death ceremonies? Shambhu Raje is Rajaram's elder brother, after all!'

They spoke in whispers but Annaji Datto, sitting nearby, heard all of it. He said, smiling and caressing his grey whiskers, 'You seem to forget that each man is destined to get what he deserves on the basis of his abilities and merit.'

Moropant said, shaking his head, 'I think it is unjust to deny Shambhu Raje an invitation to his own brother's wedding.'

Annaji was expecting the Peshwa to disagree. He said, 'No one appreciates salt in milk or an unwelcome guest during marriage festivities.'

'Annaji, this is too much! Your hatred for Shambhu Raje has spread through your veins,' Balaji commented.

'Well, only some of us who have lost their beloved daughters to his cruel lust can understand the pain and sorrow. How will you ever know?' Annaji said, his voice turning hoarse.

Annaji's bitter words silenced others. No one said another word.

Fearing Shivaji Maharaj's anger, ministers of the Ashta Pradhan conducted themselves with apparent bonhomie but the undercurrents of animosity were strong. Moropant and Annaji were unable to see eye to eye on many issues. Shivaji Raje would often avoid sending the two men on the same campaign, knowing they did not get along.

It was afternoon. The office had taken a break for lunch. Prahlad Niraji was about to leave when Annaji held his hand, indicating that he was to stay back. Then Annaji addressed Shivaji, literally stopping Raje in his steps, 'Maharaj, may I ask you to spare a few moments? We have a request to make.'

'Certainly,' Shivaji said.

'No one doubts your keen sense of justice. Even an enlightened soul like Ramdas Swami praises you. Would it be unusual if we ask for a little fair dealing from you?'

'Pant, why are you speaking in riddles? Come to the point.'

'Maharaj has never allowed relationships or emotions to come in the way of deciding what is good for the Hindavi Swaraj. You killed Afzal Khan at the base of Pratapgad, but Khandoji saved Afzal Khan's son, hiding him in the jungles. Khandoji's son-in-law had taken the help of Kanhoji Jedhe to plead on his behalf. But you did not allow your relationship with Kanhoji, someone who was a father figure to you, to come in the way of your decision. Your emotional restraint, firm convictions and purity of heart are praiseworthy. You punished Khandoji, ordering his hand and leg to be cut off.'

Balaji Avaji interrupted, 'Maharaj is in a hurry. Cut the preamble short.'

Annaji threw an angry glance at Balaji and said, raising his hand as a judge would do, 'This is what I wanted to say: I believe Shivaji Raje would not allow an iota of leeway when it comes to a crime like treason.'

Shivaji's expression was a mixture of pain and surprise. All those present, except Balaji, shivered. Annaji had boldly voiced that which no one else would have dared to murmur. They all knew that Shivaji Raje had undoubtedly realised what it was that Annaji was alluding to.

Maharaj said, 'There is no need for this drama of allusions. If you have a complaint against Shambhu Raje, please say so explicitly.'

This blunt remark silenced Annaji for a few moments. He said, recovering quickly, 'I beg your pardon, Maharaj, but according to the law of the Swaraj, the scales of justice do not differentiate between an ordinary cowherd and a Yuvraj. Well, what I want to say is that the elder Yuvraj is not exactly under house arrest at Panhala. So I mean ...'

'I have not put him under any kind of arrest,' Shivaji Raje said bluntly. 'I have asked him to look after the provinces of Panhala, Prabhawali and Dabhol.'

Annaji wiped the sweat off his face, but persisted, 'That's exactly what I want to say, Maharaj! Those who have committed treason are roaming around freely, being rewarded instead of receiving just punishment. I wonder what the common man is making of it!'

Shivaji, about to leave for his quarters, stopped in his tracks. He turned around and sat on his chair determinedly. He said, forcing a smile to his face, 'True, Shambhu Raje joined the Mughals. I was sure that the request for punishing him would be put forth by you, if no one else.'

'Maharaj, he waives the taxes of farmers and the weavers.'

'Annaji, I have looked into the matter. I had set up an independent enquiry, examined every detail of the case, and found that the plight of the farmers whose taxes were waived by the Yuvraj was terrible. He would have committed a crime, in fact, had he allowed them to be taxed.'

'But Maharaj, his behaviour since then has hardly been exemplary.'

Shivaji glanced at Annaji with surprise. He had not expected him to discuss Sambhaji's behaviour so openly. Others were in a state of dilemma, not knowing whether to run away or stay. But the curiosity to know how Raje would deal with the issue compelled them to stay.

Shivaji said, taking the bull by its horns, 'Annaji Pant, I am acutely aware of the pain caused by the death of your dear daughter. I had asked Soyrabai to enquire whether Shambhu Raje was responsible for the tragedy. I have not yet heard of any crime committed by Shambhu in that regard.'

'Raje, you were the one who treated even the daughter-in-law of the Muslim Subedar of Kalyan with such respect …'

'I am asking you, Annaji, to give me proof that Shambhu has misbehaved. If found guilty, I will see that he is punished appropriately; arrest him, if needed.'

But Annaji was not one to abandon the issue halfway. He said, 'What about Godu?'

'I did look into the events which took place on the day of Holi. Godu's accusations were corroborated by my findings. Trayambakrao and Niwasrao were caught red-handed. They tried to escape from jail and both men died while fleeing down the steep slope, falling into the deep ravine below. You are aware of the facts, aren't you?'

The tension in the air was palpable. Annaji had touched a raw chord, challenging Raje's pride. The old man was desperate to ensure Sambhaji would not return to Raigad as a result of being invited for Rajaram's marriage. Risking Raje's wrath, he continued to make accusations. Raje heard footsteps behind the curtain of the doorway that led to his private quarters. He smiled and said, a tad loudly, 'Ranisaheb, you may not be able to hear everything I say. You might as well step into the office.'

Soyrabai came in, her eyes fixed on the floor while taking a seat in a corner. Well, here is one more person who loves Shambhu, thought Raje wryly. Annaji, somewhat chastised by Raje's remarks, was now emboldened once again by the presence of his ally Soyrabai. Tension in the atmosphere was greater than before as the others shuffled their feet nervously, waiting for Raje to speak.

Shivaji, forcing his anger to subside, said in a friendly voice, 'Gentlemen, Shambhu is my son. However, I have known many of you since childhood and I can never forget sacrifices you have made for the Swaraj.'

Annaji glanced at Soyrabai. It was evident from her expression that she was on his side. He said, his voice taking on a confident tone, 'Maharaj, are we to conveniently assume that no crime was committed? That Shambhu Raje never met the Mughals? Maybe he never even left Shringarpur!'

'Annaji, bear in mind that Shambhu met the Mughals in broad daylight. It begs the question: Did his act cause any actual harm to the Swaraj?' Shivaji paused and looked around. 'Where is Moropant? Call him.'

Balaji Chitnis said, ignoring the glares of Soyrabai and Annaji, 'Raje, Shambhu is adamant by nature. Many think he is arrogant. But I can swear on Bhawani's name that he is pure at heart.'

'Why not look at evidence? That, at least, is undisputable,' Shivaji suggested.

On cue, Moropant entered the room with a bag meant for carrying secret messages. Shivaji said, opening its silken knots, 'While leaving for Karnatak, I had planted my spies all around Shambhu Raje, specifically with the intention of intercepting messages between Diler Khan and my son. My spies sent me copies of Yuvraj's letters to Khan. Later, when I returned to Panhala after concluding the campaign, Sambhaji had shifted to Sajjangad. By that time the threads of my spy network had snapped, leading to a tragedy later. But listen! This is a letter written by Shambhu Raje to Diler Khan from Shringarpur: *"It would not become me if I were to defect when my father is away, having handed over to me the responsibility of protecting my people."* Do you see? While the Mughal sardars would not hesitate to behead their own fathers, brothers and sons to grab power, our Yuvraj, in the absence of his father, is unwilling to do anything which might harm the Swaraj! This is the difference between a Mughal Shahzada and the Yuvraj of the Marathas!'

Shivaji seemed tired. He said, looking at the men assembled in the room, 'Joining Diler was no doubt an imprudent act, a misdemeanour committed in the arrogance of youth, prompted by misplaced overconfidence in his abilities. But imagine what would have happened if he had really intended to damage the Maratha Empire, betraying it and despoiling Bhawani Mata! Can you picture him coming to Raigad in my absence and trumpeting his act of treason? Can you even think of that! If that had come to pass, I would have jumped on my horse at once to ride back to Raigad. Yet, it would have taken me four days to reach here. Can you imagine the havoc that would have been unleashed in those intervening days?'

The men in the room were rendered speechless by Shivaji's emotional speech. He asked Moropant, focusing his gaze on Annaji, 'Tell me, Pant, what would you have done if such a thing had actually happened?'

'I beg your pardon, Maharaj. Such a situation would never have occurred! Yet, if it had happened, we would have fought the enemy tooth and nail.'

Shivaji laughed, saying, 'Suppose such a thing had happened when none of you were present in Raigad! All of you are often away on some work or other. Well, we may not have lost the empire, perhaps, but such an act would surely have endangered it, am I right?'

No one dared to speak. There was sorrow in Shivaji's voice when he spoke next, 'I had been thinking of dividing the kingdom between Rajaram and Sambhaji. But I see that the kingdom is already divided by the differences amongst the people in it. Instead of working to unite and strengthen the Swaraj, many are trying to secure their own personal gains first. There is much enmity and jealousy between the Maratha sardars. Look at the infighting amongst the Ashta Pradhan here. Balaji Avaji and Annaji Datto cannot see eye to eye. Meanwhile the Brahmins are forming their own groups. Not to mention the clamour of demands by the Chandraseniya Kayastha Prabhus. The Maratha people are being divided into warring factions based on their castes. If I were to divide the Empire in the midst of all this mistrust and rivalry, it would mean sinking deeper into the quicksands of disunity and corruption that threatens to swallow us all. In any case, future events will decide my course of action.'

Shivaji stood up. Those present were about to leave when he said, 'I was in the thick of battle at Pratapgad. We had just taken over the fort of

Purandhar when he was born. His mother died soon after, leaving him in my care. I remember the way he had clutched my thumb when I hugged him close to my chest. Soyrabai, Annaji ... many of you may find Shambhu short-tempered or blunt in his manners. But remember what Jijausaheb had said, "Shivba, don't be fooled by his irreverent attitude. He is a gem, a real diamond in the rough. If the need were to arise, this mad son of yours would willingly sacrifice his life for the truth and for his father's Swaraj."'

4

Sambhaji loved to roam the mountains and valleys around Panhala. He knew the ravines and routes like the back of his hand. There were spots where a thousand-strong army could watch the enemy from afar, undetected. Sambhaji would say proudly, 'There are many such places in the Sahyadris, inaccessible and impossible for the enemy to conquer. Where even sunlight fails to enter, how can that sinner Aurangzeb dream of conquest?'

Shivaji came to Panhalgad a day before Sankranti. Father and son continued their talks for three or four days, after which Shivaji left for Raigad. Sambhaji was struck once again by the large-hearted and tender nature of the elder Maharaj. Yet, despite being given the Subedari of Panhala, he felt like an outsider. He had experienced men like Hiroji Farzand and Janardan Pant working for him, along with new recruits like Bahirji Naik. Farzand was related to Sambhaji and had always been affectionate towards the Yuvraj. But Sambhaji now sensed a coldness in his demeanour. The other officials of the fort answered to the Ashta Pradhan. All in all, Sambhaji felt he was a stranger in his own home.

Sambhaji had asked his father, when he was leaving, 'Abasaheb, when shall I come to Raigad?'

Shivaji Raje had hesitated for a brief moment before replying, 'Listen, Shambhu! Stay put until I ask you to come.'

'Shall I consider it my misfortune that you have not gotten over your mistrust?' Sambhaji asked, unable to hold his tongue.

His words pierced Shivaji's heart. Maharaj said, 'Shambhu, I don't need any proof of the purity of your heart. Believe me when I say the poisonous winds blowing in Raigad are not good for your health. Pray to the Lord and let time heal all misunderstandings. I am confident that one day we will all assemble in Raigad as one family. We have much to do in the meantime.'

The days spent in conversation with his father at Panhalgad left a deep impression on Sambhaji's mind. But his nights were sleepless once again. Anxious thoughts crowded his mind. He would complain to Yesubai, 'I wonder why Hiroji Farzand Kaka has changed. When Abasaheb escaped from Agra, he was the one who stayed behind in his place, masquerading as Shivaji. I always believed he would be there for me when I needed him. But I find him avoiding me these days.'

Yesubai said, 'Yuvraj, perhaps they disapprove of your behaviour.'

'I know. They love to call me a womaniser and a drunkard, a smoker of cannabis.'

'Ignore all that, Yuvraj. You have made peace with Maharaj saheb, haven't you? He does not get influenced by these rumours. Why then should you bother about others?'

'Yesu, a king needs the trust and support of his ministers and administrators. Without them he cannot function. But often, the fence erected to protect the farm manages to destroy it!'

Meanwhile, he received news that Rajaram's thread ceremony had been performed, soon to be followed by his marriage. Yuvraj was happy to hear of it. Hoping against hope, he waited for a formal invitation, but soon realised that it would never come.

Yesubai asked, sensing Sambhaji's disappointment, 'Can't we go even if we don't get an invitation?'

'Who is going to stop me? If not me, who will attend Rajaram's wedding, the Mughal Shahzada?'

Sambhaji and Yesubai resolved to attend the wedding and made preparations for the journey. Meanwhile Hiroji Farzand, Janardan Pant, and even the clerks at Panhalgad had received their invitations. Little Bhawani, who was now two and a half years old, ran excitedly into her mother's arms and asked, 'Everyone is ready to leave for Raigad. When are we going?'

Sambhaji hugged his daughter and said, trying to restrain his sobs, 'Dear, the younger Balraje's mother does not like our presence.' Sambhaji then said to Yesubai, 'When Abasaheb was here, we were able to speak so freely! I wonder whether he is so busy that he has forgotten to invite me for my younger brother's marriage.'

'I am sure he has his reasons. Even the saints have had to suffer when it came to the troubles caused by their family members.'

That day, many palanquins and horses left for Raigad. Sambhaji and Yesubai had decided not to go, for the deliberate snub implied by the omission of a formal invitation was difficult to swallow. While young Bhawani, enjoying her new clothes, pranced about, Sambhaji was quiet, recalling how he used to play with his young brother, carrying him around the fort on his shoulders.

He said to Yesubai, 'You know Rajaram used to say, "Dadasaheb, you must come to my marriage dressed as a Mawal playing the drums." Yesu, I am eager to fulfil the promise I made to him.' He continued after a pause, 'No one would believe me today, but after Jijabai, if there was someone who loved me dearly, it was Soyrabai saheb.'

Yesubai mumbled, 'How things change!' Then she said, 'Ever since Hambirrao, younger brother of Soyrabai Ranisaheb, has been made the commander-in-chief of the Maratha forces, she is in seventh heaven. I am told that she boasts, "Since my brother is now the Senapati, who can stop Rajaram from ascending the throne?"'

Seeing Sambhaji silent, Yesu asked, 'Do you believe Hambirrao would support Soyrabai Ranisaheb in the matter of succession?'

'Why not, Yesu? Which uncle can resist the temptation to ensure that his nephew takes charge of a kingdom that boasts a treasury brimming with crores of hons? It is obviously a foregone conclusion that Hambirrao would support Ranisaheb when the need arises.'

When those who had attended Rajaram's marriage returned to Panhala, Sambhaji, out of sheer affection and curiosity, could not stop himself from enquiring about his younger brother. One of them said, 'Rajaram Raje was upset just before the ceremony. He made a fuss about your absence, Yuvraj! Finally, Hambirrao made him go through the rituals with a promise that you were expected to arrive by evening. It was then that the younger Yuvraj finally agreed.'

Sambhaji's heart was wrenched listening to how his brother had missed him.

The next morning, while Sambhaji and others sat for lunch, a servant arrived with a decorated basket. Yesubai immediately realised that the basket was a gift from Raigad. She admonished the servant silently with her eyes but the poor fellow was confused. Finally, Yesubai managed to pick up the basket and was about to take it to another room, when Sambhaji said,

'Why are you trying to hide that, Yesu? It is a gift from the wedding. Serve it here!' His tone betrayed a mixture of anger and frustration. Sambhaji took a laddoo from the basket and put half of it in Yesubai's mouth. 'Eat! Eat, I say! After all, it is from Rajaram's marriage.' He put the other half in his mouth while tears streamed down his cheeks. 'Jotyaji, Yesubai; all of you! Eat! And don't bother whether they are sweet or bitter. We have no choice but to eat them, henceforth!'

5

It was Falguni Amavasya, new moon day, and a solar eclipse was under way. Many at Panhalgad watched curiously as the sun disappeared slowly behind the moon's shadow. Sambhaji too stood gazing at the sight until Yesubai came out and held his hand. 'Come inside now! It is not considered auspicious to watch the solar eclipse.'

'Yesu, does all that mean anything now? I committed the grave sin of going over to the enemy camp. My father, the lion-hearted one, pardoned me. Pleading with me not to make such a mistake again, he hugged me. That one embrace was enough to dissolve all woes, jealousies, suspicions—everything!'

Four days had passed since the eclipse when Sambhaji returned to his quarters one evening, his face downcast and forehead creased with anxiety. Yesubai saw him standing in his room, looking out of the window, lost in thought. 'What happened?'

'Abasaheb is unwell.' Sambhaji's voice trembled as he spoke. 'Soyrabai Matoshree is taking advantage of Abasaheb's illness. She has ordered strict vigilance all around Raigad, restricting movement of people in and out of the fort.' He continued, 'The atmosphere is rife with suspicion and fear. No one can enter or leave without explicit orders. Sardar Malsavant stands guard with ten thousand men at the base of the fort. Yesu, I am worried. Trouble is brewing in Raigad.'

'Should you not rush to Raigad?'

'Yesu, I am confused. Abasaheb's failing health worries me to no end, but I don't want to precipitate a clash. You know that if I go, I won't put up with anyone trying to bar my way. But that would be interpreted as revolt, or an opportunistic attack. My defection to the Mughals did not dent the Swaraj in any manner, but I have a black spot on my forehead for life!'

'Perhaps it's better for you to stay here. I am sure we will get regular updates from Raigad. Let's wait it out then, and not take any steps in a hurry.'

Sambhaji sent an urgent message to Kavi Kalash at Sangameshwar. He also alerted his father-in-law Pilajirao Shirke at Shringarpur.

A fortnight passed. It was Hanuman Jayanti, a full moon day. Sambhaji woke at dawn and prayed to the tall idol of Hanuman.

Yesubai was anxious that morning. 'I am very worried about elder Maharaj's health! I am feeling uneasy today.'

Sambhaji's state of mind was no different. Yet he said, wanting to put Yesubai at ease, 'Don't worry about Abasaheb! He is going to live a long life. After all, he will be fifty a month from now. The Marathi soil needs him more than it needs you or me!'

That evening, Kavi Kalash came to see Sambhaji. He was accompanied by two of Sambhaji's spies who had been sent to Mahad and Raigad. The moment Sambhaji saw their faces, he knew the news was not good.

'No one is allowed to enter the fort,' one of the men said, 'But we hear that the elder Maharaj is seriously ill and bedridden. The ryots too are clamouring to see him but not even an ant can get into Raigad these days.'

The other man added, 'We heard that he is suffering from a deadly disease. Other sources, who do not wish to be quoted, whisper that the Maharaj has been poisoned by Soyrabai Ranisaheb.'

Sambhaji sighed heavily as he listened to these grim reports. He said to Kalash, 'Kaviji, things are not going well at Raigad. We need to be alert. Please send some spies who can find out exactly how Abasaheb is faring.'

On the day of Chaitra Poornima, after suffering from high fever for eight days, Shivaji Maharaj died!

6

Raigad was cloaked in grief by the sudden and unexpected death of Shivaji. It seemed that the very pillars of the fort were bent in sorrow and even the water in the tanks tasted bitter.

The spine of the Maratha Empire was broken. There were worries that enemies of the Swaraj, waiting for an opportune moment to strike, would descend on them at any moment. None of the senior members of the Astha Pradhan had been present in Raigad when Maharaj drew his last breath. Rahuji Somnath and Soyrabai ensured that news of his death was contained. They did not want the tidings to spread far. Somehow they managed to get Rajaram to perform the last rites.

Annaji Datto, who was on a campaign in Karwar, returned hastily. Moropant Peshwa too returned from Trayambakeshwar.It was important for the Ashta Pradhan to ensure that the rules of command were being followed in this time of crisis and that power remained with the throne. Annaji Pant, especially, was an anxious man. Some of his followers were asking, 'Annaji, now that Shivaji Maharaj is dead and Shambhu Raje is likely to take over, how are you going to fare?'

'Well, whatever may happen, we cannot allow Sambha to take the throne. We are all finished if that happens.'

Sambhaji had never minced words telling others how corrupt Annaji was. He was aware of the way Annaji had misused his power, issuing orders to suit his interests and filling his coffers by diverting revenue for his personal gain. He was often heard saying in public when Annaji approached, 'Here comes our minister, the one who has looted us in broad daylight!'

Sambhaji knew that while his father had worked for the welfare of all, there were many senior ministers whose primary aim was to fatten their own purses. There was no question that the revenue collected from the ryots and provinces was being pilfered for this purpose. When the representatives of the French, English and the Portuguese came to pay their respects to Shivaji, these ministers would brazenly demand gifts for themselves. Yuvraj, young and hot-blooded, could not tolerate such shameful behaviour. He would fret and fume, attracting the wrath of the senior ministers who had earned Shivaji's gratitude for their years of loyal service to the Swaraj.

Prospects for corrupt ministers like Annaji were dim. Although he was sure that Soyrabai would try her best to put Rajaram on the throne, Annaji was well aware that intrigues and conspiracies were not enough to manage a kingdom. He knew that good governance must rely on resources, both monetary and military. Annaji sent an urgent message to Hambirrao, the commander of the Maratha army, who was camped at Karad, '*I am determined to coronate your nephew Rajaramsaheb. And he would see to it that seven generations of your descendants are taken care of. But I need your explicit support to make this happen.'*

Annaji was elated by Hambirrao's quick response. *'You are the chief of the treasury and know the kingdom better than anyone else. What greater pleasure can I expect than seeing my nephew ascend the throne? An ordinary soldier like me would be elated.'*

Support in writing from Hambirrao made Annaji's resolve stronger. He had conferred with Soyrabai a couple of times but now, with the letter from Hambirrao, he was emboldened to move fast. No one knew better than Annaji the greedy eagerness Soyrabai had shown to put her son on the throne. All Soyrabai's selfish ambition needed was a little nudge, which Annaji was more than willing to provide. Rajaram's accession to the throne would ensure Annaji's position and security in the days to come.

7

Shivaji's palace seemed desolate. Yet, Annaji was not kept waiting when he called upon Soyrabai. She was shattered by Maharaj's death and her mind was racked with anxiety about her future and that of her son. However, not allowing the situation to bog her down, she had ordered a strict vigil around and inside the fort. Annaji was well aware of Soyrabai's desires, intentions and capabilities, making him confident that his plans would see the light of day.

As soon as Soyrabai stepped out of her quarters, Annaji saluted her and said, 'Maharanisaheb, it does not make sense to delay any further. The ryots are confused and the army is rudderless, sans direction and command.'

'You are suggesting that we expedite our plans?'

'Expedite? Ranisaheb, the more we try to suppress the news of Raje's death, the faster it will spread. Keeping the throne vacant is inviting trouble.'

Soyrabai's angst was clearly visible on her face. She let out a deep sigh. 'Who do you propose to ascend the throne?'

'Well! When the opportunity has walked into your arms, you ask such rhetorical questions?'

Soyrabai felt encouraged by Annaji's confidence. Yet, she could not brush off the nameless fear which enveloped her.

'Would the ryots accept Rajaram in place of Shambhu Raje as their king? Would the elders give their consent?'

'Why are you hesitating at the last moment? You have been at the elder Maharaj's side all these years. Has he ever explicitly said that Sambhaji should be made the king?'

'Well, neither did he deny it!'

Annaji wiped the sweat from his face nervously. He warned Soyrabai, 'Ranisaheb, try to recall the last days of Maharaj. What was he saying?'

Soyrabai was confused.

'Well, he was delirious most of the time. He would shout, "Call my Shambhu; call Shambhu Raje."'

'It does not that mean he was calling for him to take the throne. At death's door, one remembers and wants to be with loved ones, that's all!'

Even as he spoke these words, Annaji Datto felt suffocated. He waved his angavastram to fan himself and continued, 'Even if Maharaj had left explicit instructions for Shambhu Raje to succeed to the throne, we are not naïve to follow his wishes!'

Annaji's words were music to Soyrabai's ears. He was saying what she wanted to express.

'Maharani, you need to act fast. The delay in announcing Raje's death and declaring Rajaram as king is causing a lot of confusion and fear in the minds of people.'

'Fear? What fear?'

Annaji looked around to ensure that there was no one within earshot. 'Tongues are wagging, Ranisaheb. There are rumours that you poisoned Maharaj to fulfil your ambition!'

Soyrabai was shaken. Her mind was in turmoil now. She realised that it was crucial for her to take a firm decision without further delay.

8

The same afternoon, Ramchandra Nilkanth, Prahlad Niraji and Rahuji Somnath assembled at the office. Soyrabai was present as well. But the

Peshwa Moropant Pingle had not arrived yet, although they heard that he had set out from Nashik five days ealier. Annaji was not sure of Moropant, and was rather relieved that he had reached Raigad before the Peshwa. It was easier to drum up support against Sambhaji in Moropant's absence.

After waiting for a long time, and having sent three messengers to Moropant's haveli, an impatient Annaji stood up and said, 'Let us send a batallion to his house to find out why he has not bothered to come here. That arrogant man is not going to make an appearance otherwise.'

At that moment, Moropant Peshwa's tall and slender figure appeared at the door. He had heard what Annaji said. Glancing at the men assembled in the room, he quickly surmised that they were all opposed to Sambhaji.

'Well, gentlemen! I want you to speak up. These are tough times and the enemy is at the gate. We need to take a wise but swift decision,' Annaji began. 'Can we trust a man who, only last year, defected to the Mughals and helped them to destroy a strong Maratha fort like Bhupalgad? How can we hand the reigns of the kingdom to someone who was a traitor to his own father and his kingdom?'

No one argued. Annaji's reasoning was strong. Moropant was his usual calm and reserved self. 'I say we need to proceed with caution. What is the great hurry?'

'Hurry?' Annaji stood up. 'Are we waiting for Shambhu Raje's arrival? Are you hoping that he arrives and orders that many of us be crushed under an elephant's feet? Are you not worried for your own life? Is your future so secure?'

Annaji made a huge fuss, but none of the others openly supported him. In fact, many of them were tickled by the fact that Annaji's worry stemmed from the fact that Sambhaji, who knew all of Annaji's corrupt practises, would not hesitate to put him in his place. They shrugged their shoulders and remained mute.

The lack of response to his tantrum was too much for Annaji to bear. He grit his teeth and, caressing his whiskers with a show of bravado, said, 'Well, you may all feel blessed to wipe Shambhu Raje's sandals. Do as you wish! I will not stay here a moment longer. I would prefer to spend the rest of my days in Kashi!'

A dejected Annaji glanced at the assembly, hoping against hope, but no one said a word. Soyrabai realised that none of the ministers had declared support for Annaji, and that it was unlikely her hopes would be fulfilled. All her dreams of strutting around as a Rajmata evaporated, and the thought of walking towards Kashi in the garb of an ordinary pilgrim sent a shudder down her spine. She said, speaking to no one in particular, 'Annaji is not saying this for his own benefit. Maharaj's death has brought the kingdom to the brink of disaster. Have you considered the threat to the future of the empire if someone like Shambhu, who does not have the wisdom to differentiate good from evil, ascends the throne? I urge you to make a decision now! Not because of what Annaji said, but based on your love for the Swaraj.'

Soyrabai's words managed to turn the tide in her favour. Most of the men assembled in the room had been hurt or insulted by Sambhaji, and nursed a grudge against him.

Justice Prahlad Niraji said, 'It was out of sheer affection for his son that the elder Maharaj never spoke against Sambhaji openly. But I am willing to wager that a person with his choleric temperament will fail if he is given the charge of a kingdom.'

Ramchandra Nilkanth nodded in agreement. 'You are absolutely right. He will destroy himself and everyone around him.'

Annaji Pant realised that he was back in the game. 'That is why I urge you to hurry. Rajaram Raje is calm and composed. We need to place him on the throne before Aurangzeb knocks on our doors. This is the best course of action for all of us.'

Soyrabai got an opportunity to voice her thoughts now. 'One should not share in public what is said in private. However under these circumstances I have no option but to do so. The elder Maharaj had confided in me many times that Shambhu is a hot headed young man with many harmful habits. His behaviour has always been reckless and irresponsible. His stay at Aurangabad has only increased his debauchery in all forms, whether it be food, drink or women. If such a careless and self-indulgent person were to ascend the throne, the kingdom would be destroyed in no time.'

The atmosphere in the room had changed now. Soon they began to discuss the modalities of running the kingdom while Rajaram was coronated. Many views were aired on how to manage the threat posed by Sambhaji. Moropant Peshwa was silent.

Annaji asked, 'Peshwa, why are you not speaking?'

Moropant said, his voice calm and composed, 'I am loyal to my king and his kingdom. I am unable to understand why the elder son, who is still alive, was not called to perform the final rites of his father, and how we can think of putting the younger son on the throne, ignoring all the rules of hierarchy and ascension.'

Annaji Datto fumed, 'It is the view of most of the ministers that Rajaram should succeed Shivaji to the throne.'

'Gentlemen, you are free to decide whatever suits you but I am not going to be party to this crime.'

Moropant Peshwa's words were a powerful reprimand to all present. Soyrabai was confused and did not know how to react. Annaji Datto on the other hand was incensed, realising that Moropant might turn the tables on him.

'Peshwa, are you in your senses? Do you know what you are saying?'

'Annaji, I wish you would not get agitated,' Moropant said, without raising his voice. 'I have nothing against Rajaram but you must concede that the situation is delicate. I wonder who would lead the charge if Badshah Aurangzeb decides to descend upon the Deccan.'

'Wah! You mean to say that we are all impotent fools? Is Shambhu Raje the only valorous man amongst us?'

'That is true! It is Shambhu Raje who has the courage to lead an attack against the Delhi Badshah. No one else can compete with Yuvraj in this regard. Have you taken a look outside the fort? Thousands have gathered, shouting slogans in Shambhu Raje's support. The army is behind Shambhu. You need to recognise that times are changing and act wisely. Annaji, if you wish, I will go and convince Sambhaji to give away the throne. He will do so happily if you all demand it. But I warn you: this is not the time to act in haste and make childish decisions prompted by personal grudges.'

Moropant's blunt remarks shut everyone up. Balaji Chitnis began, 'Well, to tell the truth ...'

'I suggest you don't say a word, Balaji Pant,' Annaji interrupted him. Turning to Moropant he said, 'What's your fear regarding the army? Have you forgotten that Hambirrao, Soyrabai's younger brother, is the commander-in-chief? The army answers to him.'

Soyrabai added, 'He has already sent his written consent in support of Rajaram.'

'Peshwa, you must have noticed a strong force of fifteen thousand men standing outside the fort's main entrance. The treasury and the administration of the fort is under our control as well. The commander is on our side. The queen too is with us. Where do you stand, Moropant?

Which side are you going to support? That of Kavi Kalash?' Annaji challenged Moropant.

Annaji was in his element now, at his dramatic best. As he spoke, he raised his eyebrows and stroked his moustache, removed his turban and put it back several times while tying and untying his hair. Once again, he reiterated the benefits of putting Rajaram on the throne and the dangers of coronating Sambhaji, exaggerating the latter's vices and flaws. Then he turned his vitriolic flow of words towards Kavi Kalash.

'Let him come here once. You will see his true nature when he sits on a buffalo skin, sticking needles into small dolls and performing his tantric rituals. Only then will you realise what kind of a shaman he is!'

Those assembled in the room shuddered, imagining the scenario. Finally, even Moropant seemed to relent. But Annaji was not going to leave it at that.

'Moropant, I prefer that you give your consent in writing. Not that I doubt your words, but they have a tendency to fly away in the wind. It is always best to have things on paper.'

Soyrabai and Annaji let out secret sighs of relief. Things were moving the way they wanted. Even the date of Rajaram's coronation was agreed on. But the question still remained: what to do with Sambhaji? Would it be possible to run the kingdom even for a day if he was still at large?

Annaji thundered, 'Moropant, send orders to arrest Shambhu Raje. As long as he is free, no one would be able to live without fear.'

'Yes, issue the orders right now,' Soyrabai demanded. 'Send word to Janardan Pant to arrest Yuvraj and imprison him in the dungeon at Panhalgad. No point in dragging him to Raigad.'

Moropant smiled sweetly. 'You seem to be forgetting something, Annaji. Such orders are not issued by me or by you.'

'Oh, really?'

'No fortkeeper or subedar would take any action unless the seal of Balaji Avaji is on the paper.'

Annaji was clearly rattled. Sweat trickled down his neck. He turned to look at Balaji Avaji but he was not there. No one had realised that Chitnis, the chief secretary of the king, had long since left the room.

9

It was a dark and windy night. The lamps in Soyrabai's quarters burnt brightly. Outside the window, the loud chirping of the crickets could be heard. Annaji Datto and Soyrabai sat silently, their faces strained with anxiety.

'Ranisaheb, I wonder who could make this Chitnis understand the situation. He has always been inclined to favour Shambhu Raje.'

Soyrabai seemed fidgety. 'He has been sent the message, hasn't he? I am sure he will come. He must obey your orders.'

Within a few minutes, the tall, hefty Balaji Avaji entered the room and bowed in mujra to Soyrabai. She put on a sweet smile and said, almost pleading, 'Chitnis, the letters with your seal need to be despatched at once.

'Only over my dead body, Maharani saheb.'

'No fortkeeper will take action unless the letters carry your seal. You know that!'

Neither Soyrabai's repeated requests nor Annaji's veiled threats had any effect on Balaji. He bowed respectfully and said, 'How can I be disloyal to Maharaj? I cannot issue such orders. Sambhaji Raje is my king now.'

Soyrabai and Annaji persisted, 'But you have to write what we order you to.'

'Don't force me to. I cannot commit such a crime.' Balaji Avaji could not have put it more bluntly. 'Maharani saheb, these orders are clearly not in line with the law, or with our tradition and customs.'

Annaji tried to change his tactics, switching from threats to a tone of reconciliation.

'Chitnis, do you think we will harm Shambhu Raje? After all, the elder Maharaj treated us like his children. His son is our son too. Rajaram is not going to rule forever. Shambhu Raje is a little immature now. When he is older and wiser, we will ask him to manage the kingdom. It is up to him to then take charge or refuse.'

Soyrabai and Annaji were trying their best to conceal the anger and annoyance they felt towards Balaji Pant. It was getting late but Balaji would not change his stance.

'Balaji Pant, you are getting old. Your two sons, Khandoba and Niloba, are not going to find jobs at Janjira. Their future is in serving Soyrabai

Ranisaheb. Your stubbornness will ruin their prospects. Why do you want to be responsible for that?'

Annaji had found Balaji's weak spot. The emotional pressure of this final threat was not easy to withstand. Balaji realised that Soyrabai and Annaji were not going to rest until the orders to arrest Sambhaji were stamped with his seal. He folded his hands in supplication and said, 'I beg of you, do not compel me to commit such a crime. Please pardon me!'

Balaji remembered how, years ago, when he was a fatherless boy with no prospects, his elegant handwriting had impressed Shivaji Raje. He said, wiping his tears, 'It is my handwriting which raised an orphan like me to the position of the Chief Secretary of the Hindavi Swaraj. I am not going to use the same hand to commit treason. Tchah! Annaji Pant, if you wish, you may cut my fingers off, but I will not be forced to write that letter.'

It was past midnight. Annaji threatened Balaji with arrest and the confiscation of his property but the latter did not move an inch. Finally, Balaji said,

'If you insist, I will ask my son Abaji to write. But I am unable to come to terms with my part in this backstabbing. Shambhu Raje reposes unconditional trust in me. I wonder what he will think!'

10

Every time Sambhaji glanced at the Sajja Kothi in Panhalgad, where he had been under house arrest for a while, he would remember his father and tears would come to his eyes.

Feeling suffocated, Sambhaji decided to go for a ride. Kavi Kalash and Jotyaji Kesarkar accompanied him. They stopped on the edge of a deep ravine, observing the winding path below. Sambhaji spotted two travellers on foot, holding the reins of their horses as they guided them slowly up the steep path.

After a while, they were clearly visible. Sambhaji instantly recognised them. They were Khandoji Naik and Ganoji Kavle—spies whose job was to keep an eagle eye on the area around Panhalgad and Vishalgad up to the borders of Raigad. Yuvraj surmised that they were returning with some urgent news from Raigad.

The pair finally reached the spot where Sambhaji and his companions stood. Seeing Yuvraj, Khandoji bent low in mujra as he tried to recover his breath. Then, avoiding Sambhaji's eyes, he took a letter from his cummerbund and handed it over. The note was from Balaji but Sambhaji could see that the handwriting was not his. The letter did not contain any important news. After a hurried mujra, the two men began to walk away when Sambhaji thundered, sensing that something was amiss, 'Why are you in a hurry? And where are you off to?'

'We have to meet the fortkeeper before it gets dark,' Khandoji faltered.

Sambhaji's glare bored into them. They were unable to meet his eye. With a wave of his fingers, Sambhaji gestured them to come closer. They were shivering, and sweat trickled down their foreheads.

'Kavle, what are those papers in your cummerbund?'

'Nothing, Yuvraj! Just some regular letters. They are addressed to the fortkeepeer,' Ganoji answered hurriedly, trying to put on a casual air. But his trembling legs gave him away.

Sambhaji signalled to Kavi Kalash who rushed forward and snatched the letters from Ganoji. One of them was addressed to the fortkeeper, Vithal Trayambak, and the other to Havaldar Bahirji Naik. Sambhaji read the contents:

> *'The situation here is a matter of great concern. We shall update you whenever we can but, for the time being, don't allow Shambhu Raje to step out of the fort under any circumstances. Arrest him. Don't let him know about Maharaj. We shall send you furthers orders as and when necessary.'*

Sambhaji anger knew no bounds. The two spies did not dare to raise their eyes and started trembling more violently.

'Tell me the truth! What is going on in Raigad? Who is behind the orders to arrest me? Is it Matoshree, or is it that loyal servant of the Swaraj, Annaji Datto?'

Then, recalling the reference to Maharaj, he asked, 'And what about Abasaheb? How is his health?'

The fierce barrage of questions overwhelmed the two spies; they collapsed to the ground, quaking in fear. Tortured by the fact that they were carrying a terrible secret that they had been ordered to conceal from Yuvraj, the heir to the throne, they started crying like children. Clutching at Sambhaji's feet, they sobbed, 'Sarkar, please pardon us. We poor folks are caught in the crossfire of this fight amongst the royals.'

At a gesture from Yuvraj, the soldiers standing not far away rushed forward and arrested the two spies. Sambhaji called for an urgent meeting with Vithal Trayambak, Bahirji Naik and others. It was clear that a political conspiracy was being hatched.

Sambhaji glared at Khandoji. 'Out with the truth, Khandoba! How is Abasaheb's health?'

The spy, shivering to the core, did not know how to break the terrible news. Somehow he blurted, crying hoarsely as he spoke, 'Yuvraj, destiny has played a cruel hand. The elder Maharaj has left all of us orphaned!'

It was as if the heavens had collapsed. There was not a single soul who could hold back their tears. Even Vithal Trayambakrao, who was part of the conspiracy in a way, couldn't restrain his grief. The palace was drowned in sorrow.

Surprisingly, Sambhaji's reaction was very different. He neither shed tears nor spoke a single word. Like a huge boulder falling down a steep slope, he simply collapsed to the floor. He was not unconscious; his eyes were wide open. Yet, there was no movement whatsoever!

There was chaos all around. They tried to revive him with smelling salts. After a while, like a wounded lion who roars with pain, Sambhaji screamed 'Abasaheb!' Kavi Kalash and others rushed to hold him but Sambhaji pushed everyone aside. Clutching a pillar, he started banging his head on it while he continued to mumble, 'Abasaheb, Abasaheb!' It was as if the Lord had appeared in form of an iron pillar and Sambhaji was resting his head on his shoulders. The poignant sight left everyone transfixed. They did not know how to console Yuvraj.

After a long time, Sambhaji was quiet. He managed to sip a little water from a tumbler. But his grief was palpable as the rumbling of the earth long after an earthquake. He shouted at the spies, 'If you are trying to make fun of me, please tell me so! How can Abasaheb leave this world so easily?'

'Yuvraj, unfortunately, it is true. He had a fever for merely a week but it turned out to be the cause. Shivaji Raje is no more!'

The shock had subsided now. Sambhaji listened carefully to the spies as they explained how the fort had been sealed during the week leading up to Maharaj's death. On the day of Hanuman Jayanti, Shivaji Raje had bid farewell to the world. As the two men spoke, none present could suppress their sobs.

'Who performed the last rites?' Kavi Kalash's voice boomed in the uncomfortable silence of the room. The spy tried to evade the question by describing how the funeral pyre was laden with sandalwood.

'Who performed the last rites?' Sambhaji repeated the question.

'It was Rajaram saheb.'

Sambhaji said, to no one in particular, 'Did the pandits forget that it is the duty—nay, the right—of the eldest son to perform the last rites?'

Tears continued to flow down his cheeks. Those present were reminded of pearls flowing down a necklace when the delicate silk thread holding them snaps. Yet, he was angry too, seething with rage at the gross injustice of it all.

'What right did Matoshree and her self-serving sycophants have to perform the last rites in my absence? Is Shivaji's Shambhubal dead? Or do they feel that my hands are soiled, unworthy of offering the rites? Did they not know that I would have regarded it a blessing merely to have prayed at his deathbed? But no, I was not considered worthy even of being informed of my father's death, depriving me of the chance to offer a few flowers to the memory of his valiant soul.'

SEVEN

At Raigad

1

'It has been quite a while since we went to war. The body feels dull and stiff,' Hambirrao thought, filling his mouth with water and spitting it out. He had just completed his morning exercise routine and sat watching the sun rise. The Koyna flowed serenely by. The Maratha garrison he commanded, which had been inactive for a while, was camped nearby. Even the horses, mules and elephants were getting restless.

It was only the previous day that Hambirrao had returned to his camp at Karad from his haveli at Talbid near Satara. It was his habit to do more than a thousand push-ups every morning. He would feel relaxed only after his whole body and the floor below was drenched with his sweat.

Hambirrao was a tall, muscular man with a bull neck and thick, curled whiskers. He had earned his reputation with the prowess of his sword. There was an aura of strength around him, a commanding persona which radiated the ability to lead men in battle. In the battle against Bahlol Khan at Nesari, when Prataprao Gujar had jumped into the fray with just six men and sacrificed his life, it was Hambirrao who had galvanised the rest of the troops, ensuring that they did not retreat in fear. He had, on the other hand, managed to turn the tide, chasing Bahlol Khan and his men towards Bijapur like wild boars being hounded by hunting dogs. When Shivaji's step-brother Vyankoji Raje had raised his voice and challenged Shivaji Raje's supremacy, it was Hambirrao's daredevil attack on Tanjavur that made Vyankoji run for his life.

The elder Maharaj had been heard to say, 'You may offer me fifty firangi cannons which can destroy walls of a fort but I am not willing to exchange Hambirrao for them! He is more precious than any artillery the Europeans can devise!'

Everyone at Raigad was now waiting for word from Hambirrao. It was crucial to know which side the commander-in-chief of the Maratha forces was leaning towards. His support would be crucial to win the war of succession. As expected, Hambirrao had received requests from both sides.

As he was leaving his haveli, his wife Rakhmabai bid him goodbye, saying, 'I am sure you have received the message from Soyrabai Ranisaheb.

All said and done, it is the kinship of blood which matters in the end. Rajaram Balraje is our nephew. I hope he ascends the throne and that you will support his claim.' Hambirrao's only response to his wife's words was an indulgent smile.

When Hambirrao reached his camp at dusk, a clerk was waiting for him with a message from Panhala. He read the letter by the light of the burning torch.

> *'Warm regards from Shri Raja Shambhu Chhatrapati, to the commander in chief, Hambirrao Mohite.*
>
> *Mamasaheb, I am your nephew by blood. The Bhosale and Mohite families have been associated for three generations now. Why did Abasaheb appoint you as the commander? Not because you were Soyrabai Ranisaheb's brother, but because there was a need to fill the vacuum left by that gem of a soldier, Prataprao Gujar. Since the elder Maharaj's death, I feel orphaned. Mamasaheb, what else can I write. I pray that there are no differences amongst us, and I am sure you will take a wise decision.'*

Hambirrao was approaching his mid-fifties, but his energy and enthusiasm would have shamed a young soldier. After his exercise, he ran towards the river and dived into the water that was twenty feet deep. Swimming for a while, he reached the bank where his servants stood waiting with his clothes. After changing into them, he rode to the camp, accepting mujras and salutes from his troops on the way.

Rupaji Bhosale and Anandrao Makaji were waiting at his tent. Their weary faces showed that they had been waiting for a long time.

Rupaji conveyed the message, 'I am informed that the team from Raigad has reached Umbraj.'

'The team from Raigad?'

'Annaji Datto and Moropant Pingle.'

'What for?'

Hambirrao knew why they had come but he had posed the question deliberately.

'Well, they want to convince you to join them. I am told they want to take your help to march on to Panhala and arrest Shambhu Raje.'

Hambirrao was silent. He knew that, as commander-in-chief, he was not answerable to anyone there. At that moment, he recalled another letter which he had received from Sambhaji. He took the letter out and read it again.

'Warm regards from Shri Raja Shambhu Chhatrapati, to the commander-in-chief, Hambirrao Mohite.

I felt as if the heavens had collapsed when I heard of Abasaheb's demise. The only silver lining is the fact that three months ago, I had the privilege of spending five days with him at Panhalgad. We were able to sort out all our differences. He pardoned my misdemeanours, including my defection to the Mughals. He not only forgave me but also entrusted me with the task of vanquishing the Mughals. His sudden departure from this world has shattered me. But I am determined to fulfil his wishes.

But there are a few men who insist on putting a spoke in my wheel. Their intentions are suspect. They are corrupting Soyrabai Matoshree's mind with idea of putting Rajaram on the throne. For their personal gain, they are willing to split the kingdom. Mamasaheb, I may not be related to you the way Rajaram is, but I am the son of Shivaji, the founder of the Hindavi Swaraj. Once my path is cleared of these obstacles, I vow to finish off Aurangzeb the sinner. I have high ambitions and I am sure I can cross any sea of troubles if you are with me. You have every right to pull my ears, if ever I make a mistake or act wrongly.

Badshah Aurangzeb is growing arrogant by the day and wants to crush us by levying the Jizya tax on Hindus. My sole purpose is to ensure that we fulfil Abasaheb's vision. I look forward to your blessings.'

Shambhu Raje's heartfelt letter touched Hambirrao and he mulled over it the whole afternoon. As he sat in his tent, he was informed that two senior administrators from Raigad had reached his camp. Hambirrao peeped out of the canvas window. He could see a tired Moropant Pingle astride a horse, his face aflame from exposure to the raging sun. It was clear that he had not enjoyed the ride. Close behind him, sitting in a palanquin carried by six men, was the corpulent Annaji Datto. He too seemed tired and irritated by the long journey.

Finally the two men, huffing and puffing, entered the cool environs of the tent. Despite their exhaustion, they seemed eager to perform the task for which they had journeyed so far.

Hambirrao ordered his soldiers to leave the tent. Now he sat alone with the two sardars from Raigad. He said, smiling at Annaji,

'Annaji, looks like you left your horse behind at Umbraj.'

'No! Can you imagine him riding a horse at his age? He has been in a palanquin since Raigad. The poor bearers are dog-tired, despite the fact that we have two teams,' Moropant responded, laughing heartily.

Annaji was not pleased with the turn the conversation was taking and shifted nervously in his seat. Hambirrao quickly realised that both men were hesitating to bring up the topic they wanted to discuss.

'Pant, you have come all this way with high hopes for a favourable outcome from an important discussion. But I am sorry to have to tell you that I don't think your wishes will be fulfilled here.'

The pair had not certainly not expected an opening remark which rejected their proposal outright. In their arrogance, they had aassumed that the commander, a pea-brained soldier, would naively follow the dictates of power and be more than willing to march with his forces to Panhala. But his words put them in a quandary and their faces fell.

Annaji was furious. 'What are you blabbering? Have you not promised me already that you will take your troops wherever we ask you to? And now, when we demand action, you seem to be backing out!'

Moropant looked at Annaji, indicating that a more conciliatory approach might be wiser. Annaji's tone changed.

'What we mean, Senapati, is that … after all, it is your nephew who is going to be coronated, isn't it?'

Hambirrao smiled. 'I would like to know what makes Rajaram the right choice for the throne.'

'Well, Hambirrao, it is Shivaji Maharaj's own dying wish.' Their subdued tone suggested that they did not even expect Hambirrao to swallow this.

'Don't lie so brazenly, Pant. Had Maharaj been so sure, he would have left instructions in writing.'

'Well, neither has he said explicity that Shambhu Raje should be made the king. Listen, Hambirrao, if your nephew ascends the throne, it benefits you and us too.'

'No! I do not think so.'

Annaji was losing his temper now. 'No? What do you mean? Are you Rajaram's Mama or Kansa to his Krishna?'

Hambirrao was as cool as a cucumber despite such a direct confrontation.

'No, you listen to me! I know I would benefit more than anyone else, but that's not the point. You are all learned men while I am an ordinary soldier. I only know that when one walks with the Lord's palanquin, one gets showered with the petals meant for the Lord and feels blessed. Walking with a great man like Shivaji all my life, I have learned to follow what is right. Let me explain! When someone like Shivaji leaves the world suddenly, I look towards his Bhawani sword for directions. It is my responsibility to ensure that it is handed over to the right person. Don't try to corrupt my mind by reminding me of my nephew and my sister. I appeal to your conscience. Think for a moment! If we want to further the cause of Swaraj, there is no choice but to put Shambhu Raje on the throne.'

Hambirrao's words were like those of a judge delivering his final verdict, leaving the accused in turmoil. Annaji removed his turban and placed it on his lap. Moropant looked confused and did not what to say.

Hambirrao continued, 'You have seen Shambhu Raje as a meek son in the presence of Shivaji Maharaj. I have been witness to his avatar on the battlefield when, naked sword in hand, he cuts his way through the enemy ranks. It is a sight to behold! You are unfortunate never to have seen it. Whenever Shivaji Raje was on a campaign, he would entrust Shambhu Raje with thousands of troops. And the valiant son never let his father down. He could inspire an ordinary man, a ryot, to fight for his kingdom by the mere spurring of his horse. Tomorrow, God forbid, if we are to face Aurangzeb, we need a soldier-king like Shambhubal at Raigad.'

'What are you blabbering, Hambirrao?' Annaji Datto stood up, prepared to continue his tirade.

'Annaji Pant, I am going to act according to the principles taught by Shivaji Maharaj and Prataprao.'

'But your nephew …'

'Will you stop saying that? This is not about my nephew. Had it been my own son, I would have pushed him aside to make way for the lion's cub. Shambhu Raje is the man who deserves my salute.'

Annaji and Moropant were speechless. Evidently, they had not expected Hambirrao to sing paeans in praise of Sambhaji. Annaji gulped water from a tumbler and said, 'Please call your Diwan.'

The Diwan, Raibhan Sabnis, presented himself. Annaji's fury had returned, and he thundered, 'Diwan, Rajaramsaheb is the king of the Marathas. By his orders, I, Annajipant Prabhunikar, and the Peshwa Moropant, order you to arrest Hambirrao for committing treason. Bind him in fetters and drag him to Raigad immediately.'

Annaji thought he had fired a cannon but it turned out to be a damp squib. The Diwan barely moved a muscle. After a moment, Annaji stood up and stormed out of Hambirrao's tent. They had come from Raigad with a troop of five thousand men but they did not stand a chance against the twenty thousand loyal soldiers who stood with Hambirrao. Yet, Annaji was not one to give up. He screamed at his men, 'Come on! Attack! Enter the tent and arrest Hambirrao!'

Hambirrao stood at the door of his tent. Not a single soldier from Annaji's troops dared to step forward. Annaji, waving his hands, looked like a raving madman. Hambirrao said to his second-in-command, 'Rupaji, arrest these two and leave for Panhala immediately. Present these 'jewels' to Shambhu Raje and inform him that I shall be there by dawn tomorrow.'

2

A mountain of work was piling up. It was time to set the kingdom right. There had been too many disturbances and distractions thanks to politics and intrigue. Sambhaji's eyes were red; he had been working day and night.

A servant announced the arrival of Rupaji Bhosale. Sambhaji stepped out of his quarters. Rupaji saluted him and said, almost shouting with joy, 'Raje, we have won! The ones who were trying to arrest you are in chains now!'

'What do you mean?'

'Hambirrao arrested Annaji Pant and Moropant Pingle this afternoon at Karad. I have brought them here, tied in chains. Hambirrao will present himself tomorrow morning.'

'Fantastic! Put them in the dungeon and keep a strict eye on them. We will discuss the rest tomorrow,' a relieved and happy Sambhaji said.

It had been a lively few days at Panhala. Despite Rajaram being declared the king, the ryots considered Sambhaji as the real heir to the throne. They had flocked to Panhalgad in thousands, clamouring to meet him.

Sambhaji went back into his quarters to find Yesubai sleeping. She was tired too, from helping her husband with his work day and night. Sambhaji did not feel like waking her up but he simply could not keep the latest news to himself! The arrest of Annaji and Moropant, and the fact that the Senapati of the Maratha forces would stand by him, was indeed a turning point in their fortunes. Sambhaji's detractors and enemies, both within and outside the kingdom, would be stumped by the news. He wanted to share it with Yesu at once.

Sambhaji shook her out of her sleep and told her about the latest developments.

'Where is Hambir Mama meeting you?'

'At my private quarters, why?'

'I suggest you welcome him formally, in a durbar.'

'That is a good idea, Yesu. But we don't have a throne here.'

'Why worry about that? A throne is wherever the king stands!'

According to Yesubai's suggestion, a small durbar was set up in Panhalgad. Everyone waited eagerly for Hambirrao's arrival.

The Senapati made a grand entry. His tall, strapping figure and the string of pearls dangling from his turban made quite the impression on those assembled to greet him. He saluted Yuvraj in an elaborate fashion. Sambhaji was in tears. Yesubai wiped her tears gently. Hambirrao held Yuvraj's hands and hugged him affectionately.

They were genuinely happy to be meeting each other after a long time. Sambhaji could scarcely believe that Hambirrao had not allowed his relationship with Soyrabai Ranisaheb and Rajaram to come in the way of extending his support to him. Visibly relieved, he said, 'Mamasaheb, your presence here is truly reassuring. Going forward, you will continue to be the commander-in-chief, the Senapati of the Maratha forces.'

'Shambhu Raje, don't look at me as your Mama. Shivaji Raje used to say: let the boundaries of your relationships end at the rangoli laid around your dining plate.'

'Whatever you say, Mamasaheb, but the service you have rendered to the Swaraj has been exemplary.'

Hambirrao's affection and loyalty overwhelmed Yesubai and Sambhaji. Shambhu Raje took off his jewelled necklace and gifted it to Hambirrao, along with fine clothes.

'Mamasaheb, I want to honour another giant here today. He will be here any moment.'

'Who is it?'

'Our Hiroji Farzand Kaka. You are aware of the heights to which Abasaheb has taken Hindavi Swaraj. It is not possible for someone like me to steer the chariot alone. I have made mistakes, drunk on the arrogance of my youth. I want to ensure that I have experienced people like you to guide me. Hiroji Kaka is another.'

While the durbar was in progress, a servant announced the arrival of Ramji Naik, the emissary from Goa. He presented a message from the

Viceroy Paes de Sande, expressing his grief at the untimely death of Shivaji Raje. He also conveyed the Viceroy's wish to maintain cordial relations between the Marathas and the Portuguese. Sambhaji could picture the sea on one side and the green Konkan coast on the other. Above all he was thinking of Janjira near Murud, a fortress which curled like a poisonous snake, threatening anyone who dared to attack.

Hambirrao interrupted his reverie, saying, 'Raje, it is not advisable to stay at Panhala any longer. The earlier we reach Raigad and take charge, the better.'

'There is no need to hurry, Hambir Mama. See how the Portuguese, the French and the English are making a beeline to Panhalgad, to present themselves as our allies!'

That afternoon, Moropant and Annaji were dragged into Sambhaji's presence. Moropant's hands were tied with ropes while Annaji was bound in iron chains. Guilt was written all over the old Peshwa's face and he did not dare to meet Sambhaji's gaze.

Sambhaji rose from the throne and said, walking towards Moropant, 'Kaka, I wonder what made you join these devils. Why did you choose to toe their line?'

Moropant was devastated. He said, in a piteous voice, 'What has happened is not right. I know I made a mistake.'

Shambhu Raje gestured to a guard to free the old man from his bonds. 'Moropant is in his seventies now. Don't tie him in ropes.'

He turned his attention to Annaji Datto. Annaji had not allowed guilt or shame to show on his face. However, he fidgeted like a wild animal caught in a hunter's trap.

'As for you, Annaji Pant, you take the cake, leading the revolt against me! I am unable to understand your motives. But it would be suicidal to pardon you and let you go scot-free.'

Despite being in fetters, Annaji growled, 'Sambhaji Raje, what good can any sensible person anticipate from your ascension to the throne? The elder Maharaj is no more. And with him has gone all justice and logic. What can the Maratha Empire expect from you, with your rowdy behaviour?'

'Pant, do not pretend to be so concerned about the kingdom. Speak for yourself; what made you take such desperate measures?'

'I will tell you; provided you assure me that you have forsaken your unruly behaviour and show that there is a semblance of politeness in you.'

'Politeness is not called for when dealing with a traitor. Say what you must!'

'First release me from these iron fetters.'

'This is a small punishment for a grave crime like treason!'

'You are the one committing treason, Sambhaji Raje. I am here under the authority of the seal and signature of the king who has been appointed at Raigad. You must release me immediately!'

'Clearly, you are not willing to change!'

'Shambhu Raje, you are a sinner, with many vices and a terrible reputation,' Annaji shouted, waving his hands in the air. Yesubai rose from her seat, unable to listen to his rant. Sambhaji glanced at Hambirrao, and the Senapati shouted orders to his men,'Take this ungrateful rascal away and throw him into the dungeons.' Moropant was put in a prison cell while Annaji was thrown into a dark dungeon.

The durbar continued and matters of administration were discussed in detail. Hiroji had not yet arrived. Suddenly, a few ryots rushed in and, after a quick salute, said, 'Raje, we have been fooled. Farzand has escaped!'

'Escaped? But we had never put him under arrest! What exactly are you trying to say?'

'He has taken two large boxes full of jewels from the treasury and is on his way to the Konkan coast with fifteen of his men.'

Hambirrao was shocked that someone like Hiroji Farzand had taken such a step. He ordered a few men to follow them and report their whereabouts. Sambhaji was unfazed. He said, 'Hambir Mama, where can he hide? Let's not worry. Anyway, there are more important matters to discuss. We will have to sit here well into the night.'

Malhoji Ghorpade, Krishnaji Kank, Hambirrao, and Prahlad Niraji, who had arrived earlier to meet Sambhaji, were present for the discussion. Yesubai joined them. Sambhaji began, 'Our hopes were dented by Hiroji's act but this does not surprise me. A mansion will always attract a few mice. We must find them and squash them. I am not very worried about revolts or infighting. But we must start preparing for the eventuality of a Mughal invasion. Abasaheb had warned me of such a possibility when we met three months ago. Aurangzeb is one of the world's most powerful emperors. A single Subah of the Mughal Empire is a few times the size of our entire Swaraj.'

'Is that so?' Niraji exclaimed.

'I am not exaggerating. We have to begin reinforcing each and every Maratha fort with food supplies, ammunition and troops.'

'Once we reach Raigad, we will start the process formally.'

'We cannot wait for that. We have to start this very moment. Troubles don't arrive with a forewarning. Pant, I will need a detailed inventory of all the forts in the Swaraj within the next four days. We have to ensure that the ammunition is dry, that the wells are full of water, and that the forts are sufficiently stocked with food. I will also require a list of all the key personnel at every fort. Send your men to Rajapur tomorrow and get the inventory of the stock of foodgrains there. I want to ensure that each and every fort is ready to withstand a siege before I leave for Raigad.'

Sambhaji was aware that many sardars were sitting on the fence. He despatched personal messages to them, reminding them of his love and appealing to their loyalty. Sambhaji's unbounded enthusiasm and the promptness with which he had set about the task of defending the kingdom immediately inspired those around him.

He said, as he finally stepped out of the room, 'Let Aurangzeb know: the plateau of the Deccan was formed by mighty volcanoes. You are most welcome to arrive in a golden howdah but the men of the Sahyadris would destroy you. Your body would be mixed with the dust here and you will never see Agra or Delhi ever again. You will be finished once you step into the Deccan.'

3

Hiroji had created history in Agra, taking the place of Shivaji while Maharaj had escaped. He resembled Shivaji closely in physical appearance and had successfully fooled the guards at Agra. The fact that he might be beheaded by Aurangzeb did not stop him from saving his king's life. The same Hiroji had today decamped with contents of the treasury from Panhala.

Sambhaji was disturbed. He said, looking at Yesubai,

'I wonder what makes people like Hiroji do such things. Why do men change colour like a chameleon? Farzand Kaka's behaviour is surprising. And so is Balaji Avaji's.'

Yesubai looked askance. 'Balaji Avaji?'

'Yes! You might not be able to realise that. He lovingly calls you "daughter-in-law." But I am surprised to learn that he sent a secret message to the fortkeeper at Panhala, asking him to take immediate action and arrest me!'

Yesubai realised that Sambhaji's anger was rising.

'Yuvraj, but the letter was probably not written by Balaji. The handwriting was not his, surely? It was probably written by his son.'

That further enraged Sambhaji.

'Do you think I am naïve? All of us are aware that in Balaji's absence, his son's seal and signature is perfectly valid.'

'I still cannot believe that the orders had Balaji Kaka's consent.'

Sambhaji's was an affectionate, trusting nature. He had always reciprocated the trust and affection of those who had showered the same on him. Balaji Chitnis was one such person. During Shivaji's reign, he had been a close confidante of the family. Sambhaji was hurt by the fact that many of the administrators in Raigad had taken sides against him but he was working to ensure that the vitiated atmosphere changed slowly in his favour. To help matters, he had the staunch support of the ryots and the troops.

There were murmurs all over the kingdom, urging those in power to declare him king. The commoners were increasingly agitated by the fact that administrators were trying to oppose Sambhaji's ascension. Eventually, Raigad's troops and ryots revolted openly. They arrested those in favour of Soyrabai and, marching on the havelis of Annaji and Moropant on 16 May 1680, looted them. Taking charge of Raigad, they sent an urgent message to Panhala, 'Raje, come immediately!'

Seeing the tide turning, Sambhaji worked with renewed vigour. He immediately despatched a message to Shringarpur, asking his father-in-law, Pilajirao Shirke, to march on Raigad with ten thousand troops. Hambirrao was also on the move with five thousand men. Sambhaji had ensured that the soldiers were paid two months' salary in advance. Soon, thousands of troops on horseback, brandishing their swords and spears, were seen approaching Panhala to join Sambhaji. At the same time, hundreds of bullock carts from Rajapur were moving towards forts all over the kingdom, carrying grains and other food supplies. Everything was working in Sambhaji's favour and according to plan.

One morning Yesubai, who was performing pooja at her quarters, heard footsteps behind her. Realising that they were not Sambhaji's, and wondering who had dared to enter her quarters unannounced, she turned to see a tall, thick-moustached man smiling at her. Yesu smiled back at Ganoji Shirke, her brother.

Yesubai gestured towards the swing in her garden, asking him to wait while she finished pooja. Sitting there, Ganoji looked with admiration at his younger sister, who would now be the Queen of the Hindavi Swaraj in Raigad. He remembered their carefree childhood days, and how he used to roam the woods near Shringarpur, collecting wild flowers to make garlands for his sister. Now she was to be the Maharani of a kingdom which had crores of hons in its treasury.

'Dadasaheb, would it not have been better for you to go directly to Raigad? There are so many things to do there …'

'Yesu, don't worry about all that. Destiny is in your favour now!'

'It has nothing to do with destiny. It was my father-in-law who chose me and changed my life. Remember, how he was impressed by the shining utensils in the kitchen and surmised that I must be very meticulous in my work?'

A flicker of anxiety appeared on Ganoji's face. 'Yesu, I hope you won't forget us, once you don the Maharani's clothes.'

'Don't pull my leg!'

'Well, you know that the Shirkes of Shringarpur are not Maharajas. I just hope we too can benefit from the good fortune which shines on you now.'

'Why are you speaking in riddles, Dada?'

'Then let me put it plainly. I have heard that power corrupts the mind and tends to make you forget your loved ones.'

Yesu watched her brother closely as he continued, 'The day you are anointed Maharani, I hope we too can be awarded a small watan.'

'Watan? What are you talking of?'

'I am asking that the territory of Dabhol, which belonged to our family, be returned to us in the form of a watan.'

Yesubai was taken aback. She had not expected her brother to come asking her for special favours when Sambhaji had scarcely occupied the throne. She said, 'Things are hectic here, Dada. Give me a couple of days. Let me put in a word with Yuvraj, and we will see.'

Ganoji was back in her quarters after two days. He had stayed on at Panhala.

'So what did Yuvraj say, Yesu?'

'About what?'

'Oh, it appears that you have picked up the Bhosale style of cunningness pretty quickly,' Ganoji said, in a bitter tone. 'I am speaking of Dabhol, your hometown. We talked about it, remember?'

'I did speak to Yuvraj. He asked me to tell you to wait for a while.'

'Yesu, it looks like you have forgotten the pride of the Shirkes now that you are Bhosale's daughter-in-law!'

'Dadasaheb, why are you so adamant?'

'The fault is not ours. We were forced to give up our hereditary watandari under pressure from the great Shivaji Maharaj!' Ganoji spat out.

'Why are you blaming Maharaj?'

'He was a cunning man, your father-in-law! He promised that we would get our watandari back when I have a son. What if I don't get it even after having a son?'

'Dada, Maharaj was against the whole notion of watandari. He believed that it was the root cause of the kingdom's troubles, being a system that impoverished the ryots. He was opposed to the estate holders exploiting the poor farmer.'

'You must understand that we are not begging. Our watan was granted to us by Adil Shah of Bijapur. We are only demanding what is ours by right.'

Ganoji's angry tone spoiled the festive mood of the palace. Yesu said, trying to pacify her brother, 'I ask you to have some patience, Dada. I will speak to Yuvraj. He is busy with preparations for the coronation. Please bear with him.'

'Well, that is why I thought I should remind you. Your father-in-law died without fulfilling his promise. I hope you will help fulfil it now. Though, of course, I cannot expect people like your husband's family, descended from ryots themselves, to understand the pains of a respectable and landed Maratha family like ours.'

Yesubai lost her patience. 'Well, if you are in such a hurry, I suggest you meet Yuvraj yourself and put forth your demand.'

However, she touched his feet when he was leaving and said, 'Dadasaheb, don't hold these things against him. I hope you will be there in Raigad when he is coronated.'

Ganoji threw an unpleasant glance at her. 'Huh! You mean we should be there to see prestige and honour being showered on you while we silently suffer and bear our insults?'

4

It had been two months since the demise of Shivaji Maharaj. Kavi Kalash's advice to Sambhaji was clear: A king should not stay away from his capital for long. Hence, after ensuring that all the forts had been adequately provisioned, Sambhaji moved with his troops towards Raigad.

En route, he prayed at the Bhawani temple in Pratapgad. Sambhaji was accompanied by Hambirrao, Kavi Kalash, and the senior commander Malhoji Ghorpade. While Hiroji Farzand may have been a deserter, Kondaji Farzand, a warrior well into his sixties, had pledged his loyalty to the Yuvraj. Kondaji and Rayappa were constantly at Sambhaji's side.

Sambhaji stood on the ramparts of Pratapgad, gazing at the undulating outlines of the Sahyadris merging into each other as if they stood with their arms around each other. In the clear light of the day, he could see the peaks of distant Raigad, nearly thirty kos away. To his right were the green mountains of Mahabaleshwar.

Luckily, the wave of revolt had subsided before it turned into a hurricane. Hambirrao's strict instructions had ensured that all the commanders and provincial sardars had fallen in line and joined Sambhaji. Slowly but surely, Sambhaji was gaining control of all aspects of the kingdom's administration. Heavy responsibility often makes a man turn towards religion. Knowing that Aurangzeb was occupied with his military campaign in Rajputana, Sambhaji breathed easy and took the time to meet various Brahmins and sanyasis en route to Raigad.

Sambhaji was resting in the village of Par at the base of Pratapgad fort when a few riders arrived, announcing, 'We have found Hiroji. He has been arrested!' Hiroji had been intercepted at Chiplun and the treasure he had stolen was recovered. As Hiroji had been a veteran commander in Shivaji's day, Sambhaji decided to confront him in private rather than humiliate him in public.

Hiroji was presented at the haveli of the local Patil at Par. Sambhaji looked at Hiroji—a tall, well-built man with a pointed chin, hawk-like nose, beard tapered to a point, and bright eyes—how he reminded him of Abasaheb! Sambhaji smiled at the thought but Hiroji's face remained grim. He was clearly overwhelmed with guilt. Tears trickling down his cheeks, he said, 'Shambhubal, don't kill someone who is already dead!'

'Hiroji Farzand Bahadur! Kaka, look at the way I address you! Instead of taking care of me, you run away like an ordinary thief with jewels from the treasury? You stabbed me in my back, Kaka!'

Hiroji stood with his hands folded in supplication. 'I made a mistake, Shambhubal.'

'Farzand Kaka, all you had to was ask and I would have put the entire treasury at your feet. Why did you choose to run away like a burglar?'

After conferring with his men, Sambhaji Raje decided to pardon Hiroji's mistake.

'Let bygones be bygones. I will pardon him.'

Hambirrao interrupted. 'Raje, I understand your large-heartedness but I must remind you that you are not a Yuvraj anymore. People should not misinterpret your good nature. A king needs to ensure that people fear punishment for their misdeeds.'

Sambhaji thought for a moment. 'Let us take him to Raigad and put him under house arrest then. But don't bind him in fetters; see that he is treated with due respect.'

Noticing Sambhaji's crestfallen face, Kavi Kalash asked, 'What is the matter, Raje?'

'The mind goes numb when someone so dear is tempted to stab you in the back and run away! Farzand Kaka, or for that matter Soyrabai Matoshree, who considered me dearer than her own son at one time! I was not even allowed to attend my father's funeral!'

'Forget the past, Raje!'

'Kaviraj, it seems that I have been the target of their ill-feeling and curses for too long.'

They were crossing small ravines and rivulets. The massive fort of Raigad was visible from time to time. It reminded Sambhaji of a proud eagle's nest. When Shivaji had decided on the spot for building Raigad, he had thought of the eagle's penchant for building its nest in inaccessible places. Sambhaji's mind was filled with myriad emotions. He had spent the happiest years of his childhood there. But he was returning after three long years.

The town of Pachad was decked up to receive the new king. Horns, trumpets, drums and garlands of flowers created a festive atmosphere. As soon as the trumpets began playing at Pachad, cannons boomed from the great fort to welcome the new Raje. Raigad, drenched in sorrow ever since the death of Shivaji Raje, was now awakening to a new dawn. Men like

Rahuji Somnath, Kanhoji and Malsawant had been arrested a while ago, removing the thorns in the path of Sambhaji Raje's ascension.

Pilajirao Shirke was at Pachad to welcome his son-in-law. He had ensured that the town was well protected and that his guards stood at attention to receive Sambhaji. His face reflected the pride in the fact that his daughter's husband was to become the second king of the Hindavi Swaraj.

Sambhaji was taken aback by the reception party. The winds were surely blowing in his favour these days. He was pleasantly surprised to find all his brothers-in-law in attendance to receive him, without having been formally invited. His cousin Arjunji Bhosale, Harjiraje Mahadik and Tukoji Palkar were eagerly awaiting his arrival.

Yesubai was surprised to see her elder brother there, smiling and welcoming Sambhaji. She recalled how he had threatened not to show his face till he was promised his watandari. Sambhaji spotted Mahadji Nimbalkar, smiling and bowing in mujra. Jotyaji Kesarkar whispered to him, 'You know, Mahadji has left the Mughals once and for all!'

'Is that so?'

'Yes! He says, "When my brother-in-law is the Chhattrapati, why should I work for someone else?"'

While the trumpets, drums and horns, the fireworks and chanting of mantras by the Brahmins created a welcoming din, Sambhaji's mind turned to the haveli at Pachad where Jijabai had spent her last days. Overwhelmed by memories of his grandmother, tears of joy and sadness streamed down his cheeks. Those watching him could not restrain their tears either.

That evening, palanquin bearers dressed to their nines presented themselves. Sambhaji sat in the palanquin and moved its curtain away as the bearers lifted it and started up the path leading to the fort.

Yesubai, Hambirrao, Kavi Kalash and others followed. As soon as the palanquin reached the main entrance, Sambhaji indicated to the bearers to stop. He stepped out. There was an air of nervousness about him. He looked at the great doors leading into the fort and then, surprising everyone around him and ignoring protocol, sat down on the steps. His fair face was flushed with emotion when he looked at Pilajirao and said, 'Mamasaheb, what's the point in going to a deserted place? A temple without the Lord and Raigad without Shivaji Maharaj—they are both the same!'

The poet in him had come to life again. 'What's the point in visiting Kashi, Mathura, Vrindavan and Rameshwar? You are the unfortunate one if you have not visited Raigad!'

Finally, after a lot of cajoling, Sambhaji consented to entering the fort. At the Mahadwar, he met with a rousing welcome. Stepping out of the palanquin for a darshan at the Jagadeeshwar temple, he met many of the officials who had come to receive him.

The officials brought Malsawant before Sambhaji. He had had the temerity to tell Yuvraj, when the latter had reached out to him for support, that he was loyal to Soyrabai. He had also tried to punish those who had raided Annaji's haveli. Raje ordered the two men who had aided him in this treachery, Kanhoji and Hiroji Indulkar, to be sent to prison. Surprisingly Malsawant, despite being under arrest, was as arrogant as before. He looked at Sambhaji with contempt when Raje said, 'Good words are all very well for gentlemen but crooks only understand the language of weapons, unfortunately.' He immediately gave orders for Malsawant to be thrown off the cliff—a death sentence!

That night, Takmak Tok, a point which overlooked the sheer vertical drop of one of the highest cliffs of Raigad, was crowded with traitors, their faces covered with blindfolds as they were thrown off. They met a painful death. Vultures gathered for their feast, swooping down as soon as corpses tumbled down the rocky cliff.

Next morning, the doors of the prison at Pachad creaked open. Annaji Datto and Moropant were to be presented to Raje. They were asked to walk all the way up to the fort. Guilt was written all over Moropant's face but Annaji continued to maintain his contempt for Sambhaji. He looked at the guarded ramparts as they walked up to Raigad.

Annaji was sure of meeting the same fate as the other traitors. Both men knew their crime was even worse than theirs. They wondered if there would be any reprieve from the painful death which loomed large over them.

'We have committed crimes far worse than others,' Moropant said, 'I doubt that we can hope for a pardon.'

They were detained in the palace itself with guards posted at the door. Meanwhile, Hiroji Indulkar was presented to Sambhaji. Hiroji Indulkar was a well-loved and familiar face in Raigad. Shivaji Raje, seeing his unwavering attention to the repair and maintenance of the fort, and his tireless labour—day and night, come rain or shine, even in the biting cold of winter—used to lovingly call him a 'roaming ghost.' Those present could only rue the fact that he had fallen in wrong company and joined the revolt against Yuvraj.

Taking Indulkar's wrinkled hands in his, Sambhaji Raje said, 'These hands are worth revering. But you soiled them by joining hands with traitors.' Those in the assembly shuddered, remembering the the traitors who had been thrown off Takmak point the previous night. Sambhaji said, continuing to hold Indulkar's hands, 'You know how Shah Jahan had treated the men who built Taj Mahal? He ordered their thumbs to be cut off.'

Indulkar shivered involuntarily. Was Sambhaji suggesting that he would meet with the same punishment? But Raje smiled.

'I admire Abasaheb's foresight. If I am unable to save these beautiful hands, people would doubt my interest in poetry and music and wonder whether I value artistic abilities at all. Go! Ensure the magic of your hands remains untainted in future!'

Sambhaji's decision took everyone by surprise. Indulkar pressed Raje's hands to his chest and said, tears in his eyes, 'Who says the elder Maharaj is no more? He lives in Shambhubal now!'

5

That afternoon, Sambhaji and Yesubai prayed at the temple of Jagadeeshwar. Yesubai had asked Sambhaji not to meet Soyrabai yet, but he had visited Putalabai the previous evening. Putalabai Matoshree was devastated by Shivaji Raje's death. She looked frail and Sambhaji was concerned about her health. After hearing that she had made up her mind to jump into Shivaji's pyre and commit sati, Sambhaji was shaken to the core. He remembered how Abasaheb had managed to convince Jijausaheb not to take the extreme step when Shahaji Raje had died.

Raigad was brimming with activity. Yesaji Kank and Malhoji Ghorpade were taking stock of the foodgrain stocks and ammunition reserves while Kavi Kalash was busy setting up a library. Suddenly, Raje remembered Pandit Gaga Bhatt. He had formed a friendship with him during Shivaji Raje's coronation. Young Sambhaji had impressed the pandit with his incisive questions. 'He is a precocious child,' Gaga Bhatt had remarked. Sambhaji instructed Kavi Kalash, 'Send for Gaga Bhatt; ask him to come to Raigad. And send the gift of a thousand hons with the message.'

Kavi Kalash looked askance. Sambhaji clarified, 'Kaviraj, I want to commission a new treatise on how a king should follow religion and ethics. What better person than an authority on the subject like Bhatt to write it?'

It was evening and golden rays of the setting sun bathed the fort in a beautiful hue. The lamps had been lit when Sambhaji walked towards Putalabai's palace. Yesubai followed. Putalabai, wearing a white saree, sat next to Shivaji Maharaj's bed which was adorned with Raje's personal items. Sambhaji stepped into the quarters and hugged Putalabai affectionately. She said, in between her sobs, 'Shambhubal, he went away too early!'

Sambhaji did not have the words to console her. She regained her composure after a while.

'Shambhu Raje, it is good that you are here. I have been waiting for you. I was planning to go away with him but I was waiting for two reasons.'

'Aaisaheb, I beg you, get over your pain before you speak of such matters,' Sambhaji interrupted.

Putalabai seemed determined to speak. 'Maharaj died suddenly. The possibility of an enemy attack was very strong at the time, and in such a situation, I did not want to send my men to Mahad or elsewhere to get the clothes for sati. Had they been intercepted by the enemy, they would have known of Maharaj's death.'

'Aaisaheb, it is more than two months now … please …'

She continued, ignoring his pleas, 'There is one more reason; the tragedy occurred just a fortnight or so after Rajaram's marriage. Maharaj was in a delirious state in the last ten days. I spent day and night at his bedside. One night, he was wide awake. He asked me to come near him. What he told me is of utmost importance to you.'

A shiver went down Sambhaji's spine. Putalabai continued, her voice barely audible, 'Raje took my hand and said, "Putala, I am not likely to meet Shambhubal. But pass my message on to him. Tell him: Shambhu, I am leaving for the other world. I am sure that the Swaraj built on the sweat and toil of the ryots is safe in your hands. If only I could have hugged you tightly before leaving, my tears would have washed off all the misunderstandings between us. I would have been blessed. It is only you, Shambhu, who has the courage to challenge and defeat Aurangzeb, if he ever has the temerity to attack us. I have not lived long but destiny and blessings of the Lord have crowned me with many victories. I pray to Jagadeeshwar that you are blessed with such fortune and more."'

It was impossible to stop Sambhaji's tears now. Raje's last words had rendered him inconsolable. He said, hugging Raje's turban and sword, 'Aaisaheb, if only you had sent me a message when his health deteriorated …'

'How was I to do that, Shambhu Raje? I was helpless. What shall I say to you about the way things were being handled here during Raje's illness?'

Sambhaji had issued orders for the house arrest of Rajaram. The very thought of Soyrabai enraged him and he avoided meeting her. After seeing the dedication with which Putalabai had served the elder Maharaj, he was further incensed at Soyrabai's ambitious and scheming nature. One evening he decided to confront her on a whim and stomped his way to her quarters.

On the doorstep was young, innocent Rajaram who affectionately called out 'Dadasaheb!' The brothers rushed towards each other and hugged. Sambhaji kissed him on his cheeks affectionately. Rajaram said in a gruff voice, 'Dadasaheb, I am offended.'

'What happened?'

'You never came for my wedding.'

'I was not invited, my dear.'

'Why does a family member need an invitation?'

Sambhaji's face fell. 'Matoshree invited even the servants at Panhala. There is a limit to putting up with insults. You will understand that when you grow up.'

Sambhaji left his brother in Prahlad Niraji's care and entered the palace. The maids, seeing Raje's stern face, ran away scared. Soyrabai, shocked for a moment, recovered quickly and stood up.

'Matoshree, do you realise the extent to which you can go for the love of your son? You allowed yourself to be a mere toy in the hands of those selfish rascals.'

Soyrabai was aware of her crime. She had, under the influence of the council of ministers, played a treacherous game but it had not worked in her favour. All she had managed to achieve was to provoke Sambhaji's anger. Self-serving men like Annaji had manipulated her. But they all had played with fire and got burnt in the process. In the end, Soyrabai had incensed a lion's cub, challenging his self-esteem, inviting ignominy and defeat upon herself.

Waving a casual hand to indicate that she may sit, Sambhaji growled, 'Matoshree, whether you like it or not, whether you approve or not, I have been crowned now. At least for courtesy's sake, you can invite me or welcome me into your home!'

'Why do you expect me to welcome you? The moment you arrived, you ordered seven or eight poor souls to be thrown off the cliff. Their anguished voices still hang in the air.' Soyrabai retorted angrily.

'Are you a mother or a witch? How can a mother's heart speak so?'

'Shambhu Raje, do you have an arsenal in the place of a brain? Look at the way you explode! It extinguishes all wisdom, if there was any in the first place.'

'Why should you sympathise with those who were thrown off the cliff? What did you expect? That I would felicitate them for having committed a grave offence like treason?'

'You throw an old and loyal soldier like Hiroji Farzand into prison! Did you not think once about his age and experience?'

'He deserves to be imprisoned in the dark dungeon at Lingana for the rest of his life. And people like Moropant and Annaji deserve to be blasted off a cannon! All I have done is put them under house arrest. I have not insulted them in any way. I may not have learnt much from Abasaheb, but I have certainly understood how to behave when it comes to such matters.'

Seeing that Sambhaji's anger had subsided, Soyrabai said, 'Shambhu Raje, you and your immature friends are finding reasons to blame me. I am told rumours mills are abuzz with the allegation that I was the one who poisoned Maharaj and caused his death!'

Sambhaji did not respond immediately. He looked at the floor.

'Matoshree, I would not give any credence to such rumours. I know that your heart is pure like quartz. I know how affable and loving you have been towards my father. Nevertheless, you are blinded by love for your son. The crimes you committed against me are unpardonable.'

Soyrabai was alert. She could see a glint of fury in his eyes. He had curled his fists in anger. At that moment, Sambhaji turned to see Rajaram standing at the door, trembing with fear. Like a crystal of salt dissolving in water, Sambhaji's anger melted away. The storm had subsided.

He hugged Rajaram saying, 'Dear, who but me would take care of you, now that Abasaheb is no more?'

'Dadasaheb, I hope you will not put Matoshree in prison.'

'No. She is my mother too. I will see to it that she is not touched. But you both would be placed under house arrest.'

'What does that mean, Dada?'

'I have to ensure that no one corrupts your mind and that you are not influenced by selfish and scheming men. As a king I have to ensure this.'

'As you command, Dadasaheb.'

Sambhaji turned to leave.

'Matoshree, I promise you that I will behave in a manner befitting Chhattrapati Shivaji Maharaj's son. What has happened in the past cannot be changed, but I do pray that in future you do not behave in a manner which tarnishes the image of that great Yugapurush!'

6

Three weeks after Shivaji Maharaj's death, on the eve of Ekadashi, Putalabai committed sati. Sambhaji had tried his best to change her mind but she was determined. Finally, he relented, much against his own wishes. After her death, Sambhaji occupied himself with acts of charity for a few days.

The date for his formal coronation was fixed for 20 July 1680. Raigad was overflowing with visitors and friends. His elder sister Sakhubai and her husband Mahadji Nimbalkar had come to stay. So did Ambikabai and Harjiraje Mahadik. Ganojiraje Shirke was everywhere. He was married to Sambhaji's sister Rajkunwar, in addition to being Yesubai's elder brother. Ganoji thus commanded a great deal of respect in Raigad.

One morning, Sambhaji had a bath and sat down for pooja. Yesubai noticed that he seemed somewhat crestfallen despite the festive atmosphere in the palace.

'Yesu, I wonder how Ranubai Akkasaheb and Durgabai are faring. They are still at the enemy camp.'

'Raje, I cannot stop thinking about them. My eyes are always watching the Mahadwar desperately, waiting for their arrival. But I am sure this Bhawani sword of yours will find its strength and you will, seizing the right moment, attack and release them from captivity.'

Sambhaji was about to begin his pooja when he heard someone say, 'Shambhubal, wait a moment!' It was Ambikabai. She was older than him but the youngest of his sisters. Sambhaji was surprised to see his favourite sibling up so early.

'Shambhu Raje, you are aware that the region around Karnatak and Jinji is one of our richest territories. Yet, the question is whether we receive the revenue that is due to us in proportion to is the taxes being collected.'

Sambhaji was surprised at the directness of her allegation. 'Why? Is there any reason to doubt that we do? After all, we have an experienced and loyal administrator like Raghunath Pant Hanmante managing the province. Do you know who appointed him? It was our grandfather, Shahaji Bhosale. He has been managing the southern province for us for the past thirty years.'

Ambikabai was silent but the large vermillion dot on her forehead could not conceal its creases. Sambhaji expressed his surprise. 'Akkasaheb, why this sudden doubt early in the morning?'

'To tell you the truth, Shambhu Raje, you may be king now but to me you are first my younger brother. And it is the job of elder sisters to look after their younger brother. Despite your position and hereditary right, the officials and ministers here did not hesitate to stage a revolt, did they?'

'Akkasaheb, are you saying that the embers of the revolt are still burning? And that Raghunath Pant is one of them?'

'You guessed right! You are not aware of this fact but he has been in secret correspondence with Soyrabai Matoshree. You may investigate the matter if you want to ascertain the truth. But Raje, it is dangerous to leave such a rich province to the governance of a traitor. I have told you what I know. I leave the rest to you!'

Akkasaheb turned abruptly and left the room without waiting for Sambhaji to respond.

After finishing his pooja, Sambhaji stepped out of his quarters. There were men all around waiting to felicitate him, throwing garlands around his neck or bowing in mujra. Sambhaji's mind was not at ease. He asked, as he walked with Akkasaheb, 'Assuming that Raghunath Pant is not reliable, I wonder who I can trust to govern the southern province instead.'

Akkasaheb said, looking into Sambhaji's eyes, 'My husband Harjiraje Mahadik is a capable man. You may confer with Kavi Kalash if you have any doubt.'

Akkasaheb walked on but Sambhaji stopped. He remembered his father's words, 'Amongst my four sons-in-law, Harjiraje is a real daredevil. He has the courage, just like you Shambhu, to put his hand in a lion's mouth.'

There were many things to look into and the discussion ended there. The coronation was only two days away. Sambhaji walked hurriedly towards the office of the council. Kavi Kalash, Prahlad Niraji and others were already there. A group of farmers from the Konkan were waiting for him with a plea. The coast was ravaged with famine and they were expecting rice crops to fail that year. Sambhaji issued orders to waive their taxes. He also instructed the treasury to give them support for buying seeds and manure. The farmers, happy with the quick and just decision, bowed before leaving.

Kalash said, 'Raje, the Portuguese emissary has been waiting to meet you for the past four days.'

'Is that so, Kaviraj? It is not advisable to meet so many enemies at the same time, be they from the family or outside. My so-called family members, the Portuguese boats sailing around the Konkan coast, a deadly snake called Siddi at Janjira, and the poisonous cobra called Aurangzeb who is itching to descend on the Deccan any moment, not to mention the English … we have to save the Swaraj from all of them, Kaviraj.'

'I agree, Raje.'

'The Habshis at Janjira are happy to concede their rights to Aurangzeb. We need to put the Goans in their place before the Portuguese and Aurangzeb shake hands and become friends. We cannot ignore the artillery strength of the firangis.'

The Portuguese emissaries were presented before Sambhaji in his office. Wearing long, tubular Portuguese hat, heavy, colourful coats and trousers, the two of them bowed in mujra. Their translator, Ramchandra Shenavi, stood by their side. Sambhaji's emissaries, Ramji Thakur and Yesaji Gambhirrao, were present too. Ramchandra read the message aloud: *'Shambhu Raje, please accept salutes from the new Viceroy Conde de Alvor. We are more than eager to extend our hand in friendship.'*

Sambhaji smiled ironically. 'Well, we too are pleased to know that the Viceroy is keen to make friends with us.'

The translator continued, *'The main reason for this, Raje, is that we have common boundaries in the Sawantwadi and Kudal provinces. We have a suggestion: you need not send any soldiers to guard those borders. We, the Portuguese, will ensure that your borders are safe!'*

'Wah!' Sambhaji exclaimed but refused to comment further.

The firangis presented rich gifts to Raje before departing.

The atmosphere in Raigad was charged, with trumpets and horns playing while the Brahmins chanted mantras continuously. Many religious ceremonies were being conducted as precursors to the coronation.

Sambhaji's close friends were in conference. Yesubai was present too. He could detect from their excited and eager faces that they were discussing something important.

Mahadji Nimbalkar said, 'Shambhu Raje, it is a great honour to be here to witness your coronation. But …'

'Speak, Mahadji. Don't hesitate!'

'Raje, have you noticed the havelis on the right? The ones where the Ashta Pradhan are housed?'

'I don't understand you!'

'For the past three months, Balajipant Chitnis, Annaji Datto, Hiroji Farzand and others have been under house arrest. There are guards standing outside their gates.'

'We all feel that they cannot be in such sorrow, living in darkness, while we celebrate,' Harjiraje Mahadik said.

Sambhaji was silent for a long time. It was evident from his face that his mind was in turmoil. He said with a heavy sigh, 'I am pained too when I see the state they are in. They were all close confidantes of Abasaheb. I grew up in their arms. Hiroji Kaka is a relative. I have often toyed with the idea of pardoning them. But I also wonder whether, going forward, their loyalty can be relied on.'

No one could answer that question with confidence, and they all avoided his gaze. Yesubai said, 'Raje, you are thinking too much. Everyone makes mistakes.'

Yesubai's words pierced Sambhaji's heart like an arrow but he did not allow his emotions show.

That night Ambikabai came to his quarters to meet him. She did not say anything but her questioning eyes impelled Sambhaji to say, 'Akkasaheb, don't rush me. I have no doubts about Harjiraje's valour. But I have more than one brother-in-law. Even Ganojiraje has been demanding the same.'

'Shambhu, Ganoji has his own watan. That makes him nearly as independent as a king. All we are asking for is a subedari, under your rule, that's all!'

Sambhaji was silent. Ambikabai continued, 'Raje, don't compare Harjiraje with your other brothers-in-law. I can promise you that he will be willing to sacrifice his life, if the need arises, for the cause of the Swaraj. And he will never be a traitor.'

'I will decide at an appropriate time,' Sambhaji said, and he left the room. He saw Yesubai smiling as he entered his bedroom. 'Look at how rattled you are by Ambikabai's proposal! Raje, it is not a crime to be Chhattrapati.'

'These people are willing to dance to any tune for power and money. But it is more than likely that none of them will stand with us when we are in trouble. Abasaheb had deliberately kept relatives away from power. Instead, he found his gems in the soil. That is why the crown of our Swaraj, decked with these jewels, shines with such brilliance.'

He snapped his fingers, remembering something. 'Do you know why Abasaheb chose Raigad as the capital of his kingdom, so far away from Pune? When Mirza Raja Jaisingh and Diler Khan attacked Purandhar, Absaheb was not willing to concede defeat. The Mughals went on to ravage over seventy villages around Rajgad. It was then that Abasaheb decided he needed to move the capital away from the plains to a place like Raigad. The fort is in a sparsely populated area and is difficult to access, with its cliffs and ravines providing natural protection from enemies. There is only single route, a narrow path, that one can take to reach the top. Only the wind and the rain can reach the summit of Raigad with ease. There was one more reason: the ryots here are as dependable and as protective of us as nature herself. Raigad allows us the luxury of distancing ourselves from selfish and arrogant folks.'

Yesubai smiled. 'Raje, it is good to hear that you have been large-hearted and decided to pardon Balajipant Chitnis, Annaji Datto and Hiroji Farzand. But please bear in mind, Harjiraje has a clean chit. He has not committed any crime.'

'Do you trust him?'

'Why not? He is an intelligent man. And he is keen to do something for the Swaraj.'

'Well, it appears that luck is in his favour.'

He explained, seeing Yesubai's surprised look, 'I just received some messages from our spies. The Bengaluru province was consolidated by my grandfather Shahaji Raje. A huge city was founded there. My father and Ekoji Raje established the Maratha presence in the south. But the rich and fertile province is under threat from Chikkadevaraja of Mysore. Our jagirs are spread over Karnatak, Tanjavur, Madurai, Mysore, and Bengaluru but we face threats from the local rulers all the time. And to add to our troubles, Chikkadevaraja has now entered Trichanapalli. We must nip his ambitions in the bud. In such times, we need a daredevil, someone who can use his brains and brawn with equal ease.'

'You mean our brother-in-law?'

'Not merely our brother-in-law, but a capable, efficient and valorous Maratha subedar like Harjiraje. I have decided to send him to Karnatak.'

Later, Sambhaji was resting on his bed, lost in thought, when he suddenly recalled Yesubai's words, 'Raje, who does not make mistakes?' He said, looking at Yesubai, 'Your words pierced my heart like an arrow. I wish you had not uttered them.'

'I am sorry, Raje, I did not mean to hurt you. But wasn't it a crime to abandon a great father like Shivaji Raje and join Diler Khan, albeit for a few days?'

'No, Yesu. It was not a crime. It was the arrogance of youth. It was my foolishness. I thought I could fool Diler Khan, making him believe that I had defected, and thus, entering the enemy camp, defeat them on their own ground. I wanted to set a new standard and example of valour. It was my dream to show my father what I was capable of; to do something which no one had ever dared to do before. But as fate would have it, everything collapsed and I could achieve nothing!'

'Yuvraj, even on a full moon night, one cannot ignore the blemishes on the moon's face. This act of yours will remain a black spot on your character forever,' Yesubai bluntly said.

'What if the moon itself were to burn to ashes?'

'Don't say such terrible things, Raje!'

Sambhaji got up. A strong wind blew outside. Holding Yesubai's wrist, he literally dragged her onto the terrace. The sky was cloudy and one could barely see the crescent of the moon, partially hidden behind the mountains.

Holding Yesubai's hand near his heart, Sambhaji said, 'If my motherland demands, this moon is willing to burn itself away for Abasaheb's Swaraj. Ask the moon in the sky whether it has the courage to do the same.'

EIGHT

Raj Dand
The Royal Punishment

1

'Raje, I wonder how our guests have survived these torrential rains and the misty clouds throughout the day?' Kavi Kalash said, smiling.

'Guests?'

'Well, we have two English emissaries in Raigad: Gary and Robert! They are housed right at the edge of the fort, very close to the huge waterfalls. They have been there for the past three months. Their butler said they often get up at night, scared of the din the rain makes. Apparently, they were complaining that if they stay any longer, their bodies would sprout mould!'

'Kaviraj, come to the point!'

'Why don't you meet the poor souls?'

Sambhaji did not respond. That night, Kavi Kalash and Jotyaji Kesarkar discussed the matter for a long time. The port of Mumbai was now under control of the English, having changed hands from the Portuguese. Along with the port, the English had gained in arrogance as well. The main cause of worry for the Marathas was the English port at Surat. The English stationed at Surat were supporting the Siddi at Janjira, supplying him with ammunition and encouraging him to act as if he were invincible. He was ravaging the Konkan coast. Sambhaji had sent Kavi Kalash to tour the southern Konkan region. Kalash, braving the torrential rains, had just returned to Raigad after inspecting the area. Sambhaji had plans to set up ammunition factories at Dicholi and Kudal. This would reduce their dependence on the Dutch and the English.

The next morning, Sambhaji woke early and looked out of his window to see the valley and the ramparts of the fort covered in a thick fog. It was still dark outside and a cold wind blew. With all the administrative work that had piled up, he could barely manage the time these days to go on a tour of the fort. This morning, with a dozen guards in tow, he stepped out of his quarters. New grass grew along the paths with jasmine flowers blooming everywhere, giving out a pleasant fragrance. On the other side of the valley, the Konkan Diva fort too was waking up to a new day.

Sambhaji stopped at the Gangasagar tank to look at the blue waters reflecting the skies. Lotuses bloomed in the ponds. The sun was now peeking from behind the clouds. Despite the beautiful surroundings, Sambhaji felt miserable. The memory of Durgabai and Ranuakka languishing in the enemy camp troubled him. He turned to look westwards. Beyond the hills was the blue ocean. And somewhere on the vast Konkan shore, kissing the waves was Janjira—the fort that had captured Sambhaji's imagination for a long time now.

Sambhaji was restless. It had been three months since he took over the reins of the kingdom. Yet he had not been able to plan a campaign against the Siddi. The Abyssinian Siddis ruled over the territory from Murud to Shrivardhan along the Konkan coast. The region was also referred to as Habsan, after the 'Habshis,' as the Abyssinian race was called in local parlance. The fort stood on a huge outcrop of rock that spread over forty acres. A fisherman by the name of Rama Patil had built a wooden structure on the rocks, gaining access to the ships plying in the coastal waters and, eventually, control of the maritime trade in the area. Later, Patil became a rebel and refused to take orders from the Nizam Shah.

One of the Nizam's commanders captured the fort by entering with three ships full or soldiers who pretended to be sailors of a merchant fleet. Piram Khan, the leader, offered Rama Patil and his men some fine wine from their cargo. Once they were intoxicated, Nizam's soldiers captured the fort. Piram Khan's son Burhan Khan later built the impregnable fort of Janjira on Rama Patil's rock. But the Siddis, known to be selfish, rebellious and cruel, were nobody's friends. They managed to break away from the Nizam, keep the Portuguese, the English and the Mughals at bay, while extending a hand of friendship whenever it served their interests.

That afternoon, when Sambhaji was at work in his office, he heard a clamour outside. Stepping out, he saw a group of nearly three hundred men, drenched to their skin, screaming for justice. They were fishermen from Nagothane, Apta and Nagaon. The moment they saw Sambhaji, they fell at his feet and pleaded, 'Raje, please save us! The Habshis looted our villages two days ago. They ravaged our homes and took away our young daughters.'

'Our women are going to be ruined, Raje. The Siddi will force them to embrace his religion and sell them in the bazaars of Mumbai …' An old man wailed, as he lay at Sambhaji's feet.

Sambhaji was stunned to hear their account of the Habshi attack. Such complaints had reached him earlier too. He shouted at Kaviraj, 'Kalash, do you hear their wails? Do you recall that you were praising the English emissaries? Tell me, whose support has made the Siddi so arrogant?'

'But Raje …'

'Abasaheb used to say: just as a mouse nibbles everything once it enters the house, these Siddis are nibbling at our Konkan coast. The scheming Habshis keep the Mughal Badshah happy on one hand while befriending the English at Mumbai on the other. We need to kill this snake before it spreads poison everywhere.'

Sambhaji promised the fishermen to put the Habshis in their place. After the men had left, Sambhaji asked Kavi Kalash to present the English emissaries in his durbar.

That evening, Gary and Robert entered the durbar and saluted smartly. Gary placed a bag full of jewels, diamonds among them, at Sambhaji's feet. Hoping to attract Sambhaji's attention, he stood fiddling with his uniform. Finally Sambhaji said, in a dry voice, 'Perhaps you expected me to be wide-eyed, seeing your "priceless" gift? Please keep in mind that you can scarcely win my respect with such a lowly offering.'

The English emissary realised that Sambhaji was furious. Wiping the sweat off their foreheads nervously, they stood waiting for Raje to continue. Sambhaji turned to their interpreter, who asked,

'Raje, if I may; I wonder why you are so annoyed at us.'

'That is because you Englishmen don't have a habit of keeping your word. Did you not make a treaty with Shivaji Maharaj whereby you promised to stop supplies to Janjira? But here you are, happily ignoring the treaty by docking their ships in your port at Mumbai, supplying them with ammunition, and what not! Stop this immediately or you will see what my wrath looks like!'

Sambhaji did not stop with a mere warning. He said threateningly, to the translator, 'There is a steep ravine next to the rooms in which you are staying. There are dungeons nearby. I wonder if you have seen them.'

'No, not really, Sarkar!'

'Well, the dungeons are quite notorious. When the English stationed at Rajapur tried to help Siddi Johar during the siege of Panhala, Abasaheb had them arrested and thrown into those dark cells for nearly two years. Let your masters know: if they persist in fooling us and maintaining a friendship with the Siddi, we would be happy to host them in those dungeons!'

The English and their translator left with hasty salutes. Krishnaji Kank, impressed by the way Sambhaji had reprimanded them, said, 'You really ticked those monkeys off, Raje! I am sure they won't be able to sleep for a week.'

Sambhaji waved the compliment off casually, saying, 'Well that's just letting off steam. But kingdoms don't run on that. Kavi Kalash, Daulat Khan at Rajapur has five thousand Maratha soldiers and fifty ships. He has been itching for action ever since I took charge. Ask him to be on the alert. Tell him that if the Siddis at Janjira try anything funny, we will descend upon them. We will destroy their jetties at Mumbai too, if we are provoked.'

2

'Do whatever it takes, but you need it to rein Kavi Kalash in,' Somaji Datto pleaded.

The revenue officials had been pardoned after Sambhaji's coronation. While Balaji Avaji had taken charge of the department, the division of work amongst the officials was yet to be done. Balaji was happy to be back in his job and had plunged himself into work with dedication. They had assembled in Moropant's haveli for a discussion.

Moropant was not happy that the meeting included Annaji and Somaji Datto. Annaji had spent three months under house arrest, thanks to his ambitions! He was lucky that Sambhaji had not tortured or punished him physically. But the emotional trauma he had suffered was considerable.

'I will drop by in the evening,' That was the message the Chief Justice Prahlad Niraji had left for them. They were all waiting for him. Annaji was getting impatient. He asked a guard to find out what was delaying Prahlad Niraji.

Moropant's haveli was close to the main office and the guard returned soon. A restless Annaji was sitting on the swing outside. The guard announced, 'He is busy. The court is still in session.'

'Raje is here? I was told he left this afternoon.'

'Yes, that is right. He left this afternoon. The court is discussing the matter of Mahadji Patil of Masoor.'

'You idiot! You say Raje is not in court. Who is presiding then?'

'Kavi Kalash saheb.'

'Sitting on the throne?'

'No! He is sitting on the steps below the throne. How can he sit on the throne? He salutes it even when Raje is not present.'

Annaji smiled sarcastically. He said, looking at those present, 'How does it matter where he sits? What matters is that he is presiding over the court in Raje's absence.'

At that moment Prahlad Niraji entered the room. Annaji said, with an edge to his voice,

'Prahlad Pant, it looks like you have retired from your job. And has that Qazi Haidar, the elder Maharaj's favourite, left for his Haj pilgrimage?'

'What are you saying, Annaji?'

'Well, I wonder what Kaviraj is doing in the durbar.'

'Well, Raje has gone for an inspection of the weapons and asked Kaviraj to look into the matters of the court in his absence.' He looked at Annaji and continued, 'Raje has a thousand things to do at the same time. He has a right to allow someone else to act on his behalf. The elder Maharaj too used to do that too. However, I have every authority to oversee the judgments made by Kavi on behalf of Raje; they are subject to my approval. Only then can the decisions be implemented. Annaji Pant, that is what Sambhaji has commanded.'

'Well, you showed you true colours! Remember, we had all led the revolt together and you were sent to arrest Shambhu Raje. But you turned the tables on us and joined him. Your sweet talk and fickle loyalties ensured that you kept your post. We were the fools who suffered the consequences,' Annaji muttered.

'Let bygones be bygones, Annaji Pant,' said Prahlad Niraji. I am pitching for you, to ensure that you get the prestige your position deserves. So are Maharanisaheb and several others.'

'What prestige are you talking of? As long as we are ruled by this notorious king and his scheming friend, what justice can we expect? Misrule and injustice will reign at Raigad!'

Moropant could not remain quiet any longer. He said, looking around nervously lest someone outside overheard them, 'Enough, Annaji! I beg of you! We don't want to get burnt by your hatred for those two. We have suffered a great deal in our old age. Now let us live the rest of our lives in peace!' Moropant glanced at his son Nilopant as he spoke.

3

The date of Sambhaji's formal coronation was approaching fast. Preparations were on in full swing at Raigad. Sambhaji was naturally inclined towards religion and made several decisions with regard to the administration of the temples in the kingdom after he ascended the throne. He also ensured that Tukaram Maharaj's son Mahadoba, received his annual pension.

One day a group of men came from Karad with requests, 'Maharaj, Ramdas Swami has built a huge temple at Chaphal and is planning a great festival on the day of Ramnavami. We are short of funds ...'

'What's the hesitation?' Sambhaji interrupted. 'The elder Maharaj has already sanctioned an annual expense fund for Sajjangad and Chaphal. I have continued the tradition. Take money from the treasury for the festival. You need not ask me. I have already instructed the treasury to ensure that your expenses are met.'

'Raje, we have had trouble with some of the rogue Muslims there.'

Sambhaji's forehead creased with irritation. He ordered Kavi Kalash, 'Please instruct Vasudev Balkrishna to ensure that he provides security to Ramdas Swami and other Brahmins who assemble there for the ceremonies. Ask him to send us a detailed report once the festival is over.'

Raje had heard that Moreshwar Gosavi, who managed the temple at Chinchwad, was facing similar problems. Sambhaji issued instructions to arrange for the protection of the temple. As the day of the coronation neared, Sambhaji descended from the fort one day and went to Kelshi to pray at the tomb of Yakub Awaliya Fakirbaba. He had visited the tomb many times with his father. Instead of staying at the fort of Mandangad, which was nearby, he spent a whole week camped close to the tomb. Memories of childhood flooded his mind and praying at the tomb daily brought him a measure of peace.

The office was busy with preparations for the coronation. Yesubai received news that Khando Ballal had returned to Raigad after visiting Kashi. He had been sent to invite Gaga Bhatt to supervise the coronation.

When Sambhaji stepped out of his office, Yesubai noticed that while he was trying to put on a cheerful face, he was in fact anxious and disturbed. After dinner, she asked, 'I hope Khandoba could meet Gaga Bhatt.'

'Huh ...? Yes, he did meet him. Upon my request, Gaga Bhatt has written 'Samanvay', a treatise on how to run a kingdom in accordance with moral ethics and principles. He has sent the manuscript with Khando Ballal.'

'Is he attending the coronation ceremony? Raje, you seem to be avoiding this question,' Yesubai asked, a little hesitantly.

'He is not well, it seems.'

Yesubai was silent. Sambhaji let out a deep sigh and said, 'Ranisaheb, our unseen opponents have a far greater reach than ours. Their messages reached Gaga Bhatt even before Khandoba presented himself in Kashi.'

'Apparently, they complained that my conduct has been unbecoming of Shivaji's Yuvraj, of how my behaviour flouts the laws of religion, and how the kingdom is being run without any regard for morality ...'

Sambhaji was getting used to such aspersions. Yet, it hurt him that his detractors had managed to poison Gaga Bhatt's mind against. His friends—Jotyaji Kesarkar, Dadaji Raghunath Deshpande, and Krishnaji Kank, along with trusted aides like Yesaji Kank, Kondaji Farzand and Hambirrao Mohite—gathered at Raigad for a discussion. The first item on the agenda of the conference was the recent death of Moropant Peshwa. Moropant, ripe in age, had died of a minor ailment. Sambhaji said,

'He was a good man at heart. He did confess that he made a mistake in letting the others influence him to join the revolt.'

'Raje, we must commemorate him,' Hambirrao suggested.

'I believe his son, Nilopant, is the most capable candidate to take up the post of Peshwa,' Sambhaji said, his eyes on the future.

Everyone was delighted at Sambhaji's decision. Raje said, 'Yesaji Kaka, Kondaji Kaka, I want to share something with you. My enemies have been quite successful in spreading the rumour that I don't respect the old administrators and others who were loyal to Abasaheb all their lives, and that I treat the revenue officials with contempt. Their poisonous tongues have even reached Kashi.'

'Ignorant fools will rant but there are many veterans, like Yesaji Baba, Hambirrao and others, who don't get swayed by such rumours. Raje, why are you worried when you have men who have served the Swaraj since Shivaji Raje's times standing firm behind you?' Kondaji Farzand said.

'I am more worried about the noise from such wagging tongues than the booming of enemy cannons, Kaka.'

'You have spared the lives of those who revolted against you. You have reinstated them with honour. I can tell you this: Shivaji Raje would not have been so merciful,' Hambirrao reminded him.

Dadaji Deshpande and Kondaji said, almost at the same time, 'Raje, we must warn you: whatever you do, don't spare Annaji Datto.'

Sambhaji was not one to be influenced by such pleas. 'Kondaji Kaka, we must keep in mind that Annaji Datto's contribution in building the Swaraj was substantial.'

Balaji Chitnis joined the discussion after a while. Sambhaji said, 'Balaji Avaji, please send a messenger to Samarth Ramdas, requesting his presence at the coronation.'

The conference continued well into the night but Sambhaji, lying on his bed hours later, was wide awake. He asked Yesubai, 'What do you think? Should we pardon Annaji Pant?'

'The most important thing is to be decisive, whether your decision is harsh or otherwise.'

Sambhaji sighed heavily. 'Annaji has always been a slippery character by nature. Never easy to catch, like a slimy fish. He is good at creating the impression that he and some of his men are indispensable. I feel like a man with a twisted ankle. I cannot run fast, but if I sit, it hurts like hell.'

4

16 January 1681

Nearly a hundred thousand men from all over the Swaraj and representatives from other kingdoms had assembled in Raigad. It was after a gap of six years that a ceremony of this scale was taking place in the Maratha capital. Except for Ranubai, Sambhaji's sisters were present as well with their families. Like the tens of thousands of Varkaris who gathered on the banks of the Chandrabhaga on the day of Kartik Ekadashi, huge crowds had flocked to Raigad to witness the important event.

Sambhaji hurried towards the Sabha Mandap when he spotted a group of around fifteen Muslims waiting for him. Curious to find out who they were, Sambhaji moved towards them but Somaji Datto and Jotyaji reminded him that he was already late.

It was then he heard the shani mantra being recited by one of the Muslims:

> *'Nilanjana samabhasam raviputram yamagrajam chaya martanda sambhutam tam namami shaishcharam.'*
>
> 'You are resplendent like a blue hill; you are the son of Lord Surya and the brother of Lord Yama. You are the son of Chaya and Martanda (another name for the Sun God); Oh, the slow moving one, I pay my respects to you.'

Sambhaji stopped in his tracks. Who were these people, and why were they reciting the powerful shanti mantra meant for times of trouble? He asked them, 'Who are you?'

'Raje, we were once Brahmins. Kolhatkars from Shreebag. This man here is Gangadhar Pant from Rasool. We were all forced to become Muslims by the Habshis at Janjira.'

'Raje, please take us back into the Hindu fold. There are many like us who have suffered.'

Sambhaji glanced around for Balaji Chitnis to look into the matter immediately. Somaji Datto volunteered, 'Pant is busy with the ceremonies. I will do the needful.'

People in the durbar hall were getting restless as Sambhaji had not yet arrived. The hall was resplendent with beautiful Venetian glass chandeliers. The walls were painted with scenes from epics. It was the second coronation ceremony to be conducted there.

The throne awaited Sambhaji's arrival. Finally, the trumpets and horns blew to announce his entrance. The mace bearers announced in chorus:

> *Beware all … Maharaj! The learned, the compassionate, the Kshatriya … Shambhu Raje!*

Sambhaji entered the hall, walking with slow and purposeful steps. The onlookers cheered loudly. He was barely twenty-two! They stared in admiration at his tall and powerful physique, his dreamy eyes and the aquiline nose which reminded them of the elder Maharaj. The large jarring gems around his neck shone in the light of the lamps but the glow on his face bespoke an indescribable confidence.

Tall, graceful and smiling, Yesubai followed a few steps behind Raje. She wore a beautifully embroidered silk saree and matching jewellery. The vermillion on her forehead enhanced her radiant beauty, while the golden cummerbund accentuated her slim figure. She reminded many of the statue of Meenakshi at the temple in Madurai. Rajaram's wife Jankibai and Shambhu Raje's step-mother Soyarabai walked behind her.

Accompanying Sambhaji was an eleven-year-old boy. The dignified walk, royal garb and fine jewels were sufficient to indicate to those assembled in the durbar that he was none other than Yuvraj Rajaram, Sambhaji's younger brother.

Sambhaji walked up to the golden throne. He glanced at the crowd and then turned towards the throne again. His mind was in turmoil. Should he ascend the throne or walk away? He stood very still, unable to make up his mind. He recalled his father's words, 'Dear son, when you look at the throne, ask yourself whether you have the strength to fulfil the mountain-high dreams of the people here. You will ascend the throne not because you are entitled to it by birth but because you have the confidence to fulfil the dreams of the people you represent. But, if even for a moment you doubt your capabilities or your loyalty, don't even think of sitting on the throne. You may as well put on a hermit's clothes and walk away into the forest.'

Sambhaji glanced at the people gathered in the durbar. Energy surged through his body as he saw thousands of eyes looking at him, especially those of the ryots full of expectation. Puffing his chest out with confidence, he moved towards the throne. The very thought that it was the same throne on which Abasaheb sat brought tears to his eyes. He mumbled to himself, 'Yes, Abasaheb! I shall endeavour to keep the reputation of your honoured seal and your tradition intact, following your footsteps to the best of my ability.'

'Wah, Raje!' Kavi Kalash, Jotyaji and Prahlad Niraji, who were standing close by and had heard him, cheered loudly.

Sambhaji Raje said, his voice taking on the tone of an oath, 'I will see that the Swaraj, and its priceless forts adorning the Sayhadris like shining jewels, are never despoiled by anyone. If, while protecting it, I have to sacrifice my head, I am willing!'

With confident steps, Raje ascended the throne. At that moment, the cannons boomed, announcing the arrival of a new king. Yesubai was in tears while Rajaram, Jankibai and others were simply overwhelmed by the rousing reception.

The religious ceremonies began but cheering did not subside. There was a general clamour as celebrations and rituals continued together.

The Brahmins were being felicitated and those representing Ramdas Swami were given alms. Sambhaji took their blessings and gave them gifts of jewellery and expensive clothes. Sant Tukaram's son Mahadoba and Narayan Maharaj were present. They too were felicitated. Emissaries from other states presented themselves before the new king.

Sambhaji announced, as the celebrations were being concluded, 'I have decided to remove the restrictions placed by house arrest on Balaji Pant, Annaji and Hiroji. I intend to take the Swaraj forward using the advice, experience and dedication with which they have served the elder Maharaj.'

The elders were happy that the senior officials had been accorded due respect by Sambhaji. Soon, Annaji Datto, Hiroji Farzand, and Balaji Avaji Chitnis came out of their havelis. They wore turbans, jewellery and clothes befitting the occasion. They bowed gracefully–first to Sambhaji and then to the entire assembly. The durbar welcomed them with a loud cheer.

Sambhaji said, 'Gentlemen, the waters are no longer murky. My mind and heart are clear now. So I ask you: who shall we appoint to the post of Chitnis?'

The durbar was silent. Sambhaji laughed loudly and said, 'There is no one better qualified than Balaji Avaji, our Chitnis, whose dedication and diligence in service of the Swaraj are unmatched.'

The senior administrators were impressed by Sambhaji's straightforward humility and capacity for forgiveness. Raje requested Chitnis to step forward and accept a gift of fine robes as a token of appreciation. An overwhelmed Balaji Avaji wanted to fall at Sambhaji's feet but instead Raje held him by the shoulders and hugged him affectionately. Sambhaji had already decided to appoint Moropant's son, Nilopant, as the next Peshwa. He also proposed to entrust him with the additional responsibility of governing the Subahs of Kalyan and Bhiwandi. Sambhaji then looked at Hambirrao Mohite proudly and said, 'It takes a real man to lead an army. After the untimely death of Prataprao Gujar, you have handled the responsibility remarkably well and I wish that you would continue to hold the post of the commander-in-chief of the Maratha forces under my rule.'

Soon after, Sambhaji felicitated Prahlad Niraji and asked him to continue as the chief justice. Janardan Pant would continue to serve as Dabir or the minister responsible for external relations. Abaji Sondev was made Surnavis, the chief secretary, while Dattaji Pant was appointed the minister for internal affairs.

Annaji Datto, standing in a corner, was now an anxious man. His whole body shivered with beads of sweat appearing on his forehead. He feared for his fate as his earlier position of Surnavis had been taken away. The Surnavis was responsible for all royal edicts and commanded a great deal of prestige in the administrative council.

After staring at him for a moment, Sambhaji said, 'Pant, there is a lot of pressure on me to not unshackle you. But I believe you deserve a position in the new administration and I am happy to inform you that you have been appointed as the treasurer.'

Annaji tried to force a smile but he could not hide the resentment at having lost the important post of Surnavis.

Sambhaji did not forget to honour Rayappa, the man who had served him loyally all these years. Raje then spotted Daryasarang and Daulat Khan, standing at the rear of the durbar. They looked striking in their tall, pointed Turkish turbans, flowing green robes and short henna-stained beards.

'My Abasaheb used to say that one must learn to control the seas if one wishes to protect the forts and keep the Swaraj's flag fluttering on their ramparts. I want to honour you who protect the seas.'

He said, 'Jijausaheb showed us how a woman could manage a kingdom and a household with equal ease. She made Shivaji Raje what he was and Shivaji created the Hindavi Swaraj. The jewel in his crown was his mother.' Sambhaji turned to look at Yesubai, creating a flutter of excitement in the durbar. 'I will often be away on campaigns with my ministers to confront the enemy. I would like to hand over the reins of administration to Maharani Yesubai. This newly minted gold coin and seal is being released in her honour.'

'Abasaheb created heroes like Tanaji, Yesaji, Murarbaji, Daulat Khan, and Daryasarang out of ordinary men. Today, I am happy to honour a man who has never asked me for anything—Kavi Kalash. I am bestowing on him the title of 'Chandogamatya,' expounder of the Vedas, and I include him in my council of ministers with this special post.'

A grateful Kavi Kalash bowed, while his wife Tejasbai could not hold back her tears. The coronation of the second Chhattrapati of the Maratha Empire thus came to an end. More than a hundred thousand people had assembled in Raigad, and it was now time for them to disperse. Thousands of brahmins and sanyasis who had come to collect alms were caught in a stampede while rushing out through the fort's narrow gates. A few hundred lost their lives.

Many who were not content with the alms they had received, quickly blamed Kavi Kalash for the calamity. 'You know, Kavi Kalash, the chandal, beheaded nearly fourteen hundred men and four thousand sheep for the coronation!'

'You don't say! I have heard that he is neck-deep in occult practices!'

5

A few select men were assembled at Sambhaji's quarters. Having finished dinner, they were relaxing on the terrace at midnight. Sambhaji said, looking at Hambirrao, 'Hambir Mama, during Abasaheb's time, the territory of Sinhagad, Rajgad and Pratapgad earned a lot of fame. We must create a name in the region of Nashik, Ramshej and Trayambakeshwar.'

He stopped for a moment as he clenched his fists. 'I am told there is a likelihood of Aurangzeb marching on the Deccan. Let him! We are ready.'

Hambirrao suggested, 'In Marwari weddings, it is customary for the Mama to present a unique gift to his nephew. I too want to give you something.'

'What are you hinting at, Mamasaheb?'

'Surat!' Hambirrao almost whispered, taking everyone by surprise, and they exclaimed, 'The third time?'

'Yes! And why not? There is much to loot in the city.'

There was a general consensus on avoiding the discussion of this plan at length in public, as they wanted to keep it to themselves for the time being. But such exciting news did reach a few more ears nevertheless.

Annaji Datto and Hiroji Farzand presented a silver crown to the deity at the Jagadeeshwar temple. They had taken a vow to present a crown to the Lord if they were released from captivity. Only a few months earlier, they were royal prisoners under house arrest. They wondered at their good fortune: Sambhaji had not only released them but pardoned all their crimes. To top it all, they were inducted back into the council of ministers.

The same day, after their midday meal, senior ministers sat on the terrace of Annaji's haveli discussing various matters. Coronation was over but the palaces and havelis of Raigad still wore a festive air. Rahuji Somnath said to Farzand, pointing at a haveli next to the Peshwa's residence, 'Hiroji, do you notice the richly decorated haveli over there? Whose is it?'

'It has been built on orders from Sambhaji and is for Kavi Kalash,' Rahuji continued before Hiroji could respond.

'Well, let it be,' Hiroji said. 'It is for Raje's friend.'

'Hiroji, I am surprised at the lack of reaction from you. Are you made of stone?'

'Why, what do you mean?'

'Well, a friend is taken care of by a friend. That is all very well. But should a nephew not take care of his uncle? You may be the son of Shahaji by one of his mistresses, but you are Shivaji Raje's brother and an uncle to Sambhaji, aren't you?'

'Let it be … Rahuji.'

'Why should I? He felicitates that fellow he picked up from the banks of the Ganga and builds a haveli for him. But you, Hiroji Pant, are given an ordinary two-storeyed house to stay in! Is that just?'

Annaji, who had remained silent till now, smiled ironically. 'Hiroji, you stayed back in place of the elder Maharaj while he escaped from Agra. What a risk you took! You could have lost your life. But this is what you get for your loyalty and daring!'

Hiroji downed another tumbler of wine and said,

'Well, I did commit the crime of running away with jewels from the treasury. Shambhubal is kind; he pardoned me.'

'That may be true. But have you asked yourself whose treasure it is? After all, you too are part of the family and may claim some of it.'

It did not take much to influence the simple mind of a soldier like Hiroji. Others joined the discussion. The clerks from Ratnagiri and Devgad complained,

'Annaji, isn't Shambhu Raje insulting you by taking away your post as the Surnavis? We have nowhere to go now. If there is an accounting error of a few hundred hons, we won't have someone like you to pardon us!'

'Do whatever it takes, Pant! But we cannot allow this to continue.'

Annaji's disciples were deliberately raking up the issue. The old wounds opened up easily, and Annaji winced at the memory of the day he had learned that Sambhaji had not re-appointed him as the Surnavis. He said in a bitter voice, 'Can you guess where our second Chhattrapati was after the coronation? Paying his respects to Yakub Fakir Baba at Kelshi!'

'Well, even Shivaji Maharaj used to consider him his guru. Maharaj used to visit him often ...'

'Hiroji, you old fool! How can you compare Shivaji Maharaj with Shambhu? Mark my words, as long as the two of them, Shambhu and Kavi Kalash, are thick as thieves, old loyals like us have no place in the administration of this kingdom. That arrogant, reckless Raja and his vile advisor need to be shown their place.'

NINE

Misdemeanour

1

After Agra and Delhi, Burhanpur, on the banks of the river Tapti, was the most important city of the Mughals. Not only was it a strategic post for the army, being the gateway to the Deccan, but it had also grown into a vital trading centre. The Subedar of Burhanpur was invariably a close relative of the Badshah. Khan Jahan Bahadur Khan Kolkatash, Aurangzeb's 'milk brother', had been appointed the Subedar, and he kept a close eye on the region.

On 30 January 1681, the beautiful palaces and havelis along Burhanpur's riverfront glowed in the golden hues of the evening sun. The tall, majestic minarets of the Jama Masjid rose from the heart of the city.

Bahadur Khan Kolkatash had left for Aurangabad four days earlier to attend the marriage of his nephew. The bride was from Golconda and the marriage party had left Hyderabad with a lot of fanfare. Not wanting to fall short in the reciprocal arrangements, Bahadur Khan had taken with him an army of three thousand men out of the eight thousand troops stationed at Burhanpur. It would not do for the groom's party to pass up an opportunity for a show of strength.

The Naik Subedar, Kakar Khan, was in charge of the city in Bahadur Khan's absence. As evening fell, lamps were lit across the city. The reflections of the illuminated facades dissolved in the small waves on the Tapti's surface.

The old city had fortified mud walls, but Burhanpur had expanded in the last few years, and new localities like Nawabpura, Karanpura, Shahjahanpura, Khurrampura and others had sprung up. Bahadurpura was one such neighbourhood where a large number of rich merchants as wealthy as their counterparts in Surat and Hyderabad lived. Transactions worth crores of hons took place there in silk, gold, silver and other precious commodities.

To all appearances, the evening of 30 January was no different from other evenings. Kakar Khan had just finished his evening prayers. Two hundred armed soldiers guarded his haveli day and night as a precautionary measure. Of late, he had managed to antagonise the Hindu ryots, thanks to his harsh and discriminatory policies.

The afternoon had been quite eventful. He had received news from spies in the vicinity of Surat. They had spotted a large number of Maratha horsemen in the jungles around the city. The citizens, especially the foreign merchants based in the port, were dreading another Maratha attack. They had not forgotten the two raids on Surat by Shivaji, twelve and twenty years back. The very thought that his son Sambhaji was planning the next foray made them shiver with fear.

The Thanedar at Surat had requested for urgent reinforcement, asking Kakar Khan 'to send as many troops as possible from Burhanpur.' After the last loot of Surat, the Mughals had built a fifteen-foot-high wall around the city and increased the number of troops permanently stationed there. But the thought of a Maratha raid still made them nervous. The moment Kakar Khan received the message, he angrily thumped his fist on a table, saying, 'It is a tragedy that Bahadur Khansaheb is busy with wedding celebrations during such testing times.'

After a brief discussion with his sardars, Kakar Khan decided that afternoon to retain a thousand men in Burhanpur and send the rest with adequate ammunition towards Surat. By evening, when Khan had finished his namaaz, the troops were far away. As he was folding his prayer mat, a few soldiers rode up rapidly, tied their horses at the gates, and rushed in. 'Huzoor! The Marathas are marching on Burhanpur. We are being attacked, Huzoor!'

'What are you raving about? Marathas at Burhanpur? You idiots, their target was Surat …' Kakar Khan stopped mid-sentence. He gulped water from a tumbler, and closed his eyes for a moment as he regained his composure. Then he asked, 'Who is their leader? It cannot be Sambhaji! He was in Raigad a fortnight back, enjoying the coronation ceremonies. Even if he rode day and night, it would take him at least six days to get here.'

Kakar Khan and his sardars could hardly believe what the soldiers were saying. But their frightened faces testified to the truth of their report. Khan despatched a messenger to summon the wealthy traders of the city. By then, news of an imminent Maratha attack had spread like wildfire across Burhanpur creating panic. One of the spies reported, 'The Marathas are only a few kos away, hiding in the jungles. It is a large force, led by a commander called Hambirrao.'

'How many?'

'Nearly fifteen or seventeen thousand men, Huzoor.'

'Ya Allah!' Kakar Khan exclaimed.

He wondered what he could do. Half the force was with Bahadur Khan while he had despatched the remaining troops to Surat. He cursed himself for doing that. He yelled in desperation, 'These Marathas are despicable fellows and our spies are idiots! They fooled us by acting as if they were going to attack Surat while their real target was Burhanpur all along. Looks like Sambhaji is an even more cunning fox than his rascal father Shivaji!'

'What can I say, Huzoor! Those Marathas have been camped in the jungle on the outskirts of the city since last night. They must have prepared their meals but we could not even see the smoke from their kitchen fires. We learned that their commander Hambirrao ordered the troops to leave pieces of meat outside the villages in the vicinity, attracting the dogs there. While the dogs were feeding, they killed them with arrows. That way they have ensured that the dogs would not bark and wake the villagers.'

One of the merchants asked, 'What exactly is their intention?'

'What else?' Kakar Khan said, curling his fists in anger. 'They want to attack Burhanpur and loot the city.'

Soon, an urgent meeting was underway at Kakar Khan's quarters. The prominent merchants and mullahs of the city were present, as well as the sardars who worked under Khan. They all were scared, anticipating the worst. Many of the traders were on the verge of tears.

They pleaded, 'We know how Shivaji had looted Surat. Please help us! Do whatever it takes!'

Saying so, a few of them placed bags of silver and gold coins at Kakar Khan's feet. Khan was a seasoned soldier and a stern administrator whom Aurangzeb had trusted to implement the Jizya tax. He conferred with his his fouzdar and assessed the situation. It was a tricky one: they had only a thousand men to defend Burhanpur.

Finally Kakar Khan announced confidently, 'I have a thousand soldiers with me. Send your private guards to join them. Let me make this clear: I may die, but I will save Burhanpur!'

That gave a lot of courage to those present at the meeting. Nearly fifteen hundred guards who were in the employ of various merchant families joined Kakar Khan's forces that night. He shouted, galvanising the men, 'Let us go! Why should we waste our time waiting for the Marathas to come here?'

'What is your plan, Sardar?'

'The Marathas must be fast asleep right now. If we show some daring and manage to enter their camp, we can take them by surprise. We will burn their tents and roast the devils alive!'

'Wah!' The idea was met with cheers and applause.

At midnight, the main door of the fortified city creaked open. A thousand-strong cavalry, followed by fifteen hundred foot soldiers, exited the gate. The contingent was led by Kakar Khan who was astride a horse. Accompanied by five hundred soldiers, he rode ahead and reached a moat which had often been filled with burning logs to keep the enemy at bay.

Something stirred in the darkness of the moat and suddenly, as if it had sprung to life, out came thousands of Maratha soldiers with cries of 'Har Har Mahadev!', 'Shivaji Maharaj ki jay!', and 'Sambhaji Maharaj ki jay!' Nearly four thousand Maratha soldiers rushed forward to attack, with shouts of 'Kill!' and 'Attack!' Leading the men was Sambhaji, wearing an armoured vest and metal headgear for protection. His Bhawani sword swung in the air as he urged his men on. Like the stalks of jowar cut down by farmers in the fields, the Mughals were beheaded and struck down as the Marathas advanced.

For the Maratha troops, it was the first opportunity to fight alongside their newly coronated Chhattrapati, and their enthusiasm knew no bounds. They chased the Burhanpuris and crushed them. Kakar Khan somehow managed to save his life by retreating behind the city's fortified walls. By then, nearly four hundred of his men had been massacred while hundreds lay wounded on the ground.

Khan had closed behind him the huge doors leading into the city. However Sambhaji was aware that the loot was not inside the mud walls but on the outer periphery of the city where the rich merchants resided. He said to Kavi Kalash, 'Keep a few men here with instructions to bang on the doors. Maintain the facade of trying to break them open to enter the inner city while the rest of the troops make their way to Bahadurpura. We need to start looting the shops right away.'

'As you command, Raje.'

'And make sure that no women or children are touched. Avoid killing even a single man if you can. But spare no one if he attacks you!'

2

A good commander has to be ware even while he is asleep. Hambirrao Mohite and his men were resting in the jungles outside the city when they heard the shouts of 'Har Har Mahadev', 'Shivaji Maharaj ki jay', and 'Sambhaji Maharaj ki jay!' Hambirrao woke up and rushed out of his tent. His men too, having heard the commotion, came out to see.

Sensing that his men were excited, he said, 'Don't do anything silly. These are traps set by our enemy to fool us into thinking that Sambhaji Maharaj is here and has attacked them.' At that very moment, hearing the sound of approaching horses, the men unsheathed their swords. Soon, a pair of Hambirrao's scouts rode up, shouting, 'Mamasaheb! Shambhu Raje!'

'Shambhu Raje? Where? How is he here?'

'I saw him. He has attacked Burhanpur!'

The other man added, 'Shambhu Raje rode without stopping for five days and nights from Raigad with five thousand men.'

That was enough for Hambirrao to spring into action. Twirling his whiskers, he mounted his horse and shouted 'Har Har Mahadev!' His troops poured out of the jungles and charged towards Burhanpur, soon converging with Sambhaji's forces. The loot of Bahadurpura began. They broke down the doors of shops and pried open safes full of jewels, coins and other riches. They found passages leading to basements where most of the traders stocked their wares.

Sambhaji and Hambirrao took stock of the situation. Many soldiers were still at the doors leading into the old city, creating the impression that the Marathas wanted to enter and sack Burhanpur. Meanwhile, Sambhaji was informed that the Sikhs who resided in Karanpura could join Kakar Khan's forces. He directed his troops to that locality and soon managed to get the Sikhs to surrender. At the same time, he ensured that news of their attacks on the outskirts did not reach the old town.

Many men who took part in the raid on Burhanpur led by Sambhaji were experienced looters who had attacked Surat along with Shivaji Maharaj. They plundered the localities of Nawabpura, Shahjung, Shahjahanpura and Khurrampura. They also dug through basements and recovered hoards of wealth stored underground.

The raid was nearly over before the night ended. Sambhaji and Hambirrao sat on a boulder near the Maratha camp. Rayappa, realising that Raje would be hungry, had roasted a few corn cobs which Sambhaji and Hambirrao nibbled on.

Hambirrao looked at Sambhaji with pride. 'My nephew, you seemed quite eager to follow us!'

'A nephew should never be far behind his uncle, Mamasaheb. And don't forget! This nephew of yours has his father's blood in him. A Raja is not one who wears jewels looted by his troops but one who fights hand in hand with his men to acquire them! And secondly, I am told a coronation is akin to a king marrying his land. According to tradition the husband, after marriage, is supposed to go out and hunt to bring something home for his wife. I thought, what better way to show my gratitude than by looting Burhanpur?'

Both Hambirrao and Sambhaji laughed.

Hambirrao was on a constant vigil to ensure that news of the loot never reached the main city. The plunder continued for two days while some soldiers gathered extra horses and mules to carry the loot back into Maratha territory. On the third day, Rayappa brought news that a horse trader with two thousand Arabian steeds in his possession was willing to negotiate a deal with the Marathas.

'He had come hoping to strike a deal with Bahadur Khan but the Subedar is in Aurangabad and the trader is growing impatient.'

Sambhaji immediately left to meet the trader. He was impressed at the sight of the tall and sturdy horses. He had not seen such magnificent beasts in recent years. The trader stood with his hands folded, a little scared.

'Where did you get such lovely animals from? I am sure there are none like these in Hindustan.'

'From Arabestan, Huzoor.'

Sambhaji suddenly leaped onto a barebacked horse and pulled its reins. It neighed and lifted the hooves of its forelegs in the air.

'Raja saheb, stop! You will fall! Don't try to ride that horse!' But Sambhaji and the horse shot forth like an arrow, with Rayappa and a few other soldiers in hot pursuit. The trader sat down on the ground, slapping his forehead with his palm. Hambirrao, looking at the man, merely smiled. After a few hours, Sambhaji returned. As for the horse, it behaved as if Sambhaji had been its rider for years!

When asked what his price was, the trader fell at Sambhaji's feet and wailed, 'Huzoor, take them free of cost but spare our lives! We want to return home safely with my family and my men.'

'I don't intend to accept that offer. State your price! You have reared these animals with care and we will not use our strength to steal them from you.'

After closing the deal, Raje instructed Khando Ballal, 'Please ensure that the money is paid from our treasury and not from the loot here at Burhanpur.'

Later that day, a few spies came rushing from Aurangabad. 'Bahadur Khan Kolkatash has received news of the raid and has left the wedding celebrations to return as soon as possible. They are on their way; the horses and the men have not even stopped for water.'

Immediate instructions were issued to wind up the operation in Burhanpur. The loot in any case was over. There were no more mules or carriages available to transport it. By afternoon, the carts left Burhanpur. The total value of the loot exceeded a crore hons.

Meanwhile, Sambhaji had received several complaints from the Hindus around Burhanpur who were troubled by imposition of the Jizya tax. Kakar Khan was arrested and presented before Sambhaji. Sambhaji ordered his men to remove Khan's robe and tie him to a tree. Then he said to him, 'I warn you … don't harass the people around here with the Jizya tax.' Kakar Khan nodded meekly in reply. As soon as Sambhaji turned his back, Rayappa rushed towards Kakar Khan and tried to remove his dhoti. Sambhaji shouted, 'Rayappa, stop that! He may be a rascal but that does not mean we abandon all decency!'

Hambirrao and Sambhaji were worried that they might have to encounter Bahadur Khan on their way back. They knew the Mughals were aware of the routes Marathas had taken while returning with loot from the raids on Surat. In order to reduce the risk, they divided the Maratha force of twenty thousand men into five parts.

Hambirrao suggested, 'Shambhu Raje, I propose to return after taking Aurangabad. A troop strength of ten or twelve thousand would suffice.'

'I have five thousand men with me; that will be sufficient,' Sambhaji said.

'Be careful, Shambhubal. It might be safer to take along a larger force,' Hambirrao suggested.

Most of the loot was to be deposited at the Salher fort. They were planning to return via Dharangaon and Chopda, and the possibility of being confronted by Bahadur Khan en route was strong.

3

Bahadur Khan waited patiently a few miles from Chopda. He planned to massacre the Marathas as soon as they reached there. After a long wait, he was finally able to hear the sound of hooves in the jungle nearby. He was surprised to see that it was a small force consisting of only about five hundred men. As soon as the Mughals attacked, the Marathas shouted,

'We are only emissaries! Please don't attack.'

Bahadur Khan and his men confronted them, blocking their path. Two men, sitting atop a camel, addressed him, 'Huzoor, we are Mullah Kazi Haider and Jotyaji Kesarkar. We are emissaries on our way to Bhaganar to deliver a message to Qutb Shah from Shambhu Raje.'

Bahadur Khan took the letter and asked his spies whether the signature was that of Sambhaji. The spies confirmed that. Bahadur Khan then questioned the emissaries about Sambhaji's whereabouts.

'He would not dare to come this way, Huzoor! He knows that he is likely to meet you here.'

'Where is he then? Where is the Maratha army?'

'Well, we believe he must be well on his way towards Jalgaon or Aurangabad. We are not sure though. However we are certain that they have not taken this route.'

The two emissaries soon started pleading with Bahadur Khan to take them into his service. First, Mullah Haider requested, 'Sarkar, I am a man of your faith. Please take me into your fold and make me a sardar.' Then Jotyaji said, 'Khansaheb, even Netaji Palkar embraced Islam. If you have need of a tough commander like me, I too am willing to change my religion.'

Suddenly Bahadur Khan noticed it was getting dark and he heard horses in the valley. He indicated to his men not to move or attack until he gave the signal.Khan and his men waited, hidden by the dense undergrowth, as the Marathas came climbing up the slope. There were nearly three thousand men—mere soldiers—and they carried no loot. Bahadur Khan signalled to his men not to attack and let them go.

Jotyaji said, 'What did I tell you, Khansaheb? Shambhu Raje is not coming this way. They must have taken the route via Edlabad.'

Bahadur Khan was obsessed with the thought of confronting Sambhaji and Hambirrao, and recovering the loot. That was the only way he could protect himself from Aurangzeb's wrath. Possessed with the idea, he rushed towards Edlabad. He never even noticed when Mullah Haider, Jotyaji and their men turned in another direction and vanished.

As soon as Bahadur Khan left for Edlabad, a chain of spies sent the information to the Marathas waiting to move on with the loot. Barely three hours after Khan's departure, Sambhaji and Hambirrao crossed Chopda and moved rapidly towards Salher.

It was past midnight. The troops had been riding without a break. Despite the cold, both the men and the horses were sweating from exhaustion. Nearly five thousand riders crossed a narrow gorge. They wanted to reach their destination by dawn.

Manaji pointed towards a hill, saying, 'Raje, the hill ahead is the abode of Saptashrungi Mata.'

Sambhaji halted his horse. 'Let the others go ahead. Fifteen hundred men are enough for me.'

'Where are you planning to go? For the darshan at Saptashrungi?'

'Yes! I had made a promise to pay my respects at the temple before leaving for Burhanpur. I cannot proceed without taking Mata's blessings.'

'Raje, we are already delayed, and not yet out of danger. We can always return for the darshan on another day,' Rupaji tried to convince Sambhaji.

'It will take the whole night just to scale the steep mountain,' Manaji said.

'Well, one does not achieve success or receive blessings without making an effort, does one?'

Kavi Kalash was asked to the lead the troops with the loot while Sambhaji, along with fifteen hundred men, began the trek up the mountain. It was getting bright as they reached the summit. The local thanedar was ready to receive him. The small temple of Saptashrungi was perched on the edge of a cliff. They had to dismount near the temple and walk up the steep slope by the light of torches.

The news of Raje coming to the temple had already reached the beggars, sadhus and fakirs in the area. They crowded the temple in a frenzy of anticipation. Khando Ballal carried the bag of coins which Raje used for giving alms. Crying out 'Jay Mate Saptashrungi' and 'Allah!', they blessed Raje. Suddenly, cries of 'Deen, Deen!' were heard. Pathans, disguised as fakirs, took out swords hidden beneath their shawls and attacked Sambhaji. Raje unsheathed his sword while five fakirs lunged at him. A sword struck his shoulder, but all it could do was hit the armour. Sambhaji had not neglected to wear his armour and metal headgear. They finally came to his rescue now!

Sambhaji then pounced on the Pathans the way a lion would attack its prey. Soon, three of his assailants were on the ground. Sambhaji struck the fourth man on his shoulder with such force that his arm was severed. He fell off the cliff, unable to keep his balance. Suddenly, the fifth Pathan, hiding behind a tree nearby, jumped onto Sambhaji's back. He gripped Raje's neck with his thighs and both men fell to the ground, rolling in the dust. The Pathan was a strong man and did not allow his grip to loosen. Somehow Sambhaji managed to extricate his right hand and took a dagger out of his cummerbund. The next moment the dagger had entered the Pathan's stomach and emerged, ripping his body open near his neck. Sambhaji stood up and brushed the dust off his robes. His men rushed over to see if he was hurt. Sambhaji was unscathed.

'Well, it is all due to the blessings of Saptashrungi Mata,' he said, laughing.

Dawn broke as they continued their trek to the temple.

4

Sambhaji Raje, Hambirrao Mohite, Manaji, Rupaji, and the twenty-five thousand Maratha troops accompanying them, had performed feats of valour across Maharashtra. They had devastated favourite cities of the Badshah—Burhanpur and Aurangabad. All along the route to Raigad, at Aapta, Pen, Mahad and various other places, the soldiers were felicitated by the local womenfolk. Shouts of 'Shivaji Maharaj ki jay!' and 'Sambhaji Maharaj ki jay!' were heard wherever they went.

A durbar was held in Raigad. Sambhaji wanted to felicitate the brave soldiers. Stepping forward and walking ten steps, he presented fine robes to Hambir Mama and showered diamonds on his turban. Sambhaji wanted Soyrabai to felicitate her brother but she had excused herself, stating ill-health as a reason for not attending the durbar.

As the celebrations were drawing to a close, Sambhaji said to Prahlad Niraji, 'I hope you have taken stock of the loot.'

'It is going on, Raje! The clerks are exhausted, their eyes strained by making an inventory of this mountain of wealth. I am told a similar quantity is stocked in Salher?'

Sambhaji nodded. 'Yes, that's right.'

Suryaji said in a disappointed tone, 'It was our bad luck! We had almost captured Aurangabad. When we entered the town with seven thousand men, the place was deserted and ripe for plunder. The townsfolk were hiding in their homes. Then we heard that Bahadur Khan was marching on us. We were forced to leave!'

'Nothing is lost, Suryaji. There will be enough and more opportunities in the future.'

Sambhaji had sent his forces across the region to every corner of the Deccan. The Maratha troops, despatched towards Nagar and Nashik right up to Warhad, and some towards the borders of Bhaganar and Hyderabad in the south, were wreaking havoc in the Mughal territories. Their mandate was to create as much trouble as possible and ravage these areas. The men were encouraged by the fact their Raja was willing to fight with them, come rain or shine.

The victory at Burhanpur had been achieved a mere fortnight after the coronation. While most of Sambhaji's courtiers were appreciative of this, there were voices of dissent in the durbar. A few of the elders expressed their opinion, 'Raje, you have managed to create quite a spark but we are sure Aurangzeb is not going to watch this silently.'

'That's right!' Mullah Haider added, 'The Badshah has dismissed Bahadur Khan and appointed a new subedar at Burhanpur. And the Muslim ryots are up in arms.'

'Why so?'

'They have threatened that they will stop the Friday prayers if the Badshah is not able to find ways to protect them.'

Sambhaji said, 'Well, I agree with you. But let us keep in mind that I cannot hold back the ambitions and aspirations of young daredevils like Rupaji Bhosale, Dhanaji Jadhav, Santaji Ghorpade, Nilopant Peshwa and Krishnaji Kank. They dream of building a strong Swaraj.'

'Raje, Aurangzeb is building an army numbering hundreds of thousands of men. He is not going to take this lying down.'

Hiroji Farzand said, pride in his voice, 'The lion cub shall prove to be mightier than the lion Shivaji!'

Sambhaji smiled. 'Farzand Kaka, let me make it clear: I am not a patch on Abasaheb! Such men are born only once in a few generations. Don't even try to compare me with him. At the same time, I wish no one forgets that it is his blood which flows through my veins!' He continued, 'Know this: I will not allow a single fort—nay, a single stone from any of the forts—to be taken by Aurangzeb!'

The durbar was over but Sambhaji stayed back to talk to the ryots who had come seeking an audience. As Balaji Chitnis walked with Yesubai towards her quarters, he said, 'Shambhu Raje seemed very emotional today.'

'That is to be expected, isn't it? He is a poet in a soldier's uniform! A soldier's heart can be like a stone but a poet's heart melts at the slightest thought of seeing his men in pain.'

5

Sambhaji was resting in his quarters one afternoon when Kavi Kalash stormed in, waving his hands. He was clearly upset. 'Raje, it's a calamity! A pillar, on whom the Swaraj rested, has crumbled.'

'Don't speak in riddles! What happened?'

'Farzand has joined the Siddis at Janjira.'

'What are you saying? Hiroji or Kondaji?'

'Kondaji!'

Yesubai's face fell. She had heard Shivaji Raje sing the praises of Kondaji—the way he had climbed the walls of Panhalgad with only sixty-four Mavals and captured the near-impregnable fort. Shivaji Maharaj had called him a magician!'

Sambhaji said, trying to rein in his anger, 'We cannot believe all rumours, Kaviraj!'

'Here! You may read the letter from Dandarajpuri's subedar.'

Sambhaji read the letter and said, biting his lips to keep his voice low, 'Did he take his men too?'

'Well, eleven of them followed him. To add insult to injury, he has complained about the lack of justice here and how the administrators are creating havoc in the kingdom.'

'I wonder what makes people do this!' Yesubai asked, thinking aloud.

'Well, it is all because of the watandari system!' Sambhaji said, letting out a deep sigh. 'It is the greed for one's own watan that has been the bane of the Marathas.'

The news of Kondaji's defection spread like wildfire across Raigad. Sambhaji was deeply disturbed when Kavi Kalash said, 'Raje, you need to make a decision. All of them, be it the Brahmins or the Maratha sardars, are clamouring for their own watan—the right to hold lands where they can collect revenues. They were unable to raise their voices on this matter in front of Shivaji Maharaj, out of sheer respect and fear of his displeasure. But now you need to confront this issue once and for all.'

Sambhaji said, 'Abasaheb always said that the watandari system was the bane of the Marathas and believed that the entire kingdom would be broken into pieces if we continue the age-old practice. Let them clamour for their so-called rights. I am not going to budge an inch, as long as I am alive!'

Kondaji's betrayal had been a great shock for Sambhaji but it also made him more vigilant. He instructed Nilopant, 'Be prepared for a war on the seas. Ensure that the fort at Kulaba is adequately stocked with foodgrains and ammunition. If need be, send them more.'

Nilopant said, 'The elder Maharaj's foresight is praiseworthy. He started building the fort two years before his death.'

'But the fort is not yet complete. I must ensure that the ramparts are strong and well-protected within the next four months.'

That night Sambhaji lay awake for a long time. Seeing him smile, Yesubai asked, 'What is it, Raje?'

'Yesu, I was recalling an incident from my childhood. During the negotiations leading up to the treaty of Purandar, having lost all his forts to the Mughals, except Raigad, Abasaheb had made a request for the fort of Janjira to be handed over to us as a compensation. Mirza Raje Jaisingh had made the petition to Aurangzeb on behalf of Abasaheb. But you know what Aurangzeb said?'

Yesubai continued listening.

'Well, Aurangzeb wrote back saying Jaisingh was a fool to suggest it. He said, "Janjira is dear to us. If we make the mistake of handing the fort over to him, that mountain rat would turn into a dangerous alligator and the swish of his tail would shake the Mughal throne."'

'Raje, is Janjira such a strategic fort?'

'Yesu, I am not disappointed that we have not been able to take Janjira so far. But Kondaji's defection is a hard blow. He has doubled the Siddi's strength by his mere presence.'

6

'If by Allah's grace, I am able to ascend the throne at Delhi, I will be the Emperor but you would be in command, Sambhaji Raje! Alamgir Badshah may be my father but, keep in mind, he is your enemy and mine! It is imperative that we come together to finish off this enemy of ours.'

Kaviraj paused while reading the letter.

'Who is the author of this letter, Kaviraj?'

'Shahzada Akbar.'

'Is he Badshah's real son or a fake?'

'I have conducted my enquires, and he is indeed Aurangzeb's son, born to Dilras Banu Begum. In fact, he was considered the Badshah's favourite amongst all his sons!'

'Isn't he the one who revolted against Aurangzeb in Rajputana and joined the Rajput forces, declaring himself the Emperor of Hindustan?'

'That's right! He is the one.'

'Why does he want to meet me in the Deccan?'

'Where else can he hide from Aurangzeb's wrath?'

'Find out why he wants to come here. What are his real intentions? Who are his supporters? I need all the details.'

Sambhaji had been playing safe, but he heard that Shahzada Akbar, not waiting for a formal invitation from the Marathas, had already begun his journey to the Deccan.

Within a fortnight, another message arrived from Shahzada Akbar. He seemed to be eager for Sambhaji's help and was keen to meet him at the earliest opportunity. But his urgent pleas did not appear to move Sambhaji. Kaviraj was surprised at Raje's cool demeanour. 'Raje, you have not replied to his earlier letter either. Is it wise, not to take any action?'

'Kaviraj, I am keen to know more about him. What have you heard?'

The question took Kavi Kalash by surprise. He said, recovering quickly, 'Aurangzeb is deeply hurt by his dearest son's rebellious attitude. And he was taken aback when he heard that his son is joining the enemy camp of the Marathas. He is worried that others who are against him may also join forces with the Shahzada and will somehow find a way to stop his march into the Deccan. Aurangzeb has asked his men to stop the prince, wherever they can find him, whether in the mountains, ravines or serais. Poor Akbar is dodging all this as he moves southwards.'

Sambhaji listened quietly. Kavi said, unable to contain his excitement, 'Raje, the very fact that the dearest son of the Badshah wishes to join forces with us has made our sardars jump with joy.'

'Is that so?'

'Hiroji Farzand and others believe you will form an alliance with Akbar and attack Delhi.'

Sambhaji merely smiled. Seeing his cold reaction, Kavi said, a little agitated, 'I beg of you, Raje! We cannot sit idle. He is, after all, the Badshah's son. And he is on the run, lest he get burnt in the fire of his father's wrath. We must make the most of this opportunity.'

'Is it not important to find out whether he is running with the fire or away from it? Let us not act in haste.'

Meanwhile, Annaji Datto was fuming. Sambhaji had received several complaints about revenues that were not reaching the treasury. He has increased the audits and introduced checks and balances to ensure that there were no leakages. Moreover, Annaji could not tolerate the fact that the abhorrent Kavi Kalash was Raje's closest confidante, almost as powerful as Sambhaji himself.

Annaji's brother Somaji said in a peevish tone, 'I don't undertand why Raje bothers about all these details. The elder Maharaj too ran a tight ship and there was discipline all around but he would overlook small mistakes.'

'Well, he was truly an Emperor! He had the wisdom to understand that while carrying a potful of water, a little of it will invariably spill over. Likewise, minor errors in accounting are normal. He ignored such slips.'

'Dada, things have changed here. Yesubai Ranisaheb, instead of spending time in her mahal, is always in the office. She even handles the paperwork, amongst other things!'

Annaji sighed heavily. 'What a pity! Raje, Maharani, and that Kavi! When three devils are at work, I wonder how ordinary folks like us can survive?'

7

It was late evening and the shadows lengthened at Raigad. Sambhaji was about to wrap up the day's work and leave for his quarters when Prahlad Niraji came in.

'Raje, the Portuguese emissaries have been waiting to meet you for the past two days. The humid weather here does not suit them and they are getting quite restless.'

'Are our emissaries with them?'

Yes, Ramji Thakur and Yesaji Gambhirrao are with them.'

'Send them in,' Raje said.

The Portuguese emissaries were soon ushered in, accompanied by their translator Ramchandra Shenavi. They saluted Sambhaji. After the initial introductions, the Portuguese emissaries glanced at Kavi Kalash before saying, 'Raje, we have a message from our Viceroy which we have been instructed to deliver to you in private.'

'You may speak without fear. Kavi Kalash is my confidante. There is nothing he does not know.'

Ramchandra Shenavi read out the letter:

> *'Dear Chhattrapati Sambhajiraje,*
>
> *As you are aware, we have complained on earlier occasions of the uncultured and rough behaviour of your Subedar Moro Dadaji of Dicholi. He is both a corrupt man and a cruel administrator. I am writing to inform you that he is trying to create a rift between us, with intention of sabotaging our relations. We are told that the reason for his temerity is the fact that he is close to a senior administrative official in your court. He seems to have no fear of the consequences of his actions.'*

Sambhaji did not react immediately. When the Portuguese emissaries were about to leave, he asked, 'Who is the senior official your Viceroy was referring to?'

'We don't know,' the men said.

Sambhaji glared at his own emissaries. 'Don't you know?'

Seeing their tense faces, Raje said, 'Your reaction tells me that the person concerned is a powerful man indeed!'

Sambhaji left for his quarters. Many complaints had reached Raigad regarding the malpractices of the Subedar of Dicholi. But it was the question of the identity of the senior court official whose support had emboldened Moro Dadaji which troubled him. That evening, he sent his guards to the emissaries' haveli to summon Ramchandra Shenavi. Meeting the translator alone in the office, Raje came straight to the point. 'You refused to reply when I asked you. Tell me, who is the official supporting Moro Dadaji?'

Ramchandra Shenavi looked at the floor as he spoke, 'The person who has been visiting Dicholi regularly in connection with the ammunition factory and to collect revenues.'

'You mean Annaji …?'

'Yes! He is very close to Moro Dadaji. Annaji has lent his black money to the traders at Sawantwadi and Ponda at high rates of interest, and given Moro Dadaji the task of managing it.'

Sambhaji's guess was right. He mumbled, when Shenavi had left, 'Who else but the shameless Annaji Datto would have the gall to carry on in this manner!'

He said to Kavi Kalash, who had joined him in the office, 'I was not delirious when I took over the throne. I knew what such men are capable of. Moro Dadaji is just one of the men Annaji is using to serve his own interests. I had discovered the leaks in the treasury back when I was put in charge of it during Abasaheb's coronation. I was merely sixteen then, young and bold, and I spoke my mind! It was then that these administrators turned against me!'

He continued, 'We need to take action against the Subedar of Dicholi. Not that I trust the Portuguese completely. Their loyalties will be tested when the Mughals march on us. In any case, send out an immediate royal decree removing Moro Dadaji from the post.'

'Raje, doesn't it require the seals of the Peshwa and the Surnavis?'

'Why have I given you the title of Chandogamatya? If there is a need to send an urgent firmaan and none of the Ashta Pradhan are around, you are automatically entitled to all the powers which are bestowed on the council of ministers.'

'Raje, I am grateful for the trust you repose in me but please understand that these are matters of administration. It is better to involve your ministers in this.'

'I don't believe in protocol just for the sake of it. When I know what I am doing is for the good of the Swaraj, I don't care what others say. I am responsible for this kingdom. Whenever there is turmoil, when the throne is threatened, it is the one sitting on the throne who has to worry about his neck—not the clerks!'

8

Moro Dadaji was asked to resign and his haveli was taken over. Under the supervision of Ramaji Thakur, his seal, official papers and the keys to the local treasury were confiscated. Within an hour, he was a nobody.

The news of his dismissal reached Raigad four days later. The council of ministers were taken aback by the fact that Raje had issued direct orders of which they had no inkling. Many in the Ashta Pradhan felt insulted that their position had been challenged, and almost made redundant by such an act.

Ananji Datto was the one most severely affected. He lost his sleep and appetite, and refused to touch food for a few days. He complained to Balaji Chitnis, 'These are signs of things to come. Action will be taken without an enquiry of any sort. Anyone who is not in Raje's good books will suffer!'

Chitnis said, trying to pacify Annaji, 'Let it be, Annaji! Why make an issue of the termination of an ordinary Subedar? Raje, after all, has the right to take action without conferring with his ministers, doesn't he?'

'Balaji, don't underestimate the significance of the act. There is a deep-rooted conspiracy behind this. Certain people are being targeted. It is a ploy to prove that all the revenue officials appointed during Shivaji Maharaj's reign are useless and corrupt.'

'Who is responsible for this conspiracy?'

'Why look far for someone to blame? That rogue Kavi has put our entire administration, not to mention our religion and society, at risk!'

Hiroji Farzand had of late been assigned a number of important tasks and spent a great deal of time with the revenue officials. However, he seemed disturbed. Raje had received complaints about his lack of involvement in the task at hand.

One afternoon, he presented himself before Raje. Although well into his sixties, he was still a tall, sturdy man. He said, as he saluted sambhaji, 'Raje, if I may give you some advice ...'

'Please speak your mind freely, Farzand Kaka.'

'Shambhubal, that son of Aurangzeb's has been sending you messages but you don't seem to be responding at all!'

'That is true.'

Hiroji was annoyed at Sambhaji's lukewarm response. 'Shambhu Raje, I can tell you one thing with certainty. Had this opportunity presented itself to Shivaji Raje, he would have lost no time in seizing it. It is the whole of Hindustan, on a platter! I suggest you hold that rascal Akbar's hand, and together, attack Delhi.'

Sambhaji smiled. 'Your imagination does run wild, Hiroji Kaka. The less said about your ambitions, the better!'

'Shambhubal, I wonder why the lion's cub is so timid today?'

'Kakasaheb, you have far more experience in these matters than I so. Surely, you understand that we need to ensure that these messages are coming from Akbar and not from someone posing as the Shahzada?'

'Shambhu Raje, we have made enquiries. It is indeed the Shahzada who is reaching out for help.'

'Then we need to be sure why he wants our help. Is it for a full-fledged revolt or will it turn out to be a damp squib?'

Hiroji was quiet for a few moments. Then he left without attempting further discussion of the matter. The next morning, Prahlad Niraji taunted him. 'Hiroji, I am told you met Raje. Have you planned a royal welcome for the Shahzada?'

'What to say, Prahlad Pant! I can imagine Kavi Kalash decamping with the entire treasury of Raigad but Raje trusts him blindly. His constant presence and devious mind has made Shambhubal a dull-witted person. That really frightens me!

In fact, Sambhaji was keeping a close eye on Shahzada Akbar's progress. He sent Farzand towards Trayambakeshwar for a lookout and instructed the Subedar at Nashik, on the northern border of the Maratha Empire, to welcome both Akbar and Durgadas Rathore (the Rajput from Marwar who was helping Akbar to defy Aurangzeb) with expensive gifts of jewels and finery. A troop of Raje's soldiers had been speedily despatched to accompany the Shahzada while his spies, moving equally fast in the opposite direction, carried news back to Raigad.

Kavi Kalash said, 'Raje, you and Akbar have much in common. Both of you are twenty-four years of age and the fourth child of your fathers. The Shahzada lost his mother when he was barely two months of age while you lost your mother at the age of two. And, if you will pardon me for my insouciance, both of you revolted against your fathers.'

Sambhaji was amused at the similarities listed by Kalash. Kavi continued, 'Raje, politics is much like a game of chess. As a rule, one must not ignore a jewel when it literally walks onto your chessboard. Such a pawn can be used very effectively in the game.'

'Kaviraj, by the same analogy, it is not wise to hurry your moves. However, keeping in mind that Durgadas Rathore is accompanying the Shahzada, I ensured that we gave him an honourable reception at the borders. We must not forget that Aurangzeb, while he keeps his other sons at bay, genuinely loves Shahzada Akbar. His mother, Dilras Banu, was his true love. Aurangzeb, who ruthlessly destroyed the temples in Mathura, Somnath and Kashi, has a soft heart when it comes to some people. Shahzada Akbar may have revolted against his father but we cannot be sure how things will pan out in future. In such cases, it is better to bide our time and rely on wisdom rather than force.'

Sambhaji received news that Shahzada Akbar had reached Bhiwandi and Kalyan. He immediately sent a message asking them to halt at Sudhagad. He instructed Hiroji Farzand, 'Leave at once for Sudhagad and meet the Shahzada as an emissary of the Hindavi Swaraj. Take as many jewels from the treasury as you deem fit for an emissary of the Swaraj to honour the Shahzada.'

9

No one can predict the twists and turns of destiny. Some are born with a golden spoon in their mouth while others become Shahenshah by dint of sheer accident or true merit. However, it is always a tragedy when a man who is born to riches turns pauper owing to the vagaries of fate.

He too was a Shahzada. The Shahzada of Delhi's Badshah! He merely had to lift a finger to get a host of servants dance to his tunes. But now the time of luxury and ease had ended. He was forced to ride through valleys and ravines spending his nights in herdsmen's cottages.

He was a young man, barely twenty-four years of age. Slim, of medium height and a glowing complexion, he carried the sapphire necklace which shone brilliantly around his neck with grace. His clothes, stitched by the royal tailors of Delhi's Meena bazaar, had not yet lost their sheen. However, his mind was in turmoil.

Ironically, while the treasury in Delhi overflowed, Shahzada Akbar was roaming the wilds of the Deccan like a beggar! Gone were the days when lissome, blue-eyed maids were at his command and all kinds of entertainment were devised for him from the moment he opened his eyes each morning. The Shahenshah had long since banned music and dance but his concubines and maids knew how to take care of the Shahzada. He was, after all, preferred by Badshah Aurangzeb to the Shahzadas Azam, Muazzam and Kam Baksh. He was considered by most as the likeliest successor to the Mughal throne. Dilras Banu had died when he was barely two months old and since then Aurangzeb had taken a personal interest in his upbringing, ensuring he received the best of care and affection.

Shahzada Akbar woke up to the bleating of goats in a dense forest somewhere near Sudhagad. He could still see in his mind the tall minarets and palatial columns gleaming through his ivory-framed windows in Delhi each morning. He always felt suffocated in the open wilderness. On campaigns with his father, Shahzada's caravan alone would spread across three miles. But now he was sleeping on a bed made of grass, with calico curtains hung over the windows of his tent. Only four hundred horsemen, a few foot-soldiers and two hundred and fifty camel riders accompanied him. It was a tiny battalion, more suited to a Mughal platoon commander than a Shahzada of his stature.

Dark clouds, a constant drizzle and humid weather had welcomed him in Pali. He had not seen the sun for weeks together. The biting cold, and his fear of snakes and scorpions in jungles made his life miserable. It had been months since he reached the Deccan but Sambhaji had not yet formally invited him to Raigad. In fact, despite his repeated entreaties, there was no word from Sambhaji.

Losing his patience, he screamed at Durgadas one day, 'Don't forget that I am the future Shahenshah of Hindustan. I am surprised that an ordinary Maratha zamindar called Sambhaji dares to act so impertinently.'

'Shahzade, please be a little more patient. I am sure he will present himself soon.'

'Tchah! I am fed up. I had expected him to rush here to honour me. I had even planned to make him the Subedar of the Deccan when I ascend the throne. But now I am not interested. Even if you were to make a personal request!'

Durgadas could not hide his smile. Shahzada Akbar shouted, 'Don't be so shameless, Durgadas!'

'It is true that you were born a Shahzada. But see where you are now and in what condition!' Durgadas said. 'Without land, crown or subjects, a king is reduced to a mere caricature. What matters is the present, Shahzade.'

'I wonder why that cruel Sambhaji is not concerned about my suffering.'

'Well, he has sent a senior official of the Maratha court, Hiroji Farzand, as his emissary. He has also sent gifts of precious jewels. Not to mention five hundred cavalry for your protection! He has treated you the way one king should treat another. What more do you expect, Shahzade?'

Akbar continued his rant, 'How cruel destiny is! The long journey from the North, the endless stay in these jungles ... I am tired of this torture. I am going mad!'

'Don't blame others for your plight. The fault lies in your own idle life, filled with pleasures. The Rajputs waited for nearly ten days near Ajmer, literally poised to garland you, but you were busy sleeping. Of course your father took advantage of the situation and stumped you! Who else but you were to blame in that situation?'

Akbar was silent. Durgadas continued, 'The only man in Hindustan who is capable of challenging a mighty emperor like Aurangzeb is Sambhaji. Don't be so impatient. Watch where the wind blows and go with the flow.'

Shahzada Akbar could not argue with Durgadas's prudent advice. He was aware that Sambhaji was young and dynamic, and that he had a devoted army. Yet, a plot was taking shape in his crafty mind which he could not resist putting before Durgadas, 'What if we were to get Hiroji Farzand on our side and raise our own army?'

Durgadas was incensed by Akbar's childish plots. 'Shahzade, don't get carried away by such ludicrous plans. Keep in mind that Sambhaji's strong forts and faithful sardars will not change sides. Their loyalties are well nigh unbreakable.'

Akbar laughed out loudly. 'I can understand that it may not be possible for us to capture the forts. But as far as the loyalty of the sardars you speak of is concerned … well, time will tell!'

10

In the dim light of the lamp, Annaji Datto's swarthy faced looked even more menacing. His sharp eyes had a new twinkle in them. He had just returned to Raigad after a long visit to the Karwar and Kudal provinces. Sambhaji had been at Panhalgad for the past two months.

Annaji Datto said, looking at Hiroji, 'Whatever you may say my dear Farzand, the council of ministers had a certain prestige during Shivba's time. They had respect. Now I neither have the post of Surnavis nor do I command any respect.'

Somaji Datto added, 'Now Yesubai and Sambhaji manage everything. No one else is allowed to take any decisions.'

'Let me correct you, Somaji. The third character in this play is the vilest one. The tantric ghost … how can you forget Kaviraj?'

Annaji Datto was an anxious man these days. The termination of Moro Dadaji's job meant that Annaji's illegal activities were in danger of being exposed again. He was worried that the ill-gotten money he had lent to several people at Sawantwadi and Panaji was unlikely to be returned in the absence of Dadaji. Earlier, Rahuji Somnath had held the keys to the treasury vault but now it was under the direct and strict supervision of Yesubai. Times were tough indeed.

Rahuji Somnath said, 'Annaji, Shambhu Raje has not been in Raigad for the past two months. It is an opportune moment. Let us go for the kill!'

Hiroji Farzand lamented, 'He lacks vision. For the past three months, Aurangzeb's Shahzada has been sitting idle, getting drenched in the monsoons. It was such a golden opportunity to destabilise the Mughal Empire. Had it been Shivba on the throne, he would have seized the moment and converted our small Swaraj into a huge empire!'

'Let it be! We cannot expect anything else from the whimsical Sambhaji.'

'Shivaji, the protector of cows and Brahmins, has a son who revels in sin. He has a dirty habit of mingling with the lower castes. Look at the way he treats Mullah Haider with honour and considers the Muslim fakir, Yakub Baba of Kelshi, as his guru!'

Nilopant Peshwa could not remain quiet any longer. He stood up, red-faced with anger, and said to Annaji, 'Pant, we seem to be going too far! Mullah Haider was given the same importance by Shivaji Raje himself. Didn't the elder Maharaj consider Yakub Baba to be in the same league as his other gurus, Tukaram and Ramdas? I wonder why veteran administrators like you are unnecessarily castigating Sambhaji Raje.'

Somaji was not going to take this reprimand lying down. He taunted Nilopant, 'Well, we all know you got the post of Peshwa thanks to your hereditary status! Please sit!'

Annaji said, 'Gentlemen, my daughter lost her life because of Sambhaji Raje. However I am not saying this because of my personal tragedy … I am sure that the Hindu religion is in great danger of corruption by tantric miscreants and we need to stop it from getting further degraded.'

He continued, 'Shivaji Raje's coronation was carried out under the expert guidance of Gaga Bhatt but, for some reason, Raje invited this tantric Kavi Kalash to crown him. I am sorry to speak against the one that feeds this mouth … but this is a question of the survival of our religion! The elder Maharaj may have erred once or twice but his son has pampered this so-called Shiva worshipper beyond the limits of our endurance. Given the kind of powers granted to him, soon the real Brahmins and scholars would have to leave this kingdom!'

Nilopant Peshwa was clearly rattled by the allegations Annaji was levelling but the old man was in no mood to stop.

'Nilopant, I am willing to say it in writing: our religion and our gods are in danger as long as Shambhu Raje is on the throne. And don't stare at me as if I am ranting like a lunatic. Do you think your father Moropant would have tolerated this? Would he have allowed that scheming fraudster Kavi Kalash to take Muslim converts back into Hindu faith?'

Nilopant was evidently incensed by the barrage of questions. He said, getting up angrily, 'Do you know why those poor souls forced to adopt Islam, go to Kavi Kalash for redemption? It is because you Brahmins charge exorbitant rates, literally killing them with debt.'

As Annaji glared at him, he continued, 'Well, I am not lying, am I? Let me ask you: has Shambhu Raje made any significant changes in Shivaji's administration? There are hardly any new appointments among nearly three hundred and fifty officials, be they Brahmins, Marathas or anyone else. Even in Shivaji Maharaj's time, there were Muslims in high positions like Brahmins. Above all, Shambhu Raje has not revived the watandari system despite tremendous pressure from family members. However, in my opinion, he committed one grave error.' He continued, scanning the faces of his colleagues, 'Despite your act of treason he made the mistake of pardoning you all. You were given back your posts and treated with honour. That was his mistake!'

Without waiting for others to react, Nilopant stormed out of the room. A visibly relieved Annaji wiped beads of sweat off his brow. He also knew that Nilopant's rant had only a superficial effect on those present. Annaji was confident that he had the support of his fellow ministers. Surprisingly, even Hiroji was in favour of Annaji now.

The very fact that Sambhaji had ascended the throne rankled Hiroji. Poisonous comments like 'Hiroji, you may be an illegitimate child, but you have the Bhosale blood in you', and 'You are being treated unfairly, just the way Vidur was treated in the Mahabharata', had brought about a change of heart, slowly but surely. Reconciling himself, albeit grudgingly, to the fact that he would never be considered as a potential successor to Raje, he had developed a sort of contempt for Sambhaji. Annaji could read his mind like a book.

Hiroji mumbled, 'Let us decide once and for all. What can we expect from a son who wishes his father to die so that he may ascend the throne? From the man who allows that fraud pandit from Kashi to carry out his tantric activities? We cannot expect any justice from Shambhu Raje, Annaji! Don't worry, I am with you.'

'Wah, Hiroji!' Annaji shouted, as he looked at the others triumphantly. Then he said to Hiroji, remembering something, 'Farzand, you were sent to receive the Shahzada, weren't you? I am sure you must have struck a chord of friendship with him, having stayed with him for so long?'

'But of course! All I have to do is snap my fingers and he will come running from Pali to Raigad.'

Hiroji's comment strengthened Annaji's resolve. The thought of revenge, which had been simmering in his mind for a long time, was now boiling over, mixed with ideas for a devious conspiracy.

He asked, 'Hiroji, will the Shahzada listen to you? I want your word on it.'

'Be assured. You must take a bold decision, swiftly!'

Annaji was encouraged by Hiroji's confidence. 'You are right, Hiroji. Why wait if we have the Shahzada's support? What has Shambhu Raje ever done for me? All he did was force my daughter to commit suicide, put a stop on my earnings, remove me unceremoniously from my post, find fault with my revenue collection, and parade us all the way from Panhala to Raigad as if we were common criminals! If there is a golden opportunity to drive away such an arrogant, insensitive, injudicious and debauched Yuvraj with Shahzada Akbar's help, we must seize it!'

The very thought filled Annaji with joy.

'Annaji, how we do we make it happen?'

Annaji smiled. 'The same old game: throw Sambhaji behind bars and put Rajaram on the throne.'

The discussion continued. Shahzada Akbar would in all likelihood succeed Aurangzeb to the Mughal throne, and the idea of taking his help to remove Sambhaji seemed plausible. Annaji was now in his elements. He gave vent to his rage against Kavi Kalash, 'I say the elder Maharaj made a terrible mistake, inviting that devil for his coronation. And Sambhaji is spoiling him rotten, building a new haveli for him here as well as in Malkapur. Who the hell is he anyway? He drinks wine and eats meat! Tchah! Farzand, in the name of Lord Shiva, I take an oath to end this. It is impossible to stay any longer in such a suffocating atmosphere.'

Hiroji warned, 'Let us be careful lest we fail and are accused of treason again.'

Annaji was furious. 'Don't teach me what treason is! Sambhaji Raje joined Diler Khan. He was the one who made his father weep. He was the one who tarnished the family's name.'

Rahuji Somnath could not resist, adding, 'Raje has gone mad, believing whatever that fraudster says. We need to get out of his clutches, sooner than later.' It was late in the night but the conspirators continued to plot and plan. The lamps were refilled with oil. Someone enquired whether there was concurrence from Soyrabai's side.

Annaji said, 'Why would she refuse to support us if, when our plans succeed, she is going to be the Rajmata without so much as moving her finger?'

'But what about Balaji Chitnis?' Rahuji Somnath asked.

Annaji's enthusiasm was slightly dampened by Rahuji's question. Hiroji Farzand said, 'We presumed that Hambirrao would join us, remember? Let us not make the same mistake with Balaji now.'

Somaji Datto let out a deep sigh. 'Balaji is a devotee of Sambhaji. But we have to find a way to get him on our side if we want to succeed this time.'

'Why not finish him off?' Annaji suggested.

'Annaji, what kind of suggestion is that? Have you considered his caste?'

'What has his caste got to do with it?'

'Don't forget that, ever since Shivaji Maharaj's time, the fortkeepers have been from the Prabhu caste. If we harm Balaji, all the fortkeepers would be baying for our blood. We need to find way to convince him—with love, with wit, with affection!'

Annaji smiled. 'Farzand, your suggestion is apt. We need to win him over to our side. We will ask him to write a letter to Shahzada Akbar. I don't mind rubbing my nose on the ground in front of that Shahzada. If he helps us, we will all live happily. Forever!'

The thought of it brought tears of happiness to Annaji's eyes.

11

Evil thoughts have the power to deprive a man of peaceful rest. At an hour past midnight, sleep was far from the minds of those plotting against Sambhaji. They all got up and walked towards the residence of Balaji Chitnis. It was a dark, humid night. A dog barked somewhere in the distance. The stars were hardly visible as clouds covered the sky. Balaji came out of his room, rubbing his eyes, when the servants called out for him.

He stared at the ministers assembled in front of his haveli. Why where they here in the dead of the night?

Annaji said, 'Chitnis, we need to go immediately.'

'Where to?

'To meet Soyrabai Ranisaheb. She has called for an urgent meeting.'

Chitnis put on his sandals hurriedly. He presumed there was an urgent message from Raje at Panhala. Or else the ministers would not meet at such an odd hour. The guards outside Soyrabai's palace were surprised to see the Ashta Pradhan in the dead of the night but Annaji barked before they could react, 'What are you staring at us for? Go and wake Ranisaheb. Tell her we are here at her command.'

A little while later, Soyrabai came out. She glanced at all the men, especially Balaji. Was it the moment she had been waiting for? It was difficult for her to believe but the triumphant smile on Annaji's face gave her hope. She asked the men to step in and bolted the door behind them.

'Pant, I hope this time everyone has made up their mind.' There was doubt in Soyrabai's voice.

'Matoshree, you are going to be the Queen Mother. You cannot show fear!'

Soyrabai was clearly nervous as she fanned herself with the edge of her saree. 'Sambhaji has eyes and ears everywhere. Even if a leaf moves, he will find out.'

Annaji cleared his throat and said, 'What can I say, Ranisaheb? We had the privilege of serving Shivaji Maharaj but now everything has changed. We cannot work like this anymore. That is why we are here. Only you can save the kingdom. You must put Rajaram on the throne!'

'Careful!'

'Oh, I don't care now. Let whatever has to happen, happen now.'

Balaji Chitnis and his son Avaji looked at each other, unable to believe their ears. They felt like animals trapped in a cage. The others seemed quite unperturbed.

Annaji's directness seemed to put Soyrabai at her ease. 'I must say I was feeling suffocated here. To lead a life of an ordinary woman after being the favourite queen! There were seven other queens but Maharaj always treated me differently and with honour.'

Hiroji added, 'Ranisaheb, your days of glory can return if you wish.'

Soyrabai let out a deep sigh. 'After all, I had a queen like Jijau to guide me, as my mentor and mother-in-law. And now look at Yesu, the girl who was born yesterday! I believe she even has a seal in her name now. She orders everyone around, young and old alike. And Shambhu Raje trots around calling himself a lion cub! It is better to die than to live here anymore. My own brother Hambirrao is supporting the enemy, unfortunately. He did not welcome the possibilty that his own nephew could have been crowned. What a pity!'

Annaji was moved by Soyrabai's agony. He said, folding his hands in supplication, 'We cannot tolerate this injustice anymore, Ranisaheb! Shambhu Raje and his crony Kavi Kalash have wreaked havoc on this kingdom. We cannot allow this to continue.'

'What do you suggest, Pant?'

'We still have time. We can win back what we have lost.'

'You mean, revolt against Shambhu Raje?'

'Yes.'

'But who is going to support us?'

'A magician called Shahzada Akbar. He is Aurangzeb's favourite son. It is an opportune moment. Shambhu Raje is away in Panhala.'

Hiroji added excitedly, 'Shahzada will agree to whatever I propose. Even if we promise him half the kingdom, it will be worth it—we will get what we want.'

Soyrabai felt confidence seep into her as she heard the way the men spoke. She said, 'It does seem as if the gods are favouring us. But we must be careful and move slowly. We have to ensure that this does not leak out.'

Annaji said, 'Well, we have Balaji Pant and his son too here with us.'

Soyrabai looked at Balaji Chitnis. She could not believe that she had his support. She said, 'Chitnis, you have not spoken a word since you came in.'

Both father and son felt like rabbits caught in a hunter's net. They knew all eyes were on them. Balaji's throat was so dry that he could barely speak. He finally said, finding his voice, 'As you command, Maharanisaheb!'

'Chitnis, you and Shambhu Raje are close friends. Your children spend time at his palace. Yesubai considers your Khando and Nilo as her children.'

Rahuji Somnath spoke on his behalf, 'Maharanisaheb, Chitnis has his grouses. He does not get the respect he used to be given earlier.'

'How is that?'

'Well, Dadaji Raghunath Deshpande of Mahad is at Panhala, trying to convince Shambhu Raje to give him the post of Chitnis.'

'Is that so? And remove Balaji?' Soyrabai said, pretending to be shocked.

Rahuji added before Chitnis could speak, 'Dadaji is Kavi Kalash's friend.'

Balaji and his son, already pressured by the others planning the coup against Sambhaji, were further silenced by this new information. They promised support to Soyrabai although she did not believe them fully.

Balaji said, trying to buy time, 'Avaji had issued orders on my behalf to arrest Raje at Panhala. Since then, he has been upset with me. I am not sure how long my position will last.'

'So, what do you plan to do?'

Balaji said, 'My family ties with Shambhu Raje are a thing of the past. I cannot trust Raje anymore. I would rather lend my support to Rajaram Saheb.'

Soyrabai, Annaji Datto and the others looked at Balaji Chitnis and smiled.

12

The morning breeze at Panhala was biting cold. Kavi Kalash greeted Raje but was surprised to find him red with anger. Surely, something had happened to upset him. Sambhaji asked, 'Kaviraj, what according to you is fit punishment for an ordinary soldier or an official who commits treason?'

'The only just punishment for such a crime is death penalty, Raje!'

'What if such a criminal is a minister?'

The second question took Kavi Kalash by surprise. 'Raje, it is possible that an ordinary man could, under the influence of some personal need or greed, commit the crime. One may look at such a case with compassion, but when a minister or a senior official decides to go against the king, it is surely a dereliction of duty. The king has no choice but to make efforts to transform such a person.'

'But what if the king ignores such a crime committed by a senior minister?'

'Then the king is as ineffective as a scarecrow in the field.'

'Kaviraj, what if the senior minister, who has been pardoned once, decides to commit the crime once again?'

'If the king decides to pardon such people every now and then, he may as well abandon his throne and herd cattle.'

Sambhaji sat down with a heavy heart, repenting his earlier actions or the lack of them.

Kavi Kalash suddenly noticed a tall Rajput standing nearby. He had a striking personality, enhanced by the shapely beard. Shambhu Raje said, introducing him, 'Oh, this is Gaurav Singh. He is an emissary of Shahzada Akbar.'

Sambhaji said, 'Kaviraj, remember the day I almost died?'

'Are you talking of the poisoned fish you were about to eat?'

'Yes! I survived, thanks to the innocent kitchen workers who warned when I was about to eat the piece of fish. I threw it away, and the moment the dog ate it, he died. I realised that such an act could not carried be out by cooks. It was the work of someone in a far superior position.'

'Anyway, Gaurav Singh bears a gift, along with a message from Shahzada Akbar. It is a letter from Matoshree Soyrabai, Hiroji Farzand, Balaji Avaji Chitnis, and Annaji Datto. Read it out.'

Kavi Kalash read the letter aloud:

> *'Badshah-e-Hindustan Akbarsaheb,*
>
> *We are honoured to know a man of your valour. You have already met Hiroji Farzand. We were once fortunate to work under Shivaji Maharaj but now we are leading a life worse than those of insects. Sambhaji is a short-tempered, vengeful and debauched man. Loyal ministers like us feel suffocated serving under him. To add insult to injury, he is being advised by the ill-mannered tantric from Kanauj, Kavi Kalash. He is bent on sending us all to hell. If your honour so decides, we can easily eliminate these two devils.*
>
> *We request you to free us from them. It is up to you whether you kill them or arrest them. In exchange, we are willing to give you half our kingdom, and we ask you to allow Rajaram to ascend the Maratha throne. As for us, we loyal sardars would be content to manage a small territory with our old watans restored to us. Please release us from the clutches of Sambhaji and Kavi Kalash. We can discuss the rest of the terms when we meet in person.'*

Raje said, 'It is our good fortune that Shahzada has sent this letter to us.'

'Where are these treacherous people? Have they run away?' Kavi Kalash asked, sounding a little worried.

'No! The Shahzada has kept them guessing and tricked them into accepting an invitation to Sudhagad.'

'What about Soyrabai Matoshree?'

'She was clever enough to remain in Raigad. In case the traitors were caught red-handed, she could always deny her involvement.'

Sambhaji trembled. He wondered how the Ashta Pradhan could dream of such a treacherous act. He had, over the past year, not only run the kingdom smoothly but also forgiven their earlier crimes and reinstated them in their posts. What had made them do this, he wondered, as he banged his fists on a wooden pillar.

'Kaviraj, look at this and tell me who has written this letter.'

'It looks like Chitnis's handwriting.'

'Do you realise the depth to which this treason has percolated? This time Balaji Chitnis wrote the letter himself! What do you make of the fact that a man of such intelligence and so close to our family should participate in treason? This is no ordinary storm; a hurricane is brewing! If we don't find a way to stop it, we will get blown away like dry leaves.'

There was no point in staying at Panhalgad anymore. Kavi Kalash and Sambhaji left for Sudhagad immediately. After riding for nearly two days, they reached the base of the Sudhagad fort. Sambhaji looked up at the towering fortress, bathed in the full moon light. The traitors were holed up there!

Sambhaji reached the haveli where Shahzada Akbar and Durgadas Rathore had been put up. They embraced Sambhaji as soon as he dismounted.

'Shahzade, I am grateful for your help,' Sambhaji said, holding Shahzada Akbar's hands.

'Sambhaji Raje, your father's kingdom is one that accepts all religions without discrimination. This is why a Mughal Shahzada has come here with a Rajput and is asking for shelter,' Durgadas Rathore said.

'What an inopportune moment you have chosen! You come all the way from Delhi to seek shelter, and here we are, our ministers begging you to usurp the very throne they serve. What a shame!'

They spent the night sitting on makeshift cots outside the small haveli. Sambhaji was exhausted after a two-day ride. Seeing Raje look up at Sudhagad darkly from time to time, Akbar said, 'Don't worry, Raje! I have kept your ministers in good humour. They do not suspect anything.'

But Sambhaji was restless. He whispered to the Shahzada and Durgadas, 'Let us not wait for the morning. Send your men up there and bring those traitors here.'

'As you wish,' Akbar replied.

Sambhaji passed a restless night, lying on the cot under the night sky. Every now and then, he would wake from a fitful sleep and look towards Sudhagad. Finally he spotted a group of soldiers climbing down the fort, torches in hand. He had sent fifty of his own foot-soldiers as a precautionary measure. Soon, the men reached the base of the fort and ran towards him, shouting, 'Raje, Raje! They have escaped!' Sambhaji stood up startled. Akbar and Durgadas Rathore look bewildered too. One of the soldiers panted, 'There is a narrow path through the forest on the other side. They ran away before we could reach the fort.'

'But how did they know you were approaching? You walked through forests under the cover of night!'

'We had to cross a barren piece of land at one point. In the moonlight, it is not difficult to make out a cavalry of a thousand odd men marching through, Raje!'

'You are right!' Sambhaji said, sighing heavily. 'Annaji has an eagle eye. That old fox must have spotted you!'

A dejected Sambhaji sat down on his cot. Shahzada Akbar and Durgadas Rathore looked confused and worried. After a while, Raje said, 'Well, whatever had to happen has happened. But where will those traitors go? Annaji cannot move without a palanquin. Balaji's age does not allow him to ride a horse. The only one capable of running is Farzand Kaka. But no one will allow anyone to go ahead, so the traitors will slow each other down!'

Sambhaji called out to his men, 'Jotyaji, Rupaji! Let us move! Those traitors will still be in the ravines on the other side of the fort. Search the forests before dawn, and once you find them, tie them to a tree and inform me.'

It was a sad day for any king who had pardoned his treacherous ministers and reinstated them with full honours. The very same men had decided to stab him in the back. It was a terrible shock for Sambhaji and he was in no mood to engage in discussions of any kind with Shahzada Akbar and Durgadas. He said, 'Let us meet in another fortnight or so.'

13

The next morning Sambhaji had a quick bath before performing his morning prayers. Soon, Jotyaji and Rupaji returned. Their beaming faces told Sambhaji that the mission had been successful.

'We caught them and tied them up in a cowherd's shed. Some of our troops are posted nearby and we have asked them to guard the prisoners.'

Sambhaji asked his men to assemble below a tree. He folded his hands to salute some of the older soldiers who were too embarrassed to look into his eyes. Then he said, in a voice choking with pain, 'You are aware that the senior ministers of the Swaraj wanted me to be arrested rather than exercise my hereditary right to ascend the throne. Instead of me, they wanted a ten-year-old boy to be coronated. Not stopping at that, they sent an army to capture me at Panhala. Despite their treasonous acts, I pardoned them and treated them with honour. In the past year, what crime have I committed for them to repeat their treachery? While putting up a show of loyalty each day, they now try to get the Shahzada on their side to conspire against me! I want the ryots to decide how these traitors should be treated.'

An old man with bushy whiskers, strong despite his age, said, 'Raje, you cannot tolerate this any more! You must make a decision like a real king—harsh yet just.'

'Hang those traitors!' A few of them shouted.

Another man added, 'Have you forgotten how the elder Maharaj punished those who revolted against him? Remember how he had dealt with Chandrarao More of Jawli. He dragged his two sons to Pune and had them beheaded in a crowded bazaar!'

'I had not expected Annaji Datto to change his treacherous ways. But I am shattered by the way Hiroji Farzand Kaka has behaved. Somehow, I am not willing to believe that Balaji Chitnis could have participated in this act willingly. I don't doubt his loyalty.'

'He wrote the letter himself. He is here with the other traitors. What more proof do you want, Raje?'

Sambhaji knew he had to make a decision now. He said, turning to Kavi Kalash, 'I sentence Hiroji Farzand, Annaji Datto, Somaji, and Avaji Chitnis to death, to be trampled beneath the feet of an elephant. But I want Balaji Chitnis to be chained and brought to Raigad. Put him in prison there.'

The men were unable to understand why Raje would be so sympathetic towards Balaji. They looked at him suspiciously. Kavi Kalash kept looking at Sambhaji but did not move an inch. He said, 'Raje, I feel you must be present when the orders are executed.'

Sambhaji smiled wryly. He said, 'It seems you still don't know me, Kaviraj. I have seen these men, the ones who are traitors now, with my father for more than twenty years. What if I am tempted to change my decision when I see their faces? No, Kaviraj! I cannot relent this time. In order to stop such revolts, it is imperative that we execute the punishment meted out to them.'

'Raje, why don't you send some Maratha or a Brahmin to carry out the sentence? I am just an outsider ...' Kavi Kalash pleaded with folded hands.

'We don't have time to lose, Kaviraj. You must execute my orders at once. I am content to be labelled as a murderer as long as I preserve from harm the Swaraj so lovingly created by Abasaheb's hard work.

Kavi Kalash pleaded with Sambhaji to be excused from the task. 'I am already labelled as a tantric, as one who practises black magic. I will be considered responsible for these deaths. Please do not send me, Raje!'

'Whom else can I send? Hambir Mama is not here. Kaviraj, this time it is the king's dearest friend who has to bear the brunt!'

Kavi Kalash had no option but to go. Sambhaji asked him to take Dadaji Raghunath Desphande along with him as a witness. Kavi Kalash pleaded once more before leaving, 'Raje, think twice! No doubt treason is a grave crime, but I wonder if you would be labelled as someone who is responsible for the killing of Brahmins.'

'I don't care! I know the scales of justice do not differentiate on the basis of caste. It is the crime which needs to be punished.'

14

Sambhaji halted his horse at the base of Raigad. He looked at the Takmak Tok, the steep point from which criminals were flung to their death. The dark ragged cliff looked menacing. Sambhaji patted the his horse affectionately and dismounted.

'I will not be proceeding to the capital for another four days. I will be here at Pachad, in Jijausaheb's palace. I want to spend a few days here.'

Kavi Kalash, Rupaji, Dadaji and Jotyaji started their ascent to Raigad. Shambhu Raje turned his horse towards Pachad. The news of his arrival had reached the people even before he reached the town. The ryots were celebrating the execution of the traitors. Balaji Chitnis too had met the same punishment, and was trampled by an elephant.

Sambhaji was in deep distress. While he had ordered the punishment deep inside he felt something was amiss. Four elephants now stood at the entrance of Jijabai's palace. They were decked up to welcome Sambhaji and looked resplendent in their caparisons of fine embroidered cloth. But a glance at their bloodstained feet sent a shiver down Sambhaji's spine.

Trumpets announced the arrival of Raje at Pachad, and within a few hours, Yesubai had descended from the fort to receive him. Kaviraj's wife Tejasbai accompanied her. Kavi Kalash, who had met them halfway up the path, joined them.

Yesubai said, seeing Sambhaji's surprise, 'It was I who suggested that Kaviraj should come here. People at the fort are up in arms against him. They are blaming him for the way the traitors were put to death.'

'But the orders were issued by me. He only executed them!'

'That may be true, Raje, but a few angry men tried to burn down his haveli. I thought it was safer for Kaviraj and Tejasbai to spend some time here.'

There was a desolate air about the palace at Pachad that night. Yesubai was relieved that the traitors had been eliminated, but was distressed by Balaji Chitnis's death. Balaji's haveli was not far from Yesubai's palace and she had heard the heart-rending cries of Lakshmibai, Balajipant's old widow. Unable to bear the torture anymore, she had decided to come down to Pachad and meet Raje there.

Yesubai remembered her last interaction with Balaji. Somaji Datto and Hiroji Farzand were with him. As they saluted, Yesubai had asked whey they were on the way to Pali when Raje was at Panhala.

'Some work given by Raje, Ranisaheb,' Balaji had replied, a little hesitantly.

'What work?'

It was Hiroji who answered, 'Raje has instructed Chitnis to meet Shahzada Akbar.'

Balaji Chitnis had walked a few steps when he stopped and turned, removing his turban and placing it on his chest. 'Maharanisaheb, I am tired now ... I feel like I must retire. Whatever happens, I wish you would take care of Khandoba and Niloba.'

'And where is Avaji these days?' Yesubai had asked.

'He too is coming with us,' Hiroji replied.

'Chitnis, why are you speaking in such morose tones? You are going to meet the Shahzada for a discussion, not to wage war.'

'What for we need war? I may die just mounting or dismounting a horse. You will care for my children, I hope.'

Before Yesubai could respond, Somaji Datto had interrupted, 'We must leave; shall we?'

It was the last time Yesubai had seen Balaji. He was wiping his tears as he walked away behind Hiroji and Somaji.

Both Yesubai and Sambhaji were restless that night. The silence of Jijabai's palace weighed on them. Balaji Chitnis was no ordinary man. Shivaji Maharaj had looked upon him as a brother and never questioned his loyalty to the Swaraj. It was Balaji whom the elder Maharaj had sent as his envoy to Rajputana, to retrieve papers attesting to Shivaji's connection with the Sisodiya family. A man with a sharp intellect, he had a remarkable memory and the ability to ingest long paragraphs from treaties and reproduce them verbatim in his neat, cursive handwriting.

Sleep eluded Sambhaji as he tossed and turned in his bed. Yesubai said, 'Raje, they were not ordinary men. Whenever people recall Maharaj's visit to Agra, they will talk of Hiroji Farzand.'

Yesubai's words pierced Sambhaji's heart. He rose from his bed.

'Yesu, it was painful for me to take their lives. You cannot believe the turmoil I went through when I issued the orders. But when senior ministers in the durbar start plotting against their king, must the king write a letter of pardon and touch their feet? I arrived at the decision after much deliberation. Yesu, all these men were veterans who have served on the administrative council since Abasaheb's reign, but they committed the worst crime of all—treason. And as a king, it was my duty to see that they were punished. But I am saddened by the fact that people are blaming Kavi Kalash. He, in fact, was very reluctant to carry out the order.'

'Should you not have been a little lax when it came to Chitnis?'

'In fact, I had only instructed Kavi Kalash to arrest him. But when the guards were about to execute Avaji, Balaji Pant jumped in between and started shouting that he would allow them to touch Avaji only if he were first trampled under the elephant's feet. Kaviraj immediately sent a messenger to me, asking for my opinion. I was in a dilemma. If I let both father and son live, I realised, I must let everyone go scot-free. I had no choice but to decide to punish all those who had been part of the plot ...'

Sambhaji and Yesubai slept fitfully. At dawn, a message was delievered by a soldier who seemed to have travelled a great distance and was visibly exhausted. Sambhaji was shocked the moment he saw the beautiful cursive writing. His mind reeled with the emotions of repentance, anger and fear. He rushed into the room, shouting. 'Yesu, Yesu ...!'

'Yesu,' Sambhaji stuttered, not able to find words. 'This was sent to me but I had already left to confront the traitors at Sudhagad. This letter written by Chitnis was never seen by me, Yesu. He had tried to warn me about the plot. Oh, look at my cursed fate, Yesu! I was never to receive this in time!'

Yesubai stared at Sambhaji, wide-eyed, before reading the message.

'Salute to Shriraja Shambhu Chhattrapati from Balaji Avaji Chitnis.

The moment you left for Panhala, a plot to overthrow you has started rearing its head. Your senior ministers are once again planning to stage a coup and put Chiranjeev Rajaram on the throne. Unfortunately, the same officials whom you pardoned are once again joining hands. The plan is to meet Shahzada Akbar at Pali and take his help to throw you out, Swami.

In your absence, I have been forced to participate in this dangerous and vile plot. My son Avaji and I are being forcibly taken to meet Shahzada Akbar. They compelled me to write letters detailing our plot to the Shahzada. I have somehow managed to find time to write this and I hope it will reach you, with the blessings of the Lord, in time. My son and I feel that we are trapped in the coils of a python and are praying that you come and release us. The rest I leave to my destiny!

When the elder Maharaj died, they had forced Avaji to write a letter on my behalf. Now I too have been forced to write with a sword at my neck.

I cannot explain how I felt while writing that letter, against my wishes. But Swami, you are Saraswati's son, a man of knowledge! You may throw your tantrums but you are large-hearted. I bless you, Shambhubal and Yesurani: may you have a long and blessed life.

If I survive, thanks to the Lord's blessings, I will be at your service for as long as I live. If I don't, I will meet my Lord. I wish you good health!'

Somehow, leaning on a wooden pillar, Sambhaji sat down. He was sweating profusely. Gulping water from a silver vessel, he said, 'Yesu, what a misfortune! Now I understand why Balaji was repeatedly asking Kavi whether I had received any letters!'

Sambhaji's grief was beyond consolation. For the first time after his father's death, he once again sobbed like a child. Yesubai put a hand on his shoulder, trying to pacify.

'Swami, take charge of yourself. We will treat their sons, Khando Ballal and Nilo Ballal, as our own. We will give them a chance to serve us. We will nurture them as one cares for a tender sapling.'

TEN

The Invasion

1

In Raigad, Sambhaji and had immersed himself in work in order to forget the nightmares which tormented him. He often rode alone to the temple of Jagadeeshwar, seeking solace in the cool silence, but it eluded him. The threat of Aurangzeb's descent on the Deccan was very real and Sambhaji spent some time inspecting the ammunition stores. However, all his efforts to bury himself in work had not helped.

The image of Balaji Chitnis, with his grey eyes and loving face, would not leave his mind. Kalash had narrated in detail how the executions had been carried out. Annaji Datto had faced death without batting an eyelid. Perhaps he had known for a long time that someday he would be punished with death for treason. Balaji Chitnis, on the other hand, had met his tragic end with great agony. He had explained everything in his last letter to Sambhaji but it was never to reach Raje in time. Sambhaji felt no guilt for having put the traitors to death, but owing to their intrigues and treachery, he had been responsible for the death of a man whose loyalty and affection to the throne were undoubted. This grieved him deeply.

As he was climbing up the palace steps one day, he suddenly stopped. He realised that he had punished all but one of the traitors who had plotted against him. She was still alive and living in the royal quarters! There was a clamour among the guards, servants and other attendants when they saw a grim-faced Sambhaji enter the main hall. Terrified, they rushed to inform Soyrabai of his arrival, quickly closing the door leading to her private chambers behind them.

Reaching the door, Sambhaji growled, 'Matoshree, closing the doors and windows is not going to hide your sins. The first time I had you placed under house arrest, I had warned you to behave as a real mother would! Unfortunately, you have crossed the very limits of treachery. Instead of a Rajmata, all I see is a woman who is selfish, cunning and conniving. Why are you hiding now? Open the door!'

Sambhaji's heart burned with anger. He shouted, 'Matoshree, your deed is worse than that of Queen Kaikeyi in the Ramayana. Despite my being the true heir to the throne, you plotted with your men to arrest me! Not once, but twice, you tried to kill me! For mere selfish gain, you are willing to give away half the kingdom to Aurangzeb's son? What kind of a Matoshree are you? You don't deserve to be called one!'

The servants and guards on the other side of the door were a worried lot. At that moment, Yesubai came marching in with firm footsteps and said, holding Sambhaji's raised hand, 'Dear! You are a Raje! And you must behave like one.'

Sambhaji brushed Yesubai's hand off, saying, 'Shouldn't the Rajamata behave like one? Should our Ashta Pradhan kowtow to a Mughal emperor? Should they plot to kill me?'

'Raje, restrain yourself …'

'Let me go, Yesubai! Had she not been Rajaram's mother, I would have punished her by burying her alive!'

Yesubai shivered at the sight of Sambhaji's fury. Then she caught sight of ten-year-old Rajaram, holding onto a pillar as he stared at his elder brother, eyes wide with fear. With tears in her eyes, Yesubai held Sambhaji's hand and turned him towards Rajaram. Sambhaji, coming to his senses, rushed to him and hugged him. He said, as he wiped Rajaram's tears, 'You know dear, your tears have such strength! Just two drops and they deluge me!'

Picking him up affectionately, Sambhaji put Rajaram on his horse and rode towards the temple. Yesubai and Raigad heaved a sigh of relief.

2

Yesubai was surprised to see Kavi Kalash so early in the morning. However, it was evident he was suffering from tremendous anxiety. Yesubai could understand the reason for his distress. Ever since he had carried out executions of the traitors, Kavi Kalash had held himself responsible for the untimely and unfortunate killing of Balaji Chitnis.

'Please relieve me of my duties,' he said, prostrating before Yesubai. 'I want to go back to Kanauj.'

'Why, is anything the matter there?'

'No, Maharanisaheb. I want to retire permanently.'

Yesubai said sympathetically, 'I understand, Kaviraj. Often, when the wood burns, a few leaves get singed. Balaji Chitnis' death was the result of an unfortunate misunderstanding … because of his letter not reaching Raje in time. You don't know how troubled he is! He mumbles and shouts in his sleep every night.'

'Ranisaheb, I tried to dissuade Raje but unfortunately he was unaware of the letter then. However, now my enemies have one more reason to hate me,' Kavi Kalash said, clutching Yesubai's feet. 'Let me go; I cannot stay here anymore!'

'Kaviraj, if you leave in this manner, your enemies would celebrate while Raje will be the loser. To be frank, I need you here. You know how difficult it is to manage the tornado called Shambhu!'

She continued, 'Whether it is a play from Kalidas, a poem from the Gita Govinda, or a Sufi song, it is you he wishes to discuss it with. It is due to your influence that he has composed the Budhabhushanam in Sanskrit, and the Nakhashikha, Satasataka and Nayikabheda in the Brij dialect. He has people like Hambir Mama, Mhaloji Ghorpade, Rupaji Bhosale and others by his side on the battlefield, but only you who can accompany him when he wants to be in the garden of Saraswati.'

Kavi Kalash was silent, not knowing how to react.

'There are many opportunists who have joined Raje. They have their selfish reasons. But Raje is struggling to hold onto the old loyalists while priming the new generation to take over. At such a time, if dear friends like you go away, who will he look up to?'

'Ranisaheb, I am accused of black magic while I find dolls and lemons with pins stuck in them outside my door each day. I am really worried!' Kavi Kalash folded his hands in supplication.

'Do you think Raje gives credence to such accusations? I myself would have smashed the head of such a fraudster!'

Kavi Kalash let out a sigh of relief.

Yesubai continued, 'Shivaji Maharaj has seen you for more than twelve years. If he had believed that his Yuvraj was being influenced by someone who practises black magic, would he not have ordered his execution? Listen to me now! Forget your plans to leave for Kanauj. Raje is burdened by many battles. The Siddis at Janjira have been emboldened by the patronage of the Mughals. We have the Portuguese, Dutch and the English to worry about. There are dark clouds on the horizon. Aurangzeb can arrive here at any moment. Our administration is yet to be streamlined. Not to mention the traitors, waiting to revolt! In such times, Kaviraj, Raje needs a matured, experienced mentor and father-figure like you.'

3

Alamgir Aurangzeb departed from Ajmer in September 1681 with a huge army of nearly five lakh men, and another hundred thousand men comprising servants, cooks, water-bearers and palanquin-bearers. It was not an army. It was a city on the move.

Aurangzeb sat at a makeshift tent set up near a stream for a brief rest. He had been on the throne for more than three decades. His robust health belied his sixty-three years. Very few could withstand his penetrating gaze.

A select group of men including Kazi Abdul Wahab and Wazir Asad Khan sat with Aurangzeb.

'Jahanpanah,' Asad Khan began, 'your rule extends from Kabul in the west to Bengal and Assam in the east, and upto Burhanpur and Khandesh in the south. No one today dares to look into your eyes. You are amongst the most powerful emperors on this earth.'

Kazi asked, 'Jahanpanah, how long would we be in the South?'

Aurangzeb replied in a serious tone, 'You are not aware of the difficulty the Deccan poses. Even Emperor Akbar did not succeed in capturing it. My Abbajaan, Shah Jahan, managed to defeat the Nizam at Ahmadnagar. Golconda and Bijapur are under the control of Shia Muslims while the whole of Maharashtra is ruled by the Marathas. The terrain, while it looks deceptively simple, is not easy to capture.'

No other Mughal emperor had marched with an army of such gigantic proportions. Sitting in his howdah, Aurangzeb could see the three lakh cavalrymen, two lakh foot-soldiers, and an ocean of men, animals and carts stretching as far as the eye could see. Such an army would be a matter of pride for any emperor and certain to scare the living daylights out of any opponent. Aurangzeb believed the Shahs of Golconda and Bijapur would soon be running for cover. He imagined the 'kafir' Sambhaji would behave like a frightened mouse upon hearing of his massive onslaught. Yet, somehow, the Shahenshah felt he was not yet able to put a finger on the pulse of the Deccan.

Aurangzeb was restless. The way his favourite Shahzada, Akbar, had treated him still rankled.

The Mughals had always managed to keep hundreds of Rajput rajas and sardars under their heels. After Raja Jaswant Singh's death, Aurangzeb had refused to acknowledge his son as his heir, provoking the ire of the Rajputs who joined forces against Aurangzeb. But the wily emperor, using political and other stratagems, was able to avoid a direct confrontation. At that crucial moment, Shahzada Akbar had chosen to revolt against his father and managed to garner support in Rajputana. But once again, Aurangzeb's wiles won the day and Akbar had to run away to the Deccan to save himself. Akbar had taken the help of Durgadas Rathore, son of one of Raja Jaswant's ministers.

Aurangzeb said, when Asad Khan congratulated him on his victory in Rajputana, 'I may have won the war but a Badshah has lost his Shahzada and a father his son!'

It was not an easy task to be the Emperor's confidante. His four begums had found it impossible but Wazir Asad Khan, a cousin of Aurangzeb's, had managed to fill the post for many years. Asad Khan was not able to understand why the Emperor had taken Akbar's revolt so much to heart.

Meanwhile, Aurangzeb recalled the days of his youth. As an eighteen-year-old, he had been given the onerous responsibility of the Subedari of the Deccan by Shah Jahan. But the young Shahzada had realised that his father's true motive was to send him away. No Shahzada would wish to be far away from the throne and the riches. But Shah Jahan had rightly understood the over-ambitious nature of his young son. He had sensed that Aurangzeb—reticent, secretive and serious by nature—would likely become a threat to his throne. Shah Jahan also wanted to protect his favourite son, Dara Shikoh. He knew that if the tree called Aurangzeb developed its roots in the capital, it would one day spread deep and wide enough to destroy the walls of the palace.

But a strong tree will grow roots even in dirt. As the Deccan Subedar, Aurangzeb showed his mettle, expanding the boundaries of the Mughal province rapidly. He defeated Malik Ambar and razed the city of Khadki, renaming it Aurangabad. Aurangzeb was also confident of defeating the Shia rulers in Bijapur, hoping to earn his father's praise, but intervention by Dara Shikoh at the last moment spoilt his chances.

When Shah Jahan died, Aurangzeb had to rush to Delhi. He had always dismissed Shivaji as no more than an arrogant landlord. But he warned his thanedar before leaving for the capital, 'Be careful of that rebel! He is getting too big for his boots.'

Aurangzeb was stuck in the north for nearly twenty-five years after ascending the throne, occupied with administrative tasks and military campaigns in Kabul-Kandahar, as well as in Bihar and Bengal.

Now, sitting in his tent, Aurangzeb recalled how he had erred in not sending Shivaji and Sambhaji on the campaign in Kabul. 'I had plans to finish them off in the ravines there. What a terrible mistake I made!' Aurangzeb confessed to Asad Khan. 'The day Shivaji called the Brahmins from Kashi and coronated himself was one of the most disappointing days in my life. I rubbed my nose on the floor when I heard the news and begged Allah for forgiveness.'

'Why should an ordinary zamindar's so-called coronation upset you so much, Jahanpanah?' Asad Khan asked.

'Wazir-e-Azam, a ryot decides to ascend the throne and calls himself a Maharaja! The very thought is disturbing!'

'I am told Sambha calls himself a lion's cub!'

'Huh! He is just a mosquito.'

'How long will it take to rout him?'

Aurangzeb caressed his long white beard and raised a finger in the air.

'Just a year?' Kazi was surprised.

The Badshah merely nodded.

Apart from the enormous cavalry and the giant infantry, Aurangzeb's army boasted nearly three thousand five hundred elephants which carried the Mughal sardars. Behind them were the seventy-odd elephants of the royal zenana. It included the begums, the princesses, the Badshah's daughters-in-law and the families of the the senior mansabdars. Udepuri Begum sat in an exquisite sandalwood howdah. The Badshah's favourite daughter, Zeenat-un-Nissa, sat beside her. Hundreds of Khojas, the royal eunuch guards, and Kashmiri and Afghan women guards walked alongside. The zenana was a sight to behold with its silver- and gold-plated howdahs, not to mention the accompanying fanfare. Behind the elephants, with their swaying gait and wide eyes, walked nearly fifty thousand camels with their mounted troops. Aurangzeb's personal effects and other paraphernalia alone required fourteen hundred camels, four hundred carts and a hundred and fifty elephants. Around two hundred and fifty bazaars from Delhi followed the massive caravan.

Wherever the caravan city camped, it spread across more than twenty miles. The men accompanying the Badshah were an excited lot. 'The moment the Marathas see our vast army, they will run for cover! The mountain rats, those kafirs ... they would bury themselves in the ground in fear!'

Thousands of men went ahead of the caravan, clearing the path for the huge carriages to roll by, especially the ones carrying cannons. Aurangzeb had seventy cannons, some so large that they required twenty pairs of bulls to pull them. Elephants were put to work when they had to be transported over hills or across rivers. Apart from the huge old-fashioned cannons, the artillery was equipped with three hundred new brass cannons manned by artillery experts who were mostly of English, French, Dutch, German and Portuguese origin.

Aurangzeb was the richest of the Mughal emperors, thanks to the wealth hoarded by generations of Mughals. It had been looted from every corner of Hindustan—be it Kabul, Kandahar, Agra, Mathura, Kashi, Bengal, Orissa, Malwa or Gujarat. Confronting such wealth, and an ocean-like army with hundreds of thousands of soldiers, the Marathas looked like a small rabbit facing an elephant. In terms of their geographical extent and the size of their treasury, the Maratha kingdom was smaller than a single Subah of the Mughal Empire. There were twenty-two such provinces under Mughal rule!

Aurangzeb marched with the confidence of a conqueror certain of his victory. To add to his assurance, his arch enemy Shivaji was no more. Sambhaji had taken over a year and a half ago. Many of Shivaji's old sardars had already sworn allegiance to the Badshah. Their letters read, 'Alampanah, you rule the entire world. Please come to the Deccan at the earliest and redeem us from the cruel Sambhaji!' Aurangzeb was sure that he could simply crush Sambhaji like an insect.

One evening, the advance party had cleared a hilltop for the royal tents. Nearby Aurangzeb's tent were the royal hammams and the sentinel posts guarding his family. Aurangzeb's elephant sat down near the Badshah's tent. The khidmatgars brought a silver ladder for the Emperor to dismount. Aurangzeb stepped down slowly as he surveyed the landscape surrounding the camp. In the distance, just beyond the hills, the sun was setting. Aurangzeb looked at the massive caravan of his army, spread across dozens of miles.

While the cantonment busied itself with various tasks, Aurangzeb, along with his select sardars, performed the evening namaaz. After some discussion with the sardars, he returned to the Gulalbar—the area reserved for the royals.

It was an important evening. The Badshah had invited the royals, all his senior sardars, and a few other guests for a 'bada khana,' a feast. The guests had already arrived in the Gulalbar. The begum entered, led by Udepuri Begum. They were followed by the shahzadas, Muazzam, Kam Baksh and Azam Shah, and all his grandsons. Those in the durbar stood up on seeing the royals enter. Asad Khan stood behind Aurangzeb. To his right stood Aurangzeb's cousin, Zulfikar Khan. Aurangzeb had appointed his close relatives to key posts in the army and the administration.

The banquet was quite an event, as the Emperor rarely indulged in any form of extravagance. His interests lay in politics and prayers. He abhorred music and dance. He was rarely, if ever, known to smile. Muazzam and Azam were terrified on receiving any message from their father. Such was the fear Aurangzeb inspired that despite having been invited to a grand feast, the men in the durbar were on tenterhooks, praying to Allah lest they do something to attract the Emperor's ire.

Aurangzeb entered the durbar, acknowledging the salutes of his guests. His slim figure exuded the energy of a much younger man. His favourite daughter, Zeenat-un-Nissa, followed. Earlier, his elder daughter Zebunissa had occupied that coveted place in his affections, but the moment it became clear that she had played a role in Akbar's revolt, Aurangzeb had her imprisoned for the rest of her life in a dungeon in Salimgad fort.

After a relatively quiet dinner, Aurangzeb said, his voice tinged with pride, 'I use only two weapons in the battlefield—my sword and my intelligence. And I find the latter more effective!'

Asad Khan, encouraged by the Badshah's words, ventured, 'You remember the way Alamgir was able to make that Rajput dog Durgadas Rathore and the unfortunate Shahzada Akbar run for their lives. That battle was won without shedding a drop of blood!'

Aurangzeb said, his voice solemn, as he looked at his guests with piercing eyes, 'I have one more weapon—sharper and more dangerous than the other two.' He took a small dagger from the girdle at his waist and raised it, as he spoke. 'If someone tries to commit treachery, this dagger goes into his stomach to come out only after breaking a few ribs!'

He continued to scan the faces of those present. 'Many brave Emperors have sat on the throne at Delhi. Many of them were connoisseurs of art. Jahangir sahab spent half his life painting. But I am made of a different clay. My hands itch to hold a sword. I am hungry for the blood of enemies which flows on the battlefield. My Abbajaan, Shah Jahan sahab, wasted his entire life building beautiful tombs and palaces. Emperor Akbar used to love embracing the Rajputs. I am not in favour of fondling snakes! I am not enamoured by displays of affection from the enemy. On the other hand, I have great regard for Allauddin Khilji sahab. He knew how to treat his subjects, be they ordinary folk, dogs or horses. He treated all animals with the same contempt. I, too, rule with my sword on the common man's neck.'

Shahzada Azam was not present in the durbar. He had been sent ahead to investigate the whereabouts of Sambhaji. However, it was his eldest son Muazzam whom Aurangzeb considered the one most capable and trustworthy when it came to carrying out a dangerous mission.

'I have undertaken this campaign in the Deccan despite my age. However, it is also a test for my two capable shahzadas. It is time to decide who will ascend the throne once I step down.'

Muazzam looked at his father, surprised. Azam's wife looked around, unable to believe what she had just heard. Aurangzeb's face darkened, as he remembered something. He said, after a pause, 'In fact, neither Azam nor Muazzam have the credentials to ascend the throne. It is my misfortune that the one who really was capable turned out to be a fool. I pity him. Allah gave him all he wanted but, thanks to his stupidity, he has lost everything now.'

Aurangzeb's heart bled. The very thought of Shahzada Akbar and his treachery was difficult for him to bear. The durbar was stunned. Very rarely did they see the Badshah express his feelings so openly. Stung by the memory of Akbar's rebellion, Aurangzeb thundered, 'Anyone who tries to revolt against me will be reduced to ashes. It is only I who know the true art of treachery. When my own father turned senile, I did not hesitate to teach him a lesson. I assassinated my brothers while my sister, who took their side, was thrown into a dark dungeon. I did not allow my father to decide who the next Badshah would be. But let me make this clear: I alone am going to decide who my successor will be! The shahzada who wins this campaign, the one who crushes that ignorant Sambhaji—he is the one whom I will crown as the Emperor with my own hands.'

4

Hambirrao was in Raigad to requisition some ammunition and a pay rise for his soldiers. After a meeting with Yesubai, he was surprised to receive a message from Soyrabai requesting his audience. In the year and a half since Sambhaji's ascension, he had not met his sister even once. In fact, Hambirrao had made a few attempts to meet Soyrabai but she had refused to see him.

Hambirrao knew the reason behind his Akkasaheb's anger and refusal to meet him. He remembered the bitter words which Soyrabai had spoken: 'Why blame anyone else when he himself did not wish his own nephew to ascend the throne?'

It had been two months since Sambhaji had almost knocked down the door leading to her inner quarters. After that, the residents of Raigad had seen Soyrabai only once, when she had visited the temple. She had confined herself to her palace. Rumours of her failing health were doing the rounds. Yesubai had visited to enquire about her health and ensured that the royal physician and hakeem were looking after her.

Hambirrao was shocked when he saw his sister. Soyrabai was a pale shadow of her former self. With her white saree, creased forehead, dark circles around her eyes and an emaciated body, she resembled a nun living the life of an ascetic for years. Her voice too had lost its charm and sounded faint. She asked her brother to pull up a chair.

Hambirrao said, 'You seem so tired, Akkasaheb!'

'Let it be, Hambir! Raje is no more and I have committed a sin I shouldn't have. Why aspire to live any longer?'

'I am sorry, Akkasaheb. But I was not able to support you in any manner.'

'Oh, forget that, Hambir! I was angry at you initially, but when I look at the events dispassionately, I do realise that you did what was right. I must congratulate you!'

'I remember the day of my appointment as commander-in-chief, not long before Rajaram's marriage,' Hambirrao said. 'The elder Maharaj had said, 'I am giving you this post not because you are my brother-in-law but because of your capabilities."'

'He had the knack of spotting talent.'

They were meeting after a long time and Hambirrao felt relieved to be able to speak freely. 'The elder Maharaj had told me after meeting

Shambhu Raje at Panhala, "Hambirrao, I am now confident that the kingdom is safe in Shambhu's hands. Rajaram is a still a child."'

'I see!' Soyrabai said.

'Akkasaheb, let me say this: I may have not have taken my sister's side but I did what a loyal servant of the Hindavi Swaraj should do.'

Soyrabai said, gazing into the distance, 'You know Sambhaji was very dear to me when I came to Raigad. But when Rajaram was born, I inadvertently started thinking of his future. I was influenced by others who accused Shambhu Raje of being cruel, addicted to wine and women. I started believing in those lies. Now I know it was my greed which made me act as I did!'

Hambirrao looked around the room. 'Where is Rajaram saheb these days?'

'Whenever Shambhu Raje is at the fort, he forgets everything and everyone else. Shambhu Raje, despite the differences he has had with me, loves Rajaram the same way he did earlier. For Rajaram, he has taken the place of the elder Maharaj. Yesu too treats him like a son. He does not need me now!'

'Akkasaheb, please don't be so morose!'

'Hambirrao, I can confide in you as my younger brother. I committed terrible crimes with my eyes wide open. I don't feel like living anymore. I feel ashamed even when I go to the temple. People see me as a sly, selfish and dangerous woman, don't they?'

'Akkasaheb, you must take care of your health. You must rest …'

'Hambirrao, guilt and regret torment me all the time. Aurangzeb, who has been our enemy for three generations, is finally marching on us. It is my duty to be by Shambhubal's side, offering him solace and counsel. But I got caught in my own selfish politics and sided with the traitors! I nurtured devious thoughts of eliminating him. I feel ashamed of myself …'

Soyrabai had tears in her eyes. She had a coughing fit and a maid rushed in with a tumbler of water.

'Akkasaheb, you must pay attention to your health. Don't worry about anything else now.'

Hambirrao was about to leave when Soyrabai said to him. 'Give Yesubai my message. Tell her that I am not worried anymore, now that Rajaram is under her care.'

On 27 October 1681, the palace was rent by cries. Soyrabai's frail body lay on her bed. She had breathed her last. By the time Rajaram and

Sambhaji rushed into her room, the royal physician diagnosed that she had committed suicide by swallowing a diamond the previous night.

Sambhaji performed Soyrabai's last rites at a spot not far away from where the elder Maharaj had been consigned to flames. By evening, the ceremonies were over. The palace was full of people who had come to pay their respects.

Sambhaji said, 'She may have been wrong to think only of her son's advancement and conspire with those who wanted to finish me off. But I cannot forget the way she took care of Abasaheb in his youth and looked after me when I was a child. It would be unfair to cast aspersions that she tried to poison the elder Maharaj, whom she loved so much!'

5

'Sambhaji Raje, Aurangzeb is spreading terror across Hindustan. He has imposed the unfair Jizya tax on the Hindus. Only someone like you has the intelligence and strength to defeat a sinful bigot like my father,' Akbar said.

'The Shahzada's right, Raje. We left Delhi and Rajputana, Shahzada and I, to confer with you at Raigad and lend our support for that purpose.' Durgadas Rathore added.

Sambhaji had reached Sudhagad the previous evening and stayed the night at a haveli in the fort. He was now meeting Akbar and Durgadas at the base of the fort in the village of Dhondse. After the formalities where they had exchanged expensive clothes, Arabian steeds and precious gems, they got down to discussing business. Sambhaji looked at Shahzada Akbar. Although slightly rotund, and of medium height, he was still a rather attractive-looking prince.

'Let us meet at the fort tomorrow and discuss the details.'

'Raje, you may take Durgadas with you right now. I will come over tomorrow,' Akbar said.

'Why not today?'

'Raje, I somehow manage to survive the rains here. I am not particularly fond of the cold weather up there.'

The next morning, Sambhaji and Durgadas, after finishing their prayers, took a round of the fort. Durgadas had a pleasing personality and appearance. He was a tall man with a typical Rajputana beard. His angst was visible. Durgadas's dream was to unite all the Ranas in Rajputana under a single banner, finish Aurangzeb off and install Shahzada Akbar as the Mughal emperor. His love for Rajputana, loyalty to the Shahzada, and respect for Sambhaji was evident from his behaviour.

Raja Jaswant Singh of Jodhpur had been loyal to the Mughals and had participated in the Kabul-Kandahar campaigns. He died fighting at Khyber Pass. Instead of mourning the death of a loyal ally, the Badshah was delighted at the prospect of annexing his kingdom to the Mughal Empire. The Raja's wife was pregnant when he died. The Rajputs demanded that his newborn son Ajit Singh be declared the king of Jodhpur.

Aurangzeb laughed at the suggestion, saying, 'Why not? But on one condition. Ajit Singh and his mother should adopt the Muslim religion.'

The loyal Durgadas could not tolerate the arrogant and hurtful suggestion made by Aurangzeb. 'I will see that he is dead before I do any such thing!' Durgadas made a promise to himself as he walked away from the Mughal durbar.

The very memory of the incident made Durgadas turn red with anger. 'Our people have sacrificed their lives for the Mughals since the time of Akbar and Raja Mansingh. Three generations have passed. But Aurangzeb cannot think beyond religion. Look at the imposition of Jizya tax!'

'Why haven't the Hindus in the empire revolted?'

'Well, one day, he was on his way to the Masjid on his elephant when a few Hindus tried to appeal to him to lift the tax. Instead of hearing them out, he ordered the elephant to crush them. It was then that Rajputana erupted.'

Aurangzeb had rushed to Rajputana to crush the rebellions. He summoned Muazzam from the South and Azam from Bengal to join him. However, Durgadas found an opportunity to get Shahzada Akbar on his side. Akbar not only revolted against his father but declared himself the Emperor. He had confronted the Badshah on battlefield. Aurangzeb was not one to forgive and forget. Hence both Durgadas and Akbar had sought refuge in the Deccan. More specifically, they were looking up to Sambhaji for protection.

Sambhaji said, recalling how Shivaji had reacted to the Jizya tax, 'Abasaheb had written to Aurangzeb, asking him to repeal the tax. He said an emperor cannot discriminate among his subjects on the basis of religion. The Hindavi Swaraj had five thousand Pathans from Bijapur in its army. We have sardars like Daulat Khan and Daryasarang.'

'Don't compare Shivaji Maharaj with Aurangzeb,' Durgadas said gloomily. 'Expanding the boundaries of one's kingdom does not necessarily make one large-hearted.'

Shahzada Akbar had informed them that he would be at the fort by dawn but there was no sign of his till late afternoon. Sambhaji and Durgadas were disappointed at his lack of punctuality. Finally, in the evening, he arrived.

Hiding his irritation, Sambhaji said, 'Shahzade, if it takes so much time for you to reach here from the base of the fort, I wonder how you aspire to capture Delhi!'

Durgadas smiled. 'Shambhu Raje, if only our Shahzada could shake off the habits of his pampered life, we would have defeated Aurangzeb ten months ago.'

He continued, 'We had such a golden opportunity then! Aurangzeb's army numbered no more than ten or twelve thousand, facing more than a million Rajputs. But our dear Shahzada took fifteen days to travel twenty-one miles. He was so engrossed in dreaming of the day he would become an emperor that he forgot he needed to defeat the Badshah first. He wasted time discussing the design of the new throne with the carpenters and jewellers, and the measurements of his royal robes with the tailors. It was a golden chance but we threw it away. As for the cunning old Badshah, he was not going to sit idle. He had his way. We had no option but to run and save our lives!'

Akbar said, 'I agree that I had acted foolishly. In fact, I was fooled by my superstitious nature. An astrologer advised me that I should not travel more than a few miles each day. I later came to know that my father had bribed the astrologer and delayed my arrival in Rajputana. Well, my father is not a Badshah for nothing.'

Durgadas added, 'Raje, you would have seen all kinds of people in your life but I will wager that you have not met a man more cunning, deceitful and sly than Aurangzeb. Despite the Shahzada's delayed arrival, we were on the brink of victory. We were sure we would defeat Aurangzeb's army. One of Aurangzeb's senior sardars, Tahavvur Khan, was on our side.

Aurangzeb arrested Khan's wife, children and his father-in-law Inayat Khan. He sent a secret message to Tahavvur that night, "You are free not to join us but it you don't meet me I will ensure that your children are sold as slaves. Your wife will be thrown to my guards who will enjoy dishonouring her." Tahavvur Khan rushed to Aurangzeb's camp and, as expected, he was murdered there. Aurangzeb did not stop at that. He sent another "secret" letter to Akbar and ensured that it fell into the hands of the Rajputs. The letter said, "Dear Akbar, you have done wonders, making the Rajputs believe that you are on their side. Tomorrow my forces from one side and your army from the other will crush them.' When I read the letter, I rushed to the Shahzada's tent but he refused a meeting with me.'

'Why?' Sambhaji asked, a little surprised.

'Well, he had issued strict instructions to his guards that his sleep should not be disturbed. I shouted and screamed but to no avail. Then I rushed to Tahavvur Khan's tent but was told that he had left to meet the Badshah. After that, I had to bear the brunt of the Rajput ire. They accused me of having fallen for the trap. So we decided that it was best to run away and save our own lives. Well, the duplicity of Aurangzeb had made Akbar the victim. Aurangzeb had managed to defeat us without even unsheathing his sword. More than a million of us abandoned the battlefield. We could have easily defeated him …'

Sambhaji said, 'I am told you are the Badshah's favourite son. I believe he has been sending message after message, asking you to return. Is that true?'

'True enough. His letters are full of loving and affectionate words. But I can detect the hand of a cunning old fox by now. I am not going to fall for it.' Akbar was overcome by emotion as he continued, 'My uncle Dara was a scholar of Sanskrit, loved by both Hindus and Muslims. He was Shah Jahan sahab's favourite son too. But my father had his way in the end. I cannot forget one day when I was a child, my father had asked all of us to assemble on the balcony and watch the street below. A procession with trumpets and horns passed by. In its midst, sitting on an elephant, was a young man, bedraggled, wearing torn clothes and with dried blood on his face and limbs. He must have been a fair-skinned man once but his face was now tanned. He seemed to have been brutally beaten. He sat there with his head bowed. Behind him stood a young fourteen-year-old boy, whose eyes were filled with terror as he looked around. The moment he saw me, he tried to look away.

'I said, shouting at my father, "Abbajan, do you see him? He is Sifir!" My father replied, "Yes, I know, dear! That unfortunate man is your foolish uncle Dara and the boy is his son Sifir Shikoh." I shouted, "Who has done this to my uncle and my cousin? Who is that cruel man?" In response, my father punched me in my face and I fell down with a thud. After a couple of days, I saw my uncle's beheaded corpse on the same elephant. I heard from some friends later that my father had thrown Sifir and my uncle in a dark dungeon. One night, a few men entered the dungeon. Seeing their bloodthirsty faces, Sifir hugged his father and said, "I don't want the throne. I don't want anything. My father and I will go far away and live our lives begging for food. Don't kill my father." But they grabbed my cousin and threw him in an adjacent cell. My uncle too begged for mercy. Even a butcher kills a goat before skinning it but those devils cut off my uncle's limbs, torturing him cruelly before beheading him. Sifir could hear the screams of his father from the other cell.

'Sifir was then brought to Abbajaan's palace. After the trauma he had undergone, he was like the living dead. I saw him later, sometimes in the bazaars, or on the steps of the Jama Masjid, walking in a trance. I can never forget his face. The shahzada who had once lived a life of luxury was now roaming around like a beggar. I realised then how cruel my father could be.'

Akbar was deeply disturbed. He was silent for a long time. Sambhaji said, trying to lighten the situation, 'But I must admit your father is deeply religious, and a man who respects women.'

Shahzada laughed. 'Well, he may not have been as libidinous as my grandfather but he had his own ways.'

'Don't tell me! Your grandfather built the Taj Mahal in memory of his love. It is not a symbol of lust!'

'Don't forget he lived for another twenty-six years after building the Taj Mahal! His eyes were always preying on the sardars' wives and other women. He even tried forcing Mumtaz Mahal Begum's sister, Farzana Begum, to his bed. Naturally, my father was incensed.'

'But your father has never behaved in that manner!' Kavi Kalash said.

'You don't know, Kaviraj! My father's favourite begum is Udepuri. She used to be at my uncle's harem. Just a month after my uncle's brutal assassination, my father married Udepuri. There was another favourite of his at my uncle's harem—Ranadil. But she somehow managed not to allow Alamgir to touch her.'

Akbar was lost in memories. He said, 'One day some people from Central Asia had come to meet my father. They had a Turkish maid called Jakshi. Abbajaan fell for her and managed to get her into his harem. The son born to her, Yalangtosh Khan, is one of Alamgir's sardars.'

Akbar face now turned grim. 'My father has many faces and only Allah knows what they all are! He does portray himself as a pious servant of Islam. He reads the namaaz, hobnobs with the mullahs and maulvis, makes copies of the Quran by hand, and stitches caps to pay for the building of mosques. That is what people see and believe. But the crimes he has committed—killing his own brothers, imprisoning his father, torturing them to no end—I am sure they have destroyed his peace of mind! He possibly tries to wash away his sins by stitching caps, visiting mosques and reading namaaz. Well, it is a mystery—what we see and what he really is!'

ELEVEN

Lanjira! Lanjira!

1

'It is our good fortune that your father was not born a sailor. Else, he would have been the master of the seas as well!' The English emissary Henry Oxenden had once told Sambhaji while visiting Raigad.

Sambhaji had not forgotten Oxenden's words. In fact, the very sight of the blue seas made him increasingly restless these days. He would often ride his horse to the shore and stand there, watching the waves crash. It had been his father's dream to capture the coast from Surat till Karwar. Sambhaji wanted to fulfil that dream now.

Shivaji had explained it all in simple words. 'The Portuguese, the English and the Siddis are like the wild boar of the seas. They will chase you with the singular intention of goring your with their tusks in order to kill you. We need to be wary of them.'

Sambhaji was in conference with his sardars when a guard informed that a few ryots from Roha and Nagothane were keen to meet him. He asked for them to be sent in. The men came in and fell at Sambhaji's feet, crying, 'Raje, that cruel Siddi has kidnapped twenty-five boys from our villages!'

'What does he do with these boys, Raje? Why does he need them?' One of them wailed.

'He sells them to the English at Mumbai. Their slave trade thrives on the young boys who are easily captured in our country,' Kavi Kalash explained.

Sambhaji was lost in his thoughts. He ensured that the ryots received adequate compensation and said, trying to assuage their pain, 'I am going to put the Siddi in his place. Be assured.' The men left, nodding absent-mindedly.

Sambhaji turned to Kavi Kalash. 'Kaviraj, send a note to Mumbai's English saheb. Warn him that there will be serious consequences if he continues his slave trade. Let him decide how he wants to answer us. Tell him that we will be forced to throw him out of the port if he continues his dealings with the Siddi.'

He sent another note to the Subedar of the port at Chaul, near Raigad. 'Keep a vigil on the seas. Stop and loot the ships carrying grain to the English at Mumbai. Not one grain of rice or wheat should reach them!'

Sambhaji was now growing impatient. Like a log stuck in a whirlpool, his mind was spinning. 'Like the tall cliffs challenge the soldier in me, the huge sea, its vastness and its thundering waves challenge me too.'

Sambhaji could never forget that night in 1671. The festival of Holi had just been concluded. The fort of Raigad was awakened by loud booming noises. There was clamour and chaos all over, with men running for safety. The noise was ear-shattering. Jijabai had rushed into Sambhaji's room, followed by Shivaji. Maharaj said, 'Something is brewing at Janjira.'

Janjira was nearly sixty miles away from Raigad. It was remarkable that the noise had covered such long distances. 'We will wait for a message from Janjira,' Shivaji said, and he had stayed awake that night.

He said to Jijabai, 'Maasaheb, it is imperative to take control of the seas in future. Things are changing fast and we have no option but to put that the saffron flag on the ramparts of Janjira soon.'

Jijausaheb asked, 'Shivba, how many times are you going to attempt to capture Janjira? How much more wealth will you lose? How many men will you sacrifice at the altar of the sea?'

Shivaji answered, 'I undertand, Maasaheb! Ten years back we had captured Danda and Rajpuri. We could not take Janjira but we managed to build Padmadurg close to it. We controlled the seas from there. Despite our best efforts, Fateh Khan, the fortkeeper, did not yield Janjira.'

Sambhaji, listening to the conversation, said, 'Abasaheb, if we find that we are not able to penetrate the fort from outside, why not destroy it from the inside?'

Raje and Jijabai smiled at the words of the fourteen-year-old Shambhu Raje. Maharaj patted his back. 'Shambhubal, I have tried methods that your imagination cannot even visualise. After many attempts, I managed to win Fateh Khan over to our side. But some of his colleagues at the fort stayed loyal to their master, the Siddi. They captured Fateh Khan who had tried to escape using a sea route in order to join us and threw him into a dark dungeon for the rest of his life.'

Sambhaji listened as his father continued the conversation with Maasaheb. 'The Hindu religion forbids travel across the seven seas but if we have the captured the world, we must control the oceans. We need to build a strong navy. Our men, the daredevil Mawals who can climb any fort, will take to water like fish, I am sure!'

The day after Holi was one of the most tragic in Shivaji Raje's life. He received news of how Siddi Kasim and his brother Khairyat had divided their men into two groups—one of them attacking the Maratha fort from the seas while the other attacked from the land. They had targeted Shivaji's ammunition dump. It was that explosion which they had heard the previous night. Many men had lost their hearing due to the ear-splitting noise. Shivaji was shattered. 'I have lost everything I had gained over the past eight years.'

Sambhaji recounted his memories. Kavi Kalash asked, 'When was the first time Shivaji Raje had set his eyes on Janjira?'

'Since the beginning! It was even before Afzal Khan's death. The first time Vyankoji Pant and Moropant attacked, Siddi Khairyat was literally begging for a treaty. He agreed to hand over the stations at Rajpuri and other places. The only thing he had not given up was Janjira. Abasaheb was determined to the take the fort but Afzal Khan was nibbling at the borders on the other side and Abasaheb had to cut his short campaign mid-way.'

'Ten years later, when the Siddis realised that the Marathas were within grasping distance. Khairyat fell at the feet of Aurangzeb Badshah. He started getting ammunition, food supplies and other support from the Mughals.'

Sambhaji was determined to fulfil Shivaji's dreams. He held a discussion which included the experts in naval warfare like Maynak Bhandari. A map showing the route from Janjira to Mumbai was spread out.

'This is Mumbai,' Sambhaji said, indicating a spot on the map. 'The fort originally belonged to the Portuguese but was handed over to the English as dowry when their princess married King Charles. The English and the Janjira Siddis are both cunning foxes. Damage to the armpit can cause the arm to stop functioning. Mumbai's armpit is Khanderi,' Sambhaji put his finger on a point close to Mumbai. 'Abasaheb decided to build a fort there. The English were wise to the ploy, however, and involved the Siddis who attacked us. The Siddis built a fort at Underi, just a mile away from Khanderi.'

Sambhaji recalled the events vividly. 'Abasaheb had taken the defeat to heart. Two years before he died, he made another attempt to capture Janjira. Siddi Kasim ran to Mumbai to take shelter with the English.

Abasaheb sent fifty of his best men to find the Siddi who was hiding in the Mazgaon docks but the cunning Kasim captured them and tortured them brutally. Thus Raje's final foray failed too. In twenty-four years, he had made nearly eight attempts to take Janjira.'

Those in attendance knew that Sambhaji had planned something for Janjira. He said, as the meeting concluded, 'The coast along Janjira is crucial for our naval warfare as well as trade. Abasaheb had said once, "Shambhu, if you manage to put your flag on the walls of Janjira, it will not be long before the boundaries of the Hindavi Swaraj extend upto the Ganga and the Yamuna."'

2

Dawn broke. The outlines of the trees and the hills were getting clearer by the minute. The chirping of birds mingled with the sound of the streams gushing nearby. Sambhaji rode abreast with Kavi Kalash, followed by Rayappa. Behind them were four hundred riders. They had stayed overnight at Pachad and left before sunrise.

Soon they had reached Mahad. The mountains stood like sentinels, overlooking the small bay at Bankot which was visible in the distance. Despite the cold wind, the horses were sweating and frothing at their mouths. They had been galloping for hours on end. Reaching the bay, Sambhaji dismounted.

There was a palpable chill in the morning air. Maynak Bhandari, wrapped in a shawl, was followed by Daryasarang, Govindrao Kathe, Santhaji Pavla, and several officers of the Maratha navy. Sambhaji looked around. Several small and medium-sized boats bobbed quietly in the rippling waters of the bay. Their saffron flags fluttered in the cold breeze.

'Kaviraj, Abasaheb loved to swim in this bay. I learnt to swim here, clinging to Abasaheb's back. But he was clear about one thing; he would not teach me and expected me to learn on my own. I spent a lot of time in Raigad learning the art of warfare, mostly on my own.'

It was getting clearer now. At that moment Dadaji Raghunath Deshpande arrived with his me, all a tad breathless. They were all surprised to find that Sambhaji Raje had reached the spot before them.

Dadaji suggested, 'Raje, now that you are here, will you not partake of some refreshments at my house?'

'No, I would rather spend time here. I can always visit you later.'

Sambhaji inspected the ships that were being built near the harbour. Work was in full swing. Hundreds of carpenters were busy cutting huge logs which were being dragged to the building site by twenty bullocks at a time. Raje observed the cannons being placed on the ships that were nearly finished. Some of the vessels were huge and required around forty strong sailors to row them. Sambhaji watched the dark-skinned, well-built sailors as they went about their jobs on the boats.

Sambhaji said, shaking hands with Maynak Bhandari, 'We need to have at least fifteen huge ships ready. Let us prove that we can build them better than the ones being built at Kalyan.'

'Raje, rest assured. We are recruiting the best workers from Jaitpur and Rajapur.'

The men gathered around, curious to hear Raje speak. Sambhaji said, addressing the shipwrights and sailors, 'My dear friends, you know how Abasaheb built Sindhudurg. The foundation, drilled into the rocks at the bottom of the sea, are so strong that the fort will survive any onslaught and last for centuries. Today we have an army stronger than any other kingdom in Hindustan. But the Portuguese and English guns are longer and stronger. We need to build an artillery to match theirs. We need trained men who can man those huge cannons. That is why we have set up new factories at Kudal and Dicholi. And when the cannons are fired, we need the ships to be strong enough to take the jolts.'

Sambhaji concluded, 'The Siddis of Janjira must be crushed as one crushes a sea-snake. But we need to be careful of the Portuguese and the English.'

That afternoon they had lunch on the deck of a large ship. Raje sat down with workers, sailors and carpenters and they all enjoyed a simple meal of brown rice and fish curry together. The men's chest swelled with pride at the fact that Sambhaji sat with them.

Soon, the evening breeze began to blow. They could see a huge ship approaching the harbour. A strange animal was depicted on its green flag. The ship anchored a little distance away as it could not venture further into the bay. Small boats were soon on their way towards the ship. Rope ladders descended from the deck. Maynak Bhandari and Daulat Khan set off in a boat to receive their guest and ferry him ashore. The guest bowed elaborately before Sambhaji. He was a tall, heavily built Arab soldier.

'Welcome, Jange Khan! We were waiting for you,' Sambhaji said, hugging him affectionately. He said, addressing the men around him, 'This is Jange Khan, the Arab commander. He is a friend of the Swaraj and we are going to benefit greatly from the knowledge and skills his men will impart to our artillery and naval units.'

Jange Khan received a warm welcome. He was one of the sailors who roamed the high seas with their powerful artillery, ensuring the reached the ports of Hindustan safely. Khan planned to stay on the Konkan coast for a few months to supervise the training his men would provide to the Maratha shipwrights and artillerymen.

That afternoon, they sat down for a conference on a specially decorated deck.

'So, how is your friend the Siddi of Janjira?' Sambhaji joked.

'Raje, we could never be friends. You know we are sworn enemies. There are a lot of differences amongst the firangis, Raje. But they are united on one issue; they don't want the Marathas gaining superiority over the seas.'

'I am aware of it,' Sambhaji nodded.

That evening, on Jange Khan's request, Sambhaji dined aboard his ship. While walking across the deck, Sambhaji saw some movement in a dark corner. In the light of his burning torch he saw a few hundred men huddled together, bare-torsoed and shivering in the evening breeze. Their bodies were covered with festering wounds. It was evident that they had not had a bath for weeks. Jange Khan said, seeing Sambhaji's questioning glance, 'Oh, they are slaves, Raje! Ignore them!'

Sambhaji asked, 'Khan sahab, why don't you employ workers? Why keep slaves?'

'Well, there is nothing like having your own men, isn't it? Our slaves can work nonstop!'

'Khan sahab, isn't there any difference between a man and a horse, or a dog for that matter?'

'Raja sahab, why are you worried about these poor men? Oh, you are at a poet at heart. No doubt you are sentimental!'

'It is not that, Khan sahab. These slaves are children who belonged somewhere and were caught and sold like chickens in a bazaar. The ones sold in the bazaars of Mumbai are surely the sons of our ryots. That is why my heart goes out to them.'

Sambhaji paused for a few moments. He ordered Kavi Kalash, before Jange Khan could react, 'Pay Khan sahab whatever price he asks for but release all those men.' He turned to Khan, 'My Abasaheb was strictly against slave trade and would impose heavy penalties on the English who were caught plying it within the Swaraj. I too hate this age-old and barbaric practice.'

The dinner was a lavish spread, including a variety of meat and wines. Sambhaji tasted a little wine, saying, 'I used to enjoy wine in my youth. But since the death of my father there is only thing which I am intoxicated with—the task of fulfilling my father's dreams. To put the Siddis and the Portuguese in their place and to capture alive the terror called Aurangzeb!'

'Wah! Bahut khub!' exclaimed Jange Khan.

'We need to capture the animal called Aurangzeb who has despoiled our religion and our culture. The way a juggler or a bear-handler tames the animal by putting a rope through its nose, I wish to drag Aurangzeb through the hills and valleys of the Deccan. I pray to Ma Bhawani to give me that strength!" Sambhaji folded his hands in prayer, lost in his thoughts.

3

Sambhaji and Yesubai sat at the office in Raigad, discussing plans for a forthcoming campaign, when they heard a loud shout 'Jay Jay Raghuveer Samarth!' Soon, Diwakar Bhat presented himself. Sambhaji was overjoyed to see one of Samarth's favourite disciples.

'Please come in, Shastri Bua,' Sambhaji rose to welcome Bhat and made him sit next to him. There was a clamour amongst the servants as they rushed to get fruit and milk for him. The discussions were suspended. After all, it wasn't everyday that Samarth's ace disciple visited them from Sajjangad!

Sambhaji said, 'Shastriji, I remember Abasaheb missing Ramdas Swami's presence during the coronation. He would have been overjoyed if Swami had attended the ceremony.'

'I can understand, Shambhu Raje. But he is not keeping well these days. That is why he has sent Diwakar Gosavi.'

'Abasaheb had great respect for Tukaram Bua, Ramadas Swami, and the Fakir at Kelshi. He always sought their blessings.'

'No doubt, Samarth loved the elder Maharaj. Not to mention the fact that he had disciples like Prahlad Niraji, Nilo Sondev, Ramchandra Nilkant and, especially, Balaji Avaji Chitnis.'

Diwakar Bhat had singled out the name of Balaji Chitnis. Sambhaji felt suffocated for a moment. He said after a pause, 'I can well understand why Samarth is upset with me.'

'Maharaj, you ordered one of your finest sardars to be crushed under an elephant's feet while you give the respect that is due to men like him to an outsider, someone who is considered a fraudster. It does not become you, Maharaj!'

Diwakar Bhat had not minced words. Yesubai looked at Sambhaji nervously when Bhat asked, 'Where is that Kalash? I don't see him here. He is with you all the time, I am told.'

Sambhaji smiled. 'He has gone to Sagargad and Kothalagad. He is taking stock of the revenue collected, the ammunition stores and other security arrangements. He is with me often, it is true, but when required, I send him into battle too. He knows how to use his sword.'

'Don't tell me!' Diwakar Bhat exclaimed.

'Shastriji, you spoke of the people who were executed. Apart from Balaji Avaji and his son, all the rest were traitors and deserved to be punished. Had I not taken action, the consequences would have been calamitous.'

That softened Diwakar Bhat a bit. He realised that the complaints reaching Sajjangad may not all be true. He said, handing over a silk bag to Sambhaji, 'It's a message from Swamiji. Read it at leisure.'

'How long are you here?'

'I was planning to leave immediately but I suppose I could stay back for a few days.'

That afternoon, Sambhaji and Yesubai remained in their quarters. They read Swami Samarth's letter many times. It was as if his message, written in a poetic form, had mesmerised them. The letter read:

'Remember Shivaraya. A living example of righteousness.
His deeds are known all over.
Remember his looks. Remember his presence. His valour.
The way he spoke, walked and advised others. Taking them along.
One becomes Shiva only by forsaking pleasures. He had a single-minded focus on Swaraj.'

Even after having read it ten times, Sambhaji was not tired. He said, 'Yesu, with his words, Samarth builds such a wonderful image of Abasaheb!'

'Yesu, he is the only one who can claim to be a Shreeman Yogi, a Jaanata Raja, the real king who truly understands! No one but Shivaji Maharaj can claim these titles.'

The following lines were also enlightening.

'Beware! Don't be relaxed.
And spend time in silent contemplation.
Don't hold on to your temper. At times it is fine to be gentle.
Contemplate on the inner soul.
Pardon the deeds of the past and take your men along with you.
Let them be devoted to the task at hand.'

Sambhaji stopped for a moment. Yesubai continued reading:

'Not all stains can be washed away by water.
The minds of men too, likewise.
If your men are happy, things are fine.
If they are unhappy, you have not achieved your goal.
Understand the times and act accordingly. Shed your anger.
And never show it to others.'

Yesubai said, 'I am sure the families of those who were executed have met Swamiji at Sajjangad.'

'I am aware of the complaints that Shivaji's son is not worthy of his throne. That he spends time in the wrong company, that he is moody and does not listen to sane advice, that the kingdom is destined to be doomed … and what not.'

Yesubai said, 'Balaji Avaji was very close to Samarth. He was his favourite disciple. But I suspect the families of the real traitors have gone and complained to Samarth.'

For a long time Sambhaji was silent. He said, 'Whatever others may say, Swamiji has sent this message with his blessings. Listen to this!' He read out the remaining lines.

'Get people together. Make them work for a single cause.
And ensure that you destroy the enemy.
Hold what you have and then reach for more.
See that the flag flutters all over.'

Sambhaji was overwhelmed with emotions. He said, 'Yesu, I am fighting a perpetual battle with Aurangzeb. Swamiji is immersed in the service of the Lord. How can he be aware of these harsh realities? He has been fed all kinds of lies and rumours. I think I must write to him and explain everything.'

'That's a good idea.'

Dawn was breaking outside. The distant spire of the Jagadeeshwar temple was visible. There was no point in sleeping now. Sambhaji got up, had his bath and peformed his daily pooja before sitting down to write his letter. Khando Ballal had been asked to present himself at the office. Sambhaji dictated the letter:

'Shri Raja Shambhu Chhattrapati sends his salutations to His Holiness Sant Ramdas Swami Gosavi.

Swami has always been a great supporter of the Hindavi Swaraj and my beloved Abasaheb. The way Swami described Abasaheb is beyond compare.

Your letter reached me at the right time. I have been neck-deep in planning a sea expedition. It is true that I ordered the execution of some senior sardars who have served the kingdom since Shivaji Maharaj's time. But the reason for their death was their own treacherous intrigues and the way they plotted against the Swaraj. I grew up playing in the laps of men like Annaji Datto and Hiroji Kaka. They were pillars of the Swaraj at one time. However, when Abasaheb died and there was a serious threat of an invasion by Aurangzeb, these narrow-minded men, instead of extending their support to me, conspired to overthrow me. They started a childish campaign to put ten-year-old Rajaram on the throne. Hence they were guilty of treason. According to law, they could have been thrown over the cliff to their deaths. Yet, I neither punished them nor retired them prematurely. In fact, I reinstated them in their original posts. Despite such magnanimous gestures, they continued their scheming plots. What would a king do in such a situation?

Swamiji, I urge you to come to Raigad and look at the papers yourself. You would be pleasantly surprised to find them in perfect order. I have learned the art of administration under the tutelage of Jijausaheb. I managed the territory of Raigad for four years when I was very young. I studied the classics, Sanskrit and the works of great poets like Kalidas.

Ordering the execution of Balaji Pant was a mistake and I will repent it throughout my life. I am caring for his children as I care for my own. But the story of the others, the actual traitors, is different. Like poison spreading through one's body, it needed to be stopped in time. Else, it would have been too late.

Swamiji, our arch enemy Aurangzeb is planning to march on us with an army of nearly five lakh men and four lakh beasts. He has the enormous wealth of the Mughal Empire to support him. But I am going to make every effort to protect our newly founded Swaraj. My only aim is to see that he is defeated. If I am not able to do that, all the efforts made by Abasaheb and his dreams would be wasted.

I have no time to waste. Aurangzeb's son Shahzada Akbar has joined us along with Durgadas Rathore from Marwar. I am in touch with Raja Ramsingh of Ambar. I shall let you know of the developments.

In conclusion, Swamiji, I have been busy saving the Swaraj while you have been devoting your time and life to the service of the Lord. Who then will stop people from poisoning your ears with false complaints? I don't fear the Mughal enemy but I am worried about those who feed you with these lies.

I hear you speak of getting people together to ensure the spread of dharma. I need your blessings for this war against dharma. I may have ordered the killing of the traitors but I will always remember and cherish their good deeds and their contributions to the Swaraj. What is unpardonable is their treason, which they committed with open eyes.'

4

Sambhaji and Kavi Kalash's tents were put up near the bay at Nagothane. It was dawn and Raje had just finished his elaborate morning prayers. Kalash too was ready. Shahzada Akbar's tent was not far away. However, he had a habit of getting up late. Durgadas Rathore had often said to him, 'Akbar, you must make it a habit to get up on time when on the battlefield. Look at the way the Marathas have their breakfast astride a horse. They are ever battle-ready!'

'Durgadas, what can I do? I have the Mughal Badshah's blood in me. The Marathas lead a nomadic life, travelling like fakirs. A Badshah, on the other hand, must behave like one!'

'Shahzada, have you seen the way Sambhaji looks after his men? There is so much to learn from him!'

Shahzada Akbar laughed in response. 'Durgadas, you are partial to him as you too are a Hindu. I know you are in awe of that landlord's son. In any case, tomorrow, when I am the Badshah, I don't want to owe him any favours. I will happily grant him a Subah or two.'

All Durgadas could do was slap his forehead in disgust.

Kavi Kalash was waiting for Sambhaji to arrive. He had with him Dadaji Prabhu Deshpande of Mahad. Soon, Sambhaji, sporting a bright tilak on his forehead, arrived. The twenty-three-year-old Raje looked especially handsome this morning. Sambhaji said to Dadaji Prabhu, 'Deshpande Kaka, how are you?'

'I am at your service, Swami!'

'Be prepared for a major campaign soon!'

'As you command, Swami.' Dadaji nodded.

It was not clear to Dadaji what Sambhaji meant when he said a 'major campaign.' He waited for Raje to continue.

'Kaka, I have decided to induct you into the council of ministers.'

Deshpande responded with a bright smile. It had been his dream since a long time to be part of the council. He bowed respectfully when Sambhaji said, 'But you need to complete a task before you are appointed. No one knows the territory of Konkan, especially the coastal region, as well as you do. I want you to attack Janjira and finish off the Siddis. You would be remembered forever for this great service to the Swaraj!'

Dadaji Deshpande was confused. He said, his voice quivering a little, 'But Raje, you need to take one thing into account. Even Shivaji Raje could not break the walls of that fort. The Mughals stay away, too, while the Portuguese and English maintain a respectable distance. We need to be well-prepared if we are to attack the fort.'

'I am aware!' Sambhaji said, smiling. 'Subedar, there are wild animals in the forest but many of them can be subjugated if you hold their tail.'

'I don't understand, Raje!'

'Janjira's tail is the port at Underi, near Colaba. Take whatever support you need, but squash Underi.'

Deshpande wiped his forehead nervously with a silk handkerchief. 'Raje, the tail too is quite poisonous. At the village Thal, there is a fort that stores the best English ammunition. The Underi port is a mere half-mile away. The English are ever ready to support the Siddis and would not hesitate to retaliate.'

Sambhaji seemed to be lost in thought for a while. When he was about to leave, he held Deshpande's hand and said, 'Kaka, you know Baji Prabhu Deshpande's valour and the way he fought at Pavankhind. If you take Underi, you have a chance to recreate history.'

Kavi Kalash smiled. He knew Sambhaji had deliberately referred to Baji Prabhu Deshpande as a means of challenging Dadaji. Taking Underi would not be an easy task by any means. But Sambhaji did not simply hand over the task to Dadaji. He got involved in every aspect of the mission's preparation. Raje ensured that nearby Sagargad was adequately stocked with ammunition and foodgrains. Twenty-two ships were deployed in the bays of Nagothane and Rohada. Four thousand troops, commanded by Daryasarang, Daulat Khan and Maynak Bhandari, were ready to attack. The troops were paid two months' salary in advance to keep up their morale.

However, Sambhaji was worried. Aurangzeb was expected to arrive in the Deccan at any moment. It was imperative to capture Underi and then attack Janjira before the Mughals marched in.

Raje returned to Raigad. He was now busy coordinating several campaigns at the same time. His sardars were attacking Mughal posts in Mulher, Solapur, Ahmednagar and other places. Nearly twenty-five thousand Maratha soldiers had been deployed to ravage the Mughal territories. Then there was the question of logistics—managing the inventory of ammunition and foodgrains and ensuring that the troops were well taken care of. Messengers and spies visited Sambhaji regularly, took instructions and left.

Yesubai had taken over the role of managing the daily administration of the kingdom, just as Jijabai had done before her. She had the support of the council of ministers. One day an urgent message reached Raigad. Yesubai had already read the message when Sambhaji rushed into the office. It was not good news; Dadaji and his men had been routed at Underi.

Sambhaji cursed under his breath, 'I had told Dadaji to be careful!'

'It is not his fault, Sarkar,' the messenger said, 'Dadaji and his men had planned it well. But at the last moment, the English came to the rescue. Two hundred of our men had attacked the fort and eighty were caught alive. The merciless Siddi Kasam cut their heads off, the way a grasscutter cuts grass. He threw the bodies into the water and took away eighty heads, tied to a rope.'

'What about Dadaji Deshpande?'

'He fought with valour, Maharaj! His blood-stained sword mowed the enemy down as he moved forward. But unfortunately, he got hit in his leg as ammunition from a swivel gun brushed against it and the sulphur burnt his skin. He fell down but, luckily, he was saved by his men and is recuperating now.'

A few days later another messenger arrived. Khando Ballal's face fell as he read out the message.

'Raje, Kasam took the heads of our soldiers to Mumbai. Hanging the heads on a pole, he mocked them by poking spears into them. The Siddi's soldiers, drunk and shouting, took out a procession with trumpets and horns blowing all the way. Luckily, the English governor intervened and stopped the madness.'

Sambhaji's head reeled. He stood up. In his agitation he pulled the hooks on the walls with such force that they came off. Sambhaji could not eat that night. He could not concentrate on his prayers either. His eyes burnt with rage. His body ached for revenge. 'I am not going to stop now!' he muttered. He went into the sanctum sanctorum and touched Shivaji's wooden slippers reverently to his head.

He said to Yesubai, 'Yesu, the firangis have realised that if the Marathas conquer Janjira, they would establish their superiority over the high seas. They would never want that to happen.'

Holding the slippers to his forehead he said, 'Abasaheb, the wait is over now! I am going to lead the campaign myself. Let us see what happens!'

5

The Mughal Shahenshah rested at the palace in Burhanpur. The light of the lamps was reflected in the glass pillars and the elaborate chandeliers. Behind a screen sat Udepuri Begum, Shahzadi Zeenat-un-Nissa and other begums. Alamgir was busy discussing plans with his sardars.

Aurangzeb had returned to Burhanpur after a gap of twenty-three years but the memories of the old days were still strong. He was merely a sixteen-year-old Shahzada when he had visited his aunt in Burhanpur. To this day, roaming in the gardens, with the breeze flowing through the mango trees, he was reminded of her tinkling laughter. For it was here that he had fallen in love with Zainabadi, also known as Heera. Her tall, lissome figure, almond eyes, narrow chin and the half-opened inviting lips—the very sight of her used to make him weak in the knees. It was love at first sight. She came into his life like a whirlwind and left just as soon. A mere illness was the reason for her death. Aurangzeb could never come to terms with the loss.

The Badshah took a tour of the city to see how it had been ravaged by the kafir Sambhaji. The half-burnt havelis, looted markets and the rubble strewn everywhere pierced his heart. He could not bear to see the tortured faces of the citizens and the way impoverished merchants looked at him with vacant eyes. At the city's dilapidated cemetery, he asked an old and trusted attendant to find Heera's grave.

'If you cannot protect us from our enemies, we will stop the Friday prayers,' the maulvis had threatened. The fact that his favourite queen Dilras Banu's son, Shahzada Akbar, had joined Sambhaji was a thorn in Aurangzeb's heart. Akbar had ignored the many messages of reconciliation sent by Aurangzeb. To add insult to injury, Akbar had affronted him with taunts like 'The treasury is almost empty, the mullahs and maulvis are being insulted, you are losing control over your own administration, and your officials are corrupt. What else can the citizen expect from an old Badshah?'

Aurangzeb tried to blame his son's rebelliousness on others. He said, 'That treacherous Durgadas is helping Shahzada Akbar. We must stop him. Kill him, if you find him! But it looks like the sardars in the Deccan are useless!'

'Jahanpanah, Durgadas is a cunning fox,' Asad Khan said.

'I know,' Aurangzeb sighed. 'He had met me to propose that Jaswant Singh's heir should given the throne of Marwar. He argued with me. Jaswant Singh's queens were in captivity in Delhi then. But that wily fox managed to rescue them and escape, camouflaging them in soldier's outfits!'

'Jahanpanah, if I may ...' Asad Khan began.

'It is a dangerous situation. A wily Rajput has joined hands with the Marathas. And the Maratha leader is no less than Shiva's son—a lion's cub.'

Zulfikar Khan added, 'Alamgir, Shahzada joining forces with the Marathas is adding fuel to fire. It will not be extinguished easily.'

Aurangzeb caressed his beard with one hand while prayer beads moved in the other. He muttered a few verses from the Quran. Everyone waited with bated breath.

'Then we must snuff out the fire before it engulfs us.' Aurangzeb's outward show of anger did not reveal the inner turmoil he was going through.

Within ten days of Aurangzeb's arrival in Burhanpur, the Marathas had attacked a station managed by Lutfullah Khan Koka and killed many Mughal soldiers. The daring Marathas had shown the temerity to attack a post that was barely ten miles from Burhanpur. On the same day there had been an explosion due to an accident at the ammunition dump near the Badshah's palace. Such inauspicious signs ever since he had arrived in the city disturbed Aurangzeb.

The sixty-three-year-old Emperor displayed the energy and enthusiasm of a twenty-five-year-old youth. His physique, his discipline and his ambition were as strong as ever. As a man who controlled a huge treasury, he was ever alert. He never went to sleep at night unless he had met his spies and taken a report from them. He had been systematically collecting information from his network of spies, including a few Maratha soldiers who had defected to the Mughals. He had created a map of sorts of the Hindavi Swaraj. The map showed the exact locations of the rivers, forts, old temples and other strategic points in the kingdom. By now, Aurangzeb could point out any Maratha fort on the map.

He said to his sardars, 'I have always had the ambition to finish Shivaji's kingdom off but somehow I have not had the time in the last twenty-five years or so. It was Shivaji's good fortune that he died before I captured him. I was sure of annexing his territories quite easily. But now, it seems, things have changed. Anyway …'

Aurangzeb scanned the map as he spoke. He said, looking at Asad Khan, 'Wazir-e-Azam, tell our brother Siddi at Janjira to descend on the Konkan coast with all the men he has. Ask him to burn the Maratha territories in the region.'

'Ji, Hazrat.'

'And write to the Portuguese governor. Let him know that Goa is not near Delhi where he can call on us for help at the eleventh hour. Sambhaji can overrun their territories any day. Ask him to attack the Maratha kingdom from the south Konkan side.'

'As you command, Jahanpanah.'

Aurangzeb turned to Hasan Ali Khan. 'Hasan, my valorous soldier, there is no one who protects Islam like you. You were the one who arrested that truant Gokul Jat when you were the faujdar at Mathura. You had torn him to pieces in the public square ...'

'Ji, Hazrat.'

'You were the one who razed a hundred and seventy-six temples near Udaipur to ground. You are a true follower of Islam.'

'Just command me, Hazrat! Command me!' Hasan Ali Khan said, banging his fist on his chest as he stood up.

'Take twenty-five thousand troops with you and descend on the Konkan region from Nashik. After capturing the fort at Mahuli, destroy Bhiwandi and Kalyan as you move towards Raigad. The Siddis from Janjira, the Portuguese from the south and your men—you will reach Raigad after you ravage the entire Maratha territory that lies in between. I will pray at the fort once I see the green flag with the moon and stars fluttering on the ramparts of Raigad. Only then can I die peacefully. Ya Khuda! I have no other ambition other than this!'

The rousing and emotional speech stirred everyone. Aurangzeb looked at his men and said, 'Let us see who wins! On the one hand is the old Badshah of Hindustan while on the other we have the young, immature son of a zamindar. On one hand there is an army backed by the treasury of twenty-two provinces and a legacy of two hundred years dating from Taimur while on the other is a miniscule territory of the Marathas that they call the Swaraj!'

'We shall finish them off, Huzoor!' Zulfikar Khan growled.

'Shut up! Don't throw words around casually. Despite the presence of an imperial camp manned by five lakh Mughal soldiers, Hambirrao has the audacity to attack Lutfullah Khan's post, just a few miles from here. What does that mean?'

The sardars looked down at the carpet, not wanting to face Alamgir's penetrating stare. Aurangzeb said, letting out a deep sigh, 'It means only thing—we need to be alert! Our Deccan campaign may not be difficult, but it is not easy either. A small snake can freeze a gallant soldier in his path. A mere ant, if it enters the trunk of an elephant, can make it roll on the ground in agony like a dog! Let us not delude ourselves! Be alert!'

6

The small town of Rajpuri, nestled at the base of a hill near the coast, was literally covered with coconut, palms and other trees. From a distance the spires of the temple and the masjid's dome were visible.

Dark clouds covered the sky, giving the sea a muddy sheen. The fort of Janjira was eight hundred metres from the shore. The entire fort was visible from the small hill on the outskirts of Rajpuri. The massive fort had nineteen semicircular battlements where the Siddi sentinels stood guard. The afternoon gave way to evening when, suddenly, three cannons on the fort roared. The deafening noise shook the whole town. The Siddi had deliberately fired the cannons as a warning. Soon, around eighty small boats were seen approaching the shore, filled with Siddi troops shouting ' Allah-o-Akbar' and 'Deen Deen!'

The few Maratha soldiers stationed at Rajpuri scrambled to their horses and fled as fast as they could. The residents of Rajpuri screamed for help, shouting, 'They have come! The Siddis are here! Run!' Many were climbing the hill in a desperate bid to save themselves.

By dusk, there was chaos everywhere. The Siddis had massacred the villagers in Rajpuri and in nearby Revdanda, Koliwada, Murud and Nandgaon. Women were raped and huts burnt. They looted whatever they could lay their hands on. The few villagers who survived the attack rued the fact that Shambhu Raje's men had run away without offering any resistance.

The fort of Janjira shone in the glory of its heinous act. Torches burnt all along the walls of the fort which was a mile and a half long and nearly as wide. On one of the battlements stood Siddi Khairyat Khan and his brother Siddi Kasam Khan. They were pleased with the message they had just received.

'Kasambhai, Alamgir's message is like Allah himself talking to us!'

'I agee, Bhaijaan! We shall go ashore tomorrow. By then our troops would have reached Roha.'

'Yes, Hasan Ali Khan too would by then have taken Kalyan and Panvel, and reached there. I am confident our swords will penetrate the heart of Raigad in two days' time.'

That night, the two brothers celebrated their triumph by sipping expensive wine.

The next morning Kasam woke up at his seven-storeyed palace. He was to leave for the mainland soon. Moving the fine chik curtains to look outside, he found it to be a misty morning. The clouds had literally descended on the sea. Glancing at the hill outside Rajpuri, he had the shock of his life. For a moment he steadied himself by sitting down on his velvet bed. The hill was aglow with saffron flags! The Marathas had captured the shore and were busy laying their cannons. The soldiers who had run away the previous evening were back in full force.

The Siddis and their soldiers were now stuck at the fort. The troops who had ravaged the villages had somehow managed to find their way back to the safety of the fort.

On a stretch of flat land near the hill stood Sambhaji, staring at the fort. Beside him stood Kavi Kalash, Jotyaji Kesarkar and the veteran commander Daryasarang. Durgadas Rathore stood next to Shahzada Akbar. Jange Khan sat on a makeshift cot nearby.

'The Siddis are known to be ruthless. They are willing to do anything for money,' Sambhaji said, looking at Shahzada Akbar. 'The other day Kasam's men kidnapped a few rich Muslim merchants from Shreebag and Pen. Despite the intervention of the English emissary, the Siddis were not willing to release them until they were paid a ransom of eighteen thousand hon.'

'That devil beheaded eighty of our men at Underi,' Sambhaji continued, curling his fists in frustration. 'I am itching to take revenge.'

Not stopping at Underi, the Siddis had ravaged many small towns from Panvel to Chaul. It was then that Sambhaji had decided to go to Janjira himself. He had with him nearly twenty thousand men and three hundred boats, big and small.

The Siddi brothers had celebrated the day they had heard of Shivaji Maharaj's death. They believed their worst enemy was dead and that they had nothing to fear now. But their misplaced confidence was soon shattered when they saw Sambhaji's rise. The Siddis knew that they could never win against the Marathas in direct combat. The only solace they had had so far was the strong and impenetrable fort which protected them. The walls of the fort had withstood the ravages of the sea, despite being hammered by the waves and tides for decades. They had survived the forces of nature.

The Siddis were now a worried lot, however, as they knew that Sambhaji had recently managed to procure ammunition from the Arabs. From a distance, the Maratha fleet looked like small paper boats floating in the water. The Siddi brothers observed the boats using binoculars, and realised there were nearly three hundred of them, of various shapes and sizes, armed with guns, cannons, and jamburas or light guns, and manned by around five thousand Maratha troops. A large contingent was led by Daryasarang, and another by Maynak Bhandari, while the third was commanded by Sambhaji.

Sporadic cannon fire ensued. The green flag fluttered nervously on the fort. It was just a matter of time before a coordinated assault from the Marathas began.

The Marathas had also been emboldened by the defection of Siddi Sambal's son, Siddi Mistri, who had joined them with three hundred men. While Sambhaji was collecting information about Janjira from Mistri, the Siddi brothers were forming a fair estimate of the Maratha might by talking to Kondaji Farzand who had defected to the Siddis earlier.

Sambhaji said, looking at Shahzada Akbar, 'I have warned the Portuguese viceroy that if he does not send his troops from Chaul in our support, we will see to it that their fort at Chaul is razed to the ground!'

Duragadas looked at Sambhaji and asked, 'You think the Portuguese will lend their support?'

'Why not? If the Arabs can help us, why not the Portuguese? After all, they are using our ports and our coast for their trade.'

No one spoke for a while. Sambhaji said, after some time, 'Well, your doubts are valid, Durgadas. The new viceroy Conde de Alvor is a sweet-tongued charlatan. But I am not going to be fooled any longer. We need to build a strong fort very close to Goa. That would keep them in check.'

The discussion turned to Aurangzeb. Sambhaji asked, 'Durgadas, where has the Badshah reached?'

'He has been in Burhanpur for past two months.'

Kavi Kalash warned, 'He can descend on Maharashtra anytime.'

Akbar said, 'Abbajaan is in the Deccan after more than two decades. He was once the Subedar in his youth. His empire stretches from Kabul to Bengal in the east and extends up to Baglan-Waradh in the south. His palace is brimming with grandchildren and great-grandchildren, and the Mughal treasury is overflowing. Yet, the old man is restless and unhappy, and chooses to spend months in isolation here. Even the small children in the zenana are scared of his shadow!'

Durgadas looked at the Janjira fort and said, 'I wish Shivaji Maharaj had turned his attention to this fort much earlier!'

'You don't know, Durgadas! He made multiple attempts to capture it. Each time, victory was snatched away at the very last minute. Let me tell you about one instance. There was a fisherman called Lai Patil. On the dark night of a new moon, he managed to reach the fort and put ladders against the walls. He was waiting for Moropant Peshwa to arrive. But unfortunately, Moropant lost his way in the forest and could not reach on time. A dejected Patil had to return. When Shivaji tried to honour him, he said, "What is the point, Maharaj, when I don't have the fort?"'

Everyone was convinced that Janjira fort, the target which had eluded Shivaji despite innumerable attempts, was special. It was probably protected by forces beyond human understanding.

7

It had been two weeks since Sambhaji's arrival at Rajpuri. The cannons were being fired intermittently from both sides but the crossfire had not yielded any results for either party. The efforts from Sambhaji's side seemed weak and the troops wondered why he was not showing the kind of excitement they had expected him to display. They were worried by the fact that the Siddis, who traded with many countries, had managed to procure fine cannons from Istanbul and Portugal.

Shambhu Raje's sardars had proposed a concentrated assault more than once but they had not yet received a satisfactory answer from him. One day, Sambhaji looked at Shahzada Akbar who was sitting beside him, but Akbar seemed lost in his own thoughts. Sambhaji raised a questioning eyebrow at Durgadas who said, 'There is a concubine by the name of Roop Kanwar in the bazaars of Chaul. Shahzada was visiting her quite frequently. When he did not turn up for a few days, she came over to Murud. For the past two days Shahzada has been in her company.'

Sambhaji smiled. He said to Akbar, 'Why are you being so secretive and shy? After all, you are a Shahzada from Delhi and we understand your interests. Who is this dancer who has stolen your heart? Let's see her talent. I am curious.'

Shahzada Akbar, thrilled that Sambhaji was taking an interest in his romance, arranged for a mehfil at their camp in Rajpuri. Roop Kanwar had been born a Hindu but her mother was married to a Siddi sardar. Seeing that Sambhaji was present, she was doubly excited and performed brilliantly.

The mehfil was progressing smoothly. Sambhaji noticed that Roop Kanwar was wearing a rather splendid necklace. Curious to examine it from close quarters, he gestured to her to approach him. The moment she came near, Sambhaji pulled the necklace with a sharp tug. While the jewels were scattered all over the carpet, the other guests looked at Sambhaji in surprise. The dancing stopped.

Seeing Sambhaji's angry face, Roop Kanwar stepped back. Raje turned to Akbar and growled, 'Shahzada, you know this necklace, don't you?'

'Yes, you had presented it to me.'

'It was presented to a shahzada, not a dancer!'

For a moment, Akbar was quiet. He said, 'I am a Shahenshah in my own right. I will do what pleases me.'

Sambhaji was in a rage now. He shouted, 'If that be the case, leave now. You may go and sit anywhere you wish, and believe that you are the Badshah in Delhi.'

Durgadas, realising the gravity of the situation, quickly escorted Akbar out of the tent. Sambhaji had just stepped out with Kavi Kalash when Roop Kanwar rushed to him and fell at his feet, saying, 'Raje, don't do this!'

'I don't understand; don't do what?'

'Raje, I won't be able to face any audience after this,' she pleaded, as tears streamed down her cheeks. 'Everyone will know that Shambhu Raje walked out midway through my performance. They would presume that I am no longer beautiful or have become old, and that I don't know how to dance anymore. I plead for justice. Please don't abandon the mehfil like this.'

Sambhaji looked at Kavi Kalash but he did not say anything. At that moment Durgadas appeared. Sambhaji took a bag of gold coins out of his cummerbund and said, handing it to Roop Kanwar, 'If someone asks, tell them that I had to leave on an urgent mission. But show them the gift I have given you. It is worth ten such performances.'

Roop Kanwar bent low in mujra and left.

As they walked back to their tents, Durgadas said, 'Raje, you are familiar with the Shahzada and his childish behaviour. Why make such a fuss of it?'

Sambhaji said, 'I cannot attend such concerts, Durgadas. Instead of drumbeats I hear the booming of the cannons. It is a crime to spend even a minute more at such gatherings.'

8

'Kaviraj, I hope you have sent the despatches to Karnatak and Golconda?'

'Yes. But Raje, you are at Janjira. Why are you thinking of Karnatak?'

'Aurangzeb is here with a massive army. Our clash, whenever it happens, would be decisive. Hence we need to ensure that we have the resources to face the Mughal army. That is where Jinji, Tanjavur, and the rest of the South would come in handy. Chikkadevaraja in Mysore is a wily fellow and we need to subdue him before he thinks of joining the Mughals. When Aurangzeb descends on the Deccan, we need to put up a united front. We must send despatches to Qutb Shah, Adil Shah and others.'

The South did pose a problem but the issue of Janjira was still at hand, and unresolved. Sambhaji was often lost in thought, staring at the fort. It had been a month since they had set up camp at Rajpuri. The fort at high tide reminded him of a huge black ship floating in the water. In the slanting golden rays of sunrise and sunset, it resembled a magical kingdom. At low tide, when the water receded and a part of its foundation was revealed, the fort had an entirely different look.

Siddi Khairyat Khan and Siddi Kasam were restless in their palace within the fort. Never had they faced such a long siege. Even the narrow strip of bay between Rajpuri and the fort was now inaccessible.

Sambhaji had not launched a full-fledged attack yet. Siddi Mistry had created a wax model of the fort which Sambhaji would use while discussing with his men various strategies to enter it. They had spent sleepless nights at Sambhaji's tent trying to assess the best way to capture the fort. But they had not reached a conclusion yet.

One morning, Dadaji Deshpande entered Sambhaji's tent. He had a limp and was using a stick to walk. Sambhaji had been sure of Dadaji's victory at Underi but he had defeated at the last moment. Luckily, Dadaji had survived his injuries but his ankle was broken. Now, thanks to the support of his walking stick and more importantly, Sambhaji's encouragement, he was back on the battlefield.

Sambhaji was in conference with Dadaji, Durgadas, Maynak Bhandari and others. Dadaji voiced what others wanted to say but did not know how to. 'Raje, we are fed up of these small skirmishes. When are we going to launch a full-scale attack? Our troops are itching to see the lion's cub in action.'

Sambhaji said, as if startled from a reverie, 'Kaviraj, I sometimes wonder when and how this fort was built. Why don't you find out whether it was built on such an auspicious date that it has become impregnable?'

Kavi Kalash took Sambhaji's words seriously and enquired in the villages nearby. After a few day, he reported his findings, 'Raje, I did find out. There used to be a reputed priest called Ganesh Pandit. When the Siddis heard of him, they sent their men to his house. He was not present but his young daughter welcomed them into the house. On realising the purpose of their visit, she said she herself was well-versed in reading the almanac and could tell them the most auspicious date for laying the foundation. The Siddis returned, satisfied. The pandit, on realising what his daughter had done, muttered, "Daughter, you read the almanac well but your decision to inform them of the date was wrong. It is a huge mistake!" Well, the foundation was thus laid on such an auspicious date that it has since then become impregnable!'

Sambhaji looked at the fort. He wondered when he would walk the ramparts, if ever. The next morning, he announced to the troops assembled near his tent, 'My friends, once we finish this difficult campaign successfully, I will make sure that each one of you has a golden band around his wrist and a large bag of gold coins to take home!'

The men were ecstatic. The next day Durgadas informed Sambhaji that Shahzada Akbar too had returned. The troops waited patiently. They were sure an attack was imminent. Even the horses seemed to be tired of eating the same kind of fodder and were restless for lack of action.

Sambhaji was sitting at his tent the next day, looking at the wax model of Janjira, when he heard a commotion on the shore. He looked outside his tent to see eight or ten soldiers trying to restrain a man who wanted to meet Sambhaji. At a signal from Raje, the guards let go of him and the man approached Sambhaji. He was smeared with mud and seemed to be exhausted. The man saluted and put a small bag near Sambhaji's feet. Sambhaji asked him to open the bag. Everyone was shocked. It contained a half-burnt head. The man fell at Sambhaji's feet and wailed,

'Raje, this is Kondaji Baba's head!'

The Maratha soldiers standing nearby were pleased and broke into loud cheers. After all, a traitor deserved such an end! The man tried to silence them but they continued their celebration of Kondaji's killing.

Finally, Sambhaji stood up and shouted, 'Stop! Let me hear what he has to say.' Then he knelt and gently took out the head. He held it in his hand. The next moment he wailed, bringing tears to everyone's eyes, 'Kondaji Baba, what have they done to you!'

Sambhaji looked up at the mud-smeared man standing near him. He was in tears and could barely speak. He said, finally finding his voice, 'Raje, things were going fine, the way you and Kondaji Baba had planned. Accordingly twelve of us, including Kondaji Baba, joined the Siddis. Only we know how we managed to survive the past twelve months.'

'What happened then?'

'Raje, if only destiny and the gods had been with us, the ammunition store at Janjira would have been reduced to ashes last night. The flames erupting from the fort would have saluted you.'

'Arre! But Kondaji Baba was a very careful, diligent and alert sardar!'

'Raje, no one had suspected our motives for twelve months. We had ensured that the Siddi and his men never doubted us. Kondaji told everyone of the misgivings he had about you and convinced them that he had betrayed you. Siddi Kasam had started treating him as a dear friend! He even offered Dilruba, his favourite concubine, to Kondaji Baba. That poor lady had no inkling of the purpose for which we had entered the serpent's den.'

'Continue … don't stop!'

'Nothing went amiss till last night. We were to blow up the eight ammunition stores inside the fort. It was all planned. Babaji had bribed a few men over to our side. Even our escape boat was ready. But at the last moment, Dilruba insisted on coming with us. 'Take me with you,' she pleaded. Kondaji agreed, but a further complication was her maid Zaira, without whom Dilruba would not move an inch. An hour before the deadline, Dilruba shared the plan with Zaira. She excused herself, saying she would pack the clothes, and went straight to Siddi Khairyat Khan's palace.

'Well, it was a matter of minutes before the warning bells started ringing. Like bees swarming out of a hive, nearly two thousand soldiers streamed out and surrounded us. Three of us jumped from the ramparts; two fell on the rocks and died. Kondaji and seven others were made to stand in a line and mercilessly beheaded. Siddi Kasam himself sliced through Dilruba's neck. Kasam's men dragged the bodies and the heads, and threw them into a great bonfire they had built at the rear of the fort. Dancing and shouting to celebrate their victory, the men returned to the palace. Luckily the guards at the rear entrance were lax. I had managed to hide in a crevice in the wall. When I was sure that there was no one around, I got hold of Kondaji's half-burnt head and made for the shore. It was a huge struggle for me to get here but I knew you would be waiting to hear the outcome. Had I not survived, you would not have known of Kondaji Baba and his valour.'

No one could hide their tears. Not bothering about his mudstained dress, Sambhaji hugged the brave Maratha affectionately. The man sobbed as he said, 'Kondaji Baba used to tell us how he had captured Panhala fort with only sixty-four men and laid it at Shivaji Raje's feet. He said he wanted to capture this challenging fort and lay it at Shambhubal's feet. He said, "Let us create such an explosion that not only will it shatter the fort to pieces but fly my body high in the air to land at Shambhubal's feet. I would consider my life blessed then!"'

No one could speak a word. They were stunned into silence, hearing the soldier speak of Kondaji's last wish. Sambhaji put the half-burnt head in a palanquin. Then he placed his sapphire necklace gently around it. He ordered his men to take it with honour to Kondaji's hometown. As the palanquin and its bearers set off, Sambhaji walked up the hill and stood staring at Janjira for a long time.

Durgadas Rathore asked Kavi Kalash, 'This was planned over a year ago. Why were we not aware of the plans?'

Kavi Kalash replied, 'Even I was not aware! What you heard from the soldier just now ... I too have heard for the first time.'

9

The next day dawned to the sound of Maratha cannons booming across the bay. The villagers who lived nearby were frightened and many decided to leave their homes lest they were trapped in the crossfire. The Maratha boats, which had been waiting in the waters for weeks, now came to life and took part in the shelling. The walls of Janjira were being battered relentlessly. Siddi Khairyat Khan and Siddi Kasam Khan were not going to take the bombardment lying down. Soon, the Siddis were aiming at the boats. Many were drowned. Men had to jump into the water and cling to anything they could find to save their lives. Sambhaji directed his big cannons at the thick walls of the fort. Each cannonball weighed nearly three-fourths of a seer.

Soon, many large stones from the fort came crashing down into the sea. The strong walls were beginning to show some cracks. Many buildings inside the fort had caught fire and thick black smoke curled up into the sky. The women from the zenankhana rushed out of the rear gate and jumped into the boats anchored behind the fort.

Kasam Khan and Khairyat Khan were now galvanised into action. Their three main cannons started spitting fire. They targed the large boats and burnt them but the Marathas were not in a mood to retreat. Eventually Khairyat Khan said, 'If we knew Sambha was going to harass us, we would not have joined the Mughals. It would have been better to salute the Maratha flag and save our lives.'

The provinces surrounding the fort, particularly the towns of Murud, Tula, Mhasala, Harihareshwar and Dighi provided foodgrains and other necessaries to Janjira. Sambhaji had ensured that the supplies were cut off, leaving Janjira quite destitute. The Maratha boats in the bay kept a strict vigil, preventing the supply boats from reaching the fort. It was a total siege.

The Siddis were stuck at the fort. While Janjira remained impregnable till then and offered them shelter, they knew there was no way out of this trap. They prayed desperately to Allah and Aurangzeb for intervention, divine or otherwise!

Sambhaji was frustrated that his continuous efforts had yielded almost no results. He said, 'Kaviraj, to stay here any longer could prove disastrous. Aurangzeb may enter our territory at any moment and we need to be prepared.'

'I agree, Raje. We must get results soon, or return. The Siddis are a determined lot and will not give up so easily.'

Janjira and the Siddis were considered unconquerable but seeing Sambhaji's relentless efforts, the ryots started flocking to the Maratha camp. Their plea was simple: 'save us from these marauders!' Sambhaji was disturbed. These men believed in him but he was unable to find a way forward. Suddenly an idea occurred: if Lord Ram had built a bridge over the sea, why could he not build a path to reach Janjira? Soon, huge trees were being felled. The soldiers on the battlements of Janjira looked on in awe. Was this really happening? Were the Marathas really building a bridge to reach them? Sambhaji's soldiers continued to put huge boulders and logs into the sea. They were determined to reach the fort. But the sea was merciless. Many of the logs floated away on the waves while the boulders were unwieldy and difficult to place.

However, persistent efforts began to show results. The bridge was half done. The two main cannons of Janjira boomed. Sambhaji ordered his fleet to assemble and offer a sustained counter-attack.

The Siddis were anxious now. The troops feared that they were likely to be routed within the next few days. Kasam and Khairyat ordered their retainers to pack up the treasury, brimming over with fine clothes and jewels. The villagers had already started celebrating Sambhaji's impending victory.

Two days passed by. A few ships managed to reach the fort carrying supplies in the night. The Siddis were emboldened once again. On the other hand, a devastating piece news was about to reach Sambhaji.

That night, Sambhaji was woken up by the fortkeeper of Kothalgad. He had rushed to meet Raje along with ten riders.

'Raje, it is bad news. Aurangzeb's sardar Hasan Ali has entered Konkan from Nashik with nearly twenty thousand cavalry and fifteen thousand foot-soldiers. He ravaged the port at Kalyan and is now planning to move towards Pen and Panvel. His target is Raigad.'

'What the hell are our reconnaissance troops doing?'

'Raje,' the fortkeeper pleaded, 'what can one do while facing a tornado?'

By then, Sambhaji's sardars had gathered at Raje's tent. Sambhaji looked at Janjira in the darkness. The bridge was more than half-built. He only needed another four or five days to take over the fort. The battered walls were within grasping distance now. He could not forget Shivaji Raje's words, 'If you take Janjira, you can reach the banks of Ganga and Yamuna one day.'

Sambhaji's face was writ large with anger and frustration. He shouted, 'Kaviraj, I cannot leave till I capture the fort. I cannot retreat.'

His sardars pleaded, 'Raje, we all agree that conquest of Janjira is crucial for us. But Raigad is far more important!'

Finally, a dejected Sambhaji had no choice but to return to Raigad, leaving Raghunath Desphande to continue the siege. Before leaving, Sambhaji turned once to look at Janjira. The cool sea breeze blew. Sambhaji could see the bridge halfway across the water. The fort was so near, yet so far! He tried his best not to show his tears, lest the troops were demotivated. But his efforts were in vain. Tears streamed down his cheeks as he turned his horse.

TWELVE

Valour

1

Sambhaji returned to Raigad. En route, he had stayed at Chambhargad for a night. The spies there reported, 'Hasan Ali ravaged the areas around Bhiwandi and Kalyan and then moved towards the coast. He destroyed nearly forty villages in the Portuguese territory, presuming they were under Maratha rule.'

Kavi Kalash was despatched to supervise the ammunition factories at Kudal and Dicholi and get a sense of the Portuguese movements in Goa.

Arriving in Raigad, Sambhaji was pleasantly surprised to receive a traditional welcome from Yesubai. Wearing a yellow embroidered saree, she looked radiant. It was then that Sambhaji noticed she was nearly five months pregnant. He was overjoyed.

'Raigad has found its successor,' he said later, as they were resting in the royal quarters. 'Where are you planning to go for the delivery?'

'Why? Shringarpur, or else, to Ganojirao's place at Dabhol. My father may not be alive but my brother would be more than happy to take care of me.' Tired, Yesubai dozed off. Sambhaji stayed awake, thinking of Janjira and Aurangzeb's foray into the Deccan. Suddenly, he remembered a secret message which Khandoji had handed over to him when he reached Raigad. He got up and read the message in the light of the oil lamp. It was from Miyan Khan.

> *'Shambhu Raje, it seems four of my earlier messages have not reached you. I am worried that the messengers may have been intercepted and possibly arrested by Aurangzeb's men. I am eternally grateful to you. It is only because of you that I could get two of my daughters married.'*

Sambhaji recollected his days at Bhupalgad and the time he had spent with Miyan Khan.

> *'I am writing to you with some good news; you are the father of a lovely daughter now.'*

Sambhaji sat down on the bed reading this. He was thinking of the pregnant Durgabai …

'Your daughter is now growing up at the fort of Ahmednagar as a prisoner of Aurangzeb. But you may rest assured. Your queen Durgadevi, Ranutai, and your daughter are well taken care of. But in the end a golden cage is still a cage. Your servant Miyan Khan is at your disposal. I have managed to get an ordinary job at the fort. But I am a servant of your dear daughter, not the Badshah ...'

Sambhaji could not hold back his tears and a sob escaped his lips. Yesubai woke up to find him holding the letter in his hands and crying. Reading it, she too could not restrain her tears. Sambhaji, lying down on the bed, wondered how his daughter was faring.

The next morning, many people were surprised when Sambhaji distributed sweets. 'The delivery is still a few months away, isn't it?' someone asked. Sambhaji replied, 'Well, I can sense the child's movements in the womb, so I thought why not distribute some sweets. We shall celebrate again when he is born,' he said. No one knew the real reason for Sambhaji's happiness.

2

It had been five days since Sambhaji's arrival in Raigad but people had hardly seen him. He had not even gone to the temple. He was not ill but 'war fever' had caught hold of him and he spent day and night in discussions with Yesaji Kank, Mhaloji Ghorpade, Nilopant Peshwa, Prahlad Niraji, Khando Ballal, Manaji More and some of the younger sardars. Durgadas Rathore and Akbar were housed in a haveli nearby and they would join the discussions once a while. As always, Durgadas showed keen interest while Shahzada Akbar was only casually involved.

The conference would begin at nine in the morning and continued almost till dawn the next day. Sambhaji would rest for a couple of hours, finish his morning chores, and start the discussions again. No one outside really knew what the meetings were about but they had seen maps and wax models of forts inside the room. Sambhaji was aware that Aurangzeb's army was a vast as the ocean, and that it was approaching the Maratha kingdom swiftly.

Hambirrao arrived in Raigad and joined the discussions midway, taking everyone by surprise. 'Mama,' Sambhaji began, 'I thought you were on a campaign ...'

'Shambhubal, I am the commander of the elder Maharaj. And his favourite brother-in-law too. I have learnt a few things from him. Someone in the camp has been assigned the task of masquerading as me, feigning illness. No one knows that I am here.'

Hambirrao's presence inspired the team. While discussions were on in the capital, ryots and other men from all over the province were being inducted into Sambhaji's troops. The eighteen factories in Raigad were busy producing weapons and ammunition.

The discussions entered a serious phase on the fifth day. Kavi Kalash had returned with reports and inventories from the ammunition factories. Sambhaji and others were in office, waiting for Yesubai to arrive. Soon, they heard the palanquin bearers outside the hall. Yesubai stepped gingerly out of the palanquin.

'I am sorry, I am a little late,' she said. 'I was looking at the list of four hundred men whom we lost at Janjira. At least thirty of the families need our support to take care of their children.'

Sambhaji explained, seeing the confused looks of the others, 'Yesubai ensures that all men whose children have been orphaned are placed under the care of the state. Once they complete their education, they are free to join the troops. The mothers and wives of the deceased soldier are also taken care of.'

'There is an orphanage for such children near the elephants' stables. You should make a visit to see how the orphans are being taken care of,' Sambhaji added.

All senior sardars except Dadaji Raghunath Deshpande were present. Dadaji was busy carrying on the siege at Janjira. Sambhaji began, 'Abasaheb knew that the Sahyadris are the true protectors of the Marathas. We can, with our guerrilla tactics, ward off any attack as long as we have the mountains backing us.'

'But Raje, the wars that were waged back then were not of the scale we are facing now.'

'I am confident that the armour called Sahyadri can protect us, no matter the size of the enemy.' Raje continued, 'We cannot face the enemy on an open battlefield. It will be disastrous. Prataprao Gujar faced Adil Shah's troops in direct combat and sacrificed his life. There is no point in fighting like that. We cannot afford to lose a single fort of the Hindavi Swaraj. Not a single ship of ours must sink in the seas. We will dig a grave for Aurangzeb here in the Deccan! As Abasaheb used to say, it will take them five years to capture one fort of ours. Imagine the time they will need to take all three hundred and fifty forts!'

Nilopant Peshwa asked, 'Raje, what is our plan?'

'Wherever possible, we will attack. Where we believe we cannot, we must find a way to retreat. If the Mughals do enter the Sahyadris, we will massacre them in the valleys and gorges. But we are not going to wait for them to attack. I know we are merely seventy thousand against their five lakh, but we must continue to nibble at their numbers as well as their supplies whenever we get a chance. We will loot, burn, and ravage wherever we find them!'

Sambhaji allotted tasks to each of his sardars. Hambirrao said, 'If we look at our history, we have five enemies: Qutb Shah of Hyderabad, Adil Shah of Bijapur, the Siddis of Janjira, the Mughals, and the Portuguese.'

'We cannot afford to confront all of them at the same time. Luckily, Abasaheb has managed to convert Qutb Shah and Adil Shah into allies. I am sure all the powers in the South would come together to fight against Aurangzeb. I have been working day and night to ensure that.'

'The Siddis may not have been vanquished but they have received quite a jolt. I am sure they are a worried lot now. They will think twice before joining the Mughals.'

Yesubai added, 'We need to look at salaries for our soldiers. It is a sin if a soldier dies without being paid what is due to him.'

Sambhaji looked into the matter immediately and ensured that the treasury at Raigad was catering to the needs and demands of forts and military camps all over the Swaraj. The threat of a famine loomed large too, creating further problems.

Sambhaji had summoned Daryasarang and Daulat Khan from Janjira. He said to them, 'The Portuguese have been ruling the coast for nearly a century now. It is not easy to displace them. We are busy fighting the firangis at Chaul, Thane, Vasai, Tarapur and other places. Nilopant, where are your men engaged right now?'

'Maharaj, we occupied the Portuguese territories of Mahim and Tarapur in one stroke. But the firangis managed to recover Mahim. We are now busy fighting in the Revdanda area.'

'Wah, Nilopant! I wish Moropant Peshwa was alive to see your valour!'

Sambhaji had sent some men with material to build a fort on Anjediva island off the coast of Goa. He asked Kalash, 'Kaviraj, what is the status of the fort at Anjediva?'

'The moment we began construction the Portuguese ships arrived.'

'It was a remote island! Why don't you understand that the completion of the fort is a step towards capturing Goa itself?'

'I think Conte de Alvor realised that. That is why he contrived to halt our work.'

Sambhaji let out a deep sigh. 'We need to break the legs of this firangi too, in the same way that we have managed to handicap the Siddi. Else, that wily Portuguese fox may join the Mughals at an opportune moment.'

'Let us buy as much gunpowder as we can get from the English. It will be a long battle with the Mughals and we will need it,' Khando Ballal suggested.

'Agree! I don't mind paying twice the amount but let us get a large supply,' Sambhaji concurred.

There was much discussion on how to face the final confrontation. Hambirrao and Yesaji had suggestions which Sambhaji noted down. He said, satisfied that the plans were progressing well, 'I am happy that the infighting and gossip has reduced considerably. I am sure, thanks to Bhawani's blessings and the good deeds of Abasaheb, that we will manage to defeat the enemy. A fort does not win or lose because of the quality of its ammunition or the number of troops posted there. We can manage with damp gunpowder but if the enthusiasm of the soldiers dampens, everything is lost! We have the armour of the Sahyadri to shield us. All we need now is for the soldiers to do their job!'

Sambhaji reminisced a story Jijabai had told him of how his great-grandfather, Lakhuji Jadhav, had captured the Devagiri fort, a structure built on flat land.

'The fort has been cleverly designed to fool any attacker,' Jijausaheb had said. 'If he managed to cross the first hurdle, he would face moats and trenches. Anyone not knowing the way would either be lost in dark caves or fall into deep ravines. Going further the enemy would enter a flat, dark stretch of land. It was in fact a cleverly designed iron plate, which would be heated from below. The enemy, presuming it to be black soil, would step on it and get their feet burned. Lakhoji had carried bags of water with him which he poured on the plate before crossing it. That saved him and the men. Finally, they captured the fort.'

Sambhaji continued, 'We need to be agile and alert, and use our intelligence to defeat an enemy like Aurangzeb. Attack, retreat, and attack again! We have to try everything. But I am sure, we will win in the end. When an elephant attacks the door of a fort, it assumes that it will be able to break it open. Much later does it realise that the nails jutting out of the door are going to be it's undoing. Likewise, the old elephant called Aurangzeb will meet his fate when he rams against the gates of the Maratha Empire.'

3

Sambhaji invited Hambirrao to his private chambers. As he relaxed on a swing, he saw that Yesubai and Sambhaji were looking crestallen. He realised that something was amiss.

Sambhaij said, before Hambirrao could speak, 'Mamasaheb, sometimes I feel suffocated sitting here in Raigad.'

'Shambhu Raje, I too am equally worried.'

'But who would put balm on my battered soul? Sambhaji said, his voice full of pain. 'Mama, three of my loved ones are prisoners of the Badshah at Ahmednagar.'

'Ranu and Durga … who's the third one?'

'Well, I have been blessed with a daughter. It has been three years. I got the news quite late,' Sambhaji's voice quivered.

Hambirrao was taken aback. He gauged that Raje had managed to get information from inside sources at Ahmednagar. Sambhaji said, before he could react, 'Mamasaheb, I want to attack Ahmednagar and release my dear ones. What is the point of a Raja who cannot save his own family?'

'Shambhubal, as the commander of your army, I too am embarrassed by this fact. I have tried twice, with more than ten thousand soldiers, to take Ahmednagar. But the fort under the Nizam Shah is quite strong and unyielding. Ruhullah Khan, the fortkeeper, is a tough man. Several factors are not in our favour—the fort is under the Mughals now, the territory is far away from the Sahyadris, and the the vigil there is unabated. It is not easy.'

'Mamasaheb, we need to do something,' Yesubai pleaded.

'And if you cannot, I will lead the charge,' Sambhaji warned.

'Raje, your daredevil attitude sometimes worries me,' Hambirrao said. 'The elder Maharaj was born in Shivneri but the fort and the area around Junnar has remained under the Mughals. You must have heard how Shivaji Raje was held at Sangamner by Ranmast Khan. You need to be patient. You are the heart of the Hindavi Swaraj. You cannot put yourself at risk by undertaking such an enterprise.'

Hambirrao spent the next two days in Raigad discussing various issues. Sambhaji was elated when he heard news that the Maratha troops had ravaged Rahimatpur, a town in Adilshahi territory which was now under Mughal control. Several Mughal posts were being destroyed. Hambirrao could no longer afford to stay in Raigad and took Sambhaji's leave.

That afternoon, when Hambirrao went to take Yesubai's leave, he saw a dozen palanquins ready to leave. He noticed the palanquins were from Raigad and not Shringarpur. He remarked, 'It will be difficult to reach Shringarpur if you start so late.'

'I am not going to Shringarpur for the delivery. I will be in Gangoli, at the base.' Yesubai was in tears. She touched the feet of the elders and got into the palanquin.

Ganoji Shirke had not sent a palanquin to take Yesubai to Shringarpur. Sambhaji had barely managed to read the letter. It said: *'Yesu, I am not sending my men to bring you here. The Bhosales have not done anything for us Shirkes in any case. We were made paupers. You are most welcome to come to Shringarpur, but don't forget to carry the papers for our watan as promised by your wily father-in-law.'*

Sambhaji was lost in thought. He wondered how his little daughter was living at Ahmednagar, guarded by enemy troops. He said, as Hambirrao took his leave, 'Do something, Hambir Mama. This is not an order. Consider it an appeal from a father who is desperate to see his daughter!'

4

'The strength of the Marathas is their forts. Capture one fort after another, each day. Within six months we will capture the Deccan.'

'As you command, Hazrat,' Shahbuddin Feroz Jung said, bending in salute. The cat-eyed sardar looked at his Badshah, who asked, 'Where do you plan to start?'

'Ramshej. It's a few miles from Nashik. I will have thirty-five thousand men with me.'

'How long will it take?'

'Well, I plan to start after the morning namaaz. And we intend to spread the carpets for the afternoon namaaz on the fort itself!'

'Wah!' Aurangzeb exclaimed. 'I need to finish Sambha off before moving on to Golconda and Bijapur. And I want to complete the task in seven or eight months so that I can be in Ajmer for Hazrat Chishti's festival in time.'

'Jahanpanah, with your vast army, we will destroy these Marathas,' Wazir Asad Khan said with confidence.

Aurangzeb was in good spirits when Feroz Jung left for Ramshejshez. He was sure that this foray marked the beginning of their victory in the Deccan, leading to the capture of more forts in the days to come.

But days turned into weeks and his frustration increased. Feroz Jung was accompanied by top sardars like Rao Dalpat Bundela and Kasim Khan. Aurangzeb heard the siege of Ramshej included huge cannons and sophisticated ammunition, but it had not yielded any results.

Asad Khan said, trying to pacify his Badshah, 'It is just a matter of time, Jahanpanah.'

'Wazir-e-Azam, I am not foolish to believe your words so easily,' Aurangzeb snapped. His angry retort made the elderly commander sweat nervously. At that moment, Alamgir's cousin Zulfikar Khan came in and saluted. 'Zulfikar, what is the news from Sarja Khan in Bijapur?'

'Nothing yet, Jahanpanah.'

Aurangzeb face turned hard. He narrowed his eyes and growled, 'Zulfikar, people can be really stupid.' Then his voice took on a tinge of sadness. 'I had told the Bijapurkars that I would happily give the Maratha territory to them provided they helped me to defeat this kafir. All I expected was his support but that arrogant fool has not bothered to listen to us.'

Zulfikar Khan was distressed. He said, 'Jahanpanah, Adilshah Sikandar is a fifteen-year-old boy. I don't expect him to understand politics, but I am disappointed that a seasoned sardar like Sarja Khan should behave so.'

'I believe he barely acknowledges our messages.'

'That is true, Hazrat.'

Caressing his beard with his left hand while his right hand continued to move the prayer beads, Aurangzeb mumbled a few lines from the Quran. He said after a while in a bitter voice, 'The Shia Muslims of Bijapur and

Golconda are not going to change. Sarja Khan and the Bijapurkars are friends of Sambha while the Diwan of Golconda, Madanna, is a wily fox and a shrewd Brahmin. I have been destroying Hindu temples all the way from Somnath to Burhanpur. But do you know what is happening in Hyderabad? Qutb Shah's Diwan Madanna is building large temples there!'

'Tauba, tauba!' Zulfikar Khan said, slapping his cheeks to show his disbelief.

The Badshah looked at Zulfikar and Wazir Asad Khan, who were father and son. Squinting his eyes, as was his habit, he sighed heavily and said, 'Well, my plans, when I left the desert sands of Rajputana, were simple: to squash the mountain rat under my heel. But the Deccan seems to be a tougher place than I had anticipated. What do you say, Wazir?'

'Jahanpanah, just be patient! I expect Ramshej to fall within two days.'

'I am not talking of a single fort, Wazir-e-Azam! My life these days is ruled by doubt. I fear that there is some kind of a treaty between that traitor Adil Shah, that debauch Qutb Shah, and the devil Sambha.'

The father-son duo did not know how to react to the Badshah's appraisal of the situation and decided to keep quiet. Aurangzeb changed the topic and asked, bringing up the subject which hurt him the most, 'What is the news from my stupid Shahzada Akbar?'

'That he and Sambha are close friends now ... nothing more, Jahanpanah.'

Shahzada Akbar was very dear to the Badshah and the very thought of him opened up old wounds. Aurangzeb's eldest son Sultan had gone astray after joining forces with his cousins. He was now rotting in the dungeons. Muazzam, Azam and Kam Baksh found their father difficult to please. It was Akbar whom he truly loved but it was he who had joined hands with Durgadas Rathore and staged a revolt!

Aurangzeb recalled the bloody battles fought for the throne throughout Mughal history. 'The ascension to the throne has always been bloody. Your sons are your worst enemies. What I had to to do with my Abbajaan, Shah Jahan, what he did with my grandfather, Jahangir ... one has to revolt in order to take the throne!'

'I beg your pardon, Huzoor,' Wazir said, 'We cannot forget that your father built the wonder that is Taj Mahal.'

'Do you have any idea that the same hands which built the Taj Mahal were stained with the blood of Shah Jahan sahab's brothers? He killed not only Shahryar but his young, innocent children too.

Aurangzeb was alone with his thoughts now. Wazir Asad Khan and Zulfikar had left. Aurangzeb recalled how he had mercilessly killed his own brothers—Dara, Shuja and Murad. He was growing more anxious by the day. He knew that his sons too would fight a bloody battle to ascend the throne. He was worried that they may pounce on him at any moment. During every meal, he suspected that the food may have been poisoned.

Alamgir sighed, 'For the Mughals, the real Taj is the throne; nothing else matters!'

5

The small village of Gangoli was situated in a dense jungle not far from Mangaon. Yesubai's maternal grandfather's haveli was on the outskirts of the village. The small and beautifully built wooden palace, on the banks of a little river called Vaipurna, was an idyllic sight. Shambhu Raje loved the place. After all, it was here that he had been blessed with his son Shahu. A few miles from the haveli was the magnificient Raigad fort, which was visible in the distance, reminding Sambhaji of a huge elephant which sat with its forelegs folded. Sambhaji looked at Raigad as he fondled the one-month-old Shahu in his arms.

The stay at Gangoli had been a pleasant one. Tukaram Maharaj's son Mahadev Maharaj was a frequent visitor. He and Sambhaji often spent hours chatting on footsteps of the Vaijnath temple.

Sambhaji was distressed, recalling the way his men had been brutally killed in Mysore. He was waiting impatiently for the return of Krishnaji Konhere from Mysore. The image of Dadaji Kakde, Jaitaji Katkar and Tukoji Nimbalkar's heads hanging at Shrirangapattana sent a shiver down his spine. Raje was eager to attack Mysore and teach the arrogant Chikkadevaraja a lesson for life.

Monsoon was in full swing and the constant downpour, combined with the excessive humidity, made everyone uneasy. There was no respite from the rains. Brief spells of sunshine only added to the discomfort.

Sambhaji sat in conference with Yesubai, Kavi Kalash, Jotyaji Kesarkar and Rayappa. 'The year has brought mixed blessings. While we managed to scare the Siddis, stave off the Mughal attack for a while and have been blessed with Balraje, I am troubled by the way some of our men have suffered. I cannot get over the fact that three of our most valued sardars—Kakde, Katkar and Nimbalkar—were tortured to death. Even a seasoned warrior like Harji seems worried. The only way to stop this carnage is to attack! Yes!'

In the light of the oil lamps, Sambhaji's face glowed with intensity. He wanted revenge.

Yesubai suggested, 'Raje, the Mughal Badshah is literally sitting at our doorstep. In such a situation, would it not be suicidal to direct our attention and resources to the distant Karnatak and Tamil lands?'

'Chikkadevaraja has gotten too big for his boots. He struts around proudly proclaiming that no one can touch him. Keeping quiet would mean being disloyal to our esteemed sardars who were murdered there.'

The rains continued to batter the wooden roof. Kavi Kalash began, 'But with the Mughal Badshah at the front door, it wise to leave through the rear door ...'

'When we have a decisive battle with Aurangzeb, the loot we get from the South will help us to win,' Sambhaji pointed out.

After a long discussion, it was decided that they would wait for Konhere's return from Mysore before taking any bold steps. By the time the meeting was over, the lamps had nearly burned out. Sambhaji was about to step into his quarters when a servant came running in and announced the arrival of Krishnaji Pant Konhere. Sambhaji immediately stepped out to receive him. Everyone waited with bated breath for news from Mysore.

Krishnaji was drenched to the core when he entered. He looked weary as he had travelled continuously for nearly three days. Sambhaji offered him his own shawl. When Krishnaji had managed to dry his head, Sambhaji asked eagerly, 'Krishnaji, what is Chikkadevaraja saying? Did he agree to a treaty?'

'Let me show you,' Krishnaji said, and took out a tattered angarkha. It was evident that Krishnaji had been insulted when he proposed the treaty.

Sambhaji growled, grinding his teeth in anger, 'What did the arrogant fellow say?'

'Raje, I don't know how to put it ... I told him I represent Sambhaji Raje. "What Raje?" he questioned me. "I don't know any such person," he said arrogantly, dismissing me. "Such landlords are born and die everyday." I was insulted in the durbar ... they tore my dress,' Krishnaji said, as tears welled up in his eyes.

Everyone present expected Sambhaji to explode with anger. But he was calm. 'There are no more doubts in my mind now. The decision is made! We have to teach those in the South a lesson.'

It was clear that a campaign was underway. 'I will leave the administration and security of the kingdom under the supervision of Maharani and Hambir Mama respectively. I don't see any option but to be in the South for three to four months.'

'Raje, what about Aurangzeb?'

'I have studied him well,' Sambhaji said, as he ruffled his hands gently through Shahu's hair. 'The rains are heavy now. He will not dare step in the Konkan's mud till Dusshera. In the meantime, we will accomplish what we have set out to do!'

6

Banawar was a little to the north of Chikkamagalur. When Sardar Lingappa's urgent message reached Chikkadevaraja, he flew into a rage, throwing the message in the air, and shouted, 'Since when have we become so weak and inefficient? Sambhaji, with ten thousand troops, has reached Banawar and we had no clue about it!'

'He is a mountain rat! How did he reach there?' One of his sardars asked.

'Not only does he have thousands of his own men but that Basappa Naik too has joined him with another five thousand.'

Chikkadevaraja was not one to sit idle in such a situation. He gathered his troops and marched to Banawar. Unlike in the Sahyadris, there were no rains in the South this time of year and Sambhaji had made good time on his journey. The Diwan Madanna of Golconda had been true to his word and provided Sambhaji with another ten thousand soldiers. Harji Mahadik, Sambhaji's sister's husband, was thrilled by the fact that Sambhaji was leading the charge.

Sambhaji complimented Harji, 'Daaji, you have been making waves in the South. It is admirable ... the way you have been carrying on Abasaheb's work here.'

'Yet I have not been able to stem the tide of Chikkaradevaraja's ambitions.'

'Which is why we are here to help, Daaji.' Sambhaji suddenly remembered something and asked, 'Did my step-uncle Ekoji Raje offer help?'

'Well, did you ask him for his help?' Harji asked.

'Well, he is elder to me and far more experienced. And as Swami Samarth says, there is nothing wrong in asking for help for the cause of Swaraj.'

Neither Harji nor Sambhaji trusted Ekoji. He had come to meet Shivaji Maharaj during his Karnatak campaign but had suddenly decided to run away one night, crossing the river.

The troops, numbering nearly twenty-five thousand, gathered at Banawar and were being prepped by Sambhaji and his sardars. The army was a mix of Marathas, Qutbshahi and Karnatak soldiers. The plan, known to only a select few, was to move to Tiruchirappalli, loot the bounteous region of the Kaveri delta and return.

Basappa Naik said, 'Chikkadeva's strength has grown manifold over the last ten years. It will not be easy to attack Mysore and defeat him.'

'I agree, Basappa. It is unfortunate that Ekoji Raje shifted to Tanjavur. We were in Bengaluru for nearly forty years. Had the Marathas continued there, we would have maintained our pressure on Mysore and not allowed them to grow so powerful.'

There was a consensus that instead of attacking Mysore, it was best to loot Tiruchirappalli. The tiger was to be lured into open ground from a dense forest! While discussions were on, a messenger rushed in. 'Chikkadevaraja is on his way here with a fifteen-thousand-strong army! We expect them to arrive by evening.'

Sambhaji said, 'Well, it seems Chikkadevaraja is itching for a direct confrontation. And he wants to take us by surprise.'

Instructions were issued immediately. The troops were scattered across the hills, and placed at strategic points. It was going to be a defensive battle. Sambhaji was aware that the Mysore army was strong and well organised.

By evening Chikkadevaraja had deployed his army in a wide semicircle, with the intention of surrounding the combined Maratha forces. There had been no direct confrontation yet but there were reports of small skirmishes taking place across a large area. Chikkadevaraja was a shrewd tactician and a bold commander.

It was late afternoon and suddenly the sky was overcast. When the Maratha soldiers looked up, they realised that they were being targeted by a rain of arrows. Soon, the arrows, slicing through air, started hitting the men and horses.

No one could make out where the arrows were coming from. Like bees smoked out of a hive, they seemed to pour in from all directions, piercing the soldiers in their faces, arms, eyes and thighs. Blood spilled, men died. The Marathas and the Qutbshahi soldiers ran for their lives. Raising their shields, hiding beneath their horses, running for safety—they tried everything they could to prevent themselves from getting hit. But the destruction continued.

Sambhaji Raje tried to pacify the Hyderabadi troops. 'Don't run! Stay where you are!' He tried to rally them but to no avail. Harji asked, 'Shambhu Raje, what can we do? The arrows are slicing apart our men and animals.'

'Raje, we cannot run away like this. That is not what the Marathas stand for!'

Sambhaji, Harji and Kalash were trying to infuse some confidence but it was a losing battle against the shower of arrows. Chikkadevaraja had succeeded in his mission to create turmoil amongst the Maratha forces.

That evening, Ekoji Raje and his five thousand men joined the Maratha forces. The Qutbshahi troops were the worst affected. That night, when Chikkadevaraja's troops seemed to have taken a break for their dinner, Sambhaji was trying to console one of his soldiers who had taken an arrow to his chest. Seeing Ekoji Raje walk in, he stood up and hugged his uncle.

Sambhaji said, letting out a deep sigh, 'Please don't mind Kaka that I am forced to meet you in such strange lands.'

'Well, these are testing times Shambhubal. I am sure that with Bhawani's blessings, things shall turn out well.'

It was decided that the best course of action would be to make a quick escape. Chances of an attack in the night were fewer and they could take the cover of darkness to move as far away as possible.

Creating a diversion with mashaals to give the impression that the Marathas were busy reorganising their troops, teams led by Sambhaji, Harji, Kalash and Ekoji Raje moved their troops. It was the first instance in Sambhaji's life where he had had to retreat.

They moved towards Tanjavur, travelling without a stop overnight. It was nearly noon the next day when they decided to halt and rest. The men and animals were so tired that they soon found spots beneath the trees or near the streams for a siesta. They had barely got time the previous night to nurse their wounds. Sambhaji himself was tired. An arrow had pierced his right arm. It throbbed badly. Jotyaji Kesarkar, Kavi Kalash and Rayappa looked dull and crestfallen.

They had set up a makeshift tent where Sambhaji and his sardars rested. A man soon arrived from Chikkadevaraja's camp with the message:

> *'Marathas, it is best that you go away into the Sahyadris. What business do you have in the South? You are lucky to be alive today. Note that the territory of Mysore begins at Banawar and you are advised not to cross it. Ever! If you dare to even glance at the direction of Mysore again, your eyes will be gouged out!'*

Harji said dejectedly, 'It would have been better if we had not gone to war, better than having to run away from the battlefield!'

'I agree! Chikkadevaraja is now emboldened while our reputation has been destroyed,' Ekoji Raje added.

Ekoji suggested, 'Shambhubal, now that you are here, why not stay in Tanjavur for a while. Enjoy our hospitality. I don't want you to be away from Raigad for long, though. At least you are well protected there.'

'That is not possible, Kaka,' Sambhaji said, sounding hurt. 'I had entered the Karnatak region hoping to motivate the troops. All we have tasted so far is defeat.'

'What do you plan to do then?'

'For an army which has tasted defeat, is there a balm more soothing than a resounding victory?' Sambhaji asked.

7

A slightly worried Asad Khan entered Aurangzeb's private chamber. Aurangzeb's discerning eyes sensed his anxiety. Asad Khan said, 'Hazrat, the old commander at Ramshej fort, Suryaji Jedhe, is a determined fellow.'

'I see! Tell me, how many Marathas are at the fort?'

'Not too many ... seven hundred to a thousand.'

'And you have nearly six thousand of your troops at the base, don't you?'

Asad Khan replied, 'A little more than that, Huzoor. I mean, quite a bit more. Actually, around forty thousand.'

'Such a huge army for a miniscule fort?'

'Jahanpanah, the fort is not an ordinary one. It is old and difficult to ascend. And the Marathas under that old man Jedhe are a determined lot. They won't give up so easily. We are trying our best with cannonfire. We even tried to scale the walls with ladders but we were bombarded with rocks from the top.'

'Rocks?'

'They don't have cannons there but they are able to launch cannon balls using slings made from leather and wood. The cannon balls are quite effective, Jahanpanah.'

'What do you mean? How many of our men did we lose?'

'Well, around three thousand five hundred or so. But Feroz Jung claims he can capture the fort in a few days.'

The Emperor did not respond. He had been reading the messages from his spies and was beginning to worry that the friendship between Shahzada Akbar and Sambhaji had deepened. He had to find a way to break that bond and bring Akbar back to his side.

He had not expected twenty-four-year-old Sambhaji to pull this trick, that of befriending Akbar. Nor some other tricks: Sambhaji's men had attacked Burhanpur while he himself had stayed back at Janjira. Sambhaji's men, under Hambirrao, Rupaji Bhosale and Manaji More, had attacked various Mughal posts in the last few months. The Badshah had never imagined such a coordinated assault on all fronts.

Aurangzeb called for an urgent meeting. He said, ordering Shahzada Azam and Diler Khan to march towards Ahmednagar, 'Ravage whatever you can in the Maratha territory—whether standing crops, or the towns. Create havoc.'

Azam and Khan nodded. Aurangzeb turned to Zulfikar Khan and asked, 'What news from Ramshej?'

'Jahanpanah, Shahbuddin is determined to take over the fort. He is building a huge platform on which he is mounting cannons. He is sure that …'

Aurangzeb was happy to hear of Feroz Jung's progress. He said, interrupting Zulfikar, 'Wazir-e-Azam, I want you to give special attention to Ramshej. If need be, send more troops there. I want all the forts in Khandesh under our control.'

Asad Khan said, 'I am sorry to interrupt, your Highness, but I am not sure we should spend all our resources in Nashik and Khandesh. Instead, would it not be wiser to attack Raigad in the Sahyadris?'

Aurangzeb looked at him for a moment. 'Wazir, I appreciate your ambition but why are you so eager to push me into the pit of death? The Sahyadris are not easily overrun. Thanks to its treacherous terrain, an ordinary landlord like Shiva rose high enough to call himself a king.'

'It was in the dense jungles and gorges of the Sahyadris that Afzal Khan, a true and devout follower of Islam, was killed mercilessly by Siva. Using the Sahyadris for his protection, he dared to attack my Mamajaan, Shaista Khan, and cut his fingers off. These Marathas are known for their guerrilla warfare. An attack during monsoon would be disastrous. Small nullahs will be overflowing, turning into monsters and making it impossible for us to cross.'

'Jahanpanah, at present Sambha is busy in the Karnatak and Tamil region.'

Aware of it, Aurangzeb laughed loudly. 'Huh! Let us see if he survives the trap laid by Chikkadevaraja. We will tackle him later.'

Zulfikar said, 'Jahanpanah, I am unable to understand the reason for sending a huge army towards Nashik.'

Aurangzeb laughed again. He said, pointing at the map, 'Here! Do you see the road from Burhanpur, through Nashik and Kalyan, leading to Raigad? If tomorrow Shahzada Akbar and Sambhaji decide to join forces, and assuming Akbar gathers the courage to march on Delhi, our forces will be there to stop them! My enemies in Agra and Delhi would be happy to join hands with them. Hence we need to ensure that all stations from Nashik to Thane are under our control.'

8

'Rayappa, take care of your injuries. We have a lot of ground to cover yet,' Sambhaji said, while he nursed Rayappa's wounds.

The Marathas were camping on the banks of Kaveri, next to a dense jungle. Sambhaji was bandaging Rayappa's wounds. It had been ten days since he was injured. A special tent was set up for Sambhaji and his sardars. The town of Tiruchirappalli was visible in the distance, on the far bank of the river. It had witnessed glory during the reigns of the Chola and Pallava kings. At the centre of the town was a fort built nearly twenty years earlier.

From his tent, Sambhaji could see the fort. The small temples with its spires and the havelis of the town officials were also visible. Sambhaji was lost in thought when Ekoji Raje entered his tent. Slightly bent at sixty-five years of age, with his pointed beard and twirled moutache, he reminded Sambhaji of his father. Sambhaji stood up and bent in mujra.

Ekoji said, his tone a little disappointed, 'Shambhu, why are we rotting here in the jungles? We are just a day and a half's march away from Tanjavur. How many times have I asked you to enjoy our hospitality there! Why don't you and your troops rest for a while?'

'Kakasaheb, I would feel guilty enjoying your hospitality when I have been defeated in a battle. The way we retreated that night still rankles.'

'Then, come to Jinji,' Sambhaji heard a gruff voice. It was Harji Raje Mahadik. 'It is just two days' march from here.'

'No, that is impossible, Daaji! We are not mute animals, to swallow all insults and return home!'

Sambhaji was busy collecting information about Tiruchirappalli. He had found out that Chokkanath Naik from Madurai was currently housed at the fort. He was a weak and infirm king. Madurai was a prosperous town but the territory had been usurped in part by Chikkadevaraja, while other parts had been taken over by Ekoji Raje and Harji Raje. The troops guarding the fort town were paltry and hardly posed a threat. They had been stationed there for practical purposes by Chikkadevaraja. There were a few artillery men at the fort but no one was aware of their strength. Many believed they were quite powerful.

Sambhaji called for a meeting and asked Ekoji Raje and Harji Raje to arrange for extra fresh supply of ammunition. He said to Kalash, 'Kaviraj, send a messenger to Golconda and ask them to send five thousand more men within the next ten days.'

Sambhaji said, as he concluded the meeting, 'We need to wound the enemy before our wounds heal completely.'

9

Rayappa was to be on sentinel duty at Sambhaji's tent one morning. But he was woken before dawn by some servants and he rushed to Sambhaji's tent wondering whether everything was all right. Sambhaji looked like he had not slept at all. His eyes were bloodshot. A plan was being discussed.

'Rayappa,' he said, 'Go with your men into the villages nearby and get as much cow, buffalo and elephant hide as you can.'

Kavi Kalash was confused. He had ensured that the soldiers had sufficient footwear. In fact, a factory in Raigad, under the supervision of Yesubai, was engaged exclusively in the production of footwear for the troops.

Sambhaji clarified, seeing Kalash's surprise, 'We need the leather to make shields.'

Jotyaji and Kavi were given the task of assembling a fleet of nearly a thousand small and large boats on the river. Monsoon would soon reach the region and a sense of urgency was evident in Sambhaji's actions. He knew that once the river was in spate, it would be impossible to cross over. The men were busy preparing bows and arrows. Fresh troops from Tanjavur, Jinji, and Golconda boosted the morale of the Maratha soldiers, who knew that a battle was in the offing. Kavi Kalash had managed to procure five hundred elephants and the giant beasts stood all around the camp.

Finally, the night arrived.

Since morning, hundreds of boats had been lined up on the banks of the river. At midnight, the Maratha soldiers jumped into the boats, holding the reins of their horses who would be guided to swim across. After testing the waters, the mahouts too got the elephants to descend into the river. In the light of the lamps, Sambhaji's steely face watched Tiruchirappalli, asleep in the night.

By dawn Sambhaji's army had launched its attack on the town. The guards at the fort shouted, 'Marathas! Enemy! Enemy!' The men on the ramparts launched a counter-attack with a shower of arrows. Sambhaji's troops stood in their boats, clad in thick leather jackets and hoods which protected them from the arrows! The leather armour was oiled to make the arrows slip and fall, causing no harm.

By noon, the elephants had managed to break the walls of the town and enter. There were skirmishes on the road as the troops moved ahead. By evening Tiruchirappalli had been captured by the Marathas.

Sambhaji smiled at the victory. That evening they arrived at Srirangam. Ambika Bai descended from a palanquin and looked proudly at her younger brother. They all prayed at the Vishnu temple on the banks of the Kaveri.

As they exited the temple Sambhaji looked at the fort in the distance. Its ramparts were lit up and sentries were visible from where they stood.

'Shambhu Raje,' Harji Raje said, 'It may not be prudent to attack the fort right now. They have enough ammunition and supplies to inflict serious damage on us. Chokkanath and his men can hold us at bay for six months or more. Let us be patient and decide on the next steps.'

Mild skirmishes continued around the fort as both armies continued to tease and test each other. The Maratha troops enjoyed a dip in a nearby lake, in a respite from their intermittent attacks on the fort. A few days later, Sambhaji received news of Chokkanath's death.

The Diwan sought an urgent meeting with Shambhu Raje and requested them to carry Chokkanath's body to Madurai. Sambhaji immediately gave his permission. Then Basappa Naik took him aside saying, 'Shambhu Raje, this is an opportune moment. They will open the main gates to take the body out. We can storm the fort.'

Sambhaji gave Basappa an admonishing glare and said, 'Basappa, we are not ordinary dacoits!'

Sambhaji was alert. He knew that Ekoji Raje was despondent. He feared the king of Mysore. It was expected that Chikkadevaraja would attack anyday. Harji Mahadik and Kavi Kalash supervised the troops in the town, priming them for yet another battle.

A week passed. The clouds threatened to pour torrents.

One day, Sambhaji launched a direct attack on the fort with ten thousand soldiers. It was a steep climb of nearly a hundred yards. The walls were strong and were guarded by a moat. While the Maratha troops were busy crossing the moat, the enemy soldiers started raining arrows from above. Once again, the thick leather armour ensured that the arrows merely bounced off their bodies without causing any damage.

Over the next two days, the Maratha troops tried putting up ladders to climb the walls but were repulsed. Elephants were deployed to break open the main door. There was chaos and bloodshed everywhere as horses fell prey to arrows while many elephants were mortally wounded by the cannon balls. Their agonised trumpeting was unbearable.

On the third day, Sambhaji ordered his men to launch a shower of arrows. The soldiers defending the fort chuckled privately, knowing that the puny arrows of the Marathas were of no use against their powerful weapons. But Sambhaji had other plans. The arrows tips, wrapped with cloth and dipped in oil, burst into fires as they landed in the fort. Soon, the ammunition dump caught fire and loud explosions ensued which were heard for miles around. One of the ammunition stores was close to a tower, and it exploded bringing down the tower with it. Chaos reigned inside the fort. Cries of 'help, help!' were heard.

Sambhaji signalled to his men to stop the arrows. The fort had succumbed to Maratha might. Finally, the saffron flag fluttered on its rampart.

Sambhaji was unstoppable now and soon he had captured twenty-two forts in the Mysore, Karnatak and Tamil regions. The Maratha cavalry unleashed havoc from Dharmapuri and Hosur in the north to Madurai in south, all the way to Jinji and Velur. Even the overflowing Kaveri had not been able to stop them. The loot captured from these forts was being transported in hundreds of carts moving towards Raigad.

Chikkadevaraja did not dare to confront Sambhaji again. Many kings, earlier affiliated to the Mysore Raja, were now allies of Sambhaji Raje. They made willing contributions to the Maratha treasury. Finally, Chikkadevaraja sent a letter of entreaty to the Mughal Badshah. It said: *'Please stop this Sambha who is creating havoc in the South.'* But to his dismay, he did not receive any response from the Emperor.

Sambhaji celebrated Dusshera in Tiruchirappalli. He had not yet decided when to return to Maharashtra. Most of the amirs and senior officials in the South were now under Sambhaji's control, making Chikkadevaraja nervous. Sambhaji sent a message to him: *'It has been my father's wish that I should rule over the rich and fertile lands of the Karnatak and Tamil regions. Not to mention the presence here of my step-uncle Ekoji Raje and my brother-in-law Harji Raje. I wonder why I should return to the jungles of the Sahyadri. I might as well stay here and enjoy myself!'*

This put Chikkadevaraja in a quandary. He agreed to a treaty without putting forth any conditions. It was decided to hold a meeting after Diwali in the hundred-pillared hall of the fort. Chikkadevaraja was to come from Mysore with a ransom of two crore hons.

The day of the meeting arrived. Chikkadevaraja's eleven-year-old brother entered the hall with half the promised sum and a letter from his brother which vowed to pay the balance soon. Sambhaji was restless after having stayed in the South for so long and, now that the treaty had been executed smoothly, he decided it was time to return.

Before returning, Sambhaji came to know that Chikkadevaraja had deliberately chosen not to attend the meeting. He had heard of how Shivaji had killed Afzal Khan in such a meeting and was scared of countering the same fate.

As they left the borders of Tiruchirappalli, Sambhaji touched Harji Raje and Ambikabai's feet. Blessing him, Harji said, 'Shambhu Raje, may the Hindavi Swaraj stay strong under your command.'

Sambhaji was touched Although the problems that lay ahead were uppermost in his mind. He said, 'We are facing a famine. Daaji, if I have your support from the South, who cares if one or even ten Aurangzebs attack us!'

10

A warm welcome awaited Sambhaji when he reached Raigad. He said, complimenting Yesubai on her foresight, 'Yesu, you were right! Harji has proved himself an able subedar in the South.' Yesubai was delighted to hear that. Sambhaji was pleased that Harji Mahadik had turned out to be loyal and dependable, unlike his other brothers-in-law Nimbalkar and Shirke. He added, 'I hope Harji Daaji continues his support as he has promised.' Yesubai was taken aback by Sambhaji's scepticism but did not comment.

A couple of days later, Durgadas Rathore came to Raigad. He said, 'Raje, Shahzada Akbar is keen that we march on Delhi.'

'What? Leaving Raigad without any protection? We cannot think of leaving our capital when Aurangzeb is so close and waiting to pounce.'

'He wonders what made you go to Karnatak and Jinji.'

'That was different, Durgadas. I was sure that the monsoon would be a deterrent for the Mughal army and that they would not plan any major campaign. Secondly, the Siddis needed to be taught a lesson.'

'Raje, can the Shahzada be provided with adequate troops to achieve his purpose?'

'Durgadas, I am surprised that you don't understand. The Hindavi Swaraj may have created a name for itself but in reality we are just a small kingdom. We have never had an army exceeding seventy-five thousand men while the Mughal army is nearly eight times bigger. Durgadas, I suggest you spend some time trying to convince the Hindu kings in the north as well as the Muslim ryots who are tired of Aurangzeb's politics to join us.'

The meeting continued the next day. Sambhaji commented on Shahzada Akbar's absence. 'He is resting in the haveli, Raje. He says he is keener to see action than to discuss it! He is willing to march on Delhi anytime!'

Sambhaji laughed at Durgadas's comment. 'I wish Shahzada Akbar was true to his word. Well, a dead elephant too is worth quite a lot! After all, he is a shahzada. If we are able to put him on the Mughal throne, I am sure a lot of sardars would show allegiance to him—not because they love the Shahzada but because of their hatred for Aurangzeb.'

'Raje, we urge you to take action. We have received letters of protest from Rajputana and Malwa against Aurangzeb's jijya tax. They are looking for a messiah who can save them from Aurangzeb.'

'Durgadas, why doesn't someone like Ramsingh of Ambar take the lead?'

Durgadas had no answer and remained silent.

It had been nearly fourteen months since the Mughal Emperor had landed in the Deccan with his huge army. He was disappointed that he had not tasted any success yet, and disturbed by the constant attacks across the Mughal territory by Sambhaji, Hambirrao, Manaji, Rupaji, Nilopant and other Maratha sardars.

Meanwhile, Sambhaji had decided to initiate further discussions with Ramsingh. He said to Kavi, 'He is Mirza Raje's son. Mirza Raje was treated badly in his old age by Aurangzeb. I hope he is moved by our appeal and agrees to join us.' Sambhaji asked Kalash to bring all the earlier correspondence with Ramsingh. Then he dictated a letter:

Please accept my heartfelt greetings, Ambar Naresh Ramsingh ji!

I received your letter expressing your happiness in giving refuge to Shahzada Akbar. I am in agreement with your suggestion that all Hindu kings should come together for a larger cause. But I cannot agree to your request that we do not go against Aurangzeb. It is unbecoming of a Rajput like you. A proud Maratha cannot accept Aurangzeb's overlordship. There is no question of Shivaji's son even entertaining such a thought!

I don't need to remind you that Aurangzeb conspired to kill your son Krishna Singh. I wish a veteran ruler like you would take the initiative to unite the Hindu kings. Aurangzeb believes that we Hindus are weak and have no policies of our own. He feels that we don't have pride in our religion. But we are Kshatriyas and we will not allow anyone to treat our religion as inferior to theirs.

You are more experienced than me. I am far too young. I have heard many stories of your valour and pride in the Hindu religion. I appeal to you to show some courage and help me put the arrogant Mughal emperor in his place. It surprises me that a valorous and proud king like you can remain quiet in these troubled times.

I intend to send Shahzada Akbar and Durgadas to the North via Gujarat. I hope you will provide all the support we need to further our cause. The Emperor of Iran, Shah Abbaas, has promised Shahzada Akbar all his support. He will benefit the most if Shahzada Akbar were to ascend the throne tomorrow. My friends Kavi Kalash and Janardhan Pandit will write to you separately.'

Sambhaji sighed as he said to Kalash, 'What a pity that Shahzada Akbar loves to daydream, flying high over the mountains like an eagle, while in reality he cannot walk faster than an elephant! All he can do is then blame circumstances, his destiny, and the whole world around him!'

11

The days that followed were full of turmoil and action. The Maratha-Mughal conflict at Baglan was heating up while the Mughal troops had surrounded the fort at Salher. Ramshej refused to cave in despite persistent Mughal efforts. The proud Maratha fort stood its ground. Hambirrao and his men were creating trouble for the Mughals on the banks of river Bhima. Meanwhile, Yesubai was managing the administration of the kingdom from Raigad and Shahu Raje was growing up.

Sambhaji returned one evening after visiting a few forts in the area. That night, after dinner, he sat on the swing in the balcony, lost in thought. The previous month, Bajaji Nimbalkar of Phaltan had died. He was Raje's Mama and he missed him sorely.

Yesubai said, sounding a little concerned, 'Raje, are you not feeling well?'

'Bajaji Mama was a valorous man. It is unfortunate that he spent his whole life serving under the Mughals.'

'Let that be, Raje! What is the point in brooding over such things? His son Mahadji is on our side, isn't he?'

'Hmm,' Sambhaji muttered.

'He was walking around so proudly during your coronation. He is after all your sister's Sakhubai's husband. I am sure he will extend all the support if need arises.'

Sambhaji could not remain quiet any longer. He said, grinding his teeth in anger, 'Yesu, a wolf in a lion's clothing is a dangerous animal.'

'What do you mean, Raje?'

'It is not good news, Yesu! Mahadji has joined the Mughals.' Sambhaji continued, as Yesubai sat down on the swing, stunned, 'Mahadji has been appointed the mansabdar in his father's place. His cousin has been given a post in Khan Jahan's troops.'

'Don't they have any shame?'

'Mahadji has instigated his other cousins to turn against us too. Apparently, he believes that Shivaji and Sambhaji's "Swaraj" is not going to last for long.'

Four days later, more bad news reached Raigad. Yesubai's cousin Kanhoji Shirke had joined Aurangzeb! It was a rude shock for Sambhaji. He asked his wife, 'Yesu, what about your brother Ganojirao?'

Yesubai looked down at the floor, unable to answer confidently. Sambhaji said disgustedly, 'Physically, Ganojirao may be in the Swaraj but his mind has accepted Mughal supremacy long back!'

Sleep eluded Sambhaji that night. He lay on his bed for a long time, staring at the chandelier. 'Yesu, I sometimes feel that this land does not belong to the great saints and intellectuals it has given birth to. Instead it is corrupted by ungrateful traitors and turncoats. While we have brave soldiers who are willing to give their lives for the cause of the Swaraj, we also have those who are willing to sell their souls for a piece of land or a mere post in the enemy camp. They don't think twice before betraying their homeland.'

Sambhaji continued, his voice full of pain, 'What can I do, Yesu? Should I plan how to confront the mighty Mughal army or go after those who are defecting?' Yesubai could not control her sobs. She said, putting her head on Sambhaji's shoulder, 'Raje, please pardon me. My own cousins have turned traitors.'

Sambhaji hugged Yesubai, patting her head. 'Don't blame your family, Yesu. Look at my own Mama and his family at Phaltan. They preferred Aurangzeb's camp to our home!

THIRTEEN

Abducting the Crown

1

The Emperor seemed dejected. Taking liberty in his capacity as senior sardar, Asad Khan enquired, 'It seems Badshah Salamat is not keeping well?'

'Nothing good is happening, Wazir! That kafir's son Sambha is not going away anytime soon, it seems. In fact, he is growing from strength to strength. Shahzada Akbar has not come to his senses after all this time in the enemy camp. The Janjira Siddis, despite their outward bravado, are scared of Sambhaji. The idiot viceroy of Goa is not willing to confront the Marathas either and that adamant fort at Ramshej refuses to give in. There is no news to cheer me, Asad Khan!'

Alamgir continued, 'I used to believe that all my four Shahzadas are brave and loyal. Unfortunately, they have all turned out to be immature. Wazir, one life will not be enough if we try to capture one fort after another. Look at the situation: the Emperor is old, his shahzadas are useless, and the grandsons are even worse! All my sardars are fools. Whom shall I turn to for hope?'

'But Jahanpanah ...'

'Tell me, what happened to the message you had sent to Ramsingh in Jaipur?'

'He replied two months ago. He has promised that he will convince Sambha to retreat and that he is going to convince him to turn Shahzada Akbar over to us.'

'Look at the irony of the situation! We are forced to clandestinely take the help of a Hindu king to convince Sambhaji!'

That afternoon Shahzada Muazzam and Wazir Asad Khan met. Muazzam said, a little frustrated, 'Wazir sahab, it is because of my father's distrustful nature that we have landed in such a situation.'

'I don't understand ...'

'Both Azam and I are in our mid forties; yet my Abbajaan feels we are immature. He does not trust any of us. Do you know why he sent Azam towards Bijapur and Kolhapur instead of Raigad? Fourteen years ago, Shivaji had sent Sambhaji to the Mughal court to be made a mansabdar.

Azam and Sambhaji became friends. Abbajaan fears that if Azam is sent to Raigad, he may join hands with Sambha and stage a revolt!'

A couple of days passed. One morning a message came from Azam who had reached Panhala. The messenger read it out to Aurangzeb: *'Hazrat, Mubarak! Azam has crushed Hambir. Many of the Marathas were killed.'*

The messenger was expecting the Badshah to remove his necklace and throw it at him as a reward. But nothing of that sort happened. The Badshah simply ignored the poor man.

Ten days later, another message from Azam arrived. The Wazir read aloud: *'Abbajaan, we have given a fitting reply to the enemy. We managed to kill eight hundred Marathas and capture nearly seven hundred and fifty of them alive. It is a resounding victory.'*

The Badshah barely opened his eyes to acknowledge the message and sat moving his beads. The Wazir, unable to restrain himself, ventured, 'Badshah Salamat, it does not become you to remain silent each time Azam sends new of a victory.'

'What does he expect?'

'A reward from you, Hazrat.'

'Hmm,' Aurangzeb muttered and was silent for a while. 'Muazzam dear, can you read this?'

While a puzzled Shahzada Muazzam read the message, Aurangzeb instructed Ruhullah Khan, 'Let me know who did what. Do a thorough investigation.'

The Wazir continued to look at the Emperor, surprised, as Aurangzeb summoned the head of the treasury and said, 'Shaukat Miyan, take one lakh hons from the treasury. We will make a gift of it to Azam.'

Within four days the real news started pouring in from Panhala. Hambirrao had deliberately retreated during the first few clashes. Luring Shahzada Azam and his men into Maratha territory, he had launched a decisive attack on the Mughals. Azam, unable to repulse Hambir, had fled towards Satara after crossing the river Nira.

Aurangzeb said, waving the message in front of Asad Khan,

'Wazir-e-Azam! Do you see this? I was never convinced that these two shahzadas are capable of much. I took the money out of the treasury. But it was wise of me not to have sent it to the Shahzada who does not deserve it.'

That night Muazzam and Asad Khan had a long conversation. The Wazir said, acknowledging the wily nature of the Badshah, 'Muazzam,

I consider your father as my guru. Look at the way he made you read the message, instructed Ruhullah Khan to investigate the whole episode, and while taking money out of the treasury, did not actually give it to your brother. It is difficult to win against your father in a game of wits and strategy.'

That night Aurangzeb was a little feverish. Udepuri Begum nursed him. Muazzam too spent the night at the Emperor's bedside. The next morning, Aurangzeb looked fit and refreshed. Sensing an opportunity, Muazzam said, 'Abbajaan, one should trust one's children at the very least. You must not be so suspicious all the time.'

Aurangzeb smiled knowingly. Caressing his beard, he said, 'The one who wants to rule has to learn not to trust his own shadow.'

2

Sambhaji climbed the hill after visiting the temple of Mumbra Devi. Gazing in the direction of the Ghodbandar fort, he could see the glimmer of Thane creek in the distance. The creek extended towards his left, touching the port of Kalyan. The town of Thane and the surrounding villages were visible through the dense coconut plantations. The Thane fort stood strong with its foundations firmly laid in the sea. It was being guarded by the firangis.

Sambhaji glanced worriedly at the port of Kalyan. It was here that Mughal sardar Ruhullah Khan had taken refuge, chased by the Marathas. A few months back, Aurangzeb's sardar Ranmast Khan had attacked Kalyan and ravaged the territories of Dombivli, Ambarnath and Murbad. He had managed to take charge of the port.

'Kavi,' Sambhaji said, 'The port of Kalyan is strategically located and controls the trade to lands as distant as Africa, Java and Sumatra, not to mention great cities like Istanbul, Paris and London. Aurangzeb's control over the port is akin to having a golden goose with him!'

'I agree, Raje. It is also risky for another reason. Kalyan is on the route to twenty-five or thirty Maratha forts in Khandesh. If he cuts off access, they will suffer heavily from the lack of resources, and would become easy prey for the Mughals.'

Sambhaji nodded. As they descended the hill, Subedar Vithalrao informed them, 'We are told that there has been some misunderstanding between the Arab Jange Khan and the English navy. Apparently, the Arab sardar attacked the English ship 'President' with five of his boats and tried to burn it. The ship was strong and did not drown but the incident has irked the English. They managed to drown three of Jange Khan's boats, forcing him to retreat. Nevertheless, it has put the English on their guard. They have had quite a scare.'

Sambhaji glanced at the base of the hill. He had recently ordered the construction of a fort at the village of Parsik and work was progressing speedily. Elephants and camels were being used to ferry huge boulders. Soon, the foundation would be finished.

'Kaviraj, we have to find a way to defeat Ranmast Khan but the Portuguese viceroy is acting strange. He is a sweet-tongued devil. Remember how he sent lavish gifts and letters of congratulation when Shahu was born!' After a pause, Sambhaji asked, 'Kaviraj, have our messengers reached Goa?'

'Raje, as we speak, they must be crossing the Mandovi river and will soon reach Goa.'

'What is our message to the viceroy?'

'Raje, we have warned them not to poke their nose in our fight with the Mughals. They have been asked not to allow movement of Mughal ships in the waters controlled by them. We have threatened that if they don't follow our instructions, we will attack Goa.'

Sambhaji looked at the site of the Parsik fort as he descended. The Mumbra hill was steep, making it impossible even for sheep to graze on its slopes. A wooden platform was being built near the half-laid foundations of the fort. Sambhaji had erected cannons on it. If the Portuguese were to join the Mughals, the fort could help in sinking enemy ships as they passed through the creek. Sambhaji asked Kavi as they reached the base of the hill, 'Kaviraj, have you heard of Ranmast Khan?'

He continued before Kavi Kalash could answer, 'He was once a sardar under xAdil Shah but later joined the Mughals. When Abasaheb was returning to Panhala from Jalna, it was Ranmast Khan who had held him near Sangamner for nearly three days. Kaviraj, I am not worried about the sardars who have come from Delhi along with the Badshah but I am wary of traitors from the South who have become allies with the Mughals.'

While Sambhaji was busy supervising the construction of the Parsik fort, the bulk of his troops were engaged in multiple battles at the same time. Maratha forces were ravaging the territories around Solapur. There were skirmishes in Purandar, Shivapur and Rajgad. Sambhaji had sent his sardars, Keso Trimal, Nilo Moreshwar and Rupaji Bhosale, to attack Kalyan. While the Mughals were being attacked on several fronts, the administration of the kingdom had suffered. Hence Sambhaji decided to return to Raigad for some time.

He ordered Kavi Kalash, 'Send an urgent message to Hambir Mama at Panhala to direct his forces to Kalyan. We must defeat Ranmast Khan before monsoon begins.'

While Sambhaji was on his way to Raigad he received information that Portuguese ships were crossing Thane creek.

'What is our fortkeeper at Parsik doing?

'They are firing the cannons. We did sink a few small vessels but the creek is wide and the bigger ships managed to escape damage.'

'Let us not lose hope. Ask them to continue their bombardment.'

Sambhaji reached Raigad. Shahu was nearly a year old and would soon start crawling.

A few days later, Hambir Mama arrived with fresh reports from the battle front. Sambhaji looked at Hambirrao whom even Aurangzeb had praised as 'the bolt of lighting.' Whether it was the three-day loot of Burhanpur, the campaign in Khandesh, the attack on Akola in the Vidharbha region, the chase of the Mughals upto Murtijapur, the siege of Ahmednagar or the recent confrontation with Shahzada Muazzam at Panhala—it was Hambir Mama who had led the men. Cries of 'Hambir has come! Run, run!' were common amongst the enemy troops.

Hambirrao was accompanied by Rajaram when he came to meet Sambhaji. Sambhaji was impressed by the way the veteran warrior had been relentlessly fighting, scarcely leaving the battlefield for the past four years. His energy was infectious.

However, news from Kalyan was not encouraging. The Portuguese had not been deterred by the bombardment from Parsik. They had continued plying their ships which carried goods and ammunition for the Mughals at Kalyan. Not only that, one night, five Portuguese ships had attacked Parsik and damaged a large portion of the fort.

Sambhaji was growing restless. 'Hambirmama, I wonder why these firangi Portuguese are so keen to kowtow to the Mughals.'

'Raje, you must have heard of their secret pact. The Mughals have promised to hand over to the Portuguese whatever they capture in the Konkan region, in return for the support they are receiving now.'

'Mama, we need to break their alliance at the earliest. Leave at once and destroy the firangis.'

'As you command, Raje.'

By the time Hambirrao had reached Kalyan, Ranmast Khan had defeated the Maratha sardar Vithoji Mane.

The battle took a turn when Hambirrao marched onto Kalyan with nearly twenty thousand cavalrymen and ten thousand foot-soldiers. Aurangzeb, anticipating such an attack, had sent his cousin's son Ruhullah Khan to Ranmast Khan's aid.

It was an intense battle now. The Portuguese watched in awe from the Thane fort. The fort at Kalyan was deserted now as Ranmast Khan ran towards Titwala. The action now moved to the gorge near Titwala. One day, Hambirrao got news that Sambhaji had reached Dombivli. The Maratha troops were doubly inspired now. By next morning, the Portuguese and the Mughals had abandoned their posts on either side of the creek. Many drowned in the sea as they tried to escape. The attack on the creek was visible in the night even from distant Titwala. The Mughals were a worried lot now.

The next afternoon, Hambirrao attacked Ruhullah Khan and his troops. Many Mughal sardars like Akram Khan, Ibrahim Beg, Raja Durgasingh Madhoram and others were killed. Ruhullah Khan, now clearly frightened, decided to escape via Titwala. Little did he know that the route had been blocked by Sambhaji with twenty thousand men. Raje led the attack as soon as they saw the Mughals approach. Ranmast Khan and Ruhullah Khan were stuck in the valley. With Hambirrao attacking from the rear while Sambhaji bore down on them from the other side, the Mughals were trapped like a betel nut in a nutcracker.

The Mughals ran helter-skelter, trying to find a way to escape. Shouts of 'Har Har Mahadev', 'Jay Shivaji!' and 'Jay Sambhaji!' were heard all over. Meanwhile, the sad news of his brother-in-law Rangoji dying in battle reached Hambirrao. By the time he returned to the camp, it was late in the night.

'Hambirrao has been badly hurt,' one of the messengers reported to Sambhaji.

Sambhaji rushed to his tent and was relieved to find Hambirrao awake. He had feared the worst. 'An arrow took out a lump of flesh from my arm. That's all!'

'Mama, please take care,' Sambhaji mumbled, unable to speak further.

'Arre, my right hand is still functioning, don't worry! Hambirmama said, laughing. Sambhaji himself dressed his wounds. Seeing his worried face, Hambirrao said, 'Shambhubal, stop worrying! I was the one who led the elephant after Shivaji Raje's coronation. And don't think you ought to be worried about me because I am related to you. I never allowed my relation with Soyrabai and Rajaram to interfere with deciding whom I should support. Our relation is beyond all relations!'

Sambhaji looked questioningly at Hambirrao and he said, laughing loudly again, 'It is a relation which binds both of us to the Marathi soil and to Shivaji!'

As they sat chatting, a message arrived. Aurangzeb had asked his troops to withdraw, keeping in mind the advancing monsoon. Sambhaji said, 'Mamasaheb, destiny took my father away too early. It is you who stand like a rock behind me. I hope you will take care of yourself. Be careful!'

3

'The Delhi Badshah is strong like a rhinoceros. Compared to him the overzealous Maratha king is but a lamb. Once the rhino crushes the lamb, we will be the ones to benefit the most,' Viceroy Conde de Alvor said.

His secretary Louis Gonsalves asked, 'Why do you say that?'

'Aurangzeb will retreat with the same enthusiasm that he is showing as he advances now. We will, without making much noise, get the entire Konkan strip from Malwan to Thane under our control. Goa will become an empire,' Conde de Alvor boasted, sipping wine from a silver tumbler.

The message from Sambhaji, which the secretary had brought in, remained unopened on the table.

Conde de Alvor was a debauchee, a selfish and cunning man. All the Portuguese officials posted in Goa were corrupt. In addition to extending their country's trade, they were making money on the side, filling their own coffers. Panaji had become an important centre of maritime trade in the region. All ships going east towards Java, Sumatra and Japan would halt at Goa. For the Portuguese, Goa was not only a rich and constant source of revenue but also one of unbridled power.

The Goan viceroy had begun to consider himself equal to the Portuguese king. Besides his own army, he had many African soldiers serving under him. The magnificent edifice of the Raj Bhawan, visible across the sandy beaches of Panaji, shone brilliantly in the moonlight. All around it, coconut trees swayed in the sea breeze. There was a lovely lake meant for the use of the viceroy's family when they felt like swimming. The grounds were also dotted with many small guest quarters. All in all, it was no less than a palace, providing all manner of comforts and luxuries.

Conde de Alvor looked a typical Portuguese officer, wearing a stiff collar over a puffed shirt and loose trousers. He was short and stockily built. He stared at his subjects through his bluish eyes which did not reveal his emotions.

Remembering Sambhaji's message all of a sudden, the viceroy asked his secretary to read it out. It said: *'It has been nearly two and a half years since I took charge of the Maratha kingdom. Earlier, our emissary Ramji Thakur used to ensure correspondence between us. We have exchanged messages proclaiming our friendship. You have often reminded us that we are neighbours and have expressed the desire to maintain good relations. Yet, you act differently from what you propose in your letters. You promised that you had nothing to do with the Mughal Emperor and that, if need be, you would support the Marathas in fighting them. Unfortunately, you have not bothered to honour the promises you made. You have allowed the Mughals to ferry their ships from Surat, carrying grain and ammunition. You have also betrayed our trust in the Thane region. Please keep in mind that you will have to pay a heavy price for such betrayals.'*

The viceroy sat worried for a while. On one hand there were threats from Sambhaji. On the other, he feared the Mughals. Neither of them were pleasant allies. He said, a little frustrated, 'How are we supposed to handle this?

'Sir, you must openly challenge and confront Sambhaji. That is what the Badshah wants, doesn't he?'

'That course of action is not without its pitfalls. Sambhaji is a short-tempered fellow. He has already created a lot of trouble for us in Kulaba and Thane, destroying our properties there. And he has kidnapped two of our priests at Vasai.'

Sir, we did take revenge. After all, we were able to capture Yesaji Gambhirrao who has been in our custody for the past three months.'

Yesaji Gambhirrao was brought into the Raj Bhawan. The viceroy said, 'Yesaji, I am extending a hand of friendship yet your master insists on attacking our stations. This will not help our relations to improve.'

'Sarkar, one cannot clap with one hand. Why did you allow the ships filled with ammunition for the Mughals to pass through waters controlled by you?'

Conde de Alvor was not one to keep quiet in the face of such accusations. He said in a challenging tone, 'Why does your Raja befriend the Arabs?'

'The same reason you have secret pacts with the Mughals!' Yesaji retorted.

That silenced the viceroy for a moment. Yesaji could not resist adding, 'Viceroy saheb, I don't think you ever had any plans of making friends with Sambhaji. You are waiting with bated breath for Aurangzeb's troops to defeat the Marathas!'

'Tchah! What are you blabbering? How does that help the Portuguese in any way?'

'Well, quite a bit, actually! You have been waiting to enjoy the riches that would be yours if you were to control the strip from Vengurla to Panvel.'

Yesaji had precisely summarised the viceroy's dream but de Alvor continued, ignoring his jibe, 'Are you aware Sambhaji and his men have been creating havoc in Tarapur, Dahanu, Thane and elsewhere? He entered Chaul with six thousand foot-soldiers and two thousand horsemen, and looted the treasury there!'

Yesaji was delighted to hear that. Having been imprisoned for three months, he had not been able to get much information from the battle front. The viceroy sent back Yesaji to his prison cell and told his secretary, 'We must find a way to get Aurangzeb to defeat the Marathas. But I am not willing to confront Sambhaji openly. Look at the way he has put fear in the hearts of the Siddis!'

The secretary said, 'Sir, Sambhaji's territory has borders with our province. I am told he often visits the ammunition factories at Dicholi and Kudal, and stays at the haveli at Dicholi.'

'I know ...'

'Often, while on shikaar, or when he visits temples, he does not have too many guards with him.'

'Oh, I see! Tell our spies to be alert. Let them inform me as soon as they hear of Sambhaji's presence in this area.'

It was 12 August 1683. The viceroy's boat had reached the port of Diwadi before dawn. The Panchganga river flowed close by. It was the auspicious day of Gokulashtami. In the village of Narve, thousands had gathered for a dip in the river. People from far-off places, including Vengurla, had arrived for the occasion.

Sunrise was still an hour away. The viceroy stared at the opposite bank. As soon as it grew a little brighter, the viceroy took the brass binoculars from his faujdar and scanned the bank where the crowds were gathering. The very thought that he was peeping into Sambhaji's territory tickled him.

The viceroy recalled the recent messages he had received from Aurangzeb: '*Whatever territory we capture from the Marathas, we will be happy to offer it to the Portuguese. But if you manage to catch this kafir's son, alive or dead, I will grant you the entire Konkan belt, including Goa.*' The viceroy was desperate to take hold of the entire strip of coast upto Panvel. He knew it would rake in millions for the Portuguese. He had been dreaming of this for years now.

The spies had brought him news of Sambhaji's arrival that day. The viceroy could not contain his excitement and was already revelling in his good fortune. He was sure that he would apprehend Sambhaji and fulfil his dreams.

He had placed his soldiers at strategic points all along the riverbank. They hid themselves in the bushes and waited. It was generally known that Sambhaji was accompanied by very few guards when he visited such places of pilgrimage. It was an opportunity the viceroy did not want to miss. He was willing to take a chance even if Sambhaji were to be accompanied by eight hundred soldiers! The reward would be well worth the risk.

The sun rose, brightening the whole scene. Hundreds of pilgrims were seen on the banks, taking a dip in the river. Realising that the vivid colours of his boat may be conspicuous, he ordered an ordinary fisherman who was passing by to stop. The soldiers helped the viceroy onto the boat and managed to squeeze into the space that remained. At that moment, Conde de Alvor noticed a Muslim fakir in the boat, along with four young disciples. The fakir, wearing green robes, with dark collyrium lining his eyes, patted each of the viceroy's soldiers with the peacock-feather fan he held in his hand, and muttered, 'Allah!' The Hindu soldiers were pleased to receive the fakir's blessings.

'Where are you headed to, Fakir baba?' the viceroy's faujdar asked.

'Today is the day of ashtami ...' the fakir smiled.

The viceroy was amused. He chuckled, wondering aloud why a Muslim fakir wanted to take the holy dip. The man answered, 'We are fakirs; for us Allah and Krishna are one and the same.'

The boat soon stopped at the ghats and the men started getting out. Before leaving, the fakir took the viceroy's hand lovingly and handed him his brass ring. The Viceroy felt blessed at receiving such a token from the holy man. One of the soldiers said, 'Saheb, it is a great honour to be given such a gift by a fakir!'

As the boat moved on, Conde de Alvor exclaimed, slapping his forehead with his palm, 'Oh my god! That reminds me ... inform the soldiers to frisk all the Hindu gosavis and godmen. I am told Shivaji used to roam around disguised as a godman.'

The day passed uneventfully as hundreds of men took the holy dip. The Hindu sadhus and sanyasis were frisked by the Portuguese soldiers. Soon it was evening and the viceroy was deeply disappointed at not having accomplished his mission.

A few days later, they summoned Yesaji for a discussion. Yesaji noticed the brass ring on the Viceroy's fingers. Noticing that he was staring at it, the viceroy took the ring off and gave it to Yesaji.

Reading the characters engraved on the ring, Yesaji started laughing loudly. Snatching the ring back, the viceroy asked sharply, 'What is so funny about it?'

'I am sure your secretary can answer that.'

Loius Gonsalves read the letters on the ring—'Sambhaji'. He was stunned. Staring at the ring, he recalled the young, fair and sharp featured fakir ... with his bright, penetrating eyes ...

4

'Why? Why are are we not able to capture Ramshej?' The Badshah was in a foul mood. The imperial camp was now at Aurangabad, and the Emperor could barely sleep at night. Sambhaji had been making rounds all over the Sahyadris. He was also keeping a close watch on Ramshej. The fort, situated a few miles from Nashik, had been built in a place of religious importance. According to the Ramayan, Ram and Sita had stayed there. The fort was named after Lord Ram.

Ramshej had become a thorn in his side. The small yet stubborn fort had refused to yield to Mughal pressure. His father had captured Ramshej during his Deccan campaign and Aurangzeb was eager to see the green flag of the Mughals fluttering over it again. To capture Ramshej and then quickly take over the Trayambak, Ahivant, Markanda and Salher forts, to prevent Shahzada Akbar's march to Delhi, and to take over Konkan and arrest the kafir's son—it was a dream he wanted to fulfil at any cost. Yet, thousands of Mughal soldiers had died, but Ramshej refused to fall into his hands. With each passing day, the Badshah was getting more and more restless.

The fort had become a matter of prestige for both the Mughals and the Marathas. It was not as aesthetically appealing as many other forts but it was unyielding! Shahbuddin Khan was desperate to break its walls and enter. He had nearly thirty-five thousand soldiers under his command but they had not been able to make much headway. Khan could not understand it. The fort stood in isolation, unprotected by the hills around it. And to top that, it had barely nine hundred Maratha soldiers defending it.

The old fortkeeper, Suryaji Jedhe, was a seasoned and brave Maratha sardar. He had trained under Shelar Mama and had fought alongside his brother, Tanaji Malsure, when they captured Sinhagad.

Suryaji had received a letter from Sambhaji when the Mughals attacked: *'Suryaji Jedhe Mama, you are someone who has trained under Abasaheb. What advice can I give to someone as experienced as you? But I want to remind you of what Abasaheb used to say: that each of our forts can withstand Aurangzeb for five years and more! That way, with our three hundred and sixty forts, Aurangzeb will need a few lifetimes to win them! Jedhe Mama, I will say just just one thing—your fort is on the borders of Maharashtra. See that the old Badshah is held up at the border itself, and you shatter his dreams of ruining our Swarajya.'*

One such letter was enough for Suryaji! He had transformed Ramshej into an impregnable fortress. Like the black cobra who guards priceless treasures, Suryaji would roam the ramparts of the fort day and night. No one knew whether he even slept! His sheer determination had ensured that Ramshej was still beyond Mughal grasp.

Shahbuddin had come with the ambition to capture the fort in a few hours and read the evening prayers on the fort itself. But his hopes had been shattered by Jedhe and his men. The Mughals had attacked the main gate. They had managed to shake the door and were confident that they would be able to break in next day. But in the morning, to their utter surprise, they saw a newly built gate. The Marathas had magically transformed a battered gate into a strong new one, working overnight. The Mughal troops were now convinced that the Marathas were being helped by ghosts and spirits who protected the fort.

The area around the fort had witnessed some harrowing scenes due to frequent skirmishes between the two armies. Most of the villages in the area were abandoned now. Sambhaji was acutely aware that it was only Jedhe and his eight hundred men who remained. He had instructed Hambir Mama to look into the matter. Hambirrao planned to spring a surprise attack with eight thousand men, devastating the Mughal camp which was thirty-five thousand strong. Meanwhile, Suryaji did not allow the Mughals to make progress during the day, and the night attacks by the Maratha added to their grief. They could barely sleep at night. This had been going on for months now.

Sharif Khan, another Mughal sardar, reached Ramshej in May 1682. Five hundred elephants and a thousand bullocks carted rations and ammunition. Suddenly, the forests in the vicinity resonated with whistles and signals. Nearly seven thousand Marathas, who had been hiding in the dense undergrowth, sprung a surprise attack. The battle lasted for two hours. Jahir Khan, Faizullah Khan and many other Mughal sardars were killed.

The Mughal troops at the base of the fort rushed to help their brothers. In the battle that ensued, nearly six hundred Marathas lost their lives and another two thousand men were wounded. But they had managed to destroy the bulk of the Mughal supplies. Sensing that they had suffered heavy losses, the Marathas retreated. Sharif Khan was tickled that he had managed to stave off the attack and immediately despatched a letter to Aurangabad, praising himself for the victory.

Asad Khan was aware of the fact that the Badshah was eagerly waiting to hear good news from Ramshej. He rushed to the Emperor, without having verified the facts in the message. 'Congratulations, Hazrat! We have won!'

'What? Have we taken the fort, or you are talking of a battle at the base?'

Asad Khan said, realising his excitement had been premature, 'Ji, Huzoor! It was at the base.'

'How foolish of you!' Aurangzeb said, his eyes boring into Asad Khan, who was sweating nervously by now. 'Why don't our stupid sardars learn from the Marathas? Look at the way they repeatedly attack us and run away.'

Months passed by and Ramshej stood as invincible as before. Shahbuddin was frustrated and the Badshah was losing his patience. Shahbuddin had cut off all the routes which could be used to supply rations and other materials to the fort. Yet, Suryaji was as determined as before. He created cannons out of leather and wood to bombard the Mughal forces. The newly built cannons were even more powerful than the ones he had earlier!

Shahbuddin realised that it was no use trying to attack Ramshej from the ground and issued orders for a huge wooden platform to be built. It could hold five hundred people. Then he began a fresh attack from there. The tall platform rose threateningly in front of the fort. The Mughal bombardment continued but it hardly made a dent on the little fortress.

There were messages flying daily from Aurangabad to the Mughal troops and from Raigad to the Maratha forces. An year and a half passed. Aurangzeb's spies relayed the news that Sambhaji was planning to send huge reinforcements to Ramshej. Alamgir instructed his milk-brother, Bahadur Khan Kolkatash, 'Bhaijaan, the kafirs dared to ransack Burhanpur once. Sambha managed to escape. I want you to capture Ramshej.'

He continued, 'Your casual attitude has cost us dearly. It was your lax security at Khandesh which allowed Shahzada Akbar to escape and join the Marathas.'

Bahadur Khan lowered his eyes, ashamed to meet Aurangzeb's stare. 'Hazrat, I have been promised by Shahbuddin that he will not return till he has taken Ramshej.'

'What does he lose, giving false promises? Does he realise my prestige has been shattered to pieces? I don't want the troops to lose their morale. So the two of you must try together.'

Taking only essential items with him and leaving the rest of the caravan at Bahadurgad, Bahadur Khan moved swiftly to Nashik. The information reached Sambhaji. He instructed Rupaji Bhosale and Manaji More to move immediately with eight thousand troops. Bahadur Khan had been given nearly fifteen thousand men. The two forces met and clashed at Ganesh village, not far from the base of the fort.

The Marathas suffered heavy losses, forcing Manaji and Rupaji to withdraw. Shahbuddin and Bahadur Khan were determined not to return till they had captured Ramshej.

The two Mughal sardars sat at their tents that evening. In the distance they could see the saffron flag fluttering on the ramparts of the fort. The sun slowly descended over the western horizon, just beyond the hills. Soon, there was complete darkness. Bahadur Khan instructed his men to start a relentless attack on the fort. The Mughal soldiers, with mashaals in their hands, attacked yelling 'Allah-o-Akbar!' The Maratha sentries looked on, confident that nothing could touch the fort.

Unknown to the soldiers attacking the fort, Bahadur Khan and Shahbuddin had moved away and were instructing another Mughal battalion, numbering nearly fifteen hundred.

'Now listen to me carefully,' Shahbuddin said, as he dismounted. 'I don't want anyone to light a single lamp. I need men who can climb the walls of the fort.'

'Those who are willing to die may step forward,' Bahadur Khan challenged the men.

Nearly eight hundred men stepped forward. In the background the noise of the Mughal bombardment was audible. The Maratha sentinels on the walls were busy watching the drama unfold at the base of the fort. Suryaji Jedhe surveyed the scene for a while and said, 'I remember Shelar Mama's words. He had warned me that when you hear the hens making an unusual amount of noise, you can be sure there is something amiss.' Soon, Suryaji had assembled a select group of men who disappeared into the darkness after receiving instructions from him.

At the rear of the fort the silence, compared to the commotion on the other side, was deafening. The Mughal soldiers were quietly making their way up the rock face. Using trees and thorny bushes to pull themselves up or support their weight, they progressed towards the top.

Finally, three men reached the top. To their astonishment, they were greeted by stones from slingshots which the Marathas had trained on them. With cries of 'Allah!' and 'Run!', they started climbing back down but were hit badly. As they fell, they took a few more down with them. In the meantime, the Marathas chanted 'Har Har Mahadev!', 'Shivaji Maharaj ki Jay!' and 'Sambhaji Maharaj ki Jay!', attacking those who were trying to climb up. Soon huge rocks and mashaals started raining down on the Mughals. Of the four hundred men who had been assigned the task, merely twenty or thirty managed to survive that dark night.

Shahbuddin was tired the next day as he had not slept the previous night. He rested the whole day but his head reeled with the defeat. He would glance angrily at the distant fort and its impregnable walls from time to time, stoking his own misery.

He realised he did not want to stay any longer in this inauspicious jungle. He planned to leave at once and stop over somewhere near Nashik that night. He had just jumped onto his horse when he glanced at the wooden platform which the men had erected earlier. Rushing towards the platform, he instructed his men to surround it with bundles of dry grass. Soon, the bundles were lit and the platform started burning. Bahadur Khan ran to Shahbuddin saying, 'Have you gone mad? Why are you destroying it?'

'Khan sahab, I don't want anything to stand that was built by these sinners. We will start afresh.'

The platform burned through the night. Shahbuddin and his men turned towards Nashik. No one could see the tears rolling down his cheeks and disappearing into his white beard.

5

The skirmishes continued across Maharashtra, with both sides gaining and losing ground at various places. The sea of Mughal forces around Ramshej had not receded but the Maratha troops, like honeybees, would sting whosoever tried to scale their hive.

Bahadur Khan Kolkatash stared at the fort with disappointed eyes. One of his sardars suggested, 'Khan sahab, please don't mind my impertinence … but why waste time? Why not take advice of an exorcist?' Bahadur Khan glared at his sardar. How dare the man suggest such a ridiculous thing? Kolkatash said, 'I can subdue not only the Marathas but their ghosts too. I am going to block all their supply routes. Let me see how long they can survive.'

Bahadur Khan instructed his men to find all the supply routes. He came to know that supplies were being sent intermittently from Trambakgad where Moropant Peshwa's brother Trimal was the fortkeeper. He kept a close watch on the route from Trambakgad.

All the routes were blocked. The soldiers at Ramshej were in trouble now. Meanwhile, Rupaji and Manaji's men were still trying to find a way to enter the fort with reinforcements but Bahadur Khan's troops were always on guard. The men and horses were no longer able to use the undergound passages leading into the fort as they too had been blocked by now.

In Raigad, Yesubai could not contain her anxiety. It would be shameful to allow the men at Ramshej to die of hunger. Bahadur Khan boasted of putting the men and animals there to a slow but sure death. Shambhu Raje, in the meantime, summoned Manaji to assist him near Kalyan. Bahadur Khan waited for a victory, which he felt was within grasp now.

After a sudden shower, Ramshej and its surroundings were covered in a thick blanket of fog. Suddenly, the Mughal troops were subjected to a horrible stink, as if animal carcasses were being burnt nearby. The hideous smell made the troops restless, and soon, they started vomiting. Bahadur Khan moved the troops away for the night, lest the soldiers started falling ill.

The very next day things had changed at Ramshej. The Maratha troops looked twice as energetic and alert as they had the night before. The existing strength of the troops seemed to have increased by a few hundred. Bahadur Khan realised that the previous night's ploy had worked in favour of the Marathas. Was it intervention by ghosts, he wondered uneasily? He was desperate for a solution now.

'Don't bother about the costs. Get me a good exorcist,' he commanded.

The same day, an exorcist arrived. The man said confidently, 'Khan sahab, all I need is a snake made of a hundred tolas of gold. Then follow me to the gates of the fort. You will be surpised at how they opens on their own!'

The jewellers at Nashik were immediately put to work and soon a huge snake was fashioned out of pure gold. Reminders from Badshah continued to arrive and Bahadur Khan replied, explaining his new strategy. He mentioned that the suggestion had been made by an exorcist.

The exorcist literally danced with joy seeing the golden snake. All the soldiers were now waiting to witness the magical opening of the gates. As the exorcist, followed by Bahadur Khan, his sardars and some soldiers, reached the gate, they were suddenly attacked by a hail of huge rocks from the ramparts. One of the stones hit a sardar on his chest and he fell on the ground with a loud thud. Another stone hit the exorcist on his forehead. The snake flew from his hand. With shouts of 'Ya Allah!', the rest of the soldiers and Bahadur Khan ran away, much to the merriment of the Maratha troops on the walls.

A stinging note from Aurangzeb put Khan Jahan Bahadur Khan Kolkatash in his place. It said: *'One normally assumes that a man becomes wiser with age. But in your case it seems to have had a reverse effect. I am sure you remember how Shivaji, with a handful of men, had made you run away from Bahadurgad, leaving behind a treasury worth crores. Sambhaji has proved to be his father's son. He took your own dead animals and men and burnt them, making you and your men abandon your vigil. That allowed them enough time to provide additional men and supplies to the fort. Well, it is quite a tragedy that Siva's son turns out to be even shrewder than his father and continue to fool us … it seems to be our fate!'*

6

For the Emperor, the palace at Aurangabad now felt worse than a jail. He was never at ease, constantly fearing an attack on the palace. What had he achieved in the last year and a half, he wondered. The miniscule fort at Ramshej had not yielded yet, while repeated excursions into the Konkan region had not been very fruitful. Shahzada Akbar was adamant as before while Sambhaji remained elusive.

Siddi Kasam and Khairyat were lucky to have survived but were mortally afraid of provoking Sambhaji now. The Badshah had sent a huge supply of grains and ammunition from Surat but they were still unwilling to take the Marathas head on.

Despite veiled threats from the Badshah, the Portuguese viceroy was not willing to take up arms against the Marthas either. The English too did not dare to step out of their territory. When Sambhaji was in Tiruchirappalli, the Mysore king Chikkadevaraja had sent urgent pleas for help but now he seemed to have gone silent.

The Badshah's younger shahzada, Azam, had returned from Panhala after tasting defeat. Hambirrao had chased him to the banks of the river

Nira. Sleep eluded Aurangzeb as he recalled all the humiliating defeats the Mughals had faced. He asked Asad Khan in a querulous tone, 'Wazir, how do we reconcile ourselves to the fact that a mere twenty-five-year-old makes us look like amateurs? What is it that we lack? Resources?'

'That we have in plenty.'

'A huge army? Daredevil soldiers?'

'We have more than we need, Hazrat. The very sight of our ocean-like army is enough to put fear in the enemies' hearts.'

'The reality is very different from what you imagine, Wazir,' Aurangzeb said, in a distressed voice. 'The very thought of entering the ravines and gorges in the mountains here makes our soldiers shiver with fear.'

He stood up for a moment and then sat down again. He said agitatedly, 'I am sixty-five while that kafir's son is in his mid-twenties. On one side we have the Badshah of Hindustan; on the other is a mere landlord's son. He cannot be compared to me by any stretch of the imagination. Yet, I am not able to subdue him. That pains me, Asad Khan ...'

He continued, after a pause, 'It seems the ghost of Dara is not willing to leave me.'

'Please forget those days, Jahanpanah. It has been more than twenty years.'

'Once upon a time Rohilla Diler Khan was in Dara's camp.'

'Please be patient, Jahanpanah. It seems you are not well. Why look at poor Diler Khan with suspicion? He had been with you ever since you attacked Delhi to capture Dara. He has been at your service all these years.'

'But how can I forget that it was Diler Khan who allowed Sambha to escape? I would not have been suffering today had he managed to hold Sambhaji captive.'

'Men do make mistakes,' the Wazir said, trying to avoid the Badshah's eyes. 'No one would ever dare to suggest Siva and Sambha were deliberately allowed to escape from Agra.'

Aurangzeb let out a deep sigh and was silent for a while. The Badshah was under great stress. He had crossed the river Tapti with a lot of hope and a gigantic army of five lakh men and four lakh animals. But the rocky and thorny province he entered had left him shaken. He had been sure not only of putting Sambha in chains but also of arresting his shahzada and then marching on the Shia-ruled Bijapur and Golconda kingdoms to subdue them.

He had nursed a dream of capturing the entire Maharashtra in a matter of six months. But now, eighteen months down the line, he had nothing to show for his troubles.

'Sometimes I am tempted to give all this up and return to Delhi,' he said in a frustrated tone. 'It is clear that capturing Sambha is not as easy as we thought it would be. And destiny is not on our side.'

He contined, 'Shahzada Akbar may be foolish but he is a good man ...' Wazir Asad Khan raised his eyebrows questioningly and Aurangzeb said, making a face as if he had swallowed a bitter medicine, 'Shahzada Akbar revolted openly. I am sure the other shahzadas too are silent admirers of our enemy. Tell me frankly, Wazir! Is that true? I believe Shahzada Muazzam admires Sambha. I believe he has made a secret treaty with the Marathas. What do you say?'

Wazir knew that it was better to keep quiet than reply to his rhetorical question. He was well aware of the Badshah's suspicious nature. He had finished off all his brothers—Shuja, Murad and Dara—before ascending the throne at Delhi. He had put his eldest son Muhammad Sultan in prison for life for having supported Shuja. He had made life miserable for his father Shah Jahan. He had also sentenced his daughter Zebunissa to life imprisonment for having helped her brother Akbar. He was acutely aware that his sons would do to him what he had done to his father and brothers. This led to him keeping a strict eye on the movements of all his sons and begums. His spies had been working under them for years as washermen, cooks and other servants. The Badshah received regular updates from the palaces of his begums and his shahzadas.

But his own suspicious nature troubled him. He would at times confide to Udepuri Begum, 'Begum sahiba, what is the use of this Sultanate, all this wealth and fame? I have vaults filled with diamonds and other precious stones but that does not help me to buy peaceful sleep. Sometimes I wonder if the half-naked fakirs and beggars sleeping on the stone steps of the masjid and the dogs dozing without a care in the world are luckier than I am!'

Coming out his reverie, Aurangzeb instructed his Wazir, 'Keep a strict eye on Shahzada Azam.'

When Asad Khan looked hesitatingly at Aurangzeb, he thundered, 'Don't argue! And call Diler Khan and Azam back from their campaigns. I want them here!'

'As you command, Jahanpanah,' was all Asad Khan could say.

Udepuri Begum and Shahzadi Zeenat-un-Nissa were both worried. Asad Khan said, trying to pacify them, 'Begum sahiba, beti Zeenat, Badshah is upset that we have not had any success in the Deccan despite all our efforts. It is natural that he is becoming more and more suspicious. We need to engage him, distract him; else the ghost of suspicion will make him a lunatic. He needs to rest for a while.'

Udepuri Begum struggled to find a way to distract the Badshah from his current obsession. She finally found a solution. That evening, after the prayers, she said, 'My dear, I have never asked you for anything. Will you fulfil my one desire?'

'What is it?'

'I would like you to take me to Verul.'

'Verul? Don't you know that it is a place of pilgrimage for the kafirs?'

'Abbajaan,' Zeenat said, 'There is a unique blue bird called Nilkanth there. I wish that you see it once.'

Aurangzeb looked sharply at his daughter and his begum. Asad Khan, his son Zulfikar Khan and the Badshah's daughter-in-law Sheherbanu Begum, were present too. They were surprised at the odd request made by Udepuri Begum.

Aurangzeb said, 'Begum sahiba, no one dares to speak of the kafir temples in my presence. Why are you then so keen to take me to a place worse than hell? What is so special about the stone lingam in the caves there?'

'Hazrat, if a man concentrates and stares at the lingam for a long time, he will be able to see his future.'

The Badshah was not convinced but the proposal had been made by his favourite begum and his beloved daughter after all. He could not refuse. The next day, they left for Verul. Most of the troops stayed back in Aurangabad while a small contingent of seven thousand soldiers accompanied the Emperor's party. A few decorated elephants as well as a few thousand horses and camels completed the caravan.

The royal procession reached the caves of Verul by evening. The Badshah's forehead creased at the sight of the Kailash temple in the distance. He said, turning to Zulfikar Khan, 'Beta, remind me to build a masjid here in place of that temple once I destroy Sambha and the Marathas.'

They reached the caves. Aurangzeb stared at the Shiva Linga inside the cave for a long time. Suddenly, he sensed something and sweat broke out on his forehead. He turned to go, shouting, 'You idiots! Let us go. I don't want to be at the graveyard of these kafirs!'

The Badshah had ordered his tent to be pitched near one of the caves. He was angered seeing the statues of gods and goddesses, and the carvings of elephants in the Kailash temple. He gave orders to his men to destroy the sculptures. The men started breaking the idols and defacing the images on the temple walls. Soon, there was dust and broken stone everywhere. Udepuri felt disturbed. The work may have been done by Hindus but she felt that the carvings had something noble, something unique, in them.

She realised that Badshah was very upset about having come to Verul on her insistence. She wisely refrained from giving him any advice against despoiling the caves. Zeenat tried to pacify her father, 'Abbajaan, why do you want to sit here and supervise? Let Zulfikar manage that. You must take rest.'

That night they camped at the village of Verul. It had not been an easy task to destroy statues and carvings made of hard stone. They were the work of generations of stoneworkers and sculptors. The Mughal soldiers managed to break a few sculptures but they found it impossible to destroy some of the bigger ones. The arches and the larger temples stood as they were.

Zulfikar ordered his men to fill the caves with hay and dry grass and set fire to them. Soon, dense smoke spread across the night sky. Most of the idols survived the inferno but the beautiful paintings suffered damage. Seeing smoke and flames coming out of the caves soothed the Badshah's frayed nerves.

Udepuri asked a few days later, 'Hazrat, what did you see in the cave the other day that made you so miserable?'

'A pig! Do you think I am such a sinner that I will be a pig in my next life? Huh!' The Badshah dismissed the discussion with a wave of his hand. Udepuri remained silent.

7

There was silence in Aurangzeb's camp. He had called for a meeting of all his chief sardars—Ranmast Khan, Khan Jahan Khan, Asad

Khan, Zulfikar Khan and others. Of late the Badshah had become very suspicious and cantankerous, and no one was sure how he would react to anything.

Even a lifelong servant of his like Diler Khan was restless. He had been recalled from his campaign and was being escorted to Aurangabad by five thousand of the Badshah's men. His only consolation was that he had not been put in chains but he feared that day might arrive soon. In any case it was evident that he was literally under arrest and would soon be presented in the Badshah's court. Diler Khan had seen guards posted outside his tent at night, apparently to prevent his escape. Even the begums stayed away from the Badshah these days. The men serving his meals and the khojas under his command were always on tenterhooks.

The Badshah said, 'Tell me, Asad Khan; I have been roaming around Sambha's territory for a year and a half with a huge army. I am like a nomad. But what I have achieved? I can understand the success of his tactics in the Sahyadris, but what about Ahmednagar and Warhad where Hambir is making life difficult for us? With a troop strength of merely fifteen thousand, he is destroying our camps and stations there.'

'Hazrat, Hambir seems like a man possessed. His horses move with lighting speed; that is what my soldiers tell me,' Musad Khan stood up as he spoke.

'Sit down, you idiot! Are you praising that kafir or criticising him?' Aurangzeb thundered.

Aurangzeb looked at all the sardars in attendance. No one wanted to meet his eye.

'I have not been able to make even a dent in Sambha's realm. I have decided; I am going to return!'

It was as if lighting had struck the men. They all looked nervously at each other and then at Aurangzeb. Seeing their confused looks, Aurangzeb clarified, 'I am returning to Delhi. My Shahzada Muazzam, Bahadur Khan Kolkatash, Wazir Asad Khan—we have many capable sardars here to continue fighting.'

Aurangzeb got down from his seat. His tone had not been one of reprimand. Of late he had become despondent; it was evident to everyone. His decision seemed resolute. They all looked at Asad Khan, who was the oldest among them. Many of the sardars expressed their disappointment, exclaiming, 'Tauba, tauba, Ya Allah!' Asad Khan could not restrain himself any more and fell at Aurangzeb's feet. He wailed, 'You may be like a son to me but you are my Lord! Your strength is like that of an ocean. You cannot leave us alone, my Jahanpanah!'

'Chachajaan, don't stop me!'

'Jahanpanah, you are the protector of Islam; you are our pride. You are called a living saint—zinda peer! The moment Sambha comes to know that you have left, our troops will die a dog's death at his hands. Our dead bodies would not even reach Delhi!'

Zulfikar Khan and others followed suit; soon several sardars had fallen at the Badshah's feet. Aurangzeb realised that their pleas were heartfelt. He was quite pleased. He returned to his chair and looked at everyone present. They all sat looking devotedly at him, waiting for him to speak. They were convinced that without the Alamgir's presence and command, they were useless and in no position to fight a battle against the Marathas.

Aurangzeb said, 'You are all protectors of Islam. It is my misfortune that I am stuck here. The Shia rulers of Golconda and Bijapur are no less than the Hindu kafirs. What a pity that an ordinary landlord's son is making the Mughal Emperor dance to his tune! So tell me: will you all work wholeheartedly for the cause of saving Islam?'

'Ji Huzoor! Ji Jahanpanah!' They all shouted in unison.

'Are you ready to die for the cause of Islam, for your Emperor?'

'Ji, Hazrat! We will sacrifice ourselves!'

Aurangzeb knew he had roused the men. Yet, he was not completely satisfied. He took his crown off and held it in his hand. The Mughal crown, with its hundreds of diamonds and other gems, glittered in the light of the lamps. Holding it high over his head, he flung it with force. The crown banged against the walls and fell with a clattering noise on the floor as the jewels scattered all around.

Aurangzeb stood with his head held high. He curled his wrists and puffed his chest. The veins in his neck bulged as he thundered, 'My friends and saviours of Islam! Alamgir makes a promise today. Till I chase Sambha out of the Deccan and tear him into pieces, I shall not wear this crown on my head!'

FOURTEEN

Attack on Goa

1

Aurangzeb behaved like a man who had just recovered from a long illness and was now fully fit. He had emerged from the cave of his depression and misfortune. The sixty-five-year-old Badshah had started working on his Deccan campaign with renewed vigour. All the sardars and shahzadas were impressed at his turnaround. 'Work, work, and work; that's what has possessed Alamgir,' they said.

Aurangzeb had a clear hold on the affairs of his campaign now. He knew the minutest details of every operation. Faujdar Baloch Khan and his son Abu Muhammad were frequently seen visiting the Badshah. Many were quite surprised to see the twenty-three-year-old Abu Muhammad getting the Emperor's attention.

Aurangzeb rarely, if ever, praised anyone in public. That day, the sardars in attendance were surprised to hear the Emperor praising Abu Muhammad openly. 'Don't be fooled by his age. Look at what he has achieved!' Aurangzeb said, throwing a glance at his sardars as he pointed at Abu Muhammad.

On cue, Abu Muhammad unrolled the map he was carrying. It was a detailed map of the Sahyadris.

'Beta, tell me about the mountains.'

'Jahanpanah, the Sahyadris are full of thorny jungles, dangerous mountains, deep valleys and gorges.'

'How many entry routes do we have?"

There are a total of three hundred and sixty entry routes. Of which only sixty-five allow elephants, camels and other such animals to travel.'

'What about the rest?'

'The rest are very narrow and treacherous. Even tigers would fear to traverse such routes.'

Alamgir asked the question that was on everyone's lips, 'How did you manage to get such detailed information?'

'I have been fond of travelling in the mountains since childhood. I came here six years ago to explore the Sahyadris. With the help of many gosavis and fakirs, I traversed this difficult terrain. And in order to help travellers like me in future, I made this map.'

Aurangzeb took out his own maps. Studying them, he pointed out some of the mistakes in Abu's map, taking the young man by surprise. The Badshah then honoured Abu with gifts of fine robes and precious jewels. He said, turning to his Wazir, 'We need to progress in this direction. Find out more about these routes. Recruit men who know the routes. Pay them well.'

'Zulfikar, I am told Sambha is planning to attack the Portuguese in Goa.'

'Does he think he can survive the firangi cannons?' Asad Khan asked, laughing.

Everyone joined in his laughter except Aurangzeb. He was aware of the strength and determination of his arch enemy. He had made a plan over the past few nights. He presented the plan to his men. 'Sambha has taken a bold step, entering into the firangi territory. While he is busy there, we will enter south Konkan through Kolhapur and Belgaum, with a troop strength of fifty thousand.'

Asad Khan raised a doubt, 'Huzoor, how would we maintain such a large army on the move? We will need rations.'

'Wah! You have asked the right question! I have already instructed our Subedar in Surat to send his ships. They will cross the Arabian sea via Mumbai, Janjira and Rajapur, and move towards Panaji.'

'Jahanpanah, we must be aware of the ports and stations Sambha has created along the route. They will bombard our ships.'

'We have enough ammunition to counter them. Secondly, the Portuguese have no option but to come to our aid.'

Seeing Zulfikar shake his head and sigh heavily, Aurangzeb asked, 'What is the matter Zulfikar? You don't seem to be in agreement.'

'Hazrat, our plan is ambitious. But the moment Sambha comes to know that our troops are on the move, he would quickly withdraw and hide in Raigad.'

Aurangzeb smiled. He said, pointing to the map spread out in front of him, 'While one contingent is moving towards Goa, another would be moving rapidly towards Raigad from Panvel and Kalyan. They will meet near Mahad and then, together, they will blast the rocky capital of the Marathas to pieces.'

Seeing everyone applaud his plan, Aurangzeb warned, 'Don't be so enamoured by it. We have to ensure strict coordination if we want to achieve success. Else, nothing will happen.'

'I have one more plan,' Aurangzeb continued, as he pointed to various places on the map. 'I will descend into the Konkan with another ten thousand men. We must burn the region. But we need to be extremely alert. If we are lax, we can be sure of being attacked by the ryots. Their loyalty to the Marathas is unquestionable.'

Aurangzeb wanted to know who should lead the campaign in the south of Konkan. The unanimous candidate was Shahzada Muazzam. The tall, forty-five-year-old shahzada was well regarded for his pleasing personality and soft-spoken nature. For a brief moment, Aurangzeb's face showed surprise at the overwhelming support for Shahzada Muazzam. It was decided that he would lead the Konkan campaign.

Aurangzeb called on Dukhalas Khan, Latif Shah Dakkhani and the head of artillery, Atish Khan, who stood up. Then Alamgir said, 'The trustworthy Maratha, Nagoji Mane Mhaswadkar.' Hearing his name, Nagoji stood up, six feet tall. Aurangzeb said, looking at him with pride, 'Beta Muazzam, keep one thing in mind: there are many families in Maharashtra who have remained loyal to Adilshah, Nizamshah, and the Mughals. They have never supported upstarts like Siva and Sambha to be their king. Nagoji belongs to one such family. He will remain loyal to his master, always!'

When asked who would lead the campaign towards Kalyan-Panvel, Zulfikar Khan stood up, hoping to be given the command. Aurangzeb reined in his ambitions, saying, 'Zulfi beta, you are young. You are also my cousin and I don't want to disappoint you, but the campaign requires not only a daredevil but someone who has the nerve to behead the kafirs while razing their temples to the ground. After giving it much thought, I have decided that the person to lead this campaign will be Shahbuddin alias Gaziuddin Feroz Jung.'

Zulfikar protested, 'Jahanpanah, he has not been able to capture the tiny fort of Ramshej!'

'Zulfikar, one cannot judge a person by one failure alone.'

Shahbuddin was sent an urgent message, instructing him to take charge of the campaign in the North. He was camping in Junnar when he received Aurangzeb's message, 'Descend the Naneghat into Konkan.

Sambha should get trapped between your troops and Muazzam's. And keep in mind that Sambha is like the wind—elusive and not easy to contain.'

Muazzam was getting ready to confront the Marathas at Ramdara. He received news of Sambhaji's victory at Revdanda and Chaul near Alibag. That night Aurangzeb conferred with Muazzam. He said, 'Sambha has moved Akbar to Banda near Goa. Once you descend into Konkan from Ramdara, you must first attack Banda and arrest that stupid shahzada.'

The next morning, Aurangzeb ordered his servants and khojas to start packing. 'There is no point in sitting here in Aurangabad now,' he told Asad Khan. 'I need to be closer to the action. We will shift to Ahmadnagar.'

'Jahanpanah ...' Asad Khan mumbled as he bowed.

'Well, Siva's son has surely made me young once again!'

2

Strong winds blew at Rajapur, shaking Sambhaji's tent. Khando Ballal entered. For a moment Sambhaji was reminded of his father, Balaji Chitnis. He had the same sharp nose and light, shining eyes. Sambhaji said, as he gestured to Khando to sit, 'Khandoba, you are the Chitnis. There are battles going on at Tarapur, Thane, Chaul, Revdanda, and many other places. Should you not be holding fort in Raigad?'

'Maharaj ...'

'You can't put the whole burden on Yesubai's shoulders. Had Kaviraj been there, I would not have been worried. But given the circumstances, I suggest you return immediately to Raigad.'

Khandoba did not reply for a while. Sambhaji was concerned. Then the young Maratha said, 'I did not come here on my own volition, Maharaj. I was sent by Maharanisaheb.'

'What for?'

'She was worried about you and wanted me by your side.'

Sambhaji smiled. He knew Yesubai was concerned about his health. 'She is managing the administration of such a huge territory on her own but gets worried if she hears I am unwell!'

Seeing Sambhaji smile, Khando Ballal was a little relieved. 'I also had a personal interest in being here.'

'What about it?'

'Well, I was keen to see how the Maratha Chhattrapati makes his sword speak for his valour when he attacks the Goans!'

Sambhaji looked at Khando Ballal with pride. Memories of the way Balaji Chitnis had been put to death along with the traitors, and the confusion created because of the delayed letter, flooded his mind. Sambhaji said, his voice quivering with emotion, 'Khandoba, I remember how Balaji Kaka's death was an unfortunate and avoidable accident. The very thought breaks my heart. The traitors had held him to ransom and I never received his letter on time. Khandoji, I am the real culprit. I am the one who committed the crime!'

'Raje, no one is at fault. It is our misfortune. The time was not right for us, that's all! Raje, please forget what happened. You offered me my father's post and took care of our family. What more can we ask for?'

'Khandoji, before I left for the campaign, I had instructed the fortkeeper in Raigad to build a temple where Balaji Kaka was killed. The constant dripping of water over the Shiva Linga at the temple would represent the tears flowing down my cheeks.'

Khando Ballal rushed to touch Sambhaji's feet. 'Maharaj, thousands die doing their duty every day. No one remembers them! But the way you preserve the memory of my father in your heart gives me a glimpse of your kindness and the love you have for us.'

Sambhaji let out a deep sigh. 'The Lord's ways are mysterious! Man can never understand Him … or destiny.' As Sambhaji spoke he recalled the huge fort at Ahmednagar where, for the past three years, Durgadevi and Ranuakka had been imprisoned. He remembered his young daughter who was growing up there.

The next morning, Sambhaji asked Khando Ballal, 'So, when are you leaving for Raigad?'

Khando Ballal said, 'Raje, my father did not have the good fortune of accompanying you when you attacked Janjira. At least let me be with you on the Goa campaign.'

3

Durgadas Rathore spoke animatedly 'We should not wait any further, Raje! The Portuguese viceroy is not only cunning; we now know he is a traitor. We must attack without wasting any more time.'

Sambhaji had camped at Rajapur. Sitting in his tent were Durgadas Rathore, Shahzada Akbar, Yesaji Kank and Kavi Kalash. The sea shore was visible from the tent. Coconut trees swayed in the wind. Sambhaji looked at his seventy-year-old sardar Yesaji Kank. Sporting a stylish turban, an embroidered zari-bordered angarkha and a pure white dhoti, he had an air of confidence which came with age and experience. Sitting next to him was Krishnaji, a smart young man in his twenties. He was Yesaji's son.

'Yesaji Mama,' Sambhaji began, 'you are the commander of the foot-soldiers. I am going to ask you to undertake a dangerous campaign.'

'Raje, this old man will not think twice before jumping into a pit of fire if you command it.'

'I trust you, Mama. You were with us at Agra. And although I could not participate in the Karnatak campaign with Abasaheb, I know you played an important role.'

'Balraje, didn't Kondaji sacrifice himself for your cause? This old man too is ready, Raje, to sacrifice himself for the Swaraj.'

The discussion centred around the attack on Goa. They talked of the bays, the ports, the Portuguese palaces and churches and the firangi posts guarding them. Sambhaji was angered by the way Conde de Alvor had behaved. 'He is a selfish and a dangerous man. On one hand he sends me jewels and gifts on the occasion of Shahu's birth, while on the other, he hatched a plot to arrest me when I was visiting Narwe on an auspicious day. What should we do about him?'

'Attack Goa! Nothing else,' Yesaji Kank growled.

'Tomorrow, if Aurangzeb's forces come towards Goa, he will not hesitate to take their side. I am told he has already signed a secret treaty with the Mughals.'

Sambhaji stretched his hand towards Kalash who took out a bunch of papers. It was a copy of the secret treaty. It clearly stated that the Badshah would give all the territory he won in Konkan to the Portuguese. In lieu of this grant, the Portuguese would allow the Mughals to establish a naval force in their coastal waters.

'We need to hit him hard before he gets an opportunity to join the Mughals.'

Everyone was eager for action. The prospect of attacking Goa was an exciting one.

Despite the overwhelming enthusiasm all around, Sambhaji was worried. He knew that it would not be easy to tackle the Portuguese with their advanced artillery, their high-walled forts and naval prowess.

That night, Sambhaji composed an urgent message for the English. They had been requesting permission to start trading near Jinji. He ordered Kavi to send the permit to their harbour at Mazgaon. 'It is better to have them on our side,' Sambhaji said.

While Sambhaji and his men were walking along the beach at Rajapur late in the evening, he said, 'Yesaji Kaka, don't forget that the Portuguese have been in Goa for nearly a hundred years. Their cannons and ships are quite powerful. Our horses are of no use on water.' He paused for a moment to remove the sand from his sandals and asked, 'But what if we find a way to lure the Portuguese to the sound of our hooves?'

4

The tavern at Panaji habour was crowded with sailors, traders, foreign visitors, and such. A few strangers had been seen roaming around in the vicinity over the past two days. It was difficult to assess their ethnicity: their grey eyes made them seem like Konkanis, the long pointed beards suggested Afghani origins, and they were nearly as fair as firangis. They whispered to each other as they sat sipping wine, 'Sambha has got a huge treasure worth nearly five crores at the Ponda fort. The ammunition stock is also huge. The army is expected any day now.' Soon the whispers reached the ears of Viceroy Conde de Alvor. He muttered, 'Shiva's son has always had a fascination for Goa. He has procured construction material to build a fort at Anjadiv, I am told.'

Other spies confirmed that the number of soldiers at Ponda are few in number but surely they are up to something. The viceroy was optimistic. 'He managed to slip away two months back,' de Alvor said, 'We had nearly got him at Narwe. Let me see how he escapes this time.' The Mughal army was expected soon. But the viceroy dreamt of taking over the Ponda fort and its treasury even before they arrived. If the rain gods were on his side, he hoped to march on to Konkan too. Not to mention the Mughal Badshah's felicitation!

The viceroy raised an army of three thousand foot-soldiers, of whom nearly two thousand men were locally recruited Kannadigas. One early morning in October 1683, the army streamed out of Panaji. It was led by the viceroy himself. Three long cannons were pulled by bullocks. The soldiers marched in an orderly fashion, holding swords and rifles in their hands. They reached the banks of the river Mandovi, their feet sinking in the soft sand. It was after a long time that such an army had marched out of Goa and men from nearby villages came out in hordes to watch.

Some of his commanders advised the viceroy to avoid the port of Durbhat. 'The Maratha subedar Dulba Naik holds fort there. It is better to avoid a confrontation.'

'Let us see,' the viceroy said, not wanting to give up his new-found bravado.

To everyone's surprise, Dulba Naik came running out of the fort to meet the viceroy and hugged him affectionately. The viceroy kissed him on the cheeks. Dulba had turned traitor and joined the firangis! The viceroy was now firmly convinced that he could easily crush the Marathas and take Ponda fort.

The men marched, unsure of their final destination. They reached the base of the fort by night. Cold biting winds made the soldiers shiver. Suddenly the skies opened up and torrential rain descended on the viceroy's army. Conde de Alvor stood in the downpour, his coat and dress completely drenched. He had brushed aside the servant trying to hold an umbrella over head. Taking advantage of the darkness, he instructed his artillerymen to place the cannons on a hillock facing the fort. The bullocks struggled to pull the weight up the slope, some of them fracturing their limbs as they climbed slowly. Finally, they managed to reach the top. The viceroy said, 'The Marathas seem to be sleeping peacefuly. Let us bury them while they do!'

The cannons began their bombardment. The walls of the Ponda fort shuddered as the firangi cannonballs found their mark. Soon, the Marathas reacted. The cannons from the fort boomed. Even in the heavy downpour, the flames of the cannons could be seen as they emitted their cannonballs. Mud flew all over as the heavy artillery continued to pound both sides.

The second night didn't favour the Marathas. The ramparts were already damaged by heavy shelling, and in the pouring rain, one of the cannons fell off the fort, taking part of the wall with it. The Portuguese camp celebrated with loud cheers. But the defiant Marathas were not willing to give up. The viceroy stood in the rains, looking rather dejected. He had stood there for two days, his drenched coat having dried on him. They had been bombarding the fort for three days but it was putting up a spirited resistance. Frustrated, he pulled Dulba Naik by his collar and demanded, 'Tell me! How many Marathas are there inside?'

'Sarkar, I was told that there were only ten or twelve. I don't know if Kavi Kalash and Sambhaji have managed to get more people in through their black magic.'

'It is not black magic, you idiot! It is Sambha's foresight and planning.'

Conde de Alvor changed his strategy, getting the cannons back on ground and targeting the fort from there. The hammering proved effective and the viceroy was convinced that at any moment the Marathas would stream out of the fort. He ordered his men to fill the moat and cross it. Soon, the moat was filled with mud and rocks. Yet, the response from the fort was an unnerving silence. As the firangis climbed up the walls using ladders, the Marathas, led by Yesaji Kank, suddenly attacked shouting 'Har Har Mahadev!' While the elderly commander led the attack, his son Krishnaji started throwing the ladders back on the ground. The firangis were falling into the moat. The six hundred Marathas inside the fort and the two hundred hiding in the bushes around it were itching for a hand-to-hand combat.

Five days passed. The fort had suffered damage but the Marathas showed no signs of yielding. The rains continued although they were not heavy enough to stop the battle. The viceroy was now losing patience. Dulba Naik suggested that they retreat. 'I have not crossed the sevens seas to be repulsed by these petty Marathas,' the viceroy thundered. One day a few firangis managed to enter the fort through a hole they had made in the wall. Krishnaji Kank, watching from the top of a wall, jumped down into their midst. In the process he sprained his ankle badly and was immediately attacked by the firangi soldiers from all sides. Despite being wounded on his chest and his back, he managed to kill nearly a dozen firangis. Enemy soldiers continued to enter through the breach.

Yesaji saw his son being attacked and rushed to save him. A hundred odd Marathas came forward to support him. Heavy fighting ensued. The firangis were now trying to flee to save their lives. Krishnaji collapsed on the ground with a hundred or more cuts on his body. The men quickly brought a palanquin and rushed the unconscious Krishnaji to the inner quarter where a physician started applying some herbs on his wounds. Yesaji tried his best to soothe his son. He himself had a deep cut on his calf which bled profusely. The men tied a bandage to stem the blood flow. Manaji More said, 'Baba, you look after your son. We will push the firangis back.'

'No, that cannot be! I have promised Shambhu that I will crush the enemy. I cannot retreat so easily.'

By dawn the next day, the Portguese viceroy was seething with anger. He was not making any progress. The rain showed no signs of abating. The firangi soldiers stood ready with tall ladders and ropes tied around their waists. Suddenly, across the fields, they heard cries of 'Har Har Mahadev.' The Marathas from the fort were heard shouting, 'Raje has come! Sambhajiraje is here!'

Within a few minutes Sambhaji's men were near the fort. The viceroy ordered his men to attack but the firangis were literally frozen with fear. Sambhaji reached the gates of the fort on his horse, followed by Khando Ballal who rode behind him.

Sambhaji asked six hundred of his eight hundred men to surround the fort. The viceroy ordered his men to use their rifles but their gunfire seemed to make no difference to the Marathas. One of the Portuguese captains suggested that they retreat. 'If Sambhaji enters the river, our retreat will be cut off.' Against his wishes and hiding his tears, the viceroy gave the order to retreat. The firangis, wearied by the incessant Maratha attack, retreated hastily.

The battered firangi army reached the creek near Durbhat. A few Marathas hiding in the hills nearby attacked the retreating soldiers. The firangis opened fire but the Marathas, dodging bullets with their shields and horses, continued their attack. One of them, using his jamdaad—a curved snake-like sword—cut through the Viceroy's leather armour, inflicting a wound near his ribs. The firangis jumped into the Mandovi's waters to save their lives. Many drowned. A desperate viceroy tried spanking his soldiers with his cane but now their only concern was to save their own lives. The viceroy, smeared in mud, surveyed the damage done by the Marathas. Sambhaji and his men had managed to literally pound the three-thousand-strong firangi army to pulp. The survivors were in the river, trying to swim to safety.

5

It had been ten days since the attack at Ponda. Conde de Alvor's wound was yet to heal but he resolved to put up a show of power and invincibility. He selected the date of 25 November 1863. It was on the same day, many decades ago, that the Portuguese had taken over Goa. The viceroy decided to commemorate the old victory with celebrations.

However, Conde de Alvor was an anxious man these days. He had never expected the Marathas to repulse their attack so effectively. His own emissary had assured him that Sambhaji and his men were no match for the firangis. Such false assurances had got him into trouble.

The viceroy had earned his spurs in Spain and begun his career in Goa as Governor of Angole. The city of Panaji was surrounded by a fortified stone wall with strong ramparts. A big ammunition store and many forts on the river—Aguada, Cabu Reis de Magos and others—ensured strong protection against any attack. Yet de Alvor was now apprehensive, having tasted defeat once. His anxiety increased when a spy brought information that Maratha soldiers had been spotted hiding in the woods around Panaji.

The wily viceroy put forth a proposal for his captains, involving a sum of three hundred thousand gold coins. 'Sambhaji and his men are looting the territories all the way from Vasai and Daman upto Goa. We don't have enough troops to defend ourselves. The Mughal Emperor has promised support but that is far away. We have not got any reinforcements from Portugal despite my reminders. We need money to be able to defend our forts!'

He passed another order. All prisoners in Panaji were to be released on the condition that they would fight in the battle. The sole objective was the repulse the Maratha attack on Goa.

Meanwhile, as the city of Panaji was celebrating the festival, just a few miles from the borders of Goa, a new development was taking place. The river Mandovi breaks into two streams, a little north of old Goa. There, the Portuguese fort of St. Estevam stood on the island of Juve. It was a strong fort with high walls. Sambhaji and his men had surrounded the fort while hiding themselves in the coconut groves around it.

Khando Ballal said, 'Maharaj, just a few days back we put the firangis in their place. I wonder why they still don't come to their senses.'

'Well, let them decide when they want to. I am told a huge ship carrying grain from Surat has reached Goa. It is clear that the Portuguese are providing financial support to the Mughals in return for handing over our territories when Aurangzeb captures them. It is only when we break their spine that these rascals will keep quiet,' Sambhaji said, banging his fist on his horse's back.

By ten o'clock that night, the river's water receded. Sambhaji was waiting for the moment and rode across the river. But he took care not to allow the water to splash while crossing. Not a single lamp was lit. Soon, Sambhaji stood on the other bank caressing his horse's mane.

On cue, forty Marathas entered the water carefully. As soon as they crossed the river, they surrounded the fort of St. Estevam. The walls were very high but ladders were quickly put up. The fort was guarded by an old fortkeeper with a few firangi soldiers. The Marathas attacked the fort with Khando Ballal leading the troops. Within half an hour they had taken the fort. Soon, Khando Ballal fired cannons announcing the takeover. The booming of the cannons was followed by the Maratha cheer of 'Har Har Mahadev!' It created a commotion in the area. There was chaos all around as people ran to seek shelter screaming 'The Marathas have come!' Goa was shaken to the core. Fearing danger, numerous churches rang their bells. Bugles announced the impending Maratha invasion.

The firangis were frightened and cowered in various churches, praying for their lives. All doors and windows in the city of Panaji were shut tight that night. Led by Conde de Alvor, a few soldiers hurried towards the borders of the city carrying weapons. Within a few days the Marathas had captured a second fort. Furious now, next morning, the viceroy attacked St. Estevam with a hundred and fifty men. The Marathas confronted them head on. The defence was fiercer than they had expected and the firangis soon turned back, jumping into the river.

Some of the Marathas attacked the viceroy at St. Estevam but he was saved at the last moment by a few of his men. The river Mandovi was now rising. The high tide had begun. Sambhaji led the attack while the viceroy and his men rushed into the water. Stuck in the mud, many were sitting ducks for the Maratha arrows and bullets. Many lives were lost.

The viceroy was lucky to find a floating raft and managed to climb onto it. He rowed to the other side but Sambhaji saw him escaping. This was the man who had promised to catch Sambhaji alive and present him to the Mughal Emperor! Sambhaji looked at the distant church spires of

Goa. He knew it was the right moment to conquer this land. The firangis were terrified and their confidence was shattered. Goa held pride of place as an eminent trading post for foreigners. It had long eluded capture even by Shivaji Raje. To let go of such an opportunity would be foolish.

Sambhaji spurred his horse. The wise beast, sensing its master's command, hesitated for a moment at the edge of the river and then jumped into the current. Its hooves did not touch the riverbed. It could barely swim yet it continued to try. Soon a huge wave hit them and both were submerged. The Maratha soldiers watched as their Maharaj struggled in the rapid waters.

Sambhaji was an expert swimmer but one of his feet was stuck in the stirrups, pulling him down. Khando Ballal jumped into the river with his horse. He swam towards Sambhaji swiftly and, taking his dagger from his cummerbund, managed somehow to release Raje's foot from the stirrups. Soon, an exhausted Sambhaji and Khando Ballal reached the shore. They both sat on the ground catching their breath.

St. Estevam, now under Maratha control, was quiet. Sambhaji and his men were resting in the fort. A fire had been lit in the vast courtyard. Sambhaji sat with a warm shawl draped around his shoulders. Kavi Kalash, Jotyaji Kesarkar and others were in attendance. They had their meals sitting around the fire. Sambhaji stood up and hugged Khando Ballal, saying, 'Khandoba, you saved my life without caring for yours. I am indebted to you. I have already given you the post of Chitnis. Tell me how I should honour you.'

Khando Ballal was overwhelmed and fell at Sambhaij's feet, saying, 'Maharaj, allow me to be at your feet always. I don't want anything else.'

Khandoba gifted his horse to Sambhaji. Raje said, 'Khandoba, don't embarrass me any further. I am already indebted to you and now you are giving me your prized horse?' He continued, 'I can now understand why my Abasaheb had such faith in the Prabhu community when it came to managing treasuries of the forts in the Hindavi Swaraj. Khandoba, the loyalty of your father, Balaji Chitnis, was unstinted. The Prabhus have lived up to their reputation of brave service in the cause of the Swaraj—be it Bajiprabhu Deshpande at the Gajapur gorge, Murar Baji at Purandar, or Khando Ballal's leap into the swirling waters of the Mandovi to save my life! You have elevated the phrase "loyalty to the state". This trait alone has earned you a thousand salutes from the "Prabhu" above in the heavens!'

6

The city of Panaji was quiet. A strange silence pervaded Goa and its creeks. The bulk of Sambhaji's troops were garrisoned at Dicholi. He ordered two thousand men to move to Ponda. The fortkeeper was ordered to ensure repair of the fort on an urgent basis. The Portuguese emissary Albuquerque waited patiently for a meeting with Sambhaji but Raje deliberately delayed the appointment.

Sambhaji asked Yesaji Kank, 'Kaka, how is Krishnaji's health?'

'He is not yet out of danger. The wounds are deep.'

'Why are you here then, Yesaji Kaka?' Sambhaji was concerned.

'It is not easy to leave a battle halfway, Raje. I cannot afford to be elsewhere.'

Sambhaji did not reply. At that moment they heard a commotion on the other side of the fort. Khando Ballal came and reported that the locals were angry at the dismantling statue of the Virgin Mary. Some soldiers were also planning to burn the small church nearby.

An angry Sambhaji spurred his horse. The soldiers had just started the fire when Raje rode up and shouted, 'Stop it! Douse the fire or else I will cut off your hands.'

Soon the fire was put out. The local Hindus had incited the soldiers to destroy the church. One of them said, 'Raje, do you have any idea how we are treated here?'

'Silence! I don't want any arguments. I will not allow such deeds to be done in the name of Shivaji Maharaj.'

'But Raje, what about their ill treatment of us …?'

'An eye for an eye is not always the solution. Marathas are known to be God-loving. We are not iconoclasts and looteras!'

There were reports of riots from Bardesh and other places in Goa. The Hindu ryots, suppressed by Christian atrocities for decades, were now revolting openly. Churches were being torched. Sambhaji issued firmaans to ensure no place of worship was desecrated or destroyed. It troubled him that people were taking the law in their hands.

The viceroy assumed that Sambhaji would, after taking over Ponda, leave for Panhala. He did not know that Raje wanted to ensure a significant victory over the Portuguese before returning. Sambhaji, meanwhile, was in regular touch with spies from Raigad and sending messages to various people all over the region on a daily basis.

Reaching Dicholi, Raje composed a secret message for Shahzada Azam: *'Azam sahab, do give this a thought. Your father is old and extremely suspicious by nature. It is time to throw away the shackles. If you revolt, we will give you our complete support to take over the throne at Delhi.'*

Kavi Kalash laughed reading the message. 'Why, what is so funny Kaviraj?' Sambhaji asked.

'I was imagining the message landing in Aurangzeb's hands instead of the Shahzada's. Imagine how disturbed he would be!'

'That is precisely the intention of this "secret" message,' Sambhaji said, smiling.

He also dictated a message for Adil Shah at Bijapur: *'Don't count as blessing the fact that Aurangzeb has not yet reached the South. You may be under the false illusion that if the Marathas are defeated, the Mughals will spare you. Think of your future. We must join our forces and fight the common enemy.'*

He also wrote to Diwan Madanna at Hyderabad: *'If only I had the kind of wealth you have! I would have marched on Delhi and drowned Aurangzeb in the Yamuna. Don't think you will be safe just sitting in your domain and shutting the door to reality. The storm outside is not going to subside so easily.'*

A rider brought the sad news of Krishnaji Kank's death. Yesaji almost collapsed hearing it. He burst out sobbing loudly. No one could utter a word. Sambhaji, tears running down his cheeks, hugged Yesaji. 'Yesaji mama, contain yourself!' was all he could say.

'Balraje, I am not questioning destiny, but one thing troubles me! I am an old man who is destined to die sooner rather than later. But someone like Krishnaji, who was capable of fighting by your side for many years to come, has been taken away. What a tragedy!'

That evening many soldiers came to pay their last respects. Holding Yesaji's calloused hands, Sambhaji said, 'Mama, don't mourn the loss of Krishnaji. He has reached the heavens fighting for the cause of Swaraj. He will shine forever like the pole star.' Sambhaji instructed his men to allocate a Subah, a revenue-earning province, in Krishnaji's three-year-old son's name. He also ensured that the family would continue to receive Krishnaji's pension. The soldiers were overwhelmed seeing the instant decisions taken by Sambhaji to care for Krishnaji's family.

Tears of gratitude flowed down Yesaji's cheeks. He hugged Sambhaji affectionately, saying, 'To tell you the truth, Shambhu Raje, when I am with you, I feel I am with the elder Maharaj himself!'

7

It had been more than a month since the Marathas had entered Goa but they had not retreated yet. Aurangzeb's ships were anchored near Vengurla but the viceroy was refusing permission to dock them in Goa. He was not sure of the Mughals. He now feared that they may, in violation of the treaty, swallow Goa themselves!

Sambhaji roamed the banks of Mandovi restlessly. He was desperate to take Panaji. He would urge Kavi Kalash, Durgadas and Shahzada Akbar, 'Do something! We must capture Panaji. All we need is to get five or six hundred men inside. Once they infiltrate the city, we know how to attack from outside and take over.'

Shahzada Akbar started a correspondence with the viceroy, asking for permission to build a ship near Panaji. Once he had received the permit, Sambhaji sarted sending his carpenters, ironsmiths and a few soldiers across the river, ostensibly for the purpose of building Akbar's ship. But the viceroy smelled a rat, seeing the number of 'workers' increase, and did not allow them to stay in Panaji. Once the shahzada went to the harbour with nearly six hundred men but he was turned back. While Sambhaji was trying every trick up his sleeve, the viceroy too was vigilant.

Sambhaji was growing restless. Three thousand Maratha foot-soldiers and a thousand cavalrymen had reached Madgaon. The church there was very popular. Sambhaji gave explicit instructions to loot but not harm people or damage places of worship. One day, as Raje rested at the haveli in Dicholi, Kavi Kalash asked, 'How long do we continue the siege of Panaji? Their emissary Albuquerque is desperate to meet you.'

'We cannot trust this cunning viceroy. How many times has he gone back on his word? If he is really keen to have a dialogue, let us put forth a condition that we will talk only after he has shared half of the supplies Aurangzeb has sent in his ship docked near Vengurla.'

Kavi Kalash smiled. 'Apparently the viceroy, frightened by our siege, has decided to move his capital from Panaji to Marmagoa. He has already shifted the treasury there.'

'We will not stop at that. We will take over the provinces of Salcette and Bardesh in a few days. Then we will cross Mandovi and plant our flag in the heart of Goa.'

While they sat discussing their plans, Sambhaji heard cries of 'Raje! We want justice!' and 'Please give us a hearing.' Nearly a thousand men had gathered outside the Maratha camp. Sambhaji asked Kavi to find out what the matter was. But he could not concentrate on the papers he was reading as the commotion outside was growing. The clerk explained, 'These men are from Salcette. A few of our overzealous soldiers wanted to burn down a church there but one of our sardars, Ranoji More, stopped them. The locals are very upset.' Sambhaji stepped out. The crowd immediately fell quiet.

One of the Hindu leaders said, 'Raje, we are so happy that you have taught the arrogant Portuguese a lesson.'

An old man stepped forward and said, folding his hands in supplication, 'You don't know the situation on the ground, Raje! Do you know how we Hindus are surviving in this province dominated by the firangis? Our temples have been destroyed. They throw meat into our wells to pollute us. We are forced to convert to Chritianity. Come with us and see for yourself the pitiable state we are in!'

'I am aware. I know how the temples of Shantadurga, Mahalakshmi and Mangeshi are struggling to protect themselves.'

'That is what we are saying! If our gods are treated in such a manner, imagine our state. Don't stop us. This is our opportunity to take revenge.'

The men raised their spears and sticks in unison, cheering. Sambhaji thundered, 'Khamosh! Don't make a scene here. Goa is being attacked by Shivaji Raje's son, not Aurangzeb's shahzada. Keep that in mind!'

He continued, 'I can undertand your pain. As a Hindu raja I am willing to provide compensation for the damages you have suffered. But let me make it clear: the foundation of our temples is not built on revenge.'

Sambhaji issued orders to release some money for the reconstruction of temples destroyed by the firangis. The men left satisfied. Sambhaji was aware of the violence unleashed by the firangis in the name of Christ. But he could not allow his men to seek revenge through the same kind of violence.

8

The viceroy's wound reminded him of his humiliating retreat at St. Estevam. He could still hear the cries of 'Har Har Mahadev' across the banks of Mandovi. At night he could see the Maratha soldiers guarding the banks with torches. He had managed to hold on to Panaji but the locals were growing restless. They had sent letters to Portugal demanding a new viceroy and declaring the current one as a nincompoop! The viceroy felt as if a trap was closing in on him from all sides.

The Marathas had created havoc at all Portuguese stations from Thane and Tarapur upto Goa. An urgent message from the Francis de Costa, the governor at Chaul, arrived. It said: *'The English are openly supporting Sambhaji, providing him with rifles and ammunition. We have received no help from them despite our offer to give them twice the market price. If we don't get timely aid, we will lose everything!'*

The firangis had now completely lost faith in the Portuguese viceroy and their army. That night, hundreds of townspeople were seen joining a procession on the streets of Panaji. The viceroy asked, 'Where are these people headed?'

'To the Church of Bom Jesus. They believe only St. Xavier can save them now.'

Prayers were being held at the church day and night. They had received messages from Bardesh and Salcette. The fort at Shapora had fallen. News of these Maratha victories was instilling fear in the hearts of the people. One morning the viceregal coach carrying Conde de Alvor arrived at the church. He looked visibly shaken, his eyes had dark circles and his face drawn and pale. He looked less like a viceroy than a traveller who has been set upon, looted and beaten up in the course of his journey. He prayed in front the embalmed and beautifully preserved body of St. Xavier. The viceroy was in tears. He cried, 'Father Xavier, I am surrendering our lives to you. I am no longer the viceroy but an ordinary man praying to you to save us. Please save us from this destruction.'

They spent a few days in the church, eating and sleeping there. One day the viceroy instructed his men to release the Maratha emissary Yesaji Gambhir from custody. 'Tell him that we are open to Sambhaji's conditions. Let Sambhaji write the treaty. We will abide by it.' The viceroy waited with bated breath. Days went by. Sambhaji's men were creating havoc after entering Mhapse. They had taken over the forts of Aguada and Roshmagosh, as well as many small ones. A thousand Maratha soldiers were camped in Madgaon. The fort of San Miguel too had fallen.

The Portuguese emissary had repeatedly tried to make contact with Sambhaji without success. The siege had lasted twenty-two days now. The viceroy was completely fed up of sitting in the church. He wrote a desperate letter to the king of Portugal, 'We are in bad shape here. Our future in Goa is at stake. We don't have trained artillerymen to manage the cannons. Our ammunition store is empty. We are like a leaking ship sinking slowly.'

Then, one day, a miracle occurred. They received news that the Marathas had abandoned their camp and departed! Everyone in the church thanked St. Xavier. An urgent conference was held by the Viceroy on 10 January 1684. Fearing an attack in the future, the Portuguese decided to shift their capital from Panaji to Marmagoa.

Nearly a hundred thousand of Shahzada Muazzam's soldiers had been spotted by Sambhaji's spies near Ramdara ghat. There was a danger of the Marathas getting trapped with the Mughals on one side and the Portuguese on the other. It made sense to leave immediately for Sawantwadi.

9

The Maratha troops reached Mahad. When they turned towards Raigad, they saw an English camp in the jungles near Nategao. A few tents were pitched there. Nearly five hundred riflemen under the command of the English emissary stood there with their horses, wearing traditional tall red hats. Seeing Sambhaji's army, the emissary Smith sahab came out and bent low in mujra. He had been waiting patiently for Sambhaji to arrive.

On his request, Sambhaji entered his tent for a discussion. Ramchandra Shenavi acted as the interpreter. 'Raje, you were stuck in Goa while we were forced to stay in Mumbai.'

'How come?'

'Well, why do you want me to spell it out? Your Daryasarang, Maynak Bhandari and Nilopant Peshwa have gathered many boats near Khanderi-Underi. We believed you were planning to attack us in Mumbai.'

'I am not aware of this at all,' Sambhaji said, shrugging his shoulders nonchalantly.

'Raje, as an emissary, I am aware that nothing moves in this region without your knowledge. Our Commissioner Mr. Child too is aware of it. We wish to make a complaint to you …'

Sambhaji was silent for a moment. When he spoke again, his voice had taken on an edge, 'What are you complaining about? Your have a friend, the Siddi at Janjira; why don't you complain to him?'

'Siddi has nothing to offer. It is from your region that we get grain and other revenue.'

'But you have no qualms in making slaves of the children the Siddi's men kidnap from our villages, do you? And then you have the gall to come and request a treaty?'

'I request you to pardon us, Raje. I will ensure that you have no reason for any complaint henceforth. We are not going to encourage Siddi.'

'We too have no intention of attacking anyone.'

'But we see your ships in the bay at Thane. You have taken over the port at Sion. Our people are really worried. The Englishmen in Surat too are putting pressure on us to sign a treaty with you. On top of that, we are also being harassed by the Arabs,' Smith said.

'Oh, is that so? I am told they tried to sink your ship, the one called the President.'

'Sambhaji Raje, I know you were the one who had instigated Jange Khan to try and sink our ship. Raje, we request you not to test us further. We are ready to sign a treaty. We are here for trade and nothing else.'

Sambhaji did not respond immediately. He said, 'Wait for my decision. Till then, ensure you don't outstep your boundaries.'

That evening, as they were climbing up to Raigad, Kavi Kalash asked, 'Raje, we are ready. Why delay our attack on Mumbai?'

'Kaviraj, I was keen to attack. But now I see the shadow of Aurangzeb falling on our territory. We also have enemies within our own kingdom. If only the ones within had kept quiet, I would have captured the English governor long ago and made him our servant.'

FIFTEEN

Dhumaschakri
The Whirlwind

1

Aurangzeb, sitting in Ahmednagar fort, was a restless man. He had been waiting for news from Shahbuddin in Konkan and from Muazzam further south towards Goa. He was receiving frequent updates from messengers who rode swiftly on horses as well as camels. Alamgir would often sit in the balcony of his room from where he could see the main door of the fort. He would rush to receive any messenger who was seen at the gates. He asked his Wazir, Asad Khan, 'What do you think of Shahbuddin? Will he succeed?'

'He has been camping in Pune for a few days. I am sure he will attack Sambha's territory soon.'

'I don't understand what he is waiting for. I have explicity told him to descend into the valley and ravage Sambha's territory.'

'Jahanpanah, it is not as easy as it seems. While studying the maps, Abu Muhammad had reminded us that the Maratha troops are guarding the entrances to every single valley. The Sahyadri is their guardian angel; it protects them. A mere platoon of five hundred men can repulse the attack of a five-thousand-strong army, provided they know the terrain.'

'Asad Khan, have I come here to listen to the enemy being praised?'

'Give me a little time, Jahanpanah. We are expecting news from Shahbuddin any day now. He had sent me a message expressing his gratitude to you for pardoning him despite his defeat at Ramshej. He says he will surely win Konkan and also vowed to take Raigad, the heart of the Maratha kindom.'

The Badshah was happy to hear that. He enquired about Goa.

'Nothing significant,' Asad Khan said. 'I wonder what support the cunning viceroy can provide to the shahzada.'

Sleep eluded the sixty-six-year-old Badshah. He had just dozed off when he heard a commotion downstairs. Jumping off the bed he quickly picked up the sword lying near his pillow and looked out the window. Asad Khan stood there with a message in his hand, requesting a reluctant khoja to wake the Badshah.

'It is not possible, Wazir-e-Azam,' the khoja was trying to explain. 'Even when a shahzada was born, we would not dare to disturb his sleep.'

At that moment they heard the Badshah's voice, 'What is the matter?'

'An urgent message from Shahbuddin.'

'Come upstairs.'

The Wazir rushed up the steps. Aurangzeb scanned the message and smiled. He asked the Wazir to read it aloud. *'Jahanpanah, we are blessed by Allah and you! I managed to descend into Devghat. En-route, we decimated the Marathas guarding the valley. We also managed to destroy three other stations including one at Nizampur, only a little distance from Raigad. I was informed that Sambha was inside the haveli at the base of Raigad. We managed to burn the haveli down but the wily fox Sambha escaped and reached Raigad.'*

Aurangzeb was pleased. He ordered sherbet for everyone although it was late in the night. He was now imagining Shahbuddin and his men scaling the steep slopes of Raigad. He said, as he sipped the sherbet, 'Shahbuddin is a jewel. That is why we have given him the title of Feroz Jung.'

Another message from Shahbuddin came a few days later. *'I was stationed at Pachad when Sambha sent troops led by his best sardars including Rupa Bhosale and Hambirrao. A battle ensued but we managed to overpower the enemy, chasing them for nearly five miles. Many were killed.'*

Aurangzeb read the message and dismissed everyone present except Asad Khan. He asked, 'Wazir, what do you make of it?'

'I am thrilled, Jahanpanah. I feel confident that, within a fortnight, we will take over Raigad.'

Aurangzeb's stern face told a different tale. The Wazir was frightened. Clearly, Alamgir was not convinced. Aurangzeb said, 'You accuse me of being suspicious. I have my doubts about what Shahbuddin is saying. He says he was in Pachad. Sometimes he says he was at Rairi. Do I expect the Marathas to sit quiet when he burns down the haveli at the base of Raigad? I am also told that Hambir Mohite is far away and nowhere near Pachad. I am not sure if Shahbuddin is telling the truth. Anyway, now I need to take matters into my own hands.'

Within a few days, Abu Muhammad was sent to survey the territory around Raigad. The Badshah was eagerly waiting for his return. The young man said, as soon as he arrived, 'Your guess was right, Jahanpanah. There is nothing for us to celebrate. Raigad is a massive fort and not easily breachable. The village at the base of the fort has around eighteen workshops that are constantly guarded by nearly ten to twelve thousand Marathas. All Shahbuddin managed to loot and burn were a few shepherds' villages in the jungles near Raigad. And as far as Sambhaji is concerned, he is still somewhere near Goa.'

Aurangzeb was enraged listening to the report. Abu Muhammad continued, 'Jahanpanah, it is true that Shahbuddin managed to burn some villages near Nizampur. His troops are hiding in the dense jungles near Tamhini ghat. They have managed to inflict some damage but Raigad and the Marathas remain largely untouched so far.'

'That idiot!' Aurangzeb said, irritated at the empty boasts of Shahbuddin Feroz Jung. 'I am going to transfer him immediately.'

'Jahanpanah, I would request you not to. It is true that many of the forts are unsurmountable, but all the Marathas are not as loyal as we might tend to believe. Many are willing to trade their loyalty for a little bit of money.'

'What are you hinting at?'

'Shahbuddin may not have managed to win any territory but he has been engaging constantly with several Maratha landlords, luring them with promises of money, titles and better posts. It is only a matter of time before they defect; once they do, the forts are ours!'

'Wah! I am impressed with your foresight.'

He hugged Abu Muhammad affectionately and, taking off a beautiful necklace he was wearing, put it around his neck.

Kavi Kalash and his men rode through the gorge at Wagholi. In the distance the rear walls of Raigad was visible. Having been in Goa and South Konkan for a long time, five thousand men and animals were returning to the capital. They had reduced their speed once Raigad was in sight. Sambhaji was expected to arrive in two days. Fearing a confrontation with the Mughals, Raje had decided to send Kavi and the men ahead.

Kavi Kalash spotted a cloud of dust ahead, and soon emerged a platoon of nearly three hundred Marathas led by Shiledar Murari Dange. He said, pulling in his reins, 'We need to rush, Kaviraj! The Mughals are attacking Raigad.'

Kavi Kalash tied his loose hair at the back of his head in a knot and, spurring his horse, turned to face the caravan, shouting, 'Charge! Har Har Mahadev!' Like a great wave of water gushing through mountains, the Maratha riders rushed through the gorge. As soon as Kavi emerged from the gorge, he scanned the fort and the area around it. There was no sign of any attack. His eyes then moved towards Gangoli village, visible in the distance. Black fumes could be seen coming out of the huts there. Kavi Kalash asked Murari, 'Who is that devil?'

'One of Aurangzeb's sardars, Shahbuddin. For the past five days he has been creating havoc, burning and ruining the houses and haystacks in the nearby villages.'

'How dare he come so close to Raigad! Let's push them away.'

'Har Har Mahadev!' The troops shouted in unison. 'Chhattrapati Sambhaji Maharaj ki Jay!'

Kavi Kalash was literally flying through the air, standing on his stirrups as he led the charge. Soon, they reached the woods near Gangoli. The Mughals, not expecting such a huge army to descend on them, were terrified and started screaming, 'Sambha has come! Run!' They rushed to their horses. By then swords had been drawn and hand-to-hand combat began.

Soon, the action had spread across Gangoli, Panase, Jorgaon and Nizampur. Kavi Kalash was busy beheading as many Mughals as he could find. He knew he had to protect the capital in the absence of his Raje. The men, watching him swing his sword as if it were a gauntlet sword, were energised.

The Mughals, who had been busy looting for the past four days, had not anticipated this. By evening, when they had recovered a little, they realised that they had lost more than three thousand men while the Marathas casualties numbered two hundred or so. Shahbuddin, hiding his fear, yelled, 'We must retreat!' Seeing them flee, the Marathas were joined by villagers hiding in the jungles. The ryots came out in the fields and intercepted the Mughal troops riding on their horses. Shahbuddin's men were falling like leaves.

By evening the chase had reached Tamhini ghat. The remaining Mughals had managed to flee into the dense woods. The Marathas, tired of the pursuit, stopped for a rest. They fed their horses hay while they themselves munched on some chickpeas and jaggery saddles. They drank clear water from the streams.

Later the men, led by Kavi Kalash, entered the woods with torches in their hands. Soon, they spotted a place beside the stream where the Mughals had left their food, ammunition and other items. Kalash knew that the Mughals were hiding nearby.

The Marathas decided to call it a day. Kavi Kalash planned to enter the ghat next morning. As they were returning through the forest that night, someone shouted, 'Kaviraj, look!' Kavi Kalash followed the direction of his finger to see a row of Mughals high up in the mountains, beating a hasty retreat. Kavi Kalash laughed. He had known they would not dare to stay back and fight the next day. Kalash and his men reached Nizampur to find that one of the other platoons had caught a Mughal sardar alive. He was tied to a pole while they waited for Kaviraj to arrive.

They shouted, seeing Kavi Kalash, 'Kaviraj, behead this shaitan! Kill him!'

A Pathan in his mid-thirties, his fair face was pale with fear. Kavi asked, 'What is your name?'

'Dukhlas Khan, Huzoor!' Kalash asked his men to release him. Khan fell at his feet asking for pardon. The men around clamoured for his head, 'Kill him, Kaviraj! We want to dip our swords in his blood!'

Raising his hand, Kavi silenced them. He said, looking at Dukhlas Khan, 'Get up! And run to join your troops.'

Dukhlas Khan could not believe his ears, while the Maratha soldiers who had captured him were fuming. 'I am letting you live for one reason alone; I want you to meet your Badshah and give my message.'

'As you command, Huzoor,' the man said.

'Tell your idiotic Badshah that he need not revel in the fact that he is a direct descendant of Taimur. Ask him not to send these stupid lamb-like men to attack our capital. Let him know that if he ever dares to come to Raigad, he will not return alive. Let him come once, just once, if he dares to!'

2

The town of Banda near Goa was in turmoil when Shahzada Muazzam's army landed there. He had sent an order to the viceroy, asking him to present himself, but Conde de Alvor had not bothered to come. After Muazzam had waited for four days, the viceroy sent his emissary Albuquerque. Such violations of protocol were making the Mughal shahzada angry. But who was he to complain to?

Shahzada looked at the emissary and thundered, 'What does your viceroy think of himself? Doesn't he have any manners?'

'Please pardon us, Sarkar! The viceroy is not keeping well.'

'Huh! Don't lie. When Sambha was here with his twenty thousand men, your viceroy had to escape in a leaky boat. Then he took refuge in a church and prayed to the dead body of your patron saint. It seems you have forgotten those days quite quickly!'

'Huzoor, we ask for pardon …'

'It is the Mughal forces which saved you from further humiliation. Else, Sambha would have dug your graves by now. Seeing the approach of our massive army, he ran away. But of course, the moment you got time to breathe, you went back to your old ways!'

'I request shahzada not to get upset. The friendship between the Mughals and the Portuguese is as strong as ever. Please tell us how we can serve the Mughal sultanate.'

'The ships carrying our ammunition from Surat are not docked yet. We need space to anchor them in Panaji as agreed earlier.'

'We will get that done immediately,' Albuquerque said.

'Fine then. I will give orders for the ships to dock at Mandovi.'

'Sarkar, why Mandovi? The viceroy has suggested the smaller Kaisuv.'

Shahzada erupted. 'Your viceroy is even more cunning than I had imagined. He is worried that if we dock our ships in Mandovi, your capital Panaji would be under threat, isn't it? He changes colours like a chameleon. Even my Abbajaan could learn a thing or two from your viceroy!' Well, I am not going to tolerate his crafty tactics any longer.

Shahzada had not expected this kind of reception. Especially from someone he had come to rescue! He had been hammered by the Marathas when he had descended into Sawantwadi from Ramdara ghat. In revenge, he had burnt several villages under the Swaraj in Sawantwadi as well as in Banda and Vengurla, right upto the borders of Goa.

His Diwan now advised, 'Shahzada, Sambha has left for Raigad. I suggest we use this time to catch your brother Akbar.'

'Where is he?'

'He is stationed at Dicholi.'

'Look at the way this Portuguese viceroy is treating us!'

'Far from being grateful to us, he is honouring a secret pact he has made with Sambha.'

Muazzam was shocked to hear this. However, what the Diwan had said was true. The viceroy was now keen on peace. He had been paranoid ever since Sambhaji's attack. Hence he had agreed to give a fourth of the revenue from the Vasai and Daman territories to the Marathas. He had also promised not to allow Mughal ships carrying grain and ammunition to ply in their waters. He had already given these assurances in writing.

Shahzada Muazzam was now livid and wanted to take revenge. He decided to attack Dicholi in order to arrest Akbar, but soon learnt that his brother had left the town long back. In his rage, he ordered the beautiful haveli at Dicholi to be bombarded. He used his elephants to trample its lovely rose garden. He looted the nearby villages of Narve and Bhatgram and destroyed the Ram temple at Pimpalgaon. The spire of the Saptakoteeshwar temple was broken. His troops ravaged the Maratha territory in South Konkan bordering Goa. When he came to know that Akbar was planning to flee to Iran in a ship docked at Vengurla, he burnt down the entire port, thus making it impossible for his own ships from Surat to dock there.

The cunning viceroy had signed a treaty with Sambhaji and sent the papers to his king in Portugal, ensuring the continuation of his post in India. He was not afraid of Shahzada Muazzam now. The ships from Surat had already been looted by the Marathas. The ships that had escaped Maratha plunder had been gobbled by the Portuguese. The Mughal sardars manning the ships, on realisation that they could not dock anywhere, sold their cargo to the Portuguese at a throwaway price.

Amidst all this, Muazzam had suffered the most. He had to look after nearly forty thousand cavalry, sixty thousand foot-soldiers, three thousand camels and nineteen hundred elephants. He now realised how foolish he had been to burn the villages in South Konkan. Now there were no foodgrains to be had even if he was willing to pay. As expected, the troops suffered and most of the animals were dying.

He decided to return to Ahmednagar on 15 February 1684. He had made big plans which included the creation of a naval base at Goa, the conquest of Konkan and Raigad and the capture of Sambhaji--all his ambitions had come to naught.

They marched towards Ramdara ghat. On the way, a Portuguese emissary came with a message from the viceroy: '*The Marathas damaged properties worth twenty lakh gold coins in our territories. Otherwise we would have offered you monetary help*.'

'Why are you here?' Shahzada asked dryly.

'The viceroy has requested that you should not leave this territory. Please stay back till the monsoon sets in.'

'Why? So that we may protect you in case Sambha decides to attack once again? You want us to offer you our services without any payment? What makes that rascal, your viceroy, think we would agree?'

Albuquerque was taken aback by Muazzam's anger. He ordered his men to strip the emissary leaving barely enough cloth on his body to cover his modesty. The men were then asked to cut off his earlobes and nose. 'Send him back in that state to his Lord. Let them learn a lesson.'

The emissary was tortured and sent back. But it only provided temporary solace to the enraged Muazzam. His tired and hungry elephant lumbered on. Far ahead he could see Ramdara ghat and its steep slopes. And behind him was a huge army marching on an empty stomach!

3

Sambhaji had returned to Raigad. At dinner, Yesubai said, 'Raje, how nice would it have been if you had captured Goa!'

'Yesu, we were almost there! Goa was within our grasp but we heard that a hundred-thousand-strong Mughal army had descended on Ramdara ghat. The only option for us was to retreat.'

He continued, 'But I don't consider it a defeat. We have scared the living daylights out of the Portuguese viceroy! He signed our treaty without any objections. I am sure Aurangzeb will not be able to convince the Siddis at Janjira or the Portuguese at Goa to join him.'

'You must have heard of how Kaviraj repulsed the attack by Shahbuddin.'

'I do. I know you must have received the shahzada's letter praising Kaviraj. But I don't need anyone's endorsement. I know how loyal he is.'

After the meal, Yesubai hesitated before saying, 'You are aware that we had to take a tough decision in your absence.'

'Yes, I know,' Sambhaji said. 'You had to order the imprisonment of Rahuji Somnath, Gangadhar Pant, Vasudev Pant and Manoji More.'

'Yes,' Yesubai said, a little surprised. 'They had secretly met Shahbuddin at Mulshi. Their intention was treason.'

'You took the right decision. Rahuji and Manaji have served the Swaraj with dedication but that does not absolve them of this.'

Sambhaji was tired of Shahbuddin's efforts to lure men away from the Swaraj. The Mughal commander was known to ingratiate himself with men holding high positions in enemy kingdoms, bribing them with promise of riches. Kanhoji Shirke, Yeshwantrao Dalvi and Nagoji Mane were some of the men who, seduced by Shahbuddin, had defected earlier and joined the Mughals.

Yesubai knew Sambhaji was troubled. She said, 'Raje, don't think they are defecting against you. They are simply weak.'

'I know. The moment they see the Mughals, the idea of defecting gains ground. The Deshpandes of Supe, the Jadgales of Mysore ... they are all the same. Yesu, the only way to avoid all this is to finish off Aurangzeb once and for all.'

He continued, 'Yesu, all I have been planning for the past few years is a direct confrontation with Aurangzeb. He may be here with an army of five lakh men and four lakh animals. But I am twenty-six while Aurangzeb is sixty-five years old! Just wait and watch; I will tie a rope around this arrogant Mughal Badshah's neck and make him dance to my tune at the bazaars.'

The Mughal sardars were busy plotting against the Swaraj and trying to find people who were inclined to defect. It was an arduous task for Sambhaji to ensure that his kingdom and forts were safe. He was constantly keeping an eye on those he suspected would succumb to Mughal bribe. Aurangzeb was sparing no efforts, offering expensive gifts, titles, money, and whatever else it took to lure those who were willing to go against the Swaraj.

One day Khando Ballal reported, 'Raje, a sardar you consider pride of the Swaraj, one of our most loyal men, has left for Ahmednagar to join the Badshah. Shivaji Jedhe!'

Sambhaji could not control his fury. He shouted, 'Let that traitor know our Ramshej fort is still being guarded zealously by the old but loyal Suryaji Jedhe.

Shivaji Jedhe had ravaged his own territory before defecting. Sambhaji discovered that his brother Sarjerao too had plans to follow him. Sambhaji sent Santaji Nimbalkar to try and change his mind. Of late, the constant pressure of staving off such defections had made Sambhaji irritable. His voice had taken on an edge. With the help of Khando Ballal, Ramchandra Pant Amatya and Kavi Kalash, he made a list of all the sardars who were likely to defect. He met them, sent them letters of assurance and complimented them on their work. Soon, men like Shivaji Jedhe were tempted to return.

Hearing this, Sambhaji wrote a stinging letter to him, 'You defected without any qualms. You enjoyed all the privileges of being a well-regarded Maratha sardar while you were with us but did not hesitate to join the Mughals! Now that you feel they may not treat you with respect, you want to come back. You have destroyed the meaning of loyalty. I hope you shake off this bad habit of changing sides, the way a dancer changes her looks!'

It had been four years since Aurangzeb had come to the Deccan. The skirmishes between the Mughals and the Marathas continued unabated. Sambhaji said one day, as he was resting in his room, 'Yesu, neither is Aurangzeb winning nor are we! How long can this go on? Every time we are on the verge of victory, destiny changes its plans, leaving us empty-handed. I wonder what it has in store for us.'

4

Shahzada Muazzam's tired army was negotiating the difficult terrain at Ramdara. The steep, three-mile-long steep climb with narrow paths flanked by thorny bushes was gruellling for the soldiers. The dry coastal climate of South Konkan had not been kind to the Mughals. Diseases had taken a toll on men and beasts alike, forcing the shahzada to return. Many animals had died on the way. Food ration had shrunk rapidly. The men were losing morale. Although Sambhaji had returned to Raigad, he had left his troops behind at strategic points to spring surprise attacks, leaving Muazzam's army further weakened.

A messenger came and reported, 'It is not good news from Ahmednagar, Shahzada.'

He continued, 'Your enemies have been poisoning the Badshah's ears. They have accused you of fighting a very reluctant battle with the Marathas. They claim that you have actually signed a secret pact with Sambhaji, and that your lame and ineffective actions on the battlefield are evidence of the same.'

Shahzada was too weary to react. The mountainous terrain at Ramdara had drained him of both hope and energy. Elephants, horses and camels were dying by the dozens. The stench of their rotting carcasses trailed the army, tormenting living men and animals alike. Many vomited as they trekked along the steep slopes. To add to their misery, there were skirmishes en route when the Marathas, hiding in the bushes, attacked suddenly.

The Mughals took nearly eight days to cross the mountain range. The casualties were enormous; of the forty thousand who had set out on the journey, only ten thousand survived. The survivors were merely living ghosts. Those who had lost their horses had no money to buy them while those who had money could not find horses to buy! No one was willing to sell his horse. Many a sardar and mansabdar walked with empty stomachs like fakirs. They were a pathetic sight, limping and dragging their feet all the way.

Hearing of his son's state, Aurangzeb arranged for twenty thousand gold coins, five hundred camels, twenty-five mules, a hundred horses, and some clothes to be sent with all possible speed. But the fresh supplies hardly made a difference. The shahzada was badly affected by the misery all around him.

When a weak and emaciated shahzada on an equally skeletal horse finally reached the Badshah's tent, the ladies of the zenana stared in disbelief. His miserable state brought tears of pity to their eyes.

Wazir Asad Khan stepped forward to receive him. The shahzada was like a grandson to him. He took him to his tent and offered him some fruits. But the weak shahzada found the sweetmeats and fruits unpalatable.

The Wazir then took him to Aurangzeb's tent. The Badshah merely stared at his son, fondling his beard and his rosary. Muazzam was disappointed that despite his own misery, his father did not enquire about his health. He said, letting out a sob, 'Abbajaan, we have suffered! The weather, and …'

'Beta, wasnt't it expected? If you change your route, what else did you think would happen?'

Muazzam couldn't believe his ears. 'Abbajaan, there seems to be some misunderstanding …'

'What misunderstanding, Beta? What was our original plan? Shahbuddin was to descend into Konkan from Pune while you were to reach Mahad after taking over Kudal and Rajapur. Both of you were to meet and then attack Raigad.'

'Abbajaan, I did not have enough resources. The troops were suffering. We were tricked by the Portuguese viceroy.'

'Muazzam, don't waste my time with useless talk,' the Badshah thundered. 'Tell me, why did you move towards Ramdara instead of sticking to the original plan?'

'But ...'

'No buts! You are not blind. Who made you change your route? The one residing at Raigad? Sambha?'

This direct allegation from Aurangzeb literally broke Muazzam's back. He wanted to fall at his father's feet and cry his heart out. But he barely had the energy to do even that. He said in a quivering voice, 'Abbajaan, please pardon me! I hope you can see how I am suffering. Please don't mock me.'

'Beta, my spies can reach where even the wind cannot. I suppose a shahzada like you knows such a simple fact,' Aurangzeb said in a sardonic tone. 'I know Sambha's spies met you twice.'

'That is true, Abbajaan. But it is part of politics to try and penetrate the enemy camp. You too do that. The question is, did your shahzada fall for any of his tricks?'

'How do I know?'

'Abbajaan, if you are aware of Sambha's spies meeting me, you must be also aware of how the Maratha soldiers decimated us by attacking us in the Ramdara mountains.'

Aurangzeb growled, 'You deliberately chose not to take your troops through Mahad and Poladpur—the territory of a friend. So, tell me, where is the bribe which Sambha gave you?'

A thoroughly dejected Muazzam did not know how to respond to his father. He stood up and stormed out of the tent. As he entered his quarters, he banged the doors and windows shut, muttering, 'I was troubled when I left. I journeyed through hell to return and now I am being insulted. Ya Khuda! I seem to be destined to suffer!'

5

Sakhubai Nimbalkar was seven years older to Sambhaji. Brother and sister loved each other dearly. But Ambika Akkasaheb's husband, Harji

Mahadik, was given the Subah of Karnatak, creating a rift in the family. One day Sakhubai and her husband Mahadji Nimbalkar camped in Sambhaji's quarters, determined to get their way. Sambhaji was often at a loss when it came to solving such domestic problems.

Sakhubai said, reiterating her demands, 'We deserve the same honour as you have given the Mahadiks.'

'What have I given them that is so special?'

'You handed over the Subah of Jinji and Karnatak to Harji.'

'There seems to be some misunderstanding, Akkasaheb. I have asked him to manage the Subah of Karnatak as a subedar. He does not own the revenue collected there.'

Mahadji Nimbalkar, silent till then, smiled. 'Shambhu Raje, we don't want to play with words. The Subedar is the default owner of the province, isn't he?'

Sakhubai said in a pained voice, 'Shambhu Raje, why are you discriminating between your brothers-in-law?'

Sambhaji's face turned grave. Sakhubai continued, 'Well, maybe we are at fault. But we convinced the Nimbalkars to stop working under the Mughals. After all, my younger brother was to ascend the throne!'

'We have to suffer now, for our actions,' Mahadji muttered.

Sakhubai said, 'Shambhu Raje, we would not have said anything had you not given the Mahadiks the Subah. He managed to wring the territory out of you, using sweet words, and without having sacrificed anything. A province which is one of the richest in the Swaraj! And here we are, made to look like fools!'

'We left a high-yielding territory under the Mughals to join my brother's Swaraj. Perhaps it would have been better to serve under the Mughals than to suffer here,' Mahadji commented.

Sakhubai and Mahadji's comments were hurtful. Finally Sambhaji said, unable to stand their grumbling anymore, 'Akkasaheb, my Abasaheb used to feel that the Swaraj is a temple for the ryots. I see it the same way. However hard you may try to convince me otherwise, it is not possible for me to hand over any territory to anyone.'

'What about the Mahadiks then?'

'He is the representative of the Hindavi Swaraj and is managing the territories of Jinji and Karnatak under my command—not as a title holder with ownership of any revenue collected in the region.'

'You will know when he declares himself the owner,' Mahadji said.

'The day he tries to do that, he will be removed from the post. Let that be clear,' Sambhaji said.

Sakhubai and Mahadji did not react. They left Raigad the next day.

SIXTEEN

Attack on the Deccan

1

Aurangzeb was surprised to hear that Sahar Banu, his daughter-in-law, had requested an audience. Normally the women would convey their requests through Udepuri Begum. Sahar Banu, the beautiful daughter of the Bijapur Sultan, was married to Shahzada Azam. Her sparkling eyes were visible despite the long veil which flowed down to her waist. She said, when the Badshah asked the reason for her visit, 'Jille Subhani, your Sultanate is as pious to me as Mecca. But I do wish that there was no dispute between the Mughals and my Abbajaan's Bijapur. I have sent a message to Sarja Khan before he crossed Burhanpur. I have requested him to support the Mughal army and defeat the kafirs.'

'Excellent, my dear,' the Badshah murmured. 'You are innocent in all this but the Bijapurkars are not in their senses.'

Then Alamgir said, pointing at a messenger bag kept on a table nearby, 'The Shia rulers are under the delusion that we are innocent children who suckle their mothers' milk. When the kafirs had planned to destroy the fort in Tiruchirappally, it is the Shias who supported Sambha with ten thousand troops. And look at their temerity! My spies have intercepted innumerable letters of the flourishing correspondence between Qutb Shah, Adil Shah and Sambha. Their plan is to prevent the Mughals from entering the Deccan. Dear, I appreciate your concern and help. But if that childish Adil Shah, your father, does not show the basic courtesy of acknowledging my messages, I would have to burn down Bijapur one day.'

Sahar Banu bowed elaborately and retreated a few steps, taking care not to turn her back on the Badshah. Aurangzeb enquired casually, when he next met his Wazir, 'When do we intend to march on Adil Shah?'

'No one has dared to do so for many decades. And victory is another matter altogether.'

'What do you mean?' Aurangzeb asked, his forehead creased.

'Badshah Salamat, the city is fortified with a thick wall which is nearly two miles long. It is also surrounded by a deep moat. There is an inner wall which is even stronger than the one outside. And the walls are equipped with powerful long cannons like the 'Maalik-e-Maidan.'

The Badshah looked at the sky and did not reply. That afternoon, Zulfikar Khan came in and reported, 'Jille Subhani, it is good news. Four of Sambha's top sardars have defected to our camp. They are eager to present themselves to you.'

The Badshah gave his permission with a casual wave of his hand. Soon, Kanhoji Shirke, Jagdevrai, Arjoji and Achloji were ushered in. They prostrated themselves before the Badshah.

'What do you want?' The Badshah came straight to the point.

'Huzoor, it is not just us; there are many sardars from good Maratha families who are fed up of Sambhaji's rule. There is no justice,' Kanhoji wailed.

'What about your Hindavi Swaraj?"

'What about it, Huzoor? It is like a bubble on the surface of water. It will burst any day! True, Shivaji Raje got Brahmins from Kashi and made a huge fuss of coronating himself. But how long can a sham last?'

'What exactly do you want?'

'Nothing much, Huzoor. We are landlords and want to have the right to collect revenue in our own lands, that's all!'

'What is the point of a mere piece of paper declaring you as the owner?'

'Badshah Salamat, your seal will carry a lot of weight. It will be honoured for generations. Shivaji is just an accident, an exception!'

'Shirke, you seem to be a cunning man. How is Ganoji related to you?'

'He is my cousin, Huzoor.'

The sardars were cunning enough not to demand anything else. But the Badshah was no fool. He immediately assigned a mansab of two thousand men to each of them. The Wazir honoured them with gifts of fine clothes. The four Marathas fell at the Badshah's feet, obligated by the honours they had received. The Badshah smiled, 'If there are more people like you, tell them they are most welcome here.'

At that moment, Aurangzeb noticed an old man standing behind the four sardars. He was in his sixties, wore a narrow pointed cap, and sported a small beard. Zulfikar Khan replied, seeing Aurangzeb's questioning look, 'Jahanpanah, he is Kazi Haidar. He dispensed justice in Raigad during Shivaji's time.'

The sardars were ushered out. Only Kazi Haidar remained. Aurangzeb said, 'What were you doing for so many years in Raigad, working for the enemy?'

'I beg your pardon, Huzoor. I was honoured to work with someone like Shivaji. I handled all the cases, for Hindus as well as Muslims.'

'Tell me … how many mosques have Shiva and Sambha destroyed?'

'Not one, Badshah Salamat!' the Kazi said, keeping his voice low and respectful. 'Not just that, Shivaji gave me permission to build a mosque in Raigad, using money from the treasury. The mosque was still there when I left Raigad two months back.'

Aurangzeb asked, staring into the Kazi's eyes, 'If you find Raigad to be such a heaven, why are you here?'

'I am worried about some of the clerks and other officials there. When people don't hesitate to attack their own king, what safety can I be assured of?'

Aurangzeb was silent for a while as he fiddled with the beads of his rosary. His lips muttered lines from the Quran. He said, testing the Kazi's loyalty and intelligence, 'Tell me the truth. I am here with such a huge army. Yet, I find it difficult to catch that mountain rat. What is Sambha's real strength, that which prevents his capture?'

Kazi Haidar smiled. 'The hole where the mountain rat stays is in the Sahyadris. The soil there might seem soft but below the surface the rock is stronger than iron. Besides, they may have had their differences earlier, but today Sikandar Adil Shah of Bijapur, Qutb Shah of Golconda and Sambhaji are allies. The only way to fulfil your dream is to break their alliance.'

Aurangzeb was impressed. He honoured Kazi Haidar with gifts. When the Kazi had left, Aurangzeb instructed his Wazir to ensure that the old man was treated well and taken care of during his stay. 'Make arrangements for the Kazi to stay in the Gulalbar area. Whenever I need his counsel, he should be available.'

2

It was 26 April 1684.

Sambhaji was at the fort of Birwadi, near Roha. After long negotiations, the English were finally willing to sign a treaty. The Maratha emissary Prahlad Niraji and the English representative Smith were busy drafting the documents.

The Marathas had put pressure on the Portuguese from Goa to Vasai-Virar, and they had recently captured Kelva, Dantora, Sargao, Mahim and Sopara. The English had been worried ever since the capture of Karanja by Sambhaji. Mumbai had become the scene of a revolt against the atrocities of English officials Child and Ward, leading to the appointment of Richard Keigwin as the governor. Sambhaji managed to keep Keigwin at bay with talks on one hand and the threat of an attack on the other. Meanwhile, the East India Company officials in Mumbai had consulted their Surat counterparts whom they trusted. Keigwin then sent Captain Gary and Thomas Wilkins to Birwadi to sign the treaty. Sambhaji hosted them at the palace in Birwadi and ensured that they were well taken care of.

Prahlad Niraji said, 'Raje, it would have been great if you were able to buy the port of Mumbai.'

'I know. We have tried our best. I was willing to offer upto eighty thousand gold coins. The Mumbai port is a gold mine. But at the last moment the Englishmen from Surat intervened. They were convinced by the Siddi that selling the port would sound his death knell.'

Captain Gary complained to Sambhaji when they met that evening, 'Raje, why do you patronise Jange Khan? It is not good to hobnob with the Arabs!'

Sambhaji smiled. 'I hope you have not put any conditions on whom we can befriend.' Gary quickly changed the topic. The English were keen on obtaining permission to open trading posts and build godowns, particularly on the stretch of coast from Jinji to Madras.

Sambhaji agreed but warned the English, 'I am more than happy to allow you to increase your trade. But I hope you will not build forts under the pretext of protecting your marketplaces and godowns there. Please see that this is explicitly mentioned in the treaty.'

Sambhaji also ensured that the treaty specifically mentioned the size of the godowns, even the length, breadth and thickness of the walls, lest they be used as fortresses later. The English were given permission to build godowns at Nagothane and Pen but it was made clear that there would be no concessions on the import and export duties. The treaty also mandated the English to inform the local Maratha subedar of the number of people working in their godowns.

Finally, Sambhaji asked a question close to his heart, 'What about the young children being used as slaves, Gary saheb?'

'Raje, is it necessary to rake up this topic? Your father would tax us four times the normal rate on such slaves. You may tax us upto six times. But we need slaves for our trade.'

'Why are you dependent on us for slaves whom you can treat like dogs? Why don't you get young boys from England instead?'

Captain Gary sensed Sambhaji's fury and chose to keep quiet. Sambhaji continued, 'You lose nothing but it harms the Swaraj. The Siddis at Jinji kidnap our young children and sell them for a high price. You work these poor souls to death, whipping them like animals. They are not even allowed a bath for months on end. I will not allow such atrocities in my kingdom. And, speaking of religion, I believe a man should have the freedom to choose the religion he wants to practise.'

'I agree with the principle, Raje,' Captain Gary said.

'But your practice is different. Your priests are forcibly converting our people to Christainity. They are propagating the slave trade in the bazaars of Mumbai and other places. This inhuman practice needs to be stopped.'

Captain Gary nodded in agreement. Accordingly, the seventh item in the treaty explicitly stated: *'The English would not be allowed to indulge in trading of humans to make them slaves or convert them to Christanity.'*

The treaty was formalised. Gifts were exchanged. As the Englishmen took Sambhaji's leave, Prahlad Niraji said, 'Raje, it would be nice if we could negotiate the purchase of the Mumbai port.'

'We will. Let me first dig a grave for Aurangzeb. We will then focus on Mumbai. It is part of our territory and, by geographical rights, we must own it. It is a key trading post and we must have control over it. I am willing to pour money into this scheme. If that doesn't work, our swords shall always come in handy!

3

It was a pleasant morning. Sambhaji looked proudly at Arjoji Yadav. No Maratha sardar, however valorous, had yet achieved what Arjoji had accomplished. A master of disguise, the daring Arjoji had managed to meet Durgadevi and Ranuakka.

Arjoji had contrived the meeting by posing as a cloth merchant from Kashi. He had also brought a letter from Durgabai which Sambhaji read several times. It said:

> *'I think of you, day and night. The nights are especially painful. One can see one's own face in a mirror but not yours. I am lucky that I can see you in your daughter, Rajkumari Kamal. Swami, your daughter, the princess of Raigad, was born as a prisoner of the Badshah. But she is sweet, ever smiling, and as daring as her father. The Badshah's daughter Zeenat is nearly thirty-five years older but she loves her dearly.*
>
> *I remember your love for lotus flowers. You would always get a white lotus for me from the lake at Raigad. In memory of those happy days, I have named her Kamalja. She is eager to see her father and Raigad. Swami, it has been eight years since we met. I wonder how many more years I need to wait. But Kamalja is insistent on seeing you. I tell her that a prisoner should not have such hopes but she tells me, "Maasaheb, wasn't Krishna born in a prison? I want to meet my father once, fall at his feet, and look at the tall and imposing walls of Raigad to my heart's content." Ranuakkasaheb and I are taking care of her. I am sure we will come out of this darkness one day. Please take care of your health. Don't put yourself at risk for me. We are well taken care of here as royal prisoners. We may be served on silver plates but I yearn for our land! With the blessings of Tuljabhawani, I am sure we will meet sooner rather than later.'*

Sambhaji eyes were moist while Yesubai sobbed. Arjoji said, 'Raje, they are well taken care of. I am told Aurangzeb takes personal interest in the welfare of the children of royal prisoners. He ensures their comfort and well-being.'

'I can't believe it! To imagine a compassionate Aurangzeb is quite difficult.'

Arjoji said, 'Raje, I enquired into the matter. Aurangzeb's father, Shah Jahan, had revolted against his own father. Aurangzeb and his siblings were held as royal prisoners by Jahangir at Junnar. They were treated like dogs. Aurangzeb has never forgotten those days. This is why the Badshah ensures that royal prisoners and their children are treated respectfully.'

4

Chaos had reigned in the cantonment for the past three days. The vast Mughal caravan was on the move again. Thousands of carriages, pulled by bullocks and camels, were already streaming out of Ahmednagar. Within two days, the imperial household would leave in the direction of Solapur. No one knew what exactly Alamgir had in mind. But it was clear that he was restless.

Sitting in his office, Aurangzeb was busy reading the messages from his spies and informers. Shahzada Azam's troops were creating havoc in the Bijapur territory, having surrounded the Nagothane fort. Maulvi Sheikh ul-Islam was not happy with Aurangzeb's attack on fellow Muslims. He believed that both Shias and Sunnis were Allah's followers. He said, 'Jahanpanah, they are only immature children after all. Why are you so upset?'

'Who are you talking of?'

'Jahanpanah, Qutb Shah of Hyderabad is a reckless fool while Sikandar Adil Shah of Bijapur is barely fifteen years old …'

The Badshah was in no mood to listen. He snapped, 'I am being reminded by Chikkadevaraja of Mysore that I must first bring these two to their knees if I am to have any chance of defeating the Marathas. Secondly, I care nothing for their age. Even Khuda, I am sure, will not be happy with their juvenile behaviour. That Abul Hasan of Hyderabad—I am told that fool is fond of music to the extent that he plays the sarangi in court! Each Friday he gathers twenty thousand dancers and concubines in the square outside the Charminar and relishes their dance. How can we expect such persons to be of service to their subjects or to Allah?'

Remembering something, the Badshah asked Baramad Khan, 'Can you tell me what demands we had put forth earlier to Adil Shah of Bijapur?'

Baramad Khan scanned some old papers and said, 'We had asked them to ensure the safety and upkeep of the stations we had created within the Bijapur territory.'

'And what was his response?'

Aurangzeb looked keenly at Sheikh ul-Islam's face as Khan read out nervously: *'What gives you the right to demand permission to build your stations inside our territory? In fact, you need to remove the posts you had erected without our permission. If the Shahenshah wishes to wage war against Sambha, he may do so. But we will not allow even an inch of our land to be used for that purpose. Let me remind you that the Maratha territory of Shivaji and Sambha belongs originally to Adil Shah. The Badshah should not even glance at it.'*

Those present avoided looking at the Badshah. They did not recall anyone having insulted the Badshah so blatantly. Aurangzeb asked, 'What else did we demand? Read that.'

> *'Sarja Khan, your commander, should be removed with immediate effect and he should be asked to leave Bijapur.'*

'And what did the silly fellow reply?'

> *'This is our private affair. And Aurangzeb should know that he is our commander-in-chief. He will remain where he is. We are, in fact, planning to increase his salary.'*

'Enough!' Aurangzeb said, losing his patience.

No one dared to speak. Aurangzeb could not contain his anger any longer. 'Qutb Shah and Adil Shah—both are sly foxes. Sheikh sahab, I wonder why you are taking the side of these devils. Qutb Shah was never loyal to Allah. He sent an army of ten thousand men to help Sambha fight against the Mysore raja. And on top of that, he has Hindu pandits and ministers like Madanna and Akanna in his court. Imagine! A Muslim kingdom with Hindu prime ministers! How silly can they get, Sheikh sahab?'

'Tauba, tauba!' Those in attendance murmured.

'And that Qutb Shah is a crafty fellow! That idiot, despite his enormous wealth, behaves as if he is a minister under the Marathas. A few years back when Shiva Bhosale had gone to meet him in Hyderabad, this idiot welcomed him, putting a garland around his horse! He had also agreed to pay an annual compensation of one lakh hons to the Marathas. He has handed over all his power to the Brahmins Madanna and Akanna. He is a taint on Islam!'

Seeing Aurangzeb's ire, Wazir Asad Khan, Baramad Khan and Kazi Sheikh ul-Islam chose to remain quiet. 'If these two rascals have decided to protect the kafir Sambha, they will soon know the power of Alamgir's sword!'

At that moment, the curtain moved and a sweet voice was heard, 'Huzoor, other than the Badshah at Iran, you are the only protector of Islam in this world, isn't that so?'

'Who is that?'

Everyone turned to see the Badshah's daughter, Zeenat-un-Nissa. Her fair and beautiful face was visible through the thin veil she wore.

Aurangzeb stood up. He did not like the begums and shahzadis interfering in the matters of state. He was surprised that his favourite daughter had spoken out of turn. He did not say anything but stomped out of the room and into his private quarters. His daughter left hurriedly.

All the begums including Udepuri and Aurangabadi Begum were a worried lot. The Badshah was in a foul mood. Aurangzeb summoned his shahzadi that night after dinner and asked, 'What happened this afternoon, dear? What possessed you?'

'Abbajaan, I was talking of Islam.'

'Islam, or love?'

Shahzadi's face fell. She said, her voice quivering with fear, 'Abba, whom are you speaking of?'

'Dear Zeenat, you know how much I loved Zebunissa. But she got influenced by Shahzada Akbar and is now rotting in the dungeon at Salimgad. I wonder why you interfere in politics despite being a shahzadi!'

Shahzadi's face was clouded with fear. Aurangzeb continued, 'Dear Zeenat, let me be clear: I don't want to lose another daughter.'

'Abba, please pardon me.'

'I think you are in love ... with that kafir Sambha.' Aurangzeb stared at his daughter as he spoke.

'He is younger to me by almost twenty years. If anything, he is like a brother to me.'

Aurangzeb did not say anything. He realised that his daughter, now sobbing silently, was deeply hurt. His heart melted. He said, putting an affectionate hand on her head, 'Dear, I know your true love is for Islam; just like me. But the two Sultanates you seem to be compassionate about are our real enemies. They are helping the kafir. Hence they are Allah's enemies.'

Zeenat-un-Nissa looked at her father with a surprised expression. The Badshah handed her a message and said, 'Read this. A few days back, Qutb Shah of Hyderabad wrote to Adil Shah of Bijapur. It was intercepted by our spies.'

Shahzadi's eyes scanned the message:

'Bhaijaan Sikandar Adil Shah,

The Badshah Aurangzeb has sent his Shahzada Azam to put pressure on your territory. But you need not worry. We are sending an army of forty thousand troops for your support. Sambhaji's Hambirmama is creating havoc in Miraj, Athani, Mahimagad and other territories. He is helping you by engaging the Mughal forces. The three powers in the Deccan have decided to create a situation so dire that the Mughals are forced to retreat towards the Yamuna. Let us see how long that old fool from Delhi can last against the might and intelligence of the Deccan. Rest assured, Shambhu Raje and I stand firmly behind you.

Your brother Tanashah Abul Hasan Qutb Shah'

Shahzadi read the message, wide-eyed. She thanked her father for letting her know the truth. That night, a content Aurangzeb retired to his bed but was soon woken up by his khoja banging on the door. Aurangzeb got up, rubbing his eyes, to find Wazir Asad Khan and Baramad Khan standing there. The Wazir began, 'Badshah Salamat, it is bad news.'

'What happened?'

'Five thousand of our troops defected this night.'

'Where? To Sambha?'

'It is not that bad, Hazrat,' Wazir said, trying to console the Badshah. 'They ran off in the direction of Delhi-Agra.'

'Why? Were they not paid their salaries?'

'It has been five years since they arrived here. They are getting their salaries and were well taken care of but they were missing their families. They have never been on such a long campaign.'

'This is not good news. Today, it is five thousand; tomorrow there may be fifteen thousand, maybe even a lakh! We cannot afford to lose them.'

'Command us, Huzoor.'

'Send as many men as you want but bring those deserters back with their hands tied. There may be a hundred pillars supporting the palace. But it would be foolish to assume that a single bent pillar would not cause any danger to the palace. We need to be alert. We cannot afford such mistakes.'

5

The Badshah was successful in arresting the deserters. He was in a mood to hang all of them but he realised it was not the right time to take such harsh decisions. Not wanting the rest of the army to revolt, he decided to control his anger.

A dejected Aurangzeb said, looking at his Wazir, 'One can motivate a tired army by feeding them with good food, but when they give up because they are mentally exhausted, it is a matter of concern. Tell me Wazir, what other than food, clothing and salary do these people want?'

'They want victory, Jahanpanah.'

'What?'

'Alampanah, in the last five years, they have not experienced a single victory. Even the tiny Ramshej stands invincible. And there seems to be no indication that we will defeat Sambha. His forts seem to be made of steel.'

'Are you once again praising that kafir Sambha?' Aurangzeb glared at Asad Khan.

'It is not praise, Hazrat. We are only stating facts,' Baramad Khan interrupted. 'The Maratha army is a miracle of sorts. They never risk a direct confrontation unless they are sure of victory.'

'Then why don't you attack with a large army?'

'The moment they come to know that we are marching with a large army, they disappear. They vanish into the mountains and valleys. The moment we retreat, they find ways to attack us.'

Asad Khan added, 'There is no doubt that our men are getting demoralised. We suffered badly in the mountain pass at Ramdara. The Marathas even burnt the grass there so that our horses would get no fodder. Our troops are scared of roaming the hillsides in small numbers even in daytime.'

Aurangzeb said, 'We must find a way to break the treaty between the two Sultanates and Sambha. If we cannot win the Maratha territory at present, let us divert our attacks elsewhere. But understand that we need victories—somewhere!'

'Yes, Jahanpanah.'

'We must find a way to stop the money flowing from the Islamic states to Sambha. We must first march on the two Deccan sultanates and finish them off. Then we will capture the mountain rat. There is no other alternative.'

6

Golconda was heaven on earth. Even the neighbouring city of Hyderabad had all the comforts a man could desire. Qutb Shah was a generous patron of the arts. He loved to play the sarangi at his durbar to the applause of connoisseurs. But he was something of a disaster when it came to matters of administration and warfare.

The territory of Bhaganagar had numerous lakes and several small dams built around them. A network of canals provided water for irrigation and the fertile land made Golconda a rich state. Hyderabad was a wealthy city with wide roads. It had been twenty-four years since Aurangzeb had ascended the throne but in all those years no one had attacked Qutb Shah. The kingdom's riches had thus grown exponentially.

Tonight's mehfil was a special one. Wearing expensive Persian robes, Qutb Shah looked resplendent as he sat relishing the evening's entertainment. The jewels in the aigrette of his turban sparkled. Beautiful maidens entertained with their dance. It was a golden age for literature, dance and music. There were more than twenty thousand concubines and dancers who were accomplished artists and entertainers in Hyderabad and Bhaganagar alone. Every Friday, a few thousand of them would present their talent while Qutb Shah, sitting at the balcony and sipping wine, enjoyed their performances.

No one had heard the sound of cannons or rifles for many years. Instead, the rhythmic sound of drums and other musical instruments filled the air each evening. While those selling ammunition had no market, business was brisk in Hyderabad for sellers of flowers and garlands!

It was an evening like any other. Madanna, with the broad tilak on his forehead, entered the Rang Mahal, the hall where the performance was taking place. The prime minister, despite being a Deccan Brahmin, worked in an Islamic kingdom. Though he was second in command in name, he used all the powers available to Qutb Shah—a fact the ordinary citizens resented. But Madanna had earned his position due to his intelligence and erudition. He was well versed in Hindi, Telugu and Persian.

He would often travel across the city in a golden palanquin. He had used his position and proximity to Qutb Shah to build many Hindu temples with funds from the royal treasury. He had entertained visitors like Shivaji Raje and numerous foreign emissaries. But his visit to the Rang Mahal tonight, the first in nearly thirteen years, made those in attendance turn their heads in surprise. The performers stopped midway.

Tanashah looked at his Diwan, a little surprised. He asked, taking the pipe of the hukkah out of his mouth, 'What is it, Madanna? Were you not made the prime minister so that we are not disturbed while music and dance are going on?'

'Please pardon my intrusion, my Lord! But you know I would not come unless it was really important.'

'Speak!'

'Hazrat, there is an important message from the Mughal Badshah Aurangzeb.'

'What is the old man saying?' Tanashah said, sounding a little impatient. 'These poor singers have stopped midway. The percussion and my heart—both missed a beat. Anyway, Aurangzeb would not understand the finer arts, would he?'

'Huzoor, he warns us that if we dare to send our support to Bijapur's Sikandar Adil Shah, he would throw our throne and our crown into a dirty nullah.'

While Madanna's face had turned pale as he read out the message, Qutb Shah looked amused. He wanted to show that he cared little for the Badshah's threat. At that moment a khoja offered him a betel leaf. It was from his favourite betel farm at Machilapatnam. Qutb Shah chewed the leaf for a while, spat in a spittoon nearby, and then called a sixteen-year-old dancer standing close to him. He said, putting her head on his lap and caressing her long tresses, 'So what was Aurangzeb saying?'

Madanna repeated what he had just read out.

'How many of our forces are stationed in the Hyderabad and Golconda forts?'

'About a lakh, Huzoor.'

'Oh! Send around twenty thousand cavalrymen to Bijapur. Poor Sikandar Shah is only a fifteen-year-old lad. It is our duty to support out neighbour.'

At that moment the royal consort entered the hall. The nubile dancer resting her head on his lap quickly moved away. Tanashah growled impatiently, 'What is it, begum?'

'I have a complaint!' she said, speaking through her blue veil. 'Please pardon me, Hazrat, but these are dark days. When you don't bother to look at your kingdom or your family, your begum is forced to come to your harem and talk to you.'

'Get to the point!'

Begum threw an angry glance at Madanna. 'I do not mind your concubines being around you but I cannot have Madanna Pandit here.'

'How is that possible, begum? He is my shadow, my life.'

'And he is the one ruining my life,' she whined. 'You have blindly handed over the reins of power to him. His brother Akanna is the commander-in-chief. His nephew Ramdas is the chief revenue collector. All the key positions in the administration are occupied by his family. That is why the Hyderabadi Muslim citizens are up in arms.'

Qutb Shah looked at Madanna. 'Diwan, I have heard that many umraos and ulemas are making these complaints. For the last thirteen years, I have never asked a single question about how you run the affairs of the state. Tell me, which of the begum's allegations are false?'

Madanna was dumbstruck. He sat down on his knees, shivering. He said, in a beseeching tone, 'There is nothing false in the allegation, but Huzoor, if you had asked this question twelve or thirteen years ago, I would have changed my ways. We are poor Brahmins. And we were given a great deal of power. Naturally, the relatives took advantage of it.'

Qutb Shah's face was stern. He took a few sips of wine and said in a disappointed tone, 'My friend, I cannot blame you. Power corrupts everyone. But I never interefered. If only I had spared some time from this harem and sat in my durbar more often, we would not have seen these days.'

7

Aurangzeb's camp was sleeping peacefully. The guards were nevertheless alert. The Badshah, in order to teach Qutb Shah and Adil Shah a lesson, had camped at Brahmapuri on the banks of Bhima near Solapur. He had entrusted the task of overthrowing Qutb Shah to Azam while Muazzam was to deal with Adil Shah. His plan was to remain close to both battles and oversee matters from the Brahmapuri camp. It had been a year since Azam had laid siege to Bijapur. But no victory was in sight, making Aurangzeb restless. Kahi-e-Jahan, one of his sardars, had managed to capture Mangalvedha and Sangola from the Adilshahi territory, putting pressure on Bijapur and Karwar. That gave some solace to Aurangzeb.

Wazir Asad Khan had his tent pitched not far away from the Gulalbar area reserved for Badshah and his family. Asad Khan travelled with his begums, a hundred and eight in all. Although the Wazir was his uncle, his casual attitude had begun to irk Aurangzeb.

Ten horsemen arrived at the Wazir's tent that night. They were delivering an urgent message. The Wazir accompanied them to Aurangzeb's tent. Seeing no activity there, Asad Khan was about to turn back when he saw the Badshah at the door. The spies were too frightened to speak but Asad Khan said, 'Jahanpanah, it is bad news. The Marathas attacked our camp at Sangola and looted the treasury. Taking advantage of the darkness of the night, they created havoc and managed to run away with five hundred horses.'

'Who led the charge?'

'It was Hambirrao Mohite.'

The Badshah looked at the sky for a moment when he heard Hambirrao's name. Then he dismissed all the men except Asad Khan who sat in a corner, waiting to be reprimanded. Aurangzeb said, 'I read the Quran every day in the hope that at least one day will pass when I would not hear the names Sambha and Hambir and I would be able to eat my meals in peace.'

He continued, 'Why can't we produce one Hambir from amongst our five lakh troops? It looks like we have an army of hijras! All useless, unfit, impotent nincompoops!'

Asad Khan felt as if his spine had been broken and he refused to raise his head. The Badshah said, 'Wazir-e-Azam, you have to do a few things. First, invite Hambir here. Pay him crores of gold coins and ask him to join us. Promise him that we will make him the king in Raigad and throw Sambha into a dungeon for the rest of his life.'

'I had never thought of that, my Lord,' Asad Khan said, standing up in surprise.

'Relax! Sit down. It is not as easy as you think. Hambir is a loyal soldier. We will greet him with flowers if he comes. Else, we will keep a dagger ready. Either way, he must be dealt with. We need to find way to eliminate Hambirrao Mohite from our path.'

They discussed the plan for a long time. The Badshah wrote a letter to Hambirrao and instructed Asad Khan, 'Meet Nagoji Mane at Varud. He is the only man from whom Hambir may entertain such a proposal. We cannot afford to send one of our emissaries directly to him. And, Wazir, try to get Sarja Khan on our side.'

Asad Khan was surprised as the Badshah had earlier wanted Sarja Khan to be thrown out of Bijapur. Reading his mind, Aurangzeb said, 'I believe Sarja Khan is a weapon we can use well.'

8

The Chandni garden at Ahmednagar fort was for the use of ladies only. The begums, shahzadis and granddaughters of the Badshah enjoyed spending time at the gardens. It was Zeenat-un-Nissa's favourite place. She loved Kamalja despite the fact that she was the daughter of Aurangzeb's fierce enemy Sambhaji. Kamalja often rode her horse alongside Zeenat-un-Nissa.

One afternoon Kamalja was enjoying her horse ride. The five hundred cavalrymen guarding the fort's Buland Darwaza too were relaxed. Suddenly, Kamalja's horse jumped over the fence. Shouts of 'catch them!' rang in the air as the guards scrambled to chase them. Nearly a hundred soldiers leapt onto their horses to give chase. Kamalaja and her horse were now literally flying over the hedges. All Kamalja could see was the fort in Raigad. She had spent many sleepless nights dreaming of her father and the mighty fort. Zainuddin, the leader of Kamalja's pursuers, took his sword out and swung it over his head. Flying through the air, it struck the calf of Kamalja's horse. When the horse stumbled, Kamalja went flying over its head and crashed to the ground. Her leg was sprained, and before she could move, the soldiers had surrounded her.

The ever-alert Zeenat-un-Nissa instructed Zainuddin, 'Let this remain between us. Think of it as a childish game. We don't want Abbajaan to hear of this. Else the poor girl, like Zebu didi, would never be seen outside a dark dungeon for the rest of her life.' She ensured that the khojas, guards and other servants who had witnessed the incident were either bribed or threatened to remain silent.

That night Kamalja was being treated by a hakeem for the injury she had suffered in her 'game.' Zeenat-un-Nissa, who was present, said, 'Kamalja, you and I—we both love our fathers dearly.'

'Why did you stop my horse then? An unfortunate daughter was running away to meet her father whom she has never seen. You should have been happy. I was not trying to loot your treasury.'

'Kamalja, you are not an ordinary girl. The blood of your grandfather Shivaji and your father Sambhaji runs in your veins.'

'What difference does it make to the Badshah if I run away?'

'Well, a great deal of difference! You have spent eight years of your life at the Ahmednagar and Bahadurgad forts. You know each and every corner of these fortresses. What if you were to describe the forts in detail when you meet your father? It would be a threat to my father's life! Which is why ...'

9

'Yesu, I don't know who has cast an evil eye on our kingdom. We had barely begun to breathe easy with Aurangzeb turning his focus to the South when famine gripped us!'

'Many old men say it is the worst they have seen so far.'

'The poor are suffering. Their cattle are dying. So are our horses. That is a matter of concern. They are the strength of our army.'

The famine, which had been ravaging the territory for a few years, was at its worst in 1686–87. It had literally brought the Maratha Empire to its knees. Sambhaji had started a special cell to take care of those who were worst hit by the calamity. Nilopant Peshwa had issued orders stating that the ryots would get support from the royal treasury for seeds and farming. Village after village was being abandoned. The prolonged war with the Mughals was depleting the treasury. But Sambhaji did not reduce his support for the ryots. He demanded grain from the Portuguese at Rajapur and Goa. Now the rivers and wells were drying up. With drinking water scarce, where would the farmer get water for his animals to drink?

Reports from various parts of the Swaraj tortured Sambhaji's soul. He had already ordered tax collection to be suspended as he knew it would be an additional burden on the ryots crushed by the famine. One day, Raje ordered an urgent meeting of his Ashta Pradhan and senior army commanders. He said, looking at Mhaloji Ghorpade, 'If we don't have any men or animals left, how are we going to rule?'

The old man looked at the skies for a moment, folding his hands in reverence. 'It may be true that the rain gods are displeased … but even our men are not showing loyalty.'

'What do you mean?' Sambhaji asked.

'Support from Harji Raje in the South has been sporadic. Mahadik was given a specific task when he was sent to the South as a subedar. He is not fulfilling his duties. Chikkadevaraja has not met his promises either. Now the Mysore raja has joined the enemy.

'Fifteen thousand men from his cavalry are helping Aurangzeb in his campaign against Bijapur. Read this letter from Adil Shah, Raje,' Khando Ballal said, as he handed a letter to Sambhaji.

Sambhaji did not read the letter but said, 'I wonder why he has such love for the Mughals. Should he not help his southern brethren instead? History would have taken a different course had he done that.'

Seventeen-year-old Santaji Ghorpade hesitated a little before speaking, 'If I may, Maharaj … Harji Raje had lit up the Jinji fort for nearly a week to celebrate his having earned the title of Maharaja. He believes he is an independent king now.'

'I did hear of the celebrations. That is why I sent a strongly worded letter to Daaji. He says his enemies who are spreading such rumours. I know he is lying to me. Trouble is brewing at Jinji.'

The discussions continued for a wile. Sambhaji said, 'Aurangzeb has targeted Bijapur today; he will not spare Golconda tomorrow. It won't be long before he is on us! We had taken the initiative to rally forces in the South against the Mughals. I think we must lead another campaign into the Tamil and Mysore territories.'

Mhaloji Baba asked, 'Would not that be risky at this stage, Raje?'

'Doing nothing is not the solution. In a few months, the Krishna would be in spate. The Badshah will be engaged in Bijapur till then. Let us use that time to go into the South and see that we get our dues. We can use the opportunity to get the ryots on our side, threaten Chikkadevaraja, and conquer a few territories there.'

The following month, Sambhaji left with fourteen thousand horsemen. Mysore's Chikkadevaraja was terrified hearing the news. Most of his soldiers were in Bijapur supporting Aurangzeb. How was he to face Sambhaji? At best, he could only play a defensive game while Sambhaji managed to take back most of the Adilshahi territory in Karnatak which had been captured by Chikkadevaraja.

Sambhaji moved from Mysore and Dharmapuri to Srirangapattanam. Harji Raje was forced to come with his army from Jinji to Srirangapattanam. A fierce confrontation took place at the fort, which had a deep and wide moat protecting it. During a skirmish, Sambhaji jumped over the moat with his horse but the poor animal was dashed against the edge, dying instantly. Sambhaji's elbow was crushed, leaving him badly wounded.

A few months passed. Neither Sambhaji nor Chikkadevaraja were able to attain decisive victories. Sambhaji could not afford to move towards Golconda lest Aurangzeb enter the Sahyadris. Leaving the campaign midway, Raje was forced to return to Maharashtra. Before leaving for Raigad, Sambhaji spoke to Harji Daaji and Ambikabai Akkasaheb, emphasising the need for their loyalty to the Swaraj.

'Harji, it may be fine to complain at other times but we have Aurangzeb literally knocking at our doors. We cannot afford such tantrums from you.'

Ambikabai asked, 'Do you doubt our loyalty?'

'Let me be frank, now that you have asked a direct question. I am told that you, Harji, wish to declare yourself as an independent king.'

'What is wrong with that? It would be one more Maratha kingdom,' Harji Raje tried to justify his ambitions.

'Daaji, nothing wrong with that in principle. But a temple stands because each pillar does it job. If all aspire to be the golden dome, it will fall. We have built this Swaraj on the sacrifice of innumerable soldiers. We built our dreams on the blood shed by them, didn't we? We need to honour that, Daaji.'

Sambhaji returned with nearly ten thousand bullock carts carrying grain. But the famine was so widespread that even such a huge supply was able to feed the starving ryots only for a few weeks. Two years had gone by now. The famine continued with unabated intensity.

Village after village was desolated. Farmers were forced to eat rats. There was misery everywhere, leaving Sambhaji in tears as he travelled from one territory to another. Even the royal granary was rapidly depleting. Sambhaji had instructed all the landlords not to hoard any grain and to distribute whatever they could. Raje prayed for the longevity of his people. He believed that if they survived, they would find ways to resurrect the Swaraj. There were granaries near Karjat, Thane, Mahuli and Rajpuri. Sambhaji issued orders to open the godowns to provide grain to the needy. He had purchased four thousand tons of rice from the English. Using his friendship with Qutb Shah, he also managed to get supplies from Naldurg near Solapur, where the Shah had a huge granary.

A territory which provided nearly half of its annual supply of foodgrains to the Swaraj was the province of Jinji. Sambhaji had sent Harji Raje to manage the key province. The key to the Swaraj's survival was in the hands of Jinji now.

While the famine had ravaged homes, emptied villages and decimated familes, the traitors fared well. Aurangzeb was entertaining all the Maratha landlords and watandars who were defecting to him. Even a petty official abandoning Sambha was a reason for the Badshah to celebrate. Aurangzeb wanted to create the impression that the Swaraj was a sinking ship. He wanted to break the spirit of the Marathas. Handing over false papers promising all kinds of revenue to the defectors was a small price to pay for such a victory.

For the first time in its history, Raigad was suffering from a shortage of water. Water was now being carried up from the base of the fort. All the horses had been shifted to Pachad, Raigadwadi and other places. The nearby Kal river had almost dried up. Large holes were being dug in the riverbed and buckets were used to draw water. The water carriers were exhausted from carrying them up to the fort each day.

Only a few select soldiers remained at the fort. Most of the time, the royal family stayed at the Pachad palace. Old hands like Yesaji Kank had never seen such terrible times and wondered how they would overcome it.

Sambhaji said, his voice filled with anguish, 'Yesu, our men have fought the enemy for nearly seven years, risking their lives. What are they being punished for? Even my tears are dry now. I wonder why Maa Bhawani is testing us. Despite repeated reminders, Harji Raje is not sending us the supplies we asked for. He could have desptched the carts long back. I wonder what is causing the delay.'

'Swami, be a little patient,' Yesubai tried to pacify him.

'Yesu, I am now worried that Harji too may turn against us.'

A few days later, Raje's spies brought news from Jinji. What Sambhaji had feared had come to pass. Harji Raje had not only decided not to send supplies, but had declared himself the king of Jinji-Karnatak. He had also stated categorically that he had nothing to do with Raigad. Yesubai said, her head lowered in shame, 'It was I who had suggested the alliance with Mahadik for Ambikabai.'

Sambhaji said dejectedly, 'What a pity that while we have Aurangzeb waiting to pounce on us and the famine literally gobbling us up, Harji Raje thinks of deserting us!' However, he was determined not to let Mahadik get away with it. 'We will see to it that we get what we need from Jinji. I am Shivaji Raje's son. I have learnt not only to praise those who do well but also to trap those who try to go against us.'

Sambhaji summoned Moropant Pingle's younger brother Keso Trimal Pingle who had just returned from Ramshej fort. Sambhaji said, 'Keso Kaka, you have managed the fort of Ramshej so bravely for the past two years. I can't praise you enough for that. But I have made a mistake. Keeping aside an old hand like Hanmante, I handed over the Subedari of Jinji to my brother-in-law Harji Raje.'

'Raje, what is your command?' Keso Trimal asked.

'I have a cavalry of eighteen thousand men ready for you. Take them and move towards Jinji. The journey will take eight days. I want you to return to Raigad with supplies from Jinji within with a fortnight!'

'What if Harji Raje resists?'

'Do I need to elaborate? You are elders who have fought shoulder to shoulder with Shivaji Raje. Do I need to say more? You have to save our people from the famine. Do what it takes to make Shivaji Raje proud.'

The nearly seventy-year-old Keso stood ramrod straight and then bent in salute. Sambhaji asked Santaji to accompany Kesopant. They left immediately.

10

Aurangzeb's tent was lit with torches and oil lamps. Wazir Asad Khan had spread a map of Bijapur and the neighbouring territories in front of the Badshah. It had been a year since they had surrounded Bijapur. They had spent enormous sums of money, thousands of camels and horses in the process but had tasted little success. Alamgir said, studying the map, 'Wazir, what kind of fort does Bijapur have?'

The town of Bijapur was surrounded by a square-shaped wall, nearly two and a half miles long. It was nearly seventy feet tall and thirty feet wide. There were ten huge doors and ninety-six turrets. Each turret was connected to the next by a wide road. Cannons and zamburak, a soldier on a camel with swivel mounted gun, along with long-barrelled rifles, were placed at strategic points. The famous cannon, Maalik-e-maidan, was the pride of Bijapur. A moat, nearly seventy feet wide, surrounded the wall. The enemy would have to cross the moat first to reach the wall. Shahzada Azam had spent months trying to capture the city. In the process he had not only lost many men but spent an enormous amount of money.

'I had told Azam many times not to waste his energy on trying to break down the doors. We must find a weak spot and attack,' Asad Khan said

'Why is Azam not lighting fuses near the base of the wall?' Aurangzeb asked.

'The soil is rocky and it takes days for the diggers to dig a hole even a few feet deep.'

The campaign in Bijapur had turned out to be terribly expensive for Aurangzeb. He had lost thousands of men. Qutb Shah from Golconda had sent twenty thousand cavalrymen while Nilopant Peshwa had come to the rescue with ten thousand Maratha soldiers.

In the meantime, Sambhaji had stationed himself at Panhala. He was trying to provide support to Adil Shah from there. Kavi Kalash led the charge with nearly seven thousand men. Hambirrao, with fifteen thousand men, was creating havoc for the Mughals wherever possible.

Aurangzeb was keeping a close watch on Hyderabad. He had sent fifty thousand men under the command of Khan Jahan. Qutb Shah's forces had held them at Malkhed for nearly two months now. But Aurangzeb's luck was in his favour. Two of Qutb Shah's sardars, Muhammad Ibrahim and Sheikh Minaz, had an argument. Soon afterwards, their troops ran away.

Baramad Khan reported, 'Qutb Shah has holed himself up in the Golconda fort instead of gathering his troops. His kafir minister, Pandit Madanna, had advised him to take refuge at the distant Warangal fort.'

'Baramad Khan, send a message to Qutb Shah's begum and his mother that Madanna is responsible for all their troubles and that he must be hanged to death.'

Hyderabad was now being looted freely. The Mughal troops plundered whatever they could lay their hands on. The Badshah, still suspicious of his son, had instructed his spies to find out if Muazzam was hiding the loot elsewhere.

The Badshah soon received good news. The royal ladies had sent their men to kill Madanna and Akanna. They were both hacked to death in broad daylight. In March 1686, emissaries from Hyderabad met the Mughal Badshah. They carried Madanna's head with them. Aurangzeb, moving his hand lovingly over the head, was thrilled. A treaty was signed between Qutb Shah and Aurangzeb, under which the Mughal Emperor received a sum of one crore and twenty lakh hons. He also got the rich province of Malkhed. Qutb Shah also presented a hundred elephants to Aurangzeb.

Aurangzeb was pleased that he had managed to subdue one of his enemies in the Deccan. He moved decisively towards Bijapur now. He had summoned Muazzam from Hyderabad to Bijapur. It had been more than one and half years since the siege of Bijapur had begun. Aurangzeb now wanted to finish off the task.

11

Both the shahzadas, Muazzam and Azam, were eyeing the throne in Delhi. They were sure that the old Emperor would get tired one day and hand it over to one of them. Hence, both were over-anxious to show their valour. A few years earlier, the elder Shahzada, Muazzam, had marched to Goa to defeat Sambhaji and returned without accomplishing anything. Azam was hoping to defeat Adil Shah and earn a name for himself.

But luck did not favour Azam either. He was ordered to retreat. Azam nearly cried himself hoarse reading the message. He was losing a golden opportunity to make a bid for the throne. He wrote to the Badshah, 'Whether the rest of the army fights or not, my begum and my children and I will stay here till death. The Shahenshah may bury our dead bodies here.'

The Badshah was overwhelmed reading Azam's message. He could not believe that his shahzada was showing such tenacity and courage. He decided to honour Azam and sent a caravan of five thousand bullock carts loaded with supplies. Azam was relieved to receive such a huge reinforcement and continued his siege with fresh energy.

The Badshah, on the other hand, was getting increasingly restless. 'Anyone else in my place would have gone crazy in these seven years,' he shouted at his Wazir. He was desperate to show that he was not yet old or tired. The Wazir remarked, 'Jahanpanah, you have asked Shahzada Muazzam to support Shahzada Azam. I am not sure if the younger shahzada would like it.'

Aurangzeb said, 'I don't care what either of them think. This is a last-ditch effort. If it fails, you may as well make my grave ready.'

SEVENTEEN

Hambirgad

1

It was the month of July, 1686. Aurangzeb was camped at Rasulpur, not far from Bijapur. It had been sixty days since the arrival of the Badshah but the walls of the city stood firm. The minarets of Gol Gumbaz seemed to be mocking Aurangzeb.

The wall and the moat were the two most evident protectors of Bijapur but help from Golconda and Sambhaji's Panhala were other lifelines. The Badshah had kept a vigilant eye on both. He suspected that Qutb Shah, despite the treaty, would try and extend his support. He had sent Qutb Shah a strongly worded message, 'If you want to protect your throne, don't try to poke your nose here. '

Wazir Asad Khan had been right. The younger shahzada was irked by Muazzam's arrival. The brothers had no love for each other. Muazzam knew that if Azam managed to defeat the Bijapurkars, the credit would go to him. He did not want that and tried to find a way to make a treaty with Adil Shah. He decided to send his emissaries for this purpose. Some of his advisors asked, 'Is the Badshah aware of your plans?'

'Not yet. We will tell him at an appropriate juncture.'

Muazzam started his secret maneouvres. On the strength of his earlier correspondence with Sikandar Shah, he was able to obtain permission for his loyal servant Shah Quli to visit the Bijapur palace. The secret talks began. Shah Quli was fond of drinking wine and could not control his mouth once drunk. He said to the men manning the cannons, 'We are all friends here. Don't waste your ammunition by shelling us.' As expected, Azam's men captured Shah Quli and he was presented before the Shahenshah. After being tortured with heated rods, he blurted out the truth—that he had been sent by Muazzam.

When Muazzam was summoned to the Bahshah's tent, he feigned ignorance of the plot and said, falling at his father's feet, 'Jahanpanah, I don't know this drunkard. It is a trap to besmirch my name and destroy me.'

Aurangzeb said, not showing any emotion on his face, 'Shahzada Muazzam, you may try your best to shake off your sins but one day you will have to pay the price.'

The very next day, orders were issued to strip Muazzam of all his military responsibilities. He sat in his tent, helpless.

It had been two months since the Badshah had taken charge of the siege. Monsoon had played truant in Bijapur and the water carriers had to walk for miles to get water for the city. Aurangzeb had managed to cut off the support Bijapur was getting from the Marathas and Hyderabad. Without adequate food and water, the residents of Bijapur were suffering. The soldiers were now forced to eat horse and camel meat. The city, once verdant with flowering gardens, now lay bare.

One day, the main door creaked open and a man walked out holding a white flag. He was followed by thirty more men. They were not soldiers. They sported long white beards and wore flowing robes. They were the kazis, ulemas and fakirs of Bijapur.

Kazi Sheikh ul-Islam seemed restless. He had objected to the siege of Bijapur as an attack on Islam. He was the judicial authority of the Mughal court but the Badshah was in no mood to listen and quietly ordered him to go to his tent and rest. When he tried to argue, the soldiers grabbed his arm and took him away.

The men from Bijapur pleaded, 'Badshah Salamat, you are known as Zinda Pir. You are a true follower of Islam!'

'Come to the point!'

'Shahenshah, please pardon us for saying so but this battle is un-Islamic. You are the great Badshah of Delhi and you are torturting a small Islamic state and its citizens. We are your brothers, Hazrat.'

'Whose brother are you talking of?' Aurangzeb thundered, narrowing his eyes at the men. They all looked down at the floor immediately. 'You claim to be protectors of Islam. Then tell me, how is it that Siva's son Sambha is your friend?'

'But Jahanpanah …' They stuttered.

'Even back in Delhi, I had been hearing complaints about him. I don't know which religion you follow, but let me tell you this: I ensure that I destroy at least a hundred Hindu temples on any campaign I undertake. Besides, where was the Hindavi Swaraj of the Marathas earlier? Siva, and then his son Sambha managed to take a little from Adil Shah and some from Nizam Shah and created this so-called kingdom of theirs!'

The ulemas said, 'Hazrat, we were never in favour of what he was doing.'

'If that be the case, how is it that the Marathas are welcomed in Bijapur?'

'Sikandar Adil Shah is ignorant, Huzoor. Please pardon him.'

'Huh? He has the intelligence to make a secret pact with Qutb Shah and Sambha. He has the temerity to refuse support to Sarja Khan. You call this ignorance? Why are you here? Go to Panhala and take refuge under your godfather Sambha!'

'Hazrat, you know the Quran Sharif better than any one of us. Yet, we ask you a question: does the Quran allow one Islamic king to attack another?'

'I agree with you. I have no intention of swallowing your kingdom. Get me that kafir Sambha, and I will end my siege immediately.'

The maulvis left when Asad Khan came running, a little scared. 'Hazrat, our chief maulvi Sheikh ul-Islam has released an order stating that our attack is illegal.'

Aurangzeb read the order with disgust and, tearing it to pieces, ordered that the Sheikh be taken to Athani and thrown into the deepest dungeon there.

Kazi Haidar of Raigad was appointed in his place. Aurangzeb asked him, 'Kazi sahab, what is true religion?'

'The orders of the Badshah represent the true religion. Following his dictates is the duty of all citizens.'

The Badshah was impressed with the Kazi's answer and pleased by his ability to adapt to the changing times. That evening, at a grand ceremony, Kazi Haidar was nominated as the chief justice.

2

The maulvis had tried their best but the siege of Bijapur continued for another three months. The moat around the wall had been filled. The rains had added to the troubles of the town. There was a shortage of foodgrain. Earlier, horsemen from Bijapur would find ways to leave surreptitiously and get supplies but now it had become impossible. Even Hambirrao was unable to help as the river Krishna was in spate.

Sambhaji would visit Panhala often but the rains had made it difficult to provide any support to Bijapur. The Adilshahi territory was besieged by floods while the Hindavi Swaraj suffered from drought. Despite his best intentions, he was no longer able to help his friend at Bijapur.

On the other hand, Aurangzeb managed to procure supplies from the fifteen or twenty Subahs he now controlled. One day, he succeeded in getting his men into Bijapur. The city was already a graveyard. On 26 Septemper 1686, the sixteen-year-old Sikandar surrendered. In these times of crisis, some made merry. Sarja Khan, who had conveniently jumped the sinking ship, was honoured by Aurangzeb and made a Mughal mansabdar.

Aurangzeb now trained his guns on Golconda. The forts of Qutbshahi kindom were strong and their supplies adequate. Qutb Shah was not going to surrender without a fight. But Aurangzeb was not going to give up easily. He had a throne made which his bearers would carry around. The sixty-eight-year-old Mughal Badshah would tour the environs of the fort day and night, looking for an opportunity to enter Golconda. Once, a bearer was killed by a cannon ball. The Badshah was lucky to have escaped death by a hair's breadth.

Eventually his efforts proved fruitful when Mukarrab Khan defected and another sardar called Abdullah Fanni opened the gates, allowing the Mughal army inside the fort. On 21 September 1687, Golconda was finally in Mughal hands. The Badshah now had control over a treasury worth seven crore and annual revenues worth three crore. Sikandar Adil Shah and Qutb Shah were kept in the fort of Devgiri as royal prisoners with an annual salary of fifty thousand hons.

While the Badshah was returning to Bijapur after capturing Hyderbad, he was deeply disappointed to intercept letters written by Shahzada Muazzam to Sambhaji. Muazzam had realised that he needed to take his zenankhana if he wanted to defect. Otherwise Aurangzeb would torture them. Hence he was on the move with his zenana. Unfortunately for him, the Badshah had been informed of his defection in advance and he was caught.

Sambhaji had been elusive for seven years now. Aurangzeb gazed often at the Sahyadris and wondered when he would capture the impregnable Ramshej. Asad Khan came in one day and said, interrupting his thoughts, 'Jahanpanah, Shahzada Akbar has finally left for Iran. Thanks to Sambha, he was able to board a ship at Rajapur.'

Aurangzeb let out a deep sigh. 'Who knows where our destiny will take us? Only Allah is aware!'

3

One day, Hambirrao said, 'Shambhu Raje, we are losing so many men. How do we stop them from defecting? Aurangzeb is merrily handing over papers. We too can pacify our men by promising them their own 'watan.'

'How can we do that, Hambir Mama? It is against Abasaheb's principles. My father abolished the concept of large landholdings where the owner enjoyed the revenues. When did you start eyeing one, Mama?'

Sambhaji's casual remark pierced Hambirrao's heart. He said, 'Shambhu Raje, is that your assessment of me?' He continued, 'Shambhu Raje, why should Hambirrao want a watan for himself? If I was so greedy, I could have helped my own nephew to take over the throne in Raigad. You know how the other elders were in support of Rajaram.'

Realising his mistake Sambhaji said, 'Hambir Mama, please don't take my words to heart. It was spoken in jest.'

Hambirrao continued, not convinced, 'Even Aurangzeb had sent his spies to assess my loyalties. In anger, I ordered the barber to shave off their beards and sent them back. But your comments have put me in my place.' Hambirrao stood up and left the room in a huff.

Yesubai said, 'It is not good for the king and his commander-in-chief to quarrel. If Aurangzeb gets even a whiff of it, he will take full advantage to create a rift.'

Yesubai tried convincing Sambhaji to apologise but he was adamant. That night, Sambhaji was restless and could not sleep. He refused food the next day. He missed his morning prayers, and that was something which had not happened in years. Another day had passed when Yesubai came in and said, 'Are you aware that Mama too has not eaten a morsel for the past two days?'

Sambhaji stood up immediately. 'What are you saying? Why didn't you tell me earlier?' Sambhaji rushed to his Senapati's quarters. It was late in the night. Hambir Mama stood in the balcony. Before Sambhaji could speak, Hambirrao said, 'What do I hear, Shambhubal? Is is true that you have not eaten for the past two days?'

'That is true; but why are you suffering?'

'What of me? I am an old man. There is no need to worry about me. But you have to take the Hindavi Swaraj forward. I may or may not be there …'

Sambhaji fell at his feet, 'Hambir Mama, don't say that! The very thought of your absence is akin to the world collapsing on me.'

A cool breeze blew. Uncle and nephew walked on the grass. They sat on a flat rock and enjoyed their meal there.

'Mama, I know you supported me because you believed in Shivaji Raje's dream of the Swaraj. I am sorry I hurt you. Please pardon me.'

'Don't talk of pardon, Shambhu Raje! I am what I am because of Shivaji Raje. But it was you who gave me free rein. I am the one who should be grateful to you.'

'Mamasaheb, you have shown your valour in every battle fought for the past seven years. But I feel you must rest a little now; stay here and guide us.'

'What are you saying, Raje? Are you asking me not to be on the battlefield? Hambir is ready to fight till his last breath for Shivaji and Sambhaji.'

'Mamasaheb, our watandars are clamouring—each for their piece of land. Shall we take the plunge and break the Swaraj into pieces to pacify them?'

'Never! Let Aurangzeb try to lure them by offering false promises. Hambirrao and Sambhaji will never allow Shivaji's dream to die.'

That night, the two of them talked till the late hours.

4

Durgadas was returning to Rajputana. When he came to take his leave, he said, 'Shambhu Raje, you have done a lot for us. How do I thank you?'

'We did our best, Durgadas, but the shahzada was only interested in the pursuit of pleasure. If only he had shown some willingness to fight, we would have ensured that he captured Delhi. Aurangzeb's enemies were willing to fight under the shahzada's flag but in the end he was weak . No army, however large, would have given him courage.'

'We wasted seven years trying,' Durgadas said.

'Durgadas, why do you want to return to Rajputana? Stay here.'

'I had given my word to Jaswant Singh saheb that I would take care of his son Ajit Singh. It is my duty to serve under the Jodhpur Maharaja.' He added, 'When you defeat Aurangzeb, I shall be there to honour you. We shall celebrate your victory all the way from the banks of the Bhima till Yamuna's shores.'

5

Aurangzeb called for Sarja Khan and said in a tired voice, 'I may have brought Bijapur and Golconda to their knees but I am still unhappy. It is Sambha I want. But neither I nor my three shahzadas, twenty-two grandsons and thirty sardars have the ability to defeat him. Only a Deccan commander like you can vanquish him.'

He continued, after a pause, 'Take as many men as you want and all the resources you need. If you get me Sambha's head, I shall take you to Delhi and honour you at the Red Fort. If you cannot catch Sambha, at least capture one of the big forts—be it Raigad, Rajgad, Panhala, Pratapgad or Hambirgad.'

'Yes, Jahanpanah.'

It was midnight when Hambirrao's troops crossed the river Koyna and reached Talbid. The servants at his haveli were alert. Hambirrao would often rest there while on campaigns. Sometimes he would stop for a meal before moving on. But he stayed that night. His daughter Tarabai, who was married to Rajaram, had returned home from Raigad. Hambirrao said to her, 'Taru, see that you take care of Yesubai. She is tense these days and needs all the support she can get.'

Hambirrao and his men had barely begun their meal when he heard horses outside the haveli. He saw one of his spies at the door. The man said, after a quick salute, 'Sarkar, Aurangzeb has ordered Sarja Khan to attack our territory. We are told he is on his way.'

'What?' Hambirrao got up from his meal. He washed his hands and said, wiping them on his shawl, 'What route is he taking to get here?'

'He is expected to cross the Krishna tomorrow, heading towards Pratapgad. He has an army of twelve thousand. He has challenged his men to capture the fort in two days.'

Hambirrao and his men got ready. His wife had tears in her eyes. He had not even finished his meal. But the commander had no time for such emotions. Seeing his daughter at the gates of the haveli, he stopped. She said, 'Baba, ensure that you don't lose Pratapgad. Our Bhawani temple is there.'

The troops left crying 'Har Har Mahadev' and vanished in the darkness. They met a few spies on the way who informed that Sarja Khan had a troop strength of nearly seventeen thousand and had left Satara, making his way to Wai.

'Our main army has crossed Amba ghat into the Konkan region.'

'We cannot afford to let him swallow Pratapgad,' one of the sardars said.

'Even if we chase them, they would already have crossed Wai and will be well on their way to the gorge at Pasarni ghat. If they take the gorge, they will be in a much stronger position.'

'What do we do now?' the men asked Hambirrao.

'Let us change our route. We will go along the Koyna towards the Vasota fort. By tomorrow morning, we will be in the vicinity of Mahabaleshwar. We will then turn back and intercept the enemy.' Hambirrao knew that the route he had proposed was arduous and would take a toll on the men and the horses but he had no choice. He spurred his horse and rode on, followed by his five thousand men.

They reached the banks of Koyana and rode through waist-high grass. Hambirrao had barely slept for several nights. Fixing his legs in the stirrups, he managed to catch a few winks while riding. As he dozed, Hambirrao dreamed of Pratapgad, and the way Shivaji Raje had walked down the fort to meet Afzal Khan. Raje had killed the treacherous Khan. Now Sarja Khan had trained his eyes on Pratapgad. Hambirrao woke up and said, 'Come, we need to hurry. We cannot allow the enemy to have an upper hand.'

They managed to cover a distance of nearly thirty kos, almost a hundred kilometres in less than twelve hours. Soon they had reached Mahabaleshwar and descended on Panchgani. They were able to rest in the afternoon before continuing their journey in the evening. Naroji Bhosale, one of Hambirrao's spies, knew the routes like the back of his hand. In the meantime, half of Sarja Khan's troops were crossing the Pasarni ghat. They stopped for the night in a narrow gorge.

Sarja Khan was resting in the cool morning of Panchgani when suddenly he heard cries of 'Har Har Mahadev!' The gorge was filled with Hambirrao's men. The massacre had already begun while Khan and his men were half-asleep. The Mughal troops did not know where to run, and soon, two thousand of them were killed. The rest ran towards Wai to save their lives.

Before sunrise, Hambirrao's men had taken charge of the gorge. Sarja Khan's dream of capturing Pratapgad was shattered. The Mughal and Bijapuri troops were now moving away towards Kenjal. They were still triple the size of Hambirrao's force but he was not in a mood to spare them. 'Let us uproot Sarja Khan and his men completely. This is our chance!'

The men, tired to the bone, asked for a little respite. Hambirrao too was exhausted. He had been fighting relentlessly for years now. They had rested for barely an hour but Hambirrao said, getting up, 'Come, dear men! Shambhu Raje is waiting for us. There are many more missions to accomplish. We cannot afford to sleep any longer …'

The next morning, the banks of Krishna near Kenjalgad witnessed a battle between the Mughals and the Marathas. Blood flowed everywhere. The Marathas were far fewer in number. Men fell by the hundreds, their shields ruptured. In the distance, it seemed as if Goddess Kalubai watched from the Mandhardevi temple with her huge silver eyes. In the east, the fort of Chandan Wandan overlooked the carnage.

Sarja Khan had managed to hold his position till late afternoon but by then the Marathas had massacred nearly three thousand Mughals, while Hambirrao had lost only two hundred odd men. Seeing the enemy flee for their lives, the Marathas chased them with shouts of 'catch them!' and 'kill them!' At around four in the afternoon, Sarja Khan was seen escaping. His men followed suit. The Marathas managed to capture fifteen elephants and nearly fifteen hundred horses. Khan's men had left their rifles behind too. Hambirrao ordered the grain and other items to be loaded on to bullock carts. In the loot, they had also found diamonds and gems from Sarja Khan's tent.

The men and women of Kenjal welcomed Hambirrao. That evening the ladies performed a traditional aarti in his honour. Hambirrao, seeing the ladies, was reminded of Yesubai Ranisaheb and his own dear daughter Tarabai.

Suddenly there was a noise from the bushes nearby. A Mughal soldier with an injured leg was lying there. Having also lost one eye, he was barely able to see. But he recognised Hambirrao, sitting astride his horse. The soldier managed to crawl forward; he had spotted a hand-held cannon lying on the ground nearby. With enormous effort, he managed to light it. Within moments, the cannon ball shot towards Hambirmama while people around shouted to warn him. The cannon had found its mark and all that remained of Hambirrrao's head was a mass of flesh as he crashed to the ground. Raigad's foundation stone had now fallen in Kenjal. It seemed as if the Krishna had stopped flowing for a while. Tears flowed down Kalubai's cheeks in the Mandhardevi temple. It was a tragic end for the man who never gave up.

The men managed to put Hambirrao's mortal remains in a palanquin. His loyal horse was buried near the spot where he had died. The gems from Sarja Khan's tent lay scattered on the ground. The drops of Hambirrao's blood had turned the ordinary soil priceless while the diamonds lay there like mere pieces of rock.

The news of Hambirrao's death reached Raigad. Sambhaji was at the base of the fort inspecting the factories when the messenger arrived. He sat rooted to the spot for nearly two hours, dazed and unable to move. He would normally ride his horse all the way up to Raigad, tiring his servants and soldiers out as they struggled to keep up. But today, he walked slowly, stopping at many places. His attendants requested him to sit in the palanquin or ride his horse but he barely heard them.

He instructed Khando Ballal, 'Please ensure that his last rites are carried out as per tradition. Take whatever money you want from the treasury. Inform the Subedar at Karad accordingly.' Instead of going to his quarters, he walked to the Jagadeeshwar temple and sat outside the sanctum sanctorum. He instructed the servants, 'Tell Maharani that I need to stay here.' For two days and two nights, Sambhaji remained there.

The palace was in turmoil. Hambir Mama was Rajaram's father-in-law and Tarau's father. Yesubai tried to console Tarau as she read an urgent message which was delivered to her. Tarau said, looking at her, 'Vahinisaheb, how do you manage to keep your head above all this? What gives you the strength?'

'Tarau, we are Shivaji Raje's daughters-in-law. We have to face whatever comes our way. We are not Mughals living in the lap of luxury. Where is the time for us to sit and brood over our losses? Have you seen the daughters of the farmers? If their bullock dies, they till the soil themselves. The king too must follow the example of his ryots.'

Everyone knew the way Hambirrao's unexpected death had affected Sambhaji deeply. Steeped in sorrow, he was still unwilling to leave the temple. He had barely eaten anything in two days. All he drank was a little water.

On the third day, elders like Yesaji Kank, Mhaloji Ghorpade and Prahlad Niraji entered the temple. Yesubai accompanied them. They managed to convince Sambhaji to leave the temple. His grief was uncontrollable now, and he sobbed like a child. He said, 'I was not shattered even when my father left me. Hambir Mama did not allow me to miss my father. I had his support all this while. Now, without him, where am I supposed to go?'

'Raje, this is life! Elders have to die one day. Now we have young blood like Khando Ballal, Dhanaji, Santaji and others. We will create one more Hambirrao!' Yesaji baba tried to console him.

The mountain of work that was piling up would diminish because Hambirrao had died. Enemies like Aurangzeb were constantly trying new tricks. There was no time to mourn. Sambhaji stood up and decided to tackle things head on. He nominated Mhaloji Baba as the new commander-in-chief. Santaji Ghorpade was thrilled to see his father being given such an important post.

EIGHTEEN

Kavdi Kabri

1

The office at Raigad was busy. Sambhaji was looking into both administration and military matters, from loans for farmers to providing the resources needed for various campaigns.

Ganoji Shirke came in, without waiting to be granted permission to enter. Realising that he had something important to talk about, the other staff left. Seeing Ganoji so early in the morning, both Yesubai and Sambhaji were surprised.

Ganoji said with a heavy sigh, 'My own brother-in-law is the Chhattrapati of the Swaraj. He is the ruler of a treasury which holds crores of hons. My own sister is the Maharani but does little to help us. I have never been considered one amongst you, isn't that so, Yesu?'

'Why do you want to drag your sister into it, Ganojirao?' Sambhaji said, his face red with anger. 'Should I tell you the number of times you have secretly met Aurangzeb over the past months? Or do you need proof? Ranisaheb herself has seen all the letters to Badshah, signed by you!'

Ganoji was taken aback by Sambhaji's direct allegation. He said, recovering quickly and adopting a confrontational tone, 'Fine! I did meet Aurangzeb. But shouldn't the person wearing the crown try to understand why I have been forced to do this?'

'To get your watan, what else?' Sambhaji answered calmly.

'Exactly! Your father Shivaji Raje had promised us that one day we would manage our own territory. He had told us that he would hand over the jagir of Dabhol once I had a son. Now my son is eight years old. When are we going to get our watandari, Raje?' Ganoji was clearly in a mood to fight.

'Ganoji, why don't you try and understand the situation we are in? These are turbulent times. Aurangzeb is waiting for a chance to attack. If we are to hand over watandari rights to you at this point, there are others who will demand the same. There would be anarchy. I ask you to be patient.'

'Raje, learn something from the Badshah. He hands over the promise of a watan to whosoever meets him!'

'What is the point of such deceit? How long is he going to be here? Are you going to visit Delhi and Agra to see that the promises made to you are fulfilled? I want to live truthfully and in accordance with my ideals.'

Ganoji was in an argumentative mood. Sambhaji and Yesubai were hoping to pacify him but he was not willing to give up. Suddenly he changed tactics, showing concern for Raje and the Swaraj, 'I am willing to accept whatever you give me or don't, but I wish you would ask that vile Kavi Kalash to go away. Please save the kingdom which your father has created.'

'Huh! Who is going to take his place, Ganojirao? Seeing my plight in these troubled times, my cousin Arjun Bhosale too has changed sides. My sister's husband Mahadji Nimbalkar is with the Khan now. Harji Raje is capable but selfish. You are here in Raigad but your heart is with the Badshah. While we are trying desperately to save the Swaraj, Shivaji Raje's own son-in-law goes and salutes the Mughal Emperor.'

Ganoji Shirke was rather shaken by Sambhaji's blunt assessment of the situation. He said, making a long face, 'Do you see, Yesu? That Kalash has poisoned Raje's mind so that he is unable to distinguish between family and an outsider. He cannot appreciate a valiant man like me.'

'Ganojirao Shirke, Kalash may be a Brahmin but he fought valiantly when Shahbuddin attacked Raigad. He saved us with his bravery.'

'Are you saying that I have done nothing?'

'That is a question you have to ask yourself. I fought many battles. But can you name one where you were fighting shoulder to shoulder with me? Forget leading the fight, you were not even in the rear ranks.'

'Are you comparing me with Kalash?'

'Not at all! You are not worthy of being compared with him. He would not think twice before shedding blood for the Swaraj.'

Ganoji Shirke was not willing to take any more insults. The next day he left in a huff.

On the day of his departure, Sambhaji and Yesubai had just finished their lunch when a maid came in and announced that Ganoji had returned. Sambhaji smiled. He presumed Ganoji may have returned to talk to his sister or express regret for his actions. But to Raje's surprise, Ganoji continued to reiterate his demands. Finally, he voiced his deepest wish, 'Sambhajiraje, think carefully. Hand me my watan without any fuss, or one day, I will have to ravage Raigad.'

Sambhaji sprang to his feet. He wanted to wring Ganoji's neck but Yesubai stepped in and pleaded mercy for her brother. Seeing tears in her eyes, Sambhaji's anger dissolved.

Wishing to avert an ugly quarrel, Yesubai took her brother into the inner quarters. However Ganoji continued to press his demands and was not willing to see reason. He had come with the intention of getting his dues, come what may. Yesubai yelled at her brother asking him to rein himself in but he said, 'I had not demanded anything all this out of respect for his father. Little did the elder Maharaj know that we would be treated so shabbily! Let me tell you one more thing: that is not a king sitting on the throne in Raigad.'

'What do you mean? Who sits on the throne?'

'An inauspicious owl!'

It was more than what Yesubai could take. Her eyes were spitting fire. It was impossible for her to stand there a moment longer and listen to such insults being heaped on her husband. Before Ganoji could react, she slapped him hard. Ganoji stood up, shaken by the sudden assault. The servants could not believe what they had witnessed and stood with their mouths wide open. An incensed Ganoji glared at his younger sister. He said, looking at the sindoor on her forehead,

'Yesu, I will distribute sweets in at least fifty villages the day you are widowed! I will celebrate Diwali on that day!'

'Khamosh, Ganojiraje! Take your black face away from Raigad,' Yesubai thundered. 'I was born to great parents but unfortunately you turned out to be the black sheep—a black serpent, in fact!'

'Yesu, I shall take my revenge. It is not going to be good for you,' Ganoji hissed.

'Get out of here first. Don't spend a moment more in the pious land of my father-in-law and my husband. Huh! You talk of watan? You are but a dog at Aurangzeb's court. Go and beg to your Badshah. You won't get a morsel here in the Swaraj!'

2

'Yesu, we did not entertain Ganoji. He has now joined the Mughals and promised to build their stations in the Hindavi Swaraj. He has gone there seeking revenge,' Sambhaji said.

He continued, 'Does he not realise the danger of opening the doors to an enemy? I have given strict instructions to Kaviraj that he should take action in the Shirke territory before Aurangzeb can begin establishing his stations in Prabhavali.'

Kavi Kalash and Sambhaji barely spent any time together these days. Kalash had been given the task of managing the Malkapur province. His mission was to keep an eye on Amba ghat and ensure that the enemy—nay even an ant—did not enter the kingdom from that side. The area extending over Panhala, Malkapur and Vishalgad up to Amba ghat was a critical region. Kavi Kalash was on constant vigil, day and night.

Since the previous month, by Raje's orders, Kavi Kalash had been in the Shirke territory. He had made life miserable for Ganoji and his relatives. But it had been ten days since any news from Kaviraj had arrived, worrying Sambhaji.

That afternoon, Kalash's secretary Krishnaji Konhere reached Raigad. Without waiting for lunch or taking rest, he met Raje. Sambhaji asked, seeing his worried face, 'Krishnaji Pant, we have not received any news for ten days. How are things?'

'Ganoji's tongue is sharper than Kaviraj's sword.' Krishnaji hesitated a little. 'Ganoji says the Raja in Raigad has gone mad. He insults Kaviraj, calling him a fraud and a practitioner of black magic. He is also spreading the word that many Marathas and Brahmins are falling for the trickster.'

Yesubai asked, 'Why did Kaviraj go to Vishalgad, leaving the task that was assigned to him?'

'Ganoji is creating a poisonous atmosphere with his stories, making people forget that the real fight is between Aurangzeb and Shambhu Raje. He has managed to paint Kaviraj as a demon and a villain. To avoid further tension, Kaviraj stepped back.'

Sambhaji looked at Khando Ballal and said, 'Send a message to Kaviraj, informing him that I am coming to Prabhavali and that he must meet me within two days at Sangameshwar.'

Sambhaji knew that he was now taking the campaign into his father-in-law's territory. Sensing his inner turmoil, she said, 'Raje, don't hold back. Do what you think is right.'

'What do you mean by that? I am going to ravage my father-in-law's home!'

'Yes, if your father-in-law's home has become a refuge for the Badshah or another enemy, then it is right to burn it down, isn't it?'

She continued before Sambhaji could react, 'Raje, you have been fighting the enemy for nearly eight years now. You stoically accepted the death of Hambir Mama. Your valour is your virtue. But some people never changed, alienating themselves from the Swaraj and their king. I have only one prayer for Tuljabhawani: let nothing reduce your determination and courage. Raje, we have lost many who were dear to us. But new heroes like Santaji, Dhanaji, Khando Ballal, Manaji and Rupaji have taken their place. The enemy is at the gates, but not one of our forts is under their command. There is no reason to fear. I am sure Shivaji Raje would be happy to know that his Hindavi Swaraj is safe in your hands.'

3

Shambhu Raje said to Khando Ballal, 'Khandoba, send a message to the Goan viceroy. Tell him we don't want ammunition but foodgrains and other supplies.'

Raje said to Yesubai, 'I hope we get a good harvest this year. The past eight years have been terrible. The countless battles, destruction of fields and villages, famine—we have suffered so much! We have to end this conflict soon. Once we destroy Aurangzeb, we can focus on improving the condition of the farmers.'

Sambhaji entered the fort. Ganoji had managed to paint a dark picture of Kavi Kalash in the kingdom at large. Sambhaji knew that it would be disastrous for the Swaraj if Ganoji conspired with Aurangzeb. It was crucial to stem the rot as soon as possible.

That night Sambhaji felt an urge to visit the temple of Jagadeeshwar. For the first time, he went to the temple in a palanquin. Jotyaji Kesarkar and Nilopant sat outside while Sambhaji prayed. They heard the sound of hooves and were surprised to see Godavari approach, astride a horse.

'Godu, what you doing here?'

'I have come from the haveli. I was told Raje is here.'

Sambhaji was in a dilemma. He was keen to leave for Sangameshwar but he could not ignore Godu. Together, they walked a little distance away from the temple. Sambhaji said, 'Godu, you sacrificed everything for Abasaheb and his Swaraj. But what did we give you? Nothing but banishment!'

'What else can a discarded woman hope for? Earlier, Khan's men used to come into the villages and take away poor women as a tiger preys on lamb. Those who were later abandoned by them were treated as "despoiled." Many ended their lives jumping off a cliff or drowning themselves. But Raje …'

'But you left your home for the cause of the Swaraj.'

'I am neither married nor a widow. But I am lucky for sure. That is why I was sheltered by you and Maharanisaheb.'

She continued, 'Raje, not everyone has a selfish motive. I was attracted to you in the beginning, no doubt, but later … while under the care of Maharani, I was able to see her as my elder sister. My attraction for you dissolved by itself. But I could not marry anyone else. No one was worth it. No one could be your equal.'

'What do you want, Godu?'

She put her head on Sambhaji's feet and said, 'Raje, I have just one wish: when I die, I want you to light my pyre.'

'But isn't it only family members who have the right?'

'Aren't you one?' She asked, and her eyes shone with tears.

Sambhaji held her hand. No words needed to be exchanged. The touch spoke volumes.

That night they received a message from Keso Trimal at Jinji: *'Harji Raje is under control and we have managed to stem his ambitions for the time being. I will ensure that the revenues, rations and other support reach regularly and on time. Please take care of your health, Raje.'*

The next morning Raje was ready to depart for the Shirke territory but he was keen to visit the Ballaleshwar temple at Pali. Twenty-five palanquins and five hundred horsemen moved from Raigad towards Sudhagad. Stopping at Pachad, Raje visited Jijabai's tomb. The soldiers were getting restless. But Sambhaji rested his head on the tomb, in silent conversation with his grandmother. He said, 'Aau aaji, I shall place Aurangzeb's head at your feet before I take it to Raigad.'

That evening they prayed at the Ballaleshwar temple. After an hour's rest, Sambhaji said, 'Khando, I want a darshan of the Veereshwar temple in Asregao also.' They reached the temple early next morning. Sambhaji was overwhelmed. He had never been able to get over the death of Balaji Pant. Hence he had ordered the creation of this Mahadev temple in his honour. Raje muttered, 'Balaji Kaka, the continuously flowing water from the kalash over the Shiva Linga represents the tears that flow from my eyes for you.'

Now, having completed the darshan, they marched towards Mahad. Crossing the gorge near Chambar Khind, they would soon enter Shirke territory.

4

Sambhaji had not seen worse times in the past eight years. Each passing day was a harbinger of bad news. Saiyyad Abdul Khan had managed to bribe the fortkeeper at Sarasgad and taken charge of the fort. Sambhaji had acted immediately, ensuring that the fort was back in Maratha hands. However, the operation had cost them nearly a hundred lives. The Mughals, using bribes and treachery, also managed to take over the port of Kalyan and the forts at Mahuli, Bhiwandi, Durgadi and Malanggad. Trayambakgad too had fallen into enemy hands. Now the Mughals advanced rapidly, swallowing the territory of Nashik and Baglan along with the forts there. The enemy was moving closer to Raigad. The treasury was facing a tremendous burden as it depleted rapidly.

Sleep eluded Sambhaji. One night, there was a knock on the door, and soon, two messengers were ushered in. They were from the Shringarpur-Prabhavali region. The news was disastrous. Ganoji and the Mughal sardar Sheikh Mukarrab Khan had met secretly at Panhala. Sambhaji was unperturbed. He was now getting used to hearing bad news every day.

Yesubai said, 'Raje, according to their treaty, Ganoji is planning to give two villages near Sangameshwar and Shringarpur to Khan. He is also presenting him with a few stables. The cruel Mughal is going to station two batallions at Kondbhairav and Marleshwar.'

Sambhaji was now really worried. He said, 'Yesu, we have lost thousands of men and animals. We cannot allow their sacrifices to go waste. Allowing the Mughals to enter the Sahyadris is inviting death into our backyard. It is impossible! We cannot allow them to enter!'

Kavi Kalash, Sambhaji and Yesubai sat in conference. Kavi assured Raje, 'I have nearly ten thousand soldiers at Malkapur, ready to fight at any moment.'

'But we need to be alert. The Mughals can enter through other routes too.'

The situation was tense. The enemy had not only reached the door but they could literally hear them knocking at it. The Mughals were strengthening their stations at Kolhapur, Islampur, Karad, Shirval, Shivapur, Chakan and other places. Many Maratha landlords and Brahmins were joining the Mughals with the expectation of a watan. Aurangzeb now moved camp from Bijapur to Akluj.

The Mughals had managed to subdue Qutb Shah and Adil Shah. Their soldiers were in low spirits, wearied by eight years of battles and skirmishes. The only solution in sight was an open confrontation. The Mughal python, having swallowed the traitors of the Swaraj, was now itching to feast on its choicest enemy.

Sambhaji recalled an event from the annals of history. Nearly three hundred years ago, when Malik-ut-Tujjar had entered the Sahyadris, the fort of Vishalgad was under Shankarrai More. Realising that Malik was planning to attack Vishalgad, More reached out to the Shirkes at Shringapur for help. The Shirkes took a bribe from the Bahmani commander and promised to guide them to Vishalgad. Malik had no idea of the difficulty of the journey he was undertaking.

For two days, the Shirkes helped the Bahmani forces through the forest. But the trek soon turned treacherous as they encountered steep climbs and deep valleys. The Bahmani soldiers were unnerved at the sight of the high cliffs and thorny undergrowth, to say nothing of the fact that there was not a single village or even a hamlet on the way. They could barely pitch their tents at night on the narrow paths. They hardly managed to get a little sleep. On the third day, while the tired soldiers rested, Shirke rode ahead and secretly met Shankarrai, telling him to take advantage of the the enemy's exhaustion and attack. Shankarrai and his men rushed to the spot and massacred the resting troops. The treachery of the Shirkes had cost the Bahmani commander dearly. Nearly seven thousand of his soldiers were killed.

'Yesu, no one can trust the Shirkes.'

'Don't blame my father alone. What about your cousin Arjun Bhosale and your brother-in-law Mahadji? Aren't they in Aurangzeb's camp? I was born to a valorous father like Pilajirao, but unfortunately, I have a brother like Ganoji. Raje, give me the charge of the campaign against the Shirkes. I would like to supervise it myself.'

'This is no job for a woman.'

'There are many women who have sacrified much for the Swaraj. I will sacrifice my mother's home.'

'Yesu, you may be confident of victory but Ganoji can stoop to any level to ensure his. Besides, if you take charge of this campaign, who will look after Raigad? You are the key administrator here. I need your presence here.'

Sambhaji said, looking at Kavi Kalash, 'I am afraid, Kaviraj, that you must take charge of all these difficult and uncomfortable campaigns. Hambir Mama is no more. We lost Kondaji Baba at Janjira. Dhanaji, Santaji and Khando Ballal are busy elsewhere. No one else is capable of taking charge.'

Kavi Kalash said, 'Raje, command me!'

'Leave in the morning from Pachad. Take fifteen thousand men with you. See that you destroy the Shirke province before Aurangzeb and Ganoji come together.'

5

The entire Mughal camp was wasting away with a strange fever. The troops had never experienced such a malady before. Some of the firangi artillerymen called it the 'plague'. The news that the Badshah himself had contracted a mild fever was enough to send everyone into a tizzy. Nearly seventy thousand Mughal soldiers had died of the plague so far. The very air smelt foul and the pathetic cries of the afflicted made it worse. The whole camp resembled a graveyard.

The demon of plague was now dancing outside the royal camp. The Badshah had lost two of his grandsons. Wazir Asad Khan was suffering from fever. In a desperate bid to outrun the disease, Aurangzeb had shifted his camp four times in one month.

There was no cure for the dreaded disease. The hakeem provided herbs which at best offered some temporary relief but death within a few days was certain. The dead were buried in shallow graves as there were not enough men to dispose of the corpses. The grave diggers were dying of the same disease. The water carriers had perished long back.

The Badshah surveyed the camp, sitting at a window of his tent. In the distance he could see the domes of Bijapur which had been ravaged by the disease too. Aurangzeb felt lonely. His two favourite begums, Udepuri and Aurangabadi, were sitting near his bed. They were worried as the Badshah was feverish. They prayed to Allah to save him from the plague.

Aurangzeb said, thinking aloud, 'I had insulted the kazis and maulvis of Bijapur when they had paid me a visit. Maybe I am being punished for it.'

'There is no better servant of Allah than Jille Subhani,' Udepuri Begum said.

'But this dreaded disease is blind. Look at the way it has wreaked havoc in Bijapur. Each lane and every house in the city is in its clutches,' Aurangabadi Mahal added.

Aurangzeb said, looking up at the cloudy sky, 'Udepuri, I have managed to subdue the Bijapur and Hyderabad sultanates and their sultans are here as my prisoners. I don't know if I should celebrate my success or weep over the way the plague has broken our back.'

That moment, Zulfikar Khan came in and said, 'Jille Subhani, only two thousand today.'

'There is little cause to celebrate when two thousand die in the camp and not on a battlefield. Ask your Allah why thousands are dying here each day while that shaitan Sambha is still alive!'

It was not possible to march forward with an army emaciated by illness. Those who survived were living ghosts, incapable of fighting. Thousands lay languishing. But the Badshah was confident that he would survive to defeat his biggest enemy. Asad Khan had taken ill and Zulfikar managed the affairs in his place.

Aurangzeb said to his cousin, 'The commanders of the Mewati and Multani troops met me this morning. They complained of not having received their salary for the past two months. What is the reason for the delay?'

'Huzoor, the treasury is half-empty and we still have ...'

'What are you blabbering? Zulfikar, we won two large sultanates in the Deccan. We looted their treasury! How can our treasury be depleted then?'

'Jahanpanah, we have not been receiving the monthly share of revenue from Bengal for two months. Subedar Khurshid Quli Khan is giving all kinds of excuses for the delay.'

Aurangzeb was immediately suspicious. 'Why, is he planning a revolt?'

'No, Huzoor. He is not so foolish as to attempt that. Most of the other Subedars in Hindustan are delaying the revenues. So he thought ...'

'Speak freely. Don't hesitate.'

'He thought that while we may have won Bijapur and Golconda, the royal army is not going to find it easy to overcome Sambha and his men ...' Zulfikar was sweating nervously as he spoke.

The Badshah swallowed his anger. Despite the famine and the plague, his mind was as sharp as ever. He had been planning a coup in Raigad with the help of Zulfikar. The plan was to win Rajaram over and declare him king of the Marathas. The prince would be abducted from Raigad and then stationed in Pune under Mughal protection. Those who opposed Sambhaji would be happy to lend their support to his younger brother. Sambhaji's strength would be reduced considerably and the Hindavi Swaraj would gradually collapse.

It would be an almost impossible task to kidnap Rajaram from Raigad. But Zulfikar had assigned nineteen Pathan and Turkish soldiers to the task.

'Any news on that front?' Aurangzeb asked.

'Jahanpanah, it is proceeding as planned. Zainuddin, posing as Khawas Khan of Golconda, has departed for Raigad. He has nineteen soldiers with him.'

'Will Sambha suspect anything?'

'Zainuddin will meet Rajaram in Sambha's absence. That too, at the haveli in Pachad. It is impossible to stage a revolt in Raigad and then escape. We have got details of the Pachad haveli with the help of Mahadji Nimbalkar. There is a temple there in honour of Jijabai. The royal family often visits the place. Mahadji is Saibai's brother and knows the area very well.'

Having heard that, Aurangzeb walked towards his office with renewed enthusiasm. Zulfikar said, showing him a letter, 'It is from Sambhaji's brother-in-law Ganoji Shirke.' Aurangzeb asked, before reading the letter, 'He was to give us two places in the Konkan region to build our stations. What has come of that?'

'Ganoji is keen but he has been troubled by Kavi Kalash and Sambha. He writes: *"Alamgir Aurangzeb Bahadur, please accept salutes from Ganoji. Badshah Salamat, please don't doubt Marathas like me. We need your help. I want to make it clear that Sambhaji has lost his mind and he needs to be eliminated. Sambhaji has cruelly denied us our claim on our watan. Now he and Kavi Kalash are ravaging my territory, burning and looting villages. We have managed to save our womenfolk by putting them in the fort of Jinji which is managed by the Siddis. We are in terrible shape."*'

Aurangzeb asked, 'How big is Ganoji's army?'

Zulfikar said hesitatingly, 'Maybe around a thousand strong. Well, it is not what you would call a regular army.'

'Zulfikar, we have to march on Sambha once this plague reduces its intensity. But we will meet Mahadji Nimbalkar first. He is an insider and can help us cause serious damage in Maratha territory.'

A few khojas came running towards Aurangzeb. He surmised that either Udepuri or Aurangabadi Mahal must be the latest victim. As soon as he reached the royal quarters, he found that Aurangabadi Begum had high fever. Zulfikar sent for the chief physician but he did not arrive for a long time. A little while later, Aurangzeb received news that the physician had fallen prey to the dreaded disease and died the previous night.

'His son too is suffering,' the messenger added.

Finally the plague, not discriminating between caste, colour, rank or creed, had claimed seventy-five thousand lives. Aurangabadi Mahal was one of the casualties.

Aurangzeb sobbed after burying his favourite wife in a faraway land. Most people believed he was crying for the lost begum, but in reality, Aurangzeb was using her death as an excuse to let go of the emotions he had withheld for a long time—his frustration, his failures and his constant struggle over the best part of a decade.

After a fortnight, things were already looking better. Wazir Asad Khan had survived the disease but it had blinded Feroz Jung. After claiming thousands of lives and leaving hundreds blind or deaf, the plague finally disappeared.

Aurangzeb was getting regular updates on Sambhaji's activities. The Maratha kingdom was recovering from the famine, and sardars like Khando

Ballal, Nilopant Peshwa, Keso Trimal and Senapati Mhaloji Ghorpade were busy attacking the enemy wherever they could. There were clear signs that Sambhaji was planning a daring attack on the Mughals. Finally, on 14 December 1688, the Mughal army was on the move again. With renewed vigour and ambition, Aurangzeb moved towards Maratha territory.

6

The Mughal camp was spread over nearly twenty square miles. However, it was not the formidable sight it had been when it first pitched its tents in the Deccan. Water was scarce and the animals looked weak and scrawny. The imperial army had seen much better days.

Wazir Asad Khan, who had luckily survived the plague with his eyesight intact, stood inside the Badshah's tent. Aurangzeb caressed his mehndi-coloured beard and said, looking at his Wazir, 'Why don't you tell me frankly that our troops fear Sambha?'

'Jahanpanah, everone is afraid of the Sahyadris and of Sambha.'

'These days, you are withholding information from me.'

'Jahanpanah, how is that possible? There must be some misunderstanding ...'

'Tell me then, what is kavdi and kabri?'

The Wazir was dumbstruck. He had never imagined that the Badshah would enquire into such trivial affairs. Aurangzeb repeated his question, and the Wazir said, his face turning white with fear, 'Jahanpanah, our troops play a game in their spare time. It is played with small cowrie shells called kavdi. Each soldier throws the shells on the ground where small circles are drawn in the dust. The circles are named after different rivers. The soldier playing the game believes that if his shell falls in a particular circle, his kabar or tomb would be built there after his death. What can I say, Jahanpanah? The soldiers have lost their morale. They wonder whether they will ever see the Ganga and the Yamuna again. They fear that their dead bodies will be found lying in these unknown lands of the South one day.'

'Wazir, I am told they also bet on where the royal tomb would be erected. Tell me frankly, isn't it true?' Suddenly the Badshah asked, changing the topic, 'What is the news from Nashik and Baglan?'

'Our loyal Mahtab Khan is doing his best. He has laid siege to the fort of Trayambak for the past six months. The Marathas are starving as he has cut off all their supplies. We expect the fort to be taken within a day or two.'

At that moment thirty-year-old Momin Khan, Aurangzeb's grandson, came running and said, 'We have good news!'

'What is is? Has the kafir Sambha died? Or has he been caught?'

'No. But Dadajaan …' The grandson hesitated.

'If that is not the case, I am not interested. I am tired of hearing news of one siege after another. Nothing happens thereafter.'

Momin Khan looked at the ground, unable to face the Badshah's wrath. Aurangeb said, directing his anger at his Wazir, 'An army of five lakh men and we have spent more than eight years here! My ancestors have ruled over Hindustan for more than a hundred years but none of them would have lived through such torture. Eight years. And you ask for my patience! You are aware of how the soldiers have fared for the past eight years. They are away from their families. Not to mention the famine and the disease we have suffered. They are at the edge of their patience now. I won't be surprised if they talk of burying me alive!'

'Alampanah, they call you a Zinda Pir!'

'Any further delay can lead to a revolt within the camp. We need to keep that in mind.'

There was a constant murmur of dissent amongst the troops. Asad Khan too was losing patience. He said, 'It will be impossible to hold the troops for long. All attempts to lure Sambha out of the mountains have been futile. Even that Ganoji Shirke turned out to be a coward.'

'What a pity. We have two of Shivaji's sons-in-law in our camp and the third one wants to join us. Many of his sardars are with us; yet, Sambha is elusive. Do what it takes! I want Sambha.' Alamgir turned to Zulfikar, 'What news from Khawas khan?'

'He has reached Pachad.'

'Take the next steps, you fool! I want Rajaram. It will teach that Sambha a lesson.'

The Badshah was waiting for Mahadji Nimbalkar and Ganoji Shirke to do the needful. Aurangzeb had learnt that while the Marathas may not give up their forts willingly, it was possible to stab them in the back using their own men. He began writing messages late into the night, luring sardars in the Maratha army with promises and urging them to join the Mughals. He dangled before them examples of Mahadji and others like Mahadik, Jedhe, Mane, and Jagdale who were now happy allies of the Mughals, and reminded them that Mahadji had been made a Mughal thanedar. He asked the sardars to either convince Sambha to yield or aid them in capturing him.

Soon Mahadji Nimbalkar came from Bahadurgad, carrying with him rich gifts for the Badshah. As Mahadji bent low in mujra, the Badshah caressed his beard and said, 'Mahadji, your fortunes have changed now. Instead of remaining a mere thanedar at Bahadurgad, I feel you must take over the throne in Raigad.'

'Jahanpanah, I am better off at your feet.'

'Mahadji, I am giving you a large army to attack Raigad. Imagine the turmoil it would create when people hear of it!'

Mahadji fell at Aurangzeb's feet and candidly admitted that he would not be able to carry off that difficult task. 'But I will get the work done sitting here,' he said. He showed Alamgir copies of letters he had written to several Maratha sardars, coaxing them to join the enemy: *'Join the Mughals and seven generations after you will live in peace and luxury.'*

Mahadji was afraid of a direct confrontation with Sambhaji. This disappointed Aurangzeb. He asked Asad Khan that night, 'How many castes are there amongst the Marathas?'

'I have heard that there are around ninety-two or ninety-six castes; I am not sure.'

'I believe there are only two kinds of castes: one, those who enjoying the patronage of rulers like Adil Shah or Nizam Shah, or any such protector, under whom they have lived a life of luxury for generations; the second, those who are willing to sacrifice their lives for their land. Siva and Sambha belong to the latter.'

'Jahanpanah, are you criticising those who have joined us, instead of praising them?'

'Huh! They are fair-weather friends, here only to assuage their greed for land. It remains to be seen whether they will really help us.'

'Is Jahanpanah keen on extending a hand of friendship to Sambha?' Asad Khan asked a pointed question.

'Wazir, a year back, when Qutb Shah was in my clutches, I had sent an offer of friendship to Sambha through him. I knew of the secret pact he and Sambha had, of course. After all, in this age, what's the point in spending years on end in a distant land with lakhs of troops? I had asked him to surrender all his larger forts. In lieu of that, I promised Sambha all the land he wanted in Hindustan as his jagir. But you know what he did? He spat so hard on the emissary who had carried the letter with my offer of friendship, that the fellow dared not open his eyes for a while.'

Ganoji Shirke came two days later from Panhala and fell at the Badshah's feet. He complained bitterly, the way one would when meeting the elders at home after a long time. The Badshah cunningly extracted from an emotional Ganoji the information he was looking for—regarding Panhala, Vishalgad, Malkapur, Karad, and the ravines, gorges and jungle paths in the Sahyadris.

'Ganoji, I know your intentions are good but you hardly have an army to speak of.'

Ganoji was taken aback by the extent of the Badshah's knowledge. He said, recovering quickly, 'Badshah Salamat, I agree that I may not be able to risk a direct confrontation, but the dagger in my hand can penetrate a certain someone's back in a manner that his kingdom too will bleed.'

'Wah, Ganoji! Now I know why Shivaji chose you as his son-in-law.' Ganoji was honoured with finery and jewels. He spent two more days there in discussions. Before he departed, the Badshah not only promised him his watan but said, 'You are already in touch with Shahzada Azam. Keep an eye on Panhala, and if you ever need any money, don't hesitate to ask Azam.'

'You have been most kind to me, Badshah Salamat.'

'Don't worry. I will see that my message reaches Azam before you reach Panhala.'

7

Kavi Kalash arrived with good news. 'We will soon receive supplies from Jinji! Harji Raje has sent three thousand bullock carts filled with grain. It will reach us within a fortnight.'

Sambhaji was thrilled. 'Harji is perceptive. He must have realised how we are suffering from famine and drought. I am happy that he has helped us.'

Two days later, Krishnaji Konhere met Sambhaji. He seemed worried. 'Raje, we have received a message from Digoji Nimbalkar at Athani.

The bullock carts sent by Harji Raje lost their way and stumbled into Aurangzeb's camp by mistake.'

Sambhaji did not respond. Within a couple of days he received a message from Harji Daaji, asking whether they had received the supplies.

Kavi Kalash asked, 'Who was misguided? The men or the bullocks?'

Sambhaji smiled. 'Kaviraj, how many people do you think would be managing three thousand bullock carts?'

'At least seventy or so.'

'Can you blame the mute four-legged creatures then? These are tricks played by the men leading the carts. I know that Harji Daaji is intelligent as well as brave. This is a cunning trick he has played. He made a show of sending support to us and claimed that the carts landed there by mistake. Hence tomorrow, if the Badshah defeated us, he would be in his good books. He can claim that he was forced to show loyalty to us but he had always been the Badshah's true supporter. The "misguided" bullock carts would prove where his real loyalties lay.'

8

Aurangzeb was shocked to see Zulfikar when he reported to him in his tent. He could make out from the ashen face of his cousin that he was badly shaken. Furious, Aurangzeb did not even feel like asking what had happened.

Zulfikar pleaded, 'Jahanpanah, please pardon me! I wonder how to convey the news to you. Zainuddin and his men tried their best. They invited Rajaram and his family to the temple at Pachad but unfortunately Sambhaji and Yesubai arrived that day. They recognised our men and raised an alarm. The Maratha soldiers massacred our men. The two who survived are now prisoners at the fort.'

Aurangzeb did not utter a single word. He sat at the desk in the tent that served as his office and continued doing his work.

That afternoon, Mansoor Khan reported with his men. He was immediately presented to the Badshah, along with eight captives who were disguised as gosavis or travelling mendicants. The men were tough-looking, with ghastly reddish eyes and black faces, and they glared at the Badshah.

Aurangzeb asked, 'Mansoor Khan, who are these men?'

'Jahanpanah, we found them at a temple in Athani. They are Sambha's men, soldiers disguised as fakirs. There were at least a dozen of them. When my subedar attacked them, a few ran away.'

The Badshah asked, fiddling with the beads of his rosary, 'What was their plan?'

Mansoor Khan hesitated and looked at the others in attendance. A nod from Aurangzeb, and all except Khan vacated the office. Mansoor Khan said, looking down at the floor, 'Your death, Jahanpanah!'

The men had already been tortured; the wounds were visible on their bodies. Mansoor Khan continued, 'They are ordinary soldiers and do not hold important positions. Their intent was clear—to locate and kill their target.'

Aurangzeb asked one of the soldiers, 'What were the orders from Sambha?'

The young man answered without hesitation, 'Raje told us that Aurangzeb is a threat to our country, our religion and our gods. Our orders are to find him and kill him, wherever he is.'

Mansoor Khan said, clearing his throat, 'Jahanpanah, we are told such teams are operating in various places like Athani, Pandharpur and Mangalveda.'

It was difficult for Aurangzeb to hide his fear at this moment. He tried to conceal it with a display of anger, but deep down, he was a worried man. Nothing was working in his favour. Despite having survived the plague, his troubles were far from over. Sleep eluded the Badshah. Even the barking of a dog or the rustling of a leaf was enough to wake him. He remembered the game of kavdi-kabri. Was he destined to be buried on the banks of an unknown river? Images of the Emperor Shah Jahan, begging for water and Dara Shikoh's bloodstained head danced in his mind's eye.

The Badshah woke up next morning with a high fever. Udepuri tended to him. When the hakeem diagnosed that it was not a symptom of the plague, everyone breathed a sigh of relief. In his delirium, when he heard the words, 'Mukarrab Khan has arrived near Sangola,' Aurangzeb immediately sent for him.

The following evening, a weak Badshah lay on his bed looking at the setting sun. Sheikh Mukarrab Khan was standing at his bedside, holding a basket of fruit. He had rushed to the Emperor's camp the moment he received the message. Aurangzeb said, holding his hand, 'Mukarrab, you are my true hakeem!' A fresh surge of energy had rushed through the Badshah's body at the sight of Mukarrab.

The tall, lanky, tough-looking sardar with sharp eyes sat near Alamgir's bed. Aurangzeb said, sitting up on his bed, 'You are the ablest of my sardars, Mukarrab.'

Mukarrab was all ears for he had sensed that the Badshah had summoned him for a special purpose. 'You know that the kafir Sambha is a cunning fox. I had brought his father Siva to his knees when we signed the treaty at Purandar. But the son has made me roam the wilds of the Deccan like a fakir for the past nine years.'

Aurangzeb was overcome with emotion as he spoke. Tears gathered in his eyes. He said, 'I don't know what ill-fated moment it was in which I left for this campaign. Nothing is working in my favour.'

'Jahanpanah, you are called the Zinda Pir. You have an army of five lakh men. You are the Shahenshah of Hindustan. You cannot have tears in your eyes! What is the use of having people like me then?'

'That is why, Mukarrab, I am nominating you to take charge of the territory of Panhala.'

'I will challenge him to an open battle, catch that monkey, and bring him here.'

'Don't dream of such feats, Mukarrab. He is not one to agree to a direct confrontation. All my sardars and the three lakh soldiers who have survived are proving to be useless. That kafir dog is growing bolder by the day, sitting in the lap of the Sahyadris.'

Alamgir continued, 'We could not even capture Ramshej near Nasik. Raigad, Rajgad and Pratapgad are deep within the Sahyadris. How do we capture them? Anyway, take an army of fifteen thousand and move towards Panhala. Even Shahzada Azam will serve under your command. I will issue the orders right away. I want your target to be one and only one man: Sambha!'

'I am grateful that you have shown such faith in an ordinary soul like me, Jahanpanah. I am a dedicated soldier of the Deccan. I will send my spies ahead of the troops to Panhala at once. I have only one request—I need adequate funds.'

'Granted!'

'Let me tell you a secret, Jahanpanah. There is no race in Hindustan more greedy and selfish than the Marathas. They are willing to kill their own brothers for a little money.'

'Wah!' Aurangzeb exclaimed. He too had reached the conclusion that bribes were the only way to defeat the Marathas. Like a camel lost in the desert seeking an oasis, the Badshah rested his hopes on Mukarrab Khan. He said, patting his back, 'My dear Khan, don't bother about expenses. Take whatever wealth you need on your elephant. But come back victorious.'

Finally he warned, in a serious tone, 'Don't let your guard down even for a moment. Sambha is well known for his surprise guerrilla attacks. Do whatever it takes to capture him. That would be the best service you can render to Allah.'

NINETEEN

The Battle Cry

1

Light winds blew at Mukarrab Khan's camp. The horses and camels had got a few days' rest and were enjoying fresh fodder. Mukarrab's tent was at the centre of the camp. It was lit on all sides with mashaals and guards stood outside, their naked swords gleaming in the light. Mukarrab Khan was resting but his face was creased with worry. He would glance once in a while at the distant silhouette of the Panhalgad fort, visible through the window of his tent.

In the distance dogs started barking, and then a group of twenty-five riders rode into heart of the camp. They were led by Mukarrab's son Salim. Behind Salim was a Maratha sardar who was around forty-five years of age. His face was swollen and his body bore many wounds. One of his eyes was bloodshot, and seemed to have been injured. The sardar fell at Mukarrab's Khan's feet the moment he saw him. He pleaded, between sobs, 'Please save me, Khansaheb!'

Mukarrab asked his son, 'Who is this mad person?'

'Babajaan, he is Ganoji Shirke, Sambhaji's brother-in-law and Shivaji's son-in-law.'

'Get up, Ganojiraje,' Mukarrab Khan said, slapping his back. 'You are treated with respect in Badshah Salamat's camp. Why are you crying like a desperate woman today?'

'What can I do, Khansaheb? Sambha and Kavi Kalash have made us homeless. He is creating havoc in our territory, burning crops and killing those who guard the fields. He took over our haveli in the village of Kutre. A few of my cousins have been murdered. Their womenfolk are destitute; they have nowhere to go. Sambha came with only five thousand men but the way he can motivate the soldiers is fascinating! I am saying that despite the fact that he is my enemy. I am ashamed to say it, but he routed our troops within a few hours and vanished into the jungles.'

Mukarrab Khan pacified Ganoji. He was offered a cool drink by a servant. Khan said, 'Ganoji, Sambha is a threat to the Badshah and to landlords like you.'

'Khansaheb, the sardars and Brahmins criticise him in private but run like scared monkeys the moment Sambha and his men confront them on a battlefield.'

Ganoji was desperate. All he wanted was for Sambhaji to be killed or captured somehow. Mukarrab realised that Ganoji's hatred for Sambhaji was intense. He seemed more like Aurangzeb's brother-in-law than Sambhaji's! Long hours were spent in discussion that night.

The next morning, Mukarrab Khan received urgent messages from Shahzada Azam and the Badshah. The fort of Panhalgad shone in the morning sun. Mukarrab said, 'Ganoji, perhaps we cannot capture the lion but let us at least take Panhala.'

'What?'

'We must capture Panhala. Those are the Badshah's orders. It is important to keep the morale of the troops high. Once we capture the fort, we will have control of the plateau of Masai beyond it, as well as the distant Ghodkhind pass and Vishalgad all the way up to Amba ghat.'

Ganoji gulped nervously and said, 'Khansaheb, it is a very difficult task. The fortkeepers Vithal Trayambak Mhadkar and Prahlad Pant are old hands. They cannot be tempted to change sides.'

'Huh! Many Maratha sardars are now fed up of fighting. They want peace and a territory of their own to manage. Take as many jewels as you want from us but bribe the officials at Panhala.'

'Sarkar, Prahlad Pant is not one to be tempted.

'Don't be childhish. Here, read the letter written by him to Shahzada Azam.' Ganoji read the letter:

'Shahzada Azam,

Please save us from our king who is not only an ill-mannered idiot, but also losing his mind these days. A mere clerk, if found taking a small bribe, is caught and punished. He listens to Kavi Kalash alone and no one else. The Shirkes have lost their homes. Many more will. All the watandars are worried.

We request the Badshah to save us from this devil. Save the Maratha kingdom. Put Rajaram on the throne. Old folks like us are ready to serve under you.'

Ganoji read the letter thrice. He could not believe his eyes. Then he smiled and said, twirling his moustache, 'That's all I need! Leave the rest to me.'

Two nights passed. Ganoji and Devji Shirke visited Panhala under the cover of darkness. They returned and reported to Mukarrab Khan immediately. Ganoji said, hugging Mukarrab affectionately, 'Khansaheb, just wait for a couple of days. You won't see the saffron flag on the ramparts of Panhalgad thereafter. Prepare to take over the fort!'

2

The Mughal python was laying siege to the strong and strategically placed Panhala fort. The moment Sambhaji and Kavi Kalash received news that their second capital was in danger, they jumped on their horses and rode as fast as possible. En route, Kavi Kalash ordered three thousand of the ten thousand cavalrymen posted at Malkapur to gallop towards Panhala.

The traitors had removed the saffron flag. The fort was already half-occupied by the Mughals. However, Sambhaji and his men entered the fort from the plateau. The Mughal troops were massacred. Sambhaji managed to retrieve the fort. That night the traitors were lined up. Prahlad Pant was captured. Yesaji and Shidoji Farzand were thrown over the precipice to their death. Sambhaji had won back a strategic fort.

Kavi Kalash said, 'Raje, we managed it in the nick of time. You rushed like an arrow without caring for food and water, all the way from Vishalgad. Mukarrab Khan would have taken Panhalgad otherwise.'

'Yes, Panhala is ours again, but it really irks me that Ganoji managed to escape. It is unfortunate, Kaviraj, that Yesurani had almost unsheathed her sword to behead her brother when they last met in Raigad, but she allowed him to go unhurt. Else we would not have faced these problems today.'

'I agree, Raje. It was a mistake that cost us a great deal.'

'Well, Ganoji is not a person; he is a trait, a mask. Many landlords are hiding behind this persona. Many such men have approached us. These watandars were unhappy during Abasaheb's reign too but they could not open their mouths in fear. After his death, they conspired to label me an ill-mannered, dissolute, whimsical and mad person. I know these old folks. They have already attemped to kill me thrice. This is the fourth and the last time!'

One afternoon, Nagoji Mane came riding through the bazaars of Karad. He met the Yadav brothers, Girjoji and Arjoji. Nagoji said, teasing them, 'So, have you received the papers for your watan as promised by Sambhaji?'

'We put forth our demands a while ago. I am sure we will get his approval soon,' Girjoji said.

'You are being naïve. The Bhosales have never given anything to anyone. The Mughal Badshah is willing to entertain our requests but the Bhosales never will.'

Nagoji's ploy to poison the brothers' minds worked. Their faces fell. Girjoji said, 'Maybe we are not destined to have our own watan. We were about to get the papers when the elder Maharaj died.'

'So get your papers now, before the younger Maharaj dies.'

'Sarkar, don't say that!'

Nagoji realised he may inadvertently have blurted out a secret. He said, biting his tongue, 'I mean, no one knows what may happen, isnt it? Get your papers when Shambhu Raje is willing to issue them. Ganoji Shirke has been trying in vain. Find the Maharaj, plead and cajole. Get your work done!'

3

Ganoji was desperate now. He pleaded with Mukarrab Khan to finish Sambhaji and Kavi Kalash off at the earliest opportunity. Mukarrab Khan too was in trouble. That morning he had received a stinging message from the Badshah, 'We had high hopes in you. I am disappointed that you could not hold on to the fort. I hope I don't get the news that Sambha has captured you!'

That afternoon, Mukarrab did not have lunch. The fact that Panhalgad had slipped out of his hands was hard to digest. Each time he looked at the distant fort, the wounds would hurt.

Sheikh Mukarrab Khan had risen from a lowly foot-soldier to the rank of the commander of the Qutbshahi army. He had won laurels through hard work and tenacity. He decided now that he was not going to depend on the Maratha traitors for victory. He had managed to plant several spies who knew the territory well. He would ensure that they cross-checked the information he got from Ganoji's men.

One morning, he asked Ganoji, 'What do you say, can we manage to capture Sambhaji from the gardens at Sangameshwar? I am told that Sambha and Kalash have built beautiful havelis there.'

'How is that possible, Sarkar?'

'Did he not camp at Sangameshwar for a month last year?'

'That might not happen this year. He is a restless eagle, and one with a sharp beak, so to speak.'

Mukarrab said, ignoring Ganoji's inadvertent praise of Sambhaji, 'When he travels from Konkan to Vishalgad, which route does he take?'

'Through Sangameshwar, obviously.'

Mukarrab Khan smiled to himself. 'Ganoji, would you not expect him to halt at Sangameshwar where he has built these beautiful havelis?'

Ganoji said, without raising his voice, 'Mukarrab Miyan, don't think I am a fool. I just hope one thing does not happen.'

'What?'

'That your Badshah, disgusted with his lack of success here, decides to go back to Delhi.'

Mukarrab's face fell. But he said, patting Ganoji's back affectionately, 'I know the Badshah will place his trust in me for a few more days. After that, he may decide to go back.'

Ganoji was in tears now. He said, falling at Mukarrab Khan's feet, 'If that happens, we are doomed. Sambha will not forget how we have troubled him; we would be caught and literally burnt to death.'

'Ganoji, it all depends on what help you can provide.'

All the watandars were shaken now. The thought that the Badshah may go back to Delhi was unbearable. They knew their fate was sealed if that was to happen.

Ganoji and Nagoji were now sending secret letters to the deshmukhs and deshpandes.

> *'You may call yourself Marathas or Brahmins, but we need to look after ourselves and the generations that will follow us. A watandar is his own king. For twelve generations, we lived like kings until Shivaji and Sambhaji came along and ruined our way of life. We ruled over Raigad too once upon a time. We need to support the Khan and protect our families' future now.'*

The spies were now everywhere. Nagoji seized this as an opportunity to serve under the Badshah. He was now more eager than ever to reach out to as many people as possible in the hope of turning them against Sambhaji.

4

'Malharrao, I need to see that rampart repaired within two days. I won't leave Vishalgad till then,' Sambhaji said.

'Sarkar, please trust us.'

'I trust you, dear. It is Aurangzeb that I don't trust. I want to ensure that our forts are so strong that he spends his entire life failing to capture them.'

Vishalgad stood next to the mighty Sahyadris the way a foal stands near a mare. It had been built during Raja Bhoj's reign in the eleventh century. It was strategically placed to facilitate as well as prevent military invasions. From Vishalgad one could enter into Konkan through narrow and dangerous forest paths. Similarly, it was easy to control movements towards Amba ghat and Anuskura ghat using the fort as a base.

Aurangzeb's final assault was literally at the doorstep now. The kingdom trembled in anticipation of the onslaught the way windows and doors of a house shudder before a cyclone strikes it. All the Mughal stations from Chakan, Shirval and Satara to Karad, Islampur and Kolhapur were glaring at the Maratha Swaraj. The Mughal Badshah had no enemy left from Kabul-Kandahar in the north-west to Bengal in the east and upto Burhanpur in the south. Golconda and Bijapur were down on their knees. Aurangzeb had now turned his entire focus on Sambhaji and the mighty Sahyadris which protected him. It was clear that a massive battle was imminent. And the outcome was clear: either Sambhaji or Aurangzeb would die!

Sambhaji and Kavi Kalash stood on the ramparts of Vishalgad. Malhar Rangnath and Krishnaji Konda were with them. The once mighty Vishalgad had weakened a little. Just the previous month, one of the towers of the Munda Darwaza had crumbled. Sambhaji knew that the fort, with its strategic importance, should not be allowed to fall into the hands of the enemy.

When Sambhaji asked the masons how long it would take to repair the tower, they said at least two to three months. Sambhaji was annoyed. He erupted, 'That will not do. I need to get the work done in two days and two nights.'

Raje ordered his soldiers to go to all the villages on the route from Sakharpa to Anuskura uptil Amba ghat and collect as many men as possible. The three thousand soldiers guarding the fort kept their swords aside and lent a hand in the repair work. Bricks and stones were laid and cemented with mortar.

Sambhaji knew he had given the men an impossible deadline. He asked Kaviraj, 'Give me a realistic estimate; how long will it take?'

'I think we can manage in four days, working through the nights.'

'The enemy is at the gates. I want to give some special instructions to all my sardars, including the Senapati.'

'Don't worry about that, Raje. En route to Raigad, we will stop at Sangameshwar and hold the discussions there. We are all ready.'

'Have the messengers been sent aready? Kaviraj, we must not ask all the sardars to leave their posts. We don't want to be in a situation where, while we sit and discuss our plans, the enemy targets our undefended posts.'

'We have only summoned a few select sardars. Senapati Mhaloji Ghorpade will come from Pachad, and as you wished, Dhanaji and Santaji will attend.'

In order to ensure Sambhaji met with success against his arch enemy, Ramdas Swami's chief disciple Ranganath Swami was to come to Sangameshwar too. As per Sambhaji's orders, the repair work at Vishalgad was done with utmost alacrity. Sambhaji, looking at the ramparts, felt confident that the fort could resist an enemy onslaught for at least six months. It also had adequate stores of grain and ammunition.

'Kaviraj, once we agree on our next course of action, I am sure we will rout the enemy in no time. It is my intention to save Maharashtra from the Mughals in another month. Our ryots have suffered terribly in the past years. We need to ensure that they have funds to buy seeds, and that we dig enough wells to meet their needs. This year, the monsoon is expected to be adequate. I am sure our granaries would be overflowing by Dusshera.'

Sambhaji was sad despite his optimistic words. Kavi Kalash asked, 'Raje, why are you so despondent?'

'Kaviraj, I can bear many troubles and have overcome them. But sometimes I wonder why Bhawani tests me in this manner. Remember the siege at Janjira? No sardar was more valorous than Kondaji Baba. If only we had had ten more days there! Alas, the Mughal forces entered Maharashtra when we were on the verge of triumph. Why does destiny always cheat us at the last moment, snatching victory?'

Suddenly Sambhaji spotted two familiar faces in the distance. They were Arjoji and Girjoji Yadav. Skilled architects, the brothers had built the temple at Pachad among other buildings in the Swaraj. Sambhaji asked them, 'How did you know that you are needed here?'

'Raje, we are willing to do whatever you tell us. But there is one thing which has been pending for a long time.'

'And that is …?

'The elder Maharaj had promised to hand over the territories of Karad and Aundh as our watan. But he died suddenly and the papers were never prepared.'

'What's the hurry, Yadav?' Sambhaji said, a little disappointed.

'We are not blaming you, Sarkar. It's just that Maharaj fell ill suddenly. But now things have changed. We hear from the Shirkes that it is wise to get the papers in our name as soon as possible.' Realising that he had blurted out Shirke's name, Girjoji bit his tongue.

Sambhaji said in a dejected tone, trying to hide his disappointment, 'Come to Sangameshwar after a few days. Khando Ballal will get your work done.'

The next afternoon, Sambhaji and Kavi Kalash reached Ghodkhind, also known as Pawankhind. The gorge was situated between Pandharpani and Gajapur. On 14 July 1660, Bajiprabhu Deshpande had stood firm with his men in the heavy rains, guarding the pass and holding the enemy at bay till Shivaji Maharaj reached the Vishalgad fort. It was only when he heard the cannons boom from the fort, signalling the safe arrival of Shivaji, that a heavily wounded Bajiprabhu had allowed himself to succumb to his injuries. At the spot where he had died, in the gorge now made sacred with the new name Pawankhind, were two tombstones in honour of Bajiprabhu and his brother Fulaji. Sambhaji was overwhelmed as he paid obeisance to these two brave warriors who had laid down their lives to protect his father and the Swaraj.

They returned to Vishalgad that evening. The deep valleys and tall peaks surrounding the fortress offered natural protection. Sambhaji stopped on his way to the fort observe the Sahyadris in the light of the setting sun. He looked up towards the Munda Darwaza where a hundred torches burnt. Then, with determined steps, he began climbing up. He was to leave for Sangameshwar the next morning. There were many decisions to take.

5

Mukarrab Khan's camp was sleeping in the dead of the night. But sleep eluded him. He had been discussing their next moves with Ganoji Shirke who was confident that Sambhaji would halt at Sangameshwar before leaving for Raigad. Ganoji had also assured Mukarrab that his family would care for his troops while they were in Shirke territory. Mukarrab looked through the window of his tent at the faraway silhouette of Panhalgad. Mukarrab often shut his eyes to avoid looking at the fort but the mental image of Sambhaji could not be dismissed so easily. Neither his mind nor his body were at rest.

Suddenly, he heard horses outside his tent. Mukarrab Khan stood up and went out of his tent. Two messengers handed over a message from Wazir Asad Khan. Mukarrab's hair stood on end as he began to read the message:

> *'My dear Sheikh Mukarrab Khan,*
>
> *This is an urgent message from Badshah Salamat. That "Jagirdar" is now in the Vishalgad territory, away from the safe confines of his Raigad. He has carelessly busied himself with the repair of the fort. He is accompanied by select soldiers. It is an opportune moment for you to capture that zamindar. Needless to remind you, Alamgir Badshah is pinning his hopes on your valour, and waits day and night for the good news.'*

The very thought of the daring campaign lit up Mukarrab Khan's face. He could barely sit still in excitement. Unable to contain his eagerness, he stepped out of his tent and started waking up his men, giving orders for them to get ready. Soon Mukarrab Khan's sons, and nearly three thousand soldiers, had assembled near his tent. Ganoji Shirke and Nagoji Mane were sent for. Mukarrab Khan hugged Ganoji, saying, 'You are like a brother to me. Your information was accurate. The message from the Badshah confirms it. Come! We need to move at once.'

Then he said, turning to Nagoji, 'I want you to move towards Karad immediately. Get the thanedar at Karad to round up at least fifteen thousand troops. We never know when we will need them.'

Mukarrab addressed his men, 'My friends, remember! We have to forget sleep, food, water and every such thing. Follow me now! The journey ahead is tough but we have to jump into the swirling waters even though we might drown.'

'Khansaheb, don't lose your wisdom in your eagerness,' someone shouted from the crowd.

'Who said that?' Mukarrab Khan screamed.

An old Bijapuri sardar stood up. He said, 'Khansaheb, no one doubts your valour or your intentions. But I have travelled through mountainous terrain many times. I was an ordinary soldier in Siddi Johar's army when we chased Shivaji upto Vishalgad. I was barely twenty then. I have seen first-hand how dangerous the mountains are.'

'What do you wish to say?'

'That it is not just a mountain range; it is hell!' the old sardar said. 'The roads leading to the Amba ghat are so narrow and steep that a team of merely thirty or forty Maratha soldiers armed with just a catapult can send thousands of enemy soldiers to their graves.'

'Stop spreading these exaggerated lies!' Mukarrab Khan shouted.

'Let me tell you about Umberkhind, a dangerous gorge. Once Shiva ...'

'Stop! Don't utter another word!' Mukarrab Khan said, standing up. He stepped onto to a slightly raised mound of earth and said, 'Friends, we have to carry out this campaign not to live but to die! Those who believe in Allah and in me may come. Those who fear for their lives may rest here.'

Mukarrab Khan walked briskly to his horse and mounted it. Ikhlas Khan and Ganoji followed suit. Then they rode away. Mukarrab Khan was in no mood to stop now. Following him were two thousand of his select riders. A thousand odd foot soldiers sprinted after them, not wanting to be left behind. Khan had always maintained strict discipline within his troops.

The very thought of Sambhaji's capture tickled Ganoji. He looked at the Jyotiba Dongar, a Shiva temple they passed en route, and prayed, 'Lord, please allow the arrest of this rascal Sambha. I shall present a gold garland weighing a hundred and fifty tolas to you.'

Mukarrab Khan's luck had favoured him. It was a starlit night. He knew there was a Maratha camp at Navli. They would have to ensure that the soldiers at Navli did not alert the troops at Panhala. A contingent of three thousand men would certainly attract their attention. Ganoji guided them through the woods around Devale village, thus avoiding any attention. Mukarrab had instructed his best archers to kill any dog which started barking lest it awaken the villagers.

Mukarrab Khan was an intelligent leader. He said to his cousin, 'Go back to my camp. Lie down on my bed and call for the hakeem and the other physicians. You must not leave the tent for four days. You need to create the impression that while the troops have left for Karad, Mukarrab is ill. No one should know my plan.'

By morning, they had reached Bahirewadi, from where distant Malkapur was visible. Ganoji informed the others that once they crossed the difficult Amba ghat, their route to Sangameshwar would be relatively free of obstacles.

'But it is better to avoid Malkapur. Kavi Kalash has his stables there. Nearly seven thousand of his troops would be guarding the route to Amba ghat. I would suggest we go via Anuskura ghat. There too we might encounter the Marathas, but the Desais and Dalvis there are known to me. And no one would expect us to take that route as it needs an additional day. It is more treacherous than Amba ghat. I know the Marathas well. It is not possible to kill a Maratha with a sword in a fight. But it is easy to stab him in the back. Let us go via Anuskura ghat.'

Ganoji evidently knew the pros and cons of both the routes. Mukarrab Khan realised that choosing the Amba ghat route was akin to walking into the jaws of death. However, Anuskura ghat was perilous. Some men were sure to slip and die.

Mukarrab Khan hugged Ganoji again, overwhelmed with emotion. He kissed him on his cheeks and said, holding back his tears, 'Ganoji Raje, people say you are Shivaji's son-in-law and brother-in-law to Sambha. You might be. I don't care! But I can tell you this in the name of Allah, Ganoji! You were surely my bhaijaan in my previous life.'

6

The work at Vishalgad was over long before dawn. Battlecries in praise of Bhawani, Shivaji and Sambhaji rent the morning air. Sambhaji had not slept a wink the previous night. However, there was no time to waste now. They would have to leave for Sangameshwar without further delay.

At dawn, Sambhaji went to the masjid on the fort with Malhar Rangnath and Krishnaji Konda. It was the tomb of Malik-ut-Tujjar. No one had heard the heart-rending cries of the Bahmani commander. But the locals revered the stone on which his blood had fallen. Hindus and Muslims both prayed at his tomb, worshipping him as a Peer Baba.

Soon, Sambhaji descended on Konkan with five thousand men. They moved through dense forests, at times negotiating narrow paths covered with waist-high grass. The skies were growing brighter. Kavi Kalash, riding with Sambhaji, said, 'I am told Yesu Ranisaheb too is coming to Sangameshwar.'

'Womenfolk have their own mind. She knows this will be my final confrontation with Aurangzeb and wants to pray at the Mahadev temple there. It will also be an opportunity to confer with some of the key sardars.'

He continued, 'Many sangams, the confluences of rivers, have played a crucial role in my life many times. Like the rivers themselves, my life has been changed by these confluences. You know that the rivers Krishna and Venna meet at Mahuli. We had camped with Abasaheb there. When I returned to Mahuli years later, I was itching to do something spectacular. Something which would make my father stand up and notice me! I crossed the river and joined Diler Khan's troops there. But I realised my mistake at Bahadurgad. It is another sangam, the place where the rivers Bhima and Saraswati meet. Sangameshwar is at the confluence of the rivers Alaknanda and Varuna.' Sambhaji paused before he spoke again, 'Maharani believes her prayers will help me. To tell you the truth, I don't believe in all that now. But when men start behaving like animals, and when they resort to treachery, I suppose we have no option but to turn to the Lord.'

'I agree, Raje. Your people and their treachery make even the ghosts in a graveyard look friendly.'

Sambhaji and the men dismounted and walked down the slopes. It was impossible to ride a horse on the steep inclines. Sambhaji's horse rubbed his body against his master's as he walked, almost as if he was trying to say something. Sambhaji patted his back and caressed his mane as he walked.

Kavi Kalash said, 'Raje, I wish to say something … can I be excused from accompanying you? It is my task to protect Amba ghat. We need to be alert. Let me stay back here.'

Sambhaji was touched by his concern. 'There is no need to be so anxious. Amba ghat is well protected. Likewise, five thousand men are standing guard near Rajapur once you descend on Anuskura ghat. We have reinforced the troops in Jaydurg, Dandarajapuri, Harihareshwar and other coastal areas too. We need not worry about our forts here. Even a hawk will think twice before descending into this area, to say nothing of vultures!'

'I understand your misgivings, Kaviraj,' Sambhaji continued, 'but we need your advice at Sangameshwar.'

'As you command, Raje.'

7

The atmosphere at Sangameshwar was lively and pleasant. Once known as Ramkshetra, it was a charming town, surrounded by dense forests and dotted by the coconut trees lining the houses.

After a long gap, Sambhaji's haveli was full of people. More than two thousand soldiers were on guard duty. Despite the festive atmosphere in the town at large, the mood at the haveli was sombre. Those assembled were aware of the impending clash with the Mughals and knew they were there for a serious discussion.

The rivers Varuna and Alaknanda merged at Sangameshwar. Sometimes, at high tide, the waters would flow backwards from the Arabian sea. The mingled sea and river water would wash the steps of the Mahadev temple.

The nearby port was busy with hundreds of small boats bobbing on the waves. Two large ships were anchored at the port. The fishermen had worked hard to catch the choicest fish for their beloved Raje. More than a hundred soldiers guarded the coastline.

Yesubai and Kavi Kalash's wife Tejasbai had arrived the previous afternoon from Raigad. The priests and Ramdas Swami's disciple Ranganath Swami had begun their preparations for the pooja. Yesubai ensured that they were able to work undisturbed.

Sambhaji had reached the previous night and was welcomed by Yesubai, Senapati Mhaloji Ghorpade, Khando Ballal, Dhanaji-Santaji-Manaji and several other sardars. They were meeting Sambhaji after nearly a month. Raje's face looked weary. He had not slept for many nights. The tiring journey had taken its toll too. His eyes were bloodshot from lack of sleep.

Sambhaji was keen to lie down but he knew that his men had been waiting for him. He took his seat in the office and looked at Ghorpade, his commander. He was a tough soldier who had worked with Shivaji

Maharaj. Despite being in his seventies, he was a wily and strong man. Sambhaji said, 'Mhaloji Kaka, we have been fighting for eight years. it is time for one final confrontation with the Mughal Badshah.'

'Raje, it is thanks to your bravery that the Mughals do not dare step on this territory.'

Yesubai knew the discussion would be long. She interrupted, concerned for Sambhaji's health, 'Let him rest for a while. There is a lot of work to be done tomorrow.'

Sambhaji retired to his chambers. He was keen to talk to Yesubai but the moment he lay on bed, he dozed off. His tiredness had overtaken him and he was fast asleep within minutes.

Yesubai, Kavi Kalash and Senapati Ghorpade discussed various matters. Yesubai was worried that Sambhaji's health was deteriorating.

'Maharani, he has been on horseback for years now. But don't worry. Things should improve soon. During the Karnatak campaign he had once jumped over a moat. His poor horse died and Raje suffered a serious injury in his thigh. The bone still gives him trouble.'

He continued, 'The mad Badshah has only two ways forward: either he will leave for Delhi, or he will commit suicide and meet his Allah.'

'The poor boy has suffered so much,' Mhaloji Baba said, referring to Sambhaji. 'Even Shivaji Maharaj did not have to see such troubled times.'

Yesubai prayed to Bhawani, 'Aai, please relieve him of his troubles now! He was born at Purandar while it rained cats and dogs. He lost his mother before he could learn to say "Aai." He joined the Mughals, estranging himself from his father. Thanks to the Lord's blessings the elder Maharaj met him at Panhala. Luckily, that cleared all doubts and misunderstandings between them. But within four months of that meeting, Abasaheb died suddenly. And now, for the past eight years, he has been battling intrigue, family feuds, the treachery of his own sardars and relatives, and the Mughals! How long should he suffer? He has been fighting demons, both internal and external, for far too long! I wish it all ends soon.'

The next morning Sambhaji and Yesubai participated in the pooja. Under the supervision of Ranganath Swami, the religious rites were carried out to everyone's satisfaction.

That evening, Sambhaji called for a meeting of his sardars. He said, 'The Mughal Badshah is raving mad now. We expect him to attack us very soon. With traitors at home and the famine outside, we have been ravaged on both fronts. But we have the blessings of Shivaji and Bhawani

Mata, and the mighty Sahyadris which stand tall in our defence. I am deeply grateful to elders like Mhaloji and Suryaji Baba, and youngsters like Dhanaji, Santaji and Khando Ballal. I am grateful to all of you for bearing the hardships of the past eight years. It is time the Mughals learned what the Marathas are capable of. Our kingdom may be smaller than one Subah of his, and our treasury no match to their immense wealth. But we will show them what we are made of!'

'Raje, it is easy to tackle the lion at the door but it becomes very difficult to catch the mice at home. Our bodies and souls are yours,' Mhaloji said, overcome with emotion. 'Prataprao died while confronting Bahlol Khan. Hambirrao picked up the mantle and died at Wai even as he was making life hell for Sarja Khan. You have given me the task now. I am ready, Raje!'

The discussion centred around the preparedness of each fort.

'We have strong defences at Panhala, Shirval, Pune, Chakan, Panvel, Chaul, Harihareshwar and all the way from Sangameshwar to Vishalgad. We will not allow even an ant to enter.'

Everyone agreed that withdrawing the forces from Khandesh had been an error of sorts. Many watandars and sardars of the region had joined the Mughals. The Sawants from Sawantwadi too had gone over to the enemy. Prominent sardars like the Jedhes had defected. The Supe and Pune territories were under threat now.

'Our initial gameplan worked well. We have put the Portuguese and the Siddis in their place. But when the Mughals attack, they might offer Aurangzeb support. We will have to trim their aspirations before they rear their head once more.'

'Dhanaji, ensure that you maintain a strict vigil at Ratnagiri. There is a possibility of the firangis attacking us from Goa. My brother-in-law Mahadji and the Sawants are supporting Aurangzeb. We have to keep an eye on the Goan side.'

'Santaji, there is no need to remind you of that cunning rascal Siddi. He can turn against us anytime. You need to keep an eye on the coastal stretch from Harihareshwar to Panvel.'

Santaji looked at Yesubai, his father Mhaloji, and Khando Ballal, saying, 'Raje, leave your worries to me. I am grateful that you have given me this responsibility. I remember Khandoba had jumped into the waters of the Mandovi to save your life. If I get a chance to jump into fire and help you even a little, I would consider my life blessed.'

Shahzada Azam was stationed at Chakan with an army of twenty thousand, poised to enter Konkan. Spies had brought information that Feroz Jung was waiting for an opportune moment to attack Rajgad. As Sambhaji conferred with his men on how to tackle the two, one of the spies came running and said, trying to catch his breath as he spoke, 'Raje, we cannot confirm this yet but we heard that Raje's life is in danger here. It is advised that you leave immediately.'

Sambhaji looked grave. 'I agree that I must not be here for long. After dinner, we will make our move. By the way, where is Mukarrab Khan?'

'He is in his camp. We are told he has caught the chills and has not stepped out of his tent for the past three days.'

'What about our cavalry near Malkapur?' Sambhaji asked Kavi Kalash.

'Only four thousand cavalrymen are at Malkapur. The remaining six thousand are guarding Amba ghat and the route to Vishalgad.'

Sambhaji took stock of the situation. There were five thousand horsemen at Shringarpur nearby while five hundred soldiers were guarding Prachitgad. The route to Karad was being patrolled by a thousand horsemen. It was dangerous territory, very difficult to navigate. No enemy was likely to try that route. On the route to Goa, five thousand soldiers were on patrol. The Jaygad fort and the nearby port too were well guarded. Under the circumstances, it seemed unlikely that the enemy could reach Sangameshwar by sea or land. Yet, Sambhaji felt that it made sense to return to Raigad at the earliest.

The day ended. The woods around Sangameshwar were engulfed in darkness now. Sambhaji took leave of his sardars. Glancing at the dark forests, he said, 'If a hundred Sambhajis have to sacrifice their lives to ensure that Shivaji's flag keeps fluttering, it is worth it!'

TWENTY

Treachery!

1

The Mughals had not encountered such a treacherous, vile and impassable jungle in their lives. They had been on the move for a day and a night. They had started descending the Anuskura ghat after nightfall. Each step was difficult to negotiate.

Mukarrab Khan, Ikhlas Khan and Ganoji dismounted their horses. It was impossible to ride a horse down the slippery slopes of the ghat. The tall trees with their dense foliage obstructed the moonlight from falling on the ground. The extremely narrow, winding path with steep valleys and ravines on one side was a nightmare. In some places, the grass reached above their heads. A few horses had lost their balance and plunged into the valley below. Their heart-wrenching cries as they fell froze the blood of Mughal soldiers.

The trek was excruciatingly slow and seemed unending. A cool breeze rose from the valley but the soldiers, tense and exerting themselves every step of the way, were sweating nervously. Soon, nearly forty horses had been claimed by the treacherous path. The men seemed to be silently cursing Mukarrab Khan and the path he had chosen. He said, reading their minds, 'I had told you; only those who are willing to die should follow me.'

Mukarrab's blunt comment made them move a little faster. No one complained about their toes and knees getting bruised. Many had twisted their ankles and were limping painfully. But no one wanted to linger and help anyone else either. Cries of 'Ya Allah!' or 'Ya Khuda!' were being ignored now. Everyone feared that the Marathas, hiding in the forests nearby, might attack at any moment.

The night was drawing to a close now. It would soon be light. The soldiers, seeing the huge cliffs towering above them, nearly swooned. They had barely covered half the distance. There were sheer cliffs on one side and steep ravines on the other. The animals, sticking close to the side of the mountain, began climbing down slowly. Mukarrab Khan continued to exhort, 'Come on, you fools! You don't want the Marathas to catch up with you.'

In places the descent was so steep that the soldiers had to cover the eyes of the horses before they could force them to walk further. It was afternoon when the three thousand soldiers and animals inally descended the ghat onto flat land. The green grasslands were a delight to the eyes and they danced like children. The villagers looked at them curiously. The previous afternoon, Ganoji had sent his men ahead to inform the locals that a platoon of the Mughal troops had defected and was joining the Marathas. As per Ganoji's instructions, the villagers had arranged for food and water for the soldiers.

After resting a while, they resumed their journey.

While the path ahead was not as treacherous as the earlier one, it was still difficult to negotiate. They halted again that evening on another patch of grassland near a village. The local Sawants, Deshmukhs and Dalvis had gathered there to meet Ganoji. They had with them a fresh set of around four hundred horses which Mukarrab exchanged for his tired and wounded animals.

They were now only a night's walk away from Sangameshwar. The third torturous night began.

It was nearly midnight. A bright starlit sky guided the troops. Leading the convoy were Ganoji's men, followed closely by Mukarrab and his cavalry.

A few spies brought the message that Sambhaji had reached Sangameshwar. It was the news Mukarrab Khan had been waiting for. Sambhaji was literally within his grasp now. He had to hurry now, lest his prized quarry leaves Sangameshwar. It would be impossible for them to return empty-handed by the same path they had taken! Mukarrab Khan spurred his horse and galloped forward.

Mukarrab's son Ikhlas Khan called out to his father to stop. Ganoji had something to say. Mukarrab Khan waited for Ganoji to catch up. He said to Mukarrab, 'I will not be able to come any further.'

'Are you mad? What is wrong with you?'

'How do I put it, Khansaheb? The people here consider Sambhaji and Shivaji as their gods. If for some reason Sambha were to escape, he would not leave me alive. I cannot be seen there!'

'I will let you ride at the rear. But you have to come with us; there is no question of you not being there!'

'Sarkar, I will provide whatever support you want. But don't force me to come with you to Sangameshwar.'

Time was of the essence now, and it was too late to resolve such dilemmas. Mukarrab snapped impatiently at Ganoji, 'Shirke, don't think I am a fool. You need to be with me. Stop this childish rant!'

They rode on in the moonlight. The next morning, they received news that Sambhaji, having stayed in Sangameshwar overnight, was planning to leave for Raigad the very next day. Mukarrab Khan spurred his horse once more. There was no time to waste. His sole intention now was to force Sambhaji into a final confrontation on the banks of Sangameshwar.

2

Yesubai woke up. She had just heard noise of something having fallen in water. She looked out of the window. It was probably a tree branch. The curtains in the window moved with the breeze. The tiny bells attached to them let out a sweet tinkling noise. Yesubai had woken up sweating profusely. She had had a horrible nightmare. No one would ever have seen such a heinous 'bhaidooj' as she had dreamed—the festival where a brother meets his sister. In the dream, she had performed aarti with the traditional tray and lamp for her brother. In place of her brother, all she could see was a heap of burning coals. It was only the armlet with the snake design that she recognised as Ganoji's. Then she saw Sambhaji's bloodied head on the tray and swooned.

The previous evening, Sambhaji had asked his men to go back to their posts. He was keen to leave Sangameshwar at the earliest but he remembered he had given Arjoji Yadav his word regarding the papers granting the watan. Sambhaji had already asked them to meet him at Vishalgad three days later, but he wondered whether he should deal with the matter straight away. Arjoji was otherwise a loyal man. It was he who had managed to meet Durgabai and Ranuakka at Bahadurgad.

Yesubai had insisted that they should leave early in the morning. The palanquins bearers were asked to be ready. Sambhaji was in a dilemma. Should he listen to the demands of the local people including the Yadav brothers, or should he leave at once? He knew that the poor Yadavs had worked hard for the Swaraj for many years. Raje decided to take care of the matter and then leave.

Sambhaji woke up just before dawn. After finishing his morning prayers and ablutions, he said, looking at Yesubai, 'Why are you looking so pale? You seem to be worried. Start now. I shall ride behind you very soon.'

'Raje, it is an inauspicious day. I suggest you don't delay your departure.'

'Yesu, I am the Raja here. I have given my word to the Yadav brothers. I will meet them and leave.'

The guard mentioned that the brothers had been waiting for an audience with Raje since the previous night. 'There! You see!' Sambhaji said, 'They are already here. I cannot leave without listening to their demands.'

Yesubai burst into tears, taking Sambhaji by surprise. He said, hugging her affectionately and teasing her, 'Now come on! How can you, who rules Maharashtra with an iron hand, weep like an ordinary housewife? What happened?'

When Yesubai did not reply, he continued, 'Eight hundred men will accompany your palanquin.'

'Why so many?'

'I have another four hundred men with me.'

'No, your protection is more important.'

'I will soon catch up with you.'

They were alone. Yesubai put her head on Sambhaji's feet. Her tears wet his foot. Sambhaji was overwhelmed. Embracing her tightly, he said, 'Don't be so upset, Yesu! Don't you trust me? Do you think the Sahyadris would let Sambhaji down?'

It was getting late. The sun shone brightly upon Sangameshwar. Yesu stepped into her palanquin and the bearers were about to leave when Sambhaji shouted, 'Stop! I wanted to tell you that when you reach the river Vashishti near Chiplun by noon, I will join you for lunch.'

Yesubai smiled. She was reassured by Sambhaji's confidence. He said, 'We will reach Raigad the day after tomorrow. We have an important thing to do after we arrive.'

'What is it?'

'Mark a spot near the Chitta Darwaza. I am sure to find Aurangzeb soon. I want to bury his head there.'

3

Sambhaji had decided to spend two hours dispensing justice before leaving Sangameshwar. Santaji and a few others stayed back. They wanted to accompany when he left. It was bright outside but the February chill could still be felt inside the haveli. The meeting was being held in the garden under the warm sun. The Yadav brothers were insisting on certain demands and unwilling to make even small adjustments. Two hours passed in argument. It was nearly nine when Sambhaji heard someone shouting, 'Raje, we have been betrayed!'

A soldier came running and said, 'Raje, the enemy is entering Sangameshwar. At least seven hundred of them!'

Sambhaji shouted for his horse. His favourite steed, hearing the master's voice, came galloping. Sambhaji leaped onto him in a single movement. Kavi Kalash was ready, sword in hand, while Mhaloji Ghorpade put a pinch of tobacco in his mouth and drew his, eyes burning with rage.

While Sambhaji was planning an exit, he heard shouts of 'Allah o Akbar! And 'Deen Deen!' Soon, the Mughal troops were visible behind the trees.

Mhaloji Ghorpade shouted 'Har Har Mahadev!' while Santaji and Dhanaji followed with 'Shivaji Maharaj ki jay!' and 'Sambhaji Maharaj ki jay!' The Mughal and Maratha soldiers clashed. Swords clanged and horses neighed.

Mukarrab Khan was astride his horse when he spotted Sambhaji. His sole intention was to capture Sambhaji alive or dead. Within no time the Mughal soldiers had surrounded Sambhaji's haveli. Some of the Marathas who ran towards the river were intercepted by the Mughals. Sambhaji, with only four hundred soldiers defending him, was surrounded by a thousand or more Mughals.

The swift and unexpected attack took the Marathas by surprise, but realising that their Raje was in trouble, they flared up. Dhanaji, Santaji and Khando Ballal were in their element. Spears, swords, and whatever weapon they could lay their hands on, were being used on the enemy with cries of 'Kill, attack!' Some of the Marathas hiding behind the trees began targeting the Mughals with their spears. Their shouts gave Mukarrab Khan the impression that a much larger force was concealed there.

Meanwhile, fifty Pathans had surrounded Sambhaji. Raje had not seen such a battle for some time and he began his attack with gusto. The jamdaad, the sharp and double-edged wavy sword, was spinning in the air around him. Sambhaji's horse danced with him.

Soon, Santaji, Dhanaji and Khando Ballal rushed to Sambhaji's rescue, cutting through the crowd of Pathans. Mukarrab Khan too galloped towards Sambhaji, raising his Hyderabadi sword high. Before his sword could touch Raje, someone jumped onto his horse behind him. Khan's sword pierced his shouders. Sambhaji's back was wet with blood. The man who had sacrificed his life for Sambhaji fell to the ground. Sambhaji turned his horse to see who the braveheart was.

It was the Senapati Mhaloji Ghorpade!

Seeing their commander dead, the Marathas were now furious. Santaji had no time even to glance at his father's dead body. Meanwhile, someone had injured Mukarrab Khan's horse. It neighed loudly and fell on its side. None of the Marathas had seen Mukarrab Khan before, but his dress and bearing suggested that he was a Mughal sardar. The Marathas rushed towards him, seeing him standing on the ground. There was hand to hand combat now. Bodies were falling on ground like dry leaves. The grass in the garden had turned red with blood.

Mukarrab felt that his horse's fall was a bad omen. His soldiers pulled him back and helped him mount another horse. By then another group of fifty Marathas had entered the garden. Mukarrab saw them and presumed that there must be at least a thousand more near the haveli. He mounted the horse and turned towards the woods to see hundreds of Mughals and Pathans lying dead on the ground. He ordered his men in a low voice, 'Run … retreat!'

Sambhaji saw the Mughals pulling back. There were hundreds of dead and half-dead men on the ground. He could hear moans of 'Ya Allah' and 'Arre Deva'. The wounded horses neighed in pain. Sambhaji had not yet recovered from the shock of the enemy entering right into his house. Despite the intense vigil on land and at sea, how had they found their way here? How had they managed to traverse the dense jungles and treacherous ravines of the ghat without guidance?There was no doubt about it: treachery was involved!

There was no time to think about it now. Nearly three hundred and fifty Marathas had died in the skirmish. Sambhaji had only a hundred odd Mawals with him. Santaji, Dhanaji, Khando Ballal and other warriors waited for further instructions. Most of the soldiers had already left the previous night to ensure a smooth passage for Sambhaji. Kavi Kalash had been pierced in his arm by an arrow. Blood oozed through the wound.

A soldier came running and shouted, 'Raje, there is an army of fifteen hundred men coming this way.'

Dhanaji and the others shouted, 'Maharaj, hukum!'

For a moment Sambhaji closed his eyes and prayed to Bhawani Mata. He said, 'My friends, I understand your eagerness to fight but we must be practical. It is time to use our wits, not brute strength. We cannot linger another moment here. Go! Don't stop till you cross the Vashishti at Chiplun. Our men are camped there.'

'Raje, what about you?' Santaji said, his voice hoarse.

'Don't get trapped in your emotions. Santaji and Khandoba, move towards Chiplun. You will meet Yesubai and the other ladies on the way. Dhanaji, take your men and go to Hatkhamba. You must hold the route towards Goa.'

'What about you, Raje?' Dhanaji asked.

'I will move through the narrow paths, crossing the jungles, and reach Raigad.'

The men looked at each other. They had tears in their eyes. Sambhaji urged, 'Come on now! Move!'

'Raje, we cannot think of leaving you alone …'

'If we all try to escape together, the results would be disastrous. We may get captured. We cannot allow that. Move now! We must save the Hindavi Swaraj and dig a grave for Aurangzeb in the Deccan soil.'

Sambhaji continued, 'Why are you so worried about me?' His face was flushed with pride and self-confidence. 'A child cannot be taken away from a mother who is suckling it. Likewise, it is impossible to take Shambhu from the lap of the Sahyadris. Go now! Rest assured that I will return safely to Raigad.'

4

Sambhaji and Kavi Kalash galloped at full speed. Kalash's arm throbbed with intense pain. The blood continued to flow. But he could not imagine leaving his Raje alone. Sambhaji had only fifteen soldiers with him. Their sole intention now was to escape through the jungles and make their way home.

Kavi shouted, as he galloped. 'Raje, you go ahead. Save your life. Don't worry about me. Let me stay here.'

Sambhaji said, 'No! It is not possible. A true friend is the one who is by your side in the royal durbar and in the graveyard. I won't leave you.'

They galloped along the coast. Sambhaji glanced at the haveli of the Sardesais on the right. He realised that it made sense to stop here, and change their clothes as well as their direction to escape capture. There was no sense in continuing the ride in his royal clothes. Steering his horse into the woods, he removed all the decorations from his horse's saddle and tore away his own jewellery. They reached the steps of the haveli soon.

Rangoba Sardesai was sitting in the front room. His barber was cutting his hair. Seeing a dishevelled Raje and the injured Kavi Kalash at their door, the Sardesai men rushed forward. The ladies too came out of the inner chambers.

'Raje, what happened? What is this? What can we do, Raje?' Rangoba asked, his voice quivering with fear.

'Don't worry. But we have to move quickly. Just nurse Kavi's wound.' Sambhaji sat in front of the barber who immediately started cutting his locks and trimming his beard. The men began dressing Kavi Kalash's wound. Soon, a clean-shaven Sambhaji resembled a monk. At that moment, Rangoba's old mother came rushing in. The tall, slim and fair woman in her seventies reminded Sambhaji of Jijabai. She hugged Sambhaji affectionately.

The fifteen horsemen stood outside. Sambhaji had pulled the reins of his horse so tightly that its nostrils were bleeding. The animal was thirsty and moved towards a small lake nearby to quench its thirst. While drinking water it sensed some movement in the shrubs. A small platoon of the enemy had found its way to the haveli, chasing Sambhaji and his men.

Mukarrab Khan was there, leading a party of around seventy Mughal soldiers. Amongst them stood a terrified-looking Ganoji Shirke. Ikhlas Khan and others had divided themselves into groups and were searching for Sambhaji in the surrounding woods.

Ganoji pointed at Sambhaji's horse and shouted, 'There! That is his horse.' Sambhaji's horse, sensing trouble, neighed loudly and galloped away. He wanted to warn his master.

Sambhaji was taking leave of Rangoba's mother when he heard his favourite horse neighing. He realised that the enemy had found them. He looked at Kavi Kalash. His wound had not stopped bleeding yet. Kavi said, 'Raje, don't wait for me. You may get caught. Please go!'

There was no time for tears. Rangoba handed Sambhaji's sword to him while his mother quickly cracked her knuckles to ward off evil. Sambhaji called out to his horse which stood obediently at the steps. He leaped on to his horse when …

It was like a sudden flood. Hundreds of horses were seen galloping towards the haveli. It was surrounded. Sambhaji was incensed. Rotating his sword over his head, he spun his horse in all direcions. Fifteen hundred enemy soldiers had encircled him. Not one of them dared to step forward. Mukarrab Khan tried to throw a rope over Raje's horse while Ikhlas Khan struck its back with his jamdad, injuring it badly. Blood spurted out of the poor animal's flesh. Sambhaji had just turned to look at the wound when seventy Pathans pounced on him. The long wooden handle of a spear found its mark, hitting Sambhaji on his shoulder. His sword fell down.

It was the moment the enemy had been waiting for. Sahyadri's Shambhu was captured!

Inside the haveli, Rangoba's old mother banged her head on the wall. She fell down unconscious.

Ganoji Shirke cried out. He wiped his tears, unable to believe the sight. Was it really true? He was like a madman, raving with joy. The enemy shouted 'Allah o Akbar!' They torched the haveli and the surrounding houses.

What were they to do with the captured men? For a moment, even the Mughals were confused. They had thrown blankets over Sambhaji and Kavi Kalash, and like thieves taking away their loot, they moved silently through the woods. Mukarrab Khan stopped at the banks of the river Varuna. He decided to take seven hundred soldiers with him. The rest, including Ganoji, were asked to stay back. 'Kill anyone who tries to follow us,' Mukarrab ordered.

Sambhaji and Kavi Kalash were stunned into silence. Was it really happening or was it a dream? Ikhlas Khan had bound the two with ropes. Out of sheer vindictiveness and anger, he had slapped Sambhaji. Kaviraj, seeing Ikhlas Khan touch Raje's face, spat at him in disgust. Ikhlas Khan was enraged now and removed a whip tied around his waist. He whipped Sambhaji and Kavi before tying them on a horse's back. Their clothes had already been torn off their bodies. They were forced to wear the green dress of the Mughals.

Without their pointed beards and long flowing tresses, and now with their bald pates, numerous wounds and green clothes, no one would have believed that the two were Sambhaji and Kavi Kalash.

Ganoji laughed loudly, holding his stomach, when he saw Sambhaji in his new avatar. He said, with a taunting look, 'Wah! Look at Sambhaji Maharaj of Raigad.'

Mukarrab Khan snapped, 'Ganoji, you fool! This is no time to celebrate. Guide us forward.'

Ganoji came to his senses and said, 'Khansaheb, it is better to cross the mountains in the daytime. We are in danger of being attacked by the Marathas at night.'

'Ganoji, by the grace of Allah, we have made a great catch. We need to reach out station at Karad before nightfall.'

'Don't worry, Mukarrab Miyan. The route to Karad is through Shirke territory. Please follow me.'

Without further delay, Mukarrab Khan and his seven hundred horsemen started moving through the jungles. They crossed a wooden bridge on the river Shastri. Sambhaji, tied to a horse, looked at the waters of the river. The river flowed through his dear Yesu's Shringarpur. Tears flowed down his cheeks.

Soon, all familiar terrain was quickly left behind.

5

At Nivali, waiting patiently on a platform in a field, were eight youths. They had with them enough rotis for seven hundred soldiers. Two days earlier, Ganoji Shirke's assistant Govardhan Pant had reached Nivali. Pant informed the villagers that they had captured some miscreants who were trying to smuggle jewels from the Jaynagar port. They were told that the smugglers had been arrested on instructions from Sambhaji and were being taken to Satara. The locals, who believed that the dispute between the Shirkes and Sambhaji had finally ended, cheered hearing the good news. After all, they said, Ganoji was Sambhaji's brother-in-law.

Govardhan Pant, who was known to be a tough manager and a skinflint, was a changed person, the way he distributed gold coins among the villagers. The young men selected as guides for the onward journey were daredevils. Very rarely did anyone travel through the ghats where tigers roamed freely. Pant had also arranged for nearly two hundred fresh horses.

Suddenly, as they waited, they saw eight hundred men emerge from the undergrowth. The Mughals jumped down from their horses. They started eating the rotis along with hot chutney the moment they were handed the food. The long and tough journey had taken a toll and they were all tired to the bone. Govardhan Pant and his men segregated the horses which had been wounded and replaced them with fresh ones. The men who had brought the rotis looked at the two men tied on the backs of horses. Their fair faces looked dull and swollen, and their mouths were stuffed and bound with cloth.

Ganoji Shirke was impatient to resume their journey. Mukarrab Khan too was alert and rather frightened. He had never seen such dense jungles. When strong winds blew through the waist-high grass, it sounded like elephants were walking through it. The high cliffs looked intimidating. Suddenly, they heard horses. Soon a group of fifty or sixty Marathas were seen approaching. Where had they come from? How many more were there? The Pathans were stunned and waited for the Marathas to speak. Mukarrab's face was pale with fear. Ganoji's throat turned dry. He had spotted Suryaji Bhosale at the head of the group.

Ganoji winked at the fifteen Marathas in his group who shouted, 'Shivaji Maharaj ki jay!' Suryaji rode towards them immediately. He had recognised Ganoji. He said, 'Ganoji Bhau, where are you off to?'

'We are … we are going to … you know, Umbraj.'

'But why are you taking this route? And who are these men? I was told you had joined the Mughals.'

Ganoji patted Suryaji on his back and said, 'Blood is thicker than water, Suryaji, after all! We do have our differences with Raje, but when my own sister is the Maharani, how can I think of joining those treacherous Mughals?'

'Who are these men you have tied on horseback?'

'Those men? Oh, they are Irani traders who were trying to smuggle jewels at the Jaynagar port. I am going to throw them at Shambhubal's feet.'

'Oh, is that so? Well, Daaji, I should not delay you. Please go as swiftly as possible and descend into the valley before nightfall. The road is tough.'

Suryaji and his men were left behind as Ganoji and Mukarrab rode on.

As they started climbing the ghat, the Mughals struggled. Except for the two horses Sambhaji and Kavi Kalash had been tied to, all the other soldiers had dismounted. It was an excruciating trek. Toes bled and ankles were twisted. The animals were frothing at their mouths.

It had been more than two hours since they had started the climb. The soldiers had not slept a for nearly four day days and were exhausted. Had the Shirkes not arranged for food at various places, they would never have been able to cross the jungle. The animals would simply have dropped dead. The Mughals would have met the same fate as that of Malik-ut-Tujjar and his seven thousand men, nearly three hundred years earlier.

Many of Mukkarab's men had crossed the Ramdara ghat with Shahzada Azam. They were frightened out of their wits. Was Ganoji planning a coup, taking them through such treacherous paths? They looked at him suspiciously as they trudged along slowly. Mukarrab Khan, otherwise a sturdy soldier, was barely managing to walk, as he had already twisted his ankle twice. He asked, 'Ganoji, are you sure this route leads us to Karad? Or is this the path to hell?'

'Please have some patience, Khansaheb. It is through this path alone that we can reach Karad by evening. If we had taken any other route, we would surely have reached hell by now. Shiva and Sambha are the gods in this forest, Khansaheb.'

For the locals, the path was just another daily trek. They chuckled seeing the plight of the Pathans. Ganoji was tense all the way. He could not afford a single mistake. If for some reason Sambhaji was rescued, he knew he would not live long.

It was late afternoon. The trek seemed unending. Mukarrab too now started eyeing Ganoji with suspicion. Without waiting for any orders, the men simply sat down, unable to walk further. Ganoji said, taking Mukarrab to one side, 'Khansaheb, why take a risk? Why not behead these two here itself?'

'No! It is not possible. I have promised to take him to the Badshah.'

'What difference does it make whether he is alive or dead?' Ganoji asked, a little irritated.

'Ganoji, for past eight years, the five lakh strong army of the Badshah could not do what this Deccani Musalmaan has shown he can. I want to watch the Badshah going mad with joy when he sees Sambha.'

The soldiers were suffering the hardships of the trail but the state of Sambhaji and Kavi, tied to the horses, was far worse. The ropes bit into their flesh. Blood oozed from their wounds. They were literally beyond pain now.

Once the ghat road ended, it was only a two-hour journey to Karad where nearly fifteen thousand Mughal soldiers were camped. They had almost reached the end of the treacherous path. Kavi Kalash was aware that there was a Maratha station just ahead of Maleghat. His mouth was gagged but his teeth had been working like a mouse for past few hours and he had managed to nibble through the cloth. Soon, he could hear the Maratha soldiers in the distance. Mukarrab Khan looked at Ganoji Shirke. They had to find a way around them.

Kavi's ears pricked up. His world was ending but there was still a glimmer of hope. Finally, he managed to break open the rope around his mouth and shouted, 'Help, help! Save Shambhu Raje!'

Ikhlas Khan heard Kavi's shouts. He smashed his whip so hard on Kalash's bare head that the blood which spurted from the cut splattered on his beard. The soldiers in the station were alert and shouted, 'Who is is it? Who goes there?' Mukarrab froze with fear. At that moment, he heard Ganoji's voice, 'Sambhaji Maharaj ki jay!'

The thanedar looked closely at the men. But what was he to question when it was the Maharani's own brother leading them! He glanced at the two men tied to horses. Kavi Kalash was unconscious. Blood flowed from where the whiplash had left its mark on his head. Shambhu Raje, wearing green clothes, and with his beardless face, was unrecognisable. No one would have believed that the disfigured, swollen face was that of Sambhaji.

'Ganu Bhauji, are you on your way to meet Shambhu Raje?' The thanedar asked.

'That is right, my brother. I want to throw these two traders at Raje's feet. These Mughals too have defected and are joining our Swaraj. I am sure Raje would be happy to see them.'

'I suggest you hurry and descend the mountain before nightfall,' the thanedar advised.

They were nearing the village of Patharpunj now. The shadows were lengthening. The sun was descending rapidly into the western sky. The one who had fought to keep Shivaji's dream alive, the one who had worked for years to keep the enemy at bay, was now captured. The Sahyadris, the protector of the Marathas, were being left behind. In the distance, the burning mashaals of the Mughal camp at Karad could be seen.

TWENTY-ONE

Humiliating Parade

1

The scene was at the Dhangarwada, belonging to the community of herders near Patharpunj village. The eight men of Nivali who had accompanied Ganoji Shirke and showed him the path through the ghat were thrilled. They had been given gold earrings and money in exchange for their guidance. They were enjoying a hearty meal when they heard a few farmers talking.

'It is a terrible disaster! Shambhu Raje's brother-in-law turned traitor. They passed this way, this very afternoon. What a pity! What a tragedy!'

The boys could not believe their ears. They confronted the farmers. 'What are you blabbering? We guided Ganoji. Those men were traders, not Shambhu Raje!'

But the young men soon realised that they had committed a grave error. They had literally handed over their Raja to the enemy! One of them started banging his head on the wall while the others took off their earrings and threw them away in disgust. The very touch of the gifts they had received from the traitor was poison!

'That dog Ganoji! We got trapped by his sweet tongue.'

One of them wailed, 'I may throw my parents into a well but I can never think of harming my Shambhu Raje. How did we fall for this?'

All of them had heard stories of Shivaji's coronation from their elders. Some had visited Raigad, sitting on their father's shoulders. A few of them had danced and played with Shambhu when he was a young lad at Shringarpur. They all decided that there was only one thing to do. They had to find Ganoji and kill him. The eight of them set off on their mission with a single-minded fury. They set off for Karad.

These sons of soil had nothing to do with the landlords's demands for watans. All they knew was that Shivaji and Sambhaji were their heart and soul. They were devastated by the thought that they had played a role in the capture of Shambhu Raje.

Without stopping for food or water, they ran all the way to Karad.

The camp at Karad was quiet. The river Koyna flowed silently a little distance away. A cool breeze blew. Only the guards were awake, moving around with flaming torches. The boys walked straight up to the camp. A guard barred their way, asking, 'Who are you? Where are you going?'

'We are here to meet Ganoji Shirke, Sarkar. He has sent for us. We were the guides who led his party through the mountains.'

The guard was a little confused. Luckily, one of the soldiers recognised them and said, 'I know these boys. Take them to Ganoji's tent.'

The camp was eerily silent. Mukarrab and his eight hundred men were dead tired and fast asleep. The guards reached a tent. As soon as the boys realised that it was Ganoji's tent, they snatched the mashaals from the hands of the guards and threw them into the tent. The guards were taken aback. One of them ran off to get help, his beard singed. Soon, the entire tent was burning. Some hay kept inside for the horses had caught fire and the flames spread rapidly. There was a clamour all around as people ran helter-skelter with shouts of 'help' and 'run'.

The fire of revenge burning inside the boys was fiercer than the fire spreading through the tents. But they were inside the Mughal camp and were soon rounded up. The guards found three bodies of men who had succumbed to the fire, burnt beyong recognition. They wondered if they belonged to Ganoji and Nagoji. Who was the third, they wondered.

Mukarrab Khan had slept soundly through the chaos. The thanedar did not dare to wake him up.

The next afternoon, Mukarrab came out of his tent and stretched his sore but rested body. The eight men who had been captured the previous night were presented before him. They had been beaten up badly and their faces were swollen. Despite the beatings, their tattered clothes and whiplash marks all over their bodies, they stood with their spines straight.

Mukarrab listened to his men's narration of the events of the previous night. He was told that Ganoji and Nagoji had been burnt to death. Ignoring this piece of news, he asked, 'Where is Sambha?' He was happy to hear that Sambhaji was still in the camp and well guarded. At that moment, he saw Nagoji and Ganoji walking towards his tent. 'I thought you were burnt to death?' he asked Ganoji.

'I was aware of the tricks Sambha's men might get up to once they heard that he has been captured. I had an intuition and I slept in another tent.'

Mukarrab Khan smiled. 'I am sure the Badshah will give you your jagir in addition to bags of jewels and finery. He will reward you handsomely.'

'That is all in the future, Khansaheb. Our responsibilities are over,' Nagoji said. 'Please take Sambhaji away as soon as possible. Or else our lives are in danger.'

The guards asked what they should do with the captured men. Mukarrab Khan remembered that the boys had been of great help on the trek to Karad. He was in a mood to pardon them. He had, after all, got what he wanted. He said, 'These are jungle dwellers. Leave them in the jungle.'

The boys were released. As they were walking away, they suddenly realised that their freedom had not helped Sambhaji. They turned around and rushed back to attack Mukarrab Khan and Ganoji. But Mukarrab had nearly sixty guards outside his tent.

The boys had barely reached the tent when the guards fell upon them with naked swords. Within moments, there was blood everywhere and the boys had been beheaded. Mukarrab Khan could not believe his eyes. Nagoji and Ganoji were speechless.

The eight bodies and eight heads were thrown into the Koyna.

It was evening. The sun threw golden rays on the waters of the Koyna. Like flowers removed from a garland around the Lord's neck, eight heads floated on the golden surface of the Koyna.

2

The sun blazed brightly in the noon sky. Yesubai and her guards had reached the banks of the Vashishti. Her palanquin rested near the mango orchards bordering Chiplun. The soldiers had stopped for refreshment. Yesubai was about to sit down for her meal when she saw riders approaching at rapid speed. 'There! Raje too has come,' Khando Ballal said. But Sambhaji was not among them. The soldiers dismounted and cried, 'Ranisaheb, there has been a tragedy. The enemy has attacked!'

Yesubai stood up. The soldiers, drenched in sweat from their breakneck ride, panted, 'It happened at Sangameshwar. Nearly a thousand Mughals were there.'

'What about Raje?'

'He was attacked near the haveli. There was a big fight. But we were only a few.'

At that moment, three hundred soldiers rode up. Santaji jumped down from his horse. He looked flustered. Yesubai rushed to him and asked, 'Santaji, what happened? Where is Raje?'

'Matoshree, try to calm yourself. There was a sudden attack in the morning. But don't worry about Raje and Kaviraj. They left through a jungle route and are on their way to Raigad.'

'How could you come here leaving him, Santaji?' Yesubai asked.

'Raje ordered me to come. He was worried about you. No one was aware that the enemy was closing in on us. It was all so sudden. I have been instructed to hold the station at Chiplun.'

'Santaji, how did this happen? In the Shirke territory, where even the wind would think twice before entering, how did the enemy come this far?'

'It has to be treachery. Someone very close to us. But there is no point in thinking about it right now. We need to hurry.'

The palanquin bearers swung into action at once and started moving rapidly. Santaji was restless. He took the help of Chiplun's thanedar to ensure that the station was secure.

That evening two riders came from Sangameshwar. Their faces, black with sweat and dust, showed they had been riding without a halt. They started sobbing, unable to say what they had come to say. Finally, they spoke, 'Sardar, we were attacked by a large force of enemy soldiers. Someone said Raje and Kaviraj escaped through a narrow path in the jungles while others are saying that they have been captured.'

'Captured? Have you lost your mind?' Santaji screamed.

There was no way to know the real situation. Santaji was sure that a dastardly plot was behind it all but he could not place his finger on it. Without further delay, he ordered five hundred of his men to mount their horses. They were to leave for Sangameshwar immediately.

By the time they reached Sangameshwar, nearly thirty miles away, it was dark. The town had been ravaged. The enemy had burnt the place down to strike fear in the hearts of the residents. A few havelis and houses were still burning. There were corpses lying scattered on the streets. Not a soul was in sight. Fearing Aurangzeb's troops may attack again, the survivors had fled to the nearby jungles and were hiding there.

Seeing Santaji and his men, a few old men came forward. 'Raje and Kaviraj were taken alive!' they wailed. Santaji could not hold back the sob escaping his lips. At that moment Dhanaji Jadhav rode up with five hundred men. He said, 'Santa, I have been searching all over but I have not been able to figure out the route they have taken after capturing Raje. People are making all kinds of speculations.'

'Dhanaji, we simply cannot stand here doing nothing.'

They discussed the next move. In all likelihood, the enemy had taken the route through Amba ghat. They must be on the way to Kolhapur, they surmised. It would take them at least five hours to reach Amba ghat. The road was perilous, with narrow paths, steep hills and impassable gorges. A thousand men were despatched towards Amba ghat.

While Santaji was giving instructions a frail old Brahmin came and stood next to him. He said, 'Come with me this moment.' Santaji followed him. The Brahmin took him to a haveli nearby which had been burnt to ashes. It was the house where Kavi Kalash resided when he was in Sangameshwar. A body lay there, covered with a shawl. At some point during that nightmarish day, while fighting, running from one place to another, and carrying our orders, Santaji had forgotten that his father, the Senapati of the Hindavi Swaraj, had fallen. He removed the shawl. Seeing the body of Mhaloji Ghorpade, Santaji stumbled back.

Sobs racked his body as he took his father's corpse into his arms. Dhanaji tried his best to comfort Santaji. When his tears had subsided, Santaji caressed his father's face affectionately. He carefully lowered his head back onto the ground and said, handing over an emerald necklace to the Brahmin, 'Shastri Bua, see to it that you carry out the last rites of my father, and those of the others who died here. I have an appointment with the enemy ...'

They had been riding towards the ghat for an hour when they stopped at a stream to refresh themselves. The journey ahead was long and tiring. They decided to halt for a couple of hours. Herder families from the nearby villages brought some dry fodder for the horses. They had also cooked rotis with some chutney for the troops.

They were halfway through Amba ghat by afternoon. The Maratha troops at the station en route were surprised to see Dhanaji and Santaji. Santaji was equally surprised to see an army of nearly seven thousand Marathas there. When asked about enemy troops who had crossed the ghat the previous day, Krishnaji Konhere, appointed by Kavi Kalash, came forward and said, 'Sardar, we have been here for many days. I was posted here to ensure that no one crosses this ghat. There is no question of even a single enemy soldier making it through this place alive.'

Realising that Raje was in danger, Konhere shivered with fear. Everyone was confused now. Did Raje's captors travel this route at all? Krishnaji

Pant said, 'Wait a moment! Just a few hours back, a jeweller named Narhar Pant from Ratnagiri arrived here via Prachitgad. His daughter-in-law is from Patan.' They immediately sent for the jeweller. When asked about any travellers he saw on the way, he said, 'Yes! We did meet Daaji near Patharpunj.'

'Daaji? Who is he referring to?'

'Our Ganoji Shirke, Shambhu Raje's brother-in-law.'

Dhanaji and Santaji drew a sharp breath. 'What was Ganoji doing there?'

'He was on his way to Karad with nearly six hundred soldiers. Daaji was leading the way. Most of the soldiers were Pathans and a few were Marathas. They had two prisoners with them, tied to horses.'

'What did they look like?'

'They were very fair and quite well-built but they had been beaten badly. Their faces were covered with blood and they were bound with ropes and chains. I was told later that Ganoji had arrested two traders at the port. He said he was on his way to Umbraj.'

It was clear from the jeweller's story that all was lost. Santaji was overwhelmed with emotion. He wailed, clutching Dhanaji, 'Dhana! We have been fooled. A black cobra called Ganya Shirka has stung our Swaraj. He has taken away our Raje …!'

Not a single man present could hold back his tears. There was despair and confusion all around. Santaji said, unsheathing his sword as he wiped his tears, 'Dhanaji, we have six thousand men with us. We will attack Karad, and burn the Mughals and that rascal Gana alive!'

'Santaji, listen to me without getting excited. Even if we make haste, it will take us two days to reach Karad through these winding mountain routes. Do you think the enemy will stay put there, waiting for us to arrive?'

'What are you suggesting?'

'Karad is not far from Patharpunj. They would have reached the camp by nightfall yesterday. There are many Mughal stations like Rahimatpur, Islampur and others near Karad. The enemy must have gathered a troop strength of nearly fifteen thousand before leaving Karad.'

'Dhanaji, why are you discouraging me?'

Dhanaji hugged Santaji and said, 'Santaji, remember what Shambhu Raje said? We need to use our wits and not our emotions. Our Senapati is dead. Our Raje has been captured. We don't know whether Matoshree has reached Raigad safely or not. Let us leave two thousand men here at

Amba ghat. We will take the rest and make haste to reach Raigad. We will consult Matoshree there. Destiny has taken Raje away from us but we need to protect our capital. Our world will collapse if Raigad falls, my dear!'

Santaji wiped his tears. He realised that Dhanaji's words were wise. They left for Raigad immediately.

3

Yesubai sat near the tulsi plant, praying. Shambhu Raje had promised to reach before her. Worries creased her face.

Three horsemen reached the royal quarters. They were followed by Yesaji Kank and others. Seeing their distraught faces, Yesubai's heart skipped a beat.

The men dismounted and wailed, clutching Yesubai's feet, 'Rani Sarkar, we are doomed. The enemy has taken away our Raje!'

'What?' Yesubai screamed, unable to believe her ears. It was as if the whole world had collapsed around her. She said, holding her maid's shoulder for support, 'Who was it?'

'Mukarrab Khan.'

'Is the Maratha Raja a cow which can be caught?'

For a moment Yesubai felt as if her spine had been crushed. She sat down on the floor where she stood. She felt suffocated and giddy, and was sweating profusely. The maids rushed to fan her but she recovered quickly. At that moment Rajaram Saheb came in. He swooned when he heard the news.

Yesubai had been a pillar of strength for the Swaraj, managing its administration from Raigad for the past nine years. But now she felt she was drained of all her blood. Soon, Khando Ballal, Jotyaji Kesarkar, Rayappa and others had arrived. Rayappa wailed, 'Why did I leave my Sarkar and come here?' He could not control his sobs.

Yesubai came to know that Raje and Kaviraj had been taken through Maleghat in the Shirke territory. 'That is impossible. That dense jungle scares even the ghosts away. How could Khan travel through it? How did he know the routes?'

'What can I tell you, Ranisaheb? It was our own Dadasaheb, Ganoji Shirke, who accompanied Mukarrab Khan.'

'Even Ganoji Dadasaheb does not know the routes!'

'He was the one who provided the route maps. He arranged for men, animals and fodder too. His officer Govardhan Pant was with him.'

Yesubai wiped her tears with the edge of her pallu. She asked, 'Where are Dhanaji and Santaji?'

'We don't know, Maharanisaheb! There is chaos all over. But we are sure Dhanaji will convince Santaji to come here. They will not take any steps without consulting you.'

The news of Raje's capture sent a shiver down everyone's spine in Raigad. A crowd of nearly three thousand people, soldiers as well as ryots, gathered outside the royal palace. They wailed for their Raje. Yesubai came out. The men demanded to know where Shambhu Raje was.

Yesubai said, 'This is not the time for such displays of emotion. We are at war with Aurangzeb. It is useless to expect that luck will always be in our favour.'

'But what about Raje? Where is he?' They clamoured.

'Don't worry. Aurangzeb has not won the battle just because he has an upper hand now. Our army will soon leave Raigad, and we will attack Aurangzeb. We will snatch Raje out of that shaitaan's grip.'

The crowd cheered. Yesubai said, 'Please go back to your respective posts and keep guarding them. There is no time to waste.'

Yesubai asked, 'Khandoba, how long will it take to raise a fifteen thousand strong army?'

'We have nearly five thousand men here. But we will need some time to gather ammunition and other supplies. The bulk of our troops are deployed in various parts of the kingdom.'

'Then send your messengers and spies to the Sudhagad, Sagargad, and Birawadi forts. They should reach their destinations before dawn tomorrow.'

'Matoshree, don't worry. We will raise the army, and be ready to move at your command. I expect Santaji and Dhanaji too will arrive by then,' Khando Ballal said.

Yesubai was awake the whole night, supervising the preparations for the war. The next day, she assigned specific tasks to various men. By evening, the palace was empty by evening.

Yesubai came into the private temple in her quarters. She could not forget Ganoji's words, 'Yesu, I will not rest until you are widowed.' The very memory of the words made her shiver with fear. She cried out, 'Dadasaheb, what a gift you have given your sister! I wonder if there is any other brother in the world who treats his sister so.'

4

Mukarrab Khan felt like a thief who, having picked up the Kohinoor diamond by chance, is scared to death protecting it. In order to make sure that he reached Aurangzeb as fast as possible, he gathered nearly twenty-five thousand men from the nearby Islampur, Kasegaon, Aundh, Miraj and Rahimatpur stations.

The troops moved fast. They had left the Krishna and Koyna ghats behind. Mukarrab Khan wanted to reach the gorge of Shyamgaon by afternoon and the soldiers were ordered not to stop anywhere in between.

Bound to his horse, Shambhu Raje watched the landcapes flash past as they galloped ahead. He remembered Hambir Mama when he saw distant Vasantgad and the Talbid village at the base of the fort. He mused, 'Mama, how I wish you were alive!' Kavi Kalash knew Sambhaji's state of mind and was desperate yet helpless to find ways to comfort him. The troops were now moving towards the Mughal territory. His poetic mind recalled the words:

The Koyna cries out loud
Asking Krishna Mai
Tell me, where is the treacherous enemy
Taking Shivba's child to—

'Come on, move fast!' Mukarrab Khan and Ikhlas Khan shouted, urging the troops to hurry. They were terrified that any moment the Marathas would attack and take away their prized possession. Despite their army of thousands, the father and son were anxious and restless.

At Karad, Mukarrab had urged Ganoji and Nagoji to accompany him but they said, 'We have guided you out of the difficult terrain. Please don't ask us to follow you now. If the troops from Raigad find us, they will stone us to death.' Then the two vanished into the night, leaving Khan uneasy and apprehensive.

As they reached the gorge near Shyamgaon, Mukarrab said to his son, looking at the distant Krishna river, 'Beta Ikhlas, the fact that those two ran away proves that we are still not out of danger.'

Sambhaji scanned the horizon. They would soon leave the borders of the Swaraj. A host of old memories, anger, dejection and repentance racked his body and mind.

'Our Raja has been captured and the enemy is taking him away. Shambhu Raje has been taken alive ...' These words were being repeated in village after village. In the minds of the ryots, Shivaji and Sambhaji were akin to gods. The villagers wept, men and women alike. Many were incensed. They picked up their swords and ran towards their stables, only to remember that the famine had taken a toll on the animals. Most stables had been emptied long back; the horses that had survived were emaciated beasts.

A scorching sun bore down on the troops. Sambhaji and Kavi Kalash's mouths were gagged. Sweat trickled down their backs. Sambhaji nearly fainted in the heat.

En route, there were many Maratha villages. The ryots had rushed to the Deshmukhs and Deshpandes with appeals for help. 'Sarkar, do whatever it takes. Save Shambhu Raje!' The inamdars and watandars made an outward show of grief and fear but in reality they were filled with glee on hearing the knews. Had Sambhaji really been captured by the Mughals? These landlords, who believed Sambhaji had robbed them of their hereditary rights, were secretly celebrating the fact that he was now out of their way.

They tried to pacify the ryots, saying, 'Don't worry. Raje will be safe. We will look into the matter.'

'Sarkar, Khan has captured Raje and he will soon pass this way with an army of twenty-five thousand.'

'Did you hear that? Khan has tens of thousands of soldiers and we are expected to fight them with fifty men?' They countered. Clearly they had no intentions of helping to rescue Sambhaji.

'Sarkar, we will use guerrilla tactics. We may die, but we need to save Shambhu Raje ...'

'You will do no such thing. Khan and his men will burn our villages if you do, and we cannot afford to be so foolish. We will look into the matter. Don't worry, give us some time.'

5

Dhanaji and Santaji reached Pachad on the third day of their journey. Yesubai was already at the base of the fort with five thousand men.

Yesubai conferred with Yesaji Kank. 'We cannot afford to round up troops from all the forts and chase Khan. It would be disastrous if the Badshah sends his army and captures our forts.'

'I agree, Matoshree,' Khando Ballal nodded.

They decided to set out with a troop strength of eight thousand. Yesubai mounted her horse. Rajaram had stayed behind at Raigad. With cries of 'Har Har Mahadev,' the men began their march. On the way, they met Haibatrao, Hambirrao's brother. He was on his way to Raigad from Karad. Seeing Ranisaheb, he jumped down from his horse, and touching Yesubai's feet in her stirrups, sobbed like a child. Yesubai said, 'Now wipe your tears. We will return to Raigad only when we have Shambhu Raje with us.'

'How do we do that, Ranisaheb? Yesterday, Khan crossed Shyamgaon with nearly twenty-five thousand troops.'

'Oh, oh! Raje has gone beyond the boundaries of the Swaraj,' Jyotyaji Kesarkar and Rayappa said, wailing loudly.

Yesubai had faced many difficult situations in her life. But this one shattered her. She dismounted and looked around. Seeing her, Dhanaji and Santaji too got down from their horses. They said, folding their hands in supplication, 'Ranisaheb, don't worry. We will go ahead and bring Raje back.'

Yesubai could barely speak. She finally said, finding her voice, 'I am not sure if we can do anything now ...'

'Why do you say that, Matoshree? Let us go,' the two insisted.

'The territory beyond Karad is a flat one. There are no forests, mountains or ravines. Our guerrilla tactics won't work there. It is one thing to spring a sudden attack in the Sahyadris and another to face four lakh Mughal soldiers on open ground.'

It was a clash of wise words against the spirited enthusiasm of youth. Yesubai was right; Mukarrab Khan had gone beyond the territory where guerrilla warfare would work. It would be foolhardy to attack the Mughals head on and risk losing the forts still held by the Marathas. Yesu said, 'Only Raje would be able to guide us. The question is, how do we reach him?'

Rayappa said, between his sobs, 'Ranisaheb, don't stop me now. Let me decide how I will reach Raje.'

Khando Ballal wrote a message for Raje, stamping it with Yesubai's seal. Rayappa and his brother Devappa took leave of the party. They galloped away in the direction of Karad.

The sun was setting. The western sky and the mountains were already engulfed in darkness. In the distance, even the Lingana fort seemed broken. Dhanaji and Santaji's faces were crestfallen. Yesubai's sindoor was smeared by the sweat pouring down her face. Yesubai said, looking at the two bravehearts, 'Dhanaji and Santaji, have patience. In the process of trying to save a Maharani from becoming a widow, we should not lose the entire kingdom.'

6

It was a hot afternoon. The Badshah's camp at Asadnagar simmered in the bright sun. Aurangzeb had renamed Akluj as Asadnagar. The territory around Akluj and Daund had been ravaged by famine, and even in the usually wintry month of February, the heat was merciless. The Badshah's desperation was growing by the day. He had spent nearly a decade in the Deccan with no success. His arch enemy, the kafir Sambha, had eluded him all these years. The single biggest campaign in his life was turning out to be a disaster, his greatest dream a mirage.

The Badshah was busy giving instructions to his clerks regarding the dispatch of various letters and documents. Any interruption of his work during these hours was considered a blasphemy. Suddenly a spy entered the tent and stood in front of the Badshah after saluting elaborately. On any other day, such audacity would have led to the death of the intruder but from the way the guards murmured and smiled, Aurangzeb realised that the message was important.

The guards outside were nearly rolling in the mud with happiness. Aurangzeb, busy dictating the letters, had alert ears and picked up the laughter outside. He asked the messenger, 'What is the news?

'Badshah Salamat, it is great news.'

'Why, has something happened to that idiot Shahzada Akbar in Iran?'

'No, Alampanah. That devil Sambha has finally been caught. He is in our custody.'

'What?'

'Yes, Sambha! Mukarrab Khan has captured him in the Sahyadris.'

The Badshah asked the messenger to come closer. When he was within reach, he got up and slapped him hard. Aurangzeb's face was red with anger. He was further enraged when the messenger continued to smile. 'You fool. How dare you? Are you teasing the Badshah?' Aurangzeb was tempted to order his beheading that very instant for such temerity!

The Badshah glanced outside the tent. His sardars, amirs and grandchildren were all seen running towards his tent. Raising their hands in air, and with tears streaming from their eyes, they were shouting, 'Allah o Akbar!' The trumpets and horns were already blowing without any orders being given.

There was no longr any need to ascertain the veracity of the message. The Badshah, out of sheer happiness, put his hand on his bare head. He had not worn his crown for the past six years. Tears of joy rolled down his cheeks. He said, raising his hands in the air, 'Ya Khuda! Ya Allah! My voice must have reached you. Oh, Badshah of this earth, a million thanks to you!'

Asad Khan stepped forward to congratulate Alamgir. Aurangzeb took his hand and said, 'Asad Khan, even a man blind at birth, on receiving the gift of sight, would not be as mad with joy as I am today.'

7

The Badshah was alert. Mukarrab Khan and his troops were nearing Bahadurgad now. The years of waiting were finally over. But extreme happiness does not allow a man to sleep. The Badshah was ever watchful. His restless eyes scanned the horizon.

Along the banks of the river Bhima, there were no tall mountains. There was hardly any possibility of a surprise attack by the Marathas. But Mukarrab was vigilant. After all, he was carrying Shivaji's son as a trophy for the Badshah.

Aurangzeb asked Asad Khan many times about the strength of the troops accompanying Mukarrab Khan. 'Twenty-five thousand,' he would answer, yet Aurangzeb asked many others to confirm the same. He was not sure of his own strength.

News of Sambhaji's arrest spread cheer throughout the ranks of the Mughal army. The days of exile in the Deccan were over! They could leave for Delhi soon. Many sardars from other stations had already left for Bahadurgad to celebrate the victory.

The Badshah said to Asad Khan one morning, 'Send orders to all our stations around Akluj, Pandharpur and Daund that not a single horse should be seen in anyone's stables or gardens. The residents must be asked to send the animals away. I don't want a single Maratha soldier to have a horse handy. If a Maratha is seen on a horse, arrest him.'

Each day, instead of sitting in his office as was his daily routine, Aurangzeb would sit in the howdah of his royal elephant and scan the horizon. The only thought in his mind was, 'Let the news of Sambha's arrest not turn out to be a mirage.'

In the afternoons, Aurangzeb would go to the masjid for his prayers. A fakir who often sat there puffing on his chillum had the audacity to blow smoke while looking at the Badshah. He was not afraid of the Mughal Emperor. It was the fakir himself who had built the masjid, from coins collected over the years, one after another. Aurangzeb was often reminded of Shivaji while looking at the fakir. Shivaji too had built his army one man at a time. Now his son Sambha was ruling the Swaraj that he had created. Aurangzeb closed his eyes in prayer, 'Ya Allah, get me this devil soon.'

Sitting at his palace in Bahadurgad, Aurangzeb could see the Bhima flowing silently in the distance. There were ruins on the banks of the river which, if local legends were true, belonged to a seven-storeyed palace. People believed that there was treasure buried somewhere in the ruins of the palace but no one trying to find it had survived. Aurangzeb dismissed such stories as fanciful folklore.

Mukarrab Khan was expected in another couple of days. Aurangzeb's restlessness knew no bounds. He issued fresh orders to whip all the Marathas in the nearby villages. He had ordered nearly three hundred thousand soldiers to go into the villages and torture any Maratha who was seen walking around. The troops swarmed the villages on both sides of the Bhima. Soon, not a single soul was seen outside their homes.

8

The wait was almost unbearable. It had been eight long years of struggle, defeat and disappointments. The soldiers dreamt of returning to their homes, be it the deserts of Rajputana or the plains around Agra, Delhi and Bareilli. They wondered how their families would be when they saw them after a gap of nearly a decade. The children would have grown up.

Even the torturous campaign in the snows of Kabul-Kandahar had lasted less than ten months. Many had wished that the old Badshah would die in the Deccan but no one had had the courage to revolt openly. A soldier who had dared to talk loudly of returning to Delhi had been crushed under an elephant's feet. The celebrations in the camp now reminded one of Eid. Local tailors and jewellers did brisk business. Everyone was waiting breathlessly for Mukarrab and his prized catch.

Rayappa was devastated. He had lost someone dearer than his own life. 'Whatever happens, Raymama, see that you get the message to Shambhu Raje,' Yesubai had instructed. He and his brother Devappa had travelled day and night, riding towards Bahadurgad. They were shocked to see the destruction of the villages around the Bhima. Most of the houses were empty. The villagers had vacated their houses and run away in fear of the Mughals, hiding in their fields.

On the way, Rayappa and his brother had managed to get a water-bearer's leather bag. With their overgrown stubble and dark faces, they looked like bhistis, the Deccani water-bearers, thus merging with the locals. Rayappa tried to extract information regarding Shambhu Raje but no one was willing to speak. He was desperate to meet his Raje and would often cry when alone.

One morning they heard that a royal prisoner was being taken to the fort. Rayappa managed to join the group which was to provide water inside the fort. The demand for water was high and the bhistis were busy. The camp was agog with excitement. Drums, trumpets and horns played continuously. In accordance with the Badshah's orders, everyone stood waiting to receive Mukarrab Khan.

The chains holding Sambhaji jingled as he and Kavi Kalash were led to two dirty camels which stood ready. They did not have saddles on them. A few soldiers lifted Sambhaji and put him on the camel's back.

Sambhaji had not seen the sun for days on end. He looked around, dazed by the strong light, to see thousands of Mughal soldiers with naked swords in their hands. The imperial army's camp was spread across miles, with endless rows of cannons and tents.

Waves of men and animals moved forward. The procession started moving. It was being led by Mahadji Nimbalkar, the thanedar of Bahadurgad. It was difficult to estimate whether Aurangzeb had deliberately given the responsibility to Mahadji, who was Shivaji's son-in-law and brother-in-law to Sambhaji. Mahadji was carrying out his task diligently, but did not dare to meet Sambhaji's stare.

Sambhaji was bound with ropes and chains to the camel's back. Glancing at a Rajput sardar, Amar Singh, who was supervising the tying of ropes, he said, 'You look like a Rajput. Are you from Durgadas's territory?'

'Yes,' he mumbled.

'My friend. I pray you, in the name of your Lord, enough of this torture. Spare me this humiliation and free me.'

'But, the orders are ...'

'My friend, I am appealing to you as a Hindu brother. How can a Rajput tolerate the sight of Shivaji's lion cub dying a dog's death? Please! Help me.'

'What do you want me to do, Raje?'

'Pick up your sword and cut the knots. Don't wait!'

Amar Singh was overwhelmed with emotion. He could not bear to see the tears in Sambhaji's eyes and unsheathed his sword. As he was about to lift the sword, a strong hand held his arm and Ikhlas Khan's voice growled, 'Kyun sardarji? What is your plan?' Amar Singh's bid to release the prisoner had failed. A brief moment of opportunity had passed Sambhaji by.

Sambhaji, for whom tailors had vied with each other to stitch royal clothes and jewellers competed to provide the most exquisite designs, was now forced to wear the striped clothes of a court jester. The one who had sat on a golden throne, supervising the Maratha Swaraj, was now forced to sit like an ordinary criminal on a skinny camel. His neck, which had been adorned by diamond and emerald necklaces, was encircled by rough rope which was used to tie cattle. On Sambhaji and Kavi Kalash's heads were wooden caps of the kind used by Persians for prisoners. Their hands were raised in the air and passed through holes in wooden planks. Their necks too were stuck between wooden planks, to prevent them from turning to look around.

The townspeople were enjoying the spectacle of the two being paraded as objects of ridicule and mirth. And, leading the procession with trumpets, horns and drums, was Mahadji Nimbalkar!

From time to time, the camels were deliberately made to run fast and then turn suddenly. Sambhaji and Kavi Kalash tried frantically to clutch the camels' backs, although they were bound tightly and could not fall. Seeing their discomfort, the children and others walking alongside laughed scornfully.

Rayappa walked with the other bhistis. At one point, he had managed to get a glimpse of Shambhu Raje. The moment his eyes met his Raje's, Sambhaji smiled weakly. He had probably assumed that one of the water-bearers resembled Rayappa. Little did he know that it was Rayappa himself!

It was a pathetic sight. Within a mere nine years of Shivaji's death, the lion's cub had been caught and publicly humiliated. The men and children following the procession spat at Sambhaji, making obscene gestures. His head, showered with flowers in his durbar, was the now the target of sandals and stones. Sambhaji, the shining jewel in Shivaji's crown, tied like a log to a beast of burden, felt all his senses slowly being numbed. There was no anger, nor shame, any longer.

'Abasaheb, I will be present wherever you cannot be,' Sambhaji had once assured his father. For the past nine years, he had been running from one fort to another, ensuring that Shivaji's absence was not felt by the Swaraj. He had seen to it that the enemy was not emboldened after the death of his father.

He glanced at the clouds gathering on the horizon. The dark clouds reminded him of Jijabai's eyes, as if they were waiting to overflow with tears. He recalled that it was Jijabai who had insisted, in her practical wisdom, that Shivaji marry eight times. Her intention was to ensure that the political alliances thus formed would stand in good stead when enemies attacked the Swaraj. But the greedy watandars of Maharashtra had behaved like dogs who shifted loyalties with the smallest morsel thrown at them.

The procession moved forward. Rayappa looked at the tortured face of his master as he walked alongside. Rayappa remembered how he had once attacked a tiger with his sickle and saved Sambhaji's life. Now he watched helplessly as his master's boat was being sunk in the sea of the Mughal army. He could not bear the sight of it.

The procession reached the main gate of Bahadurgad. It was Rayappa's last opportunity. His loyal blood boiled. Snatching a sword from one of the Rajputs guarding the procession, he beheaded two soldiers standing nearby and shouted, 'Shambhu Raje!' Running towards the camel, he started attacking the ropes and chains that bound his Raje. 'Sambha's man!' the Mughal soldiers screamed and surrounded Rayappa.

He took blows on his neck, back and arms. Blood squirted from his body, and within moments, he was cut into nearly thirty pieces. The procession moved on. Rayappa's body, now literally a heap, was trampled beneath the animals' feet. It was the last blood-stained salute of a loyal soldier to Sambhaji, Shivaji and the Hindavi Swaraj. Sambhaji was stunned by the sacrifice. He bowed his head in gratitude.

TWENTY-TWO

Tragedy on the banks of the Bhima

1

The procession passed in front of a palace with the symbol of a moon and stars. The three royal prisoners inside heard the trumpets and horns. They would, had it been possible, have pierced the walls. Ever since they had heard of the arrest of Sambhaji, they wailed silently.

The procession reached the Diwan-e-Khas now. The durbar wore a festive look with all the Mughal amirs, umraos, shahzadas, begums, grandsons and sardars in attendance.

Mukarrab Khan, Ikhlas Khan and Bahadur Khan presented themselves before the Badshah. They were honoured with precious stones and fine clothes. They bowed and stepped aside. Then the Badshah glanced at the royal prisoners. Sambhaji and Kavi Kalash, bound in chains, stood in his presence. Seeing their Alamgir smile at last, many people in the durbar had tears in their eyes.

Unable to control his joy, Aurangzeb stood up, holding his rosary close to his stomach. As the durbar watched him curiously, Aurangzeb went down on his knees and put his head on the floor, thanking his Allah. His lips quivered and he seemed a little distraught from sheer happiness.

It was the first time that those who had gathered there had seen the Emperor so overcome with emotion. Only once before had the Badshah stepped down from his throne in a full durbar. Nearly seventeen years ago, when he had heard of Shivaji's coronation, he had been overwhelmed by anger and disgust, hating himself for his inability to stop it. He got off his throne in the presence of a full durbar then, mumbling to himself, 'Ya Allah! What a tragedy that the children of mere zamindars and ryots are now sitting on a throne, coronating themselves as emperors!'

Kavi Kalash watched the Badshah thanking his Allah profusely. His chest swelled in pride as he said, in his full-throated voice,

> *'Like Hanuman who stood in Ravan's court*
> *Stands Shambhu in the presence of Aurangzeb*
> *His body smeared with blood and shining*
> *He burns like a firefly, a sun on earth*

When even Delhi bends in salute seeing the lion's cub
No wonder Aurangzeb steps down his throne in salutation.'

The Badshah took a few steps forward until he was right in front of the two prisoners. They glared at him, heads held high.

Ikhlas Khan shouted, 'You fools! Don't you fear for your lives? Bow down to the Badshah.'

Sambhaji and Kavi Kalash continued to stare at the Mughal Emperor.

The Badshah had turned back towards his throne when Faulad Khan, who had been the police chief at Agra during Shivaji's time, thundered, 'You idiots, bow down. Salute the Badshah and save your life!'

But the prisoners were deaf to his suggestion. Unable to restrain himself, Faulad Khan walked up to Kavi Kalash and said, slapping his arms, 'Idiot! Salute your Emperor.'

Kalash could not take it anymore and kicked Faulad Khan in his leg. The latter fell down on the floor, taken by surprise. The Badshah turned, hearing the noise, and saw Faulad Khan struggle to his feet, gathering his dress and smiling embarrassedly.

Aurangzeb called Zulfikar who approached the throne and lowered himself to the floor, sitting on his knees. Aurangzeb whispered something in his ears. Zulfikar nodded and walked out of the durbar hurriedly. Soon afterwards, Sambhaji and Kavi Kalash were taken to the prison.

Elsewhere in Bahadurgad, sherbet was being served to all and sundry. It looked like Diwali was being celebrated in the fort. The very thought that they could return to Delhi, now that the Badshah's arch enemy had been caught, made people jump with joy.

Even amidst the joyous celebrations, there was a question in everyone's minds which made them fall silent when it arose. Would the Badshah order the execution of Sambha that very night?

'Of course!' Someone said. 'After all, he had beheaded his own brother Dara within a few days of his capture.'

'That is true. Remember how Gokula Singh, who had revolted against him in Mathura, was captured and hacked to pieces?'

'Bhaijaan, one day Allah may pardon these kafirs for revolting against Aurangzeb, but he will never forgive Badshah himself for his brutal ways,' someone else quipped.'

2

Sakhubai's temple inside her quarters was an impressive one. Mahadji reached his haveli late at night to see his wife lying prostrate in the sanctum sanctorum. She had no jewellery on and her hair was dishevelled.

Hearing his footsteps she sprang up like a wounded tigress. Her eyes burned with anger as she thundered, 'Oh, so you have come? What a daring task you have achieved today! Come, let me welcome you with a traditional lamp.' The taunt was not lost on Mahadji. As he tried to pacify her, Sakhubai continued, 'My brother Shambhu Raje was being insulted, taunted and teased by everyone in this fortress and for miles around. Did it not boil your blood?'

'Sakhu ...'

'He is the mighty Shivaji's brave son, the grandson of the pious Jijau. Did you not confront the person who arrested him?'

'Sakhu, that Badshah ... who will be able to confront him?'

Sakhubai choked while trying to speak. A sob escaped her lips.

'You wrote letters urging all the watandars to leave Sambhaji's sinking ship and join the Mughals. But you never bothered to consult me before taking these steps.'

Mahadji was speechless. Sakhubai continued, 'You could have forgotten for a moment that he was Shivaji's son but how did you forget that he was Saibai Nimbalkar's son? He was Nimbalkar's grandson too! How could you ignore that? Don't you have any allegiance to the blood that flows through your veins?'

Mahadji knew he could not counter Sakhubai's logic. A dejected and wrecked Sakhubai sat down on the floor when Mahadji said, his voice repentant, 'Sakhu, I will answer you without hesitation. This land has created many zamindars and watandars but there is only one Shivaji and one Sambhaji. Your father and your brother are one in a million. I must admit I am deeply ashamed of what I have done today.'

3

That night Zulfikar Khan presented himself to the Badshah in his battle gear. He said, 'Jahanpanah, my men have been arriving here since evening.'

'How many of them?'

'Twenty thousand soldiers. Another twenty thousand or so will come from Pune, Chakan and other areas. I will march on Raigad now.'

'Shabbash!' Aurangzeb said, anticipating a victory. 'I am sure the Marathas would be running scared since the arrest of Sambha. Don't waste a minute now.'

It was the second day after Sambhaji's procession at Bahadurgad. The sun was barely visible through the dark clouds covering the sky. Asad Khan, the Shahzadas and the sardars suspected that Sambha would be dead before nightfall. But even the Wazir was not sure of what the Badshah would do next. Asad Khan recalled how Aurangzeb had beheaded Dara and sent his head, wrapped in a box, to Shah Jahan. 'I wish I am not given the task of beheading a defenceless Sambha,' he said to his begum, wiping the sweat off his forehead nervously.

Soon it was dark. Lamps and torches burned at various places in the camp. Asad Khan heard footsteps outside his haveli. A soldier came in and announced, 'Badshah has sent Ruhullah Khan to Sambha's prison.'

Asad Khan thanked his stars that he had not been asked to carry out the task. Now everyone waited to see what Ruhullah Khan would do next.

4

Aurangzeb had often said that when Sambha and Kalash were captured, they would be treated not as royal prisoners but as mere looteras. Hence they had not been detained in the royal prison at Bahadurgad. Instead, they were taken to new prison cells that had been built of wood on an open plot of land. Outside the prison stood nearly five thousand soldiers with naked swords. Sambhaji and Kavi Kalash had been thrown into this wooden pen as if they were wild elephants being confined in a paddock.

They were bound with metal chains and their feet were in shackles. Sitting on the barebacked camels had peeled the skin off their backs, thighs and buttocks. The wounds of the whiplashes they had been subjected to burned.

Ruhullah Khan's heart melted, seeing the piteous state of the two prisoners. He said, 'Sambha dear, look at you! Where are your million gods? Where are the Maratha daredevils willing to jump in the fire to save you?'

Shambhu Raje and Kavi Kalash were silent. Their faces were creased with pain. But they glared at Ruhullah Khan without saying a word.

Ruhullah Khan said, 'I have a message from the Badshah. He wants to know where you have hidden your treasure.'

Sambhaji's lips did not move. Both he and Kalash looked at Ruhullah Khan with contempt. Ruhullah Khan then asked, 'Tell me the names of the people who profess to be loyal to the Badshah but are in fact supporting you. I need to know who they are.'

Sambhaji did not speak. Ruhullah Khan continued, 'Think about it, Sambha. You are young. If you join the Mughals, you can still save your life.'

Sambhaji and Kalash's lips were sealed. Ruhullah Khan shouted, 'You devils! The Badshah has not shown such mercy to any of his enemies. In fact, he is even known to break his promises and show his own blood relatives the path to hell. Tell me! Where is your treasure? Give me the names of our sardars who have secretly helped you!'

'What can that Badshah do to us?' Kavi Kalash challenged.

'Don't be foolish. He will unleash hungry dogs on you. They will tear you to pieces.

'Oh! It seems he will take the help of his brothers, after all!'

Sambhaji could not help but smile, hearing Kavi Kalash's taunt.

Ruhullah Khan, desperate to extract the information that Aurangzeb wanted, had to swallow the insults. He came closer to Kavi Kalash to whisper something in his ears. Kalash immediately spat on his face. This enraged Ruhullah Khan. He took out his dagger and lunged at Kalash but then, remembering the task given to him by Aurangzeb, checked himself. Ruhullah Khan knew he would be blamed if the prisoners were found dead. He put the dagger back in its sheath.

No amount of cajoling or threats seemed to be working on the prisoners. Khan said finally, in a sentimental tone, 'Sambha dear, I have two sons of the same age as yours. In their name, I ask you: why do you want to give up your precious life? Abandon this stubbornness.'

'Khansaheb, I pity your Badshah,' Sambhaji said, finally speaking.

'Why do you say that?'

'There is a royal way to deal with prisoners. But your Badshah does not know that. A street dog made to wear jewels and finery does not become an Emperor though he sits on the throne …'

'Tauba, tauba! Sambha, don't talk rubbish. Are you comparing the Janahpanah with a dog?'

'No! In fact a dog is loyal, unlike your foolish Badshah.'

Ruhullah Khan was sweating nervously. He stomped out of the prison, wondering how he was to convey Sambha's message without using the words which he had just heard.

It was late in the night. The floor in the makeshift prison was mere mud and getting cold now. Outside, thousands of soldiers guarded the prisoners with torches in their hands. An old subedar entered the prison to clean it up, followed by two assistants. He carried with him some bales of straw.

The subedar spread the straw on the ground, creating a bed of sorts. He helped Sambhaji and Kavi Kalash lie down on it. In the darkness they could not see his face, but his trembling hands conveyed affection. The old man, once Sambhaji and Kavi Kalash were made as comfortable as they could be, was unable to hold back his tears. He sat on the ground, sobbing and holding Sambhaji's feet. Shambhu Raje said, recognising him, 'My friend, Miyan Khan!'

5

Asad Khan was in conference with Aurangzeb. 'Jahanpanah, three hundred and fifty Maratha forts remain unconquered. Instead of trying to capture them, it would be wise to speak gently with Sambha and extract the information we need to take them over.'

Aurangzeb looked at Ruhullah Khan. The latter said, 'Sambha and Kalash are crooks. They have no respect for the Badshah Salamat, and are cursing him with choicest words!'

Aurangzeb realised that most of his sardars were of the opinion that he should treat Sambhaji with kindness, befriend him and use him to capture the forts. None of them were in favour of escalating the conflict, having suffered in the Deccan for nine years now. They were eager to march northwards and return home.

The Badshah was in a good mood these days. Asad Khan was his uncle and he spoke freely with him. Aurangzeb told the Wazir he was sure that one day Sambha's wife would come begging for her husband.

'And she will not come alone. She will come with the keys to the treasury. She will beg for her husband's release. I am sure she will come.'

As the days went by, Aurangzeb was frustrated that the two prisoners had not spoken a word despite the torture and insults they were subjected to. Meanwhile, his keen eye had noticed that Shahzadi Zeenat-un-Nissa had been restless ever since Sambha was captured. He was aware that she was close to Durgabai and Kamalja.

Zeenat-un-Nissa suggested one day, 'Abbajaan, his wife Durga and daughter Kamala are prisoners in the fort. If Sambha meets them, I am sure he will be more open to our ways.'

Aurangzeb looked with pride at his daughter. He remembered how Sambhaji had sent an army of fifteen thousand men to release Durgadevi and Ranubai but had not succeeded. He was sure Sambha would want to see his wife and sister. How would he react when he saw them after a gap of ten years? Sambha was sure to melt, Aurangzeb concluded. He would be willing to sign any treaty!

Udepuri asked Zeenat, caressing her face affectionately, 'What gives you the courage to speak your mind to the Badshah?'

'It is not courage, Ammijaan. I cannot tolerate seeing others suffer.' Zeenat had tears in her eyes, recalling her elder sister Zebunissa, daughter of Dilras Banu Begum, who had been imprisoned in the Salimgarh fort for life by Aurangzeb.

That night, sleep eluded Zeenat-un-Nissa. She recollected all the dark events of her life, when her father had mercilessly massacred or imprisoned members of the family. He may have been a very effective Emperor but she could not help shuddering at his cruel and evil ways. She recalled with horror the way the Sikh Guru Tegh Bahadur was beheaded fifteen years back. The memory of the gruesome killings of his disciples—Bhai Matidas, Satidas and Dayaldas—troubled her.

Dayaldas was thrown into boiling oil. His screams rent the air as he died an agonising death. His disfigured body had been kept hanging at the Chandni Chowk for days. Satidas met an even more horrific death. He was tied to a pole while two men, using iron claws, had peeled off his skin. The skin and flesh fell in clumps while Satidas died screaming in pain. Two women, in the advanced months of their pregnancy, had had miscarriages hearing his tormented cries.

The Shahzadi hoped that the suggestion she had made to her father to allow Sambhaji to meet his wife, sister and daughter would be entertained.

7

A few years earlier, it was Miyan Khan who was being held as a prisoner in Bahadurgad. He had not forgotten how Sambhaji had helped him arrange and attend his daughters' wedding. He would often visit Sambhaji under the pretext of looking after the arrangements in the prison cell. He felt blessed by this opportunity to serve him. These days, he was Sambhaji's eyes and ears in Bahadurgad.

One day he whispered to Sambhaji, 'Raje, I will do whatever it takes to release you from this hell. It is not difficult to escape from this prison, but for nearly a hundred miles around, it is Mughal territory. The Badshah has ensured that there are no Marathas managing the stables anymore.'

'Let it be, Miyan Khan. Maybe this is what Jagadamba had destined for me.'

Rayappa had sacrificed his life at Sambhaji's feet. Devappa, his brother, had carefully kept Maharani's letter hidden in his dress. He managed to meet Miyan Khan, and miraculously, the letter from Yesubai reached Raje safely despite all the precautions taken by Aurangzeb to cut him off from the world outside. Sambhaji was in tears reading it. Yesu had written:

> *'Raje, don't worry! We are raising a huge army here. We will attack Bahadurgad and release you.'*

The next line shook Raje to the core, wrenching his heart.

> *'Raje, it is my misfortune that you were taken a prisoner while in my father's territory. What a pity it is! And my ill luck. I pray you will forgive Yesu for it.'*

Miyan Khan had managed to bring two Brahmins to the prison disguised as his assistants. Raje said to them, 'Memorise what I am about to say. After you leave here, repeat the words to yourself and then take them carefully to Raigad. I am giving you my ring as a token of my identity.'

He said, instructing the men to listen carefully, 'Yesurani, don't trouble your heart unnecessarily. One has to accept destiny. But there is hope. Don't torture yourself and feel guilty.'

The next words filled Raje's eyes with tears as he continued, 'Don't blame the Shirke household for Ganoji's cowardly act. When I went to Raigad to take charge, it was your father Pilajirao Shirke who stood like a rock behind me. After all, it was that household which gave birth to Yesubai Maharani who has ruled from Raigad for eight years with a firm hand. Yesu, families are not bad. It is our misfortune that sometimes families give birth to treacherous men. After all, even the soil has insects and there are cobwebs in palaces. Wait for my instructions. Till then, see to it that our forts remain protected as before. I know you must be worried sick thinking about me. My Abasaheb engraved the Hindavi Swaraj on the map of Maharashtra. Warriors like Tanaji, Baji, Shelar Mama and many such bravehearts have sacrificed their lives for it. Be prepared to protect the Swaraj even if it means widowhood for you. See to it that you don't, under any circumstance, allow the forts to be taken over by the enemy.'

8

Durgabai, Ranubai and ten-year-old Rajkumari Kamala's eagerness knew no bounds as they left their prison to meet Raje. It had been ten long and torturous years. The previous night, when Miyan Khan told them that the Badshah had probably softened his stand, they could hardly sleep, waiting for the next morning.

They reached Raje's prison where nearly five thousand soldiers stood guard. The prison cell was dirtier than a horse stable. They saw a tattered rag spread on the floor which served as a bed. A very tired Raje and Kavi Kalash sat on the floor, their hands and legs bound in chains. Ranuakka could not hold back her tears seeing her beloved brother in such miserable state. She wailed, 'Shambhu … Balraje … Shambhu Raje!'

Sambhaji was hearing the sweet voice after a decade. He stood up instantly, forgetting his pain and exhaustion. He rushed forward to hug his sister. Kamala was seeing her father for the first time. She was taken aback, seeing his tattered dress, bald head, and the stubble on his face, but then she saw the glint in his eyes and she swelled with pride. She ran to embrace him. The mother and daughter hugged him, tears flowing down their cheeks as they sobbed loudly. The three wept, unable to bear the state to which Shambhu Raje had been reduced.

Shambhu Raje said, 'Ranuakka, these are tough times. It is our bad luck. I had every intention of feeding the treacherous Aurangzeb to the vultures, and ridding humanity of a cruel tyrant.'

'Raje, we spent the last ten years in the hope that one day we will go back to Raigad and see our brother on the throne.'

'Please pardon me, Akkasaheb and Durgarani! I could do nothing for you.'

'Shambhu Raje, don't say that. You fought hard and made life miserable for Aurangzeb. We may have been prisoners but we were well aware of the things happening around us.'

Sambhaji said, 'I tried my best to release you. We had nearly fifteen thousand troops outside Ahmednagar fort, led by Hambir Mama himself. The enemy sensed our intentions and moved you to Bahadurgad.'

There was so much to say, and so little time. Sambhaji said, 'Kamala, if we had met at Raigad you would have been welcomed with the booming of cannons.'

Ranuakka ruffled Sambhaji's hair affectionately, saying, 'These days too will pass, Raje!'

'Akka, why is destiny so cruel? I had never met my daughter and now I am seeing her in these circumstances. It would be the first time in history that a Raja meets his daughter for the first time ten years after her birth, and that too, never to see her again.'

The guard, Faujdar Dular Singh, peeped in and cleared his throat dramatically, saying, 'Hurry up!'

Shambhu Raje held Durgabai's hand and said, 'Durga, I could never give you any happiness.'

'Raje, I am Shivaji Raje's daughter-in-law and Shambhu Raje's wife. What else do I need?'

'What does this cruel Badshah want?' Ranubai asked.

'Ranuakka, he has asked me several times to give away all my forts and surrender my treasury. He wants us to leave the Deccan. If we agree, he will release all of us and give us a jagir in Hindustan where we can spend the rest of our lives in luxury.'

'Don't rescind the promise you have given to your Abasaheb,' Akkasaheb said.

Shambhu Raje smiled. 'We are meeting thanks to his generosity. If the same continues, I am sure we may meet again.'

'Shambhu Raje, we don't care about our safety. Don't, under the compulsion to save our lives, agree to his vile conditons,' Akkasaheb said, determinedly.

The guard was now banging on the door, indicating that the meeting was over. Kamala hugged her father and showered kisses on his cheeks. The four of them clung to each other and cried together.

Slowly, the three women were moving away when they heard Kavi Kalash's mournful voice, 'Ranuakka!' Ranu Akkasaheb hugged him and said, 'You have been with Raje, in rain and sun, whether you were cursed or praised. I hope you are born in your next life not as Raje's friend but as my brother.'

Kavi Kalash said, 'Ranu Akkasaheb, Durga Bhabhi, let our friends still fighting the enemy in the Sahyadris know this …'

He recited a few lines:

'We walk with our heads held high to the gallows
The nails in our soles still hurting
Friends, we never wished for long life
But we needed some more time
To be with you
While we fight and defeat the enemy.'

9

Aurangzeb may have caught Sambha but destiny had dealt him a cruel hand in the Deccan. He had lost Aurangabadi Mahal, his begum, to the plague. He had to throw Shahzada Muazzam into the dungeons for his revolt. Shahzada Akbar had escaped and was now trying to attack Hindustan with the help of the Shah of Iran. Zulfikar Khan and Shahzada Azam were in the Sahyadris but they had not met with much success.

The few moments of true happiness he had these days were spent in the company of Udepuri Begum and Shahzadi Zeenat-un-Nissa. He said to his daughter, 'Zeenat beta, I tried my best but Sambha is unwilling to relent. His wife and sister too are willing to go to the gallows rather than accept my conditions.'

A few khojas came in and spoke to Udepuri Begum, who was unwell and had been resting in the other room, leaving father and daughter to their chat. After the khojas left, she stormed into the Badshah's room and confronted Aurangzeb, 'Badshah Salamat, is there no limit to your cruelty? I was once married to the pious Dara. You killed him, and along with the throne, snatched me too! The throne made of wood and metal had no voice but I have been suffering all my life. Have I ever complained?'

'Be quiet, begum! Have you lost your mind?'Aurangzeb thundered, bristling with anger.

'Let the shahzadi hear this. She is not an innocent young girl anymore. You cannot understand the courage one needs to live with a person who has killed her husband. Look at Shahbuddin! He has threatened Sambha that if he does not hand over his forts and his treasury, he would molest his wife and sister in the bazaar! What audacity! Does he not have any shame?'

'Oh, is that the issue? I thought the heavens were collapsing!' Aurangzeb said, sitting down quietly. Udepuri was still fuming with anger. Shahzadi too was angry, having heard about Shahbuddin's threat. Aurangzeb said to his begum, 'Why are you so worried about that dog Sambha? Why are you so argumentative?'

Udepuri was not in a mood to back down. She said, 'Durga and Ranu are not just Sambha's wife and sister. They are Shivaji's family. Shivaji may have troubled you all your life but he has never allowed any of our tombs or mosques to be destroyed. You had publicly praised him after his death. Sambha too has behaved in the same way as his father.'

Aurangzeb knew he had no argument against Udepuri's comments. He immediately sent a strongly worded note to Shahbuddin, chastising the old sardar.

The days flew by. Zulfikar sent regular updates from Mahad, describing the various territories he was traversing with his troops. This enraged

Aurangeb who took his anger out on Asad Khan, 'What is your son trying to do? Is he teaching me the geography of the Deccan?' The truth of the matter was that Zulfikar did not have the courage to attack Raigad.

The Badshah was increasingly troubled by the question of what to do with Sambhaji. He said one day to his daughter, 'Zeenat, that devil Sambha has been in custody for twenty days now. I did not let even Dara live beyond a few days. The elders in the camp are laughing behind my back, calling me a coward.'

'Abbajaan, why don't you meet Sambha yourself? Why don't you use your sweet tongue instead of your sharp sword? I know the power of your words from the letters you have written to Akbar Bhaiya.'

Aurangzeb frowned. The very thought of the Badshah of Hindustan cajoling a mere mountain rat was intolerable to him.

10

Aurangzeb was in a foul mood. He shouted at the guards, 'What is happening in Bahadurgad? How can the enemy spies penetrate this place?' In truth, Aurangzeb had decided to take matters into his own hands. Under the pretext of inspecting the posts in Bahadurgad, he casually arrived at the makeshift prison where Sambha and Kalash were being held. He was accompanied by Wazir Asad Khan. He entered the room. Sambha and Kalash bore the marks of torture all over their weakened bodies and wore tattered clothes. Yet, it was remarkable the way they challenged Aurangzeb with their eyes, standing straight. Aurangzeb looked at them and said, 'Sambha, young man! It was thirty years ago that I took my brother Dara out on a procession atop an elephant, through the streets of Delhi. I had laughed at the way he was insulted by the people.'

'Badshah, you are a fool. Dara was a pious man. He was loved by both Hindus and Muslims,' Kavi Kalash said.

'You foolish poet! It is better that you hold your tongue. Else, I will have to pull out that flickering, pink serpent from your mouth,' Aurangzeb thundered.

He contined, 'Dara knew how to fool the common man. That is why many people were wailing and beating their chests in sorrow when he died.

You were paraded wearing a jester's dress through Shiva's own territory. Isn't that my victory and your defeat?'

Sambhaji said quietly, 'It is mere treachery. If you feel that this is your victory, you are living in a fool's paradise.'

'Such arrogance, such conceit!'

'Why not? Release me from my chains and let me face any of your sardars. My sword will show who the winner is.'

'Sambha, did anyone come to your rescue when you were being paraded through the streets? Save your life, you foolish fellow! Your ambitions, your prestige, your power—they are all ephemeral. Once broken, they are lost forever, like the pieces of a shattered chandelier. The world recognises a good deal. Shivaji's son-in-law understood that well. When will you learn? You too will be treated with honour in our army. Accept me as your Badshah. That parade was only a lesson to force you to come to your senses.'

Aurangzeb thought of all the desperate letters written by Zulfikar, lamenting that Dhanaji, Santaji and other Maratha daredevils were creating havoc in the Sahyadris, and that it was impossible to capture the forts, especially Raigad. The Badshah was therefore eager to convince Sambhaji to accede to his demands.

Changing his tone, he said, 'Sambha, I am at times jealous of your father, the kafir Siva. It must have taken great courage for an ordinary zamindar to establish a Maratha sultanate.'

'Badshah, my father's Swaraj is not the property of an arrogant sultan. The Swaraj is for the poor. The ryots own it.'

Aurangzeb continued, 'How fortunate Siva is to have a son like you. I am proud of you. A man gains wisdom from experience. You fought me and eluded me for eight years. This is not empty praise; I honestly wish at least one of my four shahzadas had shown the same tenacity you have!'

Sambhaji took a deep breath and said, returning Aurangzeb's stare, 'Instead of praising me with such words, it is better that you tell me what you want.'

'Where is your treasure hidden?'

'In my forts.'

'Which sardars from my army have joined you?'

'I don't know.'

'You arrogant fool! Come to your senses. Don't be influenced by this foolish poet. You may now know this, but Zulfikar Khan is in your territory with forty thousand horsemen. He must have laid siege to Raigad by now.'

'You foolish Badshah! Raigad is not a lump of clay which can be demolished.'

'Even if it is made of steel, I have asked Zulfikar to melt it.'

'It is made of stone and unbreakable at that.'

'You ignorant kafir! Save your life when you still can. My army is already in your territory and many of your men have joined us.'

'The men joining you are not true Marathas. You cannot destroy Maharashtra.'

'I need only two things from you: a list of the people who have joined you and the keys to your treasury.'

Even in that condition, Sambhaji could not help but smile. Kavi Kalash laughed loudly. The Badshah could not tolerate such open insults. He swallowed his anger and said, 'I am giving you one chance, and only one, Sambha. Hand over your forts and you can enjoy the rest of your life in any part of Hindustan you choose.'

'Wah, Badshah!' Kavi Kalash taunted.

'This is not a joke, you stupid poet! I give you my word, with my hands on the Quran.'

Sambhaji smiled tauntingly. 'You seem to be keen on taking over my forts. You want the forts without a fight, is it?'

'Yes.'

'Why don't you go up North then? There are many who would willingly to give you their forts, and their daughters and wives too. But we Marathas are different. We first anoint the stones of our forts with our blood and then spend our lives protecting them.'

11

'My Lord, I have never interfered in your campaigns for the past ten years. But we have been shifting camp too often. I am fed up now,' Udepuri complained.

'Huh! If those in the royal tents complain, what about the ordinary soldier who is out in the heat and dust?' Aurangzeb countered.

The entire camp was now frustrated. Men were looking forward to leaving for Hindustan. Sambha had been captured. What else was there to do?

'We need to capture his forts,' Aurangzeb said.

Udepuri suggested that they take Sambha to Delhi. Aurangzeb said, 'Udepuri, the destiny of Sambha is written in this soil. I am going to see to it that the end comes here.'

One night, Aurangzeb woke up with a sudden insight. Kavi Kalash was the soul of Sambha! He walked out of his palace, much to the surprise of the soldiers who scrambled to salute him. Aurangzeb turned towards Ruhullah Khan's tent. He ordered the guard to bring Kavi Kalash there.

Kavi Kalash entered the tent. Seeing Aurangzeb sitting there, he immediately surmised the reason for being summoned alone and smiled.

Till date, Aurangzeb had tried threats of instant death, false promises, and many other tactics to make Sambhaji yield to his demands. Kavi Kalash realised that the Badshah had one more trick up his sleeve.

Aurangzeb gestured to the guard to remove Kavi Kalash's fetters. Kavi said, laughing loudly, 'Well, the foolish Badshah is now trying to negotiate with a foolish poet.'

'What do you want, Kaviraj?'

'A poet scarcely even looks at a throne; in fact, he considers it to be of no use. My state of intoxication in my happiness is my kingdom. All I need is a cloth to cover my body and a friend like Shambhu Raje.'

'I want you to send letters to all the kiledars, conveying Sambha's orders to hand over the forts.'

'You're asking me to write false letters?'

'Why not? I will make you a rich man.'

'Badshah, you are a rascal! Many people including your Shahzada Akbar told me this. But today I know that you're the most disgraceful person on this earth. You can kill your own brothers for your selfish ambitions. You are a shaitan who can play with your own brother's decapitated head on your lap. What harm can you do to me, you old fox?'

'You foolish Brahmin, I am going to hang you at the gallows.'

'Huh! I will be happy to die for my dear friend Sambhaji. It would be an honour.'

Aurangzeb fumed at Kavi Kalash's response. He ordered the khojas standing outside to get a whip and asked them to lash him. Blood poured out of Kavi's body where the lashes of the whip broke open his skin. After a while, they dragged him out of the tent and threw him in prison.

12

A day before their planned departure from Bahadurgad, Faulad Khan came and whispered in Aurangzeb's ears, 'Jahanpanah, Kavi Kalash is willing to negotiate.'

Aurangzeb could not believe his ears. Although Kavi Kalash had been tortured relentlessly for many days, he had not expected him to change his mind so soon.

He was brought before the Emperor. His whole body was covered with cuts and wounds which had begun to fester. The Badshah indicated to the guards to seat Kalash near him. He asked, 'Kaviraj, tell me, which jagir do you want? Agra, Bareilly, Lucknow or Sasaram? Ask, and it will be yours.'

'I have only one thing to ask. You may cut me into pieces and feed my body to the dogs but you must treat my Raje as a king.'

The Badshah was taken aback. He asked, 'Why have you come here? To save your life or Sambha's?'

'I am not begging you. I have come to remind the descendant of Taimur that there is a difference between an ordinary butcher and an Emperor.'

Aurangzeb's servants shivered with fear. Kavi Kalash continued, 'Look at the way you have insulted him, parading him in a procession. No true emperor would have displayed the animal instincts you showed in the way you celebrated his arrest.'

'This is the way we honour kafirs, you fool!'

'I wish the Badshah would learn some etiquette from his enemies.'

'What etiquette are you talking of?'

'I have a little knowledge of history, Badshah. Mirza Jai Singh fought against you when you and Shuja were warring for the Mughal throne. There came a day when you found yourself alone facing Mirza Jai Singh in a forest. Had he not shown any mercy and finished you off then, you would not have been sitting here today.'

An enraged Badshah shouted at his guards, 'What are you waiting for? Break this fellow's legs and throw him in a nullah. Let him die there!'

The guards and the khojas were already dragging Kavi Kalash away when he turned around and said to the Badshah, 'Don't make a show of being a servant of Allah by stitching his caps. You need to stitch your brain together.'

The guards pounced on him. While he was being dragged away, Kavi Kalash sang:

'While you commit sins, your lips utter Bismillah
You stitch caps to fool your Allah
Your brain needs to be stitched,
It is you who is going mad.'

Incensed, Aurangzeb ordered his men to cut off Kavi Kalash's tongue. A huge Pathan sat on Kalash's chest. Two others held his head and one of them put his hand inside his mouth. He broke four of his teeth and then started pulling his tongue out. Kavi Kalash's eyes were white with fear. The Pathan cut off his tongue in one clean stroke. Instead of words, blood spilled out of his mouth now. He choked on his own blood while tears flowed down his cheeks. He was hardly able to breathe.

13

Aurangzeb gulped down water from a pitcher. He moved his hand over his bald head. He said, 'Udepuri Begum, I want to share my thoughts. I feel Shivaji is far luckier than me. He has a son like Sambha, a daredevil. Look at my four shahzadas! All donkeys. If I had a son like Sambha I would have asked Allah for just two things—a rosary and a carpet to read my namaaz. I would have left for Mecca-Madina with these two things tucked under my armpit.'

Udepuri had been by Aurangzeb's side through thick and thin. She said, 'My Lord, Allah has been with you. You defeated Bijapur and Golconda. Now you have Shiva's son. But I don't see any happiness on your face. What is wrong, my Lord?'

Aurangzeb did not say anything for a long time. He kept fiddling with the beads of his rosary while mumbling lines from the Quran. Udepuri said, 'You remember the battles of your youth? Even when the enemy surrounded you, attacking from all sides, you would spread the mat and read your prayers. That is when you were called Zinda Pir, the living saint.'

'Abbajaan, I too have heard this from many soldiers,' Zeenat-un-Nissa said. 'I too wonder why you don't seem happy despite having captured your arch enemy.'

'Dear, I don't understand the Maratha soil or its people. Their king is with us but they are not vanquished. Zulfikar has not met with any success. It has been a month since we caught Sambha but his wife is not willing to relinquish Raigad. We have whipped Sambha and Kavi Kalash till their flesh has peeled off but they are not willing to bend.'

Aurangzeb decided to shift his camp closer to Pune. He felt that Bahadurgad was not giving him any peace. The move took place the next day and Aurangzeb decided to establish the new cantonment between Tulapur and Koregaon Bhima. His sharp mind estimated that once he was close to Pune, he would be able to control the area and also the road to Konkan. His men too were feeling refreshed by the change of air and scenery. Aurangzeb would also be better able to monitor the progress made by Zulfikar Khan from this location.

Aurangzeb hoped that the mental and physical torture of the two royal prisoners would soon compel Yesubai to come from Raigad and fall on her knees before him.

The imperial army reached Tulapur on 3 March 1689. Tulapur was on the sangam of the rivers Indrayani and Bhima. The vast cantonment held nearly three lakh soldiers, apart from servants and other officials.

One evening, Aurangzeb summoned Miyan Khan and said, 'I suspect there are still some people in my camp who are supporting Sambha and trying to help him. Find out who they are and let me know.' Miyan Khan nodded, saying, 'Ji, my Lord.'

Days went by in Tulapur. There was no news from Zulfikar. One day, a frustrated Aurangzeb ordered Ruhullah Khan, 'Gouge that rascal Kalash's eyes out with a burning rod.'

The khojas and other servants ran to carry out the order. That evening, Kavi Kalash's eyes were gouged out, leaving behind hideous hollows.

Aurangzeb would enquire about the two prisoners everyday. Anyone else in their place would have succumbed long back, but they were not ones to yield to the pressures of torture.

One morning, Aurangzeb summoned Sambhaji to his office. He said, taunting him, 'I am sure you must have grown wiser, seeing your friend's pathetic condition. I cut his tongue off long back, letting you keep yours only so that I could listen to your words of defeat. Tell me, what can you do when fate is not in your favour? What can your millions of gods and goddesses do? I think you need a new vision.'

The Badshah gave orders for two rods to be heated. Miyan Khan was standing nearby. Aurangzeb said, 'Miyan Khan, come!'

Miyan Khan stood shivering. He knew what he was going to be ordered to do. Sambhaji's hands were tied behind his back. Aurangzeb said, looking at Asad Khan, 'I was looking for someone to carry out this task. Who can be more loyal than Miyan Khan?'

Seeing Miyan Khan hesitate, he said, 'If Miyan Khan does not want to do the job, let him be the first to get the new vision!' Miyan Khan had no choice but to pick up the heated rods. When he reached Sambhaji, he suddenly pierced his own stomach with the rods. There was an uproar as the Badshah's men ran forward with swords and cut Miyan Khan to pieces. His blood fell on Sambhaji's feet. It was his last act of gratitude.

The men then carried out the task meant for Miyan Khan. With a hideous noise, the rods were inserted into Sambhaji's eyes. Smoke came out, along with the stench of burnt flesh. Sambhaji's face twisted in agony but he refused to scream. Not a word emerged from his mouth. Aurangzeb was terribly disappointed.

14

Kesopant Trimal was camped near the fort of Jinji. He heard the terrible news that evening.

'Sambhaji has been captured.'

Keso Trimal's heart bled hearing the tragic news. His loyal blood would not allow him to sit and do nothing while his Raje languished in a Mughal prison. He was sure Harji would summon him any moment. He asked his troops to be ready. 'Aurangzeb may attack any day. We must be prepared.'

Keso Trimal's elder brother Moropant had been one of the Ashta Pradhan in Shivaji's cabinet. Kesopant had shown his valour at Ramshej. Shambhu Raje had rewarded his loyalty with an important assignment—sending him to supervise the territory of the Karnatak and Tamil provinces. Keso received a message from Harji, instructing him to leave for Pune immediately. 'Come to the fort for a discussion before you go,' Harji had said. The wiry old man immediately began ascending the fort. He was drenched in sweat by the time he presented himself to Harji Mahadik.

Harji Mahadik was sitting on a swing and looked quite happy. The sound of someone weeping could be heard from an inner chamber. It was probably

Ambikabai. After all, Shambhu Raje was her younger brother. Kesopant took a seat, a little confused. As soon as Harji glanced at the soldiers standing nearby, they rushed to arrest Kesopant. He was thrown into a dungeon. The old soldier fumed with anger. He had never in his wildest dreams imagined that when Maharashtra's Raje was captured, his brother-in-law, instead of rushing to save him, would act in such a treacherous manner.

Harji Raje wrote a letter to Aurangzeb, 'The Lord above and the Badshah on earth has blessed me. I wish you would honour me in the same manner as you have honoured Ganoji Shirke and Mahadji Nimbalkar. I may be related to Shivaji Raje but we have not lost our minds like his son. I pray that I get a chance to serve you, my Lord.'

15

Raigad was enveloped in grief. Ten years earlier, the capital had suffered a shock with the demise of Shivaji Raje. The second shock of Shambhu Raje's capture was difficult to digest. The citizens were drowned in sorrow with the knowledge that Sambhaji, at merely thirty-two years of age, was a prisoner of the Mughals.

It was as if a mountain had collapsed on Yesubai. Her grief was unbearable. Memories of Sambhaji filled her mind. She knew that a cruel emperor like Aurangzeb would torture Sambhaji and that Raje would never yield or accept any conditions for his release. While on one hand Yesubai lived in mortal fear, wondering how her husband would survive, on the other, as queen of the Swaraj, she had look into administrative and military matters, ensuring the safety of Raigad above all else.

The palace at Raigad felt immensely lonely. Yesubai roamed around the fort inspecting the troops and the ramparts while looking anxiously at the valleys below. Would Raje walk through them again one day? Thc moon, peeping through the clouds, would remind her of his face and she would be overwhelmed with emotions. Yet, she had to carry out her duties. Yesubai's primary aim was to ensure the security of the three hundred and fifty forts in the Sahyadris.

She received news that Aurangzeb had moved his camp to Tulapur. It was clear that the Badshah was planning to attack Raigad. Each day she would hear of dozens of old sardars and watandars joining the Mughal camp with the hope of some benefit or the other, the way a hungry dog runs for a piece of stale bread.

So far Shambhu Raje had ensured that through Miyan Khan and others, messages would reach Raigad from time to time. The latest message was heart-rending. Shambhu Raje had said, 'Yesurani, as I have said earlier, be prepared to protect Abasaheb's Swaraj. At this juncture, protecting the kingdom is crucial even at the cost of not being able to protect your husband.'

These were difficult times for the Swaraj. As always, there were selfish people who found ways to get their pound of flesh. Yesubai often would pray for Sambhaji to appear in Raigad through some divine intervention. One day a few traders from Pune came to meet Yesubai. 'We are told there are a lot of corrupt officials in the Mughal camp. We can save Shambhu Raje.' Yesubai did not hesitate for a moment. 'Khandoba, give them as much money as they want.'

She got up to arrange for the payment but suddenly stopped in her tracks. Was she being fooled? It was unlikely that the money would ever reach Aurangzeb's camp, she realised. Yet, the slim hope of being able to release Raje prompted her to give it to the men after all. The thieves distributed the wealth at the banks of the river Mula and decamped.

News of the ways in which Sambhaji and Kavi Kalash were being tortured reached Raigad every now and then. The real question was how long this would continue. Prahlad Niraij, Yesaji Kank and other elders were worried sick. How long could they continue to run the kingdom in Raje's name?

'To be frank, it is not wise to leave a throne without a king,' Yesaji said.

'What is your advice?' Yesubai asked.

'Dada Maharaj is going through hell. The Swaraj owes a lot to him. Let us put his son Shahu on the throne. We are all there to support him,' Rajaram Saheb said.

Rajaram had shown his maturity and large-heartedness by proposing Shahu's name but Yesubai knew that there were many people in the administration who would object. She said, 'No! Seven-year-old Shahu is too young right now. Rajaram Saheb is mature and can take on the responsibility. He must ascend the throne.'

The same day, a small ceremony was held coronating Rajaram Saheb as the third Chhattrapati of the Hindavi Swaraj. A grateful Rajaram bowed to his Vahinisaheb and took her blessings.

The days were passing by swiftly. Zulfikar Khan finally managed to lay siege to the Maratha capital. Raigad had never seen such dark days.

The officials were worried. What if the new heir to the throne too was captured by the Mughals? The Swaraj would end! Apart from a narrow path leading from the Chittadarwaza to the main entrance, there was no other way into the fort. But Yesubai was thinking of a way out. She asked the men to create a wooden platform which could be lowered from one of the ramparts. In the distance they could see the burning torches of the Mughal camp. 'We must hurry. Lower the platform. The other forts are well protected but we must save Rajaram.'

'Vahinisaheb, what about you?' Rajaram asked.

'I have decided to give myself up. You and Tarabai should leave immediately. Else, we will all get caught. The Mughals will celebrate my arrest as I am Shambhu Raje's wife. They will be a little relaxed for a few days. You must use the time to escape.'

Rajaram could not hold back his sobs. The enemy was approaching fast. Rajaram and Tarabai began descending the fort using the wooden plank and a rope.

Yesubai closed her eyes as she prayed.

16

'You fool, I am willing to accept death but not your religion. Shivaji's son is not going to be trapped by your words,' Sambhaji shouted at Aurangzeb.

'Sambha, I am going to continue ruling Hindustan for many more years. I have only one question. Tell me the names of my sardars who were feeding you information. Give me the names of the traitors and save your life!'

Sambhaji's stomach was literally touching his spine. He had not had a morsel of food for the past few days. His lips were dry. His health was extremely fragile. He said, 'I cannot answer your question.'

'Why?'

'I use my sword to fight the enemy. I don't stab my friends in the back.'

Aurangzeb was frustrated beyond words. He had not been able to extract a single morsel of information from Sambhaji. He gulped water from a jar and stormed out of the room. The Badshah was terribly confused now. Should he allow Sambha to live ... or should he honour the fatwa made by the maulvi and let him die?

17

It was the night before new moon. The banks of the Bhima were cold. The night was dark. In the distance a dog barked. In the hills, wolves could be heard howling. Miyan Khan's assistants, loyal to their master, were still looking after Sambhaji and Kalash. The two suffered immensely. They were allowed a bath only once in four days. They were subjected to lashes and beatings every now and then. The guards had literally pulled out all their hair. There was no place where their bodies did not hurt. They were now almost beyond pain!

It was past midnight. Sambhaji felt the cold breeze from the river bank in his cell. It was a gentle touch. It was his Abasaheb.

'Abasaheb, I could do nothing ...'

'Don't even think that, my dear. Each valley of the Sahyadris, the narrow mountain paths, the ravines, all the provinces of Maharashtra, every inch of the soil is grateful to you.'

'But Abasaheb, I am blamed, maligned by many.,.'

'My son, I have been watching you for the past nine years. Had it not been for destiny which has tied my hands, I would have come back breaking the doors of heaven to help you. You never allowed any obstacles to hinder you on your perilous path. Today or tomorrow, the world will know of your valour and bow down to honour you. You were able to hold the Mughal army at bay. They had a vast army, hundreds of thousands of men and beasts, but for eight years, they could do nothing to the Swaraj. Had Aurangzeb captured and ravaged the territory with weapons like the Jizya tax, the Maharashtra, made pious by Tukaram and Ramdas, would have wept in sorrow. But you never allowed that.'

Sambhaji rested his head on Shivaji Raje.

'Shambhu, my dear valiant son! You have challenged the Mughal might. Earlier, a mere message from Delhi was enough to send shivers down the

spines of the kings in the Deccan, be it the Qutbshahi or the Adilshahi dynasty. We were forced to make a trip to Agra ourselves, to meet the Emperor. I had to suffer the ignominious treaty of Purandar. But you managed to stem the tide. The brute force of the Mughals was ineffective when it clashed against you and your men. History will have to search for another example where someone has fought with such limited resources while being ravaged by the forces of nature against such a mighty army. No wonder Tukaram has written in your praise:

> *"One is blessed to have a son like Sambhaji*
> *Who raises his flag in all the three worlds."'*

Sambhaji was overwhelmed hearing his father's words. He had no eyes but he could feel his father's presence.

'Shambhu, Shivaji may have taught the Marathas how to live their lives but you have taught the ryots the value of loyalty to the soil and to their religion. I will tell the ryots not to forget Sambhaji's sacrifice while celebrating Shivaji's valour. Long back, I had sent Balaji Chitnis to Rajasthan to trace our lineage back to the Sisodiya dynasty. But Shambhu, after you, valiant men from other parts will be clamouring and vying with each other to find a link to you!'

Sambhaji cried, 'Abasaheb, your words have purified me. I am eager to embrace death now! If my death can wake Maharashra, and make the ryots pick up their spears and dig a grave for Aurangzeb here in the Deccan, I will consider such a death blessed.'

18

The chirping of the birds from the river bank could be heard. The cool morning breeze was strong now. Raje could see only darkness with his blinded eyes. The only way to sense day or night now was through the sounds and movements around him. Aurangzeb had still not cut off Sambhaji's tongue in the hope that one day he would beg for his life. Sambhaji said softly, 'Kaviraj!'

Kavi Kalash's ears were alert although he could not speak. He had lost his eyes long back. Sambhaji recalled that Kavi Kalash could not respond to his words. He moved slowly towards him and held his hand. He said, 'A man's life is ephemeral, like a bubble on the surface of water. Why should one feel sad? I am lucky that I met my Abasaheb last night. I feel blessed. I am ready to face Death now.'

Kaviraj moved forward and placed Raje's hand on his cheek. Sambhaji continued, 'Death is an adamant guest. He has been at our door for a long time. But I am not worried now. I am ready to welcome him anytime. I have just one wish which remains unfulfilled. If only I could have buried Aurangzeb's head at the Chittadarwaza, I would have smiled in death's embrace. The Portuguese viceroy had to run away in his boat. The Siddi at Janjira had to hide in his fort like a scared mouse. We did not allow the Mughals to touch even one of our forts. If I had embraced death on the battlefield I would have felt blessed. But I feel sad when it comes silently, like a frightened thief.'

That afternoon they heard loud footsteps. Sambhaji felt that death itself was visiting him. The footsteps stopped at the door. Then he heard Kaviraj struggling. It seemed that the messenger of death had caught Kaviraj. Sambhaji could not see but his entire body could feel the messenger's presence, and he shouted, 'Wait! Come here!'

Such was the tone of command in his voice, even death had to stop. Sambhaji moved towards Kalash and embraced him, wailing loudly, 'Kaviraj!' They hugged each other. Kavi could not speak. His body struggled to convey his emotions. It was a tragic sight. Even the dying Jataayu, with his feathers clipped, would not have suffered so much!

Shambhu Raje asked, 'Kaviraj, are you going away? And that too, before me? How lucky you are!'

Kaviraj's body was trembling. His tongue may have been cut but his whole body, even his breath, tried to speak. 'Yes, Rajan, I am indeed lucky. This is my chance to reach the doors of heaven first, to welcome you there with flowers. Your feet must be tired. The soft flowers will give them some rest.'

But even Raje's affectionate embrace was not to last for long. Death dragged him away, to the banks of the river.

That afternoon, Aurangzeb gave the order to tear Kavi Kalash's limbs apart, one by one. All the torture they practised on his body was a kind of preparation for what they would do to Sambhaji's body later. They threw the bloodied, dismembered body on the banks of the Bhima. The camp, spread across fifteen miles, was frozen in silence. The news of the death of

Kavi Kalash soon spread. The Maratha water-bearers, guards and servants sobbed quietly. Just ten years after the death of Shivaji Raje, they had witnessed another, more terrible tragedy.

The camp had a gallows to hang royal criminals but the Badshah had decided not to take Kaviraj or Shambhu Raje there. He had said many times that Sambha and Kalash were merely ordinary criminals and there was no need to hang them. As a result, Kaviraj's body lay in pieces upon the rocks on the banks of the river Bhima.

That evening news spread that the Alamgir himself wanted to witness the punishment being meted out to Sambhaji. When Asad Khan heard of it, he confronted Aurangzeb, 'Jahanpanah, you have yourself proclaimed that Sambha is but an ordinary criminal. Why should you honour him with your presence then?'

The Badshah did not react. His palanquin moved on towards the river bank.

19

The evening sun was about to sink behind the horizon. There was silence everywhere. A red-wattled lapwing suddenly shrieked and flew over the river. Sambhaji stood in shackles on the bank. His skin, despite a myriad of cuts, wounds and bruises, glowed in the evening sun. He could not see but he stood straight, his head held high.

It was getting dark now. Lanterns and torches lit the camp at various places. In the light of the torches, standing on the brink of death, Sambhaji's face shone with a strange radiance. Aurangzeb stepped forward slowly. Five men stood near the prisoner, each holding in their hands a small yet extremely sharp jamdaad and an axe. As soon as the Badshah glanced at them, two men stepped forward. As was customary, they began putting a hood over Sambhaji's head.

Aurangzeb shouted, 'You fools! He is blind. Where is the need for that hood?'

They threw away the hood. Aurangzeb stood near the pole to which Sambhaji was tied. He looked at his prisoner with a mixture of arrogance and glee. This was the man who had forced him to remove his crown. He had made Aurangzeb roam the Deccan like a madman, bearing insults and failures. At long last, the adamant traitor was in his clutches.

Aurangzeb said to Sambhaji, 'Sambha, you sinner! You troubled me ten times more than your father did. You didn't agree to a single wish of mine. I did not cut off your tongue, hoping to hear words of penitence from you. But your arrogant legs refuse to shiver with fear. Your queen continues to rule from Raigad. She does not come running here with the keys to the forts and begging for your life. Like the Sahyadris, the two of you are adamant and unyielding. Tell me, why should I keep you alive anymore?'

Sambhaji stood very still. He was beyond fear now, of death or anything else. Prison, the torture, the insults—it all seemed trivial now. At this moment, all he did was to pray to Jagadamba, Jagadeeshwar and Shivaji Raje.

The Badshah said, literally whispering into his ears, 'Sambha, you son of a kafir! You have tormented me for eight years. So what is wrong with my wish to praise you for your valour, and keep you a prisoner for life? I am giving you one more chance. Tell me where your treasures are hidden and give me the names of the traitors!'

The Badshah's words had no effect on Sambhaji. Aurangzeb said, 'It was with Allah's blessings that you were caught by one of my sardars who came from the Deccan. Otherwise, you are like a free bird of the jungle, like the wind in the forest—impossible to catch. I will not make the mistake of letting you go alive. If I do that, you will surely find a way to destroy me. That is something you know and I know too!'

Aurangzeb turned to look at the men holding the jamdaads and axes. The sharp edges of the weapons glinted in the rays of the dying sun. Raje mumbled 'Jagadamba, Jagadamba' in a soft voice. Memories flashed by. The sea waves … he had learnt to swim sitting on his father's shoulders … the nine-year-old boy who had stood glaring at the Mughal Emperor in the Agra court … the young Yesu at Shringarpur … hundreds of his men who had sacrificed their lives to protect the Swaraj … the people and animals who had died in the famine, yet struggled to live till their last breath … the great war they had waged for eight long years … Sambhaji recalled each and every moment of his life.

The Badshah growled once more. He dismissed the soldiers holding the weapons and gestured to a group of men who wore iron claws. At his glance, the men came forward. Two of them approached Sambhaji. One of them stood behind him, the other facing him. From the nape of his neck to the base of his spine and from his throat to his stomach, the men ripped his skin with their claws as the trumpets and horns started blowing. The men shouted 'Deen, Deen!' Skin peeled off Sambhaji's back, neck, chest and stomach. His whole body was a bloodied mess.

But Sambhaji did not allow his voice to be heard by anyone present. He did not scream or shout. Clenching his teeth, he bore the intense and almost unbearable pain. His body, now red with blood, trembled from head to toe. Like the milk which pools at the base of the Shiva Linga during worship, his blood gathered at his feet. Aurangzeb laughed hysterically, seeing Sambhaji's body now peeled the way a butcher skins a goat.

After the two men had finished their job, Aurangzeb gave the signal to the men holding the weapons. The men shivered for a moment. But they knew they had no choice but to carry out the orders of the Badshah. One of them aimed his axe at Sambhaji's neck while the other pierced his back. Soon Sambhaji was decapitated.

The khojas presented his head to the Badshah on a tray. Lifting it with his hands, while warm blood flowed down his arms and stained his beard, Aurangzeb smiled. He recalled how he had similarly held his brother Dara's head many years back.

Aurangzeb said, handing the head to Asad Khan, 'Impale this head on a spear and take it around the villages of the Deccan. Let them know that as long as Aurangzeb is alive, another Sambha will not dare to be born.'

Aurangzeb glanced at the men once more. They now attacked Sambhaji's body, cutting it into pieces. The Badshah ordered the executioners to throw the dismembered body away. Some of the pieces fell in the river, some on the rocky banks. For a moment it seemed that the Bhima shivered with grief. The distant Sahyadri seemed to be hiding its face in the all-enveloping darkness.

Aurangzeb felt that he had achieved an almost impossible task. He had finally eliminated his arch enemy—the one who had tortured him for years on end. He had made lakhs of his men suffer in the Deccan, on the battlefield and outside it, many thousands dying of plague and hunger.

A tired Aurangzeb stood at the banks of the Bhima, looking at the flowing waters. He signalled to his men to start the celebrations. A hundred horns and trumpets blew, announcing the death of Sambhaji and the victory of the Emperor. The camp danced with joy, singing, 'Sambha is dead!' It was the darkest new moon night of the year.

The Emperor looked into the waters, not sure of what he was seeing. Fear gripped him at times. He would peer into the river again and again to be sure Sambhaji was not standing there, alive and whole. But the celebrations were in full swing. There was no place for any doubt now. Sambha was finally gone. The son of the kafir was dead!

The Badshah laughed aloud. What he had achieved was almost unbelievable! But for the first time, victory frightened him. He was restless. If Sambha was really dead, who was he to fight against now?

'Badshah Salamat ... let us go!' The shouts of his men broke his reverie. Shahbuddin Khan, Ruhullah Khan, and many other sardars were rushing towards the river. They were eager to congratulate their Lord and master. 'Hazrat, the entire camp is waiting to congratulate you.'

'The Maratha zamindars and watandars are all waiting for you. Meet them,' Hasan Ali Khan requested.

'Why should I meet those Marathas? They are greedy dogs who have only come here for their share.'

'But Jahanpanah ...'

'Don't bother about those fools. Even if we chase them out today, they will come back like dogs tomorrow, licking my feet.'

'Hazrat, the soldiers have one more request. They have not seen you wearing your crown for years now. You had taken an oath that you would not wear it again till you kill Sambha. It has been five years. We have a new crown, specially made for you and studded with jewels and diamonds, which cost nearly half a crore hons.'

'What is the need for all this?' Aurangzeb asked, a little irritated.

'To celebrate your daring act. You have finished off a sinner, an enemy. It is a great achievement!'

Aurangzeb was fed up of the praise he was receiving. He was quiet for a few moments. Should he tell the truth? Then, indifferent to the presence of the others, he let the tears flow down his cheeks into his white beard. He said, his voice low and sad, 'You fools! What are you celebrating? The killer is dead and the one who died has become immortal!'

20

The following day, villages around the banks of the Bhima wore a sad, desolate look. A strange and fearful silence enveloped them. The Mughal camp slept through the day, dozing off after having celebrated the previous night with dance and music, which was normally not allowed by the Badshah.

In the village of Vadu, a few people had heard of Sambhaji's cruel murder. It was one of the villages which had been destroyed by the Mughal troops. They had looted the homes of the ryots and burnt their fields. A few men of Vadu had launched a daring attack on the Mughal troops, thus angering Ruhullah Khan who sent his men to the village. The soldiers dragged men and women from their homes and beat them black and blue. Many suffered grievous injuries, but they had no one to complain to. They lay in their homes, nursing their wounds.

It was afternoon. A washerman's wife, Jana, took a load of clothes from the village headman Damaji Patil's house and walked towards the river bank. Jana stood near the confluence of Indrayani and Bhima. She could see the fires of the Mughal camp on the other side. She had asked her father once to get her married to someone in Pachad. 'Why so far away?' he asked. She answered, 'Well, one day I may get a chance to wash Sambhaji and Shivaji's clothes. And I would feel blessed.'

But Jana was destined to stay in Vadu. As she washed the clothes that afternoon, one of the village goatherds was sitting near the bank. She was rinsing a dhoti when she noticed a strange rope-like thing was stuck to it. Jana said disgustedly, 'Looks like some dead animal.'

The goatherd said, 'Jana, it is not the intestine of an animal. It belongs to a human being …'

'What?'

'Don't you know? Last night, the Badshah killed Shivaji's son Shambhu Raje on the banks of the Bhima. He butchered him like an animal. They threw the pieces in the water. Don't touch it! The orders are strict.'

Jana turned and ran back to the village, stopping only at the gates of the Patil's house. Seeing her flushed face, the Patil's wife asked, 'What happened?'

'I am surprised how our men sitting here and twirling their moustaches do not feel ashamed that pieces of Shambhu Raje's body are floating in the river there.'The news spread through the village like wildfire. No one knew what to do. The villagers waited for Damaji Patil to return that evening. worried and teary-eyed.

'Shivaji Maharaj and his son have done so much for us. We cannot allow this!'

Damaji Patil said, 'What to do? We are surrounded by nearly three lakh Mughal soldiers. Our men and boys were beaten up badly by them. The firmaan is that no one should touch the body.'

It was decided that it was best to lie low. But Jana the washerwoman could not sleep. She broached the topic again that night while serving dinner at the Patil's house. The Patil was scared of the Mughals and did not know what to do.

Jana went to the village square and engaged the men there.

She suggested, 'If we gather Shambhu Raje's body and burn it here, what is the worst that can happen? At the most they will burn our village. It is our tradition to burn a body left unattended. And this is none other than Shivaji's son. Are our men going to sit here, wearing bangles like women and doing nothing?'

The men were roused now. They all clamoured to go to the river bank. It was pitch dark outside. Damaji Patil threatned them, 'You will regret this when the Badshah destroys your homes.'

But even his wife took Jana's side, saying, 'Are we cruel and ungrateful enough to allow Sambhaji's body to be eaten by vultures? Why were we born at all if we cannot even do this? You can sit here taking care of the village and the house. We are going!'

The women marched ahead. The men had no choice but to follow them. The Mughal camp was silent. The soldiers had celebrated till they were weary to the bone and were sleeping like the dead. The villagers picked up every piece of Sambhaji's body that they could find.

Then they came back to the village. The boys ran to collect whatever wood they could get their hands on. The preparations for the funeral began. There was only one question yet to be resolved: where were they to light the pyre?

Damaji Patil was willing to offer a plot of land but it was a mile away. Then Govind the sweeper said, 'Here, you can use my land. Burn Sambhaji's body there. The rest of you till the soil. You need your land. We are sweepers, and we have no need for any land. If tomorrow the Badshah's men come after us, we can go away.'

It was important to carry out the last rites very quickly. They were afraid that they may be attacked at any moment if the Mughals came to know what they were doing. The local priest had made the necessary arrangements. Soon, the pyre was burning. The flames burned tall and the smoke reached the sky.

The villagers could not hold their tears back now. The womenfolk wailed loudly, hugging each other. By dawn the fire had burnt out. Taking Raje's warm ashes, the villagers came to the banks of Bhima. Soon, the ashes floated in the flowing waters.

The sky was growing bright now. Birds had started chirping. The men and women of Vadu looked at each other with pride. The satisfaction of having done a brave deed glowed on their faces. The village priest stood on the river bank, his hands folded in obeisance, and said,

'Villagers, it must be owing to your good deeds that you were blessed to have Sambhaji with you in his final moments. The Indrayani flows here. It was the Indrayani which resurrected Tukaram's Abhangs without any damage. Who knows, one day we may see Sambhaji resurrected here! It has to happen … if not today, a few years or centuries later. Truth can never be buried forever. When people come to know the truth, this Vadu will be a holy place, just as Alandi or Dehu. The whole world will rush here for a glimpse of the man who sacrificed his life to protect his country, his religion and his land, the king who died a hero's death!'

Also by

VISHWAS PATIL

MAHANAYAK

SUBHAS CHANDRA BOSE

TRANSLATED FROM THE MARATHI BY

KEERTI RAMACHANDRA

Pages: 636   Price: ₹799

This iconic Marathi novel by Vishwas Patil brings originality and new ideas to the most storied of lives—Subhas Chandra Bose. Possibly the most enigmatic figure in the history of India's freedom struggle, Bose's ideological differences with the two stalwarts of the Independence movement, Gandhi and Nehru, split the Congress down the middle. And yet he held them in high esteem, just as they admired him. While Bose asserted the independence of his own values even as he sought help from the Axis powers—Nazi Germany, Italy and later Japan—during World War II, for the cause of a free India, it was seen as treasonous and dangerous by many.

Through meticulous research, Marathi writer Vishwas Patil recreates the life of a man who was twice elected president of the Congress, and quit to follow his own vision, forming the Indian National Army. His defiant nationalism provoked anger and distrust. *Mahanayak* traces Netaji's steps from India to Germany, Italy, Singapore, Japan and Burma, to paint a complex portrait of a man of immense strengths and fatal failings. Rich with details drawn from the colossal canvas of the Indian revolution, this is an immersive historical novel that reads like a fast-paced thriller.

First published in Marathi in 1998, the novel has remained a consistent bestseller, and has been translated into fourteen Indian and foreign languages.

PENTAGON PRESS

COMMITTED TO SERVE THE ARMED FORCES

MAOIST THREAT IN INDIA

A Red Corridor from Nepal to Tamil Nadu

Dr. B.P. Saha

PENTAGON PRESS

Maoist Threat in India: A Red Corridor from Nepal to Tamil Nadu
Dr. B.P. Saha

ISBN 978-81-8274-920-7

First Published in 2017

Published by
PENTAGON PRESS
206, Peacock Lane, Shahpur Jat
New Delhi-110049
Phones: 011-64706243, 26491568
Telefax: 011-26490600
email: rajan@pentagonpress.in
website: www.pentagonpress.in

Printed at Avantika Printers Private Limited.

Dedicated

to

All my fellow countrymen

who

Made supreme sacrifices

to

Combat terrorism

Contents

Nexus between the PW and the LTTE, link with foreign out-fits, manufacture of weapons and success of the Greyhounds Maoists were chased out, built new hide outs in Dandakarnaya, Bastar region. Comparative peace prevails in AP. Activities of the Maoists in UP and Karnataka states briefly discussed.

Gadchiroli, Maharastra, a liberated zone. Maoists run Janata sarkar, hold kangaroo courts, punish people arbitrarily. Repeated attack and ambush against the cops, low morale of the police. Maoists from Nepal participated in violence, heavy casualty of the cops. Fair sex Maoists in key position in the district. Police made inroads in inaccessible areas. Suffering of the Maoists for want of supply, health care, treatment for the wounded comrades. Tribal communities, the main supporters of the Maoists. Reckless extortion, villagers pay Rs.14 crores annually. Terrain, poverty and poor development helping the Maoists' growth. State's long term policy essential for peace and stability.

Female Maoists highly motivated, disciplined, dependable and hardly quit the out-fit. Their strength varies from 18 to 20 percent, possess good fighting spirit, distinguish them in guerrilla squads, leadership and deadly offensives. Represent in many committees, lead squads ably. Senior leaders prefer enlistment of fair sex, widely acceptable to comrades. In Chhattisgarh, "Chetna Natya Mandali", a cultural wing of the Maoists take leading role to recruit fair sex, generally from the tribal community. Rapid growth of the fair sex cadre. Narmada, leading the Gadchiroli unit, distributed key posts to the fellow fair sex comrades. Female Maoists attacked and killed 28 Congress leaders and activists in Sukuma district, displayed animal fury, treated the dead barbarously. Brief account of aggressive activities of the female Maoists in Jharkhand, Odisha, West Bengal. Many surrendered seeking family life.

Used for luring the youths to join the Maoist cadre, forced to be a bed partner for the under ground male Maoists, have to submit for sex on gun point, marry a comrade against her wish. Many suffer from filthy venereal diseases. Brutal assault, harsh treatment, threat to life to the hapless weaker sex Maoists and their agonies. Complaint for sexual abuses to seniors not heeded.

Contributions and sacrifices of the para military forces.

CRPF the lead force for the internal security duties. Hazardous, painstaking duties and supreme sacrifices. Its strategy to fight the Maoists. Welfare for the people in reclaimed territory. Pleaded hard for continuation of the joint operation in W B.

Preface

My venture to write this book needs explanation. During my stint in Koraput district, Odisha in 1967-68, the Naxal movement on the border of Odisha and Andhra Pradesh had been taking shape. I studied its growing threat to the law and order problem and watched sentiment of the poor and deprived people, especially, the tribal community, the administration's insouciance from detached angle. Later, in West Bengal, from 1971 to 1975, I noticed its growing influence and impact on the students, youths, a group of middle class educated persons, and the so called intellectuals and eventually, I saw its declining trend. I was curious to know why a large number of bright students joined the movement, keen for demolishing the present social and political order, stained their palms with human blood and ready for supreme sacrifice. Secondly, it was equally baffling as the victims of the extremists' target were persons from the lower strata of the society, a daily labourer, a wage earner, police constables, so called jodders (land owner), owning a small piece of land, cultivate for livelihood. In fact, why and how the capitalists, bourgeoisie, exploiters of the poor and have-not, had escaped the ultras' notice and remained beyond their reach.

Comrade Charu Mazumdar, was a dedicated leader and a follower of the Communist Party of India (Marxist), in the past. His brain child, the Naxal movement in India, originated in Naxalbari, a remote village in Darjeeling district, West Bengal in 1967, broadly, adhering to the Mao's Red book, Lenin's The State and Revolution and the Karl Marx's Manifesto. His followers and whiz-kids were either expelled from the CPI or drop-outs. Charu strictly followed the Chinese line which was disliked by many of his lieutenants. Many hard core comrades deserted him, established independent out-fits and selected separate areas of operation. Comrade Kanu Sanyal founded CPI (Marxist and Leninist) in Kolkata. In Bihar, Maoist Communist Centre (MCC), CPI ML (Liberation), Indian People's Front (IPF) and several small groups were founded. Spectre of split in the out-fit was a fatal blow to Charu and the growth of the out-fit. Charu imagined that the armed struggle, annihilation of the class enemy one by one and the revolutionary army would liberate the rural areas and thereafter encircle the towns and cities. He declared that the leadership of the revolutionary movement would be subordinate to the Chinese Community party.

Extremists' movement started in Andhra Pradesh independently having no link with Charu or with the Naxals of West Bengal. After collapse of Srikakulam uprising, splinter groups busied themselves in internal squabbles. Finally, a new out-fit, CPI (ML) People's War was established on 22, April, 1980. Its growth in the state and the MCC's influence in Bihar led to frienzed conflicts. People's War made substantial in-road in tribal belt of West Bengal, better known as "Jana Juddah" right from 1995. However, burying their differences People's War and MCC merged together and formed the CPI (Maoist).in September 2004. The People's War mooted the idea of the Compact Revolutionary Zone (CRZ) or the Red Corridor, connecting Nepal to Tamilnadu.

Birth of the CPI (Maoist) after merger enhanced strength of the new out-fit and posed a gigantic threat to the nation's safety and security. With renewed zeal and vigour it persuaded the Maoist movement aiming at destroying the class enemy, the existing social and political order, establish the classless society and the People's Government.

Terrorism is not directly connected with the Naxal or Maoist movement. In India in every second day, a cop dies fighting terror. Unlike the trans-border terrorism or the terrorist active in J&K, the Maoists are not secessionists. They are neither jihadis or religious fanatics nor demanding a separate or independent territory. In fact, after the merger the complexion of the Maoist movement has undergone a sea change. It is no longer a police or law and order problem, rather it is more a socio-economic and political problem backed by a specific ideology and political object. Admittedly, Maoists have gained trust and confidence of the rural mass, especially, the tribal communities, inspired them to get involved or participate in Maoist movement. Importantly, ultras ensure welfare of the poor, down trodden and discomfited rural populace, protect them from cruel hand of the power brokers, money lenders, middle men, exploiters and unscrupulous public servants. The oppressed rural mass are inclined to believe that the Maoists are the liberators and saviour of the poor and deprived people and capable of removing discrimination, inequality, and build the classless society, and the People's government.

Economic growth has hardly reached the rural areas. People abysmally suffer from immeasurable poverty, pangs of unemployment, archaic education, porous health care, deficient communication etc. None responds to their grievances, come forward to salvage them from harassment and malaises. Political leaders on the eve of election, make lofty promises for removing ordeals and improving their fortune.

But they disappear from the scene once election is concluded. Regrettably, under development, negligible economic growth, appalling denial, social disparity and the state's ambivalence to improve their lot has enhanced their miseries. Therefore, the problem needs to be viewed from wider perspective and fast changing social and political scenario.

Fast growth of the Maoists in seven states, Andhra Pradesh, Chhattisgarh, Maharastra, Jharkhand, Odisha, Bihar and West Bengal, and in small areas of Uttar Pradesh and Karnataka, escalated violence, modified modus operandi for deadly attacks, use of sophisticated weaponry, land mines, impregnable defence, higher standard of training, firm control on extended turf where Maoist writs run etc have alarmed the union and the Maoist ridden state governments. Again, ultras are no longer sticking to hit and run tactics, instead, they attack or ambush the security forces in large number, use automatic weapons, land mines, crafty skill, expertise in assembling and planting land mines, hitting the targets with precision. They manufacture fire arms, take part in protracted and obstinate gun battles. Undeniably, a proxy war is waged and its end is obscure.

Steady growth of the Maoist cadres, control over approximately 40 thousand Sr Km over the territory of seven states and the aim at building the Red corridor is alarming. Strength of the cadres shot up to about fifty thousands including fifteen thousands combatants and highly motivated guerrilla squads. The union government took the problem casually, followed the policy of masterly inactivity. The then union Home Minister Sivraj Patil was unable to visualize the burgeoning threat, suffered from complacency and stated,"Naxal activities is confined to only two percent of the country's 650000 villages." Evidently, he thought that the problem was too puny to react and greater attention was not called for. However, as events moved apace it took gargantuan shape and put the union and state governments before a formidable challenge. His successor admitted government's knee jerk action or complacency and stated before the floor of the Rajya Sabha,"For many years we did not properly assess the threat posed by the Left Wing Extremists. We underestimated the challenge and in the meanwhile, Naxalites extended their influence."

Resources and man power of the ultras during the last two decades have increased leaps and bounds. They have developed contact with the LTTE, learnt intricacies of assembling land mines, use of automatic weapons, successfully motivated youths, boys and girls to join the cadres, enriched the war chest, made recruitment drive purposeful. The "Bal Sena" is raised with minors, recruited either on payment of peltry sum or by coercive means. Importantly, fair sexes join the out-fit in large number. They are equally good and effective in leadership, surprise attacks, laying ambushes, and in sanguinary guerrilla onslaughts. Of late, the top brass of the Maoists prefer female Maoists to males as they are good in combats, faithful to the out-fit, obedient, amenable to rigor of discipline and seldam desert or quit the cadre.

Unprecedented growth, penetration into several states, unabated and frightful violence, gruesome killing, macabre festival of death of innocent persons are likely to topsyturvy the country's safety, security, social and human values. As a matter of fact, under estimation of the Maoists' strength and striking power has allowed the hydra-headed outlaws to circumvent the long arm of the law and indulge in atrocity and henious crime. The politburo of the out-fit has been taking important decisions, chalking out strategy, plans etc from its H Q, at Ahujhmad, meaning unknown forest, established in a remote and inaccessible wood in Baster region, Chhattisgarh. In the Maoist dominated areas, semblance of administration is virtually absent. There, writs of the Maoists loom large. They decide local disputes, hold kangaroo courts, inflict punishments including death sentence after mockery of trial.

The book is divided in ten chapters. In the first chapter introduction on the Maoist movement and its quick penetration into several states have been briefly discussed. In the second chapter various facets of the Maoist movement, reaction of political parties, the union government's co-ordinated plan, programmes and financial commitments to assist the Maoist ridden states have been high-lighted. From third to seventh chapters problems of the Maoist –stricken states, up-hill task to combat the proxy war and neutralize the pitiless ultras, and the states' painstaking efforts with limited resources to uphold the rule of law etc have been brought to fore. In West Bengal, chapter (seventh chapter), Maoist terror gained extra ordinary momentum in three districts right from the abortive attack on the Chief Minister in November 2008 and the state police's excesses and indiscreet actions have been unfolded. In fact, the police went berserk on the pretext of exposing the culprits. Ironically, it alienated the oppressed villagers and gave excellent opportunity to the Maoists to bring the aggrieved rural mass in their fold and accelerate the Maoist movement. The Left Front government under leadership of the CPM was lukewarm and indecisive to tackle the movement and asserted that the CPM and the government will solve the problem politically. However, attempt on the CM's life and escalated violence forced him to deploy para military forces after lingering reluctance. Indeed, West Bengal carries a special bearing in handling Maoist violence. Rivalry and ill-feeling between the CPM cadres and the Maoists soon reached the arid zone of acrimony. In fact, bloody confrontations and killing from both sides, hiring of professional desperadoes by the CPM called "harmad Bahini"from outside the state to counter the blood thirsty ultras, massacre at village Netai by the harmads, exodus of the CPM cadres from jungle mahal, nexus between the Maoists and Trinamul Congress on the eve of the election of the state Legislative Assembly, with a view to ousting the CPM government, arrests, deaths and surrender of several front line male and female Maoists etc are unflinching testimony analysed and focused dispassionately.

In chapter eight, the Maoist movement is penned clubbing Andhra Pradesh, Maharastra and UP together for keeping the canvas insouciant and within control. Secondly, in Andhra Pradesh, numerous events, developments and indomitable political will to wipe out the extremist menace deserve exhaustive analysis. Hence, I intend to write the second volume exclusively for Andhara Pradesh in near future. In ninth chapter, role of the fair sex Maoists to strengthen the Maoist movement, their active participation in combats, gun battle, leadership vis-à-vis the male Maoists, abuse of female Maoists by fellow male comrades etc have been elaborately depicted. Perhaps, their envious contribution to make the movement strong and viable has escaped the notice of the impartial critics, observers and scholars. In this respect, it is a significant addition to the volume which admittedly failed to get accommodated even in any casual literature. Unfortunately, facile pen of the journalists and authors have not endorsed consummate recognition to their selfless services and sacrifices to make the Red movement memorable. Contribution of the para military forces, their supreme sacrifices, especially of the CRPF and BSF to contain and curb the Red movement have hardly been recognized and lauded. Frankly speaking, relying on experience, I am candid that arduous and hazardous duties performed by them in unconducive terrain and their supreme sacrifices in combating the Red terror and the unknown enemy is unique in post independence era.

Success of the security forces, reclaim of the turf, retreat of the ultras was a sigh of relief for the peace loving people. Indeed, rule of law in jungle mahal, West Bengal, limped back, developmental works received fresh impetus. Meanwhile, influence and popularity of the Maoists among the rural mass, especially, among the tribal community indicated a sign of precipitious decline. The rural populace is no longer willing to be carried away by hollow promises and nuances of the Maoist jargon. In fact, friends and sympathizers of the past are no longer willing to provide shelter, food and information on movement of the security forces. They are tired of violence, death shrouds, savagery, repugnance to human life, and hoot and honk of the merciless Maoists.Indeed, cynical subversion of halcyon ambience, tranquillity, stability and apotheosis of mankind have reprehensibly dismayed them. Unfortunately, friendliness and spirit of co-operation gradually turned to hostility. Instances are many that frustrated villagers assaulted the ultras, chased them away and made the villages out of bound. In Jharkhand, a Maoist who raped a weaker sex was burnt alive by the miffed villagers. Many Maoist leaders want urban comfort, diverted or misappropriated fund for personal use, purchased land, bunglows, flats and sent wards to foreign country for higher education. Needless to add, these are unflinching testimony of degeneration already set in.

In Maoist violence ridden states unrest and blood shed have been reduced considerably. Lately, it is now confined to a few pockets. Even, Chhattisgarh, the epi-centre of the Maoist violence has recorded a marked decline. In Andhra Pradesh, thanks to the Greyhounds, state police and the government's determination to stamp out terrorism and free hand given to the police and administration have shown a spectacular result. Admittedly, credit goes to the dynamic police leadership, the para military forces, particularly the CRPF and the BSF and the union and state governments' ungrudging help and allocation of fund to fight the proxy war. In chapter ten, excess of the police in curbing Naxal movement in early stage in West Bengal, sign of decay of the Maoist movement, want of able leadership, threat perception, the people's disillusion, dislike for violence, fear for a new regime perpetrated by violence and bloodshed, link with foreign countries, unethical activities in the garb of revolution etc have been high lighted. Importantly, Maoists of West Bengal failing to resuscitate the people's support admitted their mistakes. They admitted that reckless killing in many cases was wrong, sought and have invited constructive suggestion and advice from rhe people for future guidance.

In pursuit of unearthing the truth and making the volume comprehensive I have visited Bokaro, Ranchi, visited a few villages of Jharkhand, interacted with the top cops, senior administrative officials handling Maoist problem, visited Odisha and selected places of Chhattisgarh. I visited Lalgarh, Dalilpur, Goaltore, Pirakata, Netai and several villages in and around Lalgarh, (West Medinapur district), the hot bed of the Maoists, Jhargram, interacted with many, victims of the police's torture and fabricated cases. I conversed with many Maoist leaders and activists, elicited their views, enjoyed their hospitality right in remote rural areas where their writs ran. I developed rapport with many leaders of the PCAPA, a frontal organization of the Maoists. I visited Netai village near Lalgarh on, the fourth day after the savage massacre unleashed by the CPM hired goons and noticed ramnents of atrocity and immeasureable agony of the family members of four house wives and five males of the village, killed by the "harmad bahini."

I interviewed Comrade Chhatradhar Mahato, one of the front line Maoist leaders, and Prasun Chatterjee, an ideologue of the Maoists inside the district jail. Their feeling was manifestly anti Trinamul Congress government which is obviously shared by the Maoists. I have taken it a research project, collected materials following the dictum of fastidious fondness of accuracy and in that goal written the book after spot visits, scanning evidence exhaustively, interacting with demoralized villagers, several Maoist leaders and hard core activists. Repeated visits to jungle mahal, West Bengal, interaction with the supporters, sympathizers of the Maoists, and cross section of the people have given me clear and deeper insight into the problem, sentiment of the people and the Maoist activities. The Maoists in West Bengal pulled much weight to topple the Left Front government led by the CPM. They wanted Trinamul Congress in power. Once the TMC formed the government, their expectation from the Trinamul Congress government knew no bound. Soon the Maoists were disillusioned and realized their mistake in backing a wrong horse. The new government's indifference to release the Maoists languishing in jail, and withdrawal of the criminal cases pending against them was a rude shock to them. They were upset, critical and wanted to retaliate. But arrests and deaths of several leaders, especially, Kishanji, the dramatis personae, and festival of surrenders by several hard core ultras demoralized them. In absence of a dynamic leader in place of Kishanj to resuscitate sagging morale of the rank and file, the leaderless Maoists in West Bengal were pushed to limbo.

In conclusion, in removing cobweb and unearthing truth I have scrupulously followed the punctilious path of truth totally free from prejudice. My painstaking endeavour will be adequately compensated if the readers find it interesting, meaningful and pragmatic.

Anandamath, **Dr. B.P. Saha**
Salt Lake, Kolkata

Abbreviations

ABVP	Akhil Bharat Vidarthy Parishad
APCLC	Andhra Pradesh Civil Liberties Committees
AP	Andhra Pradesh
Bn	Battalion
BSF	Border Secirity Force
CBI	Central Bureau of Investigation
CIF	Counter Insurgency Force
CISF	Central Industrial Security Force
Cobra	Combat Battalion for Resolute Action
CrPC	Criminal Procedure Code
CRPF	Central Reserve Police Force
EFR	Eastern Frontier Rifles (West Bengal)
Greyhounds	An armed police battalion (Andhra Pradesh)
GSD	Gramin Surakha Dal
Harmad Bahini	Goons hired by the CPM in West Bengal to counter Maoists
IAP	Integrated Action Plan
INSAS	A semi automatic assault rifle
IPKF	Indian Peace Keeping Force
IPC	Indian Penal Code
ITBP	Indo Tibetian Border Police
Jungle Mahal	Three districts West Medinapur, Bankura and Puralia of West Bengal, together called jungle mahal

JMM	Jharkhand Mukti Morcha
JMUBM	Jungle Mahal Unnayan Birodhi Pratirodh Manch
MPV	Mine Proof Vehicle
MHA	Ministry of Home Affairs, Govt of India
NHRC	National Human Rights Commission
NIA	National Investigation Agency
OSSF	Orissa Special Security Force
PCAPA	People's Committee Against Police Atrocity
PLFI	People's Liberation Front of India
PLGA	People's Liberation Guerrilla Army
PSBJM	Police Santras Birodhi Janasadharan Manch
PS	Police Station
PW	CPI (ML) Peoples War
SP	Superintendent of Police
SPO	Special Police Officer
SKGM	Sidhu Kanu Gana Militia
SSB	Sashastra Seema Bal
TD	Telegu Desam Party (Andhra Pradesh)
TRS	Telegu Rashtia Samity
TMC	Trinamool Congress Party
UHM	Union Home Ministry
UPA	United Progressive Alliance

Chapter One

Introduction

Terror or terrorism is synonymous with extreme fear and an organised system of intimidation. People who want to achieve any goal by terror, threat, intimidation or violence may be identified as terrorists. Truth be told, terrorism is anti-peace, tranquility and public order. It wants to secure objective by unleashing panic, unrest and violence. Intellectuals and critics who have been studying its various facets opine that it is bound to decay or subdue, as violence is unacceptable in a civilised society. According to scholars, it is an instrument of the weak against the strong or stronger force. Insurgency is distinctly different from terror as it grows or prospers gaining support or goodwill of the people. The insurgents generally do not molest, outrage or kill fellow citizens. In history, Chatrapati Shivaji of Maharashtra adopted guerrilla tactics and guerrilla warfare against the Mughals. Sudden and surprise attacks, ambush, hit-and-run, attack taking opportunity of the enemy's slackness and negligence, attack in small groups, cut off their supply and communication line, keep the enemy under constant pressure etcetera are tactics taken to in order to keep the enemy under fear, perplexity and suspense. Indeed, *modus operandi* of guerrilla warfare provides rewarding dividend to the band or the outfits to keep the enemy at bay. Shivaji's jungle warfare and guerrilla operation helped him to steal a march over the mighty army of the Mughals. Shivaji enjoyed substantial support of the local populace. As his actions were patriotic and far away from terrorism, people respected and trusted him, and relied on his aggressive operations aiming at throwing away the yoke of the Islamic rule. Eminent historian Sir Jadunath Sarkar's glowing tribute that he was the last Hindu nation builder is not a credulous eulogy but credit deservingly paid to a born leader of men. On the other hand, terrorists do not care for the peoples' support or good will. They want to destroy the old social and political order and dream for a classless society and establish a new order. In that pursuit, they recklessly let loose unrest, violence, rapine and bloodshed. They believe in terror, follow the doctrine of annihilation, and punish people arbitrarily, arranging trial in the so-called peoples' court. Verdicts are often enforced with unprecedented cruelty and brutality ignoring minimum respect to human lives.

Maoists in India have borrowed the aims and philosophy of the so-called liberation movement from three important testaments. The personalities who invented the new cult are considered to be generous in ushering a pragmatic political philosophy and a unique direction to the people's movement. It created an extra ordinary sensation among the political thinkers, intellectuals and enlightened personalities who have been clamouring for a new social and political order; and for uplifting the downtrodden and deprived people. However, the followers of the new political philosophy who are better known as the Maoists codified the ideal and goal of their revolutionary movement from the writings of Karl Marx's' *Manifesto,* Lenin's *The State and Revolution* and Mao-Tse-tung's *The Red Book.* In fact, greater emphasis was given in this revolutionary guidance on the doctrine of annihilation as a tool for achieving the goal. The movement known as Naxalbari Movement or Naxalite Movement was spearheaded by late Charu Mazumder, a drop out of the Communist Party of India (CPI). It started from Naxalbari, a remote village located on the foothills of the Himalayas in Darjeeling district, West Bengal. Charu Mazumdar and his lieutenants Kanu Sanyal, Jangal Santal, Souren Bose and several others worked relentlessly to build a formidable cadre and popularise the new cult. Importantly, all of them had either left the CPI (later CPM), or were expelled from the party.

Broadly, three kinds of terrorism are generally practised by the militant outfits and the extremists in India. The first kind is secessionist terrorism, wherein the people involved want to be separated from the mainland and govern the territory independently. In other words, their aim and objective is to acquire freedom by violent means and establish a separate country under its government. For example, many Nagas of Nagaland, Mizos of Mizoram and Ulfa outfit of North-East provinces have organised and established militant outfits, and they want to strengthen separatist movements following violence and bloodshed. In Punjab, a few years back, the Khalistan movement under PS Bhindranwala had wanted to be separated from the main land and run an independent state for the Sikh community. In fact, the agitation spearheaded by Bhindranwala had a special bearing as the rebels were clandestinely helped and patronised by a hostile neighbour. In Jammu and Kashmir, the militants want independence and separation from India. Here, the separatist elements have been relying much on trans-border terrorism, and receiving men, materials and resources from the hostile neighbor, Pakistan. Again, a sizeable Kashmiris living in the valley have been secretly lending support to the militants and eager to submit and welcome serenity of Pakistan.

The result has been a valley in the grip of protracted period of unrest and violence. In J&K, militancy has gained ground, widened its dimension and taken a shape of a proxy war. It has let loose unprecedented violence and blood curdling activities.

Second type is revolutionary terrorism, which is an armed struggle to throw away a government, capture power by force and grab the reins of the government. It is based on an ideology, and in pursuance of the ideology, the extremist movement originates, progresses and takes final shape. It is a lofty ideal and aims to topple a regime and establish a government based on revolutionary principle aiming at fulfilling aspiration of the oppressed and exploited mass. Admittedly, a movement based on ideology is not devoid of meaningful objective, principle and value. True, it is relied upon or entwined with violence and bloodshed, but is often pragmatised and motivated by a greater national cause. Although it is condemned in many quarters, it is supported by sizeable progressive elements and radicals because it is for the sake of greater public and national cause, and aspiration of the people.

Maoists in India initiated the movement embracing definite ideology, political and revolutionary values. They do not want separation from the main land but want to topple the existing social and political order by force and violence. Their aim is to establish a classless society and a People's government. The Himalayan kingdom Nepal has succeeded in pulling down the kingship through revolutionary process and established a new regime under the umbrella of the Communist Party of Nepal Maoists (CPN Maoists). Significantly, in the past in India, terrorism had been embraced by a group of radicals to liberate the country from the grip of the colonial rule. It was a prolonged struggle and passed through phases of confrontations, ugly outrages and heinous crimes. Needless to say, it was purely for a national cause, based on patriotism, idealism and the object of throwing away the yoke of an alien rule. It was viewed unflinchingly as national cause, which strengthened nationalism and lauded as "militant nationalism". The secret movement received support and goodwill from patriotic and liberty-minded country men from the cross-section who sincerely desired freedom. Sacrifices of the leaders, activists and followers have been lauded in glowing terms, and added into the pages of the history of the glorious national struggle. Indeed, their exemplary sacrifices were not credulous eulogies but credit and recognition deservingly paid to the national heroes. Even today, their sacrifices are spontaneously extolled and taken as a profound spirit and example of sacrifice and patriotism.

Third type is the Jehadi terrorism, which is fundamentally based on the accolades of religious orthodoxy, bias and rigidity, aiming at establishing a regime dominated by the religionists. Jehadi movement, at present flourishing in Kashmir, is a clear testimony of a movement backed by religious faith, orthodoxy and prejudices. Importantly, it is amply manifested that Jehadi movement in Kashmir is backed and patronised by the Islamic terrorist outfits active in Pakistan-occupied Kashmir...in other words, *azad* Kashmir. The outfits have made base in Pakistan and *azad* Kashmir, indulging in cross-border terrorism and proxy wars in J&K.

Inside the country, SIMI (Students Islamic Movement of India), Lashkar-e-Taiba and Islamic terrorist groups have been clandestinely pursuing militancy. They plead for Islamic rule in South East Asia—right from Asia-Minor to Philippines. Jehadi terrorism wants to divide the country in religious and communal parts, and wants to establish an Islamic state. In J&K, Jehadi elements backed by extremists from *azad* Kashmir and Pakistan and the local militants want religiously dominated Islamic and undemocratic rule, and argue for separation from India. Admittedly, mixed terrorism in J&K has only encouraged the cult of violence.

Another category of terrorism which has not been formally identified yet may be defined as state terrorism. It may sound paradoxal, but it is no use denying that the government often allows the police and the law enforcing agencies to suppress public opinion and genuine grievances by misusing government's machinery, power and authority. On the pretext of maintaining peace and order, the police and the law enforcing agency are allowed to chastise people illegally and arbitrarily, and let loose high handedness and shameful atrocities. In fact, recent excesses committed by the police in Singur, Nandigram and Lalgarh areas in East and West Medinapur districts of West Bengal to suppress the rural mass, and tribal movements are ample testimony in support of the contention. Police, on flimsy pretext, register criminal cases against the critics and opponents of the ruling party, raid their abodes at midnight, disturb the inmates, disrupt privacy, indiscriminately arrest the inmates, bring them to the police station, assault them, forcibly secure their confession and implicate them in false cases. If members of the family protest, the police resort to rough and ready methods and harass them with various excuses. Even women and minors are not spared. In police stations, they are detained in an unauthorised manner, tortured and put to all kinds of humiliations and disgraces. On fabricated evidence and baseless charges, the arrested persons are implicated in several criminal cases and forwarded to the court, praying their remand in police custody. Several criminal cases will be instituted against individuals so that the victims are dragged to the court frequently, and thereby, they are put to enormous hardships and harassment.

Secondly, the party cadres of the ruling party and hired goons may use muscle power to tame the activists of the rival political parties as well as the critics who are trying to expose misdeeds of the government and the ruling party cadres. Sometimes, premeditated attacks on the opponents are organised at the instigation of the party cadres. They are assaulted or killed, or their houses are set on fire. Unfortunately, the police are far from impartial—often indifferent to the incident or preferring to operate on the diktats of influential leaders or the activists of the ruling party. In fact, in West Bengal, the police and the administration have lost semblance of credibility and trust of the people to a large extent. People are inclined to believe that the police are the oppressive instrument of the ruling party. They operate hand in glove with the cadre and the party and try to protect interests of the ruling party while ignoring public interest. In rural areas, the insolent cadre decides village disputes, keep the political opponents under constant fear, suppress fair public sentiment and virtually run the cadre Raj (rule). About 34 years of porous rule by the left front under the leadership of the CPM is tainted with nepotism, corruption, high-handedness and politically-controlled administration which has generated boundless dissatisfaction. Many leaders of the CPM have amassed wealth, misused the government machinery. And instead of ensuring peoples' welfare, they have promoted self interest. Over and above, uncomfortable ambience of fear and threat, especially in rural areas, have cowed down the helpless people. Indeed, draconic rule has shaken the common people not to protest or oppose the ruling party's malfeasance and anti-people activities. Indeed, peoples' voice was gagged; honest public opinion was thrown to wind. Threat, coercion and muscle power worked as the decisive tool in pursuit of the so-called honest and impartial public service. In fact, countless adversities and mal-governance dismayed the people and generated abysmal discontentment. Truly, dissatisfaction piled upon dissatisfaction awaiting a spark to detonate. Of late, mass upheaval, especially of the *adivasi* (tribal) community in Lalgarh area in West Medinapur district of West Bengal is a manifestation of an oppressive, prejudiced and partisan rule which has forced a simple, docile and an inoffensive community to take to the agitational path. Undeniably, the State government's autocratic and harsh rule has culminated in mass protest, defiance of authority, agitation and revolt. In short, in support of the above contention, adequate convincing and corroborating evidence will be discussed in relevant chapters.

Beginning of the Naxalbari, Naxal or Naxalite Movement in West Bengal

A remote and sleepy village of Darjeeling district located on the foothills of the Himalayas called Naxalbari suddenly came to limelight in 1967. Poverty-stricken village—abode of deprived peasants, daily wage earners and have-nots—was fertile ground for mass upsurge. Chill penury, deprivation, discrimination and exploitation let loose by the tea planters, money lenders, contractors, local businessmen and affluent class multiplied miseries of the downtrodden. In such areas, undercurrent of growing discontentment and conflict between the rich and poor and have and have-nots had manifested more than once. Charu Mazumdar, a drop out of the CPI, followed the Chinese line of Marxism, spearheaded by the stalwart Mao Tse-tung. Mazumdar and his associates Kanu Sanyal, Jungal Santal and a few others critically examined socio-economic condition and the peoples' growing discontentment, and founded Naxalbari and its adjacent areas suitable for an upsurge by the peasants, labourers, and poverty-stricken populace. Soon, violence erupted in the areas. A few policemen, money lenders and moneyed people were killed. A few houses were set on fire. Initially, the police who rushed to the spots to maintain law and order was repulsed. The district administration failed to neutralise the upheaval with consummate success and determination. Importantly, at that juncture, the left front of the State led by the CPM was strong enough to acquire political power.

Significantly, the leaders of the extremist outfits originally belonged to the CPI or CPI (M). Either, for some reason, they were expelled from the party or they themselves quit the party. Subsequently, several of them either organised the terrorist outfits or gradually joined the newly-born Naxal cadres. Late Charu Mazumdar wrote eight articles during 1965-67. These articles contained the basic aims, objectives and ideology of Naxalism. Truly, the ideology embraced, or advocated by Charu Mazumdar, was borrowed from three testaments. It was Karl Marx's *Manifesto*, Lenin's book *State and Revolution* and the Mao's *The Red Book*. Charu's eight articles were written strictly following the above three documents. The salient points of the articles are the crux of the ideology of the Naxalite movement, which are briefly discussed below:

1. Indian economy is semi-feudal and semi-colonial. The state and ruling class represents the interests of big landlords and bureaucratic-comprador capitalists. The ruling class is a pawn in the hands of the US imperialism and Soviet social imperialism. Therefore, the basic objective of any democratic revolution has to be, "to overthrow the rule of feudalism, comprador-bureaucratic capitalism, the US imperialism and Soviet social imperialism".
2. There is no alternative to armed struggle. Parliamentary institutions should be discarded.
3. The conditions for waging armed struggle in India are ripe.
4. The main force of the democratic revolution emerges from the peasants and landless poor. They should be brought to the forefront of the armed struggle.
5. The primary stage of the revolution would be annihilation of class enemies, one-by-one.
6. Each act of annihilation would create a base. These bases would facilitate the free movement of guerrillas, which will eventually lead to the formation of liberation army.
7. The revolutionary army would liberate the areas one after another, and ultimately encircle towns and cities.
8. The leadership of the revolutionary movement in India would be subordinate to the Chinese Party.

Charu Mazumdar advocated Mao Tse-tung's philosophy, and firmly believed that revolution through arms is the solution to achieve the classless society and overthrow the existing government. He gave a call to make 1970s 'the decade of liberation'. He added: "When I say make 70s the decade of liberation, I cannot think beyond 1975. The idea of today's armed struggle was first born in the mind of one man (Mao). That idea has now filled the minds of 10 million people. If the new revolutionary consciousness born only in 1967 can permeate the minds of the 10 million people in 1970, why is it impossible then for those 10 million to rouse and mobilise the 500 million people of India in a peoples' war?"

Charu's dogmatic idea of armed struggle and doctrine of annihilation initially created much panic in several pockets of West Bengal, including the city of Calcutta. A few policemen and traffic constables were attacked and killed by small groups. *Modus operandi* of attack and annihilation was totally different from usual attacks or murder. Small groups armed with sharp, cutting weapons would attack the isolated policeman and kill them brutally. They loved gruesome killing, sprinkling of the victim's blood, dismembering of limbs from the body, chopping the head off, treating the lifeless body cruelly etc, thereby creating perceptible fear and panic. In many rural pockets, several villagers were killed branding them *jotdars* (land holders).

Unfortunately, many *jotdars* were owners of small plots or agricultural land, and their livelihood was cultivation. They were neither rich nor owners of vast lands or landed property. Yet, they became victims of the wrath of Charu's followers. Indeed, targets who were petty agriculturists or land-holders were wrongly selected. In fact, sudden uprise took the police unawares. They were unable to contain or combat the growing unrest and blood-letting onslaughts. In 1972, Shri SS Ray became the chief minister of the state. He was resolute to disarray the blood thirsty ultras, and took several positive steps to curb the burgeoning menace. The chief minister's harsh policy and crude police actions came under severe criticism. Public opinion sharply went against the government. Allegations piled upon allegations, that police killed many students and youths arbitrarily merely on suspicion. Gystapo method adopted by the police shocked sober people. It was believed that a large number of bright students became victims of police torture and bullets. Reports were galore that police retaliated and killed them mercilessly to avenge deaths of fellow policemen at the hands of the extremists.

Significantly, a sizeable group of progressive intellectuals carried sympathy and lent support to the ultras without coming openly for their cause. They provided them with moral support. A large number of bright students of reputed educational institutions of Calcutta were inspired by Charu's call, agreed to the ideology and secretly supported Mao's doctrine. They were highly inspired by the sense of duty to improve the lot of the poor and the destitute, and sincerely wanted to remove denial, deprivation and exploitation from the society. Callow youth possessed energy, courage and indomitable will to undertake risk and fight for their welfare. Many took active part in aggressive programmes and operations, and soon became the victims of police's hire-and-fire methods.

However, in a drive to strengthen the cadre and attract the bright students in its fold, secret campaigns in colleges, universities and academic circles were meticulously organised. As a matter of fact, the ideal and object of uplifting the poor, deprived and exploited people attracted many educated, enlightened persons and liberals to support the movement or join it directly or indirectly. In this pursuit, many teachers, lecturers and professors inspired the pupils to embrace the new cult and bring an exemplary change in society. They were inspired by a sense of duty to salvage the discriminated, neglected and exploited people who had been suffering in a stagnated society dominated by the richer, influential and privileged class. They were clear that old structure and order had to be demolished and a classless society, free from denial and exploitation, had to be established. Student community, indoctrinated and brainwashed projecting Mao's philosophy focused by Charu, was honest and sincere to do away with poverty, denial and exploitation from the society. In that direction, their fair or blood-letting activities frightened the rich and affluent class who were insensitive or indifferent to the miseries of the poor and the have-nots. As the movement gained momentum, the police and the administration was in a quandary. In fact, such a threat was neither anticipated nor gave them the opportunity to prepare and equip themselves well to counter the growing unrest ably and diligently. Police was deficient in manpower, training, weaponry, technique and purposeful strategy. Indeed, bogged down in conventional policing, failing to secure peoples' support and goodwill, new gigantic threats broke morale and performance of the police.

Rebellious students felt that the present educational system and teaching methods were archaic, and were contrary to Mao's principle. It was tampered with imperialistic design to fulfill the need of the ruling government. Hence, they attacked many academic centres and institutions, and indulged in full-blown vandalism. They harshly treated, even assaulted, fellow students who did not agree with Mao's philosophy or refused to toe their line. The science laboratory of the prestigious Presidency College, Calcutta, was ransacked and badly damaged. In rural areas, many colleges were attacked and properties were destroyed. Many students, including female students who responded to Charu's call, abandoned studies, went under ground and joined the Naxal cadre. Many took direct part in macabre operations and liquidation of the so-called class enemy. The terrorist outfits built up small sanctuaries in isolated pockets, and imparted training in using fire arms, handling explosives and conducting offensive operations. Training for annihilation was also organised, initially experimenting on goats and dogs, should the fear of killing and bloodshed upset a beginner. Continuous brainwash and killing practice made them mentally tough and unhesitant to attack and kill. Regrettably, many students tainted their hands with blood of traffic constables, policemen, *jotdars*, farmers and innocent people. In many cases, mere suspicion was enough to liquidate a person, who was actually totally ignorant of any political jargon or Mao's new idea of a classless society. Indeed, in many rural belt, a reign of terror destroyed halcyon ambience, safety and security of the habitants. Students or youth who did not respond to the call of the extremists were highly vulnerable. Indeed, they had to pass most of their time in considerable anxiety and fear.

After initial perplexity, the police tried to rise to the occasion and retrieve lost ground. They reorganised the intelligence machinery, created special cells, arranged suitable training programmes, identified and raided the hide-outs, aiming at neutralising the blood-thirsty militants. In fact, investigation was painstaking and hazardous, and the frightened witnesses were unwilling to co-operate and depose against dreaded ultras. Admittedly, judicial process was time consuming and hence, desired result to curb the burgeoning violence and blood curdling activities was opaque. In addition, many were sympathetic and advocated soft line to deal with the extremists. They argued that since the naxalites embraced an ideology and guided by the spirit of revolution and standing by the side of the poor and deprived mass, the police ought to treat them with compassion and dignity. After all, they should not be treated at per with the ordinary outlaws. This group was highly critical against the police's atrocious actions on the plea of quelling disorder, bloodshed and suppressing the movement. In a nutshell, adversities before the police were stumbling block to work out clue, chastise the offenders and after investigation put them for trial and thereby ensure criminal justice. Indeed, surprise attacks, brutal annihilation and the police's failure to prevent or curb violence and macabre festival of death put the state government in abysmal embarrassment. Attacks on the police, killing of police men and pungent criticism from many quarter demoralised the police. Hence, for overcoming the stigma the policemen discovered a short cut to subdue the ultras. Unfortunately, after arrest, engineering fake encounters, many students and youths dedicated to the Mao's thoughts, participated or directly supported the movement were shot dead. Needless to add, the police's illegal and gory killings tantamount to cold-blooded murder. In this connection a few concrete instances came to my notice, which were unflinchingly established by corroborative evidence. However, the incidents will be narrated in appropriate chapter.

Naxalite movement and the doctrine of annihilation received sympathy and support from a sizeable populace of West Bengal. Among them thinkers, intellectuals, progressive persons, students clandestinely supported the struggle hoping welfare and adequate attention to the poor and down trodden. From detached angle, persons possessing analytical mind and intellect visualized monumental impact of the Mao's political thought and philosophy and Charu's dedication and ability to carry the movement far and wide. They were hopeful that miserable plight of the poor and outraged people was going to end soon and they were likely to get due recognition and legitimate share in the society. Dominancy and supremacy of the rich and privileged class would soon disappear. Truly, secret support from various quarters was substantial impetus and strength for the participants and the activists of the movement Hence, in the beginning, the movement gained reckonable momentum and its success was not mean. However, indiscriminate and diabolic killings, fear and panic generated, in fact, thwarted the peace-loving and sober persons who sincerely desired for discarding bloodshed, animosity between rich and poor, have and have-nots. They denounced the so called class enemy and class struggle. Escalated violence and annihilation put the society in the grip of fear, panic and perplexity. The panic stricken people sincerely wanted to see the end of horror of violence. Even the hard core supporters and sympathisers of the doctrine and the movement criticized the Mao's gospel and Charu's ghastly call. Importantly, even the Communist China eventually disapproved Charu's inhuman discourses.

Unfortunately, the blood hound activists and volunteers often selected wrong targets, attacked and butchered an innocent or a person who had no fault. Devilish killing and agony of the members of victim's family deeply upset the common persons. This was one of the reasons that the people were gradually alienated from the Naxal movement. They strongly felt that violence and annihilation could not refurbish the society and wipe out social disparity, disorder and ensure a healthy social and political order and an exploitation free society. Broadly speaking, more and more fiend and violence added fuel to anti-naxalite public opinion. Under current of contrary public opinion had been growing fast, which was not perhaps, realised or noticed by the leaders of the movement. Attack on the educational institutions, damage or destruction of properties, coercion to the students and callow youths to join the naxal cadre put many families in abject despair. Parents were worried visualising bleak future of the wards, who were either forced or volunteered to respond to the so called revolutionary call. Arbitrary or indiscriminate killing created adverse effect and sent a wrong message to the people who cherished meaningful progress and prosperity, especially for the poor and neglected lot of the society. The sizeable intellectuals and radicals broadly accepted the movement and hoped for a radical change in the society. But soon, they realised that the ideology of the movement might be acceptable but its implementation was contrary to fairness, prudence, peace and stability. People were not going to embrace such a movement based on the cult of violence, bloodshed and destruction. As all that glitter is not gold, they were soon disillusioned and upset visualizing its ultimate fiasco. In rural areas several jotdars (land holders) were annihilated on the ground of rich and wealthy land owners, though in reality they possessed small pieces of land which were supplementing or directly supporting their livelihood. They themselves were cultivating land or engaged a few labourers to assist them. They did not earn notoriety for maltreating or exploiting the labourers or daily wage earners. In fact, the jotdars hardly came in the category of land owners or oppressive landlords. Secondly, on mere suspicion that a particular person is a police informer, either openly or secretly opposing the movement, was made a target and killed. Indiscriminate and gory killing and outrages generated adverse public criticism. Even hardcore supporters of the movement were afraid of its ultimate danger and visualising its bleak future. In Calcutta city the traffic constables and foot patrolling cops became the target of attack and annihilation. As all knew that the policemen of the lower strata were poorly paid who, by no standard could be branded as rich or affluent. Many daily wage earners, daily laborers fell in the hands of the Naxalites who were not a class enemy or anything to do with exploitation or oppressively treated others. This irrational and horrendous, hire and fire, actions had shocked the peace loving people who disapproved it and soon wanted to see the end of such a bloodletting movement. Paradoxically, the real class enemy, according to their understanding, remained beyond the reach of the so called revolutionaries.

Broadly speaking, the ultras, in spite of animosity against the capitalists, bourgeoises, reactionaries and affluent persons, could hardly lay hand on them. No doubt, they made them targets, but lamentably failed to achieve the goal. To make it explicit, it is iterated that not a single rich businessman or industrialist, who is marked as class enemy, as per Charu's definition, could be touched, chastised or annihilated. Calcutta's Burra bazaar area is a big business centre and abode of millionaires. In fact, the state's economy is virtually controlled from here. Yet, not any industrialist or moneyed person or a trader was a victim of the extremist's wrath. In urban and semi-urban areas naxal activities were confined to places inhabited by middle class or lower middle class people. In rural areas, so called jotdars, petty money lenders, village level contractors, petty public servants, like forest guards, revenue *patwaris*, excise sepoys, peons etc. were the targets. As a matter of fact, the ultras failed to take on the class enemies, bourgeoisie, anti-people elements and their sympathizers or followers. Seeing the overall performance, people who were enthused initially, were disappointed. Their good will and sympathy for the extremists and the outfit were soon jettisoned. They vehemently condemned the leadership and sincerely wanted their premature end. Interestingly, as the capitalists, bourgeoisie, exploiters were unscratched, suspicion arose that money had been playing a dubious role which dissuading the ultras to harm them. They might have compromised with them and the anti revolutionary forces deviating from the ideal and goal of the revolution. Hence it was strongly suspected that influence of the worldly temptation has queered the pitch. How far the allegation is free from finesse was a matter of debate. Nevertheless, the people were afraid of the terror, its diabolic outcome and bleak future. Secondly, barbarous killing, and grisly outrages unnerved the people. They realised that the so called revolution instead of strengthening the civil society it would only encourage the bloody conflicts, confusion and instability. Hence, they sincerely desired to get rid of such an unbearable situation and prayed for peace and normalcy. The frustrated radicals also visualised opaque future of the movement. Therefore, as events moved apace, flow of the young recruits who were once inspired by the ideology, gradually dried up. Evidently, its consequence was fatal, cadre wizened and leadership exasperatingly fragmented. Indeed, supreme sacrifice of hundreds of promising students and youths virtually went unwept, unsung and unnoticed. It was an irony that much trumpeted revolutionary terrorism soon languished in the limbo of oblivion and petered out from the very soil of its birth.

Hence, Charu Mazumdar's expectation that Red Flag would flutter from the top of the Red Fort, New Delhi, the India's capital by 1975, never materialised. His loud thinking "make 70s the decade of revolution" proved to be a hoax. He passed away in 1972 and his great mentor, Mao, followed him after four years and died in 1976. Charu did not live to see the collapse of the Soviet Union like a house of cards. Again, decay of Communism in Europe indicated unmistakably that the public opinion in favour of Communism has been hanging in balance. His pompous expectation that 500 millions of people of India would be participating in the peoples' war and the liberation army would occupy and liberate the rural areas one after another and eventually would encircle the towns and the cities, proved puerile and barren. Charu made no bone that revolutionary movement in India would be subordinate to the Chinese Communist Party. Needless to say, such an odd assertion and fatuous surrender to a foreign leader by no means is acceptable to any person who possesses self respect and patriotic spirit. Hence, leitmotif of Charu might initially attracted young and energetic persons and callow youths but dastardly killings, chilling horror, absurdity, or doubtful success and outlandish gospel soon disappointed them. As they noticed the prospect dismal, they decided to beat a hasty retreat. Secondly, in-fighting, groupism, suspicion and distrust in rank and file, developed well-nigh a vitiated atmosphere. It contaminated even many hard-core and tested member of the outfit. Regrettably, in spite of honest attempt of a few dedicated leaders its germ fained to spread like wild fire which soon hinted at a doomsday. Needless to add, the divided house became weak and directionless. Unfortunately, Charu's premature demise gave the disgruntled elements and the fence sitters opportunity to disassociate them from the scene. Charu's dream house was shattered, divided and fragmented in smaller groups and thereby made the movement aimless and innocuous. Truly, absence of the livewire degenerated the movement and henceforth the high profile Naxal movement practically was dormant in West Bengal. It languished in a few small pockets without any purpose. Sadly, its impact gallingly decayed. The peace loving people of the state heaved a sigh of relief. Several Naxal leaders came out from exile and joined the main stream of the politics and aspired to capture power through the normal democratic process. Significantly, in addition to reasons explained above, the police and administration were up-in-arms to crush the naxalite movement. The then Chief Minister of the state was firm in wiping out the movement Police was given free hand to deal with the ultras, resulting in, the overzealous police men committed excesses to tame and disarray the militants. In this respect a few instances of polices' high-handedness and excesses committed to neutralize the ultras will be narrated in appropriate chapter. In fact, harshness of the law enforcing authority in tackling the movement is one of the reasons of decay of the movement temporarily in West Bengal. In addition, the extremists gradually lost the peoples' sympathy and support. Thirdly, the leadership was disarrayed and the out-fit broke into several splinter groups under puny or self-styled leaders. Rank and file was demoralized, lost faith on the leaders and its ultimate success.

Anti-socials and Spotty Persons Reap Benefits and Defame the Movement

Chaotic condition, frightful ambience and the police's temporary failure opened the flood gate for many anti-socials, ruffians and outlaws to take advantage of the fluid situations. The ultras were in need of money and resources for spearheading and continuing with the movement. They needed money for buying food, weapons, hiring shelter or hide outs. Secondly, they had to buy arms and ammunitions at an exorbitant price. Again, a substantial amount was required for looking after the under ground cadre, for imparting training, buying equipments, communication instruments and defending criminal cases in the courts. True, they were receiving money and arms from China through the Chinese Embassy operating in Nepal but it was far from adequate. Hence, in guarded way, they had to collect fund either by threat or coercion from the rich businessmen, contractors, money lenders. In fact, they used to comply with the harsh diktats and part with money under fear and helplessness. This kind of extortion did not escape the notice of the anti socials and out laws. Soon they took the cue and exploited it with a good deal of caution. In the name of naxalites, or posing themselves as revolutionaries they resorted to extortion, collection of fund adopting coercive methods which ultimately soiled the name of the ultras and the outfit. It helped to grow the peoples' curse and anathema on the revolutionaries. In this way the movement was misused and exploited which was one of the odious blots on the revolutionary movement. In fact, it directly or indirectly smeared the movement which could not be checked or curbed by the naxal leadership. Indeed, it was responsible to a great extend to alienate the people from the lofty principle and expectation from the Mao's gospel, spearheaded by Charu Mazumdar and his whizkids.

A few dishonest and cunning policemen collected fund illegally on the plea of neutralizing the ultras and protecting the innocent people. One of the modus operandi reveals that they let loose extortion and forcing the hapless parents and guardians to pay them for protecting or helping their wards from the intricacies of the legal tangle. At odd hour of the night the police would raid houses, lay hand on the students, youths and bring them to the police station alleging them as extremists or they had link with the ultras or connection with the outfit. Police would threaten for their arrest and drastic legal action including criminal prosecution against them. The puzzled parents would plead hard high lighting the wards' innocence and request not to harm them and spoil their career. In this manner threat for prosecution and alibi advanced would complicate the matter. Finally, a deal in terms of money would be settled. The grudging parents or guardians would be forced to pay for securing the release of the boy. This kind of nefarious trickery tampered with bribery prevailed in many police stations functioning in naxal-hit areas. A specific instance came to my notice from Barasat Sub-Division, District 24 Parganas, now 24 Parganas North, West Bengal which was brought to the notice of the police hierarchy.

Meanwhile, political scenario and political development in erstwhile East Pakistan underwent a drastic change. People of East Pakistan under leadership of Bangabandhu Sk. Mujibar Rahaman revolted against the military government. Military junta cracked down on them and let loose unprecedented brutality, bloodshed, rapine etc. Millions of people with bear life crossed the border, entered into Indian territory, and took shelter. On the border territory several camps were opened to accommodate the refugees. It upset India's political condition, economy, safety and security. Influx of ten million refugees obviously generated a gigantic problem. However, the government and people generously came forward to salvage and protect them. Fortunately, several countries and NGOs sent relief materials to help the refugees. Finally, the war with Pakistan, surrender of the Pakistani Army, India's triumph and the birth of Bangladesh in the sub-continent diverted attention of the state and the people of India. Consequently, the naxal movement was relegated behind and lost importance. Thereafter much water has flown. The so-called revolutionary movement was in the limbo of oblivion. In fact, people of the state virtually forgot Charu and other leaders and its aims and object and hazy impact.

Of late, semblance of the activities of the extremists is noticed in three districts of West Bengal, West Medinapur, Bankura and Purulia. From West Bengal, no recognised Maoist leader or a formidable outfit are in the forefront and guiding or steering the extremists and movement In fact, Maoists from Jharkhand or Orissa clandestinely enter into the territory of the districts, operate conveniently, take to heels and return to the safe sanctuary crossing the state border. The police and the security forces are in considerable disadvantage to round up and disarray the blood thirsty ultras who after operation hide in Orissa or Jharkhand. Importantly, the districts are broadly inhabited by the Adivasis who have been suffering from abject poverty, neglect, unemployment and socio-economic disparity. Education, health care and minimal civic amenities in the areas are lamentably deficient. Inspite of 33 years prolonged rule under the Left Front government the area and the populace is denied of desired economic progress and development. Hence, the peoples' resentment and response to the call of the Maoists is not without any reason. The state government without fathoming the root cause of the discontentment of the people initially deployed the party cadres and used muscle power to suppress the sentiment of the aggrieved people. Secondly, police was given free hand to quell violence and chastise the Maoists and their supporters. Ironically, the police raj proved counter productive, rather hardened sentiment of the outraged people. Aggrieved people were hostile to the state government. Law and order and administration have virtually collapsed. The state government was in a quandary. Its credibility and the CPM's popularity had exasperatingly waned. Situation was volatile and was near approximation to mass upsurge.

Link with Communist China

The Communist movement in India received a fresh fillip since Charu Mazumdar initiated the armed uprising at Naxalbari in West Bengal in early part of 1967. He received support of the Communist Party of China. The Chinese Embassy in Kathmandu, Nepal coordinated with the Naxal leaders, supplied fund, arms, ammunition and gave moral support. In September 1967, Kanu Sanyal, Jangal Santhal, Souren Bose and six others at the initiative and assistance of the Chinese Embassy at Kathmandu clandestinely visited China and underwent political and tactical training for three months. As a matter of fact, Chinese Embassy in Katmandu provided adequate journey expenses and made other necessary arrangements. In fact, China took profound interest in uprising of the Naxal movement in India. On June 28, 1967, broadcast from the Peking radio amply revealed China's unflinching support for progress and advancement of the Naxalite movement. It asserted, "This is the front paw of the revolutionary armed struggle launched by the Indian people under the guidance of Mao-tse-tung's thought." In its editorial dated July 5, 1967, The *Peoples' Daily* eloquently published, "Spring thunder breaks over India .... It was absolutely correct thing. They have done it well.... The Chinese people joyfully applauded the revolutionary stand of the Indian peasants in Darjeeling areas as it does of all Marxists-Leninists and revolutionary people of the whole world." Kanu Sanyal visited Kathmandu several times and maintained close contact with the Chinese Ambassador. He took responsibility to train the extremists operating in Nepal. He also built a sanctuary in Terai district of Nepal to train guerrillas from India. He was working in tandem with Mohanchand Adhikari, the Politburo member of the Maoists of Nepal. On the initiative of both, a joint action committee was formed to coordinate the guerrilla activities in Nepal and India. In August 1970, Souren Bose again visited China as an emissary, contacted and consulted the Chinese leaders, and acquired fresh direction on tactics and implementation. In November 1970, he returned to India carrying a blue print on insurgency and accordingly, chalked out programme for accelerating insurgency. Souren Bose contacted the Naga and Mizo rebels and developed mutual understanding to smuggle arms and ammunitions from China.

Movement Gains Momentum in West Bengal; Internal Squabble Ensues

Kanu Sanyal, Dipak Biswas visited Kathmundu more than once and maintained close contact with the Chinese Embassy at Nepal. He built a sanctuary in Eastern Terai district of Nepal for arranging training to the guerrilla squad from India. He collaborated with the Maoists of Nepal operating under Mohanchandra Adhikari. He formed a joint action committee with Maoists of Nepal to organise and unleash guerrilla operation in both countries. The periodical, *Deshbrati,* published in Bengali by the CPI ML, continued publishing articles, write-up on guerrilla warfare and various lessons and strategies of the Maoists in high-falutin and exaggerated tone and fashion. It high-lighted various achievements, likely success of the class struggle, information on violence and annihilation spearheaded by the cadre at nook and corner of the state. But all were not well, cloud had been gathering in the horizon of the party's aim, future programme and on the question of leadership. Indeed, a hiatus and rivalry had already been manifested between the hardliners and the followers of the soft line. Kanu Sanyal and few others launched a new outfit. Comrade Satyanarayan Singh of Bihar revolted against Charu Mazumdar. Comrade Kanai Chatterjee and Amulya Sen with their followers remained aloof from Kanu Sanyal's new outfit. Comrade Kanai preferred small and loose federation of revolutionary groups, instead of monolith party. He argued in favour of the role of front organisations. By end of 1968, a separate group emerged, known as Dakhin Desh Group and its operational areas were Bardhaman, Hooghly, Medinapur district, Sundarbans and southern parts of West Bengal. Later its area was further extended and activities spread right into Assam and parts of Bihar.

Meanwhile, rift between Charu Mazumdar and several of his close associates sharply developed. Kanu Sanyal and several others organised a new outfit, All India Co-ordination Committee of Communist Revolutionaries (AICCCR) in October 1968. On April 22, 1969, the AICCCR was converted into a political party under the name and style of the CPI (Marxist-Leninist). On May 1, Kanu Sanyal arranged a rally at Calcutta and proclaimed, "State power could be seized only through armed revolution. Guerrilla war alone can expand the small bases of armed struggle to large extensive areas and develop the peoples' army." Meanwhile, Cultural Revolution in China modified or revised the attitude of the Chinese Communist Party. It denounced the Charu's annihilation line. Kanu Sanyal, Souren Bose, Chowdhury Tejeswar Rao, Nagabhusan Patnaik, Bhuban Mohan Patnaik supported the new line. Charu was practically isolated. Disagreement with the fellow comrades must have dismayed him. He was arrested at Calcutta on July 16, 1972 and died in police custody at City Police HQ, Lalbazar after 12 days of detention.

CPI (ML) published a Bengali periodical named, *Deshbrati*. It continued publishing on guerrilla warfare, success of the class struggle, information on annihilation etc. in hyperbolic terms. However, a hiatus among the top leaders had been growing fast. Many supported the hard line and others preferred soft line. Comrade Parimal Das Gupta and Asit Sen formed independent groups. Unfortunately, internal bickering, dissensions, lust for leadership cracked the unity and solidarity of the ambitious movement. Hence, within four months of its birth, the CPI (ML) crumbled like a house of cards.

Mao's Cultural Revolution gave a new idea and direction in steering the revolutionary movement in West Bengal. The Red Guard Movement started in China in 1966 was far from rewarding. Charu inspired by Mao's thought made it crystal clear that revolutionary movement in India would be subordinate to the Chinese Communist Party. Interestingly, subservience to an outlandish political party was not appreciated even by many hard core extremists. Yet bold writings on the walls of Calcutta city high lighting, "China's Chairman is our Chairman" and leaflets containing ilk assertion distributed freely, upset sober persons. Leaflets printed in China were extensively distributed in Assam and West Bengal. It was apparent that naxals and the naxalite movement were distinctly under guidance and control of China. It hurt sentiment of the nationalists and others who disliked foreign control on the organisations operating on Indian soil. Sober and progressive elements` were critical of the extremists for following the gospel of an alien nation and operating adhering to the ideal and instructions of a foreign country. However, Cultural Revolution in China ran out within four years of its very birth. China perhaps realised that the doctrine of annihilation and Red Guard movement was no longer rewarding.

Naxalites Seek Support from Other Countries—The Triple Entente

Naxalites or Maoists banked on the Pakistan's intelligence wing (ISI). They asserted that Kashmir is not an integral part of India. Secondly, Indian army in Kashmir is an occupation force. Execution of the notorious terrorist, Maqbool Butt, in January 1984, was vehemently denounced by the ultras. They also protested against the operation Blue Star, in the Punjab and extolled Bhindranwala as a martyr. They supported illegal infiltration of the Muslims from Bangladesh. The CPI (N), Nepal supported the ultras active in India. In fact, the triple entente of CPI (N), Nepal, the ISI of Pakistan and CPI (Maoist) of India, was a formidable combination worked in tandem against interest of India.

Compact Revolutionary Zone (CRZ) was the brain child of the Peoples War. In Maoist parlance it is a Red Corridor running from Nepal to Dharamapuri area of Tamal Nadu. It is purely an imaginary line starting from the border of Nepal and passing through the forest and tribal belt of Bihar, UP, Maharashtra, Chhattisgarh, Jharkhand, West Bengal, Odisha, Andhra Pradesh and ending right into Dharamapuri forest of Tamil Nadu. In fact, Maoists are weaving a cobweb to establish their absolute dominance and rule on the territorial belt passing through the above states, which in their parlance is branded as the Red Corridor.

Umbrella Organisation of the Ultras Initiates in South Asia

Nine Maoist organisations from India, Nepal, Sri Lanka and Bangladesh have formed a co-ordination committee with the aim of combining their efforts and spreading the idea of the "People's war" through the region and beyond. After a joint meeting held in W.B. a joint statement was issued by the Maoist Communist Centre activists on 20-21 June, 2001. The Apex body has been named the, "Coordination Committee of Maoist parties and Organisations of South Asia (CCOMPOSA)". In fact, Purba Bangla Sarbohara Party, Maobadi Punorgathan Kendra, Samyabadi Dal Marxist-Leninist (BSD-ML), from Bangladesh, Ceylon Communist Party-Maoist (CCP-M), the Communist Party of India (ML), Peoples

War (PW), the Maoist Communist Centre (MCC), the Revolutionary Communist Centre of India-Maoist (RCCI-M), the Revolutionary Communist Centre (M-L-Maoist) and the Communist Party of Nepal-Maoist (CPN-M), participated in the meeting. It is learnt that Nepal's CPN and PW of India took the initiative to organise the meeting. It is crystal clear that the Maoists are active to consolidate their strength in South Asia. Palace massacre in Kathmandu and overthrow of the kingship in Nepal have given them fresh impetus to put heart and soul to peruse the Maoist movement.

Growing Threat to Other States

Importantly, extremist movement in other states, like Andhra Pradesh, Orissa, part of Madhya Pradesh (now Chhattisgarh), Maharashtra was not borrowed from Naxalbari or Charu Mazumdar's brain wave. It was neither an off shoot of the revolutionary movement started in West Bengal nor originated from the initiative or patronage of the underground militant leaders of the state. The extremists of other states had no co ordination or joint strategy with the naxals of West Bengal. As a matter fact, extremist activities gained momentum separately and independently in each state on the initiative of the local leaders. In fact, adverse socio-economic condition, abject poverty, galling exploitation, shameful discrimination and deprivation etc. prepared ground for the revolutionary movement. Indeed, numerous shocking discriminations, social outrages, adversities influenced and inspired the local leaders to take up the causes spontaneously for the poverty stricken, discomfited and deprived rural masses. Initially, it was purely a humanitarian cause free from political ideology, doctrine, compulsion or colour. In rural areas a few school teachers carried cudgel for the down-trodden, who locally organised small groups to eradicate the evils. Eventually, self styled local leaders succeeded in mustering support and confidence of the village populace to organise a movement and hit upon a plan to operate in remote and isolated pockets. They selected targets secretly and operated cautiously out witting the police and administration. Truly, they had no link or co-operation with any major or deadly militant out-fit. In remote areas lying on the borders of Orissa and Andhra Pradesh money lenders, petty businessmen, influential persons, government officials extort or exploit the poor villagers recklessly. Money lenders charge high rate of interest, cheat the borrowers preparing false account and false demands taking advantage of the poor and illiterate villagers. Field officials of the revenue department and police men harass and extort them on any pretext, forcibly take away their domestic animals, chicken, vegetables, seasonal fruits, even trees or plants. The hapless villagers submit to all kinds of high-handedness. Unfortunately, the administration is unable to protect them though the district officials are aware of malaises. Working in that area I am inclined to say that the age old harassment and exploitation is known to the district officials. Nevertheless, for various unavoidable reasons they are unable to show mailed fist and curb the evils. In many villages primary schools have been functioning. The teachers are generally from the urban areas, many are well educated and possess good sense of standing up against social evils, discrimination and exploitation. Several of them mustered courage to expose the black sheep and came forward to appeal to the discomfited and exploited mass. Eventually, with the help of the villagers they built resistance groups. Initially, it had no political colour or support, yet it gained favorable support from the deprived and poverty stricken rural mass. Indeed, the leadership of many teachers was honest and selfless which attracted the oppressed people to respond to their calls.

Andhra Pradesh—Red Movement

Srikakulam district of Andhra Pradesh is adjacent to Koraput and Ganjam Districts of Western Orissa. Now Koraput district has been divided into four districts, Raygada, Koraput Nowrangpur and Malkangiri. In Gunjam district a new district, Gajapati adjacent to Andhra Pradesh has been created. All these places are covered by hill, jungles, and inaccessible areas. In interior places many primitive tribes have been living. Malkangiri district is a part of Dandakaranya. There is a hill called Bondha hill. Here a few hundreds primitive tribes live who are disinterested to come to the main stream of the society. It is believed that on the foothill of the Bondha hill the combat between Bali and Sugrib took place. Lord Rama's wife celebrated Sita took bath in a nearby pond. Before the Dandakaranya project and settlement of many refugees from East Bengal, the area was totally inaccessible and in rainy season the entire sub division used to be practically cut off from the district HQ. In its north western side the Bastar district, now of Chhattisgarh state, is located. Adivasis form the vast majority of the population. They are very poor, superstitious and unwilling to give up their archaic faith, habit and custom Inspire of government's persuasion most of them are disinterested to prosper in the accolade of modern science and advancement. Unfortunately, they have no definite means of livelihood. They depend on the jungle and jungle products, petulantly exploited by the money lenders, petty contractors, business men, traders and low rank government officials. A traders' class, called Kumties, whose mother tongue is Telugu, run small shops in rural areas, exploit the simple and innocent Adivasis. They lend money on high rate of interest, cheat them on various pretexts, and thereby enrich themselves. Appalling condition of the poverty stricken Adivasis moved a few teachers employed in schools functioning in rural areas. Ramalu, Vempatapu, Satyanarayana, Adibhatla Kailasam and several others working in rural belt were inspired to stand by the side of the poor and salvage them from exploitation and deprivation. They heard about the Naxalbari movement in West Bengal and thought of organising a movement in that line. In fact, they took tangible step to unite the Adivasis against the money lender and the Kumti traders. Significantly, puny attempt of a few school teachers had a snow balling effect and the initial protest movement soon generated an electrifying effect. A few drop out middle rank leaders of the CPM sincerely wanted to stretch the movement. In that pursuit P. Krishna Murthy and Chowdhury Tejeswara Rao met comrade Charu Mazumdar at Calcutta in October 1968 and conferred intending to organise the movement in Andhra Pradesh tying up with the Naxalbari movement. As follow up action another meeting was held at Guttikonda Balm cave, near Guntur in February 1969. Charu was present in the meeting. In fact, Charu and his outfit was lukewarm right from the beginning in joining hand with the growing protest movement developing in Andhra Pradesh.

However, on June 29, 1960, a committee of Communist Revolutionaries was formed in a meeting held at Vijayawada, A P, by the expelled members from the CPI(M). Comrade T. Negi Reddi, a prominent member of the group, visited Calcutta met the Naxal leaders and tried to put up a combined action plan etc with the AICCCR already launched by Kanu Sanyal. Interestingly, response from West Bengal was quite discouraging. Simultaneously, Reddi tried to tie up with the Srikakulam group which was turned down. Hence, right from the start in Andhra Pradesh, two groups operated independently. Eventually, Negi Reddi group disagreed with Charu Mazumdar, resulting in, dissension developed and the outfit was split. The break away group under Chandra Pulla Reddy formed Andhra Pradesh Revolutionary Communist Party. The Srikakulam group was on the verge of extinction.

Kondapalli Sitaramaiah of Krishna district and K.G. Satyamurthy jointly started violent activities in Warangal and Nalgonda district right from 1970. By 1973, it penetrated into Telengana region and gained momentum in Khamman and Karimnagar district. In 1977, the state committee of the outfit was reorganised. In April 22, 1980 it was converted into CPI (ML), Peoples' War Group (PWG). In 1984, the Central Organisation Committee (COC) was formed. However, internal discord forced a few members to resign or quit the COC. Hence, by i989 within five years of its birth, the COC virtually existed in paper. However, K. Sitaramaiah, the general secretary became all in all.

In March 1970, he reorganised the COC M. Lakshman Rao alias Ganapathy was made the secretary for Andhra Provincial Committee (PC). Thereafter, the PC was reconstructed. Soon estrange relation between the COC and the PC culminated in a bitter conflict and acrimony. In 1992, K. Sitaramaiah, the General Secretary and the founder father of the PWG was expelled from the party. His three trusted lieutenants were also expelled. M. Laxman Rao became the General Secretary. A fresh Central Organising Committee (COC) was formed. K. Sitaramaiah was arrested in 1993. After release, he was a changed personality gave farewell to the class war or armed struggle. He died on April 13, 2002. Dismayingly, rivalry, dissension and in-fighting in rank and file were an odious blot in the extremist movement in Andhra Pradesh. No doubt, many leaders were dedicated; fortudous and painstaking who led the movement with courage and determination, yet many were wonky, deficient and lacked patience and single minded devotion. They were unable to face the hardship of exiled and under ground living in jungle and hills devoid of civic amenities. The police's relentless hot chase made the situation worse. They were eager to return to the normal life. Their frustration piled upon frustration and many of them doubted ultimate success of the revolutionary movement. Many thought of giving up the idea of class war and securing power through the normal democratic process. Many surrendered to the police and joined the main stream of the society. Interestingly, terrorism in AP had various facets. It gained support from the poets, writers, and teachers, and from several students' wings. Ultras killed several high ranking police officers, IAS officers, former Ministers, Speaker of the legislative Assembly, MP, MLAs, political leaders etc. Several local leaders and activists of the Bharatiya Janata Party (BJP), Akhil Bharitiya Vidharthi Parisad (ABVP), the students' wing of the BJP, leaders of the Congress Party.

Annihilation was practiced in ghastly and barbaric manner. After killing heads used to be severed, kept hanging in public places for public gaze. No mercy or no consideration was showen even for children and fair sex. Brutality piled upon brutality. Indeed, bestial savagery tainted the lofty ideal of the revolutionary movement. Thousands of farmers and daily wage earners deserted villages and took shelter in towns and cities. Suitable persons were hardly available to till the land. Hundreds of acres of fertile lands left uncultivated in terror-stricken districts. Indeed, areas were in the grip of abyss suspense, terror, and perplexity. Growing violence thwarted safety and security of the innocent persons and in Maoist dominated rural areas state government's authority practically disappeared. Here, the writ of the extremists was paramount. Nevertheless, in spite of the reverses in the beginning the state police force faced the situation and curbed bloodshed and violence with consummate courage and determination. Frequent attacks and heavy toll on the rank and file of the police force failed to cow down the policemen and break their morale. Government extended all possible help to the police to combat the growing threat. A special police force, named Greyhounds, was raised. It was especially trained, equipped with latest weaponry to tackle the blood thirsty ultras. The newly built force proved equal to the task and succeeded in great extend to curb the outlaws. Other Maoist-torn states decided to raise new contingent in pattern of the Greyhounds.

Importantly, the Peoples' War Group receiving pressure from the police and the Greyhounds galvanized or modified its modus operandi from time to time to out wit the security forces and to achieve the desired result. In fact, it was not well for them. Truly, occasional reverses, surrender and desertion from the cadre often cracked its command and control and badly affected morale of the personnel and the outfit. Nevertheless, they did not give up their iron will and spirit, plan, strategy and operation. Adversities compelled them to lie low temporarily. But the core group did not lose heart, rather they resolutely continued with the struggle. To day, the movement has been contained considerably, but has not been banished or wiped out from the map of the state. Admittedly, the Red Corridor passing through Andhra Pradesh is quite vulnerable and a positive threat to democracy and rule of law.

Maoists Spread Their Network in Odisha

Odisha was a peaceful state. Nothing transpired that the ultras would penetrate in Orissa outwitting the Orissa government and its police force. Malkangiri sub-division was a part of Koraput district. Dandakaranya project had taken substantial initiative and helped and rehabilitated a large number of refugees migrated from erstwhile East Pakistan. The area was infested with dense jungle, small hills wild animals. From Malkangiri to interior places there was no all-weather road. Its extreme west point of Malkangiri is called Motu. Here, the river Sabari has demarcated Bhadrachalam district of Andhra Pradesh and Bastar district of the than Madhya Pradesh, now Chhattisgarh. In fact the western tip of Malkangiri sub division virtually works as a corridor to above three states. The extremists after operating in border areas often crossed the river and took shelter in inaccessible areas of Malkangiri. They made Malkangiri a sanctuary or safe haven to outwit the police of AP. Adivasis are the main inhabitants. Their mother tonge is not Oriya and their culture is entirely different. Dandakaranya project has constructed small colonies by the side of the road running from Malkangiri to Motu where refugees from East Pakistan have been rehabilitated. The Adivasis are very poor; depend on the jungle for livelihood. Yet they are disinterested to respond to the modern advancement. Indeed they prefer to cling on their archaic habits, custom and faith. The state government's and several NGOs' effort to drag them out of darkness to light and prosper in the accolade of progress and blessings of modern science and technology succeeded partially.

Oriya population in Koraput district including Malkangiri sub-division is very scanty. In interior places of Malkangiri the traders are generally from the Kumti community from Andhra Pradesh. They exploit the poor Adivasis and monopolized trade, money lending in the areas. The forest contractors are no better. They recklessly exploit the cheap labour and drinking habit of the poor people. Inspite of presence of the ultras, the district administration was not very serious to neutralize them. In the sub division there were four police stations. They were instructed to keep watch on the movements of the ultras from AP. Interestingly, the ultras were often moving in the villages and weekly *haats*, buying provisions. They were seen carrying arms but not interfering in any local affairs or frightening the local populace. However, secret intelligence report on their movements was sent to the government regularly. During my incumbency in Koraput district, I have not received any formal request or requisition from my counter part of AP to arrest the ultras or after apprehending them to hand them over to the police of AP.

State government was indifferent to the growing concentration of the extremists in Motu and Kalimela areas of the Malkangiri sub-division. The Chief Minister was briefed more than once on the burgeoning extremist menace in Koraput district, especially of the movements of the ultras and using Malkangiri areas as a sanctuary. However, the CM was reluctant to attach importance to the intelligence report. In an informal discussion the CM said that the extremists from AP were no doubt seen moving in Malkangiri jungle but they were neither doing any harm to the people nor indulging in any violent activities. Odisha is a peaceful state and, hence let, there be no precipitative action from the police and administration which might invite unrest or retaliatory step from them. The sleeping lion should not be provoked to rise from its torpor and unleash disturbances. However, the senior bureaucrats, in charge of law and order were not satisfied but were unable to convince the government on the impending danger. As events moved apace, the extremists from AP who had made the area a strong sanctuary gradually cultivated the local Advasis to respond against deprivation and exploitation and participate in the mass movement. They selected safe hideouts, attacked police stations, government offices, killed policemen and created abysmal fear and panic. Throbbed with chilling fear many public servants were unwilling to serve in the disturbed areas. Police and CRPF patrols were ambushed more than once. Several were killed. Kalimela police station was attacked four policemen including a sub-inspector were killed. Police was not a match with the ultras and had to retreat or withdraw instead of confrontation more than once. Truly, semblance of administration from Malkangiri practically disappeared for 72 hours following a deadly attack. Police's reverses encouraged the ultras who stepped up offensives. Police armoury of Koraput district was looted and a large quantity of arms and ammunitions went in possession of the ultras. Militancy gradually penetrated into Rayagada, Gunupur, Gajapati and interior places of Ganjam and Gajapati Districts. It also spread fast in north of the state, like Sambalpur, Deoghar, Sundargarh Keonjhar Districts. From Zee Udaygiri police station a sub-inspector was abducted and kept as a hostage for several days. The police training school at Nayagarh, a sub divisional town of erstwhile Puri district was attacked. Fourteen policemen were killed after fierce encounter. Ultras carried away 400 weapons, including light machine guns, self loading rifles and a large quantity of ammunitions. It was a daring attack, flawlessly planned and brilliantly executed. It exposed the state's monumental callousness and the police's fragile preparation to combat the militancy. It also broke morale of the police. The people obliquely looked at the government and police force. Interrogation of a few arrested ultras and seizure of literature and pamphlets revealed several sensitive clues. One of the revolting disclosures was very alarming. The Maoists hit upon a plan to liberate more than half of the territory of the state by 2011 and bring it under its control. Admittedly, a peaceful state boastfully claimed to be free from rancor and unrest failed to anticipate militancy of such a magnitude. As discussed above, the state government was slow, vacillating and myopic in visualising the coming events and prepare them to combat terror and the terrorists.

Dispassionately, it lacked desired promptitude, diligence and high spirit of public service. Perhaps, culture of red-tapism and complacency that the state being peaceful would be free from the cruel hand of the ultras had pooh-pooh the threat perception, appropriate alertness and home work from the government and its votaries The above adversities helped to open the flood gate in favour of the extremists to gain fortitude, increase striking power, mobilize cadre and penetrate well in semi-urban and rural areas. Swift growth of the extremists, link developed with other outfits operating in AP, MP, Maharashtra and Bihar and finally merger of the outfits and emergence of the formidable outfit, under the title of the Communist Party of India (Maoists), confirm unmistakably that it is posing a gargantuan threat to India's internal, safety, security and democratic values.

Critical Estimate of the Extremists Active in Odisha

The state government's ambivalence to appreciate the Maoists' beefy growth, striking power, organisation and complacency that peace of the state would remain undisturbed, eventually proved very fatal and costly. Indeed, the government's policy of adherence to the "make believe world" soon produced numerous adverse reactions on governance and public life. By the time the government woke up it was too late. The slogan that Odisha is a peaceful state, law and order is not at all a threat to the administration and the people and a sense of *déjà vu* so long manifested in various levels received a severe jolt. Its votaries were cornered and ridiculed. Police had been functioning in routine, orthodox and lackadaisical fashion. Police was hardly reformed, upgraded or modernised. In fact, dozens of proposals for galvanizing the police submitted to the Home Department of the state government gathered dust without any action. Proposal for procuring latest weaponry, latest equipments, organising training facilities, nominating police personnel for training in specialised training institutions were hardly given due importance. Again, keeping pace with the population growth, urbanisation and increasing socio-economic problems, crime and movements of the inter state criminals on account of enhanced railway traffic, communication facilities etc., the government lamentably failed to pay desired heed to upgrade and modernise the police force. The armed police battalions which are main striking power were neglected and allowed to drip. Dismayingly, watching the growth of the extremists in neighboring states the government failed to anticipate or visualise the impending danger knocking at the door. No tangible step was taken to raise new battalion or a special force to neutralise terrorism and its perpetrators if it happened to sweep Orissa. Orissa Military Police (OMP) known for its discipline, performance and deterrent was not oxygenized commensurately to take on the extremists' challenge. On the contrary, trade unionism was allowed in the police force which posed a mighty threat to discipline, performance, command and control. Officers in lower level, who were supposed to enforce discipline, demand implicit obedience and satisfactory performance were alarmed seeing growing indiscipline and insubordination. Frustration dissuaded them to put heart and soul to ensure laudable performance of the force. Many union leaders preferred ease to honest public service and displayed "do not care attitude" instead of humbleness. In many occasions disobedience and defiance of order marred the performance of the force. Indeed, in climactic situations of lawlessness ill effects of porous discipline, sloth and incohesion often were exposed. Unfortunately, the government was indifferent to the fall of the standard of the force and its growing incompetence to handle impending violence and disorder. Many police union leaders clandestinely developed link with the political leaders and leaders of several trade unions. Interestingly, political leaders encouraged union activities in police and viewed it exclusively from political angle. Incidentally, for construction of the union office, the Chief Minister allotted a piece of land in Bhubaneswar and inaugurated the foundation ceremony of the union building with much fan fair and publicity. It was crystal clear that government was less interested to improve and modernise the police force in keeping with the mounting problems. Indeed, lack of vision and speculation on coming events, the policy of masterly inactivity, and evils of complacency were flinty bottleneck which queered the pitch. Hence, sudden out break of terror strike in the state took the government in abject alarm and confusion.

Terrorism Gains Momentum in Jharkhand

Bihar has the history of unprecedented rivalry and conflict in caste, creed and community. Pride of the superior caste, creed and community, lust for possessing land, high handedness and dominance of the superior caste and muscle power of the stronger community often lead to clash, violence and bloodshed. Dalits and neglected lot are often targets of oppression and outrages. In fact, group clash, massacre, forcible occupation of land and caste conflict etc are scary blot on the state's social history. Indeed, such murky practices have been continuing from the time immemorial. Truly, it has nothing to do with the terrorist uprising or the naxalite movement. However, Charu Mazumdar's a few whiz-kids after snapping connection with him went to Bihar and independently mobilised groups and initiated movements in several pockets of the state. Poverty stricken people, Dalits, and deprived people responded well. Indeed, society honeycombed by caste that prefer to cling on their caste pride and muscle power to neutralise the rivals, and its long history, chill penury of the neglected mass has made the ground fertile for the peoples' movement. Hence, it was highly advantageous to bring the aggrieved people to come under the banner of agitation and mass movement and build a stubborn cadre. However, in the beginning it could not be attributed as a revolutionary or naxalite movement on the line of Charu's gospel. Neither it had any link or patronage from the core naxalite group operating in West Bengal. Nevertheless, as events moved apace, the movement took an ugly and ominous shape and alarmed the government.

Importantly, abject poverty and casteism created ground for an upsurge against rich, land owners, animosity between higher and lower caste people and community. This feeling helped to develop small groups to protest or resist against high handedness or atrocity often unleashed by either castes or communities. In fact, a few groups succeeded in mustering support of the rural mass and gained popularity. Among them, Indian People's Front and Maoist Communist Centre. These out fits were operating separately having no link or co-ordination with each other. Comrade Satyanarayan Singh, one of the close associates of Comrade Charu Mazumdar differed with him in 1970, left him and went to Bihar to organise extremist movement independently. He preferred mass movement instead of secret and selective killing. Comrade Kanai Chatterjee and Amulya Sen, the trusted comrades of Charu, were unwilling to follow Charu's line. They preferred a kind of loose federation of all revolutionary groups instead of a monolith party. Kanai Chatterjee insisted on the role of the front organisations. Soon they were aloof of Charu's outfit. From 1967, a separate group, known as Dakhin Desh group under their leadership surfaced. Activities of Dakhin Desh group were confined to South Bengal, including in Sundarban areas. They attempted to stretch their activities in Southern Assam and Bihar. They developed serious difference with Kanu Sanyal, the founder of new outfit, the CPI (Marxist-Leninist) launched in Calcutta on May 1, 1969. Soon both of them went to Bhojpur, Bihar and stepped up activities of Dakhin Desh group. It worked on the line of the MCC and finally in 1975, unveiling mask, they established the outfit known as the Maoist Communist Centre (MCC). It announced its aim and object that it must establish the Peoples' government through the Peoples' War. In fact, the idea and ideology was borrowed from Mao's theory of organised peasant insurrection. Unfortunately, internal dissension and squabble marred the unity and cohesion of the movement. Difference of opinion, ambition to achieve result in double quick time and rivalry centering leadership often hindered the weight, impact and progress of the movement. Charu's hard line was not accepted by many comrades. His annihilation theory and secret assassination was denounced by many comrades, resulting in split in the organisation vitiated the meaning and purpose of the peoples' movement. The high sounding CPI (ML), which was founded with a good deal of hope and aspiration crumbled like a house of cards within four months of its birth. In fact, split in the Charu's dream child continued. Exodus from the middle rank jeopardized strength and striking power of the cadre. Needless to add, it could be imagined how frustration over powered the sincere and dedicated revolutionary who was inspired by a lofty vision and imagination of a new political regime free from exploitation and deprivation. Importantly, in spite of numerous odds, Charu was firm in his belief and conviction and never succumbed to any pressure or agreed to any compromise formula. However, split and desertion of trusted comrades continued unabatedly. Comrade Parimal Das Gupta and Asit Sen disagreed with Charu, deserted him and formed separate groups.

Development in Bihar CPI (ML) Liberation

Comrade Vinod Mishra, a drop out of the Regional Engineering College Durgapur, WB, went to Bihar to motivate and mobilise the tribal of Bhojpur. He initiated a new out-fit in February 1976 under the name and style of CPI (ML) Liberation. Under his leadership, the organisation made a dent on the tribal community of Bhojpur areas. Truly, impact of the out-fit was reckonable and it lasted about 20 years. However, Vinod Mishra modified his modus operandi and planned to grab power by constitutional means and through Parliamentary process shunning violence. In 1982 he floated Indian People's Front and intended to join politics openly using the new unit as an umbrella organisation. Comrade Nagabhusan Patnaik active in border of Orissa and Andhra Pradesh followed him and preferred to return to the path of the open politics. In Bihar election for the Legislative Assembly was held in 1990, Indian People's Front contested in dozens of seats and succeeded in wining in seven seats. In Lok Sabha election held in 1991 the IPF captured one seat. The new outfit penetrated in selected places of Assam. In Assembly election held in 1991 in Assam, it captured four seats from Karbi Anglong district. Indeed, watching success and rewarding dividend received by the IPF following the constitutional process in Assam and Bihar, many dedicated and front line leaders of the naxalite movement were keen to modify the policy of terror and blood shed and return to the main stream. Broadly speaking, Binod Mishra's success tempted many hard core extremists to return to normal life and struggle for power embracing the usual political process. However, in 1998, Vinod Mishra expired. In fact, with his demise, the organisation decayed and eventually lost its mailed fist.

Private militia, Rajputs, Bhumihars, Kurmis, dalits etc. often clash to grab land and establish supremacy in their respective areas. Private militia like Ranbir Sena are raised by the rival groups, are freely used to cow down the opponents. The militia often recklessly let loose loot, arson, murder and heinous crime. Secondly, poverty, untouchability, superstition, pernicious social customs are very high in all level, especially, in uneducated and lower category of the populace. Maoist movement in Bihar is dominated by the Yadavs and persons from other backward classes (OBC). Even in their day to day affairs and operational matters caste plays a dominant role. Obviously, it creates anxiety and distrust among the motley groups, participate and enrich the cadre and active in operational field. In fact, the Adivasis form the major portion of the cadre. They are broadly, free from caste feeling and communal sentiment. Caste consciousness or dominance on caste line makes them uncomfortable. It is felt that it may encourage perfidy, disunity and destroy mutual trust and respect to each other. As a matter of fact, a caste-cum-ethnic dimension is likely to upset the tribals who work shoulder to shoulder exhibiting genuine fellowship, sincerity and dedication. Admittedly, they are, indeed, a mighty strength in Chhattisgarh, Jharkhand, Orissa, Andhra Pradesh,

WB and eastern part of Maharashtra. Hence, division or rift, lack of camaraderie on account of caste line or caste sentiment is likely to damage the unity, solidarity and goal of the revolutionary movement. It is not known whether the leadership is aware or watchful on such a malady. Truly, in Bihar such a sapling is noticed more than once which may take the shape of a mighty oak in the long run.

Successive governments in Bihar have failed to contain the Maoist activities. They have not paid adequate attention to eradicate poverty, develop extremist dominated areas economically and establish responsive administration. On the contrary, high corruption in government level, poor developmental work in rural areas, failure to ensure protection to the people, curb caste war and the blood thirsty ultras, has shaken faith of the people on the law enforcing authority and the government. Political tussle and instability of the government has worsened the situation. Controversy whether soft or hard line will be taken to tackle the ultras is a bottleneck to handle the problem firmly. Steady growth of the ultras has hardly been taken seriously by the government. Political parties either aspiring power or already in power are eager to encash political mileage from the growing threat and blood-curdling events. Subsequently, the birth of Jharkhand state bifurcating Bihar was a sigh of relief for many political parties and their activists. Jharkhand territory is more vulnerable from the point of the extremists operation and their striking power. Geographical condition, terrain and inaccessibility are advantageous for the ultras to build sanctuaries, training and hiding grounds and arrange better logistic support. In addition, it is a good recruiting ground, as many teenagers of both the sexes are willing to join the cadre being the victims of poverty and neglect. MCC is active in Chatra, Daltonganj, Hazaribagh, Palamu, Giridhi, Bokaro, Ranchi, Gumla, Lohardaga, Garhwa, Dhanbad and East Singhbhum districts of Jharkhand.

MCC had been maintaining close link with the Maoists of Nepal, known as CPN (Maoist). Both sides were receiving and sharing arms, ammunitions, explosives mutually. In April 2002, the CPN (Maoist) joined the training camp held at Aurangabad, Bihar and Hazaribagh, now in Jharkhand, organised by the MCC. They under took joint raids and attacking the targets located on the Indian territory. In September 2002, Pramod Mishra, a front rank leader of the MCC visited Nepal for consultation on the line of a joint confederation. In 2002, MCC, PWG and CPN formed the Indo-Nepal Border Regional Committee to coordinate and collate activities on either sides of the Indo-Nepal border. In 2001, CPN (Maoist) deputed Chandra Prakesh Gajurel alias Gaurab, a member of the politburo to attend the ninth congress of the PWG in Andhra Pradesh. Later he was arrested in Chennai air port when he was trying to travel abroad. The extremists of India, Nepal, Sri Lanka and Bangladesh planned to organise a Coordination Committee of the Maoist out-fits in South Asia which was expected to work as an effective Umbrella Organisation in the region. In this attempt MCC of Bihar played a pivotal role.

Importantly, Maoists assert that Kashmir is not an integral part of India and the Indian army in Kashmir is an occupation force. Several outfits maintain contact with Pakistan's ISI and work on their intelligence. Needless to add, the Maoists active in India have been maintaining link with the LTTE, CPN (Maoist) of Nepal and the Chinese Communist Party of China. In fact, their loyalty and allegiance to the mother land is questionable. The Maoists supported the separatist movement in Kashmir at the behest of Pakistan. Terrorist, Maqbool Butt of Kashmir was executed in January 1984 rigorously following the judicial process. Terrorist outfits in India protested, put up posters and condemned it. Meanwhile, the combination of the CPI (Maoist), ISI of Pakistan and CPN (Maoist) of Nepal, known as the Triple Entente is very active and is a positive threat to India's internal safety and security.

Dismayingly, today, of 38 districts of Bihar, 33 districts are in the grip of the Maoist violence. In six years back Maoists were active in 17 districts only. Impartial critics feel that Maoists violence has been increasing unabatedly. The coalition government's soft policy and lack of indomitable will to disarray the out laws is the root cause of escalated extremist violence. State government feels that since socio-economic condition is the prime reason for the Maoist aggressive activities and the peoples' sympathy and response to their call are not negligible, police action will not suffice to contain or banish the threat. Hence, to go deep into the root of the growing problem, eradication of poverty and removal of social discrimination is essential. Indeed, economic development and social justice in all level are sine qua non. Government's logic is not unsound. Nevertheless, how far the state has succeeded to pursue and implement it during its full five year tenure will be critically discussed in the relevant chapter. Frankly speaking, every year a substantial budgetary allotment is sanctioned for uplift of the poor and people of the lower strata. For the Adibasi population a separate and fat allocation of fund is sanctioned by the union government. Unfortunately, in majority of cases, the fund is not fruitfully spent for developmental works or often it remains unspent. Again, while marshalling a project fund is not purposefully utilised. On many occasions, allocated fund sanctioned for development and welfare activities is diverted for other projects violating the guide line of the union government. Many state governments are notorious defaulters in such unhealthy pursuit. Secondly, corruption plays a devious role and destroys moral fabric of the society and people. In fact, the lion portion of the fund is either misused or squandered away which defeats the very purpose of progress and development. A Minister of Bihar told me informally that only 28 percent of the fund sanctioned trickle down to the grass root level. This is likely to be the picture in majority of the states. Admittedly, corruption is a flinty obstacle to ensure desired development, especially, in backward areas. Hence, in spite of independence since 1947, rural and backward areas are still suffering from the pangs of under-development, innocuous or puny progress and economic instability.

Maoists in Jharkhand

Jharkhand has been carved out of Bihar. Now its head quarter is located in Ranchi. Jungle and jungle products, coal and iron ore mines of the state, the nature's gift bring economic prosperity of the state. Population is mainly adivasis in many districts. They depend on jungle for their livelihood. Labour is cheap. Investors, contractors, professionals are generally from other states, who flock there for enriching themselves. Their interest is business and to amass wealth by hook or by crook. In such a miry pursuit they are unhesitant to exploit the poor adivasis. Indeed, the state is favourable for agitation and mass movement encashing the anti rich, and anti affluent sentiment of the poverty ridden and exploited people. Secondly, geographical condition, acute poverty, poor economic growth and exploitation by mine owners, contractors, outsiders, traders etc are highly favourable for initiating pro mass agitation. The extremists who organised naxalite movement in Bihar and Jharkhand considered these plus points. They shrewdly selected the areas, mobilised the poor, labourers and adivasis, brain washed them and goaded them to respond to their call and join the movement. Broadly speaking, in remote areas administration is slack. Government officials harass and extort the poor and innocent people. Neither government nor the district administration cares for ensuring minimal civic amenities for the common people. Ironically, in spite of promises and propaganda the people are compelled to lead a sub standard living. Education and healthcare suffer beyond any measure. Monumental callousness and indifference of the government has abysmally increased discontentment and anti establishment sentiment. Dismayingly, the government has hardly undertaken welfare measure and initiated development measures in right earnest. Admittedly, the government lamentably failed to maintain desired control and surveillance on the growing aggressive activities of the ultras. The government's lukewarm attitude to fathom the real cause and identify the crux of the unrest has helped the extremists to entrench deeply in remote areas and spread their net work. Secondly, rivalry and jealousy of the political parties and attempt to add political overtone in any gory incident indirectly help the extremists to strengthen their base, win support of the local aggrieved populace and intensify violent movement. Hence, meaningful attempt to curb the extremists, engage in welfare and developmental activities badly lag behind. Significantly, in both states young recruits are enlisted either by money or coercion. In many cases, boys in the age group of 8 to 12 are forcibly taken away from the families either by threat or on the promise of paying a hefty amount. Recruits are trained and admitted in the cadre. Poor parents or guardians living in rural areas are unable to oppose the move or report to the right forum. They are compelled to reconcile to their lot without lodging complaint to the police or other appropriate agency.

Maoist demagogues desperately try to recruit the local youths. In that pursuit they adopt fair or foul means. Truly, pathetic economic condition, social injustice and the leaders' fervent appeal attract the youths to join the cadre. Many responding to the call, were volunteers that joined, aspiring for a perceptive social and political change. Surprisingly, the leaders' alacrity and flaccid interaction even attract the weaker sex to join the cadre. Many voluntarily enlist themselves in the squad, undergo training, hardship and take active part in operations ignoring risk and police offensives. Interestingly, the leadership encourages the fair sex to join the cadre for more than one reason. First, participation of fair sex in militancy is a startling revelation in the male dominated society, which carries high news value. Secondly, it helps to keep the flock together, as intimacy and emotional attachment of both sexes often work well. It prevents desertion and farewell to arms by the frustrated militants. Thirdly, fair sex can easily influence and allure the youth to join the cadre and aid to keep the cadre intact and thereby ensure solidarity.

In initial stage resources of the ultras was limited. Fund clandestinely received from China through the Chinese Embassy Nepal was far from sufficient. Financial crunch for purchase of arms, ammunitions, training equipments, provisions and other necessaries for the cadre was an uphill hindrance. However, soon they learnt the trick to collect fund through threat, coercion, robbery, kidnapping and extortion.

Mine owners, contractors, rich traders, moneyed persons were the targets. As it worked well, the similar *modus operandi* was applied for the politicians and corrupt public servants. Truly, it opened the flood gate of collecting money through threat and extortion. Corrupt political leaders, including the Ministers, MPs, MLAs, and many public servants are put under constant threat. They know that the administration is unable to disarray the rapacious ultras and protect them, and law abiding persons. Hence, they consider it wise to succumb to the Red threat and agree to be extorted regularly. In fact, such payment in local parlance is called "Protection money." Crime mutually agreed or agreed to be committed is an offence. Hence, this miry practice is unacceptable legally, morally and ethically. Yet it is going on. The idea of *quid pro quo* has been working well. Both sides perhaps feel happy. A few political leaders feel that it is a sigh of relief for them and for their family members.

I have come across more than adequate evidence on this count during my visit to Jharkhand. In remote rural areas even the school teachers are compelled to part with a portion of their salary. Truly, spectre of terrorism equally dither public servants, especially, who work in the interior places of the districts. They have to obey the diktats of the Maoists, pay them secretly either on specific demands or on monthly basis. In fact, the corrupt public servants are the object of threat and extortion. Regrettably, the government is fully aware of pervasive corruption in government offices and the ultras' extortion syndrome. Yet, it has been thriving with impunity and no relief is at sight for the people. Corruption in political and government level is an exasperating weakness of the government which often dissuades them to enforce law impartially and strictly. It is an open secret that the former Chief Minister of Jharkhand, Madhu Koda amassed money and wealth adopting corrupt means. He was, therefore, sacked and now facing criminal prosecution. I am told that he gained over the Maoists and used to pay them regularly to avoid their wrath. It appeared that from the steel city Bokaro and its periphery the Maoists extort annually rupees one hundred cores. From reliable source it is gathered that in the districts like Palamu, Latehar, Gumla, and Garhwa etc. the authority of the government is quailing and quivering for fear of the caddish ultras. Here writs of the Maoists loom large. After sunset, except the district HQ, the rest areas go under absolute control of the extremists where their writs are supreme.

Villagers in Maoists' Fold

In Maoist dominated territory the ultras have succeeded in convincing the villagers the need to stand up against exploitation, denial and social injustice. It is put into their heads that the present regime will not be able to change their miseries. Hence, they have to collectively organise mass upheaval to humble the reactionary forces, class enemies and establish a new era. Continued propaganda, contact, brain wash and populist measures etc have been producing positive result. Villagers come under the Maoists' fold and believe that armed struggle under their leadership is the solution to subdue all malaises. In fact, local followers and activists are trained to use fire arms, plant land mines, use explosives, and organise resistance groups to stall advance of the police and foil raids, search, arrests etc. In Saranda forest alone, about 400 villagers have been trained in carrying out explosions with improvised explosive devices (IEDs). In the forest there are ten revenue and 25 forest villages which are cut off from urban areas and the district HQ. In short, Saranda forest is one of the strongest and safest rabbit holes of the Maoists in eastern region. Inside the inaccessible forest Maoists run several training camps. Villagers' active support and assistance have made them dauntless and defiant. On several occasions the security forces have faced and engaged them but have achieved meager success. Advance of the police contingent is interrupted and delayed, as land mines have to be cleared and defused. In fact, the villagers trained by the Maoists plant land mines to thwart quick advance of the police party. Of late, the Maoists have initiated several welfare activities for the villagers. A few schools, health centers have been opened to take care of education of the children and health of the local populace. However, want of regular supply of essential commodities, medicine, services of medical practitioners and trained nursing hands pose a serious problem. It equally affects the Maoists to lead underground life short circuiting police watch, surveillance or raids.

Maoist Movement in Chhattisgarh and Maharashtra

Chhattisgarh has been separated from Madhya Pradesh in November 2000. Now Raipur is its head quarter. The state is known for its thick jungle, timber, forest products, mineral deposits and natural beauties. Population of the state is 20.08 million and its 80 percent are tribals. Poverty is deplorable. Communication is poor. For many villages located in interior places foot track is only means of communication. Civic amenities, health care, educational opportunities are virtually non-existent. Administration is unable to pull its weight in remote areas. Development and economic progress suffered from slovenly move, indecision and adverse conditions. Southern portion of the state is touching Andhra Pradesh, Orissa. Terrorists from Andhra Pradesh initially penetrated into Bastar region for spreading the terrorist net work. In that pursuit abject poverty of the tribal populace, terrain and inadequate roads and communication facilities and absence of administration proved very handy. Response of the people to the extremists' overture was, indeed, very encouraging. In rural areas administration and the police surveillance was either lackluster or porous. Nucleus of the impending class war, indoctrination of the Maoist gospel, animosity between have and have-not, the object of over throwing the existing government, are plentiful to cultivate the ground suitably. In a nutshell, the extremists considered the areas highly fertile for the revolutionary movement and establishing sanctuaries. Unfortunately, fast growth of the extremists and their penetration into rural areas was possible due to the government's indifference and for adopting the policy of masterly inactivity.

Broadly speaking, Jharkhand and Chhattisgarh are epicenter of the Maoist activities. Six districts of Chhattisgarh practically are the Red bastion of the Maoists since 1980. In Bastar region, 40000-sq km area is a free zone, where the writs of the Maoists decide matter. Here Kangaroo court or so called Peoples' Court decide the fate of many hapless persons. Abujmarh (the unknown forest) is the HQ of the Maoists, which is located inside thick and inaccessible forest. It is reported that 68.16 per cent of the Maoist related violence is reported from Jharkhand and Chhattisgarh together. Bailadila is one of the best reserves of iron ore of the country. National Mineral Development Corporation's (NMDC) business including export of iron ore depends much on Bastar region. Escalated violence and bloodshed unleashed by the extremists has severely hindered enterprises of the NMDC and the satellite industries and put them to galling financial losses. In 2007-08, within one year, due to the extremist violence the NMDC had lost rupees 200 crores. Insecurity in the mining belt has been stalling economic progress and developments. The ultras often target KVA towers which disrupt electric supply for several days. As a result, it jeopardizes industrial production and normal civic life. In 2008, three 132 KVA towers were blown off in Narayanpur. The areas including Dantewada district remained under darkness for 12 days continuously. Loss was to the extent of rupees 160 crores. Extremist attacks and casualty of the security personnel and civilians have been excruciatingly increasing since 2003. From July 2007 to July 2010 the state has faced 1948 attacks, and 435 security personnel, including 75 special police officers (SPOs) and 418 civilians had been killed. In fact, rough estimate reveals that during the period about 2000 persons were killed and security personnel figured 50 percent of the casualty. CRPF personnel are the worse sufferers. DGP of the state feels that 50000 Maoists are holed up in Bastar region, including 10000 are highly trained who can use mortars, rocket launchers and sophisticated weapons. Deployment of several guerrilla squads has substantially increased striking power of the ultras.

The state government has raised a civil militia, called Salwa Judum, ostensibly to protect the unarmed rural people. It originated in 2005, in Dantewada district. According to the Gondi language prevalent in Chhattisgarh, it means resistance group or bahini. However, to make it popular and acceptable, it is attributed as Santi Bihari, meaning army of peace. However, its birth and functioning style is under scathing criticism. Critics feel that, in practice, it is a killing squad formed by the government to do away with the ultras. Even the Apex Court has questioned its bonafide and the sanction by the state government and finally banned it.

Intensity of Maoist attacks, deployment of squads in strength, casualty inflicted on the security forces, special police officers and civilians, fast growth of the cadre is a flinty threat to safety and security of the people and the state. The state government is in a quandary to counter the threat and disarray the ultras, assert its authority and maintain law and order. In fact, out of 18 districts of the state, five districts, Kanker, Narayanpur, Bijapur, Bastar Sukma and Dantewada have turned to be the hunting ground of the Maoists. Eight other districts are also facing the Maoist brunt. It needs no reiteration that the police and para military forces have been operating and taking on the ultras under trying circumstances. They have to camp for months together inside jungle or inhabitable places, devoid of civic amenities, facing diseases, inclement weather, numerous odds and constant fear of the Maoist surprise attacks and death. Undeniably, their morale is affected. Majority of them want to avoid posting in Maoist infected areas. Of late, a sizeable police personnel have refused to join places in Maoist hit areas. State government has served notice on 78 policemen including 33 Inspectors, for refusing to join the places rocked by Maoist violence. Grounds advanced for refusal of complying with the posting order are sickness, including diabetes, high blood pressure, heart problem. Police administration is upset as such refusal has been increasing steadily. Dismayingly, the state is lamentably lagging behind to ensure development, economic progress, set up industries and open employment opportunities. However, the state has asked for Rs.4553 crores grant from the Planning Commission under the Integrated Action Plan (IAP) for developing five terrorist-torn districts. As a matter of fact, the Planning Commission has chalked out an integrated plan for development of Maoist hit areas. A financial package of Rs.13,742 crores under

IAP scheme will be spared for 83 districts of seven states. Again, out of 83 districts, 35 districts are ear marked as most vulnerable and thereby need extra attention.

From 2004, the state has initiated several packages, including financial packages for rehabilitating the surrendered Maoists Packages are very attractive for the ultras for returning to the main stream of the society giving up arms. Yet, response of the outlaws is far from satisfactory. Till October 31, 2010, a total of 2,619 rebels had surrendered. The state has committed to pay rupees three lakhs to an ultra if he or she surrenders with a light machine gun and rupees two lakhs will be paid if surrender is made with an AK 47 rifle. In fact, the above surrender figure may apparently be spectacular, but only six of them surrendered with 12 bore guns. It reveals that the stock of automatic or semi-automatic weapons are still in tact in the Maoists' arsenal. The police's rough estimate on this count discloses that 10000 thousand Maoists active in the state are either possessing light machine guns (LMGs) or have access to LMGs or AK 47 or automatic rifles. Hence the state's one of the dream policies to get back the rebels to normal life is yet to produce the desired result. Needless to add, it is a ponderous task to goad the hard core Maoists to bid adieu to arms and return to the main stream of the society accepting the rehabilitation package. Nevertheless, the police's and the administration's sincere and painstaking effort has indicated much ray of hope.

The villagers taken to the fold of the ultras by force, coercion or who join the Maoist cadre voluntarily are called "Sangham". In 2006, two armed rebels and 1032 "Sangham" members had surrendered agreeing to the rehabilitation offer. In 2007, total 90 Maoists and 77 Sangham members, in 2008, five Maoists including two armed Maoists and one Sangham member, in 2009, two Maoists and 13 Sangham members and in 2010 till 31st October, three Maoists have surrendered.

Recruitment of Minors—Hardcores Unwilling to Surrender

Recruitment and training mechanism in the Maoist cadre has a special bearing. Male children within the age group of 8 and 10 are forcibly picked up from the family either by threat or promise of a hefty sum and inducted into the squad of minors, called Bal Sangham. They are brain-washed for years and indoctrinated in the Maoist ideology. In fact, upon attaining youth they become the main fighting arms of the outfit, obdurately involved and entwined in Maoist gospel. It is very difficult to convince them of the will-o-the-wisp of the Maoist ideology tainted with violence, bloodshed and frenzied campaigns. No amount of council or persuasion will help to get them immune from the cobweb of the culture of annihilation and disorder and serve the humanity in the accolade of peace, prosperity and happiness. Hence, surrender of the hard core ultras shunning unctuous culture and gory object is a stymie. Evidently, all out attempts to salvage them from phantasmagoria is often negated. Impartial critics feel that it is a difficult proposition to win over the stubborn ultras. It needs patience, long term plan, strategy, mutual trust and congenial ambience. In fact, regular contact, clear cut commitment for rehabilitation and guarantee for their safety and future are essential.

Recruitment in the Red army is generally made in three or four levels. First, apart from the committed ultras, able bodied youths are recruited. They are paid a fixed amount regularly which may be taken as salary. Pangs of poverty and unemployment compel them to join the Maoist cadre. Secondly, adolescents as narrated above are inducted in the cadre by coercive means. After intensive training and strong doze of indoctrination they eventually turn to be the hard core Maoists. Recruits of the Bal Sena or Bal Sangham once attain youth, are up graded and inducted into the action, guerrilla or other operational squads. They are highly committed ultras who are generally above any temptation and insensitive to concession or rehabilitation. Thirdly, members of the "Sangham." are locally recruited and trained to assist the militants in carrying arms, ammunitions, provisions, maintaining communications, keeping watch on the movements of the police and the security forces, carry messages and assist the main body during operations. They are trained to use fire arms, plant land mines, resist the security forces and foil attempt of the police to surround the villages or arrest any comrade. However, they are not the permanent members of the cadre and not regularly paid. Broadly, they are the auxiliary hands of the Maoists.

Second Line of Defence

Of late, it has come to light that small groups from the villages are picked up and trained in carrying out explosions with improvised explosive devices (IEDs) Almost in every village small groups have been selected and trained. They are the sympathizers of the Maoists but do not belong to the cadre. Frankly speaking, the Maoists do not follow any hard and fast rule for the recruitment and strengthening the cadre. Here, the policy of local convenience matters. Many volunteer and rest are intimidated or forced to join. They help or assist the ultras, and are utilised as the second line of defence. However, picking up the adolescents under threat and fear, contrary to the wish of the parents, and transform them into deadly Maoists, is cruel, diabolic and unethical. Importantly, Ministry of Home Affairs New Delhi has admitted that from 2009, Maoist attacks and casualty of security personnel have been increasing. In 2010, the Maoist attacks have increased by 40 percent. State police feel that about 50000 thousand Maoists are holed up in Bastar region and 10000 thousand specially trained are hiding in the forest. They are highly motivated and intensively trained. They can use mortars, rocket launchers and capable of confronting the security force in good strength. Intelligence of the police is far from effective. In remote villages, the outsiders are immediately spotted and hence, a cop from intelligence branch is unable to cultivate any reliable source. Secondly, language is a bottle neck to contact a source, exchange dialogues and motivate him to divulge secret. Again, no local resident is courageous enough to develop contact with an outsider or a policeman for fear of life. He is fully aware of the risk. A little suspicion may cost his life or bring unperceived calamity for the family. Truly, in Chhattisgarh, the Maoists' aggressive activities have generated furore and frightening atmosphere. Even the precious diamond mine belt is under the control of the ultras.

Security forces are unable to penetrate in remote areas where the Maoists rule the roost. Massacre of 76 CRPF personnel including a Deputy Commandant of the 62 battalion is a manifestation of the Red militants' upper hand and magnitude of the traumatic situation. The state government is still to frustrate the Red offensive and restore normalcy.

Civilians in the Maoist turf are regularly targeted and attacked by the ultras for their suspected anti-Maoist activities. Ultras believe that many are informers of the police. Many tribals who form a segment of civil population are also suspected and kept under scanner. In fact, many being afraid of the ultra's attack have temporarily moved out of their abode and taken shelter in temporary camps. Fortunately, except in Chhattisgarh, no such exodus has taken place in other states. However, forty thousand tribals of the state have left their home and taken shelter in relief camps opened by the government at Dantewada and Bijapur districts. Exodus of the tribals was brought to the notice of the National Human Rights Commission, New Delhi. After enquiry the Commission has submitted a report in August 2008. This has been brought to the notice of the Lok Sabha. However, from many pockets of Jungle mahal, West Medinapur district, West Bengal, indiscriminate killing of the CPM activists and innocent villagers, arson, loot, atrocity and attack on the CPM offices have created a weird ambience which forced many CPM supporters and activists to leave the disturbed areas to avoid the wrath of the ultras and taken shelter in the district HQ Medinapur temporarily. Cacophony of the macabre festival of death panicked many peace loving people who preferred to shift to safer places temporarily. They stayed in friends' or relatives' house or in hired accommodation. No relief camp was opened. However, many have returned to their abodes already as the security forces' success have helped to restore semblance of administration in several pockets.

Maoists Active in Maharashtra, Uttar Pradesh and Karnataka

Gadchiroli, Gondia, Chandrapur, Bhandara districts are located in eastern region of Maharashtra state adjacent to Chhattisgarh state. Territory in the south is touching Adilabad, Karimnagar, Khammam and Warangal districts of Andhra Pradesh. Entire area is the hub of the Red ultras. Peoples War Group (PWG) from A P gradually sneaked into Chhattisgarh and Maharashtra and geared up militancy. The militant outfits of Andhra Pradesh supplied arms and ammunitions to the ultras operating in new areas. In fact Gondia worked as the major transit point for arms supply. Notably, Balaghat, Mandla and Dindori districts of Madhya Pradesh were badly affected by Maoist violence. In late nineties, in several encounters, 30 policemen, 15 civilians and 11 militants were killed. Gruesome murder of Transport Minister, Lakhiram Kavre in his residence at Sonepuri village, Balaghat district, in December 1999, high-lighted the gravity of the alarm bell.

In Gadchiroli district, it is strongly suspected that many extremists from Nepal joining hands with the local Maoists participated in gun battles against the security forces. Evidence is in galore that the terrorists from Nepal have been secretly maintaining active link with local ultra outfits. The then State Home Minister expressed his apprehension about involvement of the Nepali Maoists. Happily, the state has been galvanizing the police and armed forces to meet the challenge of the Red terror. The state has raised an elite force, called Alpha Hawks, who are specially trained to fight the Maoists. Alpha Hawks is the second anti-Naxal commando unit in the country. Personnel are trained in the Unconventional Operation Training Centre (UOTC) in Nagpur. This force is deployed in the terrorist torn areas including Gadchiroli district.

From south eastern part of Uttar Pradesh, especially, Mirzapur district, to Dharampuri forest of Tamilnadu state, the entire area is in the grip of the Maoist. Admittedly, from Tamil Nadu, the Maoists were maintaining link with the LTTE of Sri Lanka and procuring arms, explosives and land mines. It is believed that the Maoists had learnt use of land mines and the knowhow of manufacturing land mines locally. In Karnataka state terrorist activities are evident in Bollottu forest in Udipi, Chikmangalur and Tumkur districts. Apparently, activities of the ultras are temporarily controlled or suspended by the ultras and therefore, lull is prevailing. It is suspected that many high ranking Maoist leaders often take shelter in the state circumventing vigil and the dragnet of the police and intelligence agencies. Hence, as a matter of stratagem the ultras prefer to avoid violence in the state and keep it comparatively free from police surveillance to make it a safe sojourn for the Maoist leaders.

One of the top Maoist leaders Koteswar Rao alias Kishenji declared that they could over throw the Indian state much before the year 2050. A booklet circulated by the Maoists revealed that they are looking for it by 2050. However, some document discloses that it may be 2060. The Union Home Secretary refuting the pompous claim asserted that they are free to hope and in a democracy they have the privilege to dream. The union government is ready to enter into dialogue once the Maoists abjure violence. If they make a categorical statement on this count, the Ministry of Home Affairs is prepared to talk. The Home Secretary admitted that the armed cadres of the Maoists around 10000 thousands are highly motivated and well trained. Personnel drawn from para military forces and state police force had not been able to hit at even five per cent of the armed cadres. (*The Statesman*, March 8, 2010). Unfortunately, disagreement with the Chief Ministers on the joint strategy, line of action, coordination etc. has been gallingly hindering anti insurgency operations. Sympathy and support of many intellectuals is petulantly standing on the way.

Ultras spend a good amount as a monetary incentive to attract the new recruits. Rupees three thousands is paid to a recruit as a monthly remuneration. Poor and unemployed youngsters hailing from backward areas or insurgency hit areas join the Red cadre. Interestingly, many retired public servants develop link with the Maoists, help them for procuring arms, repairing arms and manufacturing arms locally. In 2007, right in Bhopal city, MP, police discovered a workshop, manufacturing fire arms including automatic rifles for the extremists. Two retired armours from the Indian army and a few public servants were employed for running the foundry. After massacre of 76 CRPF personnel on 6th April, 2010, in Chhattisgarh, probe disclosed that some people within the police force and retired cops clandestinely were involved in the deal. A few CRPF jawans were arrested. Some retired policemen associated with the Uttar Pradesh Special Task Force were directly involved in supply of ammunitions and magazines of Indian Small Arms System (INSAS) rifles to the ultras. Investigation transpired that the racket is spread to several urban areas and cities of UP. The suspects have been collecting ammunitions of different bores to suit different weapons. The racket is spread to Allahabad, Vanarasi, Mirzapur, Chandoli, Sonebhadra, Jhansi, Basti and Gonda district police armouries of Uttar Pradesh. It reveals that ammunitions for attack on the CRPF personnel on April 6, 2010 in Chhattisgarh had reached the hands of the ultras from the U P district police armoury. A retired Sub Inspector of the U P Police force, Yashodanand Singh, who was posted in Rampur armoury earlier is connected with the racket. He, along with two accomplices, had been arrested. Surprisingly, such a malfeasance has been continuing for the last four and a half years obfuscating supervision of the police hierarchy. The Special Task Force of UP entrusted to bust the conspiracy feels that it is not ruled out that these black sheep have developed link with the Maoists active in West Bengal.

Sonebhadra, Chandauli and Mirzapur districts of Uttar Pradesh are gradually becoming the hub of the extremists. Striking feature of the extremist movements is the involvement of the Islamic terrorists Harkat-ul-Islami-Jehadi (Huji) and the Lakshar-e-Taiba. It is not very clear if the Maoists have been operating in tandem with the Islamic terrorists. The surprise attack on the CRPF camp at Rampur in early morning of January 1, 2008, murder of CRPF personnel is a clear testimony of the nexus of the Maoists and the Islamic jihadi elements. True, the Maoists have not accepted the responsibility of the repeated blasts before the gory incident reported from Rampur, UP. Yet the modus operandi and magnitude of the crime suggests in that direction. Importantly, prior to this attack, serial blasts on 23 November 2007, in the court premises in Lucknow, Vanarasi and Faizabad and subsequent arrests of top militants in Lucknow unambiguously corroborate that the terrorists have been spreading their net work in UP. Government intelligence agencies claimed that prior warning was given to the UP police and the CRPF

HQ about the impending attack on the CRPF camp at Rampur. In fact, the militants meticulously planned and cunningly entered into the camp as candidates for enlistment in the force when recruitment drill was in progress. The ultras suddenly attacked the personnel and killed several of them, looted arms etc. Modus operandi of the operation is similar to that of the plan and execution generally taking place in Jammu and Kashmir. Police's rough estimate discloses that about 60 to 80 ultras only are active in UP. They are aided and abetted by more than 200 over ground supporters (OGS). In fact, number of the OGS has been alarmingly increasing. Many activists try to cultivate innocent persons and lure them to work as OGS. Culprits arrested for the blast cases have followed an extra ordinary modus operandi. After execution of the blasts they immediately joined normal duties so that none could suspect their sinister design. Several terrorists from Bangladesh directly participated in the operation. They operate receiving logistic support from the OGS elements. Immediately after execution of the dreaded task they disappear from the scene leaving no clue. Some travel to far away places or return to Bangladesh. As a result, investigation is unable to catch them and demolish the conspiracy. Interrogation disclosed that one of the arrested accused persons, named Ansari was responsible for the dreadful incident in the Sankat Mochan Temple at Vanarasi. He worked as a labourer in Calcutta Electric Supply Corporation. It is crystal clear that the ultras have been modifying their plans, mode of operation and execution. Secondly, while selecting the persons for final assault, they are not sticking to stereotyped or conventional skill or practice. Here they engaged outsiders who did not belong to the cadre and the outfit not paying them regularly. In fact, in reality, they are mercenaries or hired goons. Incidentally, the Ulfa in North East has adopted the practice of "out sourcing". Even they engage minor boys on negligible remuneration.

Interestingly, the Maoists had put candidates in three districts in UP for contesting election for the state Assembly in April/May 2008. They asked the voters to vote for their candidates. Extremists are traditionally known as election baiters and ask the people to boycott vote. Paradoxically, here the Maoists deviating from the past had jumped into the election fray. Kameshwar Baitha, sub-zonal commander of the Maoist out-fit facing 12 criminal cases and lodged in Garhwa jail, Jharkhand had submitted his candidature in BSP's ticket. Baitha, a 55 years old rebel, planned to wage a war for the oppressed people. From the jail he declared that he was no longer a Maoist, but only a BSP worker. So long he was active in Jharkhand, now he wanted to consolidate his hold across the border of Chhattisgarh and UP. Strangely, the Maoists did not react on Baitha's sudden good bye to the outfit which tentamounts to a betrayal.

The Maoists are targeting the Special Economic Zone (SEZ). Maoists consider it a kind of global imperialism which is a mighty threat to the Red movement. Hence, such move ought to be circumscribed right in the beginning. Ministry of Home Affairs New Delhi has secretly warned the states. Intelligence report revealed that the Maoists have seriously decided to take on SEZs and their promoters as they believe that the success of the attack is very crucial to the survival of the movement in the twenty first century. CPI (Maoist) leader Varavara Rao stated that decision to oppose the setting up of SEZs was taken at the Ninth Unity Congress of the CPI (Maoists) that was held at a secret location in late February 2007, and a resolution was passed. "We are opposing SEZs because these are nothing but implementation of the World Bank's constitution." Maoists organise annual conference of the outfits. About three hundred delegates from India and foreign countries attend the conference which last for two or three days. It is held in a secluded place surrounded by jungle and hills. The foreign delegates travel by air, rail and roads. Intelligence report contains details of the venue, tentative time and number of the participants. The foreign delegates can easily be identified and trailing them exact location of the conference venue can easily be pin-pointed. Yet, for reasons unknown, the government is far from decisive to round up the delegates, organisers, activists and oppose or take steps to abnegate the unauthorised conference adhering to law. Indeed, the union and state government's ambivalence or faineance to tackle the growing menace with consummate firmness and diligence has only bloated the crooner of catastrophe. As a matter of fact, the government or political leaders considers pros and cons of political ramification, public sentiment and voters' reaction before initiating actions. Hence, action or policy relied on political pussy footing is often likely to be a precipice and may be contrary to national interest.

Death shrouds, the so called ready justice, so called peoples' court, torture and atrocity on the innocent villagers have been alienating the peace loving people from the Maoist influence. Members of the families who have been oppressed or killed by the ultras are extremely bitter against them. Indeed, ultras' wrath if responsible for the loss of an earning member of the family, their agony and suffering is well-nigh unbearable. The family's near and dear and the local people are abysmally perturbed seeing their opaque future. Visualising that they have to eke out miserable existence, the persons who were once sympathetic or heralding the Maoists' cause are inclined to modify their stand. Frankly speaking, deepening fanatical bigotry of annihilation of the class enemy and the peoples' war has been accelerating erosion in the Maoist influence and its turf. Hence, in more than one place, the disillusioned villagers denied to respond to the Maoists' diktat. They organised resistance groups and repulsed the Maoist attacks, brought out protest processions and displayed determination to negate the extremists' high handedness. In Jharkhand the angry villagers in process of defending themselves killed two extremists. A rebel was assaulted and set on fire for raping a girl. In Bihar, a group of disillusioned villagers reacted badly and went to the extent of attacking and killing two extremists. Ultras realising follies has initiated damage control exercise in some pockets.

CHAPTER TWO

The Extremists Challenge – Government's Determination to Combat, New Forces Raised and infra-structure Built, Joint Operation against the Ultras

Maoists feel that Indian ruling classes are mere agents of imperialism, not having any meaningful social and political base among the Indian people. All that is required is to arm the Indians and launch the people's war to achieve the revolutionary liberation.

CPM said, it is working to change, "The co-relation of class forces" among the Indian people by using both parliamentary and extra-parliamentary methods in order to bring about a revolutionary change. This, the Maoists see as the legitimisation of the parliamentary democracy in India and hence, their hostility and attacks are on the CPM.

The task of mobilising the people and changing the co-relation of class forces amongst the people cannot be replaced by seeking submission of the people through the terror of the gun. The CPM asserted that the Maoist's view lacks substance, rather faulty.

On June 22, 2009, the central government banned the CPI (Maoist) under the Unlawful Activities (Prevention) Act and asked the Maoists hit states to take step to ban the Maoist outfit active in the state. Prior to the declaration, Andhra Pradesh and Chhattisgarh governments have already banned the Maoist outfit in the states. In fact, right from the beginning the CM of WB, Buddhadeb

Bhattacharjee said that they would tackle the Maoist problem politically. In July 2008, he stated before the state Legislative Assembly that the state government had no plan to ban the CPI (Maoists), that his party would fight them politically. Comrade Prakash Karat, the General Secretary of the CPM Politburo stated that banning the Maoists would not serve any purpose. They would shift operations to other places. Importantly, the Left Front government led by the CPM in West Bengal did not ban the Maoist out-fit in spite of the Union government's advice. Truly, it is a mystery, why the LF Front government headed by the CPM dithered to ban the Maoist outfit. However, in this regard speculation and inferences have surcharged the political climate of the state.

First, the ideological compulsion perhaps dissuaded the CPM to ban the Maoist outfit in WB. Indeed, the CPM's political ideology and the Maoist's aims and objects are akin. One cannot deny or ignore the other. However, the method of implementation may differ but goal is the same. Critics quip that they are facets of the same stone and sail in the same boat. One school feels that the CPM is projecting itself as the party of the have-nots. Party has been brain washing the cadres on the same line. Hence, any action against the sister organisation fighting for the benefit of the poor and have-nots will ridicule the party, the workers and activists who will look at the leadership obliquely. The other group feels that action against the Maoists will alienate the tribal population of West Medinapur, Bankura and Purulia. The tribal populace is a major vote bank in this belt. They vote en masse in favour of the CPM candidates thinking that the CPM is the party for well being and welfare of the deprived and exploited people. About 40 MLAs in CPM ticket win from this belt and strengthen the CPM to establish comfortable majority in the state Legislative Assembly. It may be noted that Chatradhar Mohato, the founder father of the People's Committee against Police Atrocities (PCAPA), a frontal organisation of the extremists in Jangal Mahal challenged the state government for a massive public agitation if they dared to ban the Maoist outfit.

After attack on the convoy of the Chief Minister Budhadeb Bhattacharjee, on November 2, 2008, in West Medinapur, the CM thought of following Andhra and Chhattisgarh model to tackle the Maoists. He after meeting the Prime Minister and Union Home Minister on May 20, 2012 in New Delhi, told the media, "We have to give it (ban) a serious thought." Interestingly, the CPM state secretariat discussed the issue at an emergency meeting held a few days earlier. Yet, the CPM bosses were evasive, perhaps preferred to follow the policy of masterly inactivity. In 2005, Andhra Pradesh renewed the ban on the Maoists, after a MLA and eight others were killed by the Maoists. Ministry of Home Affairs put some pressure on the CM of West Bengal to follow the footstep. CM no doubt, felt the hit but failed to persuade the party hierarchy. Significantly, after attempt of assassination on him and the Central Minister, he readily deployed several armed battalions and requested the MHA to spare CRPF and other para military forces. As a sequel to the attempt on the CM, the state police went berserk. Arbitrary arrests, raids in mid-nights, inhuman torture, fabrication of criminal cases, and damage to the poor villagers' belongings continued, virtually, a reign of terror was let loose. CM posted with intelligence and official records, read the police's high-handedness, learnt through the news papers, criticism by the intelligentsia, yet failed to rein the police. His gospel and routine reaction to tackle the Maoists politically ended in a fiasco. Perhaps, his retaliatory spirit and fatuous arrogance gave the police a free hand to teach the poor villagers a lesson.

In way back 1960/1970, the Marxists, now the CPI (Maoist) declared the left-radicals their class enemy. Comrade Kanu Sanyal severed connection with Comrade Charu Mazumdar and founded the CPL (ML) on April 22, 1969 in Calcutta. He had no link with the Communist Party of China or Mao Zedong. CPM after coming to power in West Bengal maintained a safe distance from the Communist Party of China. In fact, Maoist attacks over a decade killed about 100 CPM leaders and activists, yet the LF government under the CPM's stewardship soft paddled the whole episode. Gorged with enjoying ease, comfort and perks of parliamentary democracy the CPM gave up the toilsome and hazardous revolutionary process. To them, impending conflict between the revolution, people's war, etc. and political ascendancy, struggle for capturing power etc., practically is given good bye. Perhaps, the CPM, for smooth sailing, is disinterested to rub the differences in the arid zone of acrimony. CPM's alibi on this count is not acceptable to the Maoists.

On the other hand, the CPM attempted to generate public opinion against the Maoists and isolate them from the masses through campaigns in grass root level. Cadres were deployed to stir anti Maoist sentiment. Diplomatic trickery adopted to infiltrate into the lower level of the Maoists. At a later stage, CPM organised a private militia in West Medinapur, better known "Harmad Bahini" to counter and displace the Maoists from three districts of W.B. Police was used to aid the party cadres and "Harmad Bahini" against the Maoists. They also tried to woo the tribals to their side. But the CPM's Minister attempts lamentably failed.

Andhra Pradesh government's ban order on the Maoists out-fit in 2005 in the state was preceded by the US state department's decision to include the Maoist out-fit in its list of terror organisations in the world. It was purely a coincident. Maoists used the Washington's decision in their advantage and unleashed propaganda that Washington and India together hatched up a conspiracy to perpetuate the pro-imperialist policy to denounce and suppress the people's legitimate movement. They accused the Congress led UPA government, New Delhi for thriving in the accolade of pro-imperialist design. It gave the CPM a God sent opportunity. They joined the blotted chorus and thereby tried to come close to the Maoists. Perhaps, to prove their bonafide and hatred against the U S's policy of imperialism, the CPM withdrew her support from the UPA government opposing extensively the Indo-US nuclear deal. However, in May 2011, in the Legislative Assembly election the people of WB rejected the CPM and a new party, Trinamul Congress, formed the government.

Various developments discussed will throw light on the CPM's duplicity. The readers may draw idea as to why the CPM was reluctant to impose ban on the Maoists.

M. Koteswar Rao Alias Kishanji's Interaction with the Media

Muppala Koteshwar Rao, alias Kishanji, aged 55 years, hailed from Andhra Pradesh, number two in the Maoist hierarchy, a member of the politburo and Chief of the Central Military Commission of the Maoist outfit, spoke to the media and highlighted on the Maoist movements. He was executing operational plans in West Bengal, co-coordinating with rebels of Jharkhand and Orissa. From hideouts in Lalgarh or in its periphery, he was directing the operations, recruiting youths for the cadre, procuring arms and ammunitions, maintaining contact with the media and projecting the stand of the Maoists. He was, in fact, the live wire for the Maoist movements and successes in West Medinapur, Bankura and Purulia districts of West Bengal. His physical presence in Lalgarh areas and able leadership from 2007 to till his death on 24 November 2011 was inspiring for the Maoist cadres and also memorable for his substantial contribution in the Maoist movement. He was symbol of terror before the local populace, much wanted Maoist leader in the police's records. His frank outburst before the media was interesting and threw much light on the Maoist movements He was killed at Burishole jungle in an encounter, about 10 kms away from WB and Jharkhand border at about 6 PM on 24 November 2011. His body was carried to Andhra Pradesh and cremated in his native village Padapally, district Karim Nagar, Andhra Pradesh.

Kishanji said that the Indian government under Prime Minister Manmohan Singh is Pro-American and its decisions were based on advises from the US intelligence agency. He iterated that American intelligence was a larger threat to internal security of India. Importantly, capitalist economy was facing crisis all over the world. Soon the malady would engulf India. Secondly, the Maoists supported the Islamic upsurge, as it was basically anti-US imperialism movement. Admittedly, Islamic fundamentalism has been spreading its wings over the globe. Its indiscriminate killing of common people was condemnable and not in keeping with Maoist principle. Nevertheless, Islamic upsurge should not be opposed as its basic aim is anti-US nature. Hence, instead of opposing it, it should be allowed to flourish and muster strength. Maoists did not support the nature of attack on Victoria Terminus railway station Mumbai since majority of the victims were Muslim.

Maoists support the militant out-fits active in North East and the LTTE. Secondly, the demand for the Azad Kashmir was justified. The politburo had entrusted him to collaborate with the militant out-fits of the North East and the Communist Party of Bangladesh. Negotiation with the Communist Party of Bangladesh had shown some progress. Kishanji asserted that the Maoists support all nationality movements and the movements in the North East as it fell in that category. The glittering prospect of impending revolution was knocking at the door. CPI (Maoists) has established themselves as major alternative party in the country. Formidable mass base already built in eight states and likely to expand its control in several other states was abundant manifestation of the coming revolution. Grievances of the deprived people had reached the culminating point. The mound of explosives was more than ready awaiting only a spark to detonate. True, the out-fit was not free from internal problems and dissensions. However, discords would be sorted out soon with the people's support.

As regards the political parties, The Bharatiya Janata Party (BJP) is a communal fascist force. The Communist Party of India (CPM) is a social fascist force. Both are their enemies. In fact, BJP's internal squabble is a big threat to the party and responsible for its decay. It instigates communal fracas and spreads violence. However, it had received befitting reply in Kondamal, Orissa. The lesson they got should be enough to caution them for the future. The Congress party is the first and foremost enemy of the Maoists. The politburo was contemplating to ban it in Maoist dominated seven states. WB government planned to start joint operation in Lalgarh, west Medinapur, to suppress the legitimate people's movement. The ruling Left Front in WB, is, no doubt, guilty of it, yet, the RSP, Forward Block and CPI cannot wash their hands off. Appeal made to the common people who had their conscience alive and human right activists to come forward and protest against the state sponsored terrorism in Lalgarh.

He was candid that arms were not the last say in liberating people from the oppressive rule. It is the people and their indomitable will and determination to throw away the yoke of the despotic dominancy always work. Struggle, sacrifice and final emancipation by the Vietnamese is a bright example. A small country could humble the super power, the United States and forced them to quit. Over and above, protracted warfare drained the US's exchequer and severely hurt its economy. Heavy casualty on the US army raised the citizenry's cry spontaneously to abandon the war and recall the troops. In fact, US's elephantine appetite of imperialism received a flinty set back before the fortitude and resoluteness of the freedom loving people.

In Lalgarh people's war against the state had shown unprecedented success. People were up-in-arms against the proposed land acquisition policy of the state and attempted to grab fertile agricultural land in Singur and Nandigram. Truly, people of Singur inspired the people of Nandigram to unite and resist the state's anti-people land acquisition move. The Left Front government working under the CPM's stewardship was aware that the local people would oppose with all strength the alienation of agricultural land. Still, the CPM had implicit faith on the party cadres and its machinery. They were sanguine that the party cadres and the workers' contact and influence on the rural people would suffice to goad the farmers to agree to the proposal.

Alternatively, muscle power of the party's goons would be enough to settle the matter. The proposed chemical hub at Naya Char would be resisted by the people. Kishanji asserted that they had good influence on the mass in Nadia district. Its undercurrent had been travelling fast in Murshidabad, Malda and Bardhaman districts. Revolutionary spirit had already established firm foot hold there. With regard to the advance of the joint forces in the Maoist belt in Jangal Mahal he said that entry inside a few kilo meters does not mean victory and debacle to the Maoists. It was a protracted people's war. There are different policies and methods, people would show how they welcome troops. He came down heavily on the intellectuals, accused them saying that they had supported the armed struggle in Singur and Nandigram. It was a mystery why they were silent when the joint forces unleashed murky outrages.

The union government's decision to pump thousands of para military forces, organise joint and co-ordinated actions in jungle mahal, revamp the intelligence unit etc to check the people's movement would be assessed and appropriate counter measures would be initiated. Very often many black sheep join hands with anti-movement forces. They must take note that they would never be forgiven. Informers would be severely punished. Presumption that combined operation would be a cementing force to flush out the Maoists from Jangal Mahal and compel them to take to heels, was totally misconceived. Inspire of presence of a large number of para military forces the Maoists had been ruling 1300 kms, zone the liberated areas, in Lalgarh for the last nearly ten months. People wanted withdrawal of the combined forces immediately. It was note worthy that on August 17, 2009, thousands of local people brought out a procession in Lalgarh areas defying the prohibitory order promulgated under section 144 of the Criminal Procedure Code, and held a public meeting at Gohamidanga, ignoring the presence of paramilitary forces camping nearby. The security forces were not in a position to enforce the prohibitory order. The people were no longer afraid of police atrocity, rather determined to pursue the people's movement.

The call for negotiation across the table giving up arms was unacceptable. Maoist leadership was not opposed to talks, especially, if it was a development issue. He reiterated that there was no question of giving up arms. However, should there be any move for dialogue the pre condition for the talk had to be accepted. First, all political prisoners had to be released unconditionally. Secondly, the terrorist tag imposed on the Maoists had to be withdrawn. He added that he had been staying in Lalgarh and had no intention to quit the place leaving the discomfited people to their fate. True, the Maoists had reverses in Andhra Pradesh, but it is a temporary phase. Mass base in Andhra Pradesh was very strong. It had been flourishing there for the last thirty years. Hence, the Maoists would bounce back soon. In Uttar Pradesh the Maoists have no base. However, attention was being paid to the state. Greater concentration had to be paid to Muslim population and trade union sector of the state. In Punjab once the Communist Movement gained ground. Hence, fresh attention had to be paid there. Finally, he said that Lalgarh would teach the WB government a good lesson. People's war was going to achieve a spectacular success soon.

Kishanji camped in jungle mahal and preferred to stay with the cadres, interacted with rural mass. Being one of the top Maoist leaders, he discarded urban comfort, proved himself a leader of men and a genuine comrade. Indeed, he was an inspiring leader, shared weal and woe with his men. Admittedly, his death cast a thick shadow on the Maoist movement and mass upheaval in West Bengal. For the Maoists, a beacon light was extinguished.

Failure of the Left Trade Unions for Advancement of the Maoist Movement

All India Trade Union Congress (AITUC), the Left–affiliated the largest trade union in the country is lukewarm at the progress of the Maoist movement. Its general council meeting held in Delhi on 6 and 7 May 2007, high lighted the crusade of growing Maoist surge in India. It asserted that rapid expansion of the Maoist movement across the country due to the UPA government's (Manmohan Singh, PM of the UPA government) pro-rich economic policies, coupled with the left parties failure to consolidate and expand their support base. Dismal stagnation of the Left parties in other states except West Bengal, Kerala and Tripura is the root cause of the Maoists' penetration into poverty-stricken backward states. Indeed, the Maoists zealously have been trying to fill the vacuum and achieved reckonable success. Alarming note that extremism has already put its foothold in 168 districts and gained sympathy and support of a sizeable rural populace and radicals had upset the participants of the convention. Secondly, gorged with the success of quick advancement and favourable response of the have-nots and the Red army's unabated ascendance have upset the speakers and the participants. Larking fear that the infatuated ultras might demolish the existing democratic order was abundantly manifested in deliberations. It was conceded that if organised democratic movement, struggle of the peasantry fails to gain a meaningful shape, political extremism is bound to gain strength and sweep the poverty-stricken territory spreading over under developed rural areas.

The General Secretary of the AITUC admitted that failure of the Left, the Trade Unions to provide a platform to the poor and deprived people and burgeoning discontentment among the under privileged people have been indirectly aiding terrorism. The Communist Party of India (CPI) was sympathetic to the Maoist movements. Interestingly, The CPI is unable to condemn the Maoist movement outright, as the critics quip that the CPI is the facet of the same stone. It was hinted that assuming, India attains the high growth rate of more than nine percent, the beneficiary is only 0.2 percent of the population. Inspite of pompous claim that 47 millions jobs have been created during the Xth Plan, the rate of unemployment increased to 3.06 percent. Manufacturing sector has lost over three percent jobs and annual growth of employment in the organised sector and public sector were equally deceptive. In sum, totality of the discussion revealed that economic, political, social failure including failure of the trade unions and the UPA government's fragile and pro-rich economic policy have given impetus to the alarming growth and expansion of the extremism. Broadly speaking, office bearers and speakers were ambivalent whether the AITUC carried cudgel for the Maoists and their aggressive movements, or not in agreement to over throw the government by the peoples' armed movement.

Maoist Empire: Rs.1500 Crores Worth of War Chest

Impression gained ground that the Maoists have been fighting for the poor and exploited people must be suffering from the pangs of want, penury, peltry fund and inadequate resources. They must be ill-fed, ill-clothed, and ill-equipped and deprived of civic amenities. In fact, clinging on the ideology their sacrifices for the sake of have-nots is exemplary. Comrade Charu Mazumdar, the founder father of Naxal movement in India hardly paid attention to mobilise fund and other resources for spear-heading the movement. His whiz-kids depended upon the Chinese Embassy, Nepal, for money and weapons. However, soon it dried up. Thereafter, they depended on subscriptions secretly collected from the shopkeepers, money lenders, landholders (jotdars). Yet, it was far short of the need. Secondly, they were reluctant to pay unless pressurised or coerced. As the organisation was growing plenty of fund was required for the Red army and for buying weapons, explosives, provisions, etc. Era of Charu Mazumdar and the Naxal movement tampered with idealism was replaced by the maxim that necessity knows any law. Hence, the path of abduction and extortion found to be highly rewarding. Today, the Maoists recklessly extort the mine owners, civil and forest contractors, industrialists, business men, moneyed persons, transport owners, public servants, school teachers, etc. and collect unbelievably a hefty sum. Informal estimate reveals that annual collection of fund is to the tune of rupees one thousand five hundred crores. Every year the target of collection is raised by 15 percent. Frankly speaking, today, the Maoist Empire is rich and wealthy. Their war chest is no longer puny. Beefy money power and abundant resources is a substantial impetus to proceed with protracted insurgency.

Modus operandi of extortion is not identical in all Maoist infested territory. Terror is stepped up in areas which leaves message that either obey the Maoist diktat or get ready for death penalty. In addition to extortion, robbery, loot, levy from the poppy cultivators, trucks carrying rice, paddy, vegetables, timbers, truck and bus owners are freely indulged in. I visited the industrial town Bokaro, Jharkhand, conducted an enquiry secretly, and interacted with many victims. It revealed that the Maoists' annual collection was rupees 100 crores approximately from that area. Civil and forest contractors, mine owners, industrial and business groups, transport owners were the worse victims. Levy at the rate of rupees five on a sack of vegetables, rupees fifty for a truck load consignment, rupees 500 to 5000 on running factories and business and rupees 1000 to 5000 per month on the bus or truck owners is collected. Levy at the rate of rupees one crore per acre is collected from the illegal poppy cultivators.

A civil contractor from Singhbhum disclosed that every contractor has to cough up money adhering to the Maoist demands. Quantum of payment some times is brought down after negotiation. A business man cunningly tried to circumvent the demand of the ultras. Consequently, he was abducted and threatened for murder. However, he secured his release paying heavy ransom. Buses and trucks are set on fire if payment as per levy, either attempted to dilly-dally or delayed. In 2010, twenty trucks carrying coal and bauxite were set on fire for delaying or defaulting to pay the levy.

Andhra Pradesh, Jharkhand, Bihar contribute about 40 percent of the total collection. From mineral rich Jharkhand, 300 to 400 crores of rupees is collected annually. Many government servants secretly pay to the ultras. Even school teachers are not spared. Orissa contributes approximately ten percent of the illicit collection. Several crores of rupees are extorted from Maharastra, Karnataka and Tamilnadu, where Maoist control is confined to only in few districts. West Bengal is not cash rich. Since the ultras are trying to consolidate and expand in WB the local Maoists receive financial aid from the central fund. However, brick kiln owners, country made liquor shops, illicit distillers, stone crushing units, sponge iron factories, contractors, businessmen contribute regularly. In Jangal Mahal the school teachers are forced to pay. In this way, the Maoists collect about eight to ten lakhs per month In 2007, comrade Soumen Bose, Secretary of the WB chapter was arrested Several documents, including annual expenditure statement recovered from him which revealed that annual expenditure in WB was less than rupees one crore. In 2009, Amitava Bagchi, a politburo member was arrested and an annual expenditure return was seized from his possession, which revealed that the annual budget for the state was rupees twenty crores. In fact, sudden increase in budget expenditure was a clear sign that the Maoists had accelerated their activities, strengthening and equipping the cadre and preparing for obstinate confrontations. Importantly, major portion of the fund come from the business men. In abandoned mines in Purulia, Bankura and Medinapur West districts, they engage labourers to extract copper, lid, lime stone generally used in cement industries. In fact, they are the targets of the ultras, threatened and compelled to pay levy. Several Maoists arrested already have confessed and confirmed the above modus operandi of extortion. Police has prepared a list of business men who have been paying levy conceding to the Maoists' demand. Interrogation of the victims has confirmed that as their lives are in danger they succumb to the threat and pay reluctantly. Enquiry transpired that owners of many private firms, petrol pump dealers, and brick kiln owners and contractors have been paying levy. Ultras negotiate for the levy and often issue ultimatum if their demand is not complied with. As a matter of fact, more than 65 percent fund allotted to WB comes from other states. Bihar and Jharkhand are the prime contributors.

Maoists have been forcing the farmers of remote villages to take up opium cultivation. After the harvest, the Maoists will take away major portion of the crop which will be sold for raising fund. If the farmers decline to agree they will be brutally tortured or put to death. Funds are used for buying arms, ammunitions, satellite phones, printing literature and paying to the cadres. Police tried to cut off the extortion racket and warned the payees against obliging the ultras. However, as the police is unable to ensure their safety and protection, the helpless business men have no option but to submit to the Maoists' diktats.

Fund Collection from Odisha

Orissa, now Odisha, no doubt, is a poor state, but is rich in minerals, especially, in coal, iron ore, manganese ore, timbers and forest products. Hence, lust for fund provokes the Maoists to focus on the state for mopping up a beefy fund. Fear psychosis works well as it is an excellent handle to force the people to part money or valuables against their will. Under imminent fear of life, even an immeasurably stringy person will not hesitate to succumb to the illegal demand of the ultras. The ultras build an ambience of terror and uncertainty to perpetuate their sinister design. Malkangiri district, an erstwhile revenue sub division of Koraput district, is one of the Maoist hit districts. In January 2010, the Maoists attacked a guest house, a petrol pump, a control room and looted many moveable properties valued lakhs of rupees owned by a multi-national company and set it on fire. Incidentally, this company was in the pay roll of the Maoists. Yet it had to face the wrath of the ultras. People said that it was an open secret that the company clandestinely and regularly had been paying to the ultras. However, if payment of levy is either suspended or higher demand is not conceded, the Maoists chastise the defaulters with extreme harshness. Levy is fixed, separately for an individual, contractors, organisations, business men, money lenders, etc.

Persons and units who support secretly or show sympathy are listed and identified as "their men." They are treated leniently and given concession. Local contractors and units have to pay six percent of the total cost of the project whereas, others who are not in the list have to pay levy at the rate of 15 percent. Bus and truck owners and associations have to pay monthly. In case of default in payment, vehicle will be burned and driver or the owner will be abducted and killed. In Raygada district in Odisha, police arrested an employee of the local engineering college. From his possession, thirteen lakhs of rupees was recovered. Probe disclosed that he was going to hand over the money to the Maoists at a particular point. Incident corroborates that the Maoists, sword hangs over every body's head. Educationists and poorly paid school teachers are not spared. In April, 2009, Maoists looted rupees 99 lakhs from a nationalised bank at Malkangiri.

Mining belt of the state, Keonjhar, Sundergarh, Angul districts and Talcher sub division is a special area for collection of levy. Maoists collect levy from the mine owners, contractors, labour contractors and persons involved in mining business. The sordid practice is known to the police. But police is unable to protect them and foil attempts of the ultras.

Poppy Cultivation

Poppy cultivation is encouraged by the Maoists. It accrues double benefit. Levy is collected per acre from the growers. Secondly, commission is collected from the sale proceeds and the purchasers. Maoists in return, protect the cultivators and crop from the evil eye of the police, excise officials and local rowdies. Illegal cultivation of poppy on hundreds of acres of land near the Balimela reservoir in Malkangiri district is in practice. In fact, poppy cultivation is lucrative and highly money-minting. Maoists have introduced a strong set up to collect levy, and maintain proper account of collection and expenditure. Right from the central committee down to the local guerrilla squads the set up function with precision. Collection is made by a selected trusted cadres as per the guide line clearly defined. Finally, collected fund is deposited with the designated comrades. Substantial portion of the fund is utilised to buy weapons, ammunitions, dry rations, medicines including anti-malaria and anti-biotic drugs, vitamins, vaccines, etc. Cadres are paid salary which varies from rupees 250 to three thousands per month. Persons operate from home are not paid. Grass root cadres are allowed to spend small amount. Money collected is handed over to the authorised person of the central committee selected by the high command. Indeed, mode of collection and deposit is well organised. Persons connected with it have to work under constant watch and rigorous supervision.

Poppy Cultivation in Jharkhand

In Jharkhand, poppy cultivation under the control of the Maoists flourishes in more than 200 acres. In fact, rigour of regimentation, Spartan discipline and ideological indoctrination help to keep the flock together. Cadres are aware that disobedience of order, disloyalty or betrayal may cost life. In fact, once a person joins the cadre is unable to quit and return to the main stream. Nevertheless, when a cadre's expectation is belied and his frustration reaches extreme point he takes risk and deserts the outfit. In May 2008, the Maoists looted rupees four crores from a bank at Ranchi. The region leader Kundan Pahan sent only one crore to the central committee. He pleaded that the balance amount was retained for buying arms and ammunitions. The central committee was very up set. However, he spent a substantial amount for buying luxury goods, expensive shoes, dresses, motor bike etc. A young rebel arrested from a remote village in Bundu Block, Ranchi. He was wearing costly apparel, putting on Reebok shoes and possessing a high-end mobile phone. Indeed, in spite of rigid discipline and regimentation, the cadres are unable to give up the desire for good living and greed for luxury goods.

Front line Maoist leaders prefer to live in urban areas in the accolade of comfort and civic amenities, on the pretext of maintaining contact with radicals, intellectuals, media, journalists and for the purpose of publicity. However, Kishanji was an exception. He was living with the comrade's right inside Jungal mahal. Evidently, the party exchequer has to spend a substantial amount for their food, lodging, transport and other necessaries. Leaders occasionally visit the temporary camps in remote jungles or inside the sanctuaries. During my visit to Jharkhand, affluence of the Maoists living inside the camps surprised me. Camp was a puny township inside dense jungle and inaccessible place. It had VIP room, conference hall, dining hall, dormitory in a wide campus. Temporary electric supply through generator and water supply drawing water from the nearby stream through pipe line was arranged. In short, paradigm of bourgeois culture was exasperatingly manifested belying the object of establishing a people's government based on Marxist ideology and wanton sacrifices.

Modus operandi of the Maoists to collect fund every month by extortion or coercive means in Jharkhand is high lighted for satisfying curiosity of the readers. Extortion and fattening fund is spelt out as follows:

1. A petrol pump owner—Rs.25,000
2. Stone crusher, mechanically-operated—Rs.16,000
3. Stone crusher, manually-operated—Rs.8,000
4. A brick kiln owner—Rs. 15,000
5. Two percent levy from coal siding and construction of road.
6. Ten percent from non-metal road and auction of railway track.
7. Five percent on construction of building, canals and railway track.
8. Rupees ten per ton from bauxite mines.
9. Two percent from other sources aiming to collect Rs.70,000.

Surprisingly, almost all political leaders including Ministers, Member of the Parliament, Legislative Assembly secretly pay protection money regularly to the Maoists. Surprisingly, the revolutionaries battling for the cause of the poor and exploited people are not immune from stigma of extortion, blood shed and fiend. Mystery that several down-trodden are the victims of the Maoist bullets, but wealthy persons and bourgeois are either going unnoticed or untouched is *res ipsa loquitur*. Regrettably, deviating from the cardinal principle of revolution and instead, embarking upon crime and violence for establishing much cherished people's government, may crumble the movement and alienate the people. Nuances of Maoist jargon will serve no purpose if the peoples' good will, trust and support are not secured.

Placating the Maoists—Aim, Political Gain

Ambivalence of the successive union and state governments to tackle the extremists with consummate firmness and determination is not free from artifice. Frankly speaking, the secret will be exposed if plausible explanation is analysed. Such step by the political leaders is a calculated sinister design to secure political gain, especially, for winning the election. On the eve of election many political leaders sought support of the Naxalites, opened negotiations, showered good will gestures and high-falutin promises. A popular party before the general elections for the Parliament and the state Legislative Assembly promised to declare cease fire against the extremists, placated them promising concessions, opened dialogues for mutual benefits. The shrewd Naxalites taking opportunity of protracted negotiation ably reorganised, regrouped and reequipped to chalk out strategy and strike with renewed vigour. Interestingly, negotiations abruptly ended in many cases without any positive result.

In 1982, Chief Minister of Andhra Pradesh, actor turned politician, N.T. Rama Rao, adroitly played the negotiation card to secure support of the Naxalites for winning the Assembly election. He called the Naxalites true patriots who were misunderstood by the ruling classes. Later, M. Chenna Reddy, Chief Minister of Andhra Pradesh, from the Congress party followed the similar foot-step. In 1989, he declared that they were patriots. Subsequently, Dr. Rajasekhar Reddy, Chief Minister of the state, praised and carried cudgel for them. However, N. Chandra Babu Naidu, Chief Minister and son-in-law of Late NTR took them as out laws and wanted to deal with them firmly. The extremists were very sore with him and made an attempt to assassinate him, which fortunately failed. In many states, political leaders and the parties pampered the extremists and entered into a secret understanding for electoral gains and political mileage. In such a miry pursuit, political ideology, probity and spirit of impartial public service are thrown in wind. The spirit of *quid pro quo* for abominable political gain renegades the party's image. Political leaders are aware that such unholy pact is contrary to political ethics and public sentiment. Impartial critic's quip that the unprincipled political leaders fail to appreciate that short term political gain generates claustrophobic impact on the mass. Unfortunately, such pretentious political understanding on the eve of election is widely practised in Bihar and Jharkhand. In short, the extent of paranoia that grips the political leaders for their greed for building vote bank and cling on power and authority is a manifestation of pervasive, dishonest and abrasive political manoeuvre. No doubt, its baneful influence encourages evils of national life and subverts elegancies of democratic values, aspiration of the people and spirit of ungrudging public service. Importantly, the Chief Minister of Bihar, Nitish Kumar is lenient in tackling the Maoists for fear of incurring displeasure of a section of populace who are sympathetic to the Maoist cause. He was lukewarm for participating in the "Operation Green Hunt." Sibu Soren, the then CM of

Jharkhand was very eager for opening a dialogue with the Maoists and on this pretext, he wanted to suspend the operation by the security forces.

Muppala Lakshman Rao alias Ganapathy, the General Secretary of the out-fit addressed the delegates of the party's "Unity Congress" was held in January-February 2007, in a place situated in the border of Bihar and Jharkhand. Statement of the General Secretary was formally published on April, 24, 2007. It runs as follows, "The general direction of the Congress is to intensify the peoples' war and to take the war to all fronts. Destruction of the enemy forces has come into the immediate agenda in these areas, without which it is very difficult to consolidate our gain. Or to advance further the police and central forces, and teach how dangerous it is to enter our areas." Ganapathy admitted that reverses in Andhra Pradesh are quite serious. It had adverse effect on the revolutionary movement in the country as a whole. However, the base areas have to be established in backward areas in central and eastern India already selected by the party. It is the out-fit's immediate task to liberate the vast areas and establish Maoist rule. Hence, the focus of the movement is being shifted to Dandakarnaya and Bihar-Jharkhand. He asserted that destruction of the enemy forces has come into the immediate agenda. Armed struggle has to be expanded in territory controlled or dominated by them. The guerrilla war has to be taken to a higher level and expanded to as many states as possible. As the struggle has to be intensified in backward areas Andhra Pradesh may be left in large for the present moment. Truly, the Greyhound's intensive combing operations and incessant offensives has forced the Maoist to curtail their activities in Andhra Pradesh and shift in border areas of Odisha and Chhattisgarh.

Ganapathy's resolve soon proved deadly and true. On June 29, 2008, in Balimela reservoir, Malkangiri, Orissa, 38 Greyhound commandos were killed by the Maoists. After a few days one anti land mine vehicle carrying personnel of Orissa police was blasted by land mine in Malkangiri district. Seventeen police men from Orissa police were killed. Ganapathy was re-elected as the General Secretary of the out-fit in 2007.

Comrade Kanu Sanyal's Reaction

Comrade Kanu Sanyal, ranked next to comrade late Charu Mazumdar for the Naxalbari movement and later general secretary of CPI (ML), was candid that the CPI (Maoists) has deviated from the true path shown by the veteran revolutionaries. He did not subscribe to the on going Maoist movement of individual annihilation of class enemies. He stated, "the Maoists have been following the same old Charu Mazumdar line, which I have vehemently opposed in the past. People have to take up arms struggle after mobilising the masses." He added, "who did not believe in winning over the masses were carrying out the campaign through killing of class enemies and terror would not be able to liberate the country. Any armed struggle carried out without mass support base would not succeed. Armed movements in Russia, China, Vietnam, Cambodia and Cuba were successful as those were carried out on the basis of mass struggle after mobilisation." In his time it was not easy to procure weapons. Now the Maoists had developed connection with the outsiders. They were purchasing modern weapons easily. Confiscation of enemy properties and extortion did not take place from 1969 to 1972. The then Chief Minister of WB, S.S. Ray, on the plea of taming the Naxalites allowed the police to adopt rough and ready method. Later the CM. of the Left Front Government in WB, unfortunately, followed the same path. (*The Hindustan Times*, March 2, 2008). On the merger of the PW and the MCC, he said that unity move among other revolutionary groups had gathered momentum. Attending a rally in Anantapur town, AP, he stated that the revolutionary parties would come together on single platform. NDA and UPA, governments had been serving the imperialist interests. Armed struggle was the only means to bring the revolution. Comrade Kanu Sanyal differed with comrade Charu Mazumdar, left him and founded CPI (ML) on first of May, 1969 in Kolkata. He was expelled from the Charu's outfit. He clandestinely visited China and received training for three months. Till his last breathe he clung on the revolutionary ideal and led an abstemious life. He died in 2011, in his beloved native place, village Hatighisa, near Naxalbari, West Bengal.

Merger of the CPI (ML) People's WAR and the MCC

Kondapalli Sitaramaiah reconstituted the state committee in Andhra Pradesh after collapse of the Srikakulam uprising. It was converted into CPI(ML) Peoples War on 22nd April 1980. After several months protracted negotiations between the central committee of the CPI (ML) People's War (PW) and the Maoist Communist Centre (MCC) merger of the two was formalised on September 21, 2004, and formally started operating from November 2004. The resolution was made at the end of a three-day Convention against Imperialism held at Binani Bhavan, North Kolkata, a few kilometers away from the Writers building where Chief Minister often voiced crusade against the extremists. A PW activist present at the convention told "The leadership of both under ground parties have agreed to merge and take into their fold the two other Naxalite forces. A formal announcement of the merger might be made in November on the anniversary of the Russian revolution. We are ready to carry on with our anti-imperialist and anti-feudal movement at the level of mass movement." About 500 delegates from 160 political and cultural organisations from across the country as well as from Nepal and Bangladesh participated in the convention.

As a part of the convention's resolution, a 26 member, "preparatory committee" including seven conveners was formed to undertake the unity process with the various out-fits in the country and representing the students, peasants, dalits and minorities. Mr GN Saibaba, the general secretary of the All India People's Resistance Forum, a mass organisation maintaining close link with the PW, stated, "The idea is to meet many more out-fits across the country working towards the same goal. We would complete the process in a few months from now." In fact, Andhra Pradesh faction of CPI (ML), and CPI ML (Naxalbari), an erstwhile faction of CPI–ML (Red Flag) in West Bengal were going to join soon.

Henceforth, the new out-fit is called the Communist Party of India, CPI (Maoist). PW and MCC insiders described the effort as a part of the strategy to form a nationwide united front. It may be pointed out that animosity between two out-fits knew no bounds. For example, three members of a family at village Khaninia, in Masauhi, sub division, Patna district, invoked displeasure of the MCC. They were suspected of maintaining link with the PW. Secondly, they were close relatives of Jainandan Yadav, who was a gangster and a contact person of the PW. Sadly, without verification, on mere suspicion, the MCC killed three members of the family. Significantly, in pursuance of the merger, conflict and hostility between the CPI (ML) People's War, and the MCC was reconciled. Rancour, revenge and liquidation of the rival activists were buried. Resolve and promise for unity, establishment of the people's government through the people's war and annihilation of the class enemy were strongly reiterated. In August the Chief Ministers of nine states, where the Naxalites were active gathered in a conference. After deliberations it was decided that the unification of two out-fits should be stopped as it could pose a bigger threat to India's unity and integrity. However, belying the wish of the CMs the merger took place without any hindrance. PW's general secretary M L Rao, alias Ganapathy was selected as the general secretary of the new out-fit. It was decided to form provincial committees in 21 states. PW was already active in 13 states. MCC was strong in Bihar, Jharkhand and part of Uttar Pradesh. Ganapathy and the MCC's General Secretary, Kishan, issued a joint statement reiterating that the People's Guerrilla Army of the CPI-ML People's War (PLA) and the People's Guerrilla Liberation Army (PGLA), of the MCC had merged to form the People's Liberation Guerrilla Army (PLGA), the mighty left commando force operating in the Red corridor. The Maoist leaders decided to convert the existing 14 guerrilla zones into base areas, where alternative government would be formed in the long run. The new out-fit would accommodate the CPI (ML), Janasakti of Andhra Pradesh, and CPI (ML) Naxalbari. However, Maoists were not interested on CPI (ML) factions and the leaders and activists those who had taken the path of parliamentary democracy and the participated in elections. They accused the CPI and the CPI (Marxists) and other left wing parties as revisionists and asserted that no genuine Marxist and Leninist would lay down arms and take part in politics and contest in election. Secondly, no talk for peace would be initiated or any dialogue would be entered into with any state including the Left Front government of W.B. as they had deviated from the basic principle and ideology of Marxism They strongly felt that only arms struggle is the remedy to achieve the goal. They candidly stated, "Naxalism is not a problem, it is a solution." They supported Maoist movement in Nepal. Their aim and object is to create a Red Zone or Red Corridor right from the Himalayan kingdom, Nepal, in the north down to Tamilnadu in the south.

Meanwhile, militants of Bangladesh, Sri Lanka, Nepal and India jointly established an international organisation under the name and style of, "Co-ordination Committee of Maoist parties and organisation in South Asia." Terrorists of LTTE, Sri Lanka, had developed expertise in planting and blasting land mines. Ultras of the PW and MCC learnt the skill of using land mines. Indeed, the spectre of land mine blasts was a chilling threat to the security personnel. It put them in abysmal panic as they lacked resources to identify and neutralise it on the ground. Merger of two out-fits had increased their strength, resources, power of offensives and morale. Hence, it was not good news for the security forces. Truly, threat was grave, it was likely to cost heavily. The swift growing development indicated that the pan-Indian Naxal network from Nepal border to south India might step up violence and provide a new dimension to the Maoist movement. Admittedly, PW and MCC are the largest terrorist outfits in terms of strength of the cadre, net works, weapons and guerrilla army. Combined striking power of both was too formidable to tackle by the security forces. It was feared that two dozens of smaller terrorist groups were likely to join the newly emerged the CPI (Maoist). The Janasakti group, quite active in Andhra Pradesh had already opened negotiation to join.

Besides, it is feared that about 6000 under ground terrorists and their sympathizers in 15 states would join them. Combined strength of the People's Guerrilla Army and the People's Liberation Guerrilla Army, would pose a deadly threat to the state governments, particularly in Bihar, Jharkhand, and Andhra Pradesh. A substantial fund extorted through levies had fallen in its coffer. It would enhance capacity to buy sophisticated weapons, good quantity of ammunitions, explosives, grenades, landmines etc. Cadres between 30000 to 40000 thousands, 15 to 20 thousands guerrillas, and 70000 thousands strong, the people's militia, were behind the Maoist movement. In village level guerrilla zones, Revolutionary Peasant Committees already formed had been looking after the civil administration.

Sri Rama Krishana, the secretary of the PW said, "We do not believe that the suffering masses can be liberated through negotiations. Our ultimate goal is to capture power through revolution." He added that they support the Maoists active in Nepal, Peru, Philippines, Turkey and elsewhere. Evidently, peace and normalcy may not return to areas dominated by the Maoists. As apprehended, merger has stepped up violence and blood shed. Immediately after merger, two banks in Giridhi and Dhanbad respectively were looted. In Palamau, a block of offices were blasted, a land mine was exploded in Bokaro and nine trucks carrying bauxite in Gumla district were torched. It is feared that the cadres with renewed zeal and vigour would unleash unrest and blood letting activities. In a nutshell, the merger is viewed with profound suspense, fear and impending torrent of unrest and atrocity. Swift growth of the Maoists, their vulnerability, de facto control over a large patch of territory, where the Maoist writs run is a flinty threat to the nation's safety, security and solidarity. Analysts feel that the Maoist movements will not die down. Their fast growth, pangs of social and economic disparity, support of the radicals, agony of poor and deprived people, hunger for political power and authority etc will keep the movement alive in spite of setbacks and temporary reverses.

Top Maoists Leaders in Police Dragnet; Strength of the Politburo Slips Down Drastically from 13 to 7

The highest decision making body of the Maoists, is the politburo. It was formed in 2004, with two members, Sushil Roy and Narayan Sanyal. It was recast during the party Congress held in 2007, inside the forest situated on the border of Bihar and Jharkhand. However, offensives by the police and the security forces have succeeded in arresting several top leaders. Two top leaders. C. Rajkumar alias Azad and Kishanji were killed in gun battle. As stands today, thirteen members of the politburo have slipped down to seven only. Crisis of the leadership is a mighty set back for the Maoists. In addition, several leaders of the middle and lower ranks, including the women Maoists have surrendered to the police. In WB, after death of Kishanji, the Maoists are totally isolated. In fact, no leader worthy of his name is available to lead the ultras, and revive the movement. Police's success has compelled many leaders to take to heels and languish in safer hide-outs. In Andhra Pradesh Greyhounds' incessant combing operation, has forced the Maoists to cross the border and take shelter in Dandakaranya, and Bastar region in Chhattisgarh. On July 2, 2010, Cherkuri Rajkumar alias Azad was killed in an encounter in Adilabad district. Azad was a member of the politburo, used to co-ordinate with the members of the Central Committee and Politburo. He attempted to assassinate the former Chief Minister of Andhra Pradesh, C. Chandra Babu Naidu. A reward of Rs.12 lakhs was declared by the state government for his arrest. He took active part in expanding the organisational net work. Another Maoist N. Janardhan Reddy was also killed with him. From the spot one AK 47 rifle and a 9 mm pistol were recovered. Immediately, after merger of the PW and MCC, comrade Sushil Roy was arrested in September 2004. It soon followed by arrest of Narayan Sanyal. In September 2007, member of the Central Military Commission, Misir Besra was arrested in Giridhi, Jharkhand. Then Malla Raji Reddy was arrested from Angamally, near Kochi, Kerala. Promode Mishra, alias Banbihanji, was in police net in May, 2008, from Dhanbad town. In March, 2009, Asutosh Tudu from Rourkela and in August Amitava Bagchi alias Anilji were nabbed. In October 2009, Kobad Gandhi was arrested in Delhi. One of the central committee member V. Subramanyan was missing since June 2009, from Delhi. Later he along with Vijay Kr Arya, and Purnandu Sekhar Mukherjee were arrested in April from Bihar. State Secretary, Himadri Sen Roy alias Soumen, the General Secretary of the CPI (Maoist) West Bengal, was arrested from Barasat W.B.

W.B. Women Maoist leader Chandrakala Tewari was caught in Kashipur railway station US, Nagar Uttarakhand. Murali Satya Reddy and Arun Ferriera were arrested from Nagpur. Vernon Gonsalves and Sridhar Srinivas were in police net from Bombay. Incidentally, an agricultural scientist-turned-Maoist Ravi Sharma and his wife Anuradha were arrested. Comrade Ajit Chakraborty, alias Tara Master, a top leader was arrested from Hridaypur 24 Parganas North, WB. Earlier he was arrested in 1971 but escaped from the Presidency jail Kolkata, However, he was rearrested in 1983 but again escaped from Cooch Bihar jail W.B. in 1986. His accomplices including Juthika alias Rina Sarkar alias Krishna, a squad member were arrested along with him. She was looking after the party's women front. Woman Maoist Soni Sori aged 36, was arrested in Delhi on October 4, 2011 by Delhi police. Comrade Azad's death noticed a pall of gloom in the rank and file of the Maoists. Indeed, it was a fatal blow to the Maoist movement. In addition, deaths, arrests, surrenders have immeasurably affected the progress of the movement. As a matter of fact, crisis in leadership was gallingly apparent. Strength of the politburo has dropped down from 13 to 7 members only.

Top Leaders Enjoy Urban Comfort

Close observation reveals that the Maoist armed cadre and guerrillas stay deep inside the dense forest. Their temporary camps are not easily traceable or accessible. Therefore, security forces are not in a position to initiate offensives. Interestingly, most of the top Maoist leaders and members of the central committee dwell in towns and cities, not sharing hardship and adverse living condition of camp life. As many as 37 members of the Maoist Central Committee stay in urban areas. Top leaders and members of the central committee occasionally visit the camps halt for 3 or 4 nights and return. Cadres suffer from malaria, fever, stomach ailments for want of purified drinking water. Over and above, unhygienic ambience, mosquito and snake bites, unknown diseases are rampant. Top leaders hardly pay attention to the welfare of the cadres deployed in the field. In fact, the leaders' temporary visits do not improve their lot. Leaders plead that urban net work is essential to plan and organise operations and build support base for the outfit. Secondly, through the urban contact procurement of weaponry, ration, medical care for sick and injured comrades, good will of the intellectuals, media coverage etc. are possible and convenient. In addition, it is easier to embark upon purposeful propaganda campaign and develop contact and cultivate the media, bag support of the like minded persons, students, trade unionists and radicals. It helps to infiltrate into the NGOs, human right groups, students, labour organisations and gradually get them into the outfits' fold. A conducive ambience is essential to popularise the Maoist cult, inspire the people for mass movement aiming at establishing the People's Government. In that pursuit, the leaders have to stay in cities and towns for the greater interest of the outfit and the movement.

Unmistakable evidence reveals that the senior leaders are comfort seekers, reluctant to stay in camps inside the jungles. Even for temporary stay in camps they want VIP treatment and urbanised comfort. They spend lavishly to make their living in urban areas smooth and comfortable. Nevertheless, a question arises why the middle class educated persons either directly joining the movement or patronizing it taking risk of arrest, confinement in prisons and threat to life, which needs pensive analysis.

Prison to Parliament

A former zonal commander from Palamu and Garwah of Jharkhand was arrested from Bhabua district in 2006 and lodged in Sasaram jail. He contested from Palamu Parliamentary constituency and was elected by a margin of twenty three thousands five hundreds thirty eight votes. He was associated with the Maoist movements for 27 years, wanted in 80 criminal cases including murder, arson, abduction etc. He joined the extremist movement to fight against the land owners' atrocity. He said, "Naxalism is an idea which talks about a classless society where there will be no oppression and tyranny. But if there is a choice between violence and democracy I will always choose democracy. Maoists have to understand that to change the system one has to first be in the system. Rudderless violence and inflicting fear among people can never be the solution. Nepal is a classic example about the choices facing the Maoists." It may be recalled that Satya Narayan Singh of the MCC gave up violence, floated a political party and contested election.

Instructions to the Maoists Detained in Jails

General Secretary Muppala Lakshman Rao alias Ganapathy issued a 17 pages letter in September 2013 directing to use all legal and illegal ways to free the Maoists from jails. He stated that jails must turn into centers of political training and struggle. Comrades must keep revolutionary spirit in tact. It should be noted that the jailed leaders of Naxalbari movement who after being freed had created a mighty revolutionary storm that has led to the formation of today's CPI (Maoist). He instructed further: (1) Jailed Maoists to fill the vacuum; (2) Tell comrades that they must try to come out of the jails to join the party outside; (3) Party must send money and materials to the jailed leaders; (4) Total leaders and cadres jailed country wide would be 25 thousands; (5) Cut down daily needs of the cadres for the sake of the political prisoners; (6) Since 2010, outfit had lost comrades Kishanji and Azad, while Kobad Gandhi, Amitabha Bagchi and Saheb Chatterjee were already in police net. Therefore, comrades had to intensify the movement. Incidentally, on January 17, 2011, three senior leaders escaped from the Chaibasa jail, Bihar, cutting ventilators of the rooms, which might be an example for other comrades languishing in prisons.

Prime Minister's Observation

Prime Minister Manmohan Singh had declared from the Red Fort in New Delhi on 15th August 2006 that Maoism was the country's biggest security threat. He stated unambiguously, "Naxalism and Left-wing terrorism pose the greatest threat to national security and the state cannot and will not allow its authority to be challenged." In several forums, he reiterated his stand and made it clear that the government would not leave any stone unturned to disarray the extremists. The Maoists obviously did not take it lightly. As a mark of protest the Maoists gave call for "Bharat Bandh" on July 2, and observed protest week from June 26, 2008 in six states including Andhra Pradesh and West Bengal. They decided to step up violence to show their might and firmness in carrying out the peoples' struggle. In the event of Bharat Bandh, the states took exhaustive precaution to avert any untoward incident.

Perhaps, seeing the PM's will to wipe out the Maoists, the MHA swung into action. The union Home Secretary and the then National Security Advisor N.K. Narayanan (later Governor of WB) held several rounds of talk in September and October 2007, drafted a blue print, and instructions for the Maoist ridden states. Eight districts were identified for anti-Naxalite operations combined with a high pitched development programme. This was the first time that the centre has decided to take the problem head on. A senior official of the MHA said, "It is time to take the battle right into the Naxal strongholds and stay there rather than conduct operations at the fringes and let them disappear into the deep forests." Centre will fund for major expansion of social infrastructure and arrange increased police presence and equipments in these districts.

Plan on security side: A) Focus on core policing; B) Make trained manpower available; C) Provide policemen firearms and equipments like bullet proof vests and night vision devices; D) Fortify police stations, police posts and police pickets; E) Systematic combing of interiors, security forces to camp in forests and keep Naxalites on the run; F) Intelligence to be generated at police station levels, create special post of SP (Operations) in each district.

On the development side: 1. District hospitals to be upgraded as multi-specialty hospitals; 2. District to have higher education institute till post-graduate level; 3. Get schools and health centres to function efficiently; 4. Open Navodaya schools and industrial training institutes in districts; 5. Each of the two clusters of contiguous districts to have law college, medical college, engineering college and management institute; 6. Land records to be computerized; 7. Mandatory for district administration to collect land revenue so far given the least priority to reassert the presence of the State with concessions for weaker sections and poor; 8. Focus on stopping illicit opium farming and felling of trees; 9. Construct sports complex at block levels in each district; 10. Hundred village haats identified, 50 in each cluster.

Eight districts identified as follows:

1. Bihar State—Aurangabad and Gaya districts.

2. Chhattisgarh—Dantewada and Bijapur districts.
3. Jharkhand—Chatra and Palamu districts.
4. Odisha—Malkangiri and Rayagada districts.

On the Prime Minister Manmohan Singh's advice, the National Security Council held its first meeting on Naxalism in August 2007. On the PM's suggestion the central government had constituted an empowered group of Ministers (EGOM) with representation from the chief Ministers of seven Maoist affected states. In October the Prime Minister convened a meeting with the Chief Ministers of the seven states shortly after the conference of the Director General of Police of the states. In fact it was the first conference of Chief Ministers on Maoists at the level of the PM. In the conference the PM cited the performance of the Andhra Pradesh where the rebels were on the run. He said that the states needed to do much more to check Naxalite violence which had killed 350 persons in the first half of the year. Chain of developments and the PM's reaction indicated importance attached in dealing with Left-Wing extremism by the Union Government.

Integrated Action Plan (IAP)

In 2010, the centre had initiated development programme in the Maoist strongholds through the Integrated Action Plan (IAC). This is an initiative of the central government for areas affected by the Left Wing extremism. Its aim is to bridge the development deficit through infrastructure creation. Though various projects are in progress, but opinion is divided on whether the three year old programme has bridged the "trust deficit"—the objective out lined by the PM. Official statistics revealed that 90 per cent of the projects under the IAP for 78 Naxal affected districts across the country have been completed. However, in spite of the success a revamped IAP is likely to be implemented again from April 2013. Under the programme, villages in Maoist torn districts should be given priority for construction of high quality roads, anganwadi centres, schools and health centers and provide drinking water facilities. In addition panchayat bhawan, community hall, rural roads, livelihood activities, skill development, minor irrigation works, electricity, health centers, construction of toilets etc should be taken up in right earnest. In fact, 64000 projects so far under taken in 378058 habitations. However, 25 per cent of the posts of medical staff in newly created public health centers are lying vacant. Many new schools have only ad hoc and untrained teachers. In fact, examining pros and cons the Planning Commission aims at making good of the deficiencies by narrowing down the focus area from districts to blocks. Interestingly, a new approach is adopted which is likely to see participation of civil society and locals in decision making has the backing of Rural Development Ministry and the Planning Commission.

Officials feel that the new approach has consolidated the progress of work already done. An official in charge of the implementation of the projects said that focused approach and dedicated monitoring has worked satisfactorily and produced the desired result. Total 78 districts are covered by the IAP. A committee comprising the District Magistrates, Superintendent of Police and the District Forest Officer monitor the progress of the projects. In 2010-11, a sum of rupees 25 crores per district, in 2011-12, 30 crores per district has been allocated. In fact, total 3300 crores has been sanctioned by the central government from 2010-11, to 2012-13. The union government decided to extend the IAP for four more years with an annual allocation of rupees of one thousand crores. According to the proposal each of the 82 IAP districts would be given rupees five crores. Again remaining 590 crores of rupees will be distributed among the districts on the basis of population and areas. The nine states under the plan are AP, Bihar, Chhattisgarh, Jharkhand, M P, Maharastra, Odisha, UP and West Bengal. The Planning Commission directly will supervise in 82 selected tribal and backward districts for accelerated development. Originally, the scheme was covering 60 districts in 2010-11 and 2011-12. Now it is extended to 82 districts. Latest report reveals that out of 100133 projects under taken by the states, 69056 projects have been completed by January 2013. Fund to the tune of Rs.4177.65 crores was spent during 2010-13. The cumulative releases towards IAP during 2010-13 were at rupees 6090 crores. Member Secretary of the Planning Commission regularly monitor progress through video conferences. It is claimed that development plan for the Red-hit areas is satisfactory.

Review and Follow-up Actions

On August 17, 2009 the Prime Minister Manmohan Singh held a meeting with the Chief Ministers of Maoist stricken states at Delhi on tackling the Maoist threat. Thereafter, the UHM, P. Chidambaram discussed the problem with the CMs and chalked out a plan to galvanise the internal security matters. Precisely, the proposed actions decided to be enforced by the Union and the state governments jointly are mentioned below : Interestingly, after the PM's meeting the ultra-left militants gave a call to create, "Thousands of Lalgarh-type Liberated Zone." Kishanji, a member of the politburo, in a telephonic interview with a leading daily newspaper, expressed his views on the government's stance on the Maoists on going movement across the country. He said that within seven months the Maoists had liberated 1300 kms zone in Lalgarh, West Medinapur district, WB. Five thousands strong, much stubborn, the People's Liberation Guerrilla Army (PLGA) were behind the movement. The civil administration in the liberated zone had come to stand-still. Hence, increase of the number of liberated zone was a matter of time. Politburo released a three pages booklet highlighting the success and further advance of the Maoist movement.

Proposed movements

1. Centre should help in imparting training in counter-terrorism, jungle warfare and intelligence gathering.
2. To quicken procurement of weapons the government should consider procurement centrally.
3. To fill over 1.5 lakhs vacancies effort should be made to recruit and train police personnel before March 31, 2010.
4. The modernisation of police forces scheme should be continued for another 5 to 10 years.
5. Strength of police stations must be augmented.
6. Roads building programmes in border areas have to be expedited.
7. Attention to be paid to porous India-Nepal border.
8. Measures to be worked out to improve policing of mega cities and desert areas.
9. Surrender-cum-rehabilitation policy should be re-vamped.
10. Allocation for coastal police stations to be upgraded.
11. High speed interception boats to be imported.
12. Territorial army training to be imparted to the fishermen.

Eight-point Action Plan

On July 14, 2010, a meeting with the CMs of the Maoist torn states was called by the PM in his residence in New Delhi. The agenda was to discuss the extremist threat, pinpoint remedial measures and initiate action to wipe out the threat. Chief Minister of WB Budhadeb Bhattacharjee stayed away from the meeting. Chief Minister of Bihar, Nitish Kumar distanced himself from the security component of the two pronged approach. He felt that it was focused too much on the security component. However, after a good deal of deliberations eight point action plan was approved which is as follows:

1. Within next two years, 400 police stations in affected districts would be fortified and up graded.
2. Centre to raise strength of the Special Police Officers from existing 13500 to 16000.
3. United command in Chattisgarh, Jharkhand, Orissa and Maharastra to be headed by the Chief Secretaries of the concerned states.
4. A retired Major General from the army to be appointed in every state; designated IG (Anti Naxalite) operation.
5. In each police station at least 40 person to be posted.
6. From seven worse affected states 35 districts were marked as high focus districts on account of level of violence.
7. Twenty more helicopters to be inducted.
8. Thirty four new India Reserve Battalions to be raised.

Discussion relying on present trend and statistics transpired that three persons are being killed every day on account of the extremist violence.

Suggestion of Using Air Force to Tackle the Maoists

Suggestion came from many quarters that Indian Air Force should be pressed in service to liberate the so called liberated zone, especially, in Bastar region. AP, Chhattisgarh, Maharashtra, Odisha and West Bengal requested for air support against the Maoists. However, this question was examined in various levels. Needless to add, air strike in a target is likely to inflict casualty. Admittedly, it is unable to pin point a particular human target and hit so that only the culprit is likely to be killed or wounded. On the contrary, the strike is sure to damage or destroy an area or inflict many casualties. Many innocent civilians are likely to be the victims of air attack. Maoists get mixed up with the civilians and take shelter in villages. Sometimes, they make a human shield with the help of villagers to protect themselves from the raids of the security forces. Therefore, it is difficult to single out the Maoists from the human mass and hit the ultras directly. After all, in war indiscriminate air strike and killing is not questioned. Here, the security forces have been dealing with the own countrymen. Therefore, no license can be granted to hit or kill any one violating the human rights and democratic values. The UHM P. Chidambaram said, "I have limited mandate." Central Cabinet Committee on security declined to endorse the use of air support. However, after exhaustive discussion the idea to use aircrafts in operations against the Maoists was given up. The Central Cabinet Committee (CCS) on security approved the proposal for coordinated offensive against the Maoists and for that 75000 central security forces would be deployed. Indian Air Force, IAF, choppers will assist in move of forces for operations, rescue and evacuation works and guard commandos on board in case of Maoist attack.

Sophisticated Technology in Using Explosives

Of late, the ultras have been using advanced technology in using explosives, planting land mines and blowing up land mine proof vehicles. Land mines are planted ten to twelve feet below the surface. Secondly, it is planted two or three days before the blast. Police patrol is unable to trace or pin point the mines. Thirdly, at the spot after the blast no trace of chemical is available. In the blast every bit of the chemical is consumed which reveals that highly sophisticated chemicals is used and handled by extra ordinary skilled person. Experts opine, "Complete consumption of explosives is a very rare happening. For that to happen one requires high-order explosives, expert and sophisticated handling, latest training and technique." The ultras have been using a substance which is deadlier and more powerful than RDX. On October 22, 2007, in Belpahari, West Medinipur, W.B., a medical van was blown up. Here, advanced technology and skillful execution was well manifested. Explosives were planted a few days before the explosion and night patrol parties could not detect it. In Malkangiri district, Odisha, an anti-mine vehicle with security personnel were mined and blown up killing the occupants. Experts feel that situation is alarming and the security forces have to gear up to cope with the new development.

Procurement of Fire Arms Using of Forged Documents

Maoists have hatched up a sinister plot to enrich their arsenal. They forge gun licenses and with the help of fake licenses purchase guns and rifles from the authorised arms dealers. Many dealers taking advantage of the detestable deal misuse guide line and make their fortune. In fact, forged licenses are so skillfully made that it is not possible to identify its genuineness ordinarily. Police of Uttar Pradesh has arrested seven forgeries from Etwah district who are suspected of having link with the Maoists. Police has seized several fake licenses and the connected documents. Maoists have been purchasing guns from the authorised gun dealers using forged licenses and dispatch the weapons to the Maoists active in Bihar. It is reasonably suspected that some of the gun dealers are directly involved in this dangerous and abhorrent trade. Police has recovered several fake licenses and seized weapons illegally stored in Raj Gun shop of the town (Etwah) and sealed the shop. Meanwhile, Bihar police has raided several hide outs in Maoist dominated areas and recovered weapons illegally received from Raj Gun Shop. Capital of the state, Lucknow is located at a distance of 30 kms from Etwah. In Lucknow there are 155 authorised arms license shops. Police suspected that some of the dealers have been selling arms unauthorisedly to the Maoists. Eventually police recovered five rifles and one double barrel gun from Jayshree Arms stores. These weapons were sold illegally to the persons possessing forged licenses. Raid on Raj Gun House unearthed that 48 rifles were sold to persons holding fake licenses. The dealer purchased five guns from Shib Traders of Kanpur who procured 25 guns illegally from other sources. Investigation reveals that the Maoists have manipulated records in the concerned offices and head quarter so cunningly that the fake licenses have received acceptance in the head quarter. It is suspected that the Maoists have built a network for procuring weapons illegally for the extremist torn states tampering with or forging gun licenses. Unfortunately gorged with the idea of enriching themselves many arms dealers jumped into the fray, joined hands with the Maoists and aided illegal business in arms supply. Indeed, the exposure of the fraud is a remarkable breakthrough in frustrating the Maoists' weapon procurement drive clandestinely short circuiting the so called draconic vigil and control of the authority.

Police armoury is the main source of weapon procurement for the ultras, in addition to snatching of arms from cops, dead, or injured security personnel. Maoists purchase weapons and ammunitions secretly from various sources. Country made guns and pistols are manufactured in Bihar, Jharkhand and West Bengal and are sold to the extremists. Weapons smuggled from Bangla Desh reach the hands of the ultras. Earlier Maoists used to buy automatic weapons and land mines through the LTTE. Now, the Maoists have built foundaries in the hide outs in Chattisgarh, Jharkhand, and with the help of the armourers retired or released from army and police manufacture weapons. They have learnt the use of land mines from the LTTE. In fact, the ultras active in Andhra Pradesh took initiative, maintained contact with the LTTE and developed expertise in using it. Now-a-days, they procure components of land mines, high grade explosives from urban areas and dispatch to the secret hide outs, where parts are assembled and kept in readiness for use. Of late, they have acquired the know-how of manufacturing the rocket launchers. Once rocket launchers are available in their hands in big scale, the threat and challenge to the security forces is going to be bloody and sanguinary. Procurement of ammunitions is not easy for them. Un-assorted ammunitions for weapons of different bore and caliber are purchased without any choice which is highly disadvantageous for them. In fact, in absence of regular flow of supply of ammunitions for particular weapons many fire arms have to remain idle. Broadly, the extremists for supply of arms and ammunitions depend on contact and secret suppliers.

Lok Sabha Election in 2009

Maoists gave a call to boycott the Lok Sabha election scheduled to be held from April, 2009. On April 16, 2009, on the first phase of polling Maoists unleashed matchless violence, captured or burnt booths, killed poll officials and security personnel, blew up vehicles. In fact, violence was unprecedented in Jharkhand, Bihar, Chhattisgarh and Maharashtra. In Rajnandgaon district, Chhattisgarh, Maoists blew up a vehicle carrying poll officials resulting in, five poll officials were killed and in exchange of fire two CRPF personnel were killed. A few polling booths were set on fire. In Dantewada and Narainpur districts, in continued gun battle five persons were injured including three security persons. In spite of terror and bloodshed in Chhattisgarh, 51 per cent votes were polled.

In Gaya district, Bihar, Maoists shot dead two policemen Polling was disrupted in 86 polling booths of which 71 polling stations fell in Maoist dominated areas. A few officials were kidnapped. About 100 ultras attacked a convoy of trucks on the Grand Trunk Road near Barachatti, Gaya district and torched eight trucks and shot a truck driver who attempted to escape. In Jharkhand, a bus carrying BSF personnel was blown up in a land mine killing eight BSF personnel and two civilians. In Malkangiri district, Odisha, Maoists set fire on three polling booths disrupting voting A CRPF patrol was attacked when they were returning to the camp after poll duty.

On the eve of the second phase of election on April 21, 2009, Maoists accelerated violence. Armed Maoists aided by the villagers seized 627 Barkakhana-Mugalsarai BDM passenger train at Hehegara halt station with more than 400 passengers and detained the train for more than four hours The villagers agitated against killing of five persons by the CRPF on 15th April near Barwadih. In the night the station building and signal cabin of Chianki railway station were blown up. In mid night five grenades were exploded by the side of the railway line at Untari Road station, Palamu district as Rajdhani Express was supposed to pass by that route soon. On that night, Maoists blew up a school building and health centre in Chatra district.

However, in spite of the boycott call parliamentary election in five phases were completed by May 13, 2009 and counting took place on May 16, 2009. Maoists failed to stop the parliamentary election though they let loose sporadic terror and killing. However, they planned post poll unrest and accordingly cadres were instigated to step up offensives to mar peace and tranquility in the Maoist stricken states. In June the politburo of the out-fit' released a circular and directed the cadres for its strict adherence. It reveals that tactical counter offensives had to be geared up diligently and strictly to "divert a section of the enemy forces from attacking the guerrilla bases and organs of the (Maoist) power." Instructions given to "advance the revolution at a rapid pace though the enemy (Central and State governments) is itching to suppress our party. They have severe difficulties in implementing this at present in every state. It has to intensify the war in respective states learn from the mistakes of the LTTE in Sri Lanka." It reiterated, "Immense possibilities are unfolding in front of our eyes to advance the revolution at a rapid pace. Industry after industry is closing down throwing out millions of workers on the streets, Poverty, homelessness, starvation and destitution has become a global phenomenon proving an excellent condition for advancing the people's struggles and revolutions everywhere."

Operation Green Hunt

In August 2009, the then Union Home Minister P. Chidambaram met the Chief Ministers of seven Maoists torn states and the police chiefs in Delhi to plan a decisive offensive against the Maoist guerrillas. Discussion hinted at joint and coordinated offensives by the police and para military forces deployed in terrorist stricken states. HM's brain child finally took the shape of "Operation Green Hunt" Importantly, CMs of two states asserted that guns alone would not achieve the desired result to disarray the ultras. In fact, social and economic development is *sine qua non* to salvage the misguided people leaned towards so called the People's war, classless society, People's government, etc. and carried away by the nuances of Maoist jargon. On February 9, 2010, the HM called a meeting of Chief Ministers of Bihar, Jharkhand, Orissa and West Bengal at Kolkata for a discussion and chalking out a comprehensive plan. Chief Minister of Orissa, and two Deputy

Chief Ministers, Sudesh Mahato and Raghubar Das of Jharkhand attended the meeting. Nitish Kumar Chief Minister of Bihar did not attend the meeting but sent Officials to represent the state. He said that Maoist menace cannot be controlled by force. CM West Bengal, requested to provide unmanned aerial vehicles (UAV) and one helicopter to WB before the start of the Joint operation. It was pointed out that helicopters have been provided already to Chhattisgarh and Jharkhand. Director Generals of Police attended the meeting highlighted the constraints, exchanged notes, demanded more para military forces and welcomed the joint operations. CMs of W.B. and Orissa, Navin Patnaik separately briefed the HM on the law and order situations.

Importantly, joint operation by state police and central para military forces in West Bengal has started right from June 2009. On the eve of lunching joint operation and the Operation Green Hunt, the HM categorically stated that while combating the ultras, the security forces have to see that innocent persons are not hurt or killed. He cautioned that collateral damage has to be minimal or avoided. Ironically, the HM's advice could not strictly be adhered to for various adverse conditions. In fact, in operations spear-headed by the security force in seven states many civilians had lost their lives. Indeed, the security forces directly or indirectly are responsible for the loss of lives. However, a dispassionate analysis reveals that some loss is unavoidable in a sanguinary operation of such a magnitude. A comprehensive report released by the Union Home Ministry indicating below number of incidents, casualties, recovery of arms, arrests etc.:

Years	*2006*	*2007*	*2008*	*2009*	*2010 (Till June 30)*
Number of incidents	1509	1569	1591	2258	1103
Number of encounters	335	276	271	308	168
Casualty of ultras	274	141	199	217	97
Arrests of the Maoists	1270	1456	1743	1954	1341
Arms recovered	584	352	1511	569	264
Death of civilians	521	460	490	591	325

On July 14, 2010, the HM met the Chief Ministers of seven states at the residence of the Prime Minister, New Delhi and reviewed the result achieved from counter insurgency operation and from the Operation Green Hunt. Analysis revealed that in spite of Green Hunt operation in Chhattisgarh, Jharkhand, Bihar and West Bengal, vigour and intensity of the Maoist attacks had increased leaps and bounds. In Jharkhand no improvement was noticed. In Andhra Pradesh, Maharashtra, violence had declined. However, in Orissa it had been reduced considerably. It was crystal clear that the impact of the Green Hunt was not enough in containing or preventing armed encounters which took the shape of a proxy war. Maoist's savage attacks, killing spree of the civilians and security personnel was an extraordinary challenge to the security forces. In initial stage the security forces lagged behind. In fact, pompous claim from many that the operation Green

Hunt had forced the extremists to retreat was far from correct. However, soon the security forces rose to the occasion, successfully tackled the ultras and forced them to take to heels.

Protest by the People

A group of intellectuals, educationists, writers, radicals and sober elements in Kolkata vehemently protested against the Operation Green Hunt and deployment of joint forces to crush the extremist movement in West Bengal. On February 9, 2010, a congregation led by renowned novelist Sm. Mahasweta Devi took to the street. A mammoth procession marched through the busy streets of the city and held a public meeting near the Metro cinema, the heart of the city. The processionists raised slogan, "Stop Operation Green Hunt, Joint forces go back, abolish the UAP Act. They burnt effigies of the Union Home Minister and the Chief Minister of W.B." They demanded that torture of innocent people in the name of combating Maoists must stop. Surprisingly, Members of the West Bengal Government Employees Union (Nabajagaran) demonstrated in the compound of the Writers Building Kolkata, protesting against the joint operation and operation green hunt. They shouted slogans against the Union Home Minister and the CM of W.B.

The intellectuals, writers, radicals and civil society vehemently objected and intensified their protest. They proposed to hit the street again on 14th April 2010 in Kolkata. This time they planned to protest against the centre and states' anti-Maoist operation across the country. Author Arundhati Roy, who earlier named by the Maoists as one of the mediators, to initiate dialogue with government for peace, jumped in the fray. She was scheduled to land in Kolkata and join the rally. They were candid that the civil society is needed to intervene; otherwise the government forces would kill thousands of innocent people. They strongly asserted that only dialogue could avert the crisis.

Other Steps to Wipe Out the Maoist Threat

Chief Minister of West Bengal Buddhadeb Bhattacharjee's convoy came under mine attack on November 2, 2008, near Medinapur town. His firm belief that the Maoist problem would be solved politically was belied. The frustrated CM decided to chastise the blood thirsty ultras by resorting to massive police action. He requested the central government to spare sufficient para military forces. Centre's response was good. State police and central paramilitary forces jointly started operations in three districts to flush out the Maoists with effect from June 18, 2009. On July 16, 2008, a meeting was held in New Delhi with the DGPs of Andhra Pradesh, Orissa, Jharkhand and Chhattisgarh chaired by the union Home Secretary. The Union Home Ministry decided to establish six counter insurgency schools to train commando forces to combat the Maoists. It has already identified eight districts, two each in Andhra Pradesh, Orissa, Jharkhand and Chhattisgarh and asked the states to initiate pilot project for the above districts. In addition, it was decided to create a specialised anti-Naxalite force within the CRPF to be named Cobra and trained in its elite training school. Centre sanctioned sufficient funds to provide critical mobility to the police forces, secure camping grounds, roads, helipads at strategic locations to enable quicker movement of forces and fulfill specific requirements in districts and other areas. It is imperative that a holistic anti Maoist measures is essential to tackle the growing menace in a focused manner. Supply of equipment's like night vision instruments, mine proof vehicles (MPV), bullet proof jackets etc. was ensured on priority basic. Roads would be improved or constructed around high risk police stations. Rupees one hundred crores was ear marked for immediate execution of the projects and rupees four hundred crores would be spent in remaining period of the Eleventh Plan. Fund was expected to be spent mainly in U P, Orissa, Jharkhand and Chhattisgarh.

Centre asked the states to raise commando coys on the line of Cobra battalion of the CRPF to meet the challenge of the Maoist guerrilla (PGLA). In fact, adhering to the instruction of the Home Ministry the CRPF took prompt action and raised Combat Battalion for Resolute Action (Cobra) to meet the internal security challenges resolutely against the Guerrilla tactics and jungle warfare. Under the scheme, additional financial assistance of rupees three crores per company would be provided to the states facing problems of militancy. During the next four years forty four India Reserve Battalions were going to be raised. The CRPF raised Cobra battalions by the end of 2009, dispatched nine battalions to six states as follows: Chhattisgarh—2, Odisha—1, Jharkhand—2, Bihar—1, Maharashtra—1, and Uttar Pradesh—2.

Martyrs' Week

Maoists observe Martyrs' week from July 28 to August 03, every year to commemorate death of comrade Charu Mazumdar who was the founder father of the Naxal movement in West Bengal. He died in 1972 as an under trial prisoner in Alipur Central jail Kolkata. Maoists have been observing his death anniversary and other revolutionary leaders with great solemnity. During the week Maoist leaders and dedicated supporters congregate inside the forest, pay floral tribute to a martyrs' column and take pledge to continue the armed struggle with renewed zeal and vigor. Leaflets are distributed and speeches are made to deride the parliamentary system of government and futility of elections to achieve societal changes. Police issue alert notice to all concern as the ultras may resort to violence following the death anniversary. Ideologues and radicals in urban areas having no direct link with the Maoists also secretly observe the martyrs week with equal devotion and sincerity. Indeed, they are not guided by any fanciful or romantic discourses but believe firmly that the goal of the revolutionaries is sure to be fulfilled in the long run. Importantly, it is not without any cogent reason why the educated middle class people, like Kobad Gandhy, Vernon Gonsalves, Saketh Rajan, Sridhar Shiriniwasan, Sabyasachi Panda, B. Anuradha, Anupama, Ravi Sarma etc. have joined the movement directly or covertly, bearing hardship and taking the risk of arrest and confinement in jail, why hundreds of radicals are supporting the movement, why they denounce the representative system of government and brand the Constitution as pestilential and is an odious blot on the people's equality and freedom, why hundreds of poverty stricken and deprived people are up-in-arms against the present social and political order, plead and aspire for the People's government. Needless to say, they may be sincere and honest in supporting the movement, yet many critics sarcastically say that they want to romanticize the movement and their dream of demolishing the present order and establish the People's government is a myth. Be that as it may, their conviction and sacrifices for the cause of the poor and neglected people cannot be undermined. It needs no reiteration that seeds of the revolution once sowed trickles down from Sirs to sons. At present they may be nowhere near the revolution which is stagnating but its significance and possibility of its fulmination in the long run cannot altogether be ruled out or denied.

National Counter Terrorism Centre (NCTC)

In February 2012, the union government has notified the setting up of a new and strong anti-terror body, National Counter Terrorism Centre (NCTC), by an executive order. The Cabinet Committee on Security (CCS) has approved the NCTC. The specialised body will derive powers from the Unlawful Activities (Preventive) Act (UAPA). It can carry out operations like arrest, search, and seizure as a part of its mandate. NCTC, a fall out over the 26/11 attack in Mumbai is authorised to collect and collate intelligence on terror groups and co-ordinate response to threats. However, for various reasons, it failed to deliver the desired result. Now the NCTC armed with the law, UAPA, is stronger and will be able to collect intelligence, collate and share intelligence inputs effectively. Importantly, MHA has put in place a nationwide encrypted network with over 500 terminals for all NCTC participants to have real time sharing information. Armed with the law the NCTC can promptly conduct searches in the extremist hide out, arrest the suspects without waiting for the state police's assistance or concurrence. But question arises how the NCTC is going to fulfill the legal procedure, take responsibility of the accused persons including the under trials, produce them before the court, escort the prisoners from jail custody to the court, conduct the to and fro journey, prosecution syndrome, marshaling of evidence etc. Secondly, law and order being the state subject, action by the NCTC may overlap and create confusion, if not undermines the authority of the state. Thirdly, NCTC is virtually a stranger in a state without any administrative support and absence of intelligence output. While conducting search, seizure etc. if there is resistance or any law and order situation develops who and how it is going to be tackled.

Tactical Counter Offensive Campaigns (TCOC), a Modus Operandi of the Maoists

Offensives undertaken by the Maoists were not under influence of sudden impulse or guided by whims or caprices. Broadly speaking, in the beginning of the extremist movement they lacked proper planning, co-ordination and command and control. They avoided direct confrontation with the security forces, preferred hit and run tactics under the control of local leadership. Their training was deficient for want of capable trainers, archaic weaponry, not well conversant with the use of land or directional mines, field crafts, etc. As events moved apace the ultras consolidated their strength, built central and state command, learnt the use of sophisticated weapons, skill of planting and busting land mines and extended their activities in seven states. Eventually, the archaic strategy of hit and run tactics was replaced by surprise attacks or ambush in heavy strength to surprise the opponent. Secondly, the out-fit has raised well trained guerrilla squads, who are core group of the fighting strength. Thirdly, they continued developing swashing tactics, training standard, fire power, intelligence net work. In training centers, they used to teach assembling of rocket launchers, land mines, skill of hitting the bullet proof vehicles used by the security forces. Rebels built small foundries manufactured firearms, procured weapons by fair or foul means. They paid extra emphasis on use of land mines, which they had learnt from the LTTE. Recruitment drive for male and female recruits has been swelling the cadres. Abundant resources and substantial fund helping them to procure automatic weapons, hand grenades, high grade explosives. Again, salary is paid to the cadres regularly. Hence they are no longer ordinary rebels who can be disarrayed by routine police actions. Magnitude of direct clashes is very horrid and alarming. In short, it is a proxy war. Its final result and dead end is obscure and unknown.

Critical study on various facets of operational strategy and its implementation by the Maoists has unfolded their new offensive approach, the key to success and loopholes. It reveals that every year from mid-March to mid-June the trees shed leaves, resulting in, the forests, especially, in central India wear a depleted look. At that juncture thickness of the forests is reduced and visibility improves considerably. In such a condition, objects can be seen clearly from a long distance. In fact, the nature's largesse bestowed indirectly is highly opportune for the ultras to step up their offensives. They meticulously plan attacks, ambush and plant land mines to out wit the patrols brought out by the security forces or police, surprise the camps of the security forces, dauntlessly engage themselves in protracted gun battle and inflict casualty on the security personnel. This kind of organised offensive in their parlance is called "Tactical Counter Offensive Campaigns" (TCOC). Truly, offensives let loose during this period is often rewarding for them. Secondly, successful attacks on the camps opened flood gate to loot arms and ammunitions, procure weapons and ammunitions from the dead or wounded security personnel. Indeed, modus operandi adopted by the Maoists has given a good dividend. The security forces are generally pinned down in camps, guard the camps, and occasionally come out for patrolling, raiding villages or hideouts in search of the suspects or the rebels. Broadly speaking, the security forces by and large followed the defensive strategy for various reasons. In aggressive strategy, the civilians, public property may be affected, innocent may be hurt or killed, and criticism or public resentment may tarnish their image. Hence, they are contented defending themselves and repulsing attacks taking cover in the camps. Undeniably, defensive or passive action plan, indecisiveness to take on the rebels indirectly encouraged the ultras to accelerate attacks and keep the security forces in abyss suspense and uneasy tenterhook.

Observing the new modus operandi the security forces has galvanized their strategy and action plans to frustrate the rebels' offensives. It was decided that instead of stagnating in the camps and repulsing the attacks, the security forces should go out and confront the rebel's right in their camps or shelter places. In fact, the counter offensive policy has proved effective and purposeful. It was no longer one sided. Importantly, in less than three months, in encounters, thirty three Maoists were killed. Needless to say, now defensive fever, suspense and panic had badly tormented the Maoists. As a matter of fact, strategy of taking the battle right into the Maoist turf discarding the previous defensive tactic has produced a spectacular result. The Greyhounds, the elite forces of Andhra Pradesh has achieved unique success following the policy of relentless raids, flush out programmes and continuous hot chase. CRPF argues in favour of "Strike-back-offence-policy."

From March to June the Maoists were seen very agile and active. Incessant onslaughts initiated by them keep the security forces under flinty pressure. From the end of 2011, Maoist violence slowly declined. In 2012, the Maoists were late in unleashing offensive campaigns. Normally, it used to be started from the first week of March. However, this year (2012) it started from March 22. Truly, they were under tremendous pressure facing reverses. They had lost several comrades, many surrendered and a few top leaders were arrested which abysmally demoralised them. In fact, pro-active strategy followed by the security forces had put the Maoists in unknown fear, immeasurable suspense and confusion. Importantly, senior and top Maoist leaders during this time assembled in secure places, deliberated on various matters, chalked out strategies, mode of operation and try to boost morale and fighting spirit of the rank and file.

From end of June to October, offensives were reduced because of monsoon, incessant rain, spate of rivers, streams, water pools. Secondly, village paths, fields and forest areas get inundated which make the movement through thick forests and water logged areas weary, arduous and time consuming. However, after uneasy lull, from November Maoists rejuvenated the cadres and guerrilla squads and increased offensives. In 2008-09, the Maoists took upper hand in Jharkhand, Chhattisgarh, Bihar and Odisha. Security forces were often out-witted and lost a large number of personnel. CRPF faced the major brunt. Casualty and injury in its rank and file was petulantly high. A pall of gloom was apparent in security forces fighting the proxy war. Luckily, their morale and fighting spirit was intact. They were determined to wipe out the Maoist led insurgency and restore the rule of law.

Significantly, the security forces modified aggressive operational policy and decisive actions to take the proxy war right into the turf of the Maoists have put them in tight spot. The ultras had to cut short several programmes, afraid of coming out of their safe shelters and execute operational plans. The hierarchy was in a mess not sure of enforcing laid down programmes. Uncertainty and fear of the security forces have compelled them to defer the five yearly congresses which were due in 2012. In fact, the Ninth Congress was last held in 2007 in a jungle situated on the border of Jharkhand and Bihar states. In West Bengal, arrests of many leaders, flurry of surrender, exodus of cadres, death of Kishanji, Sasadhar Mahato, and Lal Mohan Tudu etc. has made the rebels leaderless. In Jangal Mahal rule of law has returned. Peace loving people has indeed, heaved a sigh of relief.

Hollywood Films—Training Curriculum

Maoists often make experiment new ideas and skills in training, strategies and offensives. Admittedly, they do not have regular research centers to enrich regimentation, fire power, attack and defence tactics. Yet, they borrow ideas, lessons, strategic outputs from foreign pamphlets, literature, Hollywood movies. They gather knowledge on latest weapons, bomb making processes, warfare strategies and use of land mines. The recent astounding incident in Latehar district in Jharkhand where in an encounter, CRPF personnel was killed and thereafter, a bomb was surgically implanted inside the dead body so that it might explode if any attempt was made to salvage the corpse. Maoists had copied out this novel tactics from the Oscar winning war film Hurt Locker (2008). Police of Bijapur district in Chhattisgarh raided a Maoist training camp inside the forest of the Pidiya village and seized eight CDs of Hollywood movies. These were action films depicting commando training, bomb making process, attack and defence strategies. CDs of the movies like Behind Enemy Line, Delta Force, Die Hard, Matrix and Gods Must Be Crazy were among the recovered CDs. Apart from learning and following tactics indicated in the movies, Maoists want to pin prick sentiment of the tribal community with regard to the discrimination and exploitation on them by the westerners. The movie Gods Must Be Crazy projects African tribal characters vis-à-vis the westerners to pin-prick sentiment of the tribals which was deliberately chosen to generate hatred against the rich and affluent people of the west. Film was craftily used to strengthen anti-capitalist sentiment. Prima facie, it appears that Maoists were using the CDs for training purpose. Intelligence sources reveal the Maoists are unable to organise training camps openly short circuiting the eagle eye of the security forces. Secondly, they are short of specialised instructors for jungle warfare training. Therefore, training is imparted to small groups inside the jungle. Maoists generally watch Hollywood movies to learn bomb making processes by foreign countries and keep themselves update about new weapons, attack and defence strategies. Again, the cultural wing of the tribals, Naya Manch uses popular films as propaganda tool to brain wash the tribal.

Storing Explosives—a Sinister Design

Intelligence Bureau, government of India has cautioned the states on amassing explosives by the Maoists in violence torn states to conduct large scale attacks. Ministry of Home Affairs has informed Chhattisgarh, Odisha, Jharkhand and West Bengal that the Maoist central committee has planned to collect explosives and store in secret and secure places for initiating attacks in large scale. They also try to steal, pilfer or pinch from the explosive consignments passing through the states. They gain over the transporters of the consignments or force them to part with a substantial portion of the consignment on payment of money. Secondly, they are collecting explosives from the licensed user or authorised dealers spreading all over the country. In fact, 996 licenses have been issued to the dealers or users across the country including Assam, Arunachal Pradesh, and Bihar etc. MHA has asked the states to step up surveillance on the users of explosives, especially, operating in border areas, verify and check their stock regularly.

Money Rewards and Rehabilitation Packages—Increased Surrender

Reward for good performance is an age old practice. It is also recognition for an individual for dedicated and spectacular service to the society. A lucrative money reward is declared by the police for apprehension of an absconder, encouraging informers, reliable sources, secret agents. Indeed, substantial money rewards work well to get information against absconders, wrong-doers, outlaws. It helps to conduct search, raids in hide-outs of the wanted culprits and law-breakers. Many persons hanker after monetary incentive for secretly passing on secret information, movement of the absconders, deserters, miscreants etc. In fact, similar *modus operandi* is followed to gather intelligence about the ultras, their hide-outs and activities.

In combating the extremists, Maharashtra and Chhattisgarh states first announced rewards for intelligence or arrests of the ultras. General Secretary of the CPI (Maoist), Muppala Lakshman Rao alias Ganapathy is much wanted in criminal conspiracy and criminal cases for attempting to destroy parliamentary democracy. Above states have earlier announced reward of rupees one crore each for arrest of Ganapathy. Of late, reward money has been enhanced to rupees 2.52 crores for his arrest. Secondly, for the arrest of a politburo member reward money has been increased from 7 to 10 lakhs, to rupees 50 to 60 lakhs. For arrest of politburo members, Nambala Kesaba Rao and Kishan da alias Prasant Bose, reward for rupees 1.57 crore and 1.47 crore respectively is declared. For comrade Deo

Kumar Singh alias Arvind Ji, in-charge of Jharkhand Bihar region, reward for rupees 1.32 crore is in force.

Importantly, government of Andhra Pradesh has declared substantial money reward for collecting intelligence against the ultras and their arrest. Secondly, for the comprehensive offer of reward and rehabilitation package security forces have cultivated dependable sources and receiving reliable information. Thirdly, lavish reward has helped to shoot up number of surrenders by the ultras. Indeed, surrender graph in Andhra Pradesh is much higher than that of other states. Truly, the idea to float the bounty and its upper revision from time to time has given a positive result. The other Maoist torn states have followed Andhra Pradesh's pragmatic gesture zealously.

Recently, after the NDA government has taken over under Prime Minister Narendra Modi, the idea of raising the bounty was mooted by a CRPF officer in a meeting of states affected by the Maoists. Since it is a state subject it has to be considered by the states. The union Home Secretary accordingly suggested referring the matter to the states to work on it. It is argued in some quarter that for the arrest of Riyaz Bhatkal, a dreaded terrorist and the founder of the Indian Mujahideen and for Dawood Ibrahim, a notorious gangster, reward for rupees 25 and 20 lakhs respectively was declared. The wide gap in quantum of money reward for two sets of outlaw obviously raises an eye brow. As a matter of fact, the Maoists are biggest threat to the internal security of the country, which are miles ahead of ordinary outrages or a gangster fiend. In short, threat to national security has to be given top priority which neither should be equated with other events nor compromised.

Quantum of money reward is modified depending on the status and activities of a Maoist. Incidentally, for arrest of Maoist leader of Odisha, Sabyasachi Panda, wanted in looting of the armoury of the police training school, Nayagarh and several heinous crimes, a reward of rupees 20 lakhs was declared earlier. Later, as he was expelled from the out-fit and his violent activities were reduced considerably, money reward was cut down to rupees five lakhs. Now he is in judicial custody awaiting prosecution.

All said and done, hand some money reward offered to the ultras clicked well. Arrests and surrenders by the ultras have signally increased responding to the calls for the rewards and rehabilitation packages. Informers and sources are enthusiastically coming forward to communicate intelligence, which have given good grip to the security forces to combat the ultras.

Why Growth of the Maoists was Confined to Seven States?

It may be examined that in spite of the growth of the extremist movements for more than two decades why it is confined to only seven states. Admittedly, people living in other states are equal victims of chill penury, blatant discrimination and crass exploitation. Nevertheless, these states are broadly free from the Maoist influence and unrest. Frankly speaking, many political leaders are sympathetic to their cause and are reluctant to initiate firm action to expose and curb them. Still, the Maoists have failed to register their presence in other states and influence the poverty stricken people, bring them in their fold and organise a mass movement. A question arises whether the Maoists have really succeeded in gaining peoples' good will and support. Secondly, it is imperative that the peace loving people do not approve the Maoists' blood letting activities, violence and annihilation of poor villagers, daily wage earners, unemployed and helpless persons without giving them any opportunity to defend. Thirdly, allegation that the Maoists extort money, secretly accumulate personal wealth, top leaders live in urban areas, lead luxurious life, and in camps female cadres are abused, many comrades suffer from filthy disease, etc. have shaken faith of the people on the so called the People's war, and on the crusade in wiping out the class enemy. Fourthly, caste conflict and hatred or supremacy of a caste or community has marred the very object of a movement or the revolution. Evidently, these scars or stigma are not appreciated or approved by the common people. For example, in Bihar the Yadavs are dominating over the ultras of other castes and Adivasi cadres, in Odisha the Maoists from Andhra Pradesh have been ill treating the Maoists of Odisha and dominating over them, Christian community is backed by a politically interested group vis-à-vis the Hindus in Kondamal district, Odisha which eventually led to communal riots. Needless to add, these shortcomings are going to erode unity, team spirit, cohesion and single-minded devotion to reach the goal and fulfill aspiration of the have-not.

It needs no reiteration that the enlightened people sincerely want welfare and uplift of the deprived people and down trodden. At the same time, they dislike and vehemently oppose violence, bloodshed and anarchy. This is one of the main reasons that after initial euphoria the people do not welcome disorder, annihilation and violence oriented organisation and their horrid activities whatever lofty may be their ideal and goal. Significantly, peace, harmony and mutual respect to each other is the culture and tradition of this country. Hence any deviation from the fundamental values is unacceptable to the peace-loving people. Indeed, Maoist movement is confined to rural areas and within tribal communities. However, it has failed to influence the urban population. Admittedly, prospect of its impact on the urban areas and citizenry in coming days is quite dim. Therefore, suffice to say that its further expansion in other states at this juncture short-circuiting the strict vigil of the state administration is a myth.

Allegation of Amassing Wealth and Properties by the Maoists

To be precise, a splinter group of Maoists claimed to be the Jharkhand Prastuti Committee (JPC) has brought out a leaflet containing startling revelations on possessing wealth and properties by several Maoist leaders. Importantly, in spite of allegations made pointedly against several leaders, none has challenged or contradicted those or issued any rejoinder. A list of high profile Maoists mentioned in the leaflet who alleged to have amassed wealth by wielding their clout has shaken the people. It reveals that Maoist leader Raghunath Dangi owns two plots in Hazaribagh and Jamshedpur, a 10-wheel truck, a matador van and a brick kiln. Maoist Krishna Yadav has built a big house at Chatra and purchased a 10-wheel truck. Rama Sankar Yadav has purchased ten dumpers which are being run on rent at Khelari and built palatial building in Aurangabad and New Delhi. Tilak Ganjhu has bought three hydraulic tractors, a JCB van in benami of Nirmal Soni and Raju Dangi using the party fund. Rebel Jagdish Yadav alias Prabhat, one of the members of the Politburo and the think tank has built a house in Bokaro and running a cloth business at Gaya. Rebel Sandeep alias Vijay Yadav has purchased a residential building worth rupees 60 lakhs and 100 acres of land in Gaya district.

Rebel Vijay Kumar Arya who was arrested along with six top leaders disclosed that his son has been studying in a foreign university. He owns a big house in Patna. Another Maoist, Madan Pal has sent his daughter to Singapore for higher studies. He has been expelled from the party for contesting poll. He was a senior Maoist leader of the Bengal-Jharkhand-Orissa border committee. Police confirms that several corrupt Maoist leaders belong to border committees and some also belong to the central committee. Many have amassed personal wealth, owning properties and have been running business under assumed names. Director General of Police Jharkhand stated that the police followed up the leads and identified properties belong to many Maoist leaders.

It has been high lighted that the Maoists' war chest is quite substantial. In fact, collection through levy, extortions, robberies, protection money etc is not less than 1500 crores in a calendar year. Secret police report reveals that at least 17 Maoist leaders in Bengal and Jharkhand have been identified who have enriched themselves and accumulated money and personal properties. The belief that a group of dedicated persons inspired by the Maoist ideology fighting for the poor and down trodden enduring enormous hardship and risk is a mistaken notion. It is an irony that their so called ideological struggle is not immune from motive, personal ambition and corruption.

Indeed, with these galling short comings no outfit or a movement can carry the mass with them, topple the existing social and political order and establish the Peoples' government. Revolting disclosure that a few Maoist leaders in Bihar and Jharkhand own hundreds of acres of land, palatial bungalows located in cities across the country, purchased trucks, vehicles and run public transport buses, if true, will dismay the people who have been carrying sympathy and support covertly for the Maoist movement. Even the radicals, writers, educationists and intellectuals who have been carrying cudgel for the ultras and the progressive elements who thronged the main through fares of Kolkata city objecting to the deployment of the para military forces and joint operation demanded halt of the joint operation by the security forces in Jangal Mahal are sure to repent for showing misplaced sympathy and support to the extremists. Many political leaders are soft to the ultras and unwilling to initiate action against them with consummate firmness for fear of incurring displeasure of a section of the populace who are sympathetic to the Maoist cause, may have to regret in the long run. In Bihar, Maoist threat has penetrated well into thirty three districts of total thirty eight districts during the last seven years.

Bandyopadhyay Committee Report

Union government appointed an expert committee under D. Bandyopadhyay. IAS, former Revenue Secretary of the Union Government with 16 members. Agenda of the committee was to pin-point and analyse the situation in the country in connection with the Maoist problems. The members visited affected areas in four Maoist hit states, Andhra Pradesh, Odisha, Jharkhand and Chhattisgarh and continued probe for a period of two years. The committee submitted its report in April 2008, to the Planning Commission, government of India. Concluding remarks of the report reveals, "Extremism is an effect or a deeper malaise of failure of governance and developmental activities in the affected areas where roughly 2.4 crores tribals were evicted and displaced from hearth and homes because of large scale acquisition of land for development purpose." Crux of the report discloses that eviction of the tribals and lack of development broadly contributed to the extremist movement. (Further details of the report discussed in Chapter Five)

Attempt to Expand Maoist Cult in North-East

The Eastern Regional Bureau, the Maoist brain child founded to spread activities in North East and motivate the local populace to respond to the Maoist movement failed to make any dent. First, the organisation of the Maoists here is exceptionally weak. Secondly, local leaders and activists are not capable of taking Maoist cult to higher pedestal and inspire the people to throng under its banner and participate in the movement. Thirdly, the insurgent out-fit already active in North East are unwilling to accommodate others from out side to penetrate into their turf, influence the people and initiate any movement. Lastly, they are guided by sole idea of the state craft having varying aims and objects. Many possess divisive idea, want an independent state and maintain secret link with foreign countries. Some harp on clannish supremacy and pursue the formation of a state craft accordingly. In short, reasons high-lighted above, though not exhaustive, the local insurgent outfit are not inclined to permit the Maoists to put their foot-hold on the soil of the North East and take the people in their fold. Indeed, presence and success of the strong local insurgent's outfits is an insurmountable hurdle for other extremist organisations from outside to steal a march over them. Frankly speaking, for the Maoists, so far as the North East is concerned, buck stops here.

It is unpalatable that the Maoists who project lofty ideal and aspire for the people's government is not immune from stigma of moral turpitude, dishonesty, corruption, caste and racial conflicts and internal squabbles. Uproar for the annihilation of the class enemy and establishment of the People's government through the arms struggle, coated with the ideal of salvaging the poor, exploited and deprived people appears to be pervasive and intriguing. Its baneful spirit encourages evils of national life and subverts elegancies of a democratic government, ungrudging public service and aspiration of the people. Nevertheless, its cadre is gaining strength, earning goodwill of a sizeable rural populace and the movement has been spreading. It is therefore imperative to identify its inner secret and initiate pragmatic remedial measures. After all, police action alone is unable to handle and solve the growing Maoist threat.

Maoist Link with the ISI

A study report prepared by the Centre for Land Welfare Studies (CLAWS) and commissioned by the Ministry of Defence, Government of India has categorically pointed out that the CPI (Maoist) has external linkages with Pakistan's secret agency, Inter-Services Intelligence (ISI). The report contains exclusively a chapter captioned, "External Linkages of Indian Maoists." It disclosed that the Left Wing Extremism (LWE) should not be termed as "indigenous movement" at all. Its extensive linkages with both internal states and external powers have made it extremely formidable.

The CLAWS is based in New Delhi is an autonomous think-tank dealing with national security and conceptual aspects of land warfare including conventional, sub-conventional conflict and terrorism. The study report confirmed that the ISI as one of the most internal links with the Maoists. "The Inter-Services Intelligence (ISI) in its attempts to rope in India based militant groups has found Indian Maoists more than suitable for its agenda. Report further reveals that the Maoists have link with fraternal groups and organisations based in twenty one countries. Naxals are now part of ISI's Karachi project that aims to bleed India both militarily and economically. The Pakistan Intelligence Agency also has facilitated contacts between the Maoists and anti-India terror groups based in Pakistan like Lashkar-e-Taiba (LeT), Jaish-e-Muhammad (JeM) and Bangladesh based Harkart-ul-jihad-al-Islami (HuJI)" ISI maintains close contact with Bangladesh based Islamic Militant groups and militant outfits operate in India like Indian Mujahideen and Student Islamic Movement in India (SIMI). ISI also has been maintaining contact with the militant groups active in North and helping them to extend drug cultivation. It is also using the Naxal local network and pushing counterfeit currencies all over India. The Maoists of Nepal have been extending full support and co-operation to the counter parts in India. They are assisting in arms procurement, drug trade, training and resource mobilisation.

In June 2009, Delhi police arrested Moulana Umar Madni, a LeT activist who was assigned to set up a link between Maoists and LeT activists in border areas of

Jharkhand and West Bengal. Maoists are desperately trying to enhance their fighting potential developing link with both internal and external terrorist out-fits. Maoists cultivate the external link to procure arms, learn new tactics and mobilise the resources

Report highlighted that the government has not given due attention in countering the outreach strategy of the ultra-leftists. However, though delayed India has set up 25 joint groups on counter terrorism in various countries and regional organisations. These groups are vested with responsibility to expose the militant groups who are maintaining contacts and assisting the ultras active in India. Special attention on the activities of the ultras active in Bangladesh, Nepal and Bangladesh is emphasised. Examining pros and cons the study group has recommended, "India has to commit its full diplomatic energy in a serious way both at bilateral and multilateral levels to make sure those external sources of support to Maoists are disrupted permanently." In pursuit of countering the growing menace the think-tank has advised, "Breaking this support structure that exists, especially, in the form of increasingly extensive linkages, should be a part and parcel of India's counter Naxal strategy." Frankly speaking, the ISI in an attempt to rope in India based militant groups has discovered that the Maoists in India are more than suitable for the ISI's agenda.

It is well established that movements of the militants in North East is being promoted actively by Pakistan's ISI and Bangladesh Intelligence Service. The US Security think-tank "Stratfor" has asserted in its report, "Pakistan's ISI in co-operation with Bangladesh's Director General of Forces Intelligence (DGFI) is investing considerable resources in solidifying India's militant corridor." Report further disclosed, "There are growing indications that these two agencies are working clandestinely in Bangladesh to bring all the north east based insurgent outfits and jihadi elements under one umbrella." The think-tank has observed "both could constrain India's ability to dig itself out of the militant trap Pakistan has set". The militant outfit ULFA active in North East had been advised by the ISI and Bangladesh Intelligence Service not to hold peace talk with government of India. Report has pointed out at growing Islamisation of groups like ULFA.

On April 9, 2007, the suicide bombing attack by the ULFA cadres near Guwahati very close to a spot where Prime Minister Monmohan Singh was travelling was an example of a massive threat. Significantly, ULFA for the first time experimented suicide bombing attack. It has learnt the skill from the both LTTE and Pakistan's jihadi elements. It has unmistakably proved the ULFA's growing link with Islamist jihadi elements of Bangladesh. Stratfor, while tracing the growth of the ULFA stated, "it has gradually changed into what appears to be a money making machine with a strong willingness to do the ISI's bidding. ULFA did not have many Muslim cadres in its fold in the past but the increasing flow of Bangladesh refugees across the border has given the group more capable members willing to sacrifice their lives for the group's cause with nudging from the ISI." (*The Times of India*, April 25, 2007).

Importantly, the then Union Home Minister once stated that the Maoists have no link with the ISI which was erroneous. Precisely, the think-tanks' exhaustive reports, conclusive observation and recommendation have unearthed the truth which belies the UHM's statement.

CHAPTER THREE

Red Terror in Jharkhand State

Jharkhand State was separated from Bihar state with effect from January 2000. Its geographical area is 79714 sq km. Two third territory of the state is infested with forest, hills where access is far from easy. Its population is 2.70 crores including 1.72 crores belonging to SC/ST and other backward classes. Adivasi population is approximately 55 to 60 percent. It has 24 districts and 339 police stations, About 18 districts are facing the Red terror. Ranchi is its capital, a rapidly growing industrial town. The state is surrounded by Chhattisgarh, Orissa, Bihar and West Bengal. These states are facing the growing threat of the extremists. In fact, out of terror incidents taking place in India, 68.16 percent extremist incidents are reported from Chhattisgarh and Jharkhand states together. Casualties of the security personnel and the civilians of the two states together is 76.42 percent of total victims report from the Maoist torn states. In addition to the CPI (Maoists), five other out fits (1) Sangharsh Jana Mukti Morcha (SJMM), (2) Tritiya Sammelan Prastuti Committee (TSPC), (3) Sashastra Peoples Morcha (SPM), (4) People's Liberation Front of India (PLFI), (5) Jharkhand Prastuti Committee (JPC), are quite active.

Rough estimate reveals that the strength of the Maoist cadre in the state is approximately 6000 including 2000 armed personnel. Their age group is 14 to 26. Cadre is strengthened by sizeable fair sexes including teenagers. Broadly, the out fit has two strong training units, one is situated in Gotang, Latehar district and other is situated in Pareshnath. In the midst of thick and inaccessible jungle well-knit and fortified camps are established. It has training ground, temporary camps, tents and necessary infrastructure including medical care facilities. Mini workshop to repair weapons, assembling land mine components etc is also available. Trainees are taught various techniques of hide and seek, camouflage, laying land mines, booby traps, ambush, surprise attacks and construction of fox holes. Some fox holes are 5 to 6 feet deep and half a km long. Camps are generally established 20 to 25 kms away from the rural habitation connected by jungle foot path which are not known to the outsiders, or police personnel. Often they kill persons without verifying their alibi. After brutal killing, eyes of the victims are gorged out, hands or legs are severed, bodies mutilated beyond recognition. Savage cruelty is indulged in to create a deadly impact on the psyche of the rural people. Perhaps, pitiless ultras feel that barbarous treatment to the corpse will generate boundless panic and fear in the locality which will dissuade the villagers to go against their will and obey them implicitly. They perhaps feel that terror stricken people of the areas will be joining their fold and eventually participate in the movement. Procurement of arms and ammunitions is persuaded broadly from two sources. They surprise and attack the police stations, out post, police camps, armouries, training units, ransack the posts and carry away weapons and ammunitions. They snatch away weapons from possession of the callous policemen, guards, sentries, escorts. Under threat or coercion they compel the licensed gun holders to hand over guns and ammunitions. Secondly, they purchase weapons and ammunitions secretly from the gun dealers, middlemen and secret sources. They procure weapons from Bangladesh and Nepal with the help of the smugglers and miscreants. Flow of supply of arms and ammunitions is ensured by the parent units. Outfits active in Andhra Pradesh play a major role in supplying arms and ammunition. Earlier they were helped by the LTTE to procure weapons. More over, they used to purchase weapons from open markets of several foreign countries. Surprisingly, of late, the ultras have been manufacturing weapons and land mines in their hide outs. They employ experts and skilled persons who are capable of building foundry and manufacturing small weapons from indigenous sources.

Differences with Charu Mazumdar forced a few leaders of West Bengal to shift their area of operation in several pockets of Bihar. Immeasurable poverty, discrimination and exploitation of the rural mass appeared favorable to them to peruse their lofty revolutionary ambition. At that juncture, Maoist Communist Centre (MCC), Indian People's Front (IPF) was very active in several tribal dominated districts. Thick jungle, hills, difficult terrain, archaic communication and absence of the semblance of policing and administration were considered suitable to establish hide outs or sanctuaries and organise a formidable cadre. In the north the state is sharing its boundary with Nepal which was working as a "spring board" for many extremist out fits and divisive elements including the ultras of the Khalisthan movement of the Punjab. Again cancerous growth of caste and community conflicts, bloody encounters between private militia in the state only added fuel to the Red terror. Over and above, the state government's policy of masterly inactivity or faineancy to curb the unprecedented growth of the extremist cadres, striking power, procurement of arms multiplying resources etc indirectly helped the out fits to be obdurately strong and reckless. Out fits active in Bihar meanwhile, developed link, understanding and mutual cooperation with the ultra-outfits of Nepal, Andhra Pradesh, Orissa and Madhya Pradesh. Importantly, Chhattisgarh state had been curbed out of Madhya Pradesh after some times.

MCC and IPF were already active in Bhojpur areas of Bihar and in rural areas of southern districts which are widely inhabited by the Adivasi population. Subsequently, CPI (ML) came to the fore front. In fact, much before Bihar state was divided and Jharkhand state emerged, aggressive activities of the ultras were quite vulnerable. Growth of the extremists and escalated violence in Jharkhand were responsible due to socio-economic disparity and the government's unresponsiveness to curb or contain poverty, unemployment and exploitation. Secondly, wonky police equipped with archaic training, back dated weaponry and deficient man power was unable to gnash the outlaws and bring the situation under control. Hence, poverty stricken and deprived people spontaneously responded to the call of the ultras. In 1980, in Andhra Pradesh the Peoples' War Group (PWG) emerged and stepped up abhorrent activities. The PWG supplied arms, ammunitions, land mines and imparted specialised guerrilla warfare training. In the state two safe sanctuaries were built, cadres were trained in handling sophisticated weapons, use of explosives, planting land mines, use of the ground and organise surprise attacks. Henceforth, the ultras renewed surprise attacks in good strength, attacked police posts, snatched arms from the police personnel, killed civilians mere on suspicion. Frankly speaking, they practically let loose a reign of terror. Casualty of the security personnel, jail breaks, land mine blasts increased. People past time under abyss suspense, fear and muss. The state was taken unawares, unable to face the volatile situation with consummate ability and determination. However for better appreciation number of police personnel killed, injured and weapons looted year wise is given below.

In 2004, 45 policemen were killed, 32 injured and 49 weapons from police men were snatched or looted. In 2005, altogether 30 policemen were killed, 40 injured and 185 weapons were either snatched away or looted. In 2006, total 45 policemen were killed, 34 injured and 6 weapons were snatched away. In 2007, total 11 policemen were killed, 14 injured and 17 weapons were looted. Importantly, from January to July 2007, Maoist related violent incidents increased from 191 to 259, compared to the incidents reported during the corresponding period in 2006. However, eleven security personnel were killed and fourteen were injured. Casualty of policemen reduced marginally during the period. Laudably, suffering from deficiency of man power, obsolete training, weaponry, communication and intelligence output and heavy loss in men and materials the police men have not given up the challenge. They have been facing the ultras with courage and single minded devotion. However, merger of the PW and the MCC on 21 September 2004 and formation of the CPI (Maoist) has given fresh impetus to the extremist movements in seven states of the country.

Neglected Santal Parganas and the Ultras

Santal Parganas is a sizeable portion of eastern territory of Bihar, now Jharkhand. On its east, West Bengal state is situated. Dumka, Sahibganj, Pakur, Deoghar and Giridhi are prominent districts of the Santal Parganas. The Paharia tribe is an important sect with a population of roughly 1.25 lakhs spread all over the places. It has two sects Sourive and Mal Paharia. In addition, Santhals and Ghotwals also live here. They are simple, innocent, and peace loving, earn livelihood from agriculture. They work as daily laborers and depend much on jungle and jungle products. Truly, the extremists had no influence on them till 1991. The areas is rich in mineral and hence, attractive for the ultras who freely extort and extract levies from the miners, contractors, transporters etc. Unfortunately, development in the areas is lamentably negligible. Pathetic spectacle of poverty and ill economic progress has only produced claustrophobic impact on the people. Yet the tribals did not respond to the Maoists' crafty call. Ironically, former Chief Ministers Babulal Marandi, Sibu Soren and Deputy Chief Minister Stephen Marandi belong to Santhal Parganas and elected from this place. Yet economic development in the areas is not up to the mark. Indeed, ethnic sentiment or election promises for progress etc hardly inspired the people or the political leaders to ensure advancement with missionary zeal. In such a scenario, the Paharias are the worse sufferers. They had no political representative to focus their pitiable existence before the right forum. No member of the community has ever been elected to the Lok Sabha or the State Legislative Assembly. A Paharia Development Committee was constituted in 1995 in undivided Bihar headed by the Development Commissioner of the Santhal Parganas. It slovenly functioned and thereby failed to initiate tangible development activities. Dismayingly, after creation of Jharkhand state its activities petered out. Indeed, monumental neglect, burgeoning grievances of the innocent tribals and dubious woes let loose by the extremists gradually worked. The luckless people eventually submitted to the ultras and ungrudgingly agreed to co-operate with them.

In December 2007, shameful incident of rape of three girls of the Paharia community by the policemen triggered unprecedented restlessness. The Paharias were up-in-arms against crime and outrages by public servants. At that climactic juncture much awaited opportunity knocked at the door for the ultras to built a base in the tribal belt. They adroitly utilised resentment of the tribals against the richer class, exploiters, police and administration and inspired them to join the armed struggle. An armed encounter between the police and the extremists took place at village Pokhria, in Shikaripada area, district Dumka in which three policemen, including Officer-in-Charge of Shikaripada police station were killed. After the encounter police could arrest Manoj Dehri, an area commander of the extremist out-fit. As a follow up action they raided many places and arbitrarily arrested many without proper verification. In fact, preceding the encounter a group of the Maoists, including a few senior leaders assembled in Salbona and Lobapara villages for consultation. Subsequently, a strong group took refuge in Pahariatola of Pokaria for the night. Police on a tip-off surrounded them which culminated in a bloody encounter and death of several policemen. Unfortunately, the police's reckless excesses to round up the ultras proved counter productive. It only enhanced resentment and anathema against the police and cemented unity and resoluteness of the villagers to fight injustice and exploitation. Evidently, it opened the flood gate for the Maoists to tighten up their grip and pursue their so called struggle. In fact, Dumka district was chosen to be used as the gate way to the Santal Parganas. In 1992, the Maoist activities were first noticed in the district. But the tribal community's strong opposition failed to create the desired impact. Hence, the idea of further penetration had to be jettisoned temporarily. However, the scenario under went a drastic change once the tribals agreed to support the Maoists. The Maoists from Katoria and Dhoraiya blocks of Banka district of Bihar poured in and took tangible initiative to develop direct link with the Red corridor across Bihar and Jharkhand. The mini corridor facilitated direct and swift communication between Dhoriya, Sundar blocks of Godda, Ramgarh, Kathikund and Gopi kandar block of Dumka, Amrapara and Littipara blocks of Pakur. Santa Pal faction of the Maoist soon wizened. However, it contributed substantially to make the so called mini corridor. Unfortunately, Santal Parganas is tainted with several seething attacks and dastardly killing of innocent persons, including the weaker sex.

Former Chief Minister Babulal Marandi's Jharkhand Vikas Morcha (Prajatantrik) is founded to tame or neutralise the Maoists. It organises cultural programmes, sports and games to develop contact with the people and high-light the futility of the extremist movement. In addition, the Gramin Surakha Dal (GSD) formed by the villagers which is a village level protection group. Babulal Marandi was the life wire behind the GSD. Ultras have been threatening Marandi and his family members for daring consequence for patronizing the GSD. On October 26, 2008, at Chilkaridih under Deori police station, district Giridih; the Jharkhand Vikas Manch (JVM) organised a football match and a cultural programme in the evening. Several ultras dressed in army fatigues joined the congregation and witnessed the football match and cultural show. At about 12.10 AM four ultras climbed on the stage and looked for the members of Marandi's family members. Several others surrounded the spectators and fired at the brother of Marandi, shot and killed Marandi's youngest son who got married only four months ago. The ultras fired indiscriminately, killed 18 persons including five women, two children and injured 11 persons. Villagers could not suspect presence of the ultras as they were putting on uniform and took them to be CRPF personnel. Indeed, such a savage killing was devoid of any sense or logic as the simple and unassuming villagers had not offended them in any way. After the gory incident at Chilkaridih the Maoists started poster campaign in Giridhi and Jamui district of Bihar, broadly, aiming at demolishig the GSD. On Ist November, a group of more than 50 Maoists gathered in the main market of Giridih town and warned the GSD members. After a short break, second round of posters came out. The GSD members were asked to surrender to the Maoists. Poster campaign created a goblin ambience in the rural areas. Secondly, trial in Jana Adalat and severe punishment awarded to the villagers without verifying their alibi put the villagers in abysmal panic and consternation. Importantly, earlier Sunil Mahato, a member of the Parliament from the Jharkhand Mukti Morcha (JMM), a political party constituted for the Adivasis in the area and Mahendra Prasad, a member of the State Legislative Assembly representing the CPI (ML) Liberation, were attacked and killed.

A local contractor, Balaram Pal of Dumka district was killed. Several coal dumpers in Pannem coal mines of Amrapara were set on fire, as the management did not concede to the ultras' exorbitant demand for money. Interrogation of the arrested sub-zonal commander, Badri Rai, revealed a startling clue. He disclosed that at least 45 young girls of the Paharia and Santal tribes have been recruited in the Maoist cadre. They are mainly utilised to tantalize and mobilise persons of other tribal communities to join the cadre. In fact, induction of young fair sex in the cadre is followed zealously. They are often used as a pawn to attract the youths to join the so call peoples' movement. Women leaders in senior level have shown equal élan and leadership quality. As a matter of fact, weaker sex are encouraged to respond which enrich the cadre for more than one reasons, including for the purpose of abusing them physically. This measly episode will be discussed separately in appropriate chapter. Maoist Politburo or the Central Command issue instructions to the rank and file regularly. Intelligence report transpires that in middle of 2008, a secret meeting was held between the members of Eastern Regional Bureau and the Bihar-Jharkhand-Chhattisgarh Special Area Committee of the CPI (Maoist) to discuss the stratagem, mode of execution, expansion of the area of operation and to increase the strength of man-power. It was resolved to penetrate swiftly into the new areas, virgin territories and reclaim the areas which had gone into the control of the police and the rival factions. Secondly, it was decided to take on the police and security personnel, members of the local resistance groups and the suspected informers. In short, it was aimed at bringing the whole state under the draconic control of the Maoists.

Violence, killing, destabilisation of peace and security of the people continued unabatedly. Government's move to contain or banish it was frustrated. However, for fulfilling curiosity of the readers a few instances of violence are discussed below which will reveal the magnitude of the growing atrocity and the helplessness of the peace loving people. In 2000, the extremists attacked the house of Bhado Singh and several others of village Gurmu of Gumla district, assaulted the inmates mercilessly and occupied their land, ponds and carried away valuables. In 2001, Bhado Singh founded "Santi Sena" with the villagers to resist the extremist attacks. By 2002, Bhado Singh and his brigade gained back lost lands and ponds. It obviously increased animosity between the Santi Sena and the extremists. In 2004, the extremists were transformed into Maoists with renewed strength and striking power. The new out-fit attacked Bhado Singh's house four times and killed several members of the brigade. Inspire of fear of reprisal and loss, the Santi Sena has been resisting the Maoists which only irked them. On April 9, 2008, evening, Bhado Singh with his wife, child and others were travelling in a vehicle. On the way near Bhandra Toli jungle, about 70 Maoists blocked the road throwing a wooden log and fired at the vehicle. Singh in the driving wheel was killed along with seven others. Wife of Singh was hit by a bullet on her left shoulder but succeeded in escaping with her three years old son. Ultras burnt the dead bodies and the vehicle. It was suspected that one of the members of the Santi Sena secretly passed on the travel plan of Bhado Singh to the ultras. It was whispered that Singh had been secretly communicating with the Jharkhand Liberation Tigers, a break away faction of the Maoists. After barbarous killing, the Maoists raided nearby Kotra Kona village and searched for two activists of the Santi Sena. As they were absent, the ultras thrashed their family members and looted two licensed guns. Precisely, the attack was pre-planned and executed with extreme cruelty. A pall of gloom descended in the area. The people were shocked and panicked seeing such an atrocious event unheard in the past. Police was blamed for failing to protect the activists of the Santi Sena, in spite of prior information of likely attempt on them. Members of the Santi Sena have been helping the police to undo the Maoist activities in the area and yet the police failed to come up to the expectation.

Chief Minister's Attempts to Restore Peace

Babulal Marandi, the first Chief Minister of newly formed Jharkhand state, initiated the state sponsored the Nagarik Suraksha Samity. Its object is to counter the Maoist movement in rural areas of the state. They actively co-operate with the police and secretly pass on information to them on the Maoists' activities and movements, build a ubiquitous ambience so that the villagers are immune from influence of the ultras. On a tiff off received from them, a police contingent under Superintendent of Police of East Singbhum district, surrounded Bhitor Amda village near Ghatsila where a group of ultras had been hiding. Watching the police's arrival the Maoists retaliated firing volleys from fire arms. As the situation was untenable they tried to sneak into Orissa state crossing the border. Indeed, night long armed encounter ended in the afternoon, resulting in, bullet ridden bodies of seven ultras including one regional commander and two women of the Maoist cadre were found dead at the spot. On July 28, 2007, ultras killed five persons at Lateher. It was the result of a fall out of two rival groups of the ultras. Police party rushed to village Boda and raided several pockets. Maoists fired at the police men who returned the fire, killed three ultras and recovered their dead bodies. The Maoists, to register protest against police action gave a call for "bandh" (strike) on the following day. However, the bandh passed off peacefully. On March 1, 2008, police launched an offensive against 500 ultras who had taken shelter in the forest of Netarhat bordering

Gumla district. Later a company of the Jharkhand Armed Police (JAP) stationed at Netarhat field firing range was attacked and fired upon. A fierce gun battle continued for several hours, and several ultras were killed. Police recovered four improvised explosive devices (IEDs). At Jhumra foothill, a police contingent of Bokaro and CRPF jointly led an operation and destroyed three bunkers of the ultras, seized three rifles, two twelve bore guns, one US 3006 rifle, one country made gun, two air guns, two hand grenades, huge quantity of ammunitions and Maoist literature. Indeed, the police's decisive action forced the ultras to take to their heels.

On June 23, 2008, about one hundred Maoists surrounded village, Dantar of Chatra district, singled out two persons branding them as police informers, hacked them to death and threw the dead bodies in a ditch. Ultras blew up a primary school building and a community centre. On June 15, 2008., a bridge between Dhanbad and Giridhi was badly damaged using explosives. On June 30, 2008, a police party led by Deputy Superintendent of Police, Bundu, was returning after long range patrolling duty. In Pundidiri area near Ranchi town the ultras detonated a powerful land mine concealed under a culvert and killed the Dy SP and four police personnel and injured four others critically. On July 9, 2008, Ramesh Singh Munda, MLA and former Minister was addressing a congregation in a prize distribution ceremony of a school at Barihatu village. Suddenly, a group of ultras fired indiscriminately, killed him, his bodyguards and a student. Several were injured. Panic-stricken spectators ran helter–skelter, resulting in, a stampede. On August 30, 2008., ultras attacked a police post deployed for guarding the Barudi Dam, eight kms away from Ghatsila town. It is a tourist spot where a large number of tourists throng to visit the dam and its surrounding areas. Maoists surprised the police personnel, blasted a mine and fired indiscriminately. Eleven police men including the in charge of the camp were killed. Previously, the ultras attacked the nearby village, Digha and killed two villagers.

On August 18, 2008, a splinter group of the extremists, Peoples 'Liberation Front of India, forced one hundred eleven owners of the crusher plants to shut down the plants. They set fire on the plant of Ramesh Mehta, located at village Sijua, under Ichak Police Station, district Hazaribagh. The miscreants had been collecting levy from the owners illegally. As the owners refused to oblige them anymore, the miscreants took the harsh step to teach them a lesson. In October 2008, three top Maoists including the self-styled sub zonal commander Rajendra Singh Kharuar were arrested from Garwah district; six guns, 50 gelatins and a large quantity of explosive were seized.

Madan Pal alias Jugal Pal, one of the top Maoists of Jharkhand was arrested on July 28, 2007 by the police of the Bihar state near Patna. Maoists declared bandh on August 1, 2007 protesting against the arrest and let loose violence. A group of heavily armed ultras surrounded Bendi halt and Demu railway station in

Lataher district. Stations are important railway link known as Coal India Chord (CIC) for dispatching coal. Ultras destroyed the station building, communication equipments and official records. They abducted the station master of Lataher railway station at gun point and released him after a few hours. In Ranka block of Garwah district, two buses proceeding to Daltanganj were ambushed near hilly patch of Bhaduaghati. Ultras fired at the buses. Driver of one bus, Arvind Panday, received bullet injuries in both hands and abdomen but managed to drive the bus right to Ranka police station. The other bus coming from Raighar to Daltanganj was attacked. The driver lost control, hit a tree and the bus fell into a ditch. Twenty five passengers of both buses were injured. After an hour, two trucks laden with bauxite from Chhattisgarh proceeding to Garwah were attacked near the same spot. Driver of one of the trucks, Anuj was killed. They set fire on the forest rest house at Marumaad in Betla forest. A private mobile service tower at Konwai village under Panki police station of Palamau district was blown up. In fact, life in rural areas became stand still. However, bandh had no effect on cities and urban areas. In Giridih ultras looted the armoury of the Home Guards Training Centre, over powered a passenger train and reached Dhanbad mingling with a wedding party. It was suspected that behind such daring actions clandestine assistance of local persons was evident.

In 2002, seventeen cops were killed at Bikilsog, under Monoharpur police station. In 2004, 29 cops were killed at Balva under Gua police station. In 2007, eleven CRPF personnel were killed in Jeraikela. On March 10, 08, dreaded Maoist and zonal commander Rakesh Paswan, wanted in several murder cases was arrested from Palamau district. On April 1, 2008, eight Maoists including a woman Maoist were killed in two separate operations in Garhwa jointly organised by the police and the CRPF. A huge cache of arms and ammunitions were seized. On April 2, 08, a police vehicle was hit by a land mine, 14 persons were injured. Four headless bodies were dumped in Arka area near Ranchi town. It was suspected that they were murdered in some unknown place, carried and dumped at the place. CRPF discovered a huge number of land mines, planted on the road stretching over one km patch near the steel city Bokaro. On April 16, 08, ultras gave a call of 24 hours bandh protesting against killing of eight comrades earlier. Rebels blew up two metres railway line in Giridih district. On April 19, 2008, rebels attacked a convoy of trucks on the NH 33 running from Jamshedpur to Ranchi, attempted to burn three trucks, fired and killed two khalashies. On April 26, 2008, in Dumka district in a protracted encounter with the security forces two rebels were killed and one was captured. OIC of the police station and two cops were injured who later succumbed to injury.

On May 7, 2008, one SI and two cops traveling in a jeep was ambushed near Vishnugarh, Hazaribag, and the SI was killed. On May 11, 2008, OIC of Chari P S, Hazaribag district and one CRPF personnel were killed. Another OIC Vijay Kumar Thakur was ambushed and killed in Dahidag forest area when he proceeded to raid a hide-out. On June 1, 2008, after prolonged gun battle at village Sundermahto, Hazaribag district, four Maoists including Arjun Yadav were killed. He was wanted in several murder cases and for killing MLA Mahendra Pratap Singh. On July 29, 2008 in a night long gun battle a self-styled Maoist, sub zonal commander and two women Maoists were killed in Vishnugarh jungle. On May 25, 2008, rebels partially damaged a bridge on the NH 33, using can bombs. Intensity of blast was too deafening. Police seized two live bombs from the spot. Later police nabbed three leaders of Jharkhand Liberation Tigers (JLT) a splinter group of the ultras. On May 21, 2009, the ICICI bank officials were carrying cash collected from Bishnupur and Sakchi branches and proceeding to Ranchi in a bank's delivery van under armed escort provided by a private security agency. Maoists on the way over powered the van, looted cash rupees five crores and 1.30 kg gold. They took six security personnel travelling in the van as hostages. Rebels fired at the police chasing them and injured two cops.

The area is very close to Saranda forest, West Singbhum district, one of the strong hide-outs of the Maoists. Forest here is thick and inaccessible. Inside the forest Maoists run a training camp. Security forces raided the training camp on June 10, 2009 known as Jharkhand Avon. Interestingly, the name has been copied from the Shakespeare's birth place in UK. It is a frontal organisation of the Maoists active in Maoist dominated districts across Jharkhand and Odisha. The out-fit claimed that they are a non-governmental cultural organisation that works towards spreading awareness of the tribals among various social problems pervading the tribal hinterland of Jharkhand, Odisha and part of W.B. They deny any connection with the Maoists. However in combing operation by the CRPF and state police jointly two suspects Nirbhik and Suraj were arrested and Naxal literature seized. Police team when returning to HQ with the arrested suspects in a land mine blast near Serenda under Goilkera police station, eleven police men including two sub inspectors and one Inspector of CRPF were killed. Security forces fought gallantly and forced the ultras to retreat. It was suspected that Maoists attacked the police team and killed cops for rescuing the arrested duo. Another suspect, Jeetan was arrested from Ranchi who was involved in the carnage of killing 20 persons including Babulal Marandi's son.

On January 17, 09, a powerful land mine was planted on the high way near Monica police station of Latehar district. A top Maoist leader, Rajesh Toppo was killed in an encounter near Tamar. He was responsible for killing R S Munda, the MLA of Tomar, and the Dy SP of Bundu, looting rupees five crores and one kg of gold of the ICICI bank when the valuables were being escorted to Ranchi. On April 11, 2009, five hundred ultras were holed up in Jarko hill, Arki block of Khunti district. In nearby forest, in a prolonged encounter of six hours five CRPF personnel were killed and three injured. Ultras took away one AK rifle and four INSAS rifles. In this particular belt the ultras are very active and earned notoriety for attacking police party on several occasions. Notably, Saranda forest is thick and inaccessible.

Here, the Maoists run training camps. On September 27, 2010, Jharkhand and Orissa police jointly undertook a massive operation to flush out the Maoists, demolish training camps and hideouts. Operation continued for four days and exchange of fire lasted for 48 hours. Twelve Maoists were killed, six training camps and a bunker were destroyed and huge cache of arms, ammunitions, explosive and land mines were seized. Three security personnel including one from elite Cobra force and two from Jharkhand police force lost their lives. The fleeing Maoists set fire on two stationary trucks in Sundergarh district Orissa. In fact, to make the operation effective helicopter was used.

On March 6, 2009, Adivasi leader Kailesh Chandra Hembrem was shot dead at Jaduoratola, East Singhbhum district. On June 12, 2009, near the steel town Bokaro, in two separate incidents eleven policemen were killed and four rifles were looted. On June 12, 2009, on receipt of information that the Maoists had committed a robbery in the State Bank of India Phusro market branch Bokaro, a police contingent rushed to reinforce the local police. On the way at village Sadubeda, seven kms short of Phusro, the ultras triggered a land mine. Powerful blast hit the vehicle and pushed it several feet high in the air. Nine policemen were killed and twenty eight were wounded. Interestingly, a young girl of the Maoist squad led the attack. On June 16, 2009, the police patrol party was ambushed at Beherakhand. Four cops were killed and two injured. On September 30, 2009, Francis Induwar, an Inspector of the Special Branch of Police, was kidnapped. On October 6, 2009, his headless body was found near road side ditch by the side of Ranchi Jamshedpur high way. It was a dastardly act executed savagely following the Taliban pattern. On September 8, 2009, Maoists killed five villagers at Pundigiri about 60 miles away from Ranchi town. On August 19, 2009, they abducted eight persons including three employees of Hindalco Bauxite Mining Co. in Gumla district and torched six dumpers, two tractors and two earth removing machine.

Maoists called a day long bandh on August 9, 2010. It was the Adivasi Day which is celebrated with profound respect and solemnity, especially, in Jharkhand and Odisha. Bandh disrupted normal life and traffic was completely paralysed. The President of Majhi Pargana Mahal, Bahadur Soren of the tribal community Ghatsila block expressed anguish and said, "Calling bandh on the Adivasi Day was not right, we decry the decision." Baiju Murmu head of the Santhal community and socio-cultural and religious head stated, "Bandh has marred our celebrations to mark the Adivasi Day." (*Hindustan Times*, August 10, 2010) Needless to say, bandh has hurt sentiment of the community. In fact, under current of growing estrangement against the Maoists was an encouraging signal for the security forces.

Attempts made to liberate the Saranda forest socially and economically both by the union and state government are laudable. Saranda forest is the second most important rebel hub on Orissa Jharkhand border. Both governments are up-in-arms to take up welfare and development works in 56 villages (six gram panchayats) of Saranda forest, known Saranda Action Plan (SAP). Union Rural Development Minister Jairam Ramesh visited Saranda, observed the problems in detail for execution of the programmes efficiently. Special emphasis is given on electrification, construction of roads, improvement of communication, NREGA, Indira Awas Yogona, old age pension, residential schools. Minister clearly said that security operations and development activities must go hand-in-hand. However, Chief Minister Arjun Munda said, "The central government is responsible for the Maoist menace in Jharkhand. The Union government is not providing adequate support to fight the Naxalites. Its development plan is not effective to remove the root cause of Naxalism in Jharkhand. Faulty policy is not giving any dividend." Later the Minister declared Jhumra Action Plan (JAP) and Saryu Action Plan. JAP will cover all villages of Bokaro, Ramgarh and Hazaribad districts. Cost of the project is Rs.250-300 crores. The project will focus on rural roads, Indira Awas Yojona, drinking water and irrigation facilities and formation of self-help groups. The Saryu Action Plan is meant for Latehar district. Minister hopes that Naxalism will disappear once development reaches the villages People are happy that the problems of the Saranda forest and rural areas have drawn attention of the union government.

Police arrested Kobad Ghandy, a prominent Maoist leader, Bhusan Jadav and Chatradhar Mahato. Maoists demanded their immediate release and called for "bandh" for 48 hours in Bankura, West Medinipur, Puralia districts of West Bengal, Jharkhand and part of Orissa. Call was given to boycott impending Assembly Election in Jharkhand. They attacked railway stations, damaged or destroyed government properties, snapped road and railway communication in many places. On November 24, 2009, in Gumla district land mine blast killed three CRPF personnel and injured seven persons. Five school buildings in different places were blown up. At Pratappur in Chatra district and at Pipra village, Palamau district respectively, two school building were destroyed planting dynamite. Regrettably, the Maoists nurse grudge against schools as school buildings are frequently used for establishing temporary police camps to chastise the ultras.

State Assembly Election 2009

In first phase of the State Assembly election altogether 6.5 million voters were supposed to elect 26 MLAs from 470 candidates. Fortunately, it passed off peacefully. On November 30, 2009, movement of a contingent of the Paramilitary force was held-up near village Amjore, in East Singhbhum district, blocking the road by tree trunk. A group of youngsters were returning home playing a football match. Police requested them to remove the obstacle intending to open the traffic. As they attempted to clear the hurdle, a landmine which was kept concealed exploded killing three of them and injuring five seriously.

The second phase of polling in 14 constituencies was by and large peaceful. However, in 21 polling stations in Tamar, Giridih districts, not a single voter came forward to cast vote. Voters boycotted election protesting against nothing or negligible development in the constituency. In Giridih, one personnel of the CISF was killed in a land mine blast. On December 8, 2009, a BSF patrol was ambushed near Sarasdangal forest in Dumka district. Two personnel were killed and a carbine, a SLR and 35 rounds of ammunitions were looted. In Latehar district two school building were blown up. In fact within one year, 15 government run school building were blasted and destroyed. On September 25, 2009, in an encounter in Saranda forest, West Singhbhum district, a cop of Monoharpur police station was killed and two were injured. It was suspected that four ultras were killed though their bodies could not be traced. Arms, ammunitions and land mines were seized. Police destroyed a training camp of the ultras. On July 26, 2010, in Khunti, an encounter lasted for 12 hours. Security forces killed two ultras and recovered huge quantity of arms and ammunitions. However, dreaded Maoist Kundan Pahan could give a slip to the security personnel.

From village Kajibigha district Palamau, three Maoists were arrested including the area commander. Three rifles, a pistol and one hundred bullets were recovered from them. In police training school at Nayagarh, Orissa, Maoists looted the armoury and killed 15 cops. Police while trailing the ultras an encounter took place at Bhitar Amda and Rani Jharna jungle on the border of Orissa and Jharkhand. Seven senior Maoists including the area commander of Mayurbhanj-Gudabandha-Dumaria zonal commander were killed. Villagers of Bhitar Amda, Jharkhand, were alarmed visualising likely revenge by the ultras. Truly, the villagers alerted the leaders of the Nagarik Suraksha Samity about presence of the senior Maoists including the diehard leader Vikas, in the village on the night of February 13. Hence, the villagers were sanguine of bloody backlash from the ultras and therefore, several families of village Bhitar-Amda, decided to quit the village and migrate to safer places for avoiding wrath of the blood thirsty ultras. Police met the frightened villagers and persuaded them not to leave the village and assured them adequate protection. However, the unrelenting villagers were aware of the police's limitation and the Maoists' Machiavellian spirit to nullify the police's surveillance or dragnet. On December 14, 2010, in an encounter in the forest of Ledakocha under Gurabandha police station, Sm. Sobha wife of hard core Maoist leader, Rajesh Munda, was arrested. She was the second in command of the Red squad of Dumaria unit. Earlier on June 27, 2006, Shyam Kisku, the local dramatis personnie and one of the master minds of several attacks and murders was arrested. Indeed, Kisku and Sm Sobha was a prize catch. On November 22, commander of the Dalma squad was shot dead in an encounter at Birdih under Ghatsila police station.

Violence and Attempt to Disrupt the Lok Sabha Election of 2009

Maoists gave a call to boycott the Lok Sabha poll. The first phase of the Lok Sabha poll held on April 16, 2009 was marred by blood bath. A group of polling officials, proceeding in two buses under the BSF escort towards village Dudhimasi under Chandwa police station of Latehar district, was blown up by blasting a powerful land mine. Five BSF jawans, one driver and a helper of a bus were killed and several were injured. Later, three wounded BSF personnel died in the hospital. Polling was suspended in three booths. In Giridih district ten persons were killed. A bomb was lobbed on a vehicle near Dadi-Srirampur village. An executive magistrate and a constable detailed for the election duty were injured. A car bomb of 22 kgs was detected under a culvert of the main road linking Dumri and Giridih. Polling officials could not reach the polling booths located at South Dumri areas as the ultras threatened to blow up their vehicles en route. Polling in Bermo areas of Giridih district could not take place as the villagers shied away from casting votes submitting to Maoists' boycott call. Ultras burnt EVMs (EV machine) in Sonwa block of Chaibasa district As a result, polling in Jompai area had to be cancelled. In Jamshedpur parliamentary constituency, a part of the steel town, a fierce gun battle between the ultras and the CRPF lasted for several hours. In Patamda block, a school building in Bota village where polling booth was going to be set up was blasted. A polling party near the Dimna Lake, Jamshedpur was ambushed. Fortunately, the officials narrowly escaped. A polling party returning after poll came under fire in Aam and Kanchikund area. A deadly gun battle continued and three constables were injured. Reinforcement was dispatched from Dumka.

Panchayat Poll in Jharkhand 2010

In Jharkhand three-tier Panchayat poll was going to be held after 32 years. It exhibited unprecedented enthusiasm amongst the rural voters. First phase of the five phased Panchayat poll was held on November 27, 2010, in one third of total 13324 thousands polling booths in 77 blocks. Ultras issued a writ and directed the people to boycott election. Yet, 64 to 69 percent voters turned up to exercise their democratic right braving the Maoist threat. From Seraikela-Kharsawan district voters' turnout was 79 per cent which was the highest. Even, Sahibganj, considered to be an under-developed district, reported 47 per cent turn out. In Topchanchi and Tundi, Dhanbad district, the Maoists are very active. Nevertheless, turn out of the voters in large number corroborates that the people prefer democratic values to Maoist threat. Maoist writ had hardly had impact on their determination to exercise their legitimate right. Importantly, female voters in large number were seen standing in the queue for a long time ignoring hot sun and other hardship. Indeed, they displayed extraordinary zeal and eagerness to cast their votes. The Chief Minister and the Chief of the state Police congratulated the people for ensuring incident free poll. Political leaders and parties in order to gain support of the Adivasis banked on the slogan of, "Jungle, jal and jamin." Perhaps, leaders thought that the catchy slogan would create an enviable impact on the simple tribal to bag their votes. However, to-day, perception and psyche of the tribal have undergone a drastic change. They, like others, demand development in villages, education, employment, health care and other basic facilities for them. Deviating from archaic expectation, they prefer representative from their community who will take tangible initiative to focus their problems and secure remedial measures. Truly, to-day, they cannot be carried away by pompous propaganda and hollow promises. The shrewd politicians no longer are able to fool them assuring to build a castle in the air.

Railways and Railway Properties, a Soft Target

Railways, railway properties and rolling stock are soft targets before the Maoists which are being exploited recklessly. Maoists give call for bandh at the drop of a hat and indulge in violence and wanton destruction of railway properties. In March, 2006, the Maoists hijacked a local passenger train from Palamu district. For them it was a new experiment. Intelligence report alerted that more train hijacking would take place in near future. On December 10, 2006 at 10 am, 628 Dn Barwadih-Mughal sarai passenger trains with fifty passengers were hijacked. However, the rebel gave up guarding the train at 1.30 pm and left the passengers unharmed. In 2008, the railway had lost properties valued 220 crores on account of blast on railway track, damage or destruction of rolling stock, signal equipment, station building and other assets. On October 6, 2007, in pursuance of the bandh call for 24 hours in West Bengal, Jharkhand and Orissa border, services of many express and passenger trains, including Barkakhana Palamau express, Barkakhana Mughal Sarai passenger, Garwah-Singrauti express were suspended temporarily. On August 1, 2007, thirty Maoists in groups attacked Demo and Bendi railway stations in Latehar district. They asked the railway employees to vacate the premises, fitted dynamite sticks to power panels, telephones, other instruments and exploded. Grenades and crude bombs were used to destroy the station buildings, control room and signal unit. Several passenger trains on the Barkakana-Garwah road under Dhanbad division were cancelled as a precautionary measure. However, services of goods trains were maintained under police escort. As a prelude to the boycott call for the Lok Sabha poll in April 2009, the railways had to face the brunt of Maoist attacks. On April 22, 2009 at 7.30 AM, about 200 armed guerrillas hijacked 627 UP Barkakana Dihari-Mughalsarai passengers train with 700 passengers from Hehegara station, Latehar district. The driver of the train was taken as a hostage for four hours. Thereafter, the train with passengers was allowed to proceed. In midnight more than 100 armed Maoists attacked Untari road railway station and blew up the main station building. Blast triggered just five minutes before the Ranchi-New Delhi Rajdhani Express scheduled to cross Untari road railway station. Near Kundua forest in Dumka district, exploding improvised explosive device Maoists blew up railway track between Gomia and Dumari railway stations lying in East Central railway. Another group blasted railway line between Hehegara and Chhipadohar stations, Latehar district.

Supply of Arms, Ammunitions, Explosives, Landmines

Procurement of arms, ammunitions, explosives and land mines in Jharkhand is generally from four major sources. First, arms and ammunitions are looted from the police posts once the posts are over run or captured. After ambush of a patrol or a moving column arms and ammunitions are taken away from the dead or injured security personnel. After over powering an isolated cop, arms and ammunitions from his possession are snatched away. Secondly, arms smuggled from the Maoists of Nepal are carried through the land route reach the hands of the ultras of the state. Similarly, arms and ammunitions smuggled from Bangladesh into West Bengal are conveniently dispatched to the terrorist out-fits. ULFA extremists who have taken shelter in Bangladesh play a major role in supplying weapons. Thirdly, weapons are purchased from the deserters of the army. Fourthly, in the beginning, the extremist out-fit of Andhra Pradesh ensured supply of arms, ammunitions, explosive and components of land mines to other states. Main source of the ultras of Andhra Pradesh in this murky drive was LTTE of Sri Lanka. In addition, they used to purchase weapons from the open market of Combodia, Thailand and other places of the Far East. However, procurement of ammunitions for weapons of different bore was an uphill task. In this pursuit, they secretly contact policemen of the reserve lines, army deserters, army units deployed in disturbed areas and dishonest arms dealers and purchase ammunitions against high premium. In many places of Bihar, like Monghyr, country made guns are manufactured surreptitiously. In fact, the outlaws have easy access to them. Of late, the Maoists procure sophisticated equipments, like bullet proof jackets, wireless sets, and night vision instruments etc. adopting devious tactics. A firm, titled Sekhar Construction, received contract for constructing a road between Daltonganj and Panki, a barrage in Palamau district. Maoists allowed the firm to run the construction work and complete the project if the firm arranged communication gadgets for the armed squads. The project Director Naresh Sharma succumbed to the pressure and placed order with a shop in Delhi for supply of many electronic goods for them but in reality, to oblige the Maoists. The consignment of air cargo was booked through the Indian Air Lines for Ranchi in the name of Sandeep Ji. The state police got the scent and succeeded in seizing 60 motoroller, wireless sets, 60 latest radio sets, 54 battery sets, 10 transistor, 2 world band receivers, 6 micro cassette recorders and many bullet proof jackets. Investigation disclosed that the consignee, Sandeep Ji was a member of the central committee of the CPI (Maoists). Moreover, the Maoists have been organising mini workshops for repairing weapons. Recently, on the border of Latehar and Palamau districts a mini repairing workshop has been discovered. Two guns, five pistols and a few ammunitions have been seized and two persons arrested by the police. It reveals that the culprits belong to the breakaway group of the Maoists.

Effect on Tourism Industry in the State

Chota Nagpur's captivating natural beauty, flora and fauna attract tourists from all over the country. Ranchi used to be a pleasant hill station. Enchanting water falls, hills, romantic woods and majestic animals are additional attraction for the tourists. Of late, outrages and insecurity unleashed by the extremists have been dissuading the tourists and the animal lovers to visit the state's tourist spots. Frequent bandh, disruption of communication, attacks on the passengers' buses, bomb blasts, kidnapping, horror unleashed by the pitiless ultras are reasons for the startling fall in tourist flow and its consequent negative impact on the tourism industry. Burudih Dam, near Ghatsila and its tantalizing beauty around it, has been tempting the tourists to visit the spot for sightseeing, picnic, merry making and spending holidays. Hoteliers, small traders, transport owners and poor people take it as a boon for better livelihood. Truly, it adds to economic prosperity and development in the area. Unfortunately, attack and annihilation of eleven cops deployed to ensure safety, security of the Dam, protection to the local populace and the visitors has given a blow to the inflow of the enthusiastic tourists. The thwarted visitors are hesitant to visit the places and become an easy prey of the extremists. Secondly, the Range Forest Officer of Betla range, Palamau Tiger Reserve was shot dead by the ultras. Neterhat, a picturesque hill station has faced the Maoists' fury. Forest rest houses in Garu, Marasmar and Chipadohar range had been blown up. The state forest department has stopped booking for public in the areas for security reason. Similarly, tourists have stopped visiting the Hazaribag National Park, Cannary hills, Hazaribag town which always considered to be attractive tourist hubs in normal times. Today, deserted look in the town and its periphery even in peak tourist season smacks of the state's helplessness to keep tourism intact and build a conducive ambience for the tourists to visit.

Saranda reserve forest is extolled for its highest density of sal trees in Asia and habitation of rare and majestic wild animals, to day, has turned practically to be a forbidden place for the tourists. Here, forest rest houses in Meghatiburu, Kiriburu which once used to be great attraction for the tourists, are now under gloom and decay. No tourist is seen even near the fringe of the forest. Truly, the entire forest has gone under the control of the so called liberated zone where the Maoists whims and caprices are paramount. Government's authority has practically disappeared from the area. The then Chief Minister Sibu Soren inaugurated a three-day tourism fair in Deoghar, in order to woo the tourists to visit the tourist spots of the state. Such programs are no doubt routine. However, the CM's gesture has failed to produce the desired result. Undeniably, atrocity let loose by the rapacious and blood thirsty Maoists have frightened the tourists to visit the tourist spots of the state. Sibu Soren in capacity of the CM was keen for dialogue with the ultras hoping to sooth their feeling and neutralise their grievances. But response from the ultras was far from positive. On the contrary, they stepped up violence and bloodletting activities. Indeed, the tourism industry in the state received a mighty set back and the Maoists are squarely responsible for it. Earlier Chief Ministers Babulal Marandi, Madhu Koda and Arjun Munda expressed desire for a dialogue with the ultras but of no avail.

Fund Collection—Illegal and Dubious Means

Money is indispensable to run any movement or agitation. The Maoists also feel the pinch and therefore, they collect or mobilise fund and enrich resources resorting to bank robbery, abduction, extortion and levying on the industrialists, miners, labour contractors, miners, manufacturers, traders, business men etc. Fund is procured by threat and issuance of ultimatum for daring consequence, if the Maoists' diktats are not adhered to. Secondly, they collect so called "Protection money" from the rich and moneyed individuals on assurance of immunity from wrath of the Maoists to the individuals and members of their family. In fact, safety and no harm syndrome works well since the targeted persons are helpless and get no tangible aid or assistance from the police and administration to avoid or negate the Maoists' writ. The hapless persons are candid that defiance of the ultras' demand is sure to invite an unperceived calamity either on them or to the members of the family. Hence, they find no alternative but to succumb to the ultras' ultimatum and oblige them with lingering reluctance. Indeed, collection of levy, protection money, extortion by threat or intimidation etc. is substantial source of income. Maoists find it an easy way to fill the coffer and inflate their fiscal resources. Threat perception works so deterrent that the ministers, members of the parliament and the legislative assembly and many public servants secretly pay protection money regularly seeking immunity from the ultras' rage. Ironically, the victims deny such cowardly and shameful act, but the sinister design of *quid pro quo* has been silently operating and inflating the ultras' financial resources. Regrettably, the so called "Protection Money" not only strengthening the resources of the extremists but also exposing indirectly the government's weakness and lamentable failure to weed out the Red terror and unmask the soily faces of its perpetrators. Frankly speaking, apart from intelligence report, I have received unflinching evidence on this count during my visits to Ranchi and several terror torn places of Jharkhand. I visited the steel town Bokaro and conducted a discreet enquiry contacting reliable persons from the cross section of the society. I received enough testimony that mine owners, forest and labour contractors, reputed traders and moneyed citizens are forced to pay to the Maoists regularly in keeping with their demands. They are aware that violation or rejecting the ultras' demands is sure to invite a catastrophe and therefore, it is wise to submit to the coercive and extortive tactics. From various sources, it was gathered that from this belt the ultras collect more than one hundred crore of rupees every year. Unfortunately, levy is collected from many persons who are not rich or affluent. Sometimes targets are arbitrarily selected. Their bonafide or capacity to pay is hardly verified. Yet, they are compelled to pay to save themselves from the ultras' vengeance. As a matter of fact, many school teachers working in rural areas are the victims of extortion. In Andhra Pradesh the ultras have been following this miry practice with impunity.

It needs no reiteration that appeasing and buying clandestinely the state's enemy instead of disarraying or trampling them only exposing the government's hesitation to deal with the swift growing threat to the country. Indeed, circumstances and gigantic growth of the extremists make one to believe that both union and state government lack indomitable will and single minded devotion to fight the terror and banish the growing menace. Again, the ultras have been collecting huge fund exploiting the cannabis cultivation and its sale precede. On the floor of the Parliament, the Minister of State, Ministry of Home Affairs, informed the House that the Maoists collect levy from the licensee cannabis cultivators, protection money from the narcotics traders, safe passage money from the narcotics smugglers. As a matter of fact, such detestable practice is widely followed by the ultras in Andhra Pradesh, Bihar and Orissa. Though the exact quantum of collection is obscure but it is not at all a paltry sum. Publications from several national newspapers reveal that the Maoists' illicit collection of fund is to the twin of fifteen hundred to two thousand crores annually. (*The Times of India*) Needless to say, unsavory harassment and reckless extortion from the common persons has been alienating the people from the fold of the ultras, who once sympathized and supported the ultras' cause. They eagerly hope that poverty and exploitation of the poor and have-nots will be rounded up soon and the helpless people are going to see the sun shine after tears.

Attack on Mobile Towers in Rural Areas

Maoists frequently modify their tactics, communication line, code words, signals and use of instruments. They minutely watch the movements, secrecy of operation, modus operandi, communication system, travel route and stratagem of the security forces. Thereafter, they promptly adapt themselves with the changed situation, modify their *modus operandi*, technique and chalk out fresh operational plan in keeping with the coming events and developments. Mobile phones are used for maintaining contact and communication. Generally, messengers are widely used to communicate with other camps and carry messages from one place to other. Importantly, the police has been detecting locations of the establishments of the outfits and whereabouts of many ultras by watching and tracking the mobile signals. GPRS—mobile hand sets are quite useful to intercept conversations through the mobile phones. It can identify the towers and with its assistance the speakers' location can also be traced out. These sets are issued officially to all senior officers and Officer-in-Charge of the police stations of the Maoist affected areas. Special training courses have been organised for the police officers to operate the sets. Happily, the police have successfully nabbed many ultras within short span putting the mobile phones under round the clock surveillance. Success of the police has obviously irked the Maoists. The alarmed Maoists in a co-ordination meeting held on September 30, 2008 in a secret place of Jharkhand issued an express order to the rank and file of Jharkhand, Chhattisgarh, Orissa, Bihar and West Bengal to dispense with the mobile phones as it is giving enough lead to the police and helping to compromise with their secret locations and movements. Incidentally, even the ordinary villagers have learnt about its weakness and using this gadget in tracing out ultra's location and whereabouts. In Jharkhand and Bihar, the police have supplied such instruments to many villagers who help the police in unearthing the ultras' movements and location of their camps, training centers etc. Hence, the bellicose Maoists hit upon a plan to attack and destroy the mobile operators' towers installed in the villages to provide cellular services in rural areas. In fact, misadventure disrupted communication link which eventually snapped contact with the people of rural areas. No doubt, it is contrary to public interest, yet, the Maoists are firm in their celluloid agenda. On October 8, 2008, the ultras destroyed four towers in Eraura and Ketaki villages lying on the border of Jharkhand and Bihar. In this respect Bihar is the worse sufferer.

Maoists' Mini Township Inside Sancturies

It is astonishing that the Maoists inside the sanctuaries run a parallel administration and establish a mini township with civic amenities. A video cassette of a Maoist camp functioning inside the dense forest in Jharkhand was shown to me lasted about thirty minutes. In fact, right in the sanctuary an area is cleaned up and on the flat ground the Maoists have built a small and cozy township. It was planned with a good deal of care. Several tents or make shift structures are either pitched or built around the compound. Sufficient space is available right in the centre of the camp. In every tent or structure sign boards are displayed to ensure its identity. One of the structures is marked as a VIP room or guest house. In two separate big tents tags of conference hall, dining hall respectively are prominently shown. With the help of generators temporary power supply is available in the complex. Secondly, through pipe line water is supplied to dining hall, bathing places etc. Water is drawn from the nearby stream through the pipe line which is likely to be quite long. Indeed, I was amazed seeing the picture of the township, its meticulous planning and engineering. I was equally baffled seeing courage, confidence and painstaking effort by the ultras to establish such a stable arrangement ignoring constant vigil of the police and intelligence branch, fear of surprise raids and the mailed fist of the security forces. One has to ponder how lengthy water pipes, generators, cables etc., were transported to such inaccessible place short circuiting flawless and round the clock police watch and surveillance.

Officials admitted that it is located in an inaccessible spot surrounded by thick forest. Jungle foot path which leads to the Maoists' camp is known only to the local tribal. Movement of any outsider in the periphery of the camp is rigorously screened and strictly prohibited. Moreover, none is courageous enough to trace out the foot path, reach near the camp and collect intelligence. The luckless person if detected will be immediately killed. Hence, no information or intelligence on existence of the sanctuary reaches the police. Under adverse conditions collection of intelligence or prospect of raid on the camp is ruled out. Indeed, here buck stops. The cassette has opened the ponderous box and brought out firsthand account on the Maoists'organisational ability, dauntlessness and administrative acumen to run a parallel establishment out-witting the security forces and the state government. In sum, clue will substantially help the security forces to come down heavily on the ultras and wipe them out. The cops who procured the cassette taking risk deserve fulsome praise and appreciation.

Recruitment and Training—Bal Dasta or Bal Sena

Maoists recruit physically strong youths from age group of 18 to 26. Either they coax them to join the outfit against peltry monthly salary or use coercive tactics to seek their consent for enlistment. Generally the recruits are from poor families and tribal community often unwilling parents are threatened or put to unknown danger if they disagree to spare the youth. Throbbed with fear and panic the helpless parents finally submit to the diktats of the ultras. In addition, Maoists raise a cadre called Bal Dasta or Bal Sena. Recruits either boys or a girls within the age group of 8 to 12 are inducted in the cadre. Maoists direct families that either a boy or a girl from every family has to be spared to join the outfit. If the parents fail to oblige the Maoists, they forcibly take away the ward. In many cases parents and family members object to such a barbarous practice and defy the ultras, resulting in, they are brutally tortured or killed. Complaint to the police is futile as police is unable to protect them. However, aggrieved villagers more than once mustered courage and jointly protested against the Maoists' high-handedness. In a village near Jamshedpur the villagers jointly resisted the Maoists' demand to part with a ward to join and enrich the cadre. Indeed, the Maoists had to retreat before the combined strength of the determined villagers.

As arrests, deaths and desertions in the cadres have been increasing and the Maoists are in back foot, they have intensified the recruitment drive and determined to fill the vacuum and strengthen the Bal Dasta. The adolescents are indoctrinated in Maoist ideology and put in rigorous training. After attaining maturity they are put in fighting or guerrilla squads. Indeed, forcible abduction of the adolescents has been continuing. Helpless parents are compelled to succumb to the threat of the Maoists. In some cases, ultras pay some money to the parents to silence them. Unfortunately, except rumour or whisper the local police have no specific clue on such detestable venture of the ultras. Recently, report that 30 or 40 children are either taken away or abducted from the parents' custody from Lohardaga; Gumla and Simdega districts alarmed the people and the police. The police have launched a massive drive to rescue the victims.

Police actions have not deterred the ultras. Instead, the Maoists issued a fresh writ demanding either a boy or a girl has to be spared from each family to join the cadre. It startled the parents and the villagers. Rumour has surcharged the atmosphere. The panic stricken villagers rushed to the police stations requesting protection for the wards and the family members. Meanwhile, the Maoists 'attempt to abduct eleven children including five girls from Sonua area, West Singbhum district, increased panic. Luckily, the police and the villagers jointly have foiled the sinister attempt. Police nabbed Motra Chaki alias Samuel, a Maoist who been master minding the plots to abduct children to increase the strength of the Bal Dasta.

Fresh report that 30/40 children have already been taken away or abducted from Gumla, Lohardaga and Simdega districts has put the police in a quandary. They geared up search operations and raids to rescue them. The horrid news forced the frightened villagers to rush to the police stations seeking safety and security of the wards. Many decided to leave the wards in the police stations and in custody of the police. DIG of police has confirmed that 42 children including 16 girls have been left in police stations under police custody. Boys have been lodged in Francis Induwar police picket and the girls in Kasturba Gandhi residential school. They are provided with bed, dresses, food, books, reading materials and stationery. Police escorts are arranged for their to-and-fro journey to schools. Importantly, many complaints are pouring in requesting police protection. Recently, fifteen parents from village of Kisko block, Lohardaga district met the Superintendent of Police, Lohardaga and appealed to him to provide their wards safe-shelter and keep them either in the police stations or in the police pickets so that Maoists fail to lay hands on them. Infect, fear is looming large that the ultras may force them to part with the wards or kidnap them. The badly shaken villagers have been passing moment in the grip of nyctophobia. Police confirm that fresh reports are trickling down to the police stations almost every day.

Maoists have established training centers in Gotang, Latehar and inside the dense forest of Parasnath hill. Training camps are surrounded by jungle and hills and well organised. Tent houses for the VIPs, senior leaders meeting hall for the cadres, medical inspection room, ration store, kitchen etc. have made the camps viable. Here range firing practice courses for the recruits and cadres in using fire arms, hand grenades etc. are taught.

Vigilante Groups' Meaningful Activities, and Anti-Maoist Protest

Maoists 'strategy is to cow down every body by threat, fear and gruesome annihilation. Panic stricken persons are compelled to obey their harsh diktats. Even mild protest or reluctance to submit to them is dealt with utmost severity. The pitiless ultras show no compassion or mercy even on most deserving cases. Hence, simmering discontentment is often manifested against the Maoists and their so called ideal and beefy promises are obliquely viewed. In Jharkhand several voluntary organisations have surfaced who appeal to the ultras to give up bloodshed and insist upon peace and normalcy. The vigilante units are often ruthlessly treated by the ultras. Nevertheless, risk to life has not dissuaded them to put up resistance against the dreaded ultras. The dauntless persons have been raising slogans to stop violence, unrest and the macabre festival of death. Nagarik Surksha Samity (NSS) is a tribal youth vigilante group has been performing meaningful role in that pursuit. Being a tribal organisation it enjoys free access into the community and can make useful interaction with the fellow tribals. Maoists are hostile to the non-governmental organisations (NGO). Maoists gunned down Dhanai Kisku, the general secretary of the NSS at Mosaboni, 60 kms away from the steel town, Jamshedpur. He entered into a road side tea stall for a cup of tea. Four ultras arrived in two motor bikes and sprayed bullets aiming at and killed him at the spot. Again Adivasi leader Kailesh Chandra Hembram was shot dead at Jadugoratola in East Singhbhum district. On December 29, 2009, an anti-Maoist rally was held in Singhbhum district, about 155 kms north east of Ranchi. A large number of participants were school pupils within the age group of 10 to 16 years. They raised slogans "Shall kill or get killed." Significantly, in many villages students and youngster's *suo motu* have organised small groups to guard the villages against likely attacks of the ultras. After night fall, they guard the villages throughout the night by batches and thereby try to frustrate the Maoists' entry into the villages and resuscitate sagging morale of the horror stricken villagers. In process they have to neglect studies. Yet, they were inspired by the sense of duty and have set a unique example before the discomfited people.

In village Lango, eleven extremists were lynched by the villagers in 2009. They tolerated the extremists' highhandedness and harassment enough and finally lost patience and decided to react. Indeed, it was a fatal blow to the extremists who could not imagine that the villagers could chastise them. On February 14, 2009, the Nagarik Suraksha Samity, a village resistance group challenged the Maoists in Baitarmada village, East Sighbhum district and aided the state police personnel and the CRPF to put up a stub-born resistance. In an encounter seven hard core Maoists were killed and eight weapons and a good quantity of ammunitions were seized. Importantly, vast majority of the rural mass are not faithful supporters of the Maoists. They are unwilling to submit. However, the threat perception compel them to obey the diktats of the extremists. Indeed, similar resistance against the extremists are reported from Bihar and West Bengal. Nuances of Maoist jargon impressed the poor and exploited villagers in the beginning, who hoped for a better future. But soon they were disillusioned and realised that the ultras are cruel, pitiless, who bank on extortion, violence etc. Their lofty promises for mass upheaval and matchless change in social and political order appeared to be a hoax. Secondly, often their demands are too high or oppressive which is difficult to be complied with. Hence, the outraged villagers are compelled to resist or neutralise them shedding fear and danger of likely retaliation.

Joint Operation on the Border of Jharkhand and West Bengal

The Union Home Ministry proposed a joint and co-ordinated operation against the Maoists active in Chhattisgarh, Jharkhand, Bihar, Orissa and West Bengal. It is called "Operation Green Hunt." A meeting was held in Kolkata for discussion and to chalk out a common plan and programme for lunching joint operation. However, some of the participant states were lukewarm for the joint operation. They emphasised more on development and economic prosperity in trouble torn-districts instead of relying solely on the police action. However, details of the operation green hunt will be discussed separately in relevant chapter. Broadly, joint operation in the first phase on the border of Jharkhand and West Bengal to flush out the ultras has produced satisfactory result. In fact, operation carried out in entire forest terrain on 40 kms stretch of Jharkhand bordering West Bengal has given desired result. The joint forces discovered an abandoned hide out in the Kanaisole hill in Belpahari area of West Bengal. It was later destroyed by the security forces of West Bengal. In Jharkhand, during operation a huge cache of arms had been recovered from many hide outs. Secondly, the security forces succeeded in entering deep into the jungle and in many inaccessible spots. Importantly, joint operation was backed by the helicopters which gave rewarding dividend. A makeshift helipad could be successfully constructed right inside the Saranda forest, West Singbhum district which is one of the impregnable hide outs of the Maoists. After all, Maoists' area of operation is spreading over several states having common border and ilk socio-economic problems of the rural mass. Hence, operations to confront and neutralise terrorism by one or two states in isolated manner is likely to end in fiasco. It may be noted that from January 2003 to October 2009, in Jharkhand alone 339 security personnel had been killed by the ultras. In fact, enormity of the threat and its probable repercussion on the country's security has to be appreciated. Needless to say, success of the extremists is likely to jeopardize the sovereignty of the country. All said and done, joint and co-ordinated operation is essential to disarray the Maoists and restore peace and rule of law.

Constraints of the Police to Combat the Ultras

Police forces of the states suffer from insurmountable odds and deficiencies. Its manpower is sadly inadequate, training is archaic, and weaponry is old, stereotyped and not suitable for tackling the extremists. Many police stations are located in rented building, neither secure nor fortified. Quarters are hardly available. Prolonged hours of duty put them under stress and strain. Above all, financial crunch is a flinty bottle neck to modernise the police force. Luckily, the government of India is fully aware of the short comings and initiated several steps to modernise the state police suitably to tackle the extremists with consummate ability and striking power. A central plan to pump rupees 3300 crores in phase manner to the extremist hit states for wiping out terrorism is undertaken in right earnest. It has transpired that the states are badly lagging behind in health care, child care, education, electricity and water supply, road construction. In Jharkhand, 15 per cent of the state budget is ear marked for spending for the child care though it is much higher in many other states.

Steps Initiated by the Police to Curb Extremism

Unflinching testimony discussed above reveals that the extremist movement has been gaining momentum belying the general perception. Strength of the terrorist cadre, areas of their influence, control, surprise attack, targets and areas of operation and fire power have been increasing leaps and bounds. They have modified their modus operandi, tactics, stepped up open and surprise attacks in heavy strength and enhanced resources including collection of fund, weaponry, explosives and components of land mines. They have acquired the skill of manufacturing small arms and the know-how of assembling landmines. Truly, merger of the PW, once active in Andhra Pradesh and the MCC active in Bihar and Jharkhand, resulted in, the formation of the CPI (Maoist), has made the ultras more resourceful, aggressive and dauntless. The hit and run tactics practiced earlier is no longer given emphasis or followed exclusively. Attacks on the security personnel and casualty on either side have alarmingly increased. In some areas, broadly, war like situation is prevailing. In the so called liberated areas, authority of the state government and rule of law has practically disappeared. Here writs of the Maoists are supreme. It needs no reiteration that the government's wishy-washy policy or indifference to nib the growing menace at the bud has made the ultras formidable who are emboldened to let loose strident offensives. However, the police in spite of numerous odds, loss and sacrifices have been relentlessly trying to curb the burgeoning violence and disarray the misguided extremists. Broadly speaking, it has galvanized the police, intelligence cells, reorganised meaningful training, procured latest weaponry, initiated several pragmatic programmes to frustrate the sinister design of the ultras, and kept the morale of the personnel quite high. Above all, enforcement of the rehabilitation scheme and welfare schemes in right earnest for the benefit of the disillusioned drop outs or deserters from the cadre has been helping the police to outwit the extremists and contain bestial savagery let loose by the merciless ultras.

Paradigm Shift of the Maoists in Strategy and Offensives

Police has been keenly watching the terrorist organisations, training, movements, modus operandi, areas of operation and plans to widen their agenda. Of late, paradigm shift in their recruitment drive, tactics, focus on key areas and dauntless attacks in strength in spite of loss of men have helped the police to unearth and identify many new clues which practically remained either obscure or unknown in the past. Evidently, new clues and materials are positive signal for the police to gear up anti-Maoist operations with consummate preparation and courage. First, it was believed that the ultras will confine their activities in rural areas, exert control on the rural population, convert the territory into a liberated area and eventually will go for a massive mass upsurge. In that process they will organise the so called peoples' war and topple the elected government. Admittedly, in many rural pockets of Jharkhand the ultras have entrenched themselves firmly, brought villagers under their influence and established their defacto rule. However, initially, towns and urban areas were not immediate targets or places for operation. Of late, the ultras are showing departure from the above practice, trying to penetrate into urban and greater urban areas and step up activities. Strike in targets close to state HQ Ranchi, district HQ Palamau, Latehar, Giridhi, Dumka and Ghatsila, a tourist spot, are clear testimony of increased urbanised movements initiated by them. Secondly, concentration in good number on the interstate border, joint and concerted attacks on the police, police camps, security forces, political activists, volunteers who are trying to oppose the ultras are clear manifestation of their modified strategy and mode of increased attack or defence. In fact, their indomitable will shows that so called mass upheaval is no longer a fancy. Ultras find trans-border operation is rewarding as they can conveniently escape to other state after strike and befool or misguide the security forces trailing behind. They select targets, high-light their controversial success or sacrifices for the so-called cause of the have-nots, sensationalise events and bank on pompous propaganda and publicity. They avidly try to gain sympathy and support of the impoverished and exploited people either by threat or cunning devices.

As the cadre is gaining strength ultras have hit upon a plan to organise hyper active frontal organisations to take on the opponents and the security forces. In that pursuit they select secure places situated on interstate border areas and recruit highly dedicated volunteers. Selection of the cadre is made with great care, given superior training and equipped with sophisticated weapons. Members of these crack units are motivated to initiate risky, surprise and deadly attacks, loot weapons, plant land mines, hold the so called peoples' court and recklessly indulge in atrocious reprisals. They identify the soft targets which are either partially or not at all under the watch or surveillance of the security forces. In fact, thin or negligible resistance, possibility of safe return on completion of the task, chances of success etc. are meticulously examined while selecting and attacking the target. They find railway is the easy and soft target. Secondly, disruption of railway services creates an adverse impact on the morale of the people and the railway employees. In Jharkhand, CIC section of the railways which is virtually the life line for carrying or transporting minerals, including coal, iron ore etc., is a soft target from the ultras' point of view.

Plan to intensify attacks on police patrols, police posts, temporary camps, snatch weapon from isolated policeman, loot weapons from police units, break jails, over power the jail wardens or guards, release the prisoners are in the Maoists' priority list. In tribal belts for reasons like erosion of soil, construction of dam, change of course of the streams, rivulets or rivers, road construction, industrial development, mining, plantation, forest conservation, etc., often lead to displacement of the people. Rehabilitation of the displaced people is a Herculian task. Admittedly, the administration lags behind to provide desired relief promptly to them. Consequently, it generates discontentment which is often exploited by the interested persons and political organisations. The Maoists adroitly mobilise the aggrieved people intending to spearhead a mass movement with their active support and participation. Of late, the Maoists encourage unauthorised opium cultivation as it helps to collect a substantial amount from this sordid venture. In fact, in remote rural areas illegal opium cultivation is indulged in freely. Indeed, clandestine plantation short circuiting vigil of the Excise department fetches handsome dividend. Maoists are well conversant with intricacies of the secret deal and limitation of its perpetrators, collect cut money or share from the cultivators, traders and investors by coercion or threat for instant death. Indeed, the Maoists encourage illegal cultivation since it is rewarding to fatten their coffer and financial resources.

The modified strategy to keep the mass in their fold, earn their good will and paralyze the local administration on any pretext is a palpable departure from their earlier policy and the mode of its execution. Frequent call for bandh or herbals, sometimes continuous bandh for 48 hours or 72 hours, disruption of traffic, shutting down private and government establishments, banks, business units, blocking or damaging educational institutions and paralyzing normal life etc. are abundant manifestation of the present modified or shifted strategy of the Maoists. Arguably, bandh or strike etc. cause enormous hardship to the common people who spontaneously build a hiatus between the extremists and the people. Admittedly, such undesirable move is blissfully anti-people. As a matter fact, the Maoists perhaps are insensitive to public reaction, rather they plead that it confirms the Maoists' presence, highlights their strength and generates awareness among the poor, deprived and exploited people. Secondly, they instigate prisoners confined in jails to plan jail-break and escape, organise hartals, hunger strike and indulge in ruckus inside the jail to discredit the jail authorities and the state government. Maoists feel that apart from news value such abrasive tactics unnerve the government and force them to follow the defensive line in chastising the ultras. Secondly, success in such pursuits carry ebullient message for the ultras, their activists and followers. It boosts their morale and provides fresh impetus to continue with the struggle. Thirdly, it makes the people to believe about their growth, striking power, invincibility and the dream of the mass upheaval in the long run.

Above all, paradigm shift in revamping their organisation, armed squads, guerrilla units, reckless striking capacity are formidable challenge before the police and the security forces. Truly, police is unable to prepare or organise promptly and viably in keeping with the swift changing aggressive plan, strategy and surprise strikes of the Maoists. Constraints of red tape-ism, bureaucratic ethos and ambivalence in higher level in decision making often queer the pitch.

Guerrilla Units, Guerrilla Zones and Liberated Areas

Guerrilla units are specialised units, much superior to the ordinary Maoist squads. They are specially trained, equipped with sophisticated weapons, possess flinty striking power and deployed to undertake daring and risky task. Guerrilla Zone is treated as liberated zone. Here writs of the Maoists run. In fact, three or four districts together constitute a zone. Elimination of the class enemies is followed here dogmatically. Fanatical bigotry to pursue the Marxist lesson of annihilation overzealously of the so called class enemy is abundantly manifested in the liberated zone. Depending on the success of the zone it is de-linked from the provincial committee and designated as Guerrilla Zone Committee. Armed squads operating in Guerrilla zone are called as the units of the Peoples' Liberation Army (PLA). The district secretary is the commander of the PLA. A guerrilla zone is identified as the so called "Maoist State." where the Maoist rule and administration prevails. In its state the Maoists collect tax, donation, impose levy and collect money by force or coercion. Extortion from the people is another way of mobilising fund. Significantly, merger of the Peoples' War Group (PW) and the Maoist Communist Centre (MCC) resulted in, unification of the Peoples' Guerrilla Army and the Peoples' Guerrilla Liberation Army (PGLA). Its flag projects hammer, sickle and AK 47 rifle. As events moved apace the Maoists modified the nomenclature of the PGLA and call it the People's Liberation Guerrilla Army (PLGA).

In fact, reason for conversion of the PGLA to PLGA is obscure. Perhaps, it is easier for the rural mass to understand and recognise it. Interestingly, the Maoists often change or modify their move, strategy, and refurbish the organisation depending on the situation, development and turn of events. It is understood that conversion of the PGLA to PLGA is one of the shrewd steps to come closer to the rural mass. Broadly speaking, formation of Guerrilla Zone and its functioning style is based on several cardinal principles. A good deal of labour, energy, persuasion and the so called think tank's advice are taken into consideration. In initial stage village committee or village protection squads are utilised for formation of the peoples' militia. Often, able bodied youths are either cajoled or forced to join the militia. Eventually, from small group it takes the shape of a platoon with thirty heads. Once a platoon is formed, eye is set on formation of a company with three platoons which is a standard pattern of formation of combat forces. Importantly, guerrilla warfare is not an isolated or astray movement but a continuous process to achieve the revolutionary goal. Needless to say, Maoists' guerrilla units have already proved their formidability and put the security forces in back foot more than once. Guerrilla zone being considered as "Maoist State" has separate characteristic and operate under a few important directives for effective performance. First, village protection squads or village committees take the form of peoples' militia. Secondly, once platoons formed formation of Companies must follow. Thirdly, guerrilla warfare should not be an isolated adventure or a knee-jerk action. Fourthly, it must be a continuous and ongoing process without abandoning it on the midway. Fifthly, it must operate under a central command, like recognised armed forces. PW of Andhra Pradesh after a good deal of deliberations spreading over 15 to 16 years organised Guerrilla Zone Committee (GZC). By 1996, Dandakaranya Guerrilla Zone, North Telangana Guerrilla Zone, South Telangana & Nallamala Zone and Andhra-Orissa border zone etc. were established and put in operation. Interestingly, for communicating or sending messages, the PWG had established comprehensive courier network. Secondly, the leaders active in the field adopt pseudo names to outwit the police and the intelligence agencies. Thirdly, the leaders identify themselves in different names in different places.

The PW functioned under rigid hierarchical control. It had Central Committee. In addition, it had a Central Military Commission which functioned under the Central Committee. It was like Army HQ. It had various important functions, like procurement of arms, manufacture of arms, fixing targets, issuance of directive to the guerrilla units, movement of the guerrilla units from one zone to other, higher training. Importantly, extremists of the Andhra Pradesh developed link with the LTTE of Sri Lanka right from mid-seventies. LTTE, Naga insurgents and ISI were main suppliers of arms, ammunitions and explosives. Procurement of arms followed some unique principle. In fact, procurement of arms was on the basis of 1:8 ratio. It meant, if one piece was required 8 pieces would be procured. This was practised anticipating likely loss. Secondly, 35 per cent of fund arranged to be spent for procuring arms. Later on, rocket launchers, improvised land mines etc., are manufactured indigenously by unscrupulous lathe workshop and foundry owners. On September 8, 2006, police of AP, intercepted vehicles and seized 42 rocket launchers, 1000 empty rocket shells and 35 improvised land mines. Enquiry disclosed that these deadly weapons were manufactured locally at Padi, Korattur and Mogappir, located in suburb of Chennai. Such illegal and clandestine manufacture of arms, trading and supply has been going on since 2003.

Escalated Violence

Deployment of central forces in good strength, joint operations and pragmatic schemes to disarray the Maoists has not deterred the ultras. Horrid violence and killing continued unabatedly. In fact, years 2007 to 2009, was marred by worse violence and bloodshed. A few incidents are mentioned for the information of the readers. On November 12, 2009, MLA Ram Chandra Singh belonging to RJD party with six supporters was abducted by the Maoists. Their vehicle was stopped and on gun point they were taken to an unknown place. Later some of them except the MLA were released. Convoy of former Speaker of the Legislative Assembly, Namdhari Singh was attacked. Seven cops and four civilians were killed. Luckily, the former Speaker was unhurt. Maoist looted ten fire arms, 2000 rounds and a wireless set. On December 4, 2011, Maoists attacked Farida police out post in Palamau district and looted arms, ammunitions confining the cops in a room. Another group kept the outpost surrounded. Gun battle continued for several hours when the security forces went to liberate the cops and regain the outpost. On January 21, 2012, in two land mines hit the police party travelling in an anti-land mine vehicle near Ghalo jungle, Bhandaria block, Garhwa district. Due to impact of the blast the vehicle tossed high in the air. About fifty ultras fired at the vehicle and cops who tried to come out of the vehicle. Later the vehicle was set on fire, driver and a sub Inspector were burnt alive. Many cops were killed and injured. On February 5, 2012, four ultras were killed in a protracted gun battle at project site of CCL of Piparwar, Chatra district. Later about 100 rebels attacked the site at 11.30. PM, burnt 18 vehicles, dumpers, heavy machineries used in mining work. After strong resistence the ultras retreated. Two dead bodies of the rebels, two American made automatic rifle with 250 rdx, two hand grenades, a walky talky and a wireless set, can bombs were recovered from the spot.

On April 3, 2013, Maoists blew up two storeyed panchayat bhawan in Lohardaga district. On the same day, they attacked a police van in Gumla and killed four police men On July 2, 2013, at about 2 pm about 60 Maoists ambushed the convoy of the Superintendent of Police, district Pakur near a culvert under construction. Amarjit Singh, SP along with his driver and three guards were killed. He was returning to the HQ after attending a meeting. He successfully led several operations in Latehar, Gumla, Palamu, west Singbhum. On 3. 7. 2013, the People's Liberation Front of India (PLFI) a breakaway group from the Maoist out-fit kidnapped three officers of the State Bank of India, Panki branch, Latehar district. On August 2, 2013, two officials were released. Later the branch Manager managed to escape. In protest bank staff boycotted works.

Internal Feud, Offensives—the Splinter Groups

Members of the Tritya-Sammelan Prastuti Committee (TSPC), a breakaway fraction from the main out-fit were founded in 2002. Maoists and the splinter group were at daggers drawn burying the past comradeship. Maoists in Jharkhand were in receiving end from the security forces and the estranged comrades, defected and joined the rival group. On March 28, 2013, at Lakarmanda village, near Kunda, district Chatra, a group of Maoists were proceeding to Latahar. They intended to escort Sandeepji, a member of the Maoist central committee, who was supposed to return to Bihar after attending a meeting in Jharkhand. A group of 150 TSPC activists surprised the Maoists in a place, located on the border of Chatra, Palamu and Gaya districts known as the transit corridor. The tri-junction was considered to be the safe haven for the ultras for entering into Bihar and Jharkhand. A fierce gun battle between two groups continued and ten Maoists were killed and thirty Maoists were captured by the TSPC. Account of eye witnesses revealed that the Maoists were preparing mid-day meals in the village. They were taken unawares, had hardly had opportunity to defend them. Maoist Lalesh Yadav, Bihar Jharkhand special area commander, two sub-zonal commanders were killed. Seven deceased were identified by their relatives and remaining three dead bodies left unidentified. Fate of the abducted extremists was not known. Importantly, Lalesh Yadav was involved in the sensational operation in surgical insertion of live explosives devices in the dead bodies of slain CRPF jawans in Latehar district in January last.

Revolutionary Democratic Front (RDF), another frontal group of the Maoists claimed that the deceased were drugged and thereafter were shot dead. RDF's President demanded a judicial probe to unearth the truth and appealed for the release of the abducted comrades. RDF accused the security forces that they had aided the TSPC to kill and abduct the Maoists. However, they failed to substantiate the allegation. IGP of Bokaro had pooh poohed the unfounded charges. Police recovered a large number of arms and ammunitions from the spot. It was a flinty setback for the ultras which undermined their unity, strength, and striking capacity. It is feared that clash and killing were likely to escalate in future as infantine emotion of both sides to avenge loss and influence was very miffy. Fanatical bigotry of both groups had pushed them to the arid zone of acrimony. After a few months, TSPC had killed two hard core Maoists in Chatra district. Dead bodies were found near a river bridge, about 150 kms north east of Ranchi. Five or six accomplices of the deceased persons were in the custody of the TSPC. This was another major blow to the out-fit after they killed ten Maoists in March 2013. However, internal feud reached its climax as both sides were obdurately keen to take revenge.

Dispassionate probe revealed that the ten Maoists slayed belonged to other backward classes. TSPC was formed against hegemony of Yadavs in Naxal ranks, by the tribal Maoists, belonging mainly to Oraon, Ghanju, Turi and Badai castes. Non-tribal were basically from Yadav community. Hence, in-fighting, internecine quarrel and blood shed exposed divisive germs in tribal and non-tribal groups. It was called tribal-non-tribal feud. The breakaway faction, TSPC in Jharkhand carried the banner of caste rivalry and caste animosity amongst the extremists who have been seemingly fighting a war for establishing the classless society. It was learnt that the abducted Maoists were going to be tried in so called, Jana Adalat. A spectacle would be made out of it to thwart the peace loving villagers. However, the foot soldiers would be asked to join the breakaway group. Unwilling so called prisoners would be severely punished with sentences varying from death to chopping of limbs of the body. Radicals admitted that cleavage developed due to internal squabbling was a flinty blow to unity and solidarity in the Maoist out-fit. It has push the Maoist movement in Jharkhand in reverse gear. Caste cum ethnic dimension would invariably mar the object of mass upsurge. Maoists gave call for bandh for two days for killing of their comrades by the TSPC. They alleged that the security forces formed a nexus with the TSPC for killing their leader Lalesh Yadav and other activists. Bandh evoked mixed response.

The People's Liberation Front of India (PLFI), one of the breakaway factions of the Maoists in Jharkhand is bent upon harming the Maoists, lure away its activists and admit them in their fold. Rivalry often generates into a bloody clash. They are trying to influence the local juveniles to nurse antigovernment spirit and hatred against the Maoists and other break away groups. In that pursuit PLFI in the garb of NGOs has established several schools in rural areas and enlisted minors. Its aim is to brainwash the green horns, school students, divert their simple and unbiased head and heart against the government, the existing social order and fractions of the Maoists. Such schools have been functioning in Girda, Simdega district, at Rania in Gumla and Karva in Khunti districts respectively. In remote villages situated on the border of Bihar and Odisha many schools have already been set up. Incidentally, Girda is located at a remote corner of the district, suffering from scanty economic growth and development. In fact, in violence affected districts in border belt attendance of the students in the schools is excruciatingly low. In other places schools established by the PLFI are receiving good response and functioning satisfactorily. PLFI have been providing fund. Commanders and activists of the out-fit often take special classes to teach the pupils.

Srinivas alias Taka and five members of the PLFI were arrested by the security forces from border areas after a joint raid was conducted by Jharkhand and Odisha police. Police seized one automatic rifle, carbine, AK-47 rifle and currencies. Taka during interrogation divulged the strategy of opening schools and brain washing the students. The supremo of the outfit, Dinesh Gope has instructed the cadre to concentrate on social services and earn goodwill and trust of the people. Indeed, the PLFI's move to establish schools and influence the students to follow their line has obviously irked the Maoists. It has increased acrimony between the two. Broadly speaking, intensity of the turf war among the Maoists and the splinter groups is likely to jeopardize peace, tranquility and security in the area. Alarming situation and growing conflicts may deteriorate law and order and escalate violence and bloodshed.

On April, 6, 2013, another splinter group clashed with the security forces. After brief encounter at Tupudana near Ranchi, four ultras were arrested including a girl student from Delhi University. Miss Riya Nayak was associated with the out-fit for the last one and half years. Police seized a huge cache of arms and ammunitions including six rifles, five country made pistols and fifty rounds from possession of the arrested ultras.

Rebels' Diabolic Method to Plant Explosives in Human Bodies

On January 7, 2013, in Ambatikar jungle, Latehar district, on receipt of information a CRPF contingent rushed to round up a group of Maoists. Ultras cunningly lured the CRPF personnel to walk into an ambush. They fired from the hill top and tree top at the CRPF personnel. In gun battle and incessant fire lasting over three hours ten CRPF men were killed. Rebels tore opened bodies of the dead cops and implanted IEDs (Improvised explosives devices) bombs weighing 1.5 kgs and stitched the dead body properly abolishing sign of inducting a bomb in a human body. This crude method was adopted by the LTTE. On January 10, 2013, a slain body was sent to Rajendra Institute of Medical Sciences at Ranchi for autopsy. Doctor detected that the body was stitched with surgical precision which arose suspicion. They immediately contacted the CRPF authority. Experts from the bomb disposal squad examined and detected an IED implanted beneath the ribs of the slain jawan. Explosive was fitted with a solar panel trigger. Instant explosion was possible either by pull of the stitches or coming in contact with light. Alert doctors' keen observation averted a catastrophe. It was unimaginable that a devious and diabolic method could be used to kill people. Admittedly, it created unprecedented and horrendous panic.

The real-time vital scanner (RTVS) identified the bomb. Maoists surgically inserted bomb inside the dead cop and stitched it cunningly which was possible to be detected only by an expert. Importantly, the slain cop was recovered from the encounter site by a patrol and eventually dispatched to the medical college, Ranchi by air. Luckily it did not explode during the journey. In the ambush ten CRPF personnel, one cop from Jharkhand Jaguar armed force and four civilians were killed. It was suspected that nine Maoists were also killed. However, no dead Maoist was left at the encounter site. Admittedly, such a capricious and devilish technique used to kill a person was unheard in the past.

People's Irk Against the Ultras

An area commander of the PLFI, Amar Khes aged 22, raped a minor girl in village Ghattari, under Tetaitangar police station, Semdega district. Accused subsequently along with a team stormed into the village to collect levy. Villagers caught him and assaulted mercilessly. The panchayat after so called trial convicted him and awarded death penalty. In fact, villagers laid a trap and caught him. But other members managed to escape. Finally, Amar Khes was taken to the out skirt of the village and set on fire.

Counter Measures by the State Police

Jharkhand state police's comprehensive counter measures to contain and banish the extremist violence needs analytical study. In fact, the gargantuan threat and dimension of the problem is beyond comprehension of the common persons. Indeed it is not a simple law and order problem which can ordinarily be tackled by the police. Fortunately, the police has realised the magnitude of the growing menace and shown adequate and consummate response. They have prepared four point purposeful action plan to frustrate the ultras. Police has identified eleven key areas where Maoists are active and attempting to penetrate deep into usages of the rural mass and establish their defacto control. Broadly, these are Tehpur Gurpa, Lebrahi-Mitar near Chatra, Daltanjganj, Latehar, Pareshnath hill, Jhumra, Dalma hills, Dungra and Pabda hill and Gua near Kiriburu. First, security front, focuses at ten fundamental points. Emphasis is given on strengthening and fortification of police stations, refurbishing the intelligence machinery, recruitment, specialised training, welfare of the police personnel, and modernisation of the police and utilisation of the fund fruitfully, community policing. In addition, attention is essential for utilisation of optimum man power and its purposeful deployment, co-ordination with extremist torn states and the union government, and enhancement of morale of the rank and file. Furthermore, surrender of the ultras, their rehabilitation, and investigation of the criminal cases related to outrages, prosecution of the offenders and successful marshaling of evidence against the accused persons have to be given extra importance.

Police Stations Open to Hazards

Majority of the police stations in rural areas are located in open ground without any boundary walls, strong room for storing arms, ammunitions, valuable seized properties. Watch towers, morcha, bunkers, sentry posts, defensive or shelter posts etc. are not constructed. In sum, police stations are exposed to unknown hazards and attacks by miscreants. Frankly speaking, extremist violence and attack on the police post was not imagined in the past and therefore, security and risk perception was badly neglected. In Jharkhand, today, 145 police stations are vulnerable from the point of extremist attack. Unfortified police stations, deficient in security cover, shortage of man power, poor communication facilities, porous resistance capability against surprise attacks etc., indirectly encourage the ultras to target the police posts. Hence it is imperative that the police stations are made secure and provided with adequate infra-structure to nullify any attempt to attack or over run a police post. The archaic belief and legacy that the docile rural mass are afraid of the police and take them as an engine of oppression, and therefore, will not be hostile or resort to violence or aggressive steps against police, no longer holds good. Hence, in keeping with the changed scenario the police have to be modernised to face any untoward situation, neutralise hazards and foil attack by the extremists.

Many police stations and out posts are located in rented accommodation right in thickly populated areas which are insecure and open to hazard. Family quarters in police station campus are lamentably inadequate. Police personnel are compelled to keep their family in private accommodation which is located far away from the police stations. Needless to say, it is highly disadvantageous to respond to emergent calls and for performing round the clock duties. For to and fro journey, time is wasted and travelling put them under constant stress and strain. It is very risky in insurgency areas. Admittedly, it affects performance and morale of the cops. Hence, along with improving security and fortification of the police posts, sufficient family quarters and barracks for the unmarried personnel should be constructed either inside the campus of the police posts or in nearby secure place.

Security of the Cops Essential

Admittedly, manpower of the police stations and out posts is unbelievably low which hinders to repulse the Maoist attacks and to protect the people living nearby. People are reluctant to co-operate with the police as the police is often harsh and use rough and ready method. Therefore, a spirit of selfless public service and a conducive public relation to bridge the hiatus has to be sincerely cultivated to bring the people close to the police. Mass contact programme, involvement of the members of the public in police public relation, welfare of the people, prompt and sympathetic response to public grievances etc. should be persuaded in right earnest. The idea of community policing must get top priority. Modernisation of the police should not be a knee jerk action under pressure or expediency rather it should be a continuous process. Fund allotted for the purpose should be meaningfully utilised.

Rehabilitation Packages

Disillusioned and misguided ultras who are willing to return to the main stream should be encouraged. Benefits of the rehabilitation package should be extended to them promptly. It needs no reiteration that their lives are under constant threat and danger. Therefore, their safety and protection has to be ensured and for that purpose the police have to play a crucial role. Example of satisfactory rehabilitation, safety and protection for them and their family members and social recognition may inspire or provoke several other Maoists to give up terrorist call, surrender and embrace normal living. Recruitment in police force has to be discreet. Able bodies youths having aptitude for serving the people unselfishly, ready to face hardship and hazard should be enrolled. Specialised and in-service training to tackle problems entwined with swift changing social and political scenario and the extremist threat should get top priority. Co-ordination, mutual help and exchange of intelligence with the extremist torn states has to be persuaded with missionary zeal. Finally, investigation of the criminal cases has to be done flawlessly and skillfully so that it may stand the scrutiny of the trial court. Evidence should be marshalled diligently to neutralise the defence. In short, successful prosecution, expeditious trial and exemplary conviction will disarray and demoralise the outlaws. Truly, good number of convictions will break their morale and shatter the dream of building a castle of the so called classless society, in the air. Lastly, expeditious trial is *sine qua non.* In that pursuit the judiciary has to come forward and help to curb the growing Maoist menace.

Intelligence—How it is Cultivated and Utilised

Often it is accused that intelligence failure is the root cause of the police's shabby performance or to prevent an ugly incident. People are inclined to believe it without knowing its intricacies. Admittedly, advance intelligence helps the police to prepare plan, chalk out strategy and programme for preventing any unseemly incident and frustrate sinister design of the notorious elements. Successful policing much depends on reliable intelligence. However, collection of intelligence is highly specialised, not at all easy and simple. First, the officers who collect intelligence must be well trained in the trade, must possess aptitude and skill to cultivate dependable source, must enjoy trust and confidence of the source or informer. Secondly, right and reliable source to be cultivated who is free from dupery and must not craftily guide the intelligence officer. Adequate fund is needed to gain over a source or an informer. Thirdly, some are permanent sources and some are used for a fixed work or target. Both should be free from bias and vindictiveness and must not misguide the police. Indeed, mutual trust between the two is the key of the success in intelligence gathering and its pragmatic utilisation. All said and done, such an exercise is time consuming, needs patience, perseverance and single minded devotion. Thirdly, the intelligence officer must develop expertise, must acquire the skill and acumen to single out the correct information, differentiate between information, rumor or hearsay and information tampered with exaggeration or overzealousness. He must have access into areas, develop regular contact and interact with the source either incognito or discreetly. Except the source, others living in the locality should not know his real identity and the purpose of his visit.

The tribal people generally dwell in isolated villages, small pockets or hamlets, connected through village roads, footpaths. Movement in that area is far from smooth. Community plays a crucial role in accepting an outsider and permitting him in social intercourse. Their physical appearance, language, dialect, custom and culture are quite distinctive vis-à-vis the people belonging to other communities living in semi-rural, rural and urban areas. Hence, presence of an outsider in the village is immediately spotted and the villagers are curious to know his identity and purpose of visit. In fact, if an intelligence officer steps into any village inhabited by tribal, is exposed immediately and kept under watch. He is unable to interact freely due to language barrier, constant watch and reluctance of the villagers to be intimate and enter into conversation freely. In Maoist dominated areas visit of an outsider is immediately known and the news travel from mouth to mouth. Indeed, he is exposed to Maoist wrath and his life comes under grave danger. Under such hazardous circumstances and insurmountable odds cultivating and hooking up a genuine and reliable source is not at all an easy task. In short, visit by an outsider in rural areas dominated by tribal community, and to gain their trust and confidence is not a cake walk. Indeed, constraint and hazard of building a dependable source or an informer, especially, from the Adivasi community is an up-hill task.

Stepped-up Initiative to Disarray the Ultras

Chief Minister Arjun Munda, on April 18, 2011, stated that in Jharkhand 550 Naxals had been killed and 4090 arrested during the last ten years. Eighteen districts were affected and 14 districts were Maoist ridden disturbed territory. In affected 118 police stations man power has been increased substantially. Under the new scheme 13000 additional personnel would be inducted in the police force. Five Indian Reserve battalions have already been raised. A battalion only with the youths from tribal community would be raised by 2011 and deployed in forest. Fourteen additional coys of Jharkhand armed police (JAP), twelve bomb disposal squads, two battalions of special auxiliary forces (SAP) recruited from ex-service men and 22 coys STF, better known as Jharkhand Jaguar Force, have been raised. Again, 18 new coys of the STF were soon going to be added in the armed wing of the police. In Netarhat a school for jungle warfare training has already been established. Chief Minister was candid that government would ungrudgingly extend adequate help and provide fund to the police department to combat the Maoists for restoring peace and rule of law. He invited the ultras for dialogue twice. Yet, response from other end was deceptive.

Police has already revamped the Intelligence Branch of the state. In addition, it has created the Special Naxal Intelligence Cell. In police station level, intelligence staff posted for upward flow of intelligence. Inter-state intelligence support team has been activated to exchange and collate intelligence received from other sources and states. Modernisation of the Intelligence Wing has been initiated emphasising on mobility, communication and transport facilities in all level. Focus is given on Tech-Intelligence and Human-Intelligence and developmental activities. Greater attention is given on training, jungle warfare, weaponry, interrogation of the culprits and the suspects, follow up action on the clues elicited from the suspects, co-ordination meeting with the counter parts of other states, operational co-operation, adequate security arrangements and security cover to ensure timely completion of the development schemes and negate possible attempts to stall execution of the projects. Importantly, several Blocks of Palamu and Chatra districts have been brought under Pilot Projects. Sufficient police has been deployed there to ensure safety and security so that prompt execution and time bound completion of the projects are not hindered.

It is encouraging that the police force is overhauled significantly keeping pace with the ultras' fiendish activities, operational skill and striking power. Operational strategies have been modified and care taken for their flawless execution. First, action plan is initiated and prepared in district and area wise. Secondly, three tier force structure is used and applied to counter the ultras. Thirdly, operation is organised basing on specific intelligence report. Fourthly, special care is taken on night movement of the personnel, group or a contingent. Security forces are motivated and deployed to lay ambush, organise surprise attacks and inflict heavy blow on the ultras. In fact, offensive so long was one sided and the security forces have been facing the brunt of the catastrophe. Co-ordination in operations with neighboring states, district and police station level is insisted upon so that collective thrust may produce desired result. Interstate joint operation is an effective tool to disarray the extremists. In 2007, the state has conducted 41 interstate joint operations participated by Bihar, Chhattisgarh, Orissa, Uttar Pradesh and West Bengal. In fact, Jharkhand and Bihar together initiated operation on 23 times. Jharkhand and West Bengal organised 13 joint operations. Truly, high profile joint operations enriched by collective wisdom of the participating states have phenomenally put the ultras in back foot. Cacophony of the apparent mailed fist has put them in abysmal worry as it is likely to uproot them soon.

Strength of the police cadre has been increased. New recruits are put under rigorous training and discipline. Government has been sanctioning fund ungrudgingly and its swift and meaningful utilisation is encouraging. By 2007, altogether 15729 persons were enlisted and trained. Serving personnel have undergone in-service training by batches. Four armed battalions, including one Mahila (female) battalion are raised. Extra attention is paid to keep morale of the personnel high and in that pursuit several incentives are offered, which are special allowance, comprehensive insurance cover, out of turn promotion, lump sum compensation in case of death or injury received in anti-Maoist operation, free treatment for the injured at a place of his choice with an attendant. In fact, rupees ten lakhs as ex-gratia payment, salary including allowances for the remaining years of service, employment to one dependent of the family, free education to two wards till they attain 24 years age, marriage expenses for the female child etc., will be given to the family members of the deceased incumbent. Truly, largesse is piled upon largesse, which is inspiring the rank and file to accept the extremists' challenge.

A comparative figure from 2004 to 2007 reveals that the incidents of attacks, violence, killing of civilians and police personnel, looting of arms, etc. had steadily increased. In 2004, total 279 violent incidents reported. It shot up to 478 in 2007. In 2004, 106 civilians and 45 police men were killed and 32 injured. By 2007, killing spree of civilians was shocking which cost 175 lives. However, after initial set back the police rose to the occasion, arrested 350 and 413 ultras in 2004 and 2007 respectively, seized huge cache of arms, ammunitions, land mines, detonators, substantial quantity of explosives and recovered illegally collected levy money rupees fifty lakhs. Dispassionately, in spite of numerous hurdles and pull backs the police are resolutely fighting the hydra-headed monsters, who are desperate, pitiless and carry no regard for law and human lives. Above all, the viable police leadership has succeeded satisfactorily in resuscitating sagging morale of the police personnel to face and frustrate the gory challenge. In short, impelled by impetuosity, the police have been displaying indomitable will and matchless fortitude to crush the monstrous out laws.

Jharkhand—Maoists' Haven

In Maoist dominated territory, the ultras have succeeded in convincing the villagers to stand up against poverty, exploitation, discrimination and social injustice. It has been put into their heads that the present regime will not be able to nullify their miseries and modify or improve their lot. Therefore, they have to unitedly organise the mass upheaval to defeat the reactionary forces, class enemy and establish a new social order. Continued brain wash, propaganda and regular contact have produced positive result. In fact, villagers gradually have come in Maoists' fold and believe that armed struggle under the leadership of the Maoists is the solution to banish social malaises. Villagers are advised that as a part of the struggle self defence and active assistance to the rebels are essential. Enthusiastic followers and sympathizers are trained to use fire arms, plant land mines, organise resistance group to stall advances of the security forces, foil raids, arrests etc.

Saranda Forest—an Impregnable Sanctuary

It reveals that in Saranda forest about 400 villagers have been trained in carrying out explosions with improvised explosive devices (IEDs). In this forest there are about ten revenue and 25 forest villages which are cut off from the urban or rural areas. Inside deep forest, Maoists run training camps. Villagers support the ultras; assist them in repulsing the security forces. Advance of the security forces is stalled as land mines are planted on the ground. In a recent offensive, 12 Maoists and three security personnel were killed. Security forces while dogging the ultras had to remove and neutralise eight land mines in a patch of 2.5 kms. Villagers trained by the Maoists, had planted the land mines. Hence, operation against the Maoists right inside the forest is risky, critical and time consuming. The forest is thick and inaccessible. Its flora and fauna creates a natural barrier which is extremely suitable for a sanctuary.

Extortion, Protection Money paid by CM

Resources in initial stage were limited for the ultras. Fund clandestinely received from China and other sources was insufficient. Financial crunch was a mighty bottle neck for purchasing arms, ammunitions, training equipments, provisions and other necessities. However, soon they learn the trick to amass money through threat, coercion, robbery, extortion and levy on the mine owners, forest and labour contractors, rich traders etc. Similar *modus operandi* was applied to politicians and corrupt public servants. Threat on life, kidnapping of children or family members, attack on rendezvous etc. opened flood gate for mopping up substantial fund. Corrupt political leaders including Ministers, MPs, MLAs and corrupt public servants succumb to the Red threat and agree to be extorted regularly. School teachers working in remote villages are compelled to pay a portion of their salary. Such illegal payment is called "Protection Money." Many corrupt public servants are the targets of extortion. It is an open secret that the former Chief Minister of Jharkhand, Madhu Kora amassed wealth by corrupt means. He came under Maoist scanner and used to pay "protection money" regularly to the Maoists to avoid chastisement and physical harm. Now he is facing criminal prosecution. Undeniably, the spectre of terrorism has rapped many corrupt political leaders and public servants on knuckles. During my repeated visits to Jharkhand I have received adequate evidence on this count. Intelligence report of the state and central Intelligence units are unanimous on payment of protection money by politicians, public servants. During visit to steel city Bokaro and its periphery, I learnt reliably that the Maoists collect approximately rupees one hundred crores annually. Regrettably, the government is fully aware of pervasive corruption in various levels including the political personalities and the ultras' extortion and levy syndrome. Yet, no relief or cleansing drive is initiated to banish it.

Maoist Authority and Writs Absolute

It is crystal clear that in districts, like Palamau, Sarguja, Gumla, Daltanganj etc., Maoist writs run. After sun set except the district HQ, the rest areas go under absolute control and mercy of the ultras. Surprisingly, sanctuaries established in dense forest or inaccessible areas, mini town ship with civic amenities are available. Facilities of dining hall, conference hall, VIP room, store room, medical inspection room (MI), etc. have enriched it. Water supply through pipe lines, generation of electricity through generators and supply of electricity to the rooms and campus etc., have given the taste of real town ship right inside the thick forest. In short, fair dwelling opportunity tampered with good town planning ensuring urban comfort virtually in a forbidden area deserves appreciation. Evidently, well net internal arrangement is run and maintained by experienced and competent persons. It confirms ability and engineering skill of the Maoists.

Fair Sex Maoists Play Important Role

Significantly, responding to the call of the Maoist demagogues many youths and girls volunteer to join the cadre. The leaders' alacrity and flaccid interactions attract the youths and fair sex to avidly respond. Many volunteer and enlist themselves to join the outfit, undergo training and take active part in fiendish activities. Interestingly, in Jharkhand and Chhattisgarh large number of fair sex embrace the life of extremists. The Maoist leaders encourage the fair sex to join the cadre for more than one reason. First, participation of the weaker sex in insurgency is a startling revelation and carries high news value. Secondly, fair sex often attracts the youths to join the outfit. Thirdly, it helps to keep the flock together as intimacy and emotional attachment of both male and female work well to prevent desertion and to abandon the armed struggle. Of late, fair sex Maoists are taking active part in operations. In that context, an exhaustive report has been discussed exclusively in Chapter Nine for consumption of the readers.

Red Corridor in Three States?

An idea of Red corridor from south of Chhattisgarh to Jharkhand and Orissa was published in a national daily on April 15, 2013. Impartial examination revealed that it was far from correct. It is misleading as to why the proposed Red Corridore from Nepal to Tamilnadu is not persuaded or adhered to. Instead, whisper is gaining currency for a mini Red Corridore restricting it to only three states. However, interrogation of arrested Maoists has disclosed a new clue. According to them, a narrow but contiguous strip that runs from southern tip of Chhattisgarh to central Jharkhand is used by the Maoists for speedy and safe movement. In fact, Maoists have managed to build a reasonable support base among local populace along Chhattisgarh-Odisha border right up to Gumla district of Jharkhand. Bihar-Jharkhand-North Chhattisgarh special area committee has strengthened itself in Odisha's heavily forested Nuapada district. In fact, three hundred strong team operators in Gaya, Aurangabad, Chatra, Gumla, Palamau, Garwa and Latehar districts are very active and vulnerable. To-day, it is the strongest Naxalite belt in Bastar, Dandakaranya, Jharkhand and south Bihar region. As a matter of fact, belying speculation, the Maoist politburo is still firm in its original idea of the Red Corridore from Nepal to Tamilnadu.

Setback to the Maoist Movement

Of late, unusual developments have added comatose dimension to the Maoist movement and simultaneously, given new substance to the law and order authority in handling the growing Maoist menace. Indeed, the Maoist leaders active in Jharkhand and Bihar have admitted that success of the security forces is a fatal blow to the Maoists. It has further hit the sagging morale of the activists, accelerated erosion in the cadre and indicated the somber future of the out-fit. A statement of a Maoist leader appeared in website reveals that security forces in Jharkhand has inflicted a major damage on the extremist organisation in 2011-12, more than that in other states of the country. The central committee of the out-fit has sent it to all comrades across the country. It has high-lighted that the People's Liberation Front of India (PLFI) and Jharkhand Jana Mukti Parishad have killed a large number of the Maoists and helping the state government to crush the People's War Truly, several splinter groups who severed connection with the main stream are hostile to the Maoists and working with all might to expose and disarray the present Maoist group. Statement further reveals that thirty comrades who had been actively resisting the security forces and expanding the extremist network in and around Jharkhand border and who were members of Jharkhand-Bihar-North Chhattisgarh special area committee had been killed . In addition in 2011-12, the cadre has lost 43 activists operated in Naxal affected states. Loss of the cadre is a flinty blow to the Maoists which has placed the much cherished movement in a shamble. In fact, upset Maoist central command has instructed the cadre to observe Martyr's Memorial Week from July 28 to August 3, 2012 for paying obeisance to those who had lost their lives fighting or in fake encounters. Sacrifice of the comrades deserves to be high-lighted among the rank and file to resuscitate low morale of the comrades. Instruction issued that supreme sacrifice of Akali Devi who was killed along with her minor son in an encounter should be narrated and circulated zealously so that it may inspire and invigorate the cadres. Supreme sacrifice and heroic deed of Ramko Hichami alias Ranita should be projected who fought against the CRPF Cobra force and killed three of them in a gun battle in Gadchiroli district, Maharashtra.

Central Committee's circular reveals that death of comrade MK Rao alias Kishanji in an encounter in Jangal Mahal is an immeasurable setback for the outfit. In the circular it has been admitted that two state level leaders in Chhattisgarh, one regional committee leader in Assam, three senior members of the cadre, at Lalgarh, West Bengal, were killed. In addition, five activists in Assam and eleven in Chhattisgarh were shot dead by the security forces. The committee has brought out a list of the slain comrades faced death in the hands of the security forces. After death of Kishanji in WB, no suitable leader is available to fill the vacuum. Moreover, arrests, deaths and surrender of many comrades have unnerved the central leadership. Critics quipped that festival of surrender in WB has demoralised the rank and file of the out-fit. In a nutshell, the ultras are helplessly in defensive position, lost vigour and determination to reorganise, retaliate and neutralise the onslaught of the security forces. They are equally worn out to counter and eliminate the dissident or rival groups.

Admittedly, the police and para military forces have been tackling the Maoist problem with remarkable ability. Their indomitable will, determination, courage and painstaking effort to fight the blood thirsty ultras are matchless and exemplary. Still, there is no reason to be complacent assuming that the Maoists days are numbered. Dispassionate analysis reveals that temporary setback of the Maoists should not be considered as the decay or end of the Maoists. It is not ruled out that the ultras are likely to reorganise, regroup and reappear with consummate courage, resoluteness and fury. In sum, the security forces have been working under unprecedented strain, stress, hazards and risk. Yet, their morale is high. Casualties and temporary setback have not demoralised or deterred them to fight the proxy war. I had an opportunity to discuss the Maoist threat with former Chief Minister Arjun Munda in a seminar held in Delhi. I am happy to note that he is well informed, well-meaning and determined to curb and neutralise the Maoists from the state. He expressed full faith on the state police and para military forces operating to disarray the ultras.

In Jharkhand and Bihar several Maoists are possessing money and properties like houses, bungalows, lands etc., sent wards to foreign countries for higher education etc. Allegation by the fellow Maoists has created a flutter and exposed tainted faces of the so called revolutionaries. Evidently, corruption and degeneration already set in among the Maoists is a flinty threat to the Maoist movement. In this respect details have been discussed in Chapter Two, for satisfying curiosity of the readers.

CHAPTER FOUR

Red Terror and Maoist Violence in Chhattisgarh

Chhattisgarh, now a separate state, born on November 1, 2000 carving out of Madhya Pradesh its population is 20.88 million. Tribal communities form nearly 80 per cent of the entire population of the state. Six districts of the state are in the grip of the Maoists. Abujhmarh (unknown forest) is the HQ of the Maoists, is surrounded by dense jungle and natural barriers which has made the Maoists' hide out practically impregnable. Topography and terrain is far from plain and smooth. Thick jungle, tall trees, countless small mounts, uneven ground etc. have made the areas inaccessible. In the midst of the deep forest, small villages of the tribal communities are located. Broadly, many villages are connected with small hamlets. No regular village roads are available to approach the villages. Villagers use the foot paths created automatically due to movements of the inhabitants. Many villages are not recorded in the district land records. Even revenue officials have not visited the unrecorded habitations. Tribal people strictly cling on their culture and ethos. Chill penury, unemployment, deficient or negligible health care, exploitation by traders and money lenders, etc. have been pushing them towards ruin. Over and above, malnutrition, disease and pestilence often take heavy toll of the hapless people. Jungle is their livelihood. They prefer to live in the accolade of their age old culture and heritage. Harassment and exploitation by petty government officials add to their grief. Truly, they eke out a miserable existence. Admittedly, partly for their blind and obstinate attachment to their age old social customs, habits and practices and partly of the government's insouciance, blessings of the modern advancement have hardly improved their lot.

Success of the security forces in Andhra Pradesh, especially, the "Greyhounds" a specially trained and elite anti-terrorist forces have compelled the ultras to shift their bases from Andhra Pradesh to favorable terrain in Bastar region. The region is being the home of the poverty-stricken and exploited tribal community, the ultras have easily earned good will and support of the local populace. In fact, a large portion of Bastar region is claimed to be the "Liberated Zone" where the authority of the ultras is absolute and their writ runs. Broadly speaking, Jharkhand and Chhattisgarh are the epicenter of the Maoist activities. Six districts, Narayanpur, Bijapur, Bastar, Kanker, Sukma and Dantewada of Chhattisgarh state are practically the Red bastion. In Bastar region, a large portion of the territory is a part of 40000 sq. km of the imaginary red corridor. In fact, area is a free zone where writs of the Maoists decide matters. Chhattisgarh and Jharkhand together accounted for 68.16 percent of total Maoist related violence and 76.42 percent of total casualties of security personnel and the civilians. Ministry of Home Affairs (MHA) confirmed that out of 18 districts of Chhattisgarh, 13 districts are hit by the left wing extremism since 1980.

Bailadila is one of the country's best reserves of iron ore. National Mineral Development Corporation (NMDC) is the prime mining unit. Export of the iron ore much depends on the Bastar region. Violence and bloodshed unleashed by the extremists has severely hindered the NMDC's mining industry and the satellite industries. In 2007-08 within one year due to violence NMDC had lost nearly 200 cores of rupees. Insecurity in the mining belt has been stalling economic progress and development of the mining industry. The ultras often target the KVA towers resulting in, electric supply in the areas is either disrupted or shut down for days together jeopardizing production and normal civic life. In 2008, three 132 KVA towers were blown off in Narayanpur district. Consequently, two districts including Dantewada district remained under darkness continuously for 12 days. Financial loss was to the extent of rupees of 160 crores. Extremist attacks and casualty of the security personnel and civilians have been increasing alarmingly since 2003. CRPF personnel are the worse sufferers. In 2009, by July 146 security personnel including a Superintendent of police were killed. Sadly, 700 civilians had lost their lives. Director General of Police of the state felt that 50000 Maoists were holed up in Bastar region and 10000 thousands were trained and highly motivated to take part in guerrilla warfare. They are hiding in the forest, can use mortars, rocket launchers and sophisticated weapons. Guerrilla squads are formed in small groups of 10 to 15 persons. However, squad's strength is modified depending on a situation.

Intensity of the Maoist activities including attack and annihilation of the security personnel and civilians has alarmed the state and union government Complacency of the union government taking it purely a law and order problem and it is state's responsibility to tackle it, has allowed to grow and intensify the ultra-left extremists violent movement. However, gravity of the problem has finally forced the union government to alter its policy. Union Home Minister P. Chidambaram admitted in the Rajya Sabha, "For many years we did not properly assess the threat posed by the left wing extremists. We under estimated the challenge and in the meanwhile, Naxalites extended their challenge." In the Parliament he said, "today they (Naxalites) pose a grave challenge...we are preparing to take on the grave challenge."

Success of security forces in Andhra Pradesh, especially, of the "Greyhounds" a highly trained and advanced anti-terrorist forces have compelled the ultras to shift their bases and training centers from Andhra Pradesh to latent terrain in Bastar region, Chhattisgarh. The region being the home of the poverty stricken and exploited tribal community, the Maoists have easily earned profound goodwill and support from the tribal populace. In fact, a large part of Bastar region is claimed to be the "Liberated Zone" where the Maoists, authority is absolute. The swift growth of the extremists has unnerved the state government. Deployment of the Maoist squads in heavy strength, casualty inflicted on the security personnel, special police officers and civilians has put law and order machinery of the state in a quandary. In fact, out of 18 districts six districts have turned to be the hunting ground of the Maoists. From July 2007 to July 2010 the security forces had faced 1948 attacks, 435 security personnel including 75 SPOs and 418 civilians had lost their lives. The police and para military forces have been working under immeasurable strain and stress and matchless hazards. They have to camp inside jungle or inhabitable places for months together, devoid of minimal civic amenities, face inclement weather, suffer from malaria, dysentery and other topical diseases, and spend moment under abyss suspense, fearing surprise attacks, fierce encounters and ugly death. Truly, they have been discharging duties under constant danger, risk and uncertainty. Hardly, there is any whet or stimulus to resuscitate their sagging morale. Cops representing rank and file are unwilling to work in insurgency infected areas. Indeed, number of high and low police officials have declined to accept assignments in Maoist hit areas. State government has served notice to 78 police personnel including 33 Inspectors for refusing to join the units located in places rocked by Maoist violence. Broadly, grounds for noncompliance of the posting order are sickness, including diabetics, high blood pressure, heart problem etc. Unfortunately, such incidents are increasing every month. Significantly, the state is lamentably lagging behind in development, economic progress, growth of the industry and employment opportunities. However, the state has requested the union government and the Planning Commission for a grant of rupees 4553.00 crores under the Integrated Action Plan (IAP) for development of the terror-torn districts.

Surrender of the Maoists—Rehabilitation Package

From October 2004, with the object of alluring the extremists to give up arms, surrender and return to the main stream of the society, the state has initiated several packages including financial aid for rehabilitating the surrendered extremists. Packages are attractive. State has committed to pay rupees three lakhs to a Maoist, if he or she surrenders with a light machine gun (LMG), rupees two lakhs, if one surrenders with a AK 47 rifle. However, response from the ultras was lukewarm. In fact, by 31st October 2010, altogether 2619 ultras had surrendered. No doubt surrender figure is apparently good but only six of them had surrendered with 12 bore guns. Analysis reveals that stock of the automatic and semi-automatic weapons which are in possession of the ultras is still intact. It is safely presumed that sizeable member of the cadre either possesses or have access to light machine guns and automatic weapons including AK 47 rifles. Hence, the state's dream project to rehabilitate the outlaws is yet to produce the desired result. The village level Maoists cadre, better known as Sangham, is recruited at adolescent stage. They are part of the Maoist cadre, trained and take part in armed confrontations. In 2005, 1378 Sangham members and 13 hard core Maoists surrendered, in 2006, five Maoists and 1032 Sangham members surrendered. In 2007, 90 Maoists including one armed Maoist and 77 Sangham members, in 2008, five Maoists including two armed Maoists and one Sangham member, in 2009, two Maoists and 13 Sangham members and in 2010, till 31 October only three Maoists surrendered.

Poor response and meager surrender figure apparently indicates that the scheme has lamentably failed. The Police chief admitted that the police had not made much head way in persuading armed Maoists to surrender. The police has to create for Maoists an ambience in their dominated pockets that they are vulnerable, likely to be apprehended or killed if they do not surrender. Police were unable to infiltrate in Maoist ranks or file and cultivate reliable sources to collect intelligence, secretly interact with the rebels, instigate or persuade them to surrender. The relative advantage of the surrender and prospect of the package remains foreign to a rebel since none can contact him and explain the benefits and merits of returning to the main stream for leading a normal life.

Maoists' formidability, reckless barbarity and killing spree are dreadful for peace loving persons. The Red Zone covering areas of Bastar region is infested with countless hideouts, cordoned or ringed by deadly landmines. Hence, ordinarily, to develop secret link with any ultra short-circuiting insurmountable hurdle and the outfits' internal vigil and intelligence is virtually impossible. It is difficult to convince the hard core Maoists the will-o-the-wisp of Maoist ideology tainted with violence, destruction and bloodshed. No amount of council or persuasion will help them to get immune from the frenzied cobweb of annihilation and unrest and serve the humanity in the accolade of peace, prosperity and happiness. Hence, surrender of the hard core ultras shunning unctuous culture is a stymie. Indeed, all out attempt to salvage them from phantasmagoria is often negated. Negotiators feel that it is a difficult proposition to win over the hard core ultras. It needs patience, long-term plan, sound strategy, mutual trust and favorable ambience.

Similarly, it is equally hard to launch direct assault ignoring strong obstacles or resistance to rescue a dissentient ultra. Furthermore, the state government is unable to spell out a long time firm policy of ensuring protection, safety and security of the surrendered out laws and their family members. Over and above, clear indication is missing explaining the ways and means to neutralise wrath or retaliation of the fellow truculent Maoists. Frankly speaking, the state lacks iron will and determination to follow up the surrender policy and generate an atmosphere of mutual trust and confidence among the hostile ultras. Secondly, the government's well-meaning endeavour to rehabilitate aggrieved ultras has failed to gain desired publicity that it is going to benefit the ultras profusely if surrender bait is embraced. On the contrary, the blow hot and blow cold policy, administrative gamut, red-tapism and monumental lethargy of the government employees dissuade the Maoists to respond to the call.

Counter-insurgency Movement in Chhattisgarh; Salwa Judum (Vigilante Groups)

State government has initiated a new plan and programme, called Salwa Judum to combat the growing threat of the Maoists. Broadly, it is an effort to arm the villagers to oppose and counter the blood thirsty Maoists. It has been organised in 2005, in Dantewada district on an initiative of Mahendra Karma, a local influential person. In the Gondi language spoken in Chhattisgarh, it means a resistance group or "Bahini". In an endeavour to make it popular or acceptable it is attributed as Santi Bahini, in other words, Army for Peace. In 1991, the Jan Jag ran, an organisation at the behest of the local civilians was formed to counter the ultras. It took up the instances of 'right abused' by the ultras. Truly, it is a civil militia ostensibly formed to protect the unarmed rural people. But in practice, it is a combatant squad armed and sponsored by the state government to foil attacks of the militants. As event moved apace, the idea of Salwa Judum took a concrete shape. Participants in the new unit are mainly from the tribal community. Adivasi villagers facing wrath of the Maoists used to be shifted to the camps temporarily opened by Salwa Judum. Adivasi youths are recruited in the unit on payment of rupees fifteen hundred per month. Later remuneration was enhanced to Rs.3000 per month. As per the Police Act 1861, they are called Special Police Officer (SPO). Under Section 17 of the said Act, they may be recruited temporarily. However, they enjoy the same power normally a police officer is entitled. In Dentewada and Bijapur districts several camps are opened under the protection of the Salwa Judum. Along with security forces the SPOs also resist the Maoists, guard the camps, patrol areas, collect intelligence and perform miscellaneous duties. Importantly, they are exposed to hazards and chances of injury or death for them is not ruled out.

On June 26, 2010, a bus carrying passengers and SPO were attacked and blown off by the Maoists. Eleven SPOs travelling in the bus were killed. However, on the pretext of countering the extremists, its members often commit excesses, indulge in high handedness, assault or kill the rival villagers to fulfill personal grudge. Complaints against their excesses have upset the sober persons. It is felt that the long rope given by the government has made them insolent who often take the law in their hands. Indeed, its birth, arrogance of the members and functioning style tampered with stridence, etc. have come under scathing criticism Critics quip that it is the state's killing apparatus. Teenagers and civilians are put in the vanguard to counter the Maoists and face bullets. State defends it pleading that as a matter of policy the government's private army is intended to protect its own force as also to minimise the possibility of police disaffection. Significantly, on a writ petition, the Supreme Court has strongly criticized the state's unprecedented move to disarray the Maoists. "You are playing with the so called SPOs. What will happen if they turn against the state? God save the country. You are playing." The Bench observed that far from addressing the bread and butter issues raised by the Maoists the state has for years pursued a scorched earth policy that is designed to kill the left radicals as much as the teenaged activists of the Salwa Judum The government has set tribal against the tribal, civilian against civilian. The experiment has been as sinister as it is suicidal. As a part of the Salwa Judum it is the innocent civilians facing the brunt.

From the so-called liberated areas Maoists forced the families to spare one youth from each family for enlistment in the ultras' cadre. In case of refusal, ultras would assault the inmates and compel them to pay a fine of rupees five hundred. Many youths join the cadre to save the family members from harassment and extortion. At Konta town situated on the border of Andhra Pradesh, 180 youths, including girls were forced to join the Maoist cadre. They said that option before them was clear. Either they joined the Maoists or the Salwa Judum. Disobedience to submit to the Maoist call, was sure death. They were shaken watching the outfit's diabolic rules, Spartan discipline and denial of personal freedom and free expression. Secondly, fear of arbitrary punishment and cruel death abysmally demoralised them. In fact, after training many against their wish are detailed to take part in armed encounters against the security forces. Many are detailed to kill cops or civilians. Truly, many are disinterested to take part in blood curdling activities. Soon their patience is worn out. Defying draconic surveillance and control many desert and go underground. Many deserters join the Salwa Judum to work as SPOs. The new assignment provides them protection from the Maoists' vengeance and gives them financial support. In fact, suspense and fear of grim reprisal always haunt them. They are aware that the Maoists would invariably retaliate and take life for the betrayal.

Impartial people feel that the government sponsored the extra constitutional force has indirectly given impetus for a brutal civil war between the extremists and armed civilians backed by the state. It is widening the hiatus between the poor, discomfited people and the democratically elected government. Oppressed villagers complained and the media has unearthed several instances of atrocity let loose by the Salwa Judum. Several villages on the southern border of the state adjacent to Andhra Pradesh had been burnt down by the activists of the Salwa Judum intending to destroy the potential supporters of the Maoists. The perpetrators of the outrages feel that if the villagers remain in villages and forests they will be forced to support the ultras. Therefore, the villagers should take shelter in camps established by the state enjoying protection of the police and Salwa Judum till normalcy is restored. The state and the activists of the unit assert that it is a spontaneous movement against terror unleashed by the cruel ultras. However, the critics call it a lawless authority armed by the state, guilty of scorching villages, killing resistors and abusing women. The villagers afraid of attack and frenzied outrages, desert the village and take shelter in forests. Many have escaped into Orissa and Andhra Pradesh for fear of life. Five years on, scores of families are still on heels, hiding in jungle undergoing an untold hardship and poverty. Rough estimate reveals that more than 600 villages and its population over three lakhs had been shifted out of their homes for making the anti-Maoist operation effective. A widow aged 30 years narrated her woe how her husband was shot dead by the activists of the Salwa Judum in presence of the police in an attempt to clear the village. The frightened villagers quit the village, taken shelter in the forest. Now she is living with her six year old daughter in thatched hutments deep inside the forest bordering Andhra Pradesh and struggling for existence. After three years she returned to the native village only to see everything was burnt and destroyed. Another widow aged about 50 stated that they were forced to stay in state camp at Errabore. One evening her husband and son were picked up from the camp by a group from Salwa Judum and were killed without any rhyme or reason. Several other villagers of the camp met the same fate. The grief-stricken mother is carrying a photo of his teen aged son and shows to the persons asking help and redress. She said that the camp was later attacked by the Maoists and she with others fled from the camp.

Gaganpalli village, district Dantewara, was emptied out of its residents and burnt down by a gang of armed men. The attack was a part of common strategy that Salwa Judum adopted to combat the Maoists in the region. A government school teacher said that the ultras began to control village matters, harassing villagers and killing persons branding them police informers. As a result, their good will, support and sympathy for the poverty stricken villagers received a jolt. The alarmed people wanted to get rid of them and desired peace. State felt that the ultras can easily influence the innocent villagers and bring them in their fold if they are allowed to stay in the villages. Hence, shelter in the camps will forbid them from the contact and influence of the ultras. Needless to add, it would be easier for the police and the security forces to combat the extremists if they are isolated from the contact of the ultras.

A few well-meaning persons initiated welfare activities to help the displaced persons from Chhattisgarh who have taken shelter in the villages in Andhra Pradesh.

Schools are established to teach the students of the displaced families. They are working against violation of human rights. Unfortunately, they are misunderstood both by the police and the extremists. Police suspect them to be the patrons or sympathizers or link men of the ultras and operate on their behalf to spread the Maoists role and influence. They communicate intelligence, movement of the security forces and other details of the impending operation. The ultras feel that they are cleverly working as informers or agents of the police. Indeed, their bonafide is doubted by both. Neither the police nor the ultras spare them, chastise or kill them on mere suspicion. Truly, they are in a cleft stick, unable to establish genuineness of their missionary zeal. However, they assert that deployment of troops for flushing out the extremists from forests is unrewarding. Troops will be stuck for years together but Maoists will not be wiped out. On the contrary, the area will be militarised. Secondly, the rule of the criminals is likely to creep in and spoil the simple and docile tribal. However, residents want peace, a halcyon ambience and want to live without threat to life. *The Statesman* daily, Calcutta in an editorial commented that the formation of citizens' resistance groups (Salwa Judum) carried within it the seeds of destruction. It is a suicidal move from the very start as it envisaged the pitting of ordinary folk against the Maoists. This has only steeled the determination of the latter.

Red terror has badly affected more than nine states including Chhattisgarh. Importantly, nobody was displaced from the disturbed areas and accommodated in temporary camps organised by the government except in Chhattisgarh. Indeed, no state has organised any private or public militia to disarray the militants in pattern of the Salwa Judum. In Chhattisgarh the SPOs are given pompous name of Kaya commandos following the name of a tribe in Dantewada region. Arms and ammunitions distributed to the private militia are not often judiciously used to oppose the Maoists. Frankly speaking, complaints of misuse of power and weapons on the pretext of countering the ultras were in galore. Puffed up activists of the Salwa Judum did not restrain themselves in oppressing the innocent villagers Many were trigger happy and their actions were palpably illegal, violation of human rights tainted with reckless excesses. The National Human Rights Commission (NHRC) had received many complaints of horrendous excesses and conducted enquiries. Prima facie NHRC was convinced of many devilish excesses and submitted a report to the union government in August 2008. A relevant portion of the report is quoted, "National Human Rights Commissions had probed the alleged human rights violations by Salwa Judum and pointed out to incidents of burning and killing on which FIRs were not registered and cases of high-handedness of the SPOs or civilians armed with weapons to fight naxals recorded...." People's Union for Civil Liberties (PUCL) and the People's Union for Democratic Rights (PUDR), prepared a long list of persons, mostly tribals who were killed by the security forces or the activists of Salwa Judum.

Referring to the report, the Minister of State for Tribal Affairs submitted a written reply to the Lok Sabha, which revealed that 40000 people were in relief camps in Dantewada and Bijapur districts. Camps had accommodated the panic stricken people who had temporarily moved out for fear of terrorist attacks. Civilians of the areas are regularly targeted and attacked by the ultras mere on suspicion of anti-Maoist activities. As tribals form a segment of civil population they are also affected by such threat. As a matter of fact, the Minister virtually defended the state government. Spate of attacks on the members of the Salwa Judum by the Maoists and loss of lives upset the state government. Hence, union and state government decided to deploy armed personnel, Sashastra Seema Bal (SSB) for protecting the activists of the Salwa Judum. Intelligence input revealed that the activists of the unit are mainly from tribal community. Maoist threat, attacks and deaths would dissuade them to join the Salwa Juduam. Hence, for the interest of success of the unit armed protection for them was essential. However, in the tangled web of the fast changing insurgency scenario in the state the role of the private militia has only upset the intellectuals, democrats, impartial and progressive elements. Meanwhile, Sociologist Nandini Sundar, historian Ram Chandra Guha, former public servant EAS Sharma and many others filed a writ petition before the Apex Court challenging it. Finally, the Apex Court intervened and ruled on July 5, 2011, that the Salwa Judum is unconstitutional and ruled to disband it. Observation of the Supreme Court runs as follows: "We do not under estimate the enormity of the problem (Naxalism). But the state should not encourage the common men by arming them to fight Naxalites...unless legal power is vested, you cannot arm people." Unfortunately, in an ambush by the Maoists in Darba forest on May 25, 2013, Mahandra Karma, the founder father of Salwa Judum and 27 Congress leaders and activists were killed.

Former Prime Minister's Observation and Unabated Violence

Nearly 40000 sq km at the expense of forests in Chhattisgarh's border with Orissa, Jharkhand and Andhra Pradesh, is the secret abode of roughly 10000 Maoists. Former Prime Minister Manmohan Singh stated that the Maoists are accused of hundreds of killings, kidnapping and looting in the swathes they control. MHA's report reveals that in 2007 Maoists had killed 418 civilians and 214 security personnel. In 2006, the number was 501 and 133 respectively. Ganapati aged about 60, the General Secretary of the CPI (Maoists), Kishanji, aged about 50, the general secretary of the erstwhile MCC, and now a member of the politburo, are live wire in co-coordinating with other units, plan operations and inspire the guerrilla squads to strike. They command roughly 20 guerrilla squads, ready to operate in 165 districts. They have been leading the ultras secretly from behind. On June 6, 2008, the Maoists destroyed two 220 KV power supply towers near Bodali. Consequently, four districts of Baster region, Dantewada, Bijapur, Narayanpur and Jagdalpur plunged into darkness. The people had to live about a week without electricity. At least 1400 villages had to face black out. National Mineral Development

Corporation (NMDC) faced a loss of rupees two crores per day for stopping production and failing to dispatch iron ore. Railways had to bear a loss of rupees 1.5 crore per day. The Maoists have modified their earlier modus operandi. Now they destroy towers in remote and inaccessible areas where the state employees need to travel at least ten to fifteen kms on foot to reach the damaged tower. Earlier, the Maoists blasted power towers plunging the entire Bastar region into darkness for 12 days.

State's Development Programme in the Eye of the Critics

The state government's official release reveals that in fiscal year 2009-10, the state recorded the highest growth rate 11.49 percent in the country. BJP government has been ruling the state since December 2003. It claimed that the state is on the move and that by 2020, it would be among top three states in the country. The state was formed on November 1, 2000, and hence completed a decade in its present form. The tribal community forms the vast majority of the population of the state. A senior Minister of the state government stated that the state has been growing fast and is far ahead of Jharkhand and Uttarakhand, though the three states were formed almost simultaneously. According to him, the public distribution system (PDS), health care and expansion of roads have shown a spectacular progress. In fact, upward trend of the outlay of the state has superseded past records. From rupees 1312.27 crores in 2001-02, it has shot up to rupees 13230 crores in 2009-10. Indeed, the state's trumpeted claim on boundless progress irked the impartial critics. They stated that the day the state was born number of families below the poverty line (BPL) was 1.87 million. But in 2010, it increased to 3.62 million. Now 70 percent people live on the state's subsidized rice scheme—Chief Minister's Food Assurance Scheme. In fact, supply of rice at rupees two per kilo gram for the persons belonging to the BPL category is preventing starvation death. Critics question that if economic progress and prosperity had flooded the state why the number of BPL families has increased so drastically

All India Adivasi Mahasabha, an umbrella organisation of tribal bodies pooh-pooh the growth story. Abyss neglect in development for decades is pathetic and this is one of the reasons that the Maoists have been growing rapidly. On the eve of the BJP government came to power, the Maoists had strong control in a few pockets in Bastar region. Now, their wide spread network and striking power is threatening even the urban areas. Violence at the behest of the ultra-left party had claimed over 2100 lives since BJP came to power. Corruption in public life is a deep-rooted malaise, hindering development work and welfare activities. Complaints are galore that to get enrolled and to get a job card under the National Rural Employment Guarantee Act (NREGA), the government officials and the contractor have to be bribed. Indeed, without payola none can expect any relief from the government offices. Secondly, Health care and medical facilities in remote areas, especially, in rainy season, is hardly available. Death from water borne disease is rampant. In 2010, 65 persons died in Dantewada and Bijapur district during monsoon. Local people feel that death toll is much higher. Public welfare and meaningful public service as often talked by the political leaders is a myth. Admittedly, the state government has not initiated any tangible step to stall the cancerous growth, the corruption in public life.

Abject poverty, unemployment and opaque future force the weaker sexes to submit to human trafficking. Young girls are tempted to work as domestic helps in cities on assurance of fat salary. Here middlemen play an abhorrent role, take away the girls or young women from the families on false promises. Once they fall into the trap the helpless women are pushed in the flesh trade. Pangs of poverty and socio-economic disparity compel the impoverished families to succumb to the temptations and lavish promises showered by the crafty middle men. Poor, neglected and exploited families of ten districts of the state are the victims of the organised sex racket. Unfortunately, the government is not equal to the task to eradicate the obnoxious harlotry, wipe out pervasive and baneful influence of the unscrupulous middlemen and flesh traders. It needs no reiteration that the odious blot is destroying the moral fabric of the families and the society and ruining many promising lives. Regrettably, neither the government nor the NGOs achieved any positive result in combating the social malady. Frankly speaking, social and economic adversary, sufferings of the have-nots and the government's sterile exercise to govern diligently have opened floodgate for the extremists to appear as the saviours of the poor and the socially oppressed people. Therefore, frustrated people seeing no remedy respond to the assurance of the extremists and believe that substantial improvement and bright future in their cursed fortune is knocking at the door in the hands of the new benefactors.

Recruitment and Training, Abduction of Minors and Formation of Bal Sangham

Recruitment and training mechanism in the Maoist cadre has a special bearing. It is unique in one sense as hunt for the recruits and induction of fresh blood in the cadre is practiced deviating from the conventional method. Recruiting ground is generally rural areas. Male and females are enlisted with great care. Minors aged about 8 to 10 years are forcibly taken away from the families, indoctrinated in revolutionary spirit, ideal of classless society and people's war. They are called Bal Sangham. They are repeatedly brain washed for months or years together on the social conflict between the have and have-nots, denial, discrimination of the poor and exploitation by the higher or affluent class of the society. Sufferings and deprivation meted out to the down trodden are grilled into their head. Rigid regimentation shapes them to be physically and mentally tough, energetic and industrious. They adapt themselves to live in jungle, adverse and unhygienic condition. Their endurance capacity is cultivated to unbelievably high degree. In majority of the cases, parents are threatened or terrorized to spare their wards. In some cases a paltry sum is paid to compensate the families. Physical and small arms training continue for several years. From the Bal Sangham hardy and capable boys are inducted into the middle level and trained to handle fire arms, explosives etc. From the middle level hand full are singled out and put to special training for handling sophisticated and automatic weapons like LMG, AK-47, INSA rifles, SLR and planting land mines, etc.

It is revealing that the Maoist cadre has a fair share of weaker sexes who are well trained and take part in operations. They are generally recruited from the poor tribal families. It is reliably learnt that taking advantage of the upper hand of the Maoists in Lalgarh areas of West Bengal, the Maoists had recruited at least twenty girls within the age group of 16 to 20. Late Kishenji, member of the politburo recruited all of them from poverty ridden tribal families of six tribal villages situated on the eastern side of Lalgarh. Interestingly, after enlistment the girl recruits were sent to Chhattisgarh for arms training. Intelligence reports confirmed that "Abujhmarh" in Chhattisgarh was the temporary training ground for specialised training. Special Task Force of Kolkata police arrested Anu alias Kalpana Maity, a top most female Maoist leader. During interrogation she confessed that the rebels had used Lalgarh as a resourceful base for the recruitment in the cadre. She confirmed recruitment of girls from Lalgarh areas by Kishenji. In 2003, she participated in the attack of the Bandwan police station and killing of the Officer-in-Charge. Dilip Mahato, a key link man of the ultras after arrest divulged that four or five trained females had returned from training centre to their villages in Lalgarg area, WB, and mixing with the villagers. Their main task was to keep watch on the movements of the security forces in and around Lalgarh. Critics mockingly said that female Maoists from West Bengal would be seen in Bastar region fighting the security forces.

In short, recruits from Bal Sangham eventually are upgraded and placed in the formidable combatant groups. Finally watching performance of the trainees many are placed in the guerrilla squads. In fact, standard pattern of recruitment and training discussed above is generally followed. Instructors for imparting training are chosen from senior members who have back ground of the army or the armed forces. In addition, villagers are taken to the cadre temporarily. Able bodied persons and youths are enlisted in the cadre by threat or coercion They are locally trained to assist Maoists in carrying arms and ammunitions, provisions, maintaining communication, keep watch on the movement of the police and security forces, resist them or take part in encounters as second line of fighting force. However, they are not permanent members of the cadre. They are called "Sangham" and taken as auxiliary hands.

In October 2009, the ultras forced the villagers to spare five boys and girls from each village for enlistment in the armed group. In a report it was pointed out that the Maoists had systematically carried out attacks on schools, intentionally damaged and destroyed structures to stir panic and fear among the local community. Importantly, the security forces often occupy school buildings and convert them to temporary camps. It irks the Maoists who attempt to destroy the school buildings. In Bihar and Jharkhand the Maoists have destroyed a large number of school buildings so that security forces may not establish temporary camps there. In this respect UN's one of the top officials remarked, "Combat is no place for children.... The shifting nature of conflict has put many children on the front lines. Very often children become collateral damage during military operations." (*The Hindustan Times*, May 23, 2010).

In Chhattisgarh, the Maoists have issued whip to many tribal families to send a male child from each family to join them or face death In February 2008, about 30 Maoists visited village Malaida, district Rajnandgaon and asked the tribals to support their movement by sending a child from each family to join the outfit. They said that they would give the children arms training, involve them in the movement and take care of their livelihood. Demand made the villagers abysmally perplexed and frightened. After a few days the Maoists again visited the village and threatened the inmates that they would be killed if they fail to obey the instruction. The village is located on the border of Rajnandgaon, Chhattisgarh and Balaghat, Madhya Pradesh. About thirty families, around 150 villagers with fifty children live in the village. Throbbed with panic the villagers decided to flee the village on that night. They covered a distance of 10 km, reported the matter to the police station and took shelter in the relief camp in Panchayat building of Khairagarh Development Block. They were given food and ensured security. The villagers, in spite of assurance of safety and security, were not willing to return to their village, Malaida. They informed the District Magistrate and the Superintendent of Police about their unwillingness to return.

Training is generally arranged locally inside the jungle using available resources. Centrally arranged training center has not yet come to notice. Of late, it has come to light that in Saranda forest, Jharkhand, small group of villagers are trained in planting explosives with improvised explosives devices (IEDs). Broadly from every village handful individuals are picked up and trained in this exercise. They are followers of the Maoists, not belong to the cadre. Again, villagers in good number are taken under control and used for performing miscellaneous duties. Many volunteer to join, others are coxed or forced to join and assist the ultras. Training ground is selected right inside deep forest. On fear of police raid, training ground is shifted from place to place. Fixed duration of training is not strictly followed. In fact, depending on the urgency of the operation, often the trainees are deployed to assist the hard cores Deserters from the army and security forces are employed temporarily to train the recruits. Emphasis is given much on the physical training, weapon training, unarmed combat, field craft and use of the ground etc.

Counter-terrorism and Jungle Warfare College

Counter-terrorism and Jungle Warfare College (CTJWC) at Kankar, Chhattisgarh, was founded in 2005. A retired Brigadier from the Indian army was appointed as the first Director of the Institute. In fact, stereotyped lessons, archaic training and obsolete weaponry given to the police are far from adequate to face the extremists. It needs no reiteration that specialised training and latest weaponry are essential to tackle the burgeoning militancy. Latest jungle warfare equipments including sophisticated surveillance system, armoured watch towers, superior quality of bullet proof vests, night vision goggles, sensitive communication instruments are badly required to dog the ultras and combat them with consummate courage and diligence. Director of the Institute felt that early warning and surveillance system is highly useful to foil surprise attacks. Police stations and out posts are often victims of surprise attacks. Often they are taken unawares either not alert or unprepared to put up stubborn resistance. In one sided assault policemen are compelled to submit or face ignominious death. It is seen that often armoury is looted, and arms and ammunitions are carried away. Hence, to avert such a catastrophe, early warning and surveillance system, if introduced and practiced sincerely, may give desired dividend. In fact, early warning surveillance screen can be used around the police station premises. Any suspicious movement will reflect on the screen installed inside the police station. Broadly speaking, if the experiment brings success the police administration may adopt it ungrudgingly.

Jail-break in Dantewada District

Daring jail-break of the Dantewada district jail on December 16, 2007, escape of 298 prisoners, including 110 Maoists and loot of the armoury had dumb founded the state government. Plot was pre-planned, organised well in advance and executed with precision. Ten hard-core Maoists, 298 prisoners, including convicts and under trials out of total 373 prisoners participated in the misadventure. It was winter Sunday, before the evening meal the miscreants found it opportune to operate. On holidays, reduced number of guards used to be deployed to ensure security of the jail. Rebels over powered the guards, looted the armoury, fired indiscriminately, injured three guards and decamped with 12 SLRs and ammunitions. Date and time of the attack and escape was selected with a good deal of care. News of the jail break and escape of large number of notorious prisoners shocked everyone. Town's men apprehended that the escaped out laws might commit heinous crime and disturb safety of the peace loving people. Outrages likely to be unleashed in the area may be well-nigh unbearable. District administration was taken aback and denied any security lapse. However, a large number of security personnel were pressed into service to trace out the fugitives and apprehend them. Admittedly, the district was the Maoists hot-bed. Hence, abundant precaution and flawless security arrangement was *sine qua non* to foil any possible jail break or escape of the prisoners. The alibi of the district administration was untenable. *Prima facie*, complacency of the higher authority, lack of imagination for any untoward incident in a Maoist dominated district and monumental callousness to detail adequate security guards were the root cause of the disaster. It was suspected that many escapees had crossed the border and taken shelter in Bhutan and Bangladesh.

Weapon Supply; Link with the Policemen

Several retired police officers and serving CRPF personnel have been maintaining contact clandestinely with the link men who supplied arms and ammunitions to the Maoists. Special Task Force (STF) of Uttar Pradesh police learnt that supply of arms and ammunitions to the Maoists have been going on for the last four and half years. Several CRPF jawans and retired police personnel of UP police force were involved in this sordid racket. STF arrested a few CRPF jawans and a retired sub inspector of UP police with his two associates for supplying ammunitions and magazines of Indian Small Arms Systems (INSAS) rifles to the Maoists. The SI was posted in Rampur district and was one of the in charges of the police armoury. Ammunitions of different bores to suit different rifles used to be collected and sent to the ultras through two secret contact men. Interrogation disclosed that one Akash a civil contractor from Maunath Bhajan district and Ashis from Varanasi were the vital link between the Maoists and the CRPF jawans. Top brass of the police disclosed that the racket spread to Allahabad, Varanasi, Mirzapur, Chandoli, Shonbhadra, Jhansi, Basti and Guna districts. Officials working in armouries are involved. Indeed, UP police has soiled the good name of the police. In gory massacre of 76 CRPF personnel in Dantewada district, ammunitions were procured form UP police armouries. However, once Akash and Ashis happened to be in police net the mystery would be unearthed. Investigation did not rule out the possibility of their connection with the Maoists of West Bengal.

Illegal arms trade and mushroom growth of mini arms factories in Bihar, Ranchi, Bhopal and West Bengal is a mighty threat to the safety and security of the country. Of late, Ranchi district has turned to be a hotbed of this dangerous trade. Police has been burning midnight candle and finally nabbed several activists of the People's Liberation of India (PLFI) outfit from Tupudana, involved in illegal arms trade. For running a mini arms manufacturing factory police arrested four persons. Interrogation of the culprits revealed that Ranchi district has turned to be a safe haven for illegal sale of arms and ammunitions. In fact, arms are infiltrating into the district from Nevada and Monghyr, Bihar. Consignments are sent to the secret agents of the ultras operating in Jharkhand and Chhattisgarh who ensure safe deposit to the Maoists.

Bailadila Mine (Dantewada District)

Literary meaning of Bailadila is hump of an ox lives in dread of the Reds. Twin settlements of Bacheli and Kirandul in Bailadila range of hills located in deep in southern part of Bastar jungle. Bailadila mine produces superior quality of iron ore. National Mineral Development Corporation (NMDC) runs the mines, exports a large quantity of iron ore. Belying the pale records of other public sectors it is a profit making public sector. Complex of the NMDC is a twin mining township and about fifty thousand people live here. In fact, township is the target of Maoist attacks. On any pretext the Maoists declare bandh for 4 to 5 days continuously, stalling normal work of the plant, disrupt railway services and thereby halt dispatch of iron ore, threaten or intimidate the workers who are eager to perform duties. Maoists indulge in lawlessness and horrid violence. The Central Industrial Security Force (CISF), a para military force guard the complex and is responsible for safety and security of the plant and its employees. Dismayingly, the robust security arrangement has not deterred the ultras who often assault the complex, unleash gruesome violence and stall essential public services. Throbbed with panic and fear, the people often are compelled to take shelter in safer places.

As the Maoists intensified their atrocious activities the CISF has reinforced its man power, procured latest weaponry and equipments, improved fire power and galvanized resources. Now they possess Light Machine Guns, bullet proof watch towers, night vision glasses. In fact CISF has made preparation in befitting scale to meet the onslaught with consummate courage and resoluteness. About 1000 personnel had been deployed which is more than five times compared to the record of 2005. In February 2006, Maoists attacked and killed eight CISF jawans, looted 14 self-loading rifles and 14 tons of explosives. In October 2006, they destroyed a conveyor belt crippling production for 45 days. In April 2008, the rebels stopped two buses, forced the passengers to get down, shouted pro Maoist slogans and set the vehicles on fire. Terrified passengers were forced to walk right to their destination. In October 2009, a CISF vehicle was blown up in Bacheli mining complex killing a Sub Inspector and four jawans. In January 2009, 20 trucks owned by a private contractor were burnt. In May 2009, in Sukma, a privately owned pipeline company carrying iron ore slurry was blown apart In January 2010, two pressure bombs exploded in a pump house injuring several workers. Later the pump house was destroyed.

Financial loss of the NMDC was too high to bear. In 2009-10, Bacheli alone faced loss of rupees 480 crores. Dispatch of iron ore was badly affected for 80 days. Ultras damaged train tracks and stalled movements of trains transporting iron ore. Frequent bandh calls brought the normal life to a grinding halt. Various development programmes like construction of roads, buildings, repair of public installations etc. were suspended due to unrest. In the so called liberated zone, the Maoists had been virtually running a parallel administration. They issue instructions, extort money, hold kangaroo courts, punish or kill persons on mere suspicion. The police chief admitted that the state was forced to accept the Maoists control and domination over sizeable areas. However, steps are afoot to reclaim the areas and establish the government's authority and the rule of law. Simultaneously, welfare and development programmes have been undertaken in right earnest to improve the economy and lot of the people.

Maoist Camp in Cities for Procuring Deadly Weapons and Rocket Launchers

On the initiative of Maoist High Command Central Technical Committee was formed. Politburo member Basavraj and a central committee member, Deoji were given responsibility for consolidating it. From 2002 to 2006, technical units were established in Pune, Indore, Bhopal, Bhubaneswar and Rourkela under Sadanala Ram Krishna alias Sadula's supervision. From 2008 onwards Sadanala formed a team in Kolkata and Thane, Mumbai and started procuring raw materials and components of weapons. Some of the components were processed in local workshops in and around Kolkata. Many components were processed by local mechanics and work men who were given designs, diagrams or samples of certain parts. Several firms in Kolkata and Mumbai were contacted for the purchase of component parts and assembled tools. The finished products, assembly tools and related items were being sent to Raipur, Chhattisgarh by road transports. From Raipur consignments used to be dispatched to Dandakarnya areas and places of Maoist control including Abujhmad, the HQ of the Maoists in Chhattisgarh. Here, the weapons and land mines etc. were assembled with the help of their Mobile Assembly Units and there after distributed to other units. Maoists purchased a flat in fake name in Birati near Dum Dum airport, Kolkata and procuring and manufacturing components, diagrams of weapons and rocket launchers with the help of local engineers and skilled workers. In the locality they identified themselves as businessmen who had to travel frequently to other places for promoting business. Consignments of uniform, explosives and components of weapons used to be dispatched to Raipur regularly. Operations were controlled from Kolkata city providing logistic, financial and other supports and arranging safe hide-outs.

The National Investigating Agency raided the flat in February 2012, and during investigation seized incriminating documents, explosive materials, prohibited ammunitions, Maoist literature, several diagrams and literature on rocket launchers, weapons, and documents for transporting consignments to Raipur by road transport and cash rupees 96 lakhs 66 thousands. They also seized several finished components of rocket launchers and other area weapons (mortars) and 79 wooden crates in the godown of the transporter in Kolkata and Raipur. Transporters Preeti Road Lines and Pal Goods Transport, Raipur, were involved. NIA sent several seized items seemed to be the components of weapons along with diagram and supportive literature to the Ordinance Factory Board, Kolkata for opinion. Experts opined that those are components of rocket launchers, rocket propelled grenades, 51 mm mortars and other weapons. Maoists had been running such anti-national activities clandestinely for the last 6/7 years which has shocked the people. NIA arrested two Maoists and Dipak Kumar from the flat. In March 2012, Sadanala Ram Krishna was arrested from College Street, Kolkata. Local associates Sambhu Charan Pal and Bapi Mudi were arrested. Involvement of engineer Asim Kumar and Haranath Bhattacharjee had come to fore who used to supply design of the rocket launchers. Maoists opened the hub at Birati with their help who operated as their local contact persons. Maoists used to get grenade cells manufactured from two factories. One was located in Belilious road, Howrah and the other was in Akshay Mukherjee Road, Baranagar, Kolkata. A transport company located at Jorasako, Kolkata used to transport materials regularly to Raipur, Chhattisgarh. NIA has submitted charge sheet against the culprits before the City Sessions Court on August 23, 2012.

Institute of IED Management, Pune

Training Institute for neutralising Improvised Explosives Devices (IEDs) and land mines has been established at Pune, Maharastra, at the initiative of the CRPF. In fact para-military forces have lost 130 personnel during last five years being victims of IEDs, explosions and land mine blasts. In addition, many are badly wounded, maimed, handicapped or physically crippled. In fact, in Chhattisgarh, all operations are made on foot. Dirt tracks are laced with land mines which cause ninety percent of average 100 deaths of the security personnel every year. On March 23, 2012 at Gadchiroli, Maharashtra, a CRPF vehicle was ripped apart due to explosion and 13 CRPF men were killed. IED and land mine blasts have taken heavy toll of security personnel in Chhattisgarh. CRPF has deployed 70000 thousands combatants in Maoist strife torn areas. They are anxious to enhance its capability to strengthen anti-IED operations, neutralise land mines and reduce casualty by suitably training the rank and file. For that purpose the above training institute is opened to train the personnel to neutralise the menace. The object of training is to train the personnel in identifying, neutralising and handling explosive, the IEDs and landmines and frustrate the sinister design of the ultras. Maoists secretly and craftily plant landmines or explosives beneath roads, culverts and bridges. Sometimes it is put 12 to 15 feet below the surface. CRPF possess limited persons trained in this highly skillful discipline to identify land mines or explosives concealed under the ground and kept in readiness to blast either directly or through the remote control device. Hence, to overcome such ordeal and to train sufficient number of persons to earn expertise in this trade more than 200 retired junior commissioned officers and noncommissioned officers from the army were hired on contract basis. In this pursuit, the CRPF hired experts on contract from the army-run college of Military Training. Indian army has a big establishment, like Engineering Corps to handle, detect and neutralise mines and explosives. They clear mine fields efficiently and foil the enemy's' intriguing plan. Evidently, under tutelage of the army experts the trainees will be shaped well to assist the comrades to counter the Maoists. It was expected that the army instructors' experience and skill is likely to be an additional advantage for combating CRPF engaged in an obstinate fight and proxy war in Maoist hot bed. Unfortunately, the hired personnel were not able to show the kind of result that was expected of them. Many CRPF officials who received training under them were not satisfied and opined that their capability and performance was below the standard. They recommended that their contract should be terminated. Secondly, they should be replaced by the young CRPF officers who had already undergone training in the institute to perform duties of instructors. The dismal performance and result has upset the authority of the CRPF. In fact, services of two dozens of hired ex-army personnel were discontinued. In short, whatever may be the reason, the ex-army personnel perhaps were unable to show their best under varied environment, different culture, command and control.

Liberated Zone in Chhattisgarh; Preparation to Flush Out Ultras

Admittedly, out of 620 districts in India approximately ninety five districts are affected by the Maoist terror. Bastar region, ten times the size of Kashmir valley, includes the Maoist liberated zone—the sprawling out bounds, a sizeable portion of 40000 sq km, and the so called liberated territory. Here the head quarter of the Maoists the "Abujhmarh" (the unknown forest) is functioning. Bastar region is India's richest territory in mineral deposits, yet it is home for its poorest people. A paradox may stir sentiment of the progressive people. Nevertheless, assurance of rule of law, economic development and social justice needed to be watched. A sharp-edged conflict between new India and the other India was about to start. Sixty thousands security personnel would slug it out in the Amazon like jungle. A nationality co-ordinated multi-state conglomerate of different armed forces contingents would elbow its way into the rebel's strong hold, where governance and rule of law did not exist. Indeed, longest anti-insurgency battle was about to start. The state was determined to demolish 42 years extremist domain. Panic-stricken inhabitants lost presence of mind, spend moments in abject fear awaiting a dooms day. They have been desperately running from pillar to posts for collecting identity cards, which would prove their genuineness and save them from merciless torture from the angry and jaded policemen. National commander, a top cop, stated, "A multi-pronged approach is under way. It is a retrievable war. It has gone beyond repair."

In Bastar region, especially, in southern portion, the Maoists have established their de facto rule. Semblance of the state's authority and rule of law has practically disappeared. Here, writs of the Maoists are paramount. Guns in the hands of gun-toting ultras might roar at any time on any pretext. Bullet ridden body of a guiltless villager might roll on the ground without receiving any chance to prove his innocence. In the so called liberated zone of Dantewada and Bijapur districts the

Maoists have been running schools, distribute grains to the villagers, repair dams for irrigating lands and collect taxes. Villagers were forced to pay levy for buying medicines, clothes, provide shelter and food for the ultras. Demand for rupees five hundred if not honoured, a boy or a girl from the family has to be spared to join the Maoist cadre. In fact, it is as good as paying tax if a member of a family is spared and enlisted in the Maoist cadre. According to police, in many remote areas of Bijapur and Dantewada districts a cop is unable to visit for fear of attack and annihilation. In Dantewada district 644 tribal villages were wiped out and land remained under control of the Maoists. The ultra out-fit planned to redistribute land to the villagers who submitted to them. All government establishments were either abandoned or withdrawn. Government run schools, post offices, health centers were taken over by the Maoists. The police stations somehow functioned without facilities of telephone, electricity or communication. Wireless set for limited time could contact the district police HQ. Cops of the police station were practically isolated, mentally prepared for any eventuality and helplessly submitted to their lot. On November 2, 2007, the Maoists in good number laid an ambush at Pamed, Dantewada. The outnumbered policemen frantically asked for reinforcement. But no force could be dispatched as the nearest contingent available was at a distance of 200 kms. Hapless eleven cops were killed tragically. Three police stations located in remote areas might be attacked and over run at any time. Around National High Way 43, five camps were opened under the protection of CRPF. A drive was made to recruit boys and girls as Special Police Officer (SPO). They were part of Salwa Judum, deployed to guard the camps and patrol the areas armed with .303 rifles. The youngsters responded well to join the Salwa Judum. SPOs were paid monthly remuneration from the public exchequer. Indeed, it was a positive incentive and financial support to them and to their families. However, eventually Salwa Judum was declared illegal and unconstitutional by the Apex Court.

Right up to 2007, in Bastar region, the Maoists were formidable. In the so called liberated zone their writs were absolute. Police and administration was in limbo of oblivion. State government was puzzled and lost presence of mind. The union government adopted the policy of "masterly inactivity." In fact from January to October 2007, 134 security personnel were killed. In a battle enemy is known and identifiable. Here, the invisible enemy mixing with local populace and enjoying their patronage have been operating. Unfortunately, the local people under influence of the Maoists often misguide the security forces. Maoists are cunning and pitiless, well conversant with the terrain, can easily give a slip to the security forces if attacked or surrounded. Truly, the security forces have been contesting the undeclared war facing numerous constraints. Yet they are firm in their duties showing indomitable will, indefatigable energy, elephantine strength and single minded devotion Fortunately, as events moved apace, deployment of para military forces, comprehensive strategy and economic development in the areas have considerably improved the situation. Broadly speaking, major portion of the so called liberated zone has been reclaimed and rule of law has been restored.

Importantly, the Union Home Minister P. Chidambaram spelt out the centre's two-pronged strategy of police action and development. First, armed offensive to push the rebels away is only one part of the strategy since they will not allow development. The other is to deliver quick and heavy doses of governance to the people. The state governments are told to keep the personnel and equipments ready to move in, once the security forces are able to restore civil administration in the trouble-torn areas. In pursuance of the policy, fifty thousand security forces are mobilised for five states. In Bastar region, in addition to state armed battalions, sufficient para military forces are deployed. Personnel are educated and trained to undergo a capsule course to know the custom, ethos, culture, traditions and language of the tribal populace. Critics said that Bastar is preparing for a war. Truly, a multi-pronged approach, joint and co-ordinated operations are expected to produce the desired result. Supremacy of the Maoists in southern Bastar region of Chhattisgarh, broadly, the so called liberated zone, is a formidable challenge before the security forces. Areas highly inaccessible and deep inside the jungle, known in Maoist parlance as "Abujmarh", are being used as temporary HQ. Special training for handling modern weapons, rocket launchers, mortars, land mines and explosives used to be imparted here. Recruits from other states were sent here for undergoing training. Security forces made preparation is consummate scale. They are specially equipped to operate in the jungle and hills for protracted offensives. Several helipads are constructed in strategic places for quicker movements, supplying provisions, equipments, arms, ammunitions and evacuating sick and wounded persons. GPS gadgets, satellite phones, night vision instruments are given to the contingents to aid patrolling, fast movement and prompt communication. SPOs are recruited to assist the security forces for collecting intelligence, and perform duties of guides.

Exulted comrade Koteshwar Rao alias Kishanji stated, "We will overthrow the Indian government much before 2050." He added that the Maoists had their own army and with their help they would capture the state much before 2050 A.D. Reacting to Kishanji,s wishful thinking the then Union Home Secretary G.K. Pillai stated that they were free to dream. However dialogue with the Maoists was welcome if they abjured violence. Interestingly, mystery of the comrade's self-deluding rhetoric for over throwing the democratically elected government and capturing power by 2050 or earlier needs critical analysis. In fact, positive response from the able bodied unemployed youngsters hailing from violence-hit rural areas to join the Maoist cadre and the movement is a source of substantial cheer for the top brass of the out-fit. In pursuance of attracting more unemployed youths in the cadre, the Maoist out-fit has been shelling out Rs.3000 per month as a salary for a cadre. In addition, a cut from the extortion money collected is also distributed as an incentive. As a matter of fact, abject poverty and lack of employment opportunity has been compelling many youths to join the cadre. Maoists are financially sound since their ill-gotten collection exceeds rupees 1500 crores annually. In the Red corridor, the Maoists have established their own rule. The state's authority and administration is either collapsed or stand still. The innocent and peace loving villagers, therefore, feel that the Maoist rule in the long run is sure to shine brilliantly and the state's authority will not re-appear. Hence, stark reality of poverty and unemployment force the frustrated youths to join the cadre. They are aware of the risk, yet three thousand rupees per month for a hungry family is a God-sent blessing. A large number of surrenders and desertions from the out-fit are unflinching testimony that lucre of monetary incentive compels them to join the terrorist cadre. True, after enlistment they are trained and indoctrinated in CPI (Maoist) ideology, yet often it fails to tame them. Here, the question of survival is paramount. Self and the family's two square meals and livelihood is the top priority. Fear of death, rigor of hard and regimented life in forest, police's torture, punishment and the long arm of the law often dissuade them to take up arms and participate in the macabre festival of death. Nevertheless, they want to get rid of poverty and in that pursuit any avenue may be fair or foul is suitable for their existence.

Comrade Kishanji claimed that they had strongest base in Chhattisgarh, "Old Bastar is our main base and five districts are under our control. We have one lakh militia in Chhattisgarh." He hinted that a paradigm shift in their aggressive operations had been producing desired result. From guerrilla attacks to launching mobile attacks was a part of the new strategy. In mobile attacks, 400-500 Maoists encircled a team of 100 or more security personnel, attacked them with full fury and wiped them out. Development projects were taken up by the government to attract local people and secure their support. It is paradoxical that in absence of the State's power and authority, execution of any project is a hollow dream. It would be hindered at every level. As a matter fact, destruction prior to development is desirable to achieve the goal. This is in keeping with the motto and ideology of the Maoists.

Escalated Violence in Maoist-Dominated Districts

The year 2007, witnessed highest number of casualty in the police and security forces in Chhattisgarh and Jharkhand together. It accounted for the country's 68.16 percent of the Maoist related incidents and 76.42 percent of total casualties amongst the security personnel and civilians. Indeed, Maoist related incidents and casualty of the security personnel indicated above high-lights the magnitude of the Maoist violence in Chhattisgarh. As many as 11 districts of the States were badly affected by Maoist violence. In fact, casualty inflicted on the security forces has surpassed past records. Meticulous planning for the operations, perfect and timely execution was really stunning. Secondly, distinct shift in strategy, attacks in good strength, sustained and continued exchange of fire for hours together discarding previous hit and run tactics and their sparkling success must have floundered the strategists of the MHA, police and the para military forces. Swift change of the Maoist strategies often puts security forces in disadvantage. Inter-state coordination exercises periodically worked out in Delhi often proved inadequate. State government had banned the Maoist out-fit. Ban order was further extended up to April 12, 2010 under Section I; Sub-section (3) of the Chhattisgarh Special Public Security Act 2005. It included six satellite units of the state, (1) Dandakaranya Adivasi Kishan Masdoor Sangh, (2) Krantikari Adivasi Mahila Sangh, (3) Krantikari Adivasi Balak Sangh, (4) Krantikari Kishan Committee, (5) Mahila Mukti Manch, (6) Santang Sarkar. The Union Government had banned the CPI (Maoist) under Unlawful Activities (Prevention).

Modus Operandi of the Maoists in Chhattisgarh

Significantly, the Maoists' *modus operandi* is important to know and to chalk out plan and strategy in curbing out the outfit's aggressive activities. In addition to the standard guide line like selecting a sanctuary in remote and inaccessible areas, place of operation should be far away from the sanctuary. The ultras must earn good will and trust of the local populace. The out-fit introduces new methods and operational technique after carefully studying the local conditions, resources, watch and surveillance of the police and sentiment of the local people. In fact, the hit and run tactics adopted in the past has been replaced by ambush, direct and surprise attacks in heavy strength to over power and wipe out the security forces. Secondly, they use human shield to outwit the security personnel and neutralise fire. A good number of villagers including minors and women are kept in front, hide themselves behind the innocent villagers and thereby make the advance of the security personnel ineffective. As the security forces want to avoid casualty on the civilians, the Maoists, if surrounded, try to escape taking cover of the human shield. Thirdly, the Maoists put a herd of cows and calves in front and take cover behind them. Maoists know that people respect cows and Hindus take them as one the religious symbols. Therefore, security forces will not hurt or kill a cow while chasing or counter attacking the ultras. This weakness is shrewdly exploited by the Maoists. Fourthly, under coercion minor boys and girls are recruited, trained and enlisted in the cadre contrary to the wish of the parents. The parents are afraid of the Maoists' threat and ugly consequences if their demand is not adhered to. Therefore, the aggrieved parents do not report the matter to the police. This savage practice has been helping the Maoists to enrich the cadre by bubbling youths and fresh blood. To get the hint of the security forces advance, they use the children who graze cattle in the field to alert the Maoists. Small detonators are fixed in arrows. The cowherds are instructed to shoot arrow aiming top of a tree. It produces mild explosion. Sound of explosion is a signal for the ultras that the security personnel are nearby or approaching them. They use poisoned tipped arrows against the cops and security men. Numerous booby traps are laid. In making booby traps, they follow the technique adopted by the Viet Cong Guerrillas. In addition, tracks are laced with land mines. All operations are made on foot. Hence, patrolling, raids, encirclement or drive for hunt by the security forces avoiding or neutralising booby traps and land mines is not only risky but time taking. Senior police officers said that ninety percent of casualty of policemen is due to land mines blasts. In an average 100 policemen are the victims of land mines every year. In many areas, within 100 kms there is no police station. It has no telephone, no electricity and no other means of communication. Roads are imaginary or in rainy season just navigable. In short, a primitive condition is prevailing in rural areas hindering good governance.

Relief to the Landless Persons by Ultras

Maoists are keen to earn goodwill and support of the poverty stricken people of the locality. Importantly, in areas dominated by them, they have taken recourse to so-called land reforms and enforcing provisions of land Ceiling Act and Money Lending Abolition Act. In Surguja and Raighar districts of Madhya Pradesh (now Jharkhand) they have followed it up and earned support and sympathy of many landless and poor people. They issued notices to landlords having vast chunk of land and asked them to implement the Land Ceiling Act and distribute surplus land among the poor villagers. They succeeded in getting surplus land distributed from three big landlords of two villages. The local administration admitted that the Ultras had asked the big landlords to keep land which they could cultivate and distribute the remaining surplus lands to the common villagers. The outfit formed two village level committees to pin-point the details of wealth and holdings of the landlords. They moved in villages and studied land holdings of the rich land lords. In Kosmai and Chandosi villages about four kms from Palamu district, the committees have shown positive progress. Admittedly, the land distribution drive has made a dent among the landless and deprived people. Much exultation was noticed among the land less who welcomed the move. In short, good wishes of the poor and backward people showered on the extremists knew no bounds. (*The Times of India*, December 28, 2001.)

Reaction of the World Nations on Increased Growth of the Maoists

The United Nations has expressed concern for recruiting and deploying minors by the Maoists in India. The Annual Report prepared by the Secretary General Ban Ki-moon disclosed that several creditable reports indicate that children are being abducted or forcibly recruited from the schools The Report is going to be submitted to the Security Council for necessary action. Maoists plead that children are used only as messengers and informers. But in reality they are trained to use non-lethal and lethal weapons including land mines, Report elaborated that children are being used recklessly by the armed Maoists in many districts of Chhattisgarh for hazardous and risky works.

Unprecedented growth of the extremists, establishment of the Red Corridor or The Compact Revolutionary Zone (CRZ), unabated violence and bloodshed has come to the notice of the world community and the United Nations. Merger of the PW and the MCC has given fresh impetus to the Maoist movements. Many pockets have turned to be the liberated zone where writs of the Maoists loom large. The United Nations on the ground of maintaining peace has been carefully monitoring the activities of the Maoist outfit. As increased militancy is a global phenomenon, the UN Security Council analyses the entire gamut, pin-point the flows and advise the affected country to deal with the problem with consummate ability, determination and mobilising resources. In fact, the UN's advice is not an interference or encroachment into the domain of a sovereign country. The Counter Terrorism Committee was set up in the UN after the terrorist attack in the USA in September 11, 2001.

Watching the step forward of the terrorists, the Counter Terrorism Committee of the UN has prepared a report and submitted it to the Security Council. In addition, a group of delegates from the UN visited India, met and interacted with officials across the security spectrum. They studied the situations from Indian perspective, exchanged ideas with persons who are directly involved in handling the problems. The draft report prepared is a revolting disclosure on short comings in tackling the extremist menace. It also pointed out at the deficient counter-terrorism structures and how it is disarrayed. Observation reveals that by sheer geography India is one of the biggest theatres of terror group in the world. At least its 70000 people have lost their lives on account of terrorism. Majority casualty is in Jammu and Kashmir. The Committee felt that India has no comprehensive counter terrorism legislation. Two anti-terror laws, TADA and POTA lacked purposeful teeth and subsequently both were repealed. In fact, in absence of suitable and effective counter terrorism legislation the long arm of the law is unable to circumscribe the hydra-headed monster. Secondly, Indian law enforcement structure lack a national counter-terrorism data-base, up and running data-base which facilitates to know or get information about terrorist related events, presence of the new suspects, movement of the ultras and other vital ever changing information. Lastly, the delegation found major gaps between the work of the prosecution agencies and the investigating units at the union as well as in state level.

Law and Order—State Subject, Delayed Trials, Porous Border

Combating terrorism is generally within the purview of the states since law and order is the state subject. Union government may provide required assistance on the state's request or consent. Truly, prosecutions against the terrorists pend in the courts indefinitely. Want of expeditious trial for various reasons, half hearted or indifference to just enforcement of the Court's verdicts often undermines the authority of the courts and the law. It nullifies the impact of the law and emboldens the law breakers to defy the law. Interestingly, foreign or foreigner hands working in patronising and escalating terrorism is often used shrewdly as an alibi by the interested persons or organisations which delays investigation and trials pending in the courts. India's land border is 15100 kms and coast line is 7500 kms long. Porous border is a threat to its safety and security. Uninterrupted infiltration crossing the border illegally outwitting the border sentinels is a gigantic problem. Border check posts are insufficient, not suitably equipped and deficient in communication. The committee on behalf of the UNO felt that India's counter terrorism structures are unsatisfactory which need immediate overhaul. Report is alarming that India is not adequately prepared to take on the terrorists, disarray them and make it a terrorist free country.

New Cult of the Maoists; Gonds Under the Influence of the Extremists

The Maoists has been emphasising on a new cult, "The Democratic Revolution." Its object is to seize the state power by protracted armed struggle. However, struggle against feudalism, imperialism, capitalism and bureaucratic outrages will continue. Nationalities fighting for self-determination will be supported. Untiring effort will be made to mobilise and organise the weaker sex as a formidable force of the revolution.

The Gond tribe is the main tribal community in Bastar region. Both male and female enjoy equal right in the society. Their stable food is rice. Drinking juice from "Mahua" seeds is a part of their culture. They suffer from abject poverty, diseases, exploitation, and high handedness of the government officials. Majority of them are illiterate, never enrolled in a school, or fought for their rights as citizens. Unemployment is the main problem of the community. Light of the so called economic reforms and developments have hardly reached their villages. Children are half naked and bare footed, have not joined the school for study. Villagers are unable to tell when they were born and what their present age is. They are unable to think of their future and how they can improve their lot. In such a condition, the Maoists easily gain them over assuring immunity from hunger, poverty and outrages of the richer classes, money lenders and subordinate public servants. Being simple and unassuming people they are not aware of diplomacy or trickery, they follow the ultras and often give them shelter, food and carry out their instructions unhesitatingly. They do not know the difference between the Maoists and the present democratic government. Election or casting votes is practically a festival for them. From direct experience I am inclined to narrate an incident that it provides an opportunity of marry making and drinking on the occasion of exercising franchise. Political parties through the activists visit the tribal villages, cultivate the Mukhia (head man) giving money and liquor bottles so that the voters of the village vote for a particular candidate without any deviation. On the polling day, party activists would bring a truck and with the help of the Mukhia, transport the voters to the respective polling booths. After casting votes they would be transported back to the village. I asked the members of a group who returned to village after casting votes in their language, "You went to cast votes, what you received in return." They exuberantly replied, "Ayyga (Sir), we received one bottle of liquor and rupees ten per head." Indeed, their joy knew no bounds. Many of them profusely praised the leaders and the activists for such a grace shown to them. But I was dismayed seeing the exploit and abuse of the democracy.

A few critics and local journalists commented that the entire nation is responsible for the sad plight of the tribal. After independence, the government left tribal unattended and uncared for. Ironically, substantial fund is allocated by the planning commission under plan head for various programmes, projects, for popularising education and urbanisation of the back ward areas. Unfortunately, it hardly trickles down to the right level. Deputy Chief Minister of Bihar in an informal chat told me that only 28 per cent of the sanctioned amount reaches the grass root level. Lion share of the fund is misappropriated or siphoned away at various levels. Hence, exercise on economic development remains in paper and suffering of the people continues without any desired relief. Of late, union government has sanctioned substantial fund for developing the tribal areas so that the Maoist activities can be curbed and the innocent populace are rescued from the influence of the ultras. In fact, marshalling of developmental projects in remote tribal areas has been facing numerous obstacles. A significant portion of the fund placed at the disposal of the contractors or suppliers for execution of the projects is going into the pockets of the Maoists. They demand levy on every project and under threat collect a beefy amount. Consequently, projects are either not executed or abandoned on the mid way. Pensive analysis reveals that poverty, poor education and unemployment are main hindrances of the tribal community. Hence, the government has to take exhaustive measures to identify malady and solve problems which will help to disassociate the Gonds from the clutch of the left-wing extremists.

Die-hard Maoists and Insurmountable Problems

In Chhattisgarh in 2006, altogether 715 Maoist related incidents were reported and 388 persons were killed. In 2007, in 582 incidents 369 persons had fallen to the Maoists' bullets. However, from July 30, 2008, to July 30, 2009, total 122 persons were killed in 364 incidents reported. In 2010-11, intensity of the Maoist attacks and loss of life of security personnel shot up. On April 6, CRPF's 76 personnel including 2 officers were ambushed and killed in Dantewada district On May 17, 2010, 36 security personnel including 12 Special police officers were killed in the same district. On June 29, 2010 in Narayanpur district 27 CRPF personnel were killed. In June 9, 2011, in land mine blasts, 18 security personnel lost lives. On August 18, 2011 in Bijapur district.11 security personnel were annihilated. Admittedly, the Maoists were very active from 2007 to 2011, and killing spree during the period was a clear testimony of their success and lack-luster performance of the security forces including the CRPF.

Anti-government propaganda through the frontal out-fits created an impression among the radicals, free-thinkers, independent and spirited personalities in favour of the extremists. Again, since support and sympathy of the urban mass has been decaying, the Maoists thought it prudent to infiltrate into the NGOs, human right groups, students organisations, labour unions etc., and try to build a favorable opinion on the Maoists' goal and idea of the Peoples' war etc. In fact, they were keen for developing contact with the people and thereby popularise their movement. Police of Chhattisgarh seized several documents from the Maoists which contained detailed plan, strategies and guide lines for infiltrating into the NGOs, human right units, students units, labour unions etc. Documents reveal that the Maoists have stepped up activities in that direction as well as antigovernment propaganda to frustrate the anti-Maoist offensives by the security forces. Politburo members Kobad Gandhi was arrested from Delhi. He and Peasant Bose were seen moving frequently in Cochin and Hyderabad. Four other members were arrested from Ranchi, Patna, Kolkata and Rourkela. General Secretary, Ganapathy was suffering from knee ailment. A tour operator of Raipur was arrested who admitted that he had transported Ganapati and Peasant Bose from Raipur to border of Baster jungle many times. He had no opportunity to identify them since their photos were either not published or displayed in public places. It was not clear if the police really possessed photos of the Maoist leaders. In early 2008, the state police seized a video cassette. It contained details of the Maoist Party Congress held in Bheem Bandh, district Jumai in Bihar, in 2007. Photos of Ganapati and several other front rank leaders were available in the video cassette. However, the Maoists anticipated large scale offensives in Chhattisgarh as the security forces are trying to reclaim the so called liberated areas and establish rule of law. Maoists hiding in urban areas had unleashed high falutin antigovernment propaganda to discredit the initiatives taken by the security forces. On August 6, 2009, 18 out-fits including those who nurse soft corner for the Maoists held a secret meeting in Delhi to discuss, highlight and accuse the security forces for violation of human rights. In fact, it was a ploy to curb the offensives planned by the security forces. It was nothing but a diplomatic trickery to demoralise the police and the security forces so that their indomitable will, flinty resoluteness and high morale to neutralise the ultras either to receive a set back or is reduced. Among the outfits, Democratic Students Union, Peoples' Democratic Front of India, Revolutionary Democratic Front participated in the meeting. Importantly, Nepali Maoist leaders, Pushpa Kamal Dahal alias Prachanda stated, "Indian Maoist is ideologically the same as their Nepali counterpart. Politically, we are the same." He added that the state's repression on the Maoists and so-called operation Green hunt in India has to be stopped. Problems can be solved only through dialogues and negotiations. He admitted that the Nepali Maoists had a relationship with the CPI (Maoist) when they had been operating from underground.

On October 29, 2001, PW held a convention in Rajnandgaon district, near border of Maharashtra and passed a resolution to step up violent activities in different parts of Chhattisgarh, adjoining Jharkhand and Bihar. It was followed up and spurt in violence marred peace and tranquility of the state. Killing of two policemen in a land mine blast in Bijapur district confirmed expansionary activities. Resolution passed in the convention iterating that area of influence had to be widened and if needed, rival extremist groups had to be wiped out. District police raided a hide out where convention was being held and after 14 hours long encounter killed one commander, seized documents, strategy papers and copies of resolution both in Hindi and English. On December 12, 2001, in Bhagwanpur village, Surguja district MCC held a kangaroo court and tried 3 suspects for four hours in presence of about 5000 people. The suspects were charged for extorting money misusing the name of the outfit. Finally, they were held guilty and area commander of the MCC Mandeep Singh shot them dead in presence of the gathering.

Indeed, highest number of casualties in police and central forces deployed in Chhattisgarh in combating the Maoists was reported in 2007. Law and order being the state subject the central government was lukewarm to the growing terrorism in the state. The then Union Home Minister Shivraj Patil was unresponsive to the state's problems to face the ultras. Frankly speaking, the union government and the states have, for too long, played "passing the pillow" when it comes to take on the extremists effectively. However, as the situation was falling through the fingers, finally the Prime Minister Manmohan Singh felt the heat and described Maoist terror as, "a virus that needs to be chocked and crippled." His alarm bugle provoked four Maoist torn states to share information and co-ordinate each other to fight the menace. The distinctive character of the Maoist movement which is based on ideological terrorism has hardly been assessed from wider perspective. Truly, it is a socio-economic-political problem, therefore, it is improper to handle assuming it purely a law and order matter. In our national upsurge militant nationalism was welcomed to drive away the colonial rule. Hence, it is imperative that the dimension of the Maoist uprising has to be viewed and tackled from wider perspective. It needs no reiteration that the "compact revolutionary zone" is a reality and has been gaining momentum. Therefore, before it gains the shape of a mighty phantom both Union and the state governments have to handle it with consummate zeal and determination. However, finally, the union government woke up. In August 2007, at a meeting of the National Security Council held in the capital, several points having direct bearing on the problem were discussed National Security Advisor M.K. Narayanan and Union Home Secretary Madhukar Gupta after discussion chalked out a set of guide lines for the states. By October 2007, a blueprint to wage a war against the Maoists was expected to be finalised. The union government decided to pump sufficient fund and fire power to reclaim areas presently was under the Maoists' domination. In the first round, eight districts across four states were identified for focusing anti-Maoist operations combined with a high pitched developmental programme. Centre would fund for major expansion of social infrastructure and arrange increased police presence and equipments. A planned process of de-ruralisation and simultaneous urbanisation, industrialisation and purposeful public services should be initiated. Later, the new Union Home Minister P. Chidambaram reiterated that the state governments have greater responsibility and role in tackling the Maoists than the centre. According to the mandate, the center's role is to provide para-military forces to the states for carrying out anti-Maoist operation.

A few instances mentioned below will throw light on the Maoists' robust gain and the police and administration's monumental callousness and wonky performance to disarray the outlaws.

1. On March 15, 2007, In Dantewada district, a police camp was stormed by 300 Maoists. After protracted gun battle 55 policemen were killed. It was learnt that ammunitions ran short and therefore the police men had to surrender helplessly. The spot was near the border of Andhra Pradesh. Maoists looted weapons and escaped to Andhra Pradesh.
2. On October 29, 2007, in an attack five policemen were killed in Pamalway area, Bijapur district.
3. On November 2, 2007, a 17 member police team from Pamed police station, Bijapur district was in a search operation. A strong group of Maoists attacked the party, In exchange of fire 15 police men were killed.
4. On November 29, 2007, at Konta, Dantewada district, close to border of Andhra Pradesh a land mine blast ripped through a jeep killing ten policemen. The victims belonged to Mizo armed police battalion. As Mizos are good in jungle warfare they were specially deployed in Bastar region. Explosion was so powerful that flung parts of the mutilated bodies were thrown to 300 to 400 meters away from the spot. Weapons of the deceased were carried away by the Maoists.

On February 18, 2008, Maoists ambushed a police party near Tarkel village under Mirtur police station in Bijapur district. In an encounter lasted about two hours three police men, three CRPF men and three ultras were killed. Maoists were in olive green uniform and looted the weapons of the dead. In another encounter in Bhairamgarh police station area of the same district ten ultras including three woman Maoists were killed. When reinforcement was proceeding towards the spot another encounter took place near Easmeta jungle. On September 4, 2008, a jeep with CRPF and police men was proceeding from Samri Kusmi. A landmine near village Chunchuna hit the vehicle killing 3 CRPF and a cop and wounded six persons. On August 29, 2008, a vehicle carrying security personnel proceeding from Konda to Narayangarh was blown up and killed six CRPF and five cops including a sub Inspector of police. On September 29, 2008, at village Marikodar under Mardoom police station, district Danteweda, a land mine hit one of the vehicles of the convoy and killed Deputy Commandant of the CRPF and three personnel. On October 5, 2008, in Narayanpur district one cop was killed in a land mine blast. On April 9, 2009, in an ambush in Dantewada district, a Deputy Commandant of the CRPF was killed and 14 cops were wounded.

On April 10, 2009, in Chintagufa area about 100 Maoists attacked a CRPF patrol, in a prolonged gun battle for three hours nine CRPF men including an officer were killed and eight were injured. Three Maoists were also killed. On April 12, 2009, the Maoists planted a land mine under a culvert over Gorala nala, in Bijapur district. When attempt was made to defuse, it exploded and killed one CRPF personnel, a cop and two villagers. On that day, the Maoists fired at the chopper carrying the Director General of the CRPF. However, it landed safely in Dantewada district. On May 6, 2009, one JCO of the CRPF, a cop, five SPOs, and four others total eleven persons were killed in a landmine blast near Sirguda village, Dantewada district. They were returning to the base camp after delivering ration to Bhaji police station.

On July 12, 2009, at Madanwada, Rajnandangaon district, two CRPF personnel went behind a bush to relieve themselves were killed. A convoy of security personnel rushed towards the spot. They came under heavy fire. About 200 Maoists took part in the gun battle which lasted for three hours and 25 police men were killed. Supdt of Police of the district Vinod Kumar Choubay and SHO of Madanwada were proceeding towards the spot were ambushed and killed. After an hour at Sitagaon, 60 km away from the district HQ, in a land mine blast six policemen were killed. It was an ill-fated day for the police. A pall of gloom hung over the police and district administration. Admittedly, morale of the force received a mighty jolt.

Border road organisation started road construction work at village Modakpal, district Bijapur. CRPF personnel were deployed to protect the workers engaged in construction work. On October 20, 2008, a CRPF patrol was attacked by 70/80 armed Maoists. They triggered a powerful land mine. In a protracted gun battle twelve CRPF men were killed and six were wounded critically. A Maoist in uniform was killed. The wounded jawans were air lifted for better treatment. The incident demoralised the police personnel and the district administration. Many cops declined to work in Maoist hit areas and refused to join the duty post. Several were suspended for disobedience of order. However, election for the state Legislative Assembly was held properly in spite of violence and attempt to disrupt it.

On October 31, 2008, in between Remaband and Gulumpodo village, district

Narayanpur, when a police party was returning to the base camp, the Maoists triggered a land mine blast resulting in, 17 security personnel were wounded. On November 25, 2008, after performing election duties a police party was returning to the HQ. The Maoists triggered a powerful land mine near Mardapal and Kondagaon areas, Bastar district. The deadly blast killed seven policemen of the special task force and injured two cops. On December 6, 2008, a police contingent attacked a camp of the Maoists in Kanker district and after gun battle they killed two Maoists including a female ultra. Police seized a huge cache of arms and ammunitions. In another incident Maoists suspected a person, named Avinash as police informer and murdered him slitting his throat. On May 11, 2009, near Risagaon–Mandgiri hillock at Dhamtari, about 150 Maoists ambushed a convoy of 3 vehicles. In a fierce encounter12 police men and a civilian were killed. On June 20, 2009, five CRPF personnel were killed and 10 were injured in a land mine blast near village Kokonara, district Dantewada.

Baliram Kashyap, a former MP from Bharatiya Janata Party and his family members were in the hit list of the Maoists. They supported the Salwa Judum which irked the Maoists. On September 26, 2009, his two sons went to the temple for offering prayer and puja. While coming out of the temple the Maoists fired at them. Both were hit by bullets. Tansen aged 33 died in the hospital and the other recovered after prolonged treatment. On January 11, 2010 four armed Maoists including two women were killed in an encounter at Jagargunda forest, Dantewada district. In fact, the police organised an operation called 'Hill Grant' in Dantewada district. Again in September 2009, operation "Red Hunt" was initiated in the same district. Relentless combing operations succeeded in killing thirty Maoists. However, one Assistant Commandant and six elite commandos of the CRPF were killed. Police arrested six Maoists on November 27, 2009 from Jharabahi village and three from Benur area and seized a huge quantity of explosives and Maoist literature. CRPF and police jointly demolished a Maoist camp in Kokoda Juganar jungle under Bade Donger police station and recovered a large quantity of ammunitions, explosives, grenades, detonators, personal computer, tents, clothing, medicine etc. Joint forces defused two powerful improvised explosive devices from Kankar district.

Assembly Election in 2013

Maoists gave a boycott call for the Assembly election in 2013. Being the Maoist torn areas, polling was conducted from 7 am to 3 pm. under tight security. In 90 constituencies 143 candidates were in fray. Eighty five thousand police and para-military forces were deployed for election duties. For the first phase 4142 polling booths were set up. Indeed, the voters ignored the boycott call and turned out in good number to exercise their right of franchise. First phase of election held on November 11, 2013, in 12 constituencies in Bastar division and six constituencies in Rajnandgaon district, 70 per cent voters cast their votes braving the Maoist threat. CRPF personnel were killed in a blast in Dantewada district. After exchange of fire IEDs were recovered from places closed to polling booths. On November 12, 2013, Maoists attacked a BSF convoy. In a land mine blast two BSF personnel and a driver of the vehicle were killed near Kerlapal camp in Sukma district. In a separate attack a Dy Commandant of the CRPF received injuries. In a blast in Kanker district, a CRPF jawan was wounded. The second phase of polling was bloated in lesser violence. However, centering polling, twenty six violent incidents and two deaths were reported. Despite sporadic unrest, turn out of the voters was highly satisfactory. Importantly, in Lok Sabha poll 2009, there were 125 attacks and 24 deaths in Maoist ridden states. In Chhattisgarh alone, there were 47 attacks and 7 deaths.

Chhattisgarh, a Hunting Ground for the Maoists

From July 2007 to July 2010 state had suffered from 1948 Maoist attacks, in which 435 security personnel, 418 civilians and 75 SPOs were killed. About 95 per cent of casualties reported from the Bastar region. The state demanded rupees 4553 crores for development of the Maoist torn districts. The Union Home Minister stated on August 4, 2010. before the Rajya Sabha Upper House) that Planning Commission was going to finalise The Integrated Action Plan (IAP) for development of Naxal hit areas. It would cover 83 Naxal affected districts in seven states. He indicated that financial package of rupees 13742 crores was proposed to be sanctioned for 35 worse hit districts by phases.

On April 6, 2010, a coy of CRPF of 62 Bn, under a Dy Commandant was returning to the base camp after routine patrolling. At about 6 AM in the midst of a jungle in Dantewada district about 500 Maoists ambushed them. In fact, the surprise was complete. Dy Commandant, one Assistant Commandant and 76 men were killed and ten were preciously wounded. Arms including LMGs, 2" Morters, were looted from the dead and wounded persons. The history of para military forces has not witnessed such a ghastly massacre. It was argued that intelligence failure was the prime cause of the catastrophe. DGP of the state refuted it and stated that the CRPF personnel failed to anticipate the danger and underestimated a potential ambush zone. There were four intelligence input on the Maoists concentration in the area Heavily armed guerrillas were spotted by the police informers which was communicated to the higher authority The sleuths had also specified the probable strength and route of the ultras. Secondly, their public relation was not up to the mark and they hardly developed local contact to get reliable information. Thirdly, co-ordination between the local police and central forces suffered from hindrances. The Dy Commandant was over confident who failed to judge the Maoist strength, skill, fire power and the ground condition. He was unable to anticipate the coming event and behaved like an inexperienced and poor professional leader and thereby soiled the good name of the CRPF.

On June 27, 2010, 26 CRPF personnel of 39 Bn including an Assistant Commandant, a cop and a SPO were killed in an ambush in a pocket of Jharaghati forest in Narayanpur district. Maoists smashed heads of ten dead, slit open throat, chopped of hands and legs of many and mutilated several dead bodies. Indeed, such a barbarity has exceeded the proverbial ghastly bestial savagery. In fact, such unprecedented cruelty has shocked the people. On July 1, 2010, three civilians were killed suspecting to be police informers. On May 8, 2010, Maoists triggered a land mine and blasted a bullet proof vehicle carrying CRPF personnel, proceeding from Awapalli to Bijapur. Eight CRPF personnel were killed and their weapons were carried away and two civilians were injured. On May 16, 2010, six civilians and a sarpanch were kidnapped suspecting them to be police spies and killed. Dead bodies were dumped in a forest area of Manpur near village Uchapur, district Rajnandangaon. In a gun battle at Kirandul, district Dantewada two Maoists were killed, two 12 bore guns, a few tiffin box bombs and Maoist posters were seized. On May 17, 2010, a bus moving from Sukma to Dantewada was blown up near Chingavaram village. Thirty six persons including 12 SPOs were killed. On August 4, 2010, in forest area of Gumiapal, near Kirandul, gun battle lasted for several hours. However, there was no casualty.

On August 29, 2010 about 100 Maoists ambushed a BSF patrol near village Bhuski under Durkondal police station district Kankar, and in a gun battle one Head constable and two BSP men, one cop and one SPO were killed. In Bijapur district police raided a hide out near village Mankeli, killed one Maoist, injured one and seized explosives. On October 9, 2010 in Padkipalli forest near village Rishidadar and Chotellora, district Mahasumund, in a gun battle, six Maoists and two villagers were killed. Police seized arms and ammunitions. Maoists used the villagers as human shield which resulted in death of two civilians. On October 8, 2010, three ITBP jawans were killed in a land mine blast when they were in patrolling duty. Meanwhile, four cops were abducted, however, after 12 days they were set free. On October 16, 2010, three state government officials travelling in a bus were abducted. But after 24 hours they were released in a remote place in Bijapur district. From Kuakonda area district Danteweda, a police patrol arrested six Maoists including the deputy commander of the local Maoists squad. They were the suspects for attacking the house of Congress party leader Awadesh Singh in July last. On September 19, 2010 seven cops were abducted from Bhopalpatnam, Bijapur, after 24 hours three cops were killed. Government opened negotiation for release of the rest.

On December 24, 2010, in Dantewada district, cops and volunteers of Salwa Judum looted rice, live stocks and other essential commodities sent for the tribal. Supdt of Police apologized for the misdeed and gave rupees thirteen thousands as compensation. Maoists hijacked a private truck from the national high way No. 43, carrying ammonium nitrate. Spot was in between Bhanpuri and Kondagaon, district Bastar. Truck was proceeding from Visakhapatam to Raipur. Maoists took the truck 50/60 kms deep inside the jungle and unloaded 16 tons of ammonium intending to use it for making landmines etc. The driver was later released. Maoists gave a call to boycott Independence Day on August 15, 2010 and intensified their violent activities. Fifty armed Maoists intercepted six trucks on the high way laden with iron ore belonging to NMDC in a place near Bhansi and Bacheli, Dantewada district and set fire on the vehicles. In Kankar district a SPO and a civilian were shot dead in the market place at Badgaon.

On June 10, 2011 in a forest area near Katekalan, Dantewada district, a mine proof vehicle (MPV) was blown up killing ten security personnel. In another incident, police contingent travelling in two vehicles were ambushed. Seven SPOs and three policemen were killed and four policemen were injured. On June 15, 2011, Maoists killed five policemen in Narainpur district. About 100 Maoists attacked a CRPF base camp situated very close to Bheji police station at about 7 A.M. Gun battle continued for three hours. Three CRPF men were killed and three were injured critically. It was claimed that ten rebels were killed. But no dead body could be traced at the spot. Maoists observed Janpituri Saptah (Peoples Revolution Week) from June 5 to June 11, In fact, from June 9 to 11, within three days, 18 security personnel were killed.

On November 23, 2010 about 150 Maoists attacked a CRPF patrol near Jagargunda area, Dantewada district. In gun battle nine rebels were killed, their weapons and dead bodies were recovered. It was suspected that 20 rebels were killed. However, in absence of the dead bodies it was incorrect to confirm exact number of casualties. In a separate incident, in Bijapur district a land mine hit a vehicle transporting CRPF personnel and killed two of them. On August 19, 2011, a police patrol near Bhadrakali, district Bijapur was ambushed. The first attack was repulsed. But in a renewed attack twelve policemen were killed. Due to power cut wireless sets were dead, resulting in report of the incident reached the district HQ after several hours. On October 7, 2011, in Bastanar under Gidam police station, Dantewada district, the rebels blasted a land mine and blew up a mini truck, killed two personnel of the SSB and injured two. On October 12, 2011, a group of Maoists came in motor bikes, stormed into the residence of a BJP MLA in village Munagapdar, Gariaband who was absent and snatched away the service revolver from the security guard. On November 16, 2011, rebels attacked a CISF patrol in Akashnagar (Bacheli) within NMDC areas, Dantewada district, killed two and injured three of the CISF elements. On December 30, 2011, in Bastar district four tribals and a post man were kidnapped and killed. Dead bodies were dumped in the outskirt of the village. They were directed to blow up a school building. As they refused to comply with the instruction, they were annihilated. In a separate incident two BJP activists were killed. On May 13, 2012, a CISF patrol detailed to protect the NMDC properties was ambushed near Kirandul, Dantewada district, by a strong group of Maoists from three sides, Six CISF men and a civilian driver were killed and their weapons were looted. On July 31, 2013, in Kankar district, a cousin of the Forest Minister, and a member of the panchayat, was abducted from their residence and later shot dead.

Choppers are used to evacuate the dead or wounded persons. On January 17, 2013, in Dantiwada district, a chopper was dispatched to evacuate injured security personnel and send them to hospital for treatment. It landed near Chintagufa, south Bastar, a highly dominated area of the Maoists. Maoists fired at the chopper and hit a state police wireless operator. Unfortunately, six IAF personnel gave up the rescue operation, left the injured cop in mercy of God and escaped for safety. Unexpected desertion leaving the injured companion created furore in all level. Fortunately, CRPF cobra commandos tracked down the helicopter and the wounded cop left behind. They acted bravely and rescued the wounded cop. They earned laurel for the heroic act and as a mark of recognition the Ministry of Home Affairs rewarded rupees five lakhs to the cobra commandos. (*Hindustan Times*, January 19, 2013).

On June 16, 2013, in a gun battle in Sukma district ten Maoists including comrade Sudhakar, the state committee member of the north Telengana special zonal committee, and his partner, Puspa and four female Maoists were killed. A reward of rupees twenty five lakhs each was declared on their heads. About fifty Maoists attacked the security forces. However, Greyhounds, CRPF and state police jointly led the counter offensive. Comrade Sudhakar's death was a big reward for the security forces and simultaneously, was a massive blow to the ultras.

On April 17, 2013, about 20 or 25 Maoists fired at a BSF helicopter which was carrying out search operation for tracing out jawans left in thick forest of Pamed, Sukma district. Heavy gathering of ultras in jungle of Pamed and Jagargunda bordering Andhra Pradesh, was noticed which demanded attention of the security forces. In fact, Maoists gathered under their tactical counter offensive campaign targeting security forces. Fortunately, the chopper was unharmed and there was no casualty.

Dastardly Killing of the Congress Leaders

Decline in Maoists attacks in 2012-13, perhaps made the security forces complacent. A feeling generated that the rebels are contained or curbed which was highly erroneous. Unfortunately, Saturday, the twenty fifth day, (May 25, 2013) of 2013, was the day of exaltation for the Maoists and side by side, "black day" for the security forces and the state government. Indeed, such a lurid killing was rarest of the rare. The Congress party of the state organised a massive "parivartan" rally to bag support of the people aiming at political gain for the coming Assembly election scheduled to be held in the month of October. Prominent Congress leaders, V.C. Sukla, Mahendra Karma, the founder of Salwa Judum, Nand Kumar Patel, the President of the state Congress party, ex-MLA Uday Mudaliar and hundreds of party workers and activists joined the rally and were moving from place-to-place to develop mass contact. In Darbha jungle, Sukma district, Bastar region, at about 3.30 Pm, roughly 400 Maoists ambushed and attacked the rally on its return journey to Jagaddalpur. At the spot 27 leaders and activists were killed, 32 were injured and several were missing. Ex-union Minister V.C. Sukla, badly wounded was dispatched to Delhi for better treatment. However, he succumbed to injuries after a few days

The catastrophe put the security forces and the state government on the dock. Accusation that the police and the intelligence had failed to assess the Maoists' threat and capacity to strike back was not devoid of rationale. Temporary lull was not enough to judge that the Maoist movement was either dried up or dead. Admittedly, in the so called liberated zone, the security forces were still unable to penetrate and flush out the rebels. Maoists were avoiding face-off with well-armed security forces unless they were confident of winning. They engage the security forces on their (Maoists) terms and turf. In fact, political vacuum works as oxygen to the Maoist movement. Abujmarh jungle, Saranda forest and Koel-Sankh in Jharkhand are practically off-limits for the state for decades. Hence, it was crystal clear that the ultras may regroup and strike hard in opportune moment. Since evidence was plenty that any kind of likely reprisal was not ruled out, adequate security for protecting the members of the rally was essential. Some critics pleaded that security lapse was responsible for the disaster. Superintendent of Police was transferred immediately. It was informally learnt that the leaders did not take advice of the security forces to walk into the jaws of the Maoists without adequate security arrangement. Relying on experience I am inclined to say that the political leaders often do not go by the advice of the security officials. They try to show that they are the government and therefore, others' advice or guidance is not needed. Their puffed up whiz-kids guided by fatuous arrogance often try to undermine security rules and show a 'don't care' attitude.

Among the slain Mahendra Kurma, Nand Kumar Patel, his son, Uday Mudaliar figured. Dead bodies of N.K. Patel and his son Dinesh were recovered from Jiram ghat jungle about half a km away from the place of ambush. Notably, Maoists nursed immeasurable grudge against Mahendra Karma, as the volunteers of Salwa Judum under his leadership killed many Maoists. Secondly, fair sex Maoists led the attack. Before their animal fury, resistance by a few security personnel was washed away. They tried to repulse the attack and fought till ammunitions were available. Women Maoists fired repeatedly at the dead Mahendra Karma. In fact, marks of more than sixty bullet wounds were seen on his dead body. They danced around the dead and rejoiced. Exuberant flippancy surrounding lifeless bodies, contrary to Indian custom and culture, was contemptuously ignored by the Maoists who performed death dance, treated the dead bodies with matchless indignities and displayed monstrous barbarity.

Abduction of the District Magistrate of Sukma

On April 21, 2012, Collector and District Magistrate of Sukma district A.P. Menon visited village Majhipara to interact with the villagers in connection with the government's scheme, Special Gram Suraj Abhiyan. Maoists surrounded him, shot dead one of his security guards and abducted him. State government opened dialogue with the Maoists through the interlocutors for securing his release. Maoists demanded release of their 17 comrades languishing in the jail, stop operation Green Hunt and return of the security forces to barracks against freeing the District Magistrate Alex Paul Menon. Maoists selected B.D. Sharma, a former IAS officer, and Professor Hargopal from Hyderabad to mediate with the government on their behalf. State appointed Sm Nirmala Buch, a retired IAS officer and S.K. Mishra to represent the state government and to mediate between the Maoists and the state government. Shri Sharma and Prof Hargopal had two rounds of talk with the Maoists and visited Tadmetta jungle in Sukma district which was one of the strong holds of the Maoists. After a good deal of negotiation and long detention the District Magistrate was finally released. It was crystal clear that the DM did not take adequate security cover to visit a village and converse with the villagers which was one of the strong pockets of the ultras. His indiscreet action put the state in abysmal embarrassment and forced the government to concede to several concessions to the Maoists. In fact, abduction of an important official functionary and unexpected opportunity to bargain with the government for extracting undue graces, obviously, boosted morale of the ultras. Simultaneously, the administration and the security forces who were in the forefront facing torrent of onslaughts and embracing supreme sacrifices on the altar of duties, were demoralised. Truly, their fighting spirit and single minded devotion received a flinty jolt. Government's authority was wryly undermined. Finally, release of the DM was secured against several illegitimate concessions to the ultras. Impartial critics commented that the government suffered from paranoia and abjectly submitted before the pressure of the outlaws.

Link with Other Terrorist Outfits

Maoists tried to tie up with other terrorist out-fits and wanted to develop a tactical understanding with the insurgent out-fits of the North East. Terrorist groups find support among disgruntled elements active within the country. Analysts believe, "Maoists are trying to expand their network by forging alliances with the secessionists. They are seeking ideological resonance and tactical understanding with the North East insurgents and have begun to lend support to their secessionist ideology." On May 19, 2010, Chief Minister Raman Singh said that the Maoists might have link with the Laskar-e-Taiba (LeT). He added that the ultras want to capture power on gun point. During the last ten years they have killed 1000 civilians and 650 police men, blown up 106 school buildings, 132 electric towers. They are the biggest threat and challenge to the democracy. With regard to the use of air power (air strike), to chastise the ultras, he said that he welcomes aerial support but he is against the use of air power or air strike against the Maoists.

People's Liberation Army of Manipur (PLA) intends to form a united front with the Maoists and Kashmir based terrorist out-fits. They have twice trained Maoist cadres in the jungles of Orissa and Jharkhand in 2009 and 2010 respectively. The combined front planned to overthrow the Indian government. Nepalese ultras admitted their link with the Maoists, "We have extended our full support and cooperation to the Indian Maoists."

The Maoists wished success of the secessionist elements active in the J&K. Secondly, their link with terrorist groups or the divisive elements of Assam or North East and Bangladesh has not yet been established. Union Home Minister has admitted before the Upper House that no fund from foreign countries is reaching the Maoists.

Human Shield and Fake Encounters

In June 2012, in Basuguda village, district Dantewada, very close to forest, Silger, on an intelligence report that a group of Maoists had assembled and trying to bring the villagers in their fold CRPF planned an action immediately. Three hundred CRPF elements and police personnel jointly surrounded the village. The Maoists with help of the villagers made a human shield to build resistance and facilitate their escape into the dense forest. In exchange of fire 19 persons including several minors were killed and six CRPF personnel were wounded. Volleys of complaints and anti-police sentiment of the people surcharged the atmosphere. People and media blamed the CRPF for committing excesses and engineering fake encounters. CRPF refuted the charges and took the stand that seven deceased were identified as Maoists. Later, two lifeless bodies were discovered that too, belonged to be the Maoist out-fit. About death of the minors receiving bullet wounds alibi of the CRPF was not convincing. However, the CRPF hierarchy issued an instruction to avoid recurrence in future and insisted upon prior reconnaissance before swing into action in similar situation. It was made clear that instruction must strictly be adhered to. Frankly speaking, such mistakes or error of judgments are not new. Even in army operations friendly or mistaken encounters and casualty without any malice take place. However, in any operation against the ultras casualty of a civilian has to be strictly avoided.

Several armed battalions have been raised both in central and state level. The Red corridor is passing through the tribal areas of Maharashtra, Chhattisgarh, Orissa, Andhra Pradesh, Jharkhand, and West Bengal. The tribal speak different languages which are not understood by the common people. Therefore, often it is difficult to interact with them, judge their sentiment and aspiration. They do not trust the interpreters and are reluctant to open their heart before them. Hence, it is examined in high level whether persons belonging to the same community will be able to appreciate their feeling and sensitivity, elicit their actual need and expectation. It is decided that tribal battalions if constituted exclusively with tribal youths and officials drawing from the tribal community will be ideally suited for the task. On receipt of the green signal, Andhra Pradesh has already raised two tribal battalions and Maharashtra has raised one. Chhattisgarh is contemplating to raise one battalion soon. It is hoped that it will serve the purpose of tackling the extremist threat already well penetrated in tribal belt.

Jungle Commando Unit

The Union government has organised a single commando unit in Chhattisgarh to combat the Maoist guerrillas. The unit will not possess any specific name and title; rather operate as a nameless force. Recruitment in the unit is strictly confined to tribal youths. Importantly, it is a concrete attempt to enlist youths from the areas where the Maoists have been operating with impunity. The object of such a move is manifold. In fact, the local tribal youths speak the language which is spoken by the Maoists; know the areas, roads, jungle foot paths. They are entwined with common culture, ethos and social conventions. They can easily collect information on the whereabouts and movement of the ultras, their contacts, supply line etc.

In Chhattisgarh the responsibility of training the new recruits is vested upon the COBRA, the elite commando unit of the CRPF. It has already trained and absorbed 300 tribal youths for a period of six months on jungle warfare in the training centre at Lanjhi forest, Bastar. Arguably, duration of training is too long. Even in advanced countries in the West, such training is imparted for a short period not exceeding two months. The Ranger school at Fort Benning, US, runs a similar training course. Its duration is only 61 days. Significantly, Bastar region's dense forest is highly suitable for imparting jungle warfare training. Again, the specially trained commandos are aware of the terrain, character and peculiarity of the jungle, bird calls, fake animal calls, and erratic behavior of the weather and instinct of the people belonging to tribal community. The newly raised armed tribal unit for combating the Maoists is considered to be a specialised wing of the para-military commandos.

Commandos can survive several days without food and water. They may eat animal meat, snakes, plant etc. In absence of drinking water they may extract water from spongy roots and drink. They use naphtha balls to light so that fire or smoke is not detected by others. Standard of their endurance is exemplary. A group of journalists watching a demonstration on their endurance test whole heartedly extolled that their toughness is near approximation to the endurance standard of the erstwhile the Spartan army. They are extremely good in unarmed combat, carry special type of weapons, daggers etc.

Majority of the recruits are from Gond tribe, who possess intimate knowledge of the local topography, villages, village paths and the local peoples' customs and habits. They can easily track down the Maoists' hide outs and guide the security forces to surround and take on the ultras. Incidentally, seeing satisfactory performance of the new experiment, Odisha has recruited tribal youths following the foot-step already set. In a nutshell, it is a novel attempt made with high hope and expectation. Without any prejudice, it may be concluded that its formidability and ability to disarray the ultras will place the para military forces in high pedestal. The CRPF commanders feel that their expertise and intuitiveness is proving to be a huge asset and will be deterrent against the ultras.

State's Firmness in Curbing the Ultras

On July 26, 2008, Members of the State Legislative Assembly were put into a closed room for an in-camera meeting to chalk out a strategy to counter the growing Maoist problem that had gripped the state. Secret meeting presided over by the Chief Minister started at 11 AM and concluded at 3 PM. Apart from the entire cabinet and the Members of the Legislative Assembly, the Chief Secretary, Principal Secretary of the Home department, Assembly Secretary and DGP attended the meeting. The Chief Minister said that the idea to hold the in-camera sitting was to enable the legislators to speak freely on the Maoist problem and pre-empt threats against any member to speak out against the ultras. He hoped that all aspects of the vexed problem would be discussed without any reservation so that the government could initiate appropriate step to combat the Maoists. Rule 163D, of the House reveals that if a member discloses any of the proceedings or part of it without permission of the Speaker he or she may face a breach of privilege motion. Indeed, such a step was very uncommon. CM's explanation was that the MLAs must have opportunity to express freely on blood curdling activities of the ultras. Threats given to them or to their family members could be brought to fore unhesitatingly in a closed door meeting Truly, the MLAs and many political leaders were under threat and run the risk of attack and annihilation. Often they were unable to expose the ultras in public forum as gun totting ultras may harm them. Therefore, in-camera meeting, an abundant opportunity was available to open the Pandora's Box and suggest consummate steps to wipe out terrorism and its activists and humble the mentors. However, details of the proceedings were not available for public consumption. Nevertheless, it was certain that exhaustive deliberations must have brought out pragmatic measures to tone up the anti-insurgency apparatus. The CM must have inspired the august gathering and security forces to save the state from the quagmire and tackle the extremists with indomitable will, courage and single minded devotion. Chief Minister Raman Singh's Prussian mind, indefatigable energy and unbending attitude to combat the outrageous elements were apparent. Needless to add, firmness of the government boosted morale of the police force and involvement of the bureaucracy who are assisting the government to banish violence and disorder.

In fact, strong hold of the Maoists is Dandkaranya forest, stretching over a portion of Andhra Pradesh, Odisha, Maharashtra and entire Bastar region of Chhattisgarh. In parlance of the Maoists, the areas is called the "Central Guerrilla base" function under control of Dandakaranya Special Zonal Committee. Its head quarter is located in Abujmarh, within Bastar region. Security forces regained their doddery control right from the middle of 2010. In this respect, incidents of attacks and killing of the security personnel and common men showed a declining trend. Broadly, Chhattisgarh accounted for 31 per cent of the Maoist attacks and 28 per cent resultant deaths. In 2011, total death in the state was 267 including 73 security personnel. In 2012, it was reduced to 146 including 45 security personnel. In 2013, till April 19, total killing was 65 persons including 9 security personnel. Most importantly, modified aggressive policy to take the battle right to the Maoists' own turf instead of awaiting attacks from the rebels has produced extra ordinary dividend. It has forced the Maoists to take defensive measures and confine operation to limited way with extra care and caution. Their pompous hope for the Red Corridor received a flinty jolt. Sporadic violence is not ruled out. Nevertheless, it is no longer a cake walk for the Maoists. In many areas which used to be domain of the Maoists, today, rule of law has returned, the Maoists are conspicuously absent and retreated and taken shelter in the hideouts. The peace loving people have heaved a sigh of relief. Their happiness knows no bound seeing sun shine after tears.

CHAPTER FIVE

Naxalite Movement in Bihar, Emergence of the MCC and IPF, Escalated Violence and Government's Helplessness

Comrade Charu Mazumdar, the founder father of the Naxal movement in West Bengal followed rigidly the Chinese line which eventually developed a rift with his fellow comrades. Meanwhile, in the Communist movement in China a paradigm shift was noticed. The new jargon pompously declared, the "Cultural Revolution" was contrary to the earlier doctrine of annihilation. Charu had been dogmatically following the Mao's doctrine and therefore, was unable to reconcile to accept the modified line. In 1972, comrade Kanu Sanyal, Souren Bose, Chowdhury, Tejeswar Rao, Naga Bhusan Patnaik and Bhuban Mohan Patnaik supported the new Chinese doctrine, the Cultutral Revolution. Comrade Kanhai Chatterjee and Amulya Sen differed with Charu and founded a separate group. In 1970, comrade Satya Narayan Sinha disagreed with Charu, revolted and decided to return to Bihar and operate independently. In fact, in Bihar several splinter groups had already been operating separately having no link with Charu or other Naxal leaders of West Bengal and Andhra Pradesh. Among the outfits active in Bihar, Indian People's Front and Maoist Communist Centre (MCC) were active in particular areas of west and south Bihar. Satya Narayan Sinha eventually took leadership of the MCC. In fact, he preferred open activities and mass movement to clandestine operation.

Meanwhile, Vinod Mishra, a dropout of the Regional Engineering College (REC) Durgapur, West Bengal, went to Bihar and organised movement in the tribal belt in Bhojpur areas. He received encouraging response and in February 1976, established a new outfit CPI (ML) Liberation. He led the Naxal movement in Bihar for twenty years. Eventually, he realised that blood bath and violent means would not help to secure power and fulfill the object of the Revolution. Hence, he decided to organise mass movements openly and acquire political power. In that pursuit, in 1982, he joined hands with Naga Bhusan Patnaik of Andhra Pradesh and floated a new out-fit, the Indian People's Front (IPF). Perhaps, CPI (ML) Liberation eventually merged with the IPF. He planned to enter in "Open Politics" using the new establishment as a tool to step up the revolutionary movements. He and the new out-fit under his control, broadly, gave up violence and were eager to thrive in the accolade of parliamentary politics. In 1990, his party participated in the Assembly election in Bihar and succeeded in capturing nine seats. In Parliamentary election held in 1991, the IPF captured one seat. He tried to spread the net-work of the party in Assam and West Bengal. However, his party could penetrate in selected areas of Assam and contested in Assembly election held in 1991 and captured four seats in Karbi Anglong district. However, his party drew blank in West Bengal. Indeed, he was a reckoning force in leading the Naxal or extremist movement in Bihar for about twenty years. Importantly, revisionism experimented gave him a rewarding dividend. He came in political eminence in the state and reached near approximation to form the government. Perhaps, he realised the futility of violence and mindless bloodshed and dismal future of the extremist movement. Class war, classless society and peoples' war appeared to him a myth.

Broadly speaking, polemic, rivalry, disagreement, despotic leadership, hard living conditions, uncertainty and distrust in the rank and file often hindered the progress and prospect of the movement. Petulant differences and cold conflicts often worked as a flinty bottleneck to enforce operational plans successfully. These were prime reasons for creating rift in leadership. Consequently, acrimony and disagreement in the main out-fit eventually contributed to mushroom growth of splinter groups under the callow or unsound leadership. Suspicion and distrust among the leaders queered the pitch which very often helped the police to gather clue of the secret hideouts, intelligence on the movement of the leaders or the groups and made it smooth to foil the striking plans. Dissension and split indirectly helped to grow smaller groups in eastern states. Many dissidents severed connection with the parent units and the originators of the movement, founded independent units and operated haphazardly. Many disagreeing with comrade Charu Mazumdar deserted him. Comrade Kanu Sanyal influenced several leaders and activists to join the CPI (Marxist and Leninist). Comrade Kanhai Chatterjee and Amulya Sen disowned CPI (ML) and preferred to build an independent unit. Chatterjee wanted a sort of loose federation instead of a rigid monolith party. He demanded positive role of the front organisations. In fact, upon these material points he differed with the leaders of the CPI (ML). He and his whiz-kids founded a new unit or a group known as Dakhin Desh group. This group confined their activities in southern parts of West Bengal, including the erstwhile Medinapur district, now Medinapur

West, Bardhaman, Hooghly districts and Sundarban areas. This group initiated steps to stretch their network in Bihar and Assam. In West Bengal, after demise of Charu Mazumdar in July 1972, several splinter groups emerged and operated independently. Parimal Das Gupta and Asit Sen organised a separate unit and operated on their own. Kanhai Chatterjee and Amulya Sen perhaps failed to make the desired dent in Dakhin Desh. In 1969, they shifted their activities to Bhojpur areas in Bihar and attempted to expand their activities on the line of Dakhin Desh group. Eventually, the group was galvanized and merged into the Maoist Communist Centre (MCC). The announced objective of the MCC was to establish the People's government through the Peoples' war. It claimed its ideology closed to Mao Tse-tung's doctrine of organised peasant insurrection. In March 1981, Amulya Sen died. Kanhai Chatterjee died in 1982, resulting in an apparent lull was noticed in activities of the outfit.

However, Pramod Mishra and Sanjay carried the banner of the MCC and kept it active in Bihar. In 1990, the MCC received fresh impetus as several radicals from the Jawahar Lal Nehru University; New Delhi came to Bihar and reactivated the MCC. The activists of the outfit penetrated in several districts including the state capital, Patna. Violence, atrocity and bloodshed let loose by the ultras have generated an atmosphere of insecurity, tension and unrest. It frightened the people and put state government in a quandary. The perplexed administration was unable to follow the right path either to contain the fast deteriorating law and order situations or crush the extremists.

The Communist Party of Nepal, CPN (Maoist) geared up activities in Nepal right from February 1996. The movement, in fact, took the shape of an upheaval. CPN (Maoist) got inspiration from Peru's Shining Path rebels. Its aim was to over throw the kingship through the revolutionary movement and establish the peasants rule. In that pursuit CPN (Maoist) received ample assistance and resources from China. By 2001, it had extended activities in 22 districts, out of 75 districts of Nepal. By 2002, puny strength of the rebels increased to several thousands. The rebels killed 1600 civilians and 700 security personnel. In fact, MCC in Bihar maintained close link with the CPN (Maoist). It used to supply arms, ammunitions, explosives, detonators etc. In April 2000 both out fits jointly organised training camps in Aurangabad, Bihar and Hazaribag, now Jharkhand. They jointly organised raids and hit the soft targets lying on the border of Indian territory. In September 2000 Comrade Pramod Mishra, MCC leader visited Nepal for consultation. Eventually, the Indo-Nepal Regional Committee was formed. Chandra Prakesh, a politburo member of the CPN (Maoist) visited India to attend the Ninth Congress of the Peoples' War Group (PWG). He was arrested in Chennai airport in February 2003. In fact, MCC of Bihar and CPN (Maoist) had been operating in tandem. Finally, PWG and MCC merged together and CPI (Maoist) was born on September 21, 2004.

During the Rashtriya Janata Dal (RJD)'s regime, in 17 districts out of

38 districts of Bihar intensive Maoist's activities and violence were noticed. Dismayingly, today, under the coalition government of the Janata Dal United and Bharatiya Janata Party under the chief ministership of Nitish Kumar, 33 districts of the state are facing Maoist outrages. In fact, South Bihar is badly affected. Broadly, 26 Assembly constituencies lying in South Bihar are virtually turned to be the haven of the Maoists. Truly, after sunset the whole area comes under the control of the ultras. Critics quip that the Maoists run a parallel government in South Bihar. Ketaki, a cluster of villages, Bedham, Jodhpur, Pathak bigha, etc., are bastions of the Maoists, where their writs run. Impartial observers feel that the NDA government's soft approach towards the Maoists is responsible for deterioration of the law and order and the increased violence. Dispassionately, Nitish Kumar's soft or compassionate handling of the extremist problem has added to the woe. Moreover, caste feud in the state is a contributing factor for the growth of the extremist movement. It may sound paradoxical yet, unflinching testimony will confirm how the caste conflict has been helping the extremists to pursue their outrageous policy. Surprisingly, even its cadre is not free from such evil. Instances are not remote that the leadership and the cadre run and work in caste line or caste sentiment. Of late, tension and enmity between the members of the Yadav and tribal activists working in the cadre is a mighty threat to the unity and cohesion of the outfit for achieving its goal. Adivasi Maoist, Lucus Tete was killed by the comrades representing the Yadav community. Indeed, caste rivalry and conflict in the outfit has alarmed the leaders as it might alienate the Adivasis enrolled and participating in the movement. Secondly, support and patronage of the Adivasi community is the prime support—force or the support base to strengthen the movement for which the Maoists are committed. Activists from the Yadav community were squarely blamed for the murder of an Adivasi Maoist. Tribal leaders were up-in-arms for the annihilation of a fellow comrade belonging to their community. As a matter fact, under current of casteism has been actively coming to fore which has generated a galling rift in the cadre. Admittedly, it is encouraging suspicion and distrust in the rank and file which in the long run may lead to fierce internal feud, bloodshed and a split in the outfit.

Conflict and Ill-feeling; Alienating the Tribal Community

Tribal community is generally the substantial support or asset of the Maoists. Abject poverty, neglect and exploitation of the tribals have stirred their anti-government and anti-affluent people sentiment which have been dexterously used by the extremists and succeeded in bringing the aggrieved tribal community in their fold. Social discrimination, chill penury, high handedness and extortion by the public servants provoke them to respond to the Maoist call. Areas dominated by the tribal population are good shelter grounds or hiding places for the ultras who easily adapt themselves to the living condition, social habits and custom of the tribal community. Nevertheless, of late, in the Maoist dominated areas of Rohtas and Kaimur districts of Bihar has shown a disturbing erosion. In fact, cleavage in relationship between the two has added a new dimension to the Maoist movement. Secondly, it has given a new handle to the police and administration to combat the Maoist threat. An armed squad of the Maoists numbered about 30/40 led by the zonal commander Suraj Singh alias Akbal Miyan, on July 31, 2011 raided the village Pipardih in Nauhatta area of Rohtas district at about 8.30 AM, dragged out Dasarath Singh Kharwar and Brij Bilas Singh Kharwar, both were adivasis, from their houses and assaulted them mercilessly in presence of the villagers. Later, their hands were tied and taken inside the jungle. Since then they are untraced. It is suspected that they were murdered. Prior to this incident, the Maoists had looted and burnt the house of Sudama Oraon, a Maoist leader, of village Madha near Rohtas police station, who had been languishing in jail. On July 30, a Maoist squad killed three family members of Sugriv Singh Kharwar, in village Banda, the President and former mukhiya of the Kaimuranchal Vikas Manch. The ultras also assaulted several villagers belonging to Adivasi community. It was unfortunate that tribal and non-tribal of the Maoist outfit are at daggers drawn. However, for the first incident Maoists suspected the villagers to be the police informers. For looting and setting fire on the house of Sudama Oraon, Maoists perhaps suspected that one of their comrades had to succumb to the pressure of the police and administration to give up arms and join the main stream of the society and thereby betrayed them. Again, in first week of August 2010, four cops were abducted by the Maoists. One of the cops belonging to tribal community was murdered. Another cop from Yadav community was left untouched. It was clear that in Bihar, Maoist leadership from Yadav clan has been dominating the movement. Truly, the above incidents antagonised the tribal Maoists and created fear and panic among the persons of the tribal community. Again rumour with its usual love for falsehood did its work. Several tribal leaders let loose whispering campaign that the Maoists would kill the fellow tribal. Secondly, caste and community consideration was going to steal the show. Therefore, panic-stricken tribals anticipating reprisal decided to desert their abodes. Exodus of the tribals from many villages of Rohtas and Kaimur districts started from July 31, 2011 which posed a serious problem for the police and the administration. Temporary shelter camps at Chernari and Lohra had to be opened for their safety. Police admitted that caste conflict and impending attacks on the Kharwars (Adivasis) is the root cause of the exodus. It has fueled commotion and perplexity which has alienated the tribal from the Maoist fold. However, the police opened dialogue with the frightened tribal intending to send them back to their villages assuring that peace and harmony would be restored.

Growing Acrimony

Union Home Ministry informed that from January to July 2011, 240 civilians had been gunned down or hacked to death by the ultras. Among the civilians killed, twenty four persons were from the tribal community. Interestingly, the Maoists carry cudgel for the tribal and claim to protect and promote their interest. However, in two districts of Bihar relation between the ultras and the tribal community was very sore. Disillusioned tribal who earlier responded to the Maoist call are no longer willing to lead an ignominious life under the influence of the Maoists. Hence, a dozen of tribals who joined the Maoist cadre surrendered before the district authorities of Rohtas district, Bihar and Sonebhadra district, UP with their fire arms. Sugriv Singh motivated several tribal cadres working for the Maoists to surrender their arms and return to normal life. Importantly, a zonal commander was killed by the aggrieved tribal. This irked the Maoists who went on a rampage, attacked several houses of the tribal community suspecting them to be the defectors. Blood thirsty Maoists looted and burnt down houses and hacked to death three relatives of Sugriv Kharwar. A reign of terror unleashed by the Maoists has only cracked relationship of the rival groups.

Maoists gave a call for observing 'Bandh' in the tribal heart land in Ghatsila areas, now Jharkhand, on August 9, 2011 protesting against police excesses. Bandh practically paralysed normal life. Importantly, 'Adivasi Day' falls on August 9, every year. The tribal community observes the 'Day' with great respect and solemnity. But the 'bandh' stood on the way to celebrate it in befitting manner which has hurt sentiment of the tribal community. Baiju Murmu head of the Desh Pargana, the socio-cultural and religious organisation of the Santhal community said, "calling the bandh on the Adivasi Day was not right." We decry the decision which has hurt our sentiment. The President of the Majhi Pargana Mahal of Ghatsila Block of the tribal community, Bahadur Soren said, "calling the bandh on the Adivasi day was not right. We decry the decision." In fact, bandh was observed in thickly populated areas of Jharkhand and Orissa. It created inconvenience to the followers to observe the Adivasi Day in befitting manner which had hit sentiment of the members of the community. Evidently, this decision was taken unilaterally without consulting the leaders of the Adivasi community. A sizeable group of the tribal community felt that this step was taken deliberately to ignore or spoil the sanctimonious Adivasi festival. Needless to say, indiscreet step has further widened the rift between them.

Upper Hand of the MCC

MCC gained reckonable momentum under leadership of Comrade Promod Mishra and Sanjay Singh right from 1990. The ultras initially unleashed violent activities in Jahanabad district. Eventually, it penetrated into Gaya, Aurangabad, Camoor (Bhabhua), Rohtas, Darbhanga, Mazaffarpur, Bettiah, Patna, Sitamari, Nalanda districts. Success of the CPN in Nepal since 1996 gave a substantial impetus to the MCC in Bihar. In fact, caste, community conflicts in Bihar was shrewdly exploited by the MCC. Often the out-fit operated in caste line and thereby acrimony among the members of the different castes culminated in unprecedented caste conflicts or caste war. In 1988, MCC killed 42 persons from the Rajput community in Senai, Jahanabad districts. In February 1992 it annihilated 17 Bhumihars at village Bhima in Gaya district. Under its active participation horrendous violence spread in several pockets, including, Dariam, Dalelchak Bhagara, Bakridh, Bara etc. Gory massacre of more than 30 persons at Dalellchak Bhagara forced the state government to ban the MCC formally. Nevertheless, the spree of annihilation continued unabatedly. In 1996, the outfit attacked Tekari police station, Gaya district, killed ten policemen, looted the armoury and set fire on official records. It set its target at Ranbir Sena, a stubborn caste oriented militant group emerged from pernicious influence of caste conflict and fraternal naxal groups who had snapped tie with the parent unit. It killed eight cadre of the "Party Unity" in Palamu district, now Jharkhand state. It killed two front rank leaders of the CPI (ML) Liberation, in Chatra district, now Jharkhand. In fact, MCC practically isolated and drove away the CPI (ML) Liberation from its strong holds.

Monstrous Rivalry and Retaliatory Killing

Inspire of strong opposition by the smaller outfits including, the CPI (ML) Liberation and occasional setbacks, the MCC intensified outrageous activities. In 1997, it killed eleven persons near Dadedih hill. It killed six policemen and a civilian in a land mine blast on October 19, 2000 in village Jagpura, district Patna. Again it killed five personnel of Bihar Military Police (BMP) on November 21, 2000 in a landmine blast at Koinbiagha Harijan tola, district Gaya. MCC killed three police personnel on August 11, 2002, at Lohradih village, district Rohtas. In addition, MCC killed many civilians suspecting them to be the police informers and for not obeying their instructions. On October 20, 2002 it killed three villagers in Nadaulai village, district Patna, on December 20, 2002, killed two villagers in Kakaria, district, Jahanabad, on April 13, 2003, killed four villagers in Kapri police station limit, on September 8, 2003, killed eleven police personnel and a civilian in a land mine blast in Rohtak district. On April 25, 2004, they shot dead three villagers and injured eleven persons in district Gaya.

On September 16, 2002, MCC killed a supporter of CPI (ML) Liberation, in village Bahadurganj, under Singauri police station limit, district Patna. On October 19, 2002, MCC killed three activists of CPI (ML) Liberation. However, grotesque killing was not one sided. On August 2, 2002 CPI (ML) Liberation killed three activists of the MCC in Mahuagoan village, Jahanabad district. MCC took revenge abducting ten activists of the Liberation out-fit and later killed two of them. On September 23, 2002 Ranbir Sena killed four MCC cadres in village Majidpur under Kinjer police station, district Jahanabad. On April 26, 2004, Ranbir Sena killed three MCC activists in Kapri police station area district Arwai. On April 1, 2003 MCC blasted railway track in Patna Gaya section and on April 16, 2003, blasted Nauhatta police station in Rhotas district. Importantly, in spite of reverses, the state police have been resolutely trying to disarray the outlaws. On September 12, 2003, the police arrested a front rank MCC leader, Ram Badan Tanti, alias Pankaji alias Navinji in Patna. On May 1, 2002, a zonal commander of the MCC was killed in an encounter with police in Nagauli village, district Patna. On July 10, 2002, five MCC cadres and cop were killed in an encounter in Bhojpur district. Again, two area commanders, Lalvrat and Deorath and sixteen cadres were killed at Bhawanipur; district Mirzapur, Uttar Pradesh, in an encounter with the UP police. As a matter fact, MCC desperately tried to spread its activities in Mirzapur, Chandauli and Sonbhadra districts of Uttar Pradesh.

Importantly, Sashastra Peoples' Morcha was formed by the drop-outs of the Maoist unit. Activists of the new organisation aimed at building armed resistance groups against the Maoists to neutralise their outrageous activities. Evidently, seething rivalry between the two reached the culminating point and finally hit the arid zone of acrimony. On April 10, 2008, the Maoists gunned down six activists of the Morcha in Rohtas district. In fact, MCC had been maintaining close contact with the Maoists of Nepal and the Peoples' War Group of Andhra Pradesh. Secondly, personnel of Oraon and Tharu tribes living on the border territory of Nepal who embraced Christianity, developed link with the MCC They exerted influence on the populace dwelling on the border belt of Champaran district of Bihar. In 2002, MCC killed 25 persons in Champaran district. Police was sanguine that the converted tribes maintained active link with the MCC and therefore, in June 2003, police asked one Christian priest to quit the district. However, after merger of the PW and the MCC the later received fresh impetus to stretch its violent activities. Secondly, it transpired that several Christian Missionaries and the activists of the MCC jointly conspired and added fuel to fire. The new invigorated outfit unleashed wanton outrages. Panic-stricken people were shocked seeing the macabre festival of death. In fact, the conspiracy resulted in assassination of BJP leaders, Bharat Yadav and Bhola Mian, on May 24, 2003 at Charapapur Banbar. Importantly, after liberation of Bangladesh in 1971, a large number of Hindi speaking Muslims from erstwhile East Pakistan clandestinely intruded into India. Majority of the intruders illegally took shelter in Eastern UP, East and North Bihar. MCC adroitly developed contact with them and eventually, a nexus between them developed which helped the extremists considerably to spread their network in the region.

Railway Properties—A Soft Target

Railways and railway properties were the targets of the ultras. On April 13, 2008, Maoists attacked Jhajha railway station on eastern railway, Jamui district. Ultras threw ten or twelve bombs on the government railway police station (GRP), functioning from the station premises and demolished the police station and the ticket booking counter planting dynamite. They killed five policemen and a railway employee, looted the armoury and decamped with six SLRs, 27 pieces of .315 rifles, two carbine and 898 rounds of ammunitions. Station was temporarily cut off and train services were stand still for several hours. On April 16, 2008, Maoists called bandh in Bihar and Jharkhand for 24 hours protesting against death of eight Maoists in an encounter with the security forces. In Aurangabad district, about two hundred Maoists attacked Fisher railway station and abducted five railway employees and kept them as hostages. However, they released them after a few hours. On May 20, 2010, Maoists blew up a railway track in Champaran district, East Central Railway, resulting in, fifteen oil tankers carrying high speed diesel belonging to Indian Oil Corporation being transported to Agra depot were derailed. Rebels set fire on one of the derailed oil tankers which soon spread to other tankers. The driver successfully detached several tankers and thereby saved 33 oil tankers. Railways faced loss of rupees 13 crores.

On April 18, 2008, about 200 heavily armed Maoists raided a patrol pump located by the side of the national high way in Gaya district, destroyed the pump and the building using dynamite. On July 26, 2008, about 100 Maoists attacked a brick kiln at village Arra, district Vaisali, burnt several huts and a tractor. They pasted poster on walls against the brick kiln owner.

On June 1, 2008, the Maoists called bandh for 24 hours in five districts of Bihar protesting against arrest of five front rank comrades from Lakhisarai district. On July 2, 2008, the Maoists blew up railway track in Saran and Muzaffarpur districts. and severely damaged down railway line running between Bara Gopal and Avtarnagar in Sonepur division. It hit train services and put hundreds of passengers in untold hardship. On July 11, 2006, in Jamui district ultras destroyed railway track between Ghorparan and Narganj railway station blasting twice within span of twelve hours. Both up and down line was damaged, high voltage overhead wire was snapped, resulting in, train services was badly stalled. On June 2, 2008, passengers travelling by Gorakpur Howrah Purbanchal Express were fired upon. Ultras blew up a portion of the railway track near Narang railway station close to Jhajha railway station. Two coaches were derailed and exchange of fire continued for some times. On July 8, 2008, local commander Bikash Das was arrested at Jamui. On previous night ultras attacked Jamui police station and the Block office. Police tried to repulse the attack and fired at the rebels. Exchange of fire continued and 200 rounds were fired from both sides. On August 21, 2008 a big group of ultras ambushed a police party travelling in a vehicle and in encounter one ASI and five auxiliary police personnel (SAP) among nine persons were killed and four were wounded at Raniganj, Gaya district. Maoists carried away four SLRs from the dead and injured policemen. Ultras ambushed a police patrol car in jurisdiction of Imamganj police station. In exchange of fire one rebel was killed and the dead body was recovered from the spot. Another dead ultra was carried away in a motor cycle. Villagers came in large number in aid of the demoralised policemen. Rebels before retreating lobbed a grenade at the crowd and fled.

Training Camp Run by the Maoists

Maoists were running a training camp near village Khaira in Jamui district surrounded by hill and jungles. In a major raid the police caught 97 suspected Maoists including several front line leaders, twenty two females including two of them with babies. Police seized generator sets, many equipments and huge quantity of Maoist literature. Several hard core Maoists including comrade Kundan Das, Chirag Das of Monghyr were arrested. It is suspected that this group was responsible for murdering K.C. Surendra Babu, Superintendent of police, Monghyr. Maoists organised training with good deal of care. Weapon training and firing of weapons get top priority. Importantly, the ultra out-fit has no standardised weapon. They procure weapons of different bore and caliber depending on availability from various sources. Weapons and ammunitions are generally collected after raids or ransacking the police posts and from possession of the dead or wounded policemen. Secondly, smuggled arms from Bangladesh and Nepal are purchased stealthily. Thirdly, earlier arms and ammunitions used to be procured from the LTTE with the help of the PW of Andhra Pradesh. In initial stage, China used to supply arms and ammunitions through the Chinese Embassy located in Katmandu, Nepal. In fact, training for zeroing and adaptation of weapons of various caliber and bore is not easy for the trainers. Indeed, the ultras faced considerable hurdle to impart training to the recruits in handling and firing weapons. In many cases they took help of the retired army and police personnel paying them handsomely. Secondly, use of explosives and assembling of land mines are highly specialised task. PW of AP acquired its expertise, probably, learnt its intricacies from the LTTE. PW eventually extended its active co-operation to the MCC and the Maoist outfits active in Odisha, Bihar, Jharkhand and Chhattisgarh to learn its know-how and effective use.

Attack on Mobile Towers

On tapping mobile phones police was collecting clues pin-pointing the location and movements of the ultras. It immensely helped the police to organise raids, intercept the advance and retreat of the ultras and raid the hide-outs. Hence, the rebels nursed grudge against tower companies and planned to demolish the mobile towers in areas where they are active so that the security forces may not trace them out or identify their location. On September 29, 2008., heavily armed Maoist guerrillas raided Bishnupur and Manjhaulia villages under Imamganj Block of Gaya district and blasted two mobile towers belonging to Reliance group. Thereafter, they blew up mobile towers of Airtel group located at villages Changani and Maigra and set fire on the BSNL tower. On October 3, 2008, four mobile towers in Aurangabad district belonging to Bharati Airtel Ltd and Reliance communication were blown up. In dead of night the ultras raided villages Ketaki and Araura under DEO Block, district Aurangabad and blasted several towers using dynamite. It snapped contact and communication in the region for a long time. Notably, in Dalelchak Baghura village, under DEO Block, Aurangabad district, massacre of 42 persons took place in 1984. The victims were hacked to death brutally. On

January 22, 2009, an Airtel tower at Maigra village under Dumaria block, Gaya district was blown up. Needless to say, the mobile towers were the targets of the Maoists as the police after watching the mobile network could pin-point the movements of the Maoists and round them up. Indeed, following the surveillance process the police have successfully nabbed several Maoists including many hard core leaders and activists. It revealed that in the last few months the security forces and the police could track down their movements and arrested approximately 200 Maoists including several leaders. Evidently, it made the Maoists angry who wanted to uproot the evil by silencing the mobile network and demolishing the mobile towers.

Violence Piles Upon Violence

On January 21, 2009, Maoists declared bandh for 24 hours in Bihar, Jharkhand, Chhattisgarh and Orissa alleging high handedness of police against tribal in Lalgarh areas of West Medinipur, West Bengal and complaining against fake encounters and killing of innocent tribal youths. On the following day (January 22, 2009) several ultras putting on military uniform intercepted eleven trucks laden with cement bags and set fire on the vehicles. The riotous incident took place near a village located between Tumba and Ranjeet ganj under Tilanthu police station of Rohtas district. Ultras also blasted a mobile tower available near the spot. On February 9, 2009, in a village in Nawada district about 100 Maoists attacked a police party, killed one SI, one ASI, four constables and four jawans of Bihar Military police and looted ten weapons The spot lies on the border of Bihar and Jharkhand close to Giridih. On March 11, 2009, about twenty Maoists attacked Nageshwar Mahato, a farmer at village Panchbigha, district Arwal, slit open his throat, and killed his wife, mother-in-law and two children. It may be recalled that in July 1987, in Madanpur areas of Aurangabad district, MCC killed fifty two Rajputs at Baghaura and Dalechak villages respectively.

Maoists gave boycott call for Parliamentary election scheduled to be held in April/May, 2009. They warned the people declaring, "Boycott the polls or face consequences. Election is just an exercise in treachery." Ahead of the Parliamentary election they intensified outrages, planned for jail break in Gaya, Jahanabad, Aurangabad, Arwal and Nawada districts. They organised a massive congregation of rebels in East and West of Chalho hill ranges. Forest paths were heavily mined to frustrate police raids. However, as a precautionary measure the police managed to organise raids, arrested 18 hard core Maoists, and diffused two land mines from Aurangabad district. Security personnel specially trained in the pattern of "Greyhounds" operating in Andhra Pradesh were pressed in counter insurgency operations. Yet, about 100 Maoists putting on military attire raided village Parasando, district Mungyer, dragged out Manoj Singh, President of Kharagpur Block unit from his residence and produced him before the Maoists' kangaroo court. In a mock trial he was held guilty and awarded death sentence. His throat was slit open and left bleeding to die painfully. The rebels following the similar modus operandi held court in Arwal district. Police in spite of sincere attempts failed to disrupt the kangaroo court and salvage the victims. It dismayed the hapless and peace loving villagers. Rebels warned the villagers against playing secretly the role of police informers. The Maoists distributed leaflets in places prior to their visits. On June 23, 2009, in Lakhisarai district near capital, Patna, about fifty rebels travelled in three wheelers, fired indiscriminately, killed a Home Guard, injured three security men, four civilians and freed an under trail prisoner, Mihir Besra. He was brought to the court from the jail, and after being presented before the court, was escorted back to the gallows. Rebels attacked the escort, over powered the guards and carried away the under trial prisoner who was a daring terrorist from Giridhi. On July 5, 2009, ultras hijacked two private passenger buses from Dumaria area of Gaya district and took ten employees of Maharani Travels as hostages. Several passengers were physically thrown out of the buses. Finally, the ultras fled into dense forest.

On October 2, 2009, Maoists killed 16 persons including five lads in village Amdaicharua under Atawali police station, district Khagaria. The victims belonged to Kauri and Kurmi community. Ultras threatened the Chief Minister Nitish Kumar demanding release of two Maoist leaders, Raviji and Dhiren. On November 12, 2009 forty-nine quintals of high grade explosives (81 bags) were seized from two houses in Mainpaura area of Gaya district.

On September 4, 2009, Maoists abducted seven employees of a Kolkata based construction company, Subhas Projects Marketing Ltd who had been constructing a road from Deoghar to Chakai in Jamaui district. The rescue operation team spear-headed jointly by the Special Task Force, Special Auxillary Police and district police came under heavy fire from a group of one hundred Maoists. Exchange of fire continued for four hours in Dumma hill. Maoists triggered three land mines. Finally security forces arrested seven Maoists including one women Maoist from Jumaui jungle and seized ten kgs of explosives and a few land mines.

Arrest of Many Frontline Maoist Leaders

Union government banned the CPI (Maoist) outfit with effect from June 22, 2009. Several terrorist ripped states followed the suit. Evidently, it generated plausible impact to handle and defuse the Maoist problem. Importantly, a group of radicals guided by infantile emotion protested against such an extreme step which according to them, is a blatant violation of the democratic right of a set of people who are inspired by an ideology to establish a new regime. Admittedly, the police succeeded in arresting a large number of recognised Maoist leaders neutralising resistence and hazards and thereby brought the movement under control. On September 20, 2007, a top Naxalite leader Tushar Kanti Bhattacharjee alias Srikant was arrested from a rented house in Patna. He joined the movement in 1974, earlier arrested and sent to jail. He was a member of the international wing of the South Asian

Forum of Naxal Organisation. In Patna he was engaged to train the cadres in manufacturing improvised explosives and use of explosives. A huge quantity of explosives, timers, pen drives, satellite phone maps and training equipments were seized from his possession. He was wanted by the police of several states for his direct involvement in heinous cases including mass murder. On March 14, 2009, Bhupendra Baitha, a self-styled zonal commander of the Maoist outfit, who was carrying a reward of rupees twenty five thousands, was arrested from Ismailpur near Gaya railway station by the special task force. On August 25, 2009, Anil, a politburo member and Kartik, a state committee leader were arrested by the task force when they were travelling from Ranchi to Patna. Maoists called bandh in five states protesting against the arrest. On second day of the bandh a group of about 100 Maoists raided village, Anki, district Aurangabad and blew up a community centre using dynamite. On August 7, 2009, seven hard core Maoists including the area commander of the Punpun-Sone area committee were arrested. Two bullet proof jackets and plenty Maoist literature were recovered. Interrogation revealed that the ultras were planning to disrupt Independence Day celebration in Magadha region.

Meera Ravidas, on December 2, 2009, a top Maoist leader was arrested from village Mahuliatand, district Nawada. On November 6, 2011, two top Maoist commanders were arrested from Rohtas district. Daroga Chowdhury alias Raja alias Bhardul was arrested from Tiura forest. A pistol, five life cartridges and two mobile phones were recovered from his possession. He was wanted in several cases, including murder, rioting and attacks on the security forces. Nirala Jadav, ex-zonal commander of the Sone-Ganga and Vindachal zone was arrested. He murdered the Divisional Forest Officer of Shahabad division. He planned jail break and tried to establish a new Maoist unit in Kaimur plateau. In August 2010, Maoist leader Chemeli Devi was arrested in Kolkata, West Bengal by Bihar and West Bengal police jointly. A female Maoist, Anjali Devi alias Bengali Chachi was arrested on January 21, 2012 from her abode at village Tariyani, district, Sheohar. From her house, arms, explosives, two can bombs, a carbine magazine, potassium nitrate, ammonium nitrate, Maoist literature, posters were seized. On April 29, 2011, police raided a village in Katihar district near border of West Bengal and arrested three leaders, (1) Pulendu Sekhar Mukherjee (69), alias Jhantu Mukherjee, alias Sahib da, secretary of the Eastern Regional Bureau including Chhattisgarh and Varanasi central committee, (2) Subramanian (55), secretary, Northern Regional Bureau, (3) Vijay Kumar Arya (50), Member Central Committee and in charge of subcommittee of mass organisations. Three leaders assembled at one place for discussion and chalking out plan for deeper and wider aggressive activities. Government of Andhra Pradesh has declared reward of rupees 12 lakhs and 3 lakhs for arrest of Subramanian and Vijay Kumar respectively. They are presumed to be the think-tank of the outfit. However, arrest was a prize catch for the police. On May 12, 2008, comrade Promode Mishra, a leader of the Maoist Central Command was arrested from a hideout in Binodnagar, Dhanbad. Bihar Police claim that within two years fifty top Naxalites were arrested. Comrade Tushar Kanti Bhattacharjee alias Srikant was arrested from a rented house in Patna He is a member of the international wing of the South Asian Forum of Naxal organisation. He was camping in Patna for the last two months for imparting training to the cadres for manufacturing improvised explosives.

Maoists Step Up Violent Activities

On December 19, 2011, a group of one hundred rebels attacked the office of road construction company Jamui, torched three heavy machines needed for road construction and kidnapped several labourers. Unconfirmed report revealed that the ultras demanded a hefty levy from the company. As the organisation refused to oblige them, the ultras attacked the establishment and set fire on the machines. On May 22, 2010, about one hundred Maoists stormed Ramvan village in Sheohar district, located about 200 kms north of Patna, shot dead five persons and set fire on dozens of shops. They blew off railway track and burnt fifteen oil tankers. On August 30, 2010 security personnel when engaged in combing operation at village Ramtalnagar under Kajtra police station, district Lakhisarai, came under surprise attack. Eight police men were killed and ten were injured. Ultras looted thirty five rifles from the dead and wounded police personnel. Six personnel of the Bihar Military Police, OC of Kawaiya out-post and three others were missing. From the missing cops four were abducted and kept as hostages. Ultras demanded release of eight comrades languishing in jail in exchange of releasing the abducted cops. In fact, the ultras issued ultimatum that non-acceptance of the proposal to release the comrades would only endanger lives of the detained cops. As a matter of fact, Rohtas district has earned notoriety for the increased ultra-left offensives. Security forces have galvanized collection of intelligence, improved alertness and ensured promptitude and responsiveness to neutralise the ultras. Police continued raiding the hide outs adhering to proper plan and strategy. On January 21, 2012 police seized one quintal of explosives, four can bombs, 400 detonators, Maoist literature and uniforms from a hide out at Gurmeta village in a joint operation organised by the CRPF's Cobra battalion and the state armed police. Block Development Officer, Manoj Singh who went to village Ladhours in Sheohar district for official duties was kidnapped by the ultras.

School Buildings—The Target of the Maoists

Maoists embarked upon a sinister plan to demolish and destroy the school premises as they felt that school premises are being used for running temporary camps of the security forces. From the temporary camps the security personnel have been conducting raids in the hide-outs established in interior places, chastising the rebels, frustrating their offensive plans and programmes. Hence, the security forces will be in discomfiture if suitable structures for establishing temporary camps are either unavailable or made unsuitable for stay. Unfortunately, within first six months of 2010, forty school buildings were either demolished or razed to the ground. On December 18, 2011, ultras razed to the ground a middle school building at Chananbar under Khaira police station of Jamui district. Operation for demolishing the building continued for long two hours. While retreating, the rebels looted several rice bags stored in the school premises for cooking mid-day meals for the pupils. On the same evening they demolished another middle school building at village Sarkanda under Charkapathar police station of the same district. In village Dhanraj, Muzaffarpur, Maoists razed a high school building to the ground using bulldozers. In Kaimur district seven school building were blown up in November/December, 2010. In January/February 2011, eight school building were blown up in one block of Gaya district. In addition, in two separate incidents the rebels kidnapped 22 labourers engaged in road construction work. However, they released them after a few hours. In this respect, Jamui and Aurangabad districts are worse hit districts. The rebels' grudge was irrational and contrary to ideal of serving the people ungrudgingly. Their logic was immeasurably unsound as they argued that since the security forces have been converting the school building as temporary camps to strengthen the anti-Maoist operations, they demolish the school buildings as a measure of retaliatory step so that no temporary shelter is available to the security personnel. In Gaya district several school building were pulled down. Rough estimate reveals that 150 school building had been demolished within one year in the state. State is trying to ensure total literacy through Sarva Shiksha Abhiyan and for that about three lakhs class rooms are needed. Importantly, schools are community gathering points for meets, health checkup camps and various social activities. In fact, one primary school building costs rupees nine to twelve lakhs, one middle school building costs 25 lakhs and a higher secondary school building costs approximately fifty lakhs. Needless to say, it had hindered education of countless rural students. It has shattered morale of the students, guardians and sensible persons. Unfortunately, the ultras persuaded the demolition drive with vengeance. Simultaneously, the police and the security forces lamentably failed to contain them and protect the school buildings. Indeed, in spite of periodic success of the security forces Jamui district became practically a safe haven for the Maoists who were striking at ease throwing open a formidable challenge to the security forces and the administration. Disruption of learning of a large number of rural school students alarmed everybody. Government came under scathing criticism for failing to protect the school buildings and studies of the school going pupils. Common people and persons who have sympathy for the Maoists were upset and were critical for ruining education of the school goers who are generally from poor and lower middle class families of the society. A sizeable villagers living in the Maoist dominated areas vehemently denounced action of the ultras for targeting the school buildings and upsetting learning and education of the poor and rural students. They appealed to the Maoists to halt such misadventure, spare the school buildings and thereby not to jeopardise studies of the pupils belonging to lower strata of the society. Significantly, hundreds of school students form Aurangabad sent open letters to the Maoists stating, "Maoist uncles what is our fault? Why are you targeting our school buildings." Appeals of the students were widely published in the newspapers and also highlighted through electronic media. However, it was not clear if appeals have produced mellowing influence on the Maoists and eventually has reduced attack and demolition of school premises. However, no fewer than 100 government school building had been razed to the ground. Consequently, thousands of boys and girls were deprived of basic education. It needs no mention that their right to education was not only disrupted but confined to the prescribed books only.

Increased Violence, Bloodshed and Loss of Security Personnel

Escalated violence, loss of security personnel and growing perception of insecurity put the peace loving persons in panic and perplexity. State government came under scathing criticism for failing to contain burgeoning danger. Intellectuals and progressive elements were up-in-arms accusing the Chief Minister Nitish Kumar and the state government for adopting a soft line in disarraying the Maoists. Critics stated that during the RJD's regime (Rastriya Janata Dal) under CM, Lalu Prasad Yadav and Rabri Devi 17 districts of the state were affected by Maoist violence. However, of late, law and order in the state has startlingly deteriorated under the NDA's (National Democratic Front) coalition government. Maoist violence has menacingly spread to thirty three districts of the state. Admittedly, in Maoist affected districts violence and outrages unleashed by the ultras have surpassed all records. The police is demoralised and the government has failed to hold the rein of the administration firmly and maintain law and order effectively. Critics without prejudice felt that the CM's soft paddling approach has encouraged the rebels to intensify their fiendish activities. It has thrown open a formidable challenge to the rebels. Police morale is low, they are unable to read the mind of the government and thereby are unable to pull their weight to chastise the ultras and root out the growing threat.

Unfortunately, in Bihar, from 2005 to July 2010, Maoists had killed 86 security personnel, 188 civilians and looted 132 weapons from the police personnel. State government conceded that 33 districts are hit by Maoist violence. However, from 2006 to 2009, security personnel had killed 50 Maoists, recovered and seized 105 fire arms, 14808 ammunitions, 6833 kgs explosives, 11319 detonators, 56 land mines and cash rupees 681148. In 2009, total 384 Maoists were arrested and 109 extremists were convicted by the courts. Again, under the state's rehabilitation package scheme, 297 Maoists surrendered. Broadly, counter measures taken by the police has given rewarding dividend. Government felt that in spite of adversary the success of the security forces is in no way puny or mean. Negating criticism the state reiterated that the government is alive to the situation and taken adequate initiative to combat the growing danger and in that pursuit raising several armed battalions, galvanising intelligence cells, infra-structure, training curriculum and equipping the police with latest weapons and riot or battle gears. Hence, if totality is judged from detached angle the success in tackling the Maoist problem is not at all gloomy.

Idea and Plan for Self-Defence

The idea of self-defence by the villagers themselves against the ultras has been gaining ground for some times. Foundation of Salwa Judum in Chhattisgarh with much fan fair was unproductive. Allegations of its wide misuse were in galore and finally the Apex Court of the Country had to intervene to ban the scheme. Therefore, it is very risky to arm the civilians whatever may be the cause. Yet, under pressure of adversities, the administration is compelled to initiate some step which is apparently not rewarding. Importantly, about 500 tribal were forced to flee their abodes situated in Rohtas, Nauhatta and Chenari Blocks and took shelter in a temporary base camp at Chenari. The hapless villagers had to face repeated attacks, merciless tortures and destruction of their properties let loose by the pitiless ultras. In July, 2011, in Kaimur forest range, the Maoists killed five villagers, injured thirteen and burnt 21 houses. Hence, as chance of protection was remote, the tribals throbbed with panic had to quit their houses in search of safe shelter and safety. Tumultuous exodus forced the state government to establish temporary shelter camps providing adequate security. District administration was in a fix to establish temporary camps, arrange adequate security camps within short notice. As situation moved apace and normalcy was restored the district administration advised them to return to their villages, ensuring consummate security and protection. Since fresh attack by the ultras was not ruled out the idea of self-defence, in addition to general security was considered essential by the administration. After a good deal of examination and assessment of the threat perception arms licenses were issued to 61 villagers to instill confidence and enabling them to defend themselves in the event of fresh attack by the Maoists. Importantly 12 villagers purchased fire arms themselves, and rest arms were supplied to the villagers by the district administration. Superintendent of Police cautioned them that licence will be cancelled for any kind of misuse of weapons and violation of rules.

Impartial critics felt that step taken may not produce the desired result. First, training to handle fire arms and practice to fire is a continuous process. It has to be arranged periodically. Secondly, weapons are needed to be cleaned regularly and kept serviceable so that in emergency it should respond promptly. Thirdly, safety of the weapons is essential. It must not fall in the hands of miscreants and the extremists. Instances are enough that the terrorists attack the gun owners and forcibly take away the weapons and enrich their arsenal. Sometimes, the unscrupulous owners sell weapons and ammunitions to the outlaws at a high premium. Lastly, residents or villages where weapons are available or stored become the target of the extremists. In short, the idea of self defence may be meaningful nevertheless, impending ordeals centering round it is too risky to ignore.

Meanwhile, unabated violence unleashed by the Maoists has upset the sober people who have been fast losing faith on the government. On November 1, 2011, Maoists abducted 15 labourers from Baltarghat under Sono police station in Jamui district. The helpless workers from outside the district had been working in a construction company along with local workers. They were kept in confinement at village Batia and after five days were released. It was disclosed that the ultras demanded levy from the proprietor of the company. As the demand was not conceded the ultras abducted the labourers to terrorise the owner and the workers. On November 24, 2011, death of top leader, Kishanji in an encounter with security forces in West Medinapur district, West Bengal was a fatal setback for the Maoists. The demoralised Maoists gave a nationwide bandh call for two days. In fact, semblance of bandh was partially noticed in five states dominated by the Maoists. The first day of the bandh was marred by several violent incidents in Bihar and Jharkhand in Dumariya, district Gaya, at about 8.30 PM, about eighty Maoists guerrillas assembled and attacked the camp of the CRPF's elite Cobra battalion and attempted to overpower the camp. Exchange of fire continued till mid night. However, it was successfully repulsed without any loss. At village Suhi, Aurangabad district, the ultras set a mobile tower on fire.

On January 5, 2012, district police and CRPF jointly organised combing operation in Chatra district, Jharkhand, close to border of Bihar to flush out ultras and demolish their hide outs. Joint venture succeeded in arresting four hard core Maoists from Hunterganj jungle. Following the example, on January 6, 2012, Special Task Force (STF) of Gaya and Jahanabad district jointly raided several hide outs and seized 30 bags of high grade explosives, chemicals, IEDs, can bombs, two fire arms, ammunitions, wireless sets, Maoist literature and cash rupees 4.72 lakhs. Secret supplier of explosives Bilai Mian and his associate Deepak Kumar were arrested.

Intelligence gathered that a notorious group had engaged a professional assassin to kill the Hon'ble Speaker of the Legislative Assembly of Bihar and the MLA of Imamganj constituency. Contract killer Chotu Khan alias Shamim Khan alias Babu Khan, perhaps was engaged for the bloody task. He was a member of the local area committee of the Maoists, initially a vegetable seller, who eventually developed link with the leaders of the underworld, Mumbai and finally turned to be a professional killer. He was wanted in 35 cases of murder, several cases of loot, extortion spreading over West Bengal, Jharkhand and Bihar. He was strongly suspected for gory crime in Sherghati AImamganj areas.

A helicopter is placed at the disposal of the state to combat the ultras. It will facilitate to fight the ultras in Kaimur and Kajra (Lakhisarai) hill, one of the hilly terrains to conduct search and combing operations. Augusta helicopter can carry 17 persons, capable of dropping forces in difficult locations and evacuate the wounded persons quickly. This will make a quantum difference to the effectiveness of anti-Naxal operations. The gesture was welcomed by the ground forces fighting the ultras.

Opium Cultivation, Link with International Narcotic Units

Of late, Bihar police has discovered unauthorised cultivation of opium in tri-jungle area of Bihar, Jharkhand and Uttar Pradesh. It is suspected that the Maoists arranged opium cultivation in ten-acres of land, clandestinely has developed link with international narcotic trade and the drug syndicate. Illicit trade brings flow of huge money which is a substantial financial resources to the outfit. Police and Cobra unit of the CRPF jointly organised operation named "Vishwas", raided village Hasri in Nauhatta police station areas and discovered a big unauthorised opium field. Hard core Maoist Ramashish Yadav used to control the narcotic cultivation and operation with Rajeswar Yadav, Ram Dular Yadav, Babu Lal Ram, and Ram Swroop Yadav. Watching the police's alertness the miscreants escaped deep into the forest. Security forces seized huge quantity of opium crop and took step to destroy it once examination by the forensic experts is completed. Importantly, poppy cultivation opens flood gate to mop up a substantial fund which is utilised to buy essential articles and arms, ammunitions, equipments etc. In fact, it is practised in organised manner maintaining contact with the foreign narcotic and smugglers units aiming at accumulating as much as fund possible to provide financial support to the starving Maoist units active in the states.

In rural areas of Barachatti in Gaya district the police discovered a big field of twenty acres where poppy cultivation was practised. Poppy triangle is nestled in three districts of Bihar from Gaya to Aurangabad and further west to Kaimur plateau; poppy smuggling is rampant in areas parallel to the national highway No.2. Under direct patronage of the Maoists poppy cultivation has been spreading fast, especially, in remote areas. Due to pro-active policing in Maoist hit states in recent times and due to arrest, death of several leaders, cadres, loss in encounters the Maoists have retreated to inaccessible areas of the dense forest and have taken up poppy cultivation. In addition to levy and extortion, poppy cultivation and levy from the poppy cultivators and smugglers are quite rewarding. It, indeed, is a positive drive to impel the shrunken finances of the Maoists.

Subhas Kushwaha, a self-styled zonal commander and two others were arrested from Wajirganj police station area in Gaya district. A SLR and a carbine were seized from them. Heavily armed Maoists raided village Nonpur, Begusarai district and blew up house of Dinesh Singh, the leader of the CPI planting dynamites. Luckily no casualty was reported. On August 25, 2009, about one hundred ultras raided village Irki, Aurangabad district and blasted a community bhawan with the help of explosives.

Lok Sabha Poll 2009; Boycott Call

In biggest democracy in the world, India's 714 million voters were eligible to exercise their right of franchise in 185552 polling centres. Ten thousand officials are deployed to conduct the polling. First phase of the Lok Sabha Poll was scheduled to be held on April 16, 2009. Maoists gave a call for boycotting the polling in five states. They warned the people giving wide publicity, "boycott the poll or face horrendous consequencs. Election is just an exercise in treachery." In fact, a day following the poll large scale violence in four states, killed nineteen persons including five polling officials. Polling was disrupted in 86 polling booths, including 71 which fell in the extremist dominated areas. Four officials were kidnapped. On April 16, 2009, Maoists fired at a polling station, Sindhupur village, Banki Bazar block, district Gaya and killed two cops and injured three female voters. They looted four rifles and EVM machines from six booths. Taking advantage of disorder the outlaws and hoodlums jumped into the fray, looted EVM machines, assaulted the voters and added to unrest. In Rohtas district more than 100 Maoists attacked a BSF camp, fired rocket launchers. In protracted gun battle it was believed that a dozen of Maoists were killed. However, no dead body could be traced out at the spot. Thereafter, in Daltanganj (Jharkhand) about 100 Maoists attacked a school building where personnel of Jharkhand armed police were camping. Exchange of fire continued for some times but none was injured.

Security arrangement was further tightened for conducting the second phase of polling, scheduled to take place on April 23, 2009. However, a day before the polling on April 22, 2009, the Maoists stepped up violence in four states including Bihar. In Gaya district a group of about 100 Maoists at about 12.30 AM, stopped a convoy of trucks at a gun point near Barachatti on Grand Trunk road, killed one driver and torched eight trucks. They blasted the Dev Block Development office in Aurangabad district.

Election for the State Legislative Assembly—Oct/Nov 2010

Election for the state assembly in Bihar scheduled to be held in October/November 2010 witnessed an unprecedented phenomenon. The Maoists gave a call for boycotting the state Assembly Election. Interestingly, leading political parties in the state, JD-U, Samata party and BJPdistributed party ticket to several candidates for contesting election whose image was already soiled for indulging in extremist activities in the past. Janata Dal (United), a leading political party, gave tickets to three Maoist leaders to contest from Gaya and Aurangabad districts. Apparently, the move was a fresh experiment to get the ultras back to the main stream of the society, but in reality, it was to outwit the political opponents and gain support of a section of voters living in rural areas and thriving already under influence of the Maoists. Several political leaders cutting across the party lines said, "Maoists too are part of the society. We all must try to win them over with love and conviction." Top leaders of the JD-U echoed the same. However, it was crystal clear that such a sympathy and tolerance was simply a ploy to please a section of rural mass and secure their vote. In electioneering campaigns candidates of JD-U encashed the so called liberal idea in their favour and appealed to the voters to support the Chief Minister Nitish Kumar. Interestingly, neither the JD-U, supremo Sharad Yadav nor the Chief Minister had issued any rejoinder or intimated alibi as to why party tickets were sanctioned to the former extremists for contesting election. However, impartial critics quipped that it is imperative that such a decision could not be issued without the approval of the party's top brass.

In fact, the boycott call gave sleepless night to the police who anticipated a large scale violence and disruption of election. Police intensified patrolling and requisitioned sufficient para military forces to assist them for conducting election peacefully and smoothly. However, participation of the candidates having the Maoist back ground was a sigh of relief as in Maoist dominated areas the ultras would be refraining from violence and blood curdling activities. Importantly, entry of the ultras in poll fray generated profound curiosity and interest in many circle. Impartial people felt that it was a diplomatic trickery to secure support of a set of rural voters, circumscribe outrages normally unleash by the extremists and isolate the political opponents, especially, the Rashtriya Janata Dal, led by former chief minister Lalu Prasad Yadav. Evidently, it was a novel experiment and an unorthodox dimension in state politics. In Lok Sabha poll held in April/May 2009, a dreaded Maoist commander, Kameshwar Baitha, languishing in jail got a ticket from Jharkhand Mukti Morcha (JMM), contested from Palamu constituency and was elected with comfortable margin. For the Assembly election Ashok Kumar Singh son of a top Maoist leader, Rammohan Singh was selected to contest from Rafiganj seat, Aurangabad district. It was whispered that the candidate's father negotiated with Maoists and secured release of four policemen kidnapped by the Maoists from Lakhisarai district in August 2010. Ticket was given to his son as recognition to his services. Secondly, Lalan Bhuiyan was fielded to contest from Kutumba reserved constituency, Aurangabad district. Seven criminal cases pertaining to Maoist activities were pending against him. The third candidate was Vinod Yadav supposed to contest from Sherghati constituency, Gaya district. Ironically, JD-U picked up the above candidates deliberately to bag support of the extremists. The constituencies going to be represented by them were located in the hot bed of the Maoists domain. However, an unpalatable precedent is set to accommodate the extremists henceforth carried forward zealously.

Chief Ministers' Reaction in an All-party Meeting

The Prime Minister Manmohan Singh invited the Chief Ministers of the Maoist torn states at his official residence, New Delhi, in July 2010, for a discussion to pin point remedial measures for curbing the Maoist menace. He was candid that Left Wing Extremism is a massive threat to the nation's safety and security. He was determined to stamp out Maoist violence from the country. Chief Minister of

Bihar, Nitish Kumar failed to attend the meeting and said that he preferred to distance himself from the security component of the two-pronged approach. He curtly commented that it was focused too much on the security component. The Union Home Minister present in the meeting informed that in 2010, till June, altogether 1103 Maoist related violence had taken place and 325 civilians were killed including 142 who were branded as police informers. He reiterated that Maoists have no right to set itself up a judge, jury and executor. In the meeting eight point programmes was discussed and resolved to its purposeful implementation. Prime Minister advised not to let inter personal issues stand in the way of forging a united front to tackle the menace.

Chief Minister Nitish Kumar strongly harped on his idea and said on many occasions, "Naxalites as a part of our society." He cautioned, "enforcement action alone is likely to accelerate alienation of such elements." Evidently, the CM differed on strategy in handling and containing the Maoist problem. However, his slogan, "Aapki sarkar Aapke Dwaar" meaning, government is at your door step, earned praise from many quarters. Under the scheme essential services like public distribution system, health, banking, NREGS offices, police office, public essential services like PDS and residential quarters are provided in one secure compound through an integrated participatory plan. It started in Sikaria area of Jehanabad in 2006. In fact, model was lauded by 13th Finance Commission team during its visit to Bihar. State government has extended it to 63 panchayats of 23 blocks of seven districts. Union government advised eight states to follow Bihar model to contain Naxalite menace. Panchayat Raj Ministry issued circular to the Chief Secretaries of eight states to enforce it diligently. It has identified 76 districts of eight states as extremism-effected, including thirty three most affected districts.

Chief Minister's Contact Mission with the People

Chief Minister Nitish Kumar feels that police action exclusively in tackling the Maoist problem is not going to produce the desired result. He argues that more on mass contact in rural areas, social and economic development for the poor and exploited people, sensitivity and responsiveness of the administration to the ordeals of the poor and prompt implementation of the developmental programmes and welfare of the rural mass are the key to gain support and good will of the rural masses. If the above steps are initiated and enforced with missionary zeal the extremists will easily be isolated. The aggrieved people will get rid of their miry influence and stand by the side of the government. The Chief Minister while undertaking tour in Maoist affected areas, visiting Block Development Offices, interacting with the common people and trying to project that the state is sincerely devoted to improve the lot of the poor and neglected mass. He organised and led the "Seva Yatra" to reinforce mass contact in rural areas. The Maoists have given boycott call to the CM's programme and warned the people not to respond and participate in the "Seva Yatra". The CM ignored the Maoist warning and boycott call and continued with his purposeful mission. The CM visited Parta village under Amba and Kutubagarh which are tainted for fiendish activities of the ultras. In spite of criticism response of the villagers was noteworthy. And the CM's kind gesture was enthusiastically responded by the rural populace.

Once he camped in Aurangabad and enquired about progress of various development works from the officials, wanted to know the reasons for delayed implementation of some projects and programmes and pulled up the defaulting officials. Maoists put posters on school and government building warning the people to boycott the CM's visit. They threatened the villagers for daring consequences if their warning was not given due notice. However, the CM was firm in his object and dauntlessly continued with his mission, visited villages, ignoring the ultras' pervasive tactics, interacted with villagers adhering to his programme. People in large number thronged in camping places, met the CM, put forth their grievances. CM's patient hearing, assurance and firmness to stick to meaningful remedial measures pleased the congregation. Broadly speaking, the CM's mass contact programme and dialogues directly with the common people indirectly worked as a setback for the extremists. In short, CM's direct contact and spontaneous response of the rural mass, whose support believed to be the mighty strength of the Maoists, has undeniably put the rebels in abysmal anxiety and despair.

CM's Reaction Watching Massacre of CRPF Personnel in Dantewada

On April 6, 2010, massacre of 76 CRPF personnel in Dantewada, Chhattisgarh has exposed galling operational weakness of the CRPF. A shock wave in the MHA was apparent for loss of so many precious lives. The then Union Home Minister, P. Chidambaram took responsibility for the set back and tendered his resignation to the Prime Minister. As expected the PM did not accept it. In fact resignation submitted ostensibly owning responsibility became a talk in political circle. Anti-HM group obliquely looked at him and questioned HM's sincerity to quit the office. HM took the plea that CRPF was under his charge and since the tragedy had taken place under his watch it was befitting for him to resign. However, the Prime Minister rejected the HM's move and thereby speculation was buried. In fact, the resignation episode gained much currency and gave handle to many leaders who said that it was a gimmick. Impartial critics feel that the HM craftily wanted to project his image and earn popularity.

Chief Minister of Bihar Nitish Kumar reacted sharply and said aiming at the HM, "I respect him. But my advice to him is to talk less, is it necessary to talk so much? I will suggest he controls his tone and tenor. Everybody knows that PM would not accept his resignation." CM added, "the government will have to focus on developments in grass root level that will bring people out of poverty.... Creditable action be taken to eradicate poverty and check corruption at the lower level." Importantly, the then Union Home Secretary, G.K. Pillai remarked that Bihar was a little soft in taking any hard action against the Maoists since Assembly election was scheduled to be held later this year. CM vehemently objected to it and said that the Home Secretary had no business to give such statement.

Union Home Minister P. Chidambaram and the Chief Minister of Bihar Nitish Kumar drew attention to the political circle for entering into harsh dialogues. In fact, Operation Green Hunt was not taken in right spirit by the CM. He did not attend a meeting held in Kolkata chaired by the Union Home Minister. On March 11, 2010, the CM hit out at the centre for threatening to withdraw central para-military forces from Bihar. Perhaps, a feeling is brewing in the Home Ministry that Bihar has not been co-operating for anti-Maoist offensives. CM said that the union government has been holding dialogues not through him. He added that the centre should not talk through newspapers. Naxalism is a very sensitive issue, instead of using forces, Naxalism should be tackled by winning hearts of the masses and launching development work. Development alone can stamp out Naxalism from the region. It appeared that P. Chidambaram requested the BJP leaders in Delhi to impress upon the CM to support the Centre's anti-Maoist operation which came out in print media. The CM was piqued at the media report and sharply reacted that the centre might withdraw the central forces deployed in Bihar. Yet, the state government is capable enough of tackling the Maoist problem meeting its own resources.

Unabated Violence and Bloodshed

On October 19, 2012 at the time of combing operation in Chakarbandha forest under Dudmaria police station, district Gaya the Maoists killed six CRPF personnel. Thereafter, security forces launched joint combing operation in the same area, seized nine pressure cooker bombs and six IEDs. Not deterred the ultras set fire on an anti-land mine vehicle at Karan Asthan near Barha-Chakrabandha, under Dumaria police station. Later CRPF destroyed bunkers of the ultras in Lutua and Dumaria.

On January 19, 2013, a tribal girl, Sarita Kharwar, fell in love with Maoist Sunil Kumar of Mirzapur, Uttar Pradesh. She was eloped and joined the outfit. She became mother of two sons. In fact both were born during her days as an outlaw. She was wanted in several heinous criminal cases including for a double murder at Deuri village, under Adhaura police station, district Kaimur. She now has surrendered with arms before the CRPF and police at Adhaura, a remote area of the district. Her husband has earlier surrendered before in UP.

On January 27, 2013, Maoists kidnapped eight labourers engaged in a road bridge construction work from Badaldiah under Khaira police station district Jamui In 2011, Maoists abducted 17 labourers at Balthar ghat and in another incident they abducted eleven labourers from Pakri ghat near Kiul River who were engaged in road bridge construction work. On February 22, 2013, six cops and two civilians were killed in a land mine blast in a remote village in Sherghati, district Gaya. Here the rebels used IED.

In Chatra district, Jharkhand, ten Maoists including seven leaders were killed in a factional feud and rivalry amongst the splinter groups. Maoists alleged that security forces, disgruntled elements and break away groups sinisterly hatched up a conspiracy and killed the Maoists on the border area of Bihar and Jharkhand. The Maoists gave a call for bandh for two days starting from April 6, 2013 in Jharkhand and Bihar, and planned fresh violence in Bihar and Jharkhand. Maoists planted a land mine under the road between Bandha Pahar and Pichaulia, within jurisdiction of Dumaria police station, Gaya district. It was planned to create panic in the area. However, intelligence collected from Maoist in custody disclosed the plot and thereby foiled their attempt. CRPF and BMP personnel jointly raided the spot and recovered 70 improvised explosive devices (IEDs), four pressure cooker bombs and 300 meters of wire. Police's prompt action averted a deadly blast and likely casualty. Keen observers feel that the Maoists are demoralised due to internal feud, uninterrupted and determined combing operations initiated by the security forces.

On July 2, 2013, at about 2 pm the convoy of Superintendent of Police, Pakur, Jharkhand, Amarjeet Balihar, was ambushed near a culvert in Kathikund Block and killed. He was returning to HQ after attending a meeting. Inspite of adequate precaution information about his movement leaked out. Death of a senior cop in an ambush badly affected morale of the cops in Bihar and Jharkhand. However, both states resolved to intensify joint operation. On December 3, 2013, at about 4.30 Pm, a police patrol party was returning after attending monthly meeting. Maoists ambushed the police party near the railway power plant, Aurangabad, and blasted a land mine by remote control device. The police vehicle was blown up to bits and seven cops were killed. On November 30, 2013, Sahibganj Patna intercity express was attacked. Three GRP cops escorting the train were killed and two cops were injured.

Caste Acrimony and Conflict Amongst Private Militia

Bihar has earned dubious distinction of mash room growth of private militia on the basis of caste, clan, groups, insane community pride etc. Bloody clash, massacre, wanton killing, land grabbing etc. are odious blot on the current social history of the state. Simultaneously, lamentable incompetence and failure of the administration to tackle and banish such social evil is a slash on the fair face of the successive state governments. It is an open secret that several private armies have been actively operating in the state. Each possessing separate object, operate independently and want to widen its authority and supremacy at the cost of the rival groups. In fact, no love lost among them was apparent who indulge in bitter rivalry, barbarous killing, man slaughter etc. Indeed, boundless hostility has shaken the very foundation of the so called the people's war. Instead of embracing peace, harmony and perusing the common goal the rival groups, unfortunately, prefer to thrive in the arid zone of acrimony. Broadly, in this measly competition thirteen private groups are quite prominent and active. In many rural areas they virtually run a parallel administration, defy the authority of the state and take law in their hands. The district administration often feels helpless to confront them and protect the unfortunate victims.

An alarming report submitted to the union government disclosing that all plains and plateaus of central and south Bihar have become a bastion of the ultra-left forces and domain of the private militia. The local police is unable to go against the fiend and enforce the rule of law effectively. Link of the private militia with the ultras is ambiguous, whether they share the Maoist ideology and ready to peruse the Maoist movement jointly is hazy. Interestingly, the union government has set up a co-ordination centre headed by the union Home Secretary to help the states to combat the extremist's active in the states. Secondly, the centre has committed to reimburse fifty percent of the security related expenditure. Yet, no tangible improvement of fast deteriorating situation was noticed in the beginning. However, as events moved apace, security forces have brought the tumultuous situation under control. The ultras are now forced to retreat instead of defending themselves and a large number of them have either surrendered or arrested. However, the union government has not initiated any purposeful programme to disarray the private militia.

It reveals that thirteen private army including, 1. Kunwar Sena, 2. Brahmarshi Seva. 3. Lal Sena. 4. Ranvir Sena. 5. Sunlight Sena. 6. Sawarn Liberation Front. 7. Bhumi Sena. 8. Ganga Sena etc. are notoriously active. Affected areas are Rohtas, Jehanabad, Sasaram, Bhojpur, Gaya, Patna, Bikaramganj, Nawada, and now Giridih, Hazaribagh, Dhanbad, Bokaro, Palamu, Chatra and Singhbhum of Jharkhand. Besides, there are several splinter groups or break away groups from the main extremist out-fits, who are at a daggers drawn For example, MCC massacred 13 activists of the Sangharsh Jana Mukti Morcha in April 2001, at village Belthu, district Hazaribag (now Jharkhand). The SJMM cadre retaliated; raided village Nawadih in dead of night on July 5, 2001, picked up eight able bodied persons belonging to Ganjhu tribe and hacked them to death. The marauders left hand bills at the spot stating they had taken revenge of Belthu massacre. On August 14, 2000, three members of a family suspected of having link with the PW were killed by the MCC at Khainia village in Masauhi sub-division, district Patna. Victims were close relatives of gangster Jainamdam Yadav and sympathizers of the PW. Police said killing was a retaliation of the murder of a mukhiya, Laldhari Yadav, who had secret link with the MCC.

Dalits, Target of the Ranvir Sena

Instances of massacre of the Dalits by the private militia, especially, Ranvir Sena is quoted to high light the magnitude of the acrimony and caste war. Unfortunately, Dalits are the worse victims. In 1997, 58 dalits were massacred in Lakshmanpur Bathe. After trial the lower court sentenced 16 accused persons to death and ten accused persons for life term. However, the High Court acquitted all of them on benefit of doubt in October 2013. In Miyapur massacre 32 dalits were killed in 2000. Trial court convicted ten accused persons. However, the High Court acquitted nine of them. In 1998, in Nagri bazaar massacre ten dalits were gunned down. Trial court ordered death penalty on three and life sentence to eight accused persons, but all were acquitted by the High Court. In 1996, in Bathanitola massacre 21 dalits were killed. Lower court pronounced death sentence to 3, and life sentence to 20 accused persons. In an appeal, the High Court acquitted all of them. In fact, as many accused persons were going unpunished, the state government enacted a special law in 1989 to curb caste conflicts and atrocities on dalits.

Police's Success—Seizure of Explosives

In 2012, police seized 49 quintals of high grade explosive and huge quantity of Maoist literature from two houses at Moinpur area of Gaya district. Again 81 bags of explosive material from a house at Chotki Nawadah mohalla and 29 bags from a house at Raja Babu market, district Gaya were seized. Subodh Kumar, the king pin who was running the racket was arrested. It transpired that stock piling of deadly explosives was going on for dispatching to Chhattisgarh, Jharkhand, UP, Odisha and West Bengal. In fact it was one of the biggest hauls of explosive successfully made by the Gaya district police.

Raids in hide-outs disclosed many clinching clues, including new training materials such as video cassettes of English movies on terrorism, espionage, guerrilla operations and surprise attacks on the targets, etc. These are exhibited in the camps as a part of the lesson to the cadres to inspire them to learn and follow the technique and skill whenever needed.

Jahanabad Jail-break

November 2005, was one of the dark days for the law and order authority of Jahanabad district, Bihar state. On November 13, 2005, the PLGA stormed the police lines of Jahanabad district and attacked the district jail, over powered the jail wardens, looted weapons and set free 398 prisoners including the state committee member of ultras, Ajay Kanu from Andhra Pradesh. They killed five guards and an inmate of the jail, kidnapped 20 members of Ranbir Sena, exploded bombs near residences of the District Magistrate and the Superintendent of Police. They blew up the railway track, snapped power and telephone lines. The town was in the grip of darkness and perplexity in absence of rule of law. Wild rumour with its usual love for falsehood increased muss and suspense for unknown danger. The citizenry throbbed with panic ran helter-skelter to save themselves from the ultras' rough and ready method. As a matter of fact, authority of the government in the town virtually collapsed awaiting a dooms day.

Distressingly, the daring attack and release of a large number of prisoners was unprecedented and happened to be the master stroke of the ultras since the Naxal movement originated in 1967. Maoists' intelligence apparatus, meticulous planning, extra ordinary skill and precision in execution of the task have baffled the security forces. Intelligence of the state and union government lamentably failed to anticipate such a gory event. Police was at a loss, none could imagine such an organised and horrendous attack by the ultras. Indeed, people got the taste of the Maoists' capacity and striking power. They realised that defiance of Maoist diktat was only to invite a catastrophe. Notably, after merger of the PW and MCC this was one of the diabolic strikes by the Maoists. Later, police arrested Satyendra Das, a self-styled area commander, who was a suspect in the jail break. He was involved in several heinous crime in Jehanabad, Aurangabad and Gaya districts.

Growing Threat of the Maoists—64 Leaders and Activists Forced to Resign

From 2008 to 2011, the Maoists were vulnerable in several districts, especially, in Gaya, Aurangabad, Rohtas districts. Security forces were unable to contain or force them to take to heels. There was panic all over. The emboldened ultras threatened the political leaders to quit the party and extend support to their movement. They kept them under constant threat and fear and made it clear that their family members would not be spared if they failed to carry out their instructions. Political leaders approached the government and requested for protection against the Maoist ultimatum. Unfortunately, state could not do much to salvage them. It was learnt secretly that on the state's initiative a few leaders opened dialogues with the leading ultras with the help of a few radicals known for their sympathy and leaning towards the ultra-left movement. State was ready to grant several concessions to the ultras if the political leaders and activists were left unharmed. As understood, secret talk failed. The Maoists were unrelenting and issued ultimatum. The demoralised security forces were not in a position to guarantee safety and security of the targeted party leaders and their whiz kids. In party level JD (U) and BJP clandestinely negotiated with a few front line leaders of the ultras. But it failed to produce any desired result. In fact, situation was slipping through fingers. Since the police and state was helpless and no solution was at sight, throbbed with panic, sixty four leaders and activists of the ruling coalition parties in Gaya district succumbed to the threat and finally quit the JD (U) and BJP parties in May 2008. In fact, 37 leaders and activists of the NDA were kidnapped from Imamgang, Banke Bazar and Dumaria Blocks of Gaya district. They were taken to Chakrabanda hill surrounded by forest and threatened for ugly consequences if they failed to resign publicly from the preliminary membership of the respective parties. The drama took place at a school premises at Imamganj in presence of the media persons. The abducted leaders and activists were freed after they agreed to abide by the Maoist diktat. Dismayingly, the state and the security forces could not avert such a catastrophe. Importantly, persons resigned were office bearers of two parties from the district unit level to block unit levels.

The Speaker of the Bihar Legislative Assembly representing Islampur constituency of Gaya district has continuously neglected the constituency. It was alleged that all developmental work had come to a grinding halt and police atrocities on women and poor persons were on the rise. In fact, mass resignation of the local leaders of JD(U) and the BJP is a severe blow to the Speaker as well as to the ruling parties. Fear and panic of the peace loving people knew no bounds. They realised that threat by the Maoists is not imaginary and could not be ignored since state was not in a position to ensure safety and security of the people.

Bal Manch: Child Soldiers in Bihar

Maoists have adopted dubious means to recruit males and females belonging to specific age group for increasing number and strengthening the cadre. Broadly, candidates are picked up from poor tribal families either by threat or coercion. However, the recruits are paid monthly stipend or salary once they join the cadre, which is an incentive for the poverty stricken families. Sometimes a lump sum amount is paid to the chief of the family. In fact, poor and unemployed youths of both sexes welcome the offer of joining the cadre since they will earn and will be able to support the families financially. Many, of course, join the cadre guided by the spirit of adventure. They hear stories of attack, defence, gun battle, use of fire arms, romance or adventure of camp life in company of young comrades including young girls. They are victims of constant brain wash that the people's government will be set up soon, class enemy will be eliminated and the exploited people will be free to steer their own destiny. Secondly, that the tribal are neglected discriminated and exploited etc. are put into their heads by repeated counseling and brain hammering exercise. They are told that they can change the present social and political order and contribute to establish the people's government which will destroy their miseries. All these factors and secret propaganda have a cascading effect on their callow and youthful mind. Secondly, they nurse abyss curiosity for a fire arm and avidly desire to possess a firearm and seek opportunity to use it as per their sweet will. This is one of reasons to inspire the youths to join the Maoist cadre. Many tribal girls either volunteer or forced to join the cadre. They receive training, learn to use firearms and soon deployed in operations. Once they are experienced and show courage and determination in combats, some of them are selected for the guerrilla squads. Women guerrillas have given a good account of themselves. Many are die hard ultras, obstinate in fighting and display able leadership. In fact, the feminine obstinacy, the natural instinct or blessing for the weaker sex carries weight in strengthening the cadre. Many of them earned laurel for matchless fortitude and able leadership in encounters vis-à-vis male Maoists.

In addition to general recruitment policy and drive, the Maoists prefer to recruit adolescents, indoctrinate them in party's ideology, make them physically tough, train them in keeping with the various facets of jungle operations. In fact, they are made formidable rebels totally entwined with culture and discipline of the out-fit. As an adolescent they are used to carry messages, watch movements of the security forces, collect intelligence, escort equipments, ration, deployed in maintenance of camps and assist the seniors for comfort in camp lives. They are given intensive training in handling the fire arms, field craft, use of explosives and fighting the security forces. Once they attain youth, some of them are trained in planting mines, handling of sophisticated weapons. In fact, they are considered to be the permanent assets of the out-fit. They are well looked after and many are forced to marry a fellow female rebel. Broadly, an ambience is deliberately created so that they cannot quit the out-fit and return to join the main stream of the society.

Recruitment of the adolescents is not done through the normal process. Maoists identify poor families possessing two or three boys and girls within the age group of eight to twelve. They ask the family members to spare a boy or a girl to join the cadre. If it is refused they kidnap the kid under threat ignoring the family's agony. Sometimes, the Maoists pay some money to the aggrieved family as a kind of compensation. They are unable to muster courage and lodge complaint either to the police or to any agency. In remote areas of Bihar, Jharkhand and Chhattisgarh the Maoists get virtually free hand to recruit or kidnap the kids putting the family members under fear and gory attack. The poor villagers are helpless, forced to succumb to the threat and hand over the kid to the ultras. In fact, the remote areas are the fertile ground for recruiting the kids with impunity. The ultras welcome such recruitment drive as the kids undergoing training will be the stubborn and permanent member of the cadre. Secondly, it is easier to mould a kid according to the requirement of the out-fit, indoctrinate the out-fit's aim, object and goal easily who are yet to learn to judge the right or wrong and protest against any gross error or malfeasance. Kids once trained and attain youth are used as foot soldiers. Many foot soldiers are utilised to assist the Peoples Liberation Guerrilla Army (PLGA). Indeed, recruitment of adolescents both boys and girls is a continuous process for the Maoists which has been going on unabatedly. However, no precise estimate of total number of children recruited so far is available, but uninterrupted recruitment for Bal Manch in Bihar and Jharkhand is a positive threat to the peace loving families, to police and security forces. This very matter was discussed in the Parliament. The Minister of State for Home submitted information to the House.

The alarmed Intelligence agencies have brought the trend to the notice of the state police organisations and requested to keep close watch on the missing children in villages allegedly recruited by the Red army to train them in subversive activities.

Information reveals that in certain pockets Maoists are taking away children by force. The main problem faced by the local police is that the parents are not coming forward and complaining about their children being kidnapped. Bihar is worse affected where representatives of the Red Army openly ask the villagers of economically backward areas to donate one child for the cause of Naxalism. Ultras have been following the similar practice adopted by the LTTE, Al-Qaeda and Lashkar-e-Taiba to build a hard-core brigade for the out-fit with the recruits of tender age. Local observers feel that it is easy and convenient to brain wash and train anyone coming from tender age group, make them highly motivated and disciplined. A senior police officer of Bihar admitted that the state police has not been able to do much against it since the parents are not coming forward to report the matter which may be for fear of the extremists and the police's inability to protect them.

The UN's Observation

The annual report of the Secretary General of the United Nations Organisation indicated that the Maoists are recruiting and indoctrinating children and constituted children's squads and associations as part of mass mobilisation. Report reveals, "Maoist armed groups have been recruiting and indoctrinating children and have constituted children's squads and association (Bal Dastas, Bal Sangham and Bal Manch) as a part of mass mobilisation programme. The information is supported by the report of the National Commission for Protection of Child Rights 2010. It is iterated that children were being recruited by intimidation and abduction. They are used as 'support roles, including as lookouts, messengers, porters and cooks.' This practice has been going on widely in Chhattisgarh, Jharkhand, Bihar, and adjoining states."

It has pointed at rampant attacks on the school buildings by the Maoists. From 2006 to 2011, ultras had destroyed 258 school buildings, mostly in Bihar, Jharkhand and Chhattisgarh. Importantly, the global body has cited and extolled the "Bal Bandhu" scheme in ten districts, each of the five Maoist torn states including Bihar. The scheme exhaustively looks into the needs of the children on education, health, nutrition, sanitation, safety aspect and local community participation.

Maoists—Attempt to Contest Election

Seeing success in Nepal to capture political power through ballot the Maoists in Bihar contemplated to participate in general election and form the government. In fact, the idea of taking part in election is being seriously thought in higher level of the Maoist outfit. As a matter of fact, the Maoists have already captured 33 percent seats in panchayat election held in 2006. Importantly, Bihar shares 714 km long porous border with Nepal. In border belt of the state, Maoists influence from Nepal is often manifested. Maoists are always disdainful towards the electoral system. Yet, they have perhaps realised that guerrilla warfare or doctrine of annihilation is hardly going to change the existing system. Therefore, it is wise that they should enter into electoral arena and capture power through parliamentary election. Faculties of the A N Sinha Institute of Social Sciences, Patna made an extensive field study on the subject and interviewed 23 top Naxal leaders and a large number of cadres over a period of six months. Study discloses the inclination of many Naxal leaders towards electoral process for capturing political power. In fact, success in Nepal has goaded several top leaders to re-consider the outfit's present policy. Critics feel that it is an irony if the Naxalites switch on to the electoral battle deviating from the firm goal of the Naxalite movement. Interestingly, a good number of hard-core leaders are disinterested to compromise and agree to accept any modified policy giving up revolutionary path. They reiterate that they are aware that the battle would take a long time but sanguine that the final victory would knock at the door as no government can for long resist the peoples' will inspired and enriched by revolutionary spirit and ideology.

Attack and Violence by Break-away Groups

Tritiya Sammalan Prastuti Committee (TSPC) is a breakaway group from the Maoist outfit. In the past they were comrades. However, now they are at a daggars drawn. Interestingly, the Maoists are at the receiving end both from the security forces and the estranged comrades defected and joined the TSPC. On March 28, 2013, Sandeepji, a central committee leader of the Maoist outfit was returning to Bihar from Jharkhand. He was attacked by the TSPC at a place lies near the border of Chatra and Gaya districts which is considered to be a safe transit point between Bihar and Jharkhand. About 150 TSPC cadres surrounded the village when the Maoists were preparing for mid-day meals. A fierce encounter took place. Ten Maoists were killed including two sub divisional commanders and regional commander of Bihar Jharkhand Special Area Committee member, Lalesh Yadav. Maoists allege that it was a planned operation with the aid of security forces. Seven deceased were identified.

TSPC was founded in 2002 against hegemony of the Yadavs active in the Naxal (MCC) outfit, by the tribal ultras belonging to mainly the Oraon, Ghanju, Turi and Badai castes. Rivalry between two factions often took ugly turn and finally it reached the arid zone of acrimony. Present abduction and killing could be attributed to tribal and non-tribal feud and the victims were the Yadavs. The abducted Maoists were likely to be tried in Jan Adalats, going to be punished varying from death penalty to chopping of limbs etc. Rest would be asked to join the breakaway faction in lieu of punishment. The incident again indicates the brewing deadly caste feud between the Maoists and the break-away factions. Importantly, in October 2001, before merger, the People's War passed a resolution in a convention at Rajnandangaon and resolved on concentrating on Central Bihar and initiating actions against all extremist organisations, especially, the MCC, the Ranvir Sena, the armed outfit of backward Yadavs and the Bhumihars respectively. Direction was issued to intensify armed struggle in new areas of operation.

Violence Torn Jamui District

Jamui district has been facing the brunt of the Maoist violence. On February 12, 2010, the Maoists killed 12 villagers on suspicion of being the informers of the police. In fact, Jamui district is considered to be the safe haven of the Maoists. On June 13, 2013, at about 1.30 pm, roughly 150 Maoists, assembled at Kendra halt station between Jamui and Manipur railway station. Maoists attacked Dhanbad-Patna intercity express and in exchange of fire one Railway Protection Force personnel, one junior commission officer of Bihar police and one passenger were killed. The Guard of the train and four railway employees were injured. Maoist looted belongings of many passengers, three automatic weapons from the RPF personnel and detained the train for about thirty minutes. Thereafter, the rebels disappeared in the jungle.

According to the keen observers the attack on the intercity express was far from a routine or isolated Maoist venture. In fact, part of Jamui district is under the domain of the rebels. Its jungle and hills provide a safe corridor to Monghyr district of Bihar and Giridih district of Jharkhand. Broadly, the area is a safe shelter ground for the rebels. Here, top brasses of the outfit assemble, organise meetings or conferences to chalk out policy matters and strategy to galvanise and rejuvenate the movement. Curiously enough, the rebels' satisfaction resorting to firing random at the train, killing three persons, carrying away three weapons was apparently a formidable display of aggressive potential of the ultras. However, it was not their sole aim. The rebels detained the train for about thirty minutes, security forces were nowhere to lunch counter attack. Yet they did not indulge in arson, killing of the hapless passengers or any barbaric notoriety for which they are known. Critics firmly believed that there was some sinister design behind the attack, primarily, to divert attention of the security forces to some other theatre of operation. It is inferred that well calculated diversionary tactics to reinforce strength in the areas domination by them and to regain their decaying influence in the region, was craftily adopted.

Police felt that a huge quantity of arms and ammunitions were being transported in the train under the escort of the women Maoists which was planned to be off loaded at Kundra. Police believed that cache of arms and ammunitions had reached safely to the Maoist hide out. Others felt that attack was a counter offensive drill for the newly recruited and trained Maoists. For above reasons the rebels, instead of going berserk kept the task confined to a limited arena. Top police brasses feel that demography and terrain in Monghyr-Jamui region hinders the security forces to undertake direct assault on the Maoist bastions. Secondly, insufficiency of armed forces is a formidable bottleneck to organise effective assaults, capture, kill or disarray the rebels. Already 8500 armed personnel and five battalions of the CRPF are deployed for anti-Maoist operations. In fact, in spite of numerous odds they have succeeded in cornering the ultras. Co-ordinated flush out operations have forced the ultras to go for tactical retreat or hide temporarily in safe Bhimbandh forest of Munger district, adjacent to Jamui and Kothia-Damuria territory of Gaya district at the tri-junction of Chatra and Palamu districts of Jharkhand. Intelligence report reveals that the attack was a part of the "induction programme" for the People's Liberation Guerrilla Army (PLGA). It was a first assignment ear marked for a newly recruited and trained group comprised mostly with teenagers and girls who were below 25 years of age. Critics quipped that it was a kind of baptism through bloodshed to the newly trained young rebels. Surprisingly, about fifty percent of the rank and file of the attackers was girls. Broadly, uninterrupted hot chase by the security forces and the rural peoples' dismay and disapproval for violence and blood bath have compelled the Maoists to act defensively. Secondly, loss of good will of the rural populace has excruciatingly eroded the peoples' support base and sympathy which used to be envious impetus and assistance for the ultras.

Jamui—A Disturbed District

Jamui is one of the major disturbed areas of Bihar. Its difficult terrain extends right up to Munger through Giridih, Jharkhand about 300 kms long. Monghyr's impregnable Bhimbandh, the densest forest of Bihar has been running continuously right up to Jharkhand border and further leading to Purulia region of West Bengal. It is a safe sanctuary and excellent hide-out for the Maoists. Secondly, areas being inaccessible and safe, training grounds have been established to train the recruits. In fact, increasing pressure by the security forces in Chhattisgarh and Jharkhand has pushed the rebels to use Bhimbandh as the safe shelter ground for lying low temporarily. Importantly, Maoists' activities in Sonebhadra and Mirzapur districts of Uttar Pradesh have been contained, resulting in, the rebels are trying to sneak into Bihar and gear up their violent activities. Broadly, better road communication facilities have been helping quicker movements of the security forces to take on the ultras. In addition, pro-active policing and joint operations by states have put the Maoists in back foot. Consequently, they are losing their support base. Keen observers contemplate that as the Maoists are failing in the present front, they may shift their activities to the northern territory of the state adjacent to Nepal. True, the ultras are likely to get help and support clandestinely from the Communist units of Nepal but it may not be very alarming as the intelligence units and the security forces are extra watchful on the impending development.

Violence piled upon violence in 2005. On January 5, 2005, Maoists triggered a landmine at the convoy of the Superintendent of Police K.C. Surendra Babu and killed him, six policemen and looted weapons from the deceased cops. Ultras attacked Madhuban police station and in exchange of fire six ultras were gunned down. In June ultras attempted to loot Central Bank and State Bank of India in Motihari. However, it was successfully repulsed by the police. In March 2006, about 500 Maoists encircled Dumaria police station in Gaya district and fired from all sides. They hurled petrol bombs and grenades. But attack was repulsed. In April, ultras ambushed the convoy of Ashok Singh, a candidate for Zila Parishad Election, set out to canvass for himself. He along with five others were killed and five persons were injured. The vehicle was set on fire and three dead bodies were thrown in flame. In May, a commander of the Maoists was killed in an encounter at Bhitra, Atri police station area, Gaya district. In December, an area commander of the ultras was killed in a gun battle at Visram village, Shivsagar police station area, Rohtas district. It was crystal clear that violence let loose by the ultras was not taken silently by the police. In fact, police displayed consummate zeal and courage to combat and neutralise the Maoists. They not only put up a brave front but also repulsed and foiled many devilish attacks, killed quite a number of ultras in direct encounters. Numerous ordeals did not deter the security forces. They displayed indomitable will and extraordinary fortitude to maintain peace, law and order. Indeed, their supreme sacrifices at the altar of duty have abysmally inspired the cops to fight and wipe out the extremists.

Significantly, many persons belonging to Oraon and Traru tribes living near the border of Nepal were converted into Christianity. They secretly maintained link with the MCC, Secondly, Christian missionaries of Bettiah, Champaran district developed contact with the MCC before the merger of the PW and the MCC. A few missionaries conspired at the behest of the MCC, and got Bharat Yadav and Bhola Mian, both supporters of the BJP, assassinated at Charapapur Banbar on May 24, 2003. The Director of Ratanpur Christian Mission and Adivasi Mission were suspected for the crime. A report was submitted to the police. Adequate evidence came to light that a strong nexus between MCC and infiltrators from Bangladesh had been working. Ultras were utilising them for procuring weapons clandestinely from Bangladesh.

Bihar: Fertile Land for the Red Movement

It cannot be accepted that the state will be absolutely free from Maoist violence in spite of reasonable success of the security forces to disarray them. Dispassionately, there may be lull temporarily if pressure from the security forces is intensified and made formidable. Nevertheless, the Maoists will not give up their struggle discarding their aim of destroying the present order and establishing the People's government. It may be debatable, yet it is a reality. Confrontations, endless actions and counter measures will inflate the volume of the history of conflicts between the security forces and the rebels. In the tangled web of bloody confrontations, unprecedented loss of men and materials, the peace-loving persons and the devoted readers of the history may be baffled. Indeed, its end is beyond any speculation. Since it is not exclusively a law and order problem, the government and the security forces have to be prepared for facing countless fiendish attacks and up-hill challenges from the Red rebels. They have to remain in readiness for matchless sacrifices. Without any prejudice, it may be reminded that abject poverty, unemployment, caste rivalry, untouchability and neglect of the dalits, ruthless conduct of the private militia, social discrimination, political instability etc. have made Bihar state a fertile ground for instigating the poverty-stricken people to come under the Maoist fold and carry the Maoist movement ahead. Hence, spontaneous support and participation of the poor and deprived people to the Maoist movement, its philosophy and goal etc. have accelerated the progress of the Maoist activities. If it is watched from the vintage point, it will transpire that sympathy and support of the people, especially, of the down trodden is a substantial support for the growth of the Red movement in the state. Broadly speaking, attack on the police camp at Goah, district Aurangabad on July 17, 2013, killing of three cops and two security guards who were guarding the construction work of a culvert and looting of thirty automatic and semi-automatic fire arms, attack on the convey of the Superintendent of Police, Pakur, Jharkhand, in June 2013, shooting down the SP, and four cops, and sporadic attack, ambush, killing and horrid violence in rebel-ridden areas are abundantly and manifestly clear that the Red movement is quite active and will not peter out or die so easily. Hence, the government and security forces have to be mentally prepared for protracted and obstinate struggle without anticipating its last mile stone and the D-day.

Importantly, during the President's rule in Jharkhand from January to July (July 12, 2013), violent activities of the rebels showed an increasing trend. During the first three month of the year (2013) Maoist related incidents reported from Bihar state were forty percent and deaths were fifty eight percent respectively, of total incidents recorded from the Maoist-torn states of the country. Nevertheless, success of the security forces to reclaim sizeable areas from control of the ultras and to put them in defensive position is a mighty setback for the ultras. Many intellectuals argue that a dialogue with the rebels may see light at the end of the tunnel. But the Ministry rules out possibility of negotiating with them. Officials say that the Maoists have countless leaders, self-styled commanders and isolated upstarts. Secondly, there are several splinter groups and are at daggers 'drawn. Groups are honey combed, possess tangent ideas and contradictory views. Hence the idea of negotiation is a futile exercise. Interestingly, internal feud, fractional quarrel, bitter enmity and arbitrary killings have put the Maoists in a quagmire. Admittedly, it is weakening their strength, solidarity and soiling their image. Simultaneously, it is eroding their rural support bank. Nitish Kumar, the Chief Minister of Bihar feels that police action is not enough to neutralise the Maoists.

It may be recalled that Prime Minister Manmohan Singh declared from the rampart of the Red Ford, Delhi on the occasion of Independence Day, 2006, that Left Wing extremism is a massive threat to the nation's safety and security. He was determined to stamp out Maoist violence from the country's soil. He called the all-party meet in New Delhi to discuss mainly on a detailed road map to tackle the Maoists. Secondly, the idea of National Counter Terrorism Centre was one of the core issues for discussion. However, on June 6, 2013, a conference of the Chief Ministers of nine Maoist affected states was held in New Delhi under chairmanship of the Union Home Minister S.K. Shinde to discuss the problems on left wing extremism. After prolonged discussion the participants agreed on a unified national policy to fight the threat. All, including the Home Minister stressed on urgent need to enhance deployment of security forces in affected areas. They discussed and pressed on "surgical operations" to take out the top leadership of the Maoist outfit. They also discussed the growing penetration of the ultras into urban areas. After protracted discussion it was conceded that the left wing extremism is the biggest threat to internal security of the country. Chief Ministers expressed desire to build a special force on the line of Greyhounds of Andhra Pradesh to take on the ultras. All pleaded for co-ordinated offensives, adequate financial help and technical assistance from the union government. Chief Minister of Chhattisgarh stressed on united and coordinated offensive along with the central forces in the tri-junction of the Bastar jungle from where the senior leaders of the out-fit generally operate. Chief Minister of Bihar Nitish Kumar said that solution of the problem by police action alone would be superficial, as the issue also has political dimensions. CMs felt that there is a lack of co-ordination between the state police and the CRPF.

Bandapadhya Committee Report

Union government set up a committee under D. Bandapadhya, an IAS, officer for analyzing the situation in the country in connection with the Maoist problems. There were sixteen members in the committee who are considered to be the experts. The committee members visited affected areas stretching over two years in four Maoist violence ridden states, Andhra Pradesh, Odisha, Jharkhand and Chhattisgarh, and submitted report before the planning commission in April 2008. "Development and challenges in the extremist affected areas" is the caption of the report. Concluding observation of the report reveals: "Extremism is an effect or a deeper malaise of failure of governance and development activities in the affected areas where roughly 2.4 crores tribal were evicted and displaced from hearth and homes because of large scale acquisition of land for development purpose."

Report created flutter and many state governments faced scathing criticism for displacing the tribal from their lands enjoyed by them for generations on the pretext of rural development.

Journalists—Targets of the Maoists and Police

Journalists working in rural areas are called, "Foot soldiers" of journalism. They have to work sacrificing urban comfort, facing physical hazards and wrath of the spotty, devious persons and law breakers. They also expose monumental callousness, indifference and inaction of the public servants and the police. They often write against the extremists, expose their misdeeds and thereby earn their displeasure. In the state several sensational stories were published high lighting wrong doing, extortion episode, internal feuds, accumulation of personal wealth by the ultras etc. have irked them. Hence, Maoists seek opportunity to retaliate and teach lesson to the media persons. Journalist Upendra Chaurasia was caught and mercilessly thrashed by the Maoists at Kachanpur village near Deo police station, Aurangabad district. He received multiple fracture injuries and was admitted to Patna medical college in critical condition. In another incident, a journalist from local Hindi daily was kidnapped who went to cover an incident of violence unleashed by the ultras. In fact, the Maoists killed a villager, torched five vehicles and let loose large scale violence. However, he was released after long detention. General Secretary of Bihar working journalists union and member of the Indian Press Council appealed to the Central committee of the Maoists leadership to make their position clear as their harsh action have not gone down well with the masses. In fact, very often the journalists are threatened for ugly consequence for their reports published exposing atrocities unleashed by the ultras.

Police is also hostile to the journalists since they unearth many incidents of police excesses, negligence and high-handedness. A dozen of media persons were harassed, tortured and falsely implicated in imaginary criminal cases. A Bureau chief of the local Hindi daily was nabbed and badly assaulted by a senior police officer in Khagaria district. In another incident, a journalist was caught and tortured. He was asked to disclose his source after he published a report on corruption in several development schemes. Six local journalists were implicated in cases of dacoities in railways in Jhajha. In Aurangabad district police has started a criminal case for treason against a local journalist branding him a Maoist. Inaction or misdeeds of the police personnel if brought to light, adverse public opinion obfuscates image of the government. The embarrassed government had to face severe criticism on the floor of the state assembly. Obviously, it makes the government unpopular. Unfortunately, in several districts of Bihar the field journalists are targets of both the Maoists and the police. Government assured on the floor of the House that cases against journalists would be withdrawn.

Maoist Leaders Amassing Wealth

Many Maoist leaders, deviating from the ideology and rigorous discipline of the outfit have been amassing money, accumulating wealth and assests in shape of house, flats, bunglows, land, etc. A Maoist leader has sent his ward to a foreign country for higher education spending substantial amount. In Ranchi, one leader has diverted a portion of extorted or looted money for the outfit and used it all for his personal comfort. Top leaders want to stay in urban areas enjoying urban comfort and facilities instead of sharing ordeals with the comrades camping in forests, unhealthy hide-outs, and inhospitable sanctuaries embracing malaria, water-borne diseases, and snake bites, absence of medical care and fear of surprise police raids. Broadly speaking, protracted insurgency or a proxy war, eerie suspense, delay and uncertainty of the success hit morale of the rank and file once inspired by lofty ambition of fulfilling revolutionary goal. Under such circumstances degeneration sets in. The ideal organisation of the past and its dedicated leadership at that juncture, are susceptible to frustration and paranoia. No wonder, down fall of the Maoist movement is inevitable if pocked or tainted due to the follies of the comrades sunk in worldly temptation and maggoty vices. Rival groups of the out-fit have brought out and circulated leaflets exposing the ills practised by some leaders.

Present and Future of the Red Movement

Importantly, internal squabble and rivalry among the splinter groups have brought out many startling allegations of misuse of fund, accumulation of personal wealth, opening bank accounts, fixed deposits in banks, purchase of land, flats, bunglows, sending wards to foreign countries for higher education etc. It reveals that many Maoists have badly deviated from the beefy ideal of the revolutionary movement. In this respect details are focused in Chapter two, for consumption of the curious readers.

Ministry of Home Affairs, Government of India, after critical analysis has iterated that three Maoist violence ridden states, Chhattisgarh, Jharkhand and Bihar together account for over eighty percent of Left Wing Extremist (LWE) violence in the country. Maoists, for operational purpose have divided Bihar and Jharkhand into eight zones. This arrangement is being adhered to for the last two decades. But due to unrelenting pressure of the security forces the Maoists have lost absolute control on four zones in Bihar during the last two years. First, the Magadh zone, comprising Jahanabad and Aurangabad, secondly, Vindhyachal zone covering border areas of Uttar Pradesh, Bihar and some portion of Jharkhand, thirdly, the Jamui zone comprising Jamui district and some selected areas of the border touching Jharkhand and lastly, Madhya zone comprising border belt of Bihar and Jharkhand, are not in firm grip of the rebels. In above four zones Maoists are already in defensive posture, unable to come out openly for a massive operation. Security forces are camping in strategic locations, are very alert to foil any attempt by the ultras. In fact, security forces have substantially improved their training, weaponry, fire power, tactics and intelligence output. Secondly, mass contact in village level, assurance of safety and creating an ambience of security, improvement of road communication and semblance of rural development programmes have placed them in higher pedestal. Thirdly, programmes for economic and rural developments are working positively to alienate the ultras from the rural mass. Fourthly, threat perception is no longer deterrent for the people as they realised that nuances of Maoist jargon for the so called people's war, people's government are illusory and not likely to see the light of the day. Hence, people are coming forward to co-operate with the police and the administration. Frankly speaking, people want peace and stability and hence not interested to welcome the perpetrators of blood bath and gory violence. It is reiterated that after savage attack to derail Rajdhani Express near Gaya in March 2005, and daring attack on Jahanabad district jail in November 2005, the Maoists' attacks were smaller, scattered, intermittent and sporadic which were not so deadly to upset the administration. In fact, several small incidents, occasional attacks on railways in Jamui-Monghyr installations, death of a few security personnel have not dissuaded the security forces to tackle the ultras firmly. Indeed, continuous modernisation programmes, new specialist contingents either raised or going to be founded, heavy incentive and beefy compensation to the security personnel have enhanced morale of the security forces to fight the pitiless outlaws with courage and determination. However, as explained above recurrence of devilish attacks and annihilation at any moment is not at all ruled out.

The Prime Minister Manmohan Singh asked the states to take all possible steps to contain and banish the Maoist menace. In fact, from January 2005 to May 2010, civilians and security forces together 10268 persons were killed. In many pockets rule of law has disappeared and writs of the Maoists are supreme. Hence, magnitude of the horrid Maoist threat needs to be taken with utmost seriousness. Impartial critics feel that government of Bihar has not been throwing its weight whole heartedly to contain or eliminate the growing Red threat. Chief Minister Nitish Kumar is not in favour of decisive action to silence the appalling forces and root out the ultras from the state's soil. He asserted, "Naxalites as a part of our society," and warned, "Enforcement alone will lead to alienation of such elements." He skipped a meeting of Maoist torn states called by the Union Home Minister, at Kolkata to discuss the intricacies of joint operation. People of Bihar, without any prejudice, feel that law and order in the state has deteriorated. Soft line taken by the government to tackle the Red movement and its perpetrators has queered the pitch. In fact, increasing trend of the Maoist violence is apparent, since in other states Maoist violence is either under control or declining fast. Unfortunately, Bihar has failed to keep pace with other states. In 2012, altogether 130 Maoist related incidents reported, twenty five persons including six ultras were killed. But in 2013, violent incidents shot up to 160, and sixty persons including 16 cops were killed, and no casualty from the Maoists was reported. If records of last two years are compared, it will transpire that, of late, violence in Bihar has increased by 41 per cent. Three districts, Jamui, Gaya and Aurangabad accounted for 60 per cent of total violent incidents reported in the state during the last two years. Jamui seems to be the safe haven of the Maoists. However, there is no reason to be disappointed. Spurt in Maoist violence is a temporary phenomenon and undoubtedly well within the grip of the security forces. Maxim, that as the darkest cloud has silver lining, the security forces will be successfully disarraying the appalling forces and have the last laugh.

CHAPTER SIX

Odisha in the Grip of the Maoist Terror

People of Odisha or Orissa are God-fearing, cling on the religion, Hindu culture and heritage, entwined with the Faith and blessings of the Lord Jagannath. Tribal or Adivasis constitute 22.13 percent of the population of the state. Broadly, in spite of poverty and puny industrial progress the state used to enjoy halcyon ambience of peace and stability. The police functions in the accolade of the rural mass's need in keeping with rural ethos and usages. Its prime focus is on conventional policing and professionalism. Frankly speaking, relying on the above back ground neither the government nor the people believed that violence and bloodshed can mar peace and tranquility of the state and no extremist movement can spread its wing on its soil. Hence, inspite of the growing unrest let loose by the extremists in Srikakulam, Khannam, Karimnagar, Warangal districts of Andhra Pradesh, close to the border, the government of Odisha failed to anticipate growing influence and movement of the Naxals in its soil, intelligence report that armed Naxals of Andhra Pradesh had taken shelter in Malkangiri areas of Koraput district and seen moving in weekly hats and villages, yet the state had not attached consummate importance to the development. The then Chief Minister stated that the Naxals were physically seen moving in Malkangiri areas but not indulging in outrages and hence it was imprudent to disturb them.

Meanwhile, extremist movement had been gaining momentum fast in several states, especially, in Andhra Pradesh, Bihar, and Bastar region of Madhya Pradesh. In fact, several incidents made it clear that extremist violence was going to engulf the western districts of the state soon like wild fire. Nevertheless, the state government preferred faineance to required preparation to face the impending threat, rather lamentably failed to visualise the growing phantom knocking at the door. No tangible action was taken to increase man power in the police force, galvanize training, intelligence wing and modernise the police and build a stubborn anti-insurgency police cadre. Merger of the People's War and the Maoist Communist Centre (MCC) in September 2004 and birth of the CPI (Maoist) gave a formidable push to the extremist movement in the country. Complacent and unprepared state virtually gave a free hand to the Maoists to expand their network to Koraput, Malkangiri, Raygada, Gajapati, Ganjam districts of western Odisha. Soon the Maoist activities were noticed in Mayurbhanj, Keonjhar, Sundargarh, Deoghar, Sambalpur, Bargarh and Bolangir districts. In February 2004, Naxals raided the district armoury of Koraput and looted about 500 weapons and large quantity of ammunitions. Panic and fear of insecurity loomed large in the state. It stirred the sleeping lion from its torpor and forced the government to initiate steps to combat the spectre of the extremist violence.

Ganjam and Koraput districts are touching eastern fringe of Andhra Pradesh. Now Koraput district has been divided into four districts. Malkangiri, the erstwhile revenue sub division of Koraput has been up graded to a full-fledged district. Malkangiri is a part of Dandakarnaya and its north western corner, Bastar region, now a part of Chhattisgarh, is situated. Chhattisgarh state is separated from Odisha by a narrow river, Sabari. In its south west corner Andhra Pradesh is located separated by river Sileru. Malkangiri, a part of Dandakaranya is enriched by dense forest, abode of wild animals and nature's bounty. Roads and communication is very poor and many pockets are cut off during rainy season. Tribal community forms the main component of the sparse population. Many take pride claiming that they have come down from the linage of King Bali and Sigrib, the legendary figures of the great Epic, The Ramanaya. Local people believe that the great battle between King Bali and his brother Sugrib was fought on the valley near the Bhanda hill. Poverty was immeasurably loathsome. Dandakarnya project has taken up rehabilitation programmes for the refugees migrated from East Pakistan, now Bangladesh. It has improved or built roads and bridges, culverts, established schools, health centers and indicated a semblance of urbanisation. I served in Koraput district, visited Malkangiri circle and its extreme western border point, Motu, many times. I interacted with many persons belonging to the tribal community, who claimed to be the descendants of King Bali and Sugrib. Here, meeting point of two rivers is picturesque, generate a feeling of abyss peace, tranquility and sense of withdrawal from the worldly temptations. People living here are simple, unassuming, God fearing and truthful.

Now, the state has thirty districts. Fourteen districts are Maoist rapped. Among them nine districts are included in security related expenditure scheme introduced by the union government. The union government reimburses all security related expenses of nine districts. In 1967, several splinter groups of the Naxalites became active in Parvatipuram agency areas of Srikakulam, tribal areas of Khammam and Warangal districts, Andhra Pradesh. They had no link with the founder father of

Naxal movement, Charu Mazumdar of West Bengal. Local leaders, Nagi Reddy, Naga Bhusan Patnaik, Surjya Patnaik were active in Andhra Pradesh. However, Odisha was free from Naxal activities. Ultras after operating in Andhra Pradesh often used to step into Malkangiri areas crossing the river. In fact, they made Malkangiri a safe shelter ground and a sanctuary. Many armed extremists used to move in weekly markets, villages, but not interfered in affairs or indulged in any disturbance. Intelligence reports regularly reported the extremist's movement. But the government followed the policy of non-interference, since their stay or movements in Odisha were not detrimental to peace or posing any threat to the state's law and order. In south of Raygada sub-division, now upgraded to a district, Parvatipuram agency area of Srikakulam district is located. Earlier it was a strong hub of the Naxalites. By the end of 1968, the ultras had been entering into Narayanpatna and Raygada areas of Odisha crossing the border. The rebels unleashed campaigns to influence the tribals and bring them in their fold living there. A constable of Odisha police was killed near Raygeda. Thereafter, fiendish activities of the rebels gained momentum in this belt. Soon it spread to Parlakhemdi subdivision of Ganjam district, now Gajapati district. From 1968 to1980, Naxal activities and leadership was radar-less, marred by internal feuds and mushroom growth of splinter groups. However, the CPI (ML) People's War (PW) was born in April, 1980. The new outfit stepped up outrageous activities in Andhra Pradesh, which soon spread into districts situated in western part of Odisha.

Escalated violence put the unprepared state government in a quandary. Neither the state had adequate resources nor well trained and well equipped police force to face and tackle the sudden flurry of blood curdling activities let loose by the fierce ultras. Indeed, excruciating delay and monumental callousness allowed the extremists to make a substantial dent in tribal areas and influence the tribal community for an impending upsurge. Hence, the helpless government instead of confrontation adopted the policy of conciliation. The Chief Minister Naveen Patnaik perhaps wanted to kill time for preparing and refurbishing the police force and the administration and therefore, shrewdly decided to placate the ultras temporarily. After a meeting of the representatives of nine states held in Hyderabad on 21, September 2004, the CM decided to review all cases related to extremist violence pending or under judicial trial. Government announced initiatives for the development of the trial areas and welfare of the tribal community to boost the peace process. As a gesture of liberality the government declared that it would withdraw prosecutions against 156 accused persons charged and prosecuted in 34 cases for extremist activities. In addition, prosecution against six hard core Naxals including three women ultras arrested on September 16, 2004 by Malkangiri district police would be withdrawn. CM said that the decision was taken at a high level meeting aiming at restoring peace in tribal belt of the state. According to the CM, the government expected that the extremists would reciprocate refraining from violence and bloodletting activities. He thought that good sense would prevail upon them and they would return to the main stream of the society. In fact, protesting against arrest of 18 ultras belonging to different out-fits, by the police of Malkangiri, a pro Naxalite outfit, called "Daman Pratirodh Manch" active in southern Odisha, threatened for agitation. On September 30, 2004, it demanded that the government should withdraw all cases pending against the tribals. They alleged that the police had engineered false cases, harassed the innocent tribals on the plea of neutralising the outlaws and restoring normalcy.

Dispassionately, the state's conciliatory policy to circumscribe the growing terrorism was not without any rationale. Indeed, years neglect and complacency to curb the blood thirsty ultras had made the outfit powerful and formidable. Rank and file of the outfit has swelled, ultras procured sophisticated weapons, land mines, explosives, improved training standard and striking power. Over and above, the ultras owned the heart, good will and support of the poor villagers who often ungrudgingly provided shelter and food to them. The ultras adroitly gained trust and confidence of the tribal community, made them to believe that they were the liberators capable of salvaging them from poverty, inequality, exploitation, high-handedness and corrupt practices indulged in by the government officials. Regrettably, the government has lamentably failed to check the growing hiatus between the have and have-not and undertake positive steps for rural development. Grievances piled upon grievances that the government had hardly taken purposeful steps to improve or jubilate the rural economy and socio-economic condition of poverty stricken rural mass. In short, the spectre of the militancy grew immeasurably flabby. Yet, the government was insouciant to perceive or judge the threat and take consummate measures to neutralise it. Truly, a sense of paranoia often grips the rulers who suffer from the unfailing sense of reality and exact possibilities of time to rise to occasion and strike. Presumably, the CM was fully aware of the government and the police's limitation at that juncture to take the extremists head on. Perhaps his wisdom guided him to mark time, equip the police force, refurbish the intelligence wing, make flawless preparation and finally, meet the challenge. As a matter of fact, he had no option at that critical time but to prefer soft line and conciliatory tactics to confront the ultras later and in opportune moment in full fury.

Special feature of the state should be mentioned in appropriate paragraph to satisfy curiosity of the readers. Till independence in 1947, twenty eight native kings had been ruling several small principalities independently. Rulers were from Rajput clans hailed from central India. In majority of the native states, especially located in north and north-west Odisha, a large number of Marwari and Gujarati business communities from Rajasthan and Gujarat have settled permanently. They are traders, running small industries and money lending business. In remote villages of Bolangir, Kalahandi, Bargarh and Sambalpur districts, business communities from outside the state have settled permanently and living there for generations. They have built puce houses running shops, trading in raw materials, groceries, timbers, bidi leaves and money lending business. The native rulers encouraged them to settle permanently and run business. Truly, they were controlling the economy of the areas. Regrettably, business dealing of majority of the traders with the customers and consumers, who are broadly, tribals are far from fair and honest. Galling instances of cheating and dupery are in galore. Tribals are generally illiterate or unable to check weight and measures and intricacies of accounts. Dismayingly, they are the easy targets of the traders. For example, if an innocent tribal buys a kg of rice, the shop keeper cunningly will supply 750 or 800 grams and thereby cheats him and gains wrongfully. The money lenders by manipulative skill or tampering with documents will gradually grab his properties including land. Traders amass money and wealth dishonestly at the cost of the poor tribal. Unfortunately, not a single so called progressive individual or NGO organised protest or agitation against such dishonesty and exploitation and tried to salvage the poor tribal from cruel hand of the trader community. (Incidentally, during my stint, I organised many raids in weekly hats and markets, arrested and prosecuted many dishonest traders.)

In course of time, literacy and awareness developed in tribal community. Yet, no large scale agitprop is noticed against dishonesty and exploitation indulged in by the dishonest traders in this belt. In fact, it is not clear if the Maoists have taken the tribal community in confidence and organised any movement along with them either covertly or openly against the cunning traders flourishing in Sambalpur, Bargarh, Bolangir, Kalahandi. For the northern belt the traders in question have come from outside and settled permanently in the state. In southern and western districts the traders generally belong to Ganjam and Koraput districts. They are sons of the soil, but their mother tongue is Telugu. Among the traders Kumties are small shop keepers and money lenders. They are moneyed, run shops and business in remote places of the tribal settlements. They have earned notoriety for cheating and exploiting the tribals. Maoists extorted many Kumti traders, attacked and killed many. Ganjam district, a portion of erstwhile Golconda state and later a part of Vizag division, Madras presidency, was added to Odisha in 1935. Growing Maoist threat in northern areas posed a mighty threat. Several police men and personnel of the para military forces were killed. Yet, the traders and business community who came from distant places and settled in the state, were virtually free from the wrath of the Maoists. As a matter of fact, the mystery of so called kindness of the extremists in treating the dishonest traders vis-à-vis the poor and deprived tribals is really not understood. Critics quip that perhaps money power acts as a flinty protective wall and hence the culprits are going escort free. Truly, it is strange that the ultras have been killing poverty-stricken persons, daily wage earners, laborers, and hawkers, petty traders who eke out a miserable existence and somehow arrange their livelihood over coming insurmountable odds. Yet, moneyed persons, land owners, money lenders, hoarders, black marketers and persons prospering at the cost of the poor and deprived persons are escaping notice of the Red revolutionaries. Indeed, this kind of double standard is manifested right from the time of comrade Charu Mazumdar. Broadly speaking, paradoxes noticed in the Maoist movement have provoked the sober persons who really want to see the success of the movement, to look obliquely at the movement and its leaders. Importantly, many power hungry leaders quit the out-fit and jumped into the fray of contesting election and grab political power.

Naxal movement generated in Andhra Pradesh and after failure of Srikakulam uprising, crept into Odisha and gradually contaminated Koraput district in 1968. (In those days Malkangiri and Raygada sub-divisions were integral part of Koraput district.) The Naxal leaders and cadres were broadly from Andhra Pradesh. They penetrated into the tribal belts of Koraput and Ganjam districts and tried to influence and motivate the tribal community to participate in Naxal movement. Even today, the top and middle rank leadership who organise and guide the Maoist movement in Odisha belong to Andhra Pradesh. Monoj alias Modam alias Balakrishnan hails from Andhra Pradesh is the prime leader and all in all for the Maoist activities in Odisha. He is the chief of the Andhra Orissa Border Zonal Committee (AOBZ). Under his instructions operations in the state are organised and take shape. Rough estimate reveals that the strength of the armed cadre of the Maoists is 500 to 600 persons. In addition, number of sympathizers and patrons are ten to fifteen thousand scattered all over the state. Women cadre is approximately fifteen percent of the whole armed cadre. Many Maoists from Chhattisgarh have joined the state cadre and operate in Malkangiri (Dandakarnaya) areas. Tribals are the main strength of the cadre. Oriya speaking persons are microscopic minority in the cadre. Complaints are in galore that the Maoists from Andhra Pradesh dominate over the Oriya Maoists, often maltreat and torture them which has been fomenting discontentment in rank and file operating in Odisha. Many Oriya Maoists were compelled to quit the out-fit. Even, the Oriya Maoist leader, Sabyasachi Panda, the hero of Nayagarh police training institute armoury raid, who has recently been expelled from the out-fit, had vehemently complained on high handedness and use of rough and ready method by the Maoists of AP, against the Oriya Maoists. Importantly, after death of Kishanji in West Bengal, Maoist Sabyasachi Panda was selected in his place. But it fizzled out for some unknown reason. It is crystal clear that the Maoist movement in Odisha is guided and controlled by the leaders from Andhra Pradesh. In remote forest of Malkangiri, the Maoists run a training centre. Recruits are generally from the tribal community of Odisha, Jharkhand and Chhattisgarh.

In north eastern side of the state, Mayurbhanj, Keonjhar and Sundargarh districts are located, adjacent to Jharkhand state. These districts are minerally rich and source of earning substantial revenue from the districts is bright. Angul, Sundargarh and Sambalpur districts are rich and viable for coal mine industry. In these places, many industrial groups open establishments for mining business, transport, trading and subsidiary industries. A large number of workers come from outside the state for employment. In fact, the state's economy largely depends on the mining industries. Again, northern portion of Jajpur district closed to Keonjhar district is infested with dense forest and possess substantial deposit of iron ore. Maoists find the forest is suitable for building hide-out and pursue the Maoist movement. Frequent labour trouble and industrial dispute indirectly help the Maoist movement to grow. First, disgruntled labour component, hostility between the have and have-nots, exploitation by the money lenders, traders etc. often aid the outbreak of the extremist movement. Secondly, easy collection of levy or extortion from the mine owners, contractors, business groups etc. open flood gate for filling the ultras' war chest. Thirdly, impact of the administration is far from strong which encourages the ultras to stretch their mission. Fourthly, forest and tribal population can easily be persuaded to come in their fold. Lastly, close contact with the Maoists active in Jharkhand and West Bengal can easily be maintained. The police's hot chase can easily be neutralised short circuiting surveillance and crossing the border secretly and taking shelter in other states. As a matter of fact, local condition and sentiment of the local people is highly favorable for mustering support of the poor, neglected and aggrieved people. Hence, agog with joy of plundering the heart of the tribal community and spear-heading the Maoist movement in massive scale, the Maoists are firmly entrenched in this area, stepped up recruitment drive and goaded the people to come under their influence. Simultaneously, they increased violence, attacks and killing the security personnel.

East-West Corridor

The Greyhounds' tough combing operation in Andhra Pradesh forced the People's War group to shift their many bases and training grounds to Dandakaranya and Bastar region crossing the border. Odisha's Malkangiri, a now a district, Madhya Pradesh's Baster district, now Chhattisgarh state, are parts of Dandakaranya. In fact, hot chase by the security forces in Andhra Pradesh has forced the ultras to sneak into Malkangiri, Koraput, Raygada, Ganjam and Gajapati districts of Odisha and six districts of Madhya Pradesh, now Chhattisgarh state, consolidated their hold, increased dominance and violent activities. The ultras hit upon a plan to establish a corridor from east to west from Jharkhand to Chhattisgarh via Odisha through the unfrequented jungle and hilly tracks. The idea is to build a corridor for easy contact with the counter parts of other states, facilitate quicker movements from one state to other, take shelter in the forest and if needed, escape outwitting the police and the security forces. In March 2008, a hard core ultra along with Dhanu Govinda were arrested from Meghpal forest, Sambalpur district. Comrade Dhanu Govinda was the founder member of the Sambalpur-Deoghar-Sundargarh Zonal Committee of the CPI (Maoist). He received training in Saranda forest, Jharkhand. He organised several armed operations in this belt, wanted in fifteen heinous cases like, murders, arson, abductions, encounters with police etc. Interrogation revealed that the jungle track has already been laid for building a link with Chhattisgarh. Unfrequented link roads are usually used by the armed cadres, guerrillas. In real sense these are not regular public thoroughfares for the public. But the ultras identify the target villages and other mile stones so that the cadres can move from one place to other under cover of the forest. However, informal verification disclosed that the Maoists attempted to build a link corridor from east to west through three states right to Chhattisgarh. But it came to the notice of the intelligence wing, resulting in, the attempt was foiled. However, fresh initiative to rebuild the corridor is not ruled out. Police has therefore kept it under close watch.

Pompous claim that it is a peaceful state and blind faith that violence will not be accepted by the peace loving people was exasperatingly belied. The government was taken unawares and was shocked receiving the horrid news of raid on Koraput district police armoury on February 6, 2004 at about 9.30 pm by the People's War group. About three hundred armed ultras simultaneously raided the district police armoury, town and sadar police station, district treasury and the district jail. Above targets are located in koraput town within radius of less than half a km. They also attacked the head quarter of the third battalion of Orissa special armed police, which is located about two kms south of the Koraput town by the side of the national high way. Ultras also raided Laxmipur police station, situated fifty kms east of Koraput town by the side of the state high way running from Koraput to Raygada. Ultras blocked both high ways so that no reinforcement could reach the troubled spot. One cop performing duty in the district armoury was killed. In fact raids continued for more than two hours with impunity. Ultras looted the armoury and decamped with 500 weapons and countless ammunition. A CRPF contingent coming from upper Kolab to Koraput town was ambushed. Three CRPF personnel were killed and three received injuries. Needless to say, attacks on several places at a time was planned with a good deal of care and observation and executed with precision. Dismayingly, there was no resistance from the police and the OSAP, an armed force of the state police. Admittedly, it was a rude shock for the state government. Perhaps, it forced the government to realise that complacency was too dear to uphold safety and security and ensure good governance. Therefore, exhaustive preparation to disarray the extremists with courage and determination is the right step.

Church's Patronage for the Ultras?

In tribal belt in Central India the Christian Church plays ostensively philanthropic role for uplifting the tribals from poverty, illiteracy and social inequality. They also provide relief to neutralise disease, pestilence and epidemic. Unconfirmed report reveals that rupees 12000 crores annually is pumped into India by the western countries for the so called welfare activities in tribal areas. Fund is spent and distributed through the Church. About four thousand missionaries are employed for propagating Christianity. In the garb of welfare and charity, the secret mission is to convert persons in Christianity from the tribal community and other castes or religion. In Chhattisgarh number of Christian missionaries active in the field is the highest. Broadly speaking, allegation that the missionaries clandestinely operate to convert the tribals is not at all unfounded. During the last five years astounding growth of Christianity in Nagaland, Manipur, Mizoram is a robust threat to the country's integrity and solidarity. Again, suspicion that many Christian missionaries secretly work as intelligence agent of the foreign intelligence organisations is not ruled out.

In Kandhmal district of Odisha, two tribal communities, Kondh and Panna are main fragments of the population. Entire Panna community has embraced Christianity. Their living condition has improved, rather better than other tribal communities. They receive financial help from the Christian organisations. The Kondh community cling on Hinduism or Tribal religion, are generally land holders. Members of the Panna community try to encroach or grab land of the Kondas. In fact, communal clash between two communities for reasons, including land grabbing often take place. In case of conflicts the ultras take the side of the Pannas on the plea that the Kondhs possess excessive land. They instigate the Pannas to demand and take part in land distribution movement. They also coerce or force others to alienate the so called surplus land and embrace Christianity. Ultras resolutely campaign to bring the Pannas in their fold and thereby enrich the cadre. Importantly, in this area majority of the Maoist cadres belong to Christian community.

Communal riot between two communities broke out in 2008, unabatedly continued for several months. It noticed unprecedented violence, arson loot, murders and free use of fire arms by the outlaws. The Hindu religious leader Laxmananda Saraswati was killed. Maoists aided and abetted disturbance from behind. Later, a hard core rebel, Ramesh Tama alias Dasrath was arrested. He confessed that he was involved in killing the Hindu monk He belonged to village Thakilod, Bijapur district, Chhattisgarh, joined the Maoist out-fit about six years ago and functioned as the commander of Kasipur-Niyamgiri area commander (KNAC). This unit operates in the border areas of Raygada, Koraput and Kalahandi districts. He was arrested along with two comrades from Baigor forest under Raygada police station.

Maoists of Kondamal encourage the Christian converts to forcibly occupy land from the Kondhs and attack Hindu families. Bisop Charles Soreng from Hazaribag, Jharkhand, in an interview on May 6, 2012, stated, which was published in Sathyadeepam, a Catholic weekly, from Kochi, "In this (the tribals) fight for equal opportunities and rights, the Maoists are coming to the aid of the tribals, especially in glaring cases of denial of justice and right." The Bishop admitted that the Maoists are sympathetic to the Church and support the priests in carrying out their missionary activities. He added that the Maoists do not attack the priests who are working for getting justice for the poor. "We do not advocate violence, but Maoists are making a point by targeting our corrupt system which marginalises and renders the tribals outcaste in the society. The root cause of the Maoist menace is against rampant corruption in the society. High rate of unemployment among poor youths makes Maoism an attractive option for them. Corruption and government apathy are two main factors that have helped the Maoists to become so formidable a force." However, the spokesperson of the Kerala Catholic Bishops' Council (KCBC) said that Bishop's opinion need not be those of the Church. These could be his personnel thoughts.

Suspicion on the link between the Maoists and the Church in Odisha has been verified from various sources. None could throw any direct light on the episode. In fact, that the Maoists have aided the recent unrest and bloodshed in Kondamal is corroborated by the Maoist cadres' statements recorded by the investigating officers after their arrest recently. During interrogation they have divulged tangible clues including the undercurrent of discontentment brewing on account of harsh and offensive treatments meted out to the Maoists of Odisha by the Maoists from Andhra Pradesh. Speculative assessment centering round the communal violence in Kondamal is broadly, based on rumour. In fact, rumour with its usual love for falsehood betrays the truth and misguides the people.

Maoists have set up the following five committees to accelerate the movement. 1. Andhra Orissa Border Zonal Committee (AOBZ) is the main group, 2. Orissa Bengal Border Committee, 3. Orissa Jharkhand Border Committee, 4. Odisha Chhattisgarh Border Committee, 5. Orissa State Organising Committee (for the heartland of the state, Kondamal district comes within it). The satellite units operate in close co-operation. However, leadership of the movement is in the hands of the Maoists from Andhra Pradesh. A good number of Maoists from Bastar region operate in Malkangiri and Koraput areas in tandem with the local Maoists. Procurement of weapons largely depends on the looted weapons from the police posts and police personnel. In fact, weapons seized from the surrendered and arrested Maoists in majority of the cases bear the marks of the police armoury. *Modus operandi* of attack and ambush is similar to that of the Maoists active in Bastar region. The police post or a patrol is attacked by a large number of Maoists. Emphasis is given on the use of land mines and explosives. Maoists gain over the villagers and bring them in their fold, use them to gather information on movements of the security forces, use villages located in remote areas as temporary shelter ground, cajole or coerce the villagers to work as second line of defence, operate as human shield to foil police's raids, help to escape if the police dragnet comes closer. In fact, the Maoists seek their assistance in all possible ways under threat or fear of annihilation in perpetuating their so called revolutionary mission. Admittedly, the Maoists have succeeded in establishing their defacto dominance and supremacy in Kalimela, Motu of Malkangiri district, Narayanpatna of Raygada district,

Khaprakhol, Lathor of Bolangir district and Nuapara of Kalahandi district. In these places Maoists' writs run. None is bold enough to defy them or ignore their lurid signal.

As the danger has been looming large the state government undertook comprehensive plan, programme and ensured their diligent execution to thwart the Maoist misadventure. Message was tough and clear. The ultras must be rapped on knuckle and the authority of the government has to be restored. Indeed, it was not merely nuances of administrative jargon but business like resoluteness of the government. Work started in right earnest. Able bodied, energetic youths were recruited, put in specialised training courses under competent instructors who have earned expertise in jungle warfare and anti-Maoist combats. Several armed police battalions and India Reserve Battalions (IRB) are raised. A special training school is established for imparting training including in-service training to all ranks. Bomb squads and anti-mine squads to detect and neutralise or defuse bombs, land mines and explosives have been expanded and galvanized. A paradigm shift from the archaic practice and technique of collection of intelligence cultivating source and building a reliable network has been modified. Following the Andhra Pradesh model the Special Intelligence Wing is set up which has produced the desired result. Secondly, creation of the Special Operation Group (SOG) in the pattern of the Greyhounds of Andhra Pradesh is a pragmatic step. It is an excellent striking force capable of humbling the Maoists and influence them to modify their mind set, give up arms and join the main stream of the society. In addition, the District Volunteer Force, elements of mixed armed and district police is a separate operation wing, work in tandem with the SOG. Fortification of the police stations, improved security and communication facilities initiated on priority basis. Steps taken to increase the existing manpower of the police stations, improve civil policing, provide vehicles, telephones, Mine Proof Vehicles (MPV), night vision glasses and apparatus, bullet proof jackets etc. Compensation for the police personnel in case of death or injury has been appreciably enhanced. Besides, to keep morale of the police personnel intact, incentives are liberally committed or sanctioned. Old model weapons, like .303 rifles, muskets, stun guns are discarded. Now, cops are armed with automatic or semi-automatic weapons, better equipments and assault weapons to face the ultras. Steps have been taken to fill all vacancies existing in lower and middle order of the force. Finally, the strength of the police force of the state has been enhanced to satisfactory level. All these factors together have helped to resuscitate sagging morale of the police personnel and put the security forces in higher pedestal. Importantly, state announced a lucrative rehabilitation package for the ultras if they surrender giving up violence. Discussion with senior officers reveals that the police and security forces are adequately trained, armed with sophisticated weapons, plan operations relying on creditable intelligence and see that execution is effected flawlessly. Of late, many villagers are co-operating with the police and secretly furnishing information on whereabouts of the ultras. Police hierarchy is candid that the police now can suitably strike, retaliate or neutralise the loud sounding chatters of the revolution and its perpetrators who love offensive and lurid phrases, obsessed in demolishing the present social and political order and dreaming the so called the People's government. Needless to add, the state government so long watching the jaw-open hydra, ready to swallow the social and political order, is in comfortable position, as they visualise that the catastrophic end of the ultras is knocking at the door.

People's War (PW) originated in Andhra Pradesh, eventually extended its atrocious activities in Odisha. It established several bases in western territory of the state, recruited cadres from the tribal community, other backward classes (OBCs) and trained them to use fire arms, attack police posts and ambush security forces. Recruits from the tribal community and other backward communities (OBCs) form the bulk of the Maoist cadres. In fact, they are the main flow of the Maoists' to flourish the rank and file. The Maoist leadership is extra cautious to nurse and protect the main stream of the constituency. Broadly, a few instances of attacks and annihilations are mentioned to appreciate how the extremists have been gaining support of the rural mass and how fear psychosis has forced a section of poor and deprived rural populace to fall in line with them. On September 9, 2000, PW attacked Kalimela and Motu PSs of Malkangiri district, killed six cops and wounded two. In exchange of fire two ultras were killed. On December 2, 2001, a group of fifty PW cadres blew up Poteru Police Out-Post, Malkangiri and attacked the house of Arabindo Dhali, the Minister of Textiles, representing the BJP. Another group of about one hundred attacked Motu police station and in protracted gun battle five cops lost their lives, twenty two were injured and two ultras were killed. On August 11, 2002, in a land mine explosion in Gunpur, Raygada district, seven security personnel were killed and five were wounded. On December 5, 2002, in a land mine blast concealed under a culvert in Raygada Berhempur highway eighteen police men of Orissa Special Armed Police force were injured. On March 30, 2003, in an encounter near village Gudena, Malkangiri, three ultras were killed by the security forces. On March 31, 2003, a member of the Panchayat Samity, Malkangiri was killed by the PW group. On April 24, 2004, the PW killed Daku Majhi, an independent candidate contesting election for the state Assembly and injured his two brothers in Muniguda forest, Raygada district.

In March 2006, the Maoists raided R. Udaigiri sub jail, Gajapati district, looted weapons from the wardens, set free 40 prisoners, kidnapped the superintendent of the sub-jail and the officer-in-charge of the local police station and kept both of them as hostages. They were marshalled before the Maoist people's court for deciding their fate. Fortunately, after detention for a few days they were released. The incident badly affected morale of the government officials performing field duties. On July 16, 2008, a contingent of Special Operation Group (SOG) and the district volunteer force together were proceeding from district H.Q., Malkangiri to village 126 through the Kalimela Motu road on receipt of an information that residence of BJP activist, Subala Bal was ransacked and set on fire, a jeep and a tractor were burnt by the Maoists. Ultras blocked the road near the village dumping trees, tree trunks etc. As the cops tried to clear the blockade, a powerful land mine concealed underneath the tar road blasted. It ripped through the anti-land mine vehicle (AMV), flung the vehicle about 30-40 feet high in the air and killed twenty cops travelling in the vehicle right at the spot. It was a severe blow to the security forces and the district administration.

Mobile phone towers were set and put in operation by private companies for ensuring speedy communication and attract the mobile phone users. In fact, after intercepting conversations over the mobile phones the police can identify the location of the ultras and their movements. It helps the cops to organise raids, arrest the ultras, recover weapons, explosives and demolish hideouts. This device is successfully utilised by the police. It enraged the ultras and therefore, they took steps to destroy the mobile phone towers. The object was to destroy communication and prevent the security forces from finding out clues on location of the camps and their whereabouts. In June 2007, the ultras blew up three mobile phone towers in Malkangiri district. Again, on July 3, 2008 another tower in Bandhugaon block of Koraput district was destroyed. Similarly, another tower was demolished in Raygada district. MHA instructed to build towers right inside the compound of the police stations or in secure place where the ultras cannot step in. However, in absence of sufficient space in the compound of the police stations and in absence of suitable secure place, the district administration faced considerable difficulties to enforce the MHA's instructions.

Setback for the Elite Force, the Greyhounds

A contingent of the Greyhounds, an elite anti-Naxal forces of Andhra Pradesh has achieved a reckonable success in containing the Maoists active in the state, visited Malkangiri district to work out a clue on the fiendish activities of the Maoists in Balimela areas under Chitrakonda police station. They are specially trained and equipped to combat the extremists and are efficient in jungle warfare. Across the Balimela reservoir the Maoists declared the areas as "Liberated Area." The Greyhounds crossed the reservoir in a motor boat and wanted to comb the areas to flush out the rebels. Their aim was to reach a cluster of villages which could be negotiated by boats. On June 29, 2008, sixty personnel of the elite force and a few cops of the Odisha police crossed the reservoir in a motor boat and raided the villages. Operation failed to produce desired result as the villagers, particularly the male members deserted the village and took shelter in the jungle. It was believed that the information leaked out much before the operation and the Maoists got enough time to plan meticulously and strike back. In fact, topography of the so-called liberated area, was unknown to the elite force. Regrettably, deviating from cardinal principle of operation in an insurgency area, the force commander without reconnaissance and cultivating the local source undertook operation in feverish haste.

Strength of the Greyhounds was approximately sixty. They were carrying heavy baggage and heavy weapons. As operation failed to gain any tangible success they decided to return to Chitrakonda crossing the reservoir from Alampakka point at about 10 AM. Sixty four persons including a civilian and cops of Odisha police boarded the motor boat. They failed to ensure proper watch at the time of retreat and were unable to anticipate that the Maoists were following them from a distance. No sooner had the motor boat reached half way of the reservoir than about one hundred Maoists opened fire at the boat from the bank. The cops were off the guard and were helpless to defend themselves. Neither they could advance nor retreat ignoring incessant fire. Bullets hit the motor boat and the occupants. From the capsized boat many cops fell into water receiving bullet injuries. Eight cops swam ashore inspite of bullet injuries. Seventeen cops could be rescued. Nine with bullet wounds were admitted in hospital. Thirty four Greyhounds were missing. One brutally murdered cop with chopped hands was later traced out from the jungle. Admittedly, the catastrophe was avoidable if cardinal principle of operation in the Maoist strong hold was strictly adhered to. In fact, almost entire contingent boarded the motor boat without arranging protection on the bank and to repulse the rebels since counter attack was not ruled out. Unfortunately, 36 personnel from the Greyhounds contingent were killed. Evidently, it was a flinty setback for the Greyhounds. It demoralised the security forces deployed for counter insurgency operations. Needless to add, much exulted ultras celebrated it lavishly. Their morale received extra ordinary boost and they hoped for greater success in future.

In November 2008, security forces killed one Maoist in Gajapati district. In protest, on December 5, 2008, the Maoists called "Bandh" for two days in southern districts of the state. On first day of the bandh shops, markets, offices, educational institutions were shut down. Vehicular traffic was disrupted. In fact, normal life for two days was totally out of gear. On August 9, 2008, two top ranking Maoists including the second-in-command of the extremist left wing's Orissa state committee were arrested by Raghunathpur police near Para dip. Comrade Jag alias Prasanna Pal and Robin alias Ranjan Rout after arrest confessed that they were involved in Nayagarh police armoury raid. On September 25, 2008, at Birmitrapur, thirty miles from Rourkela, a car having registration number of Chhattisgarh was checked at night. A substantial quantity of ammunitions was seized from the vehicle and four occupants of the car suspected to be Maoists were arrested.

For murdering the Hindu monk, Swami Laxmananda Saraswati and four others right inside their ashram at Jaleshpata, Kondamal district on August 23, 2008, three culprits were arrested from Tumribandh area, about 135 kms west of the district HQ. Two guns, two black masks and three black dresses were seized from their possession. They confessed that they belonged to the Maoist cadre. Prior to the arrest the Maoist outfit accepted responsibility of the murder of the pontiff. Significantly, following murder of Swami Laxmananda and his four disciples in August 2008, a gory communal riot between the Hindus and the Christians in the district broke out. Loot, arson, attacks, assaults in large scale marred peace and normalcy of the district. Members of both communities suffered wantonly. Ashok Sahu, President of the Hindu Jagaran Samukhya, a BJP candidate for the state Legislative Assembly from Kondamal constituency made the murder of the pontiff a major issue in election campaign. He alleged that conspiracy to murder the Swami was hatched in Beticola Church at Raikia Block of the district. Regrettably, communal fracas took ugly turn and continued several days unabatedly. In the district, polarisation in Hindu and Christian communities on religious line alarmed the sober people and the administration. Orissa State Committee of the CPI (ML) Liberation, at Bhubaneswar railway station, protested against fiendish attacks and outrages against the minority, the Christians in Kondamal district.

On February 11, 2009, Maoist Benudhar Majhi alias Tridev, the zonal commander of the Sambalpur-Deoghar-Sundargarh zone was arrested. A .303 rifle, a 9 mm pistol, sixty rounds of .303 ammunitions were recovered from his possession. Twenty criminal cases including murders were pending against him. On February 23, 2009, Maoists attacked and ransacked a small town, Govindapally at about 11 PM. Operation continued till wee hours of the following day. Ultras brutally executed a contractor, burnt a police out post, a forest office and several government vehicles.

On February 28, 2009, about thirty Maoists attacked Chandiposh railway station, at about 2.15 AM, located about 35 kms away from Rourkela, destroyed the tele communication system and abducted the station master. Another group of forty ultras including women ultras attacked Bhalulata railway station at about 3.40 AM they dragged out the station master and two others, blew up the main office building, signal and control room using dynamite. The station was completely destroyed and train services were paralysed. After about one hour Maoists released the abducted station master and two employees. Incidentally, attack was a part of the Maoists' 24 hours "bandh" call with effect from February 28, 2009, as two top leaders including the central committee member comrade Asutosh Soren were arrested at Rourkela on March 1, 2009. In addition, Maoists called bandh in four states protesting against arrest of seven Maoists in Bihar, Odisha, Jharkhand and West Bengal, demanding their release immediately. Bandh was complete in Jharkhand and in other states it was observed partially. In West Bengal, response was negligible in three districts of Jangal Mahal.

Maoists planned to take over Odisha state by 2010. Accordingly, they made exhaustive preparation, geared up recruitment drive, training, procured weapons, land mines, high grade explosives, indoctrinated the recruits in the Maoist ideology and tried to bring the poverty-stricken Adivasis in its fold. They galvanised the guerrilla squads and made them equipped and fit to ably confront the security forces. Dandakaranya Contagious Region (DCR) comprises Odisha, Jharkhand, a part of Chhattisgarh and Andhra Pradesh. Comrade Ashutosh Soren, aged 39 years was the head of the Maoists military unit for the eastern region. He read up to class six, used to write revolutionary poetries which is sung by the Maoist cadres across the Maoist hinterland. He was instructed to build two more impregnable strong holds in pattern of the Saranda forest, right on the border areas of Odisha and Jharkhand. Maoists claimed that the DCR had extended its network to 25 districts of the state. The Barbara forest in Mayurbhanj district was tentatively selected to establish a sanctuary. However, the police's dragnet had been effectively coming close to him. Finally, police of Rourkela district nabbed him which was a sigh of relief for the police and the administration.

On March 18, 2009, Rabi Oram aged about 35, a trade union leader affiliated to the CITU was abducted. Later his dead body was found in a forest. He was suspected to be a cadre of the CPM. Maoists suspected him to be an informer of the police. On March 19, 2009, Prabhat Kumar Panigrahi, a local leader of the Hindu organisation, RSS was killed by the Maoists. At about 2 AM about twenty Maoists attacked the house at Rudiguma where he had taken shelter. Ultra chased him out and shot him dead, left Maoist posters at the spot. They blocked the road to prevent the police from reaching the spot. Earlier Panigrahi was arrested by the police suspected for his involvement in communal violence erupted in Kondamal district in 2007-08. He was released from the jail on March 14, 2009. Maoists kept watch on his movements and killed him branding it a revenge killing. On March 25, 2009, an activist of the RSS was killed by the Maoists in Baliguda, Kondamal district. On March 29, 2009, in Simlipal areas, Mayurbhanj district, armed Maoists blew up three forest beat houses, destroyed staff quarters, torched vehicles and wireless control room. They attacked Chahala guest house, chastised about twenty tourists from West Bengal staying there. Ultras including several female Maoists misbehaved with the tourists, forcibly removed ornaments from the body of the female tourists, stole cash, cell phones and other valuables and asked them to quit the guest house and leave the place immediately. Needless to say, the Maoists who are inspired by revolutionary ideal, unfortunately, indulged in crime failed to check lust for money and ornaments. Regrettably, they even did not spare the helpless weaker sex.

On March 29, 2009, Nanda Kumar Kartami, a BJP leader was killed by a group of Maoists in Malkangiri district. On April 3, 2009, Maoists looted rupees 9.9 lakhs from a delivery van carrying and escorting cash from State Bank of India, Malkangiri to the State Bank of India, Chitrakonda branch, Malkangiri district, a badly extremist torn area. Somnath Madkami, a candidate from Samrudha Orissa Party, contesting the Lok Sabha poll 2009, was travelling in a jeep with his wife. Both of them were abducted, taken inside a jungle. Later she was released and the dead body of Madkami with bullet wounds was recovered from the jungle.

Attack on the Asia's Biggest Bauxite Mine at Damanjori

Asia's biggest bauxite mine under care of the Nalco is located on Panchapatmali hill top, Damanjori, Koraput district. It is strongly guarded by the Central Industrial Security Forces (CISF). On Sunday, April 12, 2009, at about 9 PM, four to five hundred Maoists attacked it. CISF personnel bravely faced them and tried to repulse the attack. Gun battle continued for several hours Eleven CISF personnel and four Maoists including a woman Maoists were killed. Reinforcement reached the spot. CISF with all strength forced the Maoists to retreat. Eighty to ninety employees were trapped inside the complex awaiting a dooms day. Meanwhile, commandos were pressed into the operation. Helicopters were used to locate the position of the ultras. Police and CISF jointly foiled their attempt and chased them away. In every point, especially, in Narayanpatna areas the retreating ultras fought skillfully. Protracted exchange of fire proved that the ultras were well-trained and motivated to engage a well-trained and well-equipped armed forces. CISF gave a very good account and successfully foiled the attempt to loot the armoury and the magazine. While retreating, the Maoists hijacked a truck loaded with explosive. However, after travelling a short distance, they abandoned the truck. The bloody encounter has brought out the Maoists' ability to muster a sizeable group of armed men, their organisational ability, to chalk out comprehensive plan, and its precise execution. It also exposes their fortitude, physical and mental determination to take on a strong contingent of para-military forces for a protracted and desperate encounter. Needless to add, it reveals their high morale, high standard of leadership and implicit faith on the much cherished dream, the People's government and the classless society.

On June 18, 2009, Maoists had blocked the road placing trees at Jogipalur, 9 kms from Narayanpatna Block. Nine personnel of Orissa Special Security Force (OSSF), a specially created force drawing persons from the ex-service men, were pressed in service. Orissa Disaster Rapid Action Force (ODRAF), who are supposed to clear the road obstructions soon reached Jogipalur. Suddenly a sound of blast created panic among them. In fact, without clearing the road they made U-turn and rushed back about 15 kms to a safer place, Laxmipur. The OSSF personnel in a jeep reached near a culvert close to Jogipalur and tried to remove the road obstruction. A powerful land mine hidden blasted and blew up the jeep with its nine occupants. All including the driver were killed. Later from near the spot a life land mine was recovered. On June 20, 2009, in Malkangiri district twenty Maoists hijacked a bus but allowed the passengers to escape. They demanded revival of the bus service to remote Bejingwada area. At Malkangiri three left wing extremists fired at a police party and fled on bicycles. They took shelter in Ketriguda village. Police chased them and surrounded the village. In an encounter two Maoists were killed and the third succeeded in fleeing.

On July 11, 2009, the Maoists gave a call for "bandh" for 48 hours in six states except Maharashtra, protesting against the joint operation by the police and the central forces in jungle mahal in West Bengal. MHA issued alert notice to the states. On July 11, 2009, about twenty Maoists including women cadres travelled in two tractors and attacked the forest beat house at Nuapada and destroyed it. However, none was either injured or killed. On July 18, 2009, a group of armed Maoists in Rourkela killed a S.I. of police and a CRPF personnel. On September 10, 2009, Maoists blew up a police outpost and the abandoned CRPF camp in Bonai sub-division, Sundargarh district. Maoists damaged or blew up railway track in eight places between Rourkela and Bursuan-Bimlagarh-Patasahi section. Police arrested twenty Maoists suspected them for committing the crime. Maoists retaliated declaring "bandh" in Sundargarh district. However, bandh passed off peacefully. On August 29, 2009, a group of Maoists attacked K. Balang police station and the nearby CRPF camp. After exchange of fire the ultras took to heels. Meanwhile, report revealed that five railway officials from Topadihi railway station were missing. Rumour floated that they were abducted by the Maoists. However, people heaved a sigh of relief when they returned after several hours.

On August 25, 2009, a group of eighty including fifteen women Maoists attacked Roxy railway station, 80 kms away from Rourkela, triggered a powerful explosion, torched eight dumpers and heavy vehicles parked for railway construction work. Another group attacked Bhalulata railway station, 25 kms from Rourkela, attempted to blow up the station building, but somehow failed. This was second attempt on the very station. Meanwhile, police arrested three leaders which incensed the Maoists and therefore, they stepped up violence. In Raygada district ultras killed four civilians. On November 13, 2009, the Deputy Commandant and five CRPF personal were travelling in a jeep from Malkangiri, district HQ to Kalimela. A landmine planted by the Maoists underneath a culvert near Gompagudda hit the vehicle, killed the Dy Commandant and three others. On April 4, 2010, a police contingent moving in a minibus and while passing through Gavindapally ghat, district Koraput, the Maoists blasted a landmine which hit the vehicle. It tossed up about 20 feet high in the air. Nine cops were killed and 15 were critically injured. On September 25, 2010, in Baipadiguda block, district Koraput, N.P. Panda, President of the RJD for the block was gunned down. This was the seventh killing in Koraput district within a month.

Female Maoist Padma wife of comrade Rama Krishna was arrested from the jungle of Narayanpatna, district Koraput. Two other women Maoists Iswari Andaluri of Vizag, Andhra Pradesh and Puni Mandingi of Koraput were arrested from the same area. Police seized Maoist literature, maps of several towns including Jahanabad of Bihar. On November 4, 2010, police of Malkangiri district gunned down four Maoists in Karlakuta village. Maoists declared bandh for one day protesting against the police's excess. Subsequently, they killed a peon of the state government. On November 25, 2010, ultras killed a contractor. On November 28, 2010, an ambulance carrying five persons including two women and a child was blown up by a land mine blast on the highway proceeding from Kondamal towards Bhanjanagar. Driver and occupants were killed. On January 2, 2011, security forces raided a Maoist camp inside Raighati forest under Tomka police station in Jajpur district In protracted gun battle five Maoists including a woman Maoist were killed. Police seized twelve fire arms including a SLR an Insas rifle, .303 ammunitions and camp kits. On January 12, 2007, police raided an arms manufacturing unit in Rourkela. A small firm Utkal Engineering Work was ostensibly running a small foundry business but it was secretly manufacturing weapons for the Maoists. Police seized a scanner, laser printer, barrels for manufacturing guns, laptop, lathe and welding machines. Five suspects including three women from Adilabad district, Andhra Pradesh were arrested.

Review of Violent Incidents in 2010

In 2009, the Maoists killed 61 persons including 28 civilians. In encounters with the security forces 28 rebels were killed. However, responding to the call of the government only twenty rebels surrendered. In 2010, Maoists killed 75 persons including 53 civilians. In encounters with the security forces only twelve ultras were killed. But 44 Maoists surrendered. The year noticed frequent call for 'bandh' road blocks, use of land mines to blow up culverts, attacks on the police patrols and Mine Proof Vehicles (MPV), annihilation of civilians and destruction of mobile towers to disrupt communication. Notably, the police made a mark arresting several hard core Maoists. Yet, the Maoists were stubborn and impelled by impetuosity of establishing the People's government stepped up violence and atrocious activities.

Throughout the year increasing trend of violent activities unleashed by the Maoists was a worry for the police. Peace loving persons living in Maoist torn districts were afraid of noticing steady increase of the Maoist fiendish activities, loss of lives, the state's insouciance to disarray the extremists and restore normalcy. The Maoists' secret plan to take over the state by 2010, bring it under their absolute control and transform it to a so called liberated state, created a flutter. Anxiety in every level of the government and security forces loomed large. However, security forces kept their morale high, geared up intelligence apparatus and prepared themselves with consummate determination to disarray the pitiless ultras. The Home Department of the state released a "White Paper" explaining actions initiated, the government's endeavour and single minded devotion to curb the menace, neutralise the rebels and success of the security forces already achieved.

In February 2011, ultras fired at a running passenger train moving from Barsuan to Rourkela near Pattasahi, district Sundargarh. Volleys of bullets hit the passenger train. Fortunately, no passenger was hit. In the same month about fifty ultras including women ultras attacked a police outpost at Subarnagiri under Kotagada police station, Kondamal district, and ransacked the outpost. On May 2, 2011, Maoists gunned down Ganesh Khosla, contractor in Bandhugaon, Koraput district. In the same week they attacked a patrol of the India Reserve battalion in Kalangabadi forest, under Daringbari police station, killed one and injured four jawans. In April, in a landmine blast in Koraput district, eleven personnel of the elite Special Operation Group (SOG) were killed. A Panchayat Office in Malkangiri district was blown up. Maoists asked Penta Majhi aged 24, son of the village headman to join the Maoist outfit. As he declined to oblige he was mercilessly assaulted and burnt alive.

On June 27, 2011, a male Maoist aged 24 and a girl Maoist aged 15 surrendered to the police in Jajpur district. A training camp of the Maoists was discovered near Kerubadi, Daringbari in Kondamal district during aerial survey. It was situated on the border of Ganjam and Kondamal districts. On September 25, 2011, police and cobra force of the CRPF organised a joint operation and fell on the rebel trainees like a thunder. Gun battle continued but 30 to 40 rebels undergoing training managed to escape. A large cache of arms, kit bags, CDs booklets, and documents were seized. Documents disclosed valuable information on their future plans, strategy and mode of execution of the plans and programmes. On September 24, 2011, MLA Jagabandhu Majhi aged 39, of Biju Janata Dal elected from Omarkote and his security officer were shot dead at village Gona, Nowrangpur district when the MLA was attending a public function. Importantly, in 2004, he was attacked and wounded precariously. A bullet hit his waist and incapacitated him permanently. He was therefore using a wheel chair for his movement.

On January 21, 2012, District Volunteer Force of Raygada while busy in combing operation in Hanumanthpur area of Chandrapur block was fired upon. In a fierce encounter, Subhas, a hardcore Maoist was killed. A large quantity of arms and ammunitions were recovered from the spot. On January 24, 2012, Odisha State Committee member Girish was arrested from Attabira, district Bargarh. A fire arm, 12 live cartridges, sketch map of Bargarh district police armoury were seized from him. In 2007, he was arrested in Bokaro but escaped from Chibasa jail. However, from police angle the arrest was a prize catch. On February 9, 2012, a commandant of a battalion of the Border Security Force and four personnel were travelling in a jeep. In a landmine blast near Chitrakonda, Malkangiri district, the jeep was ripped into pieces. All occupants including the Commandant were killed. For the rebels it was a grand success and a positive encouragement to continue with the movement.

Maoists Raided the Police Training Centre, Nayagarh

Nayagarh district, an erstwhile sub-division of Puri district is a small town. It is one of the training centers for training the police personnel of lower ranks. Before independence, the territory used to be ruled by a native king. Several structures of the training centre for training centre were inherited from the abolished joint forces deployed under the British Political Agent. The institute has an armoury stored with a large number of weapons of different caliber and a huge quantity of ammunition. After recruitment police personnel are trained here under competent instructors. Trainees are neither fit to tackle law and order situation nor the instructors are competent or empowered to lead them in case of crisis. The armoury is guarded round the clock by armed sentries. It is a routine static guard generally manned by a head constable and four constables. Training centre functions independently, located about one km away from the town. It has nothing to do with the local law and order problem or vested with any responsibility for maintaining law and order, collection of intelligence or keep watch on the growing Maoist menace. Hence, none believed that it might be the target of the ultras.

The Maoists adroitly judged its location, porous security of the centre, store house of arms and ammunitions, half trained or half-baked trainees' inability to use fire arms, absence of competent leadership to counter any attack. Over and above, from the northern and western sides of the institute convenient escape routes towards jungle and hills are available. Sabyasachi Panda, a science student and a drop out of the Puri College joined the Maoist out-fit. He eventually became the Secretary of the Bansadhara Division of the Maoists' Andhra-Orissa-Border Special Zonal Committee. On February 16, 2008, at 1 AM, 400 to 500 Maoists entered into the town in three groups, surrounded the main complex of the training centre and attacked the armoury. Feeble resistance offered by the sentries was silenced soon. Ultras looted 400 weapons including light machine guns, automatic weapons, 9 mm pistols and a large quantity of ammunitions. In exchange of fire fourteen policemen lost their lives. Police claimed that operation lasted for about two hours. Main object of the ultras was to loot the armoury, collect weapons and ammunitions. After operation the ultras fled towards Gasama hill range. Simultaneously, the ultras attacked Daspalla police station located about 30 kms away from Nayagarh town and looted weapons. Regrettably, the police was disastrously out-witted.

On the following morning a contingent of the Orissa Special Operation Group (SOG) dogged the rebels under the command of Assistant Commandant Pramod Satpathy. It confronted the rebels at the foot hill of the Gasama hill range. In a fierce gun battle a constable by his side fell dead receiving a bullet. In the midst of incessant fire he advanced alone, shot down a few Maoists and finally he was shot. Later his dead body recovered. He had several stabbing wounds in the stomach, eyes were badly damaged. The rebels chopped off one of his legs, perhaps attempted to gouge out his eyes. In short, rebels brutally treated the dead. State government lauded him posthumously for his exemplary courage, spectacular leadership and supreme sacrifice. Police recovered eighty percent of the looted weapons and ammunitions. However, no automatic weapon and 9 mm pistol was recovered. Many weapons were burnt by the rebels. Perhaps they were unable to carry or transport them to the nearest hide-out. Indeed, surprise attack on the armoury, killing of 14 Cops and savage killing of the Assistant Commandant left a shock wave in the state. Upset MLAs discussed the barbarous attack on the floor of the Legislative Assembly. State government gave up complacency showed determination to fight the menace. The Chief Minister in feverish haste announced several measures to curb the growing menace including increase of man power in police, raise new armed battalions, refurbish the intelligence units, training standard of the anti-insurgency forces.

Maoists later circulated a booklet in the state containing 28 pages. According to it, the name of the operation was "Operation Rope Way." It further disclosed that only 193 Maoists including fifty female cadres formed the squad. Fair sex ultras were in the forefront for the raiding the armoury. They looted eleven AK-47 rifles, 75 SLRs, 250 Insas rifles, 6 LMGs, sixty five 9mm pistols, several .303 rifles, muskets and about two lakh rounds of ammunitions. Resistance lasted only for ten minutes. Cops would not have suffered any casualty had there been no resistance. It negated the government's claim that twenty ultras were killed in encounter in Gasama forest on the following day and eighty percent of the looted weapons were recovered.

Importantly, the police failed to recover a single automatic weapon or 9 mm pistol or light machine gun. In fact, the police's failure was a stark incompetence and failure. Critics stated that the police delayed the counter operation, not sure on the actual strength of the ultras and lacked indomitable will and resoluteness to gain back the lost ground. Perhaps no senior officer led the counter operation. Secondly, back up support to the deceased Assistant Commandant was inadequate. Frankly speaking, such a surprise and massive attack, loss of so many lives, number of automatic weapons reaching the hands of the rebels and absence of a senior officer right at Nayagarh immediately after the incident put the police in a quandary. Presumably, the spectre of matchless attack, violence and loss of lives perplexed the police administration and hence they took time to regain composure and determination to chase the blood thirsty ultras. Indeed, possession of a large number of sophisticated weapons and countless ammunitions must have enhanced morale, fighting spirit and fire power of the exulted ultras. Evidently, it has threatened safety and security of the peace loving people, shaken the state's much hyped claim to contain the Maoist menace. Admittedly, success has encouraged the Maoists, active in seven states and instilled into them certain decisive doctrines, imparted to them certain powerful illusions and hopefulness to pursue their struggle relentlessly to achieve the goal. Agog with joy the out-fit must have celebrated it in befitting manner. Critics free from prejudice eulogized the main architect, Sabyasachi Panda for his wondrous plan, flawless execution and successful retreat.

Informal report reveals that the Maoists collected about 1000 weapons including automatic weapons and light machine guns from the Nayagarh operation. During retreat the Maoists discarded a large number of .303 rifles grading them unfit for rapid fire. Central Intelligence officers feared that a major portion of the looted automatic weapons were likely to be transferred to Jharkhand and West Bengal. The Maoists of the above two states were short of automatic weapons A few months back M.L. Rao alias Ganapathy, the General Secretary of the politburo, issued instructions to raise fund and raid the police armouries, collect weapons for increasing fire power. Analysts remarked observing the Nayagarh attack that intelligence network of the Maoists was superior to the official intelligence establishments. Surprise attack of such a magnitude and loss of several lives rung alarm bell throughout the state. District police was in a tizzy as intelligence lamentably failed to alert them. That the crooner of catastrophe had been knocking at the door, regrettably, had escaped everybody's notice. Unfortunately, the security forces had no opportunity to face and repulse the ultras and foil their well-organised attack. Ultras travelled in four or five big vehicles and a bus hijacked from a civilian for the movement. Yet the district police was in dark. It is not clear if the state Intelligence Department had received any inkling on the impending attack and alerted the district police. Maoists took it to be a soft target and were sanguine of the police's monumental callousness to counter and foil the attempt. In fact, such a robust haul of weapons and ammunitions from the police armoury by one stroke was unknown in the past. In no violence ridden state the Maoists have achieved in snatching away such a herculean and inglorious success. In keeping with astrological prediction it may be commented that the star of the Maoists was in meridian splendour. Faineancy and complacency of the administration only helped to accelerate it. A senior public servant of high esteem stated that so far as curbing the Maoist threat, the disastrous episode in Nayagarh has compelled the government to wake up from its torpor and prepare plan and mobilise resources to tackle the burgeoning Maoist threat. Indeed, it was a blessing in disguise for the peace loving people of the state.

Polling for the Lok Sabha in the state was scheduled to be held on April 16, 2009. Disturbance was expected in Malkangiri district. On the day of polling Maoists set fire on three polling booths, destroyed EVM machines and documents needed for conducting election, resulting in, polling in three booths was disrupted. On November 14, 2012, in an encounter in Baliaguda forest under Mohana police station, Gajapati district, five Maoists were killed. Operation was conducted jointly by the Special Operation Group and District Volunteer force. In November 2012, CRPF and police jointly raided four villages in Bonai sub-division, Sundargarh district and arrested thirty suspects, recovered one rifle, three pistols and thirty rounds of ammunitions. They were suspected to be involved in murder of police Sub-Inspector, Ajit Bardhan and loot of explosive on July 16, 2009. Arrested persons were produced before the Court. Local people protested alleging that the arrest was arbitrary and demanded their immediate release. A big crowd demonstrated before the Sub-Collector of the sub division. Local MLA and a BJP leader led the demonstration. Women folk in good number assembled in front of the Chandiposh Gram Panchayat office and protested and demanded release of the arrested persons immediately. Supdt of Police of the district stated that the arrested persons belonged to the village militia of the Maoist out-fit.

Why Docile and Unassuming Tribals Take Up Arms

Tribals of Odisha are very simple, docile and law abiding. They co-operate with the public servants, obey and respect them. Relying on my long stint in Odisha, I am candid that they are truthful, assist the public servants and confess wrong deeds if committed, without pressure or coercion. They are poor and eke out their miserable existence under numerous difficulties. Yet, they prefer to a simple living free from stigma. In several cases I have seen that after committing crime the culprit would appear before the police station and confess his guilt. Their wedlock takes place in a simple ceremony. Dowry is neither demanded nor paid. Dowry related crime is practically absent in police record. Hence, it was a surprise for me when I find that simple and humble persons free from greed and ambition, take up arms, kill innocent persons, cops and indulge in death dance. Importantly, many become diehard Maoists, take active part in armed encounters, kill a fellow villager, set fire on houses and destroy properties. Even the gentle weaker sex of the community join the Maoist cadre unhesitatingly, participate in violence, barbarous torture and annihilation. Hence, a question arises why passive and docile people support or join the blood thirsty Maoists, take up arms, kill innocent persons and commit horrid crime. In fact, district gazetteers recorded by the then District Magistrates in nineteen century have written various facets of social custom, habits, heritage, religion, character of the tribal community and historic back ground of the districts. Pen pictures are very comprehensive and useful and it works as a viable guidance to the district officials. However, it is learnt that inspite of many good trends some tribes are tough and aggressive in nature. Kondhs are capable of asserting their rights, may unite for a greater cause, may turn violent, if needed. Rivalry and jealousy among the tribal communities are not at all remote. They are victims of superstition, blind religious belief and blind faith. Many tribal communities, especially, of Kondmal, Koraput and part of Sambalpur districts, practice human sacrifice. Importantly, tribal community of Sambalpur district revolted and participated in Sepoy Mutiny and Revolt in 1857 AD, against the British administration. Leader of the mutineers, Surendra Sai of Sambalpur was arrested and confined in jail in Ranchi till his death. Reports disclosed that the members of a particular tribal community were not free from criminal habits. Taking various points together it is clear that though they are simple and unassuming, they love to live independently, want to live in the accolade of their customs, culture and traditions. Therefore, it is natural that the lovers of liberty is likely to respond to the call of ultras who promised to establish the People's government, protect human dignity and promise the end of exploitation and discrimination.

Again, socio-economic development to uplift the tribal community vis-à-vis others is lamentably neglected. Government has, no doubt, initiated many reforms to remove their poverty and bring them to the main stream of the society. Yet, it is either inadequate or implemented lackadaisically. In the rural areas where they generally live has hardly got the touch of urbanisation and blessing of modern amenities. They feel that they are badly neglected and see no ray of hope for progress and prosperity. Younger generation has been gaining awareness for better life, seek modern amenities and wider avenue for improving their lot. They want to get rid of stagnation, aspire social recognition and demand equal rights. Hence, the call of the Maoists provided suitable impetus, generated beefy hope to shake off their age old miseries. As a matter of fact, their response was encouraging and positive. It amply proves that neglect, deprivation and indifference to socio-economic development will force the oppressed communities to respond and join hands with the ultras. Fortunately, many political leaders have understood the secret and not willing to treat the Maoist threat purely a law and order problem. They advocate for the socio-economic development among the tribal and tribal settlements.

Arrests and Surrender of the Maoists in Odisha

Continued pressure from the security forces has produced rewarding dividend. In fact, several hard core Maoists surrendered to the police and returned to the main stream of the society. Secondly, many ultras were unable to bear hard living condition inside the jungle devoid of civic amenities. Thirdly, diseases like malaria, unknown fever, water borne diseases, mosquito and snake bite, rigorous regimentation, harsh treatment by the senior cadre mates and dim prospect of achieving the People's government etc. forcing the Maoists to give up the so called revolutionary ideas and join the normal life. Relentless dogging, surprise raids by the security forces, fear of arrest and death in encounters etc. demoralise the cadres who want to get rid of underground and isolated life In fact, they want normal living and therefore prefer to surrender. Again, rehabilitation scheme offered by the government for the surrendered Maoists is quite lucrative which tempts the ultras to respond to the offer for surrender. Of late, complaints are in galore that the Maoist leaders from Andhra Pradesh dominate over the Maoists of Odisha. They plan operations and execute them without giving due importance to the Maoist leaders of Odisha. Over and above, they ill treat them, use rough and ready methods and at every stage they want to assert their supremacy. In fact, harsh and discriminatory treatment have demoralised the Maoists of Odisha who are eager to throw away the yoke of subservience and prefer free living to draconic domination by the Maoists from Andhra Pradesh. Significantly, the front line Maoist leader from Odisha, Sabyasachi Panda has openly complained against the high-handedness by the Maoists of Andhra Pradesh. Moreover, a sense of *déjà vu* has already gripped the psyche of the cadres that the lofty dream of the People's government and classless society is no better than a conjecture.

Nirmala, a woman Maoist, in April 2012, surrendered to the police in Malkangiri district as she was unable to bear hardship and secluded life of a rebel. In May, Raiman Pangi alias Ramesh, Deputy Commander of the Maoist unit, resident of village Datunguda, under Chitrakonda police station, surrendered to the police in Malkangiri district. Prasant Majhi alias Susanta, the body guard of comrade Sabyasachi Panda surrendered before the Gajapati district police. Deba Padiami hails from Kalimela area, district Malkangiri surrendered. He and Raiman complained of harassment and torture in the hands of the Maoists from Andhra Pradesh. Deba Padiami was the area commander of Kalimela-Motu, Maoist Dalam for the last three years.

Subhashree alias Mili Panda, wife of rebel Sabyasachi Panda was released by an order passed by the Gunpur court. She said that her husband might give up arms and surrender if criminal cases pending against him were withdrawn. Panda was directly involved in Nayagarh police armoury raid episode and kidnapping of two Italian tourists in March 2012.

Ramash Tama alias Dasrath, a resident of Thakilod village under Bijapur district, Chattissgarh had joined the outfit six years ago. He was the commander of Kasipur-Niyamgiri, Area Commander (KNAC). The KNAC operates in bordering areas of Raygada, Koraput and Kalahandi districts. He was arrested along with two comrades Chintamani Majhi and Mumbula Majhi alias Abhilash from the forest, Baigor, about 40 kms away from the district HQ, on the border of Raygada and Koraput district. During interrogation, he had confessed to his involvement in killing of Laxmananda Saraswati, the Hindu leader, in Kondmal district and also in Nayagarh police armoury raid.

Sumitra Mullick aged about twenty, a cadre of Ghumsar division, surrendered before the Superintendent of Police, Ganjam district. She hails from Glilima village under Badagada police station and had worked for two years under Sabyasachi Panda. She complained about exploitation and torture in the camps by senior leaders including Sabyasachi Panda. She was going to be rehabilitated adhering to the policy of the government. Odisha State Committee member, Girish aged 45, was arrested from Attabira, District Bargarh. He was directly involved in several operations in Sundargarh, Deoghar, Sambalpur belt. Padma wife of top Maoist leader Rama Krishna was arrested from jungle near Narayanpatna along with two women ultras, Iswari Andaluri and Puni Mandingi. Needless to add, arrests of the above Maoist leaders were prize catch for the police. Sriramalu Srinivas aged 38, a most wanted Maoist leader, special zonal committee member of AP-Orissa border unit, was arrested by Malkangiri police. Andhra Pradesh government declared reward of rupees ten lakhs for his arrest.

A Few Important Events—Police's Failures and Successes

On December 16, 2007, James, aged (24) alias Pawan Lohar alias Chhotu was arrested with his assistant Uddhhaba. From his possession 2400 rounds of ammunitions for SLRs, 9 mm pistols,.303 rifles and three huge land mines each weighing ten kgs and a Motorola Global Positioning System (GPS) were seized. He was wanted in 24 criminal cases including murder of several cops. He was an expert in using explosives and land mines. It was believed that majority of explosions in Odisha and Jharkhand were planned and executed by him. On April 30, 2007 in a gun battle near the weekly market in MV 79, district Malkangiri, the CRPF gunned down a Maoist and captured a female Maoist. Five CRPF personnel and several civilians were injured. About thirty Maoists fired at a CRPF patrol. In exchange of fire which lasted about one hour one looted AK-47 rifle was recovered from the dead Maoist. However, the Maoists could decamp with one AK-47 rifle and a good quantity of ammunitions.

On April 28, 2007, a group of thirty Maoists including female ultras putting on uniform and armed with automatic weapons raided the forest range office in Khalasuni forest at about 11 pm. They looted a very high frequency (VHF) set, a camera, a walkie talkie and a global positioning system (GPS). Spot was very close to Kisinda police station. But the police did not take the risk of going to the spot in midnight fearing ambush. In April 2007, the police of Deoghar district raided a Maoist camp at Ranigula and gunned down four Maoists including leader Sushant Meher alias Toofan. The Maoists suspected three villagers who gave clue of the camp to the police and nursed grudge against them. After a few months the Maoists retaliated and shot three villagers of village Ranigula dead. On June 21, 2007, at about 2 am, a group of twenty Maoists attacked Durlaput railway station, set fire on the Station Master's office and burnt official documents. Maoists blasted an engine of a goods train using explosives and snatched away the communication set from engine driver. On July 16, 2008, in Malkangiti district, Maoists blew up a MPV vehicle and killed 17 cops belonging to Special Operation Group (SOG), a dedicated anti-Naxalite force. On August 28, 2007, Maoists of Malkangiri division declared bandh protesting against alleged excesses by security forces in neighbouring state Andhra Pradesh. They triggered a landmine targeting a CRPF patrol in Kalimela area. Fortunately, 17 CRPF personnel had a narrow escape. However, bandh was observed, shops and establishments remained closed.

In February 2008, Maoists attacked the camp of a construction company in Harichandanpur near Ghatgaon, Keonjhar district, and set fire on two vehicles and kidnapped two persons. Again twelve Maoists including five female ultras attacked a temporary camp of the Geological Survey of India (GSI), near same place and burnt a van, a drilling machine and pressure pump. Fifteen employees of the GSI could manage to escape. About two weeks ago the camp was set up for survey purpose. A few days before the attack, the Maoists fixed a poster near the camp urging the GSI to stop the survey work. The Maoists called 48 hours bandh in Odisha, Jharkhand, Bihar in August 2009, protesting against arrest of their leaders. On the national high way they stopped traffic and torched eight dumpers engaged for construction work. On May 9, 2011, they exploded a land mine on Panchayat office under Podia block, Malkangiri district and destroyed the building. In October, 2010, a godown adjacent to the Niliguda Panchayat building where food materials were stored for distribution to the people under the Public Distribution System (PDS) was destroyed. In January 2011, the Maoists torched four vehicles of a contractor at Baragada, district Ganjam. On January 9, 2011, in an encounter, the police killed nine Maoists near Kashipur in Raygada district.

On November 26, 2010, Manoranjan Mishra, Inspector in Charge of Sheragada police station, district Ganjam was shot dead when he was returning home in a motor bike. On October 13, 2009, in village Pandab under Chandua police station, Mayurbhanj district, Maoists attacked a religious congregation and killed three security personnel detailed to protect a former member of the Parliament and looted four rifles.

In addition to violent activities, the Maoists have taken to disrupt development works initiated by the state government for uplifting rural economy. It is imperative that development and economic progress would help the deprived people to give up patronage to the ultras. In fact, road communication projects to build roads and improve communication with remote and forest areas are essential to establish wider contact with the rural people. Ultras studied the government's move and therefore, threatened the private contractors who were executing the projects to demolish the infra-structure and shut down the projects. On June 16, 2007 the Maoists attacked two sites at Chitrakonda area, Malkangiri. In the first blast at Popotai village, two road rollers were blown up and three pieces of heavy machinery were damaged badly due to explosion. The other site located at ten kms away was attacked. During the last two months three blasts had taken place which panicked the contractors. Consequently, the road construction projects came to grinding halt. In Kalimela two contractors engaged by the Rural Development Department were severely assaulted by the Maoists before the project started functioning. Earlier the Maoists warned the contractors against carrying out the work. Evidently, the contractors did not pay any heed to the warning. In fact, the Maoists wanted no rural road development mainly for two reasons. First, good roads and improved communication would facilitate quick movement of the security forces. Secondly, blessing of rural development would encourage the poor rural populace to remain away from influence of the Maoists. Ultras were afraid that rural development and economic prosperity would alienate the people from the extremists. Hence, the Maoists were determined to thwart and stall the rural development projects.

On October 13, 2009, Maoists gunned down three cops at Bandap, under Chandua police station, 35 kms away from Baripada, Mayurbhanj district. In April 2010, Maoists blew up a bridge using explosives on a forest road at Mathalomba about 66 kms away from the district HQ. Koraput. About ten Maoists took part in the operation. Luckily, no cop or any civilian was hurt. However, traffic was disrupted and the police took several hours to restore it. On August 27, 2011, two rebels including a girl aged fifteen surrendered to the Superintendent of Police, Jajpur district. On August 23, 2013, hard core leader Madhab alias Golla Ramalu was killed in a gun battle near Muchkund area. He was wanted in several heinous crimes. State declared reward of rupees four lakhs for his arrest. On August 27, 2013, at about 9 AM, Maoists ambushed a convoy of three vehicles of the BSF, on the national high way, NH-26, near Pottangi police station, proceeding from Koraput to Vizag. A land mine planted under a culvert, triggered off. It hit the second vehicle and tossed the vehicle up in the air. It killed four BSF personnel instantaneously and injured three jawans. Exchange of fire continued for some times. As the rebels were firing from the hill top, they managed to escape unhurt. It is believed that the Maoists avenged the killing of their leader Madhav.

On December 25, 2013, at about 2 AM about fifty Maoists stormed into Podia block office with high power explosives, under Kalimela police station, district Malkangiri. Building was set on fire, documents and records were burnt. Maoists left posters which condemned killing of 13 Maoists in an encounter with the security forces in September at Silakota, Malkangiri district, near border of Chhattisgarh. Rebels killed four persons including a contractor and a village ward member as a retaliatory step in early December. On December 12, 2013, Maoists killed an old man aged 65, father of a panchayat member. Meanwhile, within three weeks the Maoists abducted ten villagers, killed two of them and set fire on two passenger buses for transporting personal effects of the security personnel. On December 25, 2013 after an encounter in Kondmal district, two rifles, and a huge cache of explosives were seized. BSF established several camps in the area to prevent Maoist attack. On December 26, 2013, Kosa Madhi aged 38, secretary of the local panchayat of village Sangal under Kalimela police station was abducted and tried in a kangaroo court. On December 30, 2013, his dead body was found by the road side near the village. Rebels gave call for bandh for an indefinite period from December 28, 2013 protesting against ongoing police operation and demanding withdrawal of the central forces. On December 28, 2013, Rebels triggered a dynamite blast and damaged a portion of the bridge over the Potteru river which connects Padia block with Kalimela. About fifty Maoists at about 2.30 am assembled near the bridge. After the blast, they left posters condemning the security forces and the state, Rebels while returning attacked the house of a special police officer (SPO) at village, Sangel which is about two kms away from the bridge, and in his absence looted his belonging. On September 14, 2013, relying on a specific intelligence report that Maoists were hiding in Silakuta forest, near Padia, Superintendent of Police, Malkangiri with the personnel of the special operational squad and district volunteer force surrounded the rebels. In a fierce and hour-long encounter thirteen rebels including a woman were killed and the rest escaped. Number of fire arms, including one AK-47 rifle, ammunitions, and Maoist pamphlets were recovered. However, no dead body was found at the spot. Maoist squad belonged to Kalimela dalam led by Rakesh. It was an inimitable success for the security forces after nine Maoists were killed in Raygada and five killed in Jajpur-Keonjhar border in encounters in 2011. On March 23, 2013, Maoist leader Sriramula Srinivas alias Sudarsan, aged 55, was arrested from Wyra forest by the police of Khammam district, Andhra Pradesh. He was a top functionary of Andhra-Orissa Border Special Zonal Committee. He was wanted in several sensitive cases including assassination attempt on former Chief Minister, Chandrababu Naidu near Tiruputi and killing of the former Home Minister, A. Madhava Reddy. A reward of rupees twenty lakhs was announced for his arrest. Truly, his arrest was a big relief for the people and security forces of Odisha and Andhra Pradesh.

Security forces intensified joint operation in Maoist torn states which put the rebels in uncomfortable situation. Impact of the combing operation topsy-turvies the ultras. The upset district committee leader of Malkangiri, Poonam Chander warned the state government for retaliation. He declared that indefinite bandh call given and observed in Malkangiri and Koraput would continue till central forces were withdrawn. Rebel Dev Kumar Singh, the chief of the Bihar-Jharkhand-north-Chhattisgarh special area committee mobilised three hundred strong team operators from Gaya, Aurangabad, Chatra, Gumla, Palamau, Latehar and kept them in readiness in deep forest of Nuapada district of Odisha for violent activities. It is believed that it is one of the strongest Naxalite belt in that region.

People's Protest Against the Maoists

All is not well for the ultras. In fact, distrust, anger and anti-Maoist spirit has been gaining momentum. People are no longer willing to be carried away by rosy pictures, lofty promises and dream of the people's government whispered by the Maoists. Frustrated villagers have tolerated the ultras enough, now learnt to defy them, protest against their misdeeds and mustered courage to chastise them. In Malkangiri areas the tribal community living in and around Sunabeda sanctuary, close to Nuapada district and border of Chhattisgarh, banned entry of the rebels into the wild life habitat. In fact, restriction imposed by the villagers irked the ultras, resulting in, clashes between the Maoists and the villagers broke out. Rebels could not reconcile to the united resistance by a simple and docile community. (*The Telegraph*, December 29, 2013.) They were upset, failed to understand why the villagers were hostile and alienated them from their influence or control.

Rebel Maoist Leader Sabyasachi Panda

A dropout of Puri College, joined the extremist out-fit about five years back. He was made in charge of operations in northern areas of Odisha and eastern fringe of the state adjacent to West Bengal. He planned and executed many operations in Mayurbhanj, Sambalpur and Kondamal region. Nayagarh police armoury raid and its execution was his brain child which proved his high class planning skill and execution capacity. In Maoist uprising in Kondamal district and murder of the Hindu monk, Laxmananda Saraswati he was directly involved. After Maoist politburo member, Koteswar Rao alias Kishanji, in charge of Jangal Mahal, West Bengal was killed in a gun battle, the high command suggested name of Sabyasachi Panda to fill the vacancy.

On March 14, 2012, he was responsible for abducting two Italian tourists, Paolo and Colangelo from Phulbani and Ganjam border. Sri Panda, Secretary of Odisha State Organising Committee (OSOC) submitted 13-point demand for the release of both. It included the demand for release of several Maoists detained in jails. Abduction of the foreigners created several complications including diplomatic relation between two countries. The government preferred negotiations for their release. Two interlocutors were engaged to open dialogues. After a good deal of negotiation Colangelo was released on March 25, 2012 and the other was set free on April 12, 2012. It was not known to public as to the quantum of concessions given to the Maoists for the release of two foreigners.

Sabyasachi was expelled from the Maoist outfit in August 2012 following differences with the top leaders. After expulsion he floated Odisha Maobadi Party (OMP). The area of operation for the new out-fit is about 70 kms radius centering Khondamal. He accused the Maoist leaders from Andhra Pradesh for exploiting, harassing and ill-treating the Maoists of Odisha. In October he led an operation with a small group on the border area of Kondmal and Ganjam district. In a surprise move the security forces surrounded the camp and in exchange of fire three rebels were killed. Sabyasachi Panda escaped and later criticized the police action. A pistol of Italian make was recovered from the spot. Perhaps, it belonged to the abducted Italian tourists and later it was used by Shri Panda. His wife, Subhasri alias Mili Panda, one of the rebels and a prima donna of the Maoist women cadre, released by the Gunpur Court, has given hint on her husband's impending surrender. In fact, speculation is ripe that his surrender is a question of time. Incidentally, she is no longer willing to take up arms, on the contrary, expressed her keenness to join parliamentary politics and contest election. However, Panda was unable to out-wit the security forces and pursue belligerence with a handful of followers. Finally, he was arrested by the police. In short, with his arrest, activity of the Odisha Maobadi party has come to an end.

Odisha Maobadi Party (OMP)

Govinda Majhi aged 24, alias Pradip, a trusted deputy of Sabyasachi Panda, was killed in an encounter with the state police in Karanjadua forest near Kendupadar village in Mohana area of Gajapati district. From the spot the police recovered several fire arms including an Italian-make pistol, two loaded magazines, a SBML gun, Maoist literature and personal belongings. It was suspected that Sabyasachi Panda was hiding in the jungle. Police believed that Govinda was the main architect of the kidnapping episode of two Italian tourists. He was wanted in 46 criminal cases including murder, kidnapping, extortion etc. The new out-fit faced crisis as its cadre was thinning out due to desertion, surrender and arrest of the activists. Sabyasachi was fighting a lone battle to keep the flock together. However, its prospect was bleak. Moreover, the police's hot chase has made life of the fugitives well-nigh unbearable. Cadres realised that it was a sinking boat. Hence, it was wise to abandon. Observers speculated that surrender by Sabysachi Panda was a question of time.

Abduction of the District Magistrate, Malkangiri

In parlance of the rebels Malkangiri is called the cut off area. It is believed that the Maoist general secretary, Ganapathy is hiding in the jungle. BSF and CRPF made several attempts to reach the spot but have failed. However, they have not given up hope. In February 2011, Shri R.V. Krishna, Collector and District Magistrate of Malkangiri district and junior engineer Pabitra Majhi were abducted by the Maoists. A shock wave swept the state and perplexed the people. A question arose that inspite of tight security how the Maoists succeeded in abducting him. The entire bureaucracy was baffled and raised finger at the so called flinty security cover. Government explored all possible avenues to secure their release. Three interlocutors were engaged to open dialogue with the Maoists and to know their terms and conditions. Dandapani Mohanty, one of the interlocutors, maintaining link with the extremists and wanted in several criminal cases was entrusted to proceed with the work. His son was charged for supplying weapons to the ultras and has been languishing in jail custody. After a good deal of negotiations terms and conditions for their release were settled. One of the conditions agreed upon that the government would not take any coercive measure against the Maoists unless they indulge in unlawful activities. Police would stop combing operation and raiding the hide-outs. Lastly, in exchange of releasing the Collector, the state had to concede to release of hard core Maoist Ganti Prasada Rao alias Prasadam who was arrested by Odisha police from Visakhapatnam in 2010. Women Maoist Padma wife of Maoist Ramakrishna and Maoist Sriramulu Srinivas were also released. In July 2013, Ganti, a poet and convener of the Martyr's committee of friends and relatives, a group representing kin of the Maoists was killed in a shootout with the police. He was shot by some unknown persons. Subsequently, he died in a hospital at Nellore.

Finally, the District Magistrate and junior engineer were set free after nine days captivity. However, Maoists were seen moving with arms and ammunitions violating the agreement. Secondly, they issued threats to blow up gram panchayat and school buildings in remote areas, in Malkangiri. Thirdly, they were implementing training programmes inside forest of Malkangiri district and showing defiance to law and authority. One day without any provocation suddenly the Maoists opened fire at a police patrol. The patrol had to return fire for self defence, resulting in, a female Maoist was killed. Police action irked the mediators who wrote to the Chief Minister for resuming the combing operation violating the agreement. DGP defending the police action stated that the ultras were responsible for breaching the agreement. They were moving with arms in public places, threatening the people, imparting training to the cadres right inside the forest of the district and fueling law and order problems. As they were resorting to violence the police had no option but to take action for the interest of maintaining peace and normalcy.

It is told that the District Magistrate maintained excellent public relation and he was popular. Unlike senior bureaucrats he was responsive and keen to serve the people sincerely and diligently. Perhaps, wide public contact and goodwill turned his head, he thrived in make believe world that he was equally acceptable to the ultras and free from their anger and acrimony. In fact, for his release the government had to succumb to pressure and granted many undue concessions to the Maoists. Broadly, the bureaucracy was very anxious to secure release of the District Magistrate. Many senior officers pulled their weight and impressed upon the Chief Minister to get him free even at the cost of some improper concessions. Unfortunately, public servants often over zealously act imagining that his honest and selfless service will be reciprocated by the people. According to them, even the extremists are not devoid of head and heart who will surely appreciate sincere and welfare oriented services of a public servant. Indeed, such a phantasm often provokes them to perform indiscreetly for which public interest is hurt beyond any repair. It needs no reiteration that public service tampered with honesty, dedication and inscrutable moral law is welcomed. However, in that pursuit one should not be indiscreet, rash and foolhardy. As a matter of fact, reprehensible chorus that security lapse was responsible for the egregious episode surcharged the atmosphere and put the police under pungent criticism. However, eventually it transpired that there was no flaw in security arrangements; abduction of the DM was not for the lapse of the security personnel.

Abduction of the MLA in Koraput District

MLA Jhina Hikaka, an Adivasi belonging to Biju Janata Dal elected from Laxmipur constituency, district Koraput, was abducted by the Maoists on March 24, 2012, when he was travelling in a car from Koraput to Laxmipur. His security guards were with him. Maoists at about 4 AM stopped the car on the state high way and abducted him. News of abduction shocked everybody. Government tried to explore various possibilities to secure his release. The Maoists active in the areas took responsibility for the abduction and agreed to release him on several conditions, including that he had to resign from the Legislative Assembly. Family members of the MLA put pressure on the government to secure his release at any cost. After protracted negotiations, he was set free on April 26, 2012 at Belipeta in Narayanpatna area, of Koraput district, very close to of Andhra Pradesh border. Condition was imposed that he must resign from the Assembly within 15 days of his release. Chief Minister was tight lipped on the question of his resignation.

However, political leaders cutting across the party line, was against his resignation from the Legislative Assembly. MLA J. Hakaka was ambivalent on probable resignation. Meanwhile, the Maoists were going to release a fresh audio tape over the resignation which would remove confusion over the issue. Surprisingly, the Maoists thereafter did not insist upon resignation of the MLA, neither the MLA resigned. Critics feel that both sides had arrived at a secret understanding and finally, allowed the matter to rest. Government and political leaders were non-committal, did not pursue it further.

Admittedly, poverty, inequality, exploitation and deprivation are root causes for the steady advancement of the Maoist movement in Odisha. In addition, poor or peltry socio-economic growth in rural areas has given impetus to the rural mass to support the movement. Again, tenuous or lukewarm response from the government establishments, wishy-washy policy of the government, excruciating failure to provide relief to the aggrieved people and precipitous decline in public services etc. goaded the frustrated people to see a ray of hope in the Maoist's promises packed with vision, energy, promises and uncommon political ideology. People have lost hope on politics and political leaders and pay no regard to their high falutin promises often announced for the welfare and advancement of the people. In this respect interaction with many innocent and peace loving villagers has brought out a gloomy picture. Unflinching testimony gathered from Malkangiri district, Odisha revealing genuine grievances of the people may upset the impartial persons. Incidentally, Balimela Dam was constructed in 1970. For construction of the Dam more than thirty villages had to be abandoned and the habitants had to be ousted with assurance for suitable rehabilitation, compensation and adequate irrigation facilities. Many villagers who had lost their hearth and home for construction of the Dam have not been rehabilitated suitably, compensated for the loss, extended irrigation facilities. Unfortunately, the areas still remained under developed. One of them said, "We have lost our villages for the Dam but we have not got anything in return. It provides irrigation to far away villages located in Andhra Pradesh. But the local people are deprived." In Doraguda village and its periphery thousands had been re-settled. No primary school, no pacca approach road to villages, no electricity and drinking water are available. Villages in Odisha affected by the Dam construction have hardly been developed. One senior person in anguish stated, "Politicians promise a lot and show up only at times of elections." Needless to say, in such situations, the Maoists have a distinct edge over the government and others to win the heart of the poor and deprived people.

Ambition of the Maoists

As discussed above, CPI (Maoist), active in Odisha planned to capture the state and make it a liberated zone by 2010, where their writs will be paramount. Importantly, repeated success of the Maoists in the state right from 2000 to 2010, and the state government's insouciance to disarray the ultras made them confident of capturing a major portion of the state and bring it under their control. They perhaps realised that Odisha was a soft target, resistance by the police and administration was far from formidable. In fact, they aimed at the districts where poverty stricken tribals have been living and eke out a well-nigh unbearable existence. As already explained, lack of seriousness and indomitable will to curb outrages let loose by the appalling forces indirectly helped the Maoists to escalate attacks on the police men, police armouries, loot weaponry, kill cops and civilians with impunity. However, though late, the government woke up, galvanized and increased the man power in police, raised new battalions, enhanced the strength of the striking force, improved the intelligence output. Mandate was made clear and unambiguous that the Maoist menace has to be wiped out and rule of law has to be restored.

True, initially the police was not well prepared, lacked training in jungle warfare, short of sophisticated weaponry, deficient in man power and intelligence output etc. However, as events moved apace the police retrieved the lost ground and confronted the ultras with courage and firmness. Police foiled many fiendish attempts of the Maoists, forced them to take to heels, raided many hide outs, arrested several ultras and in protracted gun battles killed many Maoists. In fact, police's success forced many outlaws to surrender and return to the main stream of the society. Many police personnel sacrificed their lives on the altar of duty. The Central para-military force, CRPF, BSF, CISF took part in operations, ably assisted the police and administration and disarrayed the ultras and earned laurel for the supreme sacrifices of many officers and men. Dispassionately, spectacular performance and supreme sacrifices of many police personnel have enriched the history of the Orissa Police. Frankly speaking, state police's envious and matchless performance coupled with efficient assistance and co-operation by the central para military forces has negated the so called high hope and avidity of the rebels to bring a substantial portion of the state under their absolute control. The monumental ambition and fatuous arrogance of the Maoists to establish the Maoist empire is reduced to the shape of a phantasmagoria.

Undeniably, the police's shortcoming is trumpeted and good work and sacrifices go unheralded. Dispassionately, in tackling the Maoist menace the Orissa police have given an excellent account of themselves. Police hierarchy's pragmatic leadership to motivate the rank and file to combat the blood thirsty ultras and to keep their fighting spirit and morale high is laudable and exemplary. A brief survey of the extremist related events, police's reverses and successes and supreme sacrifices on the altar of duty is sure to wizen the public grievances and act of malfeasance against the police and stir favorable sentiment and good will of the people on the custodian of law and order. In fact, from 2005 to 2008, in 190 extremist related incidents, altogether 54 civilians and 81 police personnel including 36 Greyhounds of Andhra Pradesh were killed. In exchange of fire 45 extremists were killed, 471 ultras were arrested, 1108 weapons including automatic weapons were seized. In addition, a large number of ammunitions, hand grenades, gelatin sticks, detonators, petrol bombs and substantial quantity of explosives were recovered.

From 2009 increasing trend of extremist violence in seven states was a gigantic threat. Nevertheless, the police succeeded in trimming the Maoists and containing them in small pockets. Indeed, the whetted appetite of the Maoists to liberate a substantial portion of Odisha by 2010, has been badly bruised. To-day, the Maoists are in defensive and a large number of them have either surrendered giving up arms or are in police net. From 2009 to November 2012, in 472 incidents, 132 civilians and 89 security personnel including CRPF, BSF, CISF officers and men had lost lives. In eighty incidents of exchange of fire, 65 Maoists were killed. Police arrested 718 Maoists, seized 290 fire arms, 524 IED, 1438 detonators, 1426 gelatin sticks, 22 hand grenades and huge quantity of explosives. Above testimony is irrefutable that the security forces' untiring effort, dedicated service, single minded devotion and supreme sacrifices to disarray the blood thirsty out laws and re-establish peace and rule of law in Maoist hit areas has put the police of Odisha in high esteem and higher pedestal.

High Level Conference in Delhi in June 2013

Massacre of 28 leaders and activists of the Congress party in May 2013, in Sukma district, Chhattisgarh was a rude shock to the political parties. The Prime Minister Manmohan Singh took stock of the situation and decided to take tangible step to curb the Maoists. Accordingly, he called for all party conference at New Delhi on June 10, 2013. He asked the Chief Ministers of nine Maoists stricken states to attend the meeting for exhaustive discussion and explore pragmatic measures to tackle the Maoist threat. Chief Minister of Odisha Naveen Patnaik participated in the meeting. He highlighted that Naxal problem is a national concern, the menace has to be crushed firmly to uphold democracy and the rule of law. He added, "this requires liberal central budgetary allotment for ensuring adequate and equitable deployment of police forces, improve roads, communication, helicopter support, health care, education, public distribution system and other basic requirements." Maoists are taking advantage of inaccessible forest areas and their safe hide outs. Moreover, the porous boundary facilitates the ultras to escape from one state to another after committing acts of violence. This calls for well co-ordinated joint efforts for seamless operations against the Maoists across the state borders. He stressed on adoption of two-pronged strategy including firm enforcement of law and accelerated development. Again equitable deployment of central forces in Maoist-hit areas is essential. Secondly, neighboring states should join hands to help each other to effectively tackle left wing extremism. In fact, the CM's two-pronged strategy was accepted by other Chief Ministers present in the conference.

Prior to the conference under the chairmanship of the Prime Minister, the Union Home Minister on June 6, 2013, conferred with nine CMs for more than two hours. Participants agreed on a unified national policy to fight the threat. Subsequently the Prime Minister discussed elaborately aiming at preparing a detail road map to tackle the Maoists.

In sum, numerous odds faced, hesitation, indecisiveness of the state in initial stage, the growth of the Maoists was a robust threat. However, the state government after many vicissitudes finally resolved to assert its authority and neutralise the extremists. The Chief Minister Naveen Patnaik realised the gravity of the impending danger, wisely planned and prepared to fight the evil. His meaningful gesture to provide additional man power to the police organisation, seeking services of central para military forces, increase resources, incentives, compensation in case of death or injury, etc. have motivated and inspired the police men to fight the proxy war. Secondly, welfare and development programmes and their purposeful and prompt implementation in Maoist hit areas aiming at socio-economic up lift etc. have been alienating the poverty stricken and deprived people from the Maoist influence. His gumption, profound ideas and impetuosity are positive contributions to isolate the Maoists in the state. Over and above, the comprehensive rehabilitation package for the Maoists who surrender voluntarily indicates his sound and sagacious aplomb. Without any prejudice I am inclined to add that these are not fulsome flattery but eulogy deservingly paid to a progressive personality who has ungrudgingly taken up the challenge of the Maoists and unleashed welfare measures for the poor and down trodden.

Maoist movement in Odisha, if observed from vantage point, several relevant materials will surface which are useful to tackle the Maoist growth in the state. First, Naxal or Maoist movement was neither originated nor imported in the state. The extremists of Andhra Pradesh initially used the western territory of the state for making their hide-outs or sanctuary. Secondly, Leaders from Andhra Pradesh took initiative, penetrated well into the tribal belt, won heart of the tribal populace and started the extremist movement in western districts of Odisha. No local leader from the state worthy of his name took the leadership, spread Maoist gospel and cult of violence to achieve classless society and the People's government. Leaders from Andhra Pradesh organized the movement, recruited and built the cadre and inspired the tribal population to volunteer and participate in the movement. Even, to-day, leaders from Andhra Pradesh dominate over and guide the movement. The external authority and dominance generated a lot of discontentment and therefore, a crack is apparent between the Oriya Maoists and others. The birth of Odisha Maobadi party is a galling example of the internal squabble. Thirdly, untiring effort of the extremists from Andhra Pradesh has successfully united the Tribal population, brought them under influence of the extremists and motivated to respond to the call of the ultras. Frankly speaking, tribal communities are the substantial and major strength and main arms of the Maoist cadre. They are in the forefront and facing brunt of the security forces. Indeed, participation in the movement by persons from other communities is hardly noticed. Unlike West Bengal, intellectuals, students, educated and enlightened persons have not come out openly to support the movement, providing moral support, financial help and trying to build public opinion in favour of the Maoists. It is not understood if the persons belonging to aforesaid categories are indifferent to the Maoist movement or built a hiatus deliberately between them and the Maoists. Truly, every movement or upsurge for its success needs support of the intellectuals and progressive elements. Maoists of the state if deprived of the same, the future of the movement is uncertain and may hang in balance. Broadly speaking, as it stands to-day, the Tribal communities of the state under a few leaders from the neighboring state are spear-heading and taking the Maoist movement forward. A critic sarcastically commented that it may be called the Tribal Movement in the name of the Maoists. Hence, various facets, psyche, ethos of the participants, pressure from outside and resources available to strengthen the movement etc. have to be taken into account. In the end, the personalities who are vested with the responsibility of curbing the movement and disarraying the ultras may dispassionately examine the points elaborated above. Perhaps, it may be useful in handling the Maoist problem.

CHAPTER SEVEN

West Bengal: The Birth Place of the Red Movement

Comrade late Charu Mazumdar, the founder father of the Naxal movement, which originated in village Naxalbari, district Darjeeling, West Bengal could not live to see his brain child's prosperity, impending cracks or splits. He failed to visualise its future, galling desertions by many trusted comrades and excruciating emergence of several splinter groups. Indeed, insurmountable short comings which were beyond his comprehension put the movement in abject confusion and uncertainty. Comrade Kanu Sanyal's volte face and foundation of a new outfit CPI (Marxist and Leninest) on April 22, 1969 at Calcutta was a flinty blow to Charu. Meanwhile, death of Charu in 1972, and the state government's blood and iron policy initiated by the then Chief Minister S.S. Ray to disarray the Naxal movement put the ultras in precarious state. Many leaders and activists went underground. Truly, abyss suspense followed by an uneasy lull pushed the movement in isolation.

From 1977 to May 2011, the Left Front under leadership of the CPM ruled the state. It let loose its insolent cadres to chastise the political opponents and members of the public who demanded fair and legitimate governance. Truly, the cadre's muscle power backed indirectly by the police crushed the honest public opinion. Party's exasperating influence and control were blatantly inducted in education, administration, law enforcing agencies and social order simultaneously; appalling impact of the CPM dominated rule put the ultra-left movement in limbo of oblivion. The panic stricken people lost courage to protest or resist the cadres' high-handedness and government's party dominated misrule. Truly, the protracted LF rule in WB led by the CPM was lackluster, unresponsive and oppressive.

The extremists under the People's War (PW) were active in several districts of Andhra Pradesh. The Maoist Communist Centre (MCC) was active in many districts of Bihar. PW organised many small groups in remote areas of erstwhile Mednipur district, Bankura and Purulia districts short circuiting vigil of the CPM and the local administration. Admittedly, the PW better known as 'Jana Juddah' in three districts, gained influence on the poverty stricken tribal population. In undivided Medinapur district, the Majur Krishak Sangram Samity (MKSS), a frontal organisation of the People's War persuaded the rural population living in nooks and corners of the state to take part in armed movement against the CPM's oppressive rule, the party cadres' goblin spirit and high handedness. CPM bemused with power and authority presumed that the Naxals were fully disarrayed and the party's control through the cadres in Jangal Mahal was firm and unchallenged. On December 13, 2001. PW circulated a hand bill threatening "direct action" against senior officials and leaders of the CPM, if 36 PW activists arrested alleging for murder of the secretary of the local CPM committee were not released. Message generated a shock wave among the activists and supporters of the CPM. Meanwhile, merger of the PW and the MCC in September 2004, and birth of CPI (Maoist) added wider dimension to the extremist movement in seven states, including West Bengal. The new out-fit deputed several leaders from Andhra Pradesh and Jharkhand to West Bengal to rejuvenate the moribund ultra-left movement in the state. In three districts, poverty stricken tribal population was virtually landless, suffering from hunger, scanty medical care, unemployment, porous civic amenities, shabby educational facilities and negligible social opportunities. Their substandard living exposed the state government's monumental callousness or faineance to ensure their uplift and welfare. Cadres' rough and ready methods and wanton outrages made the hapless tribal community abysmally upset. Hence, the aggrieved people promptly responded to the Maoist call. Undeniably, local CPM leaders' follies and outrages by the cadres were responsible to force the tribal to enter into the fold of the Maoists. A journalist after visiting Lalgarh observed, "the people were either deaf or mute if asked about the Maoists." In fact, anti CPM and anti-UF tirade was adroitly exploited by the Maoists in their favour and took exhaustive steps to consolidate their hold and influence in jungle mahal. The new outfit created a positive impression and earned admiration of the poor and deprived people. In no time peltry strength of a few hundred of the Maoists shot up to roughly a few thousands. It initiated tangible steps to procure arms and ammunitions, land mines, trained up many able bodied persons to handle fire arms, planting explosives, participate in ambush, surprise attacks and to keep watch on the movements of the security forces. Frankly speaking, the unprecedented growth of the Maoists was possible due to complacency of the state government and the policy of masterly inactivity followed by the union government. The state's assertion that the growing problem would be tackled politically was a hoax and finally ended in fiasco.

Activities of the People's War in WB Before Merger with the MCC

People's War outfit tried to expand its activities in other districts of West Bengal. In the district of Nadia, it accelerated its movement. A group of selected youths was sent to Dandkaranya to undergo training in combats, handling fire arms, use of explosives etc. On return, the group geared-up aggressive activities in Karimpur, Nakasipara, Chapra, Fazil nagar and Santipur areas. Police intelligence report revealed that the PW had been preparing for armed uprising in the district. CPM's outrages on the local people spontaneously built an ambience of discontent, resulting in, the aggrieved people gleefully responded to the PW's call. A few incidents of the CPM cadres' high handedness further soiled the image of the ruling party. A group of muscle men occupied illegally a piece of land owned by a poor farmer. PW activists stood by him, forced the CPM cadre to retreat. It enhanced image of the PW and helped them to earn trust of the poor and neglected people. Simultaneously, anti-CPM sentiment in the area loomed large.

In panchayat election in 1998, CPM's debacle in the areas provoked many shrewd local political leaders to maintain contact clandestinely with the PW. They planned to invite and use the PW as "Naxal Brand" to frighten the people and to gain back their decayed influence. Local CPM leader, Asit Sarkar used the PW to keep the people under constant suspense and fear. Eventually Sarkar deserted the CPM and joined the PW. An unholy and secret pact between the PW and the CPM was agreed upon. CPM with help of the PW would occupy areas in Garbeta of West Mednipur, Bankura and Hooghly districts ousting the rival political parties and reestablish their control. In return, PW would be allowed to build its organisation in Santipur and its periphery. Ironically, the CPM after achieving the object betrayed the PW and let loose the police against them.

The angry PW decided to avenge the betrayal and in that pursuit chalked out a hit list figuring eleven names. Minister Susanta Ghose from Garbeta, several local CPM leaders and one leader from BJP were mentioned in the list. Meanwhile, on January 4, CPM resorted to a mass massacre in Choto Angania, near Garbata, which further irked the PW. It circulated a leaflet accusing the CPM leaders for atrocity and murders and announced to take revenge. CPM leader Sudhir Sarkar was murdered by the PW at Belpahari. Local BJP leader Swarup Sarkar was killed on September 9, 1999. BJP retaliated sharp, killing one CPM leader and three others. On February 24, 2004, a land mine was triggered by the PW at Dadali forest which killed eight EFR (Eastern Frontier Rifles) personnel. In second blast reported from Lalgarh forest on October 14, six EFR personnel were killed. On the following day, a cop of the Intelligence branch was killed in the market of Lalgarh in presence of a big crowd. Soon three government tourist lodges and costly machineries of a road contractor in Kankarajhore were set on fire. PW established armed training camps on Lakisini mountain ridge, in Kankrajhore near border of

Jharkhand. From above events it was crystal clear that PW with its limited resources was equally formidable in jungle mahal.

Jangal Mahal—The Cradle Land of the Maoists

Lalgarh, a small town, West Medinapur district West Bengal was the epicentre of Maoist activities. Koteshwar Rao alias Kishanji, from Andhra Pradesh, a member of the politburo of the Maoists was in command of the rebels. He was an idol of the tribals and his followers. Truly, he was the dramatis personae of the Maoist movement in Jangal Mahal. His leadership achieved several plus points including extension of areas brought under the control of the rebels. In fact, his writ ran without any challenge, reinforced the strength of the cadre, initiated many encounters, earned trust and goodwill of the local tribal populace. He liberated a sizeable area from control of the CPM cadres. Indeed, CPM cadres were determined not to cede an inch of territory. Hence, deadly clash between the two was inevitable. CPM had been dominating over the areas following hire and fire tactics which alienated the innocent tribal. Cadres killed many persons who had nothing to do with the Maoist movements. Nexus of the cadres with the local police to enforce law and order favouring the ruling party, affluence of the local CPM leaders, construction of big buildings in remote villages and their changed lifestyle etc. irked the poor people.

Hence, the Maoists got a favourable ground to chastise and expel the cadres from Jangal Mahal. Cadres were unwilling to give up their control and supremacy. However, the Maoist guerrillas were too formidable to humble the cadres. In confrontations the cadres were the bad losers. According to the CPM, by October 2009, seventy local CPM cadres, activists, and persons showing allegiance to the party were killed by the Maoists. A few example of turf war revealed the magnitude of the bloody contests. In fact, a large number of the CPM cadres and supporters deserted the villages, and took shelter in towns or safer places. Broadly, the Maoists established unquestioned supremacy in jungle mahal. In September 2009, 15 CPM male cadres from Keshpur were deputed to resist the ultras. Soon they were untraced Their family members were upset, Their lady wives demonstrated before the CPM leaders and threatened them for ugly consequence if their male folk failed to return. In October 2009, the armed cadres of the CPM tried to capture Chapashol area, about 18 km west of district HQ. Gun battle continued for two hours. Cadres finally retreated. In fact, from various developments alienation of the CPM from the rural mass was near completion. Rumour with its usual love for falsehood, gained currency that the Maoists soon were going to establish their rule in Jangal Mahal.

The Idea of Red Corridor

The idea of Red corridor was originally planned by the People's War in Andhra

Pradesh. The MCC in Bihar agreed to it. It entailed to expand operations from Telengana plateau to Nepal through the tribal belts of Odisha and Bihar. It also planned to form the Compact Revolutionary Zone (CRZ) covering the states including W.B., and part of North-East where the Maoists were active. But the changed scenario in Nepal forced the Maoists to modify the plan in 2009. In the modified plan WB prominently figured not only as a corridor but also as an operational base. Importantly, the recent Maoist operations were planned by the Bengal-Jharkhand-Orissa regional committee. In WB it was executed by West Medinapur-Bankura-Purulia Zonal Committee. Significantly, the Maoists have remarkably succeeded in contacting and penetrating well in the tribal community, landless peasants, daily-wage earners. They made an envious rapport and motivated them to respond to the Maoists' call. The deprived people, in addition to support, assisted the Maoists providing shelter to the fugitives, food, medical care, collecting intelligence and sending alert notice on the movement of the security forces. Admittedly, grand success of the ultras in Jangal Mahal lied in gaining heart of the tribal, poor and land less peasants and generating an anti-CPM spirit. Regrettably, abject poverty, exasperating economic backwardness, unemployment, under development and deplorable civic amenities failed to sensitize the leaders and the protracted LF rule to initiate fruitful steps to improve the lot of the tribal. Rather, abject poverty, malnutrition, crass exploitation and galling socio-economic disparity increased like snowball which forced the frustrated and luckless people to submit to the lofty assurance and promise of the Maoists hoping for better days. District survey report of Bankura district revealed that 8126 families of the district had been carrying on with only one meal a day. Needless to add, that such a revolting disclosure only made the state government uncomfortable.

Birth of CPI (Maoist)—Escalated Violence

Leaders of PW and MCC underground out-fits together in three days convention decided to bury their differences, agreed to merge and thereby birth of the CPI (Maoist) materialised in September 2004. It was decided to announce the merger formally in November adhering to sanctity of the anniversary of the Russian revolution. Importantly, the Andhra Pradesh fraction of CPI-ML (Janasakti) and CPI-ML (Naxalbari) West Bengal jointed the new out-fit. Convention for three days was held in Binani Bhawan in North Calcutta and resolution was passed that anti-imperialist and anti-feudal movement at the level of mass movement would be persuaded in right earnest. A 26-member "preparatory committee" including seven conveners was formed to undertake the unity process with the various out-fits in the country and representing students, peasants, dalits, and minorities. Mr GN Saibaba, the general secretary of the All India People's Resistance Forum—a mass organisation maintaining close links with the PW said, "The idea is to meet many more outfits across the country working towards the same goal. We would complete the process in a few months from now." Indeed, lured with the idea of toppling the present order and establishing the People's Government, unprecedented glee and resoluteness surcharged the ambience. About 500 delegates from 160 political and cultural organisations across the country as well as from Nepal and Bangladesh participated in the convention. Interestingly, the process of unification of the out-fits took place a few kilometers away from the Writers' building, Kolkata, where Chief Minister, Buddhadeb Bhattacharjee held his office and voiced crusade against the extremists more than once. He categorically stated that he would settle the growing Maoist problems politically.

Merger and birth of the CPI (Maoist) gave a substantial impetus to the Maoist movement in seven states including West Bengal right from 2005. In 2006, in 1509 Maoist related violent incidents, 678 persons including 101 security personnel were killed. In 2007, incidents increased to 1585 and 696 persons were killed. In 2008, in 1591 incidents 721 persons were killed. In 2009, right up to June 30, altogether 1128 incidents reported and 455 persons were killed. In West Bengal during first six months of 2009, in 56 incidents 34 persons were killed. In fact, escalated violence and aborted attack on the Chief Minister of WB, Buddhadeb Bhattacharjee on November 2, 2008 put the police and administration in a quagmire. The CM's alibi that the Maoists would be tackled politically received a flinty jolt. Inspite of repeated advice from the union government to ban the outfit in WB, the LF government was non-committal. However, the CM invited the Maoists more than once for a dialogue, but they declined. As a matter of fact, the LF government's ambivalence indirectly intensified the ultra-left movement in WB, red terror received fiendish momentum and people were shaken seeing likely horror of bloodshed and macabre festival of death. The dauntless Maoists held the ninth party congress of the outfit in 2007, inside the forest situated on the border of Bihar and Jharkhand. The meeting was called, "unity congress." In fact, Muppala Laxman Rao alias Ganapaty was re-elected as the general secretary of the party. In his message to the delegates he stated that the people's war against the state had to be intensified on all fronts. Destruction of the enemy was the immediate agenda in areas where the Maoists had a strong presence. However, West Bengal was not declared a war zone at the congress. Maoist Himadri Sen Roy, alias Somen, the secretary of WB was present in the congress. On February 23, 2008, he was arrested from a railway station in north 24 parganas, WB. He master minded killing of CPM leaders Rabi Kar and Mahendra Mahato in Purulia, Prabal Sen Gupta Officer-in-Charge of Barikul police station, Bankura and Nilmadhab Das, OIC of Bandwan police station, Purulia. Importantly, in 2005, the politburo member of the Maoists, Sushil Roy was arrested by the police. Both arrests were prize catches for the police.

Unfortunately, violence piled upon violence. On July 9, 2005, two local CPM leaders and sixteen others were injured in a booby trap in Purulia district. On December, 2005, a member of the CPM district committee and his wife were killed in village Bandwan, Purulia. On February 26, 2006, four persons were killed in a land mine blast at Naakrachhara. Later a police jeep was blown-up killing two security personnel and two civilians at Naakrachhara village, district West Medinapur. On September 21, 2006, in a bomb blast two personnel of bomb disposal squad were killed and 29 persons including several journalists were injured at Jhitka, West Medinapur. On May 28, 2007, a group of Maoists putting on mask attacked the house of Upen Mahato at village Jamda under Binpur police station and fired at Manik Mahato, and killed Upen, father-in-law of Manik. However, Manik escaped through the back door. It was suspected that Maoists and Jharkhand party (Naren group) jointly planned the attack. Local CPM activists and supporters resisted the attack and gun battle lasted for about three hours. Both sides used fire arms. One AK-47 rifle, a few rifles and ammunitions were recovered from the spot. On June 7, 2007, at Lakat near Lalgarh a mine hit a police jeep. Eight cops travelling in the jeep luckily were unhurt. Exchange of fire for about one hour continued without any casualty. On November 19, 2007, about three meters of railway track was blown up near Bhimgarh railway station, Birbhum district. It disrupted railway traffic for several hours. In November 2007, about fifty armed Maoists including six women Maoists attacked the house of local CPM committee member, shot him dead and razed his house and three other houses of the locality to the ground at village Bhikharicheliana, district Purulia.

Maoists blasted Bholabheda gram panchayat office in Belpahari. Thereafter, within 24 hours ultras went on rampage at Baita and destroyed the gram panchayat office in Lalgarh block. CPM's zonal secretary of Binpur alleged that operation was jointly carried out by the Maoists and Jharkhand party (Naren group). But the Jharkhand party firmly refuted the allegations and complained that the police raided Palasboni, Sinduria, Gajgiri and Kalaboni villages, broke opened many houses, harassed many activists and supporters, assaulted a woman aged eighty who had to be admitted in Belpahari hospital.

On November 2, 2008, a land mine blasted aiming at the convoy of the Chief Minister and one of the union ministers accompanying him, at Bhadutola, Salboni, near Medinapur town which alarmed the police and the people. It was a providential escape for the VIPs. The land mine was planted on the state highway very close to a culvert. It was connected by wire carried to a distance of about 1200 yards over the paddy field. Broadly, the administration and the CPM so long had been tackling the Maoist problems lackadaisically, now realised that the long arm of the Red rebels was not at all puny, rather their jaws were sharp and deadly to bite. People's liberation guerrilla army took the responsibility of attacking the CM's convoy. State Secretary of the Maoists, Kanchan sent letters to the media admitting their direct role in the attack. Police came under scathing criticism for porous security cover for the VIPs and monumental callousness to prevent the attack. Indeed, the much denounced police decided to recover its badly bruised image. In that murky pursuit, police went berserk and unleashed a reign of terror. Police indiscriminately registered criminal cases, arrested persons, mercilessly tortured them, raided houses in mid night, picked up females, adolescents, innocent persons on mere suspicion. Police assaulted three women brutally without any evidence against them. One of them, Chhitamoni aged 38, lost her left eye. Police raided house of a respected retired teacher Khemananda Mahato aged 62, at Boropolia village, dragged him out, charging him for conspiracy to kill the Chief Minister. People of the locality fumed in anger, spontaneously condemned the police. Police assaulted nine women of village Chotapalia, who were admitted into primary health centre for treatment. On November 4, 2008, in the evening, police arrested three school lads aged below 15, who were returning to home after attending to a village music show. They were produced before the Court branding them Maoists who attempted to blow up the Chief Minister's convey. Luckily, the Court on the very face of it disbelieved the complaint, questioned the adolescents, and set them free on the third day. Unfortunately, police raided a large number of houses during odd hours, broke house hold articles, beaten up male and female inmates. Truly, an ambience of police brutality frightened every one. Able bodied persons fled their abodes and concealed themselves in jungle. I interacted with several women victims, three released adolescents, the humiliated school teacher and many villagers who were roughed up by the police. They assembled in Dalilpur play ground. I was shocked hearing their woes. Regrettably, police overzealously acted mere on inference and suspicion, recklessly used rough and ready method. In fact, without working out proper clue, the police imagined that Maoists with the help of the villagers were behind the blast. In that blind pursuit, police ignored laws and rules, human dignity and compassion even for the weaker sex and the adolescents.

Reasons for the Mass Upsurge in Jangal Mahal

Interestingly, the name jungle mahal has not been connoted in official or revenue record of the government. In the beginning of the Maoist movement the journalists, NGOs, social activists etc., had been visiting the disturbed areas of three districts and called it, "Jungle Mahal." It gained currency and earned popularity. Since then it is exuberantly and affectionately called and known as jungle mahal. News of police atrocity spread like wild fire in jungle mahal. It magically united the aggrieved tribal people and communities to protest against the police excesses and the government. Indeed, it was a blessing in disguise that a strong and unprecedented fraternity grew which was entirely anti-CPM and anti-LF government. Villagers decided to boycott the police and debar their entry into the villages. Hundreds of males and females came out on the street armed with their traditional weapons, bows and arrows and participated in the agitation. They dug the roads towards Jangal Mahal, damaged many culverts, and blocked roads felling tree trunks, branches, dumping boulders; bricks etc. thereby completely shut ingress and outgress into the jungle mahal. Public transport services were paralysed preventing movement of the people, vehicular traffic which effected supply of essential commodities. As a matter of fact, jungle mahal was cut off for several days from outside and the district HQ. News of police brutality and terror tactics gained wide currency through the print and electronic media. Unity and solidarity of the tribal community in the jungle mahal at that juncture, indeed, was exemplary.

I continued visiting Lalgarh, Goaltore, and other villages, heard grievances of the villagers, interacted with Chatradhar Mahato, convener of the PCAPA and several leaders and collected first hand account of fast deteriorating situations. Pensive analysis revealed that police brutality severely jeopardized the peoples' faith on the administration. Truly, the police-public relation reached the arid zone of acrimony. Secondly, influence of the Maoists on the tribal community increased leaps and bounds and their relationship was cemented beyond any doubt. Dispassionately, I am inclined to add that the police's barbarity after November 2, 2008, provoked or inspired the poverty stricken, deprived and leaderless tribal community to unite which spontaneously took the path of mass upsurge in Jangal Mahal. Indeed, upsurge was matchless and unknown in Jangal Mahal. It paralysed the district administration and put the UF government in a quandary. It opened the flood gate for the Maoists to get the oppressed tribal community in their fold. At the same time, harassed and chastised tribal people were keen to come under a protective umbrella to avoid or neutralise the police's harshness and excesses. Frankly speaking, mass upheaval in Lalgarh was not a contribution of any brilliant political philosopher or any outstanding revolutionary. But it was follies of the police, overzealousness and brutality unleashed by them which queered the pitch. Secondly, lamentable indifference of the police hierarchy and the state government to tame the police and direct the policemen to discharge duties adhering to police ethics and spirit of impartial public service was squarely responsible for the excesses. It was a mystery why the Writers' building was ambivalent inspite of the media's relentless effort exposing the police's excesses, loud cry of the victims and hue of the liberals and intellectuals. Chief Minister, known for his love and attachment to culture and poetic passion was surprisingly silent to prevent the police from committing excesses and misusing power. Thirdly, years neglect of the state to improve deplorable socio-economic condition of the tribal community and evils practiced by the CPM cadres on the helpless tribal and the administration's failure to ensure fair and impartial treatment to the deprived and exploited community multiplied miseries. I am candid that the police's harsh actions and fatuous arrogance was responsible for turning a low profile agitation to a gargantuan shape. The spectre of violence got the opportunity to raise its ugly head under direct assistance and support of the pitiless ultras. Hence, call of the Maoists and their assurance for social justice was avidly responded by them. Consequently, the People's Committee against Police Atrocity (PCAPA), a frontal organisation of the Maoists, was born for pursuing the movement.

Indeed, it was the God sent opportunity that the gun-toting Maoists emerged as the saviors of the outraged tribal populace. The Red brigade had conquered the heart of the people and roused boundless anti-government sentiment. In fact, the people's spontaneous welcome transformed every tribal village into dens of the Maoist guerrillas. As a gesture of friendship the Maoists stood by their side firmly and instigated them to defy the government and the present order. Every day, people's disdain and defiance of the government increased and grip of the ultras on the rural mass became stronger. In short, Maoists' control and influence in Jangal Mahal reached its pinnacle totally free from any challenge. Maoists with renewed zeal and vigour stepped up the annihilation spree targeting the local CPM leaders, cadres and personnel of the security forces. Ultras torched the CPM controlled panchayat offices at Dahijuri and Dharampur, vandalized and damaged CPM leader Anjur Panday's house at Dharampur who was the uncrown CPM king in the areas. His words were law in the locality. In fact marked eclipse of the CPM's power and authority emboldened the supporters of the Maoists and the activists of the PCAPA to attack and ransack the CPM establishments and houses of the CPM cadres with impunity. Anuj Pandey abandoned his abode and took shelter in Medinapur town hoping better days. Local CPM leaders and cadres realised that they were not a match with the Maoist plan, strategy, skill in attacks, ambush, fire power and indomitable will etc. Secondly, the government's help to protect them through the police was uncertain and fragile. Thirdly, assurance of the leaders from Alimuddin Street (party's HQ in Kolkata), carried hardly any force. Hence, they thought it wise to quit Jangal Mahal and take shelter in secure places.

Tribal Population Up-in-arms

On November 6, 2008 about 1000 bellicose men and women assembled at Lalgarh to march and raid Lalgarh police station. Importantly, women took the lead, forcibly entered into the campus of the police station, shouted slogans against the police's atrocity, smashed window panes of the thana building, broke a portion of the boundary wall. Police fired a few rounds in the air to disperse the angry mob. However, police denied firing and stated that the mob reached the police station to hand over a memorandum. On December 6, 2008, a large number of fair sex demonstrated before the Additional District Magistrate at village Chotopalia demanding employment under 100 days' work scheme. Meanwhile, an elected member of the panchayat of CPM resigned protesting against police's torture against adivasi women etc. On September 2, 2009, the joint forces arrested two suspects from Memul. Several hundred women protested, dug up roads, blocked felling tree trucks, branches, boulders, etc. at Lakat, Dhanghori, Purunapani, Dharampur, Kantapahari etc. and paralysed the traffic. Police charged them for a conspiracy of sedation, arrested several protesters and produced them before the Chief Judicial Magistrate.

In the evening at Bansberh near Sijua under Salboni police station, in an encounter security forces killed two Maoists. Reacting to the incident about 100 tribal women staged a demonstration in front of the Kantapahari camp of the joint forces and vehemently protested alleging outrages unleashed by the security forces. Police lathi charged to disperse the mob. It appeared that the PCAPA was behind the agitation.

Maoists had consolidated their control in Jangal Mahal and pursuing their cherished goal of establishing Red corridor from Nepal to Tamilnadu. Local political leaders stated, "this movement is now not under control of tribal organisations. Currently Maoist leaders are dominating the movement and they may intensify the stir if the state government does not come forward to settle the impasse." Intelligence report revealed that the Maoists were organising meeting frequently in Laljol forest. Several leaders from Jharkhand were seen in the areas. Fresh recruitment drive and reinforcement of the squads were continuing. They have already established strong bases in Lalgarh, Belpahari, Binpur and formed many squads. As a matter of fact, roughly 700 sq km forest of West Medinapur district came under their control. In short, the Maoists were preparing for a decisive action to occupy Jangal Mahal and establish the People's government and their rule.

Target on CPM Cadres—Panic in Rank and File

Killing spree and exodus of the CPM local leaders and cadres from jungle mahal unnerved the top brass. Since the situation was slipping through the fingers and cadres were losing faith on the party and the leadership, they hit upon a plan to hire armed goons and insolent elements from Jharkhand, Bihar, UP, to counter the Maoists. Leaders, ignorant of ground reality, planned to salvage the situation employing armed mercenaries. Meanwhile, CPM mobilised armed party cadres, goons (Harmads) from Keshpur, Garbeta, Amarbag, Goghat etc. and assembled them at Saora and Enyatpur. Soon in a gun battle with the Maoists CPM lost many cadres. However, the loss was denied by the party and the police. But the local people confirmed the gun battle and casualties on CPM side. They said that the dead bodies were hurriedly removed under cover of darkness. Needless to add, it demoralised the cadres who hence forth, preferred escape to confrontation with the ultras.

On June 11, 2009, Salku Soren of Kankradanga, a CPM activist was abducted by a group of Maoists. Later his dead body with stab injuries was recovered from the nearby jungle. On February 14, 2009, Sujit Panda, the secretary of the local DYFI committee was killed in the same area. It was alleged that PCAPA was responsible for the murder. On June 16, 2009, PSBPC abducted the secretary, Badal Ahir of the local committee of the CPM and Chaitan Soren, an activist. After three days, their dead bodies were recovered from Patharpara forest, near Goaltore. On October 1, 2009, a shop keeper was gunned down at Kantapahari village, under Lalgarh police station. The deceased was supplying provisions to the police camp and therefore suspected to be an informer of the police.

On December 10, 2009, the Chief Minister submitted a report on the floor of the State Legislative Assembly. It revealed that from January 1 to November 13 of the current year the Maoists had killed 69 persons including 47 CPM leaders and activists and 15 TMC activists. CM highlighted that the ultras had been killing the local CPM cadres and activists, damaged or destroyed the party offices and forced the CPM supporters to quit Jangal Mahal. CM directly accused the TMC for the first time that TMC had been patronizing the Maoists. He stated, "while the Jharkhand party is patronizing the Maoists in Jharkhand, TMC in Bengal is doing the same." CPM decided to resist the Maoists for preserving party's existence. Following the CM's statement the House noticed fracas and angry exchange of words between the MLAs.

In December 2008, the state CID had submitted a report that during the current year that Maoist violence and deaths had increased leaps and bounds. From 2003 to November 25, 2008, altogether 118 extremist related violence reported in the state. However, till November 2008, number of Maoist attacks were 27, and 80 persons were killed, including 31 leaders and activists of the CPM. In land mine blast 28 persons lost life and 46 persons were wounded. In direct confrontations four ultras were killed and 63 fire arms were recovered. On the eve of Lok Sabha poll in 2009, the state anticipated escalated violence and therefore, demanded additional para military forces. Later, massive presence of combined forces in and around Lalgarh had failed to deter the Maoists. Rebels were contacting villagers at regular intervals, arranging meetings and kept the ambience tense in the Maoist dominated areas.

Over and above, the Maoists meticulously proceeded with the expansion plan and strategy. At the same time, there was no let up in the annihilation spree on the CPM cadres. On July 1, 2009, Maoist action squad numbering about forty took shelter in Baxibund forest which stretched right to Salboni, Sarenga, Belpahari and fringe of Jharkhand border. After a few days, about 100 Maoists came out of the forest and held a meeting with the villagers of Shirsi at 3 pm. They held a kangaroo court and passed death sentence to Baren Mahato, a kendu leaf dealer and Guru Charan Mahato, a ration shop dealer. Both were taken inside the forest and on the following morning their bullet ridden bodies were recovered. Maoist posters were available by the side of the life less bodies. Ultras ransacked deceased Guru Charan's shop, residence and the CPM office of Shirsi. After three days, the Maoists again entered into the village, held the people's court and directed four local CPM leaders to quit the party or face death. The dithered CPM activists announced their resignation from the party formally to save their lives. The local people blamed the police for inaction to protect them. Shop keepers shut down shops protesting against double murder and the police's indifference. Importantly, the joint forces made no attempt to counter the killers and prevent cold blooded murders.

On July 2, 2009, Maoists triggered a land mine blast about 300 yards away from the office of BDO of Binpur I. The state armed police contingent was stationed nearby. Apparently, it was planned to create a panic in the area and put the joint forces in perplexity. Importantly, operation by the joint forces reached 13-day. Yet, no salutary result of the aggressive action came to light. Not a single leader either from the Maoist cadres or from the PCAPA was arrested. Police prepared a long list of wanted Maoists but of no avail. On the contrary, Maoists were very active in Belpahari, Ranibandh areas. However, joint forces had reclaimed Lalgarh and started combing operation in 22 villages to flush out or nab the ultras. Secondly, in many pockets and jungle where the state police did not dare to enter and face the ultras, fortunately, the joint forces had registered their presence in those vulnerable areas. The joint forces hailing from other states, not knowing the local language and topography of the areas, short of intelligence output and local contact had to face insurmountable hurdles and numerous odds at every step.

Killing Spree CPM Cadres and Activists—Main Targets

Maoists considered the CPM and its cadres as the formidable hurdle to take the revolutionary movement ahead. Therefore, they made them prime targets, unleashed gory attack and annihilation with a view to rooting them out from Jangal Mahal. Examples of reckless chastisement and brutal killing, though not exhaustive are appended below to satisfy curiosity of the readers. On April 3, 2008, a member of the CPM zonal committee was shot dead at village Bomragarh district Purulia. Another activist was injured and admitted to district hospital. On April 13, 2008, three CPM cadres including secretary of the local branch committee, Mukul Tewari, were abducted from Garmal, near Salboni and shot. In addition, seven CPM activists were abducted but they managed to escape. On April 20, 2008, the secretary of the local committee was shot dead by three Maoists at village Rangametia, Purulia. Khetrapal Majhi aged 44, a primary school teacher and resident of village Fosko was shot dead when he was returning home after attending panchayat committee meeting. On May 4, 2008, Ganapati Bhadra, a member of the CPM zonal committee was shot dead at village Bhomragarh, Purulia. Activist Rampati Majhi was attacked, received bullet injury and admitted to Purulia sadar hospital. On May 9, 2008, Maoists suddenly came out of jungle near village Andhera and fired indiscriminately at a procession organised by the CPM. Mamatha Mondal aged 32 was killed and eight persons were critically wounded. On 3110.08, CPM leader Indrajit Mura was shot dead at village Kashmar. CPM committee member Mendalal Mistry was killed. His throat was slit. Later his dead body was recovered from Mohisapuri jungle under Khoirashore police station, district Birbhum. On June 15, 2008, Biswanath Mandi aged 46, a member of the CPM zonal committee, was shot dead right in his house at Goaltore. On January 30, 2009, Nandalal Pal, a member of the zonal committee was shot dead at village Murar near Lalgarh. Four cyclists came and pumped bullets in his body, left Maoist literature near the dead body and fled On February 3, 2009, Haradhan Majhi, a member of the local committee was shot dead at Besra, Purulia. His son and grandson were injured.

On April 10, 2009, Ashim Mondal, aged 45, a former member of the CPM local committee was attacked at village Bhulaveda and was shot dead. The victim was secretly working for Gana Pratirodh committee, jointly formed by the police and the CPM and against the PCAPA. After killing the assailant Maoists shouted slogans, "Maobad zindabad". On April 22, 2008, Sridhar Das was shot dead at village Tantipara, Rajnagar, Birbhum by three Maoists came in motor bikes, fired, shouted slogans and fled. In protest CPM gave a call for bandh for 12 hours. On June 22, 2009, Maoists blew up the panchayat office at Chara, near Kirakata intending to disrupt supply line of the security forces deployed in Lalgarh area. On July 11, 2009, two CPM cadres were abducted from Chandragram under Kotawali police station and shot them dead. Another group raided and torched the house of Sudarsan Das, near Salboni who was zonal committee member. About 50 armed rebels, including 7 women rebels raided villages, Chapasholi, Bagghora, Sundarlata and Sirshi under Chandragram panchayat within sadar block, dragged out many villagers and assaulted them mercilessly. They demanded rupees two lakhs from Baren Mahato who refused to pay. A kangaroo court was held at village Shirshi. Throbbed with panic the CPM cadres and activists submitted written under taking that they had quit the CPM. Many kept the undertaking hanging on the wall of the residence or on the trees to prove their bonafide. A large number of them deserted home and Jangal Mahal and took shelter in urban areas. Exodus of the CPM cadres and activists badly upset the top brass of the CPM.

On July 14, 2009, Tarini Mahanto and Swapan Deb Singh were abducted from their residence. Later their dead bodies with bullet injuries were discovered from Mohultala forest under Salboni police station. On July 15, 2009, CPM leader Gangadhar Mahato was shot dead near Hatkhola crossing under Burra bazaar police station, Purulia. On July 18, 2009, Jaladhar Mahato, a zonal committee member was shot dead near village Andharizole by seven rebels who came riding motor bikes. Ashok Ghosh, a CPM activist was shot dead at Goaltore. Importantly, CPM's panchayat pradhan of Dharampur surrendered to the Maoist and promised to quit the party. On August 19, 2009, at about 10 AM, a group of armed Maoists along with villagers raided village Dharua, surrounded CPM office at Sisirdanga and demolished it. On August 20, 2009, Maoists with a group of villagers jointly demolished the zonal office of the CPM, located about 12 Kms from Dharampur. Ultras attacked the camp of the joint forces at Gohamidanga and fired at Kantapahari police camp. On August 26, 2009, about five hundred Maoists attacked the house of Ratan Mahato, a member of the CPM local branch committee at village Belasole under Salboni police station, dragged him out of his house and assaulted him brutally. He was admitted to hospital where he succumbed to injuries. Ultras set fire on a house of a CPM leader at village Jamdohara and ransacked houses of three CPM cadres.

Ananda Mahato, aged 30, a CPM cadre and Kanai Murmu of the Jharkhand party (Naren group) were abducted and taken to Madhupur jungle under Belpahari police station. Later their bullet ridden bodies were recovered from the bank of Kapatkata canal. On September 7, 2009, Satish Singh aged 48, and Sashanka Sekhar Roy, a ration shop owner, both CPM activists were killed. Sibu Pratihar was tortured to death inside the court lock up at Khatra Bankma. It was suspected that the Maoists already in custody killed him. On September 9, 2009, about 40 Maoists entered into the house of Ramdas Murmu aged 52, and Baneswar Murmu, both CPM activists, at village Habra under Saranga police station, Bankura, abducted and taken them to nearby jungle and shot them dead. Ranjit Sardar aged 31, an active Maoist squad member was found dead with bullet injuries in Kundan Pahari forest under Belpahari police station. It was suspected that he was killed by the "Harmads." On September 11, 2009, about eight Maoists came in motor bikes and guned down Krishna Kunder, aged 72, the Sabhapati of CPM Krishak Sabha and CPM zonal committee member. On September 14, 2009, Kartik Mahato a teacher of Belatikri primary school under Lalgarh police station was dragged out from the class room and shot dead. After a few hours Sambhu Mahato was gun down at Buripada under Salboni police station His friend tried to escape but was shot who died later. Nirmal Sardar aged 40, was shot dead near his house at Talpukuria under Salboni police station. Himadri Mahato was kidnapped and remained untraced.

In second week of December 2009, four local CPM leaders and a supporter of the CPM were gunned down by the Maoist guerrillas. The secretary of CPM branch committee was killed in Salboni area. In Bandwan, district, Purulia, another CPM leader was killed. In Lalgarh, the ultras raided Jhitka forest beat house and destroyed and burnt all official documents. They pasted posters on walls, lamp posts or on trees, asked the villagers to assist or join the movement. Joint forces raided Kanundi, Notundi and Chandpara, assaulted many villagers on the allegation of harboring the rebels. On July 30, 2009, two cops Kanchan Giri and Sabir Mollah were abducted from Brindanpur chowk. Police intensified manhunt for rescuing them but failed. Obviously, it demoralised the police considerably. In December 2009, two CPM activists were abducted from Bhandarpur and Hatimasan villages respectively under Goaltore police station. Maoists set fire on the house of local CPM leader in Hatimason village. They abducted four persons including S. K. Hansda suspecting them for maintaining link with the joint forces. Hansda was killed and rest were set free. Information from the police revealed that by December 2009, about 100 persons were murdered in jungle mahal since joint forces started operation in Lalgarh right from June 18, 2009. Vast majority of the victims were CPM activists or affiliated to the CPM. However, a small number belonged to JMM and its splinter groups.

On September 21, 2009 the Maoists attacked the CPM office at Enayatpur, West Medinapur district. CPM cadres in full fury resisted the attack. An obstinate gun battle followed which lasted several hours and put the villagers in abject panic. Local police helplessly watched the swift moving events. Spot was located about 30 kms away from Lalgarh. CPM cadres fortified the building placing sand bags, installing girders, barricades and stock piling arms and ammunitions. Cadres holed up in the office, summoned insolent comrades, action squads, reinforced strength and put up a flinty resistance In exchange of fire three villagers were injured and admitted to hospital. Police behaved like mute spectators. Neither they were bold enough to repulse the Maoists nor keen to neutralise the CPM's musclemen. In fact, police was soft with the law breakers and afraid of going against the interest of the ruling party.

Unabated Violence and the State's Helplessness

Operation by Joint forces was yet to deliver desired result. CPM complained that 43 CPM cadres were killed by the Maoists within 90 days in 2009, inspite of presence of 17000 central and state security forces in Jangal Mahal. Director General of Police W.B., said that within six months after the joint forces started operation eighty persons were killed. Sixty CPM cadres and activists were killed since November 2008. The Maoists killed 15 activists of the JMM (Jharkhand Janamukti Morcha), ten of Jharkhand party (Aditya group) and ten of Jharkhand party (Naren group). Death toll since joint forces entered into Lalgarh was 120. DG said that since June 2009, security forces nabbed 300 suspects including forty hardcore extremists. In fact, violence and killing was going on unchecked. In an average twenty persons were being executed every month.

On March 24, 2008, five Maoists were putting up posters in the Chief Minister's constituency. Five women were arrested from Bagha Jatin area Kolkata. One was the wife of a lecturer of the University Science College and holder of post graduate degree. They were members of the Nari Mukti Sangha, a women wing of the CPI (Maoists) Kolkata. On April 13, 2008, three CPM cadres including a branch committee secretary were killed by the Maoists at Garmal, Salboni. Two security guards of the state Armed police guarding a branch of State Bank of India at Dohijuri, were shot dead. Their weapons were looted. On May 11, 2008, at Sirka, Purulia, Maoists killed one BSF personnel and injured eleven using a landmine. On May 26, 2008, Maoists came in motor bikes, fired and killed one EFR personnel and injured one S.I., one jawan and looted weapons. On October 22, 2008, Maoists blasted four landmines and destroyed a vehicle of the health department killing a doctor, nurse and the driver near Choukisole forest, Belpahari. Maoist leader Kanchan said that medical staff were not their target and he sought apology for the mistake. The medical team was returning after attending patients. On December 22, 2008, at Berada, Purulia, a group of twenty Maoists attacked and killed two constables, injured one and looted their weapons. On February 25, 2009, at Barabhum railway station, Purulia, Maoists attacked the RPF pay escort, fired and killed two RPF personnel, injured two and looted their arms. Biramdi railway station was set on fire in 2007. It was re-built in February 2009. On April 21, 2009, two CPM activists were killed at village Nadaria near Lalgarh and two others were abducted. Police tried to reach the spot and recover the dead bodies, but failed as repeated blasts dissuaded the police to proceed further. On April 22, 2009, nine cadres were abducted from their homes at Saluka and taken to a jungle. They were beaten mercilessly and one died.

On March 24, 2009, a training camp of the Maoists was discovered. They had set up a control room connected with a wireless set. Here weapon target practice was going on regularly. Pamphlets for imparting training in Bengali, Hindi were recovered. On March 19, 2009, CPM leader Durga Dashwali of village Amdubi and Sontosh Mahato of village Bhulbheda were shot dead near Belpahari. Sudip Hembram was wounded. In April 2009, about 50 Maoists appeared at Bhuiyapara, village Saluka and asked the villagers to boycott election. One of them brought out a diary, read the names of local CPM leaders, branded them anti-people and declared punishment against them. They brutally assaulted several villagers and prohibited them to be taken to health centers for treatment. On April 24, 2009, at village Sukurdi, under Balarampur police station, a village fair and Chau dance was going on. About 5000 people gathered to witness dance. Maoists suddenly appeared and attacked Baikanthu Mahato, a member of zonal committee and Bhibhuti Sarkar, secretary Darda local committee, killed both of them and badly wounded three cadres who attempted to save the victims. Brutal double murder in presence of thousands of people panicked every one.

Maoists set up a People's Court at Lalgarh in May 2009. Interestingly, the Maoists so long had been operating clandestinely. Now they have decided to come out in open. On May 31, 2009, they held the first public meeting at Kantapahari school ground, Lalgarh. Many ultras were carrying fire arms freely. Local action squad members, Karan Hembram, Arjun, Surya and Bablu Ranbaj were present in the meeting. Meeting continued from 6 pm to 8.30 pm, Maoist leaders, Bikash, Tara and Rakesh addressed the gathering and lambasted the CPM. Leaders, Kishanji, Dipak Das alias Chandra Rao, Akash, Sasadhar Mahato and his wife Suchitra were present at a distance. In fact, for the first time Maoists used their banner in public place. Leaders declared that it would now enter in urban areas adopting the same method they had applied in rural areas and creating mass organisations. They would not allow the Jindal Steel plant to come up at Salboni.

On June 3, 2009, Maoists attacked three policemen at Pirolgari crossing, Bankura when they were taking lunch in a road side eatery, fired indiscriminately, killed them and looted their weapons. Another group attacked a cop and NVF who were guarding Bangiya Gramin Bikash Bank, killed them and carried away their weapons. On July 11, 2009, two CPM cadres were abducted from a place close to Kotwali police station and gunned them down. Another group raided the house of Sudarsan Das, a member of the zonal committee at Salboni and torched the house. Fifty armed Maoists including 7 women Maoists raided Chapashole, Bagghora, Sundarlata and Sirshi villages under Chandra gram panchayat in West Medinapur sadar block, dragged out several persons, assaulted them mercilessly. They killed Baren Mahato and Gurucharan Mahato. On July 14, 2009, Maoist leader Bikash held a meeting at Kakradara village. He sought participation of the villagers to fight against the joint forces and appealed for armed intervention and continuing the struggle. A procession was held from Kakradara village to Adharjota. Prior to it, they held a meeting at Bhulgaddai village very close to Dharampur police camp. On September 7, 2009, Maoists killed two cadres, and a ration dealer in Salbani. On September 9, 2009, a group of forty Maoists entered into the houses of two CPM activists at village Habra, Bankura, dragged them out and took them to forest and shot them. On September 15, 2009, Kartik Mahato, a teacher was pulled out of the class room of Belaliki primary school, Lalbagh and shot them dead. Meanwhile, Kishanji said, "we will over throw Indian government much before 2050." However, the Union Home Secretary refuted it.

On April 3, 2010 the Union Home Minister held discussion with the CM of WB in Writers building. He urged the CM to take stern measures so that law and order was maintained. He visited Lalgarh on April 4, 2010, held a meeting in Lalgarh police station, met villagers and heard their grievances. In fact, response from the people was spontaneous and warm. He termed the Naxals cowards who were hiding in forest and not responding to dialogue inspite of invitation. They had killed 57 civilians alone in first three months of 2010. He stated that anti naxal drive was a long-drawn-out affair in WB and other states including Odisha and Jharkhand. It could take 2 to 3 years to defeat the extremists He appealed to the people, "Drive out the Naxals from your area and do not provide any moral and material support to them. They are killing you and continue to kill and they have no place in the society." Significantly, retired Indian Police Service Officers organised a seminar in New Delhi on April 23, 2010. The subject of discussion was, "Maoist threats—challenges and response." Discussion revealed that till April 23, 2010, Maoists had killed 116 civilians including 101 were tribals. Hence their plea for fighting for the tribals was a myth.

On October 1, 2009, three CPM activists were abducted and taken inside Ranja jungle. A mock court was held. SLRs were forced into their mouth and shot. It was alleged that they ostensively left the CPM but maintained contact with the "Janaganer committee." secretly. On October 20, 2009, about 25 Maoists including women Maoists and PLGA travelled in motor cycles at about 1.30 pm. They were divided in three groups, raided Sankrail police station, shot dead sub Inspector Dibakar Bhattacharjee, ASI Swapan Roy right inside the police station and kidnapped OIC Atindra Nath Roy from his quarters, damaged radio transmission system, looted 6 rifles, 4 revolvers, one 9mm pistol and two motor bikes. Another group looted rupees 9.5 lakhs from the State bank of India functioning nearby. Maoists planted land mines in Kesiapeta, Guptamoni and Balibhasa to prevent entry of security personnel into the police station. Three women Maoists took leading part in the operation. On November 8, 2009, the ultras attacked EFR personnel patrolling in Gidhni bazar and killed four of them and carried away their weapons.

On June 16, 2010, in a protracted encounter in Ranjha forest security forces killed eight Maoists including three women Maoists and five PLGA. A huge cache of arms was seized. In fact, after joint forces started operation in June 2009, total 20 Maoists and 45 security personnel were killed till June 15, 2010. Maoist Sidhu Soren secretary of the PCAPA, wanted in 20 criminal cases and a woman Maoist were killed in an encounter in Metala forest on July 26, 2010. Maoist Uma Kanta Mahato wanted by the CBI in Gnanswari express train sabotage, was killed in an encounter in Mohanpur forest on August 27, 2010. A kangaroo court was held at Chakua village on August 26, 2010, and death sentence was passed on three CPM activists. They were taken to Kalabani and shot dead. Heads and faces of the victims were disfigured by hammer blows. Three cadres were let off after they submitted written undertaking for disassociating them from the CPM. On August 31, 2010, Sm Chhabi Mahato and constable Paritosh Dey of Salboni police station were abducted. Her dead body was recovered from a pit at Bhangabundh, Salboni. Cop's dead body was recovered from the bank of a canal near the police station. Another body was found on the roof of Kumarpur primary school. On October 4, 2010, Maoists killed three leaders of the Forward Block in village Chirugara near Bagmundi, Purulia. On November 22, 2010, within 24 hours, two bullet ridden bodies found from Dhanghori, under Sankrail police station. Before it, two persons were killed at Kharikashuli, under Salboni police station. On the following morning headless and bullet-ridden body of Ganesh Ahir was traced from Paluidanga, Binpur. On the same night Sushil and Paresh were abducted from their abodes and shot dead. On December 17, 2010 from village Darda, seven persons including woman panchayat chief Sm Chapala Gorai were abducted and killed. Dead bodies were thrown in a paddy field, near village Baghbinda, Purulia. Victims were activists of the Forward Block. On February 15, 2011, Maoists attacked EFR camp at Silda, Bankura and killed 24 EFR personnel and looted 45 fire arms, including SLR, AK-47, INSAS rifles. Several women Maoist took active part in the operation. It was a daring attack on a temporary and unfortified camp in broad day light. In fact, location of the camp was erroneously chosen for which the police hierarchy was responsible. On May 19, 2010, in a landmine blast near a bridge in Tetulia located between Ramgarh and Goaltore, five CRPF personnel including a Dy Commandant were killed and two cops were injured. Gnaneswari express train bound for Mumbai was sabotaged between Khemashuli and Sardina railway station, near Jhargram on May 28, 2010. Altogether 162 innocent passengers were killed. The gruesome tragedy was universally condemned. On July 16, 2012, Bikram alias Bhanu/Surya and alias Arnab Dam was arrested from Biramdi in a joint raid. He was central committee leader, secretary of the Maoist of WB, Jharkhand-Orissa border committee He was involved in 80 criminal cases, killed CID officer Partha Biswas and school teacher Soumitra Basu.

Maoist leader Kanchan alias Sudip Chongdar, secretary of the Maoist state committee, stated that many members of the state unit did not approve violent means to pursue the movement, preferred by Kishanji. They wanted to participate and contest in Lok Sabha election in 2009, but not approved by Kishanji. Covert support to TMC was not approved by Kanchan and many others. He pointed out many times to Kishanji that this was not the line of the Maoists. Sushil Roy, a member of the politburo, Himadri Sen Roy alias Somen, Telugu Deepak alias Venkateswar Reddy and Durjan Hembram were arrested. In short, after their arrests only four members Ashim Mondal alias Akash, Manesaram Hembram alias Bikash, Sasadhar Mahato and Madhai Patra remained functional. But they were facing hot chase from the security forces. The panel had thinned out precariously which was affecting operations and operational activities.

On November 24, 2011, security forces in a gun battle in Burishole jungle at about 6 pm shot dead Koteshwar Rao alias Kishan Ji. Conflict lasted about thirty minutes. Two AK-47 rifles were recovered from the spot. One of his guards Suchitra Mahato was injured. After autopsy his dead body was sent to his native place, village Padapally, Karimnagar district, AP for cremation. Death of Kishanji was a major set-back for the ultras. In fact, no suitable leader was readily available to fill the vacuum.

State Government's Soft Line and Vacillation; Kishanji's Claim—War Begins, First Prisoner of War Released

Daring Maoist attack on Sankrail police station (West Medinipur district) on October 20, 2009, shooting down two officers right inside the police station, looting of arms and ammunitions, abduction of the Officer-in-Charge and dacoity on the Kesiapeta branch of the State Bank of India, exposes ineptitude and lamentable failure of the state government to disarray the Maoists. The Maoist leader Koteswar Rao alias Kishanji's diktat to the government and melodrama for freeing the OC branding him a POW smacks of performance and good governance.

Flushing out operation deploying 17 coys of central forces and sufficient state police force continued from June 2009, came under severe criticism. Regrettably, inspite of deployment of a large force, shooting spree, arson, abduction, land mine blasts have been increasing with impunity. Kishanji's frequent meeting with the media persons, telephonic conversations with the journalists, appearance before the TV camera, junior leader Bikash's dauntless movements displaying fire arms, inter action with the persons congregate to hear him reveal slapdash defiance by the outlaws and the police' inability to arrest Kishanji and his blood thirsty whiz-kids. Dispassionately, state's vacillation to curb the ultras and restore normalcy is disappointing.

Evidently, steady growth of the Maoist cadre for the last 20 years, especially, in West Bengal is not without any reason. Ironically, majority of the naxal leaders initially belonged to the CPI/CPM cadre. As events moved apace, either they were dropout or expelled from the party who eventually joined the naxal cadre. Significantly, the LF government after coming to power in 1969 and again in 1977, had released a large number of naxals languishing in the jail. Truly, right from beginning, the CPM adopted a soft policy to tame the naxals. Inspite of fast penetration of the Maoist cult in tribal belt, growth of the cadre, escalated violence and expansion of the Red Corridor right from Nepal to Tamilnadu, the state government was non-committal. Merger of the Jana juddah (PW) and MCC, formation of CPI (Maoist), Maoists' fiendish activities in three districts of WB have not alerted the government. In fact, consummate preparation to neutralise the ultras was given low priority.

Sickening assertion of the CM and the CPM that the problem will be tackled politically has failed to produce rewarding dividend. Crux of the Lalgarh unrest has hardly been pin-pointed, Indeed, scanty or casual attention on socio-economic dimension, police's high-handedness to suppress burgeoning discontentment of the tribal community and treating it an ordinary law and order problem have generated adverse public opinion. Police's excesses have helped emergence of the Peoples' Committee against Police Atrocities (PCAPA), fueled agitation, deadly clash between Maoists and CPM cadres and supremacy of the Maoists in Jangal Mahal. Now, Maoists are more aggressive, stepped up gory annihilation and unleashed a reign of terror. Kishanji's threats and challenges give impression, as if, he is above the law and uncrowned king of the so called liberated areas. From June 2009, till date, more than sixty persons have fallen due to the Maoists' daggers and bullets. Killing spree, dreaded violence, divisive tendency, etc. in the state have been increasing unabatedly. Panic stricken people from Lalgarh areas have been deserting abodes seeking safe shelter in urban areas. Dismayingly, watching the state's half-hearted, slovenly and complacent move, people are inclined to disbelieve the government's beefy assurance to disarray the ultras. Gurkha Jana Mukti Morcha (GJM) has been demanding a separate Gorkhaland, raised an armed wing, Gurkha Lathal Force and running virtually a parallel administration in the hills. GJM chief has declared that from November 7, the Home Rule will be introduced and GJM will be collecting state government taxes as a mark of its separation. Undeniably, all these developments are manifestation of misrule and indifference of the government to ensure effective and good governance. Frankly speaking, the state is in the grip of near anarchy. Faineancy, complacency or unsound strategy to curb the Maoists' grisly threat has emboldened them. Kishanji's declaration that Jangal Mahal soon would be a liberated zone needs to be taken seriously.

Truth of the story of abduction of the OC AN Dutta from his quarters without any resistance, CM's quixotic gesture and hurried release of the OC after much fanfare has to be taken with a pinch of salt. OC heard sound of gun shot from his quarters and learnt about bank robbery. Yet he neither rushed in aid of his colleagues, nor cared for the safety of the PS, arms and ammunitions, stored there. He did not communicate with anyone using his mobile phone seeking help to avert the catastrophe. He did not try to take to heels, though a Home guard personal staying in his quarters could do so. Contrary to trained and experienced police officer's reaction under such condition, he simply allowed himself to be abducted. Judging the chain of events one is inclined to believe that he was ready to oblige the Maoists either under pressure or threat. Critics sarcastically said that he volunteered to be their guest.

Maoists branded him as a prisoner of war and detained him in an unknown place. Maoist supremo Kishanji's terms for the release of the OC through the media was strange and yet accepted by the CM. Home Secretary defended the CM saying, "government has gone for a compromise with the Maoists, would do so in similar situations in future too." (*The Statesman*, October 24, 2009.) On October 23, 2009, Krishanji while releasing the OC said, "Dutta would be considered the first prisoner of war (POW) in the radical movements in India." Earlier he said, "The war has begun". His arrogance and bravado reveals that he is all in all and decides the destiny of the nation. CM succumbed to the pressure, accepted major demands instead of mobilising strength and resources to crush the upstart and his party. Importantly, abduction of two policemen, Kanchan Garai and Sabir Ali on July 30, 2009, has hardly evoked genuine anxiety of the government for their safety and release. Admittedly, government has not taken exhaustive and purposeful step to rescue them. Truly, CM's concern, promptitude to secure the OC's release and quixotic gesture to oblige a deadly leader of a banned outfit know no bounds. Sadly, a fraction of exuberance if shown for rescuing two kidnapped constables it would have enhanced morale of the policemen. OC had a stint in Banspahari outpost under Belpahari PS which is Maoist infested area. It gave him abundant opportunity to come in close contact with the Maoists. His cowardly conduct as an in charge of the thana, demeanor during interrogation are questionable. As police stations in Jangal Mahal are targets of ultras, he had not fortified the PS raising temporary defence and sentry posts by placing sand bags, wooden or brick barriers mobilising local resources. Broadly speaking, OC's sense of immunity from the Maoist attack was not free from suspicion. Meak surrender, Maoists' good treatment to him, government's hush-hush handling, Kishanji's appearance before press and TV, OC's ostensible release suggest a dubious game plan. Many felt that the OC's release episode and CM's generous action hints at a nexus between the OC and the ultras. It was not ruled out that he was set secretly to strengthen mutual understanding and exchange intelligence with the Maoists.

State government's soft line—an observation from detached angle

Plea of the government of West Bengal that the Maoists would be dealt politically has only facilitated the increase of the Maoist strength, their fire power, tendency to defy the rule of law and offensive *modus operandi*. Gorged with the government's soft or luke warm attitude Kishanji and his lieutenants came to lime light and gained undeserved recognition. Local people believed that he was the real power in the jungle mahal and could salvage the discomfited persons. Incidentally, Kanchan and Sabir's mothers, of two abducted constables directly appealed to Kishanji for their sons' release. Regrettably, the state did not ban the outfit. Even, the union government's ban order had not been notified formally nor enforced earnestly. On October 22, 2009, joint forces reached within 200 metres of Kishanji in Lakkhanpore Purnapani forest and were about to nab him either dead or alive. At that juncture, CM directed to halt the operation, thereby nullified the likely success. Later CM declared in full throat, "I will teach Maoists a lesson." (*The Statesman*, October 25, 2009) Evidently, CM's indiscreet stand badly hit morale of the armed personnel engaged in a desperate struggle at Lalgarh.

Needless to add, CM's soft line and abject submission had encouraged the PCAPA activists to detain and damage extensively the Delhi-bound Rajdhani Express at Banstala railway station on October 27, 2009 and forced the passengers to detrain under abysmal hardship, fear and suspense. In fact, the startling incident has exposed the state's helplessness. The invigorated Maoists accelerated deadly strikes in Jangal Mahal and put the government in a quandary. It needs no reiteration that the CM's soft line, indecisiveness and short of single-minded devotion were flinty bottle-neck against the joint forces' triumph. Importantly, a cabinet colleague (Kshiti Goswami) stated in public that the joint forces were not given free hand to operate. One of the Left Front partners, CPI, through its mouth piece requested the Union Home Minister, "to take a patient and sympathetic approach to deal with the Maoists." (*The Statesman*, October 2, 2009) Carrying cudgel for the ultra-left militants, CPI said, "Maoists kill a policeman and a political activist, there is hue and cry but every day many die undeserved death". Needless to say, it was an excuse to rationalise violence and annihilation by the extremists. Indeed, the CPI and CPM's reprehensible chorus certainly was an impetus for the ultras. It boosted their morale and enhanced unrest and bloodletting activities.

In sum, the CPI and CPM nursed soft corner for their expelled and wayward brethren. CM adhering to the party line, soft paddled the Maoist menace and tried to thrive blaming the political opponents. Instead of preparing a comprehensive plan and programme and its effective implementation CM Buddhadeb Bhattacharjee preferred to exploit the situation politically in party's advantage. In a healthy democracy, bureaucracy is expected to function impartially upholding public interest and administrative rectitude. Protracted Left parties rule dominated by the CPM has politicised the bureaucracy and contaminated them to serve the party's interest. Unfortunately, party had been put above the government and public interest. CM's fragile counter measures lacking indomitable will and determination to root out the militants has only upset the peace loving people. As the threat of the extremists gained momentum the CM was expected to give up political bias and blame-game and allowed free hand to the security forces and administration to crush the Maoists. In short, he is guilty of gross insouciance since he failed to come up to expectation and not enforced the rule of law impartially and without fear or favour.

Attempt to Expand Bases in West Bengal

People's War out-fit had set up bases in parts of Malda, Murshidabad and Nadia districts. Guerrilla squads consisting five members for each were formed in selected villages of three districts. Comrade Animesh Chakraborty, wanted in two murder cases was entrusted with the responsibility of organising guerrilla squads. He secretly contacted the media reporters and informed about formation of guerrilla squads in many strategic places including Harish Chandrapur, Gazole and Habibpur of Malda district. However, its authenticity could not be verified. Meanwhile, formation of the CPI (Maoist) added wider dimension to the Red movement in West Bengal.

As Lalgarh movement gained momentum the Maoists zealously stepped up their influence and established support bases in Malda, North and South Dinajpur districts separately. They called the new territory, "Gaur Banga" intending to connect three districts with Jangal Mahal through the forest region. However, clue on the sinister design for expansion was unearthed, as four youths from Malda were arrested from Lalgarh on August 20, 2009. They took part in Maoist agitation in Lalgarh. From their possession two fire arms, six cartridges, ten gelatin sticks and military uniform were recovered. One of them, Subal, a graduate from Gaur college Malda came in contact with a local Maoist, Srimanta, who trained them in using fire arms and participating in armed combat. He confessed that ten persons formed a squad and took active part in armed operation. Secondly, support bases were set up already in Bamangola, Gazol, Harirampur and Karandighi. These hideouts were very conveniently located so that the Maoists could take shelter if the security forces intensified combing operation in the area. Maoists carefully developed the support bases aiming that their influence could be spread out in the districts and could be utilised as "spring board" for the North Bengal. Secondly, as these areas have a river link to Jharkhand and Bihar, the Maoists found it easy and safe to slip in and out of West Bengal. Lastly, the districts are situated adjacent to the international border with Bangladesh, which facilitated them to cross over to Bangladesh for procuring weapons clandestinely or concealing themselves short circuiting surveillance and man-hunt by the security forces of India. It was a startling disclosure that the Kamptapuri insurgents often used to take shelter in these hideouts.

In Birbhum district Maoists formed an action squad. Three female Maoists were active in the squad: Barun Das alias Surya, Samiran Ruidas, Uttam Barui of the squad carried out 7 to 8 operations from 2007 to 2010, including murder of CPM leaders and activists, derailment of trains etc. In Nadia district Maoists geared up activities. The zonal committee secretary of Kalna and Murshidabad, Tazim Sk was arrested from Chhapra, Nadia district.

Operation by Joint Forces

June 18, 2009, deserved to be remembered by the peace-loving people of Jangal Mahal as the central para-military forces and the state armed forces started operation jointly in Lalgarh to flush out the Maoists and reclaim territories already under the Maoist domination. The State Home Secretary reiterated that huge areas covered by 18 police stations across West Medinapur, Bankura and Purulia must be free from the grip of the Maoists apart from driving them out of Lalgarh. He informed that more than 100 Maoists armed with automatic weapons, improvised explosive devices were hiding in jungle around Lalgarh. Their leader Kishanji was present. However, no time frame had been set for the operation. He added that it was difficult to distinguish between the PSBPC and the Maoists. State government appealed urging the villagers to stay away from the ultras and help the government to restore peace and normalcy. People were welcomed to enter into dialogue to sort out their everyday problems. A strong contingent marched towards Pirakata about 13 kms north of Lalgarh. They faced blockade by 3000 supporters of the PSBPC, mostly women who formed a human barricade in the afternoon, at Malida, about four Kms from Pirakata. The agitators and many local villagers blocked the thoroughfare placing tree trunks, branches, boulders etc. Joint forces cleared obstacles and dispersed the agitators busting tear gas shells, resorting to lathi charge and chastising any one coming on the way. Many received injuries and took to heels. CRPF launched combing operation. From a house top PSBPC activists fired at CRPF personnel and fled. Force camped at Pirakata for the night. Cobra (Combat battalion for resolute action) a specially trained CRPF battalion was associated with combing operation for back-up. Significantly, the state government agreed for deploying of central para military forces after lingering reluctance as the ultras were growing fast and the government's authority was slipping through its fingers. Criticism that joint operation failed to deliver the desired result in the beginning was refuted by the Home Secretary. He stated that its success was not puny at all. They had arrested 67 Maoists including 26 hardcore. He informed that second phase of operation was going to commence with renewed vigour after August 15. Secondly, development work side by side would be geared up and greater attention would be paid to ensure meaningful and responsive public relation.

Leaders of the PSBPC threatened that the tribals would resist entry of the security forces into Lalgarh at any cost. They congregated in groups armed with bows and arrows and other traditional weapons and demanded that they would not budge an inch from the path of agitation till their 23 points charter of demands were accepted and complied with. Kishanji, a member of the Politburo of the Maoists stated that both union and state government would be held responsible if there happened to be bloodshed in Lalgarh. Nevertheless, the joint operation alarmed the Maoists and demoralised the PCAPA and other out-fits backed by the Maoists. They realised that the central forces were well trained, armed with modern weapons, guided by single minded devotion and their operations were business like. Therefore, many Maoists shifted to Jharkhand, especially, in and around Latehar. Here, apart from several safe hide-outs accessibility to Chhattisgarh was easy. Meanwhile, state government deputed a group of senior officials to Lalgarh to review the situation and prepare a comprehensive proposal for economic development in the areas. The team interacted with the villagers, heard their grievances. On return to HQ the team recommended a special package for socio-economic development. Secondly, it pointed out the need to fill up the existing vacancies in government establishments functioning in the affected areas and to create employment opportunity for the local people, repair and construction of roads, bridges, improve health care, ensure supply of drinking water, build sufficient infra-structure etc. It suggested that mobile medical vans could be deployed where health care centre could not be constructed immediately. Lastly, seeing porous rationing system which was one of the main grievances, recommendation was made to take pragmatic steps to galvanize it.

It was heartening to note that the Maoist movement forced the state government to initiate steps for welfare of the tribal. Needless to say, it stirred the sleeping lion from its torpor to undertake plan and programme for socio-economic development in the criminally neglected tribal belt. The state formed a task force comprising eight departmental secretaries to oversee development work in jungle mahal. Impartial critics felt that success of the joint operation would much depend on how purposefully and expeditiously the developmental schemes were implemented by the state.

Protest Against Deployment of Central Forces and Joint Operation

Deployment of central forces and joint operation failed to produce any tangible result in initial stage. State government came under scathing criticism. However, as events moved apace, scenario was perceptively changed. Joint operation substantially isolated the Maoists They were compelled to retreat from Lalgarh, Goaltore, Kantapahari and shift activities to Binpur, Belpahari, Gopiballavpur areas and right to the border area of Jharkhand. A group of radicals, intellectuals and progressive elements of the civil society protested against the joint operation and demanded withdrawal of central forces. Admittedly, Maoists get moral support from many intellectuals, radicals, teachers, students and liberals residing, especially, in urban areas and in Kolkata. The contact persons and the leaders of the out-fit who generally stay in towns and cities maintain link with the intellectuals, radicals and media personnel to perpetuate the Maoist cult, cultivate them and try to gain favorable opinion for the movement. They seek their patronage directly or indirectly to carry the movement forward. Secondly, they try to develop covert access to the media persons so that the movement could gain wide publicity and its message might be carried far and wide. Admittedly, the Maoists get sympathy and inspiration from them who might not carry the cudgel for the Maoists directly but they sincerely desire to see that the movement reaches its pinnacle without much hindrance. Movement must provide positive relief to the down trodden, demolish the opponents, anti-revolutionaries and rap the bourgeoisie on knuckles. They reject the idea to chastise the rebels and suppress the movement by brute force. They feel that the movement is based on ideology aiming at destroying the present order tainted by denial and exploitation. However, they do not want blood shed but want ultimate success of the movement. Operation by central forces and operation "Green Hunt" were unacceptable and unpalatable to them. Hence, they mustered courage to communicate their meaningful message to the rebels.

Significantly, majority of the "pro-change" radicals, singers, painters, intellectuals and persons from various walks of life were up-in-arms against the protracted misrule and repressive measures practiced by the LF government to crush the peasants' and the land less farmers' genuine movements in Singur and Nandigram. In fact, they, in large number hit the streets of Kolkata, protested and demanded immediate withdrawal of the central forces. The mammoth gathering and spirited march inspired the civil society to unite and fight against the state's high-handedness. Indeed, it generated robust antigovernment public opinion and put the government in immeasurable discomfiture. The congregation resolved to build strong public opinion, appealed to the progressive elements to join the chorus to stop anti Maoist operation and ask the central forces to return to the barracks. They emphasised that instead of using force dialogue could easily solve the problem.

Renowned writer and novelist Mahasweta Devi was vocal against the joint operation and demanded withdrawal of the central forces. She stated, "government needs to pay heed to the PCAPA's just demands." The convener of the assembly said that civil society must intervene otherwise the government would kill thousands of innocent people. Secondly, nexus between big corporate houses and the government was working to evict the poor and deprived tribals of their ancestor's land so long enjoyed and cultivated by them. A group of intellectuals issued a statement revealing that the anti-Naxal operation was aimed at killing the common people and destroying forest lands. It was a crafty design to issue licence to the corporate houses to loot the country's natural resources.

It was distressing that the government was trying to suppress the mass upsurge deploying thousands of well-equipped security forces. The TMC supremo Mamata Banerjee initially pressed for firm action against the ultras. However, after studied silence for a few days she blamed the CPM for using the joint forces for wrong reasons. However, she was not averse to the joint operation. In the meantime, Chhatradhar Mahato was arrested and Maoist ideologue Prasun Chatterjee, was arrested from Kolkata which irked the intellectuals and prominent persons of the civil society. Sm Arundhati Roy, a noted writer based in Delhi planned to organise a viable protest movement against the joint operation in Lalgarh. She said that the CPM had no right to criticize or denounce the ultra-left movement. Importantly, the Maoist politburo decided to authorise her on their behalf to mediate or participate in dialogues, if the state government agreed to it. However, a galaxy of intellectuals in Kolkata intensified protest movement for withdrawal of the central forces.

Maoists were demanding that the government should give up operation by joint forces immediately. Protest by the radicals and progressive elements surcharged the atmosphere, rallies taken out in Kolkata by many noted intellectuals and persons from cross section of the society. It enthused them to press the demand hard. In short, cry to stop operation by the joint forces and withdrawal of central forces eventually gained support from many quarters. Members of the West Bengal Government Employees Union (Nabajagaran) demonstrated right in the compound of the Writers Building demanding that joint operation and the operation Greenhunt should be discontinued. They chanted slogans against the Union Home Minister for convening a meeting at Kolkata intending to curb the Maoist movement.

Excesses by the Combined Forces?

Complaints against the combined forces poured in. It was alleged that they asked many villagers in Lalgarh areas to quit their abodes. They forced about two hundred villagers to leave the villages. Perhaps, such step was taken for operational necessity and safety of the villagers. It irked the PCAPA who warned the police to stop harassing the people or face violent resistance. Inspite of the lofty claim of impregnable security cover, a CPM leader was killed right in Jhargram town. Maoists abducted five CPM activists and killed them. In fact, murder of the CPM cadres continued unabatedly short circuiting the so called security cover. Police authorities stated that the combined forces took time to study and adapt with the condition. However, they achieved some major successes in Lalgarh, Salboni and Goaltore areas and gained foot hold in other parts of Lalgarh. The rebels temporarily retreated, but regrouped and increased activities in Jhargram, Binpur, Nayagram and Gopiballavpur areas. Police felt that it was a tactical retreat but they would certainly strike back in opportune moment. Maoists' arsenal was too rich to capture or destroy. Many ferocious leaders, like Bikash, Sasadhar Mahato, Suchitra Mahato, Akash etc. were very active and operating from underground. They were capable of launching major offensive and put the security forces in a tizzy. Maoists still possessed 20 guerrilla squads and two platoons comprising 21 to 30 well trained guerrillas who were itching for renewed strike.

Secondly, "Gana Militia" raised by the PCAPA backed by the Maoists was often resisting the movements of the combined forces. Happily, security forces' hard blow to wipe out two PLGA squads in Ranjha and Metala forests encouraged the district administration. Nevertheless, the Maoists were firm and monstrously desperate to proceed with the revolutionary goal. Police felt that the Maoists after tactical retreat from Lalgarh areas stepped up their activities in other areas of Jangal Mahal where impact of the joint forces was either scanty or weak. Admittedly, the Maoists, no doubt, retreated temporarily but neither given up violence nor their revolutionary object of capturing power through the barrel of gun.

Criticism that joint operation failed to produce the desired result in initial stage, was refuted by the Union Home Secretary. He stated that its success was not puny at all. They had arrested 67 Maoists already, including 26 hard cores. He informed that second phase of operation was going to commence with renewed vigour after August 15. Simultaneously, programme for development work, would be geared up and greater attention would be paid to ensure healthy and responsive public relation and meaningful public service. For improving the police forces, state government decided to sanction rupees 75 crores to develop infrastructure of thirty police stations including eighteen police stations coming within Maoist infested areas in West Medinapur, Bankura and Purulia districts. In new police station building, boundary wall etc. would be constructed and sufficient number of police personnel would be posted. State allotted 141 acres of land at Salboni for setting up the HQ for the Combat Battalion for Resolute Action (Cobra). State further decided to set up three police training schools to train Counter Insurgency Forces (CIF) following the model of Greyhounds of AP, at Salua, Purulia and Siliguri. From the union government side, Cabinet Committee of Economic Affairs (CCEA) approved a Planning Committee proposal to sanction rupees 137.42 billion to initiate development projects in Maoist affected district of nine states. Importantly, the Superintendent of Police of the district would be associated with the decision making body. Maoists criticized the move and remarked, "The huge allotment was not to solve basic problems of the people. The decision making committee was nothing but an effort to put a "developmental mask" to their Fascist repressive measures."

Allegation of Nexus Between the CPM and Security Forces, Maoists and the TMC

Volleys of complaints from Medinapur West district surcharged the political atmosphere that a nexus between the combined security forces and CPM backed goons and insolent activists clandestinely operating against the Maoists. CPM goons (Harmads) misguiding the security personnel, goaded them to chastise the rebels, push them out of jungle mahal and brought the area under the CPM's control. In fact, people whispered that it was a combined operation by the security forces and the CPM to terrorise the political opponents, scare them away to quit the areas and helping indirectly to re-establish the CPM's control and domain. Sober persons felt that the vacuum created due to retreat of the Maoists and areas reclaimed by the joint forces' toil, was indirectly going into the hands of the CPM. The state government had been misusing the joint forces for regaining the party's lost control in that area. According to them, success of the joint forces had been benefiting the ruling political party CPM.

Chief Minister Buddhadeb Bhattacharjee and the Left Front partners claimed that the Trinamool Congress party had been maintaining close link with the Maoists in Jangal Mahal. Its supremo Miss Mamata Banerjee's patronage had encouraged the Maoists to indulge in violence, annihilation of the CPM cadres and let loose a reign of terror. The Chief Minister in a public meeting addressed at Egra, West Medinapur, accused the TMC of being hand in glove with the Maoists in tracking down and killing CPM leaders and activists. CPM leaders brought out several allegations against the TMC and vehemently accused her and her party for secretly maintaining link with the Maoists. One of the former CPM MP, Md Salim accused her as the "Official Translator" of the Maoist leader Kishanji. (*Hindustan Times*, February 10, 2010) The episode of detaining the prestigious train Rajdhani Express by the activists of the PCAPA enjoyed support and patronage of the TMC. In fact, the CM and CPM leaders let loose reckless propaganda alleging that nexus between the two was primarily responsible for the Maoists' triumph in Jangal Mahal. However, TMC firmly denied the allegations.

On December,10, 2009, the CM on the floor of the Legislative Assembly stated, "While the Jharkhand party is patronising the Maoists, the TMC is doing the same in West Bengal." Upon the CM's assertion, a noisy squabble disturbed normal functioning of the House and silenced the CM's voice. MLAs of the TMC refuted the allegations and charged the government for soft-pedaling the Maoist problem. On February 5, 2010, Jogneswar Mahato, a supporter of the TMC was abducted allegedly by the CPM Harmads (muscle men) from village, Chhoto Kalshivanga, under Salboni police station. A few days ago, TMC activist Mongal Mahato was abducted from Banstala village under Jhargram police station by the joint forces on the instigation of the CPM Harmads. Since then, both were untraced. TMC supremo, Mamata Banerjee demanded immediate release of the abducted activists. Secondly, she accused the state government for utilising the joint forces for helping the CPM in reestablishing the party's influence and reclaiming the areas dominated by the ultras. Maoists unleashed a vigorous campaign against the security forces. In a press meet, the politburo member of the Maoists, Kishanji stated that if the government failed to rescue and release two abducted TMC activists, the government would face consequence and people of Jangal Mahal were ready to take appropriate action. He demanded answer from the CM for such a heinous crime. He added that on the plea of the operation "Green Hunt" the police and CPM goons jointly working to abduct and kill activists and supporters of the opposition. Referring to the recent abduction, he said that it was pre-planned action to chock voice of the protesting people of Jangal Mahal who would not tolerate such a diabolic act. In fact, by, "the people of Jangal Mahal," he meant the Maoists active in jungle mahal. Truly, the rebels and the TMC came close to organise a strong opposition against the CPM. Interestingly, Kanchan, alias Sudip Chongdar, the secretary of Maoist state committee disclosed that neither he nor many members of the committee agreed with Kishanji for extending support to Miss Mamata Banerjee covertly in ousting the CPM government. He asserted that he pointed out to Kishanji many times that this was not the line of the Maoists. Indeed, Kanchan's revolting disclosure gave strong inference that there was a mutual understanding between the Maoists and the TMC in Jangal Mahal to fight the CPM jointly.

Allegation that the CPM-led state government had been misleading the combined forces to consolidate the party's hold in the jungle mahal was not altogether hollow. Broadly speaking, Maoists' and Mamata's similar allegation against the CPM on this count added a new dimension to anti Maoist tirade. Significantly, Maoists of Nepal came out in support of the Indian comrades and declared their support against the operations let loose by the security forces in Jangal Mahal. Maoist leader of Nepal, Pushpa Kamal Dahal alias Prachanda stated, "Indian Maoists are ideologically the same as their Nepali counterpart. Politically we are also the same." He added that the state's repression on the Maoists and so called operation Green Hunt in India had to be stopped. Problems could be solved through dialogues and negotiations. He admitted that the Nepali Maoists had a relationship with CPI (Maoist) when they were operating from underground.

Truly, the Maoists started campaigning against the abduction episode in nooks and corners of Jangal Mahal to build public opinion against the CPM. Maoists announced that it was decided not to attack "errant" Trinamool leaders and workers. In case of their misdemeanor the matter should be left to the TMC leaders to take appropriate action against the black sheep. Finally, the Maoist leaders categorically announced that the Maoists would not attack, chastise or kill any TMC activist or supporter even if they oppose or confront the Maoists. They made it clear that since the TMC was anti-CPM and fighting against the insolent elements engaged by the CPM, such support was essential. Notably, the people obliquely looked at the state government for its indecisiveness to tackle the Maoist problem. Admittedly, allegations of unholy rapport between Maoists and the TMC led by Mamata Banerjee, the then union railway minister and a part of the UPA coalition government in Delhi, had substantially sullied the impartial image of the operation green hunt. The union Home Minister refuted the allegations and categorically said that the joint forces were impartial and totally free from any extraneous pressure. However, security forces proved useful in the long run and succeeded in containing the rebels in terror ridden states. Several leaders of the outfit were either arrested or surrendered, much areas have been reclaimed and the rule of law was established. Jungal mahal in West Bengal now has seen peace and stability. Horror of the past now is confined in bitter memory. Indeed, people have heaved a sigh of relief.

It was believed that during discussion with the Union Home Minister, P. Chidambaram held in the Writers building, Kolkata on February 9, 2010, CM Bhattachariya hinted at the purported nexus between the Maoists and the TMC. On conclusion of the meeting the UHM met the media personnel along with the CM. On the question of the nexus he said that the CM and the Union Railway Minister ought to have discussed the matter. In fact, CM looked visibly embarrassed. However, the UHM categorically stated that no political party that believed in parliamentary democracy could collude with the Maoists who had been fighting against both union and state governments. They believe in armed liberation struggle and call the parliamentary system a pigsty. Hence, no political party who has been prospering in the accolade of parliamentary democracy can join hand with the Maoists. In short, the UHM virtually endorsed a clean chit to the TMC. Journalists sought clarification on the joint operation and the TMC supremo's stand on it. UHM defended the union railway minister Miss Mamata Banerjee and stated, "She told me that the operations in West Medinapur are not yielding result that were hoped for. I told her that we would try to make the operation as effective as possible. She is concerned that the innocents should not be affected by the operation and we are making sure that happens." He further added, "our purpose is not to kill any one. They are our own people. The objective of the operation is to reclaim the areas that are now dominated by the Maoists and reestablish civil administration. Our operations are careful, calibrated and controlled."

The UHM had strongly refuted the CPM's canard on Trinamul's link or nexus with the Maoists. The CM and the CPM failed to place any tangible evidence in support of the allegations. The CPM leaders argued that more than 100 CPM local leaders, cadres and supporters were killed by the Maoists. Several CPM offices and residences of the local party leaders were either damaged, destroyed or set on fire. Hundreds of CPM cadres, supporters had to quit the Jangal Mahal for fear of life and taken shelter in safer urban areas.

Broadly speaking, entire area which once used to be controlled and dominated by the CPM had gone under control by the Maoists. Indeed, barrel of the gun menacingly worked. Existence of the CPM was precariously hanging in balance. Paradoxically, the activists and supporters of the TMC in Jangal Mahal were free from the Maoists' vengeance. They were indulging in party activities without any fear or hindrance. The CPM argued that these are enough testimony to infer that the Maoists and the TMC had entered into a mutual understanding to bundle out the CPM from the Jangal Mahal. On November 10, 2009, the state Home Secretary stated that there was no information about links between the TMC or any of the mainstream political parties and the Maoists. Home Secretary's denial came about an hour after the TMC supremo, Mamata Banerjee threatened on November 9, 2009, at a rally held at Metro Square, Kolkata to file a defamation suit against the CM for his malicious allegations, and Home Secretary further stated that the information was from political channels.

TMC's Beefy Assurance to the People of Jungle Mahal

In election campaigns for the state Legislative Assembly 2011, Miss Mamata Banerjee in public meetings assured that if TMC happened to come to power the criminal cases instituted against the Maoists would be scrutinized, cases not supported by evidence would be either dropped or withdrawn and the Maoists in custody would be released. Secondly, operations by the joint forces would be discontinued. Needless to say, the beefy promises from the TMC supremo obviously had some soothing effect on the Maoists. They must have hoped for a better deal if change of the guards in the state happened to materialise after the election. Admittedly, there was no love lost between the Maoist and the CPM. However, Maoists were not hostile or inimical to the TMC. The activists and supporters of the TMC could move freely, work for the party easily. They knew that they were not the targets of the Maoists. The TMC was voted to power in May 2011 and Mamata Banerjee occupied the office of the Chief Minister. Unfortunately, as events moved apace the people noticed that the new government was not eager to release the Maoists languishing in jails and withdraw the criminal proceedings not supported by convincing evidence. In a well-attended public meeting held on August 31, 2011 in Lalgarh in which I participated. Sm Nimadi wife of Chatradhar Mahato and Sm Laxmimoni wife of slain Maoist leader Lal Mohan Tudu in their speeches blamed the new government for not adhering to her promises. In an interaction with me she expressed her feeling that the Chief Minister had betrayed the people of the Jangal Mahal. She told me that Mamata Banerjee before coming to power promised to release her husband, Chatradhar Mahato. Now she was not paying any heed to her repeated requests made through various channels. Nabarun Bhattacharjee son of Sm Mahaseta Devi, a dramatist present in the meeting blurred out and said," CPM deployed Harmad bahini, now TMC using "jallad bahini" (butchers) Significantly, I formally met Chatradhar Mahato, Prasun Chatterjee and two Maoist leaders detained in Medinipur central jail and interacted with them. They were disappointed seeing the CM's volte face. They helped the TMC to oust the CPM from power and hoped that the new government would show magnanimity in considering their grievances. Indeed, in Jangal Mahal during my repeated visits many pro Maoist sympathizers informed that their expectation from the new government badly belied.

Extortion Slur Against CPM and TMC

Allegations of high-handedness and extortion against the TMC activists posed a big threat to local populace aspiring to see the end of the CPM rule. Dispassionate enquiry revealed that TMC and its allies unleashed high-handedness in many rural areas in organised manner. Activists picked up persons, demanded money and in case of refusal the victims were tortured cruelly. The insolent elements forcibly carried the man or woman to Ramchandrapur crossing the river Dulung. In the village they had formed a village committee, demanded money from the helpless persons brought before them. If anyone declined to pay they were put to inhuman torture. Extortionists introduced a novel method to extort money. A fixed scale was made. A farmer possessing one bigha of land had to pay rupees one hundred and one kg of rise every month. Persons owning bigger piece of land had to pay higher amount. Maoists and CPM had been extorting money regularly from the public servants and schools teachers. School teachers were forced to pay 25 per cent of their monthly salary. Business men were forced to pay at an increased rate. TMC activists were forcibly collecting money from the traders, contractors and from selected public servants. Needless to say, it upset the villagers who were dreaming for better days. However, the TMC authority denied the allegation.

In sum, events and circumstances discussed above vis-à-vis the Union Home Minister's remarks on the vexed question of nexus between the Maoists and the TMC, needs to be accepted with abundant caution. Dispassionate analysis reveals that in the initial stage the Maoists and TMC reached an understanding to tackle the CPM cadres and supporters and chase them out of Jangal Mahal. It was going on well. But soon a rift developed and the so called friendship landed in arid zone of acrimony. It may be observed that accusations and counter accusations, attack and killing of the TMC activists marred their relation. TMC, stepping into power resolved to curb ultras, establish rule of law in Jangal Mahal and in that pursuit perhaps the CM and TMC decided to allow the security forces to operate firmly in ousting the Maoists. Paradoxically, TMC shut its eyes to the lofty promises made in pre-poll days for winning over heart of the ultras.

CPM Hired Desperadoes to Disarray the Maoists

Administration and the police lamentably failed to protect and save people from the Maoists' wrath in Jangal Mahal. People lost faith on the police. Throbbed with fear they were compelled to submit to the diktats of the ultras. In fact, alienation of the people from the administration virtually reached the culminating point. Even presence of the central forces and operation by joint forces had not improved the situation during first four months of the flush out operation. Not a single

Maoist leader of importance was arrested. Truly, setback piled upon setback for the CPM. According to the CPM, seventy cadres, including local leaders and persons showing allegiance to the CPM were killed by the Maoists who dauntlessly unleashed violence and blood curdling activities. Rule of law practically vanished. CPM cadres withdrew from Lalgarh, Binpur, Belpahari and taken shelter in Medinipur town or in semi-urban areas. A pall of gloom noticed in rank and file of the party. Indeed, exodus upset the CPM leadership. Fear of impending collapse of the local unit in Jangal Mahal dismayed the party leaders. Excessive dependence on the police that they would be playing the saviours' role vis-à-vis the Maoist attacks fell flat. Many panic stricken cadres submitted written undertaking to the Maoists declaring that they had either resigned or severed all connection with the CPM. Evidently, its cascading effect on the cadres, supporters and sympathizers were too hard to keep their morale high and strong. In fact, the shaken CPM hierarchy visualised a dooms day for the party. Hence, CPM hit upon a plan to avert catastrophe, hold the ground and recapture the lost areas by engaging the hired "Harmad Bahini." The personnel of the bahini were notorious desperadoes, professional killers, trigger happy gunmen, hired from Jharkhand, Bihar and Garbeta areas of West Medinapur. They were a band of pitiless and fierce mercenaries, physically tough, professional killers and cruel out laws. CPM considered them to be a consummate match to confront the blood thirsty Maoists. The "harmads" were deployed in groups of 20 to thirty in villages. Camps were opened either in houses of the party men or in make shaft structures. Arms and ammunitions and provision were supplied to them. Men and women of the villages were forced to provide domestic help, procure water, cook their means, wash utensils, cloths etc. for the harmads.

CPM was sanguine that contest between the hired goons and the Maoists was likely to be bloody and deadly. CPM's nostomania to re-establish supremacy in Lalgarh with the help of Harmads added fuel to fire. In this murky pursuit CPM hoped that police and the joint forces would cooperate with the harmads to put the Maoists in back foot. However, sober people were disturbed as they anticipated fiendish clashes and loss of lives which was going to destroy peace and halcyon atmosphere in Jangal Mahal. As expected, from August 2010 murderous clashes and death toll increased leaps and bounds. In fact, no direct and accurate number of clashes and killing was available as both sides denied to divulge the truth and hushed up the lifeless bodies. Police was indifferent and remained aloof from the gory events. However, secret report of the intelligence branch was the only source to get some clue on clashes and deaths. It disclosed that during the first twenty days of the month (August) sixty five persons including forty Harmads and twenty five Maoist guerrillas were killed. Both sides neither admitted nor denied it. Intelligence officers believed that the rival groups secretly buried the dead bodies in jungle.

Both sides possessed countless firearms. Secret reports highlighted incidents of numerous gun fights and annihilations. According to the secret report, in the month of May, 2010, 10 Harmads and 7 ultras total 17 were killed. In July it jumped up to 37, including 15 Harmads and 22 Maoists. Unprecedented spurt in bloody fights and death panicked the people. Maoists asked reinforcement from Jharkhand units. A band of 70 Maoists soon reached. They were pitted to hold Lalgarh at any cost. A secret report sent to the MHA disclosed that 71 camps of the Harmads were operating in Jangal Mahal. In 17 camps manufacturing of fire arms started employing experts from Monghyr, Kishanganj. These units used to supply weapons to other camps. In addition, sophisticated firearms were also purchased to arm the Harmads. In last week deadly confrontation took place in Pingboni, Bhalukbasa, Dharua and Lakhanpur near Goaltore. Both sides lost many men. The killed Harmads were identified. They belonged to Kishanganj, Monghyr of Bihar and Jamshedpur, Jharkhand. The killed Maoists were local youths. However, in a combat at Bakshibah under Kotwali police station, with the joint forces, a few Maoists were killed, who belonged to Jharkhand. Police failed to rise to the occasion. Truly, law and order was slipping through their fingers. Rumour gained currency that central forces and joint operation was far from deterrent. Maoists were free to strike at will.

State Government's Ambivalance

The state government was surprisingly not taking notice of the CPM's sinister plan to organise the "Harmad Bahini," employing professional killers and desperadoes. Intelligence reports regularly reached the Chief Minister, who was also the Home Minister. Hence, it could be inferred that either the government followed the policy of the masterly inactivity or agreed to follow the party line. CPM was obdurate to regain control in jungle mahal and in that pursuit never cared fair or foul means. Therefore, the party ungrudgingly spent money to hire goons, establish camps, employ outsiders to manufacture indigenous weapons, keep the police indifferent to maintain law and order. Unfortunately, the government's cavalier disregard to maintain rule of law and expose the offenders obviously shocked the people. Dispassionately, the CPM's misadventure and abhorrence to disarray the Maoists with the help of hired gunmen was unacceptable. It was not only unethical but tantamount to a criminal conspiracy to suppress a political movement tampered with political ideology. Indeed, pungent accusation that the state sponsored terrorism spear headed by the LF government was not imaginary at all.

Nevertheless, CPM was firm in its miry mission to push out the Maoists from Lalgarh. Fortunately, opportunity knocked at the door soon. To start with the joint operations was far from rewarding. However, after teething trouble, the joint operations chased out the ultras from many pockets and reclaimed areas so long dominated by the Maoists. In fact, success of the joint forces was the God sent opportunity for the CPM to fulfill its ambition. The areas liberated by the joint forces had noticed immediately omnibus presence and brisk activities of the CPM cadres and activists. In fact, more the joint forces chastised and forced the Maoists to take to heels exuberance of the cadres knew no bounds. Undeniably, forward march of the joint forces ushered a favorable wind for the CPM in Lalgarh. Watching the changed scenario the local CPM leaders boastfully said, "It is now a matter of days before we enter into Lalgarh and establish control there again." They gleefully organised colourful processions carrying party flags, impressive banners, festoons and chanted slogans. They imagined that display would boost morale of the moribund cadres, activists and supporters. Secondly, recovery and re-control on turfs was assumed to be a stupendous victory for the party. It was going to compensate their inglorious retreat made a few months back.

Ironically, success of the joint forces in flushing out the Maoists, reclaiming areas and re-establishing the rule of law was a blessing in disguise for the demoralised CPM cadres. Indeed, it was a grand opportunity for the CPM cadres to return to Lalgarh, renew their political activities, re-motivate and reactivate the Village Resistance Groups (VRG) and other satellite units. New units in Radhanagar, Majhi, Marwa were going to be established immediately. In fact, the party pumped fresh fund to meet the expenses. Villagers received monetary incentive and therefore, enthusiastically jointed the VRGs. On October 10, 2010, local leaders including Anuj Pandey and cadres agog with joy organised an impressive procession and formally enter into Lalgarh. Celebration was boundless. However, impartial critics commented that the so called victory of the CPM was achieved under secret care and protective arms of the ruling party's subservient police.

CPM cadres were afraid of surprise attacks by the Maoists. They were seen moving in small groups in Purnapani, Ajnashuli areas, very close to Lalgarh. CPM asked the higher authority of the joint forces to flush out the splinter groups and make Lalgarh fully safe and secure. Frankly speaking, the CPM indirectly demanded that forces must operate adhering to their direction and interest of the party. It irked the TMC supremo and the political opponents. On October 6, 2010, in a rally held in Medinapur, Mamata Banerjee demanded immediate withdrawal of the central forces and threatened to hit the road with party colleagues. Sri Subhendu Adikary, MP of the TMC led two rallies at Manikpara and Jamboni demanding immediate withdrawal of the joint forces. He said, "with help of joint-forces armed goons of the CPM are entering in villages and torturing the villagers." The Congress party so long was aloof on the withdrawal of joint forces. On October 5, TMC held a big rally. It marched from Lalgarh to Dharampur reiterating their demand.

Importantly, the security forces gunned down 14 armed ultras within one month and arrested several local leaders. It damaged morale of the Maoists. Being unable to withstand growing pressure of the security forces many Maoists responded to the palmy rehabilitation scheme and surrendered to the police or to the administration. Luckily, semblance of rule of law was reappearing in reclaimed areas. Restoration of normalcy instigated the CPM cadres and supporters to return promptly aided by the Harmads and reestablish their control and influence in the liberated areas. As the Maoists' reappearance and onslaught was not ruled out the CPM retained the mercenaries and utilised them to strengthen the local units. CPM organised campaigns, public rallies and mass contact programme. As a matter of fact, the party geared up activities with renewed zeal and energy. Critics quipped that the CPM ripped abundant benefit from the joint operations.

Meanwhile the Maoists warned the CPM that the CPM was unleashing violence on the people, especially, on the supporters of the opposition as they were afraid of losing power. If they were unable to restrain themselves the Maoists would teach them a lesson. Maoist leader Gour Chakraborty stated that the state sponsored terrorism was poll oriented violence (Assembly poll), exposed the CPM's anti-people move to remain in power by force. He added that the power mongers needed to stop atrocity on the people immediately. Police had been arbitrarily arresting, torturing people brutally and even misbehaving with the women protesters. In December 2009, comrade Bikash, the zonal secretary of Maoists, from an undisclosed location informed the media that they had decided to raise the peoples' militia with fifty thousand persons in three districts of Jangal Mahal. Secondly, they would extend further the area of domination in the state, step-up attacks against the enemies including security personnel and the persons working in collusion with the police. He admitted that two members of the night patrol party organised by the local resistance group were killed by the Maoists.

An impression gained ground that the CPM's return to Lalgarh was due to success of the joint forces. Indeed, anti-Maoist whispering campaigns unleashed by the security forces and other parties and co-operation directly or indirectly extended by the joint forces to the CPM cadres indirectly went in favour of the CPM. Even the Maoists believed it. However, Maoist leader Akash played it down and paid scanty attention to anti-Maoist rallies organised in Mednipur, Jhargram, Belpahari areas. The Maoists announced, "There is no mercy for the CPM or Congress. We will give the security forces and CPM backed goons a fitting reply." The TMC supremo Mamata Banerjee complained that blessing of the joint forces worked to regain the lost ground by the CPM. Many went further and alleged that the CPM was using joint forces as a shield against the Maoists in re-affirming their control and influence.

Authorities of the joint forces firmly refuted the accusation and reiterated that the role of the security forces was limited to flush out operation and restore normalcy in Jangal Mahal. They had nothing to do with the CPM's reentry into Lalgarh. Broadly, return of the CPM cadres and their hired muscle men who earned notoriety for brutal killing alarmed the people. Secondly, the Maoists might be isolated temporarily but not wiped out. They might return again once security forces were sent back to barracks. Thirdly, intolerance and spirit of vengeance of the CPM cadres was a threat to the peace loving people. They were afraid that Lalgarh's blood soaked history might be repeated once the cadres aided by armed goons regained their control. Hence, lasting peace in the area was illusory.

In fact, success of the joint forces was recklessly exploited by the CPM cadres. Undeniably, forward march of the joint forces ushered a favorable wind for the CPM in Lalgarh. Truly, perverse jubilation for the return of the CPM provoked the Maoists to be more stubborn and revengeful to destroy the CPM cadres. The impartial villagers and the sympathizers of the Maoists were afraid visualizing the CPM cadres' frenzied campaigns and retaliatory spirit. They felt that crooner of catastrophe was knocking at the door. Lalgarh was going to be bloated with pathetic and ghastly tales of bloodshed and butchery of innocent human lives. CPM was aware that return of the Maoists was certain and likely conflict would be obstinate and bullet for bullet. Hence, CPM planned to strengthen its arsenal with sophisticated weapons, improve fire power, mobilise muscle men and cadres in good number. Susanta Ghosh, the Pachimanchal development Minister, was entrusted with responsibility to procure automatic weapons, light machine guns etc. equip cadres and Harmads properly to beat back the Maoists. CPM set up a camp at Bejdanga with 100 cadres and harmads. Admittedly, the CPM was deficient in guerrilla warfare and therefore, they had to depend on the security forces for repulsing the PLGA, a valiant squad lauded for Spartan discipline and surprise attacks. It is regrettable and unprecedented that the political party steering the government, procured fire arms illegally, armed the cadres, hired professional gunmen, instigated them to participate in sanguinary gun battles and disarray the Maoists. Regrettably, the party's role like bandits or killers, was not only illegal and unethical but also a positive threat to equity, fair governance and democratic values. Dismayingly, the government was excruciatingly indifferent to prevent the impending threat to the peoples' safety and security and break down of the law and order.

PCAPA was worried anticipating erosion in their support base. They appealed to the villagers including the tribal community of Radhanagore, a Maoist strong hold, not to sacrifice interest of the tribal succumbing to the temptation of money, perks etc. and the CPM's pressure tactics. They tried to prick sentiment of the community in the name of late reverend tribal leaders, Sidhu, Kanu, Birsa Munda, etc. Over and above, they hit upon a plan to unite the tribal community and stir anti security forces and anti-CPM sentiment. At their behest a Students' Society was founded on July 21, 2010 with tribal students. Ostensively, it was formed to strengthen movement against alleged atrocities let loose by the police. But in reality it was made to keep the Maoist influence alive. A large number of students from tribal communities joined the new unit, brought out rallies in nooks and corners of Jangal Mahal protesting against the joint forces, arrests, police action and harassment to the women folk. A women's organisation named, "Nari Izzat Bachao

Committee" was formed to protest against rape, molestation and torture on the weaker sex. Many tribal women joined the new unit, displayed unity, organised mammoth meetings, participated in protest marches in massive scale. Frankly speaking, the PCAPA was alarmed watching progress made by the joint forces, corresponding decay of the Maoist influence in Lalgarh and their losses confronting the well trained security forces. Hence, the Maoists adopted a new stratagem to form small units in the villages to keep the movement alive. Indeed, the mushroom growth of the new units were expected to carry cudgel on their behalf.

Atrocity Unleashed by Hired Harmad Bahini

In pursuit of using band of hired armed desperadoes to neutralise the Maoists, on CPM's instruction several temporary camps were opened. In each camp twenty to twenty five armed men were kept. Fire arms and ammunitions were supplied to them by the party. Broadly, their duty was to patrol and guard the areas, confront and repulse the Maoists. Villagers were instructed under threat to look after their comfort, provide domestic services including cooking, cleaning of utensils, washing cloths etc. Regrettably, the camp dwellers were very rude and rough, used to assault persons on any pretext and kept the villagers under abject fear and submission. They built an ambience of terror and sent messages that no mercy would be shown in case of defiance of their wish or instruction.

Massacre in Netai

In village Netai, located about 7 kms away from Lalgarh, a camp of Harmads was opened in a double storyed building of Rathin Dandapat, a local CPM leader. About 3000 persons live in the village, number of voters is 1300. Similar camps were opened in Sigua, Belatikgri, Khosguri situated within five kms radius of Netai. Twenty Harmads were staying in the camp armed with firearms, moving in the area brandishing firearms, threatening and harshly treating the villagers. They came from Jharkhand, Bihar and not adapted with local language. They allotted domestic work to males and females of the village under threat. For example, duty of preparing breakfast was allotted a group of males, duties of cleaning of utensils and washing clothes was given to separate groups of females by rotation. Interestingly, for their dinner, task for baking sixty six chapaties (baked roti) every evening was given to a group of house wives. Villagers were grudgingly obeying them as they were helpless before the pitiless goons. Finally, the Harmads directed the villagers to depute lads and youths to attend arms training under their care and supervision. They forced the families to spare lads and youths to participate in arms training. In fact, after 3 or 4 days training majority of the trainees were unable to take physical strain and fell sick. But the Harmads were firm in their murky mission and threatened the parents for ugly consequence for disobedience of instruction.

Villagers were very upset visualising future of the wards. Threat and boorish conduct compelled the villagers to unite and protest collectively. Hence, mustering courage, on January 7, 2011, at 9 am, about 200 villagers including roughly fifty house wives, assembled in front of the camp and reasoned with the Harmads against deputing the wards for arms training. Dialogues gradually gained higher tone. One of the Harmads started beating Habul Roy and Dhruba. Intolerant muscle men were not agreeable to listen to the persons assembled, soon lost cool and many of them fired at the congregation. Members of the crowd attempted to run away for life for avoiding bullets. The camp existed in the midst of the village, surrounded by huts and low roof thatched houses, road was narrow and congested, hardly a cart could pass. Nine persons including four women received bullets and fell on the ground, about 25 persons received bullet injuries and altogether thirty-nine persons were injured. Seven died at the spot. One male and a lady later died in the hospital.

After three days of the incident I visited the spot and shocked seeing how cruelly nine innocent persons were gunned down having no fault of theirs. I could see marks of bullets on walls of many houses. Secondly, along with bullet marks, small pieces of human flash were still sticking on the wall of the club room. I was candid that such a barbarous firing on a peaceful and unarmed crowd without any provocation was unheard in a civilised society. Police visited the spot at about 4 pm on that day. No senior district official visited the village before my visit. The Harmads shut down the camp and fled. Government denied any knowledge or connection with the party sponsored Harmad Bahini. State police was luke warm to expose the culprits. Finally, CBI investigated the case submitted charge sheet against 20 accused persons, including Anju Panday, the Lalgarh zonal committee secretary and Rathin Dandapat, the house owner. Trial was in progress. I must confess that such a gruesome event I have never come across in my long stint in the police. It only reminded me the odious history of the Bestial savagery which followed the French Revolution.

Left Front was crushed in the Assembly election. New government under Miss Mamata Banerjee took over on May 20, 2011. Atrocity unleashed by the "Harmad Bahini" was exposed. Testimony of countless horrendous outrages indulged in by the CPM muscle men were dug out. Revolting disclosure of manifold ills practiced by the ruling party shocked the people. An elected government's action to hire professional gun men to counter the Maoists, gave them a long rope to chastise and brutally kill innocent villagers, is unparalleled in the history of human civilisation. Dismayingly, the Chief Minister claimed himself to be an enlightened person, anxious for welfare of the common people, has proved lamentably unworthy.

Welfare for the People—Gesture of the Maoists

Significantly, Maoists devoted to welfare activities for the poor villagers to earn their good will. In village Sereng Swakra, district Bankura the Maoists had been running a primary school, named Keherwal Primary school. It was a primary co-education school having residential facilities. One hundred twenty boys and girls students were in its roll. Fifty students used to get residential facilities including free board and lodging. Other pupils were given lunch only. School's monthly financial budget was rupees twenty five thousands only. School was not receiving any financial aid from the government. However, the Maoists were forcing local traders, businessmen, timber merchants and stone dealers to subscribe every month. Secondly, the rich farmers and well-to-do persons were compelled to spare a fixed quota of rice regularly. Intelligence report revealed that two influential villagers from villages, Churku and Haramagara, respectively were keeping close contact with the Maoists for running the school. Interestingly, since 2003, the school was functioning under care of the ultras. Yet the local administration was in dark about it. However, critics felt that the local administration deliberately ignored its existence to avoid the Maoists' displeasure. However, the local people welcomed it and appreciated such a kind gesture of the ultras.

Voluntary organisations founded by the Maoists ran health centers, coaching classes for the school students, repaired roads, embankments, supplied drinking water in remote villages. They got support and co-operation from the villagers. A group of journalists visited such health centers functioning in Lalgarh, Jhargram, Gopiballabpur, Nayagram, Salboni, Belpahari, Binpur, all were strong holds of the Maoists. Qualified doctors attended the centers once in a week and treated the patients. Either fee of rupees five was charged from each patient or deserving poor patients were treated free. Villagers dug wells, repaired roads, building etc. voluntarily. Villagers of Bandordoni, Chheraboni, Tentuldanga, Balarampur and Murakuti built 1.5 km long "veri bandh" (an embankment built locally) within 23 days.

Truly, in Chhattisgarh the Maoists initiated several welfare measures including health care for the villagers which were enthusiastically welcomed by the villagers. Ultras issued notices to the big land lords to implement the Land Ceiling Act and distribute surplus land among the poor. Maoists succeeded in getting surplus land distributed. Importantly, many land owners co-operated and responded to the call of the ultras in this pious pursuit.

Liberal Rehabilitation Package for the Ultras

The state government on July 28, 2010 declared the rehabilitation package for the ultras who volunteered to surrender and return to the main stream of the society. A surrendered Maoist was supposed to get a lump sum amount of rupees 1.5 lakhs which would be deposited in the bank in shape of fixed deposit in the name of the surrendered ultra. Again if he surrendered with a machine gun, AK-47 rifle, pistol, satellite phone, additional amount of rupees twenty five, fifteen, three thousands and fifteen thousand respectively would be paid to him. In addition, he or she would be paid rupees two thousands per month for next three years. Needless to say, it was an incentive to the wayward extremists for discarding violence and outrages and got them established in normal life. Importantly, Andhra Pradesh introduced a lucrative rehabilitation package in 1995 and received over whelming response. The state revised and enhanced the quantum of the monetary aid thrice. Taking the cue from the AP, Jharkhand and Chhattisgarh introduced it in 2004. Bihar and Maharashtra started it in 2005. Odisha followed the suit in 2006. Many hard core ultras of AP avidly accepted the offer and surrendered giving up arms and bloodletting activities. However, financial package in West Bengal was not so attractive, resulting in, response from the Maoists was petulantly poor.

Jharkhand has revised the package which clicked very well and allured one hundred rebels to surrender. In addition to monetary incentive, for purchase of land and construction of a house additional amount would be paid. Over and above, free treatment for the ultra and his or her family members, free education for the children right up to matriculation standard would be provided and extra grant for solemnizing marriage of the daughter or a girl in the family would be sanctioned. The Chief Minister's "Kanya Dan" yojana played a vital role. In Bihar from 2006 to July 2010, accepting the package, 160 Maoists had surrendered. In Maharashtra from 2005 to 2010, total 320 rebels surrendered. In West Bengal after TMC took the rein of the government the situation underwent a sea change. CPM's Harmad Bahini disappeared, clashes between the Maoists and the CPM muscle men stopped. The demoralised CPM cadres and activists lost courage and energy to stand against the rebels and the TMC activists. Soon a festival of surrender by hard core ultras virtually threatened the very existence of the Maoists in Jangal Mahal.

Secret Support to the Left Wing Extremism in West Bengal

Undeniably, the Naxal movement in WB received support and patronage from many radicals, intellectuals, educationists, students and social activists. It may be recalled that from 1968 to 1971, a large number of radicals and bright students from reputed educational institutions took active part in Naxal movement. Many brilliant students highly dedicated to the ideology of the movement firmly believed in doctrine of annihilation. They unhesitatingly tainted their hands with human blood. Dastardly murders in their hands and destruction of public properties, college laboratories etc. shocked everyone. Dismayingly, many intellectuals gave them moral support, many regularly subscribed to their copper and inspired them from behind to carry the banner of the Naxal movement ahead. The state government under Chief Minister S. S. Roy's strong actions disarrayed the Naxals and pushed the movement to limbo. However, all said and done, it did not die.

Remnant of the Maoist movement in low profile survived at a great cost. Many diehard pro-Maoist students had been silently operating in many universities of WB. A group of students of Jadavpur University were clandestinely trying to bring the friends and fellow students into their fold. In that pursuit a few teachers were actively behind the scene. In November 2011, Maoist posters were seen in the campus. Intelligence report revealed that many squad leaders operating in Jangal Mahal were students belonged to Jadavpur University. United Students' Democratic Front (USDF), was a pro-Maoist student body. In fact pro-Maoist student organisations decided to hold a conference in College Street area, on Wednesday, November 9, 2011. More than once, Maoist posters were seen on the walls of the City and Presidency University, Coffee House, entry gate of Ashutosh College, Metro railway stations and many district towns like Uttarpara, Nadia and in public places. From August 1, 2011, massive Maoist poster drive was noticed in Kolkata and its suburb. Posters were pasted on conspicuous places of Sealdah railway station North and south, Belghoria, Titagarh, Agarpara, and Sodepur railway stations. In metro railway stations, Jatindas park, Netaji bhawan, Rabindra sarobar, Esplanade and in Calcutta University, Presidency University and coffee house posters were seen. In College square, four posters were seen by the side of the Vidyasagar statue. Eight posters were seen on the walls of Barisha Housing complex, opposite Barisha College. In fact, poster drive created a good deal of panic in the city. Secret report revealed that several pro-Maoist student groups were behind the mischief.

Abhisekh Mukherjee alias Raju, alias Aranya, ex-student of Jadavpur University, secretary of the Maoists unit for Calcutta area, was assigned the task of goading the persons to support the Maoist movement and get the students involved in it. He was co-coordinating all programmes in the city, used to spread the outfits' political agenda among the labourers. He was receiving rupees three lakhs per month to meet expenses. He and his two close associates, Sunil Mondal and Subhas Roy were arrested. His wife, an ex-student of Jadavpur University held a press conference in the campus of the University on July 2, 2010. She was an activist of pro-Maoist organisation, Matangini Mahila Samity. She was arrested for organising an eviction movement in Nonadanga near Kolkata. Impartial critics felt that a large number of Maoist sympathizers hailed from Jadavpur University. It was virtually a breeding ground for the rebels. Surprisingly, Maoists supported the terrorist active in Kashmir valley.

Signs of Decay of the Maoist Influence in Jangal Mahal

Maoists, once the darling of the rural populace, used to enthusiastically act on the lurid signal of the Maoists, of late, was hardly responsive to the ultras and reluctant to assist them providing food, shelter, collecting intelligence and shielding them from the police's long hand. In fact, nuances of the Maoist jargon no longer inspired them and opposed the government's effort to reestablish rule of law. Protracted unrest, dastardly killings, excruciating bandhs, kangaroo courts, break down of the law and order and uncertainty, abjectly upset and demoralised them. Now they sincerely desired to see the return of normalcy and wanted to live in peace and harmony. Many villagers were sore with the Maoists as they had faced humiliation and brutality in their hands and were compelled to live under constant terror. In fact, earlier, villagers used to supply cooked food to the jaded ultras either willingly or under coercion. Rice, dal, vegetables, sometimes fish or chicken were liberally given to feed the ultras. Many receiving hot chase from the police used to get safe shelter in the villages. Villagers used to misguide the police and often foiled police raids and thereby protected fugitives. However, of late, situation is drastically changed. Villagers refuse to give food or shelter to the Maoists in Lalgarh, Salbani, Goaltore. Rebels consume food supplement tablets and oral rehydration solution (ORS) failing to get proper food in rural areas or in the hide-outs. A good number of people from Mahato community assembled in Salboni and decided that henceforth none would support the Maoists or extend any kind of help to them. On December 28, 2011, five suspected young Maoists were caught by the villagers of Ghritakham. They came to paste posters. They belonged to the village but had been absconding for a long time. One country made pistol and many posters and leaflets were recovered from them. In the posters appeal was made to take revenge for killing of Kishanji and Sasadhar Mahato. Villagers mercilessly assaulted and handed them over to the police.

Supporters of the Maoist movement lamented the incident and said that earlier, with the support of the villagers the Maoists had increased their influence. Now the situation has been reversed. Villagers were bigger threat to the Maoists. In many villages peace loving villagers were up-in-arms and jointly resisted the Maoists. Administration offered many incentives to encourage the villagers for resisting the ultras. The Vivek gram award was given to seven villagers of Radhanagar for resisting a group of Maoists who came to the village demanding their support. Joint forces felt that as the villagers were alienated from the ultras, the aggrieved people coming forward to inform on the Maoist whereabouts, location of their hideouts, movements, etc. In short, hostility of the villagers indirectly helped the security forces to get proper intelligence to tackle the terror. Death of Kishanji, and non-availability of a competent leader in his place inspite of rigorous search had damaged morale of the rank and file operating in Jangal Mahal. Again, either Killed or arrests of several top leaders, annihilation of Rajkumar Azad, arrest of Kobad Gandhi had added to woe. Now strength of the Maoist politburo has been reduced to seven only from thirteen, which was a major setback for the out-fit. Admittedly, the rural populace was abysmally disillusioned and realised that success of the Maoists was a myth. In many villages, on their own formed village defence parties to guard, protect and patrol the villages against the Maoist attacks. On March 23,

2008, five Maoists including a woman Maoist attacked and fired at a village defence patrol party at village Test, district Murshidabad. A boy accidentally received bullet injury. Villagers chased and caught hold of a rebel while others managed to escape. The rebel named Baan alias Swapan, belonged to Birbhum district, and was an active member of the Maoist squad operating in the zone.

A national workshop was held at Delhi on August 13, 2011. Sixty Collectors from the Maoist-ridden districts, and many dignitaries attended the workshop. The Prime Minister, Union Home Minister and other Ministers attended and addressed the gathering. Workshop was on the theme of appropriate development strategy for effective implementation of rural development scheme in Maoist affected districts under Integrated Action Plan (IAP). Deliberations highlighted that most violent movement in India is not terrorism or insurgency but left-wing extremism, while 26 persons were killed in terrorist violence and 46 persons killed in insurgency including 27 in J&K, 297 persons were killed in Maoist violence during first six months of the year. In fact, death in Maoist violence is approximately ten times more than that of terrorism. It was agreed that formidable challenge before the government is left wing extremism, not terrorism or insurgency. However, it was decided to add twenty more districts to the list of the IAP.

As stood on December 31, 2011, 42 Coys of CRPF was deployed in Jangal Mahal in addition to armed police of West Bengal as follows, West Medinapur district-31 Coys, Bankura-2 Coys, Purulia-7 Coys. In 2010, total killing in jungle mahal was 425. Luckily, in 2011, it was reduced to 51 persons. The break up was 22 from CPM, 14 from TMC, 2 from Forward Block, 1 from JMM, 2 from PCAPA, 1 from state police and 1 from India Reserve battalion were killed. In 11 big or notable encounters total 110 Maoists and their link men were arrested, 12 automatic weapons, 100 fire arms, 44 land and directional mines and 400 kg explosives were seized.

Interaction with Maoist Leaders

It is unfair to hasten to conclusion on the Maoist plan, programme, their cherished goal and inner strength relying on media reports, communication from the government sources, hearsay and gossip. It is therefore, essential to interact with the leaders, cadres active on the field to unearth the truth. In that pursuit I have visited the spot where the CM's convoy was attacked and Lalgarh, Goaltore, Ramgarh, Dalilpur, Netai and many villages of Jhargram subdivision several times and interacted with Maoist leaders, insolent cadres and innocent male and female villagers. I have met members of the bereaved families, lady wives of unfortunate victims killed either by the Maoists or by CPM goons or police. In fact, harrowing tales from their mouth immeasurably shocked me which I believed would move even steel hearted persons. I have recorded statements of the wives of the victims, many hapless souls, members of the discomfited families and aggrieved villagers.

In one of my visits to Goaltore, I met the PCAPA leader Chatradhar Mahato who was surrounded by a group of his followers. I understood that several of his companions were either Maoist cadres or sympathizers of the rebels, but none was a fair sex. I noticed that he was a popular leader and villagers were obedient and carried out his instructions ungrudgingly. He belonged to Adivasi community, was respectful to social activists and frank in conversation. I knew his antecedents that he was one of the top leaders of the PCAPA, a frontal organisation of the Maoists, brother of dreaded Maoist Sasadhar Mahato, himself a Maoist and operating on the instructions of the Maoists. He organised meetings, rallies, bandhs mobilised villagers on behalf of the rebels. He and his followers participated in many ruckus and unrest.

He complained that poverty had crippled noble rage of the Adivasi community. They were exploited, discriminated and deprived at every stage. The protracted CPM rule in WB lamentably failed to uplift them and ensure their welfare. CPM cadres' rough and ready method and egregiousness had only enhanced their miseries. State was indifferent to their cause, not sincere to treat the community at per with others. Secondly, unemployment for the Adivasi youths was acute and devastating. Yet, hardly any tangible step was initiated by the government to improve or banish it. Public servants working in the field harassed and exploited them on any pretext. Police was too harsh to treat them. They acted on the direction of the local CPM leaders, registered false cases, arrested and tortured the innocent persons. Administration was lukewarm, fairness and justice for them was remote.

I asked him the ways and means to demolish the mound of eels and cleanse the public life. He replied that they have to fight for their rights and that the People's government was essential, exploitation and discrimination had to be wiped out. His followers present, as per my perception, were within the age group of 18 to 30, belonged to either lower middle class or peasantry, physically not strong and sign of poverty was clear in their attire and bearing. Several of them argued that the existing social and political system could not improve their lot. Therefore, classless society and the people's government were needed which was the pragmatic solution. Some of them drew my attention to a person sitting by the side of the village road and selling potato. Importantly, in that belt potato grows in abundance and cultivation of potato is one of the major sources of livelihood. It provides temporary and seasonal employment. Unfortunately, the cultivators hardly get fair return for the crop which was not commensurable with their investment, labour and other expenditure. First, there is no market where the farmers can sell crop directly circumventing the middle men, brokers and hoarders. Secondly, there was no storage and transport facility to dispatch the crop to a wholesale market. Therefore, the small potato growers are bound to sell potato in small quantity to a middle man at a low rate. Enquiry transpired that sale price was rupees 3 to 3.5 per kg. The middle men after buying in small quantity, store potato temporarily and send a truck load to whole sale market to Kolkata and fetch rupees 13 to 14 per kg. Finally, the retailers sell potato to the consumers at rupees 18 to 20 per kg.

Chakradhar Mahato pointed out that it was one of the instances of crass exploitation and denial to the poor farmers. Unfortunately, inspite of repeated appeals neither the district administration nor the government paid any heed to salvage the potato growers from the cruel hands of the middle men, hoarders, money lenders, transporters. They felt that in the people's government where the people's will is paramount exploitation of the poor will have no room. He informed me that after a week he was going to address a gathering in a village near Goaltore. He requested me to attend it and hear the speakers. On that very day I reached the place from Lalgarh at about 12.30 noon along with a small group and noticed that in the venue people were gathering slowly. Chatradhar requested us to take lunch arranged by them since meeting was going to start after one hour. In nearby school building lunch for us was served. In fact in a remote village where resources were limited, a sumptuous lunch highly impressed us. Interestingly, two armed cops patrolling the areas were asked to join us for lunch. In fact, the Maoists who were after blood of the cops invited them for a meal burying animosity delighted me.

I returned to the meeting venue. It was a small open space by the side of a road. Here, hardly 200 persons could be accommodated. In one side of the space facing the road, on a small platform, a few chairs were placed for the speakers. About 20 yards behind the dais, a small group of 10 to 12 persons were loitering and talking in low voice. From distance I realised that they were not part of the congregation. Secondly, bearing of two persons was distinctly different. In fact, their magnetic countenance forced me to go near them and exchange a few words. A person aged about 35, tall, well-built and energetic drew my attention. He looked stubborn, his eyes were piercing, neither fear nor pity could shake him. I asked his welfare intending to elicit his views on the proposed meeting. He was indifferent, as I pressed for his reaction, with lingering reluctance, he spoke a few words and disappeared. By then, I was sanguine that the person who was disinterested to enter into conversation and suddenly disappeared, was none but Sasadhar Mahato, the dauntless Maoist leader of Jangal Mahal. However, his companions freely exchanged words. They were highly critical of the protracted CPM rule and made the government responsible for the miserable plight of the people of jungle mahal. They accused the police for unleashing atrocity on the poor people who were struggling for their rights. They showed determination to topple the CPM government, destroy the class enemy and establish the people's government.

On Chatradhar's pursuance I sat on the dais and heard the speakers. Crux of the speeches was an alarm bell to the CPM. They said that being the followers of the Marxist ideology, CPM had been patronizing the capitalists, clinging on parliamentary democracy and indulging in anti-people activities. Hence, CPM was the immediate target, it cadres and supporters should either be annihilated or chased out of Jangal Mahal. CPM offices and establishments should be destroyed, Maoist movements must be intensified and the people's government must be stalled demolishing the archaic social and political order. In short, enmity against the CPM was so bitter and intense that the well-organised CPM cadres having indirect backing of the police and the government was not in a position to face or counter the fiendish campaigns and annihilation let loose by the Maoists.

In sum, my presence in the meeting and inter action with Chatradhar Mahato and other Maoists was fruitful. It gave me useful insight to know their mind, aims, object and acrimony against the CPM. I was convinced that PCAPA establishment was a *de facto* Maoist organisation and Chatradhar was a part and parcel of the Maoist out-it. Their expectation from the TMC was high. Therefore, they were unhesitant to build comradeship with the TMC in pursuit of ousting the CPM from power. Comrade Kishanji was eager to cement good relation with the TMC hoping to extract a pound of flesh if Mamata Banerjee happened to come to power. But he was not aware that there was a fly in the cup of honey. Within six months the TMC formed the government he was shot dead by the security forces.

The Left Front government's catastrophic defeat in general election held in April/May 2011 and formation of the new government by the Trinamul Congress (TMC) under leadership of Mamata Banerjee visibly changed the political scenario in the state. Mandate was loud and clear. It disastrously rejected the CPM and its allies. Anti-Maoist operation by the joint forces in Jangal Mahal was halted awaiting instruction from the new government. Evidently, a status quo was maintained. Newly elected Chief Minister appealed to the Maoists to give up violence and come forward for a dialogue. From Jangal Mahal four MLAs from TMC and one MLA from CPM were elected. In Nayagram, Salboni and Sankril TMC had a visible presence. But in Jhargram, Lalgarh, Binpur and Gopiballavpur the TMC's influence was meager. Maoist backed out-fits often organised meetings, rallies in many pockets. It was believed that TMC MLA from Gopiballavpur avoided confrontation with the ultras. TMC MLA from Nayagram hardly stayed in his constituency. As a result, Maoists and their satellite out-fits tried to gain back the ground very fast.

Genocide in Jangal Mahal; Maoists, CPM Goons and Cops Unleash Brutality and Killing

Hired goons (Harmad Bahini) used in jungle mahal by the CPM was unprecedented in a democratic country. They created panic, unleashed fear and atrocity. As the CPM cadres were no match with the head hunting ultras the CPM hired a large number of notorious desperados and trigger happy out laws from Jharkhand, Bihar and ill-reputed places. A band of dacoits lived within the jurisdiction of Onda police station, district Bankura were hired and deployed in and around Jhargram town. In Jhargram town the CPM formed a RG party, ostensibly to protect the townsmen from the Maoist attack and patrol the town during night. In reality the Harmad Bahini was detailed to counter the Maoist attack and to guard the CPM Zonal committee office which was safe shelter for the wanted criminals and spotty comrades of the party. The hired goons were instructed to catch and chastise the political opponents and force them to quit jungle mahal. The purpose of detailing the Harmads was to cow down the people and build an ambience of terror. It was a message to the political rivals, their activists and muscle men that the area was under the control of the CPM cadres and any attempt to flout their authority or influence would be brutally dealt with. In fact, the object was to ensure dominance over the turf and repulse any attempt of the Maoists to capture the area.

In each municipal ward of Jhargram town a camp of the Harmad Bahini was established. Firearms including sophisticated weapons were supplied to them from the party. A group of 50 to 55 Harmads used to come out of the camp at about 10.30 pm and patrolled the town till the sun rise. For transferring weapons from one camp to other a white Tata Sumo without registration number was frequently used. Scared shop keepers used to shut down shutters after sunset. Markets, roads, bus stand, railway station looked deserted by 7 PM. Harmads earned notoriety for insolence, rough and ready method and fire at a person without any provocation. Local CPM leaders used to coddle them, looked after the camps, their deployment and comfort.

In addition, many physically tough muscle men possessing criminal records from border areas of West Bengal and Jharkhand were picked up and sent them to Jhargram to join the camps. These mercenaries were very rough and rude and used to treat the people harshly, created an atmosphere of fear and panic. Harmads often took part in patrolling with the cops and security forces. On the advice of the local CPM leaders the harmads and CPM goons assisted the security forces to identify the roads, locality and the suspects. In fact, the CPM used the Harmad Bahini almost parallel to the security forces. Interestingly, the security forces welcome help or guidance of the local CPM goons and Harmads. First, the area of operation was foreign to them They were not well conversant with the local language, ignorant of the roads, village paths and location of villages. Truly, none was readily available to supply information or guide them to identify the vulnerable spots, where the Maoists were strong, might attack or ambush the patrol. Hence, the security forces avidly wanted their assistance and co-operation.

Frankly speaking, friendly relation and mutual understanding between the goons and security forces was a big relief to the local police. They thought it wise to keep their camaraderie undisturbed since they were virtually working as the first line of defence and would face the brunt of the Maoists before others. Being on the front they were going to be the immediate target of attack, face the enemy's bullet, injury and likely casualty. The local police had been thriving upon the mutual co-operation and friendliness of security forces and the outlaws. In many occasions the security forces provided cover to the Harmads and while patrolling took them as guides. Frankly speaking, assisting and extending guidance by the Harmads to the security forces tantamount to a control by a caucus.

The unholy friendship of both irked the other political parties. The TMC supremo vehemently criticized the CPM for misguiding the security forces and re-establishing their influence on the turf which were reclaimed by the security forces from the Maoist control. It was true that many areas regained by the security forces from the Maoist clutch by hard toil and sacrifices were promptly occupied by the CPM cadres. In fact, CPM reestablished their control and influence on the regained territory, deserted party or panchayat offices, celebrated it organising meetings, processions, unbridled exuberance and fan-fair. Comrade Anuj Pandey returned to his half burnt house, re-opened the CPM party office and initiated steps to re-establish his lost authority. As a matter of fact, success of the security forces in flushing out and reclaiming the Maoist controlled turf ultimately went in favour of the CPM. Paradoxically, the triumph of the forces in flushing out and pushing back the Maoists was indirectly the triumph of the CPM. Success of the security forces had given golden opportunity to the CPM to re-establish their control and authority on the territory which had to be deserted in the past leaving on the mercy of the Maoists. Importantly, the Chief Minister planned to visit Jangal Mahal on October 2, 2010, and to address the party cadres for the celebration of victory for re-capturing the areas from the Maoists and re-establishing the party's control. The secretary of the state CPM, Biman Basu, was going to participate in the jamboree of the victory celebration. Eye witnesses confirmed that euphoria of the CPM cadres and activists knew no bound. Again, following re-entry into areas freed from the Maoist control, flurry of the CPM's political activities increased considerably which paled the past records in insignificance in Jangal Mahal.

The authorities of the central forces were totally out-witted to fathom the diplomatic trickery of the CPM to prosper politically at the cost of the central forces. By the time they understood the CPM's crafty success it was too late. Later, their damage control exercise and firm denial to help or rescue the CPM, friendly gesture to the Harmads failed to make a dent. It failed to convince the political opponents of the CPM and a section of the people about their bonafide actions and neutrality of the central forces. The government of India was highly embarrassed. CPM after watching that use of Harmads had worked well in keeping with the plan the party arranged more Harmads and established many camps under them. At Salboni a camp was built in the CPM party office. In Humgarh, Goaltore, on the initiative of the brother of a minister a big camp and in the residence of the MLA of Nayagram at village Kotkainasia, a camp of the Harmads were functioning. In station para, Jhargram bus stand, near the railway station, and in Raghunathpur camps were operating. In many camps stock-piling of arms, ammunitions, bombs, etc. perturbed the peace loving people. Camps were shifted frequently depending on the situation. Such decisions were taken by the CPM leaders of Jhargram town. Existence of the camps of the harmads was within the knowledge of the police chief and district administration.

Complaints poured in that the joint forces on the pretext of flushing out the ultras, assaulted many innocent villagers, killed many and unleashed terror. After killing they had buried dead bodies and thereby destroyed evidence. A journalist accused the joint forces that they had massacred 20 villagers in a place about ten kms away from Jhargram town on the plea of gun battle with the Maoists. In two pick-up vans the dead bodies were transported from the village to the bank of the Kansabati river and buried the dead bodies in the river bed. Panic stricken villagers deserted the villages and taken shelter in temporary camps opened by the TMC. Harmads remained behind the security forces and set fire on many houses of villages, Badarbani, Sowarbani, Khemdi, Gandula, Kudlihai and Sevayatan. According to the TMC supporters the local police did not take any action to stop arson, killings and violence. Rather shamefully police was behind the genocide.

Allegations created furore. Indeed, the vortex of adverse public opinion pushed the CPM to the brink of precipice. The wonky CPM acted political pussy footing visualising reaction of the people in the impending Assembly election. Local print media and NGOs were up-in-arms, demanded immediate enquiry to pin-point responsibility to take exemplary action against the offenders and disband the harmad bahini. Broadly, the allegations could be divided in three categories. First, the Maoists abducted many persons either from the public place or from their abodes on suspicion. Victims' bullet ridden dead bodies were later discovered from the jungle or from isolated places. They abducted and killed CPM activists or patrons. Secondly, the CPM;s armed cadres along with cops in midnight abducted persons from their residence, known for their anti-CPM bias, silencing resistance of the family members. Thereafter, either the victim was untraced or his dead body was recovered from jungle or road side after 2 or 3 days. In some cases immediately after abduction the members of the family heard sound of gun-fire. Later his dead body was found nearby or in the hospital morgue. In many cases the police picked up persons from their residences during night. Later their dead bodies with bullet injuries were traced out either from jungle or from deserted places. Thirdly, the Harmads and police jointly abducted persons and later shot them dead and dumped the dead bodies in abandoned places. In addition, the harmads either damaged or set fire on houses of many persons who joined the anti-CPM tirade. In sum, Maoists abducted and killed persons on suspicion. Cops either jointly with the CPM armed cadres or goons/Harmads or independently killed persons on suspicion that they had link with the ultras. Harmads hired by the CPM killed many persons who were anti-CPM and pro-Maoists.

However, the CPM denied the charges. Police hierarchy was non-committal. Government ignored criticism which only increased disappointment of the people.

Gana Sunani—A Public Hearing

Shocking allegations corroborated by many victims' widows, parents, near and dear one generated strong anti CPM public opinion. Police was put on the dock. Several NGOs demanded that the government should come out with the truth. A NGO in pursuit of unearthing the truth and mobilising honest public opinion organised the," Gana Sunani" meaning public hearing in the playground of Jhargram town for two days. Its aim was to hear the aggrieved persons and record their statements for taking follow up action. On December 16, 2010 a team was formed with teachers, students, advocates and progressive persons to examine and record statements of the complainants. A few thousands men, women and persons from various walks of life spontaneously gathered. Friends and relatives of the victims and many sufferers appeared to narrate their woes and co-operate with the "Gana Sunani". Congregation of countless women was very conspicuous. Many of them had lost husbands, sons, brothers or were victims of torture, mischief, damage or destruction of properties. It was a pathetic spectacle, the town has never seen such a colossal assembly of aggrieved men and women who appeared mustering courage and ignoring threat of the CPM cads to lodge complaint and seek justice. Incidentally, the local Member of the Parliament Subhendu Adikary helped the organisers to make the Gana Sunani a success. A group of intellectuals from Kolkata were present and gave moral support to the outraged family members.

On the request of the NGO I chaired the sessions on both days, heard the complainants, and after cross-examination recorded their statements. Statements of twenty persons were recorded by me. Other teams recorded many statements. Upon conclusion of the sessions the statements were examined from legal angle. Thereafter, on behalf of the NGO, the renowned novelist Mahasweta Devi filed a the public interest litigation, Writ Petition (No.WP 2333(W) of 2011 before the High Court, Calcutta seeking an enquiry under my supervision (because of my experience in CBI), fix responsibility and initiate appropriate legal action against the culprits and issue direction for financial compensation to the victims' family. The High Court did not agree to entrust the enquiry to a retired IPS officer. Instead, the Court ordered that the serving police officers of West Bengal have to conduct enquiry and submit report for further action. Court has approved the prayer for monetary compensation to the victim's families. Later, I learn that the government has sanctioned monetary compensation to the members of the victims' families. Regarding allegation of nine missing persons abducted and killed the Hon'ble Court ordered that investigation should continue to find out what has happened to them and their whereabouts.

Statements were startling revelation. In fact, stories disclosed are ordinarily not believable. People were stunned knowing the secret annihilation of persons without any fair enquiry or scrutiny or giving them any opportunity to defend. They were highly shocked seeing the police's beastly role in the genocide. However, they appreciated the pragmatic actions of the NGO to expose the brutality and cold blooded murders by the armed cadres, hired goons, cops and the head hunting Maoists. Much jubilation was noticed in the camps of the political opponents of the CPM. Truly, it surcharged the political atmosphere of the state since election for state Legislative Assembly was knocking at the door. However, relevant portion from the statements are quoted below to satisfy curiosity of the readers.

Sm Bimla Mahato aged 32, wife of Pradip Mahato of village Nandanapur, police station, Jhargram:

> "On October 22, 2010, at about 9.30 pm, my husband aged 40, was called out of the house by unknown persons. Within a few minutes I heard sound of gun fire. I hurriedly reached the spot and noticed my husband lying dead."

Sm Sampatti Mahato, aged 50, w/o Bikram Mahato of village Indrabani. PS Jhargram:

> "In the month of Ashar (July), at about 5.30. am my husband was going to attend the call of nature. Police arrived and surrounded our house and shot him dead. Police threw the dead body near the bamboo grove. Police and harmads were together and left the spot in one vehicle. Dead body kept in the morgue was not handed over to us as we failed to pay charges for the morgue."

Sm Manika Mahato aged 31, w/o Uttam Mahato, of village Chunpara PS Sankrail.

> "On November 4, 2010 at about 4 am police men and Harmads came together and misbehaved with us. As my husband protested he was forcibly carried away. About one km away, his dead body with bullet injuries was found by villagers. My father-in-law lodged a complaint to the police station. I do not know the progress of the case."

Sm Chabi Mudi aged 22, wife of Ajit Mudi, a school teacher of village Jobnikata, PS Jhargram

> "On September 22, 2010, my husband travelled in a bus for going to the BDO's office at Jhargram to receive his salary. At about 2 pm at Radhaknagore a group CPM goons stopped the bus, dragged him out and abducted him. Since then my husband is untraced. My father-in-law reported the matter to the PS.

Smt Mira Mahato aged 60 w/o Banamali Mahato, village Ajnasuli PS Lalgarh.

> "About a year back 30/40 harmads at about 7 pm 30/40 Harmads arrived and set my house on fire, looted our ornaments, money and valuables.

Samsun Neha Bibi, aged 35, w/o Sakandar Khan of village Jaikrishnapur, PS Salboni.

> "On February 5, 2010, at about 9.30 am my husband went to buy cows in a cycle. He carried Rs 18, 000. Later I learnt that he was abducted and killed by the harmads. Dead body is still untraced. I reported it to the PS on February 6, 2010."

Tarak Mahato, aged 42 son of late Rabindranath Mahato of village Jhumpara, PS Sankrail.

> "About one and half month back at about 4 am, hearing noise I came out of my room and noticed about 100 people gathered. Policemen travelled in two vehicles were present. Miscreants threw bombs and fired at me which hit my right leg. I lost my senses. I was taken to Medinapur hospital. Later I was taken to SSKM hospital Calcutta and my right leg was amputated."

Sm Sailabala Naik stated that her son Nirmal Naik aged 24 was called out on the plea of attending a meeting. Since then he was untraced. Later she learnt that Nirmal was killed. She reported the matter to the police mentioning names of four miscreants.

Sm Rupali Dutta aged 23 w/o Kaushik Dutta of village Manikpara PS Jhargram.

> "My husband working as a mechanic, used to take metre reading from houses. On April 9, 2010, at about 8 am he went to village Lalgaria for taking metre reading. I learnt that my husband and his friend Paban Mahato were abducted by a group of miscreants, carried away forcibly inside the jungle on the following day both dead bodies were recovered from the jungle. My husband was a TMC activist. His motor bike, phone and money were taken away."

Probe disclosed that Kaushik and Paban were abducted and killed by the Maoists suspecting them to be police informers. I examined Smt Aparna Mahato aged 24, w/o Prabal Mahato of village Manikpara PS. She stated that her husband was owning a small pan (beetle) shop and maintaining the family in extreme hardship. He went with his friend Kaushik. Thereafter he did not return home. On October 10, 2010 she learnt that both of them were murdered in Bangara Chapaldanga forest.

My sadness knew no bounds imagining two young widows' pathetic survival with widowhood and a small child in their lap, and had to struggle for the rest of their life. Chill penury, ungraciousness of the society and opaque future of the child would be a mighty threat to their existence. Their sombre future may not shake the society and the ultras who have been clamoring for the welfare and betterment of the people. Almost similar complaints from the mouth of Smt Anushree Kar, Sm Shafali Mahato, Smt Baisakhi, Nilima Mahato, Danesh Fatama,

Smt Nilima, Sri Surajit Mahato and many others, put the audience in immeasurable pain and despair. I was indeed inspired seeing bravery and determination of the women complainants who appeared to expose the culprits. Mournful fate has not dissuaded them to demand equity and justice.

Notably, violence and annihilation are dreaded disease. They disrupt a society by spoiling or attacking norms which holds the society together. Regrettably, the ultras' pompous and unpalatable political ambition responsible for premature and brutal death of countless persons and abyss agony for their near and dear are contrary to the society's interest and welfare and, therefore, have to be defeated at all cost. The CPM's detestable action to hire desperados who chastised and killed people, is unheard in a civilised country. The party's thinly veiled attempt to deny the allegations has perturbed the people. Alibi would not immune them from the peoples' anger. After all, inscrutable moral law is supreme in public life. Police's camaraderie with the Harmads and appalled actions discarding professional ethics is highly deplorable. The police hierarchy's cavalier disregard to check the subordinates who came down to the level of outlaws is a slur in the history of Indian police. Even the colonial police in the past never possessed such a miry record.

Trinamool Congress (TMC) and the Maoists in West Bengal

The name 'Jangal Mahal' in West Medinapur district has not been coined formally or recognised by any legitimate authority. In fact it gained currency automatically and travelled from mouth to mouth. The local populace call it jungle mahal since it is left unattended and uncared for by the administration, indirectly allowed to be dominated or controlled by the extremists. Here, the Maoists enforced their rule, decided the local problems, conflicts, held kangaroo courts and delivered justice arbitrarily. In such matters Maoist writs were paramount. Truly, the name has no connotation. The local habitants have accepted it ungrudgingly and the media played a big role to circulate and popularise the new name.

On the eve of the state Assembly election in April/May 2011, operation by the joint forces was either reduced or suspended in absence of the government's clear direction. Secondly, anti-Maoist joint operation with Jharkhand and Odisha came to a grinding halt The Left Front government's catastrophic defeat in general election held in April/May 2011, and formation of the new government by Trinamool Congress party in May 2011, under leadership of Miss Mamata Banerjee visibly changed the political scenario of the state. Mandate was loud and clear. It disastrously rejected the CPM and its allies. The Chief Minister of the new government, herself holding the "Police" portfolio has not ordered renewal of the joint operation and fresh offensive against the ultras. In fact, status quo and temporary lull prevailed in terror torn areas. CM invited the Maoists for a dialogue, giving up violence. On the government's initiative a team of civilians was formed to negotiate with the Maoists headed by a social activist, Sujata Bhadra. The team politically possessed left background and enjoyed access to the Maoist leaders. Maoist leader Kishanji was agreeable to enter in dialogue with the team. Maoists demanded withdrawal of the central forces, release of the Maoists already in custody and suspension of the joint operation. Meanwhile, alarming report received that the Maoists were regrouping in three districts of Jangal Mahal, consolidating their position in villages, reinforcing their resources, recruiting teenagers on the line of Bal Vahini. The recruits were detailed at the markets, near the camps of the security forces for collecting intelligence on the movement of the security forces. Reliable information received that the Maoist Central Committee in a meeting held in February last resolved to follow the Lalgarh model. In that goal, twelve people's militia squads, 40 to 50 village safety groups and four guerrilla base camps would be set up. With increased strength the ultras would disrupt the state's development works and upset the new government's progressive and developmental programmes.

State's gesture for suspension of fresh offensive and joint operation along with the neighboring states and call for a dialogue was a sigh of relief for the peace loving people Nevertheless, uneasy suspense was apparent whether peace talk was really going to be materialised and Maoists were going to give up arms and return to normal life. Sober persons feel that the Maoists are guided by definite political ideology. They cannot discard it and embrace the parliamentary democracy. Hence, the proposed peace talk might not produce the desired result. Government's anxiety to solve the problem in feverish haste and accommodate the Maoists in any capacity might create "Nepal like situation." Indeed, quixotic approach instead of a well calculated step might upset the peace process. Significantly, Jharkhand, Odisha and Chhattisgarh already expressed concern for halting the joint operations against the rebels. They apprehended that WB was likely to turn to be a safe haven for the ultras. If mailed fist of the security forces was slackened the ultras might sneak into West Bengal and gained back the lost ground. In fact, the DGPs of three states in a meeting chaired by UHM had raised this point before the Union Home Minister who had been co-coordinating the joint operations.

Election pledges to release political prisoners including the Maoists and withdrawal of criminal prosecutions against them might be a conciliatory step to curb the Maoist problem. Yet its dark side might not be ignored. The released rebels might not shed sentiment which once inspired them to join the out-fit embracing the Maoist ideology, might take up arms at any moment. MHA has already asked the state to refer the cases against political prisoners having Maoist records, to the Ministry before any decision taken for their release. MHA emphasised that the detained Maoist leaders' activities had been spreading over a few states and therefore, their release had direct bearing on containing the Maoist movement. Hence, unilateral decision to release them may be suicidal. (*The Statesman*, August 3, 2011) Truly, even it is good for WB, may be a flinty threat for other Maoist-hit states. Dispassionately, soft line adopted by the

CM Mamata Banerjee was likely to encourage the ultras and ravage further sagging morale of the security forces. Secondly, the policy of conciliation might not guarantee the farewell to arms by the rebels. It may be recalled that the then Chief Minister of Jharkhand Sibu Soren's soft line to neutralise the ultras ended in a fiasco, which should be a lesson for other states and sober persons.

State's Strategic Shift

State government's strategic shift banking on soft line to quell Maoist unrest may be well intended. Nevertheless, its wider ramification needs unbiased and pensive analysis. Growing strength of the Maoist cadres, penetration into sixteen states and 165 districts, deadly striking power, substantial resources, ambition of the leaders to topple the elected government and usurp power and authority by violence etc., are formidable threat to the democracy and the rule of law. CM's conciliatory note perhaps had not been taken in right spirit by the Maoists. Inspite of repeated calls for dialogue, response of the Maoists was lukewarm. Neither they had shun violence and bloodshed nor showed interest to come down to the negotiation table. In the meantime, they refurbished and reinforced the squads, stock piled fire arms, ammunitions and modified the strategy to surprise the security forces. Impartial critics felt that the design to delay the peace talk was a ploy to outwit security forces. The joint forces were in great suspense that the ultras might re-appear with renewed vigour and strength and obfuscate partial success already achieved by the security forces. From June to November 2011, suspense prevailed in *Jangal Mahal.* Security forces awaited order from the government to resume operation and disarray the Maoists. Meanwhile, the interlocutors headed by Sujato Bhadra failed to show any positive result. Maoists called off cease fire offer and showed U-turn in November 2011. Maoist leader Akash said that neither the government nor the mediators kept their promises.

Suspension of operations by the combined forces generated adverse conditions for the security forces. CRPF pointed out that the state police was reluctant to co-operate for raids in the hideouts of the rebels and detaining them. They even dissuaded the CRPF to undertake offensive action. Situation was very grim as the armed rebels, who were pushed back earlier re-grouped and preparing for stringent blow. CRPF camps were vulnerable as they were confined in the camps, not going out and initiating aggressive actions. Fear of attacks on the CRPF camps loomed large. Local police officers who use to work as guides and supplied intelligence were withdrawn. Indeed, standard procedure for operation in disturbed territory was not adhered to. In this context a report published in *The Hindustan Times* on August 24, 2011 might be seen.

Return of the Red Terror in Jangal Mahal

Maoists returned to Jangal Mahal. Peace loving people were alarmed visualising the impending horror of violence and macabre festival of death. On August 23, 2011 Tapan Deswal, aged 24, was abducted from Tamajuri area and shot dead. The dead body with three bullet marks was lying on the road near Tongaveda under Belpahari police station. A Maoist poster left at the spot disclosed that he was a police informer. It revealed that the deceased was previously attached with the rebels and later broke out. In fact it was the first killing after TMC government was formed on May 20, 2011. On August 24, 2011, Rabindranath Mishra, an activist of the TMC was killed at village Dhangri, under Jhargram police station. On September 20, 2011, Lal Mohan Mahato of Pukuria under Jhargram police station was killed. Maoists blamed that deceased was a member of the Bhairab Bahini, a vigilante group of TMC. On September 25, 2011, Babu Sen, a popular social activist and a co-coordinator of the JMM was shot dead near Binpur. It was suspected that the Maoists were behind the murder.

On August 11, 2011, Maoists ambushed a CRPF patrol and fired indiscriminately at Lakhimpur, Salboni and injured a CRPF personnel critically. The spot was very close to an arms training camp of the Maoists. Police later seized two Insas rifles, a SLR, a .303 rifle, 220 rounds of ammunitions remotes, batteries, chargers, flash guns, 60 kgs of explosives, mines, gelatin sticks, etc. Several leaders including Bikash, Akash, Suchitra, Tola Hembrem and others managed to escape. It appeared that the Maoists made both CPM and TMC their targets. On November 4, 2011, two TMC activists Ajit Singh Sardar and his son, Baku Singh Sardar of Ghatberia village, Purulia district, were taken to nearby jungle and shot dead. On November 5, 2011, Manik Mandi, the branch secretary of the CPM was shot dead at Kukrahupi, Jamboni. On November 6, 2011, a group of TMC activists when holding meeting at village Masandihi, near Jhargram the Maoists fired at the gathering from nearby Adarisole forest. Rup Chand Soren, an activist received bullet injury. On November 16, 2011, police seized 13 country made rifles, 200 rounds of ammunitions, 85 kgs explosive from Berabaddorha under Kotawali police station. Meanwhile, Akash blamed the state government for failing to fulfill promises made by the TMC supremo in pre-election campaigns. Political observers stated that the Maoists did not want peace process to continue as they had re-grouped themselves in Jangal Mahal and ready for a show down. Their vacuous assurance for negotiation for the peace and good bye to insurgency had to be taken with a pinch of salt.

Chief Minister had already announced several welfare measures for the people of Jangal Mahal. TMC faced constraints in taking the rein of Jangal Mahal politically. Four MLA from TMC and one from CPM were elected from jungle mahal. In Nayagram, Salboni, Sankril areas TMC's presence is visible. But in Jhargram, Gopiballavpur, Binpur and Lalgarh the TMC's existence was conspicuously puny. Here TMC could organise meetings and rallies in some pockets only. TMC had therefore, organised several vigilante groups to enhance its influence.

TMC MLA from Gopiballavpur avoided confrontation with the Maoists. MLA of Nayagram hardly stayed in his constituency.

Media commented that the Maoists were back in *Jangal Mahal.* It revealed that the Maoists had established ten camps around Lalgarh where 1200 rebels assembled. For their movements they normally proceeded from Dahijuri situated in south west of the district, crossed the Kansabati river via Basantpur and took the Baghara route on way to Bhulagara and such adjacent areas as Bonishol, Karamsole and Lakhanpur which had thick forest cover. If they were intercepted by the security forces they followed the same route for tactical retreat. In fact, the state government waited about five months expecting response from the Maoists. Its worn-out patience called for decisive action. On November 15, 2011, comrade Akash sent a letter expressing interest in holding talks provided joint operation was suspended and frontal organisations were allowed to organise meetings and rallies in Jangal Mahal.

State's appeal for peace and welfare of the people had hardly been reciprocated by the Maoists. Dismayingly, they were non-committal for discarding violence and ensuring farewell to arms. In one hand they were interacting with the interlocutors presumably for a honorable solution, on the other, unleashed escalated unrest and annihilation of the innocent villagers. Regrettably, they had not yet disclosed what they actually wanted. In fact, the mystery of despicable double standard unfolded their devious style of functioning. Critics felt that they had insurmountable constraints to accept peace and social harmony. First, the cadres accustomed to live in jungles and sanctuaries under enormous hardship, constant suspense, fear of police raids and regular brain wash for armed revolution and grab power by the barrel of gun might not be agreeable for them to return to normal life. Secondly, peace is likely to bring unemployment for the cadres. Thirdly, easy flow of hefty amount by threat and coercion would be missing in a normal civil society. Fourthly, unless leaders were elected by the people their position in the government or in the society would be innocuous. Lastly, shabby compromise sacrificing the ideology might ridicule them in the people's estimation and destroy their political credibility. In fact, pensive analysis leads one to believe that peace and normalcy is a monumental detriment for the Maoists to pursue their cherished goal. Hence, ostensively they might talk about peace, cease-fire and dialogue for a honorable settlement but in reality, fundamental duress of the outfit would dissuade them to prosper in the accolade of normal social and political order and halcyon ambience. In a nutshell, they are unable to give up the Maoist ideology and the quest for power by force uprooting the parliamentary democracy. On the expected negotiation, the intellectuals were candid that no purpose was being served by the current, "on to-day, off tomorrow" style of negotiations. Interestingly, manifested stagnation of the peace talk at the initiative of the interlocutors was obliquely viewed by the sober people.

In 2011, 22 CPM activists, 14 TMC, 2 Forward Block, 1 JMM, 2 PCAPA, activists, one state police and one Indian Reserve Battalion (IRB) personnel and a few civilians were killed. Altogether 11 deadly encounters with the Maoists took place. In fact,110 Maoists and their link men were arrested, 12 automatic weapons, 100 fire arms, 44 land directional mines, about 400 kgs explosives were seized. However, in 2011, number of killing was reduced to 51 only. It was crystal clear that attempt to bring the Maoists down to the negotiation table was likely to be a futile exercise. Hence, the state government was in no mood to relax its vigil. In fact, watching diplomatic trickery of the Maoists to kill time on the pretext of joining the peace talk, the government decided no letup in forward offensive against the rebels. In addition to state armed police, as stood on December 31, 2011, 42 coys of CRPF were deployed in Jangal Mahal. In West Medinapur district, 31 coys, in Purulia district 7 coys including Naga coys, 2 coys exclusively for the Ayodhya hill and in Bankura 2 Coys of the CRPF were placed. As fierce confrontations were inevitable, the state requested the union government to send additional 1300 CRPF personnel for tackling the situation in jungle mahal. Finally, renewal of operations by the joint forces after talk failed in November 2011, produced a salutary result. The hope of the Maoists for liberating the Jangal Mahal was belied. They were unable to resist the determined pressure of the joint forces, and thereby forced to retreat and take shelter in safer sanctuaries in deep jungle and remote areas. It was bolt from blue for them that the life wire of the Maoist movement in Jangal Mahal, Koteshwar Rao alias Kishanji, was killed in a protracted gun battle with the security forces on November 24, 2011 at about 6 PM, in Burishole jungle, West Medinapur. From the spot two AK 47 rifles, a water bottle and a small bag were recovered. Kishanji was a member of the politburo, in charge of operation for WB, Jharkhand and Bihar. After post mortem examination his dead body was sent to his native place, village Padapally, district Karimnagar, AP, for cremation.

Death of Kishanji in an encounter was an astounding success for the security forces. It was extolled by the peace loving people suffered from the rebels' outrages. Simultaneously, it abysmally demoralised the rebels. Their woe further aggravated when no suitable successor in his place could be selected. Talk was in the air that either Sabyasachi Panda from Odisha or Smt Suchitra Mahato wife of slain leader Sasadhar Mahato could step into the shoes. Finally, no able Maoist leader filled the vacuum. Needless to say, the leaderless and effete rebels lost heart to face the joint forces. Though they promised to avenge the death of their beloved leader but in practice, they failed to re organise and neutralise growing pressure of the joint forces. In fact, they planned attack in a few isolated occasions but it failed lamentably to make a dent. On December 9, 2011 when the security forces started combing Barobaru forest near Jhargram on receipt of specific information, the Maoists fired at them. A fierce gun battle continued for a few hours and finally the jaded rebels took to heels. This was the last obstinate gun-battle with the security forces took place after Kishanji's death.

On January 22, 2012, Maoists planned to attack the police out post located near Kolaikunda air field on the Republic Day (January 26, 2012). In a raid in Akhrasole forest many documents, plan for an explosion in national high way No.6 etc. fell in the hands of the police and thereby impending attack was either suspended or given up. Under leadership of Prasanta Bose, a member of the central committee, and in presence of comrades Akash, Madan Mahato and Sabyasachi Panda, a meeting was held in Laboni forest, Belpahari. They discussed the strategy to make the units operating in Jangal Mahal viable to win back support of the rural mass. It was resolved to launch a movement against delayed procurement of paddy by the government and minimum support price fixed by the Union Government which was contrary to the interest of the farmers. In fact, galling erosion in mass support in rural areas, especially, in Jangal Mahal was discussed. Persons, especially, the Adivasi community who once gave implicit support to the Maoist movement, had been alienating themselves from the ultras, needed exhaustive probe. Indeed, under current of unfriendly sentiment of the disillusioned people who were once sympathetic and supportive to their cause, arrests of several leaders and surrenders by many hardcore Maoists, had enhanced their anxiety, fear of split or collapse of the movement. They had been noticing that belying the friendly gesture, of late, the villagers were refusing to give cooked food, safe shelter, information on movement of the security forces etc. to the Maoists. Situation had been drastically changing. Ultras and their link men had been facing resistance from the villagers. In fact, leaders assembled, were inclined to believe that loss of mass support and unacceptability of their political goal had been looming large. In short, rebels were fast losing their grip over the common people, and therefore, modification of the strategy and the *modus operandi* to pursue the movement to right direction was *sine qua non*. Impartial critics educated a sizeable rural populace to look at the Maoists' loud cry for the revolution, people's war, people's government, and call for the upsurge by the poor and deprived people etc. from wider perspective. They whispered and campaigned silently that hyperbolic Maoist jargon was a hoax and hypocritical, unable to demolish the existing order and wipe out miseries of the down trodden. Six rebels of the Sidhu Kanhu Gana Militia were killed inside Metala forest which was a major setback for the rebels.

In 2009, Maoists' punch was quite deterrent and its impact felt in nooks and corners of jungle mahal. Security forces came under scathing criticism for failing to contain the Maoist menace. However, from 2010, situation in favour of the security forces was changing very fast. Comrade Sasadhar Mahato, considered to be a high profile and dauntless Maoist, was killed in an encounter which was a terrible shock for the rebels. A pall of gloom was apparent in rank and file. Meanwhile, 'drive for hunt' and 'encirclement' by the security forces isolated and cornered the rebels. Their morale touched its lowest ebb and the radar-less middle rank leaders lost presence of mind, failed to inspire the cadres and guide the movement ably. Indeed, arrest and loss of several front rank leaders had already given a flinty blow to the outfit. For example, Venkateswar Reddy, alias Telugu Dipak was arrested in March 2010, Cherikuri Rajkumar alias Azad was shot dead by the Andhra police in July 2010. Comrade Kobad Gandhi was arrested in September, 2009 and Mohan Biswakarma, a technocrat of the Maoists was arrested from Delhi. Ram Krishna Sadanala was arrested from Kolkata in July 2012. With death of comrade Azad six members of the Maoist politburo, of the strength of total thirteen, were either killed or languished in jails. In fact, on February 23, 2010, Lal Mohan Tudu President of the PCAPA was gunned down at Kantapahari. On July 26, 2010, in an encounter Sidhu Soren, secretary of the PCAPA wanted in 20 murder cases was killed in four hours long gun battle in Metala forest. He was also the general secretary of the Sidhu Kanu Gana Militia (SKGM). From the spot one SLR, one Insas rifle, two .303 rifles, two twelve bore guns, three 9mm pistols, gelatin sticks, magazines were seized. On June 16, 2010, eight Maoists including three women and five PLGA Maoists were killed in an encounter in Ranjya forest and one was physically captured. In fact, within one year after joint operation was afoot, 45 security personnel and twenty Maoists were killed. Uma Kanta Mahato of PCAPA who was wanted by the CBI in Gyaneswari express train sabotage case was killed in a gun battle in Mohanpur forest near Jhargram. On August 31, 2010, Maoist Bibhuti Mahato of Banspahari surrendered to the police at Belpahari police station. Comrade Ajit Sit, head of the Jamboni squad was arrested.

Comrade Abhay was placed in place of deceased C. Rajkumar alias Azad. He was appointed as the spokesperson of the central committee. On November 27, 2011, he stated that the Maoists vowed to fight the central government's unified action plan (UAP). He hinted that the coming days might be more gruesome than the past. Operation Green Hunt was a part of the fascist repressive campaign by the central and state governments. He admitted that since 2004, they had a list of 1500 martyrs. Significantly, 300 Maoists martyrs embraced supreme sacrifice from May 2009 to July 2010. Eight top comrades including politburo member Azad as well as 10 state level comrades either been killed or detained in jails. Many comrades from district level either arrested or killed. Loses have affected the party and the movement badly. Perhaps, many Maoists realised that it is futile to fight the security forces facing hardship, ordeals, risks and hazards. Evidently, progress made by the security forces might wipe out the ultras from Jangal Mahal. Comprehensive mandate and the people's support to the TMC government, especially, from Jangal Mahal revealed that the people were no longer willing to take up the cause of the ultras. Precisely, Maoists could see the dim prospect of the extremist movement and therefore, thought it wise to return to normal life.

Frolic of Surrender

A distinct sign of demoralisation in the rank and file of the Maoists was apparent. Indeed, death of the life wire, Kishanji in an encounter and lack of an able leader in his place had shaken the Maoists. In fact, the crisis of leadership badly affected morale of the cadres. Simultaneously, arrest of many cadres, retreat of the ultras due to mounting pressure by the security forces, made the writing on the wall abundantly and manifestly clear. Secondly, tribal community, once the pillar of support and co-operation was no longer standing by their side. Thirdly, watching bad days of the Maoists, local people mustered courage to inform the police on the Maoists' hideouts, movements, attempt for procuring fire arms, ration etc. Security forces confirmed that as the Maoists were on the run intelligence were pouring in which helped them to conduct raids, arrests and recovery of weapons, explosives, etc. Perhaps, Maoists realised that over throw of the elected and parliamentary form of government was beyond their capacity. The leaders' high-falutin promises to establish the people's government was a thinly veiled attempt to gain over the cadres. Furthermore, a large number of arrests and surrenders panicked the cadres. The Maoists, the keen observers of events, visualised the security forces ultimate success and the impending dooms day for the movement. Ironically, want of competent leadership to resuscitate sagging morale of the cadres was a flinty hurdle for the Maoists. Admittedly, many Maoists guided by selfish motive decided to give up arms and return to the main stream of the society.

Surrender in Galore

Dreaded female Maoist Jagari Baski who was one of the members of the security ring for Kishanji, and seen by the side of the slain leader and her Maoist husband Rajaram with their seven years old son walked into the Writers building, Kolkata and surrendered before the Chief Minister. It was a great surprise for all and celebration for many. Many dreaded Maoists followed the suit. Soon Durjadhan Raj Kumar and his wife Akari alias Lalita, in charge of the Purulia squad surrendered. On January 12, 2012, in public meeting at Jhargram, Maoists Lambodar Majhi, Karan alias Sanjay Kaibarta, Bhajahari Mahoto from Purulia and Suhadev Mahato from Salboni surrendered before the Chief Minister. On February 8, 2012. Maoist Chiranjit Mahato and his wife Anima surrendered before the IG Western Range. They attacked the EFR camp at Silda. On March 6, 2012, Maoist Ramesh Singh Sardar alias Tapan and his wife Sibani Laya alias Sheema who belonged to Audhya squad surrendered before the district police chief. On March 10, 2012, Maoist Suchitra Mahato wife of slain leader Sasadhar Mahato went to the Writers Building with her newly married husband Prabir Garai and presented before the Chief Minister. She was one of the close aides of Kishanji and found by the side of the dead Kishanji. She and her husband were interviewed by the journalists and electronic media extensively. She stated that she wanted to lead normal life. Surrender of Suchitra Mahato was a substantial gain for the police which was celebrated with much exuberance in many quarters. Maoist central leaders once considered to make her the supreme leader in Jangal Mahal in place of deceased Kishanji. Hence, her surrender was viewed with extra ordinary significance. On July 16, 2012, Comrade Bikram alias Bhanu alias Surjya alias Arnab Dam, secretary of CPI (Maoist) for WB-Jharkhand-Orissa border committee, was arrested from Biramdi, Purulia district, border of W.B. and Jharkhand. One AK-47, rifle, two magazines, 30 rounds and a camera were seized from his possession. He was involved in 80 cases including murder of seven Forward Block activists on December 16, 2012 at Bagbindya village, under Jalda police station, Purulia. He confessed to have murdered Partha Biswas a CID officer and Soumitra Basu, a school teacher. He admitted that the Maoists were in back foot due to continuous raids, search operations and arrests of the leaders. However, it was a prize catch and a fatal blow to the Maoists. On July 13, 2012, squad members Raju Murmu and Sujata alias Champa Hembram were arrested from Bankura. One of the squad leaders, Subodh Hasda alias china surrendered before the Court at Jhargram. His three lieutenants, who were members of the squad were arrested from jungle under Binpur police station. On February 4, 2012, comrade Narayan Sanyal, a member of the politburo who master-minded loot of 200 rifles, 1000 rounds of ammunitions from the home guard training centre at Pachamanba, near Giridih, Jharkhand, on November 11, 2005 was arrested. Broadly, instances discussed above not exhaustive but were unimpeachable testimony to show how the table turned and the Maoists in Jangal Mahal were in quagmire.

Triumph of the Security Forces—Maoists on Heels, Not Wiped Out

A good number of arrests and surrenders by hard core Maoists put the outfit in critical logjam. Secondly, Maoists' hunt for picking up a competent leader to lead the movement and their disappointment to get it had abysmally demoralised the cadres. The effete and leaderless cadres were in dark about their duties and steps needed to keep the movement alive. Over and above, triumph of the security forces broke their morale and they were not in a position to reorganise, invigorate and renew the fast decaying movement. Thirdly, government under took several comprehensive projects to improve roads, health care, open up employment opportunity, economic progress in the areas and bring an overall socio-economic development in Jangal Mahal. Thirdly, people were very cross with the Maoists and no longer willing to help or co-operate with them. Violence, bloodletting activities and annihilation of the innocent persons were disapproved by people. They were keen to see the end of odious tyranny, violence, and fear of death. Broadly speaking, people of Jangal Mahal were frustrated enduring protracted unrest, insecurity and blood curdling episodes. They sincerely desired the end of Maoist violence and restoration of peace and order. Truly, from 2012, peace and rule of law gradually returned to jungle mahal. Undeniably, pyrrhic success goes to the credit of the security forces. Their painstaking effort, plodding industry, envious performance ignoring risks and hazards, and examples of supreme sacrifices paid a matchless dividend. At the same time, the state government's uncompromising stand and free hand given to the security forces humbled the ultras and led to the monumental success. Meanwhile, law and order were limping back to normalcy. Fear psychosis which had been haunting the people indicated its gradual decline. Seeing improvement of the situation, night train services through Jangal Mahal which were suspended after Gyaneswari express train tragedy, on May 28, 2010, was resumed with effect from January 13, 2012. The radicals and intellectuals who waffled endlessly in support of the extremists were perturbed visualising gloomy prospect of the Maoist movement. However, critics feel that the Maoists, no doubt, were isolated and cowed down, but not wiped out. They might furtively operate awaiting better days, reappear and take up arms. After all, an ideology propounded by eminent personality, Mao Tse-tung is immortal and bound to prosper inspite of temporary setback.

Maoists firmly believed that Miss Mamata Banerjee, the Chief Minister would recognise their support and graciously reciprocate their services. However, except inviting them for a dialogue and appealing to shun violence and return to the main stream of the society the CM had not taken any other tangible step. The interlocutors' mission for a conciliatory talk with the rebels had hardly shown any satisfactory progress. Secondly, a review committee was set up under chairmanship of a retired High Court Judge to examine the question of premature release of the Maoists languishing in jails. The committee after careful examination of individual cases recommended release of 78 rebels from the jails.

The interlocutors visited Jangal Mahal and the district jail, discussed with many rebel leaders. Broadly, majority of the rebel leaders welcomed the talk. In fact, repeated dialogues indicated a ray of hope. However, soon a bottleneck developed and threatened the progress. Interlocutors had no access to the underground leaders to know their mind. Rebels detained in jails demanded that a few leaders should be released to participate in the talk with the government.

It may be recalled that The Lalgarh Manch was formed by a civil society in April 2009, about two months before the central forces were deployed in Lalgarh and joint operation started. The TMC, being in opposition appreciated its move. Importantly, the Manch's many activists took part in Lalgarh agitation Section 144 of the Cr P C was promulgated in Lalgarh and hence they were not allowed to enter into Lalgarh. Many were detained by the police as they attempted to violate the prohibitory order. The Lalgarh Manch demanded that the government must announce the names of the extremists killed in police action. Secondly, the members of the organisation should be permitted to visit Lalgarh to study the ground situation. UHM P. Chidambaram stated that ten Maoists were killed in police action in the second half of 2009. The Manch intensified its demand for disclosing the names of the deceased and to trace out their dead bodies. State government was evasive in meeting the demand. The Manch decided to bring out a procession in Kolkata on August 29, 2009. and submit a memorandum to the Governor. TMC supported the Manch's proposed agitation. Interestingly, later one of the leaders of the Manch was picked up by the TMC government as an interlocutor to negotiate with the Maoists in 2011.

Perhaps, patience of the Maoists was exhausted seeing no positive assurance from the TMC government. Inspite of repeated dialogues the interlocutors failed to achieve any encouraging result. CM might have remembered that the Maoists declared her along with CM Buddhadeb Bhattacharjee, Biman Bose, Pranab Mukherjee as class enemy. Kishanji in a press release condemned Mamata Banerjee and her party in a manner that obliterated differences between the TMC and the CPM. Kishanji disclosed that the Maoists had given support to the TMC in anti-land acquisition movement in Nandigram, East Mednipur district. Importantly, initially Mamata Banerjee demanded immediate withdrawal of the joint forces from jungle mahal. But ever since the TMC joined the central cabinet led by the Congress party she was surprisingly silent. The Maoists were angry, yet preferred to back the TMC for greater interest of mutual help if the TMC happened to form the state government in near future. As a mark of friendship, the Maoists never killed any TMC activist. Significantly, TMC gained two third majority in the state Assembly and its popularity reached its zenith. Finally, success of the joint forces and reverses in the Maoist out-fit perhaps made her firm not to bow down to the pressure of the Maoists. Interlocutors' monumental failure to achieve any positive result might be one of the reasons for the government to ignore the Maoist demands. CM did not accept the recommendation for the premature release of 78 rebels. Thus the lofty move of the peace talk ended in a fiasco.

Poverty-stricken Adibasi community in jungle mahal was the main support base of the Maoists. In fact, fifty percent of Adivasis are living below the poverty line, followed by the Dalits, who are thirty two percent. A sizeable number of Dalits living below the poverty line reside in urban areas. Adivasis and Dalits house hold have the lowest annual income at Rs.20000 and Rs.28500 respectively. (Census Report of 2001) Their social custom, culture and traditions are entirely different, Vast majority of them still cling on blind religious faith, superstition and reluctant to prosper in the accolade of modern advancement. However, they are simple, law abiding and maintain a spectacular community relation. Maoists capitalised their poverty-stricken agonies, social short comings and finally succeeded in taking them into their fold.

In conclusion, dispassionate analysis reveals that Maoist movement is a rural based insurgency with little support in the urban areas. It is yet to graduate to the level of a mass uprising. However, its prospect to attain the level of the mass upsurge in the long run both in rural and urban areas is really doubtful. The think tank has laid down a few pieces of advice to contain or demolish the Maoist movement. First, drying up the swamp by exhaustive combing and flush out operations, by gaining of such areas like, Bastar, Malkangiri etc. absolute control to be ensured. Secondly, administration can adopt the "outsider-in" approach by stabilizing the moderately affected areas and then trying to converge on the most troubled regions. This may yield greater dividend, as it would be possible to deploy government resources judiciously and thereby improve the lot of the disaffected and win them over. Finally, watching many events and public sentiment in jungle mahal from vantage point I may add that the government must show sound judgment, practical sense, pragmatic imagination and unfailing attention to prosaic details in handling the problem. It needs no reiteration that instead of police action, greater attention has to be paid on socio economic development, improvement in public services, greater employment opportunity and protection to the people from the public servants' high-handedness, lust for payola and extortion. In conclusion, the TMC government under Mamata Banerjee deserves credit for restoring peace and normalcy in jungle mahal. The developmental programmes under taken to improve the socio economic condition of the people of jungle mahal is very encouraging. Employment of tribal youths in police force is an extra ordinary gesture and pragmatic step of the government.

Exclusive Interview with Chatradhar Mahato

Chatradhar Mahato was arrested on September 26, 2009, from village Birkand near Lalgarh under Unlawful Activities (Preventive) Act (UAPA) and detained in Medinapur jail. TMC formed government in May 2011. In fact, death of Kishanji, alias Koteshwar Rao demoralised the Maoists considerably. Simultaneously, success of the security forces put the Maoists in defensive position. CM's invitation for a peace talk and suspension of anti-Maoist operation was not responded by the Maoists. Hence, dead-lock continued. However, from end of 2011, violence showed a declining trend and normalcy was gradually limping back. Many Maoist leaders and activists who had been languishing in jail custody hoped that the new government would consider their release quixotically adhering to pre-election promises. Chatradhar Mahato was weaving cobweb of his early release as recognition for his services to oust the CPM from jungle mahal. However, as events moved apace, expectation of the détentes was belied. The new government was lukewarm to the question of release of the Maoists.

Chhatradhar perhaps thought that as the PCAPA had contributed substantially to the CPM's debacle in the Assembly election, the new government would treat them kindly and reciprocate their useful services. He was mentally prepared to agree to any condition awaiting his release. His family members were hoping against hope for his early release. Meanwhile, the government sponsored interlocutors were negotiating with the Maoist leaders. Dismayingly, protracted negotiation failed to produce the desired result. Chatradhar secretly cultivated many political leaders to get their support. It was not known what transpired between them. Perhaps he expressed his willingness to withdraw from the movement and return to normal life if released from the jail. Interestingly, he aspired to be a member of the Legislative Assembly and accordingly, from jail he contested election held in May 2011, but was defeated. Hence it was apparent that he wanted to thrive in the accolade of politics and wanted a political platform. Government, the shrewd judge of events, watched the decaying movement of the Maoists, progress made by the security forces, recapture of turf so long remained under the Maoist domination, growing unpopularity of the ultras and their alienation from the rural mass. Hence it was not felt expedient for the state to fulfill the pre-election promises promptly and release the Maoists. Meanwhile, the Maoists attempted to build pressure on the government activating the frontal organisations, PCAPA, Nari Izzat bachao Committee, DSABGM etc. However, it failed to break ice. On the contrary, it made the government stubborn to deal with the outlaws. Chatradhar's wife Niyati and members of the family moved from pillar to post pleading Chatradhar's release. She was eager to accept any terms and conditions for it. Maoists kept her under close surveillance and cautioned her not to agree to any settlement without their prior consent.

In the office room of the Jailer Chatradhar Mahato and Prasun Chatterjee were brought who took seat facing me. In smiling face both of them greeted me. Chhatradhar possessed good health, added weight, looked fresh and energetic. For the first time I met Prasun Chatterjee who looked good and presentable. I enquired about their health and welfare. Both responded well.

> I said, "Perhaps you know our mission to meet you here"
>
> He replied, "Yes comrades meet me often and inform various developments."
>
> "I have come to negotiate your release. If you agree to terms and conditions prima facie I may convey the same to the right authority for follow up actions"
>
> "My out-fit's approval is essential to consent to any settlement."
>
> "Your wife is waiting outside. She is very keen to see you free and live happily with the family."
>
> "It is quite natural. I also want freedom and peaceful life and domestic comfort."
>
> "What hinders you, if you are asked to give up association with the Maoists, abandon insurgency and return to the main stream of the society?" After a pause he said, "I can do it, but the party's approval here is essential."

He vehemently complained that the legal Advisory Body to examine the merit of detention and pass the final order was lamentably slow. Adjournment of hearing without sufficient ground was often allowed. On the last sitting adjournment had to be granted as the Judge was absent. In such a fashion, light would not be seen at the end of the tunnel.

He spitted venom against the CPM and the state government. He accused that the government was not serious for the welfare and advancement of the tribal community. They were deprived, discriminated and exploited at every stage. State had undertaken no comprehensive plan and programme to salvage them from social and political evils. Politicians promised profusely on the eve of the election but forget conveniently once election fever waned. CPM was the worst enemy of the poor and have-not. The party cadres practiced rough and ready methods, they were oppressive and atrocious. Police operated as per the instructions of the local CPM leaders. They started false cases, concocted evidence, arrested arbitrarily and brutally tortured the innocent persons. None could get fair treatment and substantial justice from the government. Public servants from revenue, forest, public works departments harassed the villagers, demanded bribe or extorted on any pretext. Villages were in shamble, without supply of drinking water, deficient in health care, public transport services, education and employment opportunities. He repeatedly said that the CPM government must be uprooted. In fact, in one stroke he expressed his grievances. He was firm and frank in his utterances totally free from finesse.

> I asked, "how do you propose to banish the above evils?"
>
> "For that, revolution is the key. It will destroy the existing political order, annihilate the class enemy and establish the people's government."
>
> "Do you think, following the doctrine of annihilation and blood bath, the social and political order can be refurbished or re-organised?
>
> "Why not, China has established the people's government, recast the social and political order and made herself economically and militarily sound"
>
> I asked, "why a poor labourer, a daily wage earner, who has no money, no land, no property, is being made a target and killed?"
>
> He replied, "Many are police informers and work against our interest"
>
> I pointed out "I have met several victims' widows below 25 years, with one or two children having no earning member or any means to support them. Who is going to be accountable for such grim tragedies?"
>
> "Do you think about their future and future of the hapless victims' off springs? Do you agree, in absence of proper care and up-bringing their career is likely to be affected or ruined. Eventually, they may turn to be anti-socials or criminals."
>
> "How the Maoists are going to fulfill obligations and take responsibility to rehabilitate them?"
>
> Chatradhar was quiet for few seconds and replied," These are manifestations of pre-revolution events. For greater achievement minor sacrifices are inevitable."

Frankly speaking, I could see hidden fire in him. Before parting, I asked him, "Will you accept the proposal to sever connection with the Maoists and secure your release?" He was non-committal and suddenly blurred out, "Mamata Banerjee has betrayed us."

I could read his mind, full of grievances against the current political regime. He had no complaint against the jail authorities. He said that he had been using time reading newspapers, books etc. Prasun Chatterjee said that his detention was blatantly wrong. He had not violated any law or committed any crime. Government has shown cavalier disregard to law and ethics and kept him in confinement without any trial.

I was happy to see them healthy and agile. I wished them well and came out. Chatradhar's wife was anxious to know the result of our conversation. Unfortunately, negotiation was stuck on the mid way. Perhaps, threat by the Maoists to the family members of Chatradhar dissuaded him and his local advisors to work contrary to the diktat of the ultras. Truly, none ventured to antagonize the Maoists and carry cudgel for Chhatradhar.

Local activists of the TMC attacked Chhatradhar's house, threatened his family members not to agitate against his detention. In fact, judging the fast changing scenario in jungle mahal, and keenness of the people to get rid of terror-stricken ambience, the government perhaps thought it futile to step up the idea of negotiation and peace-talk.

Mushroom Growth of Vigilante Groups in Jungle Mahal

Alarming growth of Maoists, murder of CPM activists, writs of the Maoists, the police's inability to neutralise the ultras etc. perplexed the ruling party, especially, the CPM. It realised that the cadres were the target of annihilation who were fast losing faith on the leadership and the party's hold and authority was under threat. Hence, in pursuit of resisting and neutralising the Maoists the CPM initiated several steps including floating of new satellite units enlisting party cadres and reliable villagers. The object of the new units was to organise parallel units to unleash anti-Maoist propaganda, build anti-Maoist public opinion and outwit the Maoists in gaining local support and sympathy.

On the patronage of the government the local CPM formed a new unit, (1) Gana Pratirodh Manch. Villagers were either coxed or forced to join the new unit. Truly, it failed to make any positive dent in jungle mahal since the people were hostile to the CPM and change of the political guard was in the cards. After TMC formed the government it lost its bite and faced a natural death. Later the CPM formed Santras Bodhi Pratirodh Committee to mobilise the people against the Maoists.

(i) People's committee against police atrocity (PCAPA) was formed in November 2008, ostensively to redress grievances of the people but in practice, its task was to keep the Maoist movement alive. Duties assigned to misguide or neutralise the security forces and clandestinely push the Maoist movement ahead. Indeed, it indulged in disorder, violence, abductions, arsons, murders, bandhs etc.

New units formed after defeat of the LF government: Nari Izzat Bachao Committee.

(ii) After TMC formed the government, Nari Izzat Rancho Committee was founded at the behest of the Maoists. A large number of fair sex from the tribal community either joined or patronized it. They took part in meetings, processions and antigovernment agitations. In fact, strength of the unit was reckonable and its response was encouraging. The impetuous members were guided by single minded devotion and were critical of the new government for failing to adhere to election promises. In initial stage, Sm Jyotshna Mahato was the secretary of the unit. Later she showed volte face and joined the Trinamul Congress.

The new ruling party (TMC) in addition to the offer of peace talk tried relentlessly to build anti Maoist public opinion. TMC understood the Maoists' sinister design for forming organisations and jack up agitations through the new units from behind. Therefore, it decided to recalcitrant the ultras and in that pursuit, formed several units.

(iii) In August 2011, Jana Jagaran Manch was formed. On November 6, 2011, its members were holding a meeting at Masandihi area. Maoists fired at them. Rup Chand Soren, an activist received bullet injury. Meeting was disrupted and the panic stricken participants took shelter in nearby houses.

(iv) In November 2011, Gram Rakhi Bahini (village Defence Army) was formed in grass root level to counter the rebels. The Chief Minister during her visit to Purulia on November 12, 2011, gave a call for forming resistance groups. In sixty villages of Ayodhya hill, Purulia district, the Gram Rakhi Bahini was organised. Unofficially they were equipped with arms but the TMC denied it. They used to screen entry of outsiders into the villages and maintained surveillance on the movements of the ultras.

(v) Jungle Mahal Unnyan Birodhi Pratirodh Manch (JMUBM) was founded by Maoist, Aghoor Hembrem who defected from the parent Maoist outfit and established this anti-Maoist vigilante unit. He organised anti Maoist agitation in Aydhoya hill. Chief Minister Mamata Banerjee profusely praised him. She said that he put a brave face to sever tie with the Maoists and built the new unit. As he was a target of the Maoists, he was provided six security personnel for his protection.

(vi) Jungle Mahal Santi Committee was founded. Posters on the walls of the houses were displayed urging the local people to rise against boorish treatment, barbarous torture, indiscriminate killing etc. unleashed by the "band party," meaning the Maoists. Local people mockingly called the Maoists, "band party." In the posters anti Maoist feeling was highlighted, and written, "We want peace, roads, drinking water, development" but why the "band party" creating obstacle to the developments?

(vii) On TMC's initiative, a unit was formed with insolent elements, called, "Bhirab Bahini." They used muscle power and preferred to settle scores by rough and ready method.

The frontal organisations of the Maoists vehemently criticised and opposed the Bhirab Bahini. Nari Izzat Bachao Committee wrote to the CM Mamata Banerjee on October 16, 2011, on the eve of her visit to jungle mahal to ban Bhirab Bahini and Gana jagaran Manch for the interest of restoring peace and beginning of the peace talk. Dr Vinayak Sen, a pro Maoist, quipped about the Gana jagaran Manch. He said that it was similar to Salwa Jadum operated in Chhattisgarh and banned by the Apex Court.

(viii) Meanwhile, CPM formed Santras Birodhi Pratirodh Committee to counter the Maoists and spear head agitation by the people of the tribal community. It used to threaten the villagers not to attend any meeting and participate any bandh.

(ix) In January 2009, under influence of the Maoists, a committee named "Janogoner Committee" was formed to prepare ground for initiating agitations. Similar committees were formed in Bankura and Purulia districts. The new unit held several public meetings in Maoist strong holds in three districts. Frankly speaking, extended activities of the Maoists in Lalgarh areas had brought the territory practically under their control where semblance of administration and law and order was absent. Truly, it transformed into a police free zone. Maoists set up control room, wireless network and established a training camp in Harulia–Kumarbandh. Trees were cut down, bushes were cleared. A field range for target practice (testing of weapons) was made for undertaking practice regularly.

In close vicinity several strong hide-outs were built. People used to see them patrolling in sizeable strength with arms abandoning earlier practice of deploying squad with meager strength. In fact, Lalgarh gained considerable strategic importance and therefore Maoists established training ground there. State police wanted to reclaim the areas but was at a loss seeing the expanded strength and influence of the Maoists and ungrudging support of the tribal populace. State government issued stern warning to the rebels as the state had to ensure safety and security to the people for the Lok Sabha poll scheduled to be held in May 2009.

(x) After attack on the CM's convoy, the police's excesses stirred sentiment of the tribal community. The leaderless people in a double quick time formed a committee named, Police Santras Birodhi Janasadhran Manch (PSBJM), in December 2008 to proceed with the agitation. Chatradhar Mahato was selected its secretary. Road blockade in Lalgarh and adjacent areas continued. The body urged the people to boycott the police socially and stop their entry into the villages. One of the leaders Chatradhar Mahato said that 15000 people from tribal community carrying their traditional weapons with bows and arrows assembled at Dharampur under the banner of the PBSBM. Other organisations, Lodha Sabar Samity, Jana Surakha Samity were coming in a procession from Kantapahari and other places to join. The congregation declared that blockade would continue till the police publicly apologized for the excesses committed.

(xi) Chatra Samaj was formed in June 2009. Interestingly, the United Students' Democratic Federation (USDF), a Kolkata based naxalite students out-fit decided to join hands with Jharkhand Students' Federation (JSF) and Chatra Samaj to form a united forum named All Bengal Students' Union (ABSU). These organisations were pro Maoists and keen supporters of the Left Wing Extremism, expressed solidarity with the PCAPA.

(xii) Durniti-O-Samrajyaba Agrashan Birodhi Ganatantrik Manch (DSABGM), an umbrella organisation of the Maoists was founded in August, 2011 planning to organise fresh Maoist movements in jungle mahal. Its secretary Ashok Jivan Ghosh was trying to rope students, teachers, intellectuals from Kolkata to back the agitation. In a mammoth gathering in the school compound of Lalgarh Ram Krishna Vidyalaya on August 31, 2011, several speakers criticised the TMC government under leadership of Mamata Banerjee for arrests, police raids, banning processions, slapping criminal cases etc. on innocent villagers. ADPR participated in the meeting and shared the dais. Dramatist Nabarun Bhattacharjee, son of renowned novelist Sm Mahaseta Devi, present on the dais vehemently criticized the government. He said that the CPM's "harmad" bahini is replaced by the TMC's jallad (butcher) bahini." In fact, the out-fit was eyeing to found committees across the state to contest panchayat election, and contemplating to shift its HQ from West Mednipur to Kolkata. I addressed the gathering, interacted with father of Chatradhar Mahato who presided over the meeting. Sm Laxmimoni Tudu wife of late Maoist leader Lal Mohan Tudu, Sm Niyati Mahato wife of Chatradhar Mahato and several local participants addressed the gathering. I had the opportunity to elicit their feeling. Women formed about forty percent of the gathering who were innocent house wives, having no link with the Maoists. They preferred peace and were keen to live happily with family. They were afraid of the pitiless rebels and therefore, were compelled to obey them. They were highly critical of the new government for not fulfilling its pre-election promises.

(xiii) Lalgarh Manch was founded by a civil society from Kolkata. Its object was to take up the causes for the tribal population of jungle mahal. They were not allowed to enter into Lalgarh area as prohibitory order under section 144 CRPC was promulgated in Lalgarh.

(xiv) In addition, several splinter groups came forward to support the movement. People's Cultural and Literary Forum and Matangini Mahila Samity were active and supported the movement. MS Dibalina Chakraborty, a former student of Jadavpur University and a member of Nandigram Zonal Committee convened a press conference in the campus of the university.

(xv) The Manch Rebel organised poster drive in large scale in Kolkata from August 2011. Maoist posters were noticed in Sealdah main and south stations, Belghoria, Khardah, Titagarh, Sodepur, Agarpara railway stations. Posters were seen right on the walls of Calcutta university, Jadavpur university, Presidency University, Coffee house and in several metro stations, near Pandit Vidya Sagar statue inside college square, Barisha Housing complex. It was also seen in many places of greater Kolkata, Nadia, Uttarpara etc. It was seen in good number in market places of Salt Lake, Kolkata. It was suspected that many squad leaders active in jungle mahal were students of Jadavpur University. Activists of United Students Democratic Front (USDF) and several pro Maoist student organisations proposed to hold a conference in College street, Kolkata on November 9, 2011. ADPR criticized the TMC government alleging that it has planned to build a "Thangari Bahini" (Torture force) with ten thousand recruits who would be utilised to cow down the people by muscle power.

(xvi) Police of Lalgarh and the local CPM leaders jointly formed an anti-Maoist committee aiming at frustrating agitations spear-headed by the ultras. However, it was far from purposeful and failed to produce any tangible result.

Maoists raised a hue and cry against vigilante groups aiming at curbing the Maoist movement. The new government (TMC) announced that a special police force was going to be raised with 10000 youths belonging to jungle mahal. Obviously, it was an attempt to provide employment to the tribal youths which made the Maoists uncomfortable. They distributed leaflets warning the villagers, especially, the youths of dire consequences, if one happened to join the special police force.

Sordid competitive spirit to form vigilante groups and their mush room growth hardly served any useful purpose. Interestingly, Maoists, CPM, TMC and the police were in the fray. Political parties were keen to cling on their power, authority and influence on the local people outwitting the political rivals. Maoists were equally anxious to maintain their ground. Unfortunately, police only followed the instruction of the ruling party on the pretext of police community relation. However, as event moved apace, the security forces gained upper hand, and the rule of law gradually regained its foot hold, the vigilante groups lost importance, decayed and faced natural death.

People's Committee Against Police Atrocity (PCAPA)

PCAPA was one of the frontal organisations of the Maoists operated in jungle mahal. It was founded on November 16, 2008, immediately after attack on the Chief Minister's convoy, in November 2, 2008. Lal Mohan Tudu, and Sidhu Soren, committed Maoists, became its President and secretary respectively. Chatradhar Mahato, brother of dreaded Maoist leader Sasadhar Mahato was made the convener. After the abortive attempt on the convoy of the Chief Minister the police unleashed wanton excesses which forced the aggrieved villagers to form the above organisation. As per the convener the oppressed and under privileged rural population of the region wanted a nonpolitical platform from where they could raise concerted voice and fight for their rights. He added that 82 innocent villagers had been languishing in jails in Jharkhand and West Bengal for raising voice and protesting against corrupt police forces. Happily, people had been joining the new unit in large number shunning party affiliation. Triumph of the Maoists forced the CPM cadres and activists to pull their rein and operate defensively. PCAPA took control of two strong-holds of the CPM, Dharampur and Senjuti located on the outskirt of Lalgarh. Its insolent elements attacked and razed Kolaimuri police camp under Salboni police station. It issued ultimatum to the police administration to disband the police camp at Koima. Lal Mohan Tudu said, "We want all police camps in the area to be withdrawn. They only help the CPM in attacking our supporters." Superintendent of Police refused to comment. However, the police did not take the matter lightly. Police issued alert notices to all concerned and asked them to repulse any attempt to damage or over run any camp, inducted a big contingent of police force to disarray the new out-fit. PCAPA, in fact, attempted to reorganise the tribal units, keep the tempo of the Maoists' violence going, disarray the CPM cadres and keep the Red's influence and control intact. Administration was alarmed watching growth of the unit. Leaflets were distributed urging the people not to join the unit. Importantly, office bearers of the PCAPA were directly involved in the Red movement. They were propagating the Maoist ideal right from the grass root level and succeeded in building a formidable support base for the extremists. Frankly speaking, the out-fit was operating on the secret instructions of the Maoists. Sidhu Soren developed expertise in planting and exploding land mines. He was made the Chief Executor of the operation war. However, evidence was adequate that the leaders were directly linked with the Maoists and operating on the secret instructions of the Maoists.

PCAPA was formed ostensively to redress grievances of the people but in practice, its task was to keep the Maoist movement alive. Duties assigned to them to misguide or neutralise the security forces and clandestinely push the Maoist movement ahead. It carried cudgel for the Maoists, indulged in violence, disorder, abductions, arson, murders, bandhs etc. Immediately after formation it organised indefinite blockade in West Medinapur, Bankura and Puralia districts of jungle mahal and stopped entry of vehicular traffic, including police vehicles into the districts. It arranged a public meeting at Lodhasuli near Jhargram protesting against arrests, police raids, harassments and police excesses. About three thousands males and females from the tribal community armed with bows, arrows and traditional weapons attended the meeting. Chatradhar Mahato cautioned the government that the move to stop the tribals to take part in processions, meeting carrying their traditional weapons would force them to initiate greater mass movement. Since it is an integral part of their culture and heritage any attempt to curb it would be opposed with all strength. The congregation cheered it with beating of drums, shouting slogans, danced brandishing bows and arrows. An ultimatum was issued to three sponge iron factories functioning in jungle mahal to shut down factories within seven days as high grade pollution from smoke and chemical discharge had been accelerating health hazard.

Thereafter road blockades programme started. Agitators damaged roads, culverts or chocked public thoroughfares placing tree trunks, branches, stone boulders, heaps of bricks etc. completely shutting ingress and egress of vehicles. They decided to boycott the police and stop entry of cops into the villages. Disruption of the movement of traffic continued for several days. Even carts carrying food grains were not allowed to proceed which put the common people in untold hardship.

Wanton Outrages by the PCAPA

It recklessly unleashed outrages, murdered singling out CPM cadres, supporters and villagers on mere suspicion. On December 27, 2008, in a rural fair at Bhimpur, two PCAPA activists were killed by the joint forces in a gun battle. On February 14, 2009, Sujit Panda aged 32, a CPM Zonal committee member, of Binpur I, Lalgarh was shot dead by the PSBPC. On April 7, 2009, Maoists attacked house of Chandi Karan a member of the CPM Zonal committee. Local people resisted the attack and caught two suspects who belonged to the PCAPA and handed them over to the Binpur police station. A gun and a country made pistol were recovered from them. As a retaliatory step PCAPA abducted nine CPM cadres from village Baradanga under Sarenga police station, district Bankura. CPM cadres attempted to rescue them. But a strong group of tribal women and children armed with bows and arrows made a human wall and blocked the road and thereby frustrated the attempt. In June 2009, it made a recruitment drive at Lalgarh on behalf of the Maoists. Secondly, it called a meeting at Lalgarh and threatened to make the local Vodafone towers inoperative if the company refused to dismiss two employees who were office bearers of the local CPM. They demanded that the company must take their supporters in the places of the persons after dismissal. Chatradhar Mahato complained that CPM plotted to kill four PCAPA activists who had been missing for the last four months. On June 1, 2009, at about 7 PM, a mob armed with bows and arrows attacked the medical officer assigned for general duty, attendants, and class IV employees of Odolchua primary health centre in Belpahari block and forced them to leave the place. Mob snapped electric connection of the health center, destroyed lifesaving vaccines of polio, chicken pox, measles and T B. On June 6, 2009, the medical officer of Chilkigarh block hospital was kept under lock and key for 12 hours by the activists of the PCAPA. MO Manoj Munda of Binpur rural hospital was forced to rush to Jhargram sub divisional hospital to attend to a patient of the unit. On June 8, 09, PCAPA activists assaulted doctors, nurses and other staff performing duties in Belpahari, Lalgarh, Binpur, Salboni health centers. About 80 panic-stricken government doctors, nurses and other staff working in different hospitals and health centers in jungle mahal wanted to quit jungle mahal.

On June 9, 2009, PCAPA and CPM activists clashed at Debgram near Lalgarh. Bows, arrows, bombs, fire arms were freely used and many were injured. PCAPA demanded release of nine comrades arrested in June and detained in Jharkhand jail. They pressed their demands, cut roads in many places and disrupted traffic. They declared that agitation would continue till the comrades were released. On September 5, 2009, police shot dead Hamenta Deb Singh and Jaladhar Mohato two activists of the PCAPA and arrested two others. The outfit called bandh for 12 hours protesting against killing. Bandh was well responded at Lalgarh, Salboni, Binpur, Belpahari, Ramgarh. It was observed partially in Bankura and Purulia districts. In many places people demonstrated and protested vehemently. Fourteen women demonstrators were arrested. On December 10, 2009 Chatradhar Mahato called a press conference and criticised police action. On the same day, Maoists killed four CPM cadres. Another was killed at Bandawan, Purulia. On December 11, 2009, a CPM activist was killed within Salboni police station jurisdiction.

On January 3, 2010, its activists kidnapped Anath Singh and Hiteshwar Singh from Shyamnagar, Belpahari area who were activists of Gana Pratirodh Committee, the CPM sponsored out-fit. Both were taken to nearby jungle and beheaded. On the following day their life less bodies were recovered. PCAPA took responsibility for the murder and stated that they were informers of the police. On December 30, 2009, the PCAPA militia removed several pandrol clips from the railway track lying between Jhargram and Jamshedpur stations damaging about 400 meters of track near Gidhni railway station, South Eastern railway. Local people suspecting the foul play, informed the station master. Purusattam express bound for Delhi was promptly stopped and thereby a catastrophe was averted. On October 20, 2009, they set fire on a timber laden truck on Ramgarh Goaltore road near Kadasoli forest. In second week of December 2009, police shot dead a PCAPA activist on suspicion that he was harboring the rebels. On January 2, 2010, joint forces opened fire and killed three PCAPA activists who participated in a rally at Joynagar and Tilbjoni villages under Lalgarh police station. Mob fired at the police. The joint forces after lathi charge and firing tear gas shells fired 20 rounds from rifles. On April 2, 2010, PCAPA took out a procession at Lalgarh and Salboni under its banner opposing the proposed visit of the Union Home Minister P. Chidambaram to Lalgarh on April 4, 2010. Rallies were held in five places defying prohibitory order promulgated under section 144 Cr.P.C. Processionists shouted slogans, "Chidambaram go back", waved black flags and asked to observe, "Black Day" on April 4, 2010.

In the meantime, CPM formed Santras Birodhi Pratirodh Committee to counter the Maoists and to spear head agitations by the tribal community. Nirmal Sardar, aged 40, an activist of the PSBJM was murdered. His bullet ridden body was found in a jungle close to Talpukuria village under Belpahari police station. Chatradhar Mahato blamed the CPM for the gruesome murder, called a meeting and bandh for 24 hours in the locality. CPM backed Santras Birodhi Pratirodh Committee threatened the villagers not to attend the meeting and to participate in the bandh. Men and women in large number from the tribal community attended the meeting and observed the bandh. CPM, however, denied its involvement in the crime.

On the allegation of misappropriating rice allotted for the mid-day meals scheme for the students of Boita school under Lalgarh police station, PCAPA activists garlanded the members of the managing committee of the school with shoes and paraded them through the village. They held a rally at village Bamal defying the prohibitory order. About 2000 supporters, mostly women participated and demanded withdrawal of the combined forces. The joint forces opened fire to disperse the agitated crowd and shot Biplap Sahoo dead, an activist and injured ten others near a camp at Salboni. All these incidents took place after the anniversary week observed by the PLGA.

Maoist armed wing PLGA observed the anniversary week for the establishment of the People's Liberation Guerrilla Army from Ist December to December 8. Its object was to strengthen the PLGA. Comrade Bikash, the secretary of West Medinapur-Bankura-Purulia Zonal Committee issued a press release. Leaflets were distributed in various parts of the Zone. Police felt that preparation was afoot to gear up violent activities. On December 1, 2009, school teacher Satya Kinkar Mandi, another leader of JMM and an activist of Gana pratirodh Committee were gunned down at village Sirishboni under Goaltore police station.

Chadradhar Mahato, the convener and later secretary of the PCAPA was arrested on September 26, 2009 from village Birkand near Lalgarh. State Home Secretary said that he was arrested after his link with the Maoists was confirmed. PCAPA called bandh for two days protesting against the arrest. Bandh was total in West Medinapur, Bankura and Purulia districts and partially observed in Jharkhand and Odisha. On October 3, 2009, there was a blast in between Kantadih and Urma railway station in Adra division, followed by second blast between Poisata and Mahadevshal railway stations, in Chakradharpur division. It disrupted train services for about ten hours.

On April 25, 2009, about fifteen thousand men and women of the adivasi community armed with bows and arrows and their traditional weapons assembled at Esplanade, Kolkata city led by Chatradhar Mahato. A procession marched from the College Squire covering a long distance, joined the meeting venue at Esplanade. A sizeable number of adivasis from West Medinapuar, Bankura and Purulia arrived and participated in the meeting. In fact, traffic in Central Kolkata went out of gear. Adivasi leaders addressed the congregation and demanded development and economic progress for the adivasi community.

Police complained that whenever the police raided a village and tried to nab an ultra they faced stiff resistance from the villagers backed by the PCAPA. Its leaders refuting the allegation stated, "Our movement is against police atrocities. We are not Maoists. Sidhu had no link with the Maoists." Indeed, when joint forces were advancing towards Lalgarh more than ten mines were blasted to arrest their advance. In addition, police had to defuse more than twenty land mines planted right on the track. Whatever might be the alibi, it was imperative that the PCAPA were operating adhering to the diktats of the Maoists and enforcing their instructions. On April 22, 2009, PCAPA submitted 23 point charter of demands including withdrawal of criminal cases and banning of the police's entry in selected villages. The state Home Secretary stated that their genuine demands would be reviewed sympathetically. But demand of prohibiting police's entry into villages could not be accepted. However, anticipating that the ultras might foment fresh trouble, the state decided to seal the border with Jharkhand. Simultaneously, stern warning was issued to the ultras to shun violence and come forward for a dialogue.

Meanwhile, Lal Mohan Tudu, President of the unit, was gunned down by the security forces on February 15, 2010, near his house at village Narcha. In his place Kanai Hasda was selected. Sidhu Soren, the general secretary of the PCAPA was killed on July 26, 2010 in an encounter with the security forces in Metala forest near Goaltore. After arrest of Chatradhar Mahato on September 26, 2009 Asit Mahato was put in his place. PCAPA had 33 members in its central committee. Arrests and casualty of the office bearers used to be filled in promptly from the list of the members. The armed wing of the out-fit, Sidhu Kanhu Gana Militia was formed in October 2009, headed by Sidhu Soren. It was also called "People's

Militia." After he was killed, the vacancy was promptly filled in placing Tota Hembram. PCAPA in a congregation paid "Lal Salam" to four slain leaders of the out-fit to commemorate their memory. They raised four columns in the names of the departed leaders: (i) Uma Kanta Mahato, the main accused in Gyaneswari Express train sabotage (ii) Lal Mohan Tudo (iii) Sidhu Soren and (iv) Sarabala Mahato. They asked the villagers to attend the ceremony. However, after arrest of Chatradhar Mahato activities of the PCAPA showed a declining trend. Right from beginning of the 2010, the success of the joint forces and later death of Kishanji, was an alarm bell for the Maoists. Morale of the Maoists received another fatal blow after Maoist Sasadhar Mahato, a dreaded leader was killed in an encounter in March 2011. Meanwhile, the TMC formed the government in May 2011. Indeed, the political scenario of the state abruptly changed. It was not clear as to how the new government was going to counter the Maoist threat.

CPM Government's Insouciance in Tackling the PCAPA

Allegations poured in that joint forces had been harassing the family members of the Maoist leaders and activists. On August 20, 2011, the family members of Chatradhar Mahato were attacked either by the joint forces or insolent elements of the TMC. PCAPA called Bandh on August 24, 2011 against terror and attack let loose by the joint forces. Again, goons of the TMC attacked the house of the leader of Jhargram Students' Federation. As he was not present in his house, they assaulted his brother. PCAPA observed bandh for 24 hours on September 19, 2011 protesting against high handedness by joint forces and for carrying out incessant raids in Bersa jungle, Ayodha hilla in search of Maoist leader Bikram.

Increased criticism against the state government for reluctance to initiate firm action against the Maoists was the talk of the time. Even abortive attempt on the Chief Minister failed to generate positive reaction in government level. Meanwhile, pressure from the union government to disarray the ultras and restore the rule of law in the Maoist dominated areas, coupled with growing peoples' demand to save and protect the hapless people from the Maoists' wrath ultimately forced the government to come to its senses. Secondly, the CPM cadres and supporters were the targets of the Maoists. In fact, several cadres were attacked and killed, many houses and party offices were either set on fire or ransacked. Exodus of the cadres and supporters from jungle mahal put the left parties and state government in abysmal anxiety. The cadres so long relied on the party's help and protection by the police. Unfortunately, police failed to curb the blood thirsty ultras and protect the cadres. Hence, triumph of the Maoists forced the CPM cadres and activists to pull their rein and work for the party either defensively or indifferently. The party leadership realised that if protection to the cadres was not ensured they might shift allegiance to other party or quit the party which was likely to be a fatal blow to the party. Lastly, the peace loving people of jungle mahal might not vote for the

Left Front and thereby vote bank in three districts might be drastically eroded. In fact, fear that the party's strength and people's support for the CPM might peter out and put the CPM in log-jam finally worked and forced the Chief Minister to agree to the joint operation.

Interestingly, the Maoists so long had been facing counter operations initiated by the state police force, who were ill trained, armed with archaic weapons and deficient in jungle operations. Hence the Maoists were not facing any flinty resistance and hence there was no threat to their rapid growth. However, the central paramilitary forces are well trained, well equipped and sufficiently experienced in tackling the terrorists. CRPF and BSF battalions have been commendably fighting the cross border terrorism in Jammu and Kashmir. Hence, joint operation frightened the Maoists as they visualised obstinate contest and do or die confrontations. Therefore, they raised their voice against joint operation through various forums. Truly, PCAPA is the brain child of the Maoists and one of the active forums for anti-joint operation and antigovernment initiative in jungle mahal. The PCAPA took active part in agitations to stop and withdraw joint operation.

Tribal Agitations and Mass Upsurge in Jungle Mahal

Failure to prevent attack on the CM's convoy put the police in disgrace and scathing criticism. Police thought to retrieve the lost ground by harsh police actions. However, wanton excesses unleashed by the police on the pretext of neutralising the Maoists back fired. On November 5, 2008, the police organised an operation into Chhotopelia, Borapelia, Banshberia and Kantapahari. Arbitrary raids, indiscriminate arrests, brutal torture, rough and ready method in treating the villagers only increased resentment of the local people. In fact, police conducted raids in 35 villages, arrested countless innocent people including four school lads, assaulted and injured many women, damaged many huts and virtually created a reign of terror. Hence, instead of normalising the situation it enhanced anger and discontentment of the aggrieved people who spontaneously rose up and organised resistance groups in many pockets of jungle mahal. From November 7, about 10,000 tribals, males and females armed with their traditional weapons, bows and arrows, joined the agitation. They either dug up or blocked the main roads by felling trees, tree trunks, branches, boulders, bricks etc. and thereby completely stopped traffic towards Lalgarh. Their aim was to boycott police and administration and prevent entry of the police to Lalgarh and its adjacent places. In fact, news of angry protest and demonstration spread like wild fire from place-to-place. The tribal community spontaneously displayed an unprecedented unity and determination to silence the police's horrendous excesses. Movement of the vehicular traffic was completely paralysed. Police personnel were unable to move inside to maintain law and order. Indeed, ambience was highly tense and explosive; a clear indicative of a likely outburst at any moment was imminent.

On November 11, I attempted to reach Lalgarh from Medinapur town. Leaving the high way, we took left turn and driving about 12 kms towards Lalgarh we had to stop as the road was dug up and the culvert was damaged. We had to leave the vehicles, crossed the obstacle and walked some distance. Inter action with many agitators and villagers including weaker sex gave unmistakable impression that a civil war was knocking at the door. Needless to say, the agitators had received impetus and support from the Maoists to intensify the agitation. Frankly speaking, the police's barbarous excesses were the root cause of exemplary unity and spirit of protest movement displayed by the tribal community. Undeniably, the police's folly and excesses led to the upheaval of a community who are simple, unassuming, and inoffensive and law abiding. Luckily, villagers helped us to reach Lalgarh through village paths and jungle. It was a great opportunity to inter act with the people, know their sentiment, impact of the Maoist movement and the police and the district administration's apathy.

Tribal communities from Jharkhand and Bihar pledged their support to the movement. Many intellectuals, educationists and progressive elements vehemently criticized the government and the police for brutal excesses. Agitation and road blockade continued for about a month. Meanwhile, angry protest spread to Bankura and Puralia districts. Regrettably, the police hierarchy never initiated any tangible step to dissuade the erring policemen to indulge in excesses. Similarly, the Chief Minister and the state government failed to curb police excesses and pull up the delinquent police personnel. Simultaneously, the CM was indifferent to take cognizance of the growing upsurge. Indeed, exposure by the print and electronic media, cry of the impartial people and steady growth of public opinion lamentably failed to sensitise the CM. He was ambivalent and did not feel it prudent to direct the police to refrain from treating the people harshly and halt all kinds of aberrance and obnoxious excesses.

Meanwhile, the PCAPA circulated a charter of demands to stir the agitation. One of the demands was that the Superintendent of Police West Medinapur district should say, "Sorry holding his ears" for the excesses committed by the police. On the information that a large contingent of CRPF and other central forces were going to be deployed soon for joint operation, convener Chhatradhar Mahato reacted sharply and said, "By sending a large contingent of security forces to Lalgarh the government intends to repeat barbarism perpetrated in November 2008." On the question that the tribals were carrying weapons while demonstrating, he stated, "traditional weapons have a religious association for the tribals, just a Kripan for the Sikhs." However, he indicated that they were willing to enter into dialogue with the government if invited.

CPM, in the meantime, in a conference held in Birbhum district resolved to dislodge the Maoists who should be prevented from developing contact with the people. Secondly, people should be sensitised on anti-Maoist sentiment and atrocities let loose by them. CPM blamed the opposition parties, especially, the Trinamul Congress party for the spurt in Maoist violence on the territory lying on the border of West Bengal and Jharkhand. They alleged that the TMC had been providing shelter, clandestinely patronizing the Maoists and fueling unrest. According to them, police arrested two Maoists on suspicion from Rampurhat near Jharkhand border. But the TMC leaders defended them pleading that the suspects were supporters of the TMC, not Maoists and therefore arrest was malafide.

Flurry of protest movement spear headed by the PCAPA took gargantuan shape, broadly, for the police's reckless excesses and high-handedness. The entire tribal community was up-in-arms which provided extra ordinary boost to the Maoists to undertake deadly offensives. Unfortunately, outrages, instead of ushering peace and stability, united the tribal community for a determined and stubborn mass agitation. The Maoists adroitly capitalized the peoples' sentiment, provided leadership from behind and made their presence felt in jungle mahal. Police and central forces started co-ordinated operation against the Maoists from June 20, 2009. Prior to the joint operation the Maoists warned the government for provoking them for going for a large scale and protracted violence. The Maoists said," the guerrilla war has began and it would not be an easy battle for the security forces." One of the top Maoist leaders, Koteswar Rao alias Kishanji warned that the government had to pay dearly for trying to suppress the peoples' movement by police action. Kishanji, a land mine expert trained by the LTTE, stated, "The joint forces would have to face public resistance in many places. Let them come and experience it." Admittedly, keeping pace with the joint operation the Maoists struck back with consummate vigour and resoluteness. On June 19, 2009, the Maoist attacked a police patrol and injured eight policemen. In a fierce gun battle and a land mine blast at Kandasole area, a villager and an activist of the PCAPA were shot dead. Kishanji warned, "Those who are responsible for the violence will not be able to escape the people's anger." Undeniably, PCAPA, a brain child of the Maoists performed well to mobilise the tribal population and keep the strident movement agile.

CHAPTER EIGHT

Extremist Growth in Andhra Pradesh, Birth of the CPI (ML) People's War (PW), Government's Ambivalence, the Idea of the Red Corridor, Maoist Threat Contained, Maoist Activities in Maharastra

The Naxal movement in Andhra Pradesh originated in mid-sixties. It had no link with the Naxals or Naxal movement flourishing in West Bengal. Comrade Charu Mazumdar was lukewarm to the extremist movement growing fast in Andhra Pradesh. However, a brief history of the growth of the extremists, their activities, internal dissensions, jealousy and split will throw sufficient light on its progress and hindrances. In this respect sickening details of jealousy, rivalry, squabbles, conflicts have been depicted in chapter one. Curious readers may go through the relevant portion of the chapter to know the developments. In fact, abject failure of the uprising in Srikakulam, dissension, in-fighting and exasperating obduracy of the leaders of the frustrated groups collapsed the extremist movement in the state. Fragmented groups were in moribund state. Lust for power and ego clashes of the group leaders accelerated the fall of the disarrayed groups. At that juncture comrade K. Sitaramaiah played a crucial and well-meaning role, brought many dissidents and rival groups together and re-organised the movement. Under his leadership some amount of stability returned and concrete shape of the out-fit was noticed.

The CPI (ML) People's War, was formed on April 22, 1980 on his initiative. Since then, the People's War (PW) persuaded the extremist movement in Andhra Pradesh and gained considerable success. Soon the PW penetrated in Odisha, Bastar region, Madhya Pradesh and part of West Bengal. In three districts of West Bengal it was known as "Jana Juddha" In Bihar, rivalry and bloody conflict between the PW and the Maoist Communist Centre (MCC) marred the movement and soiled its image. Eventually, PW and several splinter groups active in Andhra Pradesh burying differences merged with the MCC. Merger formed the new out-fit, the CPI (Maoist) in September 2004. It gave a significant boost to the extremist movement, better known as the Maoist movement. Morale of the extremists received fresh and mighty push. The invigorated combined strength increased the canvas of operation, man power and resources and gained formidability. They discovered that terrain in many pockets was eminently suitable for building hide-outs, training ground and recruitment centers for the cadres. Secondly, the tribal population was responsive and suitable for carrying the banner of the Maoist movement. Hence, they zealously stepped up activities in tribal areas of Dandakaranya, Odisha and Bastar region, Madhya Pradesh, in tandem with the local rebels. Thirdly, in many villages located in remote areas vigil of the police and the administration was either slack or absent. Therefore, activities of the extremists could easily be followed up without any check. Moreover, poverty stricken and exploited tribal community could easily be inspired to come under influence of the ultras. In fact, the ultras were wise enough to judge the local condition and sentiment of the deprived people. As a matter of fact, the PW's increased influence over the rural mass worked well. Fiendish activities, annihilation of many VIPs, abduction of several public servants etc. threatened the safety, security and rule of law. Over and above, the state's perplexity either to placate or disarray the ultras indirectly helped them to enhance their influence and control on the poor and repressed rural mass. Truly, writs of the ultras ran over vast area and put the police and administration in back foot. Finally, the state government woke up and decided to curb the Maoists' threat at any cost. Specialised and competent security forces were raised, intelligence network galvanized and rural developmental programmes were taken up and marshalled in right earnest.

PW succeeded in extending its turf in three states and let loose violence, blood curdling activities. It killed innocent persons, cops, threatened safety and security and created an ambience of panic and fear. In fact, failure of the police and administration to curb flagrance and maintain law and order posed a flinty threat to the people. Hence, rural mass throbbed with panic and fear were forced to support and show allegiance to the rebels. Meanwhile, the police sincerely tried to regain control and restore rule of law. A new force, especially trained and equipped to combat the rebels, called the "Greyhounds" was raised. Truly, the Greyhounds' relentless raids on the hide outs of the ultras, encirclement of the camps, demolition of the training camps and successful encounters forced many ultras to give up arms, go underground or get mingled with the local crowd. In addition, many hard-core ultras unable to face pressure of the Greyhounds and felt insecure hurriedly shifted to Dandakaranya, Malkangiri and Bastar region. Admittedly, the Greyhounds' commendable performance brought a comfortable respite for the people and administration in Andhra Pradesh. But the migrated rebels intensified unrest and the movement in new territory. In inaccessible forests they established sanctuaries, training grounds and motivated the tribal mass to join the movement. Indeed, many pockets became virtually "liberated area" where writs of the ultras loomed large.

Outrages unleashed by the PW:

> Jealousy, detestable competition for leadership and lust for power smeared unity and progress of the out-fit in the state. The Central Organising Committee (CPC) was formed in 1984. As a sequel to the internal squabble, comrade K.G. Satyamurthy, a dalit and a senior member alleged that members from the upper caste had been dominating the PW. Soon, he and two senior members were expelled from the out-fit. Notably, founder father of the PW, comrade K. Sitaramaiah was expelled from the party in June 1992. Unfortunately, reckless excesses, matchless cruelty and unprecedented atrocity indulged in by the PW is an odious blot on the history of the so called Maoist revolutionary movement. In fact, successive state governments' conciliatory policy or steps to placate the extremists, withdrawal of the ban order etc. instead of decisive action, only encouraged the ultras. Under current of blow hot blow cold policy water downed loss, toil and sacrifices of the security forces. Needless to add, the effete security forces lost heart to out-wit the rebels and keep the situation under control. Evidently, the encouraged ultras' wanton outrages and blood shed shocked the people, who gradually lost faith on the government. During the tenure of the then Chief Minister Chenna Reddy from 1989-91, the PW increased its strength and influence leaps and bounds. PW during the period had killed 400 innocent persons, 55 cops, increased its influence and widened its turf for operation.

Patronage of the Political Parties

NT Rama Rao, a popular cine actor, turned politician founded Telugu Desam Party (TDP). He and his party triumphed and he was elected as the Chief Minister of the state. His tenure from 1983 to 1989, noticed saga of the PW's progress and penetration in a wide section of the rural mass. He complimented the PWs as patriots and pampered them in many ways. However, behind his kind gestures, his hidden design was to secure their support, win the poll battle and remain in political power. Astonishingly, 17 newly elected MLAs of the TDP had secret link with the People's War group. Later several MLAs were inducted into the cabinet who were very friendly with the ultras. Frankly speaking, NTR's so called liberal policy gave free hand to the PW to develop and increase their strength. In his incumbency violence let loose by the PW knew no bounds. PW killed 334 civilians,

54 cops, acquired sophisticated weapons including AK-47 rifles, land mines and high grade explosives. Significantly, within weeks after NTR took the rein of the government PW executed the escape of comrade K. Siraramaiah from Osmania General Hospital, Hyderabad. People were alarmed. Perhaps, later NTR realised his follies and therefore, finally banned the PW in 1987.

The Congress Party Rules the State (1989-94)

TDP was defeated in election and the Congress party formed the government of A P in 1989. The Congress Party was equally keen to muster support of the PW for winning election battle for the State Legislative Assembly in 1989. Sordid understanding between the Congress party and the PW surprised the people. It was equally disturbing that the PW who is guided by an ideology and fighting for the cause of the deprived and down trodden has joined hands with the Congress, who is not free from the capitalists' control. In election held in 1989, in forty constituencies the cadres of the PW secretly supported and worked for the Congress candidates. TDP brought many allegations against the Congress candidates and tried to expose the nexus between the Congress and the PW. However, belying all complaints the Congress party defeated the TDP and returned to power in December 1989. M. Chenna Reddy became the Chief Minister. Interestingly, as recognition to the services rendered by the PW in succeeding in election, the new government lifted ban over the PW immediately, imposed by the NTR. He blatantly adopted the soft policy and made the security forces ineffective in tackling the extremists. In public functions, the Chief Minister used to criticise the police actions taken against the PW. Before a group of journalists the CM obliquely told the senior police officers present, "We are trying to create law out of lawlessness but you people are creating lawlessness out of law. (*The Hindu*, December 29, 1989) The CM approved the idea of functioning of the "People's Court" (Praja Court) mooted by the extremists.

CM ordered to disband the special police force formed by the NTR government to counter the insurgency. Under his order 170 notorious extremists detained in the jail were set free. Many of them were charged for committing heinous crime including murder. In fact, police arrested many of them after a good deal of risky and painstaking effort. CM decided not to enforce the Disturbed Areas Act. As a result, it helped the ultras to spread its influence and control in rural areas. Allegation that many Congress MLAs maintained link clandestinely with the PW was not unfounded. Secondly, basing on the support of the ruling Congress party, the PW planned to chastise or eliminate the CPI(M) activists. The Congress and PW jointly addressed a meeting in November 1990. Meanwhile, the lifting of the ban order upset the sober people and the security forces. But unprecedented exuberance was noticed among the PW activists and their perpetrators. Many underground ultras came out, paraded on the streets rejoicing, dancing and brandishing fire arms. People were afraid of watching the insolent ultras moving in groups carrying fire arms. Many PW leaders suo motu addressed the media personnel. In villages, aggressive posture of the fierce ultras carrying deadly weapons put the villagers in abyss fear and panic. The record of their brutality and cold blooded murder of innocent persons on any pretext unnerved the rural people. In absence of any authority to tame them the thwarted people marked moment anticipating the dooms day. As a matter of fact, CM M. Chenna Reddy's short stint from December 1989 to April 1992 is tainted with the state's abhorrence of pampering the ultras, indecisiveness to neutralise violence and stark deterioration of the law and order. The police and the public servants' morale was broken. Regime, in fact, noticed uninterrupted violence, loss of 400 lives of civilians and 55 cops. Ultras were emboldened to defy law, step up unrest and bloodletting activities. Instead of peace and stability, people were shocked to see growing insecurity, egregiousness and macabre festival of death.

Ultras were emboldened to defy law, stepped up unrest, blood bath and committed crime practicing extreme cruelty. Often a suspect was murdered in front of his wife and children, after beheading the victim his head was kept handing in front of his house. Brutality was deliberately practiced so that ghastly episode might travel from mouth to mouth and caution the people not to antagonise the ultras and ignore their diktat. PW destroyed pump sets used in farm lands for irrigation purpose, set fire on standing crops, took away live stocks, tractors, vehicles. Consequently, thousands of farmers lost livelihood and compelled to flee the villages along with families and took shelter in urban areas. Thousands hectors of agricultural land remained uncultivated which had adverse impact on the rural economy of the state. In many villages PW forced the officials to hand over the official land records, summoned the land owners before the Praja court and passed decrees. The new incumbent Chief Minister N. Janardhan Reddy re-imposed ban on the PW in May 1992 as situation was going out of control.

TDP again returned to power in 1994 receiving mandate of the electorates. Right from the beginning the TDP sought support of the PW for winning election. It distributed party tickets to forty candidates to contest election who had either link with or support of the PW. In pursuit of keeping the ultras in good humour, the TDP government lifted the band from the PW on June 2, 1995. The CM N.T. Rama Rao adhering to commitment and pledges tried to treat the PW leniently. His quixotic steps soon back fired. Unfortunately, bonhomie did not last long. During the first year of the TDP's government the extremists killed more than one hundred civilians and twelve cops. The government came under scathing criticism. In fact, violence piled upon violence. Meanwhile, the son-in-law of the NTR, N. Chandrababu Naidu became the Chief Minister in August 1995. As law and order was slipping through fingers he re-imposed ban on the PW on July 23, 1996. Indeed, his firm actions made him unpopular and target of the PW. The infuriated PW made an assassination attempt on the CM (N.C. Naidu near Alipiri, Tirupati, on October 1, 2003. CM was unhurt and miraculously survived. One

Minister and a MLA accompanying him were critically wounded. General election for the Lok Sabha and the state Assembly was held in April/May 2004. In election campaigns the PW helped the Congress party and the Telangana Rashtriya Samiti (TRS). In rural areas PW prevented the rival parties from entering into the villages and campaign. The Congress Party Returns to Power; Dr. Y S Rajasekhar Reddy Becomes the Chief Minister in May 2004; Peace Talk with the PW:

> The new CM right from the start adopted soft line to deal with the extremists. On June 15, the government announced that the police would suspend all operations in Naxal infested areas for three months. Secondly, ban order on the PW was allowed to lapse on July 22, 2004. Police was withdrawn from many villages. A draft for holding dialogue with the PW was prepared after consultation with ten eminent persons who were pro extremists. Draft contained terms and conditions for discussion. On behalf of the PW three persons signed it. Clause 7, of the draft revealed that the ultras had agreed not to roam in villages and public places carrying weapons. The draft agreement was a well-guarded secret. However, the government took steps to hold talk with the ultras. The state secretary of the PW Rama Krishna declined to obey clause 7 and stated that they would not lay down arms. He claimed that armed struggle is a part of their ideology and not at all an issue for discussion.

PW activists and guerrillas fully armed and putting on uniform came out from Nallamala jungle on October 11, travelled to Guttikonda Bilam (cave) in Guntur district, under police escort to inaugurate a stupam commemorating the visit of comrade Charu Mazumdar in 1968. Ultras got wide publicity through the print and electronic media. People saw hurly burly and insolence of the armed ultras. On September 23, 2004, the Home Minister sent a formal invitation letter to Mr. Varavara Rao, the emissary of the out-fit for direct and face-to-face talk on October 2. Similar invitation was sent to the other ultra out-fits, like Janasakti and others. The Home Minister asked the PW to suggest the venue for the talk. The CM, Dr. Y.S.R. Reddy's gesture to allow the ban order to lapse was lauded by the ultras and their patrons. The H M, felt that neither the PW nor the security forces would carry weapons as discussion was going to be held in a conducive atmosphere. However, police would be present to ensure safety and security of the VIPs. The secretary of the PW made it clear that merger of the PW and the MCC had no bearing on the peace talk. PW leaders were highly enthused on receipt of the opportunity to show strength to the public and to interact with the people directly for the first time. PW announced that its activists would carry weapons in the rally. The government warned that anybody carrying arms inside the city would be arrested. PW asked the government to shift the date of the meeting which was conceded. Thirty rooms of the state guest house Manjeera, in Hyderabad city were booked for the leaders and the activists. Incidentally, the state guest house was inaugurated by the former CM, N.C.B. Naidu. Presence of the police around the guest house was conspicuous. Many absconding ultras carrying heavy rewards on their heads and guerrillas were seen moving freely in the guest house.

Watching the government's move for a dialogue and free movement of the ultras, a section of the people were inclined to believe that the ultras were capable of delivering goods, look into their grievances and provide suitable relief. Stream of visitors from dalit organisations and many parents whose wards were missing, stood in the queue anxiously with petitions in hands hoping to meet the leaders to get some relief. Ironically, a Minister of the state government sought an interview which, however was not granted. About 700 applications from the aggrieved persons were received. However, the much awaited meeting started at 11 AM on October 15, 2004, at Manjeera guest house. PW's emissary G. Kalyan Rao declared that opening remarks from the government and the Naxal out-fits would mark the inauguration of the peace talk. The Home Minister led the nine-member government team. PW leader Rama Krishna headed six-member team. Amar, the leader of Janasakhati with five member-team participated. Home Minister made last minute consultation with the Chief Minister. He was assisted by three Ministers. Several mediators, civil rights activists, academicians, lawyers, retired bureaucrats and prominent journalists were invited to help both sides. However many underground leaders skipped the meeting. The group's top leader Chandrama addressed the gathering. Speaker after speaker vehemently criticized the former CM, N.C.B. Naidu. They alleged that he and his government was accused of killing 1400 innocent persons in fake encounters. A spokesperson of the PW cautioned the government that participation in the peace talk should not be taken a weakness or lack of strength of the ultras, He stated, "We are talking peace from a position of strength and the government must take that into account."

The eleven-point agenda for the talks mainly focused on distribution of land to the landless and reversal of the policy related to the World Bank and unconditional release of the political prisoners including the prisoners serving life sentence. Demand made that salaries of the constables have to be substantially increased. The ultras stressed that 27000 thousand acres of urban land already allotted to the VIPs, multi-nationals and encroached by the illegal land grabbers should be taken back and re-distributed to the poor and landless persons. Comrade Rama Krishna the chief negotiator submitted a list of 43 powerful encroachers including media baron, Ramoji Rao of the ETV channel, Girish Sanghi of Vaartha, Srini Raju (TVG), Ramalinga Raju of Satyam, former CM N.C.B. Naidu, several MNCs, relators and owners of Telegu film industry. It was a master stroke which cornered the government and helped the ultras to earn profuse good will of the cross section of the people. Several names mentioned in the list already figured in the hit-list. The HM kept informing the Chief Minister on the crux of the talk. The CM out right rejected the demands of reclaiming the urban land already allotted, release of the prisoners and hike salary of the constables. Finally, meeting ended without any conclusive decision.

In fact, populist demands made them virtually the darling of the poor and the dalits. It was a majestic spectacle that a large number of poverty stricken and deprived persons congregated to ventilate their grievances seeking intervention from the PW and appropriate remedy. Truly, gumption of the ultras to gain popularity and penetrate into the heart of the neglected people worked well. The government was badly embarrassed. The ultras addressed several public meetings. In a meeting they advised the aggrieved persons to approach the dalams, intimate their problems for proper solution. Leaders addressed the gathering trying to steal their heart, projected the out-fit in a manner that the ultras were viable alternative to take the rein of the government.

In short, their message was loud and clear. The state's appeasement policy to buy peace failed to produce any tangible gain. Critics sarcastically commented that the state was practically rapped on knuckles in an attempt to bring them to terms. Undeniably, the incorrigible and pitiless ultras were firm in the object of destroying the class enemy, go for the people's government through violence and bloodshed. In sum, the state's endeavour to bring peace and tame the ultras through dialogues and negotiations ended in a fiasco. It only exposed the government's weakness, ridiculed the government in the eye of the peace loving people, demoralised the security forces and public servants.

Union Government's Refusal to Participate in Peace Talk

Watching initiative for the peace talk with the PW taken by the government of Andhra Pradesh a question arose in many circles as to why the union government was not taking the leading role for holding such talks or participate in it. Pointing at the Andhra Pradesh's steps for peace talk with the PW, the Union Home Minister, Shivraj Patil was asked to clear his stand on the matter. In a press conference the Union Home Minister categorically stated that the state was at a liberty to decide the matter. He reiterated, "We do not want to advise the state. Whatever you are doing, if done in a proper manner, we will stand by you." However, he said that talk should be unconditional. In fact, Jharkhand, Bihar and Chhattisgarh demanded that the union government should go for dialogues with the ultras for a solution since Naxal menace had been spreading fast. CM Arjun Munda of Jharkhand sought the centre's involvement in the talks. He well come the Andhra Pradesh's good intention and pragmatic initiative. Home Minister of Chhattisgarh stated that dialogue with the ultras under the union government's initiative was desirable. Chief Minister of Odisha declared his intention to invite the ultras for a talk The Union Home Minister Shivraj Patil stated, "You (states) are in a better position to handle the matter ... the centre's and the state's area of jurisdiction was clearly demarcated. If need be we will stand by the state." However, critics felt the UHM diplomatically avoided to take the responsibility on its shoulder.

On September 22, 2004, union Home Minister Shivraj Patil held a meeting with Chief Ministers of nine extremist ridden states in New Delhi. In discussion he made it clear that various economic and social disparities and discriminations have to be eliminated and in Naxal affected areas performance of the administration should be improved and trust of the people on the administration have to be markedly improved.

After merger of the PW and MCC and birth of the CPI (Maoist) the question of entering into dialogue with the government was examined in the out-fit's forum. The newly provisional central committee resolved not to encourage the state units to indulge in talks with any of the state governments in future. Henceforth, the party would ignore all offers for talks and instead would intensify the armed struggle to convert their 14 guerrilla zones into base areas where a people's democratic government would be formed which would be free from all forms of exploitation. A top Maoist leader stated, "We will then increase the areas of our bases, merge several such bases, thereby increasing the area of influences of the people's government till the entire country is liberated." The committee criticized the Andhra Pradesh government and the centre for not being sincere enough in solving the problems of the poor.

PW Extra Active in North Telangana

PW gained substantial strength and made a dent in northern territory of Telengana. They had been running a parallel government where their writs were paramount. In fact, rule of law from the area practically disappeared, as if, the government had abdicated its authority and allowed the ultras to run the show. Government officials were afraid of visiting rural areas, instead they shut themselves up in towns or urban places. Rural development programmes were either neglected or stalled. Deprived and exploited people avidly responded to the ultras' call. The ultras' strongholds are the poorest regions in the state smeared by poverty, exploitation, high child mortality and unemployment. Poverty and unemployment force the youths to join the extremist cadre. On the pretext of enforcing social justice the PW activists were treating people harshly, convening kangaroo court and imposing penalty on the villagers arbitrarily. Guerrilla squads were collecting revenue from the villagers and initiated steps for the welfare of the people. Tanks were renovated, roads were repaired, school buildings were either repaired or constructed. Through the village panchayats they were settling local disputes. Decisions taken by the panchayats were final. Defiance of its order was meted with severe punishment including death. Many are inclined to believe that the ultras will continue to thrive and grow because of socio-economic condition and political instability in Telengana. Unfortunately, political leaders prefer to be in good books of the ultras and seek their help for personal and political purposes. A senior police officer commented, "Almost all elected representatives of North Telengana take help of the Naxals during polls."

In fact, eighteen odd Naxal groups were active and operating in Andhra Pradesh. However, PW was largest and strongest. Its area of operation, strength of the cadre, guerrilla squads, weaponry, resources, influence on the rural mass etc. were too formidable to tackle. Rough estimate revealed that it had 1300 full time underground guerrillas, several thousand militant cadres, countless supporters and sympathizers. In fact, growth of the PW, increasing strength of its man power and sudden spurt in violence put the unprepared police in discomfiture. The sabre-rattling police and the administration lacked experience and resources to counter the ultras with crusading zeal and consummate resolve. Perhaps, the police thought that bullet for bullet to humble the ultras would normalise the tumult. In that pursuit the police committed excesses and sometimes went berserk. From 1988 to 2001, as many as 1034 extremists were killed. Yet, it failed to control the unabated violence, bloodshed, attack on the police posts and death of the cops. Existence of the political parties in Naxal dominated areas was at stake. MPs, MLAs and political leaders were unwilling to take the risk of visiting vulnerable areas of the constituencies without taking heavy armed escort.

From 1988 to 2001, the PW and other extremist groups had killed 243 leaders and activists belonging to TDP, Congress, CPI, CPM and MCPI. PW murdered former MLA A.K. Ranga Das right inside his house and cut his body into pieces. Former Speaker D. Sripada Rao, former Minister T. Hayagrivachari of P.V. Narshima Rao's cabinet were killed. A Madhava Reddy, Minister of Panchayat Raj and former Home Minister in TDP government, was killed in a land mine blast. Chenna Reddy, a sitting MLA, M.S. Reddy, MP from Ongole, K.N. Reddy, a former MP from Adilabad, C.N. Reddy, MLA were killed. Several senior police officers, K.S. Vyas, DIG of the Police Academy, Superintendent of Police of Mahabbobnagar, a Deputy Supdt of Police, Additional IGP were killed. Addl IGP was shot dead near his residence right in Hyderabad city. It was a daring action which shocked the people and demoralised the cops. Many political leaders lost faith on the security forces and secretly negotiated with the leaders of the PW for safety and protection for themselves and the members of the family. In that pursuit many clandestinely paid "protection money" to the out-fits. In fact, almost all representatives of the people from North Telengana were eager to placate the ultras. It is believed that they took help from the ultras either directly or indirectly to win the election battle. Critics sarcastically stated that the veteran actor and founder of the TDP, NTR opened the pandora's box and utilised the PW to cow down the political opponents. Unfortunately, other political parties and leaders only followed his footsteps. Regrettably, the gainers were the extremists.

Since 1967, police arrested thousands of extremists for committing murders, looting banks, destroying public properties and unleashing a reign of terror. Most of the arrested offenders were prosecuted. Unfortunately, none was convicted. Among numerous reasons for such a setback was unwillingness of the witnesses to come forward to depose. In fact, witnesses were so terrorized that they lacked courage to depose against the ultras. Secondly, the police was unable to build an ambience of safety and security, guarantee that no witness would be harmed if they speak against the extremists. Thirdly, investigation by the police was not exhaustive and flawless. Investigating officers could not move freely in terror stricken areas, visit places, interrogate the witnesses, seize vital materials, collect evidence and work out clues without any hindrance. Therefore, investigation suffered from many faults which went against the prosecution.

Virasam

The Revolutionary Writers Association, Virasam, was founded by well-known Marxist poet S. Srinivasa Rao in 1970. It was a group of five poets who wrote several poems inspiring the people to rise in revolt against the state. After PW came to lime-light, this organisation worked as its live wire and mouth piece. Rivalry among the Brahmin and Dalit members of the unit often surfaced. Comrade K.G. Satymurthy who was expelled from the PW alleged that the upper caste members had been playing the dominant role in the out-fit. A whisper was apparent that the upper caste members had conspired to drive away the dalit members from the out-fit. Virasam eulogized the Srikakulam uprising and justified many unpalatable actions of the PW. The organisation undertook the task of indoctrination of students and unemployed youths and inspired them to come within the fold of naxalism.

Eventually, Virasam became the life line of the PW and its dedicated youths took the leadership of the underground squads. However, internal feud and rivalry among the top leaders exposed the weakness of the party. President of the organisation, Kalyan Rao, a dalit and Varavara Rao, a senior leader and a Brahmin, quarreled openly. Varavara Rao resigned on May 6, 2005. In fact, crisis was averted when top leaders intervened and settled the differences amicably. The organisation with missionary zeal penetrated into the intellectuals, progressive elements and the students community and succeeded in unleashing propaganda on the aims and object of Naxalism and the usefulness of the PW in fighting the cause of the poor and down trodden.

Jana Natya Mandali

It used to organise street plays, folk songs, drum beating etc. which made a positive impact on the rural youths. It earned popularity and helped to bring number of youths in its fold. Troupes used to move around the state and high-lighted the ultras' struggle for the classless society and the People's government and mustered support for the movement. A ballad on, "Annihilation of the class enemies" created a deep impression on the poor and rural mass.

Radical Students Union (RSU)

A group of students of Osmania University, Hyderabad, having left leaning founded the unit. K.V. Raghunath Reddy, later Governor of West Bengal, Jaipal Reddy, later a member of the union cabinet supported the establishment. Critics say that they were practically the God-fathers of the organisation. Later it was converted into Progressive Democratic Students Union (PDSU), a wing of the CPI (ML).

AP Civil Liberties Committee (APCLC)

Authors, Advocate, lecturers, teachers having Naxalite leaning formed this organisation. Its object was to provide legal aid to the extremists either arrested or prosecuted or fighting the legal battle. Secondly, it wanted to act as the frontal organisation of the extremists. It unleashed pompous propaganda in favour of the PW and tried to create a favorable public opinion for the out-fit. It let loose tirade against the police actions, especially, criticizing fake encounters with the sole object of demoralizing the police. It posed itself a great champion of the human rights, but in reality, it espoused the causes of the extremists. In the trial courts they defended the ultras and tried to corner the prosecution lawyers and advocates and make them ineffective. Leaders of the unit justified the dastardly killing on the ground of violence on retaliation. They took the plea that violence was inevitable for the unlawful terror and countering the conspiracy hatched by the state for killing the ultras. They adopted many sinister tactics to frustrate the prosecution and the progress of the trial. Truly, it was a pro extremist organisation in the garb of protecting the civil liberties.

Significantly, a large number of radical students of Osmania University, Hyderabad supported the Naxal movement. Conflict and campus violence between pro and anti-extremist groups marred academic ambience of the university. Unfortunately, several bright students lost lives. Nevertheless, extremists made an inroad in the student community and a group of students became sincere and dedicated followers of the extremist movement. Regional Engineering College (REC) Warangal, Kakatiya University, Warangal, Osmania University Hyderabad were tainted by horrid campus violence and blood bath. Several student leaders were killed by the ultras.

Importantly, ban order re-imposed on August 17, 2005 on the Maoists was reviewed by the cabinet. It was further extended till August 16, 2008, on the CPI(Maoist) and its frontal organisations. The Andhra Pradesh Public Security Act was extensively used for tackling the ultras. Broadly, the frontal organisations are: 1. Radical Youth League (RYL). 2. Rythu Coolie Sangham (RCS). 3. Radical Students Union. 4. Singareni Karmika Samakhya (SIKASA). 5. Viplava Karmika Samakhya (VIKASA). 6. All India Revolutionary Students Federation (AIRSF). In addition there were many small groups who supported the Maoist movement.

Hope for the Second Peace Talk Belied

After the first public peace meeting with the PW held in October 2004, during the time of the CM Dr.Y.S. Rajasekhar Reddy, the encouraged ultras did not reduce blood letting activities. They perhaps thought that the government was already rapped on knuckles and would initiate a compromise formula. They hoped against hope and thought that the Chief Minister would soon call the second peace talk. Meanwhile, situation in the state underwent a positive change. The state tightened its grip vis-a-vis the Maoist violence. Success of the security forces, especially, notable performance of the Greyhounds put the Maoists in back foot. Maoists shifted many training centers to Dandakaranya and Bastar region. Incessant raids by the Greyhounds forced them to take to heels and build new hide-outs in Baster region, Malkangiri, Odisha. Hence, the state got breathing time to re-organise and resolved to show mailed fist to the outlaws. Since January, 63 ultras were killed in encounters, many ultras surrendered in Warangal, Guntur and Kurnool districts. In fact, Offensives by the Greyhounds turned to be a nightmare for the extremists. In the changed scenario the government decided to ignore the call for the second peace talk. It upset the Maoists. The Maoist emissaries P. Varavara Rao and two others blamed the CM for not coming to the negotiation table. They vehemently criticized the government for allowing the Greyhounds to pursue the combing operations untiringly. They demanded that government should stop combing operations, arrest of the Maoists and sit for a dialogue. They brought many allegations that the government was vindictive, following the path of confrontation adopted by former CM C.B. Naidu, unwilling to listen to the grievance of the Maoists and the down trodden. However, jugglery of overture failed to make a dent on the government. CM made it clear that he was not interested to resume the second round of the so called peace talk.

Nexus Between the PW and the LTTE

PW maintained close link with the LTTE of Sri Lanka. In fact, LTTE sold the idea of raising the guerrilla squads. They briefed and supplied know how of organising guerrilla squads. LTTE trained a handful of physically fit and determined PW cadres in jungle warfare. From the group LTTE picked up stubborn and willing cadres to be enlisted in guerrilla squads. Special training was given to the guerrillas to handle heavy weapons, mortars, hand grenades, technique of laying ambush and attacking advancing column of the security forces. They also taught intricacies of assembling, planting and defusing land mines. In fact, the idea of using land mines in large scale by the PW was virtually borrowed from the LTTE. It gave the clue of procuring AK-47 rifles and automatic weapons from the foreign market. Initially LTTE supplied a few consignments of automatic small arms, hand grenades, land mines, training pamphlets. The then Prime Minister Rajiv Gandhi's misadventure in Sri Lanka, dispatch of the IPKF (peace keeping force) in feverish haste, immeasurable loss of men and materials and national prestige gave a mighty boost to the LTTE. PW being the beneficiary of receiving largesse from the LTTE was equally encouraged to zealously pursue the extremist movement. PW watched the porous performance of the IPKP on the soil of Sri Lanka and realised that army was not invincible. They were sanguine that dedicated, determined and well trained cadres, armed with sophisticated weaponry could easily counter and push the armed forces back. Admittedly, PW received adequate aid and assistance from the LTTE which gave them robust impetus to inspire the cadres and proceed with the movement. A weapon specialist from the LTTE and a retired army officer was deputed to train the PW cadres, to teach the intricacies of land mine technology, secret of planting land mines and IEDs. For that a training camp operated in Kariguntla in Bastar region. Needless to say, PW–LTTE axis gave the PW reckonable combat superiority over the police and para military police forces.

Nexus of the PW and the LTTE received attention of the union government at a later stage. In 1989, in a land mine blast in Ambatipalli, Karimnagar district six BSF personnel were killed which alarmed the union government to take the threat seriously. A meeting of senior police officers of AP, MP, Odisha and Maharastra was held in Mumbai in July 1989 to discuss the growing impact of the axis. Coast guard was alerted. Police raided several places to arrest the king pins and demolish the nexus. It also revealed that private smugglers were buying automatic weapons from the LTTE and selling those to the PW at a higher rate. In this connection a notorious smuggler was arrested. From raids conducted in Adilabad district in August 1992 police seized ten rocket launchers supplied by the LTTE.

Connection with the Extremist Outfits of Foreign Countries

Many extremists out-fits are active globally and trying to develop contact, consolidate the groups, build a strong global organisation and establish them as one of the reckoning powers. Brussels, the capital of Belgium is the undeclared HQ of the world extremists. Workers Party of Belgium took the lead to maintain contact, exchange programmes, advice and issue guidance. In May 1996, an international seminar was organised at Brussels. It was attended by sixty representatives from forty countries. Representatives of the PW attended the seminar, inter-acted with the representatives of the CPP of the Philippines, PCP of Peru, MLPD of Germany, TKP (ML) of Turkey, AKP of Norway, Communist party of Japan, FACMLN of Mexico, Marxist-Leninist Organisation of Senegal, PTB of Belgium etc. (*The Hindu*, August 3, 1997). Philippines showed keen interest to maintain regular contact with the PW, exchange notes. The idea of patronizing a chain of the extremist out-fits in the Far East was discussed. PW showed eagerness to development rapport with the PCP of Peru. PW wanted overseas support and in that pursuit they wanted to cultivate the Indians settled abroad. They somehow learnt that the Indians settled in foreign countries carry sympathy for the left wing extremism. In short the PW was very enthusiastic to build an overseas network. However, PW constituted an International Bureau to develop or consolidate contact with the likeminded organisations active in foreign countries.

Manufacture and Procurement of Arms

LTTE's main source of procuring arms was police posts, police personnel either slayed or injured. Ultras procured arms and ammunitions after raiding the police stations, police posts and ambushing police parties, killing or injuring the cops. Secondly, they collected automatic small arms, grenades, land mines from the LTTE, on payment. Thirdly, they purchased weapons from the Naga insurgents and from the open market in Combodia. They used to manufacture guns, pistols, single barrel improvised guns, crude bombs, rockets, improvised explosive devices (IEDs) using materials available locally. In interrogation many leaders admitted that 35 per cent of the fund used to be spent for procuring arms. They appointed retired or released trained and experienced armourers from the Indian army. LTTE built a wide network of building arms in other states deputing experts from the armed cadre based in A.P. Such crafty steps were taken to avoid suspicion and to deceive the police of A.P.

On September 2006, the state police intercepted a truck coming from Chennai, seized 42 rocket launchers, 1000 empty rocket shells and 35 improvised land mines. Investigation revealed that manufacture of these deadly weapons had been continuing in lathe workshops and foundries in suburbs of Chennai since 2003. On January 10, 2007, police raided Bhaskara Engineering Workshop. Satnam Nagar, Bhopal city and seized accessories of revolver, grenades, dies, tools and arms manufacturing manual. From the laptop detailed literature on how to make different types of explosives mixing different kinds of chemical, designs, notes, index and references, designs of rocket launchers could be possessed. Police arrested five Maoists connected with the workshop hailed from Guntur and Warangal districts of A.P. On January 12, 2007, in Rourkela police raided Utkal Engineering Workshop and seized a scanner, laser printer, barrels for manufacturing rifles, lap top, lathe and welding machines, and arrested five technicians including three women who belonged to Adilabad district, A.P.

From reliable source it was learnt that the Maoists' Central Military Commission (CMC) decided to allot rupees thirty crore exclusively for developing process of manufacturing rocket launchers, mortars and hand grenades for use in guerrilla zones in AP, Chhattisgarh, Odisha, Bihar and Jharkhand. These are area weapons which give the ability to strike at security forces with an advantage of not being spotted. Intelligence report revealed that the decision to allot funds for fabrication of ordnance was taken at a meeting of the CMC held in February 2007, in Bhimbandh wild life sanctuary, Munger district. Police believed that four or more fabrication units are operating in four states including in a south Indian state. Parts of the weapons are made in each of these units and later sent to the right destinations for assembling and final shape. This practice is followed to maintain secrecy and to deceive the police. Of late, raids in manufacturing units functioning in Chennai, Bhopal and Rourkela and arrest of the mechanics have forced the Maoists to shift the units to Bihar, Jharkhand and Chhattisgarh and operate under supervision of the central technical team.

Interestingly, the PW was often perforated by internal squabbles, dissensions and sordid competition for leadership. Secondly, surrender of many senior leaders created a big vacuum in the out-fit. It indirectly helped the security forces to put heavy pressure on the ultras. Mukku Subha Reddy, one of the three members of the central committee surrendered to the police on April 9, 1989. He worked 22 years effectively remaining underground. He was B.Tech from Warangal University and worked as the secretary of the state committee for a short period. He disapproved killing of innocent person, destruction of public properties, looting of banks etc. He stated that the extremists have alienated the people and lost their sympathy and support. Malapati Venkateswar Rao alias RK, a provincial commander, worked 23 years with the extremists, surrendered to the police on April 23, 1993. He was disillusioned with the party's anti-people activities. He appealed to the comrades to give up the path of armed struggle and devote to the welfare of the people. Nimmaluri Bhaskar Rao, a member of the provincial committee, spent 22 years sharing weal and woe of the party, surrendered before the Chief Minster on March 25, 1994. He was frustrated seeing the party's anti-people activities. Comrade Pilla Venkatawar Rao, a key strategist of the PW, surrendered to the police in Hyderabad on April 15, 2004 after 20 years association with the party. He said that influence of the movement dwindled and continuous erosion of the mass base had been increasing due to failure of the top leadership.

Instances of Outrages

A few instances of horrid outrages let loose by the PW are mentioned below for assessing magnitude of violence, annihilation, destruction of public properties. Ironically, the high-falutin propaganda that the people's movement is based on terror, bloodshed and damage and demolition of public properties and attempt to destroy existing social and political order. Comrade late Charu Mazumdar said, "He who has not dipped his hand in blood of class enemies can hardly be called a Communist." Hence, his followers and disciples evidently put heart and soul to achieve the goal of forming the People's government by violent means and blood bath. Indeed, after 47 years (1967 to 2014) of the Naxal/Maoist movement one can easily fathom their so called success and justification of killing approximately 25 thousands innocent civilians. Broadly, erosion in their support base, people's despair, hostility and success of the security forces to isolate them etc. are unimpeachable testimony that the progress of the Maoist movement received flinty set back. Much exultation after the merger of the PW and MCC and birth of the

CPI (Maoists), was apparent but it soon wizened. The ultras' brutal and reckless executions, in reality, dragged the people's movement into swamps of blood. Aura of matchless violence, bloodletting activities and destruction of public properties etc. shocked and alienated the people. Throbbed with fear and uncertainty, many sympathizers of the ultras, wanted to get rid of them. They sincerely desired peace and stability and restoration of the rule of law.

On April 29, 1982, student leader S. Jaganmohan Reddy was eliminated in Warangal as he wanted to depose before the court against the ultras. Several students of Osmania University and activists of ABVP were attacked and shot. On January 16, 1990 Raghavendra Reddy, a member of the National Council of BJP, was killed. On April 20, 1995, Pujari Manikyam, Vice President of Warangal district BJP, was attacked by a strong group of PW. He boldly defended and killed three ultras till he was axed to death. On March 27, 1999, the state secretary of BJP, Maisaiah Goud was shot dead. P. Purushotam Rao of the TDP, a sitting MLA, and his three gun men, Venkata Raju, Malakonda Reddy, both trade union leaders and Bathula Bhishma Rao, a member of the CPM regional committee, Bhadrachalam, were killed.

On December 27, 1987, PW ambushed and abducted five IAS officers from Gurthadu, East Godavari district. They demanded release of eight PW leaders detained in jail. CM NTR was upset. However, negotiation by a group of IAS officers known for carrying sympathy for the ultras, finally succeeded in securing release of the hostages agreeing to the release of eight PW prisoners. In fact, the government was compelled to succumb to the pressure of the ultras. As a matter of fact, the ultras discovered kidnapping an effective tool to put the government in knuckles and get their demands fulfilled.

On October 9, 1990, PW set fire on a crowded coach of the Kakatiya Fast passenger train near Hyderabad, resulting in, 47 passengers including women and children were roasted alive. Several railway stations, trains were attacked, damaged and passengers were killed. On November 16, 1997, a DSP, a circle Inspector and four constables were killed in an ambush in Medak district. On June 10, 1998, a SI, and 12 constables were killed in a land mine blast in Warangal district. On March 18, 2008, in an encounter in Khammam district with the Greyhounds 14 Maoists including 3 women Maoists were killed. The spot was very close to the border of Chhattisgarh. On May 24, 2009, top Maoist leader and a member of the politburo and in charge of the Maoist activities in Karnataka, Sudhakar Reddy was killed in an encounter in Warangal district. He attempted to kill former CM C.B. Naidu and suspected for killing former Home Minister, A Madhava Reddy. He was most wanted Maoist and state declared reward of rupees 20 lakhs for his arrest. He was a gold medalist in post graduate from Osmania University. One of his associates K. Venkatiah was also killed. On March 12, 2010, one of the top Maoists Shakamuri Appa Rao alias Ravi Vankanna was killed in Nallamala forest. Comrade Solipeta Kondal Reddy was killed in Warangal district. On June 13, 2010,

Comrade Chandrashakar Gorabale was arrested at Aiza, Andhra Pradesh. On July 2, 2010, top Maoist leader Cherukuri Raj Kumar alias Azad was killed in an encounter in Adilabad district. Maoists and their sympathizers voiced protest for Azad's killing. They alleged that police killed him in a fake encounter. Leader Ganti Prasada Rao alias Prasadam was shot by unidentified persons in Nellore. He died in a hospital at Nellore on July 5, 2013. On January 7, 2014, Gudsa Usendi alias G.V. Prasad and his wife Raji from Warangal district surrendered to the police. He was one of the top leaders, suspected for killing Mahendra Karma, V.C. Sukla and Congress leaders in May 2013 in Chhattisgarh. A reward of rupees 20 lakhs was declared for his arrest. On December 17, 2010 in a gun battle in village Cherrvuri near the border of Odisha, three Maoists were killed and one cop was injured.

CPI ML-Janashakti kidnapped a woman from her residence in village Rudrangl, district Karimnagar suspecting her to be a police informer, mercilessly assaulted her and finally hacked her to death. On July 29, 2004, about one hundred PW attacked Eturunagaram police station, Warangal district. Ultras came in two tractors, encircled the PS, used directional mines, grenades, crude bombs. In exchange of fire 2 CRPF personnel and one cop and two civil police, a forest guard and the priest of the temple located behind the PS building were killed. Bombs were thrown on the quarters of the Circle Inspector and SIs located inside the PS campus. Buildings were badly damaged. PW used directional mines for the first time. On September 28, 2010, Maoists from Andhra Pradesh abducted seven cops from Bijapur district, Bastar region, killed three of them and released the rest after negotiation. On August 15, 2005, in an ambush in Narayanpet, Mahaboobnagar, one MLA and eight civilians were killed. On March 12, 2005, ultras attacked Chilakaluripet police station and killed CI and three cops.

The Road Transport Corporation is virtually the communication life line of the state. Its extensive network and services connects the rural areas with the capital, cities and business centers. Unfortunately, the buses are the easy targets of the ultras.

Buses ply in rural areas without any security cover or armed escort. In fact, buses are the easy targets of the ultras. Ultras damaged or torched about 1200 buses of the corporation which created untold hardship to the passengers from rural areas. More than five hundred government building, including Mandal Revenue offices, Electricity Board office at Vijayawada and court building at Kamareddy, Nizamabad district were blasted.

Right from 1968 to 1980, Naxals killed 234 persons and in police actions 199 extremists were killed. From 1981 to 1990, PW killed 568 persons, 59 cops and in encounters police killed 282 ultras. In sum, from 1968 to October 2006, altogether 2968 persons and 538 cops were killed and in police actions 2612 ultras were killed. In fact, PW recklessly damaged or destroyed public properties, created abyss insecurity and a reign of terror. Incidents high-lighted are unflinching testimony of the magnitude of violence, destruction and loss of human life in the hands of the so called liberators of the poor, exploited and deprived people. From April 1980 to September 2004, till the merger and formation of the CPI (Maoist) PW attacked, partially damaged or fully damaged 94 railway stations, 290 telephone exchanges, 1200 state owned RTC buses and approximately 500 government buildings. In addition, PW blasted several private owned factories and thereby affected livelihood of thousands factory workers and denied employment to the jobless youths.

Success of the Greyhounds in Disarraying the Ultras?

Greyhounds, an elite commando force raised by the state in and around 1980. Training for the elements is of high order and they are equipped with latest sophisticated weapons. They are physically strong, proficient in jungle warfare and possess indomitable will to fight the ultras even in adverse conditions. Their morale, striking capacity to humble the ultras, endurance and perseverance to dog the outlaws is remarkably high. They are experts in tracking the extremists, raid hide outs, arrest the holed up ultras and demolish the safe shelters. Their incessant raids have built a flinty pressure which forced many Maoists either to surrender or take shelter in other states. They persuade the policy of "eliminate, arrest and surrender", and their relentless hot chase has rapped the ultras on knuckle which is working as a proverb in the state. In fact, their very presence in a place is a nightmare for the extremists. After the Greyhounds have taken the field the extremists are on the heels. They have shut down many training grounds in the state, migrated to Dandakaranya and Bastar region. From Warangal, Guntur and Kurnool districts many ultras have surrendered. Within first six months of 2005, 63 extremists were killed in encounters with the security forces. It is formally claimed that Maoist violence has sharply declined in the state. In fact, the cadre strength of the Maoists has declined from 1133 in 2004, to 474 in 2008. During the same period over 6500 sympathizers and propagandists of ultras were arrested and 2300 persons surrendered. Number of Maoist related incidents have dipped from 708 in 2004, to less than 100 in 2008. Importantly, almost all top leaders active in the state including M. Lakshmana Rao alias Ganapathi, the general secretary of the out-fit, do not feel secure to live in AP. State police, specialised forces work side by side with the Greyhounds. Contingents use satellite imagery and advanced snooping devices to track the Maoists' movements, especially, in the forest areas. Indeed, combination and mutual assistance of the elite commando force and the police has proved deterrent to pitiless ultras. They are no longer is the unchallenged authority in the so called liberated pockets or areas. Frankly speaking, the Maoists have to reckon with the mailed fist of the Greyhounds. Admittedly, the Greyhounds' incessant combing operation has given spectacular result to isolate the Maoists.

Fortunately, the state is no longer indifferent to the development of the tribal habitats, and welfare of the tribal community. Government has made a concerted effort to win over the tribal population who earlier used to provide shelter, food and assistance to the Maoists. Employment opportunity is opened for the tribal youths, various facilities provided and rural development programmes initiated. Secondly, lucrative rehabilitation package for the surrendered ultras has opened the flood gate for them to give up arms and return to the main stream of the society. In fact, before many extremists, prospect of the classless society and the people's government appears to be bleak. People's support and sympathy have been fast evaporating. Idealism and beefy promises are no longer effective to keep the flock together. Hence, the top leaders are anxious apprehending its head-long fall in near future. Glittering light lit by the security forces and government of Andhra Pradesh should be a signal for the extremists to discard violence, uphold the democratic banner and participate in democratic process.

Ramakrishna, the secretary of the PW, stated, "We do not believe that the suffering masses can be liberated through negotiations. Our ultimate goal is to capture power through armed revolution." Admittedly, merger of the PW and MCC and birth of the CPI (Maoist) has strengthened the extremist movement, increased the number of full time party activists which was roughly 30 to 40 thousands and guerrilla squads (PLGA) around 15 thousands strong. Its arsenal and striking capacity has increased, financial resources considerably improved. It has extended its activities to 49 districts. Over and above, its morale shot up and reached its pinnacle. The top leaders were firm that it was a question of time to achieve their goal. Truly, from 2007 to 2010, Maoist violence increased in the Maoist torn states. In Andhra Pradesh from 1990 to October, 2006, altogether 2357 persons, 483 cops were killed by the ultras and 2154 extremists were killed in encounters. Frankly speaking, CM Dr. R.S. Reddy's high hope for honorable solution from the peace talk lamentably failed. On the contrary, it helped the ultras to develop wider mass contact and build an ambience of trust and confidence that they could serve the poor and deprived people meaningfully in keeping with their hope and expectation, if rein of the government is given to them. In short, to-day, Andhra Pradesh has contained the Maoist threat and violence to a large extend. Security forces' sacrifices and painstaking effort has produced spectacular result. Nevertheless, the threat is not going to widen soon, none can predict when the ultras will give up arms and outrages, embrace peace and submit to the rule of law.

Comparative Peace, Maoist Movement Contained?

In Andhra Pradesh now the Maoist movement is comparatively quiet. In the so called the liberated territory claimed by the ultras the rule of law has been restored. Telangana, the erstwhile a princely state taken over by the Indian army for anti-Indian activities, later turned to be the safe haven of the PW. Here the extremists are deeply entranced and posed a robust threat to peace and order. However, now it is a separate state carved out of Andhra Pradesh. As already discussed that many political leaders and political parties used to be great patrons of the ultras, sought their help and assistance to cow down the political rivals and win over election battle. After formation of the new state, the ultras have been watching and awaiting the new government's gesture for the concessions promised to the extremists on the eve of coming to power. First, the TRS's commitment for releasing the Maoist leaders from jails and withdrawal of criminal cases pending against them is still hanging in balance. The Chief Minister K. Chandrasekhar Rao finds numerous constraints to run the government and wide hiatus between quixotic announcements and practical difficulties to govern in keeping with the people's hope and aspiration. Hence, it is a matter of watch and observation how long the Maoists have to wait and how soon their patience is going to be exhausted. Therefore, lull in Maoist activities in the state is not the sign of permanent peace and tranquility. Needless to add, protracted struggle, ordeals of underground life, fear of the police's raids and arrest, surrenders by many comrades have substantially taken out the revolutionary steam. Secondly, the rural mass are no longer willing to stand by the side of the Maoists, rather they obliquely look at the ultras for failing to fulfill their beefy assurance of a classless society and the people's government. Hence the Maoists in Andhra Pradesh who proved themselves formidable, conquered the heart of the rural mass and reached near approximation to the zenith of power are in back foot. To-day, they are considerably jaded and worn out, not on firm ground and facing unfavorable public opinion. Simultaneously, the Union government's right assessment that it is a colossal threat to the safety and security of the nation and meaningful steps initiated to disarray the ultras and demolish the movement has turned the table. The union government's ungrudging support to raise commando forces, build infra-structure, liberal sanction of funds, co-ordination with the states etc. have produced desired result. Over and above a good doze of governance, rural developmental programmes and their speedy implementation have badly isolated the ultras. Hence, it is difficult for the Maoists to impel the sagging morale of the comrades and revive the tempo of the movement afresh.

The top political leaders of the state have learnt from experience that conciliatory policy to tame the ultras is far from rewarding. They were candid that the ultras are perfidious, unreliable and devoid of scruple. CM Dr. Y.S.R. Reddy's exuberance to gain over the PW through dialogues, concessions and friendly gesture was a ghastly miscalculation Sad plight of the successive Chief Ministers right from NTR to Chandrababu Naidu to placate the appalling forces, attempt to buy peace at the cost of the public interests are galling examples of abject political disaster. It was crystal clear that the pampered head hunting ultras eager for coming close to the top leaders, want to gain publicity and popularity, made a desperate attempt to assassinate Chandrababu Naidu. Hence, memory is still fresh. The cautious leaders are not going to repeat the same mistake. They are clear that attempt to win over the ultras is politically erroneous and unproductive, rather it is wise to follow the straight forward policy and allow the police and administration to tackle the problem independently strictly adhering to administrative rectitude, accountability and public interest. Needless to add, it is obvious that there is a wide hiatus between expectation and the government's limitation to accept demands and fulfill promises made to win the poll battle which the ultras are unable to concede.

Undeniably, at present, the ultras in Andhra Pradesh are in receiving end. Many training units had to be shut down. A large number of the Maoists have taken to heels failing to withstand hot chase of the security forces, especially, the Greyhounds. Many have crossed the border and taken shelter in Dandakarnaya and Bastar region. Indeed, the Greyhounds' uninterrupted raids, combing operations, encirclement, drive for hunt offensives, demolition of the hide outs, arrests, shooting down many hard core Maoists in encounters etc. have broken the back bone of the rebels. Surrenders by many hard core comrades have further accelerated the impending catastrophe. The effete ultras see the writing on the wall and realised that they are fighting the losing battle. Frankly speaking, the 'Greyhounds phobia' has fallen on the nerve of the ultras and badly affected their spirit and morale. Admittedly, formidability of the security forces, especially, the mailed fist of the Greyhounds to root out the ultras is laudable. Secondly, the state government's indomitable will and determination to wipe out the ultras has worked very well. Moreover, free hand absolutely free from interference given to the security forces to deal with the problem backed by high standard of professionalism has given fresh impetus to the security forces. The exulted security forces diligently performing duties tampered with experience, skill and single minded devotion. Lastly, the people are tired of violence, bloodshed and the barbarity of the ultras in treating the people. Therefore, they want peace, safety, security and halcyon ambience. Hence, the plus points together high-lighted have given a spectacular result and created a strong adverse impact on the Maoists. Erosion in support base has considerably upset the ultras. Their fatuous arrogance is broken into pieces. Peace, security and rule of law have come back, and the peace loving people have heaved a sigh of relief.

Punch and outrages of the Maoists in Andhra Pradesh are in diminishing. trend. Their retreat from the field and decaying influence on the rural mass are quite evident. As discussed already, three major factors are responsible for the decline of the extremist movement in AP. Importantly, inimitable success of the security forces, the government's resoluteness to disarray the ultras and stamp out the movement, the alienation of the rural mass and their demand for peace, safety and security are relevant and meaningful for the decay of the Maoist movement on AP's soil. However, there is no reason for complacency. It may be noted that the Maoists are down but not out. It is like a sleeping volcano which may be quiet for some times but may erupt violently at any time. Hence, the security forces, and the government have to be alert and maintain watch and surveillance regularly on their activities.

Extremists Build Bases in Uttar Pradesh

As a part of the strategy to establish the Red Corridor, the extremists have initiated steps to extend their movements in the eastern territory of Uttar Pradesh. Indeed, extremist violence has spilled into Sonebhadra, Chandauli and Mirzapur districts of Uttar Pradesh. They were gaining strength and planning for "major strikes." Among the targets for attacks, they have zeroed on the government offices, camps of the security forces, explosive go downs owned by industry units at Sonebhadra and Mirzapur. From 2001 to October 2004, more than fifty extremist-related violence reported from above three districts. People's War, MCC and CPI ML-Liberation, unleashed underground operations, trying to build bases. Observation of the intelligence cell revealed that recruitment drive started from the weaker section and rural youths with help of many NGOs. Secondly, training of the recruits was taken up earnestly in a few selected pockets inside the jungle. In fact, they have already gained much strength, improved training standard and built a strong cadre. Invincibility of attacks, ambush etc. on the police patrols and camps of the security forces unmistakably prove that the ultras were formidable and could strike at will. For example, ambush and attack on the police party on 20, November, 2004, and killing of 17 PAC (Provincial Armed constabulary) personnel was enough testimony of the ultras' deadly offensive. The police party proceeded towards Nuaghar in a vehicle for combing operation. A land mine planted under the road hit and blew up the vehicle carrying the cops and killed them.

CPI-ML Janashakti, an extremist out-fit vulnerable in AP was equally active in eastern UP. They had been operating in tandem with the PW. Comrade K. Rajanna, former secretary of the Central Committee of the Janashakti was arrested from Barabanki, UP, in September 2006. His brother comrade K. Amar alias Devendra, secretary of the central committee of Janashakti was arrested from Karimnagar, AP in April 2005. Incidentally, Amar represented the Janashakti in the peace talk held in Hyderabad, AP, in October 2004. While pin-pointing the reasons for the growth of the extremists and later the Maoists, opinion of many senior police officers was sensational and highly relevant. The police authority felt that the extremist movement is not connected with the law and order problem. It has direct bearing on socio economic problem, denial and disparity to the poor and down trodden and indifference or lackluster performance of the public servants for speedy implementation of the developmental programmes for the welfare of the rural populace. Police top brass blamed the revenue and forest departments for the growing dissatisfaction among the tribal community. Systemic uprooting of the tribal from their ancestor's land, encroachment of the forest land and no help or remedy to protect their interest has made their life well-nigh unbearable. Fear of losing their land, social identity and tribal culture has been always haunting them. Top brass are afraid that likely peril is knocking at the door and none is there to protect and salvage the tribal community from the threat and impending doom. They added that lack of tangible steps to remove poverty and denial, develop areas economically and growing unemployment etc. has created a favorable ground for the extremists to penetrate into tribal territory and bring the tribal community within their fold.

It was pointed out that lack of development as many as in 252 villages, the home land of the tribal community, spread over three districts projected a grim picture of neglect, scanty or porous development, substandard living of the people and taint of exploitation. Again, absence of missionary zeal of the administration to uplift the deprived people from injustice, social and economic malaises has only added fuel to fire. Evidently, the extremists have identified the fertile ground suitable for their purpose, cultivated the aggrieved people and developed a 'support base' right in tribal community. Simultaneously, ultras developed contact and rapport with persons belonging to other backward castes who are at the receiving end of harassment, discrimination, neglect and injustice and victims in the hands of both feudal lords and officials. The senior public servants and the impartial critics are unanimous that if developmental activities are not accelerated it will lead to large scale Naxal indoctrination among the local people, especially, the tribal communities. Admittedly, fast growth of the ultras and their blood curdling activities has put the state in a quandary. The state has already considered a special proposal for developing the affected areas. State Revenue Minister felt that delay in disposal of land related cases are providing handle to the ultras to strengthen their network and drawing the have-nots under the ultras' influence. He stated that the government has planned to constitute special courts for expeditious disposal of the revenue cases. Secondly, the state government was keen to sanction a special package for the public servants as an incentive, working in three districts facing risks and hazards. The union government has already included three districts in the Naxal-affected list. Minister expected that the union government should share the cost of sanctioning 'encouragement allowances' to its employees. Importantly, many Maoists from Nepal clandestinely cross the border and take shelter in UP. Many Maoists, especially, the wounded Maoists enter into the state and get admitted in hospitals for better medical treatment. In a special drive organised, several wounded Maoists from Nepal admitted in Lucknow Medical College and Hospital and private hospitals were arrested and handed over to the government of Nepal.

Attack on the CRPF Camp at Rampur, UP; Terrorists or Maoists Involved?

Islamic terrorist out-fits, Harkat-ul-Islami Jehadi (Huji) and Laskar-e-Toiba (LeT), have established support base and spread extensive network in Utter Pradesh. Rough estimate reveals that sixty jihadi terrorists are active in UP supported by 200 over ground supporters (OGS). Again strength of OGS has been increasing alarmingly. In addition, separate groups are brain washing the innocent persons to get enlisted in the OGS for providing support to the Huji and LeT. On November 23, 2009, serial blasts in the court premises in Lucknow, Varanasi and Faizabad and death of many persons have shocked the sober people. Terrorists have planned wisely and executed the operation with precision. In fact, operations were similar to what they have been doing in J&K and to some extent in the North East. During investigation several suspects were arrested. Interrogation disclosed the rapid spread of the terrorist network in UP. The modus operandi adopted by the terrorists is likely to baffle the police intelligence. Surprisingly, number of terrorists who have been operating in UP are hailing from Bangladesh. They receive logistic support from the local OGS to execute the task and immediately after operation return to Bangladesh leaving no clue. Secondly, many on arrival take employment in the state much before the operation and develop friendship with the locals. After committing the crime they join duties immediately so that none can suspect them.

On January 1, 2008, a group of terrorists in the morning attacked the camp of the CRPF at Rampur UP. CRPF personnel were conducting ground test for the recruitment of constables. Terrorists posing themselves as candidates arrived and suddenly attacked the CRPF personnel. Indeed, surprise attack abjectly out-witted them who had no opportunity to defend themselves. Eleven cops were killed and several were critically wounded. Intelligence agencies claimed that hint of the probable attack on the camp was indicated well in advance to the CRPF, HQ and the state police. It was warned that the terrorists might enter into the camp as candidates and attack the CRPF personnel.

Initially, it was suspected that the Maoists were responsible for the attack and killing. However, probe revealed that the Huji and LeT planned and executed the operation. Police arrested the miscreants and submitted charge sheet against fifteen terrorists. The government of UP under the Chief Minister Akhilesh Yadav moved the trial court to withdraw prosecution against the culprits which was a blatant attempt of placating the minorities and keeping the minorities vote bank intact.

Maoists Spread Network in Karnataka

In Karnataka, terrorists and Laskar-e-Toiba, one of the Islamic terrorist out-fits are quite active. Critics commented that Bengalaru has earned laurel as "Information Technology Hub" is likely to be transformed as the "International Terrorist Hub". Print media has reported that Karnataka has turned to be the haven of the terrorists. In 2001, the Union Home Ministry drew attention of the state government that as per intelligence report the terrorists are hyper active in Hubli and Gulbarga districts of the state. Therefore, strong action should be initiated to curb terrorist activities. Frankly speaking, the report is not clear whether it is pointed at the Maoist movement and its perpetrators aspiring to establish the People's government or a hint at the terrorist's active in the J&K and other places.

After murder of former Prime Minister Rajiv Gandhi terrorist Sibsaran, the main accused in Rajiv Gandhi's murder case and two other terrorists belonging to the LTTE, took shelter in Bengalaru city. Md Arif Ansar, accused of attacking the

Red Fort, Delhi, admitted during interrogation that Laskar-e-Toiba had established a hideout in the city and conspiring to kill Azim Premji, the chief of the WIMCO and Narayan Murthy of INFOSIS. He confirmed that the terrorists had been spreading their network in Karnataka. Several violent incidents confirmed that the terrorists were vulnerable and going to step up outrages further. In 1985, police arrested two terrorists from Punjab who took shelter in outskirt of Bengalaru. Many arms and ammunitions were seized from their possession. In May 2000, the terrorists damaged churches using explosives in Gulbarga, Hubli and J.J. Nagar. In that connection police arrested several suspects who were connected with the banned organisations. On September 29, 2002, ISI agent Imam Ali and four terrorists were killed by the police in an encounter. In November 2002, police arrested Vijay Murti, Sibsaran, the LTTE activists, seized bombs and grenades and foiled their conspiracy to kill a few political leaders. In 2005, Delhi police killed three Laskar terrorists who were planning for bloody violence in Bengalaru city. On December 28, 2005, terrorists attacked the Indian Institute of Science. In the campus scientist M.C. Puri was killed and five persons were wounded. In October 2006, from Mysore two Pakistani citizens representing AL-Badar were arrested.

Growing unrests were unflinching testimony of ferocious activities of the terrorists in Karnataka. Pensive analysis revealed that Maoists were not involved in these disturbances. Nor they had any link with the terrorists. The state government was far from firm to initiate effective steps to neutralise the terrorists. Government contemplated to raise anti-terrorist commando force to counter the terrorists and wipe out terror. But paucity of fund stood in its way. Impartial critics commented that the state was in two minds to raise new force and shoulder extra financial burden. State preferred to take the help of the union government for fund and involve them to fight the terror. However, it is crystal clear that the Maoists have penetrated well into selected areas of the state. They have adopted altogether a crafty and pervasive strategy so that their activities might not come under the scanner of the police and the intelligence branch.

Comrade Sudhakar Reddy, a member of the Maoist central committee was made the in-charge for the Maoist movement in Karnataka state. Reddy, a post graduate and a gold medalist from Osmania University, hailing from Mahaboobnagar district, AP, expert in jungle warfare was killed in a gun battle in Warangal district. Comrade Sambasivudu, the designated secretary for the Maoist committee, Karnataka, surrendered to the police on February 16, 2009, in Hyderabad. In fact, the Maoists have been operating covertly in Karnataka following a novel strategy. They do not want to stir Maoist movement in the state in large scale and thereby come under surveillance of the police and the administration. Instead, they prefer selective targets and operate discreetly as they want to make the state a safe haven and a quiet shelter ground or hiding abode for the comrades who are dogged by the security forces in Maoist torn states. In fact, many comrades "wanted or declared absconders" in other Maoist hit states search for a safe and secure hide-out for avoiding hot chase of the police. Indeed, they prefer to enter into the state incognito avoiding fan fare or publicity, mark time and prepare for fresh operation. In safe shelter, they lie low temporarily, watch developments awaiting favorable time and opportunity to return to the original areas of operation. As a matter of fact, Maoists adroitly want to keep the activities of the out-fit as low as possible in Karnataka to out-wit the police and neutralise surveillance of the intelligence units. Frankly speaking, it is not ruled out that in coming days Karnataka may be one of the hot beds of the Maoist fury and egregiousness.

Gadchiroli (Maharastra)—A Liberated Zone for the Maoists

Gadchiroli, Gandia, Bhandara and Chandrapur are officially declared vulnerable by the government of Maharastra. Gadchiroli district is located in remote south east corner of the state. Ninety percent of the territory of the district is covered by hills and jungle. Many villages are inaccessible and not recorded in the land and land revenue records of the state. Here tribals form the majority of the population. Chill penury, poor education, porous health care, lamentable communication facilities are the main malaises, which are compounded by indifferent economic growth and negligible development. The district was too backward not seen economic progress right from independence. Maoists virtually run a parallel government in the district, which was in their parlance, “Janata Sarkar”. They attempted to establish self-rule in the district. Interrogation of several arrested Maoists has disclosed that the ultras have established 22 units. The units have 208 office bearers including 162 men and 38 women, which function through 325 village units having altogether 7825 members. Village units provide crucial logistical support to the party’s PLGA. It maintained 167 units of “Gram Raksha Dal” who submit reports to the out-fit. Head of the local units used to take orders directly from the party’s politburo. This was the picture in 2008. However, later the scenario has been drastically changed. Security forces have taken upper hand, arrested or killed many ultras in gun battles. Therefore, the Maoists were compelled to disband many PLGA units being unable to face the police pressure.

Maoists claimed that major portion of the territory of the district was under their control where their writs were paramount. Truly, semblance of the district authority was practically nonexistent. Hapless people had no option but to submit to the diktats of the ultras. Panic-stricken rural mass knew that it was futile to lodge any complaint to the police or to the district officials for help or protection. Hence, for them it was the ‘Hobson choice’ to obey the head hunting ultras. Maoists had been deciding village disputes, summarily disposing of complaints, holding kangaroo courts, punishing the people arbitrarily, even inflicting death sentence. Execution of the guilty persons used to be implemented brutally in public view to terrorize the people so that the people might not muster courage to defy the Maoists’ desire. In fact, surprise attacks, ambush, land mine blasts and death of a large number of security personnel had affected morale of the cops. Police hierarchy and the state government initiated several steps to motivate and uplift morale of the effete security personnel to curb the ultras with consummate zeal, courage and determination.

Burgeoning Maoists' violence forced the anxious state government to modernise and increase the strength of the police force. The special anti Naxal commando forces, the Greyhounds, built and organised by the Andhra Pradesh government and its spectacular success has given the impetus to the Maoist-hit states to build a purposeful commando force to take on the extremists. Maharastra raised a special commando contingent, called "Alpha Hawks." It is one of the dedicated anti-Naxal commando forces in the country. Its elements are specially trained in the state's Unconventional Operation Training Centre (UOTC). In first attempt, 500 personnel were trained and equipped with latest sophisticated weapons. Its HQ is located in Nagpur. Personnel are given palmy incentives, including special pay, extra perks to make the job attractive. Maoist units were maintaining close contact with many action units of the Maoists active in Nepal.

As the situation was slipping through fingers, Alpha Hawks was deployed in Gadchiroli. In 2009, the Maoists went berserk, stepped up violence, inflicted heavy casualty on the security forces and civilians. Administration was unable to check the swift moving events. Peace loving people was upset seeing deterioration in law and order. Diabolic threat of the Red movement and the administration's poor response to counter it was a stern warning to the people. A few climactic incidents are high-lighted below to assess the gravity of the growing Maoists' threat. On February 1, 2009, at about 11 AM the Maoists ambushed a police contingent of 15 near village Markagaon, inside Dhanora jungle, district Gadchiroli. Cops were aware of the congregation of the Maoists and their likely plans for attacks. Previously, near Markagaon village the Maoists attempted twice to put the cops in a trap. Police succeeded in foiling the attempts and forced the Maoists to take to heels. On the fateful day, Maoists burnt a vehicle on the road which was cunningly used to drag the cops to rush into the jungle, comb the areas to flush out the ultras. Maoists in heavy strength ambushed the cops, fired and injured four cops. At that juncture, the cops had ample opportunity to retreat, reinforce and renew offensive with double vigour. Instead, inspired by courage and call of duty they decided to fight and silence the attackers. Unfortunately, the cops were over powered before the numerically superior strength of the Maoists. After fierce gun battle, all cops were killed. Ultras took away 8 AK, 2 Insas and 4 self-loading rifles, one pistol, one 2 inch mortar and ammunitions from the dead cops. Woman Maoist Narmada led the attack and under her instruction the ultras gouged out eyes and cut away limbs of the dead cops.

On May 21, 2009 near Tabilota, Dhanora Tehsil in northern part of Gadchiroli district a police party of sixteen including five women cops were ambushed. Cops travelled in two vehicles, left vehicles near a village and walked on the Dhanora-Murumgaon road to reach a particular point in search of the ultras. Suddenly the ultras surprised them in heavy strength. In gun battle cops including an Inspector were killed. Investigation revealed that five dalams from Rajnandangaon district and several Maoists from Nepal took part in the assault. In fact direct involvement of Nepali Maoists in ambush and attack disclosed a new dimension of the Maoist movement in Maharastra, Baster and Dandakarnaya region. Secondly, this was the first instance that women cops were killed in that area. On October 8, 2009 at Lahiri near Border of Chhattisgarh about 300 Maoists ambushed a police patrol. Cops including 40 jawans of elite C-60 force fought four hours. Unfortunately, eighteen cops including one SI were killed and equal number were injured. Patrol party claimed to have killed many Maoists though no dead body was recovered from the spot. Later, the ultras dragged out Suresh Halame aged 30, from his house at village Malewada and beheaded him suspecting him to be a police informer. In October 2009, on the eve of the Assembly election scheduled to be held on October 13, 2009, near village Tadgaon, in a gun battle six ultras were killed. Meanwhile, the Maoists gave a call for boycotting the election. On September 8, 2009, at Bhamragarh, south of the district, in a land mine blast Maoists killed 17 cops. On October 4, 2010 in a powerful IED blast in a market place at Perilimili village four cops including one Inspector and one constable of CRPF were killed. On May 5, 2011, six members of a marriage party were killed in Gondia district.

Attacks on security personnel and killing of civilians had been going on unabatedly. In fact, from January 2010 to December 2012 the Maoists had killed 85 civilians including three women and two school students. In first three months of the 2013, 12 civilians were killed on suspicion that they were police informers. The year 2011 was comparatively peaceful. It was presumed that either the ultras had temporarily withdrawn from the scene or killing time to regroup for fresh offensive. Indeed, a sense of relief was noticed everywhere. Many commented that effective action by the security forces must have tamed the Maoists.

Simultaneously, good sense must have prevailed on the Maoists who detached themselves from violence and longing for peace. Paradoxically, the year 2012 and first six months of 2013, was blotted with matchless violence. It belied all sober speculation for normalcy and unnerved the local populace. On April 2, 2012 Maoists abducted Bapu K Enka, aged about 50 and Arjun Talandi aged 55 from Joganguda village, district Gadchiroli branding them as police guides. They shot both of them dead in front of the villagers and beheaded Arjun Talandi, which put the villagers in abysmal fear and panic.

On March 27, 2012 in Gadchiroli district in IED explosion a patrol vehicle of the CRPF was ripped apart which killed 13 CRPF personnel. On April 26, 2012 ultras abducted 12 civilians from village Markegaon and beheaded Ramu Naroti, aged 31 and Deosai Usendi aged 34 accusing them as police informers. However, rest were released without any punishment. On January 20, 2013 in an encounter near Govindgeon police killed six Maoists. On March 12, 2013 the anti-Maoist unit C-60 came under heavy fire when they were combing Sindesur jungle in protracted gun battle, four Maoists, a cop and two civilians were killed. On April 3, 2013,on receipt of intelligence that about 100 Maoists were holding a meeting in Bhatpur jungle, a contingent of elite anti Maoist force, C-60 reached the spot and surrounded the ultras. In exchange of fire lasting about two hours seven ultras were killed. Luckily, the cops had no casualty. On July 7, 2013 in a gun battle near Etapalli six women Maoists in uniform were killed. From their possession one .303 carbine, three rifles and a good quantity of ammunitions were seized.

In Gadchiroli and Gondia districts from January 2002 to February 2009 the Maoists killed 70 cops. Admittedly, from the beginning of the Naxal movement till merger of the MCC and the People's War, the state police was in cul-de-sac Police was not adequately trained in jungle combats, skill to foil ambush, detect land mines and defuse them. They were shabbily equipped, their weaponry were archaic and the personnel not physically fit or trained for protracted gun battle, field craft and combing operations and deficient in physical endurance etc. Intelligence officers were not conversant with tribal and local languages, not cultivated reliable sources, lacked proper means to communicate etc. However, as events moved apace the Maoists' attacks and violence gained momentum. However, in keeping with development training of the armed forces was galvanized, automatic weapons, night vision instruments and anti-land mine devices were provided. Intelligence machinery was refurbished and strengthened, communication network improved. Secondly, sufficient para military forces were deployed. Thirdly, co-ordinated strategy and joint operations with the security forces of nearby Maoist hit states were planned. The union government came forward to assist the states ungrudgingly including liberal allotment of funds. Modernisation of the police forces with the central assistance was undertaken in right earnest. In fact, pragmatic steps helped the police to regain the lost ground and helped to prepare to tackle the Maoists ably with consummate zeal and effectiveness. Admittedly, success of the Maoists and loss of the security forces was not one sided. In encounters loss of man power of the Maoists, recovery of weapons, land mines from them, arrests and surrenders of the rebels, demolition of many hide outs, training centers etc. was quite deterrent for the outlaws. Needless to add, success of the security forces to kill ultras and repulse attacks of the ultras generated a sense of déjà vu and fear psychosis in the rank and file of the Maoists. Indeed, their lofty dream to build the Red corridor received a mighty jolt. Unfortunately, rural development in the district lamentably lagged behind. In fact, communication and educational facilities, health care services, unemployment and social security were far short of the desired standard. High handedness, extortion and outrages by the lower level public servants, especially, from the police, revenue and forest departments and exploitation by the petty traders, money lenders made the life of the innocent villagers well-nigh unbearable. Regrettably, neither the government nor the high officials of the district initiated any tangible step to protect the oppressed villagers from harassment and exploitation.

As already narrated that on February 1, 2009 about 150 Maoists led by woman Maoist Narmada aged 44, assisted by another woman Maoist, Taraka alias Vimlaa ambushed a police party. Cops defended heroically for ninety minutes. Finally, 15 cops lost their lives. A pall of gloom was noticed in the police force. However, inspite of the grim tragedy, morale of the police force was intact. They became more stubborn and pledged to avenge the death of their colleagues and disarray the head hunting ultras. MHA's sharp reaction to the catastrophe was to assist the security forces in all possible ways deserved appreciation and called a conference of the DGPs of Maharastra, Chhattisgarh, Odisha, Jharkhand and Andhra Pradesh in New Delhi. The Union Home Secretary presided over the meeting. Discussion held to give final shape to the co-ordinated action plan to neutralise the Maoists. Emphasis was given on exchange of intelligence output, strategy of deployment of the central forces, special training, improvement of quality of investigation etc. Indeed, all agreed that joint operation was essential as it was going to give desired result.

Importantly, in Gadchiroli and Bastar region the women Maoists are in the fore front of the Maoist movement. They have been holding many key posts and heading number of units. Interestingly, strength of women cadres have been steadily increasing. In fact, the Maoists' hierarchy encourages the weaker sex to join the cadre for many distinct advantages. They find them highly dedicated, equally competent, effective and skillful in operations vis-à-vis males. Narmada skillfully led the operation on February 1, 2009 near Makagoan jungle, successfully ambushed and killed 15 cops, looted their weapons. The police contingent who rushed to reinforce the advance party was tempted to walk into the trap. Maoists adopted the similar modus operandi and lured them to enter into the jungle. Luckily, the cops visualised the sinister game plan and abandoned the idea to enter into the jungle. It was a joint operation by the units of North Bastar and Gadchiroli district security forces. After Shivanna, a deadly Maoist was killed in an encounter in Chhattisgarh in 2007, Narmada took over the charge of the district. She preferred the fair sex Maoists to head the local units. In fact, several local squads comprising 10 or 15 armed Maoists were placed under the command of women Maoists. In this area, physically tough girls aged 15 to 20 are plentifully available who willingly join the Maoist out-fit.

Roughly 40 thousands sq km territory on the border touching Maharastra, Chhattisgarh and Andhra Pradesh virtually is a liberated zone. However, the Maoists in this area suffered badly, faced many setbacks and remained in limbo during the last two years. Several Maoist leaders were either killed or arrested. Camps were raided and destroyed. Several dalam (squad) commanders and 250 activists surrendered. Two dalam commanders and 15 hard core Maoists were captured from Bhamragarh areas in the last week of January 2009. Top leaders, Murali Satya Reddy and Arun Ferriera were arrested from Nagpur. Vernon Gonsalves and Sridhar Srinivas were arrested from Mumbai. True, ordeal piled upon ordeal on the Maoists, yet, redeeming feature for them was that they enjoyed support and good will of the local tribal populace. Gond tribe constitute majority of the population of the district who are landless, suffer from chill penury and victims of exploitation. Sizeable Maoists active in the areas belong to Gond tribe. Hence, under current of fraternity often works. Over and above, the Maoists have initiated many steps and welfare measures to improve the lot of the tribal. On their intervention Kendu leave contractors were forced to pay better daily wages to the tribal workers Secondly, they introduced new policy of land reforms, compelled the rich and powerful land owners to adhere to the laws ensuring payment of legitimate dues to the tribal which was so long being denied contemptuously to them. In short, the Maoist writs have considerably helped the marginalised section of the society to get better deal and protest against exploitation by money lenders, traders and harassment by the public servants. Even observation of the representatives of the Planning Commission and in its report submitted has acknowledged the positive contribution of the Maoists to help and protect the poverty-stricken tribal in Gadchiroli district. Side by side, arrests, surrenders, death in encounters have increased confidence, spirit and morale of the security forces. Simultaneously, it has shown a positive ray of hope for restoring normalcy in the district. As a matter of fact, lull in Maoist activities was not taken lightly by the higher authorities of the security forces as it may be a ploy to regroup, reorganise and prepare for fresh attacks.

Statistics of events, casualties etc. from 2004 to 2008 are given below:

	2004	*2005*	*2006*	*2007*	*2008*
1. Police men killed	6	18	3	3	6
2. Civilians killed	10	26	39	24	15
3. Maoists killed	4	3	22	7	11
4. Maoists arrested	155	300	79	123	112
5. Maoists surrendered	100	83	65	39	146

Broadly speaking, uneasy lull in the district for several months, provoked Maoist leader Satyanarayan Reddy alias Kosa, Secretary of the Dandakaranya Special Zonal Committee (DKSZC) to issue instructions containing 24 pages, addressed to the district leaders. It revealed, "There has been hardly any output from Gadchiroli division. We have been on the back foot for quite some time. Why has there been a dearth of recruits for the PLGA? Ambush after ambush has failed. Policies of development (by the state) have tried to gain favour of the people. I want companies and platoons from DKSZC to join hands and strengthen our base."

Perhaps, the above instructions from the secretary inspired the local squad under woman Maoist Narmada to ambush the police contingent on February 1, 2009 near Village Markegaon and killed 15 cops. The gruesome incident badly bruised the image of the police and district administration. Critics said that the temporary quietness made the security forces complacent. However, annihilation of 15 cops was an abundant manifestation that the Maoists in the district have neither given up arms and blood curdling activities nor returned to the main stream of the society. Rather, the horrendous attack was a clear testimony to regain the lost ground by the ultras. Indeed, it was crystal clear that the Maoists may lie low temporarily but will not give up their movement and revolutionary goal.

Police successfully made inroads in many Maoist dominated areas, faced resistance and after gun battles, arrested ultras, recovered weapons, explosives and killed many. Yet the Maoists were not wiped out. They attacked the security forces and in gun battles killed many security personnel. On January 20, 2013, police patrol confronted a group of ultras in a forest near Govindgaon village in Aheri Taluk In a protracted gun battle six Maoists including two female Maoists were killed. Jalku Lakda aged 43, a member of South Gadchiroli Divisional Committee and commander of Aheri dalam, wanted in 59 criminal cases and his wife were killed. Police seized 2 SLRs, two .303 rifles, ammunitions and Maoists literature from the spot.

The Maoists were badly handicapped due to scanty supply of ammunitions, poor facilities for treatment by specialised physicians, lack of competent surgeons and non-availability of life saving drugs to treat a patient in critical condition. Secondly, comrades received bullet injury in gun battle needed immediate operation. Extrication of bullets from bodies, amputation of limbs, blood transmission etc. is often essential to save a life. Truly, these facilities are not available in jungle hide outs. To make good such difficulties the Maoists kidnap physicians at gun point from urban areas, take them to the hide-outs and force them to treat sick or wounded comrades. In fact, once the task is achieved they are escorted back to their places. If any physician declines to obey the ultras his life is at stake. Hence, many succumb to the pressure and agree to go to the hide outs to treat a wounded or moribund Maoist. Such hush hush business and quid pro quo often not escape the police's surveillance. It helps the police to locate the hide outs and organise raids. In Gadchiroli district lack of able physicians and surgeons is a genuine problem even for the common persons. Maoists, to overcome the hurdle often forcibly bring physicians from distant town's right into the hide outs. For example, in a small rural place called Hemal Kasa, 275 km away from Nagpur, located on the border of Chhattisgarh and Andhra Pradesh, social activist Prakesh Amte and his wife Mandakini settled here about 35 years back, much before the Naxal movement started. Their motto was to serve and medically treat the poor and exploited persons of the areas. In fact, they were inspired by the ideal of rendering ungrudging medical service to the poor and the down trodden. Truly, both of them were highly respected in the area for their magnanimity, missionary zeal and selfless public service. It was an open secret that both were taken to the hide outs more than once under threat to treat the ultras. On interrogation by police neither they admitted nor denied the episode since their survival depended much on the wish of the Maoists.

Gadchiroli, the hot bed of the Maoist activities in the south east Vidarbha region was under heavy pressure from the security forces. Since 2010 the Maoists were in back foot and faced considerable loss. Truly, success of the security forces was due to clandestine help given by the tribal living in the region. Maoists suspected that many villagers were police informers who had been secretly passing information on the movements of the ultras to the police. Hence, the Maoists being bottled or isolated by the growing pressure unleashed by the security forces, often turn their anger to the local tribal. On suspicion they had killed twenty two tribal in 2010. During the first six months of 2011, they had killed 28 civilians. In fact, some killing was so brutal that a shock wave travelled from village to village and has completely de-moralised the peace loving people. On July 18, 2011 Maoists abducted the village head man of Korchi Tehsil along with two others. After two days their dead bodies were discovered on the road. Investigation revealed that two victims were shot and head of the third was crushed by stone boulders. The village head man was against the developmental projects in the village proposed by the Maoists. Police was unable to pin point the reasons of acrimony between the ultras and the civilians and the resultant killing.

Uneasy calm in the district was a clear indication of an impending disquiet before a monstrous storm. Intelligence officers were candid that the ultras were re-grouping, geared up recruitment drive taking youths from the tribal community and putting them under rigorous training. Training camps were organised in May and August 2010. Jana militia and dalam level formation were galvanized. Secondly, the Maoist raised a platoon and a company in pattern of the Indian army. Activities were stepped up in small pockets at Gondia and in large part of Gadchiroli. They reiterated that much emphasis on temporary decline in aggressive activities should not be given undue importance. Rank and file was advised to cheer up and prepare for a bigger and wider movement. Surprisingly the rural development programmes, improvement of roads and communication network and government sponsored welfare works etc. were unpalatable to the ultras. Meanwhile, dragnet by the security forces to nab the Maoists was coming closer every day. In fact, pro-active discourses by the security forces either blocked or checked many unfrequented jungle corridors used by the ultras to move in or out of the Maoist dominated areas. Needless to say, it put the Maoists in uncomfortable situation. Their movements were considerably restricted. Admittedly, it gave a good opening to the security forces to reach inaccessible places, organise raids and chastise the rebels. All said and done, impartial assessment reveals that the Maoists might lie low for the present but are sure to surface soon with renewed energy and resolve.

Gadchiroli is a prize territory for the Maoists for extortion and enlistment of young males and females in the out-fit. Poverty-stricken villagers earn livelihood from collection of kendu leaves, bamboo trees, forest products etc. Rough estimate reveals that the poor villagers have to pay rupees fourteen crores annually to the Maoists. In addition, a substantial amount is collected from levy imposed on labour and forest contractors, transporters, traders etc. Inspite of reverses, the Maoists were obdurately trying to ensure their presence and strengthening their grip on the district. Security forces are fully aware of the head hunters' activities and their lust for money. They are fully alive to the situation and hence, leaving no stone unturned to disarray the appalling forces. State with the help of central forces planned to reclaim the lost areas. A massive mobilisation of armed personnel roughly 4600 cops under command of senior officers were deployed covering areas of twenty police stations. Police called it Operation Area One "Op Area 1" Operation was expected to be obstinate and bloody. The tribal people living in the areas were afraid of being sandwiched between the security forces and the ultras. Security forces liked to collect intelligence on the locations, movements of the ultras, approach roads towards the Maoist camps and other details of the ultras from the villagers. Sometimes they used the villagers as guides In that pursuit police used rough and ready method. Maoists on the other hand suspected the villagers as police informers, never trusted them, tortured or even put them to death. Hence, the villagers were in log-jam. Maoists were preparing to counter the security forces. Divisional secretary of the Maoists, Anand Gedam instructed the local tribal to form village committees to resist the state power and asked them to remain in readiness for an armed confrontation with the security forces. Pamphlets were widely distributed which created some impression on the tribal. However, the peace loving villagers were apprehensive that confrontation between the security forces and the Maoists was sure to disrupt normal life. They were afraid of torture, outrages and bloodshed.

True, lull prevailed, comparative peace returned to the district. However, sporadic violence had marred the peace. Occasionally, when violence erupted the security forces felt indignant as they were accused for their lapses or complacency. It gained support that temporary quietness never indicate that the Maoist movement in the district has dried up or disappeared. In the current year (2013) since January to October, security forces killed 23 left wing extremists in several operations. In June the Maoists killed three civilians including vice president of Lloyds Metals and a sarpanch of a village near Surajagarh. On October 16, 2013, fifty anti Maoists commandos of SAG were resting in a school building after conducting combing operation in nearby jungle. Maoists came out of the jungle and suddenly attacked them Exchange of fire continued for one hour. Three commandos were killed and two were injured. On October 17, 2013, a police patrol near Tendulwahi jungle was attacked. In a gun battle a woman Maoist was killed. No cop was either killed or injured.

Mass Resignation of the Elected Representatives

Mass resignation of the elected representatives in the district is alarming. In many pockets of the district writ of the Maoists run and the administration is unable to contain the growing unrest. The elected representatives in rural areas are under constant threat of the Maoists. They were cautioned and given ultimatum that unless they resign from the posts their lives including lives of their family members would be in danger. In fact threat was not at all hollow as security forces are unable to ensure their safety and security, especially, the persons living in remote areas not connected by good road and suffering from absence of the police's surveillance network. Truly, threat worked drastically which forced seventy one elected representatives to resign from their posts. The resigned representative was one Zill Parishad member, four Panchayat Samiti members and 66 village Panchayat members. Administration failed to persuade them to give up their resolve inspite of assurance for adequate protection. Above incidents generated fear and panic among the peoples' representatives working in rural areas of Bihar, Jharkhand, Chhattisgarh and Odisha. They were highly demoralised and thought to quit the assignments. In short, surge of Maoist violence only accelerated fear, panic and uncertainty of the common people which have not spared their elected representatives.

As discussed, the terrain of the area is distinctly different from other states and highly favorable for the Maoists. Secondly, living condition of poverty-stricken and deprived tribal is immeasurably deplorable which force them to be lured easily by the Maoist. Here, socio economic development is slow and far from encouraging. Thirdly, local people prefer to live in the accolade of their archaic habits, ethos, and traditions. Indeed, they are lukewarm to the modern scientific and technological progress and advancement. Hence, it is a herculean task to change their mind-set so easily. Interacting with many persons from the tribal community, dispassionately, I feel that the Maoist movement in this belt is not going to wizen early. Hence, the state government has to draw and follow a long term policy, initiate exhaustive developmental activities and persuade the tribal to respond to modern progress and prosperity. Special emphasis has to be given on the employment of the tribal youths including the fair sex. The community has to be protected from the exploitation by the contractors, middle men, money lenders and government servants. Relying on experience, I am candid that the public servants discharging duties in the field excruciatingly harass and extort the poor tribal on flimsy pretext. This creates discontentment and force the victims to develop hatred against the public servants and the administration. Simultaneously, it gives an excellent handle to the Maoists to draw the aggrieved persons to their fold. In short, unless the mound of eels is eradicated the Maoist movement in this particular territory cannot be curbed. As it stands to-day, action by the security forces is far from enough to banish the Maoist menace. A proxy war is on, unfortunately, its end is obscure.

CHAPTER NINE

Maoist – Fair Sex Cadres, their Sexual Abuses: Contributions and Sacrifices of the para Military Forces

Women admired for their gentleness, tranquility, love and affection, indeed, are placed in envious pedestal of the Indian society. However, bloated rhetoric in support of the weaker sex is hardly appropriate in respect of the female cadres of the Maoists. Frankly speaking, people are inclined to believe that weaker sex is deficient in armed combats, handling firearms, physical exertion and endurance vis-à-vis males. The archaic belief that females are unable to tolerate physical hardship, face hazards and defend themselves, unfortunately work against them Broadly, it is partly due to physical inequality and social environment in which she is brought up, kept aloof from manly duties and vested with domestic responsibility. Secondly, as they live under male dominance, their mental and physical strength, courage and determination fail to develop. Significantly, the female Maoists operating in the red corridor or areas controlled by the ultras have proved themselves equally dedicated, physically tough, spirited, good in combats, gun battles, lying ambush etc. Maoist hierarchy is candid that the fair sex Maoists are very motivated, submit to discipline and obedience implicitly and possess excellent fighting spirit. Moreover, they are dependable and their desertion from the out-fit is much less than that of the male Maoists.

In each state, strength of the female cadres of the Maoists varies from 15 to 20 percent. They are generally recruited from poor tribal families, either by coercion or on payment of a nominal amount. Recruits are put in intensive physical and weapon training and then detailed in the squads. Once experience gained in combats, fortitude and fighting spirit is shown, many are allotted to guerrilla squads. In course of time, many lead squads, organise surprise attacks, ambush the police patrols, over run and ransack police camps, loot arms and ammunitions. In Bastar region, Chhattisgarh, the hot bed of the Maoist movement, the women cadres have been actively participating in deadly offensives. Their strength has exceeded the number of the male Maoists active in the region. Their spectacular performance has provoked the hierarchy to select them in decision making in zonal level. Some of them have been inducted in the special zonal committees. In fact, Chhattisgarh and Dandakaranya is a fertile ground for recruitment of the able bodied tribal girls. Recruits are hardworking, habituated to live in jungle and secluded places, possess high degree of endurance and can put up with ordeals. Secondly, they may easily get mingled with the local tribal people, speak same language, share ilk culture and inspire the girls and young females to join the cadre. Being broadly part of the local community they can maintain effective watch and surveillance on the movements of the security personnel in the area and alert the comrades to escape if raids by the security forces happen to loom large.

Previously, women cadres used to assist the male Maoists or deployed for innocuous tasks. Of late, the scenario has been drastically changed. In fact, female Maoists are given special preference for important tasks. A large number of females are deployed in operations and in guerrilla squads. Desertion rate of the male Maoists is high. They do not hesitate to quit the out-fit on suitable opportunity. But desertion by female Maoists seldom takes place. Therefore, Maoist leaders prefer the female recruits to males. Close observation reveals that in 2010, women constituted about 40 percent of the Maoist cadre in Bastar region. But from beginning of the year it has shot up to approximately 60 percent. In recent drive for enrollment, number of the female candidates was much higher than the males. In divisional committees they are representing in 25 percent posts. In Dandakarnaya Special Zonal Committee which covers Bastar region, the women Maoists have been leading twenty committees. Hence, it confirms the women Maoists' appreciable performance and high standard of competence. Sujata, a hard core female Maoist is heading the Dandakaranya state military commission, Niti is the chief of the north Bastar divisional committee, Madhavi is the chief of the west Bastar divisional committee, Kosi heads the committee for Mangtar area.

Maoist leadership encourages the enlistment of fair sex to enrich the cadre. Leaders feel that the policy adopted is beneficial for the out-fit, First, the local sentiment gains ground if the weaker sex is patronized or projected. Secondly, it helps to gain sympathy and support of the local women folk who can play a positive role to influence the fellow weaker sex to help the Maoists and support the movement. They may easily confide with the women folk of the villages and enthuse them to provide shelter, food and treat the jaded or wounded Maoists sympathetically. They may be utilised to collect intelligence, outwit the police if they raid the villages in search of the ultras. Thirdly, fair sex ultras enjoy wider acceptability in the cadre and are treated warmly and equally. Women Maoists are better suited for routine duties in the camps. Evidence is abundant that in operations many have shown exemplary leadership, courage, skill and fighting spirit. They take on the security forces in a spirit of vengeance and are ready for supreme sacrifice. Admittedly, they have distinguished themselves in bloody combats, purposeful organisational ability and leadership quality. Regrettably, according to the impartial observers, female Maoists are ferocious, pitiless and treat cruelly the wounded and even the dead enemy. In several cases their frenzied barbarity in treating the wounded or dead security personnel and the innocent villagers is shocking. Bastar region is the tribal dominated area where sex ratio is 1023 females per 1000 males. The national average is 940 females against 1000 males. The long history of atrocities on tribal women has made easier for the extremists to bring the tribal fair sex and populace in their fold.

A good deal of study reveals that female Maoists generally do not quit the out-fit or withdraw from the movement. They are highly committed, firm in their decisions and are obdurately attached to the out-fit. Critics quip that spirit of "feminine obstinacy" influence them to be decisive, unshakable and indomitable to complete a task assigned to them. They get fully absorbed in Maoist way of life, often marry the fellow Maoist, become mother and take the jungle camp as their home and hearth. This is one of the reasons that strength of the female cadres have been steadily growing. In Chhattisgarh "Chetna Natya Mandali" a cultural wing of the Maoists has been playing a pivotal role in recruiting fair sex for the out-fit. Recruits, mostly tribal girls, are physically tough who easily adapt themselves in regimentation and isolated camp life inside remote jungle.

Women ultras are deputed for reconnaissance and watching the movements of the security forces. On pretext of driving away animal herd they reach close to the camps of the security forces, watch the location of the camp, its loop holes, movements of the contingents and on return submit details of their observation to the leaders. Many are trained in nursing, as pharmacists, signalers and wireless operators. A book captioned, "Mahila Sawaal Par Drishtikon," published by the Maoist central committee, spouts progressive ideas about women, and denounces patriarchy and religion. Sometimes women are deputed to sabotage or harm the security personnel or damage or destroy the camps. In Bijapur district a female approached a camp of the CRPF and requested for medicine for her sick child. She was obliged but her movement was not free from suspicion. After a few days she appeared carrying a large bowl of local meat for the members of the camp. She profusely thanked them for giving medicine previously. CRPF personnel were too cautions to respond to her gesture. After she left it was discovered that meat was mingled with deadly poison.

Admittedly, their martial arduousness, presence of mind in diplomacy and combat is a substantial boost to the movement. Indeed, their meteoric rise and active participation has accelerated the speed of the movement in many pockets which is a cause of concern for the security forces. Truly, rapid growth of the Maoist female cadre is a formidable threat to the country's safety and security. A few instances of operational successes under their leadership will substantiate their importance and utility in the out-fit.

Narmada aged 44, a college dropout from Andhra Pradesh, a prima donna in pursuing the movement in northern territory of Chhattisgarh and in eastern portion of Maharastra is one of the promising female leaders. In February 2009, she, assisted by female Maoist, Taraka alias Vimlaa led a squad of about 150 Maoists and ambushed a police party. They tempted the police personnel to walk into an ambush near village Marke jungle, Gadchiroli district, Maharastra. In that pursuit, Narmada used a police informer and compelled him to furnish false intelligence to the police. The police party wanted to verify the secret information, waited for two days before rushing into spot. A team of 15 police personnel reached the spot taking standard precaution. But they were outnumbered before the superior strength of the Maoists. They fought bravely and determinedly to repulse the attack. Gun battle continued for about ninety minutes. Unfortunately, ammunitions of the police personnel ran short, made them helpless and forced them to surrender abjectly. All were killed, some bodies were mutilated. Ultras carried away eight AK-47 rifles, 4 SLRs, 2 Insas rifles, 2 pistols and one 2"mortar-launcher from the dead cops. A police party was dispatched to reinforce the contingent. They were attacked and lured to enter into deep of the jungle. However, the cops understood the crafty design of the ultras and therefore did not penetrate further to fall into the trap. It was a joint operation by the north Bastar and Gadchiroli district units of the Maoists.

Narmada married Maoist leader Sudhakar alias Kiran who was working in the publicity wing of the out-fit. Her deputy Taraka Vimlaa, a tribal girl from the district married a senior Maoist leader Bhupati. After Shivanna, a senior leader was killed in an encounter with the police in 2008, Narmada stepped into his shoes and has been leading the party's Gadchiroli unit. Being the incharge of the unit she distributed key posts of the local units to women leaders. Majority of the local unit which is 12 or 15, are put under the charge of the women Maoists. Women Maoist Ramko Hichami alias Ranita fought against the Cobra forces of the CRPF at Makadhuvva village, Gadchiroli district. In combat she displayed exemplary courage and killed three cobra commandos and injured four others. Finally she was killed. The central committee of the Maoists lauded her heroic deed and supreme sacrifice and asked the rank and file to give a befitting tribute to the bereaved soul. In fact, the central committee's initiative to high-light her contribution was a clever device to encourage the fair sex cadre and to resuscitate sagging morale of the comrades.

Female Maoists Active in Chhattisgarh

On April 16, 2013, in Sukma district, Chhattisgarh, in a fierce gun battle with the security forces ten Maoists were killed. About fifty Maoists participated in the fight and fifty percent of the attackers were women. Among the dead four were women Maoists. Puspa, a hard core female Maoist perhaps led the fighting squad. She was wanted in several heinous crime. A reward of rupees fifteen lakhs was declared for her arrest. However, Sudhakar, one of the top leaders and Puspa were killed.

On May 25, 2013, at Jiram valley in Sukma district, Chhattisgarh, about 400 hundred Maoists including 200 female Maoists ambushed and attacked a convoy of the Congress party. The Congress leaders and activists in vehicles went for public contact mission. In the convoy, Mahendra Karma, the founder father of the erstwhile Salua Judum and former union minister, Vidya Charan Sukula, Nanda Kumar Patel, the president of the Congress party, Chhattisgarh, his son and about one hundred party activists participated. Except a few gun men for Mahendra Karma and V.C. Sukla security cover was inadequate as it was a political congregation. Savage attack took them unawares. Incessant firing killed 28 persons including Mahendra Karma. V.C. Sukla was wounded. Being out numbered many raised hands and begged for their lives. Mahendra Karma came out of the car, raised hands and appealed for mercy. Maoists nursed strong grudge against him for founding Salua Judum and for anti-Maoist movements. Personal security guards of Mahendra and others returned fire with all might till ammunitions were available. Unfortunately, their feeble resistance only cost their lives. No serenity or pity shook the ultras. Women Maoists pumped fifty bullets in Mahendra's body and stabbed him recklessly. Guided by animal fury women Maoists made a ring around Mahendra and other dead bodies and with extreme barbarity rejoiced the blood bath and indulged in devilish dance around the lifeless bodies. Indeed, extreme scoff, harshness and disrespect to the dead bodies are repugnant to decency and culture. It mocks at human values and civilisation Here barbarity committed, perhaps, may pale the odious Bestial savagery in insignificance Truly, Indian weaker sex who are placed in high esteem and heralded for their gentleness, love, affection and innocence cannot imagine such atrocious conduct from the fellow fair sex who are pursuing the peoples' movement idolized for revolutionary spirit and object of welfare of the down trodden. Frankly speaking, the grisly massacre created a claustrophobic impact on the peace loving people and the security forces fighting the dreaded ultras adhering to discipline and professional ethics. Senior police and para military force officers who have been facing and tackling the ultras are candid that the women cadres have been actively participating in operations, including ambush, assaults and encounters. According to them, women cadres are more active, brutal and ferocious. The gory incident and unprecedented cruelty displayed in Jiram valley is an unflinching example set by the pitiless and head hunting ultras. Such a barbarity and macabre festival of death was an exception even in mediaeval history. Later, critically wounded V.C. Sukla was sent to Delhi for better treatment where he succumbed to injuries. In Chhattisgarh, among the dreaded female guerrillas, Meenakka, Sharda, Kamala, Basanti, Ganga are very active and have been leading many bloody operations.

Sarita Kharwar aged 32, a woman belonged to the tribal community fell in love with a fellow Maoist, Sunil Kumar hailing from Mirzapur district, Uttar Pradesh. Eventually, they entered into wed-lock. She gave birth to two sons. Her husband surrendered to the police in UP. On January 19, 2009, she surrendered to a contingent of the CRPF in Kaimur district with two sons aged 8 and 4 respectively who were born in her days as an outlaw. She was wanted in several hideous criminal cases including a double murder at village Deuri under Adhaura police station.

Fair Sex Maoists in Jharkhand

Maoists' attack on the Dhanbad Patna intercity express in June, 2013, in Jamui district, Bihar, was far from a routine assault. In fact, majority of the assailants were teen aged girls. The train was stopped near Kundar halt station by about 150 Maoists. Volleys of bullets hit the bogies of the train. A few Railway Protection Force personnel returned fire and wanted to repulse the attack. In exchange of fire one RPF constable was killed and two passengers were injured. Ultras looted weapons from the RPF personnel. They detained the train for twenty minutes and then took to heels. Girl ultras belonged to People's Liberation Guerrilla Army (PLGA). Intelligence report reveals that it was first assignment for the girls and a part of induction programme in the guerrilla squad. Secondly, it was a kind of baptism through bloodshed for the new group. Eye witnesses confirm that girl Maoists were agile and dauntlessly played the aggressive role in conducting the operation.

In July 2013, about sixty Maoists ambushed the convoy of the Superintendent of Police, Pakur district, Jharkhand at Katithikund near a bridge and killed Amarjeet Balihar, the S P and five cops. In fact, fifty percent of the attackers were female Maoists who took leading role in the operation. Enquiry disclosed that about 20/25 female Maoists from Birbhum district, West Bengal, took part in the operation. After completion of the task they had returned to Birbhum. On December 14, 2010, Sobha wife of dreaded Maoist Rajesh Munda was arrested from Ledakocha forest under Gurabandha police station, Jharkhand after a fierce encounter. She was second-n-command of the Red squad of Dumaria unit. Riya Nayak a student of Delhi university had been working in the People's Liberation Front of India (PLFI), a splinter group of the Maoists. She was arrested after a brief encounter at Tupudana near Ranchi on April 6, 2013. Alaka Devi along with her minor son was killed in an encounter in Gumla district.

Fair Sex Maoists Active in West Bengal

Women Maoists had taken leading role in several bloody operations, killed cops and built an ambience of terror in jungle mahal. Comrade Koteswar Rao alias Kishanji, a member of the politburo and in-charge of eastern part including West Bengal, made a drive in 2009-10 to recruit physically fit girls from poor tribal families living in Kankradara, Rautara, Dhyanghohora, Bomshol, Salboni, Hadali, Lalgarh and Goaltore areas, West Medinapur district. He recruited about twenty tribal girls within age group of 16 to 20. Twelve of them were sent to Abujhmad, Dantewada, Chhattisgarh for training. The plan was to put them in action squads on completion of training. A contact divulged to the police that 4 or 5 girls after training had returned from Chhattisgarh to their villages, mingling and inter acting with the villagers. They were keeping watch on the movements of the security forces.

Meanwhile, Female Maoist Anu alias Kalpana Maity wife of Maoist Akash alias Ashim Mondal, one of the dreaded female Maoists active in eastern region was arrested by the state special task force (STF). She was in charge of the Ayodhya squad W.B., and participated in attacks on Sildha EFR camp and Sankrial police station. On October 20, 2009 about 25 Maoists including three women PLGA under her leadership travelled in motor bikes and attacked Sankrail police station, shot dead SI Dibakar Bhattacharjee, ASI Swapen Roy right inside the police station and kidnapped the Officer-in-Charge Atindra Nath Roy from his quarters and looted 6 rifles, 4 revolvers, one 9 mm pistol, ammunitions and two motor bikes. Women Maoists looted rupees 9.5 lakhs from the local State Bank of India. They planted land mines on NH 6, to prevent reinforcement, if sent to salvage the officers of the police station. She confessed to have taken leading part in killing the Officer-in-Charge of Bandwan Police Station, Nilmadhab Das in 2003, using automatic weapons. On November 8, 2009, women Maoists attacked a police patrol and killed four EFR personnel in Gidhni bazaar, jungle mahal. On February February 15, 2010, female Maoist Raimoni Soren led a deadly attack on EFR camp at Sildha and killed 24 EFR personnel and looted their weapons. Kalpana Maity participated in the attack and killed several EFR personnel.

Shibani Laya alias Sheema wife of Maoist Ramesh Singh Sardar alias Tapan was a member of the Ayodhya Squad, district Purulia. Earlier, she was forced to marry Maoist Bidyut. Subsequently, she married Maoist Ramesh Singh. On March 6, 2012, both of them surrendered before the S P Purulia. On February 8, 2012, Anima Mahato wife of Maoist Chiranjit was one of the active participants in Silda EFR camp attacked on February 15, 2010, surrendered along with her husband before the IG Western Range. Both of them were associated with Sukdev squad. Eliciting clue from her police arrested Maoist Sunil Murmu and female Maoist Panumani from Laudaha village, Lalgarh. They were members of the Sukdev squad and participated in attack of Silda EFR camp. Bela Sarkar alias Usha, sister of comrade Gour Chakkaborty, a spokesperson of the Maoists, already in custody, participated in Silda operation.

Secret report revealed that 19 Maoists including eight females aged between 20 to 25 years, formed the squad in Ayodha hill. Kalpana headed the squad and assisted by Sikha Majhi, Chhabi Singh Sardar, Anita, Champa and others. The squad kidnapped Partha Biswas, an Inspector of Intelligence branch and teacher Saumajit Bose on March 11, 2010, killed and buried them in the jungle of Ayodha hill. After about two years their dead bodies could be dug out receiving a clue from an arrested Maoist.

Suchitra Mahato wife of comrade Sasadhar Mahato, a prima donna among the female Maoists, enjoyed confidence of Kishanji. She was perhaps the aid-de-camp of the Kishanji who was killed in an encounter in Burishole jungle at about 6 PM on November 24, 2011. At that juncture, Suchitra was by his side and received gunshot injury. In fact, a protection group for Kishanji was formed by 12 to 15 women Maoists who used to encircle him and worked as body guards. Jagari Baska, Anu, Basanti, Jyanti, Suchitra were part of the group. Importantly, a joint photo of Suchitra with Jyotshna Mohato, the secretary of Nari Izzat Banchao Committee, a women's' unit and a frontal organisation of the Maoists operating in the jungle mahal, was traced out from the bag of the deceased Kishanji. Subsequently, Sasadhar Mahoto, her husband was killed in a gun battle. Thereafter, she married Prabir Garoi on February 25, 2012. She dramatically appeared before the Chief Minister in Writers building, Kolkata on March 10, 2012 and announced that she had surrendered. She presented herself before the media and electronic media and explained reason for quitting the Maoist movement.

A squad of nine members including three women was very active and moving in Lalgarh and Goaltore areas under leadership of female Maoist Santa. She was arrested in November 2011. Thereafter, Sita and Bhima, took the command of the squad. It revealed that the squad developed expertise in using directional mines against the security forces. In Ranjya forest, about seven miles away from Salboni, in an encounter with the security forces eight Maoists including three hard core female Maoists of the PLGA were killed. Female Maoist Juthika alias Rina alias Krishna, was looking after the party's women front in Galakata Bhatjangola, district Nadia. She was also a member of a squad and participated in an incident of rifle snatching in Bhutpara, Nadia. Kumkum Singh's father Ajit Singh and his aide Balu Singh belonged to village Ghatbera, Balarampur, district Purulia were killed by the Maoists for their allegiance to a political party, the TMC. She took vow to take revenge of her father's murder. She virtually waged a war against the Maoists from her village. Eventually she contested election for the state Legislative Assembly on behalf of the Trinamul Congress.

It was a matter of anxiety that fair sex in good number have been joining the Maoist squads. In 2009, in Birbhum, three females were enlisted in the action squad. After death of Kishanji, crisis of leadership of the Maoists operating in eastern region was apparent. It created a wide vacuum. The leaderless ultras faced numerous adversaries. Simultaneously, the mailed fist of the security forces and volte face of the local populace put the Maoists in considerable discomfiture. Meanwhile, under Miss Mamata Banerjee, the Chief Minister, the new government initiated several tangible steps to curb the ultras. She gave free hand to the security forces to tackle the Maoist problem. Security forces succeeded in arresting several leaders, killed six front line leaders including Kishanji and Sashadhar Mohato in encounters which demoralised the Maoists. Consequently, several leaders lined up to surrender giving up arms. A member of a squad Sujata alias Champa Hembrem was arrested on July 13, 2012 from Bankura. Adari Murmu alias Dipa was arrested on July 22, 2012 from Tulakendu village, very close to the border of Odisha. She was working with Ranjan Munda and Sasadhar Mohato. She was given responsibility to organise women squads. Panumani Murmu of the Tota squad involved in Silda camp attack was arrested.

Hard core female Maoist Jagri Baske and her husband Rajaram came to writers building, Kolkata met the Chief Minister in November 2011 and surrendered. Jagri belongs to village Bakdoba, West Medinapur, left home at the age of 16 inspired by Maoist ideal and their spirit of selfless services. She took part in several attacks and stained her hands in human blood. She married a fellow Maoist, became mother of a son. She was worried imagining the son's future and decided to return to normal family life. On July 29, 2012 Sikha Hansda and Champa Hembram, female Maoists of Ayodhya squad surrendered to the police. Akari alias Lalita with her husband Durjodhan Rajkuwar alias Sujan surrendered to the Purulia district police on November 19, 2011. Anima Mahato and her husband Chiranjit Mahato surrendered before the IGP Western Range on February 8, 2012. She participated in Silda camp attack. Soma Mandi alias Sobha, alias Uma, a squad commander went to the police lines Medinapur West and surrendered on August 28, 2010. She carried a bag of currencies.

Instances of kidnapping teen-aged girls have been resented by the hapless villagers. Police was equally anxious to curb such crime and enjoy trust and confidence of the people. Sukurmoni Soren aged 13, of village Bagdubi, district Bankura, was lured away by the Maoists to join the cadre. She was put in rigorous training in the hide out at Lithira forest of the district against her will. After training she was placed in Ranibandh squad. She had been resenting physical hardship and secluded camp life being cut off from home. She felt suffocated and sought opportunity to escape. Finally, she left the camp and remained in hiding. Meanwhile, on her parents' complaint the police was relentlessly trying to rescue her. Luckily, they traced her out on November 22, 2010, and restored her to parents.

Sita, a girl aged 17, joined the Maoist guerrilla squad to avenge her father's murder. Goons of the CPM murdered her father suspecting him to be a Maoist. Her father had no connection with the Maoists, yet he was killed mere on suspicion. Sita was also not an extremist. But she joined the PLGA to kill the armed cadres of the CPM to take revenge of her father's death. In course of time she became one of the dreaded female Maoists. The incident is an eye opener that an indiscreet and brutal action forced a sober girl to join the Maoist and take up arms.

Female Maoists Active in Odisha

Nirmala of Andhra Pradesh played a crucial role in spear heading the Maoist movement in Malkangiri area. She surrendered in April 2012 before the police at Malkangiri. Padma wife of Sadanala Ramakrishna alias "Ra K", a much wanted Maoist in four states and for his arrest government of Andhra Pradesh declared reward of rupees thirty lakhs. She was arrested on November 14, 2011 from village Dudhwari, Simliguda block, district Koraput, Odisha. Iswari Andaluri, a dreaded woman Maoist from Andhra Pradesh and Puni Mandigni of Odisha were arrested from Narayanpatna jungle, Koraput, Odisha. On August 27, 2011 a girl Maoist aged 15, surrendered to the S P of Jajpur district, Odisha. On August 25, 2009, a group of 15 women Maoists triggered a powerful explosion in Roxy railway station, near Rourkela. On July 11, 2009 a squad of women Maoists came in two tractors set fire on the forest beat house at Nuapara and destroyed it.

Incidentally, 20 tourists including women from W.B., occupied Chahala guest house near Simlipal jungle, Mayurbhanj, Odisha. Maoists chastised them, women Maoists snatched away ornaments from the female tourists, forcibly took away cash, mobile phones from all, threatened them to leave the guest house and get lost immediately. Sumitra Mullick aged about 16 surrendered before the SP Ganjam. She complained against Maoist leader Sabyasachi Panda for ill-treating and harassing her. Women Maoists gunned down three cops including two security guards detailed for security duties of Sudam Marandi, the senior JMM leader at Bandap under Chandua police station, district Mayurbhanj. Subhashree Panda alias Mili Panda wife of Maoist Sabyasachi Panda, a hero of the police armoury raid, Nayagarh, surrendered to the police. She was unable to bear pangs of underground living and hardship of running from pillar to post to avoid police raids and arrest. She expressed her desire to lead a normal life, wanted to join politics and contest election. Her husband separated himself from the Maoists and founded Odisha Maobadi party independently. Later he was arrested by the police.

Female Maoists Active in Other Places

Woman Maoist Chandrakala Tewari aged 40, wife of Prashant Sanglikar alias Rahi, area commander for Uttarakhand, was arrested on February 5, 2009, from Kasipur railway station, near Haldwani town under Kunda police station. She was given the task of organising and preparing ground for developing the movement in Uttarakhand. Woman Maoist B. Anuradha wife of Ravi Sharma, a technical advisor of the Maoists was arrested from Nagpur. She used to teach in Nagpur University and organised many Dalit and students movements in Nagpur. She was the unit secretary of the Maoists for Maharashtra. She went underground right from 1990, took shelter in Gondia-Balaghat forest and contacted malaria. As local treatment did not respond she was shifted to a private hospital in Mumbai where she died. In August female Maoist leader, Chemeli Devi was arrested in Kolkata, West Bengal, by police from Bihar and West Bengal in a joint operation. On January 21, 2012,

Anjali Devi a female Maoist alias Bengali Chachi was arrested from her house at village Tariyani, Sheohar district. From her possession arms, explosives, two can bombs, a carbine magazine, potassium nitrate, ammonium nitrate, Maoist literature, posters were seized. In Bihar Sarita Ganjhu alias Babita Bhokta, a woman commander of the Maoists' Koleshwari sub zone operating on the Jharkhand-Bihar border was very active and wanted in several criminal cases. Bihar government declared reward for rupees fifteen lakhs for her arrest. Finally she was killed in an encounter. Truly, many fair sex Maoists distinguished themselves as rebels and put the state government in abyss suspense and discomfiture. In that respect, Sujata, Puspa from Chhattisgarh, Subhasree alias Mili Panda, Puni Mandigni from Odisha and several others may be mentioned.

Impartial analysts feel that the top Maoist leaders' liberality to recruit the fair sex in the out-fit is not immune from finesse. It is not an innocent gesture to motivate the weaker sex to join the movement rather it is a sinister design and intriguing move to make the out-fit attractive and a tool to lure the males to jump into the fray of the extremist movement. First, weakness of a man for fair sex is well known. Man by nature is a polygamist and hence young fair sex can easily exploit males to join the out-fit. In other words, tantalizing charm of a fair sex works well to bring a male under her clutch. It is one of the perverse ways to hook recruits and inflate the cadre. Secondly, once emotional attachment grows between male and female, a deep fraternity automatically develops and they become an integral part of the out-fit. Often they enter into wed lock and take the camps as means of permanent settlement. After marriage many couples get off-spring and live happily. Interestingly, union of a male and a weaker sex neutralizes lustful eyes of many male comrades notorious for advances and sexually assaulting the female comrades.

In the camps inside the jungle the Maoists are often victims of malaria, fever, water born disease, snake bite etc. As a preventive measure, the Maoists carry mosquito coils, preventive medicines, and anti-venom serum. Malaria and snake bite have been taking a heavy toll of the comrades. A hard core leader Rahul Tewari died as a king cobra bit him. In 2007, 15 Maoists including a few senior leaders were victims of snake bites in Gadchiroli, Gondia and Chandrapur jungle. Female Maoist, Vasanti after surrender stated that after such tragedies Maoists made it compulsory for all dalams to keep stock of anti-venom serum.

Indeed, rural development programmes, road building activities, excessive or pro-active policing have considerably disturbed the social base of the local villagers. It has equally hurt social base of the Maoists. Relentless combing operation and hot chase by the security forces have forced the male Maoists to take to heels and search for safe shelters. Thirdly, migration of able bodied persons to other states seeking livelihood coupled with above adversaries are greatly responsible for the reduced over ground frontal activities of the Maoists. Over and above, dearth of potential males to fill the squads in lower level has further obfuscated the source of inducting fresh blood. In a nutshell, endless discords have provoked the Maoist hierarchy to divert their choice on the weaker sex, resulting in, steady growth of the female cadres has been taking place. In sum, to-day, the female cadres have been playing a crucial role in strengthening the Maoist movements.

Broadly, many girls join the Maoist out-fit being inspired by ideological zeal. Secondly, many are recruited from poor tribal families by threat or coercion and indoctrinated into Maoist philosophy. After training they are motivated to participate in armed movement. However, many recruits soon get disillusioned being victims of high-handedness, abuses and disgraces. They are often used to lure the males to join the cadre. Thirdly, they are forced to work as mates for the underground male cadres. Regrettably, majority of the weaker sex are forced to submit to the fellow comrades for satisfying their sexual lust. In fact, underground life provides ample opportunity to the male comrades to advance towards the female ultras. Some times on threat or gun point fair sex Maoists are compelled to submit to forced sex. Often, they catch filthy venereal diseases. Unfortunately, many are forced to marry the comrades against their wish. Sometimes, local leaders or party bosses decide the knot. Often suspicion and conjugal discord develops and marriage hangs in balance. Females are severely ill-treated, brutally assaulted and threaten to be killed. Cry and complaints to the higher authority yield no relief. Rather it may cost her life. Comrades in higher pinnacle are disinterested to interfere. Secrecy and authoritarianism in steering the man management often produce adverse result. Senior leaders know that for the interest of running the show this kind of indulgence to the sex-deprived men has to be allowed and complaint of the dishonored females has to be ignored. In sum, plight of the hapless women Maoists is well-nigh unbearable. An abstract from the writing of an eminent human right activist and a long time sympathizer of the Naxal insurgency is quoted which is self-explanatory. "Girls are being dragged into the movement to provide mates for the underground cadres. Some of them were still minor and had not attained marriageable age. Those women who joined the underground movement on their own due to ideological zeal were also compelled to satisfy the carnal desires of dalam members."

Sexual Diseases Afflict the Extremists

Fair sex Maoists are often victims of sexual abuses. Unfortunately, the culprits are their male colleagues and comrades. Reckless and forced sex has been transmitting filthy venereal diseases to many female Maoists. Several suffered from AIDs and eventually died. Indeed, the putrid phenomenon has upset the Maoist leadership who is in a quandary to find out suitable solution either to check or eradicate the malaises. Police raided a camp of the Maoists in Gadchiroli district in the beginning of 2009 and seized many documents. Many literature contained firm instructions issued to the male comrades to refrain from forced sex with female comrades. Stern warning was given to the offenders for any kind of intimidation, advances or forced sex. Leaders were candid that such outrages have to be curbed with all strength.

One of the literatures revealed, "We should not encourage such anarchism. If any one likes any one, they should approach their seniors to get married."

Often unwilling female comrades are forced to submit for sex by threat or on gun point. Clinching evidence has come to light that arrested female Maoist, Sushila Gawde, aged 32, had been suffering from syphilis. Male Maoist Ramakrishna aged 35 and female comrade Mahalaxmi, aged 30, was suffering from AIDS. A doctor from Nagpur under threat was escorted to the jungle camp of the Maoists for their treatment. Eventually, Ramakrishna died and Mahalaxmi remained under treatment and struggled for life. Sona Gawde, aged 30, was attracted to the Maoist movement and joined the out-fit when she was in teens. She married comrade Budhu Betlu, a commander of the dalam Her husband was killed in an encounter in 2006. Thereafter, several senior comrades forcibly took her to bed and sexually assaulted her. Some times on gun point she had to submit for forced sex. Her repeated complaints to the leaders were thrown to wind. In fact, her desperate protest for protection and to silence the miscreants went unheeded. After surrender to the police she narrated her woes. She disclosed that forced sex was so rampant in the camps that it was difficult to identify who was sleeping with whom in the jungle. If a female comrade conceived she was forced to abort. She added that any feeble attempt to object forced sex used to be harshly retaliated instead of punishing the offenders. Importantly, police raided a Maoist camp at Bangetudi in 2006, and seized a blue film CD, many used and unused condoms, Mala-D pills and potency boosting Ayurveda drugs. It is an irony that the Maoists who are inspired by revolutionary zeal, determined to establish the People's government ousting the present regime, blatantly and beastly indulge in promiscuous sex with the helpless female cadre mates. It must be a rude shock to many radicals who carry cudgel for the Maoists and dreaming for a glittering era, if they happen to know immoral acts and outrages recklessly practiced by the comrades aspiring to destroy the class enemy and establish a popular government. Many so called liberals argue that it is a stark reality as males and females have to live in common camps inside a dense forest, under constant suspense, numerous constraints and fear of police raids, and in such environment unhealthy permissiveness and illicit relationship among males and females is inevitable. Man by nature is a polygamist. Many fair sex suffer from nymphomania who avidly welcome a male for sex. Hence, it is nothing to be upset as it is not going to impair the Maoist revolutionary movement. Broadly speaking, how far their argument is rational from the point of inscrutable ethical and moral law is a matter of debate. However, on the very out set it is socially and morally distasteful and ridicules a movement claimed to be lofty based on idealism and the people's welfare.

Legacy of outrages on tribal females in Bastar region is highly deplorable. However, it has given good handle to the Maoists to enhance their area of control, recruitment drive for the weaker sex and to indoctrinate them in Maoist movement. Admittedly, sexual exploitation of the tribal girls is not a new phenomenon. Many tricksters and dubious public servants working in the field often exploit weaker sex of the tribal community to satisfy their sexual perversion. It is alleged that in the initial stage of suppressing the Maoist movement the administration adopted the international warfare methods of targeting women to threaten the community and break morale of the discomfited and panic-stricken people. In that pursuit rape was used as a tool to undermine dignity and honour of the fair sex and hurt them morally and socially. To my mind, relying on the field experience I am candid that it is a hoax since the Maoists do not belong to a single stock, one clan, one community or one state. However, there is no official confirmation on such obnoxious modus operandi if at all, practiced by the administration or by any individual public servant of this country.

However, a social worker claimed to be a Gandhian, working in the region for last 18 years has prepared a list of incidents of 522 atrocities including 99 rapes which took place from 2005 to 2009 in the Maoist domain at the instigation of the state machinery. Happily, the local habitants admit that situation has been changed. CRPF and BSF personnel are disciplined lot. They do not indulge in excesses while dealing with the people. Earlier the Special Police Officers (SPO) used to treat the people brutally, torture, molest or rape the females. Tribal women were the targets of both rogues and the petty public servants. Of late, ambience has undergone reckonable change. Any miry incident will be reaching the media's notice promptly and gain wide publicity. The journalists' facile pen will expose the wrong doers, generate public opinion and alert the government. Social activists operating in the region say that there is no security for tribal girls. Earlier either the Maoists used to take them away forcibly or they are trafficked as laborers to distance places like Bengalaru or Hyderabad by the unscrupulous contractors or agents. Government employment schemes hardly reach the tribal community. Police and para military forces officials assert that Maoists take away tribal boys and girls when they are 10 to 12 years old and employ them in odd tasks. Eventually, they are trained, indoctrinated and placed in squads. Females are often sexually assaulted by the high and low commanders.

Often female ultras are barbarously treated by the male ultras, arbitrarily punished, sexually abused, forced to participate in perverse or unnatural sex act or killed even on unfounded suspicion or accusation. Unfortunately, the top leaders ignore complaints, do not interfere in local commanders' action on the pretext of maintaining discipline. An unflinching testimony cited below may throw sufficient light on it. Sarala, a girl of 17, a student of a college in Khammam district, Andhra Pradesh, was profoundly inspired by the Maoist ideology and sincerity of the PW cadres aiming at social and political change. She left home on 19 February 1992 to join the PW and reached Sirsapalli in Nizamabad district and stayed in the house of a militant. After a month, Haribhushan, the district secretary of the PW, took her and introduced to Sankar, secretary of the North Telengana zone on March 22, 1992. Sankar suspected her genuiness and brutally tortured her. He instigated other comrades to assault and rape her. Under his initiative three dalams raped her. After gang rape she was shot dead. Propaganda was let loose that as she was working clandestinely for the police, she had been suitably punished. Similar brutalities are not unknown in the ethos and culture of the extremists, which have only blackened image of the Maoist movement and alienated the sober, peace loving people and supporters from them. As a matter of fact, jungle rule prevails in the hide outs and sanctuaries. Harsh treatment by the senior leaders meted to the junior comrades is one of the reasons for desertion of the male Maoists. Indeed, fair sex Maoists are the worse victims of torture, abuse and male chauvinism.

All said and done, the contribution of the fair sex Maoists in sustaining the Red movement is not at all mean or insignificant. Maoist movement may not be acceptable in a democracy. People may feel that the rebels are misguided and dominated by haughty and desperate elements. Their dream for People's war, People's government and elimination of class enemies will never materialise. Peace loving people of the country will never accept violence and bloodshed. The Red terror has only upset and frightened the people and hence the movement is confined to a few small pockets of seven states. Of late, its growth is negligible, rather it is decaying fast. Moreover, the rebels are abysmally disillusioned and are doubtful about its ultimate success. People, once was very friendly to the ultras have been distancing themselves from the head hunting ultras. Dispassionately, inspite of numerous adversaries, sacrifices and criticism, contribution of the women Maoists is laudable. It has cemented the cadre and given fresh impetus to the rebels to continue with the struggle. The idea to topple a democratically elected government and the doctrine of annihilation may not be palatable. Admittedly, it is unethical and unacceptable in a civilised society. Nevertheless, the female Maoists have made a mark as dedicated comrades, painstaking and courageous fighters who deserve recognition without any prejudice. People may be critical and look obliquely at them, but my plastic mind may not wizen in obscurantism or get lost in cul-de-sac. Needless to say, the devil has to be given his due.

Security Forces and the Maoist Movement

Rise of the Naxal movement in West Bengal under the leadership of Comrade Charu Mazumdar and its growth in other states was initially tackled by the state police force and the state police armed battalions. As events moved apace the ultras gained strength and posed a mighty challenge to many states. The affected states requested help and assistance of the union para military forces. Andhra Pradesh raised special battalions, Greyhounds, specialised in jungle warfare and guerrilla tactics. However, West Bengal was reluctant to take help of the central para military forces on the plea of tackling the problem politically. Chief Minister asserted that state police was enough to neutralise the ultras. Radicals and many intellectuals opposed the idea of deployment of the central forces. After an aborted attempt on the Chief Minister the state government was shaken and agreed to deploy central para military forces from June 2009. At that juncture a group of radicals and intellectuals protested, came out on the street, brought out protest march, street procession. Meanwhile, CRPF deployed in Jharkhand and Chhattisgarh, BSF in Odisha put the Maoists in precarious position. In West Bengal CRPF came under criticism for failing to show the desired result during the first six months of its deployment. But the table was turned soon. Once the central forces succeeded in tightening the grip the Maoists were on the run. Critics realised the utility of the central forces. The local populace once were hostile to the central forces realised their mistakes and welcome the CRPF and other central forces. In jungle mahal, West Bengal, rule of law was limping back. People demanded that CRPF should stay in jungle mahal till the ultras are fully disarrayed. In Chhattisgarh people appreciate the welfare activities for the villagers initiated by the CRPF. Broadly speaking, people acknowledge toil, determination of the security and supreme sacrifice of the forces to fight the terror.

To-day, the Central Reserve Police Force (CRPF) is the lead force tasked with internal security duties. They are fighting the Naxal/Maoists in central and eastern India, insurgents in North East and the terrorists in Jammu and Kashmir. There was a time when the ultras were killing three persons every day. From 2007 to 2011, on every second day an Indian cop died fighting terror. During this period 130 CRPF personnel were killed to IED explosion in addition to casualties in attacks, ambush, gun battle etc. Nevertheless, the CRPF personnel did not lose their heart. Radicals and intellectuals were critical for using CRPF along with state forces to curb the ultras and their blood curdling activities. In many places of deployment the local people did not welcome CRPF, rather a section of people was hostile to them. In West Bengal a group of intellectuals led by eminent novelist Sm Mahaseta Devi vehemently protested against deployment of the CRPF in jungle mahal, thronged on the street and marched through the main thoroughfare. Criticism piled upon criticism against them for failing to show positive result from June 2009 to December 2009. Inspite of numerous odds, CRPF kept its morale high, remained firm in their duties. They strictly followed the strike-back-offence policy and gradually achieved spectacular success. In June 2007, 27 coys of the CRPF were deployed in jungle mahal, West Bengal. By December 31, 2011, it was increased to 42 coys. In 2012, the state requested for deploying additional 1300 personnel. Increased demand for the CRPF unmistakably proves CRPF's capability and envious performance to neutralise the ultras.

Constraints and difficulties of the CRPF are not generally known to the people. On receipt of urgent notice CRPF has to move in double quick time to a new place. The area and people are unknown, miscreants are unidentifiable, climate is unconducive, terrain is difficult and hazardous. Temporary camps have to be established in a hurry, badly lacking in minimal civic amenities. Local people are either indifferent or hostile. Local language is hardly known to them to interact with the locals. Indeed, it is a big hurdle. Perhaps they have never worked in the area, topography is totally foreign and unable to distinguish a friend or a foe. They have no time or opportunity to build intelligence network and cultivate local sources. For that they have to depend blindly on the local police. In fact, under insurmountable adversaries the CRPF have to discharge duties, face the head-hunting ultras and aid the local administration to maintain law and order.

In Jharkhand, Chhattisgarh, Malkangiri, Gadchiroli areas the security forces have to work in hilly terrain, thick forest, Amazon like jungle, no road or pathways or reliable local guides are available. In Chhattisgarh, The Maoist dominated turf, and their head quarter, the Abujhmad—the unknown forest, is virtually inaccessible to the outsiders and impregnable to the security forces. Happily, the CRPF have considerably succeeded in reaching many remote corners of inaccessible spots surrounded by the hide-outs of the ultras, dense jungle and habitats of pro Maoist tribal community. Of late, Indian Space Research Organisation's (ISRO) satellites have given an edge to the CRPF to penetrate effectively into deep interior and expose the ultras and their safe shelters which were earlier unknown to the security forces. In fact, access to the images is likely to work as a tremendous multiplier. Satellite images have helped the security forces to initiate operations. With its help CRPF and state police jointly surprised a Maoist training camp functioning in Daringbari, Kondmal district, Odisha, demolished the camp, seized weapons and training materials. Jharkhand police has planned operation in massive scale with the aid of the spy satellites.

On Government of India's initiative CRPF raised elite combat battalion, Cobra (Combat battalion for Resolute Action) to meet the internal security challenges mainly from the point of guerrilla tactics and jungle warfare technique used by the left wing extremists. Union government asked the states to raise commando coys on the line of the Cobra battalions of the CRPF to meet the growing threat of the ultras. Centre proposed to set up six counter insurgency schools with the assistance of the CRPF in Odisha, Andhra Pradesh, Chhattisgarh and Jharkhand. Broadly, the union government has been depending much on the CRPF for organising specialised training in jungle warfare, guerrilla tactics for the security forces of other states. It is, indeed, a recognition for a force. Undeniably, the CRPF has been facing the main brunt of the terrorists, the secessionists in J&K, and bloody violence of the extremists in eastern and central India. In fact, efficient handling of the ultras, indomitable will to curb the ultras and loss of personnel in attacks, ambush, land mine blasts and gun battles in pursuit of maintaining internal security has placed the CRPF in higher pedestal.

In Bastar region, Chhattisgarh, the iconic heart of the Maoist insurgency, Dantiwada, Bijapaur, Sukma, Narayanpur, Kankar, districts in two years back were virtually the liberated zone where the writs of the Maoists were supreme. In this region the head quarter of the Maoists, called Abujhmad, has been functioning. Indifference of the state has indirectly allowed to grow the Red terror. Along with disappearance of the rule of law the parallel government of the dauntless Maoists had been operating. Fortunately, deteriorating situation forced both the union and state governments to meet the threat with consummate preparation and determination. Deployment of central para military forces in massive scale, joint action by state police and central forces soon produced the expected result. The welter of porous interstate co-ordination between the Maoist ridden states and security forces was successfully liquidated. The state police was no longer wobbly. Indeed, solidarity of both forces gave a fresh impetus and courage to fight the ultras. The shambolic situation indicated a positive note of improvement. Maoists were losing grip fast on the so called liberated territory, preferred retreat to hang on the dominated turf. Normal life slowly returned to many disturbed districts. In Dantiwada district a hive of schools, colleges, hostels, market places, booming business etc. brought back a bubbling life. Hoardings of sexy cine actress, business advertisements, wall-posters on cultural activities reminded the noise and bustle and the hectic past.

A huge educational hub is coming up at Geedam, a tiny town situated very close to Dantiwada which was unimaginable a few years back. Meanwhile rural development programme and its forceful implementation is a substantial relief to the poor and neglected tribal. It needs no reiteration that reclaim of a sizeable portion of the Maoist controlled territory and restoration of peace in Dantiwada and many places in Bastar region was possible due to indomitable will, resoluteness and sacrifices of the security forces. The local people say that situation has remarkably improved. Maoists had been controlling them through guns, forced them to join their meetings, serve food, dig up roads, send sons and daughters for terror training. As terror wind was inclined to decline the community policing both by the state and the central forces gained momentum. Anti-Maoist public opinion became louder. The Maoists were shaken seeing erosion in their unquestioned authority. They circulated pamphlets sternly warning the villagers for not adhering to their diktats and supremacy. Maoists vehemently criticized the growth of educational hub at Geedam.

CRPF has initiated welfare activities in Baster region in big scale. It has opened 100 telemedicine camps function on Mondays and Thursdays Patients deserve greater medical care are sent to the All India Institute of Medical Sciences, Raipur branch. CRPF distribute foot balls, sports goods to boys, girls and students to motivate them in sports and games. Personnel also play and inter act with them freely. They distribute solar panel, medicine and other stuff to the tribal to gain their good will. In fact, extensive welfare activities have drawn the CRPF close to many villagers. Many are very popular with the students, youths and villagers. One of the officers of a Cobra battalion is treated as a darling of the local tribal community. Reputation that CRPF and central forces are disciplined persons, compassionate in treating the people, good in conduct and behavior and do not use rough and ready method has travelled far and wide. Evidently, it has helped to reduce the hiatus between the security forces and the local tribal community. Near hostility spirit of the villagers has been reduced considerably. Majority of them co-operate with the cops, pass on information and try to help the security forces. Grudge against the security forces for the excesses and high handedness committed by the SPOs no longer up set the peace loving villagers. Banks and post offices have been functioning smoothly which was unthinkable a few years back. Several schools have been built by the NMDC. The rural job scheme, National Rural Employment Guarantee Act (NREGA) has been working fairly well. Job seekers' crowd is noticeable.

Improvement in law and order, access of the security forces right into the Maoist dominated territory and reclaim of their turf is quia ipsa loquitur. Right from 2010 the Maoists are in back foot. In 2009 and 2010, total 908 and 1005 persons respectively were killed in Maoist violence. In 2011 and 2012 it was reduced to 611 and 415 respectively. In 2009, there were 2258 attacks but it declined to 1415 in 2012. Admittedly, now semblance of rule of law is apparent in many parts of Bastar region. Chief Minister of Chhattisgarh has stated, "We are coming up with social, health and educational schemes for the tribals and have got clear results on the ground."

The CRPF officers working in the field and facing the ultras directly earn valuable experience. They organise patrols, combing, drive for hunt operations basing on ground reality. The field officers' assessment often helps to prepare meaningful strategy in higher level to frustrate the ultras. A particular example will suffice to confirm how field experience is useful for preparing the larger strategy. A meeting with the Maoist ripped states was organized by the MHA in New Delhi. During deliberations an officer representing the CRPF pointed out the idea of raising bounties for catching the top Maoists. The proposal was broadly appreciated by the participants. However, since it is a state subject the state governments have to decide the question. Therefore, the Union Home Secretary advised to refer the matter to the states to work on it. Importantly, the government of Andhra Pradesh has declared maximum reward money for intelligence and arrest of the ultras. It is reviewed and enhanced from time to time so that persons are encouraged to put heart and soul and work out the clue. Truly, it has produced very good result. To-day, reward for rupees 2.52 crores for arrest of L.R. Rao alias Ganapathy, the top man of the Maoist politburo, has been declared.

Unfortunately, CRPF has come under scathing criticism for indiscreet actions and loss of man power. On April 6, 2010, at about 6 AM, a CRPF patrol of the 62 battalion under a Dy commandant was ambushed at Termitola, Dantiwara district, by a strong group of Maoists. In fact, surprise was complete and the CRPF personnel had no opportunity to defend themselves. Seventy six personnel including the Dy Commandant and an Assistant commandant were killed. Their weapons including LMGs, mortars were taken away. The blow was fatal and the CRPF came under pungent criticism. The Union Home Minister shouldering responsibility for the debacle wanted to resign. But the Prime Minister did not accept it. The print media was in up-in-arms. In an editorial, a national daily remarked that it was an unquestionable tactical failure and to continue such ineffective operations only added to the clout the Maoists wield. DGP of Chhattisgarh blamed the CRPF for the failure. CRPF felt that intelligence output furnished by the state police was deficient. The Congress party demanded the Chief Minister's resignation. The General Secretary of the AICC of the state said that the police Chief did not deserve to continue. Dispassionately, the Dy Commandant ignored the cardinal principle of jungle warfare. Secondly, CRPF suffered from developing contact with the local people. Thirdly, porous or lukewarm co-ordination with local police was one of the reasons for the catastrophe. However, instead of entering into a debate it was clear that the ambush zone was not taken seriously by the field commander. Moreover, chance of a surprise attack in the Maoist infested areas was not given consummate heed. Unfortunately, further misery for the CRPF waited. On June 29, 2010, in Narayanpur district, elements of 39 CRPF battalion were ambushed and 26 CRPF personnel were killed. In fact, for such massive losses within quick succession competence of the CRPF was obliquely looked at. Press media commented that the CRPF had not learnt lesson from the massacre of 76 cops of the 62 Bn in Dantiwada district. Similar massacre in Narayanpur district exposed the CRPF's monumental incompetence and utter lack of tactical appreciation of the ground. In its editorial a national daily hinted at deploying army. It argued whether army could remain unutilized when authority of the Indian state is being so daringly challenged.

In June 2012, on receipt of information that in Basuguda village, close to Silger forest, Dantiwara district, a group of Maoists have gathered and inter acting with the villagers. Maoists were brain washing them and goading them to come under their fold. Acting on the information, about three hundred CRPF and police personnel jointly surrounded the village and asked the Maoists to surrender. Maoists with the help of the villagers including minors, promptly built a human shield around them, refused to surrender. After repeated warning the attempt of the security forces to arrest them was resisted. Many tried to escape using cover of the human shield and fired at the cops. In exchange of fire nineteen members including several minors who formed the human barrier, were killed. In the encounter CRPF played the major role and six CRPF personnel were injured. The villagers who formed human shield were not the Maoists. Perhaps seeing advance of the security forces the Maoists forced them to make a barrier around them so that they could escape out witting the advancing cops. Indeed, action of the CRPF and shooting down innocent villagers including minors on the plea of rounding up the Maoists was untenable. It was illegal and inhuman and contrary to ethics of dealing with a peaceful crowd. Criticism against the CRPF surcharged atmosphere. Impartial public opinion badly went against them. Undoubtedly, it is an odious blot on the performance of the CRPF. Its head quarter has assured to initiate action against the black sheep and stop such recurrence in future.

Trinamool Congress under leadership of Miss Mamata Banerjee formed the government in West Bengal in May 2011. The new government was ambivalent to decide about the fate of the joint operation by the security forces. In pre-election campaigns the Trinamool Congress (TMC) supremo Miss Banerjee promised many concessions to the Maoists including release of the Maoists languishing in jails, withdrawal of prosecutions against the ultras etc. Critics were inclined to believe that a nexus between the Maoists and the TMC had been manifestly operating to oust the Left Front government from the state. The new Chief Minister appealed to the Maoists to give up violence and join the main stream. No clear instruction was issued to the security forces either to suspend or give up operation against the Maoists. In fact suspense piled upon suspense and time was running out. A team of interlocutors was set to enter into dialogue with the ultras. Watching indecisiveness of the government and lull in joint forces operation the shrewd Maoists attempted to re-organise the movement in jungle mahal and resorted to violence. On August 24, they killed a local TMC leader. Again on September 20, 2011, Maoists killed another leader of the TMC near Jhargram town. The second killing indicated the return of the spectre of terror in West Bengal. CM warned the Maoists and kept the security forces under greater suspense.

Evidence was clear and comprehensive that the Maoists were regrouping and reorganising for massive strike. Cacophony of impending unrest alarmed the administration and put the security forces in abyss anxiety. They were afraid that the positive gain achieved by the joint forces by virtue of plodding industry, perseverance and sacrifices was going to be belied due the state's indifference or indecision. Truly, suspension of the raids, combing or encircling hide outs, dispatching fighting patrols, firm control on the reclaimed turf etc. was going to energise and re-activate the hydra headed monster.

The Union Home Minister stated, "Left-wing extremism was the most violent movement in the country and that the CPI-Maoist was the most violent organisation." He added further, "although the number of incidents and number of casualties seem to indicate a decrease in the level of violence, this is largely attributable to the changed situation in W.B." In short, admission of the Union Home Minister signified the meaningful contribution of the joint forces including the central forces to curb the ultras in W.B. Hence, return of the Maoist terror alarmed the security forces and the administration. Senior officials in charge of operations were firm that under no circumstances good work done would be allowed to be undone.

Union Home Minister P. Chidambaram was equally disturbed and issued a note of caution that the Maoists were increasing their strength in jungle mahal. Prior to that, senior officials of the CRPF deployed in jungle mahal had urged the state government to resume joint operation once again without wasting time. They pleaded that in absence of joint operation the area of domination secured already was gradually facing the threat of the Maoists. In fact, state forces working shoulder to shoulder were unable to participate in operations as the state lacked clear cut policy to curb the outrages unleashed again by the ultras. The state's ambivalence and absence of decisive instructions the central forces were compelled to withdraw from spear-heading offensive field duties. They had to restrict themselves to routine patrolling and killed time languishing in camps awaiting order. Admittedly, inaction and idleness provided handle to the Maoists to return with renewed vigour, re-capture the lost turf and re-establish their authority.

On August 11, 2011, in heavy exchange of fire in Laxmanpur jungle several CRPF personnel were wounded and subsequently one of them succumbed to injuries. Inspector General of the CRPF complained to the higher authority of the police of W.B. that lack of intelligence-based operation resulted in the gun battle and death of a cop. He informed the higher authority that the joint forces were grossly under utilised and only performing routine maneouverings instead of intelligence based night operations. Consequently their area domination was lamentably weakened. Secondly, in addition to regrouping the Maoists were obstructing rural development works initiated by the state government. They were resisting the public servants to distribute essential commodities to the villagers through the public distribution system. Thirdly, the Maoists were planning to attack the camps of the security forces in massive strength. They were selecting soft targets to attack, like police stations located in isolated places, police patrols, small police contingents and CRPF camps. IG made it clear that the ultras were mustering strength and preparing grounds to renew the onslaught. Hence, unless they are checked and disarrayed it would be difficult to control and repulse their impending attacks. IG reminded the state the usefulness and deterrence of the joint operations and requested the state government to give free hand and allow the joint operation to commence without further loss of time. At the spot of gun battle held on August 11, 2011, the Maoists left behind many materials which confirmed that they had been camping there for several days. Yet, the state was lukewarm to the growing menace. Perhaps the state still believed to tame the Maoists through dialogues, negotiation and initiatives taken by the interlocutors.

In jungle mahal right from 2011, the Maoists were in defensive state. Security forces have pushed them deep into the forest. In a well-planned encounter, Kishanji, the member of the Maoist politburo and the dramatis personae of the eastern theatre of the Maoist battle command and a dreaded Maoist leader, Sasadhar Mahato were killed. Here the CRPF played a crucial role. Since then, the leaderless Maoists in jungle mahal had lost the grip fast. As the Maoist activities dried up and triumph of security forces was manifestly clear the peace loving people heaved a sigh of relief. Ironically, there was no love lost between the CRPF and the people of the jungle mahal. However, as events moved apace, the unfriendly people appreciated the CRPF's positive role. They demanded that the central forces should not be withdrawn from jungle mahal till the outlaws are neutralised and normalcy is fully restored. I interacted with many villagers living near the CRPF camps. They categorically stated that presence of the CRPF has prevented the ultras from raiding the villages, assault them and extort money, loot ration, force them to cook meals and supply food and abduct the youths to join the Maoist training camps. They are candid that temporary CRPF camps are deterrent to keep away the Maoists which have been indirectly providing security to the village and villagers.

Border Security Forces deployed in Malkangiri area, Odisha have been tackling the Maoists effectively along with the state police. A Commandant of a battalion along with a few personnel was killed in a land mine blast near Chitrakonda. CISF successfully repulsed the Maoist attack to loot the armoury at Damanjory, Nelco plant, in Korapur district Odisha. In a protracted gun battle they pushed back the Maoists, saved the armoury and the explosive store and lost eleven cops. CISF has been maintaining security of the NMDC plant in Bastar region, repulsed several attacks and in that pursuit lost many of their comrades. Railway Protection Force (RPF) has been facing the Maoists frequently. They escort the trains, protect the passengers and encounter the Maoists. In Jharkhand they fought the Maoists more than once, lost a few personnel and their weapons were looted. In sum, contribution of other para military forces, like ITBP, SSB in tackling the ultras is in no way mean. Details of their activities are not discussed here due to lack of space which is sincerely regretted.

Frankly speaking, now the Maoist atrocity has been contained to a great extent. Sporadic violence and attack on the security forces in Jharkhand and Chhattisgarh disturbing the peace. However, dispassionate examination of the Maoist activities makes it clear that the Maoist movement is on the wane and the Maoists are in cul de sac. Nevertheless, it is illusory to imagine that the Maoists and their movement would be wiped out soon. Truly, none can predict the decay or death of the hydra-headed monster as the cult of Maoism is aimed at eradication of the poverty, ensuring equality, human rights and the advancement of the poor and deprived people.

In a nutshell, success in fighting the proxy war and taming the pitiless ultras greatly goes to the credit of the state police and the central forces. Among the central forces to share credit CRPF is in the front seat. Dispassionately, the nation should pay glowing tribute to the state police and central para military forces for their fortitude, single minded devotion and supreme sacrifices for fighting the head hunting ultras. Undeniably, cops' good work goes often unheralded and unrecognised. Critics may sarcastically question the lavish eulogy showered on the security forces. Needless to say, my observation is based on direct evidence, spot visits, examination of the eye witnesses and local villagers and many Maoists. Indeed, my pensive analysis is totally free from prejudice and recorded strictly adhering to the punctilious path of truth.

CHAPTER TEN

Police Excesses in West Bengal, Maoist Movement Declining, Threat Perception

Comrade Charu Mazumder's call for the annihilation of the class enemy received positive response from radicals, a set of intellectuals, teachers and student community. Many bright students from reputed colleges, like Presidency College, Kolkata, colleges of Nadia, Murshidabad, Birbhum joined the movement suspending studies. They firmly believed that the Red flag was going to be fluttered over the Red Fort New Delhi by 1975. They agreed that a revolutionary has to stain his hand with blood of the class enemy. Hence, youths and students sincerely and devoutly joined the Naxal cadre. They were baptized assigning the task of killing a class enemy. Many proved themselves worthy of the task of brutally killing many human being. In Calcutta city many traffic constables were attacked and barbarously killed. The perplexed police failed the stop bloodletting and disarray the ideologically groomed blood thirsty cadres. Perhaps police realised that conventional policing was not enough to contain the movement. Police therefore, followed the policy of hire and fire, bullet for bullet.

Allegations of false encounters and gunning down the suspects are often heard. In Madhya Pradesh, Rajasthan and Punjab, the police on the ground of controlling the dacoity-menace often kill dreaded criminals in the so called encounters. In J&K security forces often gun down the trans-border terrorists for illegal infiltration or attacking the security forces. Needless to act, annihilation in fake encounters is contrary to professional ethics, probity and humanity. Secondly, such reckless killing tantamount to cold blooded murder which is highly condemnable and not acceptable in a civilised society.

Torrent of the Naxal movement in West Bengal under Comrade Charu Mazumdar's leadership posed a gigantic threat to the law and order authority. Its deadly impact both in Calcutta city and many rural pockets of the state put the police and administration in abject bewilderment. Both Calcutta and West Bengal police were not prepared, their intelligence machinery awfully lagged behind to tackle the spectre of the blood thirsty fanatics and killers. Secondly, the outlaws and the killers neither had any past record nor were history sheeters. Therefore, police faced considerable difficulties in identifying and tracing out the culprits. Secondly, history of the Naxal movement, its organisation, aims and object was scantily known to the police. Police generally keep records; maintain watch, surveillance, on the suspects, out laws and convicts released from the jails. The comrades for the Naxal movement were fresh from the society, educational institutions, or various organisations, were ordinarily not out laws or suspects. No details of their antecedents were available in police file. Hence, it was very difficult for the police to distinguish between a Naxal and an ordinary criminal and to initiate suitable action.

With these adversaries the police was in a quandary to handle the growing extra ordinary threat to peace and social order. In Kolkata city many traffic constables and cops were murdered in broad day light by the Naxals. Assailants, generally, in a group attacked armed with knives, daggers, choppers, and stabbed the target repeatedly, disfigured the body or in some case severed limbs, head, cut limbs into pieces. Sometimes the severed head was kept hanging in public place. A horrid scene was created deliberately to thwart the people and to generate panic in the area. Indeed, such savage killing was not heard or seen by the peace loving people. Truly, the police was taken unawares to handle such an unprecedented and bloodletting movement supported by the radicals, students, educated, and the so called progressive persons.

The perplexed police failed to curb the movement, stop butchery and instill confidence among the people. In fact, seeing gory deaths of the colleagues, retaliatory spirit goaded them so settle score with the ultras but was unable to know the where about of the leaders and the devoted activists and the hide outs. However, many cops working in the field and in the police station level suo motu decided to follow the aggressive policy. They believed that tit for tat would be deterrent to disarray the Naxals. In many cases during raid if an ultras was picked up or arrested otherwise, the suspect was taken to unknown place on the plea of interrogation and on the way he was shot dead and the dead body was either thrown or shown as encounter death. This monstrous practice adopted by a handful of overzealous police officers. But from 1972, the government under the Chief Minister S.S. Ray it took ugly turn. The secret killing of the Naxals was given a covert legitimacy by the police chief and the Chief Minister. Unfortunately, cops working in police stations overzealously persuaded it to contain or wipe out the movement. In a selected and informal gathering the Police Chief of West Bengal forcefully stated, "If a mad dog enters into your drawing room what you will do?" As none gained courage to reply in fear of discipline, he continued, "Shoot it down." Mind and stand of the police chief was very much known to the cops. Hence, cops working in the field were impelled by the idea of eliminating the ultras and thereby made his jurisdiction immune from Naxal menace.

Initially, Naxal attacks were one sided and the cops were the only victims. But soon the table turned. The police hierarchy and government's view emboldened the cops to single out the Naxals mere on suspicion and gun them down. This obviously frightened the Naxals who were anxious of their security. Parents, guardians of the youths and students who embraced the Naxal cult were worried of the safety and future of the wards visualising the cops' ruthless and barbarous measures in neutralising the Naxal movement. In fact, the large number of unnerved youths and students went underground to save themselves from the cruel hand of the cops. Many escaped to other states to avert the police's wrath. In process many bright students possessing envious academic records were killed. Exodus of many youths and students from many renowned educational institutions of West Bengal upset the parents, teachers, educationists and intellectuals. A few instances mentioned below are enough testimony to corroborate the savage killings let loose by the cops on the pretext of curbing the Naxal movement.

A group of eight Bengali students, male and weaker sex within the age group of 18 to 22 escaped from West Bengal and took shelter in the pilgrimage town Puri, Odisha. Local police caught them suspecting them to be extremists and brought them to the town police station for interrogation and to take follow up action. The local police faced difficulties to interrogate them as they were not well conversant with Bengali language. I was enjoying holidays in Puri. The Superintendent of Police, Puri contacted and requested me to help the interrogating officers to overcome language difficulties. In fact, I was requested to act an interpreter and help the police to elicit the truth. Reaching the P S, I noticed six youths and two girls from middle class families. From wearing apparel and vermillion marks on the forehead of the girls I realised that they entered into wed lock not before a week. They admitted that they had married two colleagues and pointed at their husbands. Since such early marriage in educated and progressive families hardly celebrated in West Bengal, I asked them the secret of their early and hurried marriage. They were reluctant to divulge the truth.

Protracted interrogation revealed that they were inspired by the new political idea of the classless society and the People's government and therefore, responding to the call of the comrade Charu Mazumdar they had joined the movement. They hoped to bring a change for the society discarding the existing political and social order. They were actively working as Naxal cadres, moving from place to place adhering to the instructions of the party bosses. They were trained to kill cats, dogs, goats and finally detailed to assist the squad ear marked for killing a man or woman. They took the lessons sincerely and were in readiness to kill person on receipt of instruction. They rehearsed many times before going for an operation with the squad. Both girls were reading in Higher Secondary class and the boys were reading in colleges. They joined the movement suspending studies and defying vehement opposition of the parents.

I asked, "Who was your mentor and briefed you the ideology of the Naxalism?" One of them appeared to be taking the leading role, replied, "A senior student of the college was the source and the contact person who used to brain wash us regularly. We were charmed by his oratory and the picture he projected for the welfare of the poor and down trodden."

"What was the reason for untimely and hurried marriage for the couples present?"

"Police was after us, we are likely to be liquidated by the police at any time."

The married youths replied," We are intensely in love. We may be the victims of the police's bullets at any moment. Therefore, we wanted to be united as early as possible to get the taste of love and wedded life."

"Why all of you have left West Bengal and taken refuge in Odisha?"

"Police was chasing us desperately and with vengeance. If they happen to catch us they will shoot and kill us like rabbit dogs. We want to live mingling with the common people. We want a safe shelter to avoid the dragnet of the revengeful police. We beg, please do not hand over us to West Bengal police."

They looked very stubborn and carried no regret for joining the Naxal movement. But they were very scared of the police's barbarous killing which was cold blooded murder. I understood from conversation that they were keen to give up or withdraw from the Naxal movement and wanted to live happily and therefore taken shelter in Odisha assuming that they were safe and beyond the reach of the West Bengal police.

I realised that they were spirited and sincerely guided by the vision of bringing a new era for the betterment of the poor and deprived people. However, they were not much conversant with the Mao's thought and political philosophy. In fact, their tender age, inexperience and ardent desire to improve the lot of the poor and have-not was adroitly exploited by the leaders of the Naxal movement.

I was dismayed thinking the obfuscated future of the youths. Their fervent appeal for not handing them over to the cops of the W.B. and their genuine fear that they would be annihilated if they happened to fall in the hands of the cops of their own state, indeed, was disturbing. I was certain that it would equally shake the right thinking persons. Unfortunately, it was beyond my capacity to protect them from impending fear and danger. After all, Odisha police was legally bound to hand them over to the W.B. police on receipt of formal requisition from them under the Criminal Procedure Code (CrPC).

After a few days I enquired from the SP about the fate of the suspects interrogated by me. He informed that four cops of W.B. headed by an SI (Sub inspector) arrived, took charge of the suspects and left for West Bengal. The team discussed the growing Naxalite problem with the officers of the Town PS, Puri. They expressed disgust for detailing them for escorting the ultras from other state to W.B. However, they whispered that their burden would be lightened soon as the suspects were going to be executed during the transit at a suitable place. They added that the police had been informally following the practice of liquidating the Naxals to control the Naxal movement. They believed that this modus operandi produced good dividend. They were highly critical of the existing procedure of investigation, prosecution and delay in judicial process. They said that stultifying legalism is a mighty bottle neck to the criminal justice system and to ensure relief to the aggrieved persons seeking justice. The cops of Odisha police were shocked hearing the hint of a sinister design driving at the cold blooded murder. In fact, mystery was unveiled before them why the suspects vehemently begged for not delivering them to the WB police. Subsequently, exhaustive verification disclosed that Calcutta and WB police had been following the illegal and horrendous practice of killing Naxals in fake encounters. It was amply corroborated from adirect evidence high-lighted below.

On the eve of the Parliamentary election in 1971, a battalion of the Orissa Military Police (OMP) commended by me was air lifted from Jharsuguda airport, Odisha, and dropped in Kolaikunda aerodrome, Medinapur district, W.B. We were directed to proceed to Contai sub division for performing election duties. At Kolaikunda airport a police officer of the district received me. We were travelling in a police jeep. On the way an Inspector of police met me and briefed me about the topography, Naxal threat and the police's problem to tackle the ultras. He narrated three or four incidents how he neutralised the ultras' outrages. He said that ultras were killing innocent persons and cops without any rhyme or reason. If a Naxal was arrested no witness was willing to come forward and depose before the court. Hence, to keep the area safe and free from the Naxal menace, counter killing of the ultras was the appropriate remedy. However, I was unable to appreciate his logic. I firmly told him that the cops being the custodian of the law and order cannot play the role of a criminal or commit crime. Instead of agreeing with me he said that Naxal calamity could not be contained by normal policing. The police must modify its mode and style of functioning. Police had to adopt the policy of hire and fire to disarray the Naxals. Suddenly, he was excited and stated, "I have executed four Naxals. After they were caught, I fired at them from a revolver and killed them. This is the reason in my jurisdiction, the ultras are hardly active." I was at a loss hearing him and unable to reconcile how a police officer could justify or took credit after committing cold blooded murder. I was equally up set seeing that police training, discipline, professional ethics and sense of benign duty to protect life and property of a person, had no influence or impact on him. After all, he was required to respect the inscrutable moral law and expected to be conscious of the Divine punishment. After some times, he took leave from me and went for other duty. The journey became bitter to me. As I went up the ladder, I saw many police officers hardly sympathetic to public cause and indifferent to serve the people with the motto of selfless and honest public service.

Adhering to the request of the government of W.B., the Orissa Military Police (OMP) personnel were deployed in Howrah town, Salt Lake and Barasat town in 1970. Naxalite violence in these places was in its peak. Attack, ambush and annihilation of men and cops continued unabatedly. Barasat, a part of greater Calcutta was in the grip of urbanisation. Here violence and blood bath put the people under fear and panic. Cops of Barasat police station were under boundless pressure. Police was unable to arrest the right culprits, in spite of painstaking and sincere effort. In nights they were raiding hide outs of the ultras but success was negligible. The frustrated cops obdurately tried to arrest the deteriorating law and order situation by fair or foul means. Once in a wee hour local police with the help of the OMP platoon surrounded a double storied building on receipt of reliable intelligence that two young Naxals armed with fire arms had taken shelter on the first floor of the building. However, before the cops reached the first floor the Naxals got the scent, went up the roof and tried to escape climbing down catching the rain water pipes. Reaching the ground both of them ran to out-wit the cops. The OMP personnel under the Subadar (platoon commander) cordoned the building already chased and caught one of them. The other managed to escape. The Subadar firmly holding the suspect's hand brought him near the building. At that juncture the Circle Inspector of Police arrived. Without verifying the matter, he instructed the Subadar to shoot down the arrested suspect. Subadar declined to carry out the CI's instruction and replied, "We do not shoot and kill an accused in custody. My Commandant's order in this respect is very clear."

The CI retorted, "If you are reluctant to obey me, very well, I will myself finish the task." Within a few seconds, he dragged out his pistol from the holster and shot the accused. The Subadar was still holding the hand of the injured suspect who was struggling for life. The unbearable and matchless barbarity dumb founded the Subadar and other cops present. The lifeless body was dropped on the ground. The CI left the scene without uttering a word. The other cops sent the dead body for autopsy and prepared records to give it a pretentious encounter killing.

The Subadar formally brought the incident to my notice. I submitted a detailed report to the Inspector General of Police Odisha. He in turn drew it to the attention of the IGP West Bengal. Fortunately, the then IGP (Ranjit Gupta, IP) sent a reply condemning the murky incident and expressing his sincere regret. Frankly speaking, the above incidents are unflinching testimony of the police's excesses and brutality in tackling the Naxals and the Naxal movement in W.B. As a matter of fact, fast growth of the Naxal cadre and dreaded violence unleashed by the ultras topsy-turvies the unprepared police. Being unable to handle the problem professionally, the police took the path of counter violence to disarray the ultras.

Maoist Movement Decaying?

Birth of the CPI (Maoist) in September 2004, indicated a new era in the Maoist movement in India. From 2005 the Maoist movement gained extra ordinary momentum. Its impact on the radicals, intellectuals, thinkers and the poverty stricken rural mass was reckonable. It put both union and violence ridden state governments in abyss anxiety. The bogey of the liberated zone and the Red corridor is a formidable threat to combat the swift growing Maoist movement. In fact, by the middle of 2010 it reached its zenith and soon followed by a sharp fall. Its meteoric rise was welcomed by radicals, a group of intellectuals and the supporters of the ultra-left movement. However, its quick fall brought a sense of relief to the sober and peace loving people and the people who cling on democratic values.

Its rapid growth, influence and control on the rural mass, especially, the tribal population has been highlighted already. Frankly speaking, a revolutionary movement is based on firm ideology and must follow several cardinal principles. It must be instinctive and enjoy spontaneous support and patronage of the people. The leadership must be the symbol of morality, ethics and tampered with patriotic spirit and free from stigma. True, the extremists and the Maoists succeeded in making a dent on the poor and neglected rural populace, especially, the tribal communities in several states of the Central India. It is equally important to pin point why it is unsuccessful to penetrate into other states where the sizeable people live below the poverty line and their suffering knows no bound. In this context, in addition to many reasons, the deficiency of the extremists to win over heart of the people needs dispassionate examination.

Violence and Outrages Disliked by the People

Maoists assert that the classless society and the people's government can be achieved through the barrel of the gun. Comrade Charu Mazumdar said, "If a revolutionary does not make his hand red with the blood of enemies then he is not a Communist." The high-falutin propaganda on annihilation of the class enemy and establishment of the people's government excited the down trodden and a section of the rural mass. They imagined that the meridian splendor is knocking at the door through the hands of the perpetrators of the Maoist revolution. However, exuberant flippancy soon evaporated. Sober and peace loving people were mortally frightened knowing Maoism is the synonym of violence and bloodshed. Leaders' rebellious utterances and insolent forays further scared the people. Indeed, people belonging to the land of peace and ahimsa by no means can welcome violence, killing and massacre. They are unable to reconcile that unrest and bloodbath can bring or guarantee a good government and welfare of the people.

Erosion in the People's Faith

People who have been keeping information of the political developments of the

Communist countries in the world see a wide gap between the lofty ideal of the Marxist movement and its ground reality. True, the Marxism although is placed on the higher pedestal of humanism. However, there are instances that after acquiring political power it has opened the flood gate for the worst type of tyranny. Unfortunately, immorality of misguiding the people promising a fair and the people's government is too patent and injustice is too cynical. It is an irony that the people once carried high opinion and trusted the Maoists as the saviour of the poor and down trodden, now are dismayed and take them as tricksters and perpetrators of outrages and violence. Poor and exploited people's implicit faith and respect on the Maoists is a ghastly miscalculation.

Fear of the People for a New Regime

The aim of the Compact Revolutionary Zone (CRZ) or the Red Corridor right from Tamilnadu to Nepal, classless society and the people's government have scared and confused the people. Since it is not explained or defined, they are afraid of some unknown danger. People are unable to visualise its structure, shape and likely performance. None is sure how far the new government, if at all, materialised will be honest, competent and viable to serve the people. Uncertainty and fear of an authoritarian or oppressive regime haunt them. Secondly, the makers of the new government may be good as dedicated comrades but their ability and sense of responsibility to run a government has not been tested. It is an uphill task to fit a new regime for governing a country after six decades of the democratic rule where individual freedom, freedom of speech and reign of the law is paramount Undeniably, the people are apprehensive that their fundamental rights, blessing of the *Habeas Corpus* and the rule of law may be circumscribed. The cult of a new government deviating from the democratic values may demolish the existing social and political order. A reign of terror and anarchy may prevail, destroy peace, happiness and stability of the society. Admittedly, art and skill of running a government needs a long course of preparation or practical education for the rulers. Simultaneously, surging up of the masses to adapt themselves in the new political ideology and culture is equally important. Admittedly, "Democracy is a philosophy of life and outlook on the world. The authority of the state and its laws is derived from general agreement among citizens upon the main postulates of philosophy of life." A question, therefore, may arise how far it is possible for an individual to express his opinion freely and practice liberty without any interference or control. Taking holistic view the impartial critics feel that experiment of a new political ideology tampered with cult of violence practiced by the head hunting Maoists may be catastrophic.

Wanton Cruelty and Killing Shock the People

In pursuance of the revolutionary goal, the extremists have let loose attack, arson, extortion, kidnapping, abduction and dastardly killing. After murder, the ultras gorge out eyes, dismember limbs, treat the dead and wounded with extreme indignity. In Sukma district, Chhattisgarh after savage killing of 28 Congress leaders and activists, the Maoists including the fair sex Maoists barbarously treated the dead and injured, rejoiced the so called success vulgarly and danced devilishly around the dead bodies. Indeed, brutal killing, boundless cruelty and animal fury have shocked the people. The Bestial savagery indulged in by the head hunting ultras has unveiled their monstrous face. It has shocked the people and alienated them from the Maoists.

People's Disillusionment

Progress of the PW in Andhra Pradesh and in Bastar region, MCC's progress in Bihar, and the Maoist writs running in the so called liberated zone in Chhattisgarh and alarming success after merger of the PW and the MCC in 2004, convinced many about the potential of the Maoists to reach the goal. The support base built on the rural mass enthusiastically supported the movement. A big section of the rural mass was inclined to believe that the dream of the Maoists is going to be fulfilled soon and foundation of the people's government is a matter of time. They assisted the ultras in many ways, providing food, shelter, communicating intelligence on the movement of the security forces and protected them against the police raids taking risk and building human shield. For the sake of the ultras they tolerated police harassment, torture, criminal prosecution and some of them even faced death. Paradoxically, ignoring gratitude the ultras brutally killed many tribal on mere suspicion without giving the victims any opportunity to defend. Brutal killing of the fellow tribal, dishonour to the tribal fair sex, kidnapping of adolescents from tribal families to join the Maoist militia etc. upset the tribal people. Indeed, under current of discontentment has been brewing which eventually took the shape of hostility.

Unethical and Immoral Activities Upset the People

Blatant and reckless sexual exploitation of the fair sex Maoists have dismayed even the radicals and the devoted supporters of the Maoist movement In Bihar several Maoist leaders secretly acquired money and properties, purchased land, bungalows, sent son or daughter to foreign countries for higher study. In Jharkhand a leader siphoned a portion of booty looted from a bank for his personal use. Again, conflict between the tribal Maoists and the higher caste Maoists, especially, the Yadavs created a wide rift in the Maoist out-fit in Bihar. The leaders living in urban areas enjoying urban comfort are unpalatable to the Maoists active in the field. In Andhra Pradesh, sickening details of rivalry and acrimony between the higher caste ultras and the lower caste ultras has shaken faith of the people on them. In Odisha, supremacy of the Maoists from Andhra Pradesh on the Maoists of Odisha has led to an ugly situation. Consequently, a rift developed and the Odisha Maobadi party was born. Rich war chest of the outfit, collection of approximately rupees 1500 crores annually by extortion, robbery, ransom, levy etc. is obliquely looked at by the impartial people. Stigma of immorality, caste conflict, and many leaders' lust for money and wealth to enrich them dishonestly has shaken faith of the people. News of the mound of eels have been travelling from mouth to mouth of the people who once regarded the Maoists as the harbinger of an new era and expected a clean society, honest and welfare oriented government. As events moved apace neither the ultras modified odious activities nor gave up outrages, extortion, kidnapping and dastardly killing. Moreover, they failed to indicate the probable time and date of establishing the people's government. In short, disappointment piled upon disappointment. The discomfited people considered it wise to maintain distance from the ultras. In short, the ultras' brutality and indiscriminate killing without distinguishing a friend or a foe has generated deep resentment among the members of the support base which has culminated in indifference or hostility of the rural mass.

Security Forces and Their Mailed Fist

The steady growth of the extremists in several states was initially taken casually by the union as well as the concerned state governments. Perhaps, they thought that the movement by a few upstarts without the people's support will face a natural death. However, it was badly erroneous. The then Prime Minister Mon Mohan Singh visualising the burgeoning threat inspired the union and state governments to face the challenge. The union cabinet decided to spare thirty thousand para military forces, sanctioned sufficient fund and built purposeful infra-structure to combat the menace. Government of West Bengal was reluctant to deploy central forces on the plea that the state will tackle the problem politically. Bihar was dragging its feet to take decisive action against the outlaws. However, situation soon noticed a sea change. Finally, W.B. government agreed to deploy central forces. A joint operation, Green Hunt, was organised and eventually produced good result. The security forces reclaimed much territory so long remained under the Maoist control. Many top leaders were arrested, killed in gun battles and surrendered. Pressure has forced the Maoists to take to heels. The security forces' mailed fist, freer or more intrepid spirit dithered the Maoists and compelled them to abandon the ground. They have realised that retreat is the best way to avoid the flinty punch of the security forces. In Andhra Pradesh the Greyhounds are virtually nightmare to the ultras.

From 2010, the Maoists are badly isolated and unable to pull their weight. In fact, inimitable success of the security forces and simultaneously pathetic spectacle of the down fall of the Maoists, has convinced the people that beefy propaganda for the people's government is a hoax. More and more news of setback for the Maoists pouring in, galling erosion in the Maoist support base is abundantly manifested. Ironically, now the rural mass is eagerly coming forward to co-operate with the security forces. Interestingly, contrary to the past conduct, the villagers, who once supported the Maoists, are passing on intelligence to the police against them. As a matter of fact, success of the security forces is one of the prime reasons for the decline of the Maoist movement.

Government's Pragmatic Steps

Significantly, the union government's pragmatic decision that in addition to combating the ultras, a doze of good governance, refurbish and uplift of the rural economy, construct houses, roads, schools, improvement in public services like public distribution system, health care, education and employment opportunity etc. have to be initiated in right earnest. Maoist torn states have zealously taken up rural development works, various welfare measures and steps to place the have-nots in equal footing vis-à-vis the solvent people. Meaningful steps for confidence building that the rural mass is no longer ignored or neglected, rather being brought at per with others will go a long way to defeat and silence the cry of the Maoists carrying cudgel for the poverty stricken, discriminated and exploited rural mass. Needless to add, rural economic progress, socio economic development, employment opportunity will dissuade the rural mass to respond to the Maoist call. Broadly speaking, rural development projects and their forceful execution have strengthened the people's confidence on the government's meaningful gesture and therefore, find it futile to cast their lot with the ultras.

Cadres leading a substandard living in remote jungle, have to put up with fear of malaria, pestilence, water born disease, snake bite etc. They are under constant fear of police raids, arrest, torture and death. Strict regimentation, rigorous discipline, harsh treatment by the senior comrades often demoralise them. Moreover, they do not know the end of the ordeals and when their cherished dream of the people's government is going to be materialised. They security forces decisive actions, strange volte face of the villagers and obscure future now put them in abject frustration. Evidently, the increased rate of desertion and surrender of the cadres is an eloquent testimony of decadency of the Maoists strength and striking capacity.

Maoists' Review Report—Mistakes Admitted

Interestingly, the Maoists have brought out a review report admitting set back of the Maoist movement in jungle mahal, West Bengal. The three-page review report dated October 20, 2014, was published on the occasion of the 10th anniversary of the CPI (Maoist) by the Eastern Regional Bureau of the Maoist central committee. Report in introspect has high-lighted many important internal matters of the out-fit operating in West Bengal. Of late, the report has been circulated secretly in Jhargram sub division of jungle mahal. Maoists claim that the movement in jungle mahal is historic and admitted that they have committed "five mistakes" in pursuing the movement. However, they have invited constructive criticism and suggestion from the people for avoiding recurrence of such mistakes in future.

One of the striking admissions is the leadership's 'lack of clarity on Mamata's class character,' that led to the misconception that the movement would benefit from the release of the political prisoners once the TMC supremo Mamata Banerjee happened to come to power. Secondly, the West Bengal leaders' response to the peace talk ignoring advice of the central leaders was a scurrilous fall in a trap. The central leaders took the stand that the party should participate in 'peace talk' after mutual cease fire and release of the political prisoners. Unfortunately, the leaders of WB, were over enthused to trust the newly elected TMC government and the Chief Minister They consented to the peace talk short circuiting the advice of the central leaders.

Thirdly, they confessed that some of their killings were wrong. In fact, the Maoists wanted to override violence and atrocity unleashed by the CPM cadres. Sordid competitive spirit provoked them to declare crusade against the CPM cadres with equal barbarity. The review reveals. "we over reacted to the CPM atrocities and repeated their mistakes like killing people without issuing public declaration and by secretly dumping the bodies."

Maoists alleged that the TMC government conspired with UPA II (union government) under Prime Minister Manmohan Singh to kill comrade Kishanji on November 24, 2011, and disclosed the idea of peace talks. Importantly, lack of clarity on TMC chief Mamata Banerjee's politics misguided them. Maoists and people under their influence were often deputed to attend TMC's programmes. They were directly or indirectly came under influence of Mamata Banerjee which eventually circumvented the original plan of using her for the benefit of the Maoists. Error of judgment cost them heavily. In review the Maoists have expressed their sincere regret and iterated, "We feel earnestly sorry for our mistakes and our party is publicly self-criticising before the people of W.B., with an open mind. We pledge not to repeat the mistakes."

Self-criticism, regrets for the mistakes committed and desire for the people's constructive inputs to energize the movement etc. are unflinching testimony of the Maoists head long fall and galling alienation from the people of the jungle mahal. Effete leaders' laments and fervent appeal to the people reveal their helplessness to return to the field and revive the movement. Sadly, it only corroborates precipitous decline of the Maoist movement.

Of late, radicals and orthodox supporters of the Maoist movement are inclined to doubt the ultimate success of the movement. A hiatus has been growing very fast between the ultras and the intellectuals, youths and students. They are indifferent to the movement, thrive in sordid influence of materialism and avidly hanker after building their career. It is crystal clear that people are unwilling to live in a terror-torn society where tension, violence, bloodshed and chaos loom large. Undeniably, the peoples' support in favour of the movement has been waning fast. Lastly, the Maoists have lamentably failed to produce a competent leader possessing sterling qualities to hold firmly the rein of the out-fit. Indeed, the leader's cadre has been thinning out due to arrest and death. Unfortunately, the vacuum is going unfilled. It is alarming that the strength of the members of the Maoist politburo has come down from thirteen to seven only. In sum, a dynamic leader may stem the rot, stall the cancerous growth and put the movement back firmly on the rail. Alas, the Maoists have miserably failed in that pursuit.

Instances and developments discussed immune from any prejudice are unflinching testimony to corroborate that the Maoist movement has been declining and the chance of its revival at this juncture is a stymie. Undeniably, the review note issued by the Maoists in West Bengal is an axiom in support of the above contention.

Maoist Threat—Threat Perception

The tangled web of the Maoist revolutionary movement in India is distinctly different and bloated by a few exasperating pock marks. Maoism in India is a political movement guided by an ideology borrowed from outside the country. Outlandish cult is based on violence and bloodshed and its aim is to over throw the existing social and political order, usurp and establish a new regime unknown on Indian soil. Secondly, understandably the police and security forces being the government's instrument of force resisting the ultras involved in protracted proxy war are the target of attack and annihilation. Secondly, political leaders and activists are also the equal target. Many JMM, CPM and BJP cadres were attacked and killed. Thirdly, countless simple and innocent villagers, the nucleus of the people's army support base are attacked, killed brutally, punished arbitrarily by the kangaroo courts. Fourthly, many act in the garb of the movement indulged in by the Maoists tantamount to heinous crime which are contrary to the sanctity and ethics of the revolutionary spirit.

The Maoist movement is confined to a few states of the central India. Poverty stricken and deprived rural mass, especially, the tribal population is the main support base of the Maoists. The movement spear headed by radicals, intellectuals and the supporters of the ultra-left movement. It was experimented in urban areas which gradually shifted to the rural areas. Notably, the Maoists are not secessionists and the Maoist movement is not a separatist movement. Maoists want to root out the existing parliamentary system of democracy and in its place want to establish classless society and the people's government. The Maoists bank on violence and blood curdling activities. Here the target is the fellow countrymen. Ironically, the so called class enemy is their brethren, may be innocent having no thinnest connection with politics. Broadly speaking, the Maoist threat has to be judged from wider perspective entwined with the above relevant points which will focus the magnitude of the Maoist threat in near future.

Crime Committed by the Ultras and the Police's Apathy

Ultras attack on persons and properties, loot, murder, abduct, kidnap, collect levy, commit robbery etc. Victims are innocent people. Most of the crime is committed in the Maoist dominated areas or remote areas where presence of the police is either absent or very thin. Frankly speaking, the police is unable to protect the victims, investigate the complaints and prosecute the offenders. The police's unavoidable lapse indirectly allows the ultras to intensify unlawful activities. In fact, helplessness of the police and the administration to curb crime and protect the people has been compelling the people to submit to the diktats of the ultras. Escalated criminal activities of the Maoists jeopardising normalcy and halcyon atmosphere of the society, disturbing social and economic growth, was rampant.

The ultras dauntlessly indulge in crime, punish the villagers whimsically. Sometimes, they send advance demand note asking to hand over cash or deliver a minor member of a family for joining the cadre. Yet, the police is unable to prevent the crime and save the shaken and frightened people. Reason for such a tragedy sometimes is known to the police. Nevertheless, the police lamentably fail to expose the outlaws. Often it is heard that the victim's family members do not report the matter to the police station. They know that the cruel hand of the ultras is very long. Police cannot guard them round the clock and indefinitely. Cops are exposed to the ultras' threat and often are unable to defend themselves. Therefore, it is unwise to inform the police and thereby face their wrath.

It is crystal clear that the police is unable to prevent and investigate crime and protect the victims from atrocity of the head hunting ultras. Evidently, the police is failing to perform their bounden duties, prevention and detection of crime and prosecute an offender. Indeed, inaction and dereliction of duties of the police is tolerated with lingering reluctance since the Maoist threat and fiend loom large. As a matter of fact, this kind of threat will not diminish even the Maoist movement is brought under control in a particular state. A long time planning is essential to tackle the problem and demolish the threat. Culprits, absconders, abettors, harbourers, have to be arrested, investigation have to be finalised and prosecution to be lunched before the trial courts. Finally, the wings of the growing phantom has to be clipped so that it cannot raise its ugly head and gnash again. In short, continued Maoist threat has be given due care and consummate importance.

Threat of the Outlaws and Anti-socials

Many notorious anti socials and outlaws taking cue from the ultras extort money from the traders, shop-keepers, contractors, owners of illicit business. Secondly, claiming themselves falsely as part and parcel of the out-fit they collect money subscription on the pretext of strengthening the movement. This evil practice is very acute in places once dominated by the ultras and subsequently were compelled to quit or desert due to flinty pressure of the security forces. Relying on direct evidence I may add that in 1971-72, after Naxals were brought under control in Kolkata city and its periphery many caddish anti-socials had been secretly extorting money from the people on the plea of reviving the movement. In fact, they had no link with the Naxalites which was not known to the people. Yet, the cowed down people were forced to succumb to fear and met their palpably illegitimate demand. Markedly, even the menace is contained or wiped out such a threat either from the former ultras or from the anti-socials and spotty elements, mafia group is likely to loom large. Hence, along with combating the Maoist threat crime by the ultras and outlaws has to be curbed and destroyed. Needless to add, the police have to prepare and galvanise suitably the crime control devices. In short, the police have to perform the duel responsibility in pursuit of neutralising the Maoist threat.

Link with the Out fits of Foreign Countries

People's War (PW) developed link with the LTTE, ISI, and extremists of Peru, Chile, Philippines and several other countries. They are eager to co-operate with the Maoists active in India. Importantly, PW learnt the know-how of assembling, planting and defusing land mines, and using deadly explosives from the LTTE of Sri Lanka. It deputed experts to Andhra Pradesh to impart commando and jungle warfare training to the PW commandos. Secondly, the Maoists of Bihar have been maintaining close link with the CPN, Nepal. Internally, close contact with the rebels of Manipur, Nagaland, Mizoram and divisive elements of the North East is a massive boost to the Maoists. The out-fits desire to see that the Maoists in India increases influence and control and establishes the de facto Maoist rule in India. At present outlandish active support is puny. However, their moral support and encouragement is substantial. It is not ruled out that their active support in the long run may intensify the Maoist movement. Indeed, their growing co-operation is likely to keep the threat in our country alive.

Firearms Manufacturing Units

Increased demand for fire arms, ammunition, explosives etc. to accelerate extremist violence has helped mush room growth of foundries, country made weapon manufacturing mini units. It is a severe threat to the safety and security of the country. Myungar district in Bihar has earned dubious distinction for manufacturing country made guns right from the days of Mughal rule. Dacoits, outlaws, rebels in central India used to procure guns from Myungar. Now-a-days, the outlaws prefer one shot-gun and pistol for committing crime. This type of weapon can easily be manufactured in local foundry by skilled workers. As demand for weapons has been increasing manufacturing units are coming up in West Bengal, Jharkhand, Madhya Pradesh, UP etc. In Bhopal, Madhya Pradesh and Rourkela, Odisha illegal manufacturing units were discovered. Near Dum Dum airport, Kolkata, manufacturing of parts and components of rocket launchers was going on clandestinely and being dispatched to Raipur, Chhattisgarh by road transport.

In UP guns were purchased with the help of fake gun licenses from the authorised gun dealers. In fact, retired armourers from police and armed forces are appointed on high salary to guide the workers of the manufacturing units. Procurement of ammunition is an up-hill task. Ammunition for weapons of uneven caliber has to be collected from various sources and places. From UP, a few retired cops are arrested for supplying ammunition to the Maoists. A few CRPF personnel are also directly involved in this racket. Evidently, suppliers of raw materials, skilled workers, middle men, sellers, purchasers of weapons and manufacturers have built a vicious circle to pursue the undesirable flourishing trade. Now it is their livelihood. Terrorists, secessionists, outlaws, anti-socials are the purchasers of the illegal and unsanctioned weapons. Assuming, the Maoist movement has reached its nadir, secret making and selling of illegal arms will not be stopped. Indeed, the threat will continue and gain fresh momentum keeping pace with the tumultuous scenario of the country.

Shift of the Theatre of Operation

Intensity of the Maoist violence has been reduced considerably. Situation in Chhattisgarh is no longer so grim. Much liberated areas have been reclaimed. Security forces have absolute control on the situation. As dragnet of the security forces in Maoist affected states is coming closer, the alarmed ultras finding no help prefer to retreat. They have realised the stark reality of insurmountable bottle neck to gain back the lost ground. Hence, they strongly feel that it is no use moving in the rodeo ring, rather it is rewarding to discover a new theatre, build infra-structure, cultivate the people's support, impel the cadres and finally gear up the Maoist movement. They prima facie find the Kerala state suitable for the movement. Jungle in western ghat may be safe and convenient for building hide-outs, sanctuaries, training ground etc. The Communist Party of India (CPM) is deeply entrenched in the state. Ideologically, the Maoists are very close to the CPM. In northern territory activities of the Maoists are noticed in mild form. Of late, failing to repulse the security forces in central India the Maoists have opened a new front in Kerala. In Mangalore a zonal committee has been formed to co-ordinate with the counter parts active in Karnataka and Tamilnadu and to increase influence in the forest land connecting the three states. Perhaps, they are intending to spread activities on the western coast of Gujarat.

It will be a mistake to equate socio-economic condition and culture of the people of Chhattisgarh, Jharkhand, Bihar, West Bengal and Andhra Pradesh with those of Kerala. In fact, Kerala is extolled for the higher rate of literacy and education. Poverty is much in lower side. A sizeable people work in foreign countries and help the country to earn foreign exchange substantially. Economic condition of the people is not at all chaotic vis-à-vis the condition of the people living the Maoist ridden states. People are peace loving and politically very conscious. They may not act under influence of the head hunting ultras. Significantly, inspite of protracted CPM rule the extremist movement is weak and sluggish. Hence, to my mind, Kerala is not a fertile ground for the Maoist violence and macabre festival of death.

Modified Modus Operandi and Increased Striking Capacity

Maoists have modified their modus operandi, given up hit and run tactics, instead they attack and confront the security forces in heavy strength and dauntlessly face protracted gun battle, They are using blessing of the advancement of science and technology in fighting the security forces. Fair sex squads are made more stubborn, combat the security forces courageously, display able leadership and are highly dedicated in duties. They are using latest sophisticated weapons, land mine, explosives and planning to make rocket launchers. In Chhattisgarh they hit a helicopter flying in the air and injured a cop. Perhaps, a mini missile was used to hit the chopper. It is suspected that soon they may possess missiles capable of hitting a target in the sky or at distant places. They have learnt from the experts the technique of planting land mine or explosive about 8 to 10 feet below the surface which ordinarily, cannot be detected. Astonishing technique of planting explosive inside stomach of a dead CRPF cop and stitching it with precision with a view to causing a massive explosion has baffled everyone. In fact, surgery was so perfect that it could be detected much late in the hospital by the surgical experts. Investigation revealed that the Maoists have learnt this flagrant trick from the LTTE.

More the security forces disarraying the Maoists they are likely to be revengeful. The frustrated ultras may venture to select and assassinate an individual who according to them has been standing on their way. Accordingly, they may chalk out a programme, carefully select the target and execute it firmly. Secondly, like the Islamic jihadis, the Maoists may form suicide squads, motivate and train minor boys or girls to join the squads, hit the targets sacrificing themselves for the so called benign cause of the revolution. The critics feel that the gory act is no doubt deterrent but will adversely hurt ambition of the Maoists to win over heart of the people.

Political Ambition

Maoists are not free from political ambition. Like political leaders the Maoists hone scalpel to secure money, power and authority. They aspire for enjoying official hallo, privilege, dogma, honour and social recognition. They know that it is possible to achieve laurel once they form the government. In a Parliamentary democracy, a citizen, high or low may occupy an envious position, may be an important functionary and symbol of the authority of the government. Detestable jealousy, abhorrent competition and base-spirited acrimony between the political leaders and political parties often upset peace, harmony and stability. It creates a pervasive and baneful influence and pollutes the social and political environment. If a leader happens to occupy any glamorous position either in the government or in the party, he has to face campaign of calumny from the ambitious party colleagues and the competitors of the rival political parties. Tug of war for power, high office and unquestioned authority etc. right within the party as well as in rival parties generates tension and acerbic ambience. Unfortunately, many unscrupulous leaders combine the characteristics of a political enfant terrible and whet their appetite for charisma, power and authority. Interestingly, many crafty leaders patiently try to reach the goal as a political pussy footing.

Many Maoist leaders' arrogant pretention to superior wisdom to serve the poor and down trodden unselfishly has to be taken with a pinch of salt. Their lust for money, political power and recognition are boundless. Leaders of the MCC, Satya Narayan Sinha, Vinod Mishra of the CPI (ML) Liberation, Bihar left the extremist out-fits and floated political party, contested election and came to political lime light. Kameshwar Baitha, a Zonal commander of the Maoists from Jharkhand, already in judicial custody, contested election from Palamu constituency and was elected. From Andhra Pradesh the former PW leader S. Jaipal Reddy was a Minister in the union cabinet. Two extremist leaders abandoned the extremists. One eventually became the Governor of a state and the other reached the high office of Vice President of India. Several Chief Ministers of AP, secured help of the PW to succeed in election battle. In West Bengal many formal Naxal leaders have joined open politics and occupied the posts of Minister, MP and MLA. Wanton evidence available that many ultras seek opportunity to secure political power discarding motto of establishing the people's government and classless society may upset the people. I am candid that most of the extremist leaders gorged with the ambition of securing political power submit to various temptations. Broadly speaking, abominal political ambition of the extremists as well as political leaders will keep tension high and the threat alive. As long as the spectre of jealousy and competition is active the Maoist threat will prevail. Peace, tranquility and stability will be marred by violence and unrest. In sum, facets of likely threat discussed above are crystal clear that virus of political ambition is not going to die, rather steering the country towards muss, uncertainty and crisis.

Finale

In 1967, the Naxal movement originated in Naxalbari, a remote village in Darjeeling district, West Bengal. Comrade Charu Mazumdar was its founding father, assisted by comrade Kanu Sanyal, and several others. Charu strictly followed Mao's diktat and the Chinese line. He was so taken by Mao's thought that he boastfully declared: "China's chairman is our chairman." He borrowed Mao's ideology and displayed fatuous arrogance in clinging on to Mao's gospel, and in the process, he alienated his several trusted lieutenants and indirectly forced the mushroom growth of splinter groups. Comrade Kanu Sanyal founded the CPI (Marxist and Leninist) in Calcutta on May 1, 1969. Charu, a Rabelais's hero living in a make-believe world that the Red flag was going to be unfurled at the Red Fort in New Delhi and millions of Indians would be marching towards Delhi responding to his call, was a myth. His lofty promises and call to the youth, students and people to join the cadre was politically an exploitative venture. He and his whizkids failed to understand that India is not China. After all, India is a complicated mosaic of diverse linguistic, ethnic and religious communities with deep-seated mutual fear and antagonism. Hence, the people cannot be taken as dumb, driven mass and dragged toward any direction in keeping with the whims of a leader. As several comrades did not subscribe to his views, desertion, split and mushroom growth of the splinter groups took place, which was a major setback to the movement. After Charu's demise, the mercurial leadership failed to keep the flock together.

Importantly, majority of the Naxals were either expelled or drop outs from the CPI. In Andhra Pradesh, many of these dropouts and teachers seeing appalling condition of the tribal community organised protests/movements in small pockets. They had no link with the Naxal leaders of West Bengal. However, after failure of the Srikakulam uprising, the movement collapsed. In April 1980, under Kondapalli Sitaramaiah's initiative, CPI (ML) People's War was founded. It was very active in AP and penetrated in parts of MP, Odisha, Maharashtra and West Bengal. In Bihar,

Maoist Communist Centre and Indian People's Front (IPF) had been operating independently. Meanwhile, a new outfit CPI (ML) Liberation was founded. MCC and CPI (ML) Liberation made a dent, and separately carried the extremist movement quite far. PW stepped up activities in three districts of West Bengal, namely west Medinapur, Bankura and Purulia. Here, PW was better known as "Jana Juddah". However, PW and MCC merged together in September 2004, and formed the CPI (Maoist). From 2000, the growth of the extremists, PW, MCC and Jana Juddah gained unprecedented momentum. Dandakarnaya, Bastar region, four districts of Maharashtra and several districts of Chhattisgarh were brought under their influence. A few districts of Chhattisgarh have earned notoriety of so-called liberated territory. Here, writs of the extremists, later the Maoists' writs, were running. In Bastar region in Chhattisgarh, headquarter of the Maoists has been functioning in an inaccessible forest called Abujhmarh (unknown forest). PW sold the idea of Compact Revolutionary Zone (CRZ) or the Red Corridor connecting Dharmapuri forest area of Tamil Nadu with Nepal, covering a forest track of several states of central India. In the Red territory or corridor, the Maoists intended to establish a classless society and the People's government, demolishing the existing social and political order.

Reasons for the poor and neglected rural population, especially the tribal community, to respond to the extremists' call and go in their fold are not far to seek. Both, the union and state governments' snide indifference to drag them out of poverty and deprivation, and monumental callousness to uplift them socially and economically enhanced their discontent and repugnance to the government's assurance for satisfactory rural development. Impartial critics feel that after more than 60 years of independence, the fate of the tribal community is still unaltered. Hence, the extremists' promise for equality, classless society and equal share in the government made a profound and credible impression on them. Moreover, welfare activities for the poor rural masses, undertaken by the ultras from their scanty resources and protection against harassment and exploitation of the money lenders, contractors and oppressive public servants etc., cemented good relationship between the ultras and the rural mass. Hence, seeing their keenness for the good of the poor and downtrodden, missionary zeal for welfare of the deprived and simultaneously, galling indifference of the government, they had no hesitation in casting their lot with the ultras. Importantly, in this unequal contest, the government lamentably lagged behind. Indeed, the government's routine and lack-luster rural developmental plan and programmes, and execution in halfhearted and slovenly manner, failed to fulfill hope and aspiration of the impoverished rural populace. Hence, the ultras' pompous whispering campaign that the government and the existing political order are unable to get rid of the comatose condition, and ensure a glittering future, worked well. The neglected people relied on the promises hoping for better days, and therefore, gleefully followed the ultras. Admittedly, the successive governments were consciously or unconsciously responsible for the poverty-stricken and helpless rural people's response to the extremists' call and implicit submission to the ultras' influence and control.

Unprecedented growth and burgeoning threat of the ultras was perhaps viewed by the union and state governments insouciantly. Union Home Minister Sivraj Patil was idly busy in watching the growth of the spectre of violence. He was unable to assess the menacing growth of the ultras, and their link with the LTTE, ISI and other outfits of foreign countries, as well as their power and capacity to de-stabilise the safety and security of the country. Indeed, his utter indifference to the growing threat was evident when he said, "Naxal activity is confined to only 2 per cent of the country's 650000 villages and not one-third of the national territory or that a mere 300 of the country's 14000 police stations". Interestingly, many state governments placated the ultras, keen to buy peace at the cost of the public interest. Chief Minister of Andhra Pradesh NT Rama Rao carried cudgel for the ultras, adroitly used them to humble the political rivals and win the election battle. Later, successive CMs of AP representing the Congress party followed similar modus operandi and tried to keep them in good humour, sacrificing the police morale and administrative rectitude. CM SR Reddy halted the police operation against the PW for three months, ignored their outrageous activities and invited them for a peace talk. Dismayingly, the peace talk failed, but it enhanced popularity and acceptability of the PW to the common people. The then CM of Odisha, seeing presence and movement of the PW in Malkangiri area, was unwilling to take any action on the ground that the PW, no doubt, had built sanctuary in Odisha, but were not disturbing peace or indulging in violence.

The CM of West Bengal, instead of taking decisive actions, asserted that the problem would be tackled politically. However, after an attempt on taking his life was made, he, after lingering reluctance, agreed to deploy central force to flush out the ultras from the Jungle mahal. However, he avoided a ban on the Maoist outfit in spite of union government's request. Meanwhile, new states Jharkhand and Chhattisgarh were born. Ultras stepped up violent activities in new states and made several districts 'liberated territory', covering approximately 40000 sq km area, aiming at building the Red Corridor or the Compact Liberated Zone (CRZ) and set up the People's government, pulling down the existing elected governments. Merger of PW and the MCC, and birth of the CPI (Maoist) in September 2004 gave ultras an extraordinary impetus. The Chief Minister of Bihar, Nitish Kumar, took soft line to handle the ultras, and was reluctant to accept the joint operation. He said, "Naxalites are a part of our society." He warned, "Enforcement action alone would lead to wider alienation of such elements." Chief Minister of Jharkhand Sibu Soren, during his brief stint, followed the soft line and wanted dialogue with the ultras to solve the problem. Frankly speaking, CMs of the Maoist-torn states took a different stand which lacked cohesion, single-minded devotion and indomitable will to rap the ultras on knuckle and wipe out unrest and bloodletting activities. Reckless killing of the cops and civilians, and punishment of innocent people on mere suspicion by the so-called people's court generated unprecedented panic, fear and insecurity. In the Maoist-dominated territory, the peace-loving people were shaken seeing near breakdown of the rule of law and abdication of the government's power and authority. They were deeply perturbed and afraid as atrocities were unleashed by the ultras and anarchy disrupted normal life.

Unfortunately, peltry rural development, deficiency in solving the socio-economic problem, inadequate education facilities, healthcare, employment opportunity, civic amenities etc. gave excellent opportunity to the ultras to get the rural masses in their fold. In such a scenario, unprecedented growth of the ultras posed a gigantic threat to internal safety and security of the country. After much analysis, I am constraint to say that insouciance and complacency of both, the union and the state governments, was squarely responsible for increasing the Maoist threat to gargantuan shape. The governments failed to visualise the growing danger and its wider ramification, and lamentably failed to nip it in the bud. Folly of the government has put the security scenario in a log-jam, facing insurmountable hurdle either to contain or liquidate the hydra-headed monster.

In fact, taking advantage of the states' ambivalence and the union government's policy of masterly inactivity, the growth of the cadres, capture of turf and fiendish activities have been continuing unchecked. In so-called liberated territory, Maoist writ ran and the administration was helpless to enforce the rule of law. Maoists developed link with the Maoists of Nepal, LTTE, ISI and several extremist outfits active in foreign countries. Surprisingly, their fund was substantial and resources were abundant. In fact, the cadre strength shot up to 50,000, including 20,000 armed cadres. Deadly guerrilla squads and fair sex cadres flourished beyond imagination. Induction of adolescents in the cadre either by coercion or consent, and their indoctrination in revolutionary spirit, training, deployment etc. markedly strengthened the outfit, its confidence and striking power to direct, confront or attack the security forces. Tactics of hit and run were modified to confrontation or attack in heavy strength, protracted gun battle and extensive use of land mines.

Finally, magnitude of the ultra-left movement, unabated violence, preparation to topple the duly elected governments, dominance over the liberated territory and preparation of the Red Corridor etc. forced the union and state governments to wake up from torpor and tackle the threat with equal strength. Prime Minister Manmohan Singh publicly declared: "It is the single biggest security challenge to the Indian states. We need to cripple Naxalite forces with all means at our command." The Parliament was rocked by the issue of neutralising the extremist menace. The then Home Minister admitted the union government's complacency and stated on the floor of the Rajya Sabha: "For many years, we did not properly assess the threat posed by the left wing extremists. We underestimated the challenge and meanwhile, Naxalites extended their influence." On the floor of the Parliament, he said: "Today, they pose a grave challenge...we are preparing to take on the challenge."

It may be appreciated that it is no longer an ordinary law and order problem which is normally tackled by the state police based on their archaic resources. Secondly, there is a paradigm shift in the ultras' tactics and offensives. Now, the invigorated ultras plan attacks meticulously, ambush the police patrols and security forces in good number, try to run over the police stations, out posts and camps, use land mines, explosives, sophisticated weapons and prefer protracted gun battle. In the changed scenario, the security forces have to consummately upgrade their training, weaponry, fire power and refurbish or modify the strategy. Greater emphasis is put on jungle warfare training and guerrilla tactics. Significantly, as on 2009, the Red Corridor covered approximately 40,000 sq km-long jungle patch through the forest land of seven states. The union government decided to sanction sufficient fund for major expansion of the security forces and for development of social infrastructure. The central cabinet committee of the union government on October 8, 2008 approved the proposal for offensive in Chhattisgarh, Jharkhand, Odisha, Maharashtra and West Bengal, deploying 30,000 Paramilitary forces. Simultaneously, it was followed by heavy doses of governance, introducing mobile medical vans, kickstarting the public distribution system (PDS), ensuring attendance of teachers at schools, and steps for a comprehensive survey to identify people living below poverty line. Over and above, the union and state governments jointly chalked out fresh strategy to curb the Maoist movement. The Prime Minister said, "Development and internal security are critically dependent on each other and highlight problems of development divides."

The Union Home Minister P. Chidambaram initiated several tangible steps to modernise the state police forces, raise new forces like Cobra, established specialised training centers, procured latest weaponry, equipments, night vision instruments, organised coordinated meetings with the states, joint operations, sanctioned sufficient fund etc. Happily, the union government's indomitable will and resolution gave a massive push to the states to fight the Maoists. Sagging morale of the security forces received a mighty boost. On the question of forming liberated zone by the Maoists, he stated, "Grand scheme to create liberated zones would not succeed. The government is duty-bound to protect its people and ensure that the civil administration's writ runs in every part of the state. Battle against the Naxalites will continue."

Broadly speaking, the situation was changing towards improvement and upper hand of the security forces was noticed right from the beginning of 2010. In AP, the security forces, especially the Greyhounds, kept the Maoists busy to defend themselves. It was noteworthy that violence was broadly contained.

Analysts feel that for curbing the threat, a security centric approach may not be the solution, and calls for a multi-pronged strategy. National Human Rights

Commission has pointed out its root in socio-economic deprivation including lack of job opportunities. The counter-terrorism committee set up by the United Nations dispatched a team to India. After visiting, the team commented that India is one of the biggest theatres of the terror groups active in the world. Secondly, India's counter terrorism structures are in disarray. It has no comprehensive counter-terrorism legislation to fight the terror.

Admittedly, merger of PW and MCC outfits reveals the sagacious aplomb of the top brass of the extremists. The invigorated new outfit, the CPI (Maoist) and its outrageous activities from 2004 to 2009 in seven states has created a frightful tension and posed mighty threat to the internal security of the country. The union government and the Maoist wrapped state governments to gave up complacency and paid special attention to counter the challenge with zeal and resolution. In addition, special attention is now being given to improve the rural economy; and in that pursuit, undertaking of several pilot projects to improve roads, communication, education, health care and employment opportunity has come about. Funds were liberally sanctioned to bring a sea change in socio-economic condition of the poor, deprived and exploited rural masses. In reality, it is a rural-based insurgency, and people living in rural areas are the sufferers. The hideouts, sanctuary, training grounds etc. are located inside the deep forests surrounded exclusively by tribal villages and hamlets. Hence, operations by the security forces have to be planned carefully so that the habitants are not harmed.

Ironically, the top leaders, instead of sharing hardships of the cadres, live in towns and cities, enjoying civic amenities. They occasionally visit the hideouts inside the forests, stay for a few days and interact with the cadres. Leaders strongly defend the practice of living in towns or cities on the ground that they have to build reliable contact with intellectuals, the youth, students, supporters of the movement and the print media to get favourable media coverage. Secondly, crux of the ideology, aims and object have to be secretly carried too far and wide to make the movement popular and acceptable to others. How far the alibi of the top leaders is prudent needs exhaustive examination. Indeed, growing hiatus between the leaders and the rank and file has been hurting the unity, solidarity and camaraderie, which ultimately jeopardises the movement. Admittedly, the leaders living in urban areas are far away from the ground reality.

The idea of forming the CRZ or the Red Corridor was mooted by the People's War (PW) in Andhra Pradesh. In the beginning, the PW contemplated on spreading operation from the Telengana plateau right up to the Himalayan kingdom of Nepal through the tribal belt of Odisha, Bihar, West Bengal, Madhya Pradesh and Maharashtra. MCC, active in Bihar, Jharkhand and Chhattisgarh were not born then, approved the idea. Initially, it faced many hurdles. Uprising of the CPN (Maoist) in Nepal stood in its way. Subsequently, the politburo partially modified the aim and objectives of the CRZ in 2009, making it wider, while purposefully covering a bigger area, right from Tamil Nadu to Nepal. Indeed, merger of the PW and MCC was a diplomatic success to make the Maoist movement more viable and effective.

Reverses and Modified Strategy

The PW's initial success in AP was, broadly, due to the successive state government's conciliatory policy, use of the PW for selfish political gain and indecisiveness to handle them. Eventually, the elite force, the Greyhounds' mailed fist, forced the PW to take to heels. Activities of the head hunting ultras were contained. Comrade Muppala Lakshman Rao alias Ganapathy, the General Secretary, said, "I agree that the losses in Andhra Pradesh are quite serious. They have a considerable impact on the revolutionary movement in the country as a whole." However, he added that establishment of base areas is selected in more backward areas in central and eastern India to gear up the movement. He hinted that backward areas of Dandakarnaya, Bastar region, Jharkhand and Bihar etc. are amply suitable for intensifying the movement. Of late, reverses in almost Maoist-torn states have forced the Maoists to modify their strategy. Leadership feels that the movement, once started in the cities, must be taken back to the cities. Comrade Ram Anna alias Narendra, a member of the Maoist Central Committee, stated, "It is the struggle that is shaking the system." It is believed that he took part in the barbarous massacre of 76 CRPF cops in Chhattisgarh. Intelligence report reveals that the Maoists are looking for a new direction. Leaders believe that the movement which started from the city, is now restricted to the jungle and must be taken back to the cities. In January 2010, General Secretary Ganapathy issued instructions, directing the cadres to turn urban areas into support centers to make good the losses of its rural strongholds. However, he realises that the task is not easy short circuiting the intense security cover and intelligence network existing in urban areas. Secondly, citizens have mixed reactions with regard to the Maoist movement. They look obliquely at the success of the movement. Thirdly, recruitment of the urban youth for the cadre is an uphill task. Ram Anna, however, is very optimistic that the mission would achieve its goal in the long run.

It may be recalled that Naxal movement started in Naxalbari, a village in remote area of Darjeeling district West Bengal, which is not at all an urban area. In AP, Chhattisgarh, Jharkhand and Odisha, the Maoist movement gained momentum broadly in rural areas. However, radicals and intellectuals living in urban areas extended moral support covertly to the ultra-left movement. In fact, in towns and cities the movement was hardly intensified. In late sixties, in metropolitan city, Kolkata, a group of students participated in the movement zealously, indulged in violence, annihilation and killed cops, jotdars (petty land holders), daily wage earners, poor laborer etc. It is a paradox that not a capitalist, hoarder, money lender, rich land lord, bourgeois was taken to task or figured in the annihilation list.

However, from early seventies panic and Naxalite terror from the city fully wizened. Ganapathy's instruction to take back the movement to the cities is misleading. Critics feel that it is an artifice to divert attention of the security forces and the administration. The Maoists neither have any organisation nor infra-structure in cities to initiate movement ignoring constant watch and surveillance of the police, intelligence units and alert citizens.

Significantly, cadres living in forest, isolated places, denied of civic amenities, facing hardship, pestilence and hazards are not appreciating the leadership in absentia, and direction communicated by the leaders living in the ivory tower. In fact, surrender of good number of Maoists in AP, WB, Odisha, Chhattisgarh and Bihar is an eloquent testimony of dissatisfaction of the cadres. Truly, the leaders are anxious broadly on two counts. First, surrender and exodus of the cadres and thereby erosion in the outfit, secondly, volte face of the tribal communities who are no longer the firm support base of the ultras, is a positive threat at present to the Maoist movement. In short, the shaken leadership has hit upon a plan to plug the erosion and in that pursuit perhaps, craftily raising the bogey of galvanizing the movement focusing on cities and urban areas. Without any prejudice, I am inclined to believe that it is a ploy to curb the exodus and neutralise disappointment fast brewing in the rank and file.

Co-ordinated Offensive Initiated by the Union Government

Co-ordinated offensives by the central and state police on the persuasion of the union Home Ministry have produced rewarding result in containing the outrageous activities of the Maoists and reclaiming substantial portion of the so called liberated areas, especially, in Chhattisgarh and Jungle Mahal, W.B. Importantly, along with the success of the joint operations the government has injected a generous doze for rural development. Security forces after hard toil take control of the so called liberated turf but they have no role on the developmental plan, programmes and their fruitful execution. In fact, relying on ground experience the security forces may suggest and identify areas needing immediate attention for development and immediate execution of the projects. Admittedly, often expected result of the development projects are either not satisfactorily achieved or lagged behind. A senior officer in charge of the operation in Chhattisgarh stated, "We are waging a futile war...the Maoists return the moment we shut down the camp." Truly, the forces disarray the rebels and reclaim an area do not have the power to develop and the authorities who have the power to develop the areas do not step out of their offices. In fact, New Delhi is worried about the states' lackluster performance. An official of the MHA said, "Bihar started governance reforms on a promising note but it appears to be floundering." Luckily, the government has considered this question and directed that the district Superintendent of police should be one of the members of the district development plan and programmes committee.

Jharkhand and Chhattisgarh are the epicenter of the Maoist movement. Here, major portion of the territory is covered by thick forest, hills, and inaccessible places, cut off from even puny towns scantily urbanised. In such conditions, the places are highly suitable for building safe hide-outs, sanctuaries and training grounds. Poverty-stricken and neglected tribal people, denied of the blessing of the modern socio economic progress reside here who eke out living with numerous difficulties. Unfortunately, the government's endeavor to improve their lot is lamentably deficient. The extremists, the shrewd judge of the wretched condition of the tribal people, succeeded easily in luring them in their fold, campaigning and whispering pompous promises to establish the classless society and the people's government. The simple and unassuming tribal people easily fell prey and carried away by the nuances of the extremist jargon and became the main support base of the ultras. Indeed, part of Dandakarnaya and Bastar region of Chhattisgarh turned to be the bastion of the ultras. Here, inconvenient terrain, Amazon like jungle, tribal population etc. are agreeable to the ultras for strengthening the organisation and the movement. Again in this belt able bodied unemployed tribal youths and fair sex are sufficiently available for enlisting them in the cadre. Conditions helped the ultras to set firmly to spear-head their activities and converted many pockets into liberated areas where their writs have been running. Ultras founded guerrilla squads, known as the People's Liberation Guerrilla Army (PLGA) who is the formidable and main striking force of the ultras. The keen observers comment that they are like Vietcong guerrillas. After the merger and birth of the CPI (Maoist), the Maoist movement gained gigantic momentum. Intelligence report reveals that M.L. Rao alias Ganapathy; the general secretary is hiding in Bastar portion of Dandakarnaya jungle, and operating from the hide outs.

In Chhattisgarh, at the initiative of the state government, a private militia, named Salwa Judum was raised. Its founder father was Mahendra Viswakarma and its duty was to protect and defend the people from the Maoist atrocity. In make shift camps many people took shelter under the protection of the Salwa Judum. Unfortunately, it committed wanton excesses, killed villagers arbitrarily. Finally, the Apex Court intervened and banned the Salwa Judum. In two states the CRPF have faced major brunt of the Maoists' fury. In an ambush 76 CRPF personal including a Deputy Commandant were killed. Massacre of 28 Congress leaders and activists including the former union Minister V.C. Shukla in Sukma district sent a shock wave. Inspite of sporadic violence, the security forces reclaimed sizeable areas from the liberated zone and have established rule of law there. In fact, totality of unrest reveals that the tide has gradually turned in favour of the state. Lull in violence torn areas, restoration of normalcy in reclaimed turf, defensive posture of the ultras and dominance of the security forces in disarraying the Maoists is a positive sign of improvement. Admittedly, bluntness of the Maoists' fiend in disturbed areas is evident and hinting at peace and stability which is res ipsa loquitur.

Maoists planned to liberate northern and western districts of Odisha state by

2010. Surprise attack and loot of arms and ammunition from the police armoury of Koraput district and loot of hundreds of weapons, ammunition and dozens of light machine guns from the police training institute, Nayagarh, smacks of the police's so called tight security and intelligence network In Kondmal district conflict between the pro Maoist Christians and the anti-Maoist Hindus led to bloody riots, loot, arson, murders including murder of a Hindu monk have put the administration in cul de sac. Markedly, Maoist leaders from Andhra Pradesh have been controlling the organisation, planning and directing operations in Odisha. In fact, harsh or shabby treatment to the Maoists of Odisha, have generated resentment. Finally, under current of discontentment soon developed a divisive tendency which broke the unity in the out-fit in the state. On the initiative of comrade Sabyasachi Panda the Odisha Maobadi party was born. The state's tangible steps to modernise the police force, raise new forces, training centers and participation in joint offensives, operation the Green Hunt and taking up rural development with missionary zeal have produced spectacular result. Maoists are isolated and lost the people's support and sympathy. Even the much disturbed district Malkangiri is quiet.

Bihar state has earned dubious distinction for violence and bloodshed among the private militia. Secondly, feud has equally soiled social unity, harmony and cohesion. Regrettably, this evil has not spared the Maoists aspiring for a classless society. In fact, caste rivalry and caste conflict between the Maoists belonging to the tribal community and the Maoists from other castes, especially, the Yadav community is a big bottle neck for the progress of the Maoist movement. Again, in-fighting among the splinter groups is a threat to the unity and solidarity of the state out-fit. Allegations against many leaders for illegally possessing money, wealth, and purchasing land, flats, bungalows, heavy vehicles and sending wards to foreign countries for higher study, extorting people on any pretext etc. have shocked the people. Alienation from the beefy ideal of Maoism and enriching themselves by corrupt practices is a wrong message to the people who have been building a cobweb to see a tainted free efficient government in the hands of the selfless revolutionaries. Indeed, the Maoists are very active in the districts touching Jharkhand. In fact, Jamui district and Jamui jungle are practically the free land for the ultras. The Chief Minister Nitish Kumar has been following soft line to tackle the Maoist threat. He may be correct in his pious pursuit. However, from the detached angle it may be questioned how far his vision is going to restore peace and bring the pitiless ultras to the main stream of the society.

In West Bengal, the left front government led by the CPM used the party cadres and muscle power to keep the party's influence in tact over the people, especially, living in rural areas. Police and administration functioned and treated the people shabbily adhering to the diktat of the local party leaders. In three districts of jungle mahal the Maoists under Kishanji, a darling of the tribal community, brought a vast area under the Maoists' grip so long remained under the CPM's control. In fact, CPM cadres and activists became their main target. Within three months of 2009, Maoists killed 43 CPM leaders and activists in jungle mahal. On November 2, 2008, after an attempt on the Chief Minister's motorcade in the outskirt of Mednipur town, the CM and his party was alarmed. Callous police to save their face went berserk, raided houses, assaulted villager, including women and adolescents brutally, arrested people arbitrarily, concocted criminal cases against innocent persons. A reign of terror was let loose by the police. It provoked the entire tribal population to be united, and to take the path of protest and agitation. Soon, it took the shape of the mass upsurge and built an unprecedented anti-government public opinion. The Maoists exploited the situation in their favour, founded several frontal organisations and vigorously backed the anti CPM and antigovernment tirade in full vigor. The tribal people of jungle mahal was up-in-arms, blocked the roads, stopped vehicular traffic, obstructed the police to enter into Lalgarh and kept the area completely cut off from the district HQ for several days.

Startling progress of the Maoists, territory snatched away from the CPM's control, annihilation of the CPM cadres and activists, exodus of the frightened comrades from jungle mahal, alarmed the CPM leaders. Misgiving that the police's allegiance to the party and protection to the party activists and supporter's vis-à-vis the Maoist threat fell flat. Cops were no match with the dauntless ultras. Moreover, the tribal people were not co-operating with the police, on the contrary, helping the Maoists providing shelter, food and intelligence on the movement of the security forces. In fact, the CPM leadership was shaken as existence of the party and party cadre was on the verge of decay. Hence, the party decided to hire goons, professional killers and gunmen from Bihar, Jharkhand and other places to confront the Maoists. Small makeshift camps were made for the stay of a group of 20 to 25 goons, weapons were supplied. The police was instructed to remain aloof. They were locally called the "harmad bahini" and supposed to protect the party cadres, patrol the area, hold the ground and fight the Maoists. Surprisingly, such an abominable step by an elected government is unknown in social and political history of West Bengal. The harmad bahini chastised the villagers, treated them brutally and forced them to look after their comfort. In village Netai, near Lalgarh, a temporary camp was opened in the house of a local CPM office bearer. The insolent harmads compelled the villagers and the house wives to cook meals for them, clean utensils, wash cloths etc. Finally, they demanded that the youths have to join physical and weapon training under them. Villagers including the women folk one morning assembled in front of the camp and protested against their high handedness and refused to send wards for training. Temper ran high. The ruthless harmads suddenly fired at the crown without any provocation, killed five men and three women at the spot. Later one male and a house wife died in the hospital. I visited the spot after three days and prepared a detailed report. On public demand the CBI investigated the case and placed charge sheet against twenty accused persons which is still sub-judice.

In West Bengal, the joint forces initially failed to deliver desired result and came under scathing criticism. A strong group of radicals, authors, teachers, intellectuals and members of the civil society demanded halt of the joint forces and withdrawal of the central forces, organised protest march etc. In jungle mahal, areas reclaimed by the joint forces were promptly occupied by the CPM cadres who quit the area a few months back in fear of the Maoists. Upon the development, many people cried foul that a nexus is apparent between the CPM and the security forces which is firmly denied by the security forces. Evidently, the CPM cadres taking opportunity of the security forces' success cleverly planned to return and reestablish their control on the turf which once had to be abandoned in fear of the Maoists. As events moved apace in W.B., the success of the security forces has silenced all criticism. In other states the security forces and the state police forces together have given good account of them, cornered the Maoists and helped to restore normalcy in violent ridden districts.

Election for the state Legislative Assembly was knocking at the door. Trinamool Congress Party (TMC) under its supremo Miss Mamata Banerjee was the main political rival of the CPM. Allegations of nexus between the Maoists and the TMC for spear-heading election campaigns in jungle mahal to defeat the CPM surcharged the political atmosphere. People's Committee against Police Atrocity (PCAPA), one of the frontal organisations of the Maoists headed by the Maoist leader Chatradhar Mahato confronted the CPM cadres, attacked and killed many of them. In May 2011, the Left Front was disastrously defeated and the TMC formed the government and Miss Mamata Banerjee became the Chief Minister. The new government invited the rebels for a dialogue. Operation of the security forces remained suspended. However, the rebels' reaction was lukewarm. A team of interlocutors was appointed by the government to negotiate with the leaders of the rebels for peace talk and settlement. However, nothing tangible came out inspite of protracted negotiation. Meanwhile the Maoists were preparing for fresh show down. Indeed, recurrence of violence and bloodshed appeared imminent. The security forces were anxious visualising that unrest was going to be unleashed by the ultras. Meanwhile, comrade Kishanji, the dramatis personae of the Maoist movement in jungle mahal, was killed in an encounter in November 2011. In February, 2012, dreaded Maoist leader Sasadhar Mahato was killed in a gun battle. Many comrades were arrested. Then came the spree of surrender of the rebels. Sm Jagari Baski, a dauntless woman Maoists, her husband, Maoist Sm Suchitra Mahato wife of slain leader Sasadhar Mahato and a large number of male and female Maoists surrendered. Maoists failed to select a suitable leader in place of Kishanji. Leaderless rebels in jungle mahal were isolated and the movement came to a grinding halt. Meanwhile the state has initiated many rural developmental programmes, enlisted hundreds of tribal youths for employment. Truly, the people of jungle mahal were tired of violence, blood bath, suspense and insecurity now, seeing peace and stability they have heaved a sigh of relief.

Fair sex Maoists have been playing a crucial role in the forward march of the Maoist movement. The top brass of the out-fit prefer fair sex in the cadre as they are highly devoted to work, well-disciplined and hardly desert the unit. Regrettably, they are forced to use their tantalizing charm to lure youths to join the out-fit. In the hide outs, they are often sexually abused against their consent either under threat or gun point. Needless to say, it has marred the lofty ideal of the revolution. Even the inscrutable moral law has not dissuaded the culprits to refrain from such a shameful crime. Details in this respect may be seen in chapter nine.

Police's good work is unheralded and its short coming is trumpeted. People hardly know the hardship, hazards and sacrifices made by the state and para military police forces in combating the protracted proxy war. Hence, role and supreme sacrifices of the police and the security forces is high-lighted in chapter nine, to beef up awareness among the people. A few instances of the cop's excesses and cruelty in treating the Naxalites are brought to fore for the consumption of the cops so that they discharge duties giving up prejudices and strictly adhering to human dignity, moral law and professional ethics.

Peace, harmony and human values are the ethos and traditions of the people of this country. In the land of Gautam Buddha and Mahatma Gandhi violence is universally condemned. Cult of Maoism based on violence and bloodshed is neither acceptable nor welcomed by the people. Comrade Charu Mazumdar's elephantine appetite for unfurling the Red flag on top of the Red Fort Delhi, through bloodshed was either obliquely viewed or laughed at by the people. However, a handful of radicals, intellectuals and persons obsessed with the idea of the people's government subscribed to the Charu's vision. They plead that through violence and bloodshed the People's government can be achieved and its favour they refer to the militant nationalism of the country which received support and patronage from the freedom hungry people. In fact, militant nationalism, a part of the national movement in India, was confined to a few pockets in urban areas. It enjoyed support and patronage of a group of intellectuals, educated people, students and patriotic youths. Its meteoric rise was, no doubt, astounding but its decay was equally depressing. A handful of nationalists attacked and killed a few bureaucrats and English men and thought it one of the surest means of achieving independence. However, it had no lasting influence and was not accepted by the people. Hence, the people are likely to maintain distance from Maoism which is entwined with disquiet, violence and annihilation.

Three important points have been pointed out for critical examination. First, the reason why the movement is stagnating in seven states and its bleak prospect to spread it in other states calls for pensive analysis. Secondly, its erosion in the support base, hostility of the rural mass once whole heartedly supported and assisted the extremists, decaying trend of the Maoist movement needs critical examination from wider perspective. Thirdly, the Maoist threat or the threat perception, its bearing on the country's safety and security, social and political life of the people and its future is very pertinent for studying the Maoist movement and pin-pointing the remedial measures to contain or curb it. However, pros and cons of the above points have been discussed in chapter ten. It may be noted that the Maoist movement may be in limbo temporarily, but may recur with renewed vigor at any opportune moment.

In conclusion, it may be mentioned that the Maoist unrest is not at all an ordinary law and order problem which can be wiped out by the police action. Importantly, the Maoists, the shrewd judge of events, have been modifying their modus operandi on offensives from time to time to out-wit the security forces. Hence, the security forces have to adjust and galvanize their plan and tactics in keeping with the swift changing situations. Dispassionately, in addition to law and order, it is a colossal political problem having its dimension equally robust. Now-a-days, political parties and political leaders of India have deviated from patriotic spirit, ideology, ethics and motto of selfless public service. Sadly, politics has come down to the level of a profession. Leaders are ambitious; hanker after money, power and authority. Sordid jealousy and odious competition mar the political ambience. Intrigue that the political rivals have to be maligned and pushed out of the scene at any cost often disturbs public peace and order. Indeed, majority of the Maoist leaders are not immune from the ambition, lust of power and authority. Their idealism and spirit of public service is likely to disappear once they are in the seat of power. This gets amply supported when many extremist leaders join open politics, contest in election, get elected and secure important assignments by fair foul means.

Maoism may be a lofty political ideology intending to eradicate miseries of the deprived and exploited people, promise them equality, equal rights and the people's government. Nevertheless, once the present order is destroyed absolute power and authority may concentrate in the hands of a few powerful and ambitious individuals. Consequently, abhorrent dictatorial and autocratic spectre may creep in and demolish individual liberty, democratic value and probity of the people's freedom of speech and the right for protest and agitation. Undeniably, examples on this count are many, which will unmistakably corroborate my fear and apprehension. Therefore, instead of jumping into the band wagon, people have to rely on the gumption of the impartial political thinkers, and judge the Maoist movement and its future from detached angle with utmost care.

Bibliography

Chakravarti Sudeep, *Red Sun*, Delhi.

Das Gupta Biplap, *Observation on Naxal Movement in West Bengal* (Selected chapters), Calcutta.

Hazen Downer Charles, *Modern Europe*, Delhi.

Sarkar Sir Jadunath, *Fall of the Mughal Empire*, Calcutta.

_____, *Shivaji and His Times*, Calcutta.

Saha Dr. B.P., *Liberation Struggle and After*, New Delhi.

_____, *Trans-border Terrorism—Internationalisation of Kashmir Tangle.*

Samanta Dr. A.K., *Late Extremist Movement in WB*, Calcutta.

Hussain M., *Assam Movement.*

Martyrs' Memorial Research Institute Hyderabad, *Maoist Insurgency.*

_____, *A perspective of Maoist Insurgency.*

Naxal Scenario in Jharkhand and State Response, Prepared by the state police of Jharkhand.

Newspapers

The Statesman

The Times of India

The Hindustan Times

The Telegraph

The Hindu

The Indian Express

Vernacular Newspapers (Bengali)

Bartaman

Ananda Bazar Patrika

Pratidin

Dainik Statesman

Hindi

Dainik Bhaskar

Dainik Jagaran

Hindustan Samachar

Index